Fyodor Dostoevsky, Collection novels Volume TWO

In this book:
The Brothers Karamazov
Crime and Punishment

Translated By Constance Garnett

Fyodor Mikhailovich Dostoyevsky (1821 – 1881), was a Russian novelist, short story writer, essayist, journalist and philosopher. Dostoyevsky's literary works explore human psychology in the context of the troubled political, social, and spiritual atmosphere of 19th-century Russia. He began writing in his 20s, and his first novel, Poor Folk, was published in 1846 when he was 25. His major works include Crime and Punishment (1866), The Idiot (1869), and The Brothers Karamazov (1880). His output consists of eleven novels, three novellas, seventeen short novels and numerous other works.

In this book:

The Brothers Karamazov

PART I

Book I. The History of a Family

Chapter 1. Fyodor Pavlovitch Karamazov

Alexey Fyodorovitch Karamazov was the third son of Fyodor Pavlovitch Karamazov, a landowner well known in our district in his own day, and still remembered among us owing to his gloomy and tragic death, which happened thirteen years ago, and which I shall describe in its proper place. For the present I will only say that this "landowner"--for so we used to call him, although he hardly spent a day of his life on his own estate-- was a strange type, yet one pretty frequently to be met with, a type abject and vicious and at the same time senseless. But he was one of those senseless persons who are very well capable of looking after their worldly affairs, and, apparently, after nothing else. Fyodor Pavlovitch, for instance, began with next to nothing; his estate was of the smallest; he ran to dine at other men's tables, and fastened on them as a toady, yet at his death it appeared that he had a hundred thousand roubles in hard cash. At the same time, he was all his life one of the most senseless, fantastical fellows in the whole district. I repeat, it was not stupidity--the majority of these fantastical fellows are shrewd and intelligent enough--but just senselessness, and a peculiar national form of it.

He was married twice, and had three sons, the eldest, Dmitri, by his first wife, and two, Ivan and Alexey, by his second. Fyodor Pavlovitch's first wife, Adelaida Ivanovna, belonged to a fairly rich and distinguished noble family, also landowners in our district, the Miusovs. How it came to pass that an heiress, who was also a beauty, and moreover one of those vigorous intelligent girls, so common in this generation, but sometimes also to be found in the last, could have married such a worthless, puny weakling, as we all called him, I won't attempt to explain. I knew a young lady of the last "romantic" generation who after some years of an enigmatic passion for a gentleman, whom she might quite easily have married at any moment, invented insuperable obstacles to their union, and ended by throwing herself one stormy night into a rather deep and rapid river from a high bank, almost a precipice, and so perished, entirely to satisfy her own caprice, and to be like Shakespeare's Ophelia. Indeed, if this precipice, a chosen and favourite spot of hers, had been less picturesque, if there had been a prosaic flat bank in its place, most likely the suicide would never have taken place. This is a fact, and probably there have been not a few similar instances in the last two or three generations. Adelaida Ivanovna Miusov's action was similarly, no doubt, an echo of other people's ideas, and was due to the irritation caused by lack of mental freedom. She wanted, perhaps, to show her feminine independence, to override class distinctions and the despotism of her family. And a pliable imagination persuaded her, we must suppose, for a brief moment, that Fyodor Pavlovitch, in spite of his parasitic position, was one of the bold and ironical spirits of that progressive epoch, though he was, in fact, an ill-natured buffoon and nothing more. What gave the marriage piquancy was that it was preceded by an elopement, and this greatly captivated Adelaida Ivanovna's fancy. Fyodor Pavlovitch's position at the time made him specially eager for any such enterprise, for he was passionately anxious to make a career in one way or another. To attach himself to a good family and obtain a dowry was an alluring prospect. As for mutual love it did not exist apparently, either in the bride or in him, in spite of Adelaida Ivanovna's beauty. This was, perhaps, a unique case of the kind in the life of Fyodor Pavlovitch, who was always of a voluptuous temper, and ready to run after any petticoat on the slightest encouragement. She seems to have been the only woman who made no particular appeal to his senses.

Immediatley after the elopement Adelaida Ivanovna discerned in a flash that she had no feeling for her husband but contempt. The marriage accordingly showed itself in its true colours with extraordinary rapidity. Although the family accepted the event pretty quickly and apportioned the runaway bride her dowry, the husband and wife began to lead a most disorderly life, and there were everlasting scenes between them. It was said that the young wife showed incomparably more generosity and dignity than Fyodor Pavlovitch, who, as is now known, got hold of all her money up to twenty five thousand roubles as soon as she received it, so that those thousands were lost to her forever. The little village and the rather fine town house which formed part of her dowry he did his utmost for a long time to transfer to his name, by means of some deed of conveyance. He would probably have succeeded, merely from her moral fatigue and desire to get rid of him, and from the contempt and loathing he aroused by his persistent and shameless importunity. But, fortunately, Adelaida Ivanovna's family intervened and circumvented his greediness. It is known for a fact that frequent fights took place between the husband and wife, but rumour had it that Fyodor Pavlovitch did not beat his wife but was beaten by her, for she was a hot-tempered, bold, dark-browed, impatient woman, possessed of remarkable physical strength. Finally, she left the house and ran away from Fyodor Pavlovitch with a destitute divinity student, leaving Mitya, a child of three years old, in her husband's hands. Immediately Fyodor Pavlovitch introduced a regular harem into the house, and abandoned himself to orgies of drunkenness. In the intervals he used to drive all over the province, complaining tearfully to each and all of Adelaida Ivanovna's having left him, going into details too disgraceful for a husband to mention in regard to his own married life. What seemed to gratify him and flatter his self-love most was to play the ridiculous part of the injured husband, and to parade his woes with embellishments.

"One would think that you'd got a promotion, Fyodor Pavlovitch, you seem so pleased in spite of your sorrow," scoffers said to him. Many even added that he was glad of a new comic part in which to play the buffoon, and that it was simply to make it funnier that he pretended to be unaware of his ludicrous position. But, who knows, it may have been simplicity. At last he succeeded in getting on the track of his runaway wife. The poor woman turned out to be in Petersburg, where she had gone with her divinity student, and where she had thrown herself into a life of complete emancipation. Fyodor Pavlovitch at once began bustling about, making preparations to go to Petersburg, with what object he could not himself have said. He would perhaps have really gone; but having determined to do so he felt at once entitled to fortify himself for the journey by another bout of reckless drinking. And just at that time his wife's family received the news of her death in Petersburg. She had died quite suddenly in a garret, according to one story, of typhus, or as another version had it, of starvation. Fyodor Pavlovitch was drunk when he heard of his wife's death, and the story is that he ran out into the street and began shouting with joy, raising his hands to Heaven: "Lord, now lettest Thou Thy servant depart in peace," but others say he wept without restraint like a little child, so much so that people were sorry for him, in spite of the repulsion he inspired. It is quite possible that both versions were true, that he rejoiced at his release, and at the same time wept for her who released him. As a general rule, people, even the wicked, are much more naive and simple-hearted than we suppose. And we ourselves are, too.

Chapter 2. He Gets Rid of His Eldest Son

You can easily imagine what a father such a man could be and how he would bring up his children. His behaviour as a father was exactly what might be expected. He completely abandoned the child of his marriage with Adelaida Ivanovna, not from malice, nor because of his matrimonial grievances, but simply because he forgot him. While he was wearying everyone with his tears and complaints, and turning his house into a sink of debauchery, a faithful servant of the family, Grigory, took the three-year old Mitya into his care. If he hadn't looked after him there would have been no one even to change the baby's little shirt.

It happened moreover that the child's relations on his mother's side forgot him too at first. His grandfather was no longer living, his widow, Mitya's grandmother, had moved to Moscow, and was seriously ill, while his daughters were married, so that Mitya remained for almost a whole year in old Grigory's charge and lived with him in the servant's cottage. But if his father had remembered him (he could not, indeed, have been altogether unaware of his existence) he would have sent him back to the cottage, as the child would only have been in the way of his debaucheries. But a cousin of Mitya's mother, Pyotr Alexandrovitch Miusov, happened to return from Paris. He lived for many years afterwards abroad, but was at that time quite a young man, and distinguished among the Miusovs as a man of enlightened ideas and of European culture, who had been in the capitals and abroad. Towards the end of his life he became a Liberal of the type common in the forties and fifties. In the course of his career he had come into contact with many of the most Liberal men of his epoch, both in Russia and abroad. He had known Proudhon and Bakunin personally, and in his declining years was very fond of describing the three days of the Paris Revolution of February, 1848, hinting that he himself had almost taken part in the fighting on the barricades. This was one of the most grateful recollections of his youth. He had an independent property of about a thousand souls, to reckon in the old style. His splendid estate lay on the outskirts of our little town and bordered on the lands of our famous monastery, with which Pyotr Alexandrovitch began an endless lawsuit, almost as soon as he came into the estate, concerning the rights of fishing in the river or wood-cutting in the forest, I don't know exactly which. He regarded it as his duty as a citizen and a man of culture to open an attack upon the "clericals." Hearing all about Adelaida Ivanovna, whom he, of course, remembered, and in whom he had at one time been interested, and learning of the existence of Mitya, he intervened, in spite of all his youthful indignation and contempt for Fyodor Pavlovitch. He made the latter's acquaintance for the first time, and told him directly that he wished to undertake the child's education. He used long afterwards to tell as a characteristic touch, that when he began to speak of Mitya, Fyodor Pavlovitch looked for some time as though he did not understand what child he was talking about, and even as though he was surprised to hear that he had a little son in the house. The story may have been exaggerated, yet it must have been something like the truth.

Fyodor Pavlovitch was all his life fond of acting, of suddenly playing an unexpected part, sometimes without any motive for doing so, and even to his own direct disadvantage, as, for instance, in the present case. This habit, however, is characteristic of a very great number of people, some of them very clever ones, not like Fyodor Pavlovitch. Pyotr Alexandrovitch carried the business through vigorously, and was appointed, with Fyodor Pavlovitch, joint guardian of the child, who had a small property, a house and land, left him by his mother. Mitya did, in fact, pass into this cousin's keeping, but as the latter had no family of his own, and after securing the revenues of his estates was in haste to return at once to Paris, he left the boy in charge of one of his cousins, a lady living in Moscow. It came to pass that, settling permanently in Paris he, too, forgot the child, especially when the Revolution of February broke out, making an impression on his mind that he remembered all the rest of his life. The Moscow lady died, and Mitya passed into the care of one of her married daughters. I believe he changed his home a fourth time later on. I won't enlarge upon that now, as I shall have much to tell later of Fyodor Pavlovitch's firstborn, and must confine myself now to the most essential facts about him, without which I could not begin my story.

In the first place, this Mitya, or rather Dmitri Fyodorovitch, was the only one of Fyodor Pavlovitch's three sons who grew up in the belief that he had property, and that he would be independent on coming of age. He spent an irregular boyhood and youth. He did not finish his studies at the gymnasium, he got into a military school, then went to the Caucasus, was promoted, fought a duel, and was degraded to the ranks, earned promotion again, led a wild life, and spent a good deal of money. He did not begin to receive any income from Fyodor Pavlovitch until he came of age, and until then got into debt. He saw and knew his father, Fyodor Pavlovitch, for the first time on coming of age, when he visited our neighbourhood on purpose to settle with him about his property. He seems not to have liked his father. He did not stay long with him, and made haste to get away, having only succeeded in obtaining a sum of money, and entering into an agreement for future payments from the estate, of the revenues and value of which he was unable (a fact worthy of note), upon this occasion, to get a statement from his father. Fyodor Pavlovitch remarked for the first time then (this, too, should be noted) that Mitya had a vague and exaggerated idea of his property. Fyodor Pavlovitch was very well satisfied with this, as it fell in with his own designs. He gathered only that the young man was frivolous, unruly, of violent passions, impatient, and dissipated, and that if he could only obtain ready money he would be satisfied, although only, of course, a short time. So Fyodor Pavlovitch began to take advantage of this fact, sending him from time to time small doles, instalments. In the end, when four years later, Mitya, losing patience, came a second time to our little town to settle up once for all with his father, it turned out to his amazement that he had nothing, that it was difficult to get an account even, that he had received the whole value of his property in sums of money from Fyodor Pavlovitch, and was perhaps even in debt to him, that by various agreements into which he had, of his own desire, entered at various previous dates, he had no right to expect anything more, and so on, and so on. The young man was overwhelmed, suspected deceit and cheating, and was almost beside himself. And, indeed, this circumstance led to the catastrophe, the account of which forms the subject of my first introductory story, or rather the external side of it. But before I pass to that story I must say a little of Fyodor Pavlovitch's other two sons, and of their origin.

Chapter 3. The Second Marriage and the Second Family

VERY shortly after getting his four-year-old Mitya off his hands Fyodor Pavlovitch married a second time. His second marriage lasted eight years. He took this second wife, Sofya Ivanovna, also a very young girl, from another province, where he had gone upon some small piece of business in company with a Jew. Though Fyodor Pavlovitch was a drunkard and a vicious debauchee he never neglected investing his capital, and managed his business affairs very successfully, though, no doubt, not over-scrupulously. Sofya Ivanovna was the daughter of an obscure deacon, and was left from childhood an orphan without relations. She grew up in the house of a general's widow, a wealthy old lady of good position, who was at once her benefactress and tormentor. I do not know the details, but I have only heard that the orphan girl, a meek and gentle creature, was once cut down from a halter in which she was hanging from a nail in the loft, so terrible were her sufferings from the caprice and everlasting nagging of this old woman, who was apparently not bad-hearted but had become an insufferable tyrant through idleness.

Fyodor Pavlovitch made her an offer; inquiries were made about him and he was refused. But again, as in his first marriage, he proposed an elopement to the orphan girl. There is very little doubt that she would not on any account have married him if she had known a little more about him in time. But she lived in another province; besides, what could a little girl of sixteen know about it, except that she would be better at the bottom of the river than remaining with her benefactress. So the poor child exchanged a benefactress for a benefactor. Fyodor Pavlovitch did not get a penny this time, for the general's widow was furious. She gave them nothing and cursed them both. But he had not reckoned on a dowry; what allured him was the remarkable beauty of the innocent girl, above all her innocent appearance, which had a peculiar attraction for a vicious profligate, who had hitherto admired only the coarser types of feminine beauty.

"Those innocent eyes slit my soul up like a razor," he used to say afterwards, with his loathsome snigger. In a man so depraved this might, of course, mean no more than sensual attraction. As he had received no dowry with his wife, and had, so to speak, taken her "from the halter," he did not stand on ceremony with her. Making her feel that she had "wronged" him, he took advantage of her phenomenal meekness and submissiveness to trample on the elementary decencies of marriage. He gathered loose women into his house, and carried on orgies of debauchery in his wife's presence. To show what a pass things had come to, I may mention that Grigory, the gloomy, stupid, obstinate, argumentative servant, who had always hated his first mistress, Adelaida Ivanovna, took the side of his new mistress. He championed her cause, abusing Fyodor Pavlovitch in a manner little befitting a servant, and on one occasion broke up the revels and drove all the disorderly women out of the house. In the end this unhappy young woman, kept in terror from her childhood, fell into that kind of nervous disease which is most frequently found in peasant women who are said to be "possessed by devils." At times after terrible fits of hysterics she even lost her reason. Yet she bore Fyodor Pavlovitch two sons, Ivan and Alexey, the eldest in the first year of marriage and the second three years later. When she died, little Alexey was in his fourth year, and, strange as it seems, I know that he remembered his mother all his life, like a dream, of course. At her death almost exactly the same thing happened to the two little boys as to their elder brother, Mitya. They were completely forgotten and abandoned by their father. They were looked after by the same Grigory and lived in his cottage, where they were found by the tyrannical old lady who had brought up their mother. She was still alive, and had not, all those eight years, forgotten the insult done her. All that time she was obtaining exact information as to her Sofya's manner of life, and hearing of her illness and hideous surroundings she declared aloud two or three times to her retainers:

"It serves her right. God has punished her for her ingratitude."

Exactly three months after Sofya Ivanovna's death the general's widow suddenly appeared in our town, and went straight to Fyodor Pavlovitch's house. She spent only half an hour in the town but she did a great deal. It was evening. Fyodor Pavlovitch, whom she had not seen for those eight years, came in to her drunk. The story is that instantly upon seeing him, without any sort of explanation, she gave him two good, resounding slaps on the face, seized him by a tuft of hair, and shook him three times up and down. Then, without a word, she went straight to the cottage to the two boys. Seeing, at the first glance, that they were unwashed and in dirty linen, she promptly gave Grigory, too, a box on the ear, and announcing that she would carry off both the children she wrapped them just as they were in a rug, put them in the carriage, and drove off to her own town. Grigory accepted the blow like a devoted slave, without a word, and when he escorted the old lady to her carriage he made her a low bow and pronounced impressively that, "God would repay her for orphans." "You are a blockhead all the same," the old lady shouted to him as she drove away.

Fyodor Pavlovitch, thinking it over, decided that it was a good thing, and did not refuse the general's widow his formal consent to any proposition in regard to his children's education. As for the slaps she had given him, he drove all over the town telling the story.

It happened that the old lady died soon after this, but she left the boys in her will a thousand roubles each "for their instruction, and so that all be spent on them exclusively, with the condition that it be so portioned out as to last till they are twenty-one, for it is more than adequate provision for such children. If other people think fit to throw away their money, let them." I have not read the will myself, but I heard there was something queer of the sort, very whimsically expressed. The principal heir, Yefim Petrovitch Polenov, the Marshal of Nobility of the province, turned out, however, to be an honest man. Writing to Fyodor Pavlovitch, and discerning at once that he could extract nothing from him for his children's education (though the latter never directly refused but only procrastinated as he always did in such cases, and was, indeed, at times effusively sentimental), Yefim Petrovitch took a personal interest in the orphans. He became especially fond of the younger, Alexey, who lived for a long while as one of his family. I beg the reader to note this from the beginning. And to Yefim Petrovitch, a man of a generosity and humanity rarely to be met with, the young people were more indebted for their education and bringing up than to anyone. He kept the two thousand roubles left to them by the general's widow intact, so that by the time they came of age their portions had been doubled by the accumulation of interest. He educated them both at his own expense, and certainly spent far more than a thousand roubles upon each of them. I won't enter into a detailed account of their boyhood and youth, but will only mention a few of the most important events. Of the elder, Ivan, I will only say that he grew into a somewhat morose and reserved, though far from timid boy. At ten years old he had realised that they were living not in their own home but on other people's charity, and that their father was a man of whom it was disgraceful to speak. This boy began very early, almost in his infancy (so they say at least), to show a brilliant and unusual aptitude for learning. I don't know precisely why, but he left the family of Yefim Petrovitch when he was hardly thirteen, entering a Moscow gymnasium and boarding with an experienced and celebrated teacher, an old friend of Yefim Petrovitch. Ivan used to declare afterwards that this was all due to the "ardour for good works" of Yefim Petrovitch, who was captivated by the idea that the boy's genius should be trained by a teacher of genius. But neither Yefim Petrovitch nor this teacher was living when the young man finished at the gymnasium and entered the university. As Yefim Petrovitch had made no provision for the payment of the tyrannical old lady's legacy, which had grown from one thousand to two, it was delayed, owing to formalities inevitable in Russia, and the young man was in great straits for the first two years at the university, as he was forced to keep himself all the time he was studying. It must be noted that he did not even attempt to communicate with his father, perhaps from pride, from contempt for him, or perhaps from his cool common sense, which told him that from such a father he would get no real assistance. However that may have been, the young man was by no means despondent and succeeded in getting work, at first giving sixpenny lessons and afterwards getting paragraphs on street incidents into the newspapers under the signature of "Eye-Witness." These paragraphs, it was said, were so interesting and piquant that they were soon taken. This alone showed the young man's practical and intellectual superiority over the masses of needy and unfortunate students of both sexes who hang about the offices of the newspapers and journals, unable to think of anything better than everlasting entreaties for copying and translations from the French. Having once got into touch with the editors Ivan Fyodorovitch always kept up his connection with them, and in his latter years at the university he published brilliant reviews of books upon various special subjects, so that he became well known in literary circles. But only in his last year he suddenly succeeded in attracting the attention of a far wider circle of readers, so that a great many people noticed and remembered him. It was rather a curious incident. When he had just left the university and was preparing to go abroad upon his two thousand roubles, Ivan Fyodorovitch published in one of the more important journals a strange article, which attracted general notice, on a subject of which he might have been supposed to know nothing, as he was a student of natural science. The article dealt with a subject which was being debated everywhere at the time--the position of the ecclesiastical courts. After discussing several opinions on the subject he went on to explain his own view. What was most striking about the article was its tone, and its unexpected conclusion. Many of the Church party regarded him unquestioningly as on their side. And yet not only the secularists but even atheists joined them in their applause. Finally some sagacious persons opined that the article was nothing but an impudent satirical burlesque. I mention this incident particularly because this article penetrated into the famous monastery in our neighbourhood, where the inmates, being particularly interested in question of the ecclesiastical courts, were completely bewildered by it. Learning the author's name, they were interested in his being a native of the town and the son of "that Fyodor Pavlovitch." And just then it was that the author himself made his appearance among us.

Why Ivan Fyodorovitch had come amongst us I remember asking myself at the time with a certain uneasiness. This fateful visit, which was the first step leading to so many consequences, I never fully explained to myself. It seemed strange on the face of it that a young man so learned, so proud, and apparently so cautious, should suddenly visit such an infamous house and a father who had ignored him all his life, hardly knew him, never thought of him, and would not under any circumstances have given him money, though he was always afraid that his sons Ivan and Alexey would also come to ask him for it. And here the young man was staying in the house of such a father, had been living with him for two months, and they were on the best possible terms. This last fact was a special cause of wonder to many others as well as to me. Pyotr Alexandrovitch Miusov, of whom we have spoken already, the cousin of Fyodor Pavlovitch's first wife, happened to be in the neighbourhood again on a visit to his estate. He had come from Paris, which was his permanent home. I remember that he was more surprised than anyone when he made the acquaintance of the young man, who interested him extremely, and with whom he sometimes argued and not without inner pang compared himself in acquirements.

"He is proud," he used to say, "he will never be in want of pence; he has got money enough to go abroad now. What does he want here? Everyone can see that he hasn't come for money, for his father would never give him any. He has no taste for drink and dissipation, and yet his father can't do without him. They get on so well together!"

That was the truth; the young man had an unmistakable influence over his father, who positively appeared to be behaving more decently and even seemed at times ready to obey his son, though often extremely and even spitefully perverse.

It was only later that we learned that Ivan had come partly at the request of, and in the interests of, his elder brother, Dmitri, whom he saw for the first time on this very visit, though he had before leaving Moscow been in correspondence with him about an important matter of more concern to Dmitri than himself. What that business was the reader will learn fully in due time. Yet even when I did know of this special circumstance I still felt Ivan Fyodorovitch to be an enigmatic figure, and thought his visit rather mysterious.

I may add that Ivan appeared at the time in the light of a mediator between his father and his elder brother Dmitri, who was in open quarrel with his father and even planning to bring an action against him.

The family, I repeat, was now united for the first time, and some of its members met for the first time in their lives. The younger brother, Alexey, had been a year already among us, having been the first of the three to arrive. It is of that brother Alexey I find it most difficult to speak in this introduction. Yet I must give some preliminary account of him, if only to explain one queer fact, which is that I have to introduce my hero to the reader wearing the cassock of a novice. Yes, he had been for the last year in our monastery, and seemed willing to be cloistered there for the rest of his life.

Chapter 4. The Third Son, Alyosha

He was only twenty, his brother Ivan was in his twenty-fourth year at the time, while their elder brother Dmitri was twenty-seven. First of all, I must explain that this young man, Alyosha, was not a fanatic, and, in my opinion at least, was not even a mystic. I may as well give my full opinion from the beginning. He was simply an early lover of humanity, and that he adopted the monastic life was simply because at that time it struck him, so to say, as the ideal escape for his soul struggling from the darkness of worldly wickedness to the light of love. And the reason this life struck him in this way was that he found in it at that time, as he thought an extrordinary being, our celebrated elder, Zossima, to whom he became attached with all the warm first love of his ardent heart. But I do not dispute that he was very strange even at that time, and had been so indeed from his cradle. I have mentioned already, by the way, that though he lost his mother in his fourth year he remembered her all his life her face, her caresses, "as though she stood living before me." Such memories may persist, as everyone knows, from an even earlier age, even from two years old, but scarcely standing out through a whole lifetime like spots of light out of darkness, like a corner torn out of a huge picture, which has all faded and disappeared except that fragment. That is how it was with him. He remembered one still summer evening, an open window, the slanting rays of the setting sun (that he recalled most vividly of all); in a corner of the room the holy image, before it a lighted lamp, and on her knees before the image his mother, sobbing hysterically with cries and moans, snatching him up in both arms, squeezing him close till it hurt, and praying for him to the Mother of God, holding him out in both arms to the image as though to put him under the Mother's protection...and suddenly a nurse runs in and snatches him from her in terror. That was the picture! And Alyosha remembered his mother's face at that minute. He used to say that it was frenzied but beautiful as he remembered. But he rarely cared to speak of this memory to anyone. In his childhood and youth he was by no means expansive, and talked little indeed, but not from shyness or a sullen unsociability; quite the contrary, from something different, from a sort of inner preoccupation entirely personal and unconcerned with other people, but so important to him that he seemed, as it were, to forget others on account of it. But he was fond of people: he seemed throughout his life to put implicit trust in people: yet no one ever looked on him as a simpleton or naive person. There was something about him which made one feel at once (and it was so all his life afterwards) that he did not care to be a judge of others that he would never take it upon himself to criticise and would never condemn anyone for anything. He seemed, indeed, to accept everything without the least condemnation though often grieving bitterly: and this was so much so that no one could surprise or frighten him even in his earliest youth. Coming at twenty to his father's house, which was a very sink of filthy debauchery, he, chaste and pure as he was, simply withdrew in silence when to look on was unbearable, but without the slightest sign of contempt or condemnation. His father, who had once been in a dependent position, and so was sensitive and ready to take offence, met him at first with distrust and sullenness. "He does not say much," he used to say, "and thinks the more." But soon, within a fortnight indeed, he took to embracing him and kissing him terribly often, with drunken tears, with sottish sentimentality, yet he evidently felt a real and deep affection for him, such as he had never been capable of feeling for anyone before.

Everyone, indeed, loved this young man wherever he went, and it was so from his earliest childhood. When he entered the household of his patron and benefactor, Yefim Petrovitch Polenov, he gained the hearts of all the family, so that they looked on him quite as their own child. Yet he entered the house at such a tender age that he could not have acted from design nor artfulness in winning affection. So that the gift of making himself loved directly and unconsciously was inherent in him, in his very nature, so to speak. It was the same at school, though he seemed to be just one of those children who are distrusted, sometimes ridiculed, and even disliked by their schoolfellows. He was dreamy, for instance, and rather solitary. From his earliest childhood he was fond of creeping into a corner to read, and yet he was a general favourite all the while he was at school. He was rarely playful or merry, but anyone could see at the first glance that this was not from any sullenness. On the contrary he was bright and good-tempered. He never tried to show off among his schoolfellows. Perhaps because of this, he was never afraid of anyone, yet the boys immediately understood that he was not proud of his fearlessness and seemed to be unaware that he was bold and courageous. He never resented an insult. It would happen that an hour after the offence he would address the offender or answer some question with as trustful and candid an expression as though nothing had happened between them. And it was not that he seemed to have forgotten or intentionally forgiven the affront, but simply that he did not regard it as an affront, and this completely conquered and captivated the boys. He had one characteristic which made all his schoolfellows from the bottom class to the top want to mock at him, not from malice but because it amused them. This characteristic was a wild fanatical modesty and chastity. He could not bear to hear certain words and certain conversations about women. There are "certain" words and conversations unhappily impossible to eradicate in schools. Boys pure in mind and heart, almost children, are fond of talking in school among themselves, and even aloud, of things, pictures, and images of which even soldiers would sometimes hesitate to speak. More than that, much that soldiers have no knowledge or conception of is familiar to quite young children of our intellectual and higher classes. There is no moral depravity, no real corrupt inner cynicism in it, but there is the appearance of it, and it is often looked upon among them as something refined, subtle, daring, and worthy of imitation. Seeing that Alyosha Karamazov put his fingers in his ears when they talked of "that," they used sometimes to crowd round him, pull his hands away, and shout nastiness into both ears, while he struggled, slipped to the floor, tried to hide himself without uttering one word of abuse, enduring their insults in silence. But at last they left him alone and gave up taunting him with being a "regular girl," and what's more they looked upon it with compassion as a weakness. He was always one of the best in the class but was never first.

At the time of Yefim Petrovitch's death Alyosha had two more years to complete at the provincial gymnasium. The inconsolable widow went almost immediately after his death for a long visit to Italy with her whole family, which consisted only of women and girls. Alyosha went to live in the house of two distant relations of Yefim Petrovitch, ladies whom he had never seen before. On what terms she lived with them he did not know himself. It was very characteristic of him, indeed, that he never cared at whose expense he was living. In that respect he was a striking contrast to his elder brother Ivan, who struggled with poverty for his first two years in the university, maintained himself by his own efforts, and had from childhood been bitterly conscious of living at the expense of his benefactor. But this strange trait in Alyosha's character must not, I think, criticised too severely, for at the slightest acquaintance with him anyone would have perceived that Alyosha was one of those youths, almost of the type of religious enthusiast, who, if they were suddenly to come into possession of a large fortune, would not hesitate to give it away for the asking, either for good works or perhaps to a clever rogue. In general he seemed scarcely to know the value of money, not, of course, in a literal sense. When he was given pocket-money, which he never asked for, he was either terribly careless of it so that it was gone in a moment, or he kept it for weeks together, not knowing what to do with it.

In later years Pyotr Alexandrovitch Miusov, a man very sensitive on the score of money and bourgeois honesty, pronounced the following judgment, after getting to know Alyosha:

"Here is perhaps the one man in the world whom you might leave alone without a penny, in the centre of an unknown town of a million inhabitants, and he would not come to harm, he would not die of cold and hunger, for he would be fed and sheltered at once; and if he were not, he would find a shelter for himself, and it would cost him no effort or humiliation. And to shelter him would be no burden, but, on the contrary, would probably be looked on as a pleasure."

He did not finish his studies at the gymnasium. A year before the end of the course he suddenly announced to the ladies that he was going to see his father about a plan which had occurred to him. They were sorry and unwilling to let him go. The journey was not an expensive one, and the ladies would not let him pawn his watch, a parting present from his benefactor's family. They provided him liberally with money and even fitted him out with new clothes and linen. But he returned half the money they gave him, saying that he intended to go third class. On his arrival in the town he made no answer to his father's first inquiry why he had come before completing his studies, and seemed, so they say, unusually thoughtful. It soon became apparent that he was looking for his mother's tomb. He practically acknowledged at the time that that was the only object of his visit. But it can hardly have been the whole reason of it. It is more probable that he himself did not understand and could not explain what had suddenly arisen in his soul, and drawn him irresistibly into a new, unknown, but inevitable path. Fyodor Pavlovitch could not show him where his second wife was buried, for he had never visited her grave since he had thrown earth upon her coffin, and in the course of years had entirely forgotten where she was buried.

Fyodor Pavlovitch, by the way, had for some time previously not been living in our town. Three or four years after his wife's death he had gone to the south of Russia and finally turned up in Odessa, where he spent several years. He made the acquaintance at first, in his own words, "of a lot of low Jews, Jewesses, and Jewkins," and ended by being received by "Jews high and low alike." It may be presumed that at this period he developed a peculiar faculty for making and hoarding money. He finally returned to our town only three years before

Alyosha's arrival. His former acquaintances found him looking terribly aged, although he was by no means an old man. He behaved not exactly with more dignity but with more effrontery. The former buffoon showed an insolent propensity for making buffoons of others. His depravity with women was not as it used to be, but even more revolting. In a short time he opened a great number of new taverns in the district. It was evident that he had perhaps a hundred thousand roubles or not much less. Many of the inhabitants of the town and district were soon in his debt, and, of course, had given good security. Of late, too, he looked somehow bloated and seemed more irresponsible, more uneven, had sunk into a sort of incoherence, used to begin one thing and go on with another, as though he were letting himself go altogether. He was more and more frequently drunk. And, if it had not been for the same servant Grigory, who by that time had aged considerably too, and used to look after him sometimes almost like a tutor, Fyodor Pavlovitch might have got into terrible scrapes. Alyosha's arrival seemed to affect even his moral side, as though something had awakened in this prematurely old man which had long been dead in his soul.

"Do you know," he used often to say, looking at Alyosha, "that you are like her, 'the crazy woman'"--that was what he used to call his dead wife, Alyosha's mother. Grigory it was who pointed out the "crazy woman's" grave to Alyosha. He took him to our town cemetery and showed him in a remote corner a cast-iron tombstone, cheap but decently kept, on which were inscribed the name and age of the deceased and the date of her death, and below a four-lined verse, such as are commonly used on old-fashioned middle-class tombs. To Alyosha's amazement this tomb turned out to be Grigory's doing. He had put it up on the poor "crazy woman's" grave at his own expense, after Fyodor Pavlovitch, whom he had often pestered about the grave, had gone to Odessa, abandoning the grave and all his memories. Alyosha showed no particular emotion at the sight of his mother's grave. He only listened to Grigory's minute and solemn account of the erection of the tomb; he stood with bowed head and walked away without uttering a word. It was perhaps a year before he visited the cemetery again. But this little episode was not without an influence upon Fyodor Pavlovitch--and a very original one. He suddenly took a thousand roubles to our monastery to pay for requiems for the soul of his wife; but not for the second, Alyosha's mother, the "crazy woman," but for the first, Adelaida Ivanovna, who used to thrash him. In the evening of the same day he got drunk and abused the monks to Alyosha. He himself was far from being religious; he had probably never put a penny candle before the image of a saint. Strange impulses of sudden feeling and sudden thought are common in such types.

I have mentioned already that he looked bloated. His countenance at this time bore traces of something that testified unmistakably to the life he had led. Besides the long fleshy bags under his little, always insolent, suspicious, and ironical eyes; besides the multitude of deep wrinkles in his little fat face, the Adam's apple hung below his sharp chin like a great, fleshy goitre, which gave him a peculiar, repulsive, sensual appearance; add to that a long rapacious mouth with full lips, between which could be seen little stumps of black decayed teeth. He slobbered every time he began to speak. He was fond indeed of making fun of his own face, though, I believe, he was well satisfied with it. He used particularly to point to his nose, which was not very large, but very delicate and conspicuously aquiline. "A regular Roman nose," he used to say, "with my goitre I've quite the countenance of an ancient Roman patrician of the decadent period." He seemed proud of it.

Not long after visiting his mother's grave Alyosha suddenly announced that he wanted to enter the monastery, and that the monks were willing to receive him as a novice. He explained that this was his strong desire, and that he was solemnly asking his consent as his father. The old man knew that the elder Zossima, who was living in the monastery hermitage, had made a special impression upon his "gentle boy."

"That is the most honest monk among them, of course," he observed, after listening in thoughtful silence to Alyosha, and seeming scarcely surprised at his request. "H'm!...So that's where you want to be, my gentle boy?"

He was half drunk, and suddenly he grinned his slow half-drunken grin, which was not without a certain cunning and tipsy slyness. "H'm!...I had a presentiment that you would end in something like this. Would you believe it? You were making straight for it. Well, to be sure you have your own two thousand. That's a dowry for you. And I'll never desert you, my angel. And I'll pay what's wanted for you there, if they ask for it. But, of course, if they don't ask, why should we worry them? What do you say? You know, you spend money like a canary, two grains a week. H'm!...Do you know that near one monastery there's a place outside the town where every baby knows there are none but 'the monks' wives' living, as they are called. Thirty women, I believe. I have been there myself. You know, it's interesting in its way, of course, as a variety. The worst of it is it's awfully Russian. There are no French women there. Of course, they could get them fast enough, they have plenty of money. If they get to hear of it they'll come along. Well, there's nothing of that sort here, no 'monks' wives,' and two hundred monks. They're honest. They keep the fasts. I admit it...H'm...So you want to be a monk? And do you know I'm sorry to lose you, Alyosha; would you believe it, I've really grown fond of you? Well, it's a good opportunity. You'll pray for us sinners; we have sinned too much here. I've always been thinking who would pray for me, and whether there's anyone in the world to do it. My dear boy, I'm awfully stupid about that. You wouldn't believe it. Awfully. You see, however stupid I am about it, I keep thinking, I keep thinking--from time to time, of course, not all the while. It's impossible, I think, for the devils to forget to drag me down to hell with their hooks when I die. Then I wonder--hooks? Where would they get them? What of? Iron hooks? Where do they forge them? Have they a foundry there of some sort? The monks in the monastery probably believe that there's a ceiling in hell, for instance. Now I'm ready to believe in hell, but without a ceiling. It makes it more refined, more enlightened, more Lutheran that is. And, after all, what does it matter whether it has a ceiling or hasn't? But, do you know, there's a damnable question involved in it? If there's no ceiling there can be no hooks, and if there are no hooks it all breaks down, which is unlikely again, for then there would be none to drag me down to hell, and if they don't drag me down what justice is there in the world? Il faudrait les inventer,* those hooks, on purpose for me alone, for, if you only knew, Alyosha, what a black-guard I am."

* It would be neccessary to invent them.

"But there are no hooks there," said Alyosha, looking gently and seriously at his father.

"Yes, yes, only the shadows of hooks. I know, I know. That's how a Frenchman described hell: 'J'ai vu l'ombre d'un cocher qui avec l'ombre d'une brosse frottait l'ombre d'une carrosse.'* How do you know there are no hooks, darling? When you've lived with the monks you'll sing a different tune. But go and get at the truth there, and then come and tell me. Anyway it's easier going to the other world if one knows what there is there. Besides, it will be more seemly for you with the monks than here with me, with a drunken old man and young harlots...though you're like an angel, nothing touches you. And I dare say nothing will touch you there. That's why I let you go, because I hope for that. You've got all your wits about you. You will burn and you will burn out; you will be healed and come back again. And I will wait for you. I feel that you're the only creature in the world who has not condemned me. My dear boy, I feel it, you know. I can't help feeling it."

* I've seen the shadow of a coachman rubbing the shadow of a coach with the shadow of a brush.

And he even began blubbering. He was sentimental. He was wicked and sentimental.

Chapter 5. Elders

Some of my readers may imagine that my young man was a sickly, ecstatic, poorly developed creature, a pale, consumptive dreamer. On the contrary, Alyosha was at this time a well-grown, red-cheeked, clear-eyed lad of nineteen, radiant with health. He was very handsome, too, graceful, moderately tall, with hair of a dark brown, with a regular, rather long, oval-shaped face, and wide-set dark grey, shining eyes; he was very thoughtful, and apparently very serene. I shall be told, perhaps, that red cheeks are not incompatible with fanaticism and mysticism; but I fancy that Alyosha was more of a realist than anyone. Oh! no doubt, in the monastery he fully believed in miracles, but, to my thinking, miracles are never a stumbling-block to the realist. It is not miracles that dispose realists to belief. The genuine realist, if he is an unbeliever, will always find strength and ability to disbelieve in the miraculous, and if he is confronted with a miracle as an irrefutable fact he would rather disbelieve his own senses than admit the fact. Even if he admits it, he admits it as a fact of nature till then unrecognised by him. Faith does not, in the realist, spring from the miracle but the miracle from faith. If the realist once believes, then he is bound by his very realism to admit the miraculous also. The Apostle Thomas said that he would not believe till he saw, but when he did see he said, "My Lord and my God!" Was it the miracle forced him to believe? Most likely not, but he believed solely because he desired to believe and possibly he fully believed in his secret heart even when he said, "I do not believe till I see."

I shall be told, perhaps, that Alyosha was stupid, undeveloped, had not finished his studies, and so on. That he did not finish his studies is true, but to say that he was stupid or dull would be a great injustice. I'll simply repeat what I have said above. He entered upon this path only because, at that time, it alone struck his imagination and presented itself to him as offering an ideal means of escape for his soul from darkness to light. Add to that that he was to some extent a youth of our last epoch--that is, honest in nature, desiring the truth, seeking for it and believing in it, and seeking to serve it at once with all the strength of his soul, seeking for immediate action, and ready to sacrifice everything, life itself, for it. Though these young men unhappily fail to understand that the sacrifice of life is, in many cases, the easiest of all sacrifices, and that to sacrifice, for instance, five or six years of their seething youth to hard and tedious study, if only to multiply tenfold their powers of serving the truth and the cause they have set before them as their goal such a sacrifice is utterly beyond the strength of many of them. The path Alyosha chose was a path going in the opposite direction, but he chose it with the same thirst for swift achievement. As soon as he reflected seriously he was convinced of the existence of God and immortality, and at once he instinctively said to himself: "I want to live for immortality, and I will accept no compromise." In the same way, if he had decided that God and immortality did not exist, he would at once have become an atheist and a socialist. For socialism is not merely the labour question, it is before all things the atheistic question, the question of the form taken by atheism to-day, the question of the tower of Babel built without God, not to mount to heaven from earth but to set up heaven on earth. Alyosha would have found it strange and impossible to go on living as before. It is written: "Give all that thou hast to the poor and follow Me, if thou wouldst be perfect."

Alyosha said to himself: "I can't give two roubles instead of 'all,' and only go to mass instead of 'following Him.'" Perhaps his memories of childhood brought back our monastery, to which his mother may have taken him to mass. Perhaps the slanting sunlight and the holy image to which his poor "crazy" mother had held him up still acted upon his imagination. Brooding on these things he may have come to us perhaps only to see whether here he could sacrifice all or only "two roubles," and in the monastery he met this elder. I must digress to explain what an "elder" is in Russian monasteries, and I am sorry that I do not feel very competent to do so. I will try, however, to give a superficial account of it in a few words. Authorities on the subject assert that the institution of "elders" is of recent date, not more than a hundred years old in our monasteries, though in the orthodox East, especially in Sinai and Athos, it has existed over a thousand years. It is maintained that it existed in ancient times in Russia also, but through the calamities which overtook Russia--the Tartars, civil war, the interruption of relations with the East after the destruction of Constantinople--this institution fell into oblivion. It was revived among us towards the end of last century by one of the great "ascetics," as they called him, Paissy Velitchkovsky, and his disciples. But to this day it exists in few monasteries only, and has sometimes been almost persecuted as an innovation in Russia. It flourished especially in the celebrated Kozelski Optin Monastery. When and how it was introduced into our monastery I cannot say. There had already been three such elders and Zossima was the last of them. But he was almost dying of weakness and disease, and they had no one to take his place. The question for our monastery was an important one, for it had not been distinguished by anything in particular till then: they had neither relics of saints, nor wonder--working ikons, nor glorious traditions, nor historical exploits. It had flourished and been glorious all over Russia through its elders, to see and hear whom pilgrims had flocked for thousands of miles from all parts.

What was such an elder? An elder was one who took your soul, your will, into his soul and his will. When you choose an elder, you renounce your own will and yield it to him in complete submission, complete self-abnegation. This novitiate, this terrible school of abnegation, is undertaken voluntarily, in the hope of self-conquest, of self-mastery, in order, after a life of obedience, to attain perfect freedom, that is, from self; to escape the lot of those who have lived their whole life without finding their true selves in themselves. This institution of elders is not founded on theory, but was established in the East from the practice of a thousand years. The obligations due to an elder are not the ordinary "obedience" which has always existed in our Russian monasteries. The obligation involves confession to the elder by all who have submitted themselves to him, and to the indissoluble bond between him and them.

The story is told, for instance, that in the early days of Christianity one such novice, failing to fulfil some command laid upon him by his elder, left his monastery in Syria and went to Egypt. There, after great exploits, he was found worthy at last to suffer torture and a martyr's death for the faith. When the Church, regarding him as a saint, was burying him, suddenly, at the deacon's exhortation, "Depart all ye unbaptised," the coffin containing the martyr's body left its place and was cast forth from the church, and this took place three times. And only at last they learnt that this holy man had broken his vow of obedience and left his elder, and, therefore, could not be forgiven without the elder's absolution in spite of his great deeds. Only after this could the funeral take place. This, of course, is only an old legend. But here is a recent instance.

A monk was suddenly commanded by his elder to quit Athos, which he loved as a sacred place and a haven of refuge, and to go first to Jerusalem to do homage to the Holy Places and then to go to the north to Siberia: "There is the place for thee and not here." The monk, overwhelmed with sorrow, went to the Oecumenical Patriarch at Constantinople and besought him to release him from his obedience. But the Patriarch replied that not only was he unable to release him, but there was not and could not be on earth a power which could release him except the elder who had himself laid that duty upon him. In this way the elders are endowed in certain cases with unbounded and inexplicable authority. That is why in many of our monasteries the institution was at first resisted almost to persecution. Meantime the elders immediately began to be highly esteemed among the people. Masses of the ignorant people as well as of distinction flocked, for instance, to the elders of our monastery to confess their doubts, their sins, and their sufferings, and ask for counsel and admonition. Seeing this, the opponents of the elders declared that the sacrament of confession was being arbitrarily and frivolously degraded, though the continual opening of the heart to the elder by the monk or the layman had nothing of the character of the sacrament. In the end, however, the institution of elders has been retained and is becoming established in Russian monasteries. It is true, perhaps, that this instrument which had stood the test of a thousand years for the moral regeneration of a man from slavery to freedom and to moral perfectibility may be a two-edged weapon and it may lead some not to humility and complete self-control but to the most Satanic pride, that is, to bondage and not to freedom.

The elder Zossima was sixty-five. He came of a family of landowners, had been in the army in early youth, and served in the Caucasus as an officer. He had, no doubt, impressed Alyosha by some peculiar quality of his soul. Alyosha lived in the cell of the elder, who was very fond of him and let him wait upon him. It must be noted that Alyosha was bound by no obligation and could go where he pleased and be absent for whole days. Though he wore the monastic dress it was voluntarily, not to be different from others. No doubt he liked to do so. Possibly his youthful imagination was deeply stirred by the power and fame of his elder. It was said that so many people had for years past come to confess their sins to Father Zossima and to entreat him for words of advice and healing, that he had acquired the keenest intuition and could tell from an unknown face what a new-comer wanted, and what was the suffering on his conscience. He sometimes astounded and almost alarmed his visitors by his knowledge of their secrets before they had spoken a word.

Alyosha noticed that many, almost all, went in to the elder for the first time with apprehension and uneasiness, but came out with bright and happy faces. Alyosha was particularly struck by the fact that Father Zossima was not at all stern. On the contrary, he was always almost gay. The monks used to say that he was more drawn to those who were more sinful, and the greater the sinner the more he loved him. There were, no doubt, up to the end of his life, among the monks some who hated and envied him, but they were few in number and they were silent, though among them were some of great dignity in the monastery, one, for instance, of the older monks distinguished for his strict keeping of fasts and vows of silence. But the majority were on Father Zossima's side and very many of them loved him with all their hearts, warmly and sincerely. Some were almost fanatically devoted to him, and declared, though not quite aloud, that he was a saint, that there could be no doubt of it, and, seeing that his end was near, they anticipated miracles and great glory to the monastery in the immediate future from his relics. Alyosha had unquestioning faith in the miraculous power of the elder, just as he had unquestioning faith in the story of the coffin that flew out of the church. He saw many who came with sick children or relatives and besought the elder to lay hands on them and to pray over them, return shortly after-- some the next day--and, falling in tears at the elder's feet, thank him for healing their sick.

Whether they had really been healed or were simply better in the natural course of the disease was a question which did not exist for Alyosha, for he fully believed in the spiritual power of his teacher and rejoiced in his fame, in his glory, as though it were his own triumph. His heart throbbed, and he beamed, as it were, all over when the elder came out to the gates of the hermitage into the waiting crowd of pilgrims of the humbler class who had flocked from all parts of Russia on purpose to see the elder and obtain his blessing. They fell down before him, wept, kissed his feet, kissed the earth on which he stood, and wailed, while the women held up their children to him and brought him the sick "possessed with devils." The elder spoke to them, read a brief prayer over them, blessed them, and dismissed them. Of late he had become so weak through attacks of illness that he was sometimes unable to leave his cell, and the pilgrims waited for him to come out for several days. Alyosha did not wonder why they loved him so, why they fell down before him and wept with emotion merely at seeing his face. Oh! he understood that for the humble soul of the Russian peasant, worn out by grief and toil, and still more by the everlasting injustice and everlasting sin, his own and the world's, it was the greatest need and comfort to find someone or something holy to fall down before and worship.

"Among us there is sin, injustice, and temptation, but yet, somewhere on earth there is someone holy and exalted. He has the truth; he knows the truth; so it is not dead upon the earth; so it will come one day to us, too, and rule over all the earth according to the promise."

Alyosha knew that this was just how the people felt and even reasoned. He understood it, but that the elder Zossima was this saint and custodian of God's truth--of that he had no more doubt than the weeping peasants and the sick women who held out their children to the elder. The conviction that after his death the elder would bring extraordinary glory to the monastery was even stronger in Alyosha than in anyone there, and, of late, a kind of deep flame of inner ecstasy burnt more and more strongly in his heart. He was not at all troubled at this elder's standing as a solitary example before him.

"No matter. He is holy. He carries in his heart the secret of renewal for all: that power which will, at last, establish truth on the earth, and all men will be holy and love one another, and there will be no more rich nor poor, no exalted nor humbled, but all will be as the children of God, and the true Kingdom of Christ will come." That was the dream in Alyosha's heart.

The arrival of his two brothers, whom he had not known till then, seemed to make a great impression on Alyosha. He more quickly made friends with his half-brother Dmitri (though he arrived later) than with his own brother Ivan. He was extremely interested in his brother Ivan, but when the latter had been two months in the town, though they had met fairly often, they were still not intimate. Alyosha was naturally silent, and he seemed to be expecting something, ashamed about something, while his brother Ivan, though Alyosha noticed at first that he looked long and curiously at him, seemed soon to have left off thinking of him. Alyosha noticed it with some embarrassment. He ascribed his brother's indifference at first to the disparity of their age and education.

But he also wondered whether the absence of curiosity and sympathy in Ivan might be due to some other cause entirely unknown to him. He kept fancying that Ivan was absorbed in something--something inward and important--that he was striving towards some goal, perhaps very hard to attain, and that that was why he had no thought for him. Alyosha wondered, too, whether there was not some contempt on the part of the learned atheist for him--a foolish novice. He knew for certain that his brother was an atheist. He could not take offence at this contempt, if it existed; yet, with an uneasy embarrassment which he did not himself understand, he waited for his brother to come nearer to him. Dmitri used to speak of Ivan with the deepest respect and with a peculiar earnestness. From him Alyosha learnt all the details of the important affair which had of late formed such a close and remarkable bond between the two elder brothers. Dmitri's enthusiastic references to Ivan were the more striking in Alyosha's eyes since Dmitri was, compared with Ivan, almost uneducated, and the two brothers were such a contrast in personality and character that it would be difficult to find two men more unlike.

It was at this time that the meeting, or, rather gathering of the members of this inharmonious family took place in the cell of the elder who had such an extraordinary influence on Alyosha. The pretext for this gathering was a false one. It was at this time that the discord between Dmitri and his father seemed at its acutest stage and their relations had become insufferably strained. Fyodor Pavlovitch seems to have been the first to suggest, apparently in joke, that they should all meet in Father Zossima's cell, and that, without appealing to his direct intervention, they might more decently come to an understanding under the conciliating influence of the elder's presence. Dmitri, who had never seen the elder, naturally supposed that his father was trying to intimidate him, but, as he secretly blamed himself for his outbursts of temper with his father on several recent occasions, he accepted the challenge. It must be noted that he was not, like Ivan, staying with his father, but living apart at the other end of the town. It happened that Pyotr Alexandrovitch Miusov, who was staying in the district at the time, caught eagerly at the idea. A Liberal of the forties and fifties, a freethinker and atheist, he may have been led on by boredom or the hope of frivolous diversion. He was suddenly seized with the desire to see the monastery and the holy man. As his lawsuit with the monastery still dragged on, he made it the pretext for seeing the Superior, in order to attempt to settle it amicably. A visitor coming with such laudable intentions might be received with more attention and consideration than if he came from simple curiosity. Influences from within the monastery were brought to bear on the elder, who of late had scarcely left his cell, and had been forced by illness to deny even his ordinary visitors. In the end he consented to see them, and the day was fixed.

"Who has made me a judge over them?" was all he said, smilingly, to Alyosha.

Alyosha was much perturbed when he heard of the proposed visit. Of all the wrangling, quarrelsome party, Dmitri was the only one who could regard the interview seriously. All the others would come from frivolous motives, perhaps insulting to the elder. Alyosha was well aware of that. Ivan and Miusov would come from curiosity, perhaps of the coarsest kind, while his father might be contemplating some piece of buffoonery. Though he said nothing, Alyosha thoroughly understood his father. The boy, I repeat, was far from being so simple as everyone thought him. He awaited the day with a heavy heart. No doubt he was always pondering in his mind how the family discord could be ended. But his chief anxiety concerned the elder. He trembled for him, for his glory, and dreaded any affront to him, especially the refined, courteous irony of Miusov and the supercilious half-utterances of the highly educated Ivan. He even wanted to venture on warning the elder, telling him something about them, but, on second thoughts, said nothing. He only sent word the day before, through a friend, to his brother Dmitri, that he loved him and expected him to keep his promise. Dmitri wondered, for he could not remember what he had promised, but he answered by letter that he would do his utmost not to let himself be provoked "by vileness," but that, although he had a deep respect for the elder and for his brother Ivan, he was convinced that the meeting was either a trap for him or an unworthy farce.

"Nevertheless I would rather bite out my tongue than be lacking in respect to the sainted man whom you reverence so highly," he wrote in conclusion. Alyosha was not greatly cheered by the letter.

Book II. An Unfortunate Gathering
Chapter 1. They Arrive at the Monastery

IT was a warm, bright day the end of August. The interview with the elder had been fixed for half-past eleven, immediately after late mass. Our visitors did not take part in the service, but arrived just as it was over. First an elegant open carriage, drawn by two valuable horses, drove up with Miusov and a distant relative of his, a young man of twenty, called Pyotr Fomitch Kalganov. This young man was preparing to enter the university. Miusov with whom he was staying for the time, was trying to persuade him to go abroad to the university of Zurich or Jena. The young man was still undecided. He was thoughtful and absent-minded. He was nice-looking, strongly built, and rather tall. There was a strange fixity in his gaze at times. Like all very absent-minded people he would sometimes stare at a person without seeing him. He was silent and rather awkward, but sometimes, when he was alone with anyone, he became talkative and effusive, and would laugh at anything or nothing. But his animation vanished as quickly as it appeared. He was always well and even elaborately dressed; he had already some independent fortune and expectations of much more. He was a friend of Alyosha's.

In an ancient, jolting, but roomy, hired carriage, with a pair of old pinkish-grey horses, a long way behind Miusov's carriage, came Fyodor Pavlovitch, with his son Ivan. Dmitri was late, though he had been informed of the time the evening before. The visitors left their carriage at the hotel, outside the precincts, and went to the gates of the monastery on foot. Except Fyodor Pavlovitch, more of the party had ever seen the monastery, and Miusov had probably not even been to church for thirty years. He looked about him with curiosity, together with assumed ease. But, except the church and the domestic buildings, though these too were ordinary enough, he found nothing of interest in the interior of the monastery. The last of the worshippers were coming out of the church bareheaded and crossing themselves. Among the humbler people were a few of higher rank--two or three ladies and a very old general. They were all staying at the hotel. Our visitors were at once surrounded by beggars, but none of them gave them anything, except young Kalganov, who took a ten-copeck piece out of his purse, and, nervous and embarrassed--God knows why!--hurriedly gave it to an old woman, saying: "Divide it equally." None of his companions made any remark upon it, so that he had no reason to be embarrassed; but, perceiving this, he was even more overcome.

It was strange that their arrival did not seem expected, and that they were not received with special honour, though one of them had recently made a donation of a thousand roubles, while another was a very wealthy and highly cultured landowner, upon whom all in the monastery were in a sense dependent, as a decision of the lawsuit might at any moment put their fishing rights in his hands. Yet no official personage met them.

Miusov looked absent-mindedly at the tombstones round the church, and was on the point of saying that the dead buried here must have paid a pretty penny for the right of lying in this "holy place," but refrained. His liberal irony was rapidly changing almost into anger.

"Who the devil is there to ask in this imbecile place? We must find out, for time is passing," he observed suddenly, as though speaking to himself.

All at once there came up a bald-headed, elderly man with ingratiating little eyes, wearing a full, summer overcoat. Lifting his hat, he introduced himself with a honeyed lisp as Maximov, a landowner of Tula. He at once entered into our visitors' difficulty.

"Father Zossima lives in the hermitage, apart, four hundred paces from the monastery, the other side of the copse."

"I know it's the other side of the copse," observed Fyodor Pavlovitch, "but we don't remember the way. It is a long time since we've been here."

"This way, by this gate, and straight across the copse...the copse. Come with me, won't you? I'll show you. I have to go...I am going myself. This way, this way."

They came out of the gate and turned towards the copse. Maximov, a man of sixty, ran rather than walked, turning sideways to stare at them all, with an incredible degree of nervous curiosity. His eyes looked starting out of his head.

"You see, we have come to the elder upon business of our own," observed Miusov severely. "That personage has granted us an audience, so to speak, and so, though we thank you for showing us the way, we cannot ask you to accompany us."

"I've been there. I've been already; un chevalier parfait," and Maximov snapped his fingers in the air.

"Who is a chevalier?" asked Miusov.

"The elder, the splendid elder, the elder! The honour and glory of the monastery, Zossima. Such an elder!"

But his incoherent talk was cut short by a very pale, wan-looking monk of medium height wearing a monk's cap, who overtook them. Fyodor Pavlovitch and Miusov stopped.

The monk, with an extremely courteous, profound bow, announced:

"The Father Superior invites all of you gentlemen to dine with him after your visit to the hermitage. At one o'clock, not later. And you also," he added, addressing Maximov.

"That I certainly will, without fail," cried Fyodor Pavlovitch, hugely delighted at the invitation. "And, believe me, we've all given our word to behave properly here...And you, Pyotr Alexandrovitch, will you go, too?"

"Yes, of course. What have I come for but to study all the customs here? The only obstacle to me is your company..."

"Yes, Dmitri Fyodorovitch is non-existent as yet."

"It would be a capital thing if he didn't turn up. Do you suppose I like all this business, and in your company, too? So we will come to dinner. Thank the Father Superior," he said to the monk.

"No, it is my duty now to conduct you to the elder," answered the monk.

"If so I'll go straight to the Father Superior--to the Father Superior," babbled Maximov.

"The Father Superior is engaged just now. But as you please--" the monk hesitated.

"Impertinent old man!" Miusov observed aloud, while Maximov ran back to the monastery.

"He's like von Sohn," Fyodor Pavlovitch said suddenly.

"Is that all you can think of?...In what way is he like von Sohn? Have you ever seen von Sohn?"

"I've seen his portrait. It's not the features, but something indefinable. He's a second von Sohn. I can always tell from the physiognomy."

"Ah, I dare say you are a connoisseur in that. But, look here, Fyodor Pavlovitch, you said just now that we had given our word to behave properly. Remember it. I advise you to control yourself. But, if you begin to play the fool I don't intend to be associated with you here...You see what a man he is"--he turned to the monk--"I'm afraid to go among decent people with him." A fine smile, not without a certain slyness, came on to the pale, bloodless lips of the monk, but he made no reply, and was evidently silent from a sense of his own dignity. Miusov frowned more than ever.

"Oh, devil take them all! An outer show elaborated through centuries, and nothing but charlatanism and nonsense underneath," flashed through Miusov's mind.

"Here's the hermitage. We've arrived," cried Fyodor Pavlovitch. "The gates are shut."

And he repeatedly made the sign of the cross to the saints painted above and on the sides of the gates.

"When you go to Rome you must do as the Romans do. Here in this hermitage there are twenty-five saints being saved. They look at one another, and eat cabbages. And not one woman goes in at this gate. That's what is remarkable. And that really is so. But I did hear that the elder receives ladies," he remarked suddenly to the monk.

"Women of the people are here too now, lying in the portico there waiting. But for ladies of higher rank two rooms have been built adjoining the portico, but outside the precincts you can see the windows--and the elder goes out to them by an inner passage when he is well enough. They are always outside the precincts. There is a Harkov lady, Madame Hohlakov, waiting there now with her sick daughter. Probably he has promised to come out to her, though of late he has been so weak that he has hardly shown himself even to the people."

"So then there are loopholes, after all, to creep out of the hermitage to the ladies. Don't suppose, holy father, that I mean any harm. But do you know that at Athos not only the visits of women are not allowed, but no creature of the female sex--no hens, nor turkey hens, nor cows."

"Fyodor Pavlovitch, I warn you I shall go back and leave you here. They'll turn you out when I'm gone."

"But I'm not interfering with you, Pyotr Alexandrovitch. Look," he cried suddenly, stepping within the precincts, "what a vale of roses they live in!"

Though there were no roses now, there were numbers of rare and beautiful autumn flowers growing wherever there was space for them, and evidently tended by a skilful hand; there were flower-beds round the church, and between the tombs; and the one-storied wooden house where the elder lived was also surrounded with flowers.

"And was it like this in the time of the last elder, Varsonofy? He didn't care for such elegance. They say he used to jump up and thrash even ladies with a stick," observed Fyodor Pavlovitch, as he went up the steps.

"The elder Varsonofy did sometimes seem rather strange, but a great deal that's told is foolishness. He never thrashed anyone," answered the monk. "Now, gentlemen, if you will wait a minute I will announce you."

"Fyodor Pavlovitch, for the last time, your compact, do you hear? Behave properly or I will pay you out!" Miusov had time to mutter again.

"I can't think why you are so agitated," Fyodor Pavlovitch observed sarcastically. "Are you uneasy about your sins? They say he can tell by one's eyes what one has come about. And what a lot you think of their opinion! you, a Parisian, and so advanced. I'm surprised at you."

But Miusov had no time to reply to this sarcasm. They were asked to come in. He walked in, somewhat irritated.

"Now, I know myself, I am annoyed, I shall lose my temper and begin to quarrel--and lower myself and my ideas," he reflected.

Chapter 2. The Old Buffoon

THEY entered the room almost at the same moment that the elder came in from his bedroom. There were already in the cell, awaiting the elder, two monks of the hermitage, one the Father Librarian, and the other Father Paissy, a very learned man, so they said, in delicate health, though not old. There was also a tall young man, who looked about two and twenty, standing in the corner throughout the interview. He had a broad, fresh face, and clever, observant, narrow brown eyes, and was wearing ordinary dress. He was a divinity student, living under the protection of the monastery. His expression was one of unquestioning, but self-respecting, reverence. Being in a subordinate and dependent position, and so not on an equality with the guests, he did not greet them with a bow.

Father Zossima was accompanied by a novice, and by Alyosha. The two monks rose and greeted him with a very deep bow, touching the ground with their fingers; then kissed his hand. Blessing them, the elder replied with as deep a reverence to them, and asked their blessing. The whole ceremony was performed very seriously and with an appearance of feeling, not like an everyday rite. But Miusov fancied that it was all done with intentional impressiveness. He stood in front of the other visitors. He ought--he had reflected upon it the evening before--from simple politeness, since it was the custom here, to have gone up to receive the elder's blessing, even if he did not kiss his hand. But when he saw all this bowing and kissing on the part of the monks he instantly changed his mind. With dignified gravity he made a rather deep, conventional bow, and moved away to a chair. Fyodor Pavlovitch did the same, mimicking Miusov like an ape. Ivan bowed with great dignity and courtesy, but he too kept his hands at his sides, while Kalganov was so confused that he did not bow at all. The elder let fall the hand raised to bless them, and bowing to them again, asked them all to sit down. The blood rushed to Alyosha's cheeks. He was ashamed. His forebodings were coming true.

Father Zossima sat down on a very old-fashioned mahogany sofa, covered with leather, and made his visitors sit down in a row along the opposite wall on four mahogany chairs, covered with shabby black leather. The monks sat, one at the door and the other at the window. The divinity student, the novice, and Alyosha remained standing. The cell was not very large and had a faded look. It contained nothing but the most necessary furniture, of coarse and poor quality. There were two pots of flowers in the window, and a number of holy pictures in the corner. Before one huge ancient ikon of the virgin a lamp was burning. Near it were two other holy pictures in shining settings, and, next them, carved cherubim, china eggs, a Catholic cross of ivory, with a Mater Dolorosa embracing it, and several foreign engravings from the great Italian artists of past centuries. Next to these costly and artistic engravings were several of the roughest Russian prints of saints and martyrs, such as are sold for a few farthings at all the fairs. On the other walls were portraits of Russian bishops, past and present.

Miusov took a cursory glance at all these "conventional" surroundings and bent an intent look upon the elder. He had a high opinion of his own insight a weakness excusable in him as he was fifty, an age at which a clever man of the world of established position can hardly help taking himself rather seriously. At the first moment he did not like Zossima. There was, indeed, something in the elder's face which many people besides Miusov might not have liked. He was a short, bent, little man, with very weak legs, and though he was only sixty-five, he looked at least ten years older. His face was very thin and covered with a network of fine wrinkles, particularly numerous about his eyes, which were small, light-coloured, quick, and shining like two bright points. He had a sprinkling of grey hair about his temples. His pointed beard was small and scanty, and his lips, which smiled frequently, were as thin as two threads. His nose was not long, but sharp, like a bird's beak.

"To all appearances a malicious soul, full of petty pride," thought Miusov. He felt altogether dissatisfied with his position.

A cheap little clock on the wall struck twelve hurriedly, and served to begin the conversation.

"Precisely to our time," cried Fyodor Pavlovitch, "but no sign of my son, Dmitri. I apologise for him, sacred elder!" (Alyosha shuddered all over at "sacred elder".) "I am always punctual myself, minute for minute, remembering that punctuality is the courtesy of kings...

"But you are not a king, anyway," Miusov muttered, losing his self-restraint at once.

"Yes; that's true. I'm not a king, and, would you believe it, Pyotr Alexandrovitch, I was aware of that myself. But, there! I always say the wrong thing. Your reverence," he cried, with sudden pathos, "you behold before you a buffoon in earnest! I introduce myself as such. It's an old habit, alas! And if I sometimes talk nonsense out of place it's with an object, with the object of amusing people and making myself agreeable. One must be agreeable, mustn't one? I was seven years ago in a little town where I had business, and I made friends with some merchants there. We went to the captain of police because we had to see him about something, and to ask him to dine with us. He was a tall, fat, fair, sulky man, the most dangerous type in such cases. It's their liver. I went straight up to him, and with the ease of a man of the world, you know, 'Mr. Ispravnik,' said I, 'be our Napravnik.' 'What do you mean by Napravnik?' said he. I saw, at the first half-second, that it had missed fire. He stood there so glum. 'I wanted to make a joke,' said I, 'for the general diversion, as Mr. Napravnik is our well-known Russian orchestra conductor and what we need for the harmony of our undertaking is someone of that sort.' And I explained my comparison very reasonably, didn't I? 'Excuse me,' said he, 'I am an Ispravnik, and I do not allow puns to be made on my calling.' He turned and walked away. I followed him, shouting, 'Yes, yes, you are an Ispravnik, not a Napravnik.' 'No,' he said, 'since you called me a Napravnik I am one.' And would you believe it, it ruined our business! And I'm always like that, always like that. Always injuring myself with my politeness. Once, many years ago, I said to an influential person: 'Your wife is a ticklish lady,' in an honourable sense, of the moral qualities, so to speak. But he asked me, 'Why, have you tickled her?' I thought I'd be polite, so I couldn't help saying, 'Yes,' and he gave me a fine tickling on the spot. Only that happened long ago, so I'm not ashamed to tell the story. I'm always injuring myself like that."

"You're doing it now," muttered Miusov, with disgust.

Father Zossima scrutinised them both in silence.

"Am I? Would you believe it, I was aware of that, too, Pyotr Alexandrovitch, and let tell you, indeed, I foresaw I should as soon as I began to speak. And do you know I foresaw, too, that you'd be the first to remark on it. The minute I see my joke isn't coming off, your reverence, both my cheeks feel as though they were drawn down to the lower jaw and there is almost a spasm in them. That's been so since I was young, when I had to make jokes for my living in noblemen's families. I am an inveterate buffoon, and have been from birth up, your reverence, it's as though it were a craze in me. I dare say it's a devil within me. But only a little one. A more serious one would have chosen another lodging. But not your soul, Pyotr Alexandrovitch; you're not a lodging worth having either. But I do believe--I believe in God, though I have had doubts of late. But now I sit and await words of wisdom. I'm like the philosopher, Diderot, your reverence. Did you ever hear, most Holy Father, how Diderot went to see the Metropolitan Platon, in the time of the Empress Catherine? He went in and said straight out, 'There is no God.' To which the great bishop lifted up his finger and answered, 'The fool has said in his heart there is no God and he fell down at his feet on the spot. 'I believe,' he cried, 'and will be christened.' And so he was. Princess Dashkov was his godmother, and Potyomkin his godfather."

"Fyodor Pavlovitch, this is unbearable! You know you're telling lies and that that stupid anecdote isn't true. Why are you playing the fool?" cried Miusov in a shaking voice.

"I suspected all my life that it wasn't true," Fyodor Pavlovitch cried with conviction. "But I'll tell you the whole truth, gentlemen. Great elder! Forgive me, the last thing about Diderot's christening I made up just now. I never thought of it before. I made it up to add piquancy. I play the fool, Pyotr Alexandrovitch, to make myself agreeable. Though I really don't know myself, sometimes, what I do it for. And as for Diderot, I heard as far as 'the fool hath said in his heart' twenty times from the gentry about here when I was young. I heard your aunt, Pyotr Alexandrovitch, tell the story. They all believe to this day that the infidel Diderot came to dispute about God with the Metropolitan Platon..."

Miusov got up, forgetting himself in his impatience. He was furious, and conscious of being ridiculous.

What was taking place in the cell was really incredible. For forty or fifty years past, from the times of former elders, no visitors had entered that cell without feelings of the profoundest veneration. Almost everyone admitted to the cell felt that a great favour was being shown him. Many remained kneeling during the whole visit. Of those visitors, many had been men of high rank and learning, some even free thinkers, attracted by curiosity, but all without exception had shown the profoundest reverence and delicacy, for here there was no question of money, but only, on the one side love and kindness, and on the other penitence and eager desire to decide some spiritual problem or crisis. So that such buffoonery amazed and bewildered the spectators, or at least some of them. The monks, with unchanged countenances, waited, with earnest attention, to hear what the elder would say, but seemed on the point of standing up, like Miusov. Alyosha stood, with hanging head, on the verge of tears. What seemed to him strangest of all was that his brother Ivan, on whom alone he had rested his hopes, and who alone had such influence on his father that he could have stopped him, sat now quite unmoved, with downcast eyes, apparently waiting with interest to see how it would end, as though he had nothing to do with it. Alyosha did not dare to look at Rakitin, the divinity student, whom he knew almost intimately. He alone in the monastery knew Rakitin's thoughts.

"Forgive me," began Miusov, addressing Father Zossima, "for perhaps I seem to be taking part in this shameful foolery. I made a mistake in believing that even a man like Fyodor Pavlovitch would understand what was due on a visit to so honoured a personage. I did not suppose I should have to apologise simply for having come with him..."

Pyotr Alexandrovitch could say no more, and was about to leave the room, overwhelmed with confusion.

"Don't distress yourself, I beg." The elder got on to his feeble legs, and taking Pyotr Alexandrovitch by both hands, made him sit down again. "I beg you not to disturb yourself. I particularly beg you to be my guest." And with a bow he went back and sat down again on his little sofa.

"Great elder, speak! Do I annoy you by my vivacity?" Fyodor Pavlovitch cried suddenly, clutching the arms of his chair in both hands, as though ready to leap up from it if the answer were unfavourable.

"I earnestly beg you, too, not to disturb yourself, and not to be uneasy," the elder said impressively. "Do not trouble. Make yourself quite at home. And, above all, do not be so ashamed of yourself, for that is at the root of it all."

"Quite at home? To be my natural self? Oh, that is much too much, but I accept it with grateful joy. Do you know, blessed father, you'd better not invite me to be my natural self. Don't risk it...I will not go so far as that myself. I warn you for your own sake. Well, the rest is still plunged in the mists of uncertainty, though there are people who'd be pleased to describe me for you. I mean that for you, Pyotr Alexandrovitch. But as for you, holy being, let me tell you, I am brimming over with ecstasy."

He got up, and throwing up his hands, declaimed, "Blessed be the womb that bare thee, and the paps that gave thee suck--the paps especially. When you said just now, 'Don't be so ashamed of yourself, for that is at the root of it all,' you pierced right through me by that remark, and read me to the core. Indeed, I always feel when I meet people that I am lower than all, and that they all take me for a buffoon. So I say, 'Let me really play the buffoon. I am not afraid of your opinion, for you are every one of you worse than I am.' That is why I am a buffoon. It is from shame, great elder, from shame; it's simply over-sensitiveness that makes me rowdy. If I had only been sure that everyone would accept me as the kindest and wisest of men, oh, Lord, what a good man I should have been then! Teacher!" he fell suddenly on his knees, "what must I do to gain eternal life?"

It was difficult even now to decide whether he was joking or really moved.

Father Zossima, lifting his eyes, looked at him, and said with a smile:

"You have known for a long time what you must do. You have sense enough: don't give way to drunkenness and incontinence of speech; don't give way to sensual lust; and, above all, to the love of money. And close your taverns. If you can't close all, at least two or three. And, above all--don't lie."

"You mean about Diderot?"

"No, not about Diderot. Above all, don't lie to yourself. The man who lies to himself and listens to his own lie comes to such a pass that he cannot distinguish the truth within him, or around him, and so loses all respect for himself and for others. And having no respect he ceases to love, and in order to occupy and distract himself without love he gives way to passions and coarse pleasures, and sinks to bestiality in his vices, all from continual lying to other men and to himself. The man who lies to himself can be more easily offended than anyone. You know it is sometimes very pleasant to take offence, isn't it? A man may know that nobody has insulted him, but that he has invented the insult for himself, has lied and exaggerated to make it picturesque, has caught at a word and made a mountain out of a molehill--he knows that himself, yet he will be the first to take offence, and will revel in his resentment till he feels great pleasure in it, and so pass to genuine vindictiveness. But get up, sit down, I beg you. All this, too, is deceitful posturing..."

"Blessed man! Give me your hand to kiss."

Fyodor Pavlovitch skipped up, and imprinted a rapid kiss on the elder's thin hand. "It is, it is pleasant to take offence. You said that so well, as I never heard it before. Yes, I have been all my life taking offence, to please myself, taking offence on aesthetic grounds, for it is not so much pleasant as distinguished sometimes to be insulted--that you had forgotten, great elder, it is distinguished! I shall make a note of that. But I have been lying, lying positively my whole life long, every day and hour of it. Of a truth, I am a lie, and the father of lies. Though I believe I am not the father of lies. I am getting mixed in my texts. Say, the son of lies, and that will be enough. Only...my angel...may sometimes talk about Diderot! Diderot will do no harm, though sometimes a word will do harm. Great elder, by the way, I was forgetting, though I had been meaning for the last two years to come here on purpose to ask and to find out something. Only do tell Pyotr Alexandrovitch not to interrupt me. Here is my question: Is it true, great Father, that the story is told somewhere in the Lives of the Saints of a holy saint martyred for his faith who, when his head was cut off at last, stood up, picked up his head, and, 'courteously kissing it,' walked a long way, carrying it in his hands. Is that true or not, honoured Father?"

"No, it is untrue," said the elder.

"There is nothing of the kind in all the lives of the saints. What saint do you say the story is told of?" asked the Father Librarian.

"I do not know what saint. I do not know, and can't tell. I was deceived. I was told the story. I had heard it, and do you know who told it? Pyotr Alexandrovitch Miusov here, was so angry just now about Diderot. He it was who told the story."

"I have never told it you, I never speak to you at all."

"It is true you did not tell me, but you told it when I was present. It was three years ago. I mentioned it because by that ridiculous story you shook my faith, Pyotr Alexandrovitch. You knew nothing of it, but I went home with my faith shaken, and I have been getting more and more shaken ever since. Yes, Pyotr Alexandrovitch, you were the cause of a great fall. That was not a Diderot!"

Fyodor Pavlovitch got excited and pathetic, though it was perfectly clear to everyone by now that he was playing a part again. Yet Miusov was stung by his words.

"What nonsense, and it is all nonsense," he muttered. "I may really have told it, some time or other...but not to you. I was told it myself. I heard it in Paris from a Frenchman. He told me it was read at our mass from the Lives of the Saints...he was a very learned man who had made a special study of Russian statistics and had lived a long time in Russia...I have not read the Lives of the Saints myself, and I am not going to read them...all sorts of things are said at dinner--we were dining then."

"Yes, you were dining then, and so I lost my faith!" said Fyodor Pavlovitch, mimicking him.

"What do I care for your faith?" Miusov was on the point of shouting, but he suddenly checked himself, and said with contempt, "You defile everything you touch."

The elder suddenly rose from his seat. "Excuse me, gentlemen, for leaving you a few minutes," he said, addressing all his guests. "I have visitors awaiting me who arrived before you. But don't you tell lies all the same," he added, turning to Fyodor Pavlovitch with a good-humoured face. He went out of the cell. Alyosha and the novice flew to escort him down the steps. Alyosha was breathless: he was glad to get away, but he was glad, too, that the elder was good-humoured and not offended. Father Zossima was going towards the portico to bless the people waiting for him there. But Fyodor Pavlovitch persisted, in stopping him at the door of the cell.

"Blessed man!" he cried, with feeling. "Allow me to kiss your hand once more. Yes, with you I could still talk, I could still get on. Do you think I always lie and play the fool like this? Believe me, I have been acting like this all the time on purpose to try you. I have been testing you all the time to see whether I could get on with you. Is there room for my humility beside your pride? I am ready to give you a testimonial that one can get on with you! But now, I'll be quiet; I will keep quiet all the time. I'll sit in a chair and hold my tongue. Now it is for you to speak, Pyotr Alexandrovitch. You are the principal person left now--for ten minutes."

Chapter 3. Peasant Women Who Have Faith

NEAR the wooden portico below, built on to the outer wall of the precinct, there was a crowd of about twenty peasant women. They had been told that the elder was at last coming out, and they had gathered together in anticipation. Two ladies, Madame Hohlakov and her daughter, had also come out into the portico to wait for the elder, but in a separate part of it set aside for women of rank.

Madame Hohlakov was a wealthy lady, still young and attractive, and always dressed with taste. She was rather pale, and had lively black eyes. She was not more than thirty-three, and had been five years a widow. Her daughter, a girl of fourteen, was partially paralysed. The poor child had not been able to walk for the last six months, and was wheeled about in a long reclining chair. She had a charming little face, rather thin from illness, but full of gaiety. There was a gleam of mischief in her big dark eyes with their long lashes. Her mother had been intending to take her abroad ever since the spring, but they had been detained all the summer by business connected with their estate. They had been staying a week in our town, where they had come more for purposes of business than devotion, but had visited Father Zossima once already, three days before. Though they knew that the elder scarcely saw anyone, they had now suddenly turned up again, and urgently entreated "the happiness of looking once again on the great healer."

The mother was sitting on a chair by the side of her daughter's invalid carriage, and two paces from her stood an old monk, not one of our monastery, but a visitor from an obscure religious house in the far north. He too sought the elder's blessing.

But Father Zossima, on entering the portico, went first straight to the peasants who were crowded at the foot of the three steps that led up into the portico. Father Zossima stood on the top step, put on his stole, and began blessing the women who thronged about him. One crazy woman was led up to him. As soon as she caught sight of the elder she began shrieking and writhing as though in the pains of childbirth. Laying the stole on her forehead, he read a short prayer over her, and she was at once soothed and quieted.

I do not know how it may be now, but in my childhood I often happened to see and hear these "possessed" women in the villages and monasteries. They used to be brought to mass; they would squeal and bark like a dog so that they were heard all over the church. But when the sacrament was carried in and they were led up to it, at once the "possession" ceased, and the sick women were always soothed for a time. I was greatly impressed and amazed at this as a child; but then I heard from country neighbours and from my town teachers that the whole illness was simulated to avoid work, and that it could always be cured by suitable severity; various anecdotes were told to confirm this. But later on I learnt with astonishment from medical specialists that there is no pretence about it, that it is a terrible illness to which women are subject, especially prevalent among us in Russia, and that it is due to the hard lot of the peasant women. It is a disease, I was told, arising from exhausting toil too soon after hard, abnormal and unassisted labour in childbirth, and from the hopeless misery, from beatings, and so on, which some women were not able to endure like others. The strange and instant healing of the frantic and struggling woman as soon as she was led up to the holy sacrament, which had been explained to me as due to malingering and the trickery of the "clericals," arose probably in the most natural manner. Both the women who supported her and the invalid herself fully believed as a truth beyond question that the evil spirit in possession of her could not hold if the sick woman were brought to the sacrament and made to bow down before it. And so, with a nervous and psychically deranged woman, a sort of convulsion of the whole organism always took place, and was bound to take place, at the moment of bowing down to the sacrament, aroused by the expectation of the miracle of healing and the implicit belief that it would come to pass; and it did come to pass, though only for a moment. It was exactly the same now as soon as the elder touched the sick woman with the stole.

Many of the women in the crowd were moved to tears of ecstasy by the effect of the moment: some strove to kiss the hem of his garment, others cried out in sing-song voices.

He blessed them all and talked with some of them. The "possessed" woman he knew already. She came from a village only six versts from the monastery, and had been brought to him before.

"But here is one from afar." He pointed to a woman by no means old but very thin and wasted, with a face not merely sunburnt but almost blackened by exposure. She was kneeling and gazing with a fixed stare at the elder; there was something almost frenzied in her eyes.

"From afar off, Father, from afar off! From two hundred miles from here. From afar off, Father, from afar off!" the woman began in a sing-song voice as though she were chanting a dirge, swaying her head from side to side with her cheek resting in her hand.

There is silent and long-suffering sorrow to be met with among the peasantry. It withdraws into itself and is still. But there is a grief that breaks out, and from that minute it bursts into tears and finds vent in wailing. This is particularly common with women. But it is no lighter a grief than the silent. Lamentations comfort only by lacerating the heart still more. Such grief does not desire consolation. It feeds on the sense of its hopelessness. Lamentations spring only from the constant craving to re-open the wound.

"You are of the tradesman class?" said Father Zossima, looking curiously at her.

"Townfolk we are, Father, townfolk. Yet we are peasants though we live in the town. I have come to see you, O Father! We heard of you, Father, we heard of you. I have buried my little son, and I have come on a pilgrimage. I have been in three monasteries, but they told me, 'Go, Nastasya, go to them'--that is to you. I have come; I was yesterday at the service, and to-day I have come to you."

"What are you weeping for?"

"It's my little son I'm grieving for. Father, he was three years old--three years all but three months. For my little boy, Father, I'm in anguish, for my little boy. He was the last one left. We had four, my Nikita and I, and now we've no children, our dear ones have all gone I buried the first three without grieving overmuch, and now I have buried the last I can't forget him. He seems always standing before me. He never leaves me. He has withered my heart. I look at his little clothes, his little shirt, his little boots, and I wail. I lay out all that is left of him, all his little things. I look at them and wail. I say to Nikita, my husband, 'let me go on a pilgrimage, master.' He is a driver. We're not poor people, Father, not poor; he drives our own horse. It's all our own, the horse and the carriage. And what good is it all to us now? My Nikita has begun drinking while I am away. He's sure to. It used to be so before. As soon as I turn my back he gives way to it. But now I don't think about him. It's three months since I left home. I've forgotten him. I've forgotten everything. I don't want to remember. And what would our life be now together? I've done with him, I've done. I've done with them all. I don't care to look upon my house and my goods. I don't care to see anything at all!"

"Listen, mother," said the elder. "Once in olden times a holy saint saw in the Temple a mother like you weeping for her little one, her only one, whom God had taken. 'Knowest thou not,' said the saint to her, 'how bold these little ones are before the throne of God? Verily there are none bolder than they in the Kingdom of Heaven. "Thou didst give us life, O Lord," they say, "and scarcely had we looked upon it when Thou didst take it back again." And so boldly they ask and ask again that God gives them at once the rank of angels. Therefore,' said the saint, 'thou, too, O Mother, rejoice and weep not, for thy little son is with the Lord in the fellowship of the angels.' That's what the saint said to the weeping mother of old. He was a great saint and he could not have spoken falsely. Therefore you too, mother, know that your little one is surely before the throne of God, is rejoicing and happy, and praying to God for you, and therefore weep, but rejoice."

The woman listened to him, looking down with her cheek in her hand. She sighed deeply.

"My Nikita tried to comfort me with the same words as you. 'Foolish one,' he said, 'why weep? Our son is no doubt singing with the angels before God.' He says that to me, but he weeps himself. I see that he cries like me. 'I know, Nikita,' said I. 'Where could he be if not with the Lord God? Only, here with us now he is not as he used to sit beside us before.' And if only I could look upon him one little time, if only I could peep at him one little time, without going up to him, without speaking, if I could be hidden in a corner and only see him for one little minute, hear him playing in the yard, calling in his little voice, 'Mammy, where are you?' If only I could hear him pattering with his little feet about the room just once, only once; for so often, so often I remember how he used to run to me and shout and laugh, if only I could hear his little feet I should know him! But he's gone, Father, he's gone, and I shall never hear him again. Here's his little sash, but him I shall never see or hear now."

She drew out of her bosom her boy's little embroidered sash, and as soon as she looked at it she began shaking with sobs, hiding her eyes with her fingers through which the tears flowed in a sudden stream.

"It is Rachel of old," said the elder, "weeping for her children, and will not be comforted because they are not. Such is the lot set on earth for you mothers. Be not comforted. Consolation is not what you need. Weep and be not consoled, but weep. Only every time that you weep be sure to remember that your little son is one of the angels of God, that he looks down from there at you and sees you, and rejoices at your tears, and points at them to the Lord God; and a long while yet will you keep that great mother's grief. But it will turn in the end into quiet joy, and your bitter tears will be only tears of tender sorrow that purifies the heart and delivers it from sin. And I shall pray for the peace of your child's soul. What was his name?"

"Alexey, Father."

"A sweet name. After Alexey, the man of God?"

"Yes, Father."

"What a saint he was! I will remember him, mother, and your grief in my prayers, and I will pray for your husband's health. It is a sin for you to leave him. Your little one will see from heaven that you have forsaken his father, and will weep over you. Why do you trouble his happiness? He is living, for the soul lives for ever, and though he is not in the house he is near you, unseen. How can he go into the house when you say that the house is hateful to you? To whom is he to go if he find you not together, his father and mother? He comes to you in dreams now, and you grieve. But then he will send you gentle dreams. Go to your husband, mother; go this very day."

"I will go, Father, at your word. I will go. You've gone straight to my heart. My Nikita, my Nikita, you are waiting for me," the woman began in a sing-song voice; but the elder had already turned away to a very old woman, dressed like a dweller in the town, not like a pilgrim. Her eyes showed that she had come with an object, and in order to say something. She said she was the widow of a non-commissioned officer, and lived close by in the town. Her son Vasenka was in the commissariat service, and had gone to Irkutsk in Siberia. He had written twice from there, but now a year had passed since he had written. She did inquire about him, but she did not know the proper place to inquire.

"Only the other day Stepanida Ilyinishna--she's a rich merchant's wife--said to me, 'You go, Prohorovna, and put your son's name down for prayer in the church, and pray for the peace of his soul as though he were dead. His soul will be troubled,' she said, 'and he will write you a letter.' And Stepanida Ilyinishna told me it was a certain thing which had been many times tried. Only I am in doubt...Oh, you light of ours! is it true or false, and would it be right?"

"Don't think of it. It's shameful to ask the question. How is it possible to pray for the peace of a living soul? And his own mother too! It's a great sin, akin to sorcery. Only for your ignorance it is forgiven you. Better pray to the Queen of Heaven, our swift defence and help, for his good health, and that she may forgive you for your error. And another thing I will tell you, Prohorovna. Either he will soon come back to you, your son, or he will be sure to send a letter. Go, and henceforward be in peace. Your son is alive, I tell you."

"Dear Father, God reward you, our benefactor, who prays for all of us and for our sins!"

But the elder had already noticed in the crowd two glowing eyes fixed upon him. An exhausted, consumptive-looking, though young peasant woman was gazing at him in silence. Her eyes besought him, but she seemed afraid to approach.

"What is it, my child?"

"Absolve my soul, Father," she articulated softly, and slowly sank on her knees and bowed down at his feet. "I have sinned, Father. I am afraid of my sin."

The elder sat down on the lower step. The woman crept closer to him, still on her knees.

"I am a widow these three years," she began in a half-whisper, with a sort of shudder. "I had a hard life with my husband. He was an old man. He used to beat me cruelly. He lay ill; I thought looking at him, if he were to get well, if he were to get up again, what then? And then the thought came to me-"

"Stay!" said the elder, and he put his ear close to her lips.

The woman went on in a low whisper, so that it was almost impossible to catch anything. She had soon done.

"Three years ago?" asked the elder.

"Three years. At first I didn't think about it, but now I've begun to be ill, and the thought never leaves me."

"Have you come from far?"

"Over three hundred miles away."

"Have you told it in confession?"

"I have confessed it. Twice I have confessed it."

"Have you been admitted to Communion?"

"Yes. I am afraid. I am afraid to die."

"Fear nothing and never be afraid; and don't fret. If only your penitence fail not, God will forgive all. There is no sin, and there can be no sin on all the earth, which the Lord will not forgive to the truly repentant! Man cannot commit a sin so great as to exhaust the infinite love of God. Can there be a sin which could exceed the love of God? Think only of repentance, continual repentance, but dismiss fear altogether. Believe that God loves you as you cannot conceive; that He loves you with your sin, in your sin. It has been said of old that over one repentant sinner there is more joy in heaven than over ten righteous men. Go, and fear not. Be not bitter against men. Be not angry if you are wronged. Forgive the dead man in your heart what wrong he did you. Be reconciled with him in truth. If you are penitent, you love. And if you love you are of God. All things are atoned for, all things are saved by love. If I, a sinner, even as you are, am tender with you and have pity on you, how much more will God. Love is such a priceless treasure that you can redeem the whole world by it, and expiate not only your own sins but the sins of others."

He signed her three times with the cross, took from his own neck a little ikon and put it upon her. She bowed down to the earth without speaking.

He got up and looked cheerfully at a healthy peasant woman with a tiny baby in her arms.

"From Vyshegorye, dear Father."

"Five miles you have dragged yourself with the baby. What do you want?"

"I've come to look at you. I have been to you before--or have you forgotten? You've no great memory if you've forgotten me. They told us you were ill. Thinks I, I'll go and see him for myself. Now I see you, and you're not ill! You'll live another twenty years. God bless you! There are plenty to pray for you; how should you be ill?"

"I thank you for all, daughter."

"By the way, I have a thing to ask, not a great one. Here are sixty copecks. Give them, dear Father, to someone poorer than me. I thought as I came along, better give through him. He'll know whom to give to."

"Thanks, my dear, thanks! You are a good woman. I love you. I will do so certainly. Is that your little girl?"

"My little girl, Father, Lizaveta."

"May the Lord bless you both, you and your babe Lizaveta! You have gladdened my heart, mother. Farewell, dear children, farewell, dear ones."

He blessed them all and bowed low to them.

Chapter 4. A Lady of Little Faith

A visitor looking on the scene of his conversation with the peasants and his blessing them shed silent tears and wiped them away with her handkerchief. She was a sentimental society lady of genuinely good disposition in many respects. When the elder went up to her at last she met him enthusiastically.

"Ah, what I have been feeling, looking on at this touching scene!..." She could not go on for emotion. "Oh, I understand the people's love for you. I love the people myself. I want to love them. And who could help loving them, our splendid Russian people, so simple in their greatness!"

"How is your daughter's health? You wanted to talk to me again?"

"Oh, I have been urgently begging for it, I have prayed for it! I was ready to fall on my knees and kneel for three days at your windows until you let me in. We have come, great healer, to express our ardent gratitude. You have healed my Lise, healed her completely, merely by praying over her last Thursday and laying your hands upon her. We have hastened here to kiss those hands, to pour out our feelings and our homage."

"What do you mean by healed? But she is still lying down in her chair."

"But her night fevers have entirely ceased ever since Thursday," said the lady with nervous haste. "And that's not all. Her legs are stronger. This mourning she got up well; she had slept all night. Look at her rosy cheeks, her bright eyes! She used to be always crying, but now she laughs and is gay and happy. This morning she insisted on my letting her stand up, and she stood up for a whole minute without any support. She wagers that in a fortnight she'll be dancing a quadrille. I've called in Doctor Herzenstube. He shrugged his shoulders and said, 'I am amazed; I can make nothing of it.' And would you have us not come here to disturb you, not fly here to thank you? Lise, thank him--thank him!"

Lise's pretty little laughing face became suddenly serious. She rose in her chair as far as she could and, looking at the elder, clasped her hands before him, but could not restrain herself and broke into laughter.

"It's at him," she said, pointing to Alyosha, with childish vexation at herself for not being able to repress her mirth.

If anyone had looked at Alyosha standing a step behind the elder, he would have caught a quick flush crimsoning his cheeks in an instant. His eyes shone and he looked down.

"She has a message for you, Alexey Fyodorovitch. How are you?" the mother went on, holding out her exquisitely gloved hand to Alyosha.

The elder turned round and all at once looked attentively at Alyosha. The latter went nearer to Lise and, smiling in a strangely awkward way, held out his hand to her too. Lise assumed an important air.

"Katerina Ivanovna has sent you this through me." She handed him a little note. "She particularly begs you to go and see her as soon as possible; that you will not fail her, but will be sure to come."

"She asks me to go and see her? Me? What for?" Alyosha muttered in great astonishment. His face at once looked anxious.

"Oh, it's all to do with Dmitri Fyodorovitch and--what has happened lately," the mother explained hurriedly. "Katerina Ivanovna has made up her mind, but she must see you about it...Why, of course, I can't say. But she wants to see you at once. And you will go to her, of course. It is a Christian duty."

"I have only seen her once," Alyosha protested with the same perplexity.

"Oh, she is such a lofty, incomparable creature If only for her suffering...Think what she has gone through, what she is enduring now Think what awaits her! It's all terrible, terrible!

"Very well, I will come," Alyosha decided, after rapidly scanning the brief, enigmatic note, which consisted of an urgent entreaty that he would come, without any sort of explanation.

"Oh, how sweet and generous that would be of you", cried Lise with sudden animation. "I told mamma you'd be sure not to go. I said you were saving your soul. How splendid you are I've always thought you were splendid. How glad I am to tell you so!"

"Lise!" said her mother impressively, though she smiled after she had said it.

"You have quite forgotten us, Alexey Fyodorovitch," she said; "you never come to see us. Yet Lise has told me twice that she is never happy except with you."

Alyosha raised his downcast eyes and again flushed, and again smiled without knowing why. But the elder was no longer watching him. He had begun talking to a monk who, as mentioned before, had been awaiting his entrance by Lise's chair. He was evidently a monk of the humblest, that is of the peasant, class, of a narrow outlook, but a true believer, and, in his own way, a stubborn one. He announced that he had come from the far north, from Obdorsk, from Saint Sylvester, and was a member of a poor monastery, consisting of only ten monks. The elder gave him his blessing and invited him to come to his cell whenever he liked.

"How can you presume to do such deeds?" the monk asked suddenly, pointing solemnly and significantly at Lise. He was referring to her "healing."

"It's too early, of course, to speak of that. Relief is not complete cure, and may proceed from different causes. But if there has been any healing, it is by no power but God's will. It's all from God. Visit me, Father," he added to the monk. "It's not often I can see visitors. I am ill, and I know that my days are numbered."

"Oh, no, no! God will not take you from us. You will live a long, long time yet," cried the lady. "And in what way are you ill? You look so well, so gay and happy."

"I am extraordinarily better to-day. But I know that it's only for a moment. I understand my disease now thoroughly. If I seem so happy to you, you could never say anything that would please me so much. For men are made for happiness, and anyone who is completely happy has a right to say to himself, 'I am doing God's will on earth.' All the righteous, all the saints, all the holy martyrs were happy."

"Oh, how you speak! What bold and lofty words" cried the lady. "You seem to pierce with your words. And yet--happiness, happiness--where is it? Who can say of himself that he is happy? Oh, since you have been so good as to let us see you once more to-day, let me tell you what I could not utter last time, what I dared not say, all I am suffering and have been for so long! I am suffering! Forgive me! I am suffering!"

And in a rush of fervent feeling she clasped her hands before him.

"From what specially?"

"I suffer...from lack of faith."

"Lack of faith in God?"

"Oh, no, no! I dare not even think of that. But the future life--it is such an enigma And no one, no one can solve it. Listen! You are a healer, you are deeply versed in the human soul, and of course I dare not expect you to believe me entirely, but I assure you on my word of honour that I am not speaking lightly now. The thought of the life beyond the grave distracts me to anguish, to terror. And I don't know to whom to appeal, and have not dared to all my life. And now I am so bold as to ask you. Oh, God! What will you think of me now?"

She clasped her hands.

"Don't distress yourself about my opinion of you," said the elder. "I quite believe in the sincerity of your suffering."

"Oh, how thankful I am to you! You see, I shut my eyes and ask myself if everyone has faith, where did it come from? And then they do say that it all comes from terror at the menacing phenomena of nature, and that none of it's real. And I say to myself, 'What if I've been believing all my life, and when I come to die there's nothing but the burdocks growing on my grave?' as I read in some author. It's awful! How--how can I get back my faith? But I only believed when I was a little child, mechanically, without thinking of anything. How, how is one to prove it? have come now to lay my soul before you and to ask you about it. If I let this chance slip, no one all my life will answer me. How can I prove it? How can I convince myself? Oh, how unhappy I am! I stand and look about me and see that scarcely anyone else cares; no one troubles his head about it, and I'm the only one who can't stand it. It's deadly--deadly!"

"No doubt. But there's no proving it, though you can be convinced of it."

"By the experience of active love. Strive to love your neighbour actively and indefatigably. In as far as you advance in love you will grow surer of the reality of God and of the immortality of your soul. If you attain to perfect self-forgetfulness in the love of your neighbour, then you will believe without doubt, and no doubt can possibly enter your soul. This has been tried. This is certain."

"In active love? There's another question and such a question! You see, I so love humanity that--would you believe it?--I often dream of forsaking all that I have, leaving Lise, and becoming a sister of mercy. I close my eyes and think and dream, and at that moment I feel full of strength to overcome all obstacles. No wounds, no festering sores could at that moment frighten me. I would bind them up and wash them with my own hands. I would nurse the afflicted. I would be ready to kiss such wounds."

"It is much, and well that your mind is full of such dreams and not others. Some time, unawares, you may do a good deed in reality."

"Yes. But could I endure such a life for long?" the lady went on fervently, almost frantically. "That's the chief question--that's my most agonising question. I shut my eyes and ask myself, 'Would you persevere long on that path? And if the patient whose wounds you are washing did not meet you with gratitude, but worried you with his whims, without valuing or remarking your charitable services, began abusing you and rudely commanding you, and complaining to the superior authorities of you (which often happens when people are in great suffering)--what then? Would you persevere in your love, or not?' And do you know, I came with horror to the conclusion that, if anything could dissipate my love to humanity, it would be ingratitude. In short, I am a hired servant, I expect my payment at once--that is, praise, and the repayment of love with love. Otherwise I am incapable of loving anyone.'"

She was in a very paroxysm of self-castigation, and, concluding, she looked with defiant resolution at the elder.

"It's just the same story as a doctor once told me," observed the elder. "He was a man getting on in years, and undoubtedly clever. He spoke as frankly as you, though in jest, in bitter jest. 'I love humanity,' he said, 'but I wonder at myself. The more I love humanity in general, the less I love man in particular. In my dreams,' he said, 'I have often come to making enthusiastic schemes for the service of humanity, and perhaps I might actually have faced crucifixion if it had been suddenly necessary; and yet I am incapable of living in the same room with anyone for two days together, as I know by experience. As soon as anyone is near me, his personality disturbs my self-complacency and restricts my freedom. In twenty-four hours I begin to hate the best of men: one because he's too long over his dinner; another because he has a cold and keeps on blowing his nose. I become hostile to people the moment they come close to me. But it has always happened that the more I detest men individually the more ardent becomes my love for humanity.'"

"But what's to be done? What can one do in such a case? Must one despair?"

"No. It is enough that you are distressed at it. Do what you can, and it will be reckoned unto you. Much is done already in you since you can so deeply and sincerely know yourself. If you have been talking to me so sincerely, simply to gain approbation for your frankness, as you did from me just now, then, of course, you will not attain to anything in the achievement of real love; it will all get no further than dreams, and your whole life will slip away like a phantom. In that case you will naturally cease to think of the future life too, and will of yourself grow calmer after a fashion in the end."

"You have crushed me! Only now, as you speak, I understand that I was really only seeking your approbation for my sincerity when I told you I could not endure ingratitude. You have revealed me to myself. You have seen through me and explained me to myself

"Are you speaking the truth? Well, now, after such a confession, I believe that you are sincere and good at heart. If you do not attain happiness, always remember that you are on the right road, and try not to leave it. Above all, avoid falsehood, every kind of falsehood, especially falseness to yourself. Watch over your own deceitfulness and look into it every hour, every minute. Avoid being scornful, both to others and to yourself. What seems to you bad within you will grow purer from the very fact of your observing it in yourself. Avoid fear, too, though fear is only the consequence of every sort of falsehood. Never be frightened at your own faint-heartedness in attaining love. Don't be frightened overmuch even at your evil actions. I am sorry I can say nothing more consoling to you, for love in action is a harsh and dreadful thing compared with love in dreams. Love in dreams is greedy for immediate action, rapidly performed and in the sight of all. Men will even give their lives if only the ordeal does not last long but is soon over, with all looking on and applauding as though on the stage. But active love is labour and fortitude, and for some people too, perhaps, a complete science. But I predict that just when you see with horror that in spite of all your efforts you are getting farther from your goal instead of nearer to it--at that very moment I predict that you will reach it and behold clearly the miraculous power of the Lord who has been all the time loving and mysteriously guiding you. Forgive me for not being able to stay longer with you. They are waiting for me. Good-bye."

The lady was weeping.

"Lise, Lise! Bless her--bless her!" she cried, starting up suddenly.

"She does not deserve to be loved. I have seen her naughtiness all along," the elder said jestingly. "Why have you been laughing at Alexey?"

Lise had in fact been occupied in mocking at him all the time. She had noticed before that Alyosha was shy and tried not to look at her, and she found this extremely amusing. She waited intently to catch his eye. Alyosha, unable to endure her persistent stare, was irresistibly and suddenly drawn to glance at her, and at once she smiled triumphantly in his face. Alyosha was even more disconcerted and vexed. At last he turned away from her altogether and hid behind the elder's back. After a few minutes, drawn by the same irresistible force, he turned again to see whether he was being looked at or not, and found Lise almost hanging out of her chair to peep sideways at him, eagerly waiting for him to look. Catching his eye, she laughed so that the elder could not help saying, "Why do you make fun of him like that, naughty girl?"

Lise suddenly and quite unexpectedly blushed. Her eyes flashed and her face became quite serious. She began speaking quickly and nervously in a warm and resentful voice:

"Why has he forgotten everything, then? He used to carry me about when I was little. We used to play together. He used to come to teach me to read, do you know. Two years ago, when he went away, he said that he would never forget me, that we were friends for ever, for ever, for ever! And now he's afraid of me all at once. Am I going to eat him? Why doesn't he want to come near me? Why doesn't he talk? Why won't he come and see us? It's not that you won't let him. We know that he goes everywhere. It's not good manners for me to invite him. He ought to have thought of it first, if he hasn't forgotten me. No, now he's saving his soul! Why have you put that long gown on him? If he runs he'll fall."

And suddenly she hid her face in her hand and went off into irresistible, prolonged, nervous, inaudible laughter. The elder listened to her with a smile, and blessed her tenderly. As she kissed his hand she suddenly pressed it to her eyes and began crying.

"Don't be angry with me. I'm silly and good for nothing...and perhaps Alyosha's right, quite right, in not wanting to come and see such a ridiculous girl."

"I will certainly send him," said the elder.

Chapter 5. So Be It! So Be It!

THE elder's absence from his cell had lasted for about twenty-five minutes. It was more than half-past twelve, but Dmitri, on whose account they had all met there, had still not appeared. But he seemed almost to be forgotten, and when the elder entered the cell again, he found his guests engaged in eager conversation. Ivan and the two monks took the leading share in it. Miusov, too, was trying to take a part, and apparently very eagerly, in the conversation. But he was unsuccessful in this also. He was evidently in the background, and his remarks were treated with neglect, which increased his irritability. He had had intellectual encounters with Ivan before and he could not endure a certain carelessness Ivan showed him.

"Hitherto at least I have stood in the front ranks of all that is progressive in Europe, and here the new generation positively ignores us," he thought.

Fyodor Pavlovitch, who had given his word to sit still and be quiet, had actually been quiet for some time, but he watched his neighbour Miusov with an ironical little smile, obviously enjoying his discomfiture. He had been waiting for some time to pay off old scores, and now he could not let the opportunity slip. Bending over his shoulder he began teasing him again in a whisper.

"Why didn't you go away just now, after the 'courteously kissing'? Why did you consent to remain in such unseemly company? It was because you felt insulted and aggrieved, and you remained to vindicate yourself by showing off your intelligence. Now you won't go till you've displayed your intellect to them."

"You again?...On the contrary, I'm just going."

"You'll be the last, the last of all to go!" Fyodor Pavlovitch delivered him another thrust, almost at the moment of Father Zossima's return.

The discussion died down for a moment, but the elder, seating himself in his former place, looked at them all as though cordially inviting them to go on. Alyosha, who knew every expression of his face, saw that he was fearfully exhausted and making a great effort. Of late he had been liable to fainting fits from exhaustion. His face had the pallor that was common before such attacks, and his lips were white. But he evidently did not want to break up the party. He seemed to have some special object of his own in keeping them. What object? Alyosha watched him intently.

"We are discussing this gentleman's most interesting article," said Father Iosif, the librarian, addressing the elder, and indicating Ivan. "He brings forward much that is new, but I think the argument cuts both ways. It is an article written in answer to a book by an ecclesiastical authority on the question of the ecclesiastical court, and the scope of its jurisdiction."

"I'm sorry I have not read your article, but I've heard of it," said the elder, looking keenly and intently at Ivan.

"He takes up a most interesting position," continued the Father Librarian. "As far as Church jurisdiction is concerned he is apparently quite opposed to the separation of Church from State."

"That's interesting. But in what sense?" Father Zossima asked Ivan.

The latter, at last, answered him, not condescendingly, as Alyosha had feared, but with modesty and reserve, with evident goodwill and apparently without the slightest arrierepensee

"I start from the position that this confusion of elements, that is, of the essential principles of Church and State, will, of course, go on for ever, in spite of the fact that it is impossible for them to mingle, and that the confusion of these elements cannot lead to any consistent or even normal results, for there is falsity at the very foundation of it. Compromise between the Church and State in such questions as, for instance, jurisdiction, is, to my thinking, impossible in any real sense. My clerical opponent maintains that the Church holds a precise and defined position in the State. I maintain, on the contrary, that the Church ought to include the whole State, and not simply to occupy a corner in it, and, if this is, for some reason, impossible at present, then it ought, in reality, to be set up as the direct and chief aim of the future development of Christian society!"

"Perfectly true," Father Paissy, the silent and learned monk, assented with fervour and decision.

"The purest Ultramontanism!" cried Miusov impatiently, crossing and recrossing his legs.

"Oh, well, we have no mountains," cried Father Iosif, and turning to the elder he continued: "Observe the answer he makes to the following 'fundamental and essential' propositions of his opponent, who is, you must note, an ecclesiastic. First, that 'no social organisation can or ought to arrogate to itself power to dispose of the civic and political rights of its members.' Secondly, that 'criminal and civil jurisdiction ought not to belong to the Church, and is inconsistent with its nature, both as a divine institution and as an organisation of men for religious objects,' and, finally, in the third place, 'the Church is a kingdom not of this world.'"

"A most unworthy play upon words for an ecclesiastic!" Father Paissy could not refrain from breaking in again. "I have read the book which you have answered," he added, addressing Ivan, "and was astounded at the words 'The Church is a kingdom not of this world. 'If it is not of this world, then it cannot exist on earth at all. In the Gospel, the words 'not of this world' are not used in that sense. To play with such words is indefensible. Our Lord Jesus Christ came to set up the Church upon earth. The Kingdom of Heaven, of course, is not of this world, but in Heaven; but it is only entered through the Church which has been founded and established upon earth. And so a frivolous play upon words in such a connection is unpardonable and improper. The Church is, in truth, a kingdom and ordained to rule, and in the end must undoubtedly become the kingdom ruling over all the earth. For that we have the divine promise."

He ceased speaking suddenly, as though checking himself. After listening attentively and respectfully Ivan went on, addressing the elder with perfect composure and as before with ready cordiality:

"The whole point of my article lies in the fact that during the first three centuries Christianity only existed on earth in the Church and was nothing but the Church. When the pagan Roman Empire desired to become Christian, it inevitably happened that, by becoming Christian, it included the Church but remained a pagan State in very many of its departments. In reality this was bound to happen. But Rome as a State retained too much of the pagan civilisation and culture, as, for example, in the very objects and fundamental principles of the State. The Christian Church entering into the State could, of course, surrender no part of its fundamental principles-- the rock on which it stands--and could pursue no other aims than those which have been ordained and revealed by God Himself, and among them that of drawing the whole world, and therefore the ancient pagan State itself, into the Church. In that way (that is, with a view to the future) it is not the Church that should seek a definite position in the State, like 'every social organisation,' or as 'an organisation of men for religious purposes' (as my opponent calls the Church), but, on the contrary, every earthly State should be, in the end, completely transformed into the Church and should become nothing else but a Church, rejecting every purpose incongruous with the aims of the Church. All this will not degrade it in any way or take from its honour and glory as a great State, nor from the glory of its rulers, but only turns it from a false, still pagan, and mistaken path to the true and rightful path, which alone leads to the eternal goal. This is why the author of the book On the Foundations of Church Jurisdiction would have judged correctly if, in seeking and laying down those foundations, he bad looked upon them as a temporary compromise inevitable in our sinful and imperfect days. But as soon as the author ventures to declare that the foundations which he predicates now, part of which Father Iosif just enumerated, are the permanent, essential, and eternal foundations, he is going directly against the Church and its sacred and eternal vocation. That is the gist of my article."

"That is, in brief," Father Paissy began again, laying stress on each word, "according to certain theories only too clearly formulated in the nineteenth century, the Church ought to be transformed into the State, as though this would be an advance from a lower to a higher form, so as to disappear into it, making way for science, for the spirit of the age, and civilisation. And if the Church resists and is unwilling, some corner will be set apart for her in the State, and even that under control and this will be so everywhere in all modern European countries. But Russian hopes and conceptions demand not that the Church should pass as from a lower into a higher type into the State, but, on the contrary, that the State should end by being worthy to become only the Church and nothing else. So be it! So be it!"

"Well, I confess you've reassured me somewhat," Miusov said smiling, again crossing his legs. "So far as I understand, then, the realisation of such an ideal is infinitely remote, at the second coming of Christ. That's as you please. It's a beautiful Utopian dream of the abolition of war, diplomacy, banks, and so on--something after the fashion of socialism, indeed. But I imagined that it was all meant seriously, and that the Church might be now going to try criminals, and sentence them to beating, prison, and even death."

"But if there were none but the ecclesiastical court, the Church would not even now sentence a criminal to prison or to death. Crime and the way of regarding it would inevitably change, not all at once of course, but fairly soon," Ivan replied calmly, without flinching.

"Are you serious?" Miusov glanced keenly at him.

"If everything became the Church, the Church would exclude all the criminal and disobedient, and would not cut off their heads," Ivan went on. "I ask you, what would become of the excluded? He would be cut off then not only from men, as now, but from Christ. By his crime he would have transgressed not only against men but against the Church of Christ. This is so even now, of course, strictly speaking, but it is not clearly enunciated, and very, very often the criminal of to-day compromises with his conscience: 'I steal,' he says, 'but I don't go against the Church. I'm not an enemy of Christ.' That's what the criminal of to-day is continually saying to himself, but when the Church takes the place of the State it will be difficult for him, in opposition to the Church all over the world, to say: 'All men are mistaken, all in error, all mankind are the false Church. I, a thief and murderer, am the only true Christian Church.' It will be very difficult to say this to himself; it requires a rare combination of unusual circumstances. Now, on the other side, take the Church's own view of crime: is it not bound to renounce the present almost pagan attitude, and to change from a mechanical cutting off of its tainted member for the preservation of society, as at present, into completely and honestly adopting the idea of the regeneration of the man, of his reformation and salvation?"

"What do you mean? I fail to understand again," Miusov interrupted. "Some sort of dream again. Something shapeless and even incomprehensible. What is excommunication? What sort of exclusion? I suspect you are simply amusing yourself, Ivan Fyodorovitch."

"Yes, but you know, in reality it is so now," said the elder suddenly, and all turned to him at once. "If it were not for the Church of Christ there would be nothing to restrain the criminal from evil-doing, no real chastisement for it afterwards; none, that is, but the mechanical punishment spoken of just now, which in the majority of cases only embitters the heart; and not the real punishment, the only effectual one, the only deterrent and softening one, which lies in the recognition of sin by conscience."

"How is that, may one inquire?" asked Miusov, with lively curiosity.

"Why," began the elder, "all these sentences to exile with hard labour, and formerly with flogging also, reform no one, and what's more, deter hardly a single criminal, and the number of crimes does not diminish but is continually on the increase. You must admit that. Consequently the security of society is not preserved, for, although the obnoxious member is mechanically cut off and sent far away out of sight, another criminal always comes to take his place at once, and often two of them. If anything does preserve society, even in our time, and does regenerate and transform the criminal, it is only the law of Christ speaking in his conscience. It is only by recognising his wrongdoing as a son of a Christian society--that is, of the Church--that he recognises his sin against society--that is, against the Church. So that it is only against the Church, and not against the State, that the criminal of to-day can recognise that he has sinned. If society, as a Church, had jurisdiction, then it would know when to bring back from exclusion and to reunite to itself. Now the Church having no real jurisdiction, but only the power of moral condemnation, withdraws of her own accord from punishing the criminal actively. She does not excommunicate him but simply persists in motherly exhortation of him. What is more, the Church even tries to preserve all Christian communion with the criminal. She admits him to church services, to the holy sacrament, gives him alms, and treats him more a captive than as a convict. And what would become of the criminal, O Lord, if even the Christian society--that is, the Church--were to reject him even as the civil law rejects him and cuts him off? What would become of him if the Church punished him with her excommunication as the direct consequence of the secular law? There could be no more terrible despair, at least for a Russian criminal, for Russian criminals still have faith. Though, who knows, perhaps then a fearful thing would happen, perhaps the despairing heart of the criminal would lose its faith and then what would become of him? But the Church, like a tender, loving mother, holds aloof from active punishment herself, as the sinner is too severely punished already by the civil law, and there must be at least someone to have pity on him. The Church holds aloof, above all, because its judgment is the only one that contains the truth, and therefore cannot practically and morally be united to any other judgment even as a temporary compromise. She can enter into no compact about that. The foreign criminal, they say, rarely repents, for the very doctrines of to-day confirm him in the idea that his crime is not a crime, but only a reaction against an unjustly oppressive force. Society cuts him off completely by a force that triumphs over him mechanically and (so at least they say of themselves in Europe) accompanies this exclusion with hatred, forgetfulness, and the most profound indifference as to the ultimate fate of the erring brother. In this way, it all takes place without the compassionate intervention of the Church, for in many cases there are no churches there at all, for though ecclesiastics and splendid church buildings remain, the churches themselves have long ago striven to pass from Church into State and to disappear in it completely. So it seems at least in Lutheran countries. As for Rome, it was proclaimed a State instead of a Church a thousand years ago. And so the criminal is no longer conscious of being a member of the Church and sinks into despair. If he returns to society, often it is with such hatred that society itself instinctively cuts him off. You can judge for yourself how it must end. In many cases it would seem to be the same with us, but the difference is that besides the established law courts we have the Church too, which always keeps up relations with the criminal as a dear and still precious son. And besides that, there is still preserved, though only in thought, the judgment of the Church, which though no longer existing in practice is still living as a dream for the future, and is, no doubt, instinctively recognised by the criminal in his soul. What was said here just now is true too, that is, that if the jurisdiction of the Church were introduced in practice in its full force, that is, if the whole of the society were changed into the Church, not only the judgment of the Church would have influence on the reformation of the criminal such as it never has now, but possibly also the crimes themselves would be incredibly diminished. And there can be no doubt that the Church would look upon the criminal and the crime of the future in many cases quite differently and would succeed in restoring the excluded, in restraining those who plan evil, and in regenerating the fallen. It is true," said Father Zossima, with a smile, "the Christian society now is not ready and is only resting on some seven righteous men, but as they are never lacking, it will continue still unshaken in expectation of its complete transformation from a society almost heathen in character into a single universal and all-powerful Church. So be it, so be it! Even though at the end of the ages, for it is ordained to come to pass! And there is no need to be troubled about times and seasons, for the secret of the times and seasons is in the wisdom of God, in His foresight, and His love. And what in human reckoning seems still afar off, may by the Divine ordinance be close at hand, on the eve of its appearance. And so be it, so be it!

"So be it, so be it!" Father Paissy repeated austerely and reverently.

"Strange, extremely strange" Miusov pronounced, not so much with heat as with latent indignation.

"What strikes you as so strange?" Father Iosif inquired cautiously.

"Why, it's beyond anything!" cried Miusov, suddenly breaking out; "the State is eliminated and the Church is raised to the position of the State. It's not simply Ultramontanism, it's arch-Ultramontanism! It's beyond the dreams of Pope Gregory the Seventh!"

"You are completely misunderstanding it," said Father Paissy sternly. "Understand, the Church is not to be transformed into the State. That is Rome and its dream. That is the third temptation of the devil. On the contrary, the State is transformed into the Church, will ascend and become a Church over the whole world-- which is the complete opposite of Ultramontanism and Rome, and your interpretation, and is only the glorious destiny ordained for the Orthodox Church. This star will arise in the east!"

Miusov was significantly silent. His whole figure expressed extraordinary personal dignity. A supercilious and condescending smile played on his lips. Alyosha watched it all with a throbbing heart. The whole conversation stirred him profoundly. He glanced casually at Rakitin, who was standing immovable in his place by the door listening and watching intently though with downcast eyes. But from the colour in his cheeks Alyosha guessed that Rakitin was probably no less excited, and he knew what caused his excitement.

"Allow me to tell you one little anecdote, gentlemen," Miusov said impressively, with a peculiarly majestic air. "Some years ago, soon after the coup d'etat of December, I happened to be calling in Paris on an extremely influential personage in the Government, and I met a very interesting man in his house. This individual was not precisely a detective but was a sort of superintendent of a whole regiment of political detectives--a rather powerful position in its own way. I was prompted by curiosity to seize the opportunity of conversation with him. And as he had not come as a visitor but as a subordinate official bringing a special report, and as he saw the reception given me by his chief, he deigned to speak with some openness, to a certain extent only, of course. He was rather courteous than open, as Frenchmen know how to be courteous, especially to a foreigner. But I thoroughly understood him. The subject was the socialist revolutionaries who were at that time persecuted. I will quote only one most curious remark dropped by this person. 'We are not particularly afraid,' said he, 'of all these socialists, anarchists, infidels, and revolutionists; we keep watch on them and know all their goings on. But there are a few peculiar men among them who believe in God and are Christians, but at the same time are socialists. These are the people we are most afraid of. They are dreadful people The socialist who is a Christian is more to be dreaded than a socialist who is an atheist.' The words struck me at the time, and now they have suddenly come back to me here, gentlemen."

"You apply them to us, and look upon us as socialists?" Father Paissy asked directly, without beating about the bush.

But before Pyotr Alexandrovitch could think what to answer, the door opened, and the guest so long expected, Dmitri Fyodorovitch, came in. They had, in fact, given up expecting him, and his sudden appearance caused some surprise for a moment.

Chapter 6. Why Is Such a Man Alive?

DMITRI FYODOROVITCH, a young man of eight and twenty, of medium height and agreeable countenance, looked older than his years. He was muscular, and showed signs of considerable physical strength. Yet there was something not healthy in his face. It was rather thin, his cheeks were hollow, and there was an unhealthy sallowness in their colour. His rather large, prominent, dark eyes had an expression of firm determination, and yet there was a vague look in them, too. Even when he was excited and talking irritably, his eyes somehow did not follow his mood, but betrayed something else, sometimes quite incongruous with what was passing. "It's hard to tell what he's thinking," those who talked to him sometimes declared. People who saw something pensive and sullen in his eyes were startled by his sudden laugh, which bore witness to mirthful and light-hearted thoughts at the very time when his eyes were so gloomy. A certain strained look in his face was easy to understand at this moment. Everyone knew, or had heard of, the extremely restless and dissipated life which he had been leading of late, as well as of the violent anger to which he had been roused in his quarrels with his father. There were several stories current in the town about it. It is true that he was irascible by nature, "of an unstable and unbalanced mind," as our justice of the peace, Katchalnikov, happily described him.

He was stylishly and irreproachably dressed in a carefully buttoned frock-coat. He wore black gloves and carried a top hat. Having only lately left the army, he still had moustaches and no beard. His dark brown hair was cropped short, and combed forward on his temples. He had the long, determined stride of a military man. He stood still for a moment on the threshold, and glancing at the whole party went straight up to the elder, guessing him to be their host. He made him a low bow, and asked his blessing. Father Zossima, rising in his chair, blessed him. Dmitri kissed his hand respectfully, and with intense feeling, almost anger, he said:

"Be so generous as to forgive me for having kept you waiting so long, but Smerdyakov, the valet sent me by my father, in reply to my inquiries, told me twice over that the appointment was for one. Now I suddenly learn--"

"Don't disturb yourself," interposed the elder. "No matter. You are a little late. It's of no consequence..."

"I'm extremely obliged to you, and expected no less from your goodness."

Saying this, Dmitri bowed once more. Then, turning suddenly towards his father, made him, too, a similarly low and respectful bow. He had evidently considered it beforehand, and made this bow in all seriousness, thinking it his duty to show his respect and good intentions.

Although Fyodor Pavlovitch was taken unawares, he was equal to the occasion. In response to Dmitri's bow he jumped up from his chair and made his son a bow as low in return. His face was suddenly solemn and impressive, which gave him a positively malignant look. Dmitri bowed generally to all present, and without a word walked to the window with his long, resolute stride, sat down on the only empty chair, near Father Paissy, and, bending forward, prepared to listen to the conversation he had interrupted.

Dmitri's entrance had taken no more than two minutes, and the conversation was resumed. But this time Miusov thought it unnecessary to reply to Father Paissy's persistent and almost irritable question.

"Allow me to withdraw from this discussion," he observed with a certain well-bred nonchalance. "It's a subtle question, too. Here Ivan Fyodorovitch is smiling at us. He must have something interesting to say about that also. Ask him."

"Nothing special, except one little remark," Ivan replied at once. "European Liberals in general, and even our liberal dilettanti, often mix up the final results of socialism with those of Christianity. This wild notion is, of course, a characteristic feature. But it's not only Liberals and dilettanti who mix up socialism and Christianity, but, in many cases, it appears, the police--the foreign police, of course--do the same. Your Paris anecdote is rather to the point, Pyotr Alexandrovitch."

"I ask your permission to drop this subject altogether," Miusov repeated. "I will tell you instead, gentlemen, another interesting and rather characteristic anecdote of Ivan Fyodorovitch himself. Only five days ago, in a gathering here, principally of ladies, he solemnly declared in argument that there was nothing in the whole world to make men love their neighbours. That there was no law of nature that man should love mankind, and that, if there had been any love on earth hitherto, it was not owing to a natural law, but simply because men have believed in immortality. Ivan Fyodorovitch added in parenthesis that the whole natural law lies in that faith, and that if you were to destroy in mankind the belief in immortality, not only love but every living force maintaining the life of the world would at once be dried up. Moreover, nothing then would be immoral, everything would be lawful, even cannibalism. That's not all. He ended by asserting that for every individual, like ourselves, who does not believe in God or immortality, the moral law of nature must immediately be changed into the exact contrary of the former religious law, and that egoism, even to crime, must become not only lawful but even recognised as the inevitable, the most rational, even honourable outcome of his position. From this paradox, gentlemen, you can judge of the rest of our eccentric and paradoxical friend Ivan Fyodorovitch's theories."

"Excuse me," Dmitri cried suddenly; "if I've heard aright, crime must not only be permitted but even recognised as the inevitable and the most rational outcome of his position for every infidel! Is that so or not?"

"Quite so," said Father Paissy.

"I'll remember it."

Having uttered these words Dmitri ceased speaking as suddenly as he had begun. Everyone looked at him with curiosity.

"Is that really your conviction as to the consequences of the disappearance of the faith in immortality?" the elder asked Ivan suddenly.

"Yes. That was my contention. There is no virtue if there is no immortality."

"You are blessed in believing that, or else most unhappy."

"Why unhappy?" Ivan asked smiling.

"Because, in all probability you don't believe yourself in the immortality of your soul, nor in what you have written yourself in your article on Church Jurisdiction."

"Perhaps you are right!...But I wasn't altogether joking," Ivan suddenly and strangely confessed, flushing quickly.

"You were not altogether joking. That's true. The question is still fretting your heart, and not answered. But the martyr likes sometimes to divert himself with his despair, as it were driven to it by despair itself. Meanwhile, in your despair, you, too, divert yourself with magazine articles, and discussions in society, though you don't believe your own arguments, and with an aching heart mock at them inwardly...That question you have not answered, and it is your great grief, for it clamours for an answer."

"But can it be answered by me? Answered in the affirmative?" Ivan went on asking strangely, still looking at the elder with the same inexplicable smile.

"If it can't be decided in the affirmative, it will never be decided in the negative. You know that that is the peculiarity of your heart, and all its suffering is due to it. But thank the Creator who has given you a lofty heart capable of such suffering; of thinking and seeking higher things, for our dwelling is in the heavens. God grant that your heart will attain the answer on earth, and may God bless your path."

The elder raised his hand and would have made the sign of the cross over Ivan from where he stood. But the latter rose from his seat, went up to him, received his blessing, and kissing his hand went back to his place in silence. His face looked firm and earnest. This action and all the preceding conversation, which was so surprising from Ivan, impressed everyone by its strangeness and a certain solemnity, so that all were silent for a moment, and there was a look almost of apprehension in Alyosha's face. But Miusov suddenly shrugged his shoulders. And at the same moment Fyodor Pavlovitch jumped up from his seat.

"Most pious and holy elder," he cried pointing to Ivan, "that is my son, flesh of my flesh, the dearest of my flesh! He is my most dutiful Karl Moor, so to speak, while this son who has just come in, Dmitri, against whom I am seeking justice from you, is the undutiful Franz Moor--they are both out of Schiller's Robbers, and so I am the reigning Count von Moor! Judge and save us! We need not only your prayers but your prophecies!"

"Speak without buffoonery, and don't begin by insulting the members of your family," answered the elder, in a faint, exhausted voice. He was obviously getting more and more fatigued, and his strength was failing.

"An unseemly farce which I foresaw when I came here!" cried Dmitri indignantly. He too leapt up. "Forgive it, reverend Father," he added, addressing the elder. "I am not a cultivated man, and I don't even know how to address you properly, but you have been deceived and you have been too good-natured in letting us meet here. All my father wants is a scandal. Why he wants it only he can tell. He always has some motive. But I believe I know why--"

"They all blame me, all of them!" cried Fyodor Pavlovitch in his turn. "Pyotr Alexandrovitch here blames me too. You have been blaming me, Pyotr Alexandrovitch, you have!" he turned suddenly to Miusov, although the latter was not dreaming of interrupting him. "They all accuse me of having hidden the children's money in my boots, and cheated them, but isn't there a court of law? There they will reckon out for you, Dmitri Fyodorovitch, from your notes, your letters, and your agreements, how much money you had, how much you have spent, and how much you have left. Why does Pyotr Alexandrovitch refuse to pass judgment? Dmitri is not a stranger to him. Because they are all against me, while Dmitri Fyodorovitch is in debt to me, and not a little, but some thousands of which I have documentary proof. The whole town is echoing with his debaucheries. And where he was stationed before, he several times spent a thousand or two for the seduction of some respectable girl; we know all about that, Dmitri Fyodorovitch, in its most secret details. I'll prove it...Would you believe it, holy Father, he has captivated the heart of the most honourable of young ladies of good family and fortune, daughter of a gallant colonel, formerly his superior officer, who had received many honours and had the Anna Order on his breast. He compromised the girl by his promise of marriage, now she is an orphan and here; she is betrothed to him, yet before her very eyes he is dancing attendance on a certain enchantress. And although this enchantress has lived in, so to speak, civil marriage with a respectable man, yet she is of an independent character, an unapproachable fortress for everybody, just like a legal wife--for she is virtuous, yes, holy Fathers, she is virtuous. Dmitri Fyodorovitch wants to open this fortress with a golden key, and that's why he is insolent to me now, trying to get money from me, though he has wasted thousands on this enchantress already. He's continually borrowing money for the purpose. From whom do you think? Shall I say, Mitya?"

"Be silent!" cried Dmitri, "wait till I'm gone. Don't dare in my presence to asperse the good name of an honourable girl! That you should utter a word about her is an outrage, and I won't permit it!" He was breathless.

He was breathless. "Mitya! Mitya!" cried Fyodor Pavlovitch hysterically, squeezing out a tear. "And is your father's blessing nothing to you? If I curse you, what then?"

"Shameless hypocrite!" exclaimed Dmitri furiously.

"He says that to his father! his father What would he be with others? Gentlemen, only fancy; there's a poor but honourable man living here, burdened with a numerous family, a captain who got into trouble and was discharged from the army, but not publicly, not by court-martial, with no slur on his honour. And three weeks ago, Dmitri seized him by the beard in a tavern, dragged him out into the street and beat him publicly, and all because he is an agent in a little business of mine."

"It's all a lie! Outwardly it's the truth, but inwardly a lie!" Dmitri was trembling with rage. "Father, I don't justify my action. Yes, I confess it publicly, I behaved like a brute to that captain, and I regret it now, and I'm disgusted with myself for my brutal rage. But this captain, this agent of yours, went to that lady whom you call an enchantress, and suggested to her from you, that she should take I.O.U.s of mine which were in your possession, and should sue me for the money so as to get me into prison by means of them, if I persisted in claiming an account from you of my property. Now you reproach me for having a weakness for that lady when you yourself incited her to captivate me! She told me so to my face...She told me the story and laughed at you...You wanted to put me in prison because you are jealous of me with her, because you'd begun to force your attentions upon her; and I know all about that, too; she laughed at you for that as well--you hear--she laughed at you as she described it. So here you have this man, this father who reproaches his profligate son! Gentlemen, forgive my anger, but I foresaw that this crafty old man would only bring you together to create a scandal. I had come to forgive him if he held out his hand; to forgive him, and ask forgiveness! But as he has just this minute insulted not only me, but an honourable young lady, for whom I feel such reverence that I dare not take her name in vain, I have made up my mind to show up his game, though he is my father..."

He could not go on. His eyes were glittering and he breathed with difficulty. But everyone in the cell was stirred. All except Father Zossima got up from their seats uneasily. The monks looked austere but waited for guidance from the elder. He sat still, pale, not from excitement but from the weakness of disease. An imploring smile lighted up his face; from time to time he raised his hand, as though to check the storm, and, of course, a gesture from him would have been enough to end the scene; but he seemed to be waiting for something and watched them intently as though trying to make out something which was not perfectly clear to him. At last Miusov felt completely humiliated and disgraced.

"We are all to blame for this scandalous scene," he said hotly. "But I did not foresee it when I came, though I knew with whom I had to deal. This must be stopped at once! Believe me, your reverence, I had no precise knowledge of the details that have just come to light, I was unwilling to believe them, and I learn for the first time...A father is jealous of his son's relation with a woman of loose behaviour and intrigues with the creature to get his son into prison! This is the company in which I have been forced to be present! I was deceived. I declare to you all that I was as much deceived as anyone."

"Dmitri Fyodorovitch," yelled Fyodor Pavlovitch suddenly, in an unnatural voice, "if you were not my son I would challenge you this instant to a duel...with pistols, at three paces...across a handkerchief," he ended, stamping with both feet.

With old liars who have been acting all their lives there are moments when they enter so completely into their part that they tremble or shed tears of emotion in earnest, although at that very moment, or a second later, they are able to whisper to themselves, "You know you are lying, you shameless old sinner! You're acting now, in spite of your 'holy' wrath."

Dmitri frowned painfully, and looked with unutterable contempt at his father.

"I thought...I thought," he said in a soft and, as it were, controlled voice, "that I was coming to my native place with the angel of my heart, my betrothed, to cherish his old age, and I find nothing but a depraved profligate, a despicable clown!"

"A duel!" yelled the old wretch again, breathless and spluttering at each syllable. "And you, Pyotr Alexandrovitch Miusov, let me tell you that there has never been in all your family a loftier, and more honest-- you hear--more honest woman than this 'creature,' as you have dared to call her! And you, Dmitri Fyodorovitch, have abandoned your betrothed for that 'creature,' so you must yourself have thought that your betrothed couldn't hold a candle to her. That's the woman called a 'creature'."

"Shameful!" broke from Father Iosif.

"Shameful and disgraceful!" Kalganov, flushing crimson cried in a boyish voice, trembling with emotion. He had been silent till that moment.

"Why is such a man alive?" Dmitri, beside himself with rage, growled in a hollow voice, hunching up his shoulders till he looked almost deformed. "Tell me, can he be allowed to go on defiling the earth?" He looked round at everyone and pointed at the old man. He spoke evenly and deliberately.

"Listen, listen, monks, to the parricide!" cried Fyodor Pavlovitch, rushing up to Father Iosif. "That's the answer to your 'shameful!' What is shameful? That 'creature,' that 'woman of loose behaviour' is perhaps holier than you are yourselves, you monks who are seeking salvation! She fell perhaps in her youth, ruined by her environment. But she loved much, and Christ himself forgave the woman 'who loved much.'"

"It was not for such love Christ forgave her," broke impatiently from the gentle Father Iosif.

"Yes, it was for such, monks, it was! You save your souls here, eating cabbage, and think you are the righteous. You eat a gudgeon a day, and you think you bribe God with gudgeon."

"This is unendurable!" was heard on all sides in the cell.

But this unseemly scene was cut short in a most unexpected way. Father Zossima Father Zossima rose suddenly from his seat. Almost distracted with anxiety for the elder and everyone else, Alyosha succeeded, however, in supporting him by the arm. Father Zossima moved towards Dmitri and reaching him sank on his knees before him. Alyosha thought that he had fallen from weakness, but this was not so. The elder distinctly and deliberately bowed down at Dmitri's feet till his forehead touched the floor. Alyosha was so astounded that he failed to assist him when he got up again. There was a faint smile on his lips.

"Good-bye! Forgive me, all of you", he said, bowing on all sides to his guests.

Dmitri stood for a few moments in amazement. Bowing down to him--what did it mean? Suddenly he cried aloud, "Oh God!" hid his face in his hands, and rushed out of the room. All the guests flocked out after him, in their confusion not saying good-bye, or bowing to their host. Only the monks went up to him again for a blessing.

"What did it mean, falling at his feet like that? Was it symbolic or what?" said Fyodor Pavlovitch, suddenly quieted and trying to reopen conversation without venturing to address anybody in particular. They were all passing out of the precincts of the hermitage at the moment.

"I can't answer for a madhouse and for madmen," Miusov answered at once ill-humouredly, "but I will spare myself your company, Fyodor Pavlovitch, and, trust me, for ever. Where's that monk?"

"That monk," that is, the monk who had invited them to dine with the Superior, did not keep them waiting. He met them as soon as they came down the steps from the elder's cell, as though he had been waiting for them all the time.

"Reverend Father, kindly do me a favour. Convey my deepest respect to the Father Superior, apologise for me, personally, Miusov, to his reverence, telling him that I deeply regret that owing to unforeseen circumstances I am unable to have the honour of being present at his table, greatly I should desire to do so," Miusov said irritably to the monk.

"And that unforeseen circumstance, of course, is myself," Fyodor Pavlovitch cut in immediately. "Do you hear, Father; this gentleman doesn't want to remain in my company or else he'd come at once. And you shall go, Pyotr Alexandrovitch, pray go to the Father Superior and good appetite to you. I will decline, and not you. Home, home, I'll eat at home, I don't feel equal to it here, Pyotr Alexandrovitch, my amiable relative."

"I am not your relative and never have been, you contemptible man!"

"I said it on purpose to madden you, because you always disclaim the relationship, though you really are a relation in spite of your shuffling. I'll prove it by the church calendar. As for you, Ivan, stay if you like. I'll send the horses for you later. Propriety requires you to go to the Father Superior, Pyotr Alexandrovitch, to apologise for the disturbance we've been making..."

"Is it true that you are going home? Aren't you lying?"

"Pyotr Alexandrovitch! How could I dare after what's happened! Forgive me, gentlemen, I was carried away! And upset besides! And, indeed, I am ashamed. Gentlemen, one man has the heart of Alexander of Macedon and another the heart of the little dog Fido. Mine is that of the little dog Fido. I am ashamed! After such an escapade how can I go to dinner, to gobble up the monastery's sauces? I am ashamed, I can't. You must excuse me!"

"The devil only knows, what if he deceives us?" thought Miusov, still hesitating, and watching the retreating buffoon with distrustful eyes. The latter turned round, and noticing that Miusov was watching him, waved him a kiss.

"Well, are you coming to the Superior?" Miusov asked Ivan abruptly.

"Why not? I was especially invited yesterday."

"Unfortunately I feel myself compelled to go to this confounded dinner," said Miusov with the same irritability, regardless of the fact that the monk was listening. "We ought, at least, to apologise for the disturbance, and explain that it was not our doing. What do you think?"

"Yes, we must explain that it wasn't our doing. Besides, father won't be there," observed Ivan.

"Well, I should hope not! Confound this dinner!"

They all walked on, however. The monk listened in silence. On the road through the copse he made one observation however--that the Father Superior had been waiting a long time, and that they were more than half an hour late. He received no answer. Miusov looked with hatred at Ivan.

"Here he is, going to the dinner as though nothing had happened," he thought. "A brazen face, and the conscience of a Karamazov!"

Chapter 7. A Young Man Bent on a Career

ALYOSHA helped Father Zossima to his bedroom and seated him on his bed. It was a little room furnished with the bare necessities. There was a narrow iron bedstead, with a strip of felt for a mattress. In the corner, under the ikons, was a reading-desk with a cross and the Gospel lying on it. The elder sank exhausted on the bed. His eyes glittered and he breathed hard. He looked intently at Alyosha, as though considering something.

"Go, my dear boy, go. Porfiry is enough for me. Make haste, you are needed there, go and wait at the Father Superior's table."

"Let me stay here," Alyosha entreated.

"You are more needed there. There is no peace there. You will wait, and be of service. If evil spirits rise up, repeat a prayer. And remember, my son"--the elder liked to call him that--"this is not the place for you in the future. When it is God's will to call me, leave the monastery. Go away for good."

Alyosha started.

"What is it? This is not your place for the time. I bless you for great service in the world. Yours will be a long pilgrimage. And you will have to take a wife, too. You will have to bear all before you come back. There will be much to do. But I don't doubt of you, and so I send you forth. Christ is with you. Do not abandon Him and He will not abandon you. You will see great sorrow, and in that sorrow you will be happy. This is my last message to you: in sorrow seek happiness. Work, work unceasingly. Remember my words, for although I shall talk with you again, not only my days but my hours are numbered."

Alyosha's face again betrayed strong emotion. The corners of his mouth quivered.

"What is it again?" Father Zossima asked, smiling gently. "The worldly may follow the dead with tears, but here we rejoice over the father who is departing. We rejoice and pray for him. Leave me, I must pray. Go, and make haste. Be near your brothers. And not near one only, but near both."

Father Zossima raised his hand to bless him. Alyosha could make no protest, though he had a great longing to remain. He longed, moreover, to ask the significance of his bowing to Dmitri, the question was on the tip of his tongue, but he dared not ask it. He knew that the elder would have explained it unasked if he had thought fit.

But evidently it was not his will. That action had made a terrible impression on Alyosha; he believed blindly in its mysterious significance. Mysterious, and perhaps awful.

As he hastened out of the hermitage precincts to reach the monastery in time to serve at the Father Superior's dinner, he felt a sudden pang at his heart, and stopped short. He seemed to hear again Father Zossima's words, foretelling his approaching end. What he had foretold so exactly must infallibly come to pass. Alyosha believed that implicitly. But how could he go? He had told him not to weep, and to leave the monastery. Good God! It was long since Alyosha had known such anguish. He hurried through the copse that divided the monastery from the hermitage, and unable to bear the burden of his thoughts, he gazed at the ancient pines beside the path. He had not far to go--about five hundred paces. He expected to meet no one at that hour, but at the first turn of the path he noticed Rakitin. He was waiting for someone.

"Are you waiting for me?" asked Alyosha, overtaking him.

"Yes," grinned Rakitin. "You are hurrying to the Father Superior, I know; he has a banquet. There's not been such a banquet since the Superior entertained the Bishop and General Pahatov, do you remember? I shan't be there, but you go and hand the sauces. Tell me one thing, Alexey, what does that vision mean? That's what I want to ask you."

"What vision?"

"That bowing to your brother, Dmitri. And didn't he tap the ground with his forehead, too!"

"You speak of Father Zossima?"

"Yes, of Father Zossima,"

"Tapped the ground?"

"Ah, an irreverent expression! Well, what of it? Anyway, what does that vision mean?"

"I don't know what it means, Misha."

"I knew he wouldn't explain it to you There's nothing wonderful about it, of course, only the usual holy mummery. But there was an object in the performance. All the pious people in the town will talk about it and spread the story through the province, wondering what it meant. To my thinking the old man really has a keen nose; he sniffed a crime. Your house stinks of it."

Rakitin evidently had something he was eager to speak of.

"It'll be in your family, this crime. Between your brothers and your rich old father. So Father Zossima flopped down to be ready for what may turn up. If something happens later on, it'll be: 'Ah, the holy man foresaw it, prophesied it!' though it's a poor sort of prophecy, flopping like that. 'Ah, but it was symbolic,' they'll say, 'an allegory,' and the devil knows what all! It'll be remembered to his glory: 'He predicted the crime and marked the criminal!' That's always the way with these crazy fanatics; they cross themselves at the tavern and throw stones at the temple. Like your elder, he takes a stick to a just man and falls at the feet of a murderer."

"What crime? What do you mean?"

Alyosha stopped dead. Rakitin stopped, too.

"What murderer? As though you didn't know! I'll bet you've thought of it before. That's interesting, too, by the way. Listen, Alyosha, you always speak the truth, though you're always between two stools. Have you thought of it or not? Answer."

"I have," answered Alyosha in a low voice. Even Rakitin was taken aback.

"What? Have you really?" he cried.

"I...I've not exactly thought it," muttered Alyosha, "but directly you began speaking so strangely, I fancied I had thought of it myself."

"You see? (And how well you expressed it!) Looking at your father and your brother Mitya to-day you thought of a crime. Then I'm not mistaken?"

"But wait, wait a minute," Alyosha broke in uneasily, "What has led you to see all this? Why does it interest you? That's the first question."

"Two questions, disconnected, but natural. I'll deal with them separately. What led me to see it? I shouldn't have seen it, if I hadn't suddenly understood your brother Dmitri, seen right into the very heart of him all at once. I caught the whole man from one trait. These very honest but passionate people have a line which mustn't be crossed. If it were, he'd run at your father with a knife. But your father's a drunken and abandoned old sinner, who can never draw the line--if they both themselves go, they'll both come to grief."

"No, Misha, no. If that's all, you've reassured me. It won't come to that."

"But why are you trembling? Let me tell you; he may be honest, our Mitya (he is stupid, but honest), but he's-- a sensualist. That's the very definition and inner essence of him. It's your father has handed him on his low sensuality. Do you know, I simply wonder at you, Alyosha, how you can have kept your purity. You're a Karamazov too, you know! In your family sensuality is carried to a disease. But now, these three sensualists are watching one another, with their knives in their belts. The three of them are knocking their heads together, and you may be the fourth."

"You are mistaken about that woman. Dmitri despises her," said Alyosha, with a sort of shudder.

"Grushenka? No, brother, he doesn't despise her. Since he has openly abandoned his betrothed for her, he doesn't despise her. There's something here, my dear boy, that you don't understand yet. A man will fall in love with some beauty, with a woman's body, or even with a part of a woman's body (a sensualist can understand that), and he'll abandon his own children for her, sell his father and mother, and his country, Russia, too. If he's honest, he'll steal; if he's humane, he'll murder; if he's faithful, he'll deceive. Pushkin, the poet of women's feet, sung of their feet in his verse. Others don't sing their praises, but they can't look at their feet without a thrill--and it's not only their feet. Contempt's no help here, brother, even if he did despise Grushenka. He does, but he can't tear himself away."

"I understand that," Alyosha jerked out suddenly.

"Really? Well, I dare say you do understand, since you blurt it out at the first word," said Rakitin, malignantly. "That escaped you unawares, and the confession's the more precious. So it's a familiar subject; you've thought about it already, about sensuality, I mean! Oh, you virgin soul! You're a quiet one, Alyosha, you're a saint, I know, but the devil only knows what you've thought about, and what you know already! You are pure, but you've been down into the depths...I've been watching you a long time. You're a Karamazov yourself; you're a thorough Karamazov--no doubt birth and selection have something to answer for. You're a sensualist from your father, a crazy saint from your mother. Why do you tremble? Is it true, then? Do you know, Grushenka has been begging me to bring you along. 'I'll pull off his cassock,' she says. You can't think how she keeps begging me to bring you. I wondered why she took such an interest in you. Do you know, she's an extraordinary woman, too!"

"Thank her and say I'm not coming," said Alyosha, with a strained smile. "Finish what you were saying, Misha. I'll tell you my idea after."

"There's nothing to finish. It's all clear. It's the same old tune, brother. If even you are a sensualist at heart, what of your brother, Ivan? He's a Karamazov, too. What is at the root of all you Karamazovs is that you're all sensual, grasping and crazy! Your brother Ivan writes theological articles in joke, for some idiotic, unknown motive of his own, though he's an atheist, and he admits it's a fraud himself--that's your brother Ivan. He's trying to get Mitya's betrothed for himself, and I fancy he'll succeed, too. And what's more, it's with Mitya's consent. For Mitya will surrender his betrothed to him to be rid of her, and escape to Grushenka. And he's ready to do that in spite of all his nobility and disinterestedness. Observe that. Those are the most fatal people! Who the devil can make you out? He recognises his vileness and goes on with it! Let me tell you, too, the old man, your father, is standing in Mitya's way now. He has suddenly gone crazy over Grushenka. His mouth waters at the sight of her. It's simply on her account he made that scene in the cell just now, simply because Miusov called her an 'abandoned creature.' He's worse than a tom-cat in love. At first she was only employed by him in connection with his taverns and in some other shady business, but now he has suddenly realised all she is and has gone wild about her. He keeps pestering her with his offers, not honourable ones, of course. And they'll come into collision, the precious father and son, on that path! But Grushenka favours neither of them, she's still playing with them, and teasing them both, considering which she can get most out of. For though she could filch a lot of money from the papa he wouldn't marry her, and maybe he'll turn stingy in the end, and keep his purse shut. That's where Mitya's value comes in; he has no money, but he's ready to marry her. Yes, ready to marry her! to abandon his betrothed, a rare beauty, Katerina Ivanovna, who's rich, and the daughter of a colonel, and to marry Grushenka, who has been the mistress of a dissolute old merchant, Samsonov, a coarse, uneducated, provincial mayor. Some murderous conflict may well come to pass from all this, and that's what your brother Ivan is waiting for. It would suit him down to the ground. He'll carry off Katerina Ivanovna, for whom he is languishing, and pocket her dowry of sixty thousand. That's very alluring to start with, for a man of no consequence and a beggar. And, take note, he won't be wronging Mitya, but doing him the greatest service. For I know as a fact that Mitya only last week, when he was with some Gipsy girls drunk in a tavern, cried out aloud that he was unworthy of his betrothed, Katya, but that his brother Ivan, he was the man who deserved her. And Katerina Ivanovna will not in the end refuse such a fascinating man as Ivan. She's hesitating between the two of them already. And how has that Ivan won you all, so that you all worship him? He is laughing at you, and enjoying himself at your expense."

"How do you know? How can you speak so confidently?" Alyosha asked sharply, frowning.

"Why do you ask, and are frightened at my answer? It shows that you know I'm speaking the truth."

"You don't like Ivan. Ivan wouldn't be tempted by money."

"Really? And the beauty of Katerina Ivanovna? It's not only the money, though a fortune of sixty thousand is an attraction."

"Ivan is above that. He wouldn't make up to anyone for thousands. It is not money, it's not comfort Ivan is seeking. Perhaps it's suffering he is seeking."

"What wild dream now? Oh, you--aristocrats!"

"Ah, Misha, he has a stormy spirit. His mind is in bondage. He is haunted by a great, unsolved doubt. He is one of those who don't want millions, but an answer to their questions."

"That's plagiarism, Alyosha. You're quoting your elder's phrases. Ah, Ivan has set you a problem!" cried Rakitin, with undisguised malice. His face changed, and his lips twitched. "And the problem's a stupid one. It is no good guessing it. Rack your brains--you'll understand it. His article is absurd and ridiculous. And did you hear his stupid theory just now: if there's no immortality of the soul, then there's no virtue, and everything is lawful. (And by the way, do you remember how your brother Mitya cried out: 'I will remember!') An attractive theory for scoundrels!--(I'm being abusive, that's stupid.) Not for scoundrels, but for pedantic poseurs, 'haunted by profound, unsolved doubts.' He's showing off, and what it all comes to is, 'on the one hand we cannot but admit' and 'on the other it must be confessed!' His whole theory is a fraud! Humanity will find in itself the power to live for virtue even without believing in immortality. It will find it in love for freedom, for equality, for fraternity."

Rakitin could hardly restrain himself in his heat, but, suddenly, as though remembering something, he stopped short.

"Well, that's enough," he said, with a still more crooked smile. "Why are you laughing? Do you think I'm a vulgar fool?"

"No, I never dreamed of thinking you a vulgar fool. You are clever but...never mind, I was silly to smile. I understand your getting hot about it, Misha. I guess from your warmth that you are not indifferent to Katerina Ivanovna yourself; I've suspected that for a long time, brother, that's why you don't like my brother Ivan. Are you jealous of him?"

"And jealous of her money, too? Won't you add that?"

"I'll say nothing about money. I am not going to insult you."

"I believe it, since you say so, but confound you, and your brother Ivan with you. Don't you understand that one might very well dislike him, apart from Katerina Ivanovna. And why the devil should I like him? He condescends to abuse me, you know. Why haven't I a right to abuse him?"

"I never heard of his saying anything about you, good or bad. He doesn't speak of you at all."

"But I heard that the day before yesterday at Katerina Ivanovna's he was abusing me for all he was worth--you see what an interest he takes in your humble servant. And which is the jealous one after that, brother, I can't say. He was so good as to express the opinion that, if I don't go in for the career of an archimandrite in the immediate future and don't become a monk, I shall be sure to go to Petersburg and get on to some solid magazine as a reviewer, that I shall write for the next ten years, and in the end become the owner of the magazine, and bring it out on the liberal and atheistic side, with a socialistic tinge, with a tiny gloss of socialism, but keeping a sharp lookout all the time, that is, keeping in with both sides and hoodwinking the fools. According to your brother's account, the tinge of socialism won't hinder me from laying by the proceeds and investing them under the guidance of some Jew, till at the end of my career I build a great house in Petersburg and move my publishing offices to it, and let out the upper stories to lodgers. He has even chosen the place for it, near the new stone bridge across the Neva, which they say is to be built in Petersburg."

"Ah, Misha, that's just what will really happen, every word of it," cried Alyosha, unable to restrain a good-humoured smile.

"You are pleased to be sarcastic, too, Alexey Fyodorovitch."

"No, no, I'm joking, forgive me. I've something quite different in my mind. But, excuse me, who can have told you all this? You can't have been at Katerina Ivanovna's yourself when he was talking about you?"

"I wasn't there, but Dmitri Fyodorovitch was; and I heard him tell it with my own ears; if you want to know, he didn't tell me, but I overheard him, unintentionally, of course, for I was sitting in Grushenka's bedroom and I couldn't go away because Dmitri Fyodorovitch was in the next room."

"Oh yes, I'd forgotten she was a relation of yours."

"A relation! That Grushenka a relation of mine!" cried Rakitin, turning crimson. "Are you mad? You're out of your mind!"

"Why, isn't she a relation of yours? I heard so."

"Where can you have heard it? You Karamazovs brag of being an ancient, noble family, though your father used to run about playing the buffoon at other men's tables, and was only admitted to the kitchen as a favour. I may be only a priest's son, and dirt in the eyes of noblemen like you, but don't insult me so lightly and wantonly. I have a sense of honour, too, Alexey Fyodorovitch, I couldn't be a relation of Grushenka, a common harlot. I beg you to understand that!"

Rakitin was intensely irritated.

"Forgive me, for goodness' sake, I had no idea...besides...how can you call her a harlot? Is she...that sort of woman?" Alyosha flushed suddenly. "I tell you again, I heard that she was a relation of yours. You often go to see her, and you told me yourself you're not her lover. I never dreamed that you of all people had such contempt for her! Does she really deserve it?"

"I may have reasons of my own for visiting her. That's not your business. But as for relationship, your brother, or even your father, is more likely to make her yours than mine. Well, here we are. You'd better go to the kitchen. Hullo! what's wrong, what is it? Are we late? They can't have finished dinner so soon! Have the Karamazovs been making trouble again? No doubt they have. Here's your father and your brother Ivan after him. They've broken out from the Father Superior's. And look, Father Isidor's shouting out something after them from the steps. And your father's shouting and waving his arms. I expect he's swearing. Bah, and there goes Miusov driving away in his carriage. You see, he's going. And there's old Maximov running!--there must have been a row. There can't have been any dinner. Surely they've not been beating the Father Superior! Or have they, perhaps, been beaten? It would serve them right!"

There was reason for Rakitin's exclamations. There had been a scandalous, an unprecedented scene. It had all come from the impulse of a moment.

Chapter 8. The Scandalous Scene

MIUSOV, as a man of breeding and delicacy, could not but feel some inward qualms, when he reached the Father Superior's with Ivan: he felt ashamed of having lost his temper. He felt that he ought to have disdained that despicable wretch, Fyodor Pavlovitch, too much to have been upset by him in Father Zossima's cell, and so to have forgotten himself. "The monks were not to blame, in any case," he reflected, on the steps. "And if they're decent people here (and the Father Superior, I understand, is a nobleman) why not be friendly and courteous with them? I won't argue, I'll fall in with everything, I'll win them by politeness, and...and...show them that I've nothing to do with that Aesop, that buffoon, that Pierrot, and have merely been taken in over this affair, just as they have."

He determined to drop his litigation with the monastery, and relinquish his claims to the wood-cutting and fishery rights at once. He was the more ready to do this because the rights had become much less valuable, and he had indeed the vaguest idea where the wood and river in question were.

These excellent intentions were strengthened when he entered the Father Superior's dining-room, though, strictly speaking, it was not a dining-room, for the Father Superior had only two rooms altogether; they were, however, much larger and more comfortable than Father Zossima's. But there was no great luxury about the furnishing of these rooms either. The furniture was of mahogany, covered with leather, in the old-fashioned style of 1820 the floor was not even stained, but everything was shining with cleanliness, and there were many choice flowers in the windows; the most sumptuous thing in the room at the moment was, of course, the beautifully decorated table. The cloth was clean, the service shone; there were three kinds of well-baked bread, two bottles of wine, two of excellent mead, and a large glass jug of kvas--both the latter made in the monastery, and famous in the neighbourhood. There was no vodka. Rakitin related afterwards that there were five dishes: fish-soup made of sterlets, served with little fish patties; then boiled fish served in a special way; then salmon cutlets, ice pudding and compote, and finally, blanc-mange. Rakitin found out about all these good things, for he could not resist peeping into the kitchen, where he already had a footing. He had a footing everywhere, and got information about everything. He was of an uneasy and envious temper. He was well aware of his own considerable abilities, and nervously exaggerated them in his self-conceit. He knew he would play a prominent part of some sort, but Alyosha, who was attached to him, was distressed to see that his friend Rakitin was dishonourable, and quite unconscious of being so himself, considering, on the contrary, that because he would not steal money left on the table he was a man of the highest integrity. Neither Alyosha nor anyone else could have influenced him in that.

Rakitin, of course, was a person of too little consequence to be invited to the dinner, to which Father Iosif, Father Paissy, and one other monk were the only inmates of the monastery invited. They were already waiting when Miusov, Kalganov, and Ivan arrived. The other guest, Maximov, stood a little aside, waiting also. The Father Superior stepped into the middle of the room to receive his guests. He was a tall, thin, but still vigorous old man, with black hair streaked with grey, and a long, grave, ascetic face. He bowed to his guests in silence. But this time they approached to receive his blessing. Miusov even tried to kiss his hand, but the Father Superior drew it back in time to avoid the salute. But Ivan and Kalganov went through the ceremony in the most simple-hearted and complete manner, kissing his hand as peasants do.

"We must apologise most humbly, your reverence," began Miusov, simpering affably, and speaking in a dignified and respectful tone. "Pardon us for having come alone without the gentleman you invited, Fyodor Pavlovitch. He felt obliged to decline the honour of your hospitality, and not without reason. In the reverend Father Zossima's cell he was carried away by the unhappy dissension with his son, and let fall words which were quite out of keeping...in fact, quite unseemly...as"--he glanced at the monks--"your reverence is, no doubt, already aware. And therefore, recognising that he had been to blame, he felt sincere regret and shame, and begged me, and his son Ivan Fyodorovitch, to convey to you his apologies and regrets. In brief, he hopes and desires to make amends later. He asks your blessing, and begs you to forget what has taken place."

As he uttered the last word of his tirade, Miusov completely recovered his self-complacency, and all traces of his former irritation disappeared. He fully and sincerely loved humanity again.

The Father Superior listened to him with dignity, and, with a slight bend of the head, replied:

"I sincerely deplore his absence. Perhaps at our table he might have learnt to like us, and we him. Pray be seated, gentlemen."

He stood before the holy image, and began to say grace, aloud. All bent their heads reverently, and Maximov clasped his hands before him, with peculiar fervour.

It was at this moment that Fyodor Pavlovitch played his last prank. It must be noted that he really had meant to go home, and really had felt the impossibility of going to dine with the Father Superior as though nothing had happened, after his disgraceful behaviour in the elder's cell. Not that he was so very much ashamed of himself-- quite the contrary perhaps. But still he felt it would be unseemly to go to dinner. Yet his creaking carriage had hardly been brought to the steps of the hotel, and he had hardly got into it, when he suddenly stopped short. He remembered his own words at the elder's: "I always feel when I meet people that I am lower than all, and that they all take me for a buffoon; so I say let me play the buffoon, for you are, every one of you, stupider and lower than I." He longed to revenge himself on everyone for his own unseemliness. He suddenly recalled how he had once in the past been asked, "Why do you hate so and so, so much?" And he had answered them, with his shameless impudence, "I'll tell you. He has done me no harm. But I played him a dirty trick, and ever since I have hated him."

Remembering that now, he smiled quietly and malignantly, hesitating for a moment. His eyes gleamed, and his lips positively quivered.

"Well, since I have begun, I may as well go on," he decided. His predominant sensation at that moment might be expressed in the following words, "Well, there is no rehabilitating myself now. So let me shame them for all I am worth. I will show them I don't care what they think--that's all!"

He told the coachman to wait, while with rapid steps he returned to the monastery and straight to the Father Superior's. He had no clear idea what he would do, but he knew that he could not control himself, and that a touch might drive him to the utmost limits of obscenity, but only to obscenity, to nothing criminal, nothing for which he could be legally punished. In the last resort, he could always restrain himself, and had marvelled indeed at himself, on that score, sometimes. He appeared in the Father Superior's dining-room, at the moment when the prayer was over, and all were moving to the table. Standing in the doorway, he scanned the company, and laughing his prolonged, impudent, malicious chuckle, looked them all boldly in the face. "They thought I had gone, and here I am again," he cried to the whole room.

For one moment everyone stared at him without a word; and at once everyone felt that something revolting, grotesque, positively scandalous, was about to happen. Miusov passed immediately from the most benevolent frame of mind to the most savage. All the feelings that had subsided and died down in his heart revived instantly.

"No! this I cannot endure!" he cried. "I absolutely cannot! and...I certainly cannot!"

The blood rushed to his head. He positively stammered; but he was beyond thinking of style, and he seized his hat.

"What is it he cannot?" cried Fyodor Pavlovitch, "that he absolutely cannot and certainly cannot? Your reverence, am I to come in or not? Will you receive me as your guest?"

"You are welcome with all my heart," answered the Superior. "Gentlemen!" he added, "I venture to beg you most earnestly to lay aside your dissensions, and to be united in love and family harmony--with prayer to the Lord at our humble table."

"No, no, it is impossible!" cried Miusov, beside himself.

"Well, if it is impossible for Pyotr Alexandrovitch, it is impossible for me, and I won't stop. That is why I came. I will keep with Pyotr Alexandrovitch everywhere now. If you will go away, Pyotr Alexandrovitch, I will go away too, if you remain, I will remain. You stung him by what you said about family harmony, Father Superior, he does not admit he is my relation. That's right, isn't it, von Sohn? Here's von Sohn. How are you, von Sohn?"

"Do you mean me?" muttered Maximov, puzzled.

"Of course I mean you," cried Fyodor Pavlovitch. "Who else? The Father Superior could not be von Sohn."

"But I am not von Sohn either. I am Maximov."

"No, you are von Sohn. Your reverence, do you know who von Sohn was? It was a famous murder case. He was killed in a house of harlotry--I believe that is what such places are called among you--he was killed and robbed, and in spite of his venerable age, he was nailed up in a box and sent from Petersburg to Moscow in the luggage van, and while they were nailing him up, the harlots sang songs and played the harp, that is to say, the piano. So this is that very von Solin. He has risen from the dead, hasn't he, von Sohn?"

"What is happening? What's this?" voices were heard in the group of monks.

"Let us go," cried Miusov, addressing Kalganov.

"No, excuse me," Fyodor Pavlovitch broke in shrilly, taking another step into the room. "Allow me to finish. There in the cell you blamed me for behaving disrespectfully just because I spoke of eating gudgeon, Pyotr Alexandrovitch. Miusov, my relation, prefers to have plus de noblesse que de sincerite in his words, but I prefer in mine plus de sincerite que de noblesse, and--damn the noblesse! That's right, isn't it, von Sohn? Allow me, Father Superior, though I am a buffoon and play the buffoon, yet I am the soul of honour, and I want to speak my mind. Yes, I am the soul of honour, while in Pyotr Alexandrovitch there is wounded vanity and nothing else. I came here perhaps to have a look and speak my mind. My son, Alexey, is here, being saved. I am his father; I care for his welfare, and it is my duty to care. While I've been playing the fool, I have been listening and having a look on the sly; and now I want to give you the last act of the performance. You know how things are with us? As a thing falls, so it lies. As a thing once has fallen, so it must lie for ever. Not a bit of it! I want to get up again. Holy Father, I am indignant with you. Confession is a great sacrament, before which I am ready to bow down reverently; but there in the cell, they all kneel down and confess aloud. Can it be right to confess aloud? It was ordained by the holy Fathers to confess in secret: then only your confession will be a mystery, and so it was of old. But how can I explain to him before everyone that I did this and that...well, you understand what-- sometimes it would not be proper to talk about it--so it is really a scandal! No, Fathers, one might be carried along with you to the Flagellants, I dare say...at the first opportunity I shall write to the Synod, and I shall take my son, Alexey, home."

We must note here that Fyodor Pavlovitch knew where to look for the weak spot. There had been at one time malicious rumours which had even reached the Archbishop (not only regarding our monastery, but in others where the institution of elders existed) that too much respect was paid to the elders, even to the detriment of the authority of the Superior, that the elders abused the sacrament of confession and so on and so on--absurd charges which had died away of themselves everywhere. But the spirit of folly, which had caught up Fyodor Pavlovitch and was bearing him on the current of his own nerves into lower and lower depths of ignominy, prompted him with this old slander. Fyodor Pavlovitch did not understand a word of it, and he could not even put it sensibly, for on this occasion no one had been kneeling and confessing aloud in the elder's cell, so that he could not have seen anything of the kind. He was only speaking from confused memory of old slanders. But as soon as he had uttered his foolish tirade, he felt he had been talking absurd nonsense, and at once longed to prove to his audience, and above all to himself, that he had not been talking nonsense. And, though he knew perfectly well that with each word he would be adding more and more absurdity, he could not restrain himself, and plunged forward blindly.

"How disgraceful!" cried Pyotr Alexandrovitch.

"Pardon me!" said the Father Superior. "It was said of old, 'Many have begun to speak against me and have uttered evil sayings about me. And hearing it I have said to myself: it is the correction of the Lord and He has sent it to heal my vain soul.' And so we humbly thank you, honoured guest!" and he made Fyodor Pavlovitch a low bow.

"Tut--tut--tut--sanctimoniousness and stock phrases! Old phrases and old gestures. The old lies and formal prostrations. We know all about them. A kiss on the lips and a dagger in the heart, as in Schiller's Robbers. I don't like falsehood, Fathers, I want the truth. But the truth is not to be found in eating gudgeon and that I proclaim aloud! Father monks, why do you fast? Why do you expect reward in heaven for that? Why, for reward like that I will come and fast too! No, saintly monk, you try being virtuous in the world, do good to society, without shutting yourself up in a monastery at other people's expense, and without expecting a reward up aloft for it--you'll find that a bit harder. I can talk sense, too, Father Superior. What have they got here?" He went up to the table. "Old port wine, mead brewed by the Eliseyev Brothers. Fie, fie, fathers! That is something beyond gudgeon. Look at the bottles the fathers have brought out, he he he! And who has provided it all? The Russian peasant, the labourer, brings here the farthing earned by his horny hand, wringing it from his family and the tax-gatherer! You bleed the people, you know, holy Fathers."

"This is too disgraceful!" said Father Iosif.

Father Paissy kept obstinately silent. Miusov rushed from the room, and Kalgonov after him.

"Well, Father, I will follow Pyotr Alexandrovitch! I am not coming to see you again. You may beg me on your knees, I shan't come. I sent you a thousand roubles, so you have begun to keep your eye on me. He he he! No, I'll say no more. I am taking my revenge for my youth, for all the humiliation I endured." He thumped the table with his fist in a paroxysm of simulated feeling. "This monastery has played a great part in my life! It has cost me many bitter tears. You used to set my wife, the crazy one, against me. You cursed me with bell and book, you spread stories about me all over the place. Enough, fathers! This is the age of Liberalism, the age of steamers and railways. Neither a thousand, nor a hundred roubles, no, nor a hundred farthings will you get out of me!"

It must be noted again that our monastery never had played any great part in his life, and he never had shed a bitter tear owing to it. But he was so carried away by his simulated emotion, that he was for one moment almost believing it himself. He was so touched he was almost weeping. But at that very instant, he felt that it was time to draw back.

The Father Superior bowed his head at his malicious lie, and again spoke impressively:

"It is written again, 'Bear circumspectly and gladly dishonour that cometh upon thee by no act of thine own, be not confounded and hate not him who hath dishonoured thee.' And so will we."

"Tut, tut, tut! Bethinking thyself and the rest of the rigmarole. Bethink yourselves Fathers, I will go. But I will take my son, Alexey, away from here for ever, on my parental authority. Ivan Fyodorovitch, my most dutiful son, permit me to order you to follow me. Von Sohn, what have you to stay for? Come and see me now in the town. It is fun there. It is only one short verst; instead of lenten oil, I will give you sucking-pig and kasha. We will have dinner with some brandy and liqueur to it...I've cloudberry wine. Hey, von Sohn, don't lose your chance." He went out, shouting and gesticulating.

It was at that moment Rakitin saw him and pointed him out to Alyosha.

"Alexey!" his father shouted, from far off, catching sight of him. "You come home to me to-day, for good, and bring your pillow and mattress, and leave no trace behind."

Alyosha stood rooted to the spot, watching the scene in silence. Meanwhile, Fyodor Pavlovitch had got into the carriage, and Ivan was about to follow him in grim silence without even turning to say good-bye to Alyosha. But at this point another almost incredible scene of grotesque buffoonery gave the finishing touch to the episode. Maximov suddenly appeared by the side of the carriage. He ran up, panting, afraid of being too late. Rakitin and Alyosha saw him running. He was in such a hurry that in his impatience he put his foot on the step on which Ivan's left foot was still resting, and clutching the carriage he kept trying to jump in. "I am going with you!" he kept shouting, laughing a thin mirthful laugh with a look of reckless glee in his face. "Take me, too."

"There!" cried Fyodor Pavlovitch, delighted. "Did I not say he was von Sohn. It is von Sohn himself, risen from the dead. Why, how did you tear yourself away? What did you von Sohn there? And how could you get away from the dinner? You must be a brazen-faced fellow! I am that myself, but I am surprised at you, brother! Jump in, jump in! Let him pass, Ivan. It will be fun. He can lie somewhere at our feet. Will you lie at our feet, von Sohn? Or perch on the box with the coachman. Skip on to the box, von Sohn!"

But Ivan, who had by now taken his seat, without a word gave Maximov a violent punch in the breast and sent him flying. It was quite by chance he did not fall.

"Drive on!" Ivan shouted angrily to the coachman.

"Why, what are you doing, what are you about? Why did you do that?" Fyodor Pavlovitch protested.

But the carriage had already driven away. Ivan made no reply.

"Well, you are a fellow," Fyodor Pavlovitch said again.

After a pause of two minutes, looking askance at his son, "Why, it was you got up all this monastery business. You urged it, you approved of it. Why are you angry now?"

"You've talked rot enough. You might rest a bit now," Ivan snapped sullenly.

Fyodor Pavlovitch was silent again for two minutes.

"A drop of brandy would be nice now," he observed sententiously, but Ivan made no response.

"You shall have some, too, when we get home."

Ivan was still silent.

Fyodor Pavlovitch waited another two minutes.

"But I shall take Alyosha away from the monastery, though you will dislike it so much, most honoured Karl von Moor."

Ivan shrugged his shoulders contemptuously, and turning away stared at the road. And they did not speak again all the way home.

THE Karamazovs' house was far from being in the centre of the town, but it was not quite outside it. It was a pleasant-looking old house of two stories, painted grey, with a red iron roof. It was roomy and snug, and might still last many years. There were all sorts of unexpected little cupboards and closets and staircases. There were rats in it, but Fyodor Pavlovitch did not altogether dislike them. "One doesn't feel so solitary when one's left alone in the evening," he used to say. It was his habit to send the servants away to the lodge for the night and to lock himself up alone. The lodge was a roomy and solid building in the yard. Fyodor Pavlovitch used to have the cooking done there, although there was a kitchen in the house; he did not like the smell of cooking, and, winter and summer alike, the dishes were carried in across the courtyard. The house was built for a large family; there was room for five times as many, with their servants. But at the time of our story there was no one living in the house but Fyodor Pavlovitch and his son Ivan. And in the lodge there were only three servants: old Grigory, and his old wife Marfa, and a young man called Smerdyakov. Of these three we must say a few words. Of old Grigory we have said something already. He was firm and determined and went blindly and obstinately for his object, if once be had been brought by any reasons (and they were often very illogical ones) to believe that it was immutably right. He was honest and incorruptible. His wife, Marfa Ignatyevna, had obeyed her husband's will implicitly all her life, yet she had pestered him terribly after the emancipation of the serfs. She was set on leaving Fyodor Pavlovitch and opening a little shop in Moscow with their small savings. But Grigory decided then, once for all, that "the woman's talking nonsense, for every woman is dishonest," and that they ought not to leave their old master, whatever he might be, for "that was now their duty."

"Do you understand what duty is?" he asked Marfa Ignatyevna.

"I understand what duty means, Grigory Vassilyevitch, but why it's our duty to stay here I never shall understand," Marfa answered firmly.

"Well, don't understand then. But so it shall be. And you hold your tongue."

And so it was. They did not go away, and Fyodor Pavlovitch promised them a small sum for wages, and paid it regularly. Grigory knew, too, that he had an indisputable influence over his master. It was true, and he was aware of it. Fyodor Pavlovitch was an obstinate and cunning buffoon, yet, though his will was strong enough "in some of the affairs of life," as he expressed it, he found himself, to his surprise, extremely feeble in facing certain other emergencies. He knew his weaknesses and was afraid of them. There are positions in which one has to keep a sharp lookout. And that's not easy without a trustworthy man, and Grigory was a most trustworthy man. Many times in the course of his life Fyodor Pavlovitch had only just escaped a sound thrashing through Grigory's intervention, and on each occasion the old servant gave him a good lecture. But it wasn't only thrashings that Fyodor Pavlovitch was afraid of. There were graver occasions, and very subtle and complicated ones, when Fyodor Pavlovitch could not have explained the extraordinary craving for someone faithful and devoted, which sometimes unaccountably came upon him all in a moment. It was almost a morbid condition. Corrupt and often cruel in his lust, like some noxious insect, Fyodor Pavlovitch was sometimes, in moments of drunkenness, overcome by superstitious terror and a moral convulsion which took an almost physical form. "My soul's simply quaking in my throat at those times," he used to say. At such moments he liked to feel that there was near at hand, in the lodge if not in the room, a strong, faithful man, virtuous and unlike himself, who had seen all his debauchery and knew all his secrets, but was ready in his devotion to overlook all that, not to oppose him, above all, not to reproach him or threaten him with anything, either in this world or in the next, and, in case of need, to defend him--from whom? From somebody unknown, but terrible and dangerous. What he needed was to feel that there was another man, an old and tried friend, that he might call him in his sick moments merely to look at his face, or, perhaps, exchange some quite irrelevant words with him. And if the old servant were not angry, he felt comforted, and if he were angry, he was more dejected. It happened even (very rarely however) that Fyodor Pavlovitch went at night to the lodge to wake Grigory and fetch him for a moment. When the old man came, Fyodor Pavlovitch would begin talking about the most trivial matters, and would soon let him go again, sometimes even with a jest. And after he had gone, Fyodor Pavlovitch would get into bed with a curse and sleep the sleep of the just. Something of the same sort had happened to Fyodor Pavlovitch on Alyosha's arrival. Alyosha "pierced his heart" by "living with him, seeing everything and blaming nothing." Moreover, Alyosha brought with him something his father had never known before: a complete absence of contempt for him and an invariable kindness, a perfectly natural unaffected devotion to the old man who deserved it so little. All this was a complete surprise to the old profligate, who had dropped all family ties. It was a new and surprising experience for him, who had till then loved nothing but "evil." When Alyosha had left him, he confessed to himself that he had learnt something he had not till then been willing to learn.

I have mentioned already that Grigory had detested Adelaida Ivanovna, the first wife of Fyodor Pavlovitch and the mother of Dmitri, and that he had, on the contrary, protected Sofya Ivanovna, the poor "crazy woman," against his master and anyone who chanced to speak ill or lightly of her. His sympathy for the unhappy wife had become something sacred to him, so that even now, twenty years after, he could not bear a slighting allusion to her from anyone, and would at once check the offender. Externally, Grigory was cold, dignified and taciturn, and spoke, weighing his words, without frivolity. It was impossible to tell at first sight whether he loved his meek, obedient wife; but he really did love her, and she knew it.

Marfa Ignatyevna was by no means foolish; she was probably, indeed, cleverer than her husband, or, at least, more prudent than he in worldly affairs, and yet she had given in to him in everything without question or complaint ever since her marriage, and respected him for his spiritual superiority. It was remarkable how little they spoke to one another in the course of their lives, and only of the most necessary daily affairs. The grave and dignified Grigory thought over all his cares and duties alone, so that Marfa Ignatyevna had long grown used to knowing that he did not need her advice. She felt that her husband respected her silence, and took it as a sign of her good sense. He had never beaten her but once, and then only slightly. Once during the year after Fyodor Pavlovitch's marriage with Adelaida Ivanovna, the village girls and women--at that time serfs--were called together before the house to sing and dance. They were beginning "In the Green Meadows," when Marfa, at that time a young woman, skipped forward and danced "the Russian Dance," not in the village fashion, but as she had danced it when she was a servant in the service of the rich Miusov family, in their private theatre, where the actors were taught to dance by a dancing master from Moscow. Grigory saw how his wife danced, and, an hour later, at home in their cottage he gave her a lesson, pulling her hair a little. But there it ended: the beating was never repeated, and Marfa Ignatyevna gave up dancing.

God had not blessed them with children. One child was born but it died. Grigory was fond of children, and was not ashamed of showing it. When Adelaida Ivanovna had run away, Grigory took Dmitri, then a child of three years old, combed his hair and washed him in a tub with his own hands, and looked after him for almost a year. Afterwards he had looked after Ivan and Alyosha, for which the general's widow had rewarded him with a slap in the face; but I have already related all that. The only happiness his own child had brought him had been in the anticipation of its birth. When it was born, he was overwhelmed with grief and horror. The baby had six fingers. Grigory was so crushed by this, that he was not only silent till the day of the christening, but kept away in the garden. It was spring, and he spent three days digging the kitchen garden. The third day was fixed for christening the baby: meantime Grigory had reached a conclusion. Going into the cottage where the clergy were assembled and the visitors had arrived, including Fyodor Pavlovitch, who was to stand godfather, he suddenly announced that the baby "ought not to be christened at all." He announced this quietly, briefly, forcing out his words, and gazing with dull intentness at the priest.

"Why not?" asked the priest with good-humoured surprise.

"Because it's a dragon," muttered Grigory.

"A dragon? What dragon?"

Grigory did not speak for some time. "It's a confusion of nature," he muttered vaguely, but firmly, and obviously unwilling to say more.

They laughed, and, of course, christened the poor baby. Grigory prayed earnestly at the font, but his opinion of the new-born child remained unchanged. Yet he did not interfere in any way. As long as the sickly infant lived he scarcely looked at it, tried indeed not to notice it, and for the most part kept out of the cottage. But when, at the end of a fortnight, the baby died of thrush, he himself laid the child in its little coffin, looked at it in profound grief, and when they were filling up the shallow little grave he fell on his knees and bowed down to the earth. He did not for years afterwards mention his child, nor did Marfa speak of the baby before him, and, even if Grigory were not present, she never spoke of it above a whisper. Marfa observed that, from the day of the burial, he devoted himself to "religion," and took to reading the Lives of the Saints, for the most part sitting alone and in silence, and always putting on his big, round, silver-rimmed spectacles. He rarely read aloud, only perhaps in Lent. He was fond of the Book of Job, and had somehow got hold of a copy of the sayings and sermons of "the God fearing Father Isaac the Syrian, which he read persistently for years together, understanding very little of it, but perhaps prizing and loving it the more for that. Of late he had begun to listen to the doctrines of the sect of Flagellants settled in the neighbourhood. He was evidently shaken by them, but judged it unfitting to go over to the new faith. His habit of theological reading gave him an expression of still greater gravity.

He was perhaps predisposed to mysticism. And the birth of his deformed child, and its death, had, as though by special design, been accompanied by another strange and marvellous event, which, as he said later, had left a "stamp" upon his soul. It happened that, on the very night after the burial of his child, Marfa was awakened by the wail of a new-born baby. She was frightened and waked her husband. He listened and said he thought it was more like someone groaning, "it might be a woman." He got up and dressed. It was a rather warm night in May. As he went down the steps, he distinctly heard groans coming from the garden. But the gate from the yard into the garden was locked at night, and there was no other way of entering it, for it was enclosed all round by a strong, high fence. Going back into the house, Grigory lighted a lantern, took the garden key, and taking no notice of the hysterical fears of his wife, who was still persuaded that she heard a child crying, and that it was her own baby crying and calling for her, went into the garden in silence. There he heard at once that the groans came from the bath-house that stood near the garden gate, and that they were the groans of a woman. Opening the door of the bath-house, he saw a sight which petrified him. An idiot girl, who wandered about the streets and was known to the whole town by the nickname of Lizaveta Smerdyastchaya (Stinking Lizaveta), had got into the bath-house and had just given birth to a child. She lay dying with the baby beside her. She said nothing, for she had never been able to speak. But her story needs a chapter to itself.

Chapter 2. Lizaveta

There was one circumstance which struck Grigory particularly, and confirmed a very unpleasant and revolting suspicion. This Lizaveta was a dwarfish creature, "not five foot within a wee bit," as many of the pious old women said pathetically about her, after her death. Her broad, healthy, red face had a look of blank idiocy and the fixed stare in her eyes was unpleasant, in spite of their meek expression. She wandered about, summer and winter alike, barefooted, wearing nothing but a hempen smock. Her coarse, almost black hair curled like lamb's wool, and formed a sort of huge cap on her head. It was always crusted with mud, and had leaves; bits of stick, and shavings clinging to it, as she always slept on the ground and in the dirt. Her father, a homeless, sickly drunkard, called Ilya, had lost everything and lived many years as a workman with some well-to-do tradespeople. Her mother had long been dead. Spiteful and diseased, Ilya used to beat Lizaveta inhumanly whenever she returned to him. But she rarely did so, for everyone in the town was ready to look after her as being an idiot, and so specially dear to God. Ilya's employers, and many others in the town, especially of the tradespeople, tried to clothe her better, and always rigged her out with high boots and sheepskin coat for the winter. But, although she allowed them to dress her up without resisting, she usually went away, preferably to the cathedral porch, and taking off all that had been given her--kerchief, sheepskin, skirt or boots--she left them there and walked away barefoot in her smock as before. It happened on one occasion that a new governor of the province, making a tour of inspection in our town, saw Lizaveta, and was wounded in his tenderest susceptibilities. And though he was told she was an idiot, he pronounced that for a young woman of twenty to wander about in nothing but a smock was a breach of the proprieties, and must not occur again. But the governor went his way, and Lizaveta was left as she was. At last her father died, which made her even more acceptable in the eyes of the religious persons of the town, as an orphan. In fact, everyone seemed to like her; even the boys did not tease her, and the boys of our town, especially the schoolboys, are a mischievous set. She would walk into strange houses, and no one drove her away. Everyone was kind to her and gave her something. If she were given a copper, she would take it, and at once drop it in the alms-jug of the church or prison. If she were given a roll or bun in the market, she would hand it to the first child she met. Sometimes she would stop one of the richest ladies in the town and give it to her, and the lady would be pleased to take it. She herself never tasted anything but black bread and water. If she went into an expensive shop, where there were costly goods or money lying about, no one kept watch on her, for they knew that if she saw thousands of roubles overlooked by them, she would not have touched a farthing. She scarcely ever went to church. She slept either in the church porch or climbed over a hurdle (there are many hurdles instead of fences to this day in our town) into a kitchen garden. She used at least once a week to turn up "at home," that is at the house of her father's former employers, and in the winter went there every night, and slept either in the passage or the cow-house. People were amazed that she could stand such a life, but she was accustomed to it, and, although she was so tiny, she was of a robust constitution. Some of the townspeople declared that she did all this only from pride, but that is hardly credible. She could hardly speak, and only from time to time uttered an inarticulate grunt. How could she have been proud?

It happened one clear, warm, moonlight night in September (many years ago) five or six drunken revellers were returning from the club at a very late hour, according to our provincial notions. They passed through the "backway," which led between the back gardens of the houses, with hurdles on either side. This way leads out on to the bridge over the long, stinking pool which we were accustomed to call a river. Among the nettles and burdocks under the hurdle our revellers saw Lizaveta asleep. They stopped to look at her, laughing, and began jesting with unbridled licentiousness. It occurred to one young gentleman to make the whimsical inquiry whether anyone could possibly look upon such an animal as a woman, and so forth...They all pronounced with lofty repugnance that it was impossible. But Fyodor Pavlovitch, who was among them, sprang forward and declared that it was by no means impossible, and that, indeed, there was a certain piquancy about it, and so on...It is true that at that time he was overdoing his part as a buffoon. He liked to put himself forward and entertain the company, ostensibly on equal terms, of course, though in reality he was on a servile footing with them. It was just at the time when he had received the news of his first wife's death in Petersburg, and, with crape upon his hat, was drinking and behaving so shamelessly that even the most reckless among us were shocked at the sight of him. The revellers, of course, laughed at this unexpected opinion; and one of them even began challenging him to act upon it. The others repelled the idea even more emphatically, although still with the utmost hilarity, and at last they went on their way. Later on, Fyodor Pavlovitch swore that he had gone with them, and perhaps it was so, no one knows for certain, and no one ever knew. But five or six months later, all the town was talking, with intense and sincere indignation, of Lizaveta's condition, and trying to find out who was the miscreant who had wronged her. Then suddenly a terrible rumour was all over the town that this miscreant was no other than Fyodor Pavlovitch. Who set the rumour going? Of that drunken band five had left the town and the only one still among us was an elderly and much respected civil councillor, the father of grown-up daughters, who could hardly have spread the tale, even if there had been any foundation for it. But rumour pointed straight at Fyodor Pavlovitch, and persisted in pointing at him. Of course this was no great grievance to him: he would not have troubled to contradict a set of tradespeople. In those days he was proud, and did not condescend to talk except in his own circle of the officials and nobles, whom he entertained so well.

At the time, Grigory stood up for his master vigorously. He provoked quarrels and altercations in defence of him and succeeded in bringing some people round to his side. "It's the wench's own fault," he asserted, and the culprit was Karp, a dangerous convict, who had escaped from prison and whose name was well known to us, as he had hidden in our town. This conjecture sounded plausible, for it was remembered that Karp had been in the neighbourhood just at that time in the autumn, and had robbed three people. But this affair and all the talk about it did not estrange popular sympathy from the poor idiot. She was better looked after than ever. A well-to-do merchants's widow named Kondratyev arranged to take her into her house at the end of April, meaning not to let her go out until after the confinement. They kept a constant watch over her, but in spite of their vigilance she escaped on the very last day, and made her way into Fyodor Pavlovitch's garden. How, in her condition, she managed to climb over the high, strong fence remained a mystery. Some maintained that she must have been lifted over by somebody; others hinted at something more uncanny. The most likely explanation is that it happened naturally--that Lizaveta, accustomed to clambering over hurdles to sleep in gardens, had somehow managed to climb this fence, in spite of her condition, and had leapt down, injuring herself.

Grigory rushed to Marfa and sent her to Lizaveta, while he ran to fetch an old midwife who lived close by. They saved the baby, but Lizaveta died at dawn. Grigory took the baby, brought it home, and making his wife sit down, put it on her lap. "A child of God--an orphan is akin to all," he said, "and to us above others. Our little lost one has sent us this, who has come from the devil's son and a holy innocent. Nurse him and weep no more."

So Marfa brought up the child. He was christened Pavel, to which people were not slow in adding Fyodorovitch (son of Fyodor). Fyodor Pavlovitch did not object to any of this, and thought it amusing, though he persisted vigorously in denying his responsibility. The townspeople were pleased at his adopting the foundling. Later on, Fyodor Pavlovitch invented a surname for the child, calling him Smerdyakov, after his mother's nickname.

So this Smerdyakov became Fyodor Pavlovitch's second servant, and was living in the lodge with Grigory and Marfa at the time our story begins. He was employed as cook. I ought to say something of this Smerdyakov, but I am ashamed of keeping my readers' attention so long occupied with these common menials, and I will go back to my story, hoping to say more of Smerdyakov in the course of it.

Chapter 3. The Confession of a Passionate Heart--in Verse

Alyosha remained for some time irresolute after hearing the command his father shouted to him from the carriage. But in spite of his uneasiness he did not stand still. That was not his way. He went at once to the kitchen to find out what his father had been doing above. Then he set off, trusting that on the way he would find some answer to the doubt tormenting him. I hasten to add that his father's shouts, commanding him to return home "with his mattress and pillow" did not frighten him in the least. He understood perfectly that those peremptory shouts were merely "a flourish" to produce an effect. In the same way a tradesman in our town who was celebrating his name-day with a party of friends, getting angry at being refused more vodka, smashed up his own crockery and furniture and tore his own and his wife's clothes, and finally broke his windows, all for the sake of effect. Next day, of course, when he was sober, he regretted the broken cups and saucers. Alyosha knew that his father would let him go back to the monastery next day, possibly even that evening. Moreover, he was fully persuaded that his father might hurt anyone else, but would not hurt him. Alyosha was certain that no one in the whole world ever would want to hurt him, and, what is more, he knew that no one could hurt him. This was for him an axiom, assumed once for all without question, and he went his way without hesitation, relying on it.

But at that moment an anxiety of sort disturbed him, and worried him the more because he could not formulate it. It was the fear of a woman, of Katerina Ivanovna, who had so urgently entreated him in the note handed to him by Madame Hohlakov to come and see her about something. This request and the necessity of going had at once aroused an uneasy feeling in his heart, and this feeling had grown more and more painful all the morning in spite of the scenes at the hermitage and at the Father Superior's. He was not uneasy because he did not know what she would speak of and what he must answer. And he was not afraid of her simply as a woman. Though he knew little of women, he spent his life, from early childhood till he entered the monastery, entirely with women. He was afraid of that woman, Katerina Ivanovna. He had been afraid of her from the first time he saw her. He had only seen her two or three times, and had only chanced to say a few words to her. He thought of her as a beautiful, proud, imperious girl. It was not her beauty which troubled him, but something else. And the vagueness of his apprehension increased the apprehension itself. The girl's aims were of the noblest, he knew that. She was trying to save his brother Dmitri simply through generosity, though he had already behaved badly to her. Yet, although Alyosha recognised and did justice to all these fine and generous sentiments, a shiver began to run down his back as soon as he drew near her house.

He reflected that he would not find Ivan, who was so intimate a friend, with her, for Ivan was certainly now with his father. Dmitri he was even more certain not to find there, and he had a foreboding of the reason. And so his conversation would be with her alone. He had a great longing to run and see his brother Dmitri before that fateful interview. Without showing him the letter, he could talk to him about it. But Dmitri lived a long way off, and he was sure to be away from home too. Standing still for a minute, he reached a final decision. Crossing himself with a rapid and accustomed gesture, and at once smiling, he turned resolutely in the direction of his terrible lady.

He knew her house. If he went by the High Street and then across the market-place, it was a long way round. Though our town is small, it is scattered, and the houses are far apart. And meanwhile his father was expecting him, and perhaps had not yet forgotten his command. He might be unreasonable, and so he had to make haste to get there and back. So he decided to take a short cut by the backway, for he knew every inch of the ground. This meant skirting fences, climbing over hurdles, and crossing other people's back-yards, where everyone he met knew him and greeted him. In this way he could reach the High Street in half the time.

He had to pass the garden adjoining his father's, and belonging to a little tumbledown house with four windows. The owner of this house, as Alyosha knew, was a bedridden old woman, living with her daughter, who had been a genteel maid-servant in generals' families in Petersburg. Now she had been at home a year, looking after her sick mother. She always dressed up in fine clothes, though her old mother and she had sunk into such poverty that they went every day to Fyodor Pavlovitch's kitchen for soup and bread, which Marfa gave readily. Yet, though the young woman came up for soup, she had never sold any of her dresses, and one of these even had a long train--a fact which Alyosha had learned from Rakitin, who always knew everything that was going on in the town. He had forgotten it as soon as he heard it, but now, on reaching the garden, he remembered the dress with the train, raised his head, which had been bowed in thought, and came upon something quite unexpected.

Over the hurdle in the garden, Dmitri, mounted on something, was leaning forward, gesticulating violently, beckoning to him, obviously afraid to utter a word for fear of being overheard. Alyosha ran up to the hurdle.

"It's a good thing you looked up. I was nearly shouting to you," Mitya said in a joyful, hurried whisper. "Climb in here quickly! How splendid that you've come! I was just thinking of you."

Alyosha was delighted too, but he did not know how to get over the hurdle. Mitya put his powerful hand under his elbow to help him jump. Tucking up his cassock, Alyosha leapt over the hurdle with the agility of a bare-legged street urchin.

"Well done! Now come along," said Mitya in an enthusiastic whisper.

"Where?" whispered Alyosha, looking about him and finding himself in a deserted garden with no one near but themselves. The garden was small, but the house was at least fifty paces away.

"There's no one here. Why do you whisper?" asked Alyosha.

"Why do I whisper? Deuce take it" cried Dmitri at the top of his voice. "You see what silly tricks nature plays one. I am here in secret, and on the watch. I'll explain later on, but, knowing it's a secret, I began whispering like a fool, when there's no need. Let us go. Over there. Till then be quiet. I want to kiss you.

"Glory to God in the world,

"Glory to God in me...I was just repeating that, sitting here, before you came."

The garden was about three acres in extent, and planted with trees only along the fence at the four sides. There were apple-trees, maples, limes and birch-trees. The middle of the garden was an empty grass space, from which several hundredweight of hay was carried in the summer. The garden was let out for a few roubles for the summer. There were also plantations of raspberries and currants and gooseberries laid out along the sides; a kitchen garden had been planted lately near the house.

Dmitri led his brother to the most secluded corner of the garden. There, in a thicket of lime-trees and old bushes of black currant, elder, snowball-tree, and lilac, there stood a tumbledown green summer-house; blackened with age. Its walls were of lattice-work, but there was still a roof which could give shelter. God knows when this summer-house was built. There was a tradition that it had been put up some fifty years before by a retired colonel called von Schmidt, who owned the house at that time. It was all in decay, the floor was rotting, the planks were loose, the woodwork smelled musty. In the summer-house there was a green wooden table fixed in the ground, and round it were some green benches upon which it was still possible to sit. Alyosha had at once observed his brother's exhilarated condition, and on entering the arbour he saw half a bottle of brandy and a wineglass on the table.

"That's brandy," Mitya laughed. "I see your look: 'He's drinking again' Distrust the apparition.

Distrust the worthless, lying crowd,

And lay aside thy doubts. I'm not drinking, I'm only 'indulging,' as that pig, your Rakitin, says. He'll be a civil councillor one day, but he'll always talk about 'indulging.' Sit down. I could take you in my arms, Alyosha, and press you to my bosom till I crush you, for in the whole world--in reality--in real-i-ty--(can you take it in?) I love no one but you!

He uttered the last words in a sort of exaltation.

"No one but you and one 'jade' I have fallen in love with, to my ruin. But being in love doesn't mean loving. You may be in love with a woman and yet hate her. Remember that! I can talk about it gaily still. Sit down here by the table and I'll sit beside you and look at you, and go on talking. You shall keep quiet and I'll go on talking, for the time has come. But on reflection, you know, I'd better speak quietly, for here--here--you can never tell what ears are listening. I will explain everything; as they say, 'the story will be continued.' Why have I been longing for you? Why have I been thirsting for you all these days, and just now? (It's five days since I've cast anchor here.) Because it's only to you I can tell everything; because I must, because I need you, because to-morrow I shall fly from the clouds, because to-morrow life is ending and beginning. Have you ever felt, have you ever dreamt of falling down a precipice into a pit? That's just how I'm falling, but not in a dream. And I'm not afraid, and don't you be afraid. At least, I am afraid, but I enjoy it. It's not enjoyment though, but ecstasy. Damn it all, whatever it is! A strong spirit, a weak spirit, a womanish spirit--what, ever it is! Let us praise nature: you see what sunshine, how clear the sky is, the leaves are all green, it's still summer; four o'clock in the afternoon and the stillness! Where were you going?"

"I was going to father's, but I meant to go to Katerina Ivanovna's first."

"To her, and to father! Oo! what a coincidence! Why was I waiting for you? Hungering and thirsting for you in every cranny of my soul and even in my ribs? Why, to send you to father and to her, Katerina Ivanovna, so as to have done with her and with father. To send an angel. I might have sent anyone, but I wanted to send an angel. And here you are on your way to see father and her."

"Did you really mean to send me?" cried Alyosha with a distressed expression.

"Stay! You knew it And I see you understand it all at once. But be quiet, be quiet for a time. Don't be sorry, and don't cry."

Dmitri stood up, thought a moment, and put his finger to his forehead.

"She's asked you, written to you a letter or something, that's why you're going to her? You wouldn't be going except for that?"

"Here is her note." Alyosha took it out of his pocket. Mitya looked through it quickly.

"And you were going the backway! Oh, gods, I thank you for sending him by the backway, and he came to me like the golden fish to the silly old fishermen in the fable! Listen, Alyosha, listen, brother! Now I mean to tell you everything, for I must tell someone. An angel in heaven I've told already; but I want to tell an angel on earth. You are an angel on earth. You will hear and judge and forgive. And that's what I need, that someone above me should forgive. Listen! If two people break away from everything on earth and fly off into the unknown, or at least one of them, and before flying off or going to ruin he comes to someone else and says, 'Do this for me'--some favour never asked before that could only be asked on one's deathbed--would that other refuse, if he were a friend or a brother?"

"I will do it, but tell me what it is, and make haste," said Alyosha.

"Make haste! H'm!...Don't be in a hurry, Alyosha, you hurry and worry yourself. There's no need to hurry now. Now the world has taken a new turning. Ah, Alyosha, what a pity you can't understand ecstasy. But what am I saying to him? As though you didn't understand it. What an ass I am! What am I saying? 'Be noble, O man!'--who says that?"

Alyosha made up his mind to wait. He felt that, perhaps, indeed, his work lay here. Mitya sank into thought for a moment, with his elbow on the table and his head in his hand. Both were silent.

"Alyosha," said Mitya, "you're the only one who won't laugh. I should like to begin--my confession--with Schiller's Hymn to Joy, An die Freude! I don't know German, I only know it's called that. Don't think I'm talking nonsense because I'm drunk. I'm not a bit drunk. Brandy's all very well, but I need two bottles to make me drunk:

Silenus with his rosy phiz
Upon his stumbling ass.

But I've not drunk a quarter of a bottle, and I'm not Silenus. I'm not Silenus, though I am strong,* for I've made a decision once for all. Forgive me the pun; you'll have to forgive me a lot more than puns to-day. Don't be uneasy. I'm not spinning it out. I'm talking sense, and I'll come to the point in a minute. I won't keep you in suspense. Stay, how does it go?"

* In Russian, silen.

He raised his head, thought a minute, and began with enthusiasm:

Wild and fearful in his cavern
Hid the naked troglodyte,
And the homeless nomad wandered
Laying waste the fertile plain.
Menacing with spear and arrow
In the woods the hunter strayed...
Woe to all poor wretches stranded
On those cruel and hostile shores!
From the peak of high Olympus
Came the mother Ceres down,
Seeking in those savage regions
Her lost daughter Proserpine.
But the Goddess found no refuge,
Found no kindly welcome there,
And no temple bearing witness
To the worship of the gods.
From the fields and from the vineyards
Came no fruits to deck the feasts,
Only flesh of bloodstained victims
Smouldered on the altar-fires,
And where'er the grieving goddess
Turns her melancholy gaze,
Sunk in vilest degradation
Man his loathsomeness displays

Mitya broke into sobs and seized Alyosha's hand.

"My dear, my dear, in degradation, in degradation now, too. There's a terrible amount of suffering for man on earth, a terrible lot of trouble. Don't think I'm only a brute in an officer's uniform, wallowing in dirt and drink. I hardly think of anything but of that degraded man--if only I'm not lying. I pray God I'm not lying and showing off. I think about that man because I am that man myself.

Would he purge his soul from vileness
And attain to light and worth,
He must turn and cling for ever
To his ancient Mother Earth.

But the difficulty is how am I to cling for ever to Mother Earth. I don't kiss her. I don't cleave to her bosom. Am I to become a peasant or a shepherd? I go on and I don't know whether I'm going to shame or to light and joy. That's the trouble, for everything in the world is a riddle! And whenever I've happened to sink into the vilest degradation (and it's always been happening) I always read that poem about Ceres and man. Has it reformed me? Never! For I'm a Karamazov. For when I do leap into the pit, I go headlong with my heels up, and am pleased to be falling in that degrading attitude, and pride myself upon it. And in the very depths of that degradation I begin a hymn of praise. Let me be accursed. Let me be vile and base, only let me kiss the hem of the veil in which my God is shrouded. Though I may be following the devil, I am Thy son, O Lord, and I love Thee, and I feel the joy without which the world cannot stand.

> Joy everlasting fostereth
> The soul of all creation,
> It is her secret ferment fires
> The cup of life with flame.
> 'Tis at her beck the grass hath turned
> Each blade towards the light
> And solar systems have evolved
> From chaos and dark night,
> Filling the realms of boundless space
> Beyond the sage's sight.
> At bounteous Nature's kindly breast,
> All things that breathe drink Joy,
> And birds and beasts and creeping things
> All follow where She leads.
> Her gifts to man are friends in need,
> The wreath, the foaming must,
> To angels--vision of God's throne,
> To insects--sensual lust.

But enough poetry! I am in tears; let me cry. It may be foolishness that everyone would laugh at. But you won't laugh. Your eyes are shining, too. Enough poetry. I want to tell you now about the insects to whom God gave 'sensual lust.'

To insects--sensual lust.

I am that insect, brother, and it is said of me specially. All we Karamazovs are such insects, and, angel as you are, that insect lives in you, too, and will stir up a tempest in your blood. Tempests, because sensual lust is a tempest worse than a tempest! Beauty is a terrible and awful thing! It is terrible because it has not been fathomed and never can be fathomed, for God sets us nothing but riddles. Here the boundaries meet and all contradictions exist side by side. I am a cultivated man, brother, but I've thought a lot about this. It's terrible what mysteries there are! Too many riddles weigh men down on earth. We must solve them as we can, and try to keep a dry skin in the water. Beauty! I can't endure the thought that a man of lofty mind and heart begins with the ideal of the Madonna and ends with the ideal of Sodom. What's still more awful is that a man with the ideal of Sodom in his soul does not renounce the ideal of the Madonna, and his heart may be on fire with that ideal, genuinely on fire, just as in his days of youth and innocence. Yes, man is broad, too broad, indeed. I'd have him narrower. The devil only knows what to make of it! What to the mind is shameful is beauty and nothing else to the heart. Is there beauty in Sodom? Believe me, that for the immense mass of mankind beauty is found in Sodom. Did you know that secret? The awful thing is that beauty is mysterious as well as terrible. God and the devil are fighting there and the battlefield is the heart of man. But a man always talks of his own ache. Listen, now to come to facts."

Chapter 4. The Confession of a Passionate Heart--In Anecdote

"I was leading a wild life then. Father said just now that I spent several thousand roubles in seducing young girls. That's a swinish invention, and there was nothing of the sort. And if there was, I didn't need money simply for that. With me money is an accessory, the overflow of my heart, the framework. To-day she would be my lady, to-morrow a wench out of the streets in her place. I entertained them both. I threw away money by the handful on music, rioting, and Gypsies. Sometimes I gave it to the ladies, too, for they'll take it greedily, that must be admitted, and be pleased and thankful for it. Ladies used to be fond of me: not all of them, but it happened, it happened. But I always liked side-paths, little dark back-alleys behind the main road--there one finds adventures and surprises, and precious metal in the dirt. I am speaking figuratively, brother. In the town I was in, there were no such back-alleys in the literal sense, but morally there were. If you were like me, you'd know what that means. I loved vice, I loved the ignominy of vice. I loved cruelty; am I not a bug, am I not a noxious insect? In fact a Karamazov! Once we went, a whole lot of us, for a picnic, in seven sledges. It was dark, it was winter, and I began squeezing a girl's hand, and forced her to kiss me. She was the daughter of an official, a sweet, gentle, submissive creature. She allowed me, she allowed me much in the dark. She thought, poor thing, that I should come next day to make her an offer (I was looked upon as a good match, too). But I didn't say a word to her for five months. I used to see her in a corner at dances (we were always having dances), her eyes watching me. I saw how they glowed with fire--a fire of gentle indignation. This game only tickled that insect lust I cherished in my soul. Five months later she married an official and left the town, still angry, and still, perhaps, in love with me. Now they live happily. Observe that I told no one. I didn't boast of it. Though I'm full of low desires, and love what's low, I'm not dishonourable. You're blushing; your eyes flashed. Enough of this filth with you. And all this was nothing much--wayside blossoms a la Paul de Kock--though the cruel insect had already grown strong in my soul. I've a perfect album of reminiscences, brother. God bless them, the darlings. I tried to break it off without quarrelling. And I never gave them away, I never bragged of one of them. But that's enough. You can't suppose I brought you here simply to talk of such nonsense. No, I'm going to tell you something more curious; and don't be surprised that I'm glad to tell you, instead of being ashamed."

"You say that because I blushed," Alyosha said suddenly. "I wasn't blushing at what you were saying or at what you've done. I blushed because I am the same as you are."

"You? Come, that's going a little too far!"

"No, it's not too far," said Alyosha warmly (obviously the idea was not a new one). "The ladder's the same. I'm at the bottom step, and you're above, somewhere about the thirteenth. That's how I see it. But it's all the same. Absolutely the same in kind. Anyone on the bottom step is bound to go up to the top one."

"Then one ought not to step on at all."

"Anyone who can help it had better not."

"But can you?"

"I think not."

"Hush, Alyosha, hush, darling! I could kiss your hand, you touch me so. That rogue Grushenka has an eye for men. She told me once that she'd devour you one day. There, there, I won't! From this field of corruption fouled by flies, let's pass to my tragedy, also befouled by flies, that is, by every sort of vileness. Although the old man told lies about my seducing innocence, there really was something of the sort in my tragedy, though it was only once, and then it did not come off. The old man who has reproached me with what never happened does not even know of this fact; I never told anyone about it. You're the first, except Ivan, of course--Ivan knows everything. He knew about it long before you. But Ivan's a tomb."

"Ivan's a tomb?"

Alyosha listened with great attention.

"I was lieutenant in a line regiment, but still I was under supervision, like a kind of convict. Yet I was awfully well received in the little town. I spent money right and left. I was thought to be rich; I thought so myself. But I must have pleased them in other ways as well. Although they shook their heads over me, they liked me. My colonel, who was an old man, took a sudden dislike to me. He was always down upon me, but I had powerful friends, and, moreover, all the town was on my side, so he couldn't do me much harm. I was in fault myself for refusing to treat him with proper respect. I was proud. This obstinate old fellow, who was really a very good sort, kind-hearted and hospitable, had had two wives, both dead. His first wife, who was of a humble family, left a daughter as unpretentious as herself. She was a young woman of four and twenty when I was there, and was living with her father and an aunt, her mother's sister. The aunt was simple and illiterate; the niece was simple but lively. I like to say nice things about people. I never knew a woman of more charming character than Agafya--fancy, her name was Agafya Ivanovna! And she wasn't bad-looking either, in the Russian style: tall, stout, with a full figure, and beautiful eyes, though a rather coarse face. She had not married, although she had had two suitors. She refused them, but was as cheerful as ever. I was intimate with her, not in 'that' way, it was pure friendship. I have often been friendly with women quite innocently. I used to talk to her with shocking frankness, and she only laughed. Many woman like such freedom, and she was a girl too, which made it very amusing. Another thing, one could never think of her as a young lady. She and her aunt lived in her father's house with a sort of voluntary humility, not putting themselves on an equality with other people. She was a general favourite, and of use of everyone, for she was a clever dressmaker. She had a talent for it. She gave her services freely without asking for payment, but if anyone offered her payment, she didn't refuse. The colonel, of course, was a very different matter. He was one of the chief personages in the district. He kept open house, entertained the whole town, gave suppers and dances. At the time I arrived and joined the battalion, all the town was talking of the expected return of the colonel's second daughter, a great beauty, who had just left a fashionable school in the capital. This second daughter is Katerina Ivanovna, and she was the child of the second wife, who belonged to a distinguished general's family; although, as I learnt on good authority, she too brought the colonel no money. She had connections, and that was all. There may have been expectations, but they had come to nothing.

"Yet, when the young lady came from boarding-school on a visit, the whole town revived. Our most distinguished ladies--two 'Excellencies' and a colonel's wife--and all the rest following their lead, at once took her up and gave entertainments in her honour. She was the belle of the balls and picnics, and they got up tableaux vivants in aid of distressed governesses. I took no notice, I went on as wildly as before, and one of my exploits at the time set all the town talking. I saw her eyes taking my measure one evening at the battery commander's, but I didn't go up to her, as though I disdained her acquaintance. I did go up and speak to her at an evening party not long after. She scarcely looked at me, and compressed her lips scornfully. 'Wait a bit. I'll have my revenge,' thought I. I behaved like an awful fool on many occasions at that time, and I was conscious of it myself. What made it worse was that I felt that 'Katenka' was not an innocent boarding-school miss, but a person of character, proud and really high-principled; above all, she had education and intellect, and I had neither. You think I meant to make her an offer? No, I simply wanted to revenge myself, because I was such a hero and she didn't seem to feel it.

"Meanwhile, I spent my time in drink and riot, till the lieutenant-colonel put me under arrest for three days. Just at that time father sent me six thousand roubles in return for my sending him a deed giving up all claims upon him--settling our accounts, so to speak, and saying that I wouldn't expect anything more. I didn't understand a word of it at the time. Until I came here, Alyosha, till the last few days, indeed, perhaps even now, I haven't been able to make head or tail of my money affairs with father. But never mind that, we'll talk of it later.

"Just as I received the money, I got a letter from a friend telling me something that interested me immensely. The authorities, I learnt, were dissatisfied with our lieutenant-colonel. He was suspected of irregularities; in fact, his enemies were preparing a surprise for him. And then the commander of the division arrived, and kicked up the devil of a shindy. Shortly afterwards he was ordered to retire. I won't tell you how it all happened. He had enemies certainly. Suddenly there was a marked coolness in the town towards him and all his family. His friends all turned their backs on him. Then I took my first step. I met Agafya Ivanovna, with whom I'd always kept up a friendship, and said, 'Do you know there's a deficit of 4500 roubles of government money in your father's accounts?'

"'What do you mean? What makes you say so? The general was here not long ago, and everything was all right.'

"'Then it was, but now it isn't.'

"She was terribly scared.

"'Don't frighten me!' she said. 'Who told you so?'

"'Don't be uneasy,' I said, 'I won't tell anyone. You know I'm as silent as the tomb. I only wanted, in view of "possibilities," to add, that when they demand that 4500 roubles from your father, and he can't produce it, he'll be tried, and made to serve as a common soldier in his old age, unless you like to send me your young lady secretly. I've just had money paid me. I'll give her four thousand, if you like, and keep the secret religiously.'

"'Ah, you scoundrel!'--that's what she said. 'You wicked scoundrel! How dare you!'

"She went away furiously indignant, while I shouted after her once more that the secret should be kept sacred. Those two simple creatures, Agafya and her aunt, I may as well say at once, behaved like perfect angels all through this business. They genuinely adored their 'Katya,' thought her far above them, and waited on her, hand and foot. But Agafya told her of our conversation. I found that out afterwards. She didn't keep it back, and of course that was all I wanted.

"Suddenly the new major arrived to take command of the battalion. The old lieutenant-colonel was taken ill at once, couldn't leave his room for two days, and didn't hand over the government money. Dr. Kravchenko declared that he really was ill. But I knew for a fact, and had known for a long time, that for the last four years the money had never been in his hands except when the Commander made his visits of inspection. He used to lend it to a trustworthy person, a merchant of our town called Trifonov, an old widower, with a big beard and gold-rimmed spectacles. He used to go to the fair, do a profitable business with the money, and return the whole sum to the colonel, bringing with it a present from the fair, as well as interest on the loan. But this time (I heard all about it quite by chance from Trifonov's son and heir, a drivelling youth and one of the most vicious in the world)--this time, I say, Trifonov brought nothing back from the fair. The lieutenant-colonel flew to him. 'I've never received any money from you, and couldn't possibly have received any.' That was all the answer he got. So now our lieutenant-colonel is confined to the house, with a towel round his head, while they're all three busy putting ice on it. All at once an orderly arrives on the scene with the book and the order to 'hand over the battalion money immediately, within two hours.' He signed the book (I saw the signature in the book afterwards), stood up, saying he would put on his uniform, ran to his bedroom, loaded his double-barrelled gun with a service bullet, took the boot off his right foot, fixed the gun against his chest, and began feeling for the trigger with his foot. But Agafya, remembering what I had told her, had her suspicions. She stole up and peeped into the room just in time. She rushed in, flung herself upon him from behind, threw her arms round him, and the gun went off, hit the ceiling, but hurt no one. The others ran in, took away the gun, and held him by the arms. I heard all about this afterwards. I was at home, it was getting dusk, and I was just preparing to go out. I had dressed, brushed my hair, scented my handkerchief, and taken up my cap, when suddenly the door opened, and facing me in the room stood Katerina Ivanovna.

"It's strange how things happen sometimes. No one had seen her in the street, so that no one knew of it in the town. I lodged with two decrepit old ladies, who looked after me. They were most obliging old things, ready to do anything for me, and at my request were as silent afterwards as two cast-iron posts. Of course I grasped the position at once. She walked in and looked straight at me, her dark eyes determined, even defiant, but on her lips and round mouth I saw uncertainty.

"'My sister told me,' she began, 'that you would give me 4500 roubles if I came to you for it--myself. I have come...give me the money!'

"She couldn't keep it up. She was breathless, frightened, her voice failed her, and the corners of her mouth and the lines round it quivered. Alyosha, are you listening, or are you asleep?"

"Mitya, I know you will tell the whole truth, said Alyosha in agitation.

"I am telling it. If I tell the whole truth just as it happened I shan't spare myself. My first idea was a--Karamazov one. Once I was bitten by a centipede, brother, and laid up a fortnight with fever from it. Well, I felt a centipede biting at my heart then--a noxious insect, you understand? I looked her up and down. You've seen her? She's a beauty. But she was beautiful in another way then. At that moment she was beautiful because she was noble, and I was a scoundrel; she in all the grandeur of her generosity and sacrifice for her father, and I--a bug! And, scoundrel as I was, she was altogether at my mercy, body and soul. She was hemmed in. I tell you frankly, that thought, that venomous thought, so possessed my heart that it almost swooned with suspense. It seemed as if there could be no resisting it; as though I should act like a bug, like a venomous spider, without a spark of pity. I could scarcely breathe. Understand, I should have gone next day to ask for her hand, so that it might end honourably, so to speak, and that nobody would or could know. For though I'm a man of base desires, I'm honest. And at that very second some voice seemed to whisper in my ear, 'But when you come to-morrow to make your proposal, that girl won't even see you; she'll order her coachman to kick you out of the yard. "Publish it through all the town," she would say, "I'm not afraid of you." ' I looked at the young lady, my voice had not deceived me. That is how it would be, not a doubt of it. I could see from her face now that I should be turned out of the house. My spite was roused. I longed to play her the nastiest swinish cad's trick: to look at her with a sneer, and on the spot where she stood before me to stun her with a tone of voice that only a shopman could use.

"'Four thousand! What do you mean? I was joking. You've been counting your chickens too easily, madam. Two hundred, if you like, with all my heart. But four thousand is not a sum to throw away on such frivolity. You've put yourself out to no purpose.'

"I should have lost the game, of course. She'd have run away. But it would have been an infernal revenge. It would have been worth it all. I'd have howled with regret all the rest of my life, only to have played that trick. Would you believe it, it has never happened to me with any other woman, not one, to look at her at such a moment with hatred. But, on my oath, I looked at her for three seconds, or five perhaps, with fearful hatred--that hate which is only a hair's-breadth from love, from the maddest love!

"I went to the window, put my forehead against the frozen pane, and I remember the ice burnt my forehead like fire. I did not keep her long, don't be afraid. I turned round, went up to the table, opened the drawer and took out a banknote for five thousand roubles (it was lying in a French dictionary). Then I showed it her in silence, folded it, handed it to her, opened the door into the passage, and, stepping back, made her a deep bow, a most respectful, a most impressive bow, believe me! She shuddered all over, gazed at me for a second, turned horribly pale-white as a sheet, in fact--and all at once, not impetuously but softly, gently, bowed down to my feet--not a boarding-school curtsey, but a Russian bow, with her forehead to the floor. She jumped up and ran away. I was wearing my sword. I drew it and nearly stabbed myself with it on the spot; why, I don't know. It would have been frightfully stupid, of course. I suppose it was from delight. Can you understand that one might kill oneself from delight? But I didn't stab myself. I only kissed my sword and put it back in the scabbard--which there was no need to have told you, by the way. And I fancy that in telling you about my inner conflict I have laid it on rather thick to glorify myself. But let it pass, and to hell with all who pry into the human heart! Well, so much for that 'adventure' with Katerina Ivanovna. So now Ivan knows of it, and you--no one else."

Dmitri got up, took a step or two in his excitement, pulled out his handkerchief and mopped his forehead, then sat down again, not in the same place as before, but on the opposite side, so that Alyosha had to turn quite round to face him.

"NOW," said Alyosha, "I understand the first half."

"You understand the first half. That half is a drama, and it was played out there. The second half is a tragedy, and it is being acted here."

"And I understand nothing of that second half so far," said Alyosha.

"And I? Do you suppose I understand it?"

"Stop, Dmitri. There's one important question. Tell me, you were betrothed, betrothed still?"

"We weren't betrothed at once, not for three months after that adventure. The next day I told myself that the incident was closed, concluded, that there would be no sequel. It seemed to me caddish to make her an offer. On her side she gave no sign of life for the six weeks that she remained in the town; except, indeed, for one action. The day after her visit the maid-servant slipped round with an envelope addressed to me. I tore it open; it contained the change out of the banknote. Only four thousand five hundred roubles was needed, but there was a discount of about two hundred on changing it. She only sent me about two hundred and sixty. I don't remember exactly, but not a note, not a word of explanation. I searched the packet for a pencil mark n-nothing! Well, I spent the rest of the money on such an orgy that the new major was obliged to reprimand me.

"Well, the lieutenant-colonel produced the battalion money, to the astonishment of everyone, for nobody believed that he had the money untouched. He'd no sooner paid it than he fell ill, took to his bed, and, three weeks later, softening of the brain set in, and he died five days afterwards. He was buried with military honours, for he had not had time to receive his discharge. Ten days after his funeral, Katerina Ivanovna, with her aunt and sister, went to Moscow. And, behold, on the very day they went away (I hadn't seen them, didn't see them off or take leave) I received a tiny note, a sheet of thin blue paper, and on it only one line in pencil: 'I will write to you. Wait. K.' And that was all.

"I'll explain the rest now, in two words. In Moscow their fortunes changed with the swiftness of lightning and the unexpectedness of an Arabian fairy-tale. That general's widow, their nearest relation, suddenly lost the two nieces who were her heiresses and next-of-kin--both died in the same week of small-pox. The old lady, prostrated with grief, welcomed Katya as a daughter, as her one hope, clutched at her, altered her will in Katya's favour. But that concerned the future. Meanwhile she gave her, for present use, eighty thousand roubles, as a marriage portion, to do what she liked with. She was an hysterical woman. I saw something of her in Moscow, later.

"Well, suddenly I received by post four thousand five hundred roubles. I was speechless with surprise, as you may suppose. Three days later came the promised letter. I have it with me now. You must read it. She offers to be my wife, offers herself to me. 'I love you madly, she says, 'even if you don't love me, never mind. Be my husband. Don't be afraid. I won't hamper you in any way. I will be your chattel. I will be the carpet under your feet. I want to love you for ever. I want to save you from yourself.' Alyosha, I am not worthy to repeat those lines in my vulgar words and in my vulgar tone, my everlastingly vulgar tone, that I can never cure myself of. That letter stabs me even now. Do you think I don't mind--that I don't mind still? I wrote her an answer at once, as it was impossible for me to go to Moscow. I wrote to her with tears. One thing I shall be ashamed of for ever. I referred to her being rich and having a dowry while I was only a stuck-up beggar! I mentioned money! I ought to have borne it in silence, but it slipped from my pen. Then I wrote at once to Ivan, and told him all I could about it in a letter of six pages, and sent him to her. Why do you look like that? Why are you staring at me? Yes, Ivan fell in love with her; he's in love with her still. I know that. I did a stupid thing, in the world's opinion; but perhaps that one stupid thing may be the saving of us all now. Oo! Don't you see what a lot she thinks of Ivan, how she respects him? When she compares us, do you suppose she can love a man like me, especially after all that has happened here?"

"But I'm convinced that she does love a man like you, and not a man like him."

"She loves her own virtue, not me." The words broke involuntarily, and almost malignantly, from Dmitri. He laughed, but a minute later his eyes gleamed, he flushed crimson and struck the table violently with his fist.

"I swear, Alyosha," he cried, with intense and genuine anger at himself; "You may not believe me, but as God is Holy, and as Christ is God, I swear that though I smiled at her lofty sentiments just now, I know that I am a million times baser in soul than she, and that these lofty sentiments of hers are as sincere as a heavenly angel's. That's the tragedy of it--that I know that for certain. What if anyone does show off a bit? Don't I do it myself? And yet I'm sincere, I'm sincere. As for Ivan, I can understand how he must be cursing nature now with his intellect, too! To see the preference given--to whom, to what? To a monster who, though he is betrothed and all eyes are fixed on him, can't restrain his debaucheries--and before the very eyes of his betrothed! And a man like me is preferred, while he is rejected. And why? Because a girl wants to sacrifice her life and destiny out of gratitude. It's ridiculous! I've never said a word of this to Ivan, and Ivan of course has never dropped a hint of the sort to me. But destiny will be accomplished, and the best man will hold his ground while the undeserving one will vanish into his back-alley for ever--his filthy back-alley, his beloved back-alley, where he is at home and where he will sink in filth and stench at his own free will and with enjoyment. I've been talking foolishly. I've no words left. I used them at random, but it will be as I have said. I shall drown in the back-alley, and she will marry Ivan."

"Stop, Dmitri," Alyosha interrupted again with great anxiety. "There's one thing you haven't made clear yet: you are still betrothed all the same, aren't you? How can you break off the engagement if she, your betrothed, doesn't want to?"

"Yes, formally and solemnly betrothed. It was all done on my arrival in Moscow, with great ceremony, with ikons, all in fine style. The general's wife blessed us, and--would you believe it?- congratulated Katya. You've made a good choice,' she said, 'I see right through him.' And--would you believe it?--she didn't like Ivan, and hardly greeted him. I had a lot of talk with Katya in Moscow. I told her about myself--sincerely, honourably. She listened to everything.

There was sweet confusion,

There were tender words. Though there were proud words, too. She wrung out of me a mighty promise to reform. I gave my promise, and here--"

"What?"

"Why, I called to you and brought you out here to-day, this very day--remember it--to send you--this very day again--to Katerina Ivanovna, and--"

"To tell her that I shall never come to see her again. Say, 'He sends you his compliments.'"

"But is that possible?"

"That's just the reason I'm sending you, in my place, because it's impossible. And, how could I tell her myself?"

"And where are you going?"

"To the back-alley."

"To Grushenka, then!" Alyosha exclaimed mournfully, clasping his hands. "Can Rakitin really have told the truth? I thought that you had just visited her, and that was all."

"Can a betrothed man pay such visits? Is such a thing possible and with such a betrothed, and before the eyes of all the world? Confound it, I have some honour! As soon as I began visiting Grushenka, I ceased to be betrothed, and to be an honest man. I understand that. Why do you look at me? You see, I went in the first place to beat her. I had heard, and I know for a fact now, that that captain, father's agent, had given Grushenka an I.O.U. of mine for her to sue me for payment, so as to put an end to me. They wanted to scare me. I went to beat her. I had had a glimpse of her before. She doesn't strike one at first sight. I knew about her old merchant, who's lying ill now, paralysed; but he's leaving her a decent little sum. I knew, too, that she was fond of money, that she hoarded it, and lent it at a wicked rate of interest, that she's a merciless cheat and swindler. I went to beat her, and I stayed. The storm broke--it struck me down like the plague. I'm plague-stricken still, and I know that everything is over, that there will never be anything more for me. The cycle of the ages is accomplished. That's my position. And though I'm a beggar, as fate would have it, I had three thousand just then in my pocket. I drove with Grushenka to Mokroe, a place twenty-five versts from here. I got Gypsies there and champagne and made all the peasants there drunk on it, and all the women and girls. I sent the thousands flying. In three days' time I was stripped bare, but a hero. Do you suppose the hero had gained his end? Not a sign of it from her. I tell you that rogue, Grushenka, has a supple curve all over her body. You can see it in her little foot, even in her little toe. I saw it, and kissed it, but that was all, I swear! 'I'll marry you if you like,' she said, 'you're a beggar, you know. Say that you won't beat me, and will let me do anything I choose, and perhaps I will marry you.' She laughed, and she's laughing still!"

Dmitri leapt up with a sort of fury. He seemed all at once as though he were drunk. His eyes became suddenly bloodshot.

"And do you really mean to marry her?"

"At once, if she will. And if she won't, I shall stay all the same. I'll be the porter at her gate. Alyosha!" he cried. He stopped short before him, and taking him by the shoulders began shaking him violently. "Do you know, you innocent boy, that this is all delirium, senseless delirium, for there's a tragedy here. Let me tell you, Alexey, that I may be a low man, with low and degraded passions, but a thief and a pickpocket Dmitri Karamazov never can be. Well, then; let me tell you that I am a thief and a pickpocket. That very morning, just before I went to beat Grushenka, Katerina Ivanovna sent for me, and in strict secrecy (why I don't know, I suppose she had some reason) asked me to go to the chief town of the province and to post three thousand roubles to Agafya Ivanovna in Moscow, so that nothing should be known of it in the town here. So I had that three thousand roubles in my pocket when I went to see Grushenka, and it was that money we spent at Mokroe.

Afterwards I pretended I had been to the town, but did not show her the post office receipt. I said I had sent the money and would bring the receipt, and so far I haven't brought it. I've forgotten it. Now what do you think you're going to her to-day to say? 'He sends his compliments,' and she'll ask you, 'What about the money?' You might still have said to her, 'He's a degraded sensualist, and a low creature, with uncontrolled passions. He didn't send your money then, but wasted it, because, like a low brute, he couldn't control himself.' But still you might have added, 'He isn't a thief though. Here is your three thousand; he sends it back. Send it yourself to Agafya Ivanovna. But he told me to say "he sends his compliments." But, as it is, she will ask, 'But where is the money?'"

"Mitya, you are unhappy, yes! But not as unhappy as you think. Don't worry yourself to death with despair."

"What, do you suppose I'd shoot myself because I can't get three thousand to pay back? That's just it. I shan't shoot myself. I haven't the strength now. Afterwards, perhaps. But now I'm going to Grushenka. I don't care what happens."

"And what then?"

"I'll be her husband if she deigns to have me, and when lovers come, I'll go into the next room. I'll clean her friends' goloshes, blow up their samovar, run their errands."

"Katerina Ivanovna will understand it all," Alyosha said solemnly. "She'll understand how great this trouble is and will forgive. She has a lofty mind, and no one could be more unhappy than you. She'll see that for herself."

"She won't forgive everything," said Dmitri, with a grin. "There's something in it, brother, that no woman could forgive. Do you know what would be the best thing to do?"

"What?"

"Pay back the three thousand."

"Where can we get it from? I say, I have two thousand. Ivan will give you another thousand--that makes three. Take it and pay it back."

"And when would you get it, your three thousand? You're not of age, besides, and you must--you absolutely must--take my farewell to her to-day, with the money or without it, for I can't drag on any longer, things have come to such a pass. To-morrow is too late. I shall send you to father."

"To father?"

"Yes, to father first. Ask him for three thousand."

"But, Mitya, he won't give it."

"As though he would! I know he won't. Do you know the meaning of despair, Alexey?"

"Yes."

"Listen. Legally he owes me nothing. I've had it all from him, I know that. But morally he owes me something, doesn't he? You know he started with twenty-eight thousand of my mother's money and made a hundred thousand with it. Let him give me back only three out of the twenty-eight thousand, and he'll draw my soul out of hell, and it will atone for many of his sins. For that three thousand--I give you my solemn word--I'll make an end of everything, and he shall hear nothing more of me. For the last time I give him the chance to be a father. Tell him God Himself sends him this chance."

"Mitya, he won't give it for anything."

"I know he won't. I know it perfectly well. Now, especially. That's not all. I know something more. Now, only a few days ago, perhaps only yesterday he found out for the first time in earnest (underline in earnest) that Grushenka is really perhaps not joking, and really means to marry me. He knows her nature; he knows the cat. And do you suppose he's going to give me money to help to bring that about when he's crazy about her himself? And that's not all, either. I can tell you more than that. I know that for the last five days he has had three thousand drawn out of the bank, changed into notes of a hundred roubles packed into a large envelope, sealed with five seals, and tied across with red tape. You see how well I know all about it! On the envelope is written: 'To my angel, Grushenka, when she will come to me.' He scrawled it himself in silence and in secret, and no one knows that the money's there except the valet, Smerdyakov, whom he trusts like himself. So now he has been expecting Grushenka for the last three or four days; he hopes she'll come for the money. He has sent her word of it, and she has sent him word that perhaps she'll come. And if she does go to the old man, can I marry her after that? You understand now why I'm here in secret and what I'm on the watch for."

"For her?"

"Yes, for her. Foma has a room in the house of these sluts here. Foma comes from our parts; he was a soldier in our regiment. He does jobs for them. He's watchman at night and goes grouse-shooting in the day-time; and that's how he lives. I've established myself in his room. Neither he nor the women of the house know the secret--that is, that I am on the watch here."

"No one but Smerdyakov knows, then?"

"No one else. He will let me know if she goes to the old man."

"It was he told you about the money, then?"

"Yes. It's a dead secret. Even Ivan doesn't know about the money, or anything. The old man is sending Ivan to Tchermashnya on a two or three days' journey. A purchaser has turned up for the copse: he'll give eight thousand for the timber. So the old man keeps asking Ivan to help him by going to arrange it. It will take him two or three days. That's what the old man wants, so that Grushenka can come while he's away."

"Then he's expecting Grushenka to-day?"

"No, she won't come to-day; there are signs, She's certain not to come," cried Mitya suddenly. "Smerdyakov thinks so, too. Father's drinking now. He's sitting at table with Ivan. Go to him, Alyosha, and ask for the three thousand."

"Mitya, dear, what's the matter with you?" cried Alyosha, jumping up from his place, and looking keenly at his brother's frenzied face. For one moment the thought struck him that Dmitri was mad.

"What is it? I'm not insane," said Dmitri, looking intently and earnestly at him. "No fear. I am sending you to father, and I know what I'm saying. I believe in miracles."

"In miracles?"

"In a miracle of Divine Providence. God knows my heart. He sees my despair. He sees the whole picture. Surely He won't let something awful happen. Alyosha, I believe in miracles. Go!"

"I am going. Tell me, will you wait for me here?"

"Yes. I know it will take some time. You can't go at him point blank. He's drunk now. I'll wait three hours-- four, five, six, seven. Only remember you must go to Katerina Ivanovna to-day, if it has to be at midnight, with the money or without the money, and say, 'He sends his compliments to you.' I want you to say that verse to her: 'He sends his compliments to you.'"

"Mitya! And what if Grushenka comes to-day--if not to-day, or the next day?"

"Grushenka? I shall see her. I shall rush out and prevent it."

"And if--?"

"If there's an if, it will be murder. I couldn't endure it."

"Who will be murdered?"

"The old man. I shan't kill her."

"Brother, what are you saying?"

"Oh, I don't know...I don't know. Perhaps I shan't kill, and perhaps I shall. I'm afraid that he will suddenly become so loathsome to me with his face at that moment. I hate his ugly throat, his nose, his eyes, his shameless snigger. I feel a physical repulsion. That's what I'm afraid of. That's what may be too much for me."

"I'll go, Mitya. I believe that God will order things for the best, that nothing awful may happen."

"And I will sit and wait for the miracle. And if it doesn't come to pass--"

Alyosha went thoughtfully towards his father's house.

Chapter 6. Smerdyakov

HE did in fact find his father still at table. Though there was a dining-room in the house, the table was laid as usual in the drawing room, which was the largest room, and furnished with old-fashioned ostentation. The furniture was white and very old, upholstered in old, red, silky material. In the spaces between the windows there were mirrors in elaborate white and gilt frames, of old-fashioned carving. On the walls, covered with white paper, which was torn in many places, there hung two large portraits--one of some prince who had been governor of the district thirty years before, and the other of some bishop, also long since dead. In the corner opposite the door there were several ikons, before which a lamp was lighted at nightfall...not so much for devotional purposes as to light the room. Fyodor Pavlovitch used to go to bed very late, at three or four o'clock in the morning, and would wander about the room at night or sit in an armchair, thinking. This had become a habit with him. He often slept quite alone in the house, sending his servants to the lodge; but usually Smerdyakov remained, sleeping on a bench in the hall.

When Alyosha came in, dinner was over, but coffee and preserves had been served. Fyodor Pavlovitch liked sweet things with brandy after dinner. Ivan was also at table, sipping coffee. The servants, Grigory and Smerdyakov, were standing by. Both the gentlemen and the servants seemed in singularly good spirits. Fyodor Pavlovitch was roaring with laughter. Before he entered the room, Alyosha heard the shrill laugh he knew so well, and could tell from the sound of it that his father had only reached the good-humoured stage, and was far from being completely drunk.

"Here he is! Here he is!" yelled Fyodor Pavlovitch, highly delighted at seeing Alyosha. "Join us. Sit down. Coffee is a lenten dish, but it's hot and good. I don't offer you brandy, you're keeping the fast. But would you like some? No; I'd better give you some of our famous liqueur. Smerdyakov, go to the cupboard, the second shelf on the right. Here are the keys. Look sharp!"

Alyosha began refusing the liqueur.

"Never mind. If you won't have it, we will," said Fyodor Pavlovitch, beaming. "But stay--have you dined?"

"Yes," answered Alyosha, who had in truth only eaten a piece of bread and drunk a glass of kvass in the Father Superior's kitchen. "Though I should be pleased to have some hot coffee."

"Bravo, my darling! He'll have some coffee. Does it want warming? No, it's boiling. It's capital coffee: Smerdyakov's making. My Smerdyakov's an artist at coffee and at fish patties, and at fish soup, too. You must come one day and have some fish soup. Let me know beforehand...But, stay; didn't I tell you this morning to come home with your mattress and pillow and all? Have you brought your mattress? He he he!"

"No, I haven't," said Alyosha, smiling, too.

"Ah, but you were frightened, you were frightened this morning, weren't you? There, my darling, I couldn't do anything to vex you. Do you know, Ivan, I can't resist the way he looks one straight in the face and laughs? It makes me laugh all over. I'm so fond of him. Alyosha, let me give you my blessing--a father's blessing."

Alyosha rose, but Fyodor Pavlovitch had already changed his mind.

"No, no," he said. "I'll just make the sign of the cross over you, for now. Sit still. Now we've a treat for you, in your own line, too. It'll make you laugh. Balaam's ass has begun talking to us here--and how he talks! How he talks!"

Balaam's ass, it appeared, was the valet, Smerdyakov. He was a young man of about four and twenty, remarkably unsociable and taciturn. Not that he was shy or bashful. On the contrary, he was conceited and seemed to despise everybody.

But we must pause to say a few words about him now. He was brought up by Grigory and Marfa, but the boy grew up "with no sense of gratitude," as Grigory expressed it; he was an unfriendly boy, and seemed to look at the world mistrustfully. In his childhood he was very fond of hanging cats, and burying them with great ceremony. He used to dress up in a sheet as though it were a surplice, and sang, and waved some object over the dead cat as though it were a censer. All this he did on the sly, with the greatest secrecy. Grigory caught him once at this diversion and gave him a sound beating. He shrank into a corner and sulked there for a week. "He doesn't care for you or me, the monster," Grigory used to say to Marfa, "and he doesn't care for anyone. Are you a human being?" he said, addressing the boy directly. "You're not a human being. You grew from the mildew in the bath-house. That's what you are," Smerdyakov, it appeared afterwards, could never forgive him those words. Grigory taught him to read and write, and when he was twelve years old, began teaching him the Scriptures. But this teaching came to nothing. At the second or third lesson the boy suddenly grinned.

"What's that for?" asked Grigory, looking at him threateningly from under his spectacles.

"Oh, nothing. God created light on the first day, and the sun, moon, and stars on the fourth day. Where did the light come from on the first day?"

Grigory was thunderstruck. The boy looked sarcastically at his teacher. There was something positively condescending in his expression. Grigory could not restrain himself. "I'll show you where!" he cried, and gave the boy a violent slap on the cheek. The boy took the slap without a word, but withdrew into his corner again for some days. A week later he had his first attack of the disease to which he was subject all the rest of his life-- epilepsy. When Fyodor Pavlovitch heard of it, his attitude to the boy seemed changed at once. Till then he had taken no notice of him, though he never scolded him, and always gave him a copeck when he met him. Sometimes, when he was in good humour, he would send the boy something sweet from his table. But as soon as he heard of his illness, he showed an active interest in him, sent for a doctor, and tried remedies, but the disease turned out to be incurable. The fits occurred, on an average, once a month, but at various intervals. The fits varied too, in violence: some were light and some were very severe. Fyodor Pavlovitch strictly forbade Grigory to use corporal punishment to the boy, and began allowing him to come upstairs to him. He forbade him to be taught anything whatever for a time, too. One day when the boy was about fifteen, Fyodor Pavlovitch noticed him lingering by the bookcase, and reading the titles through the glass. Fyodor Pavlovitch had a fair number of books--over a hundred--but no one ever saw him reading. He at once gave Smerdyakov the key of the bookcase. "Come, read. You shall be my librarian. You'll be better sitting reading than hanging about the courtyard. Come, read this," and Fyodor Pavlovitch gave him Evenings in a Cottage near Dikanka.

He read a little but didn't like it. He did not once smile, and ended by frowning.

"Why? Isn't it funny?" asked Fyodor Pavlovitch. Smerdyakov did not speak.

"Answer stupid!"

"It's all untrue," mumbled the boy, with a grin.

"Then go to the devil! You have the soul of a lackey. Stay, here's Smaragdov's Universal History. That's all true. Read that."

But Smerdyakov did not get through ten pages of Smaragdov. He thought it dull. So the bookcase was closed again.

Shortly afterwards Marfa and Grigory reported to Fyodor Pavlovitch that Smerdyakov was gradually beginning to show an extraordinary fastidiousness. He would sit before his soup, take up his spoon and look into the soup, bend over it, examine it, take a spoonful and hold it to the light.

"What is it? A beetle?" Grigory would ask.

"A fly, perhaps," observed Marfa.

The squeamish youth never answered, but he did the same with his bread, his meat, and everything he ate. He would hold a piece on his fork to the light, scrutinise it microscopically, and only after long deliberation decide to put it in his mouth.

"Ach! What fine gentlemen's airs!" Grigory muttered, looking at him.

When Fyodor Pavlovitch heard of this development in Smerdyakov he determined to make him his cook, and sent him to Moscow to be trained. He spent some years there and came back remarkably changed in appearance. He looked extraordinarily old for his age. His face had grown wrinkled, yellow, and strangely emasculate. In character he seemed almost exactly the same as before he went away. He was just as unsociable, and showed not the slightest inclination for any companionship. In Moscow, too, as we heard afterwards, he had always been silent. Moscow itself had little interest for him; he saw very little there, and took scarcely any notice of anything. He went once to the theatre, but returned silent and displeased with it. On the other hand, he came back to us from Moscow well dressed, in a clean coat and clean linen. He brushed his clothes most scrupulously twice a day invariably, and was very fond of cleaning his smart calf boots with a special English polish, so that they shone like mirrors. He turned out a first rate cook. Fyodor Pavlovitch paid him a salary, almost the whole of which Smerdyakov spent on clothes, pomade, perfumes, and such things. But he seemed to have as much contempt for the female sex as for men; he was discreet, almost unapproachable, with them. Fyodor Pavlovitch began to regard him rather differently. His fits were becoming more frequent, and on the days he was ill Marfa cooked, which did not suit Fyodor Pavlovitch at all.

"Why are your fits getting worse?" asked Fyodor Pavlovitch, looking askance at his new cook. "Would you like to get married? Shall I find you a wife?"

But Smerdyakov turned pale with anger, and made no reply. Fyodor Pavlovitch left him with an impatient gesture. The great thing was that he had absolute confidence in his honesty. It happened once, when Fyodor Pavlovitch was drunk, that he dropped in the muddy courtyard three hundred-rouble notes which he had only just received. He only missed them next day, and was just hastening to search his pockets when he saw the notes lying on the table. Where had they come from? Smerdyakov had picked them up and brought them in the day before.

"Well, my lad, I've never met anyone like you," Fyodor Pavlovitch said shortly, and gave him ten roubles. We may add that he not only believed in his honesty, but had, for some reason, a liking for him, although the young man looked as morosely at him as at everyone and was always silent. He rarely spoke. If it had occurred to anyone to wonder at the time what the young man was interested in, and what was in his mind, it would have been impossible to tell by looking at him. Yet he used sometimes to stop suddenly in the house, or even in the yard or street, and would stand still for ten minutes, lost in thought. A physiognomist studying his face would have said that there was no thought in it, no reflection, but only a sort of contemplation. There is a remarkable picture by the painter Kramskoy, called "Contemplation." There is a forest in winter, and on a roadway through the forest, in absolute solitude, stands a peasant in a torn kaftan and bark shoes. He stands, as it were, lost in thought. Yet he is not thinking; he is "contemplating." If anyone touched him he would start and look at one as though awakening and bewildered. It's true he would come to himself immediately; but if he were asked what he had been thinking about, he would remember nothing. Yet probably he has, hidden within himself, the impression which had dominated him during the period of contemplation. Those impressions are dear to him and no doubt he hoards them imperceptibly, and even unconsciously. How and why, of course, he does not know either. He may suddenly, after hoarding impressions for many years, abandon everything and go off to Jerusalem on a pilgrimage for his soul's salvation, or perhaps he will suddenly set fire to his native village, and perhaps do both. There are a good many "contemplatives" among the peasantry. Well, Smerdyakov was probably one of them, and he probably was greedily hoarding up his impressions, hardly knowing why.

Chapter 7. The Controversy

BUT Balaam's ass had suddenly spoken. The subject was a strange one. Grigory had gone in the morning to make purchases, and had heard from the shopkeeper Lukyanov the story of a Russian soldier which had appeared in the newspaper of that day. This soldier had been taken prisoner in some remote part of Asia, and was threatened with an immediate agonising death if he did not renounce Christianity and follow Islam. He refused to deny his faith, and was tortured, flayed alive, and died, praising and glorifying Christ. Grigory had related the story at table. Fyodor Pavlovitch always liked, over the dessert after dinner, to laugh and talk, if only with Grigory. This afternoon he was in a particularly good-humoured and expansive mood. Sipping his brandy and listening to the story, he observed that they ought to make a saint of a soldier like that, and to take his skin to some monastery. "That would make the people flock, and bring the money in."

Grigory frowned, seeing that Fyodor Pavlovitch was by no means touched, but, as usual, was beginning to scoff. At that moment Smerdyakov, who was standing by the door, smiled. Smerdyakov often waited at table towards the end of dinner, and since Ivan's arrival in our town he had done so every day.

"What are you grinning at?" asked Fyodor Pavlovitch, catching the smile instantly, and knowing that it referred to Grigory.

"Well, my opinion is," Smerdyakov began suddenly and unexpectedly in a loud voice, "that if that laudable soldier's exploit was so very great there would have been, to my thinking, no sin in it if he had on such an emergency renounced, so to speak, the name of Christ and his own christening, to save by that same his life, for good deeds, by which, in the course of years to expiate his cowardice."

"How could it not be a sin? You're talking nonsense. For that you'll go straight to hell and be roasted there like mutton," put in Fyodor Pavlovitch.

It was at this point that Alyosha came in, and Fyodor Pavlovitch, as we have seen, was highly delighted at his appearance.

"We're on your subject, your subject," he chuckled gleefully, making Alyosha sit down to listen.

"As for mutton, that's not so, and there'll be nothing there for this, and there shouldn't be either, if it's according to justice," Smerdyakov maintained stoutly.

"How do you mean 'according to justice'?" Fyodor Pavlovitch cried still more gaily, nudging Alyosha with his knee.

"He's a rascal, that's what he is!" burst from Grigory. He looked Smerdyakov wrathfully in the face.

"As for being a rascal, wait a little, Grigory Vassilyevitch," answered Smerdyakov with perfect composure. "You'd better consider yourself that, once I am taken prisoner by the enemies of the Christian race, and they demand from me to curse the name of God and to renounce my holy christening, I am fully entitled to act by my own reason, since there would be no sin in it."

"But you've said that before. Don't waste words. Prove it," cried Fyodor Pavlovitch.

"Soup-maker!" muttered Grigory contemptuously.

"As for being a soup-maker, wait a bit, too, and consider for yourself, Grigory Vassilyevitch, without abusing me. For as soon as I say to those enemies, 'No, I'm not a Christian, and I curse my true God,' then at once, by God's high judgment, I become immediately and specially anathema accursed, and am cut off from the Holy Church, exactly as though I were a heathen, so that at that very instant, not only when I say it aloud, but when I think of saying it, before a quarter of a second has passed, I am cut off. Is that so or not, Grigory Vassilyevitch?"

He addressed Grigory with obvious satisfaction, though he was really answering Fyodor Pavlovitch's questions, and was well aware of it, and intentionally pretending that Grigory had asked the questions.

"Ivan," cried Fyodor Pavlovitch suddenly, "stoop down for me to whisper. He's got this all up for your benefit. He wants you to praise him. Praise him."

Ivan listened with perfect seriousness to his father's excited whisper.

"Stay, Smerdyakov, be quiet a minute," cried Fyodor Pavlovitch once more. "Ivan, your ear again."

Ivan bent down again with a perfectly grave face.

"I love you as I do Alyosha. Don't think I don't love you. Some brandy?"

"Yes.--But you're rather drunk yourself," thought Ivan, looking steadily at his father.

He was watching Smerdyakov with great curiosity.

"You're anathema accursed, as it is", Grigory suddenly burst out, "and how dare you argue, you rascal, after that, if--"

"Don't scold him, Grigory, don't scold him," Fyodor Pavlovitch cut him short.

"You should wait, Grigory Vassilyevitch, if only a short time, and listen, for I haven't finished all I had to say. For at the very moment I become accursed, at that same highest moment, I become exactly like a heathen, and my christening is taken off me and becomes of no avail. Isn't that so?"

"Make haste and finish, my boy," Fyodor Pavlovitch urged him, sipping from his wineglass with relish.

"And if I've ceased to be a Christian, then I told no lie to the enemy when they asked whether I was a Christian or not a Christian, seeing I had already been relieved by God Himself of my Christianity by reason of the thought alone, before I had time to utter a word to the enemy. And if I have already been discharged, in what manner and with what sort of justice can I be held responsible as a Christian in the other world for having denied Christ, when, through the very thought alone, before denying Him I had been relieved from my christening? If I'm no longer a Christian, then I can't renounce Christ, for I've nothing then to renounce. Who will hold an unclean Tatar responsible, Grigory Vassilyevitch, even in heaven, for not having been born a Christian? And who would punish him for that, considering that you can't take two skins off one ox? For God Almighty Himself, even if He did make the Tatar responsible, when he dies would give him the smallest possible punishment, I imagine (since he must be punished), judging that he is not to blame if he has come into the world an unclean heathen, from heathen parents. The Lord God can't surely take a Tatar and say he was a Christian? That would mean that the Almighty would tell a real untruth. And can the Lord of Heaven and earth tell a lie, even in one word?"

Grigory was thunderstruck and looked at the orator, his eyes nearly starting out of his head. Though he did not clearly understand what was said, he had caught something in this rigmarole, and stood, looking like a man who has just hit his head against a wall. Fyodor Pavlovitch emptied his glass and went off into his shrill laugh.

"Alyosha! Alyosha! What do you say to that! Ah, you casuist! He must have been with the Jesuits, somewhere, Ivan. Oh, you stinking Jesuit, who taught you? But you're talking nonsense, you casuist, nonsense, nonsense, nonsense, nonsense. Don't cry, Grigory, we'll reduce him to smoke and ashes in a moment. Tell me this, O ass; you may be right before your enemies, but you have renounced your faith all the same in your own heart, and you say yourself that in that very hour you became anathema accursed. And if once you're anathema they won't pat you on the head for it in hell. What do you say to that, my fine Jesuit?"

"There is no doubt that I have renounced it in my own heart, but there no special sin in that. Or if there was sin, it was the most ordinary."

"How's that the most ordinary?"

"You lie, accursed one!" hissed Grigory.

"Consider yourself, Grigory Vassilyevitch," Smerdyakov went on, staid and unruffled, conscious of his triumph, but, as it were, generous to the vanquished foe. "Consider yourself, Grigory Vassilyevitch; it is said in the Scripture that if you have faith, even as a mustard seed, and bid a mountain move into the sea, it will move without the least delay at your bidding. Well, Grigory Vassilyevitch, if I'm without faith and you have so great a faith that you are continually swearing at me, you try yourself telling this mountain, not to move into the sea for that's a long way off, but even to our stinking little river which runs at the bottom of the garden. You'll see for yourself that it won't budge, but will remain just where it is however much you shout at it, and that shows, Grigory Vassilyevitch, that you haven't faith in the proper manner, and only abuse others about it. Again, taking into consideration that no one in our day, not only you, but actually no one, from the highest person to the lowest peasant, can shove mountains into the sea--except perhaps some one man in the world, or, at most, two, and they most likely are saving their souls in secret somewhere in the Egyptian desert, so you wouldn't find them--if so it be, if all the rest have no faith, will God curse all the rest? that is, the population of the whole earth, except about two hermits in the desert, and in His well-known mercy will He not forgive one of them? And so I'm persuaded that though I may once have doubted I shall be forgiven if I shed tears of repentance."

"Stay!" cried Fyodor Pavlovitch, in a transport of delight. "So you do suppose there are two who can move mountains? Ivan, make a note of it, write it down. There you have the Russian all over!"

"You're quite right in saying it's characteristic of the people's faith," Ivan assented, with an approving smile.

"You agree. Then it must be so, if you agree. It's true, isn't it Alyosha? That's the Russian faith all over, isn't it?"

"No, Smerdyakov has not the Russian faith at all," said Alyosha firmly and gravely.

"I'm not talking about his faith. I mean those two in the desert, only that idea. Surely that's Russian, isn't it?"

"Yes, that's purely Russian," said Alyosha smiling.

"Your words are worth a gold piece, O ass, and I'll give it to you to-day. But as to the rest you talk nonsense, nonsense, nonsense. Let me tell you, stupid, that we here are all of little faith, only from carelessness, because we haven't time; things are too much for us, and, in the second place, the Lord God has given us so little time, only twenty-four hours in the day, so that one hasn't even time to get sleep enough, much less to repent of one's sins. While you have denied your faith to your enemies when you'd nothing else to think about but to show your faith! So I consider, brother, that it constitutes a sin."

"Constitute a sin it may, but consider yourself, Grigory Vassilyevitch, that it only extenuates it, if it does constitute. If I had believed then in very truth, as I ought to have believed, then it really would have been sinful if I had not faced tortures for my faith, and had gone over to the pagan Mohammedan faith. But, of course, it wouldn't have come to torture then, because I should only have had to say at that instant to the mountain, 'Move and crush the tormentor,' and it would have moved and at the very instant have crushed him like a black-beetle, and I should have walked away as though nothing had happened, praising and glorifying God. But, suppose at that very moment I had tried all that, and cried to that mountain, 'Crush these tormentors,' and it hadn't crushed them, how could I have helped doubting, pray, at such a time, and at such a dread hour of mortal terror? And apart from that, I should know already that I could not attain to the fullness of the Kingdom of Heaven (for since the mountain had not moved at my word, they could not think very much of my faith up aloft, and there could be no very great reward awaiting me in the world to come). So why should I let them flay the skin off me as well, and to no good purpose? For, even though they had flayed my skin half off my back, even then the mountain would not have moved at my word or at my cry. And at such a moment not only doubt might come over one but one might lose one's reason from fear, so that one would not be able to think at all. And, therefore, how should I be particularly to blame if not seeing my advantage or reward there or here, I should, at least, save my skin. And so trusting fully in the grace of the Lord I should cherish the hope that I might be altogether forgiven."

Chapter 8. Over the Brandy

THE controversy was over. But, strange to say, Fyodor Pavlovitch, who had been so gay, suddenly began frowning. He frowned and gulped brandy, and it was already a glass too much.

"Get along with you, Jesuits!" he cried to the servants. "Go away, Smerdyakov. I'll send you the gold piece I promised you to-day, but be off! Don't cry, Grigory. Go to Marfa. She'll comfort you and put you to bed. The rascals won't let us sit in peace after dinner," he snapped peevishly, as the servants promptly withdrew at his word.

"Smerdyakov always pokes himself in now, after dinner. It's you he's so interested in. What have you done to fascinate him?" he added to Ivan.

"Nothing whatever," answered Ivan. "He's pleased to have a high opinion of me; he's a lackey and a mean soul. Raw material for revolution, however, when the time comes."

"There will be others and better ones. But there will be some like him as well. His kind will come first, and better ones after."

"And when will the time come?"

"The rocket will go off and fizzle out, perhaps. The peasants are not very fond of listening to these soup-makers, so far."

"Ah, brother, but a Balaam's ass like that thinks and thinks, and the devil knows where he gets to."

"He's storing up ideas," said Ivan, smiling.

"You see, I know he can't bear me, nor anyone else, even you, though you fancy that he has a high opinion of you. Worse still with Alyosha, he despises Alyosha. But he doesn't steal, that's one thing, and he's not a gossip, he holds his tongue, and doesn't wash our dirty linen in public. He makes capital fish pasties too. But, damn him, is he worth talking about so much?"

"Of course he isn't."

"And as for the ideas he may be hatching, the Russian peasant, generally speaking, needs thrashing. That I've always maintained. Our peasants are swindlers, and don't deserve to be pitied, and it's a good thing they're still flogged sometimes. Russia is rich in birches. If they destroyed the forests, it would be the ruin of Russia. I stand up for the clever people. We've left off thrashing the peasants, we've grown so clever, but they go on thrashing themselves. And a good thing too. 'For with what measure ye mete it shall be measured to you again,' or how does it go? Anyhow, it will be measured. But Russia's all swinishness. My dear, if you only knew how I hate Russia...That is, not Russia, but all this vice! But maybe I mean Russia. Tout cela c'est de la cochonnerie...* Do you know what I like? I like wit."

* All this is filthiness.

"You've had another glass. That's enough."

"Wait a bit. I'll have one more, and then another, and then I'll stop. No, stay, you interrupted me. At Mokroe I was talking to an old man, and he told me: 'There's nothing we like so much as sentencing girls to be thrashed, and we always give the lads the job of thrashing them. And the girl he has thrashed to-day, the young man will ask in marriage to-morrow. So it quite suits the girls, too,' he said. There's a set of de Sades for you! But it's clever, anyway. Shall we go over and have a look at it, eh? Alyosha, are you blushing? Don't be bashful, child. I'm sorry I didn't stay to dinner at the Superior's and tell the monks about the girls at Mokroe. Alyosha, don't be angry that I offended your Superior this morning. I lost my temper. If there is a God, if He exists, then, of course, I'm to blame, and I shall have to answer for it. But if there isn't a God at all, what do they deserve, your fathers? It's not enough to cut their heads off, for they keep back progress. Would you believe it, Ivan, that that lacerates my sentiments? No, you don't believe it as I see from your eyes. You believe what people say, that I'm nothing but a buffoon. Alyosha, do you believe that I'm nothing but a buffoon?"

"No, I don't believe it."

"And I believe you don't, and that you speak the truth. You look sincere and you speak sincerely. But not Ivan. Ivan's supercilious...I'd make an end of your monks, though, all the same. I'd take all that mystic stuff and suppress it, once for all, all over Russia, so as to bring all the fools to reason. And the gold and the silver that would flow into the mint!"

"But why suppress it?" asked Ivan.

"That Truth may prevail. That's why."

"Well, if Truth were to prevail, you know, you'd be the first to be robbed and suppressed."

"Ah! I dare say you're right. Ah, I'm an ass!" burst out Fyodor Pavlovitch, striking himself lightly on the forehead. "Well, your monastery may stand then, Alyosha, if that's how it is. And we clever people will sit snug and enjoy our brandy. You know, Ivan, it must have been so ordained by the Almighty Himself. Ivan, speak, is there a God or not? Stay, speak the truth, speak seriously. Why are you laughing again?"

"I'm laughing that you should have made a clever remark just now about Smerdyakov's belief in the existence of two saints who could move mountains."

"Why, am I like him now, then?"

"Very much."

"Well, that shows I'm a Russian, too, and I have a Russian characteristic. And you may be caught in the same way, though you are a philosopher. Shall I catch you? What do you bet that I'll catch you to-morrow? Speak, all the same, is there a God, or not? Only, be serious. I want you to be serious now."

"No, there is no God."

"Alyosha, is there a God?"

"There is."

"Ivan, and is there immortality of some sort, just a little, just a tiny bit?"

"There is no immortality either."

"None at all?"

"None at all."

"There's absolute nothingness then. Perhaps there is just something? Anything is better than nothing!"

"Alyosha, is there immortality?"

"God and immortality?"

"God and immortality. In God is immortality."

"H'm! It's more likely Ivan's right. Good Lord! to think what faith, what force of all kinds, man has lavished for nothing, on that dream, and for how many thousand years. Who is it laughing at man? Ivan For the last time, once for all, is there a God or not? I ask for the last time!"

"And for the last time there is not."

"Who is laughing at mankind, Ivan?"

"It must be the devil," said Ivan, smiling.

"And the devil? Does he exist?"

"No, there's no devil either."

"It's a pity. Damn it all, what wouldn't I do to the man who first invented God! Hanging on a bitter aspen tree would be too good for, him."

"There would have been no civilisation if they hadn't invented God."

"Wouldn't there have been? Without God?"

"No. And there would have been no brandy either. But I must take your brandy away from you, anyway."

"Stop, stop, stop, dear boy, one more little glass. I've hurt Alyosha's feelings. You're not angry with me, Alyosha? My dear little Alexey!"

"No, I am not angry. I know your thoughts. Your heart is better than your head."

"My heart better than my head, is it? Oh Lord! And that from you. Ivan, do you love Alyosha?"

"You must love him" (Fyodor Pavlovitch was by this time very drunk). "Listen, Alyosha, I was rude to your elder this morning. But I was excited. But there's wit in that elder, don't you think, Ivan?"

"Very likely."

"There is, there is. Il y a du Piron la-dedans.* He's a Jesuit, a Russian one, that is. As he's an honourable person there's a hidden indignation boiling within him at having to pretend and affect holiness."

* There's something of Piron inside of him.

"But, of course, he believes in God."

"Not a bit of it. Didn't you know? Why, he tells everyone so, himself. That is, not everyone, but all the clever people who come to him. He said straight out to Governor Schultz not long ago: 'Credo, but I don't know in what.'"

"Really?"

"He really did. But I respect him. There's something of Mephistopheles about him, or rather of 'The hero of our time'... Arbenin, or what's his name?...You see, he's a sensualist. He's such a sensualist that I should be afraid for my daughter or my wife if she went to confess to him. You know, when he begins telling stories...The year before last he invited us to tea, tea with liqueur (the ladies send him liqueur), and began telling us about old times till we nearly split our sides...Especially how he once cured a paralysed woman. 'If my legs were not bad I know a dance I could dance you,' he said. What do you say to that? 'I've plenty of tricks in my time,' said he. He did Demidov, the merchant, out of sixty thousand."

"What, he stole it?"

"He brought him the money as a man he could trust, saying, 'Take care of it for me, friend, there'll be a police search at my place to-morrow.' And he kept it. 'You have given it to the Church,' he declared. I said to him: 'You're a scoundrel,' I said. 'No,' said he, 'I'm not a scoundrel, but I'm broadminded.' But that wasn't he, that was someone else. I've muddled him with someone else...without noticing it. Come, another glass and that's enough. Take away the bottle, Ivan. I've been telling lies. Why didn't you stop me, Ivan, and tell me I was lying?"

"I knew you'd stop of yourself."

"That's a lie. You did it from spite, from simple spite against me. You despise me. You have come to me and despised me in my own house."

"Well, I'm going away. You've had too much brandy."

"I've begged you for Christ's sake to go to Tchermashnya for a day or two, and you don't go."

"I'll go to-morrow if you're so set upon it."

"You won't go. You want to keep an eye on me. That's what you want, spiteful fellow. That's why you won't go."

The old man persisted. He had reached that state of drunkenness when the drunkard who has till then been inoffensive tries to pick a quarrel and to assert himself.

"Why are you looking at me? Why do you look like that? Your eyes look at me and say, 'You ugly drunkard!' Your eyes are mistrustful. They're contemptuous...You've come here with some design. Alyosha, here, looks at me and his eyes shine. Alyosha doesn't despise me. Alexey, you mustn't love Ivan."

"Don't be ill-tempered with my brother. Leave off attacking him," Alyosha said emphatically.

"Oh, all right. Ugh, my head aches. Take away the brandy, Ivan. It's the third time I've told you."

He mused, and suddenly a slow, cunning grin spread over his face.

"Don't be angry with a feeble old man, Ivan. I know you don't love me, but don't be angry all the same. You've nothing to love me for. You go to Tchermashnya. I'll come to you myself and bring you a present. I'll show you a little wench there. I've had my eye on her a long time. She's still running about bare-foot. Don't be afraid of bare-footed wenches--don't despise them--they're pearls!"

And he kissed his hand with a smack.

"To my thinking," he revived at once, seeming to grow sober the instant he touched on his favourite topic. "To my thinking...Ah, you boys! You children, little sucking-pigs, to my thinking...I never thought a woman ugly in my life--that's been my rule! Can you understand that? How could you understand it? You've milk in your veins, not blood. You're not out of your shells yet. My rule has been that you can always find something devilishly interesting in every woman that you wouldn't find in any other. Only, one must know how to find it, that's the point! That's a talent! To my mind there are no ugly women. The very fact that she is a woman is half the battle...but how could you understand that? Even in vieilles filles, even in them you may discover something that makes you simply wonder that men have been such fools as to let them grow old without noticing them. Bare-footed girls or unattractive ones, you must take by surprise. Didn't you know that? You must astound them till they're fascinated, upset, ashamed that such a gentleman should fall in love with such a little slut. It's a jolly good thing that there always are and will be masters and slaves in the world, so there always will be a little maid-of-all-work and her master, and you know, that's all that's needed for happiness. Stay...listen, Alyosha, I always used to surprise your mother, but in a different way. I paid no attention to her at all, but all at once, when the minute came, I'd be all devotion to her, crawl on my knees, kiss her feet, and I always, always--I remember it as though it were to-day--reduced her to that tinkling, quiet, nervous, queer little laugh. It was peculiar to her. I knew her attacks always used to begin like that. The next day she would begin shrieking hysterically, and this little laugh was not a sign of delight, though it made a very good counterfeit. That's the great thing, to know how to take everyone. Once Belyavsky--he was a handsome fellow, and rich--used to like to come here and hang about her--suddenly gave me a slap in the face in her presence. And she--such a mild sheep--why, I thought she would have knocked me down for that blow. How she set on me! 'You're beaten, beaten now,' she said, 'You've taken a blow from him. You have been trying to sell me to him,' she said...'And how dared he strike you in my presence! Don't dare come near me again, never, never! Run at once, challenge him to a duel!'...I took her to the monastery then to bring her to her senses. The holy Fathers prayed her back to reason. But I swear, by God,

Alyosha, I never insulted the poor crazy girl! Only once, perhaps, in the first year; then she was very fond of praying. She used to keep the feasts of Our Lady particularly and used to turn me out of her room then. I'll knock that mysticism out of her, thought I! 'Here,' said I, 'you see your holy image. Here it is. Here I take it down. You believe it's miraculous, but here, I'll spit on it directly and nothing will happen to me for it!'...When she saw it, good Lord! I thought she would kill me. But she only jumped up, wrung her hands, then suddenly hid her face in them, began trembling all over and fell on the floor...fell all of a heap. Alyosha, Alyosha, what's the matter?"

The old man jumped up in alarm. From the time he had begun speaking about his mother, a change had gradually come over Alyosha's face. He flushed crimson, his eyes glowed, his lips quivered. The old sot had gone spluttering on, noticing nothing, till the moment when something very strange happened to Alyosha. Precisely what he was describing in the crazy woman was suddenly repeated with Alyosha. He jumped up from his seat exactly as his mother was said to have done, wrung his hands, hid his face in them, and fell back in his chair, shaking all over in an hysterical paroxysm of sudden violent, silent weeping. His extraordinary resemblance to his mother particularly impressed the old man.

"Ivan, Ivan! Water, quickly! It's like her, exactly as she used to be then, his mother. Spurt some water on him from your mouth, that's what I used to do to her. He's upset about his mother, his mother," he muttered to Ivan.

"But she was my mother, too, I believe, his mother. Was she not?" said Ivan, with uncontrolled anger and contempt. The old man shrank before his flashing eyes. But something very strange had happened, though only for a second; it seemed really to have escaped the old man's mind that Alyosha's mother actually was the mother of Ivan too.

"Your mother?" he muttered, not understanding. "What do you mean? What mother are you talking about? Was she?...Why, damn it! of course she was yours too! Damn it! My mind has never been so darkened before. Excuse me, why, I was thinking Ivan...He he he!" He stopped. A broad, drunken, half senseless grin overspread his face.

At that moment a fearful noise, and clamour was heard in the hall, there were violent shouts, the door was flung open, and Dmitri burst into the room. The old man rushed to Ivan in terror.

"He'll kill me! He'll kill me! Don't let him get at me!" he screamed, clinging to the skirt of Ivan's coat.

Chapter 9. The Sensualists

GRIGORY and Smerdyakov ran into the room after Dmitri. They had been struggling with him in the passage, refusing to admit him, acting on instructions given them by Fyodor Pavlovitch some days before. Taking advantage of the fact that Dmitri stopped a moment on entering the room to look about him, Grigory ran round the table, closed the double doors on the opposite side of the room leading to the inner apartments, and stood before the closed doors, stretching wide his arms, prepared to defend the entrance, so to speak, with the last drop of his blood. Seeing this, Dmitri uttered a scream rather than a shout and rushed at Grigory.

"Then she's there! She's hidden there! Out of the way, scoundrel!"

He tried to pull Grigory away, but the old servant pushed him back. Beside himself with fury, Dmitri struck out, and hit Grigory with all his might. The old man fell like a log, and Dmitri, leaping over him, broke in the door. Smerdyakov remained pale and trembling at the other end of the room, huddling close to Fyodor Pavlovitch.

"She's here!" shouted Dmitri. "I saw her turn towards the house just now, but I couldn't catch her. Where is she? Where is she?"

That shout, "She's here!" produced an indescribable effect on Fyodor Pavlovitch. All his terror left him.

"Hold him! Hold him!" he cried, and dashed after Dmitri. Meanwhile Grigory had got up from the floor, but still seemed stunned. Ivan and Alyosha ran after their father. In the third room something was heard to fall on the floor with a ringing crash: it was a large glass vase--not an expensive one--on a marble pedestal which Dmitri had upset as he ran past it.

"At him!" shouted the old man. "Help!"

Ivan and Alyosha caught the old man and were forcibly bringing him back.

"Why do you run after him? He'll murder you outright," Ivan cried wrathfully at his father.

"Ivan! Alyosha! She must be here. Grushenka's here. He said he saw her himself, running."

He was choking. He was not expecting Grushenka at the time, and the sudden news that she was here made him beside himself. He was trembling all over. He seemed frantic.

"But you've seen for yourself that she hasn't come," cried Ivan.

"But she may have come by that other entrance."

"You know that entrance is locked, and you have the key."

Dmitri suddenly reappeared in the drawing-room. He had, of course, found the other entrance locked, and the key actually was in Fyodor Pavlovitch's pocket. The windows of all rooms were also closed, so Grushenka could not have come in anywhere nor have run out anywhere.

"Hold him!" shrieked Fyodor Pavlovitch, as soon as he saw him again. "He's been stealing money in my bedroom." And tearing himself from Ivan he rushed again at Dmitri. But Dmitri threw up both hands and suddenly clutched the old man by the two tufts of hair that remained on his temples, tugged at them, and flung him with a crash on the floor. He kicked him two or three times with his heel in the face. The old man moaned shrilly. Ivan, though not so strong as Dmitri, threw his arms round him, and with all his might pulled him away. Alyosha helped him with his slender strength, holding Dmitri in front.

"Madman! You've killed him!" cried Ivan.

"Serve him right!" shouted Dmitri breathlessly. "If I haven't killed him, I'll come again and kill him. You can't protect him!"

"Dmitri! Go away at once!" cried Alyosha commandingly.

"Alexey! You tell me. It's only you I can believe; was she here just now, or not? I saw her myself creeping this way by the fence from the lane. I shouted, she ran away."

"I swear she's not been here, and no one expected her."

"But I saw her...So she must...I'll find out at once where she is...Good-bye, Alexey! Not a word to Aesop about the money now. But go to Katerina Ivanovna at once and be sure to say, 'He sends his compliments to you!' Compliments, his compliments! just compliments and farewell! Describe the scene to her."

Meanwhile Ivan and Grigory had raised the old man and seated him in an arm-chair. His face was covered with blood, but he was conscious and listened greedily to Dmitri's cries. He was still fancying that Grushenka really was somewhere in the house. Dmitri looked at him with hatred as he went out.

"I don't repent shedding your blood!" he cried. "Beware, old man, beware of your dream, for I have my dream, too. I curse you, and disown you altogether."

He ran out of the room.

"She's here. She must be here. Smerdyakov! Smerdyakov!" the old man wheezed, scarcely audibly, beckoning to him with his finger.

"No, she's not here, you old lunatic!" Ivan shouted at him angrily. "Here, he's fainting? Water! A towel! Make haste, Smerdyakov!"

Smerdyakov ran for water. At last they got the old man undressed, and put him to bed. They wrapped a wet towel round his head. Exhausted by the brandy, by his violent emotion, and the blows he had received, he shut his eyes and fell asleep as soon as his head touched the pillow. Ivan and Alyosha went back to the drawing-room. Smerdyakov removed the fragments of the broken vase, while Grigory stood by the table looking gloomily at the floor.

"Shouldn't you put a wet bandage on your head and go to bed, too?" Alyosha said to him. "We'll look after him. My brother gave you a terrible blow--on the head."

"He's insulted me!" Grigory articulated gloomily and distinctly.

"He's 'insulted' his father, not only you," observed Ivan with a forced smile.

"I used to wash him in his tub. He's insulted me," repeated Grigory.

"Damn it all, if I hadn't pulled him away perhaps he'd have murdered him. It wouldn't take much to do for Aesop, would it?" whispered Ivan to Alyosha.

"God forbid!" cried Alyosha.

"Why should He forbid?" Ivan went on in the same whisper, with a malignant grimace. "One reptile will devour the other. And serve them both right, too."

Alyosha shuddered.

"Of course I won't let him be murdered as I didn't just now. Stay here, Alyosha, I'll go for a turn in the yard. My head's begun to ache."

Alyosha went to his father's bedroom and sat by his bedside behind the screen for about an hour. The old man suddenly opened his eyes and gazed for a long while at Alyosha, evidently remembering and meditating. All at once his face betrayed extraordinary excitement.

"Alyosha," he whispered apprehensively, "where's Ivan?"

"In the yard. He's got a headache. He's on the watch."

"Give me that looking-glass. It stands over there. Give it me."

Alyosha gave him a little round folding looking-glass which stood on the chest of drawers. The old man looked at himself in it; his nose was considerably swollen, and on the left side of his forehead there was a rather large crimson bruise.

"What does Ivan say? Alyosha, my dear, my only son, I'm afraid of Ivan. I'm more afraid of Ivan than the other. You're the only one I'm not afraid of..."

"Don't be afraid of Ivan either. He is angry, but he'll defend you."

"Alyosha, and what of the other? He's run to Grushenka. My angel, tell me the truth, was she here just now or not?"

"No one has seen her. It was a mistake. She has not been here."

"You know Mitya wants to marry her, to marry her."

"She won't marry him."

"She won't. She won't. She won't. She won't on any account!"

The old man fairly fluttered with joy, as though nothing more comforting could have been said to him. In his delight he seized Alyosha's hand and pressed it warmly to his heart. Tears positively glittered in his eyes.

"That image of the Mother of God of which I was telling you just now," he said. "Take it home and keep it for yourself. And I'll let you go back to the monastery...I was joking this morning, don't be angry with me. My head aches, Alyosha...Alyosha, comfort my heart. Be an angel and tell me the truth!"

"You're still asking whether she has been here or not?" Alyosha said sorrowfully.

"No, no, no. I believe you. I'll tell you what it is: you go to Grushenka yourself, or see her somehow; make haste and ask her; see for yourself, which she means to choose, him or me. Eh? What? Can you?"

"If I see her I'll ask her," Alyosha muttered, embarrassed.

"No, she won't tell you," the old man interrupted, "she's a rogue. She'll begin kissing you and say that it's you she wants. She's a deceitful, shameless hussy. You mustn't go to her, you mustn't!"

"No father, and it wouldn't be suitable, it wouldn't be right at all."

"Where was he sending you just now? He shouted 'Go' as he ran away."

"For money? To ask her for money?"

"No. Not for money."

"He's no money; not a farthing. I'll settle down for the night, and think things over, and you can go. Perhaps you'll meet her...Only be sure to come to me to-morrow in the morning. Be sure to. I have a word to say to you to-morrow. Will you come?"

"When you come, pretend you've come of your own accord to ask after me. Don't tell anyone I told you to. Don't say a word to Ivan."

"Very well."

"Good-bye, my angel. You stood up for me, just now. I shall never forget it. I've a word to say to you to-morrow--but I must think about it."

"And how do you feel now?"

"I shall get up to-morrow and go out, perfectly well, perfectly well!"

Crossing the yard Alyosha found Ivan sitting on the bench at the gateway. He was sitting writing something in pencil in his notebook. Alyosha told Ivan that their father had waked up, was conscious, and had let him go back to sleep at the monastery.

"Alyosha, I should be very glad to meet you to-morrow morning," said Ivan cordially, standing up. His cordiality was a complete surprise to Alyosha.

"I shall be at the Hohlakovs' to-morrow," answered Alyosha, "I may be at Katerina Ivanovna's, too, if I don't find her now."

"But you're going to her now, anyway? For that 'compliments and farewell,'" said Ivan smiling. Alyosha was disconcerted.

"I think I quite understand his exclamations just now, and part of what went before. Dmitri has asked you to go to her and say that he--well, in fact--takes his leave of her?"

"Brother, how will all this horror end between father and Dmitri?" exclaimed Alyosha.

"One can't tell for certain. Perhaps in nothing: it may all fizzle out. That woman is a beast. In any case we must keep the old man indoors and not let Dmitri in the house."

"Brother, let me ask one thing more: has any man a right to look at other men and decide which is worthy to live?"

"Why bring in the question of worth? The matter is most often decided in men's hearts on other grounds much more natural. And as for rights--who has not the right to wish?"

"Not for another man's death?"

"What even if for another man's death? Why lie to oneself since all men live so and perhaps cannot help living so. Are you referring to what I said just now--that one reptile will devour the other? In that case let me ask you, do you think me like Dmitri capable of shedding Aesop's blood, murdering him, eh?"

"What are you saying, Ivan? Such an idea never crossed my mind. I don't think Dmitri is capable of it, either."

"Thanks, if only for that," smiled Ivan. "Be sure, I should always defend him. But in my wishes I reserve myself full latitude in this case. Good-bye till to-morrow. Don't condemn me, and don't look on me as a villain," he added with a smile.

They shook hands warmly as they had never done before. Alyosha felt that his brother had taken the first step towards him, and that he had certainly done this with some definite motive.

Chapter 10. Both Together

Alyosha left his father's house feeling even more exhausted and dejected in spirit than when he had entered it. His mind too seemed shattered and unhinged, while he felt that he was afraid to put together the disjointed fragments and form a general idea from all the agonising and conflicting experiences of the day. He felt something bordering upon despair, which he had never known till then. Towering like a mountain above all the rest stood the fatal, insoluble question: How would things end between his father and his brother Dmitri with this terrible woman? Now he had himself been a witness of it, he had been present and seen them face to face. Yet only his brother Dmitri could be made unhappy, terribly, completely unhappy: there was trouble awaiting him. It appeared too that there were other people concerned, far more so than Alyosha could have supposed before. There was something positively mysterious in it, too. Ivan had made a step towards him, which was what Alyosha had been long desiring. Yet now he felt for some reason that he was frightened at it. And these women? Strange to say, that morning he had set out for Katerina Ivanovna's in the greatest embarrassment; now he felt nothing of the kind. On the contrary, he was hastening there as though expecting to find guidance from her. Yet to give her this message was obviously more difficult than before. The matter of the three thousand was decided irrevocably, and Dmitri, feeling himself dishonoured and losing his last hope, might sink to any depth. He had, moreover, told him to describe to Katerina Ivanovna the scene which had just taken place with his father.

It was by now seven o'clock, and it was getting dark as Alyosha entered the very spacious and convenient house in the High Street occupied by Katerina Ivanovna. Alyosha knew that she lived with two aunts. One of them, a woman of little education, was that aunt of her half-sister Agafya Ivanovna who had looked after her in her father's house when she came from boarding-school. The other aunt was a Moscow lady of style and consequence, though in straitened circumstances. It was said that they both gave way in everything to Katerina Ivanovna, and that she only kept them with her as chaperons. Katerina Ivanovna herself gave way to no one but her benefactress, the general's widow, who had been kept by illness in Moscow, and to whom she was obliged to write twice a week a full account of all her doings.

When Alyosha entered the hall and asked the maid who opened the door to him to take his name up, it was evident that they were already aware of his arrival. Possibly he had been noticed from the window. At least, Alyosha heard a noise, caught the sound of flying footsteps and rustling skirts. Two or three women, perhaps, had run out of the room.

Alyosha thought it strange that his arrival should cause such excitement. He was conducted, however, to the drawing-room at once. It was a large room, elegantly and amply furnished, not at all in provincial style. There were many sofas, lounges, settees, big and little tables. There were pictures on the walls, vases and lamps on the tables, masses of flowers, and even an aquarium in the window. It was twilight and rather dark. Alyosha made out a silk mantle thrown down on the sofa, where people had evidently just been sitting; and on a table in front of the sofa were two unfinished cups of chocolate, cakes, a glass saucer with blue raisins, and another with sweetmeats. Alyosha saw that he had interrupted visitors, and frowned. But at that instant the portiere was raised, and with rapid, hurrying footsteps Katerina Ivanovna came in, holding out both hands to Alyosha with a radiant smile of delight. At the same instant a servant brought in two lighted candles and set them on the table.

"Thank God! At last you have come too! I've been simply praying for you all day! Sit down."

Alyosha had been struck by Katerina Ivanovna's beauty when, three weeks before, Dmitri had first brought him, at Katerina Ivanovna's special request, to be introduced to her. There had been no conversation between them at that interview, however. Supposing Alyosha to be very shy, Katerina Ivanovna had talked all the time to Dmitri to spare him. Alyosha had been silent, but he had seen a great deal very clearly. He was struck by the imperiousness, proud ease, and self-confidence of the haughty girl. And all that was certain, Alyosha felt that he was not exaggerating it. He thought her great glowing black eyes were very fine, especially with her pale, even rather sallow, longish face. But in those eyes and in the lines of her exquisite lips there was something with which his brother might well be passionately in love, but which perhaps could not be loved for long. He expressed this thought almost plainly to Dmitri when, after the visit, his brother besought and insisted that he should not conceal his impressions on seeing his betrothed.

"You'll be happy with her, but perhaps not tranquilly happy."

"Quite so, brother. Such people remain always the same. They don't yield to fate. So you think I shan't love her for ever."

"No; perhaps you will love her for ever. But perhaps you won't always be happy with her."

Alyosha had given his opinion at the time, blushing, and angry with himself for having yielded to his brother's entreaties and put such "foolish" ideas into words. For his opinion had struck him as awfully foolish immediately after he had uttered it. He felt ashamed too of having given so confident an opinion about a woman. It was with the more amazement that he felt now, at the first glance at Katerina Ivanovna as she ran in to him, that he had perhaps been utterly mistaken. This time her face was beaming with spontaneous good-natured kindliness, and direct warm-hearted sincerity. The "pride and haughtiness," which had struck Alyosha so much before, was only betrayed now in a frank, generous energy and a sort of bright, strong faith in herself. Alyosha realised at the first glance, at the first word, that all the tragedy of her position in relation to the man she loved so dearly was no secret to her; that she perhaps already knew everything, positively everything. And yet, in spite of that, there was such brightness in her face, such faith in the future. Alyosha felt at once that he had gravely wronged her in his thoughts. He was conquered and captivated immediately. Besides all this, he noticed at her first words that she was in great excitement, an excitement perhaps quite exceptional and almost approaching ecstasy.

"I was so eager to see you, because I can learn from you the whole truth--from you and no one else."

"I have come," muttered Alyosha confusedly, "I--he sent me."

"Ah, he sent you I foresaw that. Now I know everything- everything!" cried Katerina Ivanovna, her eyes flashing. "Wait a moment, Alexey Fyodorovitch, I'll tell you why I've been so longing to see you. You see, I know perhaps far more than you do yourself, and there's no need for you to tell me anything. I'll tell you what I want from you. I want to know your own last impression of him. I want you to tell me most directly, plainly, coarsely even (oh, as coarsely as you like!), what you thought of him just now and of his position after your meeting with him to-day. That will perhaps be better than if I had a personal explanation with him, as he does not want to come to me. Do you understand what I want from you? Now, tell me simply, tell me every word of the message he sent you with (I knew he would send you)."

"He told me to give you his compliments and to say that he would never come again but to give you his compliments."

"His compliments? Was that what he said his own expression?"

"Yes."

"Accidentally perhaps he made a mistake in the word, perhaps he did not use the right word?"

"No; he told me precisely to repeat that word. He begged me two or three times not to forget to say so."

Katerina Ivanovna flushed hotly.

"Help me now, Alexey Fyodorovitch. Now I really need your help. I'll tell you what I think, and you must simply say whether it's right or not. Listen! If he had sent me his compliments in passing, without insisting on your repeating the words, without emphasising them, that would be the end of everything! But if he particularly insisted on those words, if he particularly told you not to forget to repeat them to me, then perhaps he was in excitement, beside himself. He had made his decision and was frightened at it. He wasn't walking away from me with a resolute step, but leaping headlong. The emphasis on that phrase may have been simply bravado."

"Yes, yes!" cried Alyosha warmly. "I believe that is it."

"And, if so, he's not altogether lost. I can still save him. Stay! Did he not tell you anything about money-- about three thousand roubles?"

"He did speak about it, and it's that more than anything that's crushing him. He said he had lost his honour and that nothing matters now," Alyosha answered warmly, feeling a rush of hope in his heart and believing that there really might be a way of escape and salvation for his brother. "But do you know about the money?" he added, and suddenly broke off.

"I've known of it a long time; I telegraphed to Moscow to inquire, and heard long ago that the money had not arrived. He hadn't sent the money, but I said nothing. Last week I learnt that he was still in need of money. My only object in all this was that he should know to whom to turn, and who was his true friend. No, he won't recognise that I am his truest friend; he won't know me, and looks on me merely as a woman. I've been tormented all the week, trying to think how to prevent him from being ashamed to face me because he spent that three thousand. Let him feel ashamed of himself, let him be ashamed of other people's knowing, but not of my knowing. He can tell God everything without shame. Why is it he still does not understand how much I am ready to bear for his sake? Why, why doesn't he know me? How dare he not know me after all that has happened? I want to save him for ever. Let him forget me as his betrothed. And here he fears that he is dishonoured in my eyes. Why, he wasn't afraid to be open with you, Alexey Fyodorovitch. How is it that I don't deserve the same?"

The last words she uttered in tears. Tears gushed from her eyes.

"I must tell you," Alyosha began, his voice trembling too, "what happened just now between him and my father."

And he described the whole scene, how Dmitri had sent him to get the money, how he had broken in, knocked his father down, and after that had again specially and emphatically begged him to take his compliments and farewell. "He went to that woman," Alyosha added softly.

"And do you suppose that I can't put up with that woman? Does he think I can't? But he won't marry her," she suddenly laughed nervously. "Could such a passion last for ever in a Karamazov? It's passion, not love. He won't marry her because she won't marry him." Again Katerina Ivanovna laughed strangely.

"He may marry her," said Alyosha mournfully, looking down.

"He won't marry her, I tell you. That girl is an angel. Do you know that? Do you know that?" Katerina Ivanovna exclaimed suddenly with extraordinary warmth. "She is one of the most fantastic of fantastic creatures. I know how bewitching she is, but I know too that she is kind, firm, and noble. Why do you look at me like that, Alexey Fyodorovitch? Perhaps you are wondering at my words, perhaps you don't believe me? Agrafena Alexandrovna, my angel!" she cried suddenly to someone, peeping into the next room, "come in to us. This is a friend. This is Alyosha. He knows all about our affairs. Show yourself to him."

"I've only been waiting behind the curtain for you to call me," said a soft, one might even say sugary, feminine voice.

The portiere was raised and Grushenka herself, smiling and beaming, came up to the table. A violent revulsion passed over Alyosha. He fixed his eyes on her and could not take them off. Here she was, that awful woman, the "beast," as Ivan had called her half an hour before. And yet one would have thought the creature standing before him most simple and ordinary, a good-natured, kind woman, handsome certainly, but so like other handsome ordinary women! It is true she was very, very good-looking with that Russian beauty so passionately loved by many men. She was a rather tall woman, though a little shorter than Katerina Ivanovna, who was exceptionally tall. She had a full figure, with soft, as it were, noiseless, movements, softened to a peculiar over-sweetness, like her voice. She moved, not like Katerina Ivanovna, with a vigorous, bold step, but noiselessly. Her feet made absolutely no sound on the floor. She sank softly into a low chair, softly rustling her sumptuous black silk dress, and delicately nestling her milk-white neck and broad shoulders in a costly cashmere shawl. She was twenty-two years old, and her face looked exactly that age. She was very white in the face, with a pale pink tint on her cheeks. The modelling of her face might be said to be too broad, and the lower jaw was set a trifle forward. Her upper lip was thin, but the slightly prominent lower lip was at least twice as full, and looked pouting. But her magnificent, abundant dark brown hair, her sable-coloured eyebrows and charming greyblue eyes with their long lashes would have made the most indifferent person, meeting her casually in a crowd in the street, stop at the sight of her face and remember it long after. What struck Alyosha most in that face was its expression of childlike good nature. There was a childlike look in her eyes, a look of childish delight. She came up to the table, beaming with delight and seeming to expect something with childish, impatient, and confiding curiosity. The light in her eyes gladdened the soul--Alyosha felt that. There was something else in her which he could not understand, or would not have been able to define, and which yet perhaps unconsciously affected him. It was that softness, that voluptuousness of her bodily movements, that catlike noiselessness. Yet it was a vigorous, ample body. Under the shawl could be seen full broad shoulders, a high, still quite girlish bosom. Her figure suggested the lines of the Venus of Milo, though already in somewhat exaggerated proportions. That could be divined. Connoisseurs of Russian beauty could have foretold with certainty that this fresh, still youthful beauty would lose its harmony by the age of thirty, would "spread"; that the face would become puffy, and that wrinkles would very soon appear upon her forehead and round the eyes; the complexion would grow coarse and red perhaps--in fact, that it was the beauty of the moment, the fleeting beauty which is so often met with in Russian women. Alyosha, of course, did not think of this; but though he was fascinated, yet he wondered with an unpleasant sensation, and as it were regretfully, why she drawled in that way and could not speak naturally. She did so, evidently feeling there was a charm in the exaggerated, honeyed modulation of the syllables. It was, of course, only a bad, underbred habit that showed bad education and a false idea of good manners. And yet this intonation and manner of speaking impressed Alyosha as almost incredibly incongruous with the childishly simple and happy expression of her face, the soft, babyish joy in her eyes. Katerina Ivanovna at once made her sit down in an arm-chair facing Alyosha, and ecstatically kissed her several times on her smiling lips. She seemed quite in love with her.

"This is the first time we've met, Alexey Fyodorovitch," she said rapturously. "I wanted to know her, to see her. I wanted to go to her, but I'd no sooner expressed the wish than she came to me. I knew we should settle everything together--everything. My heart told me so--I was begged not to take the step, but I foresaw it would be a way out of the difficulty, and I was not mistaken. Grushenka has explained everything to me, told me all she means to do. She flew here like an angel of goodness and brought us peace and joy."

"You did not disdain me, sweet, excellent young lady," drawled Grushenka in her singsong voice, still with the same charming smile of delight.

"Don't dare to speak to me like that, you sorceress, you witch! Disdain you! Here, I must kiss your lower lip once more. It looks as though it were swollen, and now it will be more so, and more and more. Look how she laughs, Alexey Fyodorovitch!"

Alyosha flushed, and faint, imperceptible shivers kept running down him.

"You make so much of me, dear young lady, and perhaps I am not at all worthy of your kindness."

"Not worthy! She's not worthy of it!" Katerina Ivanovna cried again with the same warmth. "You know, Alexey Fyodorovitch, we're fanciful, we're self-willed, but proudest of the proud in our little heart. We're noble, we're generous, Alexey Fyodorovitch, let me tell you. We have only been unfortunate. We were too ready to make every sacrifice for an unworthy, perhaps, or fickle man. There was one man--one, an officer too, we loved him, we sacrificed everything to him. That was long ago, five years ago, and he has forgotten us, he has married. Now he is a widower, he has written, he is coming here, and, do you know, we've loved him, none but him, all this time, and we've loved him all our life! He will come, and Grushenka will be happy again. For the last five years she's been wretched. But who can reproach her, who can boast of her favour? Only that bedridden old merchant, but he is more like her father, her friend, her protector. He found her then in despair, in agony, deserted by the man she loved. She was ready to drown herself then, but the old merchant saved her--saved her!"

"You defend me very kindly, dear young lady. You are in a great hurry about everything," Grushenka drawled again.

"Defend you! Is it for me to defend you? Should I dare to defend you? Grushenka, angel, give me your hand. Look at that charming soft little hand, Alexey Fyodorovitch! Look at it! It has brought me happiness and has lifted me up, and I'm going to kiss it, outside and inside, here, here, here!"

And three times she kissed the certainly charming, though rather fat, hand of Grushenka in a sort of rapture. She held out her hand with a charming musical, nervous little laugh, watched the "sweet young lady," and obviously liked having her hand kissed.

"Perhaps there's rather too much rapture," thought Alyosha. He blushed. He felt a peculiar uneasiness at heart the whole time.

"You won't make me blush, dear young lady, kissing my hand like this before Alexey Fyodorovitch."

"Do you think I meant to make you blush?" said Katerina Ivanovna, somewhat surprised. "Ah my dear, how little you understand me!

"Yes, and you too perhaps quite misunderstand me, dear young lady. Maybe I'm not so good as I seem to you. I've a bad heart; I will have my own way. I fascinated poor Dmitri Fyodorovitch that day simply for fun."

"But now you'll save him. You've given me your word. You'll explain it all to him. You'll break to him that you have long loved another man, who is now offering you his hand."

"Oh, no I didn't give you my word to do that. It was you kept talking about that. I didn't give you my word."

"Then I didn't quite understand you," said Katerina Ivanovna slowly, turning a little pale. "You promised-"

"Oh no, angel lady, I've promised nothing," Grushenka interrupted softly and evenly, still with the same gay and simple expression. "You see at once, dear young lady, what a wilful wretch I am compared with you. If I want to do a thing I do it. I may have made you some promise just now. But now again I'm thinking: I may take Mitya again. I liked him very much once--liked him for almost a whole hour. Now maybe I shall go and tell him to stay with me from this day forward. You see, I'm so changeable."

"Just now you said--something quite different," Katerina Ivanovna whispered faintly.

"Ah, just now! But, you know, I'm such a soft-hearted, silly creature. Only think what he's gone through on my account! What if when I go home I feel sorry for him? What then?"

"I never expected-"

"Ah, young lady, how good and generous you are compared with me! Now perhaps you won't care for a silly creature like me, now you know my character. Give me your sweet little hand, angelic lady," she said tenderly, and with a sort of reverence took Katerina Ivanovna's hand.

"Here, dear young lady, I'll take your hand and kiss it as you did mine. You kissed mine three times, but I ought to kiss yours three hundred times to be even with you. Well, but let that pass. And then it shall be as God wills. Perhaps I shall be your slave entirely and want to do your bidding like a slave. Let it be as God wills, without any agreements and promises. What a sweet hand--what a sweet hand you have! You sweet young lady, you incredible beauty!"

She slowly raised the hands to her lips, with the strange object indeed of "being even" with her in kisses.

Katerina Ivanovna did not take her hand away. She listened with timid hope to the last words, though Grushenka's promise to do her bidding like a slave was very strangely expressed. She looked intently into her eyes; she still saw in those eyes the same simple-hearted, confiding expression, the same bright gaiety.

"She's perhaps too naive," thought Katerina Ivanovna, with a gleam of hope.

Grushenka meanwhile seemed enthusiastic over the "sweet hand." She raised it deliberately to her lips. But she held it for two or three minutes near her lips, as though reconsidering something.

"Do you know, angel lady," she suddenly drawled in an even more soft and sugary voice, "do you know, after all, I think I won't kiss your hand?" And she laughed a little merry laugh.

"As you please. What's the matter with you?" said Katerina Ivanovna, starting suddenly.

"So that you may be left to remember that you kissed my hand, but I didn't kiss yours."

There was a sudden gleam in her eyes. She looked with awful intentness at Katerina Ivanovna.

"Insolent creature!" cried Katerina Ivanovna, as though suddenly grasping something. She flushed all over and leapt up from her seat.

Grushenka too got up, but without haste.

"So I shall tell Mitya how you kissed my hand, but I didn't kiss yours at all. And how he will laugh!"

"Vile slut! Go away!"

"Ah, for shame, young lady! Ah, for shame! That's unbecoming for you, dear young lady, a word like that."

"Go away! You're a creature for sale" screamed Katerina Ivanovna. Every feature was working in her utterly distorted face.

"For sale indeed! You used to visit gentlemen in the dusk for money once; you brought your beauty for sale. You see, I know."

Katerina Ivanovna shrieked, and would have rushed at her, but Alyosha held her with all his strength.

"Not a step, not a word! Don't speak, don't answer her. She'll go away--she'll go at once."

At that instant Katerina Ivanovna's two aunts ran in at her cry, and with them a maid-servant. All hurried to her.

"I will go away," said Grushenka, taking up her mantle from the sofa. "Alyosha, darling, see me home!"

"Go away--go away, make haste!" cried Alyosha, clasping his hands imploringly.

"Dear little Alyosha, see me home! I've got a pretty little story to tell you on the way. I got up this scene for your benefit, Alyosha. See me home, dear, you'll be glad of it afterwards."

Alyosha turned away, wringing his hands. Grushenka ran out of the house, laughing musically.

Katerina Ivanovna went into a fit of hysterics. She sobbed, and was shaken with convulsions. Everyone fussed round her.

"I warned you," said the elder of her aunts. "I tried to prevent your doing this. You're too impulsive. How could you do such a thing? You don't know these creatures, and they say she's worse than any of them. You are too self-willed."

"She's a tigress!" yelled Katerina Ivanovna. "Why did you hold me, Alexey Fyodorovitch? I'd have beaten her--beaten her!"

She could not control herself before Alyosha; perhaps she did not care to, indeed.

"She ought to be flogged in public on a scaffold!"

Alyosha withdrew towards the door.

"But, my God!" cried Katerina Ivanovna, clasping her hands. "He! He! He could be so dishonourable, so inhuman! Why, he told that creature what happened on that fatal, accursed day! 'You brought your beauty for sale, dear young lady.' She knows it! Your brother's a scoundrel, Alexey Fyodorovitch."

Alyosha wanted to say something, but he couldn't find a word. His heart ached.

"Go away, Alexey Fyodorovitch! It's shameful, it's awful for me! To-morrow, I beg you on my knees, come to-morrow. Don't condemn me. Forgive me. I don't know what I shall do with myself now!"

Alyosha walked out into the street reeling. He could have wept as she did. Suddenly he was overtaken by the maid.

"The young lady forgot to give you this letter from Madame Hohlakov; it's been left with us since dinner-time."

Alyosha took the little pink envelope mechanically and put it, almost unconsciously, into his pocket.

Chapter 11. Another Reputation Ruined

IT was not much more than three-quarters of a mile from the town to the monastery. Alyosha walked quickly along the road, at that hour deserted. It was almost night, and too dark to see anything clearly at thirty paces ahead. There were cross-roads half-way. A figure came into sight under a solitary willow at the cross-roads. As soon as Alyosha reached the cross-roads the figure moved out and rushed at him, shouting savagely:

"Your money or your life!"

"So it's you, Mitya," cried Alyosha, in surprise, violently startled however.

"Ha ha ha! You didn't expect me? I wondered where to wait for you. By her house? There are three ways from it, and I might have missed you. At last I thought of waiting here, for you had to pass here, there's no other way to the monastery. Come, tell me the truth. Crush me like a beetle. But what's the matter?"

"Nothing, brother--it's the fright you gave me. Oh, Dmitri! Father's blood just now." (Alyosha began to cry, he had been on the verge of tears for a long time, and now something seemed to snap in his soul.) "You almost killed him--cursed him--and now--here--you're making jokes--'Your money or your life!'"

"Well, what of that? It's not seemly--is that it? Not suitable in my position?"

"No--I only-"

"Stay. Look at the night. You see what a dark night, what clouds, what a wind has risen. I hid here under the willow waiting for you. And as God's above, I suddenly thought, why go on in misery any longer, what is there to wait for? Here I have a willow, a handkerchief, a shirt, I can twist them into a rope in a minute, and braces besides, and why go on burdening the earth, dishonouring it with my vile presence? And then I heard you coming--Heavens, it was as though something flew down to me suddenly. So there is a man, then, whom I love. Here he is, that man, my dear little brother, whom I love more than anyone in the world, the only one I love in the world. And I loved you so much, so much at that moment that I thought, 'I'll fall on his neck at once.' Then a stupid idea struck me, to have a joke with you and scare you. I shouted, like a fool, 'Your money!' Forgive my foolery--it was only nonsense, and there's nothing unseemly in my soul...Damn it all, tell me what's happened. What did she say? Strike me, crush me, don't spare me! Was she furious?"

"No, not that...There was nothing like that, Mitya. There--I found them both there."

"Both? Whom?"

"Grushenka at Katerina Ivanovna's."

Dmitri was struck dumb.

"Impossible!" he cried. "You're raving! Grushenka with her?"

Alyosha described all that had happened from the moment he went in to Katerina Ivanovna's. He was ten minutes telling his story can't be said to have told it fluently and consecutively, but he seemed to make it clear, not omitting any word or action of significance, and vividly describing, often in one word, his own sensations. Dmitri listened in silence, gazing at him with a terrible fixed stare, but it was clear to Alyosha that he understood it all, and had grasped every point. But as the story went on, his face became not merely gloomy, but menacing. He scowled, he clenched his teeth, and his fixed stare became still more rigid, more concentrated, more terrible, when suddenly, with incredible rapidity, his wrathful, savage face changed, his tightly compressed lips parted, and Dmitri Fyodorovitch broke into uncontrolled, spontaneous laughter. He literally shook with laughter. For a long time he could not speak.

"So she wouldn't kiss her hand! So she didn't kiss it; so she ran away!" he kept exclaiming with hysterical delight; insolent delight it might had been called, if it had not been so spontaneous. "So the other one called her tigress! And a tigress she is! So she ought to be flogged on a scaffold? Yes, yes, so she ought. That's just what I think; she ought to have been long ago. It's like this, brother, let her be punished, but I must get better first. I understand the queen of impudence. That's her all over! You saw her all over in that hand-kissing, the she-devil! She's magnificent in her own line! So she ran home? I'll go--ah--I'll run to her! Alyosha, don't blame me, I agree that hanging is too good for her."

"But Katerina Ivanovna!" exclaimed Alyosha sorrowfully.

"I see her, too! I see right through her, as I've never done before! It's a regular discovery of the four continents of the world, that is, of the five! What a thing to do! That's just like Katya, who was not afraid to face a coarse, unmannerly officer and risk a deadly insult on a generous impulse to save her father! But the pride, the recklessness, the defiance of fate, the unbounded defiance! You say that aunt tried to stop her? That aunt, you know, is overbearing, herself. She's the sister of the general's widow in Moscow, and even more stuck-up than she. But her husband was caught stealing government money. He lost everything, his estate and all, and the proud wife had to lower her colours, and hasn't raised them since. So she tried to prevent Katya, but she wouldn't listen to her! She thinks she can overcome everything, that everything will give way to her. She thought she could bewitch Grushenka if she liked, and she believed it herself: she plays a part to herself, and whose fault is it? Do you think she kissed Grushenka's hand first, on purpose, with a motive? No, she really was fascinated by Grushenka, that's to say, not by Grushenka, but by her own dream, her own delusion--because it was her dream, her delusion! Alyosha, darling, how did you escape from them, those women? Did you pick up your cassock and run? Ha ha ha!"

"Brother, you don't seem to have noticed how you've insulted Katerina Ivanovna by telling Grushenka about that day. And she flung it in her face just now that she had gone to gentlemen in secret to sell her beauty! Brother, what could be worse than that insult?"

What worried Alyosha more than anything was that, incredible as it seemed, his brother appeared pleased at Katerina Ivanovna's humiliation.

"Bah!" Dmitri frowned fiercely, and struck his forehead with his hand. He only now realised it, though Alyosha had just told him of the insult, and Katerina Ivanovna's cry: "Your brother is a scoundrel"

"Yes, perhaps, I really did tell Grushenka about that 'fatal day,' as Katya calls it. Yes, I did tell her, I remember! It was that time at Mokroe. I was drunk, the Gypsies were singing...But I was sobbing. I was sobbing then, kneeling and praying to Katya's image, and Grushenka understood it. She understood it all then. I remember, she cried herself...Damn it all! But it's bound to be so now...Then she cried, but now 'the dagger in the heart'! That's how women are."

He looked down and sank into thought.

"Yes, I am a scoundrel, a thorough scoundrel" he said suddenly, in a gloomy voice. "It doesn't matter whether I cried or not, I'm a scoundrel! Tell her I accept the name, if that's any comfort. Come, that's enough. Good-bye. It's no use talking! It's not amusing. You go your way and I mine. And I don't want to see you again except as a last resource. Good-bye, Alexey!"

He warmly pressed Alyosha's hand, and still looking down, without raising his head, as though tearing himself away, turned rapidly towards the town.

Alyosha looked after him, unable to believe he would go away so abruptly.

"Stay, Alexey, one more confession to you alone" cried Dmitri, suddenly turning back. "Look at me. Look at me well. You see here, here--there's terrible disgrace in store for me." (As he said "here," Dmitri struck his chest with his fist with a strange air, as though the dishonour lay precisely on his chest, in some spot, in a pocket, perhaps, or hanging round his neck.) "You know me now, a scoundrel, an avowed scoundrel, but let me tell you that I've never done anything before and never shall again, anything that can compare in baseness with the dishonour which I bear now at this very minute on my breast, here, here, which will come to pass, though I'm perfectly free to stop it. I can stop it or carry it through, note that. Well, let me tell you, I shall carry it through. I shan't stop it. I told you everything just now, but I didn't tell you this, because even I had not brass enough for it. I can still pull up; if I do, I can give back the full half of my lost honour to-morrow. But I shan't pull up. I shall carry out my base plan, and you can bear witness that I told so beforehand. Darkness and destruction! No need to explain. You'll find out in due time. The filthy back-alley and the she-devil. Good-bye. Don't pray for me, I'm not worth it. And there's no need, no need at all...I don't need it! Away!"

And he suddenly retreated, this time finally. Alyosha went towards the monastery.

"What? I shall never see him again! What is he saying?" he wondered wildly. "Why, I shall certainly see him to-morrow. I shall look him up. I shall make a point of it. What does he mean?"

He went round the monastery, and crossed the pine-wood to the hermitage. The door was opened to him, though no one was admitted at that hour. There was a tremor in his heart as he went into Father Zossima's cell.

"Why, why, had he gone forth? Why had he sent him into the world? Here was peace. Here was holiness. But there was confusion, there was darkness in which one lost one's way and went astray at once..."

In the cell he found the novice Porfiry and Father Paissy, who came every hour to inquire after Father Zossima. Alyosha learnt with alarm that he was getting worse and worse. Even his usual discourse with the brothers could not take place that day. As a rule every evening after service the monks flocked into Father Zossima's cell, and all confessed aloud their sins of the day, their sinful thoughts and temptations; even their disputes, if there had been any. Some confessed kneeling. The elder absolved, reconciled, exhorted, imposed penance, blessed, and dismissed them. It was against this general "confession" that the opponents of "elders" protested, maintaining that it was a profanation of the sacrament of confession, almost a sacrilege, though this was quite a different thing. They even represented to the diocesan authorities that such confessions attained no good object, but actually to a large extent led to sin and temptation. Many of the brothers disliked going to the elder, and went against their own will because everyone went, and for fear they should be accused of pride and rebellious ideas. People said that some of the monks agreed beforehand, saying, "I'll confess I lost my temper with you this morning, and you confirm it," simply in order to have something to say. Alyosha knew that this actually happened sometimes. He knew, too, that there were among the monks some who deep resented the fact that letters from relations were habitually taken to the elder, to be opened and read by him before those to whom they were addressed.

It was assumed, of course, that all this was done freely, and in good faith, by way of voluntary submission and salutary guidance. But, in fact, there was sometimes no little insincerity, and much that was false and strained in this practice. Yet the older and more experienced of the monks adhered to their opinion, arguing that "for those who have come within these walls sincerely seeking salvation, such obedience and sacrifice will certainly be salutary and of great benefit; those, on the other hand, who find it irksome, and repine, are no true monks, and have made a mistake in entering the monastery--their proper place is in the world. Even in the temple one cannot be safe from sin and the devil. So it was no good taking it too much into account."

"He is weaker, a drowsiness has come over him," Father Paissy whispered to Alyosha, as he blessed him. "It's difficult to rouse him. And he must not be roused. He waked up for five minutes, sent his blessing to the brothers, and begged their prayers for him at night. He intends to take the sacrament again in the morning. He remembered you, Alexey. He asked whether you had gone away, and was told that you were in the town. 'I blessed him for that work,' he said, 'his place is there, not here, for awhile.' Those were his words about you. He remembered you lovingly, with anxiety; do you understand how he honoured you? But how is it that he has decided that you shall spend some time in the world? He must have foreseen something in your destiny! Understand, Alexey, that if you return to the world, it must be to do the duty laid upon you by your elder, and not for frivolous vanity and worldly pleasures."

Father Paissy went out. Alyosha had no doubt that Father Zossima was dying, though he might live another day or two. Alyosha firmly and ardently resolved that in spite of his promises to his father, the Hohlakovs, and Katerina Ivanovna, he would not leave the monastery next day, but would remain with his elder to the end. His heart glowed with love, and he reproached himself bitterly for having been able for one instant to forget him whom he had left in the monastery on his death bed, and whom he honoured above everyone in the world. He went into Father Zossima's bedroom, knelt down, and bowed to the ground before the elder, who slept quietly without stirring, with regular, hardly audible breathing and a peaceful face.

Alyosha returned to the other room, where Father Zossima received his guests in the morning. Taking off his boots, he lay down on the hard, narrow, leathern sofa, which he had long used as a bed, bringing nothing but a pillow. The mattress, about which his father had shouted to him that morning, he had long forgotten to lie on. He took off his cassock, which he used as a covering. But before going to bed, he fell on his knees and prayed a long time. In his fervent prayer he did not beseech God to lighten his darkness but only thirsted for the joyous emotion, which always visited his soul after the praise and adoration, of which his evening prayer usually consisted. That joy always brought him light untroubled sleep. As he was praying, he suddenly felt in his pocket the little pink note the servant had handed him as he left Katerina Ivanovna's. He was disturbed, but finished his prayer. Then, after some hesitation, he opened the envelope. In it was a letter to him, signed by Lise, the young daughter of Madame Hohlakov, who had laughed at him before the elder in the morning.

"Alexey Fyodorovitch," she wrote, "I am writing to you without anyone's knowledge, even mamma's, and I know how wrong it is. But I cannot live without telling you the feeling that has sprung up in my heart, and this no one but us two must know for a time. But how am I to say what I want so much to tell you? Paper, they say, does not blush, but I assure you it's not true and that it's blushing just as I am now, all over. Dear Alyosha, I love you, I've loved you from my childhood, since our Moscow days, when you were very different from what you are now, and I shall love you all my life. My heart has chosen you, to unite our lives, and pass them together till our old age. Of course, on condition that you will leave the monastery. As for our age we will wait for the time fixed by the law. By that time I shall certainly be quite strong, I shall be walking and dancing. There can be no doubt of that.

"You see how I've thought of everything. There's only one thing I can't imagine: what you'll think of me when you read this. I'm always laughing and being naughty. I made you angry this morning, but I assure you before I took up my pen, I prayed before the Image of the Mother of God, and now I'm praying, and almost crying.

"My secret is in your hands. When you come to-morrow, I don't know how I shall look at you. Ah, Alexey Fyodorovitch, what if I can't restrain myself like a silly and laugh when I look at you as I did to-day. You'll think I'm a nasty girl making fun of you, and you won't believe my letter. And so I beg you, dear one, if you've any pity for me, when you come to-morrow, don't look me straight in the face, for if I meet your eyes, it will be sure to make me laugh, especially as you'll be in that long gown. I feel cold all over when I think of it, so when you come, don't look at me at all for a time, look at mamma or at the window...

"Here I've written you a love-letter. Oh, dear, what have I done? Alyosha, don't despise me, and if I've done something very horrid and wounded you, forgive me. Now the secret of my reputation, ruined perhaps for ever, is in your hands.

"I shall certainly cry to-day. Good-bye till our meeting, our awful meeting.--Lise.

"P.S.--Alyosha! You must, must, must come!--Lise."

Alyosha read the note in amazement, read it through twice, thought a little, and suddenly laughed a soft, sweet laugh. He started. That laugh seemed to him sinful. But a minute later he laughed again just as softly and happily. He slowly replaced the note in the envelope, crossed himself and lay down. The agitation in his heart passed at once. "God, have mercy upon all of them, have all these unhappy and turbulent souls in Thy keeping, and set them in the right path. All ways are Thine. Save them according to Thy wisdom. Thou art love. Thou wilt send joy to all!" Alyosha murmured, crossing himself, and falling into peaceful sleep.

Book IV. Lacerations
Chapter 1. Father Ferapont

ALYOSHA was roused early, before daybreak. Father Zossima woke up feeling very weak, though he wanted to get out of bed and sit up in a chair. His mind was quite clear; his face looked very tired, yet bright and almost joyful. It wore an expression of gaiety, kindness and cordiality. "Maybe I shall not live through the coming day," he said to Alyosha. Then he desired to confess and take the sacrament at once. He always confessed to Father Paissy. After taking the communion, the service of extreme unction followed. The monks assembled and the cell was gradually filled up by the inmates of the hermitage. Meantime it was daylight. People began coming from the monastery. After the service was over the elder desired to kiss and take leave of everyone. As the cell was so small the earlier visitors withdrew to make room for others. Alyosha stood beside the elder, who was seated again in his arm-chair. He talked as much as he could. Though his voice was weak, it was fairly steady.

"I've been teaching you so many years, and therefore I've been talking aloud so many years, that I've got into the habit of talking, and so much so that it's almost more difficult for me to hold my tongue than to talk, even now, in spite of my weakness, dear Fathers and brothers," he jested, looking with emotion at the group round him.

Alyosha remembered afterwards something of what he said to them. But though he spoke out distinctly and his voice was fairly steady, his speech was somewhat disconnected. He spoke of many things, he seemed anxious before the moment of death to say everything he had not said in his life, and not simply for the sake of instructing them, but as though thirsting to share with all men and all creation his joy and ecstasy, and once more in his life to open his whole heart.

"Love one another, Fathers," said Father Zossima, as far as Alyosha could remember afterwards. "Love God's people. Because we have come here and shut ourselves within these walls, we are no holier than those that are outside, but on the contrary, from the very fact of coming here, each of us has confessed to himself that he is worse than others, than all men on earth...And the longer the monk lives in his seclusion, the more keenly he must recognise that. Else he would have had no reason to come here. When he realises that he is not only worse than others, but that he is responsible to all men for all and everything, for all human sins, national and individual, only then the aim of our seclusion is attained. For know, dear ones, that every one of us is undoubtedly responsible for all men--and everything on earth, not merely through the general sinfulness of creation, but each one personally for all mankind and every individual man. This knowledge is the crown of life for the monk and for every man. For monks are not a special sort of men, but only what all men ought to be. Only through that knowledge, our heart grows soft with infinite, universal, inexhaustible love. Then every one of you will have the power to win over the whole world by love and to wash away the sins of the world with your tears...Each of you keep watch over your heart and confess your sins to yourself unceasingly. Be not afraid of your sins, even when perceiving them, if only there be penitence, but make no conditions with God. Again, I say, be not proud. Be proud neither to the little nor to the great. Hate not those who reject you, who insult you, who abuse and slander you. Hate not the atheists, the teachers of evil, the materialists--and I mean not only the good ones--for there are many good ones among them, especially in our day--hate not even the wicked ones. Remember them in your prayers thus: Save, O Lord, all those who have none to pray for them, save too all those who will not pray. And add: it is not in pride that I make this prayer, O Lord, for I am lower than all men...Love God's people, let not strangers draw away the flock, for if you slumber in your slothfulness and disdainful pride, or worse still, in covetousness, they will come from all sides and draw away your flock. Expound the Gospel to the people unceasingly...be not extortionate...Do not love gold and silver, do not hoard them...Have faith. Cling to the banner and raise it on high."

But the elder spoke more disconnectedly than Alyosha reported his words afterwards. Sometimes he broke off altogether, as though to take breath and recover his strength, but he was in a sort of ecstasy. They heard him with emotion, though many wondered at his words and found them obscure...Afterwards all remembered those words.

When Alyosha happened for a moment to leave the cell, he was struck by the general excitement and suspense in the monks who were crowding about it. This anticipation showed itself in some by anxiety, in others by devout solemnity. All were expecting that some marvel would happen immediately after the elder's death. Their

75

suspense was, from one point of view, almost frivolous, but even the most austere of the monks were affected by it. Father Paissy's face looked the gravest of all.

Alyosha was mysteriously summoned by a monk to see Rakitin, who had arrived from town with a singular letter for him from Madame Hohlakov. In it she informed Alyosha of a strange and very opportune incident. It appeared that among the women who had come on the previous day to receive Father Zossima's blessing, there had been an old woman from the town, a sergeant's widow, called Prohorovna. She had inquired whether she might pray for the rest of the soul of her son, Vassenka, who had gone to Irkutsk, and had sent her no news for over a year. To which Father Zossima had answered sternly, forbidding her to do so, and saying that to pray for the living as though they were dead was a kind of sorcery. He afterwards forgave her on account of her ignorance, and added, "as though reading the book of the future" (this was Madame Hohlakov's expression), words of comfort: "that her son Vassya was certainly alive and he would either come himself very shortly or send a letter, and that she was to go home and expect him." And "Would you believe it?" exclaimed Madame Hohlakov enthusiastically, "the prophecy has been fulfilled literally indeed, and more than that." Scarcely had the old woman reached home when they gave her a letter from Siberia which had been awaiting her. But that was not all; in the letter written on the road from Ekaterinenburg, Vassya informed his mother that he was returning to Russia with an official, and that three weeks after her receiving the letter he hoped "to embrace his mother."

Madame Hohlakov warmly entreated Alyosha to report this new "miracle of prediction" to the Superior and all the brotherhood. "All, all, ought to know of it" she concluded. The letter had been written in haste, the excitement of the writer was apparent in every line of it. But Alyosha had no need to tell the monks, for all knew of it already. Rakitin had commissioned the monk who brought his message "to inform most respectfully his reverence Father Paissy, that he, Rakitin, has a matter to speak of with him, of such gravity that he dare not defer it for a moment, and humbly begs forgiveness for his presumption." As the monk had given the message to Father Paissy, before that to Alyosha, the latter found after reading the letter, there was nothing left for him to do but to hand it to Father Paissy in confirmation of the story.

And even that austere and cautious man, though he frowned as he read the news of the "miracle," could not completely restrain some inner emotion. His eyes gleamed, and a grave and solemn smile came into his lips.

"We shall see greater things!" broke from him.

"We shall see greater things, greater things yet!" the monks around repeated.

But Father Paissy, frowning again, begged all of them, at least for a time, not to speak of the matter "till it be more fully confirmed, seeing there is so much credulity among those of this world, and indeed this might well have chanced naturally," he added, prudently, as it were to satisfy his conscience, though scarcely believing his own disavowal, a fact his listeners very clearly perceived.

Within the hour the "miracle" was of course known to the whole monastery, and many visitors who had come for the mass. No one seemed more impressed by it than the monk who had come the day before from St. Sylvester, from the little monastery of Obdorsk in the far North. It was he who had been standing near Madame Hohlakov the previous day and had asked Father Zossima earnestly, referring to the "healing" of the lady's daughter, "How can you presume to do such things?"

He was now somewhat puzzled and did not know whom to believe. The evening before he had visited Father Ferapont in his cell apart, behind the apiary, and had been greatly impressed and overawed by the visit. This Father Ferapont was that aged monk so devout in fasting and observing silence who has been mentioned already, as antagonistic to Father Zossima and the whole institution of "elders," which he regarded as a pernicious and frivolous innovation. He was a very formidable opponent, although from his practice of silence he scarcely spoke a word to anyone. What made him formidable was that a number of monks fully shared his feeling, and many of the visitors looked upon him as a great saint and ascetic, although they had no doubt that he was crazy. But it was just his craziness attracted them.

Father Ferapont never went to see the elder. Though he lived in the hermitage they did not worry him to keep its regulations, and this too because he behaved as though he were crazy. He was seventy-five or more, and he lived in a corner beyond the apiary in an old decaying wooden cell which had been built long ago for another great ascetic, Father Iona, who had lived to be a hundred and five, and of whose saintly doings many curious stories were still extant in the monastery and the neighbourhood.

Father Ferapont had succeeded in getting himself installed in this same solitary cell seven years previously. It was simply a peasant's hut, though it looked like a chapel, for it contained an extraordinary number of ikons with lamps perpetually burning before them--which men brought to the monastery as offerings to God. Father Ferapont had been appointed to look after them and keep the lamps burning. It was said (and indeed it was true) that he ate only two pounds of bread in three days. The beekeeper, who lived close by the apiary, used to bring him the bread every three days, and even to this man who waited upon him, Father Ferapont rarely uttered a word. The four pounds of bread, together with the sacrament bread, regularly sent him on Sundays after the late mass by the Father Superior, made up his weekly rations. The water in his jug was changed every day. He rarely appeared at mass. Visitors who came to do him homage saw him sometimes kneeling all day long at prayer without looking round. If he addressed them, he was brief, abrupt, strange, and almost always rude. On very rare occasions, however, he would talk to visitors, but for the most part he would utter some one strange saying which was a complete riddle, and no entreaties would induce him to pronounce a word in explanation. He was not a priest, but a simple monk. There was a strange belief, chiefly, however, among the most ignorant, that Father Ferapont had communication with heavenly spirits and would only converse with them, and so was silent with men.

The monk from Obdorsk, having been directed to the apiary by the beekeeper, who was also a very silent and surly monk, went to the corner where Father Ferapont's cell stood. "Maybe he will speak as you are a stranger and maybe you'll get nothing out of him," the beekeeper had warned him. The monk, as he related afterwards, approached in the utmost apprehension. It was rather late in the evening. Father Ferapont was sitting at the door of his cell on a low bench. A huge old elm was lightly rustling overhead. There was an evening freshness in the air. The monk from Obdorsk bowed down before the saint and asked his blessing.

"Do you want me to bow down to you, monk?" said Father Ferapont. "Get up!"

The monk got up.

"Blessing, be blessed! Sit beside me. Where have you come from?"

What most struck the poor monk was the fact that in spite of his strict fasting and great age, Father Ferapont still looked a vigorous old man. He was tall, held himself erect, and had a thin, but fresh and healthy face. There was no doubt he still had considerable strength. He was of athletic build. In spite of his great age he was not even quite grey, and still had very thick hair and a full beard, both of which had once been black. His eyes were grey, large and luminous, but strikingly prominent. He spoke with a broad accent. He was dressed in a peasant's long reddish coat of coarse convict cloth (as it used to be called) and had a stout rope round his waist. His throat and chest were bare. Beneath his coat, his shirt of the coarsest linen showed almost black with dirt, not having been changed for months. They said that he wore irons weighing thirty pounds under his coat. His stockingless feet were thrust in old slippers almost dropping to pieces.

"From the little Obdorsk monastery, from St. Sylvester," the monk answered humbly, whilst his keen and inquisitive, but rather frightened little eyes kept watch on the hermit.

"I have been at your Sylvester's. I used to stay there. Is Sylvester well?"

The monk hesitated.

"You are a senseless lot! How do you keep the fasts?"

"Our dietary is according to the ancient conventual rules. During Lent there are no meals provided for Monday, Wednesday, and Friday. For Tuesday and Thursday we have white bread, stewed fruit with honey, wild berries, or salt cabbage and whole meal stirabout. On Saturday white cabbage soup, noodles with peas, kasha, all with hemp oil. On weekdays we have dried fish and kasha with the cabbage soup. From Monday till Saturday evening, six whole days in Holy Week, nothing is cooked, and we have only bread and water, and that sparingly; if possible not taking food every day, just the same as is ordered for first week in Lent. On Good Friday nothing is eaten. In the same way on the Saturday we have to fast till three o'clock, and then take a little bread and water and drink a single cup of wine. On Holy Thursday we drink wine and have something cooked without oil or not cooked at all, inasmuch as the Laodicean council lays down for Holy Thursday: "It is unseemly by remitting the fast on the Holy Thursday to dishonour the whole of Lent!" This is how we keep the fast. But what is that compared with you, holy Father," added the monk, growing more confident, "for all the year round, even at Easter, you take nothing but bread and water, and what we should eat in two days lasts you full seven. It's truly marvellous--your great abstinence."

"And mushrooms?" asked Father Ferapont, suddenly.

"Mushrooms?" repeated the surprised monk.

"Yes. I can give up their bread, not needing it at all, and go away into the forest and live there on the mushrooms or the berries, but they can't give up their bread here, wherefore they are in bondage to the devil. Nowadays the unclean deny that there is need of such fasting. Haughty and unclean is their judgment."

"Och, true," sighed the monk.

"And have you seen devils among them?" asked Ferapont.

"Among them? Among whom?" asked the monk, timidly.

"I went to the Father Superior on Trinity Sunday last year, I haven't been since. I saw a devil sitting on one man's chest hiding under his cassock, only his horns poked out; another had one peeping out of his pocket with such sharp eyes, he was afraid of me; another settled in the unclean belly of one, another was hanging round a man's neck, and so he was carrying him about without seeing him."

"You--can see spirits?" the monk inquired.

"I tell you I can see, I can see through them. When I was coming out from the Superior's I saw one hiding from me behind the door, and a big one, a yard and a half or more high, with a thick long grey tail, and the tip of his tail was in the crack of the door and I was quick and slammed the door, pinching his tail in it. He squealed and began to struggle, and I made the sign of the cross over him three times. And he died on the spot like a crushed spider. He must have rotted there in the corner and be stinking, but they don't see, they don't smell it. It's a year since I have been there. I reveal it to you, as you are a stranger."

"Your words are terrible! But, holy and blessed father," said the monk, growing bolder and bolder, "is it true, as they noise abroad even to distant lands about you, that you are in continual communication with the Holy Ghost?"

"He does fly down at times."

"How does he fly down? In what form?"

"As a bird."

"The Holy Ghost in the form of a dove?"

"There's the Holy Ghost and there's the Holy Spirit. The Holy Spirit can appear as other birds--sometimes as a swallow, sometimes a goldfinch and sometimes as a blue-tit."

"How do you know him from an ordinary tit?"

"He speaks."

"How does he speak, in what language?"

"Human language."

"And what does he tell you?"

"Why, to-day he told me that a fool would visit me and would ask me unseemly questions. You want to know too much, monk."

"Terrible are your words, most holy and blessed Father," the monk shook his head. But there was a doubtful look in his frightened little eyes.

"Do you see this tree?" asked Father Ferapont, after a pause.

"I do, blessed Father."

"You think it's an elm, but for me it has another shape."

"What sort of shape?" inquired the monk, after a pause of vain expectation.

"It happens at night. You see those two branches? In the night it is Christ holding out His arms to me and seeking me with those arms, I see it clearly and tremble. It's terrible, terrible!"

"What is there terrible if it's Christ Himself?"

"Why, He'll snatch me up and carry me away."

"Alive?"

"In the spirit and glory of Elijah, haven't you heard? He will take me in His arms and bear me away."

Though the monk returned to the cell he was sharing with one of the brothers, in considerable perplexity of mind, he still cherished at heart a greater reverence for Father Ferapont than for Father Zossima. He was strongly in favour of fasting, and it was not strange that one who kept so rigid a fast as Father Ferapont should "see marvels." His words seemed certainly queer, but God only could tell what was hidden in those words, and were not worse words and acts commonly seen in those who have sacrificed their intellects for the glory of God? The pinching of the devil's tail he was ready and eager to believe, and not only in the figurative sense. Besides he had, before visiting the monastery, a strong prejudice against the institution of "elders," which he only knew of by hearsay and believed to be a pernicious innovation. Before he had been long at the monastery, he had detected the secret murmurings of some shallow brothers who disliked the institution. He was, besides, a meddlesome, inquisitive man, who poked his nose into everything. This was why the news of the fresh "miracle" performed by Father Zossima reduced him to extreme perplexity. Alyosha remembered afterwards how their inquisitive guest from Obdorsk had been continually flitting to and fro from one group to another, listening and asking questions among the monks that were crowding within and without the elder's cell. But he did not pay much attention to him at the time, and only recollected it afterwards.

He had no thought to spare for it indeed, for when Father Zossima, feeling tired again, had gone back to bed, he thought of Alyosha as he was closing his eyes, and sent for him. Alyosha ran at once. There was no one else in the cell but Father Paissy, Father Iosif, and the novice Porfiry. The elder, opening his weary eyes and looking intently at Alyosha, asked him suddenly:

"Are your people expecting you, my son?"

Alyosha hesitated.

"Haven't they need of you? Didn't you promise someone yesterday to see them to-day?"

"I did promise--to my father--my brothers--others too."

"You see, you must go. Don't grieve. Be sure I shall not die without your being by to hear my last word. To you I will say that word, my son, it will be my last gift to you. To you, dear son, because you love me. But now go to keep your promise."

Alyosha immediately obeyed, though it was hard to go. But the promise that he should hear his last word on earth, that it should be the last gift to him, Alyosha, sent a thrill of rapture through his soul. He made haste that he might finish what he had to do in the town and return quickly. Father Paissy, too, uttered some words of exhortation which moved and surprised him greatly. He spoke as they left the cell together.

"Remember, young man, unceasingly," Father Paissy began, without preface, "that the science of this world, which has become a great power, has, especially in the last century, analysed everything divine handed down to us in the holy books. After this cruel analysis the learned of this world have nothing left of all that was sacred of old. But they have only analysed the parts and overlooked the whole, and indeed their blindness is marvellous. Yet the whole still stands steadfast before their eyes, and the gates of hell shall not prevail against it. Has it not lasted nineteen centuries, is it not still a living, a moving power in the individual soul and in the masses of people? It is still as strong and living even in the souls of atheists, who have destroyed everything! For even those who have renounced Christianity and attack it, in their inmost being still follow the Christian ideal, for hitherto neither their subtlety nor the ardour of their hearts has been able to create a higher ideal of man and of virtue than the ideal given by Christ of old. When it has been attempted, the result has been only grotesque. Remember this especially, young man, since you are being sent into the world by your departing elder. Maybe, remembering this great day, you will not forget my words, uttered from the heart for your guidance, seeing you are young, and the temptations of the world are great and beyond your strength to endure. Well, now go, my orphan."

With these words Father Paissy blessed him. As Alyosha left the monastery and thought them over, he suddenly realised that he had met a new and unexpected friend, a warmly loving teacher, in this austere monk who had hitherto treated him sternly. It was as though Father Zossima had bequeathed him to him at his death, and "perhaps that's just what had passed between them," Alyosha thought suddenly. The philosophic reflections he had just heard so unexpectedly testified to the warmth of Father Paissy's heart. He was in haste to arm the boy's mind for conflict with temptation and to guard the young soul left in his charge with the strongest defence he could imagine.

Chapter 2. At His Father's

FIRST of all, Alyosha went to his father. On the way he remembered that his father had insisted the day before that he should come without his brother Ivan seeing him. "Why so?" Alyosha wondered suddenly. "Even if my father has something to say to me alone, why should I go in unseen? Most likely in his excitement yesterday he meant to say something different," he decided. Yet he was very glad when Marfa Ignatyevna, who opened the garden gate to him (Grigory, it appeared, was ill in bed in the lodge), told him in answer to his question that Ivan Fyodorovitch had gone out two hours ago.

"And my father?"

"He is up, taking his coffee," Marfa answered somewhat drily.

Alyosha went in. The old man was sitting alone at the table wearing slippers and a little old overcoat. He was amusing himself by looking through some accounts, rather inattentively however. He was quite alone in the house, for Smerdyakov too had gone out marketing. Though he had got up early and was trying to put a bold face on it, he looked tired and weak. His forehead, upon which huge purple bruises had come out during the night, was bandaged with a red handkerchief; his nose too was swollen terribly in the night, and some smaller bruises covered it in patches, giving his whole face a peculiarly spiteful and irritable look. The old man was aware of this, and turned a hostile glance on Alyosha as he came in.

"The coffee is cold," he cried harshly; "I won't offer you any. I've ordered nothing but a Lenten fish soup to-day, and I don't invite anyone to share it. Why have you come?"

"To find out how you are," said Alyosha.

"Yes. Besides, I told you to come yesterday. It's all of no consequence. You need not have troubled. But I knew you'd come poking in directly."

He said this with almost hostile feeling. At the same time he got up and looked anxiously in the looking-glass (perhaps for the fortieth time that morning) at his nose. He began, too, binding his red handkerchief more becomingly on his forehead.

"Red's better. It's just like the hospital in a white one," he observed sententiously. "Well, how are things over there? How is your elder?"

"He is very bad; he may die to-day," answered Alyosha. But his father had not listened, and had forgotten his own question at once.

"Ivan's gone out," he said suddenly. "He is doing his utmost to carry off Mitya's betrothed. That's what he is staying here for," he added maliciously, and, twisting his mouth, looked at Alyosha.

"Surely he did not tell you so?" asked Alyosha.

"Yes, he did, long ago. Would you believe it, he told me three weeks ago? You don't suppose he too came to murder me, do you? He must have had some object in coming."

"What do you mean? Why do you say such things?" said Alyosha, troubled.

"He doesn't ask for money, it's true, but yet he won't get a farthing from me. I intend living as long as possible, you may as well know, my dear Alexey Fyodorovitch, and so I need every farthing, and the longer I live, the more I shall need it," he continued, pacing from one corner of the room to the other, keeping his hands in the pockets of his loose greasy overcoat made of yellow cotton material. "I can still pass for a man at five and fifty, but I want to pass for one for another twenty years. As I get older, you know, I shan't be a pretty object. The wenches won't come to me of their own accord, so I shall want my money. So I am saving up more and more, simply for myself, my dear son Alexey Fyodorovitch. You may as well know. For I mean to go on in my sins to the end, let me tell you. For sin is sweet; all abuse it, but all men live in it, only others do it on the sly, and I openly. And so all the other sinners fall upon me for being so simple. And your paradise, Alexey Fyodorovitch, is not to my taste, let me tell you that; and it's not the proper place for a gentleman, your paradise, even if it exists. I believe that I fall asleep and don't wake up again, and that's all. You can pray for my soul if you like. And if you don't want to, don't, damn you! That's my philosophy. Ivan talked well here yesterday, though we were all drunk. Ivan is a conceited coxcomb, but he has no particular learning...nor education either. He sits silent and smiles at one without speaking--that's what pulls him through."

Alyosha listened to him in silence.

"Why won't he talk to me? If he does speak, he gives himself airs. Your Ivan is a scoundrel! And I'll marry Grushenka in a minute if I want to. For if you've money, Alexey Fyodorovitch, you have only to want a thing and you can have it. That's what Ivan is afraid of, he is on the watch to prevent me getting married and that's why he is egging on Mitya to marry Grushenka himself. He hopes to keep me from Grushenka by that (as though I should leave him my money if I don't marry her!). Besides if Mitya marries Grushenka, Ivan will carry off his rich betrothed, that's what he's reckoning on! He is a scoundrel, your Ivan!"

"How cross you are! It's because of yesterday; you had better lie down," said Alyosha.

"There! you say that," the old man observed suddenly, as though it had struck him for the first time, "and I am not angry with you. But if Ivan said it, I should be angry with him. It is only with you I have good moments, else you know I am an ill-natured man."

"You are not ill-natured, but distorted," said Alyosha with a smile.

"Listen. I meant this morning to get that ruffian Mitya locked up and I don't know now what I shall decide about it. Of course in these fashionable days fathers and mothers are looked upon as a prejudice, but even now the law does not allow you to drag your old father about by the hair, to kick him in the face in his own house, and brag of murdering him outright--all in the presence of witnesses. If I liked, I could crush him and could have him locked up at once for what he did yesterday."

"Then you don't mean to take proceedings?"

"Ivan has dissuaded me. I shouldn't care about Ivan, but there's another thing."

And bending down to Alyosha, he went on in a confidential half-whisper.

"If I send the ruffian to prison, she'll hear of it and run to see him at once. But if she hears that he has beaten me, a weak old man, within an inch of my life, she may give him up and come to me...For that's her way, everything by contraries. I know her through and through! Won't you have a drop of brandy? Take some cold coffee and I'll pour a quarter of a glass of brandy into it, it's delicious, my boy."

"No, thank you. I'll take that roll with me if I may," said Alyosha, and taking a halfpenny French roll he put it in the pocket of his cassock. "And you'd better not have brandy, either," he suggested apprehensively, looking into the old man's face.

"You are quite right, it irritates my nerves instead of soothing them. Only one little glass. I'll get it out of the cupboard."

He unlocked the cupboard, poured out a glass, drank it, then locked the cupboard and put the key back in his pocket.

"That's enough. One glass won't kill me."

"You see you are in a better humour now," said Alyosha, smiling.

"Um! I love you even without the brandy, but with scoundrels I am a scoundrel. Ivan is not going to Tchermashnya--why is that? He wants to spy how much I give Grushenka if she comes. They are all scoundrels!

But I don't recognise Ivan, I don't know him at all. Where does he come from? He is not one of us in soul. As though I'd leave him anything! I shan't leave a will at all, you may as well know. And I'll crush Mitya like a beetle. I squash black-beetles at night with my slipper; they squelch when you tread on them. And your Mitya will squelch too. Your Mitya, for you love him. Yes you love him and I am not afraid of your loving him. But if Ivan loved him I should be afraid for myself at his loving him. But Ivan loves nobody. Ivan is not one of us. People like Ivan are not our sort, my boy. They are like a cloud of dust. When the wind blows, the dust will be gone...I had a silly idea in my head when I told you to come to-day; I wanted to find out from you about Mitya. If I were to hand him over a thousand or maybe two now, would the beggarly wretch agree to take himself off altogether for five years or, better still, thirty-five, and without Grushenka, and give her up once for all, eh?"

"I--I'll ask him," muttered Alyosha. "If you would give him three thousand, perhaps he-"

"That's nonsense! You needn't ask him now, no need! I've changed my mind. It was a nonsensical idea of mine. I won't give him anything, not a penny, I want my money myself," cried the old man, waving his hand. "I'll crush him like a beetle without it. Don't say anything to him or else he will begin hoping. There's nothing for you to do here, you needn't stay. Is that betrothed of his, Katerina Ivanovna, whom he has kept so carefully hidden from me all this time, going to marry him or not? You went to see her yesterday, I believe?"

"Nothing will induce her to abandon him."

"There you see how dearly these fine young ladies love a rake and a scoundrel. They are poor creatures I tell you, those pale young ladies, very different from--Ah, if I had his youth and the looks I had then (for I was better-looking than he at eight and twenty) I'd have been a conquering hero just as he is. He is a low cad! But he shan't have Grushenka, anyway, he shan't! I'll crush him!"

His anger had returned with the last words.

"You can go. There's nothing for you to do here to-day," he snapped harshly.

Alyosha went up to say good-bye to him, and kissed him on the shoulder.

"What's that for?" The old man was a little surprised. "We shall see each other again, or do you think we shan't?"

"Not at all, I didn't mean anything."

"Nor did I, I did not mean anything," said the old man, looking at him. "Listen, listen," he shouted after him, "make haste and come again and I'll have a fish soup for you, a fine one, not like to-day. Be sure to come! Come to-morrow, do you hear, to-morrow!"

And as soon as Alyosha had gone out of the door, he went to the cupboard again and poured out another half-glass.

"I won't have more!" he muttered, clearing his throat, and again he locked the cupboard and put the key in his pocket. Then he went into his bedroom, lay down on the bed, exhausted, and in one minute he was asleep.

Chapter 3. A Meeting with the Schoolboys

"Thank goodness he did not ask me about Grushenka," thought Alyosha, as he left his father's house and turned towards Madame Hohlakov's, "or I might have had to tell him of my meeting with Grushenka yesterday."

Alyosha felt painfully that since yesterday both combatants had renewed their energies, and that their hearts had grown hard again. "Father is spiteful and angry, he's made some plan and will stick to it. And what of Dmitri? He too will be harder than yesterday, he too must be spiteful and angry, and he too, no doubt, has made some plan. Oh, I must succeed in finding him to-day, whatever happens."

But Alyosha had not long to meditate. An incident occurred on the road, which, though apparently of little consequence, made a great impression on him. Just after he had crossed the square and turned the corner coming out into Mihailovsky Street, which is divided by a small ditch from the High Street (our whole town is intersected by ditches), he saw a group of schoolboys between the ages of nine and twelve, at the bridge. They were going home from school, some with their bags on their shoulders, others with leather satchels slung across them, some in short jackets, others in little overcoats. Some even had those high boots with creases round the ankles, such as little boys spoilt by rich fathers love to wear. The whole group was talking eagerly about something, apparently holding a council. Alyosha had never from his Moscow days been able to pass children without taking notice of them, and although he was particularly fond of children of three or thereabout, he liked schoolboys of ten and eleven too. And so, anxious as he was to-day, he wanted at once to turn aside to talk to them. He looked into their excited rosy faces, and noticed at once that all the boys had stones in their hands. Behind the ditch some thirty paces away, there was another schoolboy standing by a fence. He too had a satchel at his side. He was about ten years old, pale, delicate-looking and with sparkling black eyes. He kept an attentive and anxious watch on the other six, obviously his schoolfellows with whom he had just come out of school, but with whom he had evidently had a feud.

Alyosha went up and, addressing a fair, curly-headed, rosy boy in a black jacket, observed:

"When I used to wear a satchel like yours, I always used to carry it on my left side, so as to have my right hand free, but you've got yours on your right side. So it will be awkward for you to get at it."

Alyosha had no art or premeditation in beginning with this practical remark. But it is the only way for a grown-up person to get at once into confidential relations with a child, or still more with a group of children. One must begin in a serious, businesslike way so as to be on a perfectly equal footing. Alyosha understood it by instinct.

"But he is left-handed," another, a fine healthy-looking boy of eleven, answered promptly. All the others stared at Alyosha.

"He even throws stones with his left hand," observed a third.

At that instant a stone flew into the group, but only just grazed the left-handed boy, though it was well and vigorously thrown by the boy standing on the other side of the ditch.

"Give it him, hit him back, Smurov," they all shouted. But Smurov, the left-handed boy, needed no telling, and at once revenged himself; he threw a stone, but it missed the boy and hit the ground. The boy on the other side of the ditch, the pocket of whose coat was visibly bulging with stones, flung another stone at the group; this time it flew straight at Alyosha and hit him painfully on the shoulder.

"He aimed it at you, he meant it for you. You are Karamazov, Karamazov!" the boys shouted laughing, "Come, all throw at him at once!" and six stones flew at the boy. One struck the boy on the head and he fell down, but at once leapt up and began ferociously returning their fire. Both sides threw stones incessantly. Many of the group had their pockets full too.

"What are you about! Aren't you ashamed? Six against one! Why, you'll kill him," cried Alyosha.

He ran forward and met the flying stones to screen the solitary boy. Three or four ceased throwing for a minute.

"He began first!" cried a boy in a red shirt in an angry childish voice. "He is a beast, he stabbed Krassotkin in class the other day with a penknife. It bled. Krassotkin wouldn't tell tales, but he must be thrashed."

"But what for? I suppose you tease him."

"There, he sent a stone in your back again, he knows you," cried the children. "It's you he is throwing at now, not us. Come, all of you, at him again, don't miss, Smurov!" and again a fire of stones, and a very vicious one, began. The boy on the other side of the ditch was hit in the chest; he screamed, began to cry and ran away uphill towards Mihailovsky Street. They all shouted: "Aha, he is funking, he is running away. Wisp of tow!"

"You don't know what a beast he is, Karamazov, killing is too good for him," said the boy in the jacket, with flashing eyes. He seemed to be the eldest.

"What's wrong with him?" asked Alyosha, "Is he a tell-tale or what?"

The boys looked at one another as though derisively.

"Are you going that way, to Mihailovsky?" the same boy went on. "Catch him up...You see he's stopped again, he is waiting and looking at you."

"He is looking at you," the other boys chimed in.

"You ask him, does he like a dishevelled wisp of tow. Do you hear, ask him that!"

There was a general burst of laughter. Alyosha looked at them, and they at him.

"Don't go near him, he'll hurt you," cried Smurov in a warning voice.

"I shan't ask him about the wisp of tow, for I expect you tease him with that question somehow. But I'll find out from him why you hate him so."

"Find out then, find out," cried the boys laughing.

Alyosha crossed the bridge and walked uphill by the fence, straight towards the boy.

"You'd better look out," the boys called after him; "he won't be afraid of you. He will stab you in a minute, on the sly, as he did Krassotkin."

The boy waited for him without budging. Coming up to him, Alyosha saw facing him a child of about nine years old. He was an undersized weakly boy with a thin pale face, with large dark eyes that gazed at him vindictively. He was dressed in a rather shabby old overcoat, which he had monstrously outgrown. His bare arms stuck out beyond his sleeves. There was a large patch on the right knee of his trousers, and in his right boot just at the toe there was a big hole in the leather, carefully blackened with ink. Both the pockets of his greatcoat were weighed down with stones. Alyosha stopped two steps in front of him, looking inquiringly at him, The boy, seeing at once from Alyosha's eyes that he wouldn't beat him, became less defiant, and addressed him first.

"I am alone, and there are six of them. I'll beat them all, alone!" he said suddenly, with flashing eyes.

"I think one of the stones must have hurt you badly," observed Alyosha.

"But I hit Smurov on the head!" cried the boy.

"They told me that you know me, and that you threw a stone at me on purpose," said Alyosha.

The boy looked darkly at him.

"I don't know you. Do you know me?" Alyosha continued.

"Let me alone!" the boy cried irritably; but he did not move, as though he were expecting something, and again there was a vindictive light in his eyes.

"Very well, I am going," said Alyosha; "only I don't know you and I don't tease you. They told me how they tease you, but I don't want to tease you. Good-bye!"

"Monk in silk trousers!" cried the boy, following Alyosha with the same vindictive and defiant expression, and he threw himself into an attitude of defence, feeling sure that now Alyosha would fall upon him; but Alyosha turned, looked at him, and walked away. He had not gone three steps before the biggest stone the boy had in his pocket hit him a painful blow in the back.

"So you'll hit a man from behind! They tell the truth, then, when they say that you attack on the sly," said Alyosha, turning round again. This time the boy threw a stone savagely right into Alyosha's face; but Alyosha just had time to guard himself, and the stone struck him on the elbow.

"Aren't you ashamed? What have I done to you?" he cried.

The boy waited in silent defiance, certain that now Alyosha would attack him. Seeing that even now he would not, his rage was like a little wild beast's; he flew at Alyosha himself, and before Alyosha had time to move, the spiteful child had seized his left hand with both of his and bit his middle finger. He fixed his teeth in it and it was ten seconds before he let go. Alyosha cried out with pain and pulled his finger away with all his might. The child let go at last and retreated to his former distance. Alyosha's finger had been badly bitten to the bone, close to the nail; it began to bleed. Alyosha took out his handkerchief and bound it tightly round his injured hand. He was a full minute bandaging it. The boy stood waiting all the time. At last Alyosha raised his gentle eyes and looked at him.

"Very well," he said, "You see how badly you've bitten me. That's enough, isn't it? Now tell me, what have I done to you?"

The boy stared in amazement.

"Though I don't know you and it's the first time I've seen you," Alyosha went on with the same serenity, "yet I must have done something to you--you wouldn't have hurt me like this for nothing. So what have I done? How have I wronged you, tell me?"

Instead of answering, the boy broke into a loud tearful wail and ran away. Alyosha walked slowly after him towards Mihailovsky Street, and for a long time he saw the child running in the distance as fast as ever, not turning his head and no doubt still keeping up his tearful wail. He made up his mind to find him out as soon as he had time, and to solve this mystery. Just now he had not the time.

Chapter 4. At the Hohlakovs'

ALYOSHA soon reached Madame Hohlakov's house, a handsome stone house of two stories, one of the finest in our town. Though Madame Hohlakov spent most of her time in another province where she had an estate, or in Moscow, where she had a house of her own, yet she had a house in our town too, inherited from her forefathers. The estate in our district was the largest of her three estates, yet she had been very little in our province before this time. She ran out to Alyosha in the hall.

"Did you get my letter about the new miracle?" She spoke rapidly and nervously.

"Yes"

"Did you show it to everyone? He restored the son to his mother!"

"He is dying to-day," said Alyosha.

"I have heard, I know, oh, how I long to talk to you, to you or someone, about all this. No, to you, to you! And how sorry I am I can't see him! The whole town is in excitement, they are all suspense. But now--do you know Katerina Ivanovna is here now?"

"Ah, that's lucky," cried Alyosha. "Then I shall see her here. She told me yesterday to be sure to come and see her to-day."

"I know, I know all. I've heard exactly what happened yesterday--and the atrocious behaviour of that-- creature. C'est tragique, and if I'd been in her place I don't know what I should have done. And your brother Dmitri Fyodorovitch, what do you think of him?--my goodness! Alexey Fyodorovitch, I am forgetting, only fancy; your brother is in there with her, not that dreadful brother who was so shocking yesterday, but the other, Ivan Fyodorovitch, he is sitting with her talking; they are having a serious conversation. If you could only imagine what's passing between them now--it's awful, I tell you it's lacerating, it's like some incredible tale of horror. They are ruining their lives for no reason anyone can see. They both recognise it and revel in it. I've been watching for you! I've been thirsting for you! It's too much for me. that's the worst of it. I'll tell you all about it presently, but now I must speak of something else, the most important thing--I had quite forgotten what's most important. Tell me, why has Lise been in hysterics? As soon as she heard you were here, she began to be hysterical!"

"Maman, it's you who are hysterical now, not I," Lise's voice carolled through a tiny crack of the door at the side. Her voice sounded as though she wanted to laugh, but was doing her utmost to control it. Alyosha at once noticed the crack, and no doubt Lise was peeping through it, but that he could not see.

"And no wonder, Lise, no wonder...your caprices will make me hysterical too. But she is so ill, Alexey Fyodorovitch, she has been so ill all night, feverish and moaning! I could hardly wait for the morning and for Herzenstube to come. He says that he can make nothing of it, that we must wait. Herzenstube always comes and says that he can make nothing of it. As soon as you approached the house, she screamed, fell into hysterics, and insisted on being wheeled back into this room here."

"Mamma, I didn't know he had come. It wasn't on his account I wanted to be wheeled into this room."

"That's not true, Lise, Yulia ran to tell you that Alexey Fyodorovitch was coming. She was on the lookout for you."

"My darling mamma, it's not at all clever of you. But if you want to make up for it and say something very clever, dear mamma, you'd better tell our honoured visitor, Alexey Fyodorovitch, that he has shown his want of wit by venturing to us after what happened yesterday and although everyone is laughing at him."

"Lise, you go too far. I declare I shall have to be severe. Who laughs at him? I am so glad he has come, I need him, I can't do without him. Oh, Alexey Fyodorovitch, I am exceedingly unhappy!"

"But what's the matter with you, mamma, darling?"

"Ah, your caprices, Lise, your fidgetiness, your illness, that awful night of fever, that awful everlasting Herzenstube, everlasting, everlasting, that's the worst of it! Everything, in fact, everything...Even that miracle, too! Oh, how it has upset me, how it has shattered me, that miracle, dear Alexey Fyodorovitch! And that tragedy in the drawing-room, it's more than I can bear, I warn you. I can't bear it. A comedy, perhaps, not a tragedy. Tell me, will Father Zossima live till to-morrow, will he? Oh, my God! What is happening to me? Every minute I close my eyes and see that it's all nonsense, all nonsense."

"I should be very grateful," Alyosha interrupted suddenly, "if you could give me a clean rag to bind up my finger with. I have hurt it, and it's very painful."

Alyosha unbound his bitten finger. The handkerchief was soaked with blood. Madame Hohlakov screamed and shut her eyes.

"Good heavens, what a wound, how awful!"

But as soon as Lise saw Alyosha's finger through the crack, she flung the door wide open.

"Come, come here," she cried, imperiously. "No nonsense now! Good heavens, why did you stand there saying nothing about it all this time? He might have bled to death, mamma! How did you do it? Water, water! You must wash it first of all, simply hold it in cold water to stop the pain, and keep it there, keep it there...Make haste, mamma, some water in a slop-basin. But do make haste," she finished nervously. She was quite frightened at the sight of Alyosha's wound.

"Shouldn't we send for Herzenstube?" cried Madame Hohlakov.

"Mamma, you'll be the death of me. Your Herzenstube will come and say that he can make nothing of it! Water, water! Mamma, for goodness' sake go yourself and hurry Yulia, she is such a slowcoach and never can come quickly! Make haste, mamma, or I shall die."

"Why, it's nothing much," cried Alyosha, frightened at this alarm.

Yulia ran in with water and Alyosha put his finger in it.

"Some lint, mamma, for mercy's sake, bring some lint and that muddy caustic lotion for wounds, what's it called? We've got some. You know where the bottle is, mamma; it's in your bedroom in the right-hand cupboard, there's a big bottle of it there with the lint."

"I'll bring everything in a minute, Lise, only don't scream and don't fuss. You see how bravely Alexey Fyodorovitch bears it. Where did you get such a dreadful wound, Alexey Fyodorovitch?"

Madame Hohlakov hastened away. This was all Lise was waiting for.

"First of all, answer the question, where did you get hurt like this?" she asked Alyosha, quickly. "And then I'll talk to you about something quite different. Well?"

Instinctively feeling that the time of her mother's absence was precious for her, Alyosha hastened to tell her of his enigmatic meeting with the school boys in the fewest words possible. Lise clasped her hands at his story.

"How can you, and in that dress too, associate with schoolboys?" she cried angrily, as though she had a right to control him. "You are nothing but a boy yourself if you can do that, a perfect boy! But you must find out for me about that horrid boy and tell me all about it, for there's some mystery in it. Now for the second thing, but first a question: does the pain prevent you talking about utterly unimportant things, but talking sensibly?"

"Of course not, and I don't feel much pain now."

"That's because your finger is in the water. It must be changed directly, for it will get warm in a minute. Yulia, bring some ice from the cellar and another basin of water. Now she is gone, I can speak; will you give me the letter I sent you yesterday, dear Alexey Fyodorovitch--be quick, for mamma will be back in a minute and I don't want--"

"I haven't got the letter."

"That's not true, you have. I knew you would say that. You've got it in that pocket. I've been regretting that joke all night. Give me back the letter at once, give it me."

"I've left it at home."

"But you can't consider me as a child, a little girl, after that silly joke! I beg your pardon for that silliness, but you must bring me the letter, if you really haven't got it--bring to-day, you must, you must."

"To-day I can't possibly, for I am going back to the monastery and I shan't come and see you for the next two days--three or four perhaps--for Father Zossima--"

"Four days, what nonsense! Listen. Did you laugh at me very much?"

"I didn't laugh at all."

"Why not?"

"Because I believed all you said."

"You are insulting me!"

"Not at all. As soon as I read it, I thought that all that would come to pass, for as soon as Father Zossima dies, I am to leave the monastery. Then I shall go back and finish my studies, and when you reach the legal age we will be married. I shall love you. Though I haven't had time to think about it, I believe I couldn't find a better wife than you, and Father Zossima tells me I must marry."

"But I am a cripple, wheeled about in a chair," laughed Lise, flushing crimson.

"I'll wheel you about myself, but I'm sure you'll get well by then."

"But you are mad," said Lise, nervously, "to make all this nonsense out of a joke! Here's mamma, very a propos, perhaps. Mamma, how slow you always are, how can you be so long! And here's Yulia with the ice!"

"Oh, Lise, don't scream, above all things don't scream. That scream drives me...How can I help it when you put the lint in another place? I've been hunting and hunting--I do believe you did it on purpose."

"But I couldn't tell that he would come with a bad finger, or else perhaps I might have done it on purpose. My darling mamma, you begin to say really witty things."

"Never mind my being witty, but I must say you show nice feeling for Alexey Fyodorovitch's sufferings! Oh, my dear Alexey Fyodorovitch, what's killing me is no one thing in particular, not Herzenstube, but everything together, that's what is too much for me."

"That's enough, mamma, enough about Herzenstube," Lise laughed gaily. "Make haste with the lint and the lotion, mamma. That's simply Goulard's water, Alexey Fyodorovitch, I remember the name now, but it's a splendid lotion. Would you believe it, Mamma, on the way here he had a fight with the boys in the street, and it was a boy bit his finger, isn't he a child, a child himself? Is he fit to be married after that? For only fancy, he wants to be married, mamma. Just think of him married, wouldn't it be funny, wouldn't it be awful?"

And Lise kept laughing her thin hysterical giggle, looking slyly at Alyosha.

"But why married, Lise? What makes you talk of such a thing? It's quite out of place and perhaps the boy was rabid."

"Why, mamma! As though there were rabid boys!"

"Why not, Lise, as though I had said something stupid! Your boy might have been bitten by a mad dog and he would become mad and bite anyone near him. How well she has bandaged it, Alexey Fyodorovitch! I couldn't have done it. Do you still feel the pain?"

"It's nothing much now."

"You don't feel afraid of water?" asked Lise.

"Come, that's enough, Lise, perhaps I really was rather too quick talking of the boy being rabid, and you pounced upon it at once. Katerina Ivanovna has only just heard that you are here, Alexey Fyodorovitch, she simply rushed at me, she's dying to see you, dying!"

"Ach, mamma, go to them yourself. He can't go just now, he is in too much pain."

"Not at all, I can go quite well," said Alyosha.

"What! You are going away? Is that what you say?"

"Well, when I've seen them, I'll come back here and we can talk as much as you like. But I should like to see Katerina Ivanovna at once, for I am very anxious to be back at the monastery as soon as I can."

"Mamma, take him away quickly. Alexey Fyodorovitch, don't trouble to come and see me afterwards, but go straight back to your monastery and a good riddance. I want to sleep, I didn't sleep all night."

"Ah, Lise, you are only making fun, but how I wish you would sleep!" cried Madame Hohlakov.

"I don't know what I've done...I'll stay another three minutes, five if you like," muttered Alyosha.

"Even five! Do take him away quickly, mamma, he is a monster."

"Lise, you are crazy. Let us go, Alexey Fyodorovitch, she is too capricious to-day. I am afraid to cross her. Oh, the trouble one has with nervous girls! Perhaps she really will be able to sleep after seeing you. How quickly you have made her sleepy, and how fortunate it is!"

"Ah, mamma, how sweetly you talk! I must kiss you for it, mamma."

"And I kiss you too, Lise. Listen, Alexey Fyodorovitch," Madame Hohlakov began mysteriously and importantly, speaking in a rapid whisper. "I don't want to suggest anything, I don't want to lift the veil, you will see for yourself what's going on. It's appalling. It's the most fantastic farce. She loves your brother, Ivan, and she is doing her utmost to persuade herself she loves your brother, Dmitri. It's appalling! I'll go in with you, and if they don't turn me out, I'll stay to the end."

Chapter 5. A Laceration in the Drawing-Room

BUT in the drawing-room the conversation was already over. Katerina Ivanovna was greatly excited, though she looked resolute. At the moment Alyosha and Madame Hohlakov entered, Ivan Fyodorovitch stood up to take leave. His face was rather pale, and Alyosha looked at him anxiously. For this moment was to solve a doubt, a harassing enigma which had for some time haunted Alyosha. During the preceding month it had been several times suggested to him that his brother Ivan was in love with Katerina Ivanovna, and, what was more, that he meant "to carry her off from Dmitri. Until quite lately the idea seemed to Alyosha monstrous, though it worried him extremely. He loved both his brothers, and dreaded such rivalry between them. Meantime, Dmitri had said outright on the previous day that he was glad that Ivan was his rival, and that it was a great assistance to him, Dmitri. In what way did it assist him? To marry Grushenka? But that Alyosha considered the worst thing possible. Besides all this, Alyosha had till the evening before implicitly believed that Katerina Ivanovna had a steadfast and passionate love for Dmitri; but he had only believed it till the evening before. He had fancied, too, that she was incapable of loving a man like Ivan, and that she did love Dmitri, and loved him just as he was, in spite of all the strangeness of such a passion.

But during yesterday's scene with Grushenka another idea had struck him. The word "lacerating," which Madame Hohlakov had just uttered, almost made him start, because half waking up towards daybreak that night he had cried out "Laceration, laceration," probably applying it to his dream. He had been dreaming all night of the previous day's scene at Katerina Ivanovna's. Now Alyosha was impressed by Madame Hohlakov's blunt and persistent assertion that Katerina Ivanovna was in love with Ivan, and only deceived herself through some sort of pose, from "self-laceration," and tortured herself by her pretended love for Dmitri from some fancied duty of gratitude. "Yes," he thought, "perhaps the whole truth lies in those words." But in that case what was Ivan's position? Alyosha felt instinctively that a character like Katerina Ivanovna's must dominate, and she could only dominate someone like Dmitri, and never a man like Ivan. For Dmitri might--at last submit to her domination "to his own happiness" (which was what Alyosha would have desired), but Ivan--no, Ivan could not submit to her, and such submission would not give him happiness. Alyosha could not help believing that of Ivan. And now all these doubts and reflections flitted through his mind as he entered the drawing-room. Another idea, too, forced itself upon him: "What if she loved neither of them--neither Ivan nor Dmitri?"

It must be noted that Alyosha felt as it were ashamed of his own thoughts and blamed himself when they kept recurring to him during the last month. "What do I know about love and women and how can I decide such questions?" he thought reproachfully, after such doubts and surmises. And yet it was impossible not to think about it. He felt instinctively that this rivalry was of immense importance in his brothers' lives and that a great deal depended upon it.

"One reptile will devour the other," Ivan had pronounced the day before, speaking in anger of his father and Dmitri. So Ivan looked upon Dmitri as a reptile, and perhaps long done so. Was it perhaps since he had known Katerina Ivanovna? That phrase had, of course, escaped Ivan unawares yesterday, but that only made it more important. If he felt like that, what chance was there of peace? Were there not, on the contrary, new grounds for hatred and hostility in their family? And with which of them was Alyosha to sympathise? And what was he to wish for each of them? He loved them both, but what could he desire for each in the midst of these conflicting interests? He might go quite astray in this maze, and Alyosha's heart could not endure uncertainty, because his love was always of an active character. He was incapable of passive love. If he loved anyone, he set to work at once to help him. And to do so he must know what he was aiming at; he must know for certain what was best for each, and having ascertained this it was natural for him to help them both. But instead of a definite aim, he found nothing but uncertainty and perplexity on all sides. "It was lacerating," as was said just now. But what could he understand even in this "laceration"? He did not understand the first word in this perplexing maze.

Seeing Alyosha, Katerina Ivanovna said quickly and joyfully to Ivan, who had already got up to go, "A minute! Stay another minute! I want to hear the opinion of this person here whom I trust absolutely. Don't go away," she added, addressing Madame Hohlakov. She made Alyosha sit down beside her, and Madame Hohlakov sat opposite, by Ivan.

"You are all my friends here, all I have in the world, dear friends," she warmly, in a voice which quivered with genuine tears of suffering, and Alyosha's heart warmed to her at once. "You, Alexey Fyodorovitch, were witness yesterday of that abominable scene, and saw what I did. You did not see it, Ivan Fyodorovitch, he did. What he thought of me yesterday I don't know. I only know one thing, that if it were repeated to-day, this minute, I should express the same feelings again as yesterday--the same feelings, the same words, the same actions. You remember my actions, Alexey Fyodorovitch; you checked me in one of them"...(as she said that, she flushed and her eyes shone). "I must tell you that I can't get over it. Listen, Alexey Fyodorovitch. I don't even know whether I still love him. I feel pity for him, and that is a poor sign of love. If I loved him, if I still loved him, perhaps I shouldn't be sorry for him now, but should hate him"

Her voice quivered and tears glittered on her eyelashes. Alyosha shuddered inwardly. "That girl is truthful and sincere," he thought, "and she does not love Dmitri any more."

"That's true, that's true," cried Madame Hohlakov.

"Wait, dear. I haven't told you the chief, the final decision I came to during the night. I feel that perhaps my decision is a terrible one--for me, but I foresee that nothing will induce me to change it--nothing. It will be so all my life. My dear, kind, ever-faithful and generous adviser, the one friend I have in the world, Ivan Fyodorovitch, with his deep insight into the heart, approves and commends my decision. He knows it."

"Yes, I approve of it," Ivan assented, in a subdued but firm voice.

"But I should like Alyosha, too (Ah! Alexey Fyodorovitch, forgive my calling you simply Alyosha), I should like Alexey Fyodorovitch, too, to tell me before my two friends whether I am right. I feel instinctively that you, Alyosha, my dear brother (for are a dear brother to me)," she said again ecstatically, taking his cold hand in her hot one, "I foresee that your decision, your approval, will bring me peace, in spite of all my sufferings, for, after your words, I shall be calm and submit--I feel that."

"I don't know what you are asking me," said Alyosha, flushing. "I only know that I love you and at this moment wish for your happiness more than my own!...But I know nothing about such affairs," something impelled him to add hurriedly.

"In such affairs, Alexey Fyodorovitch, in such affairs, the chief thing is honour and duty and something higher--I don't know what but higher perhaps even than duty. I am conscious of this irresistible feeling in my heart, and it compels me irresistibly. But it may all be put in two words. I've already decided, even if he marries that--creature," she began solemnly, "whom I never, never can forgive, even then I will not abandon him. Henceforward I will never, never abandon him!" she cried, breaking into a sort of pale, hysterical ecstasy. "Not that I would run after him continually, get in his way and worry him. Oh, no! I will go away to another town--where you like--but I will watch over him all my life--I will watch over him all my life unceasingly. When he becomes unhappy with that woman, and that is bound to happen quite soon, let him come to me and he will find a friend, a sister...Only a sister, of course, and so for ever; but he will learn at least that that sister is really his sister, who loves him and has sacrificed all her life to him. I will gain my point. I will insist on his knowing me confiding entirely in me, without reserve," she cried, in a sort of frenzy. "I will be a god to whom he can pray--and that, at least, he owes me for his treachery and for what I suffered yesterday through him. And let him see that all my life I will be true to him and the promise I gave him, in spite of his being untrue and betraying me. I will--I will become nothing but a means for his happiness, or--how shall I say?--an instrument, a machine for his happiness, and that for my whole life, my whole life, and that he may see that all his life! That's my decision. Ivan Fyodorovitch fully approves me."

She was breathless. She had perhaps intended to express her idea with more dignity, art and naturalness, but her speech was too hurried and crude. It was full of youthful impulsiveness, it betrayed that she was still smarting from yesterday's insult, and that her pride craved satisfaction. She felt this herself. Her face suddenly darkened, an unpleasant look came into her eyes. Alyosha at once saw it and felt a pang of sympathy. His brother Ivan made it worse by adding:

"I've only expressed my own view," he said. "From anyone else, this would have been affected and over-strained, but from you--no. Any other woman would have been wrong, but you are right. I don't know how to explain it, but I see that you are absolutely genuine and, therefore, you are right."

"But that's only for the moment. And what does this moment stand for? Nothing but yesterday's insult." Madame Hohlakov obviously had not intended to interfere, but she could not refrain from this very just comment.

"Quite so, quite so," cried Ivan, with peculiar eagerness, obviously annoyed at being interrupted, "in anyone else this moment would be only due to yesterday's impression and would be only a moment. But with Katerina Ivanovna's character, that moment will last all her life. What for anyone else would be only a promise is for her an everlasting burdensome, grim perhaps, but unflagging duty. And she will be sustained by the feeling of this duty being fulfilled. Your life, Katerina Ivanovna, will henceforth be spent in painful brooding over your own feelings, your own heroism, and your own suffering; but in the end that suffering will be softened and will pass into sweet contemplation of the fulfilment of a bold and proud design. Yes, proud it certainly is, and desperate in any case, but a triumph for you. And the consciousness of it will at last be a source of complete satisfaction and will make you resigned to everything else."

This was unmistakably said with some malice and obviously with intention; even perhaps with no desire to conceal that he spoke ironically and with intention.

"Oh, dear, how mistaken it all is!" Madame Hohlakov cried again.

"Alexey Fyodorovitch, you speak. I want dreadfully to know what you will say!" cried Katerina Ivanovna, and burst into tears. Alyosha got up from the sofa.

"It's nothing, nothing!" she went on through her tears. "I'm upset, I didn't sleep last night. But by the side of two such friends as you and your brother I still feel strong--for I know you two will never desert me."

"Unluckily I am obliged to return to Moscow--perhaps to-morrow--and to leave you for a long time--and, unluckily, it's unavoidable," Ivan said suddenly.

"To-morrow--to Moscow!" her face was suddenly contorted; "but- but, dear me, how fortunate!" she cried in a voice suddenly changed. In one instant there was no trace left of her tears. She underwent an instantaneous transformation, which amazed Alyosha. Instead of a poor, insulted girl, weeping in a sort of "laceration," he saw a woman completely self-possessed and even exceedingly pleased, as though something agreeable had just happened.

"Oh, not fortunate that I am losing you, of course not," she collected herself suddenly, with a charming society smile. "Such a friend as you are could not suppose that. I am only too unhappy at losing you." She rushed impulsively at Ivan, and seizing both his hands, pressed them warmly. "But what is fortunate is that you will be able in Moscow to see auntie and Agafya and to tell them all the horror of my present position. You can speak with complete openness to Agafya, but spare dear auntie. You will know how to do that. You can't think how wretched I was yesterday and this morning, wondering how I could write them that dreadful letter--for one can never tell such things in a letter...Now it will be easy for me to write, for you will see them and explain everything. Oh, how glad I am! But I am only glad of that, believe me. Of course, no one can take your place...I will run at once to write the letter," she finished suddenly, and took a step as though to go out of the room.

"And what about Alyosha and his opinion, which you were so desperately anxious to hear?" cried Madame Hohlakov. There was a sarcastic, angry note in her voice.

"I had not forgotten that," cried Katerina Ivanovna, coming to a sudden standstill, "and why are you so antagonistic at such a moment?" she added, with warm and bitter reproachfulness. "What I said, I repeat. I must have his opinion. More than that, I must have his decision! As he says, so it shall be. You see how anxious I am for your words, Alexey Fyodorovitch...But what's the matter?"

"I couldn't have believed it. I can't understand it!" Alyosha cried suddenly in distress.

"He is going to Moscow, and you cry out that you are glad. You said that on purpose! And you begin explaining that you are not glad of that but sorry to be--losing a friend. But that was acting, too--you were playing a part as in a theatre!"

"In a theatre? What? What do you mean?" exclaimed Katerina Ivanovna, profoundly astonished, flushing crimson, and frowning.

"Though you assure him you are sorry to lose a friend in him, you persist in telling him to his face that it's fortunate he is going," said Alyosha breathlessly. He was standing at the table and did not sit down.

"What are you talking about? I don't understand."

"I don't understand myself...I seemed to see in a flash...I know I am not saying it properly, but I'll say it all the same," Alyosha went on in the same shaking and broken voice. "What I see is that perhaps you don't love Dmitri at all...and never have, from the beginning...And Dmitri, too, has never loved you...and only esteems you...I really don't know how I dare to say all this, but somebody must tell the truth...for nobody here will tell the truth."

"What truth?" cried Katerina Ivanovna, and there was an hysterical ring in her voice.

"I'll tell you," Alyosha went on with desperate haste, as though he were jumping from the top of a house. "Call Dmitri; I will fetch him and let him come here and take your hand and take Ivan's and join your hands. For you're torturing Ivan, simply because you love him--and torturing him, because you love Dmitri through 'self-laceration'-with an unreal love--because you've persuaded yourself."

Alyosha broke off and was silent.

"You...you...you are a little religious idiot--that's what you are!" Katerina Ivanovna snapped. Her face was white and her lips were moving with anger.

Ivan suddenly laughed and got up. His hat was in his hand.

"You are mistaken, my good Alyosha," he said, with an expression Alyosha had never seen in his face before--an expression of youthful sincerity and strong, irresistibly frank feeling. "Katerina Ivanovna has never cared for me! She has known all the time that I cared for her--though I never said a word of my love to her--she knew, but she didn't care for me. I have never been her friend either, not for one moment; she is too proud to need my friendship. She kept me at her side as a means of revenge. She revenged with me and on me all the insults which she has been continually receiving from Dmitri ever since their first meeting. For even that first meeting has rankled in her heart as an insult--that's what her heart is like! She has talked to me of nothing but her love for him. I am going now; but, believe me, Katerina Ivanovna, you really love him. And the more he insults you, the more you love him--that's your 'laceration.' You love him just as he is; you love him for insulting you. If he reformed, you'd give him up at once and cease to love him. But you need him so as to contemplate continually your heroic fidelity and to reproach him for infidelity. And it all comes from your pride. Oh, there's a great deal of humiliation and self-abasement about it, but it all comes from pride...I am too young and I've loved you too much. I know that I ought not to say this, that it would be more dignified on my part simply to leave you, and it would be less offensive for you. But I am going far away, and shall never come back...It is for ever. I don't want to sit beside a 'laceration.'...But I don't know how to speak now. I've said everything...Good-bye, Katerina Ivanovna; you can't be angry with me, for I am a hundred times more severely punished than you, if only by the fact that I shall never see you again. Good-bye! I don't want your hand. You have tortured me too deliberately for me to be able to forgive you at this moment. I shall forgive you later, but now I don't want your hand. Den Dank, Dame, begehr ich nicht,"* he added, with a forced smile, showing, however, that he could read Schiller, and read him till he knew him by heart--which Alyosha would never have believed. He went out of the room without saying good-bye even to his hostess, Madame Hohlakov. Alyosha clasped his hands.

* Thank you, madam, I want nothing.

"Ivan!" he cried desperately after him. "Come back, Ivan! No, nothing will induce him to come back now!" he cried again, regretfully realising it; "but it's my fault, my fault. I began it! Ivan spoke angrily, wrongly. Unjustly and angrily. He must come back here, come back," Alyosha kept exclaiming frantically.

Katerina Ivanovna went suddenly into the next room.

"You have done no harm. You behaved beautifully, like an angel," Madame Hohlakov whispered rapidly and ecstatically to Alyosha. "I will do my utmost to prevent Ivan Fyodorovitch from going."

Her face beamed with delight, to the great distress of Alyosha, but Katerina Ivanovna suddenly returned. She had two hundred-rouble notes in her hand.

"I have a great favour to ask of you, Alexey Fyodorovitch," she began, addressing Alyosha with an apparently calm and even voice, as though nothing had happened. "A week--yes, I think it was a week ago--Dmitri Fyodorovitch was guilty of a hasty and unjust action--a very ugly action. There is a low tavern here, and in it he met that discharged officer, that captain, whom your father used to employ in some business. Dmitri Fyodorovitch somehow lost his temper with this captain, seized him by the beard and dragged him out into the street and for some distance along it, in that insulting fashion. And I am told that his son, a boy, quite a child, who is at the school here, saw it and ran beside them crying and begging for his father, appealing to everyone to defend him, while everyone laughed. You must forgive me, Alexey Fyodorovitch, I cannot think without indignation of that disgraceful action of his...one of those actions of which only Dmitri Fyodorovitch would be capable in his anger...and in his passions! I can't describe it even...I can't find my words. I've made inquiries about his victim, and find he is quite a poor man. His name is Snegiryov. He did something wrong in the army and was discharged. I can't tell you what. And now he has sunk into terrible destitution, with his family--an unhappy family of sick children, and, I believe, an insane wife. He has been living here a long time; he used to work as a copying clerk, but now he is getting nothing. I thought if you...that is I thought...I don't know. I am so confused. You see, I wanted to ask you, my dear Alexey Fyodorovitch, to go to him, to find some excuse to go to them--I mean to that captain--oh, goodness, how badly I explain it!--and delicately, carefully, as only you know how to" (Alyosha blushed), "manage to give him this assistance, these two hundred roubles. He will be sure to take it...I mean, persuade him to take it...Or, rather, what do I mean? You see it's not by way of compensation to prevent him from taking proceedings (for I believe he meant to), but simply a token of sympathy, of a desire to assist him from me, Dmitri Fyodorovitch's betrothed, not from himself...But you know...I would go myself, but you'll know how to do it ever so much better. He lives in Lake Street in the house of a woman called Kalmikov...For God's sake, Alexey Fyodorovitch, do it for me, and now...now I am rather...tired...Good-bye!"

She turned and disappeared behind the portiere so quickly that Alyosha had not time to utter a word, though he wanted to speak. He longed to beg her pardon, to blame himself, to say something, for his heart was full and he could not bear to go out of the room without it. But Madame Hohlakov took him by the hand and drew him along with her. In the hall she stopped him again as before.

"She is proud, she is struggling with herself; but kind, charming, generous," she exclaimed, in a half-whisper. "Oh, how I love her, especially sometimes, and how glad I am again of everything! Dear Alexey Fyodorovitch, you didn't know, but I must tell you, that we all, all--both her aunts, I and all of us, Lise, even--have been hoping and praying for nothing for the last month but that she may give up your favourite Dmitri, who takes no notice of her and does not care for her, and may marry Ivan Fyodorovitch--such an excellent and cultivated young man, who loves her more than anything in the world. We are in a regular plot to bring it about, and I am even staying on here perhaps on that account."

"But she has been crying--she has been wounded again," cried Alyosha.

"Never trust a woman's tears, Alexey Fyodorovitch. I am never for the women in such cases. I am always on the side of the men."

"Mamma, you are spoiling him," Lise's little voice cried from behind the door.

"No, it was all my fault. I am horribly to blame," Alyosha repeated unconsoled, hiding his face in his hands in an agony of remorse for his indiscretion.

"Quite the contrary; you behaved like an angel, like an angel. I am ready to say so a thousand times over."

"Mamma, how has he behaved like an angel?" Lise's voice was heard again.

"I somehow fancied all at once," Alyosha went on as though he had not heard Lise, "that she loved Ivan, and so I said that stupid thing...What will happen now?"

"To whom, to whom?" cried Lise. "Mamma, you really want to be the death of me. I ask you and you don't answer."

At the moment the maid ran in.

"Katerina Ivanovna is ill...She is crying, struggling... hysterics."

"What is the matter?" cried Lise, in a tone of real anxiety. "Mamma, I shall be having hysterics, and not she!"

"Lise, for mercy's sake, don't scream, don't persecute me. At your age one can't know everything that grown-up people know. I'll come and tell you everything you ought to know. Oh, mercy on us! I am coming, I am coming...Hysterics is a good sign, Alexey Fyodorovitch; it's an excellent thing that she is hysterical. That's just as it ought to be. In such cases I am always against the woman, against all these feminine tears and hysterics. Run and say, Yulia, that I'll fly to her. As for Ivan Fyodorovitch's going away like that, it's her own fault. But he won't go away. Lise, for mercy's sake, don't scream! Oh, yes; you are not screaming. It's I am screaming. Forgive your mamma; but I am delighted, delighted, delighted! Did you notice, Alexey Fyodorovitch, how young, how young Ivan Fyodorovitch was just now when he went out, when he said all that and went out? I thought he was so learned, such a savant, and all of a sudden he behaved so warmly, openly, and youthfully, with such youthful inexperience, and it was all so fine, like you...And the way he repeated that German verse, it was just like you! But I must fly, I must fly! Alexey Fyodorovitch, make haste to carry out her commission, and then make haste back. Lise, do you want anything now? For mercy's sake, don't keep Alexey Fyodorovitch a minute. He will come back to you at once."

Madame Hohlakov at last ran off. Before leaving, Alyosha would have opened the door to see Lise.

"On no account," cried Lise. "On no account now. Speak through the door. How have you come to be an angel? That's the only thing I want to know."

"For an awful piece of stupidity, Lise! Goodbye!"

"Don't dare to go away like that!" Lise was beginning.

"Lise, I have a real sorrow! I'll be back directly, but I have a great, great sorrow!"

And he ran out of the room.

Chapter 6. A Laceration in the Cottage

HE certainly was really grieved in a way he had seldom been before. He had rushed in like a fool, and meddled in what? In a love-affair. "But what do I know about it? What can I tell about such things?" he repeated to himself for the hundredth time, flushing crimson. "Oh, being ashamed would be nothing; shame is only the punishment I deserve. The trouble is I shall certainly have caused more unhappiness...And Father Zossima sent me to reconcile and bring them together. Is this the way to bring them together?" Then he suddenly remembered how he had tried to join their hands, and he felt fearfully ashamed again. "Though I acted quite sincerely, I must be more sensible in the future," he concluded suddenly, and did not even smile at his conclusion.

Katerina Ivanovna's commission took him to Lake Street, and his brother Dmitri lived close by, in a turning out of Lake Street. Alyosha decided to go to him in any case before going to the captain, though he had a presentiment that he would not find his brother. He suspected that he would intentionally keep out of his way now, but he must find him anyhow. Time was passing: the thought of his dying elder had not left Alyosha for one minute from the time he set off from the monastery.

There was one point which interested him particularly about Katerina Ivanovna's commission; when she had mentioned the captain's son, the little schoolboy who had run beside his father crying, the idea had at once struck Alyosha that this must be the schoolboy who had bitten his finger when he, Alyosha, asked him what he had done to hurt him. Now Alyosha felt practically certain of this, though he could not have said why. Thinking of another subject was a relief, and he resolved to think no more about the "mischief" he had done, and not to torture himself with remorse, but to do what he had to do, let come what would. At that thought he was completely comforted. Turning to the street where Dmitri lodged, he felt hungry, and taking out of his pocket the roll he had brought from his father's, he ate it. It made him feel stronger.

Dmitri was not at home. The people of the house, an old cabinet-maker, his son, and his old wife, looked with positive suspicion at Alyosha. "He hasn't slept here for the last three nights. Maybe he has gone away," the old man said in answer to Alyosha's persistent inquiries. Alyosha saw that he was answering in accordance with instructions. When he asked whether he were not at Grushenka's or in hiding at Foma's (Alyosha spoke so freely on purpose), all three looked at him in alarm. "They are fond of him, they are doing their best for him," thought Alyosha. "That's good."

At last he found the house in Lake Street. It was a decrepit little house, sunk on one side, with three windows looking into the street, and with a muddy yard, in the middle of which stood a solitary cow. He crossed the yard and found the door opening into the passage. On the left of the passage lived the old woman of the house with her old daughter. Both seemed to be deaf. In answer to his repeated inquiry for the captain, one of them at last understood that he was asking for their lodgers, and pointed to a door across the passage. The captain's lodging turned out to be a simple cottage room. Alyosha had his hand on the iron latch to open the door, when he was struck by the strange hush within. Yet he knew from Katerina Ivanovna's words that the man had a family. "Either they are all asleep or perhaps they have heard me coming and are waiting for me to open the door. I'd better knock first," and he knocked. An answer came, but not at once, after an interval of perhaps ten seconds.

"Who's there?" shouted someone in a loud and very angry voice.

Then Alyosha opened the door and crossed the threshold. He found himself in a regular peasant's room. Though it was large, it was cumbered up with domestic belongings of all sorts, and there were several people in it. On the left was a large Russian stove. From the stove to the window on the left was a string running across the room, and on it there were rags hanging. There was a bedstead against the wall on each side, right and left, covered with knitted quilts. On the one on the left was a pyramid of four print-covered pillows, each smaller than the one beneath. On the other there was only one very small pillow. The opposite corner was screened off by a curtain or a sheet hung on a string. Behind this curtain could be seen a bed made up on a bench and a chair. The rough square table of plain wood had been moved into the middle window. The three windows, which consisted each of four tiny greenish mildewy panes, gave little light, and were close shut, so that the room was not very light and rather stuffy. On the table was a frying pan with the remains of some fried eggs, a half-eaten piece of bread, and a small bottle with a few drops of vodka.

A woman of genteel appearance, wearing a cotton gown, was sitting on a chair by the bed on the left. Her face was thin and yellow, and her sunken cheeks betrayed at the first glance that she was ill. But what struck Alyosha most was the expression in the poor woman's eyes--a look of surprised inquiry and yet of haughty pride. And while he was talking to her husband, her big brown eyes moved from one speaker to the other with the same haughty and questioning expression. Beside her at the window stood a young girl, rather plain, with scanty reddish hair, poorly but very neatly dressed. She looked disdainfully at Alyosha as he came in. Beside the other bed was sitting another female figure. She was a very sad sight, a young girl of about twenty, but hunchback and crippled "with withered legs," as Alyosha was told afterwards. Her crutches stood in the corner close by. The strikingly beautiful and gentle eyes of this poor girl looked with mild serenity at Alyosha. A man of forty-five was sitting at the table, finishing the fried eggs. He was spare, small, and weakly built. He had reddish hair and a scanty light-coloured beard, very much like a wisp of tow (this comparison and the phrase "a wisp of tow" flashed at once into Alyosha's mind for some reason, he remembered it afterwards). It was obviously this gentleman who had shouted to him, as there was no other man in the room. But when Alyosha went in, he leapt up from the bench on which he was sitting, and, hastily wiping his mouth with a ragged napkin, darted up to Alyosha.

"It's a monk come to beg for the monastery. A nice place to come to!" the girl standing in the left corner said aloud. The man spun round instantly towards her and answered her in an excited and breaking voice:

"No, Varvara, you are wrong. Allow me to ask," he turned again to Alyosha, "what has brought you to our retreat?"

Alyosha looked attentively at him. It was the first time he had seen him. There was something angular, flurried and irritable about him. Though he had obviously just been drinking, he was not drunk. There was extraordinary impudence in his expression, and yet, strange to say, at the same time there was fear. He looked like a man who had long been kept in subjection and had submitted to it, and now had suddenly turned and was trying to assert himself. Or, better still, like a man who wants dreadfully to hit you but is horribly afraid you will hit him. In his words and in the intonation of his shrill voice there was a sort of crazy humour, at times spiteful and at times cringing, and continually shifting from one tone to another. The question about "our retreat" he had asked, as it were, quivering all over, rolling his eyes, and skipping up so close to Alyosha that he instinctively drew back a step. He was dressed in a very shabby dark cotton coat, patched and spotted. He wore checked trousers of an extremely light colour, long out of fashion, and of very thin material. They were so crumpled and so short that he looked as though he had grown out of them like a boy.

"I am Alexey Karamazov," Alyosha began in reply.

"I quite understand that, sir," the gentleman snapped out at once to assure him that he knew who he was already. "I am Captain Snegiryov, sir, but I am still desirous to know precisely what has led you--"

"Oh, I've come for nothing special. I wanted to have a word with you--if only you allow me."

"In that case, here is a chair, sir; kindly be seated. That's what they used to say in the old comedies, 'kindly be seated,'" and with a rapid gesture he seized an empty chair (it was a rough wooden chair, not upholstered) and set it for him almost in the middle of the room; then, taking another similar chair for himself, he sat down facing Alyosha, so close to him that their knees almost touched.

"Nikolay Ilyitch Snegiryov, sir, formerly a captain in the Russian infantry, put to shame for his vices, but still a captain. Though I might not be one now for the way I talk; for the last half of my life I've learnt to say 'sir.' It's a word you use when you've come down in the world."

"That's very true," smiled Alyosha. "But is it used involuntarily or on purpose?"

"As God's above, it's involuntary, and I usen't to use it! I didn't use the word 'sir' all my life, but as soon as I sank into low water I began to say 'sir.' It's the work of a higher power. I see you are interested in contemporary questions, but how can I have excited your curiosity, living as I do in surroundings impossible for the exercise of hospitality?"

"I've come--about that business."

"About what business?" the captain interrupted impatiently.

"About your meeting with my brother Dmitri Fyodorovitch," Alyosha blurted out awkwardly.

"What meeting, sir? You don't mean that meeting? About my 'wisp of tow,' then?" He moved closer so that his knees positively knocked against Alyosha. His lips were strangely compressed like a thread.

"What wisp of tow?" muttered Alyosha.

"He is come to complain of me, father!" cried a voice familiar to Alyosha--the voice of the schoolboy--from behind the curtain. "I bit his finger just now." The curtain was pulled, and Alyosha saw his assailant lying on a little bed made up on the bench and the chair in the corner under the ikons. The boy lay covered by his coat and an old wadded quilt. He was evidently unwell, and, judging by his glittering eyes, he was in a fever. He looked at Alyosha without fear, as though he felt he was at home and could not be touched.

"What! Did he bite your finger?" The captain jumped up from his chair. "Was it your finger he bit?"

"Yes. He was throwing stones with other schoolboys. There were six of them against him alone. I went up to him, and he threw a stone at me and then another at my head. I asked him what I had done to him. And then he rushed at me and bit my finger badly, I don't know why."

"I'll thrash him, sir, at once--this minute!" The captain jumped up from his seat.

"But I am not complaining at all, I am simply telling you...I don't want him to be thrashed. Besides, he seems to be ill."

"And do you suppose I'd thrash him? That I'd take my Ilusha and thrash him before you for your satisfaction? Would you like it done at once, sir?" said the captain, suddenly turning to Alyosha, as though he were going to attack him. "I am sorry about your finger, sir; but instead of thrashing Ilusha, would you like me to chop off my four fingers with this knife here before your eyes to satisfy your just wrath? I should think four fingers would be enough to satisfy your thirst for vengeance. You won't ask for the fifth one too?" He stopped short with a catch in his throat. Every feature in his face was twitching and working; he looked extremely defiant. He was in a sort of frenzy.

"I think I understand it all now," said Alyosha gently and sorrowfully, still keeping his seat. "So your boy is a good boy, he loves his father, and he attacked me as the brother of your assailant...Now I understand it," he repeated thoughtfully. "But my brother Dmitri Fyodorovitch regrets his action, I know that, and if only it is possible for him to come to you, or better still, to meet you in that same place, he will ask your forgiveness before everyone--if you wish it."

"After pulling out my beard, you mean, he will ask my forgiveness? And he thinks that will be a satisfactory finish, doesn't he?"

"Oh, no! On the contrary, he will do anything you like and in any way you like."

"So if I were to ask his highness to go down on his knees before me in that very tavern--'The Metropolis' it's called--or in the marketplace, he would do it?"

"Yes, he would even go down on his knees."

"You've pierced me to the heart, sir. Touched me to tears and pierced me to the heart! I am only too sensible of your brother's generosity. Allow me to introduce my family, my two daughters and my son--my litter. If I die, who will care for them, and while I live who but they will care for a wretch like me? That's a great thing the Lord has ordained for every man of my sort, sir. For there must be someone able to love even a man like me."

"Ah, that's perfectly true!" exclaimed Alyosha.

"Oh, do leave off playing the fool! Some idiot comes in, and you put us to shame!" cried the girl by the window, suddenly turning to her father with a disdainful and contemptuous air.

"Wait a little, Varvara!" cried her father, speaking peremptorily but looking at them quite approvingly. "That's her character," he said, addressing Alyosha again.

"And in all nature there was naught That could find favour in his eyes--or rather in the feminine- that could find favour in her eyes--. But now let me present you to my wife, Arina Petrovna. She is crippled, she is forty-three; she can move, but very little. She is of humble origin. Arina Petrovna, compose your countenance. This is Alexey Fyodorovitch Karamazov. Get up, Alexey Fyodorovitch." He took him by the hand and with unexpected force pulled him up. "You must stand up to be introduced to a lady. It's not the Karamazov, mamma, who...h'm...etcetera, but his brother, radiant with modest virtues. Come, Arina Petrovna, come, mamma, first your hand to be kissed."

And he kissed his wife's hand respectfully and even tenderly. The girl at the window turned her back indignantly on the scene; an expression of extraordinary cordiality came over the haughtily inquiring face of the woman.

"Good morning! Sit down, Mr. Tchernomazov," she said.

"Karamazov, mamma, Karamazov. We are of humble origin," he whispered again.

"Well, Karamazov, or whatever it is, but I always think of Tchermomazov...Sit down. Why has he pulled you up? He calls me crippled, but I am not, only my legs are swollen like barrels, and I am shrivelled up myself. Once I used to be so fat, but now it's as though I had swallowed a needle."

"We are of humble origin," the captain muttered again.

"Oh, father, father!" the hunchback girl, who had till then been silent on her chair, said suddenly, and she hid her eyes in her handkerchief.

"Buffoon!" blurted out the girl at the window.

"Have you heard our news?" said the mother, pointing at her daughters. "It's like clouds coming over; the clouds pass and we have music again. When we were with the army, we used to have many such guests. I don't mean to make any comparisons; everyone to their taste. The deacon's wife used to come then and say, 'Alexandr Alexandrovitch is a man of the noblest heart, but Nastasya Petrovna,' she would say, 'is of the brood of hell.' 'Well,' I said, 'that's a matter of taste; but you are a little spitfire.' 'And you want keeping in your place;' says she. 'You black sword,' said I, 'who asked you to teach me?' 'But my breath,' says she, 'is clean, and yours is unclean.' 'You ask all the officers whether my breath is unclean.' And ever since then I had it in my mind. Not long ago I was sitting here as I am now, when I saw that very general come in who came here for Easter, and I asked him: 'Your Excellency,' said I, 'can a lady's breath be unpleasant?' 'Yes,' he answered; 'you ought to open a window-pane or open the door, for the air is not fresh here.' And they all go on like that! And what is my breath to them? The dead smell worse still! 'I won't spoil the air,' said I, 'I'll order some slippers and go away.' My darlings, don't blame your own mother! Nikolay Ilyitch, how is it I can't please you? There's only Ilusha who comes home from school and loves me. Yesterday he brought me an apple. Forgive your own mother--forgive a poor lonely creature! Why has my breath become unpleasant to you?"

And the poor mad woman broke into sobs, and tears streamed down her cheeks. The captain rushed up to her.

"Mamma, mamma, my dear, give over! You are not lonely. Everyone loves you, everyone adores you." He began kissing both her hands again and tenderly stroking her face; taking the dinner-napkin, he began wiping away her tears. Alyosha fancied that he too had tears in his eyes. "There, you see, you hear?" he turned with a sort of fury to Alyosha, pointing to the poor imbecile.

"I see and hear," muttered Alyosha.

"Father, father, how can you--with him! Let him alone!" cried the boy, sitting up in his bed and gazing at his father with glowing eyes.

"Do give over fooling, showing off your silly antics which never lead to anything! shouted Varvara, stamping her foot with passion.

"Your anger is quite just this time, Varvara, and I'll make haste to satisfy you. Come, put on your cap, Alexey Fyodorovitch, and I'll put on mine. We will go out. I have a word to say to you in earnest, but not within these walls. This girl sitting here is my daughter Nina; I forgot to introduce her to you. She is a heavenly angel incarnate...who has flown down to us mortals...if you can understand."

"There he is shaking all over, as though he is in convulsions!" Varvara went on indignantly.

"And she there stamping her foot at me and calling me a fool just now, she is a heavenly angel incarnate too, and she has good reason to call me so. Come along, Alexey Fyodorovitch, we must make an end."

And, snatching Alyosha's hand, he drew him out of the room into the street.

Chapter 7. And in the Open Air

"THE air is fresh, but in my apartment it is not so in any sense of the word. Let us walk slowly, sir. I should be glad of your kind interest."

"I too have something important to say to you," observed Alyosha, "only I don't know how to begin."

"To be sure you must have business with me. You would never have looked in upon me without some object. Unless you come simply to complain of the boy, and that's hardly likely. And, by the way, about the boy: I could not explain to you in there, but here I will describe that scene to you. My tow was thicker a week ago--I mean my beard. That's the nickname they give to my beard, the schoolboys most of all. Well, your brother Dmitri Fyodorovitch was pulling me by my beard, I'd done nothing, he was in a towering rage and happened to come upon me. He dragged me out of the tavern into the market place; at that moment the boys were coming out of school, and with them Ilusha. As soon as he saw me in such a state he rushed up to me. 'Father,' he cried, 'father!' He caught hold of me, hugged me, tried to pull me away, crying to my assailant, 'Let go, let go, it's my father, forgive him!'--yes, he actually cried 'forgive him.' He clutched at that hand, that very hand, in his little hands and kissed it...I remember his little face at that moment, I haven't forgotten it and I never shall!"

"I swear," cried Alyosha, "that my brother will express his most deep and sincere regret, even if he has to go down on his knees in that same market-place...I'll make him or he is no brother of mine!

"Aha, then it's only a suggestion! And it does not come from him but simply from the generosity of your own warm heart. You should have said so. No, in that case allow me to tell you of your brother's highly chivalrous soldierly generosity, for he did give expression to it at the time. He left off dragging me by my beard and released me: 'You are an officer,' he said, 'and I am an officer, if you can find a decent man to be your second send me your challenge. I will give satisfaction, though you are a scoundrel.' That's what he said. A chivalrous spirit indeed! I retired with Ilusha, and that scene is a family record imprinted forever on Ilusha's soul. No, it's not for us to claim the privileges of noblemen. Judge for yourself. You've just been in our mansion, what did you see there? Three ladies, one a cripple and weak-minded, another a cripple and hunchback and the third not crippled but far too clever. She is a student, dying to get back to Petersburg, to work for the emancipation of the Russian woman on the banks of the Neva. I won't speak of Ilusha, he is only nine. I am alone in the world, and if I die, what will become of all of them? I simply ask you that. And if I challenge him and he kills me on the spot, what then? What will become of them? And worse still, if he doesn't kill me but only cripples me: I couldn't work, but I should still be a mouth to feed. Who would feed it and who would feed them all? Must I take Ilusha from school and send him to beg in the streets? That's what it means for me to challenge him to a duel. It's silly talk and nothing else."

"He will beg your forgiveness, he will bow down at your feet in the middle of the marketplace," cried Alyosha again, with glowing eyes.

"I did think of prosecuting him," the captain went on, "but look in our code, could I get much compensation for a personal injury? And then Agrafena Alexandrovna* sent for me and shouted at me: 'Don't dare to dream of it! If you proceed against him, I'll publish it to all the world that he beat you for your dishonesty, and then you will be prosecuted.' I call God to witness whose was the dishonesty and by whose commands I acted, wasn't it by her own and Fyodor Pavlovitch's? And what's more,' she went on, 'I'll dismiss you for good and you'll never earn another penny from me. I'll speak to my merchant too' (that's what she calls her old man) 'and he will dismiss you!' And if he dismisses me, what can I earn then from anyone? Those two are all I have to look to, for your Fyodor Pavlovitch has not only given over employing me, for another reason, but he means to make use of papers I've signed to go to law against me. And so I kept quiet, and you have seen our retreat. But now let me ask you: did Ilusha hurt your finger much? I didn't like to go into it in our mansion before him."

* Grushenka.

"Yes, very much, and he was in a great fury. He was avenging you on me as a Karamazov, I see that now. But if only you had seen how he was throwing stones at his schoolfellows! It's very dangerous. They might kill him. They are children and stupid. A stone may be thrown and break somebody's head."

"That's just what has happened. He has been bruised by a stone to-day. Not on the head but on the chest, just above the heart. He came home crying and groaning and now he is ill."

"And you know he attacks them first. He is bitter against them on your account. They say he stabbed a boy called Krassotkin with a penknife not long ago."

"I've heard about that too, it's dangerous. Krassotkin is an official here, we may hear more about it."

"I would advise you," Alyosha went on warmly, "not to send him to school at all for a time till he is calmer and his anger is passed."

"Anger!" the captain repeated, "that's just what it is. He is a little creature, but it's a mighty anger. You don't know all, sir. Let me tell you more. Since that incident all the boys have been teasing him about the 'wisp of tow.' Schoolboys are a merciless race, individually they are angels, but together, especially in schools, they are often merciless. Their teasing has stiffed up a gallant spirit in Ilusha. An ordinary boy, a weak son, would have submitted, have felt ashamed of his father, sir, but he stood up for his father against them all. For his father and for truth and justice. For what he suffered when he kissed your brother's hand and cried to him 'Forgive father, forgive him,'--that only God knows--and I, his father. For our children--not your children, but ours--the children of the poor gentlemen looked down upon by everyone--know what justice means, sir, even at nine years old. How should the rich know? They don't explore such depths once in their lives. But at that moment in the square when he kissed his hand, at that moment my Ilusha had grasped all that justice means. That truth entered into him and crushed him for ever, sir," the captain said hotly again with a sort of frenzy, and he struck his right fist against his left palm as though he wanted to show how "the truth" crushed Ilusha. "That very day, sir, he fell ill with fever and was delirious all night. All that day he hardly said a word to me, but I noticed he kept watching me from the corner, though he turned to the window and pretended to be learning his lessons. But I could see his mind was not on his lessons. Next day I got drunk to forget my troubles, sinful man as I am, and I don't remember much. Mamma began crying, too--I am very fond of mamma--well, I spent my last penny drowning my troubles. Don't despise me for that, sir, in Russia men who drink are the best. The best men amongst us are the greatest drunkards. I lay down and I don't remember about Ilusha, though all that day the boys had been jeering at him at school. 'Wisp of tow,' they shouted, 'your father was pulled out of the tavern by his wisp of tow, you ran by and begged forgiveness.'

"On the third day when he came back from school, I saw he looked pale and wretched. 'What is it?' I asked. He wouldn't answer. Well, there's no talking in our mansion without mamma and the girls taking part in it. What's more, the girls had heard about it the very first day. Varvara had begun snarling. 'You fools and buffoons, can you ever do anything rational?' 'Quite so,' I said,'can we ever do anything rational?' For the time I turned it off like that. So in the evening I took the boy out for a walk, for you must know we go for a walk every evening, always the same way, along which we are going now--from our gate to that great stone which lies alone in the road under the hurdle, which marks the beginning of the town pasture. A beautiful and lonely spot, sir. Ilusha and I walked along hand in hand as usual. He has a little hand, his fingers are thin and cold--he suffers with his chest, you know. 'Father,' said he, 'father!' 'Well?' said I. I saw his eyes flashing. 'Father, how he treated you then!' 'It can't be helped, Ilusha,' I said. 'Don't forgive him, father, don't forgive him! At school they say that he has paid you ten roubles for it.' 'No Ilusha,' said I, 'I would not take money from him for anything.' he began trembling all over, took my hand in both his and kissed it again. 'Father,' he said, 'father, challenge him to a duel, at school they say you are a coward and won't challenge him, and that you'll accept ten roubles from him.' 'I can't challenge him to a duel, Ilusha,' I answered. And I told briefly what I've just told you. He listened. 'Father,' he said, anyway don't forgive it. When I grow up I'll call him out myself and kill him.' His eyes shone and glowed. And of course I am his father, and I had to put in a word: 'It's a sin to kill,' I said, 'even in a duel.' 'Father,' he said, 'when I grow up, I'll knock him down, knock the sword out of his hand, I'll fall on him, wave my sword over him and say: "I could kill you, but I forgive you, so there!"' You see what the workings of his little mind have been during these two days; he must have been planning that vengeance all day, and raving about it at night.

"But he began to come home from school badly beaten, I found out about it the day before yesterday, and you are right, I won't send him to that school any more. I heard that he was standing up against all the class alone and defying them all, that his heart was full of resentment, of bitterness--I was alarmed about him. We went for another walk. 'Father,' he asked, 'are the rich people stronger than anyone else on earth?' 'Yes, Ilusha,' I said, 'there are no people on earth stronger than the rich.' 'Father,' he said, 'I will get rich, I will become an officer and conquer everybody. The Tsar will reward me, I will come back here and then no one will dare--' Then he was silent and his lips still kept trembling. 'Father,' he said, 'what a horrid town this is.' 'Yes, Ilusha,' I said, 'it isn't a very nice town.' 'Father, let us move into another town, a nice one,' he said, 'where people don't know about us.' 'We will move, we will, Ilusha,' said I, 'only I must save up for it.' I was glad to be able to turn his mind from painful thoughts, and we began to dream of how we would move to another town, how we would buy a horse and cart. 'We will put mamma and your sisters inside, we will cover them up and we'll walk, you shall have a lift now and then, and I'll walk beside, for we must take care of our horse, we can't all ride. That's how we'll go.' He was enchanted at that, most of all at the thought of having a horse and driving him. For of course a Russian boy is born among horses. We chattered a long while. Thank God, I thought, I have diverted his mind and comforted him.

"That was the day before yesterday, in the evening, but last night everything was changed. He had gone to school in the morning, he came back depressed, terribly depressed. In the evening I took him by the hand and we went for a walk; he would not talk. There was a wind blowing and no sun, and a feeling of autumn; twilight was coming on. We walked along, both of us depressed. 'Well, my boy,' said I, 'how about our setting off on our travels?' I thought I might bring him back to our talk of the day before. He didn't answer, but I felt his fingers trembling in my hand. Ah, I thought, it's a bad job; there's something fresh. We had reached the stone where we are now. I sat down on the stone. And in the air there were lots of kites flapping and whirling. There were as many as thirty in sight. Of course, it's just the season for the kites. 'Look, Ilusha,' said I, 'it's time we got out our last year's kite again. I'll mend it; where have you put it away?' My boy made no answer. He looked away and turned sideways to me. And then a gust of wind blew up the sand. He suddenly fell on me, threw both his little arms round my neck and held me tight. You know, when children are silent and proud, and try to keep back their tears when they are in great trouble and suddenly break down, their tears fall in streams. With those warm streams of tears, he suddenly wetted my face. He sobbed and shook as though he were in convulsions, and squeezed up against me as I sat on the stone. 'Father,' he kept crying, 'dear father, how he insulted you!' And I sobbed too. We sat shaking in each other's arms. 'Ilusha,' I said to him, 'Ilusha, darling.' No one saw us then. God alone saw us; I hope He will record it to my credit. You must thank your brother, Alexey Fyodorovitch. No, sir, I won't thrash my boy for your satisfaction."

He had gone back to his original tone of resentful buffoonery. Alyosha felt, though, that he trusted him, and that if there had been someone else in his, Alyosha's place, the man would not have spoken so openly and would not have told what he had just told. This encouraged Alyosha, whose heart was trembling on the verge of tears.

"Ah, how I would like to make friends with your boy!" he cried. "If you could arrange it--"

"Certainly, sir," muttered the captain.

"But now listen to something quite different!" Alyosha went on. "I have a message for you. That same brother of mine, Dmitri, has insulted his betrothed, too, a noble-hearted girl of whom you have probably heard. I have a right to tell you of her wrong; I ought to do so, in fact, for, hearing of the insult done to you and learning all about your unfortunate position, she commissioned me at once--just now--to bring you this help from her--but only from her alone, not from Dmitri, who has abandoned her. Nor from me, his brother, nor from anyone else, but from her, only from her! She entreats you to accept her help...You have both been insulted by the same man. She thought of you only when she had just received a similar insult from him--similar in its cruelty, I mean. She comes like a sister to help a brother in misfortune...She told me to persuade you to take these two hundred roubles from her, as from a sister, knowing that you are in such need. No one will know of it, it can give rise to no unjust slander. There are the two hundred roubles, and I swear you must take them unless--unless all men are to be enemies on earth! But there are brothers even on earth...You have a generous heart...you must see that, you must," and Alyosha held out two new rainbow-coloured hundred-rouble notes.

They were both standing at the time by the great stone close to the fence, and there was no one near. The notes seemed to produce a tremendous impression on the captain. He started, but at first only from astonishment. Such an outcome of their conversation was the last thing he expected. Nothing could have been farther from his dreams than help from anyone--and such a sum!

He took the notes, and for a minute he was almost unable to answer, quite a new expression came into his face.

"That for me? So much money--two hundred roubles! Good heavens! Why, I haven't seen so much money for the last four years! Mercy on us! And she says she is a sister...And is that the truth?" "I swear that all I told you is the truth,"cried Alyosha.

The captain flushed red.

"Listen, my dear, listen. If I take it, I shan't be behaving like a scoundrel? In your eyes, Alexey Fyodorovitch, I shan't be a scoundrel? No, Alexey Fyodorovitch, listen, listen," he hurried, touching Alyosha with both his hands. "You are persuading me to take it, saying that it's a sister sends it, but inwardly, in your heart won't you feel contempt for me if I take it, eh?"

"No, no, on my salvation I swear I shan't! And no one will ever know but me--I, you and she, and one other lady, her great friend."

"Never mind the lady! Listen, Alexey Fyodorovitch, at a moment like this you must listen, for you can't understand what these two hundred roubles mean to me now." The poor fellow went on rising gradually into a sort of incoherent, almost wild enthusiasm. He was thrown off his balance and talked extremely fast, as though afraid he would not be allowed to say all he had to say.

"Besides its being honestly acquired from a 'sister,' so highly respected and revered, do you know that now I can look after mamma and Nina, my hunchback angel daughter? Doctor Herzenstube came to me in the kindness of his heart and was examining them both for a whole hour. 'I can make nothing of it,' said he, but he prescribed a mineral water which is kept at a chemist's here. He said it would be sure to do her good, and he ordered baths, too, with some medicine in them. The mineral water costs thirty copecks, and she'd need to drink forty bottles perhaps: so I took the prescription and laid it on the shelf under the ikons, and there it lies. And he ordered hot baths for Nina with something dissolved in them, morning and evening. But how can we carry out such a cure in our mansion, without servants, without help, without a bath, and without water? Nina is rheumatic all over, I don't think I told you that. All her right side aches at night, she is in agony, and, would you believe it, the angel bears it without groaning for fear of waking us. We eat what we can get, and she'll only take the leavings, what you'd scarcely give to a dog. 'I am not worth it, I am taking it from you, I am a burden on you,' that's what her angel eyes try to express. We wait on her, but she doesn't like it. 'I am a useless cripple, no good to anyone.' As though she were not worth it, when she is the saving of all of us with her angelic sweetness. Without her, without her gentle word it would be hell among us! She softens even Varvara. And don't judge Varvara harshly either, she is an angel too, she, too, has suffered wrong. She came to us for the summer, and she brought sixteen roubles she had earned by lessons and saved up, to go back with to Petersburg in September, that is now. But we took her money and lived on it, so now she has nothing to go back with. Though indeed she couldn't go back, for she has to work for us like a slave. She is like an overdriven horse with all of us on her back. She waits on us all, mends and washes, sweeps the floor, puts mamma to bed. And mamma is capricious and tearful and insane! And now I can get a servant with this money, you understand, Alexey Fyodorovitch, I can get medicines for the dear creatures, I can send my student to Petersburg, I can buy beef, I can feed them properly. Good Lord, but it's a dream!"

Alyosha was delighted that he had brought him such happiness and that the poor fellow had consented to be made happy.

"Stay, Alexey Fyodorovitch, stay," the captain began to talk with frenzied rapidity, carried away by a new day-dream. "Do you know that Ilusha and I will perhaps really carry out our dream. We will buy a horse and cart, a black horse, he insists on its being black, and we will set off as we pretended the other day. I have an old friend, a lawyer in K. province, and I heard through a trustworthy man that if I were to go he'd give me a place as clerk in his office, so, who knows, maybe he would. So I'd just put mamma and Nina in the cart, and Ilusha could drive, and I'd walk, I'd walk...Why, if I only succeed in getting one debt paid that's owing me, I should have perhaps enough for that too!"

"There would be enough!" cried Alyosha. "Katerina Ivanovna will send you as much more as you need, and you know, I have money too, take what you want, as you would from a brother, from a friend, you can give it back later...(You'll get rich. you'll get rich!) And you know you couldn't have a better idea than to move to another province! It would be the saving of you, especially of your boy and you ought to go quickly, before the winter, before the cold. You must write to us when you are there, and we will always be brothers...No, it's not a dream!"

Alyosha could have hugged him, he was so pleased. But glancing at him he stopped short. The man was standing with his neck outstretched and his lips protruding, with a pale and frenzied face. His lips were moving as though trying to articulate something; no sound came, but still his lips moved. It was uncanny.

"What is it?" asked Alyosha, startled.

"Alexey Fyodorovitch...I...you," muttered the captain, faltering, looking at him with a strange, wild, fixed stare, and an air of desperate resolution. At the same time there was a sort of grin on his lips. "I...you, sir...wouldn't you like me to show you a little trick I know?" he murmured, suddenly, in a firm rapid whisper, his voice no longer faltering.

"What trick?"

"A pretty trick," whispered the captain. His mouth was twisted on the left side, his left eye was screwed up. He still stared at Alyosha.

"What is the matter? What trick?" Alyosha cried, now thoroughly alarmed.

"Why, look," squealed the captain suddenly, and showing him the two notes which he had been holding by one corner between his thumb and forefinger during the conversation, he crumpled them up savagely and squeezed them tight in his right hand. "Do you see, do you see?" he shrieked, pale and infuriated. And suddenly flinging up his hand, he threw the crumpled notes on the sand. "Do you see?" he shrieked again, pointing to them. "Look there!"

And with wild fury he began trampling them under his heel, gasping and exclaiming as he did so:

"So much for your money! So much for your money! So much for your money! So much for your money!"

Suddenly he darted back and drew himself up before Alyosha, and his whole figure expressed unutterable pride.

"Tell those who sent you that the wisp of tow does not sell his honour," he cried, raising his arm in the air. Then he turned quickly and began to run; but he had not run five steps before he turned completely round and kissed his hand to Alyosha. He ran another five paces and then turned round for the last time. This time his face was not contorted with laughter, but quivering all over with tears. In a tearful, faltering, sobbing voice he cried:

"What should I say to my boy if I took money from you for our shame?"

And then he ran on without turning. Alyosha looked after him, inexpressibly grieved. Oh, he saw that till the very last moment the man had not known he would crumple up and fling away the notes. He did not turn back. Alyosha knew he would not. He would not follow him and call him back, he knew why. When he was out of sight, Alyosha picked up the two notes. They were very much crushed and crumpled, and had been pressed into the sand, but were uninjured and even rustled like new ones when Alyosha unfolded them and smoothed them out. After smoothing them out, he folded them up, put them in his pocket and went to Katerina Ivanovna to report on the success of her commission.

Book V. Pro and Contra

Chapter 1. The Engagement

Madame Hohlakov was again the first to meet Alyosha. She was flustered; something important had happened. Katerina Ivanovna's hysterics had ended in a fainting fit, and then "a terrible, awful weakness had followed, she lay with her eyes turned up and was delirious. Now she was in a fever. They had sent for Herzenstube; they had sent for the aunts. The aunts were already here, but Herzenstube had not yet come. They were all sitting in her room, waiting. She was unconscious now, and what if it turned to brain fever!"

Madame Hohlakov looked gravely alarmed. "This is serious, serious," she added at every word, as though nothing that had happened to her before had been serious. Alyosha listened with distress, and was beginning to describe his adventures, but she interrupted him at the first words. She had not time to listen. She begged him to sit with Lise and wait for her there.

"Lise," she whispered almost in his ear, "Lise has greatly surprised me just now, dear Alexey Fyodorovitch. She touched me, too, and so my heart forgives her everything. Only fancy, as soon as you had gone, she began to be truly remorseful for having laughed at you to-day and yesterday, though she was not laughing at you, but only joking. But she was seriously sorry for it, almost ready to cry, so that I was quite surprised. She has never been really sorry for laughing at me, but has only made a joke of it. And you know she is laughing at me every minute. But this time she was in earnest She thinks a great deal of your opinion, Alexey Fyodorovitch, and don't take offence or be wounded by her if you can help it. I am never hard upon her, for she's such a clever little thing. Would you believe it? She said just now that you were a friend of her childhood, 'the greatest friend of her childhood'--just think of that--'greatest friend'--and what about me? She has very strong feelings and memories, and, what's more, she uses these phrases, most unexpected words, which come out all of a sudden when you least expect them. She spoke lately about a pine-tree, for instance: there used to be a pine-tree standing in our garden in her early childhood. Very likely it's standing there still; so there's no need to speak in the past tense. Pine-trees are not like people, Alexey Fyodorovitch, they don't change quickly. 'Mamma,' she said, 'I remember this pine tree as in a dream,' only she said something so original about it that I can't repeat it. Besides, I've forgotten it. Well, good-bye! I am so worried I feel I shall go out of my mind. Ah! Alexey Fyodorovitch, I've been out of my mind twice in my life. Go to Lise, cheer her up, as you always can so charmingly. Lise," she cried, going to her door, "here I've brought you Alexey Fyodorovitch, whom you insulted so. He is not at all angry, I assure you; on the contrary, he is surprised that you could suppose so."

"Merci, maman. Come in, Alexey Fyodorovitch."

Alyosha went in. Lise looked rather embarrassed, and at once flushed crimson. She was evidently ashamed of something, and, as people always do in such cases, she began immediately talking of other things, as though they were of absorbing interest to her at the moment.

"Mamma has just told me all about the two hundred roubles, Alexey Fyodorovitch, and your taking them to that poor officer...and she told me all the awful story of how he had been insulted...and you know, although mamma muddles things...she always rushes from one thing to another...I cried when I heard. Well, did you give him the money and how is that poor man getting on?"

"The fact is I didn't give it to him, and it's a long story," answered Alyosha, as though he, too, could think of nothing but his regret at having failed, yet Lise saw perfectly well that he, too, looked away, and that he, too, was trying to talk of other things.

Alyosha sat down to the table and began to tell his story, but at the first words he lost his embarrassment and gained the whole of Lise's attention as well. He spoke with deep feeling, under the influence of the strong impression he had just received, and he succeeded in telling his story well and circumstantially. In old days in Moscow he had been fond of coming to Lise and describing to her what had just happened to him, what he had read, or what he remembered of his childhood. Sometimes they had made day-dreams and woven whole romances together--generally cheerful and amusing ones. Now they both felt suddenly transported to the old days in Moscow, two years before. Lise was extremely touched by his story. Alyosha described Ilusha with warm feeling. When he finished describing how the luckless man trampled on the money, Lise could not help clasping her hands and crying out:

"So you didn't give him the money! So you let him run away! Oh, dear, you ought to have run after him!"

"No, Lise; it's better I didn't run after him," said Alyosha, getting up from his chair and walking thoughtfully across the room.

"How so? How is it better? Now they are without food and their case is hopeless."

"Not hopeless, for the two hundred roubles will still come to them. He'll take the money to-morrow. To-morrow he will be sure to take it," said Alyosha, pacing up and down, pondering. "You see, Lise," he went on, stopping suddenly before her, "I made one blunder, but that, even that, is all for the best."

"What blunder, and why is it for the best?"

"I'll tell you. He is a man of weak and timorous character; he has suffered so much and is very good-natured. I keep wondering why he took offence so suddenly, for I assure you, up to the last minute, he did not know that he was going to trample on the notes. And I think now that there was a great deal to offend him...and it could not have been otherwise in his position...To begin with, he was sore at having been so glad of the money in my presence and not having concealed it from me. If he had been pleased, but not so much; if he had not shown it; if he had begun affecting scruples and difficulties, as other people do when they take money, he might still endure--to take it. But he was too genuinely delighted, and that was mortifying. Ah, Lise, he is a good and truthful man--that's the worst of the whole business. All the while he talked, his voice was so weak, so broken, he talked so fast, so fast, he kept laughing such a laugh, or perhaps he was crying--yes, I am sure he was crying, he was so delighted--and he talked about his daughters--and about the situation he could get in another town...And when he had poured out his heart, he felt ashamed at having shown me his inmost soul like that. So he began to hate me at once. He is one of those awfully sensitive poor people. What had made him feel most ashamed was that he had given in too soon and accepted me as a friend, you see. At first he almost flew at me and tried to intimidate me, but as soon as he saw the money he had begun embracing me; he kept touching me with his hands. This must have been how he came to feel it all so humiliating, and then I made that blunder, a very important one. I suddenly said to him that if he had not money enough to move to another town, we would give it to him, and, indeed, I myself would give him as much as he wanted out of my own money. That struck him all at once. Why, he thought, did I put myself forward to help him? You know, Lise, it's awfully hard for a man who has been injured, when other people look at him as though they were his benefactors...I've heard that; Father Zossima told me so. I don't know how to put it, but I have often seen it myself. And I feel like that myself, too. And the worst of it was that though he did not know, to the very last minute, that he would trample on the notes, he had a kind of presentiment of it, I am sure of that. That's just what made him so ecstatic, that he had that presentiment...And though it's so dreadful, it's all for the best. In fact, I believe nothing better could have happened."

"Why, why could nothing better have happened?" cried Lise, looking with great surprise at Alyosha.

"Because if he had taken the money, in an hour after getting home, he would be crying with mortification, that's just what would have happened. And most likely he would have come to me early to-morrow, and perhaps have flung the notes at me and trampled upon them as he did just now. But now he has gone home awfully proud and triumphant, though he knows he has 'ruined himself.' So now nothing could be easier than to make him accept the two hundred roubles by to-morrow, for he has already vindicated his honour, tossed away the money, and trampled it under foot...He couldn't know when he did it that I should bring it to him again to-morrow, and yet he is in terrible need of that money. Though he is proud of himself now, yet even to-day he'll be thinking what a help he has lost. He will think of it more than ever at night, will dream of it, and by to-morrow morning he may be ready to run to me to ask forgiveness. It's just then that I'll appear. 'Here, you are a proud man,' I shall say: 'you have shown it; but now take the money and forgive us!' And then he will take it!

Alyosha was carried away with joy as he uttered his last words, "And then he will take it!" Lise clapped her hands.

"Ah, that's true! I understand that perfectly now. Ah, Alyosha, how do you know all this? So young and yet he knows what's in the heart...I should never have worked it out."

"The great thing now is to persuade him that he is on an equal footing with us, in spite of his taking money from us," Alyosha went on in his excitement, "and not only on an equal, but even on a higher footing."

"'On a higher footing' is charming, Alexey Fyodorovitch; but go on, go on!"

"You mean there isn't such an expression as 'on a higher footing'; but that doesn't matter because--"

"Oh, no, of course it doesn't matter. Forgive me, Alyosha, dear...You know, I scarcely respected you till now--that is I respected you but on an equal footing; but now I shall begin to respect you on a higher footing. Don't be angry, dear, at my joking," she put in at once, with strong feeling. "I am absurd and small, but you, you! Listen, Alexey Fyodorovitch. Isn't there in all our analysis--I mean your analysis...no, better call it ours--aren't we showing contempt for him, for that poor man--in analysing his soul like this, as it were, from above, eh? In deciding so certainly that he will take the money?"

"No, Lise, it's not contempt," Alyosha answered, as though he had prepared himself for the question. "I was thinking of that on the way here. How can it be contempt when we are all like him, when we are all just the same as he is? For you know we are just the same, no better. If we are better, we should have been just the same in his place...I don't know about you, Lise, but I consider that I have a sordid soul in many ways, and his soul is not sordid; on the contrary, full of fine feeling...No, Lise, I have no contempt for him. Do you know, Lise, my elder told me once to care for most people exactly as one would for children, and for some of them as one would for the sick in hospitals."

"Ah, Alexey Fyodorovitch. dear, let us care for people as we would for the sick!"

"Let us, Lise; I am ready. Though I am not altogether ready in myself. I am sometimes very impatient and at other times I don't see things. It's different with you."

"Ah, I don't believe it! Alexey Fyodorovitch, how happy I am!"

"I am so glad you say so, Lise."

"Alexey Fyodorovitch, you are wonderfully good, but you are sometimes sort of formal...And yet you are not a bit formal really. Go to the door, open it gently, and see whether mamma is listening," said Lise, in a nervous, hurried whisper.

Alyosha went, opened the door, and reported that no one was listening.

"Come here, Alexey Fyodorovitch," Lise went on, flushing redder and redder. "Give me your hand--that's right. I have to make a great confession. I didn't write to you yesterday in joke, but in earnest," and she hid her eyes with her hand. It was evident that she was greatly ashamed of the confession.

Suddenly she snatched his hand and impulsively kissed it three times.

"Ah, Lise, what a good thing!" cried Alyosha joyfully. "You know, I was perfectly sure you were in earnest."

"Sure? Upon my word! She put aside his hand, but did not leave go of it, blushing hotly, and laughing a little happy laugh. "I kiss his hand and he says, 'What a good thing!'"

But her reproach was undeserved. Alyosha, too, was greatly overcome.

"I should like to please you always, Lise, but don't know how to do it." he muttered, blushing too.

"Alyosha, dear, you are cold and rude. Do you see? He has chosen me as his wife and is quite settled about it. He is sure I was in earnest. What a thing to say! Why, that's impertinence--that's what it is."

"Why, was it wrong of me to feel sure?" Alyosha asked, laughing suddenly.

"Ah, Alyosha, on the contrary, it was delightfully right," cried Lise, looking tenderly and happily at him.

Alyosha stood still, holding her hand in his. Suddenly he stooped down and kissed her on her lips.

"Oh, what are you doing?" cried Lise. Alyosha was terribly abashed.

"Oh, forgive me if I shouldn't...Perhaps I'm awfully stupid... You said I was cold, so I kissed you...But I see it was stupid."

Lise laughed, and hid her face in her hands. "And in that dress!" she ejaculated in the midst of her mirth. But she suddenly ceased laughing and became serious, almost stern.

"Alyosha, we must put off kissing. We are not ready for that yet, and we shall have a long time to wait," she ended suddenly. "Tell me rather why you who are so clever, so intellectual, so observant, choose a little idiot, an invalid like me? Ah, Alyosha, I am awfully happy, for I don't deserve you a bit."

"You do, Lise. I shall be leaving the monastery altogether in a few days. If I go into the world, I must marry. I know that. He told me to marry, too. Whom could I marry better than you--and who would have me except you? I have been thinking it over. In the first place, you've known me from a child and you've a great many qualities I haven't. You are more light-hearted than I am; above all, you are more innocent than I am. I have been brought into contact with many, many things already...Ah, you don't know, but I, too, am a Karamazov. What does it matter if you do laugh and make jokes, and at me, too? Go on laughing. I am so glad you do. You laugh like a little child, but you think like a martyr."

"Like a martyr? How?"

"Yes, Lise, your question just now: whether we weren't showing contempt for that poor man by dissecting his soul--that was the question of a sufferer...You see, I don't know how to express it, but anyone who thinks of such questions is capable of suffering. Sitting in your invalid chair you must have thought over many things already."

"Alyosha, give me your hand. Why are you taking it away?" murmured Lise in a failing voice, weak with happiness. "Listen, Alyosha. What will you wear when you come out of the monastery? What sort of suit? Don't laugh, don't be angry, it's very, very important to me."

"I haven't thought about the suit, Lise; But I'll wear whatever you like."

"I should like you to have a dark blue velvet coat, a white pique waistcoat, and a soft grey felt hat...Tell me, did you believe that I didn't care for you when I said I didn't mean what I wrote?"

"No, I didn't believe it."

"Oh, you insupportable person, you are incorrigible."

"You see, I knew that you seemed to care for me, but I pretended to believe that you didn't care for me to make it easier for you."

"That makes it worse! Worse and better than all! Alyosha, I am awfully fond of you. Just before you came this morning, I tried my fortune. I decided I would ask you for my letter, and if you brought it out calmly and gave it to me (as might have been expected from you) it would mean that you did not love me at all, that you felt nothing, and were simply a stupid boy, good for nothing, and that I am ruined. But you left the letter at home and that cheered me. You left it behind on purpose, so as not to give it back, because you knew I would ask for it? That was it, wasn't it?"

"Ah, Lise, it was not so a bit. The letter is with me now, and it was this morning, in this pocket. Here it is."

Alyosha pulled the letter out laughing, and showed it her at a distance.

"But I am not going to give it to you. Look at it from here."

"Why, then you told a lie? You, a monk, told a lie!"

"I told a lie if you like," Alyosha laughed, too. "I told a lie so as not to give you back the letter. It's very precious to me," he added suddenly, with strong feeling, and again he flushed. "It always will be, and I won't give it up to anyone!"

Lise looked at him joyfully. "Alyosha," she murmured again, "look at the door. Isn't mamma listening?"

"Very well, Lise, I'll look; but wouldn't it be better not to look? Why suspect your mother of such meanness?"

"What meanness? As for her spying on her daughter, it's her right, it's not meanness!" cried Lise, firing up. "You may be sure, Alexey Fyodorovitch, that when I am a mother, if I have a daughter like myself I shall certainly spy on her!"

"Really, Lise? That's not right."

"Oh, my goodness! What has meanness to do with it? If she were listening to some ordinary worldly conversation, it would be meanness, but when her own daughter is shut up with a young man...Listen, Alyosha, do you know I shall spy upon you as soon as we are married, and let me tell you I shall open all your letters and read them, so you may as well be prepared."

"Yes, of course, if so--" muttered Alyosha, "only it's not right."

"Ah, how contemptuous! Alyosha, dear, we won't quarrel the very first day. I'd better tell you the whole truth. Of course, it's very wrong to spy on people, and, of course, I am not right and you are, only I shall spy on you all the same."

"Do, then; you won't find out anything," laughed Alyosha.

"And Alyosha, will you give in to me? We must decide that too."

"I shall be delighted to, Lise, and certain to, only not in the most important things. Even if you don't agree with me, I shall do my duty in the most important things."

"That's right; but let me tell you I am ready to give in to you not only in the most important matters, but in everything. And I am ready to vow to do so now--in everything, and for all my life!" cried Lise fervently, "and I'll do it gladly, gladly! What's more, I'll swear never to spy on you, never once, never to read one of your letters. For you are right and I am not. And though I shall be awfully tempted to spy, I know that I won't do it since you consider it dishonourable. You are my conscience now...Listen, Alexey Fyodorovitch, why have you been so sad lately--both yesterday and to-day? I know you have a lot of anxiety and trouble, but I see you have some special grief besides, some secret one, perhaps?"

"Yes, Lise, I have a secret one, too," answered Alyosha mournfully. "I see you love me, since you guessed that."

"What grief? What about? Can you tell me?" asked Lise with timid entreaty.

"I'll tell you later, Lise--afterwards," said Alyosha, confused. "Now you wouldn't understand it perhaps--and perhaps I couldn't explain it."

"I know your brothers and your father are worrying you, too."

"Yes, my brothers too," murmured Alyosha, pondering.

"I don't like your brother Ivan, Alyosha," said Lise suddenly.

He noticed this remark with some surprise, but did not answer it.

"My brothers are destroying themselves," he went on, "my father, too. And they are destroying others with them. It's 'the primitive force of the Karamazovs,' as father Paissy said the other day, a crude, unbridled, earthly force. Does the spirit of God move above that force? Even that I don't know. I only know that I, too, am a Karamazov...Me a monk, a monk! Am I a monk, Lise? You said just now that I was."

"Yes, I did."

"And perhaps I don't even believe in God."

"You don't believe? What is the matter?" said Lise quietly and gently. But Alyosha did not answer. There was something too mysterious, too subjective in these last words of his, perhaps obscure to himself, but yet torturing him.

"And now on the top of it all, my friend, the best man in the world is going, is leaving the earth! If you knew, Lise, how bound up in soul I am with him! And then I shall be left alone...I shall come to you, Lise...For the future we will be together."

"Yes, together, together! Henceforward we shall be always together, all our lives! Listen, kiss me, I allow you."

Alyosha kissed her.

"Come, now go. Christ be with you!" and she made the sign of the cross over him. "Make haste back to him while he is alive. I see I've kept you cruelly. I'll pray to-day for him and you. Alyosha, we shall be happy! Shall we be happy, shall we?"

"I believe we shall, Lise."

Alyosha thought it better not to go in to Madame Hohlakov and was going out of the house without saying good-bye to her. But no sooner had he opened the door than he found Madame Hohlakov standing before him. From the first word Alyosha guessed that she had been waiting on purpose to meet him.

"Alexey Fyodorovitch, this is awful. This is all childish nonsense and ridiculous. I trust you won't dream--It's foolishness, nothing but foolishness!" she said, attacking him at once.

"Only don't tell her that," said Alyosha, "or she will be upset, and that's bad for her now."

"Sensible advice from a sensible young man. Am I to understand that you only agreed with her from compassion for her invalid state, because you didn't want to irritate her by contradiction?"

"Oh no, not at all. I was quite serious in what I said," Alyosha declared stoutly.

"To be serious about it is impossible, unthinkable, and in the first place I shall never be at home to you again, and I shall take her away, you may be sure of that."

"But why?" asked Alyosha. "It's all so far off. We may have to wait another year and a half."

"Ah, Alexey Fyodorovitch, that's true, of course, and you'll have time to quarrel and separate a thousand times in a year and a half. But I am so unhappy! Though it's such nonsense, it's a great blow to me. I feel like Famusov in the last scene of Sorrow from Wit. You are Tchatsky and she is Sofya, and, only fancy, I've run down to meet you on the stairs, and in the play the fatal scene takes place on the staircase. I heard it all; I almost dropped. So this is the explanation of her dreadful night and her hysterics of late! It means love to the daughter but death to the mother. I might as well be in my grave at once. And a more serious matter still, what is this letter she has written? Show it me at once, at once!"

"No, there's no need. Tell me, how is Katerina Ivanovna now? I must know."

"She still lies in delirium; she has not regained consciousness. Her aunts are here; but they do nothing but sigh and give themselves airs. Herzenstube came, and he was so alarmed that I didn't know what to do for him. I nearly sent for a doctor to look after him. He was driven home in my carriage. And on the top of it all, you and this letter! It's true nothing can happen for a year and a half. In the name of all that's holy, in the name of your dying elder, show me that letter, Alexey Fyodorovitch. I'm her mother. Hold it in your hand, if you like, and I will read it so."

"No, I won't show it to you. Even if she sanctioned it, I wouldn't. I am coming to-morrow, and if you like, we can talk over many things, but now good-bye!"

And Alyosha ran downstairs and into the street.

Chapter 2. Smerdyakov with a Guitar

HE had no time to lose indeed. Even while he was saying good-bye to Lise, the thought had struck him that he must attempt some stratagem to find his brother Dmitri, who was evidently keeping out of his way. It was getting late, nearly three o'clock. Alyosha's whole soul turned to the monastery, to his dying saint, but the necessity of seeing Dmitri outweighed everything. The conviction that a great inevitable catastrophe was about to happen grew stronger in Alyosha's mind with every hour. What that catastrophe was, and what he would say at that moment to his brother, he could perhaps not have said definitely. "Even if my benefactor must die without me, anyway I won't have to reproach myself all my life with the thought that I might have saved something and did not, but passed by and hastened home. If I do as I intend, I shall be following his great precept."

His plan was to catch his brother Dmitri unawares, to climb over the fence, as he had the day before, get into the garden and sit in the summer-house. If Dmitri were not there, thought Alyosha, he would not announce himself to Foma or the women of the house, but would remain hidden in the summer-house, even if he had to wait there till evening. If, as before, Dmitri were lying in wait for Grushenka to come, he would be very likely to come to the summer-house. Alyosha did not, however, give much thought to the details of his plan, but resolved to act upon it, even if it meant not getting back to the monastery that day.

Everything happened without hindrance, he climbed over the hurdle almost in the same spot as the day before, and stole into the summer-house unseen. He did not want to be noticed. The woman of the house and Foma too, if he were here, might be loyal to his brother and obey his instructions, and so refuse to let Alyosha come into the garden, or might warn Dmitri that he was being sought and inquired for.

There was no one in the summer-house. Alyosha sat down and began to wait. He looked round the summer-house, which somehow struck him as a great deal more ancient than before. Though the day was just as fine as yesterday, it seemed a wretched little place this time. There was a circle on the table, left no doubt from the glass of brandy having been spilt the day before. Foolish and irrelevant ideas strayed about his mind, as they always do in a time of tedious waiting. He wondered, for instance, why he had sat down precisely in the same place as before, why not in the other seat. At last he felt very depressed--depressed by suspense and uncertainty. But he had not sat there more than a quarter of an hour, when he suddenly heard the thrum of a guitar somewhere quite close. People were sitting, or had only just sat down, somewhere in the bushes not more than twenty paces away. Alyosha suddenly recollected that on coming out of the summer-house the day before, he had caught a glimpse of an old green low garden-seat among the bushes on the left, by the fence. The people must be sitting on it now. Who were they?

A man's voice suddenly began singing in a sugary falsetto, accompanying himself on the guitar:

With invincible force
I am bound to my dear.
O Lord, have mercy
On her and on me!
On her and on me!
On her and on me!

The voice ceased. It was a lackey's tenor and a lackey's song. Another voice, a woman's, suddenly asked insinuatingly and bashfully, though with mincing affectation:

"Why haven't you been to see us for so long, Pavel Fyodorovitch? Why do you always look down upon us?"

"Not at all answered a man's voice politely, but with emphatic dignity. It was clear that the man had the best of the position, and that the woman was making advances. "I believe the man must be Smerdyakov," thought Alyosha, "from his voice. And the lady must be the daughter of the house here, who has come from Moscow, the one who wears the dress with a tail and goes to Marfa for soup."

"I am awfully fond of verses of all kinds, if they rhyme," the woman's voice continued. "Why don't you go on?"

The man sang again:

What do I care for royal wealth
If but my dear one be in health?
Lord have mercy
On her and on me!
On her and on me!
On her and on me!

"It was even better last time," observed the woman's voice. "You sang 'If my darling be in health'; it sounded more tender. I suppose you've forgotten to-day."

"Poetry is rubbish!" said Smerdyakov curtly.

"Oh, no! I am very fond of poetry."

"So far as it's poetry, it's essential rubbish. Consider yourself, who ever talks in rhyme? And if we were all to talk in rhyme, even though it were decreed by government, we shouldn't say much, should we? Poetry is no good, Marya Kondratyevna."

"How clever you are! How is it you've gone so deep into everything?" The woman's voice was more and more insinuating.

"I could have done better than that. I could have known more than that, if it had not been for my destiny from my childhood up. I would have shot a man in a duel if he called me names because I am descended from a filthy beggar and have no father. And they used to throw it in my teeth in Moscow. It had reached them from here, thanks to Grigory Vassilyevitch. Grigory Vassilyevitch blames me for rebelling against my birth, but I would have sanctioned their killing me before I was born that I might not have come into the world at all. They used to say in the market, and your mamma too, with great lack of delicacy, set off telling me that her hair was like a mat on her head, and that she was short of five foot by a wee bit. Why talk of a wee bit while she might have said 'a little bit,' like everyone else? She wanted to make it touching, a regular peasant's feeling. Can a Russian peasant be said to feel, in comparison with an educated man? He can't be said to have feeling at all, in his ignorance. From my childhood up when I hear 'a wee bit,' I am ready to burst with rage. I hate all Russia, Marya Kondratyevna."

"If you'd been a cadet in the army, or a young hussar, you wouldn't have talked like that, but would have drawn your sabre to defend all Russia."

"I don't want to be a hussar, Marya Kondratyevna, and, what's more, I should like to abolish all soldiers."

"And when an enemy comes, who is going to defend us?"

"There's no need of defence. In 1812 there was a great invasion of Russia by Napoleon, first Emperor of the French, father of the present one, and it would have been a good thing if they had conquered us. A clever nation would have conquered a very stupid one and annexed it. We should have had quite different institutions."

"Are they so much better in their own country than we are? I wouldn't change a dandy I know of for three young englishmen," observed Marya Kondratyevna tenderly, doubtless accompanying her words with a most languishing glance.

"That's as one prefers."

"But you are just like a foreigner--just like a most gentlemanly foreigner. I tell you that, though it makes me bashful."

"If you care to know, the folks there and ours here are just alike in their vice. They are swindlers, only there the scoundrel wears polished boots and here he grovels in filth and sees no harm in it. The Russian people want thrashing, as Fyodor Pavlovitch said very truly yesterday, though he is mad, and all his children."

"You said yourself you had such a respect for Ivan Fyodorovitch."

"But he said I was a stinking lackey. He thinks that I might be unruly. He is mistaken there. If I had a certain sum in my pocket, I would have left here long ago. Dmitri Fyodorovitch is lower than any lackey in his behaviour, in his mind, and in his poverty. He doesn't know how to do anything, and yet he is respected by everyone. I may be only a soup-maker, but with luck I could open a cafe restaurant in Petrovka, in Moscow, for my cookery is something special, and there's no one in Moscow, except the foreigners, whose cookery is anything special. Dmitri Fyodorovitch is a beggar, but if he were to challenge the son of the first count in the country, he'd fight him. Though in what way is he better than I am? For he is ever so much stupider than I am. Look at the money he has wasted without any need!"

"It must be lovely, a duel," Marya Kondratyevna observed suddenly.

"How so?"

"It must be so dreadful and so brave, especially when young officers with pistols in their hands pop at one another for the sake of some lady. A perfect picture! Ah, if only girls were allowed to look on, I'd give anything to see one!"

"It's all very well when you are firing at someone, but when he is firing straight in your mug, you must feel pretty silly. You'd be glad to run away, Marya Kondratyevna."

"You don't mean you would run away?" But Smerdyakov did not deign to reply. After a moment's silence the guitar tinkled again, and he sang again in the same falsetto:

Whatever you may say,

I shall go far away.

Life will be bright and gay

In the city far away.

I shall not grieve,

I shall not grieve at all,

I don't intend to grieve at all.

Then something unexpected happened. Alyosha suddenly sneezed. They were silent. Alyosha got up and walked towards them. He found Smerdyakov dressed up and wearing polished boots, his hair pomaded, and perhaps curled. The guitar lay on the garden-seat. His companion was the daughter of the house, wearing a light-blue dress with a train two yards long. She was young and would not have been bad-looking, but that her face was so round and terribly freckled.

"Will my brother Dmitri soon be back? asked Alyosha with as much composure as he could.

Smerdyakov got up slowly; Marya Kondratyevna rose too.

"How am I to know about Dmitri Fyodorovitch? It's not as if I were his keeper," answered Smerdyakov quietly, distinctly, and superciliously.

"But I simply asked whether you do know?" Alyosha explained.

"I know nothing of his whereabouts and don't want to."

"But my brother told me that you let him know all that goes on in the house, and promised to let him know when Agrafena Alexandrovna comes."

Smerdyakov turned a deliberate, unmoved glance upon him.

"And how did you get in this time, since the gate was bolted an hour ago?" he asked, looking at Alyosha.

"I came in from the back-alley, over the fence, and went straight to the summer-house. I hope you'll forgive me, he added addressing Marya Kondratyevna. "I was in a hurry to find my brother."

"Ach, as though we could take it amiss in you!" drawled Marya Kondratyevna, flattered by Alyosha's apology. "For Dmitri Fyodorovitch often goes to the summer-house in that way. We don't know he is here and he is sitting in the summer-house."

"I am very anxious to find him, or to learn from you where he is now. Believe me, it's on business of great importance to him."

"He never tells us," lisped Marya Kondratyevna.

"Though I used to come here as a friend," Smerdyakov began again, "Dmitri Fyodorovitch has pestered me in a merciless way even here by his incessant questions about the master. 'What news?' he'll ask. 'What's going on in there now? Who's coming and going?' and can't I tell him something more. Twice already he's threatened me with death

"With death?" Alyosha exclaimed in surprise.

"Do you suppose he'd think much of that, with his temper, which you had a chance of observing yourself yesterday? He says if I let Agrafena Alexandrovna in and she passes the night there, I'll be the first to suffer for it. I am terribly afraid of him, and if I were not even more afraid of doing so, I ought to let the police know. God only knows what he might not do!"

"His honour said to him the other day, 'I'll pound you in a mortar!'" added Marya Kondratyevna.

"Oh, if it's pounding in a mortar, it may be only talk," observed Alyosha. "If I could meet him, I might speak to him about that too."

"Well, the only thing I can tell you is this," said Smerdyakov, as though thinking better of it; "I am here as an old friend and neighbour, and it would be odd if I didn't come. On the other hand, Ivan Fyodorovitch sent me first thing this morning to your brother's lodging in Lake Street, without a letter, but with a message to Dmitri Fyodorovitch to go to dine with him at the restaurant here, in the marketplace. I went, but didn't find Dmitri Fyodorovitch at home, though it was eight o'clock. 'He's been here, but he is quite gone,' those were the very words of his landlady. It's as though there was an understanding between them. Perhaps at this moment he is in the restaurant with Ivan Fyodorovitch, for Ivan Fyodorovitch has not been home to dinner and Fyodor

Pavlovitch dined alone an hour ago, and is gone to lie down. But I beg you most particularly not to speak of me and of what I have told you, for he'd kill me for nothing at all."

"Brother Ivan invited Dmitri to the restaurant to-day?" repeated Alyosha quickly.

"That's so."

"The Metropolis tavern in the marketplace?"

"The very same."

"That's quite likely," cried Alyosha, much excited. "Thank you, Smerdyakov; that's important. I'll go there at once."

"Don't betray me," Smerdyakov called after him.

"Oh, no, I'll go to the tavern as though by chance. Don't be anxious."

"But wait a minute, I'll open the gate to you," cried Marya Kondratyevna.

"No; it's a short cut, I'll get over the fence again."

What he had heard threw Alyosha into great agitation. He ran to the tavern. It was impossible for him to go into the tavern in his monastic dress, but he could inquire at the entrance for his brothers and call them down. But just as he reached the tavern, a window was flung open, and his brother Ivan called down to him from it.

"Alyosha, can't you come up here to me? I shall be awfully grateful."

"To be sure I can, only I don't quite know whether in this dress--"

"But I am in a room apart. Come up the steps; I'll run down to meet you."

A minute later Alyosha was sitting beside his brother. Ivan was alone dining.

Chapter 3. The Brothers Make Friends

IVAN was not, however, in a separate room, but only in a place shut off by a screen, so that it was unseen by other people in the room. It was the first room from the entrance with a buffet along the wall. Waiters were continually darting to and fro in it. The only customer in the room was an old retired military man drinking tea in a corner. But there was the usual bustle going on in the other rooms of the tavern; there were shouts for the waiters, the sound of popping corks, the click of billiard balls, the drone of the organ. Alyosha knew that Ivan did not usually visit this tavern and disliked taverns in general. So he must have come here, he reflected, simply to meet Dmitri by arrangement. Yet Dmitri was not there.

"Shall I order you fish, soup, or anything. You don't live on tea alone, I suppose," cried Ivan, apparently delighted at having got hold of Alyosha. He had finished dinner and was drinking tea.

"Let me have soup, and tea afterwards, I am hungry," said Alyosha gaily.

"And cherry jam? They have it here. You remember how you used to love cherry jam when you were little?"

"You remember that? Let me have jam too, I like it still."

Ivan rang for the waiter and ordered soup, jam, and tea.

"I remember everything, Alyosha, I remember you till you were eleven, I was nearly fifteen. There's such a difference between fifteen and eleven that brothers are never companions at those ages. I don't know whether I was fond of you even. When I went away to Moscow for the first few years I never thought of you at all. Then, when you came to Moscow yourself, we only met once somewhere, I believe. And now I've been here more than three months, and so far we have scarcely said a word to each other. To-morrow I am going away, and I was just thinking as I sat here how I could see you to say good-bye and just then you passed."

"Were you very anxious to see me, then?"

"Very. I want to get to know you once for all, and I want you to know me. And then to say good-bye. I believe it's always best to get to know people just before leaving them. I've noticed how you've been looking at me these three months. There has been a continual look of expectation in your eyes, and I can't endure that. That's how it is I've kept away from you. But in the end I have learned to respect you. The little man stands firm, I thought. Though I am laughing, I am serious. You do stand firm, don't you? I like people who are firm like that whatever it is they stand by, even if they are such little fellows as you. Your expectant eyes ceased to annoy me, I grew fond of them in the end, those expectant eyes. You seem to love me for some reason, Alyosha?"

"I do love you, Ivan. Dmitri says of you--Ivan is a tomb! I say of you, Ivan is a riddle. You are a riddle to me even now. But I understand something in you, and I did not understand it till this morning."

"What's that?" laughed Ivan.

"You won't be angry?" Alyosha laughed too.

"Well?"

"That you are just as young as other young men of three and twenty, that you are just a young and fresh and nice boy, green in fact! Now, have I insulted you dreadfully?"

"On the contrary, I am struck by a coincidence," cried Ivan, warmly and good-humouredly. "Would you believe it that ever since that scene with her, I have thought of nothing else but my youthful greenness, and just as though you guessed that, you begin about it. Do you know I've been sitting here thinking to myself: that if I didn't believe in life, if I lost faith in the woman I love, lost faith in the order of things, were convinced, in fact, that everything is a disorderly, damnable, and perhaps devil-ridden chaos, if I were struck by every horror of man's disillusionment--still I should want to live and, having once tasted of the cup, I would not turn away from it till I had drained it! At thirty, though, I shall be sure to leave the cup, even if I've not emptied it, and turn away--where I don't know. But till I am thirty, I know that my youth will triumph over everything--every disillusionment, every disgust with life. I've asked myself many times whether there is in the world any despair that would overcome this frantic and perhaps unseemly thirst for life in me, and I've come to the conclusion that there isn't, that is till I am thirty, and then I shall lose it of myself, I fancy. Some drivelling consumptive moralists--and poets especially--often call that thirst for life base. It's a feature of the Karamazovs, it's true, that thirst for life regardless of everything; you have it no doubt too, but why is it base? The centripetal force on our planet is still fearfully strong, Alyosha. I have a longing for life, and I go on living in spite of logic. Though I may not believe in the order of the universe, yet I love the sticky little leaves as they open in spring. I love the blue sky, I love some people, whom one loves you know sometimes without knowing why. I love some great deeds done by men, though I've long ceased perhaps to have faith in them, yet from old habit one's heart prizes them. Here they have brought the soup for you, eat it, it will do you good. It's first-rate soup, they know how to make it here. I want to travel in Europe, Alyosha, I shall set off from here. And yet I know that I am only going to a graveyard, but it's a most precious graveyard, that's what it is! Precious are the dead that lie there, every stone over them speaks of such burning life in the past, of such passionate faith in their work, their truth, their struggle and their science, that I know I shall fall on the ground and kiss those stones and weep over them; though I'm convinced in my heart that it's long been nothing but a graveyard. And I shall not weep from despair, but simply because I shall be happy in my tears, I shall steep my soul in emotion. I love the sticky leaves in spring, the blue sky--that's all it is. It's not a matter of intellect or logic, it's loving with one's inside, with one's stomach. One loves the first strength of one's youth. Do you understand anything of my tirade, Alyosha?" Ivan laughed suddenly.

"I understand too well, Ivan. One longs to love with one's inside, with one's stomach. You said that so well and I am awfully glad that you have such a longing for life," cried Alyosha. "I think everyone should love life above everything in the world."

"Love life more than the meaning of it?"

"Certainly, love it, regardless of logic as you say, it must be regardless of logic, and it's only then one will understand the meaning of it. I have thought so a long time. Half your work is done, Ivan, you love life, now you've only to try to do the second half and you are saved."

"You are trying to save me, but perhaps I am not lost! And what does your second half mean?"

"Why, one has to raise up your dead, who perhaps have not died after all. Come, let me have tea. I am so glad of our talk, Ivan."

"I see you are feeling inspired. I am awfully fond of such professions de foi* from such--novices. You are a steadfast person, Alexey. Is it true that you mean to leave the monastery?"

* Professions of faith.

"Yes, my elder sends me out into the world."

"We shall see each other then in the world. We shall meet before I am thirty, when I shall begin to turn aside from the cup. Father doesn't want to turn aside from his cup till he is seventy, he dreams of hanging on to eighty in fact, so he says. He means it only too seriously, though he is a buffoon. He stands on a firm rock, too, he stands on his sensuality though after we are thirty, indeed, there may be nothing else to stand on...But to hang on to seventy is nasty, better only to thirty; one might retain 'a shadow of nobility' by deceiving oneself. Have you seen Dmitri to-day?"

"No, but I saw Smerdyakov," and Alyosha rapidly, though minutely, described his meeting with Smerdyakov. Ivan began listening anxiously and questioned him.

"But he begged me not to tell Dmitri that he had told me about him," added Alyosha. Ivan frowned and pondered.

"Are you frowning on Smerdyakov's account?" asked Alyosha.

"Yes, on his account. Damn him, I certainly did want to see Dmitri, but now there's no need," said Ivan reluctantly.

"But are you really going so soon, brother?"

"What of Dmitri and father? how will it end?" asked Alyosha anxiously.

"You are always harping upon it! What have I to do with it? Am I my brother Dmitri's keeper?" Ivan snapped irritably, but then he suddenly smiled bitterly. "Cain's answer about his murdered brother, wasn't it? Perhaps that's what you're thinking at this moment? Well damn it all, I can't stay here to be their keeper, can I? I've finished what I had to do, and I am going. Do you imagine I am jealous of Dmitri, that I've been trying to steal his beautiful Katerina Ivanovna for the last three months? Nonsense, I had business of my own. I finished it. I am going. I finished it just now, you were witness."

"At Katerina Ivanovna's?"

"Yes, and I've released myself once for all. And after all, what have I to do with Dmitri? Dmitri doesn't come in. I had my own business to settle with Katerina Ivanovna. You know, on the contrary, that Dmitri behaved as though there was an understanding between us. I didn't ask to do it, but he solemnly handed her over to me and gave us his blessing. It's all too funny. Ah, Alyosha, if you only knew how light my heart is now! Would you believe it, I sat here eating my dinner and was nearly ordering champagne to celebrate my first hour of freedom. Tfoo! It's been going on nearly six months, and all at once I've thrown it off. I could never have guessed even yesterday, how easy it would be to put an end to it if I wanted."

"You are speaking of your love, Ivan?"

"Of my love, if you like. I fell in love with the young lady, I worried myself over her and she worried me. I sat watching over her...and all at once it's collapsed! I spoke this morning with inspiration, but I went away and roared with laughter. Would you believe it? Yes, it's the literal truth."

"You seem very merry about it now," observed Alyosha, looking into his face, which had suddenly grown brighter.

"But how could I tell that I didn't care for her a bit! Ha ha! It appears after all I didn't. And yet how she attracted me! How attractive she was just now when I made my speech! And do you know she attracts me awfully even now, yet how easy it is to leave her. Do you think I am boasting?"

"No, only perhaps it wasn't love."

"Alyosha," laughed Ivan, "don't make reflections about love, it's unseemly for you. How you rushed into the discussion this morning! I've forgotten to kiss you for it...But how she tormented me! It certainly was sitting by a 'laceration.' Ah, she knew how I loved her! She loved me and not Dmitri," Ivan insisted gaily. "Her feeling for Dmitri was simply a self-laceration. All I told her just now was perfectly true, but the worst of it is, it may take her fifteen or twenty years to find out that she doesn't care for Dmitri, and loves me whom she torments, and perhaps she may never find it out at all, in spite of her lesson to-day. Well, it's better so; I can simply go away for good. By the way, how is she now? What happened after I departed?"

Alyosha told him she had been hysterical, and that she was now, he heard, unconscious and delirious.

"Isn't Madame Hohlakov laying it on?"

"I think not."

"I must find out. Nobody dies of hysterics, though. They don't matter. God gave woman hysterics as a relief. I won't go to her at all. Why push myself forward again?"

"But you told her that she had never cared for you."

"I did that on purpose. Alyosha, shall I call for some champagne? Let us drink to my freedom. Ah, if only you knew how glad I am!"

"No, brother, we had better not drink," said Alyosha suddenly. "Besides I feel somehow depressed."

"Yes, you've been depressed a long time, I've noticed it."

"Have you settled to go to-morrow morning, then?"

"Morning? I didn't say I should go in the morning...But perhaps it may be the morning. Would you believe it, I dined here to-day only to avoid dining with the old man, I loathe him so. I should have left long ago, so far as he is concerned. But why are you so worried about my going away? We've plenty of time before I go, an eternity!"

"If you are going away to-morrow, what do you mean by an eternity?"

"But what does it matter to us?" laughed Ivan. "We've time enough for our talk, for what brought us here. Why do you look so surprised? Answer: why have we met here? To talk of my love for Katerina Ivanovna, of the old man and Dmitri? of foreign travel? of the fatal position of Russia? of the Emperor Napoleon? Is that it?"

"No."

"Then you know what for. It's different for other people; but we in our green youth have to settle the eternal questions first of all. That's what we care about. Young Russia is talking about nothing but the eternal questions now. just when the old folks are all taken up with practical questions. Why have you been looking at me in expectation for the last three months? To ask me, 'What do you believe, or don't you believe at all?' That's what your eyes have been meaning for these three months, haven't they?"

"Perhaps so," smiled Alyosha. "You are not laughing at me, now, Ivan?

"Me laughing! I don't want to wound my little brother who has been watching me with such expectation for three months. Alyosha, look straight at me! Of course, I am just such a little boy as you are, only not a novice. And what have Russian boys been doing up till now, some of them, I mean? In this stinking tavern, for instance, here, they meet and sit down in a corner. They've never met in their lives before and, when they go out of the tavern, they won't meet again for forty years. And what do they talk about in that momentary halt in the tavern? Of the eternal questions, of the existence of God and immortality. And those who do not believe in God talk of socialism or anarchism, of the transformation of all humanity on a new pattern, so that it all comes to the same, they're the same questions turned inside out. And masses, masses of the most original Russian boys do nothing but talk of the eternal questions! Isn't it so?"

"Yes, for real Russians the questions of God's existence and of immortality, or, as you say, the same questions turned inside out, come first and foremost, of course, and so they should," said Alyosha, still watching his brother with the same gentle and inquiring smile.

"Well, Alyosha, it's sometimes very unwise to be a Russian at all, but anything stupider than the way Russian boys spend their time one can hardly imagine. But there's one Russian boy called Alyosha I am awfully fond of."

"How nicely you put that in!" Alyosha laughed suddenly.

"Well, tell me where to begin, give your orders. The existence of God, eh?"

"Begin where you like. You declared yesterday at father's that there was no God." Alyosha looked searchingly at his brother.

"I said that yesterday at dinner on purpose to tease you and I saw your eyes glow. But now I've no objection to discussing with you, and I say so very seriously. I want to be friends with you, Alyosha, for I have no friends and want to try it. Well, only fancy, perhaps I too accept God," laughed Ivan; "that's a surprise for you, isn't it?"

"Yes of course, if you are not joking now."

"Joking? I was told at the elder's yesterday that I was joking. You know, dear boy, there was an old sinner in the eighteenth century who declared that, if there were no God, he would have to be invented. S'il n'existait pas Dieu, il faudrait l'inventer. And man has actually invented God. And what's strange, what would be marvellous, is not that God should really exist; the marvel is that such an idea, the idea of the necessity of God, could enter the head of such a savage, vicious beast as man. So holy it is, so touching, so wise and so great a credit it does to man. As for me, I've long resolved not to think whether man created God or God man. And I won't go through all the axioms laid down by Russian boys on that subject, all derived from European hypotheses; for what's a hypothesis there is an axiom with the Russian boy, and not only with the boys but with their teachers too, for our Russian professors are often just the same boys themselves. And so I omit all the hypotheses. For what are we aiming at now? I am trying to explain as quickly as possible my essential nature, that is what manner of man I am, what I believe in, and for what I hope, that's it, isn't it? And therefore I tell you that I accept God simply. But you must note this: if God exists and if He really did create the world, then, as we all know, He created it according to the geometry of Euclid and the human mind with the conception of only three dimensions in space. Yet there have been and still are geometricians and philosophers, and even some of the most distinguished, who doubt whether the whole universe, or to speak more widely, the whole of being, was only created in Euclid's geometry; they even dare to dream that two parallel lines, which according to Euclid can never meet on earth, may meet somewhere in infinity. I have come to the conclusion that, since I can't understand even that, I can't expect to understand about God. I acknowledge humbly that I have no faculty for settling such questions, I have a Euclidian earthly mind, and how could I solve problems that are not of this world? And I advise you never to think about it either, my dear Alyosha, especially about God, whether He exists or not. All such questions are utterly inappropriate for a mind created with an idea of only three dimensions. And so I accept God and am glad to, and what's more, I accept His wisdom, His purpose which are utterly beyond our ken; I believe in the underlying order and the meaning of life; I believe in the eternal harmony in which they say we shall one day be blended. I believe in the Word to Which the universe is striving, and Which Itself was 'with God,' and Which Itself is God and so on, and so on, to infinity. There are all sorts of phrases for it. I seem to be on the right path, don't I? Yet would you believe it, in the final result I don't accept this world of God's, and, although I know it exists, I don't accept it at all. It's not that I don't accept God, you must understand, it's the world created by Him I don't and cannot accept. Let me make it plain. I believe like a child that suffering will be healed and made up for, that all the humiliating absurdity of human contradictions will vanish like a pitiful mirage, like the despicable fabrication of the impotent and infinitely small Euclidian mind of man, that in the world's finale, at the moment of eternal harmony, something so precious will come to pass that it will suffice for all hearts, for the comforting of all resentments, for the atonement of all the crimes of humanity, of all the blood they've shed; that it will make it not only possible to forgive but to justify all that has happened with men--but thought all that may come to pass, I don't accept it. I won't accept it. Even if parallel lines do meet and I see it myself, I shall see it and say that they've met, but still I won't accept it. That's what's at the root of me, Alyosha; that's my creed. I am in earnest in what I say. I began our talk as stupidly as I could on purpose, but I've led up to my confession, for that's all you want. You didn't want to hear about God, but only to know what the brother you love lives by. And so I've told you."

Ivan concluded his long tirade with marked and unexpected feeling.

"And why did you begin 'as stupidly as you could'?" asked Alyosha, looking dreamily at him.

"To begin with, for the sake of being Russian. Russian conversations on such subjects are always carried on inconceivably stupidly. And secondly, the stupider one is, the closer one is to reality. The stupider one is, the clearer one is. Stupidity is brief and artless, while intelligence wriggles and hides itself. Intelligence is a knave, but stupidity is honest and straight forward. I've led the conversation to my despair, and the more stupidly I have presented it, the better for me."

"You will explain why you don't accept the world?" said Alyosha.

"To be sure I will, it's not a secret, that's what I've been leading up to. Dear little brother, I don't want to corrupt you or to turn you from your stronghold, perhaps I want to be healed by you." Ivan smiled suddenly quite like a little gentle child. Alyosha had never seen such a smile on his face before.

Chapter 4. Rebellion

"I MUST make one confession" Ivan began. "I could never understand how one can love one's neighbours. It's just one's neighbours, to my mind, that one can't love, though one might love those at a distance. I once read somewhere of John the Merciful, a saint, that when a hungry, frozen beggar came to him, he took him into his bed, held him in his arms, and began breathing into his mouth, which was putrid and loathsome from some awful disease. I am convinced that he did that from 'self-laceration,' from the self-laceration of falsity, for the sake of the charity imposed by duty, as a penance laid on him. For anyone to love a man, he must be hidden, for as soon as he shows his face, love is gone."

"Father Zossima has talked of that more than once," observed Alyosha; "he, too, said that the face of a man often hinders many people not practised in love, from loving him. But yet there's a great deal of love in mankind, and almost Christ-like love. I know that myself, Ivan."

"Well, I know nothing of it so far, and can't understand it, and the innumerable mass of mankind are with me there. The question is, whether that's due to men's bad qualities or whether it's inherent in their nature. To my thinking, Christ-like love for men is a miracle impossible on earth. He was God. But we are not gods. Suppose I, for instance, suffer intensely. Another can never know how much I suffer, because he is another and not I. And what's more, a man is rarely ready to admit another's suffering (as though it were a distinction). Why won't he admit it, do you think? Because I smell unpleasant, because I have a stupid face, because I once trod on his foot. Besides, there is suffering and suffering; degrading, humiliating suffering such as humbles me--hunger, for instance--my benefactor will perhaps allow me; but when you come to higher suffering--for an idea, for instance--he will very rarely admit that, perhaps because my face strikes him as not at all what he fancies a man should have who suffers for an idea. And so he deprives me instantly of his favour, and not at all from badness of heart. Beggars, especially genteel beggars, ought never to show themselves, but to ask for charity through the newspapers. One can love one's neighbours in the abstract, or even at a distance, but at close quarters it's almost impossible. If it were as on the stage, in the ballet, where if beggars come in, they wear silken rags and tattered lace and beg for alms dancing gracefully, then one might like looking at them. But even then we should not love them. But enough of that. I simply wanted to show you my point of view. I meant to speak of the suffering of mankind generally, but we had better confine ourselves to the sufferings of the children. That reduces the scope of my argument to a tenth of what it would be. Still we'd better keep to the children, though it does weaken my case. But, in the first place, children can be loved even at close quarters, even when they are dirty, even when they are ugly (I fancy, though, children never are ugly). The second reason why I won't speak of grown-up people is that, besides being disgusting and unworthy of love, they have a compensation--they've eaten the apple and know good and evil, and they have become 'like gods.' They go on eating it still. But the children haven't eaten anything, and are so far innocent. Are you fond of children, Alyosha? I know you are, and you will understand why I prefer to speak of them. If they, too, suffer horribly on earth, they must suffer for their fathers' sins, they must be punished for their fathers, who have eaten the apple; but that reasoning is of the other world and is incomprehensible for the heart of man here on earth. The innocent must not suffer for another's sins, and especially such innocents! You may be surprised at me, Alyosha, but I am awfully fond of children, too. And observe, cruel people, the violent, the rapacious, the Karamazovs are sometimes very fond of children. Children while they are quite little--up to seven, for instance--are so remote from grown-up people they are different creatures, as it were, of a different species. I knew a criminal in prison who had, in the course of his career as a burglar, murdered whole families, including several children. But when he was in prison, he had a strange affection for them. He spent all his time at his window, watching the children playing in the prison yard. He trained one little boy to come up to his window and made great friends with him...You don't know why I am telling you all this, Alyosha? My head aches and I am sad."

"You speak with a strange air," observed Alyosha uneasily, "as though you were not quite yourself."

"By the way, a Bulgarian I met lately in Moscow," Ivan went on, seeming not to hear his brother's words, "told me about the crimes committed by Turks and Circassians in all parts of Bulgaria through fear of a general rising of the Slavs. They burn villages, murder, outrage women and children, they nail their prisoners by the ears to the fences, leave them so till morning, and in the morning they hang them--all sorts of things you can't imagine. People talk sometimes of bestial cruelty, but that's a great injustice and insult to the beasts; a beast can never be so cruel as a man, so artistically cruel. The tiger only tears and gnaws, that's all he can do. He would never think of nailing people by the ears, even if he were able to do it. These Turks took a pleasure in torturing children, too; cutting the unborn child from the mothers womb, and tossing babies up in the air and catching them on the points of their bayonets before their mothers' eyes. Doing it before the mothers' eyes was what gave zest to the amusement. Here is another scene that I thought very interesting. Imagine a trembling mother with her baby in her arms, a circle of invading Turks around her. They've planned a diversion: they pet the baby, laugh to make it laugh. They succeed, the baby laughs. At that moment a Turk points a pistol four inches from the baby's face. The baby laughs with glee, holds out its little hands to the pistol, and he pulls the trigger in the baby's face and blows out its brains. Artistic, wasn't it? By the way, Turks are particularly fond of sweet things, they say."

"Brother, what are you driving at?" asked Alyosha.

"I think if the devil doesn't exist, but man has created him, he has created him in his own image and likeness."

"Just as he did God, then?" observed Alyosha.

"'It's wonderful how you can turn words,' as Polonius says in Hamlet," laughed Ivan. "You turn my words against me. Well, I am glad. Yours must be a fine God, if man created Him in his image and likeness. You asked just now what I was driving at. You see, I am fond of collecting certain facts, and, would you believe, I even copy anecdotes of a certain sort from newspapers and books, and I've already got a fine collection. The Turks, of course, have gone into it, but they are foreigners. I have specimens from home that are even better than the Turks. You know we prefer beating--rods and scourges--that's our national institution. Nailing ears is unthinkable for us, for we are, after all, Europeans. But the rod and the scourge we have always with us and they cannot be taken from us. Abroad now they scarcely do any beating. Manners are more humane, or laws have been passed, so that they don't dare to flog men now. But they make up for it in another way just as national as ours. And so national that it would be practically impossible among us, though I believe we are being inoculated with it, since the religious movement began in our aristocracy. I have a charming pamphlet, translated from the French, describing how, quite recently, five years ago, a murderer, Richard, was executed--a young man, I believe, of three and twenty, who repented and was converted to the Christian faith at the very scaffold. This Richard was an illegitimate child who was given as a child of six by his parents to some shepherds on the Swiss mountains. They brought him up to work for them. He grew up like a little wild beast among them. The shepherds taught him nothing, and scarcely fed or clothed him, but sent him out at seven to herd the flock in cold and wet, and no one hesitated or scrupled to treat him so. Quite the contrary, they thought they had every right, for Richard had been given to them as a chattel, and they did not even see the necessity of feeding him. Richard himself describes how in those years, like the Prodigal Son in the Gospel, he longed to eat of the mash given to the pigs, which were fattened for sale. But they wouldn't even give that, and beat him when he stole from the pigs. And that was how he spent all his childhood and his youth, till he grew up and was strong enough to go away and be a thief. The savage began to earn his living as a day labourer in Geneva. He drank what he earned, he lived like a brute, and finished by killing and robbing an old man. He was caught, tried, and condemned to death. They are not sentimentalists there. And in prison he was immediately surrounded by pastors, members of Christian brotherhoods, philanthropic ladies, and the like. They taught him to read and write in prison, and expounded the Gospel to him. They exhorted him, worked upon him, drummed at him incessantly, till at last he solemnly confessed his crime. He was converted. He wrote to the court himself that he was a monster, but that in the end God had vouchsafed him light and shown grace. All Geneva was in excitement about him--all philanthropic and religious Geneva. All the aristocratic and well-bred society of the town rushed to the prison, kissed Richard and embraced him; 'You are our brother, you have found grace.' And Richard does nothing but weep with emotion, 'Yes, I've found grace! All my youth and childhood I was glad of pigs' food, but now even I have found grace. I am dying in the Lord.' 'Yes, Richard, die in the Lord; you have shed blood and must die. Though it's not your fault that you knew not the Lord, when you coveted the pigs' food and were beaten for stealing it (which was very wrong of you, for stealing is forbidden); but you've shed blood and you must die.'And on the last day, Richard, perfectly limp, did nothing but cry and repeat every minute: 'This is my happiest day. I am going to the Lord.' 'Yes,' cry the pastors and the judges and philanthropic ladies. 'This is the happiest day of your life, for you are going to the Lord!' They all walk or drive to the scaffold in procession behind the prison van. At the scaffold they call to Richard: 'Die, brother, die in the Lord, for even thou hast found grace!' And so, covered with his brothers' kisses, Richard is dragged on to the scaffold, and led to the guillotine. And they chopped off his head in brotherly fashion, because he had found grace. Yes, that's characteristic. That pamphlet is translated into Russian by some Russian philanthropists of aristocratic rank and evangelical aspirations, and has been distributed gratis for the enlightenment of the people. The case of Richard is interesting because it's national. Though to us it's absurd to cut off a man's head, because he has become our brother and has found grace, yet we have our own speciality, which is all but worse. Our historical pastime is the direct satisfaction of inflicting pain. There are lines in Nekrassov describing how a peasant lashes a horse on the eyes, 'on its meek eyes,' everyone must have seen it. It's peculiarly Russian. He describes how a feeble little nag has foundered under too heavy a load and cannot move. The peasant beats it, beats it savagely, beats it at last not knowing what he is doing in the intoxication of cruelty, thrashes it mercilessly over and over again. 'However weak you are, you must pull, if you die for it.' The nag strains, and then he begins lashing the poor defenceless creature on its weeping, on its 'meek eyes.' The frantic beast tugs and draws the load, trembling all over, gasping for breath, moving sideways, with a sort of unnatural spasmodic action--it's awful in Nekrassov. But that only a horse, and God has horses to be beaten. So the Tatars have taught us, and they left us the knout as a remembrance of it. But men, too, can be beaten. A well-educated, cultured gentleman and his wife beat their own child with a birch-rod, a girl of seven. I have an exact account of it. The papa was glad that the birch was covered with twigs. 'It stings more,' said he, and so be began stinging his daughter. I know for a fact there are people who at every blow are worked up to sensuality, to literal sensuality, which increases progressively at every blow they inflict. They beat for a minute, for five minutes, for ten minutes, more often and more savagely. The child screams. At last the child cannot scream, it gasps, 'Daddy daddy!' By some diabolical unseemly chance the case was brought into court. A counsel is engaged. The Russian people have long called a barrister 'a conscience for hire.' The counsel protests in his client's defence. 'It's such a simple thing,' he says, 'an everyday domestic event. A father corrects his child. To our shame be it said, it is brought into court.' The jury, convinced by him, give a favourable verdict. The public roars with delight that the torturer is acquitted. Ah, pity I wasn't there! I would have proposed to raise a subscription in his honour! Charming pictures.

"But I've still better things about children. I've collected a great, great deal about Russian children, Alyosha. There was a little girl of five who was hated by her father and mother, 'most worthy and respectable people, of good education and breeding.' You see, I must repeat again, it is a peculiar characteristic of many people, this love of torturing children, and children only. To all other types of humanity these torturers behave mildly and benevolently, like cultivated and humane Europeans; but they are very fond of tormenting children, even fond of children themselves in that sense. it's just their defencelessness that tempts the tormentor, just the angelic confidence of the child who has no refuge and no appeal, that sets his vile blood on fire. In every man, of course, a demon lies hidden--the demon of rage, the demon of lustful heat at the screams of the tortured victim, the demon of lawlessness let off the chain, the demon of diseases that follow on vice, gout, kidney disease, and so on.

"This poor child of five was subjected to every possible torture by those cultivated parents. They beat her, thrashed her, kicked her for no reason till her body was one bruise. Then, they went to greater refinements of cruelty--shut her up all night in the cold and frost in a privy, and because she didn't ask to be taken up at night (as though a child of five sleeping its angelic, sound sleep could be trained to wake and ask), they smeared her face and filled her mouth with excrement, and it was her mother, her mother did this. And that mother could sleep, hearing the poor child's groans! Can you understand why a little creature, who can't even understand what's done to her, should beat her little aching heart with her tiny fist in the dark and the cold, and weep her meek unresentful tears to dear, kind God to protect her? Do you understand that, friend and brother, you pious and humble novice? Do you understand why this infamy must be and is permitted? Without it, I am told, man could not have existed on earth, for he could not have known good and evil. Why should he know that diabolical good and evil when it costs so much? Why, the whole world of knowledge is not worth that child's prayer to dear, kind God'! I say nothing of the sufferings of grown-up people, they have eaten the apple, damn them, and the devil take them all! But these little ones! I am making you suffer, Alyosha, you are not yourself. I'll leave off if you like."

"Nevermind. I want to suffer too," muttered Alyosha.

"One picture, only one more, because it's so curious, so characteristic, and I have only just read it in some collection of Russian antiquities. I've forgotten the name. I must look it up. It was in the darkest days of serfdom at the beginning of the century, and long live the Liberator of the People! There was in those days a general of aristocratic connections, the owner of great estates, one of those men--somewhat exceptional, I believe, even then--who, retiring from the service into a life of leisure, are convinced that they've earned absolute power over the lives of their subjects. There were such men then. So our general, settled on his property of two thousand souls, lives in pomp, and domineers over his poor neighbours as though they were dependents and buffoons. He has kennels of hundreds of hounds and nearly a hundred dog-boys--all mounted, and in uniform. One day a serf-boy, a little child of eight, threw a stone in play and hurt the paw of the general's favourite hound. 'Why is my favourite dog lame?' He is told that the boy threw a stone that hurt the dog's paw. 'So you did it.' The general looked the child up and down. 'Take him.' He was taken--taken from his mother and kept shut up all night. Early that morning the general comes out on horseback, with the hounds, his dependents, dog-boys, and huntsmen, all mounted around him in full hunting parade. The servants are summoned for their edification, and in front of them all stands the mother of the child. The child is brought from the lock-up. It's a gloomy, cold, foggy, autumn day, a capital day for hunting. The general orders the child to be undressed; the child is stripped naked. He shivers, numb with terror, not daring to cry...'Make him run,' commands the general. 'Run! run!' shout the dog-boys. The boy runs...'At him!' yells the general, and he sets the whole pack of hounds on the child. The hounds catch him, and tear him to pieces before his mother's eyes!...I believe the general was afterwards declared incapable of administering his estates. Well--what did he deserve? To be shot? To be shot for the satisfaction of our moral feelings? Speak, Alyosha!"

"To be shot," murmured Alyosha, lifting his eyes to Ivan with a pale, twisted smile.

"Bravo!" cried Ivan delighted. "If even you say so...You're a pretty monk! So there is a little devil sitting in your heart, Alyosha Karamazov!"

"What I said was absurd, but-"

"That's just the point, that 'but'!" cried Ivan. "Let me tell you, novice, that the absurd is only too necessary on earth. The world stands on absurdities, and perhaps nothing would have come to pass in it without them. We know what we know!"

"What do you know?"

"I understand nothing," Ivan went on, as though in delirium. "I don't want to understand anything now. I want to stick to the fact. I made up my mind long ago not to understand. If I try to understand anything, I shall be false to the fact, and I have determined to stick to the fact."

"Why are you trying me?" Alyosha cried, with sudden distress. "Will you say what you mean at last?"

"Of course, I will; that's what I've been leading up to. You are dear to me, I don't want to let you go, and I won't give you up to your Zossima."

Ivan for a minute was silent, his face became all at once very sad.

"Listen! I took the case of children only to make my case clearer. Of the other tears of humanity with which the earth is soaked from its crust to its centre, I will say nothing. I have narrowed my subject on purpose. I am a bug, and I recognise in all humility that I cannot understand why the world is arranged as it is. Men are themselves to blame, I suppose; they were given paradise, they wanted freedom, and stole fire from heaven, though they knew they would become unhappy, so there is no need to pity them. With my pitiful, earthly, Euclidian understanding, all I know is that there is suffering and that there are none guilty; that cause follows effect, simply and directly; that everything flows and finds its level--but that's only Euclidian nonsense, I know that, and I can't consent to live by it! What comfort is it to me that there are none guilty and that cause follows effect simply and directly, and that I know it?--I must have justice, or I will destroy myself. And not justice in some remote infinite time and space, but here on earth, and that I could see myself. I have believed in it. I want to see it, and if I am dead by then, let me rise again, for if it all happens without me, it will be too unfair. Surely I haven't suffered simply that I, my crimes and my sufferings, may manure the soil of the future harmony for somebody else. I want to see with my own eyes the hind lie down with the lion and the victim rise up and embrace his murderer. I want to be there when everyone suddenly understands what it has all been for. All the religions of the world are built on this longing, and I am a believer. But then there are the children, and what am I to do about them? That's a question I can't answer. For the hundredth time I repeat, there are numbers of questions, but I've only taken the children, because in their case what I mean is so unanswerably clear. Listen! If all must suffer to pay for the eternal harmony, what have children to do with it, tell me, please? It's beyond all comprehension why they should suffer, and why they should pay for the harmony. Why should they, too, furnish material to enrich the soil for the harmony of the future? I understand solidarity in sin among men. I understand solidarity in retribution, too; but there can be no such solidarity with children. And if it is really true that they must share responsibility for all their fathers' crimes, such a truth is not of this world and is beyond my comprehension. Some jester will say, perhaps, that the child would have grown up and have sinned, but you see he didn't grow up, he was torn to pieces by the dogs, at eight years old. Oh, Alyosha, I am not blaspheming! I understand, of course, what an upheaval of the universe it will be when everything in heaven and earth blends in one hymn of praise and everything that lives and has lived cries aloud: 'Thou art just, O Lord, for Thy ways are revealed.' When the mother embraces the fiend who threw her child to the dogs, and all three cry aloud with tears, 'Thou art just, O Lord!' then, of course, the crown of knowledge will be reached and all will be made clear. But what pulls me up here is that I can't accept that harmony. And while I am on earth, I make haste to take my own measures. You see, Alyosha, perhaps it really may happen that if I live to that moment, or rise again to see it, I, too, perhaps, may cry aloud with the rest, looking at the mother embracing the child's torturer, 'Thou art just, O Lord!' but I don't want to cry aloud then. While there is still time, I hasten to protect myself, and so I renounce the higher harmony altogether. It's not worth the tears of that one tortured child who beat itself on the breast with its little fist and prayed in its stinking outhouse, with its unexpiated tears to 'dear, kind God'! It's not worth it, because those tears are unatoned for. They must be atoned for, or there can be no harmony. But how? How are you going to atone for them? Is it possible? By their being avenged? But what do I care for avenging them? What do I care for a hell for oppressors? What good can hell do, since those children have already been tortured? And what becomes of harmony, if there is hell? I want to forgive. I want to embrace. I don't want more suffering. And if the sufferings of children go to swell the sum of sufferings which was necessary to pay for truth, then I protest that the truth is not worth such a price. I don't want the mother to embrace the oppressor who threw her son to the dogs! She dare not forgive him! Let her forgive him for herself, if she will, let her forgive the torturer for the immeasurable suffering of her mother's heart. But the sufferings of her tortured child she has no right to forgive; she dare not forgive the torturer, even if the child were to forgive him! And if that is so, if they dare not forgive, what becomes of harmony? Is there in the whole world a being who would have the right to forgive and could forgive? I don't want harmony. From love for humanity I don't want it. I would rather be left with the unavenged suffering. I would rather remain with my unavenged suffering and unsatisfied indignation, even if I were wrong. Besides, too high a price is asked for harmony; it's beyond our means to pay so much to enter on it. And so I hasten to give back my entrance ticket, and if I am an honest man I am bound to give it back as soon as possible. And that I am doing. It's not God that I don't accept, Alyosha, only I most respectfully return him the ticket."

"That's rebellion," murmured Alyosha, looking down.

"Rebellion? I am sorry you call it that," said Ivan earnestly. "One can hardly live in rebellion, and I want to live. Tell me yourself, I challenge your answer. Imagine that you are creating a fabric of human destiny with the object of making men happy in the end, giving them peace and rest at last, but that it was essential and inevitable to torture to death only one tiny creature--that baby beating its breast with its fist, for instance--and to found that edifice on its unavenged tears, would you consent to be the architect on those conditions? Tell me, and tell the truth."

"No, I wouldn't consent," said Alyosha softly.

"And can you admit the idea that men for whom you are building it would agree to accept their happiness on the foundation of the unexpiated blood of a little victim? And accepting it would remain happy for ever?"

"No, I can't admit it. Brother," said Alyosha suddenly, with flashing eyes, "you said just now, is there a being in the whole world who would have the right to forgive and could forgive? But there is a Being and He can forgive everything, all and for all, because He gave His innocent blood for all and everything. You have forgotten Him, and on Him is built the edifice, and it is to Him they cry aloud, 'Thou art just, O Lord, for Thy ways are revealed!'

"Ah! the One without sin and His blood! No, I have not forgotten Him; on the contrary I've been wondering all the time how it was you did not bring Him in before, for usually all arguments on your side put Him in the foreground. Do you know, Alyosha--don't laugh I made a poem about a year ago. If you can waste another ten minutes on me, I'll tell it to you."

"You wrote a poem?"

"Oh, no, I didn't write it," laughed Ivan, and I've never written two lines of poetry in my life. But I made up this poem in prose and I remembered it. I was carried away when I made it up. You will be my first reader--that is listener. Why should an author forego even one listener?" smiled Ivan. "Shall I tell it to you?"

"I am all attention." said Alyosha.

"My poem is called The Grand Inquisitor; it's a ridiculous thing, but I want to tell it to you.

Chapter 5. The Grand Inquisitor

"EVEN this must have a preface--that is, a literary preface," laughed Ivan, "and I am a poor hand at making one. You see, my action takes place in the sixteenth century, and at that time, as you probably learnt at school, it was customary in poetry to bring down heavenly powers on earth. Not to speak of Dante, in France, clerks, as well as the monks in the monasteries, used to give regular performances in which the Madonna, the saints, the angels, Christ, and God Himself were brought on the stage. In those days it was done in all simplicity. In Victor Hugo's Notre Dame de Paris an edifying and gratuitous spectacle was provided for the people in the Hotel de Ville of Paris in the reign of Louis XI in honour of the birth of the dauphin. It was called Le bon jugement de la tres sainte et gracieuse Vierge Marie, and she appears herself on the stage and pronounces her bon jugement. Similar plays, chiefly from the Old Testament, were occasionally performed in Moscow too, up to the times of Peter the Great. But besides plays there were all sorts of legends and ballads scattered about the world, in which the saints and angels and all the powers of Heaven took part when required. In our monasteries the monks busied themselves in translating, copying, and even composing such poems--and even under the Tatars. There is, for instance, one such poem (of course, from the Greek), The Wanderings of Our Lady through Hell, with descriptions as bold as Dante's. Our Lady visits hell, and the Archangel Michael leads her through the torments. She sees the sinners and their punishment. There she sees among others one noteworthy set of sinners in a burning lake; some of them sink to the bottom of the lake so that they can't swim out, and 'these God forgets'--an expression of extraordinary depth and force. And so Our Lady, shocked and weeping, falls before the throne of God and begs for mercy for all in hell--for all she has seen there, indiscriminately. Her conversation with God is immensely interesting. She beseeches Him, she will not desist, and when God points to the hands and feet of her Son, nailed to the Cross, and asks, 'How can I forgive His tormentors?' she bids all the saints, all the martyrs, all the angels and archangels to fall down with her and pray for mercy on all without distinction. It ends by her winning from God a respite of suffering every year from Good Friday till Trinity Day, and the sinners at once raise a cry of thankfulness from hell, chanting, 'Thou art just, O Lord, in this judgment.' Well, my poem would have been of that kind if it had appeared at that time. He comes on the scene in my poem, but He says nothing, only appears and passes on. Fifteen centuries have passed since He promised to come in His glory, fifteen centuries since His prophet wrote, 'Behold, I come quickly'; 'Of that day and that hour knoweth no man, neither the Son, but the Father,' as He Himself predicted on earth. But humanity awaits him with the same faith and with the same love. Oh, with greater faith, for it is fifteen centuries since man has ceased to see signs from heaven.

No signs from heaven come to-day
To add to what the heart doth say.

There was nothing left but faith in what the heart doth say. It is true there were many miracles in those days. There were saints who performed miraculous cures; some holy people, according to their biographies, were visited by the Queen of Heaven herself. But the devil did not slumber, and doubts were already arising among men of the truth of these miracles. And just then there appeared in the north of Germany a terrible new heresy. 'A huge star like to a torch' (that is, to a church) 'fell on the sources of the waters and they became bitter.' These heretics began blasphemously denying miracles. But those who remained faithful were all the more ardent in their faith. The tears of humanity rose up to Him as before, awaited His coming, loved Him, hoped for Him, yearned to suffer and die for Him as before. And so many ages mankind had prayed with faith and fervour, 'O Lord our God, hasten Thy coming'; so many ages called upon Him, that in His infinite mercy He deigned to come down to His servants. Before that day He had come down, He had visited some holy men, martyrs, and hermits, as is written in their lives. Among us, Tyutchev, with absolute faith in the truth of his words, bore witness that

Bearing the Cross, in slavish dress,
Weary and worn, the Heavenly King
Our mother, Russia, came to bless,
And through our land went wandering.

And that certainly was so, I assure you.

"And behold, He deigned to appear for a moment to the people, to the tortured, suffering people, sunk in iniquity, but loving Him like children. My story is laid in Spain, in Seville, in the most terrible time of the Inquisition, when fires were lighted every day to the glory of God, and 'in the splendid auto da fe the wicked heretics were burnt.' Oh, of course, this was not the coming in which He will appear, according to His promise, at the end of time in all His heavenly glory, and which will be sudden 'as lightning flashing from east to west.' No, He visited His children only for a moment, and there where the flames were crackling round the heretics. In His infinite mercy He came once more among men in that human shape in which He walked among men for thirty-three years fifteen centuries ago. He came down to the 'hot pavements' of the southern town in which on the day before almost a hundred heretics had, ad majorem gloriam Dei, been burnt by the cardinal, the Grand Inquisitor, in a magnificent auto da fe, in the presence of the king, the court, the knights, the cardinals, the most charming ladies of the court, and the whole population of Seville.

"He came softly, unobserved, and yet, strange to say, everyone recognised Him. That might be one of the best passages in the poem. I mean, why they recognised Him. The people are irresistibly drawn to Him, they surround Him, they flock about Him, follow Him. He moves silently in their midst with a gentle smile of infinite compassion. The sun of love burns in His heart, and power shine from His eyes, and their radiance, shed on the people, stirs their hearts with responsive love. He holds out His hands to them, blesses them, and a healing virtue comes from contact with Him, even with His garments. An old man in the crowd, blind from childhood, cries out, 'O Lord, heal me and I shall see Thee!' and, as it were, scales fall from his eyes and the blind man sees Him. The crowd weeps and kisses the earth under His feet. Children throw flowers before Him, sing, and cry hosannah. 'It is He--it is He!' repeat. 'It must be He, it can be no one but Him!' He stops at the steps of the Seville cathedral at the moment when the weeping mourners are bringing in a little open white coffin. In it lies a child of seven, the only daughter of a prominent citizen. The dead child lies hidden in flowers. 'He will raise your child,' the crowd shouts to the weeping mother. The priest, coming to meet the coffin, looks perplexed, and frowns, but the mother of the dead child throws herself at His feet with a wail. 'If it is Thou, raise my child!' she cries, holding out her hands to Him. The procession halts, the coffin is laid on the steps at His feet. He looks with compassion, and His lips once more softly pronounce, 'Maiden, arise!' and the maiden arises. The little girl sits up in the coffin and looks round, smiling with wide-open wondering eyes, holding a bunch of white roses they had put in her hand.

"There are cries, sobs, confusion among the people, and at that moment the cardinal himself, the Grand Inquisitor, passes by the cathedral. He is an old man, almost ninety, tall and erect, with a withered face and sunken eyes, in which there is still a gleam of light. He is not dressed in his gorgeous cardinal's robes, as he was the day before, when he was burning the enemies of the Roman Church--at this moment he is wearing his coarse, old, monk's cassock. At a distance behind him come his gloomy assistants and slaves and the 'holy guard.' He stops at the sight of the crowd and watches it from a distance. He sees everything; he sees them set the coffin down at His feet, sees the child rise up, and his face darkens. He knits his thick grey brows and his eyes gleam with a sinister fire. He holds out his finger and bids the guards take Him. And such is his power, so completely are the people cowed into submission and trembling obedience to him, that the crowd immediately makes way for the guards, and in the midst of deathlike silence they lay hands on Him and lead him away. The crowd instantly bows down to the earth, like one man, before the old Inquisitor. He blesses the people in silence and passes on' The guards lead their prisoner to the close, gloomy vaulted prison--in the ancient palace of the Holy, inquisition and shut him in it. The day passes and is followed by the dark, burning, 'breathless' night of Seville. The air is 'fragrant with laurel and lemon.' In the pitch darkness the iron door of the prison is suddenly opened and the Grand Inquisitor himself comes in with a light in his hand. He is alone; the door is closed at once behind him. He stands in the doorway and for a minute or two gazes into His face. At last he goes up slowly, sets the light on the table and speaks.

"'Is it Thou? Thou?' but receiving no answer, he adds at once. 'Don't answer, be silent. What canst Thou say, indeed? I know too well what Thou wouldst say. And Thou hast no right to add anything to what Thou hadst said of old. Why, then, art Thou come to hinder us? For Thou hast come to hinder us, and Thou knowest that. But dost thou know what will be to-morrow? I know not who Thou art and care not to know whether it is Thou or only a semblance of Him, but to-morrow I shall condemn Thee and burn Thee at the stake as the worst of heretics. And the very people who have to-day kissed Thy feet, to-morrow at the faintest sign from me will rush to heap up the embers of Thy fire. Knowest Thou that? Yes, maybe Thou knowest it,' he added with thoughtful penetration, never for a moment taking his eyes off the Prisoner."

"I don't quite understand, Ivan. What does it mean?" Alyosha, who had been listening in silence, said with a smile. "Is it simply a wild fantasy, or a mistake on the part of the old man--some impossible quid pro quo?"

"Take it as the last," said Ivan, laughing, "if you are so corrupted by modern realism and can't stand anything fantastic. If you like it to be a case of mistaken identity, let it be so. It is true," he went on, laughing, "the old man was ninety, and he might well be crazy over his set idea. He might have been struck by the appearance of the Prisoner. It might, in fact, be simply his ravings, the delusion of an old man of ninety, over-excited by the auto da fe of a hundred heretics the day before. But does it matter to us after all whether it was a mistake of identity or a wild fantasy? All that matters is that the old man should speak out, that he should speak openly of what he has thought in silence for ninety years."

"And the Prisoner too is silent? Does He look at him and not say a word?"

"That's inevitable in any case," Ivan laughed again. "The old man has told Him He hasn't the right to add anything to what He has said of old. One may say it is the most fundamental feature of Roman Catholicism, in my opinion at least. 'All has been given by Thee to the Pope,' they say, 'and all, therefore, is still in the Pope's hands, and there is no need for Thee to come now at all. Thou must not meddle for the time, at least.' That's how they speak and write too--the Jesuits, at any rate. I have read it myself in the works of their theologians. 'Hast Thou the right to reveal to us one of the mysteries of that world from which Thou hast come?' my old man asks Him, and answers the question for Him. 'No, Thou hast not; that Thou mayest not add to what has been said of old, and mayest not take from men the freedom which Thou didst exalt when Thou wast on earth. Whatsoever Thou revealest anew will encroach on men's freedom of faith; for it will be manifest as a miracle, and the freedom of their faith was dearer to Thee than anything in those days fifteen hundred years ago. Didst Thou not often say then, "I will make you free"? But now Thou hast seen these "free" men,' the old man adds suddenly, with a pensive smile. 'Yes, we've paid dearly for it,' he goes on, looking sternly at Him, 'but at last we have completed that work in Thy name. For fifteen centuries we have been wrestling with Thy freedom, but now it is ended and over for good. Dost Thou not believe that it's over for good? Thou lookest meekly at me and deignest not even to be wroth with me. But let me tell Thee that now, to-day, people are more persuaded than ever that they have perfect freedom, yet they have brought their freedom to us and laid it humbly at our feet. But that has been our doing. Was this what Thou didst? Was this Thy freedom?'"

"I don't understand again." Alyosha broke in. "Is he ironical, is he jesting?"

"Not a bit of it! He claims it as a merit for himself and his Church that at last they have vanquished freedom and have done so to make men happy. 'For now' (he is speaking of the Inquisition, of course) 'for the first time it has become possible to think of the happiness of men. Man was created a rebel; and how can rebels be happy? Thou wast warned,' he says to Him. 'Thou hast had no lack of admonitions and warnings, but Thou didst not listen to those warnings; Thou didst reject the only way by which men might be made happy. But, fortunately, departing Thou didst hand on the work to us. Thou hast promised, Thou hast established by Thy word, Thou hast given to us the right to bind and to unbind, and now, of course, Thou canst not think of taking it away. Why, then, hast Thou come to hinder us?'"

"And what's the meaning of 'no lack of admonitions and warnings'?" asked Alyosha.

"Why, that's the chief part of what the old man must say.

"'The wise and dread spirit, the spirit of self-destruction and non-existence,' the old man goes on, great spirit talked with Thee in the wilderness, and we are told in the books that he "tempted" Thee. Is that so? And could anything truer be said than what he revealed to Thee in three questions and what Thou didst reject, and what in the books is called "the temptation"? And yet if there has ever been on earth a real stupendous miracle, it took place on that day, on the day of the three temptations. The statement of those three questions was itself the miracle. If it were possible to imagine simply for the sake of argument that those three questions of the dread spirit had perished utterly from the books, and that we had to restore them and to invent them anew, and to do so had gathered together all the wise men of the earth--rulers, chief priests, learned men, philosophers, poets--and had set them the task to invent three questions, such as would not only fit the occasion, but express in three words, three human phrases, the whole future history of the world and of humanity--dost Thou believe that all the wisdom of the earth united could have invented anything in depth and force equal to the three questions which were actually put to Thee then by the wise and mighty spirit in the wilderness? From those questions alone, from the miracle of their statement, we can see that we have here to do not with the fleeting human intelligence, but with the absolute and eternal. For in those three questions the whole subsequent history of mankind is, as it were, brought together into one whole, and foretold, and in them are united all the unsolved historical contradictions of human nature. At the time it could not be so clear, since the future was unknown; but now that fifteen hundred years have passed, we see that everything in those three questions was so justly divined and foretold, and has been so truly fulfilled, that nothing can be added to them or taken from them.

"Judge Thyself who was right--Thou or he who questioned Thee then? Remember the first question; its meaning, in other words, was this: "Thou wouldst go into the world, and art going with empty hands, with some promise of freedom which men in their simplicity and their natural unruliness cannot even understand, which they fear and dread--for nothing has ever been more insupportable for a man and a human society than freedom. But seest Thou these stones in this parched and barren wilderness? Turn them into bread, and mankind will run after Thee like a flock of sheep, grateful and obedient, though for ever trembling, lest Thou withdraw Thy hand and deny them Thy bread." But Thou wouldst not deprive man of freedom and didst reject the offer, thinking, what is that freedom worth if obedience is bought with bread? Thou didst reply that man lives not by bread alone. But dost Thou know that for the sake of that earthly bread the spirit of the earth will rise up against Thee and will strive with Thee and overcome Thee, and all will follow him, crying, "Who can compare with this beast? He has given us fire from heaven!" Dost Thou know that the ages will pass, and humanity will proclaim by the lips of their sages that there is no crime, and therefore no sin; there is only hunger? "Feed men, and then ask of them virtue!" that's what they'll write on the banner, which they will raise against Thee, and with which they will destroy Thy temple. Where Thy temple stood will rise a new building; the terrible tower of Babel will be built again, and though, like the one of old, it will not be finished, yet Thou mightest have prevented that new tower and have cut short the sufferings of men for a thousand years; for they will come back to us after a thousand years of agony with their tower. They will seek us again, hidden underground in the catacombs, for we shall be again persecuted and tortured. They will find us and cry to us, "Feed us, for those who have promised us fire from heaven haven't given it!" And then we shall finish building their tower, for he finishes the building who feeds them. And we alone shall feed them in Thy name, declaring falsely that it is in Thy name. Oh, never, never can they feed themselves without us! No science will give them bread so long as they remain free. In the end they will lay their freedom at our feet, and say to us, "Make us your slaves, but feed us." They will understand themselves, at last, that freedom and bread enough for all are inconceivable together, for never, never will they be able to share between them! They will be convinced, too, that they can never be free, for they are weak, vicious, worthless, and rebellious. Thou didst promise them the bread of Heaven, but, I repeat again, can it compare with earthly bread in the eyes of the weak, ever sinful and ignoble race of man? And if for the sake of the bread of Heaven thousands shall follow Thee, what is to become of the millions and tens of thousands of millions of creatures who will not have the strength to forego the earthly bread for the sake of the heavenly? Or dost Thou care only for the tens of thousands of the great and strong, while the millions, numerous as the sands of the sea, who are weak but love Thee, must exist only for the sake of the great and strong? No, we care for the weak too. They are sinful and rebellious, but in the end they too will become obedient. They will marvel at us and look on us as gods, because we are ready to endure the freedom which they have found so dreadful and to rule over them--so awful it will seem to them to be free. But we shall tell them that we are Thy servants and rule them in Thy name. We shall deceive them again, for we will not let Thee come to us again. That deception will be our suffering, for we shall be forced to lie.

"'This is the significance of the first question in the wilderness, and this is what Thou hast rejected for the sake of that freedom which Thou hast exalted above everything. Yet in this question lies hid the great secret of this world. Choosing "bread," Thou wouldst have satisfied the universal and everlasting craving of humanity--to find someone to worship. So long as man remains free he strives for nothing so incessantly and so painfully as to find someone to worship. But man seeks to worship what is established beyond dispute, so that all men would agree at once to worship it. For these pitiful creatures are concerned not only to find what one or the other can worship, but to find community of worship is the chief misery of every man individually and of all humanity from the beginning of time. For the sake of common worship they've slain each other with the sword. They have set up gods and challenged one another, "Put away your gods and come and worship ours, or we will kill you and your gods!" And so it will be to the end of the world, even when gods disappear from the earth; they will fall down before idols just the same. Thou didst know, Thou couldst not but have known, this fundamental secret of human nature, but Thou didst reject the one infallible banner which was offered Thee to make all men bow down to Thee alone--the banner of earthly bread; and Thou hast rejected it for the sake of freedom and the bread of Heaven. Behold what Thou didst further. And all again in the name of freedom! I tell Thee that man is tormented by no greater anxiety than to find someone quickly to whom he can hand over that gift of freedom with which the ill-fated creature is born. But only one who can appease their conscience can take over their freedom. In bread there was offered Thee an invincible banner; give bread, and man will worship thee, for nothing is more certain than bread. But if someone else gains possession of his conscience--Oh! then he will cast away Thy bread and follow after him who has ensnared his conscience. In that Thou wast right. For the secret of man's being is not only to live but to have something to live for. Without a stable conception of the object of life, man would not consent to go on living, and would rather destroy himself than remain on earth, though he had bread in abundance. That is true. But what happened? Instead of taking men's freedom from them, Thou didst make it greater than ever! Didst Thou forget that man prefers peace, and even death, to freedom of choice in the knowledge of good and evil? Nothing is more seductive for man than his freedom of conscience, but nothing is a greater cause of suffering. And behold, instead of giving a firm foundation for setting the conscience of man at rest for ever, Thou didst choose all that is exceptional, vague and enigmatic; Thou didst choose what was utterly beyond the strength of men, acting as though Thou didst not love them at all--Thou who didst come to give Thy life for them! Instead of taking possession of men's freedom, Thou didst increase it, and burdened the spiritual kingdom of mankind with its sufferings for ever. Thou didst desire man's free love, that he should follow Thee freely, enticed and taken captive by Thee. In place of the rigid ancient law, man must hereafter with free heart decide for himself what is good and what is evil, having only Thy image before him as his guide. But didst Thou not know that he would at last reject even Thy image and Thy truth, if he is weighed down with the fearful burden of free choice? They will cry aloud at last that the truth is not in Thee, for they could not have been left in greater confusion and suffering than Thou hast caused, laying upon them so many cares and unanswerable problems.

"'So that, in truth, Thou didst Thyself lay the foundation for the destruction of Thy kingdom, and no one is more to blame for it. Yet what was offered Thee? There are three powers, three powers alone, able to conquer and to hold captive for ever the conscience of these impotent rebels for their happiness those forces are miracle, mystery and authority. Thou hast rejected all three and hast set the example for doing so. When the wise and dread spirit set Thee on the pinnacle of the temple and said to Thee, "If Thou wouldst know whether Thou art the Son of God then cast Thyself down, for it is written: the angels shall hold him up lest he fall and bruise himself, and Thou shalt know then whether Thou art the Son of God and shalt prove then how great is Thy faith in Thy Father." But Thou didst refuse and wouldst not cast Thyself down. Oh, of course, Thou didst proudly and well, like God; but the weak, unruly race of men, are they gods? Oh, Thou didst know then that in taking one step, in making one movement to cast Thyself down, Thou wouldst be tempting God and have lost all Thy faith in Him, and wouldst have been dashed to pieces against that earth which Thou didst come to save. And the wise spirit that tempted Thee would have rejoiced. But I ask again, are there many like Thee? And couldst Thou believe for one moment that men, too, could face such a temptation? Is the nature of men such, that they can reject miracle, and at the great moments of their life, the moments of their deepest, most agonising spiritual difficulties, cling only to the free verdict of the heart? Oh, Thou didst know that Thy deed would be recorded in books, would be handed down to remote times and the utmost ends of the earth, and Thou didst hope that man, following Thee, would cling to God and not ask for a miracle. But Thou didst not know that when man rejects miracle he rejects God too; for man seeks not so much God as the miraculous. And as man cannot bear to be without the miraculous, he will create new miracles of his own for himself, and will worship deeds of sorcery and witchcraft, though he might be a hundred times over a rebel, heretic and infidel. Thou didst not come down from the Cross when they shouted to Thee, mocking and reviling Thee, "Come down from the cross and we will believe that Thou art He." Thou didst not come down, for again Thou wouldst not enslave man by a miracle, and didst crave faith given freely, not based on miracle. Thou didst crave for free love and not the base raptures of the slave before the might that has overawed him for ever. But Thou didst think too highly of men therein, for they are slaves, of course, though rebellious by nature. Look round and judge; fifteen centuries have passed, look upon them. Whom hast Thou raised up to Thyself? I swear, man is weaker and baser by nature than Thou hast believed him! Can he, can he do what Thou didst? By showing him so much respect, Thou didst, as it were, cease to feel for him, for Thou didst ask far too much from him--Thou who hast loved him more than Thyself! Respecting him less, Thou wouldst have asked less of him. That would have been more like love, for his burden would have been lighter. He is weak and vile. What though he is everywhere now rebelling against our power, and proud of his rebellion? It is the pride of a child and a schoolboy. They are little children rioting and barring out the teacher at school. But their childish delight will end; it will cost them dear. Mankind as a whole has always striven to organise a universal state. There have been many great nations with great histories, but the more highly they were developed the more unhappy they were, for they felt more acutely than other people the craving for world-wide union. The great conquerors, Timours and Ghenghis-Khans, whirled like hurricanes over the face of the earth striving to subdue its people, and they too were but the unconscious expression of the same craving for universal unity. Hadst Thou taken the world and Caesar's purple, Thou wouldst have founded the universal state and have given universal peace. For who can rule men if not he who holds their conscience and their bread in his hands? We have taken the sword of Caesar, and in taking it, of course, have rejected Thee and followed him. Oh, ages are yet to come of the confusion of free thought, of their science and cannibalism. For having begun to build their tower of Babel without us, they will end, of course, with cannibalism. But then the beast will crawl to us and lick our feet and spatter them with tears of blood. And we shall sit upon the beast and raise the cup, and on it will be written, "Mystery." But then, and only then, the reign of peace and happiness will come for men. Thou art proud of Thine elect, but Thou hast only the elect, while we give rest to all. And besides, how many of those elect, those mighty ones who could become elect, have grown weary waiting for Thee, and have transferred and will transfer the powers of their spirit and the warmth of their heart to the other camp, and end by raising their free banner against Thee. Thou didst Thyself lift up that banner. But with us all will be happy and will no more rebel nor destroy one another as under Thy freedom. Oh, we shall persuade them that they will only become free when they renounce their freedom to us and submit to us. And shall we be right or shall we be lying? They will be convinced that we are right, for they will remember the horrors of slavery and confusion to which Thy freedom brought them. Freedom, free thought, and science will lead them into such straits and will bring them face to face with such marvels and insoluble mysteries, that some of them, the fierce and rebellious, will destroy themselves, others, rebellious but weak, will destroy one another, while the rest, weak and unhappy, will crawl fawning to our feet and whine to us: "Yes, you were right, you alone possess His mystery, and we come back to you, save us from ourselves!"

"'Receiving bread from us, they will see clearly that we take the bread made by their hands from them, to give it to them, without any miracle. They will see that we do not change the stones to bread, but in truth they will be more thankful for taking it from our hands than for the bread itself! For they will remember only too well that in old days, without our help, even the bread they made turned to stones in their hands, while since they have come back to us, the very stones have turned to bread in their hands. Too, too well will they know the value of complete submission! And until men know that, they will be unhappy. Who is most to blame for their not knowing it?-speak! Who scattered the flock and sent it astray on unknown paths? But the flock will come together again and will submit once more, and then it will be once for all. Then we shall give them the quiet humble happiness of weak creatures such as they are by nature. Oh, we shall persuade them at last not to be proud, for Thou didst lift them up and thereby taught them to be proud. We shall show them that they are weak, that they are only pitiful children, but that childlike happiness is the sweetest of all. They will become timid and will look to us and huddle close to us in fear, as chicks to the hen. They will marvel at us and will be awe-stricken before us, and will be proud at our being so powerful and clever that we have been able to subdue such a turbulent flock of thousands of millions. They will tremble impotently before our wrath, their minds will grow fearful, they will be quick to shed tears like women and children, but they will be just as ready at a sign from us to pass to laughter and rejoicing, to happy mirth and childish song. Yes, we shall set them to work, but in their leisure hours we shall make their life like a child's game, with children's songs and innocent dance. Oh, we shall allow them even sin, they are weak and helpless, and they will love us like children because we allow them to sin. We shall tell them that every sin will be expiated, if it is done with our permission, that we allow them to sin because we love them, and the punishment for these sins we take upon ourselves. And we shall take it upon ourselves, and they will adore us as their saviours who have taken on themselves their sins before God. And they will have no secrets from us. We shall allow or forbid them to live with their wives and mistresses, to have or not to have children according to whether they have been obedient or disobedient--and they will submit to us gladly and cheerfully. The most painful secrets of their conscience, all, all they will bring to us, and we shall have an answer for all. And they will be glad to believe our answer, for it will save them from the great anxiety and terrible agony they endure at present in making a free decision for themselves. And all will be happy, all the millions of creatures except the hundred thousand who rule over them. For only we, we who guard the mystery, shall be unhappy. There will be thousands of millions of happy babes, and a hundred thousand sufferers who have taken upon themselves the curse of the knowledge of good and evil. Peacefully they will die, peacefully they will expire in Thy name, and beyond the grave they will find nothing but death. But we shall keep the secret, and for their happiness we shall allure them with the reward of heaven and eternity. Though if there were anything in the other world, it certainly would not be for such as they. It is prophesied that Thou wilt come again in victory, Thou wilt come with Thy chosen, the proud and strong, but we will say that they have only saved themselves, but we have saved all. We are told that the harlot who sits upon the beast, and holds in her hands the mystery, shall be put to shame, that the weak will rise up again, and will rend her royal purple and will strip naked her loathsome body. But then I will stand up and point out to Thee the thousand millions of happy children who have known no sin. And we who have taken their sins upon us for their happiness will stand up before Thee and say: "Judge us if Thou canst and darest." Know that I fear Thee not. Know that I too have been in the wilderness, I too have lived on roots and locusts, I too prized the freedom with which Thou hast blessed men, and I too was striving to stand among Thy elect, among the strong and powerful, thirsting "to make up the number." But I awakened and would not serve madness. I turned back and joined the ranks of those who have corrected Thy work. I left the proud and went back to the humble, for the happiness of the humble. What I say to Thee will come to pass, and our dominion will be built up. I repeat, to-morrow Thou shalt see that obedient flock who at a sign from me will hasten to heap up the hot cinders about the pile on which I shall burn Thee for coming to hinder us. For if anyone has ever deserved our fires, it is Thou. To-morrow I shall burn Thee. Dixi.'"*

* I have spoken.

Ivan stopped. He was carried away as he talked, and spoke with excitement; when he had finished, he suddenly smiled.

Alyosha had listened in silence; towards the end he was greatly moved and seemed several times on the point of interrupting, but restrained himself. Now his words came with a rush.

"But...that's absurd!" he cried, flushing. "Your poem is in praise of Jesus, not in blame of Him--as you meant it to be. And who will believe you about freedom? Is that the way to understand it? That's not the idea of it in the Orthodox Church...That's Rome, and not even the whole of Rome, it's false-those are the worst of the Catholics the Inquisitors, the Jesuits!...And there could not be such a fantastic creature as your Inquisitor. What are these sins of mankind they take on themselves? Who are these keepers of the mystery who have taken some curse upon themselves for the happiness of mankind? When have they been seen? We know the Jesuits, they are spoken ill of, but surely they are not what you describe? They are not that at all, not at all...They are simply the Romish army for the earthly sovereignty of the world in the future, with the Pontiff of Rome for Emperor...that's their ideal, but there's no sort of mystery or lofty melancholy about it...It's simple lust of power, of filthy earthly gain, of domination-something like a universal serfdom with them as masters-that's all they stand for. They don't even believe in God perhaps. Your suffering Inquisitor is a mere fantasy."

"Stay, stay," laughed Ivan. "how hot you are! A fantasy you say, let it be so! Of course it's a fantasy. But allow me to say: do you really think that the Roman Catholic movement of the last centuries is actually nothing but the lust of power, of filthy earthly gain? Is that Father Paissy's teaching?"

"No, no, on the contrary, Father Paissy did once say something rather the same as you...but of course it's not the same, not a bit the same," Alyosha hastily corrected himself.

"A precious admission, in spite of your 'not a bit the same.' I ask you why your Jesuits and Inquisitors have united simply for vile material gain? Why can there not be among them one martyr oppressed by great sorrow and loving humanity? You see, only suppose that there was one such man among all those who desire nothing but filthy material gain-if there's only one like my old Inquisitor, who had himself eaten roots in the desert and made frenzied efforts to subdue his flesh to make himself free and perfect. But yet all his life he loved humanity, and suddenly his eyes were opened, and he saw that it is no great moral blessedness to attain perfection and freedom, if at the same time one gains the conviction that millions of God's creatures have been created as a mockery, that they will never be capable of using their freedom, that these poor rebels can never turn into giants to complete the tower, that it was not for such geese that the great idealist dreamt his dream of harmony. Seeing all that he turned back and joined--the clever people. Surely that could have happened?"

"Joined whom, what clever people?" cried Alyosha, completely carried away. "They have no such great cleverness and no mysteries and secrets...Perhaps nothing but Atheism, that's all their secret. Your Inquisitor does not believe in God, that's his secret!"

"What if it is so! At last you have guessed it. It's perfectly true, it's true that that's the whole secret, but isn't that suffering, at least for a man like that, who has wasted his whole life in the desert and yet could not shake off his incurable love of humanity? In his old age he reached the clear conviction that nothing but the advice of the great dread spirit could build up any tolerable sort of life for the feeble, unruly, 'incomplete, empirical creatures created in jest.' And so, convinced of this, he sees that he must follow the counsel of the wise spirit, the dread spirit of death and destruction, and therefore accept lying and deception, and lead men consciously to death and destruction, and yet deceive them all the way so that they may not notice where they are being led, that the poor blind creatures may at least on the way think themselves happy. And note, the deception is in the name of Him in Whose ideal the old man had so fervently believed all his life long. Is not that tragic? And if only one such stood at the head of the whole army 'filled with the lust of power only for the sake of filthy gain'--would not one such be enough to make a tragedy? More than that, one such standing at the head is enough to create the actual leading idea of the Roman Church with all its armies and Jesuits, its highest idea. I tell you frankly that I firmly believe that there has always been such a man among those who stood at the head of the movement. Who knows, there may have been some such even among the Roman Popes. Who knows, perhaps the spirit of that accursed old man who loves mankind so obstinately in his own way, is to be found even now in a whole multitude of such old men, existing not by chance but by agreement, as a secret league formed long ago for the guarding of the mystery, to guard it from the weak and the unhappy, so as to make them happy. No doubt it is so, and so it must be indeed. I fancy that even among the Masons there's something of the same mystery at the bottom, and that that's why the Catholics so detest the Masons as their rivals breaking up the unity of the idea, while it is so essential that there should be one flock and one shepherd...But from the way I defend my idea I might be an author impatient of your criticism. Enough of it."

"You are perhaps a Mason yourself!" broke suddenly from Alyosha. "You don't believe in God," he added, speaking this time very sorrowfully. He fancied besides that his brother was looking at him ironically. "How does your poem end?" he asked, suddenly looking down. "Or was it the end?"

"I meant to end it like this. When the Inquisitor ceased speaking he waited some time for his Prisoner to answer him. His silence weighed down upon him. He saw that the Prisoner had listened intently all the time, looking gently in his face and evidently not wishing to reply. The old man longed for him to say something, however bitter and terrible. But He suddenly approached the old man in silence and softly kissed him on his bloodless aged lips. That was all his answer. The old man shuddered. His lips moved. He went to the door, opened it, and said to Him: 'Go, and come no more...come not at all, never, never!' And he let Him out into the dark alleys of the town. The Prisoner went away."

"And the old man?"

"The kiss glows in his heart, but the old man adheres to his idea."

"And you with him, you too?" cried Alyosha, mournfully.

Ivan laughed.

"Why, it's all nonsense, Alyosha. It's only a senseless poem of a senseless student, who could never write two lines of verse. Why do you take it so seriously? Surely you don't suppose I am going straight off to the Jesuits, to join the men who are correcting His work? Good Lord, it's no business of mine. I told you, all I want is to live on to thirty, and then...dash the cup to the ground!"

"But the little sticky leaves, and the precious tombs, and the blue sky, and the woman you love! How will you live, how will you love them?" Alyosha cried sorrowfully. "With such a hell in your heart and your head, how can you? No, that's just what you are going away for, to join them...if not, you will kill yourself, you can't endure it!"

"There is a strength to endure everything," Ivan said with a cold smile.

"The strength of the Karamazovs--the strength of the Karamazov baseness."

"To sink into debauchery, to stifle your soul with corruption, yes?"

"Possibly even that...only perhaps till I am thirty I shall escape it, and then-"

"How will you escape it? By what will you escape it? That's impossible with your ideas."

"In the Karamazov way, again."

"'Everything is lawful,' you mean? Everything is lawful, is that it?"

Ivan scowled, and all at once turned strangely pale.

"Ah, you've caught up yesterday's phrase, which so offended Muisov--and which Dmitri pounced upon so naively and paraphrased!" he smiled queerly. "Yes, if you like, 'everything is lawful' since the word has been said, I won't deny it. And Mitya's version isn't bad."

Alyosha looked at him in silence.

"I thought that going away from here I have you at least," Ivan said suddenly, with unexpected feeling; "but now I see that there is no place for me even in your heart, my dear hermit. The formula, 'all is lawful,' I won't renounce--will you renounce me for that, yes?"

Alyosha got up, went to him and softly kissed him on the lips.

"That's plagiarism," cried Ivan, highly delighted. "You stole that from my poem. Thank you though. Get up, Alyosha, it's time we were going, both of us."

They went out, but stopped when they reached the entrance of the restaurant.

"Listen, Alyosha," Ivan began in a resolute voice, "if I am really able to care for the sticky little leaves I shall only love them, remembering you. It's enough for me that you are somewhere here, and I shan't lose my desire for life yet. Is that enough for you? Take it as a declaration of love if you like. And now you go to the right and I to the left. And it's enough, do you hear, enough. I mean even if I don't go away to-morrow (I think I certainly shall go) and we meet again, don't say a word more on these subjects. I beg that particularly. And about Dmitri too, I ask you specially, never speak to me again," he added, with sudden irritation; "it's all exhausted, it has all been said over and over again, hasn't it? And I'll make you one promise in return for it. When at thirty, I want to 'dash the cup to the ground,' wherever I may be I'll come to have one more talk with you, even though it were from America, you may be sure of that. I'll come on purpose. It will be very interesting to have a look at you, to see what you'll be by that time. It's rather a solemn promise, you see. And we really may be parting for seven years or ten. Come, go now to your Pater Seraphicus, he is dying. If he dies without you, you will be angry with me for having kept you. Good-bye, kiss me once more; that's right, now go."

Ivan turned suddenly and went his way without looking back. It was just as Dmitri had left Alyosha the day before, though the parting had been very different. The strange resemblance flashed like an arrow through Alyosha's mind in the distress and dejection of that moment. He waited a little, looking after his brother. He suddenly noticed that Ivan swayed as he walked and that his right shoulder looked lower than his left. He had never noticed it before. But all at once he turned too, and almost ran to the monastery. It was nearly dark, and he felt almost frightened; something new was growing up in him for which he could not account. The wind had risen again as on the previous evening, and the ancient pines murmured gloomily about him when he entered the hermitage copse. He almost ran. "Pater Seraphicus--he got that name from somewhere--where from?" Alyosha wondered. "Ivan, poor Ivan, and when shall I see you again?...Here is the hermitage. Yes, yes, that he is, Pater Seraphicus, he will save me--from him and for ever!"

Several times afterwards he wondered how he could, on leaving Ivan, so completely forget his brother Dmitri, though he had that morning, only a few hours before, so firmly resolved to find him and not to give up doing so, even should he be unable to return to the monastery that night.

Chapter 6. For Awhile a Very Obscure One

AND Ivan, on parting from Alyosha, went home to Fyodor Pavlovitch's house. But, strange to say, he was overcome by insufferable depression, which grew greater at every step he took towards the house. There was nothing strange in his being depressed; what was strange was that Ivan could not have said what was the cause of it. He had often been depressed before, and there was nothing surprising at his feeling so at such a moment, when he had broken off with everything had brought him here, and was preparing that day to make a new start and enter upon a new, unknown future. He would again be as solitary as ever, and though he had great hopes, and great--too great--expectations from life, he could not have given any definite account of his hopes, his expectations, or even his desires.

Yet at that moment, though the apprehension of the new and unknown certainly found place in his heart, what was worrying him was something quite different. "Is it loathing for my father's house?" he wondered. "Quite likely; I am so sick of it; and though it's the last time I shall cross its hateful threshold, still I loathe it...No, it's not that either. Is it the parting with Alyosha and the conversation I had with him? For so many years I've been silent with the whole world and not deigned to speak, and all of a sudden I reel off a rigmarole like that." certainly might have been the youthful vexation of youthful inexperience and vanity--vexation at having failed to express himself, especially with such a being as Alyosha, on whom his heart had certainly been reckoning. No doubt that came in, that vexation, it must have done indeed; but yet that was not it, that was not it either. "I feel sick with depression and yet I can't tell what I want. Better not think, perhaps."

Ivan tried "not to think," but that, too, was no use. What made his depression so vexatious and irritating was that it had a kind of casual, external character--he felt that. Some person or thing seemed to be standing out somewhere, just as something will sometimes obtrude itself upon the eye, and though one may be so busy with work or conversation that for a long time one does not notice it, yet it irritates and almost torments one till at last one realises, and removes the offending object, often quite a trifling and ridiculous one--some article left about in the wrong place, a handkerchief on the floor, a book not replaced on the shelf, and so on.

At last, feeling very cross and ill-humoured, Ivan arrived home, and suddenly, about fifteen paces from the garden gate, he guessed what was fretting and worrying him.

On a bench in the gateway the valet Smerdyakov was sitting enjoying the coolness of the evening, and at the first glance at him Ivan knew that the valet Smerdyakov was on his mind, and that it was this man that his soul loathed. It all dawned upon him suddenly and became clear. just before, when Alyosha had been telling him of his meeting with Smerdyakov, he had felt a sudden twinge of gloom and loathing, which had immediately stirred responsive anger in his heart. Afterwards, as he talked, Smerdyakov had been forgotten for the time; but still he had been in his mind, and as soon as Ivan parted with Alyosha and was walking home, the forgotten sensation began to obtrude itself again. "Is it possible that a miserable, contemptible creature like that can worry me so much?" he wondered, with insufferable irritation.

It was true that Ivan had come of late to feel an intense dislike for the man, especially during the last few days. He had even begun to notice in himself a growing feeling that was almost of hatred for the creature. Perhaps this hatred was accentuated by the fact that when Ivan first came to the neighbourhood he had felt quite differently. Then he had taken a marked interest in Smerdyakov, and had even thought him very original. He had encouraged him to talk to him, although he had always wondered at a certain incoherence, or rather restlessness, in his mind, and could not understand what it was that so continually and insistently worked upon the brain of "the contemplative." They discussed philosophical questions and even how there could have been light on the first day when the sun, moon, and stars were only created on the fourth day, and how that was to be understood. But Ivan soon saw that, though the sun, moon, and stars might be an interesting subject, yet that it was quite secondary to Smerdyakov, and that he was looking for something altogether different. In one way and another, he began to betray a boundless vanity, and a wounded vanity, too, and that Ivan disliked. It had first given rise to his aversion. Later on, there had been trouble in the house. Grushenka had come on the scene, and there had been the scandals with his brother Dmitri--they discussed that, too. But though Smerdyakov always talked of that with great excitement, it was impossible to discover what he desired to come of it. There was, in fact, something surprising in the illogicality and incoherence of some of his desires, accidentally betrayed and always vaguely expressed. Smerdyakov was always inquiring, putting certain indirect but obviously premeditated questions, but what his object was he did not explain, and usually at the most important moment he would break off and relapse into silence or pass to another subject. But what finally irritated Ivan most and confirmed his dislike for him was the peculiar, revolting familiarity which Smerdyakov began to show more and more markedly. Not that he forgot himself and was rude; on the contrary, he always spoke very respectfully, yet he had obviously begun to consider--goodness knows why!--that there was some sort of understanding between him and Ivan Fyodorovitch. He always spoke in a tone that suggested that those two had some kind of compact, some secret between them, that had at some time been expressed on both sides, only known to them and beyond the comprehension of those around them. But for a long while Ivan did not recognise the real cause of his growing dislike and he had only lately realised what was at the root of it.

With a feeling of disgust and irritation he tried to pass in at the gate without speaking or looking at Smerdyakov. But Smerdyakov rose from the bench, and from that action alone, Ivan knew instantly that he wanted particularly to talk to him. Ivan looked at him and stopped, and the fact that he did stop, instead of passing by, as he meant to the minute before, drove him to fury. With anger and repulsion he looked at Smerdyakov's emasculate, sickly face, with the little curls combed forward on his forehead. His left eye winked and he grinned as if to say, "Where are you going? You won't pass by; you see that we two clever people have something to say to each other."

Ivan shook. "Get away, miserable idiot. What have I to do with you?" was on the tip of his tongue, but to his profound astonishment he heard himself say, "Is my father still asleep, or has he waked?"

He asked the question softly and meekly, to his own surprise, and at once, again to his own surprise, sat down on the bench. For an instant he felt almost frightened; he remembered it afterwards. Smerdyakov stood facing him, his hands behind his back, looking at him with assurance and almost severity.

"His honour is still asleep," he articulated deliberately ("You were the first to speak, not I," he seemed to say). "I am surprised at you, sir," he added, after a pause, dropping his eyes affectedly, setting his right foot forward, and playing with the tip of his polished boot.

"Why are you surprised at me?" Ivan asked abruptly and sullenly, doing his utmost to restrain himself, and suddenly realising, with disgust, that he was feeling intense curiosity and would not, on any account, have gone away without satisfying it.

"Why don't you go to Tchermashnya, sir?" Smerdyakov suddenly raised his eyes and smiled familiarly. "Why I smile you must understand of yourself, if you are a clever man," his screwed-up left eye seemed to say.

"Why should I go to Tchermashnya?" Ivan asked in surprise.

Smerdyakov was silent again.

"Fyodor Pavlovitch himself has so begged you to," he said at last, slowly and apparently attaching no significance to his answer. "I put you off with a secondary reason," he seemed to suggest, "simply to say something."

"Damn you! Speak out what you want!" Ivan cried angrily at last, passing from meekness to violence.

Smerdyakov drew his right foot up to his left, pulled himself up, but still looked at him with the same serenity and the same little smile.

"Substantially nothing--but just by way of conversation."

Another silence followed. They did not speak for nearly a minute. Ivan knew that he ought to get up and show anger, and Smerdyakov stood before him and seemed to be waiting as though to see whether he would be angry or not. So at least it seemed to Ivan. At last he moved to get up. Smerdyakov seemed to seize the moment.

"I'm in an awful position, Ivan Fyodorovitch. I don't know how to help myself," he said resolutely and distinctly, and at his last word he sighed. Ivan Fyodorovitch sat down again.

"They are both utterly crazy, they are no better than little children," Smerdyakov went on. "I am speaking of your parent and your brother Dmitri Fyodorovitch. Here Fyodor Pavlovitch will get up directly and begin worrying me every minute, 'Has she come? Why hasn't she come?' and so on up till midnight and even after midnight. And if Agrafena Alexandrovna doesn't come (for very likely she does not mean to come at all) then he will be at me again to-morrow morning, 'Why hasn't she come? When will she come?'--as though I were to blame for it. On the other side it's no better. As soon as it gets dark, or even before, your brother will appear with his gun in his hands: 'Look out, you rogue, you soup-maker. If you miss her and don't let me know she's been--I'll kill you before anyone.' When the night's over, in the morning, he, too, like Fyodor Pavlovitch, begins worrying me to death. 'Why hasn't she come? Will she come soon?' And he, too, thinks me to blame because his lady hasn't come. And every day and every hour they get angrier and angrier, so that I sometimes think I shall kill myself in a fright. I can't depend them, sir."

"And why have you meddled? Why did you begin to spy for Dmitri Fyodorovitch?" said Ivan irritably.

"How could I help meddling? Though, indeed, I haven't meddled at all, if you want to know the truth of the matter. I kept quiet from the very beginning, not daring to answer; but he pitched on me to be his servant. He has had only one thing to say since: 'I'll kill you, you scoundrel, if you miss her.' I feel certain, sir, that I shall have a long fit to-morrow."

"What do you mean by 'a long fit'?"

"A long fit, lasting a long time--several hours, or perhaps a day or two. Once it went on for three days. I fell from the garret that time. The struggling ceased and then began again, and for three days I couldn't come back to my senses. Fyodor Pavlovitch sent for Herzenstube, the doctor here, and he put ice on my head and tried another remedy, too...I might have died."

"But they say one can't tell with epilepsy when a fit is coming. What makes you say you will have one to-morrow?" Ivan inquired, with a peculiar, irritable curiosity.

"That's just so. You can't tell beforehand."

"Besides, you fell from the garret then."

"I climb up to the garret every day. I might fall from the garret again to-morrow. And, if not, I might fall down the cellar steps. I have to go into the cellar every day, too."

Ivan took a long look at him.

"You are talking nonsense, I see, and I don't quite understand you," he said softly, but with a sort of menace. "Do you mean to pretend to be ill to-morrow for three days, eh?"

Smerdyakov, who was looking at the ground again, and playing with the toe of his right foot, set the foot down, moved the left one forward, and, grinning, articulated:

"If I were able to play such a trick, that is, pretend to have a fit--and it would not be difficult for a man accustomed to them--I should have a perfect right to use such a means to save myself from death. For even if Agrafena Alexandrovna comes to see his father while I am ill, his honour can't blame a sick man for not telling him. He'd be ashamed to."

"Hang it all!" Ivan cried, his face working with anger, "Why are you always in such a funk for your life? All my brother Dmitri's threats are only hasty words and mean nothing. He won't kill you; it's not you he'll kill!"

"He'd kill me first of all, like a fly. But even more than that, I am afraid I shall be taken for an accomplice of his when he does something crazy to his father."

"Why should you be taken for an accomplice?"

"They'll think I am an accomplice, because I let him know the signals as a great secret."

"What signals? Whom did you tell? Confound you, speak more plainly."

"I'm bound to admit the fact," Smerdyakov drawled with pedantic composure, "that I have a secret with Fyodor Pavlovitch in this business. As you know yourself (if only you do know it) he has for several days past locked himself in as soon as night or even evening comes on. Of late you've been going upstairs to your room early every evening, and yesterday you did not come down at all, and so perhaps you don't know how carefully he has begun to lock himself in at night, and even if Grigory Vassilyevitch comes to the door he won't open to him till he hears his voice. But Grigory Vassilyevitch does not come, because I wait upon him alone in his room now. That's the arrangement he made himself ever since this to-do with Agrafena Alexandrovna began. But at night, by his orders, I go away to the lodge so that I don't get to sleep till midnight, but am on the watch, getting up and walking about the yard, waiting for Agrafena Alexandrovna to come. For the last few days he's been perfectly frantic expecting her. What he argues is, she is afraid of him, Dmitri Fyodorovitch (Mitya, as he calls him), 'and so,' says he, 'she'll come the back-way, late at night, to me. You look out for her,' says he, 'till midnight and later; and if she does come, you run up and knock at my door or at the window from the garden. Knock at first twice, rather gently, and then three times more quickly, then,' says he, 'I shall understand at once that she has come, and will open the door to you quietly.' Another signal he gave me in case anything unexpected happens. At first, two knocks, and then, after an interval, another much louder. Then he will understand that something has happened suddenly and that I must see him, and he will open to me so that I can go and speak to him. That's all in case Agrafena Alexandrovna can't come herself, but sends a message. Besides, Dmitri Fyodorovitch might come, too, so I must let him know he is near. His honour is awfully afraid of Dmitri Fyodorovitch, so that even if Agrafena Alexandrovna had come and were locked in with him, and Dmitri Fyodorovitch were to turn up anywhere near at the time, I should be bound to let him know at once, knocking three times. So that the first signal of five knocks means Agrafena Alexandrovna has come, while the second signal of three knocks means 'something important to tell you.' His honour has shown me them several times and explained them. And as in the whole universe no one knows of these signals but myself and his honour, so he'd open the door without the slightest hesitation and without calling out (he is awfully afraid of calling out aloud). Well, those signals are known to Dmitri Fyodorovitch too, now."

"How are they known? Did you tell him? How dared you tell him?"

"It was through fright I did it. How could I dare to keep it back from him? Dmitri Fyodorovitch kept persisting every day, 'You are deceiving me, you are hiding something from me! I'll break both your legs for you.' So I told him those secret signals that he might see my slavish devotion, and might be satisfied that I was not deceiving him, but was telling him all I could."

"If you think that he'll make use of those signals and try to get in, don't let him in."

"But if I should be laid up with a fit, how can I prevent him coming in then, even if I dared prevent him, knowing how desperate he is?"

"Hang it! How can you be so sure you are going to have a fit, confound you? Are you laughing at me?"

"How could I dare laugh at you? I am in no laughing humour with this fear on me. I feel I am going to have a fit. I have a presentiment. Fright alone will bring it on."

"Confound it! If you are laid up, Grigory will be on the watch. Let Grigory know beforehand; he will be sure not to let him in."

"I should never dare to tell Grigory Vassilyevitch about the signals without orders from my master. And as for Grigory Vassilyevitch hearing him and not admitting him, he has been ill ever since yesterday, and Marfa Ignatyevna intends to give him medicine to-morrow. They've just arranged it. It's a very strange remedy of hers. Marfa Ignatyevna knows of a preparation and always keeps it. It's a strong thing made from some herb. She has the secret of it, and she always gives it to Grigory Vassilyevitch three times a year when his lumbago's so bad he is almost paralysed by it. Then she takes a towel, wets it with the stuff, and rubs his whole back for half an hour till it's quite red and swollen, and what's left in the bottle she gives him to drink with a special prayer; but not quite all, for on such occasions she leaves some for herself, and drinks it herself. And as they never take strong drink, I assure you they both drop asleep at once and sleep sound a very long time. And when Grigory Vassilyevitch wakes up he is perfectly well after it, but Marfa Ignatyevna always has a headache from it. So, if Marfa Ignatyevna carries out her intention to-morrow, they won't hear anything and hinder Dmitri Fyodorovitch. They'll be asleep."

"What a rigmarole! And it all seems to happen at once, as though it were planned. You'll have a fit and they'll both be unconscious," cried Ivan. "But aren't you trying to arrange it so?" broke from him suddenly, and he frowned threateningly.

"How could I?...And why should I, when it all depends on Dmitri Fyodorovitch and his plans?...If he means to do anything, he'll do it; but if not, I shan't be thrusting him upon his father."

"And why should he go to father, especially on the sly, if, as you say yourself, Agrafena Alexandrovna won't come at all?" Ivan went on, turning white with anger. "You say that yourself, and all the while I've been here, I've felt sure it was all the old man's fancy, and the creature won't come to him. Why should Dmitri break in on him if she doesn't come? Speak, I want to know what you are thinking!"

"You know yourself why he'll come. What's the use of what I think? His honour will come simply because he is in a rage or suspicious on account of my illness perhaps, and he'll dash in, as he did yesterday through impatience to search the rooms, to see whether she hasn't escaped him on the sly. He is perfectly well aware, too, that Fyodor Pavlovitch has a big envelope with three thousand roubles in it, tied up with ribbon and sealed with three seals. On it is written in his own hand 'To my angel Grushenka, if she will come,' to which he added three days later, 'for my little chicken.' There's no knowing what that might do."

"Nonsense!" cried Ivan, almost beside himself. "Dmitri won't come to steal money and kill my father to do it. He might have killed him yesterday on account of Grushenka, like the frantic, savage fool he is, but he won't steal."

"He is in very great need of money now--the greatest need, Ivan Fyodorovitch. You don't know in what need he is," Smerdyakov explained, with perfect composure and remarkable distinctness. "He looks on that three thousand as his own, too. He said so to me himself. 'My father still owes me just three thousand,' he said. And besides that, consider, Ivan Fyodorovitch, there is something else perfectly true. It's as good as certain, so to say, that Agrafena Alexandrovna will force him, if only she cares to, to marry her--the master himself, I mean, Fyodor Pavlovitch--if only she cares to, and of course she may care to. All I've said is that she won't come, but maybe she's looking for more than that--I mean to be mistress here. I know myself that Samsonov, her merchant, was laughing with her about it, telling her quite openly that it would not be at all a stupid thing to do. And she's got plenty of sense. She wouldn't marry a beggar like Dmitri Fyodorovitch. So, taking that into consideration, Ivan Fyodorovitch, reflect that then neither Dmitri Fyodorovitch nor yourself and your brother, Alexey Fyodorovitch, would have anything after the master's death, not a rouble, for Agrafena Alexandrovna would marry him simply to get hold of the whole, all the money there is. But if your father were to die now, there'd be some forty thousand for sure, even for Dmitri Fyodorovitch whom he hates so, for he's made no will...Dmitri Fyodorovitch knows all that very well."

A sort of shudder passed over Ivan's face. He suddenly flushed.

"Then why on earth," he suddenly interrupted Smerdyakov, "do you advise me to go to Tchermashnya? What did you mean by that? If I go away, you see what will happen here." Ivan drew his breath with difficulty.

"Precisely so," said Smerdyakov, softly and reasonably, watching Ivan intently, however.

"What do you mean by 'precisely so'?" Ivan questioned him, with a menacing light in his eyes, restraining himself with difficulty.

"I spoke because I felt sorry for you. If I were in your place I should simply throw it all up...rather than stay on in such a position," answered Smerdyakov, with the most candid air looking at Ivan's flashing eyes. They were both silent.

"You seem to be a perfect idiot, and what's more...an awful scoundrel, too." Ivan rose suddenly from the bench. He was about to pass straight through the gate, but he stopped short and turned to Smerdyakov. Something strange followed. Ivan, in a sudden paroxysm, bit his lip, clenched his fists, and, in another minute, would have flung himself on Smerdyakov. The latter, anyway, noticed it at the same moment, started, and shrank back. But the moment passed without mischief to Smerdyakov, and Ivan turned in silence, as it seemed in perplexity, to the gate.

"I am going away to Moscow to-morrow, if you care to know--early to-morrow morning. That's all!" he suddenly said aloud angrily, and wondered himself afterwards what need there was to say this then to Smerdyakov.

"That's the best thing you can do," he responded, as though he had expected to hear it; "except that you can always be telegraphed for from Moscow, if anything should happen here."

Ivan stopped again, and again turned quickly to Smerdyakov. But a change had passed over him, too. All his familiarity and carelessnes had completely disappeared. His face expressed attention and expectation, intent but timid and cringing.

"Haven't you something more to say--something to add?" could be read in the intent gaze he fixed on Ivan.

"And couldn't I be sent for from Tchermashnya, too--in case anything happened?" Ivan shouted suddenly, for some unknown reason raising his voice.

"From Tchermashnya, too...you could be sent for," Smerdyakov muttered, almost in a whisper, looking disconcerted, but gazing intently into Ivan's eyes.

"Only Moscow is farther and Tchermashnya is nearer. Is it to save my spending money on the fare, or to save my going so far out of my way, that you insist on Tchermashnya?"

"Precisely so..." muttered Smerdyakov, with a breaking voice. He looked at Ivan with a revolting smile, and again made ready to draw back. But to his astonishment Ivan broke into a laugh, and went through the gate still laughing. Anyone who had seen his face at that moment would have known that he was not laughing from lightness of heart, and he could not have explained himself what he was feeling at that instant. He moved and walked as though in a nervous frenzy.

Chapter 7. "It's Always Worth While Speaking to a Clever Man"

AND in the same nervous frenzy, too, he spoke. Meeting Fyodor Pavlovitch in the drawing-room directly he went in, he shouted to him, waving his hands, "I am going upstairs to my room, not in to you. Good-bye!" and passed by, trying not even to look at his father. Very possibly the old man was too hateful to him at that moment; but such an unceremonious display of hostility was a surprise even to Fyodor Pavlovitch. And the old man evidently wanted to tell him something at once and had come to meet him in the drawing-room on purpose. Receiving this amiable greeting, he stood still in silence and with an ironical air watched his son going upstairs, till he passed out of sight.

"What's the matter with him?" he promptly asked Smerdyakov, who had followed Ivan.

"Angry about something. Who can tell?" the valet muttered evasively.

"Confound him! Let him be angry then. Bring in the samovar, and get along with you. Look sharp! No news?"

Then followed a series of questions such as Smerdyakov had just complained of to Ivan, all relating to his expected visitor, and these questions we will omit. Half an hour later the house was locked, and the crazy old man was wandering along through the rooms in excited expectation of hearing every minute the five knocks agreed upon. Now and then he peered out into the darkness, seeing nothing.

It was very late, but Ivan was still awake and reflecting. He sat up late that night, till two o'clock. But we will not give an account of his thoughts, and this is not the place to look into that soul--its turn will come. And even if one tried, it would be very hard to give an account of them, for there were no thoughts in his brain, but something very vague, and, above all, intense excitement. He felt himself that he had lost his bearings. He was fretted, too, by all sorts of strange and almost surprising desires; for instance, after midnight he suddenly had an intense irresistible inclination to go down, open the door, go to the lodge and beat Smerdyakov. But if he had been asked why, he could not have given any exact reason, except perhaps that he loathed the valet as one who had insulted him more gravely than anyone in the world. On the other hand, he was more than once that night overcome by a sort of inexplicable humiliating terror, which he felt positively paralysed his physical powers. His head ached and he was giddy. A feeling of hatred was rankling in his heart, as though he meant to avenge himself on someone. He even hated Alyosha, recalling the conversation he had just had with him. At moments he hated himself intensely. Of Katerina Ivanovna he almost forgot to think, and wondered greatly at this afterwards, especially as he remembered perfectly that when he had protested so valiantly to Katerina Ivanovna that he would go away next day to Moscow, something had whispered in his heart, "That's nonsense, you are not going, and it won't be so easy to tear yourself away as you are boasting now."

Remembering that night long afterwards, Ivan recalled with peculiar repulsion how he had suddenly got up from the sofa and had stealthily, as though he were afraid of being watched, opened the door, gone out on the staircase and listened to Fyodor Pavlovitch stirring down below, had listened a long while--some five minutes--with a sort of strange curiosity, holding his breath while his heart throbbed. And why he had done all this, why he was listening, he could not have said. That "action" all his life afterwards he called "infamous," and at the bottom of his heart, he thought of it as the basest action of his life. For Fyodor Pavlovitch himself he felt no hatred at that moment, but was simply intensely curious to know how he was walking down there below and what he must be doing now. He wondered and imagined how he must be peeping out of the dark windows and stopping in the middle of the room, listening, listening--for someone to knock. Ivan went out on the stairs twice to listen like this.

About two o'clock when everything was quiet, and even Fyodor Pavlovitch had gone to bed, Ivan had got into bed, firmly resolved to fall asleep at once, as he felt fearfully exhausted. And he did fall asleep at once, and slept soundly without dreams, but waked early, at seven o'clock, when it was broad daylight. Opening his eyes, he was surprised to feel himself extraordinarily vigorous. He jumped up at once and dressed quickly; then dragged out his trunk and began packing immediately. His linen had come back from the laundress the previous morning. Ivan positively smiled at the thought that everything was helping his sudden departure. And his departure certainly was sudden. Though Ivan had said the day before (to Katerina Ivanovna, Alyosha, and Smerdyakov) that he was leaving next day, yet he remembered that he had no thought of departure when he went to bed, or, at least, had not dreamed that his first act in the morning would be to pack his trunk. At last his trunk and bag were ready. It was about nine o'clock when Marfa Ignatyevna came in with her usual inquiry, "Where will your honour take your tea, in your own room or downstairs?" He looked almost cheerful, but there was about him, about his words and gestures, something hurried and scattered. Greeting his father affably, and even inquiring specially after his health, though he did not wait to hear his answer to the end, he announced that he was starting off in an hour to return to Moscow for good, and begged him to send for the horses. His father heard this announcement with no sign of surprise, and forgot in an unmannerly way to show regret at losing him. Instead of doing so, he flew into a great flutter at the recollection of some important business of his own.

"What a fellow you are! Not to tell me yesterday! Never mind; we'll manage it all the same. Do me a great service, my dear boy. Go to Tchermashnya on the way. It's only to turn to the left from the station at Volovya, only another twelve versts and you come to Tchermashnya."

"I'm sorry, I can't. It's eighty versts to the railway and the train starts for Moscow at seven o'clock to-night. I can only just catch it."

"You'll catch it to-morrow or the day after, but to-day turn off to Tchermashnya. It won't put you out much to humour your father! If I hadn't had something to keep me here, I would have run over myself long ago, for I've some business there in a hurry. But here I...it's not the time for me to go now...You see, I've two pieces of copse land there. The Maslovs, an old merchant and his son, will give eight thousand for the timber. But last year I just missed a purchaser who would have given twelve. There's no getting anyone about here to buy it. The Maslovs have it all their own way. One has to take what they'll give, for no one here dare bid against them. The priest at Ilyinskoe wrote to me last Thursday that a merchant called Gorstkin, a man I know, had turned up. What makes him valuable is that he is not from these parts, so he is not afraid of the Maslovs. He says he will give me eleven thousand for the copse. Do you hear? But he'll only be here, the priest writes, for a week altogether, so you must go at once and make a bargain with him."

"Well, you write to the priest; he'll make the bargain."

"He can't do it. He has no eye for business. He is a perfect treasure, I'd give him twenty thousand to take care of for me without a receipt; but he has no eye for business, he is a perfect child, a crow could deceive him. And yet he is a learned man, would you believe it? This Gorstkin looks like a peasant, he wears a blue kaftan, but he is a regular rogue. That's the common complaint. He is a liar. Sometimes he tells such lies that you wonder why he is doing it. He told me the year before last that his wife was dead and that he had married another, and would you believe it, there was not a word of truth in it? His wife has never died at all, she is alive to this day and gives him a beating twice a week. So what you have to find out is whether he is lying or speaking the truth when he says he wants to buy it and would give eleven thousand."

"I shall be no use in such a business. I have no eye either."

"Stay, wait a bit! You will be of use, for I will tell you the signs by which you can judge about Gorstkin. I've done business with him a long time. You see, you must watch his beard; he has a nasty, thin, red beard. If his beard shakes when he talks and he gets cross, it's all right, he is saying what he means, he wants to do business. But if he strokes his beard with his left hand and grins--he is trying to cheat you. Don't watch his eyes, you won't find out anything from his eyes, he is a deep one, a rogue but watch his beard! I'll give you a note and you show it to him. He's called Gorstkin, though his real name is Lyagavy;* but don't call him so, he will be offended. If you come to an understanding with him, and see it's all right, write here at once. You need only write: 'He's not lying.' Stand out for eleven thousand; one thousand you can knock off, but not more. just think! there's a difference between eight thousand and eleven thousand. It's as good as picking up three thousand; it's not so easy to find a purchaser, and I'm in desperate need of money. Only let me know it's serious, and I'll run over and fix it up. I'll snatch the time somehow. But what's the good of my galloping over, if it's all a notion of the priest's? Come, will you go?"

* i.e. setter dog.

"Oh, I can't spare the time. You must excuse me."

"Come, you might oblige your father. I shan't forget it. You've no heart, any of you that's what it is! What's a day or two to you? Where are you going now--to Venice? Your Venice will keep another two days. I would have sent Alyosha, but what use is Alyosha in a thing like that? I send you just because you are a clever fellow. Do you suppose I don't see that? You know nothing about timber, but you've got an eye. All that is wanted is to see whether the man is in earnest. I tell you, watch his beard--if his beard shakes you know he is in earnest."

"You force me to go to that damned Tchermashnya yourself, then?" cried Ivan, with a malignant smile.

Fyodor Pavlovitch did not catch, or would not catch, the malignancy, but he caught the smile.

"Then you'll go, you'll go? I'll scribble the note for you at once."

"I don't know whether I shall go. I don't know. I'll decide on the way."

"Nonsense! Decide at once. My dear fellow, decide! If you settle the matter, write me a line; give it to the priest and he'll send it on to me at once. And I won't delay you more than that. You can go to Venice. The priest will give you horses back to Volovya station."

The old man was quite delighted. He wrote the note, and sent for the horses. A light lunch was brought in, with brandy. When Fyodor Pavlovitch was pleased, he usually became expansive, but to-day he seemed to restrain himself. Of Dmitri, for instance, he did not say a word. He was quite unmoved by the parting, and seemed, in fact, at a loss for something to say. Ivan noticed this particularly. "He must be bored with me," he thought. Only when accompanying his son out on to the steps, the old man began to fuss about. He would have kissed him, but Ivan made haste to hold out his hand, obviously avoiding the kiss. His father saw it at once, and instantly pulled himself up.

"Well, good luck to you, good luck to you!" he repeated from the steps. "You'll come again some time or other? Mind you do come. I shall always be glad to see you. Well, Christ be with you!"

Ivan got into the carriage.

"Good-bye, Ivan! Don't be too hard on me!" the father called for the last time.

The whole household came out to take leave--Smerdyakov, Marfa and Grigory. Ivan gave them ten roubles each. When he had seated himself in the carriage, Smerdyakov jumped up to arrange the rug.

"You see...I am going to Tchermashnya," broke suddenly from Ivan. Again, as the day before, the words seemed to drop of themselves, and he laughed, too, a peculiar, nervous laugh. He remembered it long after.

"It's a true saying then, that 'it's always worth while speaking to a clever man,'" answered Smerdyakov firmly, looking significantly at Ivan.

The carriage rolled away. Nothing was clear in Ivan's soul, but he looked eagerly around him at the fields, at the hills, at the trees, at a flock of geese flying high overhead in the bright sky. And all of a sudden he felt very happy. He tried to talk to the driver, and he felt intensely interested in an answer the peasant made him; but a minute later he realised that he was not catching anything, and that he had not really even taken in the peasant's answer. He was silent, and it was pleasant even so. The air was pure and cool, sky bright. The images of Alyosha and Katerina Ivanovna floated into his mind. But he softly smiled, blew softly on the friendly phantoms, and they flew away. "There's plenty of time for them," he thought. They reached the station quickly, changed horses, and galloped to Volovya "Why is it worth while speaking to a clever man? What did he mean by that?" The thought seemed suddenly to clutch at his breathing. "And why did I tell him I was going to Tchermashnya?" They reached Volovya station. Ivan got out of the carriage, and the drivers stood round him bargaining over the journey of twelve versts to Tchermashnya. He told them to harness the horses. He went into the station house, looked round, glanced at the overseer's wife, and suddenly went back to the entrance.

"I won't go to Tchermashnya. Am I too late to reach the railway by seven, brothers?"

"We shall just do it. Shall we get the carriage out?"

"At once. Will any one of you be going to the town to-morrow?"

"To be sure. Mitri here will."

"Can you do me a service, Mitri? Go to my father's, to Fyodor Pavlovitch Karamazov, and tell him I haven't gone to Tchermashnya. Can you?"

"Of course I can. I've known Fyodor Pavlovitch a long time."

"And here's something for you, for I dare say he won't give you anything," said Ivan, laughing gaily.

"You may depend on it he won't." Mitri laughed too. "Thank you, sir. I'll be sure to do it."

At seven o'clock Ivan got into the train and set off to Moscow. "Away with the past. I've done with the old world for ever, and may I have no news, no echo, from it. To a new life, new places, and no looking back!" But instead of delight his soul was filled with such gloom, and his heart ached with such anguish, as he had never known in his life before. He was thinking all the night. The train flew on, and only at daybreak, when he was approaching Moscow, he suddenly roused himself from his meditation.

"I am a scoundrel," he whispered to himself.

Fyodor Pavlovitch remained well satisfied at having seen his son off. For two hours afterwards he felt almost happy, and sat drinking brandy. But suddenly something happened which was very annoying and unpleasant for everyone in the house, and completely upset Fyodor Pavlovitch's equanimity at once. Smerdyakov went to the cellar for something and fell down from the top of the steps. Fortunately, Marfa Ignatyevna was in the yard and heard him in time. She did not see the fall, but heard his scream--the strange, peculiar scream, long familiar to her--the scream of the epileptic falling in a fit. They could not tell whether the fit had come on him at the moment he was decending the steps, so that he must have fallen unconscious, or whether it was the fall and the shock that had caused the fit in Smerdyakov, who was known to be liable to them. They found him at the bottom of the cellar steps, writhing in convulsions and foaming at the mouth. It was thought at first that he must have broken something--an arm or a leg--and hurt himself, but "God had preserved him," as Marfa Ignatyevna expressed it--nothing of the kind had happened. But it was difficult to get him out of the cellar. They asked the neighbours to help and managed it somehow. Fyodor Pavlovitch himself was present at the whole ceremony. He helped, evidently alarmed and upset. The sick man did not regain consciousness; the convulsions ceased for a time, but then began again, and everyone concluded that the same thing would happen, as had happened a year before, when he accidently fell from the garret. They remembered that ice been put on his head then. There was still ice in the cellar, and Marfa Ignatyevna had some brought up. In the evening, Fyodor Pavlovitch sent for Doctor Herzenstube, who arrived at once. He was a most estimable old man, and the most careful and conscientious doctor in the province. After careful examination, he concluded that the fit was a very violent one and might have serious consequences; that meanwhile he, Herzenstube, did not fully understand it, but that by to-morrow morning, if the present remedies were unavailing, he would venture to try something else. The invalid was taken to the lodge, to a room next to Grigory's and Marfa Ignatyevna's.

Then Fyodor Pavlovitch had one misfortune after another to put up with that day. Marfa Ignatyevna cooked the dinner, and the soup, compared with Smerdyakov's, was "no better than dish-water," and the fowl was so dried up that it was impossible to masticate it. To her master's bitter, though deserved, reproaches, Marfa Ignatyevna replied that the fowl was a very old one to begin with, and that she had never been trained as a cook. In the evening there was another trouble in store for Fyodor Pavlovitch; he was informed that Grigory, who had not been well for the last three days, was completely laid up by his lumbago. Fyodor Pavlovitch finished his tea as early as possible and locked himself up alone in the house. He was in terrible excitement and suspense. That evening he reckoned on Grushenka's coming almost as a certainty. He had received from Smerdyakov that morning an assurance "that she had promised to come without fail." The incorrigible old man's heart throbbed with excitement; he paced up and down his empty rooms listening. He had to be on the alert. Dmitri might be on the watch for her somewhere, and when she knocked on the window (Smerdyakov had informed him two days before that he had told her where and how to knock) the door must be opened at once. She must not be a second in the passage, for fear which God forbid!--that she should be frightened and run away. Fyodor Pavlovitch had much to think of, but never had his heart been steeped in such voluptuous hopes. This time he could say almost certainly that she would come!

Book VI. The Russian Monk.
Chapter 1. Father Zossima and His Visitors

When with an anxious and aching heart Alyosha went into his elder's cell, he stood still almost astonished. Instead of a sick man at his last gasp, perhaps unconscious, as he had feared to find him, he saw him sitting up in his chair and, though weak and exhausted, his face was bright and cheerful, he was surrounded by visitors and engaged in a quiet and joyful conversation. But he had only got up from his bed a quarter of an hour before Alyosha's arrival; his visitors had gathered together in his cell earlier, waiting for him to wake, having received a most confident assurance from Father Paissy that "the teacher would get up, and as he had himself promised in the morning, converse once more with those dear to his heart." This promise and indeed every word of the dying elder Father Paissy put implicit trust in. If he had seen him unconscious, if he had seen him breathe his last, and yet had his promise that he would rise up and say good-bye to him, he would not have believed perhaps even in death, but would still have expected the dead man to recover and fulfil his promise. In the morning as he lay down to sleep, Father Zossima had told him positively: "I shall not die without the delight of another conversation with you, beloved of my heart. I shall look once more on your dear face and pour out my heart to you once again." The monks, who had gathered for this probably last conversation with Father Zossima, had all been his devoted friends for many years. There were four of them: Father Iosif and Father Paissy, Father Mihail the warden of the hermitage, a man not very old and far from being learned. He was of humble origin, of strong will and steadfast faith, of austere appearance, but of deep tenderness, though he obviously concealed it as though he were almost ashamed of it. The fourth, Father Anfim, was a very old and humble little monk of the poorest peasant class. He was almost illiterate, and very quiet, scarcely speaking to anyone. He was the humblest of the humble, and looked as though he had been frightened by something great and awful beyond the scope of his intelligence. Father Zossima had a great affection for this timorous man, and always treated him with marked respect, though perhaps there was no one he had known to whom he had said less, in spite of the fact that he had spent years wandering about holy Russia with him. That was very long ago, forty years before, when Father Zossima first began his life as a monk in a poor and little monastery at Kostroma, and when, shortly after, he had accompanied Father Anfim on his pilgrimage to collect alms for their poor monastery.

The whole party were in the bedroom which, as we mentioned before, was very small, so that there was scarcely room for the four of them (in addition to Porfiry, the novice, who stood) to sit round Father Zossima on chairs brought from the sitting room. It was already beginning to get dark, the room was lighted up by the lamps and the candles before the ikons.

Seeing Alyosha standing embarrassed in the doorway, Father Zossima smiled at him joyfully and held out his hand.

"Welcome, my quiet one, welcome, my dear, here you are too. I knew you would come."

Alyosha went up to him, bowed down before him to the ground and wept. Something surged up from his heart, his soul was quivering, he wanted to sob.

"Come, don't weep over me yet," Father Zossima smiled, laying his right hand on his head. "You see I am sitting up talking; maybe I shall live another twenty years yet, as that dear good woman from Vishegorye, with her little Lizaveta in her arms, wished me yesterday. God bless the mother and the little girl Lizaveta," he crossed himself. "Porfiry, did you take her offering where I told you?"

He meant the sixty copecks brought him the day before by the good-humoured woman to be given "to someone poorer than me." Such offerings, always of money gained by personal toil, are made by way of penance voluntarily undertaken. The elder had sent Porfiry the evening before to a widow, whose house had been burnt down lately, and who after the fire had gone with her children begging alms. Porfiry hastened to reply that he had given the money, as he had been instructed, "from an unknown benefactress."

"Get up, my dear boy," the elder went on to Alyosha. "Let me look at you. Have you been home and seen your brother?" It seemed strange to Alyosha that he asked so confidently and precisely, about one of his brothers only--but which one? Then perhaps he had sent him out both yesterday and to-day for the sake of that brother.

"I have seen one of my brothers," answered Alyosha.

"I mean the elder one, to whom I bowed down."

"I only saw him yesterday and could not find him to-day," said Alyosha.

"Make haste to find him, go again to-morrow and make haste, leave everything and make haste. Perhaps you may still have time to prevent something terrible. I bowed down yesterday to the great suffering in store for him."

He was suddenly silent and seemed to be pondering. The words were strange. Father Iosif, who had witnessed the scene yesterday, exchanged glances with Father Paissy. Alyosha could not resist asking:

"Father and teacher," he began with extreme emotion, "your words are too obscure...What is this suffering in store for him?"

"Don't inquire. I seemed to see something terrible yesterday...as though his whole future were expressed in his eyes. A look came into his eyes--so that I was instantly horror-stricken at what that man is preparing for himself. Once or twice in my life I've seen such a look in a man's face...reflecting as it were his future fate, and that fate, alas, came to pass. I sent you to him, Alexey, for I thought your brotherly face would help him. But everything and all our fates are from the Lord. 'Except a corn of wheat fall into the ground and die, it abideth alone; but if it die, it bringeth forth much fruit.' Remember that. You, Alexey, I've many times silently blessed for your face, know that," added the elder with a gentle smile. "This is what I think of you, you will go forth from these walls, but will live like a monk in the world. You will have many enemies, but even your foes will love you. Life will bring you many misfortunes, but you will find your happiness in them, and will bless life and will make others bless it--which is what matters most. Well, that is your character. Fathers and teachers," he addressed his friends with a tender smile, "I have never till to-day told even him why the face of this youth is so dear to me. Now I will tell you. His face has been as it were a remembrance and a prophecy for me. At the dawn of my life when I was a child I had an elder brother who died before my eyes at seventeen. And later on in the course of my life I gradually became convinced that that brother had been for a guidance and a sign from on high for me. For had he not come into my life, I should never perhaps, so I fancy at least, have become a monk and entered on this precious path. He appeared first to me in my childhood, and here, at the end of my pilgrimage, he seems to have come to me over again. It is marvellous, fathers and teachers, that Alexey, who has some, though not a great, resemblance in face, seems to me so like him spiritually, that many times I have taken him for that young man, my brother, mysteriously come back to me at the end of my pilgrimage, as a reminder and an inspiration. So that I positively wondered at so strange a dream in myself. Do you hear this, Porfiry?" he turned to the novice who waited on him. "Many times I've seen in your face as it were a look of mortification that I love Alexey more than you. Now you know why that was so, but I love you too, know that, and many times I grieved at your mortification. I should like to tell you, dear friends, of that youth, my brother, for there has been no presence in my life more precious, more significant and touching. My heart is full of tenderness, and I look at my whole life at this moment as though living through it again."

Here I must observe that this last conversation of Father Zossima with the friends who visited him on the last day of his life has been partly preserved in writing. Alexey Fyodorovitch Karamazov wrote it down from memory, some time after his elder's death. But whether this was only the conversation that took place then, or whether he added to it his notes of parts of former conversations with his teacher, I cannot determine. In his account, Father Zossima's talk goes on without interruption, as though he told his life to his friends in the form of a story, though there is no doubt, from other accounts of it, that the conversation that evening was general. Though the guests did not interrupt Father Zossima much, yet they too talked, perhaps even told something themselves. Besides, Father Zossima could not have carried on an uninterrupted narrative, for he was sometimes gasping for breath, his voice failed him, and he even lay down to rest on his bed, though he did not fall asleep and his visitors did not leave their seats. Once or twice the conversation was interrupted by Father Paissy's reading the Gospel. It is worthy of note, too, that no one of them supposed that he would die that night, for on that evening of his life after his deep sleep in the day he seemed suddenly to have found new strength, which kept him up through this long conversation. It was like a last effort of love which gave him marvellous energy; only for a little time, however, for his life was cut short immediately.. But of that later. I will only add now that I have preferred to confine myself to the account given by Alexey Fyodorovitch Karamazov. It will be shorter and not so fatiguing, though, of course, as I must repeat, Alyosha took a great deal from previous conversations and added them to it. Notes of the Life of the deceased Priest and Monk, the Elder Zossima, taken from his own words by Alexey Fyodorovitch Karamazov.

BIOGRAPHICAL NOTES

(a) Father Zossima's Brother.

Beloved fathers and teachers, I was born in a distant province in the north, in the town of V. My father was a gentleman by birth, but of no great consequence or position. He died when I was only two years old, and I don't remember him at all. He left my mother a small house built of wood, and a fortune, not large, but sufficient to keep her and her children in comfort. There were two of us, my elder brother Markel and I. He was eight years older than I was, of hasty, irritable temperament, but kind-hearted and never ironical. He was remarkably silent, especially at home with me, his mother, and the servants. He did well at school, but did not get on with his school-fellows, though he never quarrelled, at least so my mother has told me. Six months before his death, when he was seventeen, he made friends with a political exile who had been banished from Moscow to our town for freethinking, and led a solitary existence there. He was a good scholar who had gained distinction in philosophy in the university. Something made him take a fancy to Markel, and he used to ask him to see him. The young man would spend whole evenings with him during that winter, till the exile was summoned to Petersburg to take up his post again at his own request, as he had powerful friends.

It was the beginning of Lent, and Markel would not fast, he was rude and laughed at it. "That's all silly twaddle, and there is no God," he said, horrifying my mother, the servants, and me too. For though I was only nine, I too was aghast at hearing such words. We had four servants, all serfs. I remember my mother selling one of the four, the cook Afimya, who was lame and elderly, for sixty paper roubles, and hiring a free servant to take her place.

In the sixth week in Lent, my brother, who was never strong and had a tendency to consumption, was taken ill. He was tall but thin and delicate-looking, and of very pleasing countenance. I suppose he caught cold, anyway the doctor, who came, soon whispered to my mother that it was galloping consumption, that he would not live through the spring. My mother began weeping, and, careful not to alarm my brother, she entreated him to go to church, to confess and take the sacrament, as he was still able to move about. This made him angry, and he said something profane about the church. He grew thoughtful, however; he guessed at once that he was seriously ill, and that that was why his mother was begging him to confess and take the sacrament. He had been aware, indeed, for a long time past, that he was far from well, and had a year before coolly observed at dinner to your mother and me, "My life won't be long among you, I may not live another year," which seemed now like a prophecy.

Three days passed and Holy Week had come. And on Tuesday morning my brother began going to church. "I am doing this simply for your sake, mother, to please and comfort you," he said. My mother wept with joy and grief. "His end must be near," she thought, "if there's such a change in him." But he was not able to go to church long, he took to his bed, so he had to confess and take the sacrament at home.

It was a late Easter, and the days were bright, fine, and full of fragrance. I remember he used to cough all night and sleep badly, but in the morning he dressed and tried to sit up in an arm-chair. That's how I remember him sitting, sweet and gentle, smiling, his face bright and joyous, in spite of his illness. A marvellous change passed over him, his spirit seemed transformed. The old nurse would come in and say, "Let me light the lamp before the holy image, my dear." And once he would not have allowed it and would have blown it out.

"Light it, light it, dear, I was a wretch to have prevented you doing it. You are praying when you light the lamp, and I am praying when I rejoice seeing you. So we are praying to the same God."

Those words seemed strange to us, and mother would go to her room and weep, but when she went in to him she wiped her eyes and looked cheerful. "Mother, don't weep, darling," he would say, "I've long to live yet, long to rejoice with you, and life is glad and joyful."

"Ah, dear boy, how can you talk of joy when you lie feverish at night, coughing as though you would tear yourself to pieces."

"Don't cry, mother," he would answer, "life is paradise, and we are all in paradise, but we won't see it; if we would, we should have heaven on earth the next day."

Everyone wondered at his words, he spoke so strangely and positively; we were all touched and wept. Friends came to see us. "Dear ones," he would say to them, "what have I done that you should love me so, how can you love anyone like me, and how was it I did not know, I did not appreciate it before?"

When the servants came in to him he would say continually, "Dear, kind people, why are you doing so much for me, do I deserve to be waited on? If it were God's will for me to live, I would wait on you, for all men should wait on one another."

Mother shook her head as she listened. "My darling, it's your illness makes you talk like that."

"Mother darling," he would say, "there must be servants and masters, but if so I will be the servant of my servants, the same as they are to me. And another thing, mother, every one of us has sinned against all men, and I more than any."

Mother positively smiled at that, smiled through her tears. "Why, how could you have sinned against all men, more than all? Robbers and murderers have done that, but what sin have you committed yet, that you hold yourself more guilty than all?"

"Mother, little heart of mine," he said (he had begun using such strange caressing words at that time), "little heart of mine, my joy, believe me, everyone is really responsible to all men for all men and for everything. I don't know how to explain it to you, but I feel it is so, painfully even. And how is it we went on then living, getting angry and not knowing?"

So he would get up every day, more and more sweet and joyous and full of love. When the doctor, an old German called Eisenschmidt, came:

"Well, doctor, have I another day in this world?" he would ask, joking.

"You'll live many days yet," the doctor would answer, "and months and years too."

"Months and years!" he would exclaim. "Why reckon the days? One day is enough for a man to know all happiness. My dear ones, why do we quarrel, try to outshine each other and keep grudges against each other? Let's go straight into the garden, walk and play there, love, appreciate, and kiss each other, and glorify life."

"Your son cannot last long," the doctor told my mother, as she accompanied him the door. "The disease is affecting his brain."

The windows of his room looked out into the garden, and our garden was a shady one, with old trees in it which were coming into bud. The first birds of spring were flitting in the branches, chirruping and singing at the windows. And looking at them and admiring them, he began suddenly begging their forgiveness too: "Birds of heaven, happy birds, forgive me, for I have sinned against you too." None of us could understand that at the time, but he shed tears of joy. "Yes," he said, "there was such a glory of God all about me: birds, trees, meadows, sky; only I lived in shame and dishonoured it all and did not notice the beauty and glory."

"You take too many sins on yourself," mother used to say, weeping.

"Mother, darling, it's for joy, not for grief I am crying. Though I can't explain it to you, I like to humble myself before them, for I don't know how to love them enough. If I have sinned against everyone, yet all forgive me, too, and that's heaven. Am I not in heaven now?"

And there was a great deal more I don't remember. I remember I went once into his room when there was no one else there. It was a bright evening, the sun was setting, and the whole room was lighted up. He beckoned me, and I went up to him. He put his hands on my shoulders and looked into my face tenderly, lovingly; he said nothing for a minute, only looked at me like that.

"Well," he said, "run and play now, enjoy life for me too."

I went out then and ran to play. And many times in my life afterwards I remembered even with tears how he told me to enjoy life for him too. There were many other marvellous and beautiful sayings of his, though we did not understand them at the time. He died the third week after Easter. He was fully conscious though he could not talk; up to his last hour he did not change. He looked happy, his eyes beamed and sought us, he smiled at us, beckoned us. There was a great deal of talk even in the town about his death. I was impressed by all this at the time, but not too much so, though I cried a good deal at his funeral. I was young then, a child, but a lasting impression, a hidden feeling of it all, remained in my heart, ready to rise up and respond when the time came. So indeed it happened.

(b) Of the Holy Scriptures in the Life of Father Zossima.

I was left alone with my mother. Her friends began advising her to send me to Petersburg as other parents did. "You have only one son now," they said, "and have a fair income, and you will be depriving him perhaps of a brilliant career if you keep him here." They suggested I should be sent to Petersburg to the Cadet Corps, that I might afterwards enter the Imperial Guard. My mother hesitated for a long time, it was awful to part with her only child, but she made up her mind to it at last, though not without many tears, believing she was acting for my happiness. She brought me to Petersburg and put me into the Cadet Corps, and I never saw her again. For she too died three years afterwards. She spent those three years mourning and grieving for both of us.

From the house of my childhood I have brought nothing but precious memories, for there are no memories more precious than those of early childhood in one's first home. And that is almost always so if there is any love and harmony in the family at all. Indeed, precious memories may remain even of a bad home, if only the heart knows how to find what is precious. With my memories of home I count, too, my memories of the Bible, which, child as I was, I was very eager to read at home. I had a book of Scripture history then with excellent pictures, called A Hundred and Four Stories from the Old and New Testament, and I learned to read from it. I have it lying on my shelf now; I keep it as a precious relic of the past. But even before I learned to read, I remember first being moved to devotional feeling at eight years old. My mother took me alone to mass (I don't remember where my brother was at the time) on the Monday before Easter. It was a fine day, and I remember to-day, as though I saw it now, how the incense rose from the censer and softly floated upwards and, overhead in the cupola, mingled in rising waves with the sunlight that streamed in at the little window. I was stirred by the sight, and for the first time in my life I consciously received the seed of God's word in my heart. A youth came out into the middle of the church carrying a big book, so large that at the time I fancied he could scarcely carry it. He laid it on the reading desk, opened it, and began reading, and suddenly for the first time I understood something read in the church of God. In the land of Uz, there lived a man, righteous and God-fearing, and he had great wealth, so many camels, so many sheep and asses, and his children feasted, and he loved them very much and prayed for them. "It may be that my sons have sinned in their feasting." Now the devil came before the Lord together with the sons of God, and said to the Lord that he had gone up and down the earth and under the earth. "And hast thou considered my servant Job?" God asked of him. And God boasted to the devil, pointing to His great and holy servant. And the devil laughed at God's words. "Give him over to me and Thou wilt see that Thy servant will murmur against Thee and curse Thy name." And God gave up the just man He loved so, to the devil. And the devil smote his children and his cattle and scattered his wealth, all of a sudden like a thunderbolt from heaven. And Job rent his mantle and fell down upon the ground and cried aloud, "Naked came I out of my mother's womb, and naked shall I return into the earth; the Lord gave and the Lord has taken away. Blessed be the name of the Lord for ever and ever."

Fathers and teachers, forgive my tears now, for all my childhood rises up again before me, and I breathe now as I breathed then, with the breast of a little child of eight, and I feel as I did then, awe and wonder and gladness. The camels at that time caught my imagination, and Satan, who talked like that with God, and God who gave His servant up to destruction, and His servant crying out: "Blessed be Thy name although Thou dost punish me," and then the soft and sweet singing in the church: "Let my prayer rise up before Thee," and again incense from the priest's censer and the kneeling and the prayer. Ever since then--only yesterday I took it up--I've never been able to read that sacred tale without tears. And how much that is great, mysterious and unfathomable there is in it! Afterwards I heard the words of mockery and blame, proud words, "How could God give up the most loved of His saints for the diversion of the devil, take from him his children, smite him with sore boils so that he cleansed the corruption from his sores with a potsherd--and for no object except to boast to the devil 'See what My saint can suffer for My sake.' "But the greatness of it lies just in the fact that it is a mystery--that the passing earthly show and the eternal verity are brought together in it. In the face of the earthly truth, the eternal truth is accomplished. The Creator, just as on the first days of creation He ended each day with praise: "That is good that I have created," looks upon Job and again praises His creation. And Job, praising the Lord, serves not only Him but all His creation for generations and generations, and for ever and ever, since for that he was ordained. Good heavens, what a book it is, and what lessons there are in it! What a book the Bible is, what a miracle, what strength is given with it to man! It is like a mould cast of the world and man and human nature, everything is there, and a law for everything for all the ages. And what mysteries are solved and revealed! God raises Job again, gives him wealth again. Many years pass by, and he has other children and loves them. But how could he love those new ones when those first children are no more, when he has lost them? Remembering them, how could he be fully happy with those new ones, however dear the new ones might be? But he could, he could. It's the great mystery of human life that old grief passes gradually into quiet, tender joy. The mild serenity of age takes the place of the riotous blood of youth. I bless the rising sun each day, and, as before, my heart sings to meet it, but now I love even more its setting, its long slanting rays and the soft, tender, gentle memories that come with them, the dear images from the whole of my long, happy life--and over all the Divine Truth, softening, reconciling, forgiving! My life is ending, I know that well, but every day that is left me I feel how earthly life is in touch with a new infinite, unknown, but approaching life, the nearness of which sets my soul quivering with rapture, my mind glowing and my heart weeping with joy.

Friends and teachers, I have heard more than once, and of late one may hear it more often, that the priests, and above all the village priests, are complaining on all sides of their miserable income and their humiliating lot. They plainly state, even in print--I've read it myself--that they are unable to teach the Scriptures to the people because of the smallness of their means, and if Lutherans and heretics come and lead the flock astray, they let them lead them astray because they have so little to live upon. May the Lord increase the sustenance that is so precious to them, for their complaint is just, too. But of a truth I say, if anyone is to blame in the matter, half the fault is ours. For he may be short of time, he may say truly that he is overwhelmed all the while with work and services, but still it's not all the time, even he has an hour a week to remember God. And he does not work the whole year round. Let him gather round him once a week, some hour in the evening, if only the children at first--the fathers will hear of it and they too will begin to come. There's no need to build halls for this, let him take them into his own cottage. They won't spoil his cottage, they would only be there one hour. Let him open that book and begin reading it without grand words or superciliousness, without condescension to them, but gently and kindly, being glad that he is reading to them and that they are listening with attention, loving the words himself, only stopping from time to time to explain words that are not understood by the peasants. Don't be anxious, they will understand everything, the orthodox heart will understand all! Let him read them about Abraham and Sarah, about Isaac and Rebecca, of how Jacob went to Laban and wrestled with the Lord in his dream and said, "This place is holy"--and he will impress the devout mind of the peasant. Let him read, especially to the children, how the brothers sold Joseph, the tender boy, the dreamer and prophet, into bondage, and told their father that a wild beast had devoured him, and showed him his blood-stained clothes. Let him read them how the brothers afterwards journeyed into Egypt for corn, and Joseph, already a great ruler, unrecognised by them, tormented them, accused them, kept his brother Benjamin, and all through love: "I love you, and loving you I torment you." For he remembered all his life how they had sold him to the merchants in the burning desert by the well, and how, wringing his hands, he had wept and besought his brothers not to sell him as a slave in a strange land. And how, seeing them again after many years, he loved them beyond measure, but he harassed and tormented them in love. He left them at last not able to bear the suffering of his heart, flung himself on his bed and wept. Then, wiping his tears away, he went out to them joyful and told them, "Brothers, I am your brother Joseph" Let him read them further how happy old Jacob was on learning that his darling boy was still alive, and how he went to Egypt leaving his own country, and died in a foreign land, bequeathing his great prophecy that had lain mysteriously hidden in his meek and timid heart all his life, that from his offspring, from Judah, will come the great hope of the world, the Messiah and Saviour.

Fathers and teachers, forgive me and don't be angry, that like a little child I've been babbling of what you know long ago, and can teach me a hundred times more skilfully. I only speak from rapture, and forgive my tears, for I love the Bible. Let him too weep, the priest of God, and be sure that the hearts of his listeners will throb in response. Only a little tiny seed is needed--drop it into the heart of the peasant and it won't die, it will live in his soul all his life, it will be hidden in the midst of his darkness and sin, like a bright spot, like a great reminder. And there's no need of much teaching or explanation, he will understand it all simply. Do you suppose that the peasants don't understand? Try reading them the touching story of the fair Esther and the haughty Vashti; or the miraculous story of Jonah in the whale. Don't forget either the parables of Our Lord, choose especially from the Gospel of St. Luke (that is what I did), and then from the Acts of the Apostles the conversion of St. Paul (that you mustn't leave out on any account), and from the Lives of the Saints, for instance, the life of Alexey, the man of God and, greatest of all, the happy martyr and the seer of God, Mary of Egypt--and you will penetrate their hearts with these simple tales. Give one hour a week to it in spite of your poverty, only one little hour. And you will see for yourselves that our people is gracious and grateful, and will repay you a hundred fold. Mindful of the kindness of their priest and the moving words they have heard from him, they will of their own accord help him in his fields and in his house and will treat him with more respect than before--so that it will even increase his worldly well-being too. The thing is so simple that sometimes one is even afraid to put it into words, for fear of being laughed at, and yet how true it is! One who does not believe in God will not believe in God's people. He who believes in God's people will see His Holiness too, even though he had not believed in it till then. Only the people and their future spiritual power will convert our atheists, who have torn themselves away from their native soil.

And what is the use of Christ's words, unless we set an example? The people is lost without the Word of God, for its soul is athirst for the Word and for all that is good.

In my youth, long ago, nearly forty years ago, I travelled all over Russia with Father Anfim, collecting funds for our monastery, and we stayed one night on the bank of a great navigable river with some fishermen. A good looking peasant lad, about eighteen, joined us; he had to hurry back next morning to pull a merchant's barge along the bank. I noticed him looking straight before him with clear and tender eyes. It was a bright, warm, still, July night, a cool mist rose from the broad river, we could hear the plash of a fish, the birds were still, all was hushed and beautiful, everything praying to God. Only we two were not sleeping, the lad and I, and we talked of the beauty of this world of God's and of the great mystery of it. Every blade of grass, every insect, ant, and golden bee, all so marvellously know their path, though they have not intelligence, they bear witness to the mystery of God and continually accomplish it themselves. I saw the dear lad's heart was moved. He told me that he loved the forest and the forest birds. He was a bird-catcher, knew the note of each of them, could call each bird. "I know nothing better than to be in the forest," said he, "though all things are good."

"Truly," I answered him, "all things are good and fair, because all is truth. Look," said I, "at the horse, that great beast that is so near to man; or the lowly, pensive ox, which feeds him and works for him; look at their faces, what meekness, what devotion to man, who often beats them mercilessly. What gentleness, what confidence and what beauty! It's touching to know that there's no sin in them, for all, all except man, is sinless, and Christ has been with them before us."

"Why," asked the boy, "is Christ with them too?"

"It cannot but be so," said I, "since the Word is for all. All creation and all creatures, every leaf is striving to the Word, singing glory to God, weeping to Christ, unconsciously accomplishing this by the mystery of their sinless life. Yonder," said I, "in the forest wanders the dreadful bear, fierce and menacing, and yet innocent in it." And I told him how once a bear came to a great saint who had taken refuge in a tiny cell in the wood. And the great saint pitied him, went up to him without fear and gave him a piece of bread. "Go along," said he, "Christ be with you," and the savage beast walked away meekly and obediently, doing no harm. And the lad was delighted that the bear had walked away without hurting the saint, and that Christ was with him too. "Ah," said he, "how good that is, how good and beautiful is all God's work!" He sat musing softly and sweetly. I saw he understood. And he slept beside me a light and sinless sleep. May God bless youth! And I prayed for him as I went to sleep. Lord, send peace and light to Thy people!

Chapter 2. Recollections of Father Zossima's Youth before he became a Monk. The Duel

I spent a long time, almost eight years, in the military cadet school at Petersburg, and in the novelty of my surroundings there, many of my childish impressions grew dimmer, though I forgot nothing. I picked up so many new habits and opinions that I was transformed into a cruel, absurd, almost savage creature. A surface polish of courtesy and society manners I did acquire together with the French language.

But we all, myself included, looked upon the soldiers in our service as cattle. I was perhaps worse than the rest in that respect, for I was so much more impressionable than my companions. By the time we left the school as officers, we were ready to lay down our lives for the honour of the regiment, but no one of us had any knowledge of the real meaning of honour, and if anyone had known it, he would have been the first to ridicule it. Drunkenness, debauchery and devilry were what we almost prided ourselves on. I don't say that we were bad by nature, all these young men were good fellows, but they behaved badly, and I worst of all. What made it worse for me was that I had come into my own money, and so I flung myself into a life of pleasure, and plunged headlong into all the recklessness of youth.

I was fond of reading, yet strange to say, the Bible was the one book I never opened at that time, though I always carried it about with me, and I was never separated from it; in very truth I was keeping that book "for the day and the hour, for the month and the year," though I knew it not.

After four years of this life, I chanced to be in the town of K. where our regiment was stationed at the time. We found the people of the town hospitable, rich, and fond of entertainments. I met with a cordial reception everywhere, as I was of a lively temperament and was known to be well off, which always goes a long way in the world. And then a circumstance happened which was the beginning of it all.

I formed an attachment to a beautiful and intelligent young girl of noble and lofty character, the daughter of people much respected. They were well-to-do people of influence and position. They always gave me a cordial and friendly reception. I fancied that the young lady looked on me with favour and my heart was aflame at such an idea. Later on I saw and fully realised that I perhaps was not so passionately in love with her at all, but only recognised the elevation of her mind and character, which I could not indeed have helped doing. I was prevented, however, from making her an offer at the time by my selfishness; I was loath to part with the allurements of my free and licentious bachelor life in the heyday of my youth, and with my pockets full of money. I did drop some hint as to my feelings however, though I put off taking any decisive step for a time. Then, all of a sudden, we were ordered off for two months to another district.

On my return two months later, I found the young lady already married to a rich neighbouring landowner, a very amiable man, still young though older than I was, connected with the best Petersburg society, which I was not, and of excellent education, which I also was not. I was so overwhelmed at this unexpected circumstance that my mind was positively clouded. The worst of it all was that, as I learned then, the young landowner had been a long while betrothed to her, and I had met him indeed many times in her house, but blinded by my conceit I had noticed nothing. And this particularly mortified me; almost everybody had known all about it, while I knew nothing. I was filled with sudden irrepressible fury. With flushed face I began recalling how often I had been on the point of declaring my love to her, and as she had not attempted to stop me or to warn me, she must, I concluded, have been laughing at me all the time. Later on, of course, I reflected and remembered that she had been very far from laughing at me; on the contrary, she used to turn off any love-making on my part with a jest and begin talking of other subjects; but at that moment I was incapable of reflecting and was all eagerness for revenge. I am surprised to remember that my wrath and revengeful feelings were extremely repugnant to my own nature, for being of an easy temper, I found it difficult to be angry with anyone for long, and so I had to work myself up artificially and became at last revolting and absurd.

I waited for an opportunity and succeeded in insulting my "rival" in the presence of a large company. I insulted him on a perfectly extraneous pretext, jeering at his opinion upon an important public event--it was in the year 1826--my jeer was, so people said, clever and effective. Then I forced him to ask for an explanation, and behaved so rudely that he accepted my challenge in spite of the vast inequality between us, as I was younger, a person of no consequence, and of inferior rank. I learned afterwards for a fact that it was from a jealous feeling on his side also that my challenge was accepted; he had been rather jealous of me on his wife's account before their marriage; he fancied now that if he submitted to be insulted by me and refused to accept my challenge, and if she heard of it, she might begin to despise him and waver in her love for him. I soon found a second in a comrade, an ensign of our regiment. In those days though duels were severely punished, yet duelling was a kind of fashion among the officers--so strong and deeply rooted will a brutal prejudice sometimes be.

It was the end of June, and our meeting was to take place at seven o'clock the next day on the outskirts of the town--and then something happened that in very truth was the turning point of my life. In the evening, returning home in a savage and brutal humour, I flew into a rage with my orderly Afanasy, and gave him two blows in the face with all my might, so that it was covered with blood. He had not long been in my service and I had struck him before, but never with such ferocious cruelty. And, believe me, though it's forty years ago, I recall it now with shame and pain. I went to bed and slept for about three hours; when I waked up the day was breaking. I got up--I did not want to sleep any more--I went to the window--opened it, it looked out upon the garden; I saw the sun rising; it was warm and beautiful, the birds were singing.

"What's the meaning of it?" I thought. "I feel in my heart as it were something vile and shameful. Is it because I am going to shed blood? No," I thought, "I feel it's not that. Can it be that I am afraid of death, afraid of being killed? No, that's not it, that's not it at all."...And all at once I knew what it was: it was because I had beaten Afanasy the evening before! It all rose before my mind, it all was, as it were, repeated over again; he stood before me and I was beating him straight on the face and he was holding his arms stiffly down, his head erect, his eyes fixed upon me as though on parade. He staggered at every blow and did not even dare to raise his hands to protect himself. That is what a man has been brought to, and that was a man beating a fellow creature! What a crime! It was as though a sharp dagger had pierced me right through. I stood as if I were struck dumb, while the sun was shining, the leaves were rejoicing and the birds were trilling the praise of God...I hid my face in my hands, fell on my bed and broke into a storm of tears. And then I remembered by brother Markel and what he said on his death-bed to his servants: "My dear ones, why do you wait on me, why do you love me, am I worth your waiting on me?"

"Yes, am I worth it?" flashed through my mind. "After all what am I worth, that another man, a fellow creature, made in the likeness and image of God, should serve me?" For the first time in my life this question forced itself upon me. He had said, "Mother, my little heart, in truth we are each responsible to all for all, it's only that men don't know this. If they knew it, the world would be a paradise at once."

"God, can that too be false?" I thought as I wept. "In truth, perhaps, I am more than all others responsible for all, a greater sinner than all men in the world." And all at once the whole truth in its full light appeared to me: what was I going to do? I was going to kill a good, clever, noble man, who had done me no wrong, and by depriving his wife of happiness for the rest of her life, I should be torturing and killing her too. I lay thus in my bed with my face in the pillow, heedless how the time was passing. Suddenly my second, the ensign, came in with the pistols to fetch me.

"Ah," said he, "it's a good thing you are up already, it's time we were off, come along!"

I did not know what to do and hurried to and fro undecided; we went out to the carriage, however.

"Wait here a minute," I said to him. "I'll be back directly, I have forgotten my purse."

And I ran back alone, to Afanasy's little room.

"Afanasy," I said, "I gave you two blows on the face yesterday, forgive me," I said.

He started as though he were frightened, and looked at me; and I saw that it was not enough, and on the spot, in my full officer's uniform, I dropped at his feet and bowed my head to the ground.

"Forgive me," I said.

Then he was completely aghast.

"Your honour...sir, what are you doing? Am I worth it?"

And he burst out crying as I had done before, hid his face in his hands, turned to the window and shook all over with his sobs. I flew out to my comrade and jumped into the carriage.

"Ready," I cried. "Have you ever seen a conqueror?" I asked him. "Here is one before you."

I was in ecstasy, laughing and talking all the way, I don't remember what about.

He looked at me. "Well, brother, you are a plucky fellow, you'll keep up the honour of the uniform, I can see."

So we reached the place and found them there, waiting us. We were placed twelve paces apart; he had the first shot. I stood gaily, looking him full in the face; I did not twitch an eyelash, I looked lovingly at him, for I knew what I would do. His shot just grazed my cheek and ear.

"Thank God," I cried, "no man has been killed," and I seized my pistol, turned back and flung it far away into the wood. "That's the place for you," I cried.

I turned to my adversary.

"Forgive me, young fool that I am, sir," I said, "for my unprovoked insult to you and for forcing you to fire at me. I am ten times worse than you and more, maybe. Tell that to the person whom you hold dearest in the world."

I had no sooner said this than they all three shouted at me.

"Upon my word," cried my adversary, annoyed, "if you did not want to fight, why did not you let me alone?"

"Yesterday I was a fool, to-day I know better," I answered him gaily.

"As to yesterday, I believe you, but as for to-day, it is difficult to agree with your opinion," said he.

"Bravo," I cried, clapping my hands. "I agree with you there too, I have deserved it!"

"Will you shoot, sir, or not?"

"No, I won't," I said; "if you like, fire at me again, but it would be better for you not to fire."

The seconds, especially mine, were shouting too: "Can you disgrace the regiment like this, facing your antagonist and begging his forgiveness! If I'd only known this!"

I stood facing them all, not laughing now.

"Gentlemen," I said, "is it really so wonderful in these days to find a man who can repent of his stupidity and publicly confess his wrongdoing?"

"But not in a duel," cried my second again.

"That's what's so strange," I said. "For I ought to have owned my fault as soon as I got here, before he had fired a shot, before leading him into a great and deadly sin; but we have made our life so grotesque, that to act in that way would have been almost impossible, for only after I had faced his shot at the distance of twelve paces could my words have any significance for him, and if I had spoken before, he would have said, 'He is a coward, the sight of the pistols has frightened him, no use to listen to him.' Gentlemen," I cried suddenly, speaking straight from my heart, "look around you at the gifts of God, the clear sky, the pure air, the tender grass, the birds; nature is beautiful and sinless, and we, only we, are sinful and foolish, and we don't understand that life is heaven, for we have only to understand that and it will at once be fulfilled in all its beauty, we shall embrace each other and weep."

I would have said more but I could not; my voice broke with the sweetness and youthful gladness of it, and there was such bliss in my heart as I had never known before in my life.

"All this is rational and edifying," said my antagonist, "and in any case you are an original person."

"You may laugh," I said to him, laughing too, "but afterwards you will approve of me."

"Oh, I am ready to approve of you now," said he; "will you shake hands? for I believe you are genuinely sincere."

"No," I said, "not now, later on when I have grown worthier and deserve your esteem, then shake hands and you will do well."

We went home, my second upbraiding me all the way, while I kissed him. All my comrades heard of the affair at once and gathered together to pass judgment on me the same day.

"He has disgraced the uniform," they said; "Let him resign his commission."

Some stood up for me: "He faced the shot," they said.

"Yes, but he was afraid of his other shot and begged for forgiveness."

"If he had been afraid of being shot, he would have shot his own pistol first before asking forgiveness, while he flung it loaded into the forest. No, there's something else in this, something original."

I enjoyed listening and looking at them. "My dear friends and comrades," said I, "don't worry about my resigning my commission, for I have done so already. I have sent in my papers this morning and as soon as I get my discharge I shall go into a monastery--it's with that object I am leaving the regiment."

When I had said this every one of them burst out laughing.

"You should have told us of that first, that explains everything, we can't judge a monk."

They laughed and could not stop themselves, and not scornfully, but kindly and merrily. They all felt friendly to me at once, even those who had been sternest in their censure, and all the following month, before my discharge came, they could not make enough of me. "Ah, you monk," they would say. And everyone said something kind to me, they began trying to dissuade me, even to pity me: "What are you doing to yourself?"

"No," they would say, "he is a brave fellow, he faced fire and could have fired his own pistol too, but he had a dream the night before that he should become a monk, that's why he did it."

It was the same thing with the society of the town. Till then I had been kindly received, but had not been the object of special attention, and now all came to know me at once and invited me; they laughed at me, but they loved me. I may mention that although everybody talked openly of our duel, the authorities took no notice of it, because my antagonist was a near relation of our general, and as there had been no bloodshed and no serious consequences, and as I resigned my commission, they took it as a joke. And I began then to speak aloud and fearlessly, regardless of their laughter, for it was always kindly and not spiteful laughter. These conversations mostly took place in the evenings, in the company of ladies; women particularly liked listening to me then and they made the men listen.

"But how can I possibly be responsible for all?" everyone would laugh in my face. "Can I, for instance, be responsible for you?"

"You may well not know it," I would answer, "since the whole world has long been going on a different line, since we consider the veriest lies as truth and demand the same lies from others. Here I have for once in my life acted sincerely and, well, you all look upon me as a madman. Though you are friendly to me, yet, you see, you all laugh at me."

"But how can we help being friendly to you?" said my hostess, laughing. The room was full of people. All of a sudden the young lady rose, on whose account the duel had been fought and whom only lately I had intended to be my future wife. I had not noticed her coming into the room. She got up, came to me and held out her hand.

"Let me tell you," she said, "that I am the first not to laugh at you, but on the contrary I thank you with tears and express my respect for you for your action then."

Her husband, too, came up and then they all approached me and almost kissed me. My heart was filled with joy, but my attention was especially caught by a middle-aged man who came up to me with the others. I knew him by name already, but had never made his acquaintance nor exchanged a word with him till that evening.

(d) The Mysterious Visitor.

He had long been an official in the town; he was in a prominent position, respected by all, rich and had a reputation for benevolence. He subscribed considerable sums to the almshouse and the orphan asylum; he was very charitable, too, in secret, a fact which only became known after his death. He was a man of about fifty, almost stern in appearance and not much given to conversation. He had been married about ten years and his wife, who was still young, had borne him three children. Well, I was sitting alone in my room the following evening, when my door suddenly opened and this gentleman walked in.

I must mention, by the way, that I was no longer living in my former quarters. As soon as I resigned my commission, I took rooms with an old lady, the widow of a government clerk. My landlady's servant waited upon me, for I had moved into her rooms simply because on my return from the duel I had sent Afanasy back to the regiment, as I felt ashamed to look him in the face after my last interview with him. So prone is the man of the world to be ashamed of any righteous action.

"I have," said my visitor, "with great interest listened to you speaking in different houses the last few days and I wanted at last to make your personal acquaintance, so as to talk to you more intimately. Can you, dear sir, grant me this favour?"

"I can, with the greatest pleasure, and I shall look upon it as an honour." I said this, though I felt almost dismayed, so greatly was I impressed from the first moment by the appearance of this man. For though other people had listened to me with interest and attention, no one had come to me before with such a serious, stern, and concentrated expression. And now he had come to see me in my own rooms. He sat down.

"You are, I see, a man of great strength of character" he said; "as you have dared to serve the truth, even when by doing so you risked incurring the contempt of all."

"Your praise is, perhaps, excessive," I replied.

"No, it's not excessive," he answered; "believe me, such a course of action is far more difficult than you think. It is that which has impressed me, and it is only on that account that I have come to you," he continued. "Tell me, please, that is if you are not annoyed by my perhaps unseemly curiosity, what were your exact sensations, if you can recall them, at the moment when you made up your mind to ask forgiveness at the duel. Do not think my question frivolous; on the contrary, I have in asking the question a secret motive of my own, which I will perhaps explain to you later on, if it is God's will that we should become more intimately acquainted."

All the while he was speaking, I was looking at him straight into the face and I felt all at once a complete trust in him and great curiosity on my side also, for I felt that there was some strange secret in his soul.

"You ask what were my exact sensations at the moment when I asked my opponent's forgiveness," I answered; "but I had better tell you from the beginning what I have not yet told anyone else." And I described all that had passed between Afanasy and me, and how I had bowed down to the ground at his feet. "From that you can see for yourself," I concluded, "that at the time of the duel it was easier for me, for I had made a beginning already at home, and when once I had started on that road, to go farther along it was far from being difficult, but became a source of joy and happiness."

I liked the way he looked at me as he listened. "All that," he said, "is exceedingly interesting. I will come to see you again and again."

And from that time forth he came to see me nearly every evening. And we should have become greater friends, if only he had ever talked of himself. But about himself he scarcely ever said a word, yet continually asked me about myself. In spite of that I became very fond of him and spoke with perfect frankness to him about all my feelings; "for," thought I, "what need have I to know his secrets, since I can see without that that is a good man? Moreover, though he is such a serious man and my senior, he comes to see a youngster like me and treats me as his equal." And I learned a great deal that was profitable from him, for he was a man of lofty mind.

"That life is heaven," he said to me suddenly, "that I have long been thinking about"; and all at once he added, "I think of nothing else indeed." He looked at me and smiled. "I am more convinced of it than you are, I will tell you later why."

I listened to him and thought that he evidently wanted to tell me something.

"Heaven," he went on, "lies hidden within all of us--here it lies hidden in me now, and if I will it, it will be revealed to me to-morrow and for all time."

I looked at him; he was speaking with great emotion and gazing mysteriously at me, as if he were questioning me.

"And that we are all responsible to all for all, apart from our own sins, you were quite right in thinking that, and it is wonderful how you could comprehend it in all its significance at once. And in very truth, so soon as men understand that, the Kingdom of Heaven will be for them not a dream, but a living reality."

"And when," I cried out to him bitterly, "when will that come to pass? and will it ever come to pass? Is not it simply a dream of ours?"

"What then, you don't believe it," he said. "You preach it and don't believe it yourself. Believe me, this dream, as you call it, will come to pass without doubt; it will come, but not now, for every process has its law. It's a spiritual, psychological process. To transform the world, to recreate it afresh, men must turn into another path psychologically. Until you have become really, in actual fact, a brother to everyone, brotherhood will not come to pass. No sort of scientific teaching, no kind of common interest, will ever teach men to share property and privileges with equal consideration for all. Everyone will think his share too small and they will be always envying, complaining and attacking one another. You ask when it will come to pass; it will come to pass, but first we have to go though the period of isolation."

"What do you mean by isolation?" I asked him.

"Why, the isolation that prevails everywhere, above all in our age--it has not fully developed, it has not reached its limit yet. For everyone strives to keep his individuality as apart as possible, wishes to secure the greatest possible fullness of life for himself; but meantime all his efforts result not in attaining fullness of life but self-destruction, for instead of self-realisation he ends by arriving at complete solitude. All mankind in our age have split up into units, they all keep apart, each in his own groove; each one holds aloof, hides himself and hides what he has, from the rest, and he ends by being repelled by others and repelling them. He heaps up riches by himself and thinks, 'How strong I am now and how secure,' and in his madness he does not understand that the more he heaps up, the more he sinks into self-destructive impotence. For he is accustomed to rely upon himself alone and to cut himself off from the whole; he has trained himself not to believe in the help of others, in men and in humanity, and only trembles for fear he should lose his money and the privileges that he has won for himself. Everywhere in these days men have, in their mockery, ceased to understand that the true security is to be found in social solidarity rather than in isolated individual effort. But this terrible individualism must inevitably have an end, and all will suddenly understand how unnaturally they are separated from one another. It will be the spirit of the time, and people will marvel that they have sat so long in darkness without seeing the light. And then the sign of the Son of Man will be seen in the heavens...But, until then, we must keep the banner flying. Sometimes even if he has to do it alone, and his conduct seems to be crazy, a man must set an example, and so draw men's souls out of their solitude, and spur them to some act of brotherly love, that the great idea may not die."

Our evenings, one after another, were spent in such stirring and fervent talk. I gave up society and visited my neighbours much less frequently. Besides, my vogue was somewhat over. I say this, not as blame, for they still loved me and treated me good-humouredly, but there's no denying that fashion is a great power in society. I began to regard my mysterious visitor with admiration, for besides enjoying his intelligence, I began to perceive that he was brooding over some plan in his heart, and was preparing himself perhaps for a great deed. Perhaps he liked my not showing curiosity about his secret, not seeking to discover it by direct question nor by insinuation. But I noticed at last, that he seemed to show signs of wanting to tell me something. This had become quite evident, indeed, about a month after he first began to visit me.

"Do you know," he said to me once, "that people are very inquisitive about us in the town and wonder why I come to see you so often. But let them wonder, for soon all will be explained."

Sometimes an extraordinary agitation would come over him, and almost always on such occasions he would get up and go away. Sometimes he would fix a long piercing look upon me, and I thought, "He will say something directly now." But he would suddenly begin talking of something ordinary and familiar. He often complained of headache too.

One day, quite unexpectedly indeed, after he had been talking with great fervour a long time, I saw him suddenly turn pale, and his face worked convulsively, while he stared persistently at me.

"What's the matter?" I said; "do you feel ill?"--he had just been complaining of headache.

"I...do you know...I murdered someone."

He said this and smiled with a face as white as chalk. "Why is it he is smiling?" The thought flashed through my mind before I realised anything else. I too turned pale.

"What are you saying?" I cried.

"You see," he said, with a pale smile, "how much it has cost me to say the first word. Now I have said it, I feel I've taken the first step and shall go on."

For a long while I could not believe him, and I did not believe him at that time, but only after he had been to see me three days running and told me all about it. I thought he was mad, but ended by being convinced, to my great grief and amazement. His crime was a great and terrible one.

Fourteen years before, he had murdered the widow of a landowner, a wealthy and handsome young woman who had a house in our town. He fell passionately in love with her, declared his feeling and tried to persuade her to marry him. But she had already given her heart to another man, an officer of noble birth and high rank in the service, who was at that time away at the front, though she was expecting him soon to return. She refused his offer and begged him not to come and see her. After he had ceased to visit her, he took advantage of his knowledge of the house to enter at night through the garden by the roof, at great risk of discovery. But, as often happens, a crime committed with extraordinary audacity is more successful than others.

Entering the garret through the skylight, he went down the ladder, knowing that the door at the bottom of it was sometimes, through the negligence of the servants, left unlocked. He hoped to find it so, and so it was. He made his way in the dark to her bedroom, where a light was burning. As though on purpose, both her maids had gone off to a birthday party in the same street, without asking leave. The other servants slept in the servants' quarters or in the kitchen on the ground floor. His passion flamed up at the sight of her asleep, and then vindictive, jealous anger took possession of his heart, and like a drunken man, beside himself, he thrust a knife into her heart, so that she did not even cry out. Then with devilish and criminal cunning he contrived that suspicion should fall on the servants. He was so base as to take her purse, to open her chest with keys from under her pillow, and to take some things from it, doing it all as it might have been done by an ignorant servant, leaving valuable papers and taking only money. He took some of the larger gold things, but left smaller articles that were ten times as valuable. He took with him, too, some things for himself as remembrances, but of that later. Having done this awful deed. he returned by the way he had come.

Neither the next day, when the alarm was raised, nor at any time after in his life, did anyone dream of suspecting that he was the criminal. No one indeed knew of his love for her, for he was always reserved and silent and had no friend to whom he would have opened his heart. He was looked upon simply as an acquaintance, and not a very intimate one, of the murdered woman, as for the previous fortnight he had not even visited her. A serf of hers called Pyotr was at once suspected, and every circumstance confirmed the suspicion. The man knew--indeed his mistress did not conceal the fact--that having to send one of her serfs as a recruit she had decided to send him, as he had no relations and his conduct was unsatisfactory. People had heard him angrily threatening to murder her when he was drunk in a tavern. Two days before her death, he had run away, staying no one knew where in the town. The day after the murder, he was found on the road leading out of the town, dead drunk, with a knife in his pocket, and his right hand happened to be stained with blood. He declared that his nose had been bleeding, but no one believed him. The maids confessed that they had gone to a party and that the street door had been left open till they returned. And a number of similar details came to light, throwing suspicion on the innocent servant.

They arrested him, and he was tried for the murder; but a week after the arrest, the prisoner fell sick of a fever and died unconscious in the hospital. There the matter ended and the judges and the authorities and everyone in the town remained convinced that the crime had been committed by no one but the servant who had died in the hospital. And after that the punishment began.

My mysterious visitor, now my friend, told me that at first he was not in the least troubled by pangs of conscience. He was miserable a long time, but not for that reason; only from regret that he had killed the woman he loved, that she was no more, that in killing her he had killed his love, while the fire of passion was still in his veins. But of the innocent blood he had shed, of the murder of a fellow creature, he scarcely thought. The thought that his victim might have become the wife of another man was insupportable to him, and so, for a long time, he was convinced in his conscience that he could not have acted otherwise.

At first he was worried at the arrest of the servant, but his illness and death soon set his mind at rest, for the man's death was apparently (so he reflected at the time) not owing to his arrest or his fright, but a chill he had taken on the day he ran away, when he had lain all night dead drunk on the damp ground. The theft of the money and other things troubled him little, for he argued that the theft had not been committed for gain but to avert suspicion. The sum stolen was small, and he shortly afterwards subscribed the whole of it, and much more, towards the funds for maintaining an almshouse in the town. He did this on purpose to set his conscience at rest about the theft, and it's a remarkable fact that for a long time he really was at peace--he told me this himself. He entered then upon a career of great activity in the service, volunteered for a difficult and laborious duty, which occupied him two years, and being a man of strong will almost forgot the past. Whenever he recalled it, he tried not to think of it at all. He became active in philanthropy too, founded and helped to maintain many institutions in the town, did a good deal in the two capitals, and in both Moscow and Petersburg was elected a member of philanthropic societies.

At last, however, he began brooding over the past, and the strain of it was too much for him. Then he was attracted by a fine and intelligent girl and soon after married her, hoping that marriage would dispel his lonely depression, and that by entering on a new life and scrupulously doing his duty to his wife and children, he would escape from old memories altogether. But the very opposite of what he expected happened. He began, even in the first month of his marriage, to be continually fretted by the thought, "My wife loves me--but what if she knew?" When she first told him that she would soon bear him a child, he was troubled. "I am giving life, but I have taken life." Children came. "How dare I love them, teach and educate them, how can I talk to them of virtue? I have shed blood." They were splendid children, he longed to caress them; "and I can't look at their innocent candid faces, I am unworthy."

At last he began to be bitterly and ominously haunted by the blood of his murdered victim, by the young life he had destroyed, by the blood that cried out for vengeance. He had begun to have awful dreams. But, being a man of fortitude, he bore his suffering a long time, thinking: "I shall expiate everything by this secret agony." But that hope, too, was vain; the longer it went on, the more intense was his suffering.

He was respected in society for his active benevolence, though everyone was overawed by his stern and gloomy character. But the more he was respected, the more intolerable it was for him. He confessed to me that he had thoughts of killing himself. But he began to be haunted by another idea--an idea which he had at first regarded as impossible and unthinkable, though at last it got such a hold on his heart that he could not shake it off. He dreamed of rising up, going out and confessing in the face of all men that he had committed murder. For three years this dream had pursued him, haunting him in different forms. At last he believed with his whole heart that if he confessed his crime, he would heal his soul and would be at peace for ever. But this belief filled his heart with terror, for how could he carry it out? And then came what happened at my duel.

"Looking at you, I have made up my mind."

I looked at him.

"Is it possible," I cried, clasping my hands, "that such a trivial incident could give rise to a resolution in you?"

"My resolution has been growing for the last three years," he answered, "and your story only gave the last touch to it. Looking at you, I reproached myself and envied you." He said this to me almost sullenly.

"But you won't be believed," I observed; "it's fourteen years ago."

"I have proofs, great proofs. I shall show them."

Then I cried and kissed him.

"Tell me one thing, one thing," he said (as though it all depended upon me), "my wife, my children! My wife may die of grief, and though my children won't lose their rank and property, they'll be a convict's children and for ever! And what a memory, what a memory of me I shall leave in their hearts!"

I said nothing.

"And to part from them, to leave them for ever? It's for ever, you know, for ever!" I sat still and repeated a silent prayer. I got up at last, I felt afraid.

"Well?" He looked at me.

"Go!" said I, "confess. Everything passes, only the truth remains. Your children will understand, when they grow up, the nobility of your resolution."

He left me that time as though he had made up his mind. Yet for more than a fortnight afterwards, he came to me every evening, still preparing himself, still unable to bring himself to the point. He made my heart ache. One day he would come determined and say fervently:

"I know it will be heaven for me, heaven, the moment I confess. Fourteen years I've been in hell. I want to suffer. I will take my punishment and begin to live. You can pass through the world doing wrong, but there's no turning back. Now I dare not love my neighbour nor even my own children. Good God, my children will understand, perhaps, what my punishment has cost me and will not condemn me! God is not in strength but in truth."

"All will understand your sacrifice," I said to him, "if not at once, they will understand later; for you have served truth, the higher truth, not of the earth."

And he would go away seeming comforted, but next day he would come again, bitter, pale, sarcastic.

"Every time I come to you, you look at me so inquisitively as though to say, 'He has still not confessed!' Wait a bit, don't despise me too much. It's not such an easy thing to do as you would think. Perhaps I shall not do it at all. You won't go and inform against me then, will you?"

And far from looking at him with indiscreet curiosity, I was afraid to look at him at all. I was quite ill from anxiety, and my heart was full of tears. I could not sleep at night.

"I have just come from my wife," he went on. "Do you understand what the word 'wife' means? When I went out, the children called to me, 'Good-bye, father, make haste back to read The Children's Magazine with us.' No, you don't understand that! No one is wise from another man's woe."

His eyes were glittering, his lips were twitching. Suddenly he struck the table with his fist so that everything on it danced--it was the first time he had done such a thing, he was such a mild man.

"But need I?" he exclaimed, "must I? No one has been condemned, no one has been sent to Siberia in my place, the man died of fever. And I've been punished by my sufferings for the blood I shed. And I shan't be believed, they won't believe my proofs. Need I confess, need I? I am ready to go on suffering all my life for the blood I have shed, if only my wife and children may be spared. Will it be just to ruin them with me? Aren't we making a mistake? What is right in this case? And will people recognise it, will they appreciate it, will they respect it?"

"Good Lord!" I thought to myself, "he is thinking of other people's respect at such a moment!" And I felt so sorry for him then, that I believe I would have shared his fate if it could have comforted him. I saw he was beside himself. I was aghast, realising with my heart as well as my mind what such a resolution meant.

"Decide my fate!" he exclaimed again.

"Go and confess," I whispered to him. My voice failed me, but I whispered it firmly. I took up the New Testament from the table, the Russian translation, and showed him the Gospel of St. John, chapter 12, verse 24:

"Verily, verily, I say unto you, except a corn of wheat fall into the ground and die, it abideth alone: but if it die, it bringeth forth much fruit."

I had just been reading that verse when he came in. He read it.

"That's true," he said, he smiled bitterly. "It's terrible the things you find in those books," he said, after a pause. "It's easy enough to thrust them upon one. And who wrote them? Can they have been written by men?"

"The Holy Spirit wrote them," said I.

"It's easy for you to prate," he smiled again, this time almost with hatred.

I took the book again, opened it in another place and showed him the Epistle to the Hebrews, chapter 10, verse 31. He read:

"It   is   a   fearful   thing   to   fall into the hands of the living God."

He read it and simply flung down the book. He was trembling all over.

"An awful text," he said. "There's no denying you've picked out fitting ones." He rose from the chair. "Well!" he said, "good-bye, perhaps I shan't come again...we shall meet in heaven. So I have been for fourteen years 'in the hands of the living God,' that's how one must think of those fourteen years. To-morrow I will beseech those hands to let me go."

I wanted to take him in my arms and kiss him, but I did not dare--his face was contorted add sombre. He went away.

"Good God," I thought, "what has he gone to face!" I fell on my knees before the ikon and wept for him before the Holy Mother of God, our swift defender and helper. I was half an hour praying in tears, and it was late, about midnight. Suddenly I saw the door open and he came in again. I was surprised.

Where have you been?" I asked him.

"I think," he said, "I've forgotten something...my handkerchief, I think...Well, even if I've not forgotten anything, let me stay a little."

He sat down. I stood over him.

"You sit down, too," said he.

I sat down. We sat still for two minutes; he looked intently at me and suddenly smiled. I remembered that-- then he got up, embraced me warmly and kissed me.

"Remember," he said, "how I came to you a second time. Do you hear, remember it!"

And he went out.

"To-morrow," I thought.

And so it was. I did not know that evening that the next day was his birthday. I had not been out for the last few days, so I had no chance of hearing it from anyone. On that day he always had a great gathering, everyone in the town went to it. It was the same this time. After dinner he walked into the middle of the room, with a paper in his hand--a formal declaration to the chief of his department who was present. This declaration he read aloud to the whole assembly. It contained a full account of the crime, in every detail.

"I cut myself off from men as a monster. God has visited me," he said in conclusion. "I want to suffer for my sin!"

Then he brought out and laid on the table all the things he had been keeping for fourteen years, that he thought would prove his crime, the jewels belonging to the murdered woman which he had stolen to divert suspicion, a cross and a locket taken from her neck with a portrait of her betrothed in the locket, her notebook and two letters; one from her betrothed, telling her that he would soon be with her, and her unfinished answer left on the table to be sent off next day. He carried off these two letters--what for? Why had he kept them for fourteen years afterwards instead of destroying them as evidence against him?

And this is what happened: everyone was amazed and horrified, everyone refused to believe it and thought that he was deranged, though all listened with intense curiosity. A few days later it was fully decided and agreed in every house that the unhappy man was mad. The legal authorities could not refuse to take the case up, but they too dropped it. Though the trinkets and letters made them ponder, they decided that even if they did turn out to be authentic, no charge could be based on those alone. Besides, she might have given him those things as a friend, or asked him to take care of them for her. I heard afterwards, however, that the genuineness of the things was proved by the friends and relations of the murdered woman, and that there was no doubt about them. Yet nothing was destined to come of it, after all.

Five days later, all had heard that he was ill and that his life was in danger. The nature of his illness I can't explain; they said it was an affection of the heart. But it became known that the doctors had been induced by his wife to investigate his mental condition also, and had come to the conclusion that it was a case of insanity. I betrayed nothing, though people ran to question me. But when I wanted to visit him, I was for a long while forbidden to do so, above all by his wife.

"It's you who have caused his illness," she said to me; "he was always gloomy, but for the last year people noticed that he was peculiarly excited and did strange things, and now you have been the ruin of him. Your preaching has brought him to this; for the last month he was always with you."

Indeed, not only his wife but the whole town were down upon me and blamed me. "It's all your doing," they said. I was silent and indeed rejoiced at heart, for I saw plainly God's mercy to the man who had turned against himself and punished himself. I could not believe in his insanity.

They let me see him at last. he insisted upon saying good-bye to me. I went in to him and saw at once, that not only his days, but his hours were numbered. He was weak, yellow, his hands trembled, he gasped for breath, but his face was full of tender and happy feeling.

"It is done!" he said. "I've long been yearning to see you. Why didn't you come?"

I did not tell him that they would not let me see him.

"God has had pity on me and is calling me to Himself. I know I am dying, but I feel joy and peace for the first time after so many years. There was heaven in my heart from the moment I had done what I had to do. Now I dare to love my children and to kiss them. Neither my wife nor the judges, nor anyone has believed it. My children will never believe it either. I see in that God's mercy to them. I shall die, and my name will be without a stain for them. And now I feel God near, my heart rejoices as in Heaven...I have done my duty."

He could not speak, he gasped for breath, he pressed my hand warmly, looking fervently at me. We did not talk for long, his wife kept peeping in at us. But he had time to whisper to me:

"Do you remember how I came back to you that second time, at midnight? I told you to remember it. You know what I came back for? I came to kill you!"

I started.

"I went out from you then into the darkness, I wandered about the streets, struggling with myself. And suddenly I hated you so that I could hardly bear it. Now, I thought, he is all that binds me, and he is my judge. I can't refuse to face my punishment to-morrow, for he knows all. It was not that I was afraid you would betray me (I never even thought of that), but I thought, 'How can I look him in the face if I don't confess?' And if you had been at the other end of the earth, but alive, it would have been all the same, the thought was unendurable that you were alive knowing everything and condemning me. I hated you as though you were the cause, as though you were to blame for everything. I came back to you then, remembering that you had a dagger lying on your table. I sat down and asked you to sit down, and for a whole minute I pondered. If I had killed you, I should have been ruined by that murder even if I had not confessed the other. But I didn't think about that at all, and I didn't want to think of it at that moment. I only hated you and longed to revenge myself on you for everything. The Lord vanquished the devil in my heart. But let me tell you, you were never nearer death."

A week later he died. The whole town followed him to the grave. The chief priest made a speech full of feeling. All lamented the terrible illness that had cut short his days. But all the town was up in arms against me after the funeral, and people even refused to see me. Some, at first a few and afterwards more, began indeed to believe in the truth of his story, and they visited me and questioned me with great interest and eagerness, for man loves to see the downfall and disgrace of the righteous. But I held my tongue, and very shortly after, I left the town, and five months later by God's grace I entered the safe and blessed path, praising the unseen finger which had guided me so clearly to it. But I remember in my prayer to this day, the servant of God, Mihail, who suffered so greatly.

Chapter 3. Conversations and Exhortations of Father Zossima. The Russian Monk and his possible Significance.

Fathers and teachers, what is the monk? In the cultivated world the word is nowadays pronounced by some people with a jeer, and by others it is used as a term of abuse, and this contempt for the monk is growing. It is true, alas, it is true, that there are many sluggards, gluttons, profligates, and insolent beggars among monks. Educated people point to these: "You are idlers, useless members of society, you live on the labour of others, you are shameless beggars." And yet how many meek and humble monks there are, yearning for solitude and fervent prayer in peace! These are less noticed, or passed over in silence. And how suprised men would be if I were to say that from these meek monks, who yearn for solitary prayer, the salvation of Russia will come perhaps once more! For they are in truth made ready in peace and quiet "for the day and the hour, the month and the year." Meanwhile, in their solitude, they keep the image of Christ fair and undefiled, in the purity of God's truth, from the times of the Fathers of old, the Apostles and the martyrs. And when the time comes they will show it to the tottering creeds of the world. That is a great thought. That star will rise out of the East.

That is my view of the monk, and is it false? Is it too proud? Look at the worldly and all who set themselves up above the people of God; has not God's image and His truth been distorted in them? They have science; but in science there is nothing but what is the object of sense. The spiritual world, the higher part of man's being is rejected altogether, dismissed with a sort of triumph, even with hatred. The world has proclaimed the reign of freedom, especially of late, but what do we see in this freedom of theirs? Nothing but slavery and self-destruction! For the world says:

"You have desires and so satisfy them, for you have the same rights as the most rich and powerful. Don't be afraid of satisfying them and even multiply your desires." That is the modern doctrine of the world. In that they see freedom. And what follows from this right of multiplication of desires? In the rich, isolation and spiritual suicide; in the poor, envy and murder; for they have been given rights, but have not been shown the means of satisfying their wants. They maintain that the world is getting more and more united, more and more bound together in brotherly community, as it overcomes distance and sets thoughts flying through the air.

Alas, put no faith in such a bond of union. Interpreting freedom as the multiplication and rapid satisfaction of desires, men distort their own nature, for many senseless and foolish desires and habits and ridiculous fancies are fostered in them. They live only for mutual envy, for luxury and ostentation. To have dinners visits, carriages, rank, and slaves to wait on one is looked upon as a necessity, for which life, honour and human feeling are sacrificed, and men even commit suicide if they are unable to satisfy it. We see the same thing among those who are not rich, while the poor drown their unsatisfied need and their envy in drunkenness. But soon they will drink blood instead of wine, they are being led on to it. I ask you is such a man free? I knew one "champion of freedom" who told me himself that, when he was deprived of tobacco in prison, he was so wretched at the privation that he almost went and betrayed his cause for the sake of getting tobacco again! And such a man says, "I am fighting for the cause of humanity."

How can such a one fight? What is he fit for? He is capable perhaps of some action quickly over, but he cannot hold out long. And it's no wonder that instead of gaining freedom they have sunk into slavery, and instead of serving, the cause of brotherly love and the union of humanity have fallen, on the contrary, into dissension and isolation, as my mysterious visitor and teacher said to me in my youth. And therefore the idea of the service of humanity, of brotherly love and the solidarity of mankind, is more and more dying out in the world, and indeed this idea is sometimes treated with derision. For how can a man shake off his habits? What can become of him if he is in such bondage to the habit of satisfying the innumerable desires he has created for himself? He is isolated, and what concern has he with the rest of humanity? They have succeeded in accumulating a greater mass of objects, but the joy in the world has grown less.

The monastic way is very different. Obedience, fasting, and prayer are laughed at, yet only through them lies the way to real, true freedom. I cut off my superfluous and unnecessary desires, I subdue my proud and wanton will and chastise it with obedience, and with God's help I attain freedom of spirit and with it spiritual joy. Which is most capable of conceiving a great idea and serving it--the rich in his isolation or the man who has freed himself from the tyranny of material things and habits? The monk is reproached for his solitude, "You have secluded yourself within the walls of the monastery for your own salvation, and have forgotten the brotherly service of humanity!" But we shall see which will be most zealous in the cause of brotherly love. For it is not we, but they, who are in isolation, though they don't see that. Of old, leaders of the people came from among us, and why should they not again? The same meek and humble ascetics will rise up and go out to work for the great cause. The salvation of Russia comes from the people. And the Russian monk has always been on the side of the people. We are isolated only if the people are isolated. The people believe as we do, and an unbelieving reformer will never do anything in Russia, even if he is sincere in heart and a genius. Remember that! The people will meet the atheist and overcome him, and Russia will be one and orthodox. Take care of the peasant and guard his heart. Go on educating him quietly. That's your duty as monks, for the peasant has God in his heart.

(f) Of Masters and Servants, and of whether it is
possible for them to be Brothers in the Spirit.

Of course, I don't deny that there is sin in the peasants too. And the fire of corruption is spreading visibly, hourly, working from above downwards. The spirit of isolation is coming upon the people too. Money-lenders and devourers of the commune are rising up. Already the merchant grows more and more eager for rank, and strives to show himself cultured though he has not a trace of culture, and to this end meanly despises his old traditions, and is even ashamed of the faith of his fathers. He visits princes, though he is only a peasant corrupted. The peasants are rotting in drunkenness and cannot shake off the habit. And what cruelty to their wives, to their children even! All from drunkenness! I've seen in the factories children of nine years old, frail, rickety, bent and already depraved. The stuffy workshop, the din of machinery, work all day long, the vile language and the drink, the drink--is that what a little child's heart needs? He needs sunshine, childish play, good examples all about him, and at least a little love. There must be no more of this, monks, no more torturing of children, rise up and preach that, make haste, make haste!

146

But God will save Russia, for though the peasants are corrupted and cannot renounce their filthy sin, yet they know it is cursed by God and that they do wrong in sinning. So that our people still believe in righteousness, have faith in God and weep tears of devotion.

It is different with the upper classes. They, following science, want to base justice on reason alone, but not with Christ, as before, and they have already proclaimed that there is no crime, that there is no sin. And that's consistent, for if you have no God what is the meaning of crime? In Europe the people are already rising up against the rich with violence, and the leaders of the people are everywhere leading them to bloodshed, and teaching them that their wrath is righteous. But their "wrath is accursed, for it is cruel." But God will save Russia as He has saved her many times. Salvation will come from the people, from their faith and their meekness.

Fathers and teachers, watch over the people's faith and this will not be a dream. I've been struck all my life in our great people by their dignity, their true and seemly dignity. I've seen it myself, I can testify to it, I've seen it and marvelled at it, I've seen it in spite of the degraded sins and poverty-stricken appearance of our peasantry. They are not servile, and even after two centuries of serfdom they are free in manner and bearing, yet without insolence, and not revengeful and not envious. "You are rich and noble, you are clever and talented, well, be so, God bless you. I respect you, but I know that I too am a man. By the very fact that I respect you without envy I prove my dignity as a man."

In truth if they don't say this (for they don't know how to say this yet), that is how they act. I have seen it myself, I have known it myself, and, would you believe it, the poorer our Russian peasant is, the more noticeable is that serene goodness, for the rich among them are for the most part corrupted already, and much of that is due to our carelessness and indifference. But God will save His people, for Russia is great in her humility. I dream of seeing, and seem to see clearly already, our future. It will come to pass that even the most corrupt of our rich will end by being ashamed of his riches before the poor, and the poor, seeing his humility, will understand and give way before him, will respond joyfully and kindly to his honourable shame. Believe me that it will end in that; things are moving to that. Equality is to be found only in the spiritual dignity of man, and that will only be understood among us. If we were brothers, there would be fraternity, but before that they will never agree about the division of wealth. We preserve the image of Christ, and it will shine forth like a precious diamond to the whole world. So may it be, so may it be!

Fathers and teachers, a touching incident befell me once. In my wanderings I met in the town of K. my old orderly, Afanasy. It was eight years since I had parted from him. He chanced to see me in the market-place, recognised me, ran up to me, and how delighted he was! He simply pounced on me: "Master dear, is it you? Is it really you I see?" He took me home with him.

He was no longer in the army, he was married and already had two little children. He and his wife earned their living as costermongers in the market-place. His room was poor, but bright and clean. He made me sit down, set the samovar, sent for his wife, as though my appearance were a festival for them. He brought me his children: "Bless them, Father."

"Is it for me to bless them? I am only a humble monk. I will pray for them. And for you, Afanasy Pavlovitch, I have prayed every day since that day, for it all came from you," said I. And I explained that to him as well as I could. And what do you think? The man kept gazing at me and could not believe that I, his former master, an officer, was now before him in such a guise and position; it made him shed tears.

"Why are you weeping?" said I, "better rejoice over me, dear friend, whom I can never forget, for my path is a glad and joyful one."

He did not say much, but kept sighing and shaking his head over me tenderly.

"What has become of your fortune?" he asked.

"I gave it to the monastery," I answered; "we live in common."

After tea I began saying good-bye, and suddenly he brought out half a rouble as an offering to the monastery, and another half-rouble I saw him thrusting hurriedly into my hand: "That's for you in your wanderings, it may be of use to you, Father."

I took his half-rouble, bowed to him and his wife, and went out rejoicing. And on my way I thought: "Here we are both now, he at home and I on the road, sighing and shaking our heads, no doubt, and yet smiling joyfully in the gladness of our hearts, remembering how God brought about our meeting."

I have never seen him again since then. I had been his master and he my servant, but now when we exchanged a loving kiss with softened hearts, there was a great human bond between us. I have thought a great deal about that, and now what I think is this: Is it so inconceivable that that grand and simple-hearted unity might in due time become universal among the Russian people? I believe that it will come to pass and that the time is at hand.

And of servants I will add this: In old days when I was young I was often angry with servants; "the cook had served something too hot, the orderly had not brushed my clothes." But what taught me better then was a thought of my dear brother's, which I had heard from him in childhood: "Am I worth it, that another should serve me and be ordered about by me in his poverty and ignorance?" And I wondered at the time that such simple and self-evident ideas should be so slow to occur to our minds.

It is impossible that there should be no servants in the world, but act so that your servant may be freer in spirit than if he were not a servant. And why cannot I be a servant to my servant and even let him see it, and that without any pride on my part or any mistrust on his? Why should not my servant be like my own kindred, so that I may take him into my family and rejoice in doing so? Even now this can be done, but it will lead to the grand unity of men in the future, when a man will not seek servants for himself, or desire to turn his fellow creatures into servants as he does now, but on the contrary, will long with his whole heart to be the servant of all, as the Gospel teaches.

And can it be a dream, that in the end man will find his joy only in deeds of light and mercy, and not in cruel pleasures as now, in gluttony, fornication, ostentation, boasting and envious rivalry of one with the other? I firmly believe that it is not and that the time is at hand. People laugh and ask: "When will that time come and does it look like coming?" I believe that with Christ's help we shall accomplish this great thing. And how many ideas there have been on earth in the history of man which were unthinkable ten years before they appeared! Yet when their destined hour had come, they came forth and spread over the whole earth. So it will be with us, and our people will shine forth in the world, and all men will say: "The stone which the builders rejected has become the cornerstone of the building."

And we may ask the scornful themselves: If our hope is a dream, when will you build up your edifice and order things justly by your intellect alone, without Christ? If they declare that it is they who are advancing towards unity, only the most simple-hearted among them believe it, so that one may positively marvel at such simplicity. Of a truth, they have more fantastic dreams than we. They aim at justice, but, denying Christ, they will end by flooding the earth with blood, for blood cries out for blood, and he that taketh up the sword shall perish by the sword. And if it were not for Christ's covenant, they would slaughter one another down to the last two men on earth. And those two last men would not be able to restrain each other in their pride, and the one would slay the other and then himself. And that would come to pass, were it not for the promise of Christ that for the sake of the humble and meek the days shall be shortened.

While I was still wearing an officer's uniform after my duel, I talked about servants in general society, and I remember everyone was amazed at me. "What!" they asked, "are we to make our servants sit down on the sofa and offer them tea?" And I answered them: "Why not, sometimes at least?" Everyone laughed. Their question was frivolous and my answer was not clear; but the thought in it was to some extent right.

(g) Of Prayer, of Love, and of Contact with other Worlds.

Young man, be not forgetful of prayer. Every time you pray, if your prayer is sincere, there will be new feeling and new meaning in it, which will give you fresh courage, and you will understand that prayer is an education. Remember, too, every day, and whenever you can, repeat to yourself, "Lord, have mercy on all who appear before Thee to-day." For every hour and every moment thousands of men leave life on this earth, and their souls appear before God. And how many of them depart in solitude, unknown, sad, dejected that no one mourns for them or even knows whether they have lived or not! And behold, from the other end of the earth perhaps, your prayer for their rest will rise up to God though you knew them not nor they you. How touching it must be to a soul standing in dread before the Lord to feel at that instant that, for him too, there is one to pray, that there is a fellow creature left on earth to love him too! And God will look on you both more graciously, for if you have had so much pity on him, how much will He have pity Who is infinitely more loving and merciful than you! And He will forgive him for your sake.

Brothers, have no fear of men's sin. Love a man even in his sin, for that is the semblance of Divine Love and is the highest love on earth. Love all God's creation, the whole and every grain of sand in it. Love every leaf, every ray of God's light. Love the animals, love the plants, love everything. If you love everything, you will perceive the divine mystery in things. Once you perceive it, you will begin to comprehend it better every day. And you will come at last to love the whole world with an all-embracing love. Love the animals: God has given them the rudiments of thought and joy untroubled. Do not trouble it, don't harass them, don't deprive them of their happiness, don't work against God's intent. Man, do not pride yourself on superiority to the animals; they are without sin, and you, with your greatness, defile the earth by your appearance on it, and leave the traces of your foulness after you--alas, it is true of almost every one of us! Love children especially, for they too are sinless like the angels; they live to soften and purify our hearts and, as it were, to guide us. Woe to him who offends a child! Father Anfim taught me to love children. The kind, silent man used often on our wanderings to spend the farthings given us on sweets and cakes for the children. He could not pass by a child without emotion. That's the nature of the man.

At some thoughts one stands perplexed, especially at the sight of men's sin, and wonders whether one should use force or humble love. Always decide to use humble love. If you resolve on that once for all, you may subdue the whole world. Loving humility is marvellously strong, the strongest of all things, and there is nothing else like it.

Every day and every hour, every minute, walk round yourself and watch yourself, and see that your image is a seemly one. You pass by a little child, you pass by, spiteful, with ugly words, with wrathful heart; you may not have noticed the child, but he has seen you, and your image, unseemly and ignoble, may remain in his defenceless heart. You don't know it, but you may have sown an evil seed in him and it may grow, and all because you were not careful before the child, because you did not foster in yourself a careful, actively benevolent love. Brothers, love is a teacher; but one must know how to acquire it, for it is hard to acquire, it is dearly bought, it is won slowly by long labour. For we must love not only occasionally, for a moment, but for ever. Everyone can love occasionally, even the wicked can.

My brother asked the birds to forgive him; that sounds senseless, but it is right; for all is like an ocean, all is flowing and blending; a touch in one place sets up movement at the other end of the earth. It may be senseless to beg forgiveness of the birds, but birds would be happier at your side--a little happier, anyway--and children and all animals, if you were nobler than you are now. It's all like an ocean, I tell you. Then you would pray to the birds too, consumed by an all-embracing love, in a sort of transport, and pray that they too will forgive you your sin. Treasure this ecstasy, however senseless it may seem to men.

My friends, pray to God for gladness. Be glad as children, as the birds of heaven. And let not the sin of men confound you in your doings. Fear not that it will wear away your work and hinder its being accomplished. Do not say, "Sin is mighty, wickedness is mighty, evil environment is mighty, and we are lonely and helpless, and evil environment is wearing us away and hindering our good work from being done." Fly from that dejection, children! There is only one means of salvation, then take yourself and make yourself responsible for all men's sins, that is the truth, you know, friends, for as soon as you sincerely make yourself responsible for everything and for all men, you will see at once that it is really so, and that you are to blame for everyone and for all things. But throwing your own indolence and impotence on others you will end by sharing the pride of Satan and murmuring against God.

Of the pride of Satan what I think is this: it is hard for us on earth to comprehend it, and therefore it is so easy to fall into error and to share it, even imagining that we are doing something grand and fine. Indeed, many of the strongest feelings and movements of our nature we cannot comprehend on earth. Let not that be a stumbling-block, and think not that it may serve as a justification to you for anything. For the Eternal judge asks of you what you can comprehend and not what you cannot. You will know that yourself hereafter, for you will behold all things truly then and will not dispute them. On earth, indeed, we are, as it were, astray, and if it were not for the precious image of Christ before us, we should be undone and altogether lost, as was the human race before the flood. Much on earth is hidden from us, but to make up for that we have been given a precious mystic sense of our living bond with the other world, with the higher heavenly world, and the roots of our thoughts and feelings are not here but in other worlds. That is why the philosophers say that we cannot apprehend the reality of things on earth.

God took seeds from different worlds and sowed them on this earth, and His garden grew up and everything came up that could come up, but what grows lives and is alive only through the feeling of its contact with other mysterious worlds. If that feeling grows weak or is destroyed in you, the heavenly growth will die away in you. Then you will be indifferent to life and even grow to hate it. That's what I think.

(h) Can a Man judge his Fellow Creatures? Faith to the End.

Remember particularly that you cannot be a judge of anyone. For no one can judge a criminal until he recognises that he is just such a criminal as the man standing before him, and that he perhaps is more than all men to blame for that crime. When he understands that, he will be able to be a judge. Though that sounds absurd, it is true. If I had been righteous myself, perhaps there would have been no criminal standing before me. If you can take upon yourself the crime of the criminal your heart is judging, take it at once, suffer for him yourself, and let him go without reproach. And even if the law itself makes you his judge, act in the same spirit so far as possible, for he will go away and condemn himself more bitterly than you have done. If, after your kiss, he goes away untouched, mocking at you, do not let that be a stumbling-block to you. It shows his time has not yet come, but it will come in due course. And if it come not, no Matter; if not he, then another in his place will understand and suffer, and judge and condemn himself, and the truth will be fulfilled. Believe that, believe it without doubt; for in that lies all the hope and faith of the saints.

Work without ceasing. If you remember in the night as you go to sleep, "I have not done what I ought to have done," rise up at once and do it. If the people around you are spiteful and callous and will not hear you, fall down before them and beg their forgiveness; for in truth you are to blame for their not wanting to hear you. And

149

if you cannot speak to them in their bitterness, serve them in silence and in humility, never losing hope. If all men abandon you and even drive you away by force, then when you are left alone fall on the earth and kiss it, water it with your tears and it will bring forth fruit even though no one has seen or heard you in your solitude. Believe to the end, even if all men went astray and you were left the only one faithful; bring your offering even then and praise God in your loneliness. And if two of you are gathered together--then there is a whole world, a world of living love. Embrace each other tenderly and praise God, for if only in you two His truth has been fulfilled.

If you sin yourself and grieve even unto death for your sins or for your sudden sin, then rejoice for others, rejoice for the righteous man, rejoice that if you have sinned, he is righteous and has not sinned.

If the evil-doing of men moves you to indignation and overwhelming distress, even to a desire for vengeance on the evil-doers, shun above all things that feeling. Go at once and seek suffering for yourself, as though you were yourself guilty of that wrong. Accept that suffering and bear it and your heart will find comfort, and you will understand that you too are guilty, for you might have been a light to the evil-doers, even as the one man sinless, and you were not a light to them. If you had been a light, you would have lightened the path for others too, and the evil-doer might perhaps have been saved by your light from his sin. And even though your light was shining, yet you see men were not saved by it, hold firm and doubt not the power of the heavenly light. Believe that if they were not saved, they will be saved hereafter. And if they are not saved hereafter, then their sons will be saved, for your light will not die even when you are dead. The righteous man departs, but his light remains. Men are always saved after the death of the deliverer. Men reject their prophets and slay them, but they love their martyrs and honour those whom they have slain. You are working for the whole, are acting for the future. Seek no reward, for great is your reward on this earth: the spiritual joy which is only vouchsafed to the righteous man. Fear not the great nor the mighty, but be wise and ever serene. Know the measure, know the times, study that. When you are left alone, pray. Love to throw yourself on the earth and kiss it. Kiss the earth and love it with an unceasing, consuming love. Love all men, love everything. Seek that rapture and ecstasy. Water the earth with the tears of your joy and love those tears. Don't be ashamed of that ecstasy, prize it, for it is a gift of God and a great one; it is not given to many but only to the elect.

(i) Of Hell and Hell Fire, a Mystic Reflection.

Fathers and teachers, I ponder, "What is hell?" I maintain that it is the suffering of being unable to love. Once in infinite existence, immeasurable in time and space, a spiritual creature was given on his coming to earth the power of saying, "I am and I love." Once, only once, there was given him a moment of active lifting love, and for that was earthly life given him, and with it times and seasons. And that happy creature rejected the priceless gift, prized it and loved it not, scorned it and remained callous. Such a one, having left the earth, sees Abraham's bosom and talks with Abraham as we are told in the parable of the rich man and Lazarus, and beholds heaven and can go up to the Lord. But that is just his torment, to rise up to the Lord without ever having loved, to be brought close to those who have loved when he has despised their love. For he sees clearly and says to himself, "Now I have understanding, and though I now thirst to love, there will be nothing great, no sacrifice in my love, for my earthly life is over, and Abraham will not come even with a drop of living water (that is the gift of earthly active life) to cool the fiery thirst of spiritual love which burns in me now, though I despised it on earth; there is no more life for me and will be no more time! Even though I would gladly give my life for others, it can never be, for that life is passed which can be sacrificed for love, and now there is a gulf fixed between that life and this existence."

They talk of hell fire in the material sense. I don't go into that mystery and I shun it. But I think if there were fire in material sense, they would be glad of it, for I imagine that in material agony, their still greater spiritual agony would be forgotten for a moment. Moreover, that spiritual agony cannot be taken from them, for that suffering is not external but within them. And if it could be taken from them, I think it would be bitterer still for the unhappy creatures. For even if the righteous in Paradise forgave them, beholding their torments, and called them up to heaven in their infinite love, they would only multiply their torments, for they would arouse in them still more keenly a flaming thirst for responsive, active and grateful love which is now impossible. In the timidity of my heart I imagine, however, that the very recognition of this impossibility would serve at last to console them. For accepting the love of the righteous together with the impossibility of repaying it, by this submissiveness and the effect of this humility, they will attain at last, as it were, to a certain semblance of that active love which they scorned in life, to something like its outward expression...I am sorry, friends and brothers, that I cannot express this clearly. But woe to those who have slain themselves on earth, woe to the suicides! I believe that there can be none more miserable than they. They tell us that it is a sin to pray for them and outwardly the Church, as it were, renounces them, but in my secret heart I believe that we may pray even for them. Love can never be an offence to Christ. For such as those I have prayed inwardly all my life, I confess it, fathers and teachers, and even now I pray for them every day.

Oh, there are some who remain proud and fierce even in hell, in spite of their certain knowledge and contemplation of the absolute truth; there are some fearful ones who have given themselves over to Satan and his proud spirit entirely. For such, hell is voluntary and ever consuming; they are tortured by their own choice. For they have cursed themselves, cursing God and life. They live upon their vindictive pride like a starving man in the desert sucking blood out of his own body. But they are never satisfied, and they refuse forgiveness, they curse God Who calls them. They cannot behold the living God without hatred, and they cry out that the God of life should be annihilated, that God should destroy Himself and His own creation. And they will burn in the fire of their own wrath for ever and yearn for death and annihilation. But they will not attain to death...

Here Alexey Fyodorovitch Karamazov's manuscript ends. I repeat, it is incomplete and fragmentary. Biographical details, for instance, cover only Father Zossima's earliest youth. Of his teaching and opinions we find brought together sayings evidently uttered on very different occasions. His utterances during the last few hours have not been kept separate from the rest, but their general character can be gathered from what we have in Alexey Fyodorovitch's manuscript.

The elder's death came in the end quite unexpectedly. For although those who were gathered about him that last evening realised that his death was approaching, yet it was difficult to imagine that it would come so suddenly. On the contrary, his friends, as I observed already, seeing him that night apparently so cheerful and talkative, were convinced that there was at least a temporary change for the better in his condition. Even five minutes before his death, they said afterwards wonderingly, it was impossible to foresee it. He seemed suddenly to feel an acute pain in his chest, he turned pale and pressed his hands to his heart. All rose from their seats and hastened to him. But though suffering, he still looked at them with a smile, sank slowly from his chair on to his knees, then bowed his face to the ground, stretched out his arms and as though in joyful ecstasy, praying and kissing the ground, quietly and joyfully gave up his soul to God.

The news of his death spread at once through the hermitage and reached the monastery. The nearest friends of the deceased and those whose duty it was from their position began to lay out the corpse according to the ancient ritual, and all the monks gathered together in the church. And before dawn the news of the death reached the town. By the morning all the town was talking of the event, and crowds were flocking from the town to the monastery. But this subject will be treated in the next book; I will only add here that before a day had passed something happened so unexpected, so strange, upsetting, and bewildering in its effect on the monks and the townspeople, that after all these years, that day of general suspense is still vividly remembered in the town.

PART III

Book VII. Alyosha

Chapter 1. The Breath of Corruption

THE body of Father Zossima was prepared for burial according to the established Ritual. As is well known, the bodies of dead monks and hermits are not washed. In the words of the Church Ritual: "If any one of the monks depart in the Lord, the monk designated (that is, whose office it is) shall wipe the body with warm water, making first the sign of the cross with a sponge on the forehead of the deceased, on the breast, on the hands and feet and on the knees, and that is enough." All this was done by Father Paissy, who then clothed the deceased in his monastic garb and wrapped him in his cloak, which was, according to custom, somewhat slit to allow of its being folded about him in the form of a cross. On his head he put a hood with an eight-cornered cross. The hood was left open and the dead man's face was covered with black gauze. In his hands was put an ikon of the Saviour. Towards morning he was put in the coffin which had been made ready long before. It was decided to leave the coffin all day in the cell, in the larger room in which the elder used to receive his visitors and fellow monks. As the deceased was a priest and monk of the strictest rule, the Gospel, not the Psalter, had to be read over his body by monks in holy orders. The reading was begun by Father Iosif immediately after the requiem service. Father Paissy desired later on to read the Gospel all day and night over his dead friend, but for the present he, as well as the Father Superintendent of the Hermitage, was very busy and occupied, for something extraordinary, an unheard-of, even "unseemly" excitement and impatient expectation began to be apparent in the monks, and the visitors from the monastery hostels, and the crowds of people flocking from the town. And as time went on, this grew more and more marked. Both the Superintendent and Father Paissy did their utmost to calm the general bustle and agitation.

When it was fully daylight, some people began bringing their sick, in most cases children, with them from the town--as though they had been waiting expressly for this moment to do so, evidently persuaded that the dead elder's remains had a power of healing, which would be immediately made manifest in accordance with their faith. It was only then apparent how unquestionably everyone in our town had accepted Father Zossima during his lifetime as a great saint. And those who came were far from being all of the humbler classes.

This intense expectation on the part of believers displayed with such haste, such openness, even with impatience and almost insistence, impressed Father Paissy as unseemly. Though he had long foreseen something of the sort, the actual manifestation of the feeling was beyond anything he had looked for. When he came across any of the monks who displayed this excitement, Father Paissy began to reprove them. "Such immediate expectation of something extraordinary," he said, "shows a levity, possible to worldly people but unseemly in us."

But little attention was paid him and Father Paissy noticed it uneasily. Yet he himself (if the whole truth must be told), secretly at the bottom of his heart, cherished almost the same hopes and could not but be aware of it, though he was indignant at the too impatient expectation around him, and saw in it light-mindedness and vanity. Nevertheless, it was particularly unpleasant to him to meet certain persons, whose presence aroused in him great misgivings. In the crowd in the dead man's cell he noticed with inward aversion (for which he immediately reproached himself) the presence of Rakitin and of the monk from Obdorsk, who was still staying in the monastery. Of both of them Father Paissy felt for some reason suddenly suspicious--though, indeed, he might well have felt the same about others.

The monk from Obdorsk was conspicuous as the most fussy in the excited crowd. He was to be seen everywhere; everywhere he was asking questions, everywhere he was listening, on all sides he was whispering with a peculiar, mysterious air. His expression showed the greatest impatience and even a sort of irritation.

As for Rakitin, he, as appeared later, had come so early to the hermitage at the special request of Madame Hohlakov. As soon as that good-hearted but weak-minded woman, who could not herself have been admitted to the hermitage, waked and heard of the death of Father Zossima, she was overtaken with such intense curiosity that she promptly despatched Rakitin to the hermitage, to keep a careful look out and report to her by letter ever half hour or so "everything that takes place." She regarded Rakitin as a most religious and devout young man. He was particularly clever in getting round people and assuming whatever part he thought most to their taste, if he detected the slightest advantage to himself from doing so.

It was a bright, clear day, and many of the visitors were thronging about the tombs, which were particularly numerous round the church and scattered here and there about the hermitage. As he walked round the hermitage, Father Paissy remembered Alyosha and that he had not seen him for some time, not since the night. And he had no sooner thought of him than he at once noticed him in the farthest corner of the hermitage garden, sitting on the tombstone of a monk who had been famous long ago for his saintliness. He sat with his back to the hermitage and his face to the wall, and seemed to be hiding behind the tombstone. Going up to him, Father Paissy saw that he was weeping quietly but bitterly, with his face hidden in his hands, and that his whole frame was shaking with sobs. Father Paissy stood over him for a little.

"Enough, dear son, enough, dear," he pronounced with feeling at last. "Why do you weep? Rejoice and weep not. Don't you know that this is the greatest of his days? Think only where he is now, at this moment!"

Alyosha glanced at him, uncovering his face, which was swollen with crying like a child's, but turned away at once without uttering a word and hid his face in his hands again.

"Maybe it is well," said Father Paissy thoughtfully; "weep if you must; Christ has sent you those tears."

"Your touching tears are but a relief to your spirit and will serve to gladden your dear heart," he added to himself, walking away from Alyosha, and thinking lovingly of him. He moved away quickly, however, for he felt that he too might weep looking at him.

Meanwhile the time was passing; the monastery services and the requiems for the dead followed in their due course. Father Paissy again took Father Iosif's place by the coffin and began reading the Gospel. But before three o'clock in the afternoon that something took place to which I alluded at the end of the last book, something so unexpected by all of us and so contrary to the general hope, that, I repeat, this trivial incident has been minutely remembered to this day in our town and all the surrounding neighbourhood. I may add here, for myself personally, that I feel it almost repulsive that event which caused such frivolous agitation and was such a stumbling-block to many, though in reality it was the most natural and trivial matter. I should, of course, have omitted all mention of it in my story, if it had not exerted a very strong influence on the heart and soul of the chief, though future, hero of my story, Alyosha, forming a crisis and turning-point in his spiritual development, giving a shock to his intellect, which finally strengthened it for the rest of his life and gave it a definite aim.

And so, to return to our story. When before dawn they laid Father Zossima's body in the coffin and brought it into the front room, the question of opening the windows was raised among those who were around the coffin. But this suggestion made casually by someone was unanswered and almost unnoticed. Some of those present may perhaps have inwardly noticed it, only to reflect that the anticipation of decay and corruption from the body of such a saint was an actual absurdity, calling for compassion (if not a smile) for the lack of faith and the frivolity it implied. For they expected something quite different.

And, behold, soon after midday there were signs of something, at first only observed in silence by those who came in and out and were evidently each afraid to communicate the thought in his mind. But by three o'clock those signs had become so clear and unmistakable, that the news swiftly reached all the monks and visitors in the hermitage, promptly penetrated to the monastery, throwing all the monks into amazement, and finally, in the shortest possible time, spread to the town, exciting everyone in it, believers and unbelievers alike. The unbelievers rejoiced, and as for the believers some of them rejoiced even more than the unbelievers, for "men love the downfall and disgrace of the righteous," as the deceased elder had said in one of his exhortations.

The fact is that a smell of decomposition began to come from the coffin, growing gradually more marked, and by three o'clock it was quite unmistakable. In all the past history of our monastery, no such scandal could be recalled, and in no other circumstances could such a scandal have been possible, as showed itself in unseemly disorder immediately after this discovery among the very monks themselves. Afterwards, even many years afterwards, some sensible monks were amazed and horrified, when they recalled that day, that the scandal could have reached such proportions. For in the past, monks of very holy life had died, God-fearing old men, whose saintliness was acknowledged by all, yet from their humble coffins, too, the breath of corruption had come, naturally, as from all dead bodies, but that had caused no scandal nor even the slightest excitement. Of course, there had been, in former times, saints in the monastery whose memory was carefully preserved and whose relics, according to tradition, showed no signs of corruption. This fact was regarded by the monks as touching and mysterious, and the tradition of it was cherished as something blessed and miraculous, and as a promise, by God's grace, of still greater glory from their tombs in the future.

One such, whose memory was particularly cherished, was an old monk, Job, who had died seventy years before at the age of a hundred and five. He had been a celebrated ascetic, rigid in fasting and silence, and his tomb was pointed out to all visitors on their arrival with peculiar respect and mysterious hints of great hopes connected with it. (That was the very tomb on which Father Paissy had found Alyosha sitting in the morning.) Another memory cherished in the monastery was that of the famous Father Varsonofy, who was only recently dead and had preceded Father Zossima in the eldership. He was reverenced during his lifetime as a crazy saint by all the pilgrims to the monastery. There was a tradition that both of these had lain in their coffins as though alive, that they had shown no signs of decomposition when they were buried and that there had been a holy light in their faces. And some people even insisted that a sweet fragrance came from their bodies.

Yet, in spite of these edifying memories, it would be difficult to explain the frivolity, absurdity and malice that were manifested beside the coffin of Father Zossima. It is my private opinion that several different causes were simultaneously at work, one of which was the deeply rooted hostility to the institution of elders as a pernicious innovation, an antipathy hidden deep in the hearts of many of the monks. Even more powerful was jealousy of the dead man's saintliness, so firmly established during lifetime that it was almost a forbidden thing to question it. For though the late elder had won over many hearts, more by love than by miracles, and had gathered round him a mass of loving adherents, none the less, in fact, rather the more on that account he had awakened jealousy and so had come to have bitter enemies, secret and open, not only in the monastery but in the world outside it. He did no one any harm, but "Why do they think him so saintly?" And that question alone, gradually repeated, gave rise at last to an intense, insatiable hatred of him. That, I believe, was why many people were extremely delighted at the smell of decomposition which came so quickly, for not a day had passed since his death. At the same time there were some among those who had been hitherto reverently devoted to the elder, who were almost mortified and personally affronted by this incident. This was how the thing happened.

As soon as signs of decomposition had begun to appear, the whole aspect of the monks betrayed their secret motives in entering the cell. They went in, stayed a little while and hastened out to confirm the news to the crowd of other monks waiting outside. Some of the latter shook their heads mournfully, but others did not even care to conceal the delight which gleamed unmistakably in their malignant eyes. And now no one reproached them for it, no one raised his voice in protest, which was strange, for the majority of the monks had been devoted to the dead elder. But it seemed as though God had in this case let the minority get the upper hand for a time.

Visitors from outside, particularly of the educated class, soon went into the cell, too, with the same spying intent. Of the peasantry few went into the cell, though there were crowds of them at the gates of the hermitage. After three o'clock the rush of worldly visitors was greatly increased and this was no doubt owing to the shocking news. People were attracted who would not otherwise have come on that day and had not intended to come, and among them were some personages of high standing. But external decorum was still preserved and Father Paissy, with a stern face, continued firmly and distinctly reading aloud the Gospel, apparently not noticing what was taking place around him, though he had, in fact, observed something unusual long before. But at last the murmurs, first subdued but gradually louder and more confident, reached even him. "It shows God's judgment is not as man's," Father Paissy heard suddenly. The first to give utterance to this sentiment was a layman, an elderly official from the town, known to be a man of great piety. But he only repeated aloud what the monks had long been whispering. They had long before formulated this damning conclusion, and the worst of it was that a sort of triumphant satisfaction at that conclusion became more and more apparent every moment. Soon they began to lay aside even external decorum and almost seemed to feel they had a sort of right to discard it.

"And for what reason can this have happened," some of the monks said, at first with a show of regret; "he had a small frame and his flesh was dried up on his bones, what was there to decay?"

"It must be a sign from heaven," others hastened to add, and their opinion was adopted at once without protest. For it was pointed out, too, that if the decomposition had been natural, as in the case of every dead sinner, it would have been apparent later, after a lapse of at least twenty-four hours, but this premature corruption "was in excess of nature," and so the finger of God was evident. It was meant for a sign. This conclusion seemed irresistible.

Gentle Father Iosif, the librarian, a great favourite of the dead man's, tried to reply to some of the evil speakers that "this is not held everywhere alike," and that the incorruptibility of the bodies of the just was not a dogma of the Orthodox Church, but only an opinion, and that even in the most Orthodox regions, at Athos for instance, they were not greatly confounded by the smell of corruption, and there the chief sign of the glorification of the saved was not bodily incorruptibility, but the colour of the bones when the bodies have lain many years in the earth and have decayed in it. "And if the bones are yellow as wax, that is the great sign that the Lord has glorified the dead saint, if they are not yellow but black, it shows that God has not deemed him worthy of such glory--that is the belief in Athos, a great place, which the Orthodox doctrine has been preserved from of old, unbroken and in its greatest purity," said Father Iosif in conclusion.

But the meek Father's words had little effect and even provoked a mocking retort. "That's all pedantry and innovation, no use listening to it," the monks decided. "We stick to the old doctrine; there are all sorts of innovations nowadays, are we to follow them all?" added others.

"We have had as many holy fathers as they had. There they are among the Turks, they have forgotten everything. Their doctrine has long been impure and they have no bells even, the most sneering added.

Father Iosif walked away, grieving the more since he had put forward his own opinion with little confidence as though scarcely believing in it himself. He foresaw with distress that something very unseemly was beginning and that there were positive signs of disobedience. Little by little, all the sensible monks were reduced to silence like Father Iosif. And so it came to pass that all who loved the elder and had accepted with devout obedience the institution of the eldership were all at once terribly cast down and glanced timidly in one another's faces, when they met. Those who were hostile to the institution of elders, as a novelty, held up their heads proudly. "There was no smell of corruption from the late elder Varsonofy, but a sweet fragrance," they recalled malignantly. "But he gained that glory not because he was an elder, but because he was a holy man."

And this was followed by a shower of criticism and even blame of Father Zossima. "His teaching was false; he taught that life is a great joy and not a vale of tears," said some of the more unreasonable. "He followed the fashionable belief, he did not recognise material fire in hell," others, still more unreasonable, added. "He was not strict in fasting, allowed himself sweet things, ate cherry jam with his tea, ladies used to send it to him. Is it for a monk of strict rule to drink tea?" could be heard among some of the envious. "He sat in pride," the most malignant declared vindictively; "he considered himself a saint and he took it as his due when people knelt before him." "He abused the sacrament of confession," the fiercest opponents of the institution of elders added in a malicious whisper. And among these were some of the oldest monks, strictest in their devotion, genuine ascetics, who had kept silent during the life of the deceased elder, but now suddenly unsealed their lips. And this was terrible, for their words had great influence on young monks who were not yet firm in their convictions. The monk from Obdorsk heard all this attentively, heaving deep sighs and nodding his head. "Yes, clearly Father Ferapont was right in his judgment yesterday," and at that moment Father Ferapont himself made his appearance, as though on purpose to increase the confusion.

I have mentioned already that he rarely left his wooden cell by the apiary. He was seldom even seen at church and they overlooked this neglect on the ground of his craziness, and did not keep him to the rules binding on all the rest. But if the whole truth is to be told, they hardly had a choice about it. For it would have been discreditable to insist on burdening with the common regulations so great an ascetic, who prayed day and night (he even dropped asleep on his knees). If they had insisted, the monks would have said, "He is holier than all of us and he follows a rule harder than ours. And if he does not go to church, it's because he knows when he ought to; he has his own rule." It was to avoid the chance of these sinful murmurs that Father Ferapont was left in peace.

As everyone was aware, Father Ferapont particularly disliked Father Zossima. And now the news had reached him in his hut that "God's judgment is not the same as man's," and that something had happened which was "in excess of nature." It may well be supposed that among the first to run to him with the news was the monk from Obdorsk, who had visited him the evening before and left his cell terror-stricken.

I have mentioned above, that though Father Paissy standing firm and immovable reading the Gospel over the coffin, could not hear nor see what was passing outside the cell, he gauged most of it correctly in his heart, for he knew the men surrounding him well. He was not shaken by it, but awaited what would come next without fear, watching with penetration and insight for the outcome of the general excitement.

Suddenly an extraordinary uproar in the passage in open defiance of decorum burst on his ears. The door was flung open and Father Ferapont appeared in the doorway. Behind him there could be seen accompanying him a crowd of monks, together with many people from the town. They did not, however, enter the cell, but stood at the bottom of the steps, waiting to see what Father Ferapont would say or do. For they felt with a certain awe, in spite of their audacity, that he had not come for nothing. Standing in the doorway, Father Ferapont raised his arms, and under his right arm the keen inquisitive little eyes of the monk from Obdorsk peeped in. He alone, in his intense curiosity, could not resist running up the steps after Father Ferapont. The others, on the contrary, pressed farther back in sudden alarm when the door was noisily flung open. Holding his hands aloft, Father Ferapont suddenly roared:

"Casting out I cast out!" and, turning in all directions, he began at once making the sign of the cross at each of the four walls and four corners of the cell in succession. All who accompanied Father Ferapont immediately understood his action. For they knew he always did this wherever he went, and that he would not sit down or say a word, till he had driven out the evil spirits.

"Satan, go hence! Satan, go hence!" he repeated at each sign of the cross. "Casting out I cast out," he roared again.

He was wearing his coarse gown girt with a rope. His bare chest, covered with grey hair, could be seen under his hempen shirt. His feet were bare. As soon as he began waving his arms, the cruel irons he wore under his gown could be heard clanking.

Father Paissy paused in his reading, stepped forward and stood before him waiting

"What have you come for, worthy Father? Why do you offend against good order? Why do you disturb the peace of the flock?" he said at last, looking sternly at him.

"What have I come for? You ask why? What is your faith?" shouted Father Ferapont crazily. "I've come here to drive out your visitors, the unclean devils. I've come to see how many have gathered here while I have been away. I want to sweep them out with a birch broom."

"You cast out the evil spirit, but perhaps you are serving him yourself," Father Paissy went on fearlessly. "And who can say of himself 'I am holy'? Can you, Father?"

"I am unclean, not holy. I would not sit in an arm-chair and would not have them bow down to me as an idol," thundered Father Ferapont. "Nowadays folk destroy the true faith. The dead man, your saint," he turned to the crowd, pointing with his finger to the coffin, "did not believe in devils. He gave medicine to keep off the devils. And so they have become as common as spiders in the corners. And now he has begun to stink himself. In that we see a great sign from God."

The incident he referred to was this. One of the monks was haunted in his dreams and, later on, in waking moments, by visions of evil spirits. When in the utmost terror he confided this to Father Zossima, the elder had advised continual prayer and rigid fasting. But when that was of no use, he advised him while persisting in prayer and fasting, to take a special medicine. Many persons were shocked at the time and wagged their heads as they talked over it--and most of all Father Ferapont, to whom some of the censorious had hastened to report this "extraordinary" counsel on the part of the elder.

"Go away, Father!" said Father Paissy, in a commanding voice, "it's not for man to judge but for God. Perhaps we see here a 'sign' which neither you, nor I, nor anyone of us is able to comprehend. Go, Father, and do not trouble the flock!" he repeated impressively.

"He did not keep the fasts according to the rule and therefore the sign has come. That is clear and it's a sin to hide it," the fanatic, carried away by a zeal that outstripped his reason, would not be quieted. "He was seduced by sweetmeats, ladies brought them to him in their pockets, he sipped tea, he worshipped his belly, filling it with sweet things and his mind with haughty thoughts...And for this he is put to shame..."

"You speak lightly, Father." Father Paissy, too, raised his voice. "I admire your fasting and severities, but you speak lightly like some frivolous youth, fickle and childish. Go away, Father, I command you!" Father Paissy thundered in conclusion.

"I will go," said Ferapont, seeming somewhat taken aback, but still as bitter. "You learned men! You are so clever you look down upon my humbleness. I came hither with little learning and here I have forgotten what I did know; God Himself has preserved me in my weakness from your subtlety."

Father Paissy stood over him, waiting resolutely. Father Ferapont paused and, suddenly leaning his cheek on his hand despondently, pronounced in a sing-song, voice, looking at the coffin of the dead elder:

"To-morrow they will sing over him 'Our Helper and Defender'--a splendid anthem--and over me when I die all they'll sing will be 'What Earthly Joy'--a little cantical,"* he added with tearful regret. "You are proud and puffed up, this is a vain place!" he shouted suddenly like a madman, and with a wave of his hand he turned quickly and quickly descended the steps. The crowd awaiting him below wavered; some followed him at once and some lingered, for the cell was still open, and Father Paissy, following Father Ferapont on to the steps, stood watching him. the excited old fanatic was not completely silenced. Walking twenty steps away, he suddenly turned towards the setting sun, raised both his arms and, as though someone had cut him down, fell to the ground with a loud scream.

* When a monk's body is carried out from the cell to the church and from the church to the graveyard, the canticle "What Earthly Joy..." is sung. If the deceased was a priest as well as a monk the canticle "Our Helper and Defender" is sung instead.

"My God has conquered! Christ has conquered the setting sun!" he shouted frantically, stretching up his hands to the sun, and falling face downwards on the ground, he sobbed like a little child, shaken by his tears and spreading out his arms on the ground. Then all rushed up to him; there were exclamations and sympathetic sobs...a kind of frenzy seemed to take possession of them all.

"This is the one who is a saint! This is the one who is a holy man!" some cried aloud, losing their fear. "This is he who should be an elder," others added malignantly.

"He wouldn't be an elder...he would refuse...he wouldn't serve a cursed innovation...he wouldn't imitate their foolery," other voices chimed in at once. And it is hard to say how far they might have gone, but at that moment the bell rang summoning them to service. All began crossing themselves at once. Father Ferapont, too, got up and crossing himself went back to his cell without looking round, still uttering exclamations which were utterly incoherent. A few followed him, but the greater number dispersed, hastening to service. Father Paissy let Father Iosif read in his place and went down. The frantic outcries of bigots could not shake him, but his heart was suddenly filled with melancholy for some special reason and he felt that. He stood still and suddenly wondered, "Why am I sad even to dejection?" and immediately grasped with surprise that his sudden sadness was due to a very small and special cause. In the crowd thronging at the entrance to the cell, he had noticed Alyosha and he remembered that he had felt at once a pang at heart on seeing him. "Can that boy mean so much to my heart now?" he asked himself, wondering.

At that moment Alyosha passed him, hurrying away, but not in the direction of the church. Their eyes met. Alyosha quickly turned away his eyes and dropped them to the ground, and from the boy's look alone, Father Paissy guessed what a great change was taking place in him at that moment.

"Have you, too, fallen into temptation?" cried Father Paissy. "Can you be with those of little faith?" he added mournfully.

Alyosha stood still and gazed vaguely at Father Paissy, but quickly turned his eyes away again and again looked on the ground. He stood sideways and did not turn his face to Father Paissy, who watched him attentively.

"Where are you hastening? The bell calls to service," he asked again, but again Alyosha gave no answer.

"Are you leaving the hermitage? What, without asking leave, without asking a blessing?"

Alyosha suddenly gave a wry smile, cast a strange, very strange, look at the Father to whom his former guide, the former sovereign of his heart and mind, his beloved elder, had confided him as he lay dying. And suddenly, still without speaking, waved his hand, as though not caring even to be respectful, and with rapid steps walked towards the gates away from the hermitage.

"You will come back again!" murmured Father Paissy, looking after him with sorrowful surprise.

Chapter 2. A Critical Moment

FATHER PAISSY, of course, was not wrong when he decided that his "dear boy" would come back again. Perhaps indeed, to some extent, he penetrated with insight into the true meaning of Alyosha's spiritual condition. Yet I must frankly own that it would be very difficult for me to give a clear account of that strange, vague moment in the life of the young hero I love so much. To Father Paissy's sorrowful question, "Are you too with those of little faith?" I could, of course, confidently answer for Alyosha, "No, he is not with those of little faith. Quite the contrary." Indeed, all his trouble came from the fact that he was of great faith. But still the trouble was there and was so agonising that even long afterwards Alyosha thought of that sorrowful day as one of the bitterest and most fatal days of his life. If the question is asked: "Could all his grief and disturbance have been only due to the fact that his elder's body had shown signs of premature decomposition instead of at once performing miracles?" I must answer without beating about the bush, "Yes, it certainly was." I would only beg the reader not to be in too great a hurry to laugh at my young hero's pure heart. I am far from intending to apologise for him or to justify his innocent faith on the ground of his youth, or the little progress he had made in his studies, or any such reason. I must declare, on the contrary, that I have genuine respect for the qualities of his heart. No doubt a youth who received impressions cautiously, whose love was lukewarm, and whose mind was too prudent for his age and so of little value, such a young man might, I admit, have avoided what happened to my hero. But in some cases it is really more creditable to be carried away by an emotion, however unreasonable, which springs from a great love, than to be unmoved. And this is even truer in youth, for a young man who is always sensible is to be suspected and is of little worth--that's my opinion!

"But," reasonable people will exclaim perhaps, "every young man cannot believe in such a superstition and your hero is no model for others."

To this I reply again, "Yes! my hero had faith, a faith holy and steadfast, but still I am not going to apologise for him."

Though I declared above, and perhaps too hastily, that I should not explain or justify my hero, I see that some explanation is necessary for the understanding of the rest of my story. Let me say then, it was not a question of miracles. There was no frivolous and impatient expectation of miracles in his mind. And Alyosha needed no miracles at the time, for the triumph of some preconceived idea--oh no, not at all--what he saw before all was one figure--the figure of his beloved elder, the figure of that holy man whom he revered with such adoration. The fact is that all the love that lay concealed in his pure young heart for everyone and everything had, for the past year, been concentrated--and perhaps wrongly so--on one being, his beloved elder. It is true that being had for so long been accepted by him as his ideal, that all his young strength and energy could not but turn towards that ideal, even to the forgetting at the moment "of everyone and everything." He remembered afterwards how, on that terrible day, he had entirely forgotten his brother Dmitri, about whom he had been so anxious and troubled the day before; he had forgotten, too, to take the two hundred roubles to Ilusha's father, though he had so warmly intended to do so the preceding evening. But again it was not miracles he needed but only "the higher justice" which had been in his belief outraged by the blow that had so suddenly and cruelly wounded his heart. And what does it signify that this "justice" looked for by Alyosha inevitably took the shape of miracles to be wrought immediately by the ashes of his adored teacher? Why, everyone in the monastery cherished the same thought and the same hope, even those whose intellects Alyosha revered, Father Paissy himself, for instance. And so Alyosha, untroubled by doubts, clothed his dreams too in the same form as all the rest. And a whole year of life in the monastery had formed the habit of this expectation in his heart. But it was justice, justice, he thirsted for, not simply miracles.

And now the man who should, he believed, have been exalted above everyone in the whole world, that man, instead of receiving the glory that was his due, was suddenly degraded and dishonoured! What for? Who had judged him? Who could have decreed this? Those were the questions that wrung his inexperienced and virginal heart. He could not endure without mortification, without resentment even, that the holiest of holy men should have been exposed to the jeering and spiteful mockery of the frivolous crowd so inferior to him. Even had there been no miracles, had there been nothing marvellous to justify his hopes, why this indignity, why this humiliation, why this premature decay, "in excess of nature," as the spiteful monks said? Why this "sign from heaven," which they so triumphantly acclaimed in company with Father Ferapont, and why did they believe they had gained the right to acclaim it? Where is the finger of Providence? Why did Providence hide its face "at the most critical moment" (so Alyosha thought it), as though voluntarily submitting to the blind, dumb, pitiless laws of nature?

That was why Alyosha's heart was bleeding, and, of course, as I have said already, the sting of it all was that the man he loved above everything on earth should be put to shame and humiliated! This murmuring may have been shallow and unreasonable in my hero, but I repeat again for the third time--and am prepared to admit that it might be difficult to defend my feeling--I am glad that my hero showed himself not too reasonable at that moment, for any man of sense will always come back to reason in time, but, if love does not gain the upper hand in a boy's heart at such an exceptional moment, when will it? I will not, however, omit to mention something strange, which came for a time to the surface of Alyosha's mind at this fatal and obscure moment. This new something was the harassing impression left by the conversation with Ivan, which now persistently haunted Alyosha's mind. At this moment it haunted him. Oh, it was not that something of the fundamental, elemental, so to speak, faith of his soul had been shaken. He loved his God and believed in Him steadfastly, though he was suddenly murmuring against Him. Yet a vague but tormenting and evil impression left by his conversation with

Ivan the day before, suddenly revived again now in his soul and seemed forcing its way to the surface of his consciousness.

It had begun to get dusk when Rakitin, crossing the pine copse from the hermitage to the monastery, suddenly noticed Alyosha, lying face downwards on the ground under a tree, not moving and apparently asleep. He went up and called him by his name.

"You here, Alexey? Can you have--" he began wondering but broke off. He had meant to say, "Can you have come to this?"

Alyosha did not look at him, but from a slight movement Rakitin at once saw that he heard and understood him.

"What's the matter?" he went on; but the surprise in his face gradually passed into a smile that became more and more ironical.

"I say, I've been looking for you for the last two hours. You suddenly disappeared. What are you about? What foolery is this? You might just look at me..."

Alyosha raised his head, sat up and leaned his back against the tree. He was not crying, but there was a look of suffering and irritability in his face. He did not look at Rakitin, however, but looked away to one side of him.

"Do you know your face is quite changed? There's none of your famous mildness to be seen in it. Are you angry with someone? Have they been ill-treating you?"

"Let me alone," said Alyosha suddenly, with a weary gesture of his hand, still looking away from him.

"Oho! So that's how we are feeling! So you can shout at people like other mortals. That is a come-down from the angels. I say, Alyosha, you have surprised me, do you hear? I mean it. It's long since I've been surprised at anything here. I always took you for an educated man.

Alyosha at last looked at him, but vaguely, as though scarcely understanding what he said.

"Can you really be so upset simply because your old man has begun to stink? You don't mean to say you seriously believed that he was going to work miracles?" exclaimed Rakitin, genuinely surprised again.

"I believed, I believe, I want to believe, and I will believe, what more do you want?" cried Alyosha irritably.

"Nothing at all, my boy. Damn it all! why, no schoolboy of thirteen believes in that now. But there...So now you are in a temper with your God, you are rebelling against Him; He hasn't given promotion, He hasn't bestowed the order of merit! Eh, you are a set!"

Alyosha gazed a long while with his eyes half closed at Rakitin, and there was a sudden gleam in his eyes...but not of anger with Rakitin.

"I am not rebelling against my God; I simply 'don't accept His world.'" Alyosha suddenly smiled a forced smile.

"How do you mean, you don't accept the world?" Rakitin thought a moment over his answer. "What idiocy is this?"

Alyosha did not answer.

"Come, enough nonsense, now to business. Have you had anything to eat to-day?"

"I don't remember...I think I have."

"You need keeping up, to judge by your face. It makes one sorry to look at you. You didn't sleep all night either, I hear; you had a meeting in there. And then all this bobbery afterwards. Most likely you've had nothing to eat but a mouthful of holy bread. I've got some sausage in my pocket; I've brought it from the town in case of need, only you won't eat sausage..."

"Give me some."

"I say! You are going it! Why, it's a regular mutiny, with barricades! Well, my boy, we must make the most of it. Come to my place...shouldn't mind a drop of vodka myself, I am tired to death. Vodka is going too far for you, I suppose...or would you like some?"

"Give me some vodka too."

"Hullo! You surprise me, brother!" Rakitin looked at him in amazement. "Well, one way or another, vodka or sausage, this is a jolly fine chance and mustn't be missed. Come along."

Alyosha got up in silence and followed Rakitin.

"If your little brother Ivan could see this wouldn't he be surprised! By the way, your brother Ivan set off to Moscow this morning, did you know?"

"Yes," answered Alyosha listlessly, and suddenly the image of his brother Dmitri rose before his mind. But only for a minute, and though it reminded him of something that must not be put off for a moment, some duty, some terrible obligation, even that reminder made no impression on him, did not reach his heart and instantly faded out of his mind and was forgotten. But, a long while afterwards, Alyosha remembered this.

"Your brother Ivan declared once that I was a 'liberal booby with no talents whatsoever.' Once you, too, could not resist letting me know I was 'dishonourable.' Well! I should like to see what your talents and sense of honour will do for you now." This phrase Rakitin finished to himself in a whisper.

"Listen!" he said aloud, "Let's go by the path beyond the monastery straight to the town. H'm! I ought to go to Madame Hohlakov's by the way. Only fancy, I've written to tell her everything that happened, and would you believe it, she answered me instantly in pencil (the lady has a passion for writing notes) that 'she would never have expected such conduct from a man of such a reverend character as Father Zossima.' That was her very word: 'conduct.' She is angry too. Eh, you are a set! Stay!" he cried suddenly again. He suddenly stopped and taking Alyosha by the shoulder made him stop too.

"Do you know, Alyosha," he peeped inquisitively into his eyes, absorbed in a sudden new thought which had dawned on him, and though he was laughing outwardly he was evidently afraid to utter that new idea aloud, so difficult he still found it to believe in the strange and unexpected mood in which he now saw Alyosha. "Alyosha, do you know where we had better go?" he brought out at last timidly, and insinuatingly.

"I don't care...where you like."

"Let's go to Grushenka, eh? Will you come?" pronounced Rakitin at last, trembling with timid suspense.

"Let's go to Grushenka," Alyosha answered calmly, at once, and this prompt and calm agreement was such a surprise to Rakitin that he almost started back.

"Well! I say!" he cried in amazement, but seizing Alyosha firmly by the arm be led him along the path, still dreading that he would change his mind.

They walked along in silence; Rakitin was positively afraid to talk.

"And how glad she will be, how delighted!" he muttered, but lapsed into silence again. And indeed it was not to please Grushenka he was taking Alyosha to her. He was a practical person and never undertook anything without a prospect of gain for himself. His object in this case was twofold, first a revengeful desire to see "the downfall of the righteous," and Alyosha's fall "from the saints to the sinners," over which he was already gloating in his imagination, and in the second place he had in view a certain material gain for himself, of which more will be said later.

"So the critical moment has come," he thought to himself with spiteful glee, "and we shall catch it on the hop, for it's just what we want."

Chapter 3. An Onion

GRUSHENKA lived in the busiest part of the town, near the cathedral square, in a small wooden lodge in the courtyard belonging to the house of the widow Morozov. The house was a large stone building of two stories, old and very ugly. The widow led a secluded life with her two unmarried nieces, who were also elderly women. She had no need to let her lodge, but everyone knew that she had taken in Grushenka as a lodger, four years before, solely to please her kinsman, the merchant Samsonov, who was known to the girl's protector. It was said that the jealous old man's object in placing his "favourite" with the widow Morozov was that the old woman should keep a sharp eye on her new lodger's conduct. But this sharp eye soon proved to be unnecessary, and in the end the widow Morozov seldom met Grushenka and did not worry her by looking after her in any way. It is true that four years had passed since the old man had brought the slim, delicate, shy, timid, dreamy, and sad girl of eighteen from the chief town of the province, and much had happened since then. Little was known of the girl's history in the town and that little was vague. Nothing more had been learnt during the last four years, even after many persons had become interested in the beautiful young woman into whom Agrafena Alexandrovna had meanwhile developed. There were rumours that she had been at seventeen betrayed by someone, some sort of officer, and immediately afterwards abandoned by him. The officer had gone away and afterwards married, while Grushenka had been left in poverty and disgrace. It was said, however, that though Grushenka had been raised from destitution by the old man, Samsonov, she came of a respectable family belonging to the clerical class, that she was the daughter of a deacon or something of the sort.

And now after four years the sensitive, injured and pathetic little orphan had become a plump, rosy beauty of the Russian type, a woman of bold and determined character, proud and insolent. She had a good head for business, was acquisitive, saving and careful, and by fair means or foul had succeeded, it was said, in amassing a little fortune. There was only, one point on which all were agreed. Grushenka was not easily to be approached and, except her aged protector, there had not been one man who could boast of her favours during those four years. It was a positive fact, for there had been a good many, especially during the last two years, who had attempted to obtain those favours. But all their efforts had been in vain and some of these suitors had been forced to beat an undignified and even comic retreat, owing to the firm and ironical resistance they met from the strong-willed young person. It was known, too, that the young person had, especially of late, been given to what is called "speculation," and that she had shown marked abilities in that direction, so that many people began to say that she was no better than a Jew. It was not that she lent money on interest, but it was known, for instance, that she had for some time past, in partnership with old Karamazov, actually invested in the purchase of bad debts for a trifle, a tenth of their nominal value, and afterwards had made out of them ten times their value.

The old widower Samsonov, a man of large fortune, was stingy and merciless. He tyrannised over his grown-up sons, but, for the last year during which he had been ill and lost the use of his swollen legs, he had fallen greatly under the influence of his protegee, whom he had at first kept strictly and in humble surroundings, "on Lenten fare," as the wits said at the time. But Grushenka had succeeded in emancipating herself, while she established in him a boundless belief in her fidelity. The old man, now long since dead, had had a large business in his day and was also a noteworthy character, miserly and hard as flint. Though Grushenka's hold upon him was so strong that he could not live without her (it had been so especially for the last two years), he did not settle any considerable fortune on her and would not have been moved to do so, if she had threatened to leave him. But he had presented her with a small sum, and even that was a surprise to everyone when it became known.

"You are a wench with brains," he said to her, when he gave her eight thousand roubles, "and you must look after yourself, but let me tell you that except your yearly allowance as before, you'll get nothing more from me to the day of my death, and I'll leave you nothing in my will either."

And he kept his word; he died and left everything to his sons, whom, with their wives and children, he had treated all his life as servants. Grushenka was not even mentioned in his will. All this became known afterwards. He helped Grushenka with his advice to increase her capital and put business in her way.

When Fyodor Pavlovitch, who first came into contact with Grushenka over a piece of speculation, ended to his own surprise by falling madly in love with her, old Samsonov, gravely ill as he was, was immensely amused. It is remarkable that throughout their whole acquaintance Grushenka was absolutely and spontaneously open with the old man, and he seems to have been the only person in the world with whom she was so. Of late, when Dmitri too had come on the scene with his love, the old man left off laughing. On the contrary, he once gave Grushenka a stern and earnest piece of advice.

"If you have to choose between the two, father or son, you'd better choose the old man, if only you make sure the old scoundrel will marry you and settle some fortune on you beforehand. But don't keep on with the captain, you'll get no good out of that."

These were the very words of the old profligate, who felt already that his death was not far off and who actually died five months later.

I will note too, in passing--that although many in our town knew of the grotesque and monstrous rivalry of the Karamazovs, father and son, the object of which was Grushenka, scarcely anyone understood what really underlay her attitude to both of them. Even Grushenka's two servants (after the catastrophe of which we will speak later) testified in court that she received Dmitri Fyodorovitch simply from fear because "he threatened to murder her." These servants were an old cook, invalidish and almost deaf, who came from Grushenka's old home, and her granddaughter, a smart young girl of twenty, who performed the duties of a maid. Grushenka lived very economically and her surroundings were anything but luxurious. Her lodge consisted of three rooms furnished with mahogany furniture in the fashion of 1820, belonging to her landlady.

It was quite dark when Rakitin and Alyosha entered her rooms, yet they were not lighted up. Grushenka was lying down in her drawing-room on the big, hard, clumsy sofa, with a mahogany back. The sofa was covered with shabby and ragged leather. Under her head she had two white down pillows taken from her bed. She was lying stretched out motionless on her back with her hands behind her head. She was dressed as though expecting someone, in a black silk dress, with a dainty lace fichu on her head, which was very becoming. Over her shoulders was thrown a lace shawl pinned with a massive gold brooch. She certainly was expecting someone. She lay as though impatient and weary, her face rather pale and her lips and eyes hot, restlessly tapping the arm of the sofa with the tip of her right foot. The appearance of Rakitin and Alyosha caused a slight excitement. From the hall they could hear Grushenka leap up from the sofa and cry out in a frightened voice, "Who's there?" But the maid met the visitors and at once called back to her mistress.

"It's not he, it's nothing, only other visitors."

"What can be the matter?" muttered Rakitin, leading Alyosha into the drawing-room.

Grushenka was standing by the sofa as though still alarmed. A thick coil of her dark brown hair escaped from its lace covering and fell on her right shoulder, but she did not notice it and did not put it back till she had gazed at her visitors and recognised them.

"Ah, it's you, Rakitin? You quite frightened me. Whom have you brought? Who is this with you? Good heavens, you have brought him!" she exclaimed, recognising Alyosha.

"Do send for candles!" said Rakitin, with the free-and-easy air of a most intimate friend, who is privileged to give orders in the house.

"Candles...of course, candles...Fenya, fetch him a candle... Well, you have chosen a moment to bring him! she exclaimed again, nodding towards Alyosha, and turning to the looking-glass she began quickly fastening up her hair with both hands. She seemed displeased.

"Haven't I managed to please you?" asked Rakitin, instantly almost offended.

You frightened me, Rakitin, that's what it is." Grushenka turned with a smile to Alyosha. "Don't be afraid of me, my dear Alyosha, you cannot think how glad I am to see you, my unexpected visitor. But you frightened me, Rakitin, I thought it was Mitya breaking in. You see, I deceived him just now, I made him promise to believe me and I told him a lie. I told him that I was going to spend the evening with my old man, Kuzma Kuzmitch, and should be there till late counting up his money. I always spend one whole evening a week with him making up his accounts. We lock ourselves in and he counts on the reckoning beads while I sit and put things down in the book. I am the only person he trusts. Mitya believes that I am there, but I came back and have been sitting locked in here, expecting some news. How was it Fenya let you in? Fenya, Fenya, run out to the gate, open it and look about whether the captain is to be seen! Perhaps he is hiding and spying, I am dreadfully frightened."

There's no one there, Agrafena Alexandrovna, I've just looked out; I keep running to peep through the crack; I am in fear and trembling myself."

"Are the shutters fastened, Fenya? And we must draw the curtains--that's better!" She drew the heavy curtains herself. "He'd rush in at once if he saw a light. I am afraid of your brother Mitya to-day, Alyosha."

Grushenka spoke aloud, and, though she was alarmed, she seemed very happy about something.

"Why are you so afraid of Mitya to-day?" inquired Rakitin. "I should have thought you were not timid with him, you'd twist him round your little finger."

"I tell you, I am expecting news, priceless news, so I don't want Mitya at all. And he didn't believe, I feel he didn't, that I should stay at Kuzma Kuzmitch's. He must be in his ambush now, behind Fyodor Pavlovitch's, in the garden, watching for me. And if he's there, he won't come here, so much the better! But I really have been to Kuzma Kuzmitch's, Mitya escorted me there. I told him I should stay there till midnight, and I asked him to be sure to come at midnight to fetch me home. He went away and I sat ten minutes with Kuzma Kuzmitch and came back here again. Ugh, I was afraid, I ran for fear of meeting him."

"And why are you so dressed up? What a curious cap you've got on!"

"How curious you are yourself, Rakitin! I tell you, I am expecting a message. If the message comes, I shall fly, I shall gallop away and you will see no more of me. That's why I am dressed up, so as to be ready."

"And where are you flying to?"

"If you know too much, you'll get old too soon."

"Upon my word! You are highly delighted...I've never seen you like this before. You are dressed up as if you were going to a ball." Rakitin looked her up and down.

"Much you know about balls."

"And do you know much about them?"

"I have seen a ball. The year before last, Kuzma Kuzmitch's son was married and I looked on from the gallery. Do you suppose I want to be talking to you, Rakitin, while a prince like this is standing here. Such a visitor! Alyosha, my dear boy, I gaze at you and can't believe my eyes. Good heavens, can you have come here to see me! To tell you the truth, I never had a thought of seeing you and I didn't think that you would ever come and see me. Though this is not the moment now, I am awfully glad to see you. Sit down on the sofa, here, that's right, my bright young moon. I really can't take it in even now...Eh, Rakitin, if only you had brought him yesterday or the day before! But I am glad as it is! Perhaps it's better he has come now, at such a moment, and not the day before yesterday."

She gaily sat down beside Alyosha on the sofa, looking at him with positive delight. And she really was glad, she was not lying when she said so. Her eyes glowed, her lips laughed, but it was a good-hearted merry laugh. Alyosha had not expected to see such a kind expression in her face...He had hardly met her till the day before, he had formed an alarming idea of her, and had been horribly distressed the day before by the spiteful and treacherous trick she had played on Katerina Ivanovna. He was greatly surprised to find her now altogether different from what he had expected. And, crushed as he was by his own sorrow, his eyes involuntarily rested on her with attention. Her whole manner seemed changed for the better since yesterday, there was scarcely any trace of that mawkish sweetness in her speech, of that voluptuous softness in her movements. Everything was simple and good-natured, her gestures were rapid, direct, confiding, but she was greatly excited.

"Dear me, how everything comes together to-day!" she chattered on again. "And why I am so glad to see you, Alyosha, I couldn't say myself! If you ask me, I couldn't tell you."

"Come, don't you know why you're glad?" said Rakitin, grinning. "You used to be always pestering me to bring him, you'd some object, I suppose."

"I had a different object once, but now that's over, this is not the moment. I say, I want you to have something nice. I am so good-natured now. You sit down, too, Rakitin; why are you standing? You've sat down already? There's no fear of Rakitin's forgetting to look after himself. Look, Alyosha, he's sitting there opposite us, so offended that I didn't ask him to sit down before you. Ugh, Rakitin is such a one to take offence!" laughed Grushenka. "Don't be angry, Rakitin, I'm kind to-day. Why are you so depressed, Alyosha? Are you afraid of me?" She peeped into his eyes with merry mockery.

"He's sad. The promotion has not been given," boomed Rakitin.

"His elder stinks."

"What? You are talking some nonsense, you want to say something nasty. Be quiet, you stupid! Let me sit on your knee, Alyosha, like this." She suddenly skipped forward and jumped, laughing, on his knee, like a nestling kitten, with her right arm about his neck. "I'll cheer you up, my pious boy. Yes, really, will you let me sit on your knee? You won't be angry? If you tell me, I'll get off?"

Alyosha did not speak. He sat afraid to move, he heard her words, "If you tell me, I'll get off," but he did not answer. But there was nothing in his heart such as Rakitin, for instance, watching him malignantly from his corner, might have expected or fancied. The great grief in his heart swallowed up every sensation that might have been aroused, and, if only he could have thought clearly at that moment, he would have realised that he had now the strongest armour to protect him from every lust and temptation. Yet in spite of the vague irresponsiveness of his spiritual condition and the sorrow that overwhelmed him, he could not help wondering at a new and strange sensation in his heart. This woman, this "dreadful" woman, had no terror for him now, none of that terror that had stirred in his soul at any passing thought of woman. On the contrary, this woman, dreaded above all women, sitting now on his knee, holding him in her arms, aroused in him now a quite different, unexpected, peculiar feeling, a feeling of the intensest and purest interest without a trace of fear, of his former terror. That was what instinctively surprised him.

"You've talked nonsense enough," cried Rakitin, "you'd much better give us some champagne. You owe it me, you know you do!"

"Yes, I really do. Do you know, Alyosha, I promised him champagne on the top of everything, if he'd bring you? I'll have some too! Fenya, Fenya, bring us the bottle Mitya left! Look sharp! Though I am so stingy, I'll stand a bottle, not for you, Rakitin, you're a toadstool, but he is a falcon! And though my heart is full of something very different, so be it, I'll drink with you. I long for some dissipation."

"But what is the matter with you? And what is this message, may I ask, or is it a secret?" Rakitin put in inquisitively, doing his best to pretend not to notice the snubs that were being continually aimed at him.

"Ech, it's not a secret, and you know it, too," Grushenka said, in a voice suddenly anxious, turning her head towards Rakitin, and drawing a little away from Alyosha, though she still sat on his knee with her arm round his neck. "My officer is coming, Rakitin, my officer is coming."

"I heard he was coming, but is he so near?"

"He is at Mokroe now; he'll send a messenger from there, so he wrote; I got a letter from him to-day. I am expecting the messenger every minute."

"You don't say so! Why at Mokroe?"

"That's a long story, I've told you enough."

"Mitya'll be up to something now--I say! Does he know or doesn't he?"

"He know! Of course he doesn't. If he knew, there would be murder. But I am not afraid of that now, I am not afraid of his knife. Be quiet, Rakitin, don't remind me of Dmitri Fyodorovitch, he has bruised my heart. And I don't want to think of that at this moment. I can think of Alyosha here, I can look at Alyosha...smile at me, dear, cheer up, smile at my foolishness, at my pleasure...Ah, he's smiling, he's smiling! How kindly he looks at me! And you know, Alyosha, I've been thinking all this time you were angry with me, because of the day before yesterday, because of that young lady. I was a cur, that's the truth...But it's a good thing it happened so. It was a horrid thing, but a good thing too." Grushenka smiled dreamily and a little cruel line showed in her smile. "Mitya told me that she screamed out that I 'ought to be flogged.' I did insult her dreadfully. She sent for me, she wanted to make a conquest of me, to win me over with her chocolate...No, it's a good thing it did end like that." She smiled again. "But I am still afraid of your being angry."

"Yes, that's really true," Rakitin put in suddenly with genuine surprise. "Alyosha, she is really afraid of a chicken like you."

"He is a chicken to you, Rakitin...because you've no conscience, that's what it is! You see, I love him with all my soul, that's how it is! Alyosha, do you believe I love you with all my soul?"

"Ah, you shameless woman! She is making you a declaration, Alexey!"

162

"Well, what of it, I love him!"

"And what about your officer? And the priceless message from Mokroe?"

"That is quite different."

"That's a woman's way of looking at it!"

"Don't you make me angry, Rakitin." Grushenka caught him up hotly. "This is quite different. I love Alyosha in a different way. It's true, Alyosha, I had sly designs on you before. For I am a horrid, violent creature. But at other times I've looked upon you, Alyosha, as my conscience. I've kept thinking 'how anyone like that must despise a nasty thing like me.' I thought that the day before yesterday, as I ran home from the young lady's. I have thought of you a long time in that way, Alyosha, and Mitya knows; I've talked to him about it. Mitya understands. Would you believe it, I sometimes look at you and feel ashamed, utterly ashamed of myself...And how, and since when, I began to think about you like that, I can't say, I don't remember..."

Fenya came in and put a tray with an uncorked bottle and three glasses of champagne on the table.

"Here's the champagne!" cried Rakitin. "You're excited, Agrafena Alexandrovna, and not yourself. When you've had a glass of champagne, you'll be ready to dance. Eh, they can't even do that properly," he added, looking at the bottle. "The old woman's poured it out in the kitchen and the bottle's been brought in warm and without a cork. Well, let me have some, anyway."

He went up to the table, took a glass, emptied it at one gulp and poured himself out another.

"One doesn't often stumble upon champagne," he said, licking his lips. "Now, Alyosha, take a glass, show what you can do! What shall we drink to? The gates of paradise? Take a glass, Grushenka, you drink to the gates of paradise, too."

"What gates of paradise?"

She took a glass, Alyosha took his, tasted it and put it back.

"No, I'd better not," he smiled gently.

"And you bragged!" cried Rakitin.

"Well, if so, I won't either," chimed in Grushenka, "I really don't want any. You can drink the whole bottle alone, Rakitin. If Alyosha has some, I will."

"What touching sentimentality!" said Rakitin tauntingly; "and she's sitting on his knee, too! He's got something to grieve over, but what's the matter with you? He is rebelling against his God and ready to eat sausage..."

"How so?"

"His elder died to-day, Father Zossima, the saint."

"So Father Zossima is dead," cried Grushenka. "Good God, I did not know!" She crossed herself devoutly. "Goodness, what have I been doing, sitting on his knee like this at such a moment! She started up as though in dismay, instantly slipped off his knee and sat down on the sofa.

Alyosha bent a long wondering look upon her and a light seemed to dawn in his face.

"Rakitin," he said suddenly, in a firm and loud voice; "don't taunt me with having rebelled against God. I don't want to feel angry with you, so you must be kinder, too; I've lost a treasure such as you have never had, and you cannot judge me now. You had much better look at her--do you see how she has pity on me? I came here to find a wicked soul--I felt drawn to evil because I was base and evil myself, and I've found a true sister; I have found a treasure--a loving heart. She had pity on me just now...Agrafena Alexandrovna, I am speaking of you. You've raised my soul from the depths."

Alyosha's lips were quivering and he caught his breath.

"She has saved you, it seems," laughed Rakitin spitefully. "And she meant to get you in her clutches, do your realise that?"

"Stay, Rakitin." Grushenka jumped up. "Hush, both of you. Now I'll tell you all about it. Hush, Alyosha, your words make me ashamed, for I am bad and not good--that's what I am. And you hush, Rakitin, because you are telling lies. I had the low idea of trying to get him in my clutches, but now you are lying, now it's all different. And don't let me hear anything more from you, Rakitin."

All this Grushenka said with extreme emotion.

"They are both crazy," said Rakitin, looking at them with amazement. "I feel as though I were in a madhouse. They're both getting so feeble they'll begin crying in a minute."

"I shall begin to cry, I shall," repeated Grushenka. "He called me his sister and I shall never forget that. Only let me tell you, Rakitin, though I am bad, I did give away an onion."

"An onion? Hang it all, you really are crazy."

Rakitin wondered at their enthusiasm. He was aggrieved and annoyed, though he might have reflected that each of them was just passing through a spiritual crisis such as does not come often in a lifetime. But though

Rakitin was very sensitive about everything that concerned himself, he was very obtuse as regards the feelings and sensations of others--partly from his youth and inexperience, partly from his intense egoism.

"You see, Alyosha," Grushenka turned to him with a nervous laugh. "I was boasting when I told Rakitin I had given away an onion, but it's not to boast I tell you about it. It's only a story, but it's a nice story. I used to hear it when I was a child from Matryona, my cook, who is still with me. It's like this. Once upon a time there was a peasant woman and a very wicked woman she was. And she died and did not leave a single good deed behind. The devils caught her and plunged her into the lake of fire. So her guardian angel stood and wondered what good deed of hers he could remember to tell to God; 'She once pulled up an onion in her garden,' said he, 'and gave it to a beggar woman.' And God answered: 'You take that onion then, hold it out to her in the lake, and let her take hold and be pulled out. And if you can pull her out of the lake, let her come to Paradise, but if the onion breaks, then the woman must stay where she is.' The angel ran to the woman and held out the onion to her. 'Come,' said he, 'catch hold and I'll pull you out.' he began cautiously pulling her out. He had just pulled her right out, when the other sinners in the lake, seeing how she was being drawn out, began catching hold of her so as to be pulled out with her. But she was a very wicked woman and she began kicking them. 'I'm to be pulled out, not you. It's my onion, not yours.' As soon as she said that, the onion broke. And the woman fell into the lake and she is burning there to this day. So the angel wept and went away. So that's the story, Alyosha; I know it by heart, for I am that wicked woman myself. I boasted to Rakitin that I had given away an onion, but to you I'll say: 'I've done nothing but give away one onion all my life, that's the only good deed I've done.' don't praise me, Alyosha, don't think me good, I am bad, I am a wicked woman and you make me ashamed if you praise me. Eh, I must confess everything. Listen, Alyosha. I was so anxious to get hold of you that I promised Rakitin twenty-five roubles if he would bring you to me. Stay, Rakitin, wait!"

She went with rapid steps to the table, opened a drawer, pulled out a purse and took from it a twenty-five rouble note.

"What nonsense! What nonsense!" cried Rakitin, disconcerted.

"Take it. Rakitin, I owe it you, there's no fear of your refusing it, you asked for it yourself." And she threw the note to him.

"Likely I should refuse it," boomed Rakitin, obviously abashed, but carrying off his confusion with a swagger. "That will come in very handy; fools are made for wise men's profit."

"And now hold your tongue, Rakitin, what I am going to say now is not for your ears. Sit down in that corner and keep quiet. You don't like us, so hold your tongue."

"What should I like you for?" Rakitin snarled, not concealing his ill-humour. He put the twenty-five rouble note in his pocket and he felt ashamed at Alyosha's seeing it. He had reckoned on receiving his payment later, without Alyosha's knowing of it, and now, feeling ashamed, he lost his temper. Till that moment he had thought it discreet not to contradict Grushenka too flatly in spite of her snubbing, since he had something to get out of her. But now he, too, was angry:

"One loves people for some reason, but what have either of you done for me?"

"You should love people without a reason, as Alyosha does."

"How does he love you? How has he shown it, that you make such a fuss about it?"

Grushenka was standing in the middle of the room; she spoke with heat and there were hysterical notes in her voice.

"Hush, Rakitin, you know nothing about us! And don't dare to speak to me like that again. How dare you be so familiar! Sit in that corner and be quiet, as though you were my footman! And now, Alyosha, I'll tell you the whole truth, that you may see what a wretch I am! I am not talking to Rakitin, but to you. I wanted to ruin you, Alyosha, that's the holy truth; I quite meant to. I wanted to so much, that I bribed Rakitin to bring you. And why did I want to do such a thing? You knew nothing about it, Alyosha, you turned away from me; if you passed me, you dropped your eyes. And I've looked at you a hundred times before to-day; I began asking everyone about you. Your face haunted my heart. 'He despises me,' I thought; 'he won't even look at me.' And I felt it so much at last that I wondered at myself for being so frightened of a boy. I'll get him in my clutches and laugh at him. I was full of spite and anger. Would you believe it, nobody here dares talk or think of coming to Agrafena Alexandrovna with any evil purpose. Old Kuzma is the only man I have anything to do with here; I was bound and sold to him; Satan brought us together, but there has been no one else. But looking at you, I thought, I'll get him in my clutches and laugh at him. You see what a spiteful cur I am, and you called me your sister! And now that man who wronged me has come; I sit here waiting for a message from him. And do you know what that man has been to me? Five years ago, when Kuzma brought me here, I used to shut myself up, that no one might have sight or sound of me. I was a silly slip of a girl; I used to sit here sobbing; I used to lie awake all night, thinking: 'Where is he now, the man who wronged me? He is laughing at me with another woman, most likely. If only I could see him, if I could meet him again, I'd pay him out, I'd pay him out!' At night I used to lie sobbing into my pillow in the dark, and I used to brood over it; I used to tear my heart on purpose and gloat over my anger. 'I'll pay him out, I'll pay him out! That's what I used to cry out in the dark. And when I suddenly thought that I should really do nothing to him, and that he was laughing at me then, or perhaps had utterly forgotten me, I would fling myself on the floor, melt into helpless tears, and lie there shaking till dawn. In the morning I would get up more spiteful than a dog, ready to tear the whole world to pieces. And then what do you think? I began saving money, I became hardhearted, grew stout--grew wiser, would you say? No, no one in the whole world sees it, no one knows it, but when night comes on, I sometimes lie as I did five years ago, when I was a silly girl, clenching my teeth and crying all night, thinking, 'I'll pay him out, I'll pay him out!' Do you hear? Well then, now you understand me. A month ago a letter came to me--he was coming, he was a widower, he wanted to see me. It took my breath away; then I suddenly thought: 'If he comes and whistles to call me, I shall creep back to him like a beaten dog.' I couldn't believe myself. Am I so abject? Shall I run to him or not? And I've been in such a rage with myself all this month that I am worse than I was five years ago. Do you see now, Alyosha, what a violent, vindictive creature I am? I have shown you the whole truth! I played with Mitya to keep me from running to that other. Hush, Rakitin, it's not for you to judge me, I am not speaking to you. Before you came in, I was lying here waiting, brooding, deciding my whole future life, and you can never know what was in my heart. Yes, Alyosha, tell your young lady not to be angry with me for what happened the day before yesterday...Nobody in the whole world knows what I am going through now, and no one ever can know...For perhaps I shall take a knife with me to-day, I can't make up my mind..."

And at this "tragic" phrase Grushenka broke down, hid her face in her hands, flung herself on the sofa pillows, and sobbed like a little child.

Alyosha got up and went to Rakitin.

"Misha," he said, "don't be angry. She wounded you, but don't be angry. You heard what she said just now? You mustn't ask too much of human endurance, one must be merciful."

Alyosha said this at the instinctive prompting of his heart. He felt obliged to speak and he turned to Rakitin. If Rakitin had not been there, he would have spoken to the air. But Rakitin looked at him ironically and Alyosha stopped short.

"You were so primed up with your elder's reading last night that now you have to let it off on me, Alexey, man of God!" said Rakitin, with a smile of hatred.

"Don't laugh, Rakitin, don't smile, don't talk of the dead--he was better than anyone in the world!" cried Alyosha, with tears in his voice. "I didn't speak to you as a judge but as the lowest of the judged. What am I beside her? I came here seeking my ruin, and said to myself, 'What does it matter?' in my cowardliness, but she, after five years in torment, as soon as anyone says a word from the heart to her--it makes her forget everything, forgive everything, in her tears! The man who has wronged her has come back, he sends for her and she forgives him everything, and hastens joyfully to meet him and she won't take a knife with her. She won't! No, I am not like that. I don't know whether you are, Misha, but I am not like that. It's a lesson to me...She is more loving than we...Have you heard her speak before of what she has just told us? No, you haven't; if you had, you'd have understood her long ago...and the person insulted the day before yesterday must forgive her, too! She will, when she knows...and she shall know...This soul is not yet at peace with itself, one must be tender with...there may be a treasure in that soul..."

Alyosha stopped, because he caught his breath. In spite of his ill-humour Rakitin looked at him with astonishment. He had never expected such a tirade from the gentle Alyosha.

"She's found someone to plead her cause! Why, are you in love with her? Agrafena Alexandrovna, our monk's really in love with you, you've made a conquest!" he cried, with a coarse laugh.

Grushenka lifted her head from the pillow and looked at Alyosha with a tender smile shining on her tear-stained face.

"Let him alone, Alyosha, my cherub; you see what he is, he is not a person for you to speak to. Mihail Osipovitch," she turned to Rakitin, "I meant to beg your pardon for being rude to you, but now I don't want to. Alyosha, come to me, sit down here." She beckoned to him with a happy smile. "That's right, sit here. Tell me," she took him by the hand and peeped into his face, smiling, "tell me, do I love that man or not? The man who wronged me, do I love him or not? Before you came, I lay here in the dark, asking my heart whether I loved him. Decide for me, Alyosha, the time has come, it shall be as you say. Am I to forgive him or not?"

"But you have forgiven him already," said Alyosha, smiling.

"Yes, I really have forgiven him," Grushenka murmured thoughtfully. "What an abject heart! To my abject heart!" She snatched up a glass from the table, emptied it at a gulp, lifted it in the air and flung it on the floor. The glass broke with a crash. A little cruel line came into her smile.

"Perhaps I haven't forgiven him, though," she said, with a sort of menace in her voice, and she dropped her eyes to the ground as though she were talking to herself. "Perhaps my heart is only getting ready to forgive. I shall struggle with my heart. You see, Alyosha, I've grown to love my tears in these five years...Perhaps I only love my resentment, not him..."

"Well, I shouldn't care to be in his shoes," hissed Rakitin.

"Well, you won't be, Rakitin, you'll never be in his shoes. You shall black my shoes, Rakitin, that's the place you are fit for. You'll never get a woman like me...and he won't either, perhaps..."

"Won't he? Then why are you dressed up like that?" said Rakitin, with a venomous sneer.

"Don't taunt me with dressing up, Rakitin, you don't know all that is in my heart! If I choose to tear off my finery, I'll tear it off at once, this minute," she cried in a resonant voice. "You don't know what that finery is for, Rakitin! Perhaps I shall see him and say: 'Have you ever seen me look like this before?' He left me a thin, consumptive cry-baby of seventeen. I'll sit by him, fascinate him and work him up. 'Do you see what I am like now?' I'll say to him; 'well, and that's enough for you, my dear sir, there's many a slip twixt the cup and the lip! That may be what the finery is for, Rakitin." Grushenka finished with a malicious laugh. "I'm violent and resentful, Alyosha, I'll tear off my finery, I'll destroy my beauty, I'll scorch my face, slash it with a knife, and turn beggar. If I choose, I won't go anywhere now to see anyone. If I choose, I'll send Kuzma back all he has ever given me, to-morrow, and all his money and I'll go out charing for the rest of my life. You think I wouldn't do it, Rakitin, that I would not dare to do it? I would, I would, I could do it directly, only don't exasperate me...and I'll send him about his business, I'll snap my fingers in his face, he shall never see me again!"

She uttered the last words in an hysterical scream, but broke down again, hid her face in her hands, buried it in the pillow and shook with sobs.

Rakitin got up.

"It's time we were off," he said, "it's late, we shall be shut out of the monastery."

Grushenka leapt up from her place.

"Surely you don't want to go, Alyosha!" she cried, in mournful surprise. "What are you doing to me? You've stirred up my feeling, tortured me, and now you'll leave me to face this night alone!"

"He can hardly spend the night with you! Though if he wants to, let him! I'll go alone," Rakitin scoffed jeeringly.

"Hush, evil tongue!" Grushenka cried angrily at him; "you never said such words to me as he has come to say."

"What has he said to you so special?" asked Rakitin irritably.

"I can't say, I don't know. I don't know what he said to me, it went straight to my heart; he has wrung my heart...He is the first, the only one who has pitied me, that's what it is. Why did you not come before, you angel?" She fell on her knees before him as though in a sudden frenzy. "I've been waiting all my life for someone like you, I knew that someone like you would come and forgive me. I believed that, nasty as I am, someone would really love me, not only with a shameful love!"

"What have I done to you?" answered Alyosha, bending over her with a tender smile, and gently taking her by the hands; "I only gave you an onion, nothing but a tiny little onion, that was all!"

He was moved to tears himself as he said it. At that moment there was a sudden noise in the passage, someone came into the hall. Grushenka jumped up, seeming greatly alarmed. Fenya ran noisily into the room, crying out:

"Mistress, mistress darling, a messenger has galloped up," she cried, breathless and joyful. "A carriage from Mokroe for you, Timofey the driver, with three horses, they are just putting in fresh horses...A letter, here's the letter, mistress."

A letter was in her hand and she waved it in the air all the while she talked. Grushenka snatched the letter from her and carried it to the candle. It was only a note, a few lines. She read it in one instant.

"He has sent for me," she cried, her face white and distorted, with a wan smile; "he whistles! Crawl back, little dog!"

But only for one instant she stood as though hesitating; suddenly the blood rushed to her head and sent a glow to her cheeks.

"I will go," she cried; "five years of my life! Good-bye! Good-bye, Alyosha, my fate is sealed. Go, go, leave me all of you, don't let me see you again! Grushenka is flying to a new life...Don't you remember evil against me either, Rakitin. I may be going to my death! Ugh! I feel as though I were drunk!"

She suddenly left them and ran into her bedroom.

"Well, she has no thoughts for us now!" grumbled Rakitin. "Let's go, or we may hear that feminine shriek again. I am sick of all these tears and cries."

Alyosha mechanically let himself be led out. In the yard stood a covered cart. Horses were being taken out of the shafts, men were running to and fro with a lantern. Three fresh horses were being led in at the open gate. But when Alyosha and Rakitin reached the bottom of the steps, Grushenka's bedroom window was suddenly opened and she called in a ringing voice after Alyosha:

"Alyosha, give my greetings to your brother Mitya and tell him not to remember evil against me, though I have brought him misery. And tell him, too, in my words: 'Grushenka has fallen to a scoundrel, and not to you, noble heart.' And add, too, that Grushenka loved him only one hour, only one short hour she loved him--so let him remember that hour all his life-say, 'Grushenka tells you to!'"

She ended in a voice full of sobs. The window was shut with a slam.

"H'm, h'm!" growled Rakitin, laughing, "she murders your brother Mitya and then tells him to remember it all his life! What ferocity!"

Alyosha made no reply, he seemed not to have heard. He walked fast beside Rakitin as though in a terrible hurry. He was lost in thought and moved mechanically. Rakitin felt a sudden twinge as though he had been touched on an open wound. He had expected something quite different by bringing Grushenka and Alyosha together. Something very different from what he had hoped for had happened.

"He is a Pole, that officer of hers," he began again, restraining himself; "and indeed he is not an officer at all now. He served in the customs in Siberia, somewhere on the Chinese frontier, some puny little beggar of a Pole, I expect. Lost his job, they say. He's heard now that Grushenka's saved a little money, so he's turned up again--that's the explanation of the mystery."

Again Alyosha seemed not to hear. Rakitin could not control himself.

"Well, so you've saved the sinner?" he laughed spitefully. "Have you turned the Magdalene into the true path? Driven out the seven devils, eh? So you see the miracles you were looking out for just now have come to pass!"

"Hush, Rakitin," Alyosha, answered with an aching heart.

"So you despise me now for those twenty-five roubles? I've sold my friend, you think. But you are not Christ, you know, and I am not Judas."

"Oh, Rakitin, I assure you I'd forgotten about it," cried Alyosha, "you remind me of it yourself..."

But this was the last straw for Rakitin.

"Damnation take you all and each of you," he cried suddenly, "why the devil did I take you up? I don't want to know you from this time forward. Go alone, there's your road!" And he turned abruptly into another street, leaving Alyosha alone in the dark. Alyosha came out of the town and walked across the fields to the monastery.

Chapter 4. Cana of Galilee

IT was very late, according to the monastery ideas, when Alyosha returned to the hermitage; the door-keeper let him in by a special entrance. It had struck nine o'clock--the hour of rest and repose after a day of such agitation for all. Alyosha timidly opened the door and went into the elder's cell where his coffin was now standing. There was no one in the cell but Father Paissy, reading the Gospel in solitude over the coffin, and the young novice Porfiry, who, exhausted by the previous night's conversation and the disturbing incidents of the day, was sleeping the deep sound sleep of youth on the floor of the other room. Though Father Paissy heard Alyosha come in, he did not even look in his direction. Alyosha turned to the right from the door to the corner, fell on his knees and began to pray.

His soul was overflowing but with mingled feelings; no single sensation stood out distinctly; on the contrary, one drove out another in a slow, continual rotation. But there was a sweetness in his heart and, strange to say, Alyosha was not surprised at it. Again he saw that coffin before him, the hidden dead figure so precious to him, but the weeping and poignant grief of the morning was no longer aching in his soul. As soon as he came in, he fell down before the coffin as before a holy shrine, but joy, joy was glowing in his mind and in his heart. The one window of the cell was open, the air was fresh and cool. "So the smell must have become stronger, if they opened the window," thought Alyosha. But even this thought of the smell of corruption, which had seemed to him so awful and humiliating a few hours before, no longer made him feel miserable or indignant. He began quietly praying, but he soon felt that he was praying almost mechanically. Fragments of thought floated through his soul, flashed like stars and went out again at once, to be succeeded by others. But yet there was reigning in his soul a sense of the wholeness of things--something steadfast and comforting--and he was aware of it himself. Sometimes he began praying ardently, he longed to pour out his thankfulness and love...

But when he had begun to pray, he passed suddenly to something else, and sank into thought, forgetting both the prayer and what had interrupted it. He began listening to what Father Paissy was reading, but worn out with exhaustion he gradually began to doze.

"And the third day there was a marriage in Cana of Galilee," read Father Paissy. "And the mother of Jesus was there; And both Jesus was there; And both Jesus was called, and his disciples, to the marriage."

"Marriage? What's that?...A marriage!" floated whirling through Alyosha's mind. "There is happiness for her, too...She has gone to the feast...No, she has not taken the knife...That was only a tragic phrase...Well...tragic phrases should be forgiven, they must be. Tragic phrases comfort the heart...Without them, sorrow would be too heavy for men to bear. Rakitin has gone off to the back alley. As long as Rakitin broods over his wrongs, he will always go off to the back alley...But the high road...The road is wide and straight and bright as crystal, and the sun is at the end of it...Ah!...What's being read?"...

"And when they wanted wine, the mother of Jesus saith unto him, They have no wine"...Alyosha heard.

"Ah, yes, I was missing that, and I didn't want to miss it, I love that passage: it's Cana of Galilee, the first miracle...Ah, that miracle! Ah, that sweet miracle! It was not men's grief, but their joy Christ visited, He worked His first miracle to help men's gladness...'He who loves men loves their gladness, too'...He was always repeating that, it was one of his leading ideas...'There's no living without joy,' Mitya says...Yes, Mitya...'Everything that is true and good is always full of forgiveness,' he used to say that, too"...

"Jesus saith unto her, Woman, what has it to do
with thee or me? Mine hour not yet come.
"His mother saith unto the servants, Whatsoever
he saith unto you, do it"...

"Do it...Gladness, the gladness of some poor, very poor, people...Of course they were poor, since they hadn't wine enough even at a wedding...The historians write that, in those days, the people living about the Lake of Gennesaret were the poorest that can possibly be imagined...and another great heart, that other great being, His Mother, knew that He had come not only to make His great terrible sacrifice. She knew that His heart was open even to the simple, artless merrymaking of some obscure and unlearned people, who had warmly bidden Him to their poor wedding. 'Mine hour is not yet come,' He said, with a soft smile (He must have smiled gently to her). And, indeed, was it to make wine abundant at poor weddings He had come down to earth? And yet He went and did as she asked Him...Ah, he is reading again"...

"Jesus saith unto them, Fill the waterpots with water.
And they filled them up to the brim.

"And he saith unto them, Draw out now and bear unto
the governor of the feast. And they bear it.

"When the ruler of the feast had tasted the water
that was made wine, and knew not whence it was
(but the servants which drew the water knew);
the governor of the feast called the bridegroom,

"And saith unto him, Every man at the beginning doth
set forth good wine; and when men have well drunk,
that which is worse; but thou hast kept the good wine
until now."

"But what's this, what's this? Why is the room growing wider?...Ah, yes...It's the marriage, the wedding...yes, of course. Here are the guests, here are the young couple sitting, and the merry crowd and...Where is the wise governor of the feast? But who is this? Who? Again the walls are receding...Who is getting up there from the great table? What!...He here, too? But he's in the coffin...but he's here, too. He has stood up, he sees me, he is coming here...God!"...

Yes, he came up to him, to him, he, the little, thin old man, with tiny wrinkles on his face, joyful and laughing softly. There was no coffin now, and he was in the same dress as he had worn yesterday sitting with them, when the visitors had gathered about him. His face was uncovered, his eyes were shining. How was this, then? He, too, had been called to the feast. He, too, at the marriage of Cana in Galilee...

"Yes, my dear, I am called, too, called and bidden," he heard a soft voice saying over him. "Why have you hidden yourself here, out of sight? You come and join us too."

It was his voice, the voice of Father Zossima. And it must be he, since he called him!

The elder raised Alyosha by the hand and he rose from his knees.

"We are rejoicing," the little, thin old man went on. "We are drinking the new wine, the wine of new, great gladness; do you see how many guests? Here are the bride and bridegroom, here is the wise governor of the feast, he is tasting the new wine. Why do you wonder at me? I gave an onion to a beggar, so I, too, am here. And many here have given only an onion each--only one little onion...What are all our deeds? And you, my gentle one, you, my kind boy, you too have known how to give a famished woman an onion to-day. Begin your work, dear one, begin it, gentle one! Do you see our Sun, do you see Him?"

"I am afraid...I dare not look," whispered Alyosha.

"Do not fear Him. He is terrible in His greatness, awful in His sublimity, but infinitely merciful. He has made Himself like unto us from love and rejoices with us. He is changing the water into wine that the gladness of the guests may not be cut short. He is expecting new guests, He is calling new ones unceasingly for ever and ever...There they are bringing new wine. Do you see they are bringing the vessels..."

Something glowed in Alyosha's heart, something filled it till it ached, tears of rapture rose from his soul...He stretched out his hands, uttered a cry and waked up.

Again the coffin, the open window, and the soft, solemn, distinct reading of the Gospel. But Alyosha did not listen to the reading. It was strange, he had fallen asleep on his knees, but now he was on his feet, and suddenly, as though thrown forward, with three firm rapid steps he went right up to the coffin. His shoulder brushed against Father Paissy without his noticing it. Father Paissy raised his eyes for an instant from his book, but looked away again at once, seeing that something strange was happening to the boy. Alyosha gazed for half a minute at the coffin, at the covered, motionless dead man that lay in the coffin, with the ikon on his breast and the peaked cap with the octangular cross on his head. He had only just been hearing his voice, and that voice was still ringing in his ears. He was listening, still expecting other words, but suddenly he turned sharply and went out of the cell.

He did not stop on the steps either, but went quickly down; his soul, overflowing with rapture, yearned for freedom, space, openness. The vault of heaven, full of soft, shining stars, stretched vast and fathomless above him. The Milky Way ran in two pale streams from the zenith to the horizon. The fresh, motionless, still night enfolded the earth. The white towers and golden domes of the cathedral gleamed out against the sapphire sky. The gorgeous autumn flowers, in the beds round the house, were slumbering till morning. The silence of earth seemed to melt into the silence of the heavens. The mystery of earth was one with the mystery of the stars...

Alyosha stood, gazed, and suddenly threw himself down on the earth. He did not know why he embraced it. He could not have told why he longed so irresistibly to kiss it, to kiss it all. But he kissed it weeping, sobbing, and watering it with his tears, and vowed passionately to love it, to love it for ever and ever. "Water the earth with the tears of your joy and love those tears," echoed in his soul.

What was he weeping over?

Oh! in his rapture he was weeping even over those stars, which were shining to him from the abyss of space, and "he was not ashamed of that ecstasy." There seemed to be threads from all those innumerable worlds of God, linking his soul to them, and it was trembling all over "in contact with other worlds." He longed to forgive everyone and for everything, and to beg forgiveness. Oh, not for himself, but for all men, for all and for everything. "And others are praying for me too," echoed again in his soul. But with every instant he felt clearly and, as it were, tangibly, that something firm and unshakable as that vault of heaven had entered into his soul. It was as though some idea had seized the sovereignty of his mind--and it was for all his life and for ever and ever. He had fallen on the earth a weak boy, but he rose up a resolute champion, and he knew and felt it suddenly at the very moment of his ecstasy. And never, never, his life long, could Alyosha forget that minute.

"Someone visited my soul in that hour," he used to say afterwards, with implicit faith in his words.

Within three days he left the monastery in accordance with the words of his elder, who had bidden him "sojourn in the world."

Book VIII. Mitya
Chapter 1. Kuzma Samsonov

BUT Dmitri, to whom Grushenka, flying away to a new life, had left her last greetings, bidding him remember the hour of her love for ever, knew nothing of what had happened to her, and was at that moment in a condition of feverish agitation and activity. For the last two days he had been in such an inconceivable state of mind that he might easily have fallen ill with brain fever, as he said himself afterwards. Alyosha had not been able to find him the morning before, and Ivan had not succeeded in meeting him at the tavern on the same day. The people at his lodgings, by his orders, concealed his movements.

He had spent those two days literally rushing in all directions, "struggling with his destiny and trying to save himself," as he expressed it himself afterwards, and for some hours he even made a dash out of the town on urgent business, terrible as it was to him to lose sight of Grushenka for a moment. All this was explained afterwards in detail, and confirmed by documentary evidence; but for the present we will only note the most essential incidents of those two terrible days immediately preceding the awful catastrophe that broke so suddenly upon him.

Though Grushenka had, it is true, loved him for an hour, genuinely and sincerely, yet she tortured him sometimes cruelly and mercilessly. The worst of it was that he could never tell what she meant to do. To prevail upon her by force or kindness was also impossible: she would yield to nothing. She would only have become angry and turned away from him altogether, he knew that well already. He suspected, quite correctly, that she, too, was passing through an inward struggle, and was in a state of extraordinary indecision, that she was making up her mind to something, and unable to determine upon it. And so, not without good reason, he divined, with a sinking heart, that at moments she must simply hate him and his passion. And so, perhaps, it was, but what was distressing Grushenka he did not understand. For him the whole tormenting question lay between him and Fyodor Pavlovitch.

Here, we must note, by the way, one certain fact: he was firmly persuaded that Fyodor Pavlovitch would offer, or perhaps had offered, Grushenka lawful wedlock, and did not for a moment believe that the old voluptuary hoped to gain his object for three thousand roubles. Mitya had reached this conclusion from his knowledge of Grushenka and her character. That was how it was that he could believe at times that all Grushenka's uneasiness rose from not knowing which of them to choose, which was most to her advantage.

Strange to say, during those days it never occurred to him to think of the approaching return of the "officer," that is, of the man who had been such a fatal influence in Grushenka's life, and whose arrival she was expecting with such emotion and dread. It is true that of late Grushenka had been very silent about it. Yet he was perfectly aware of a letter she had received a month ago from her seducer, and had heard of it from her own lips. He partly knew, too, what the letter contained. In a moment of spite Grushenka had shown him that letter, but to her astonishment he attached hardly any consequence to it. It would be hard to say why this was. Perhaps, weighed down by all the hideous horror of his struggle with his own father for this woman, he was incapable of imagining any danger more terrible, at any rate for the time. He simply did not believe in a suitor who suddenly turned up again after five years' disappearance, still less in his speedy arrival. Moreover, in the "officer's" first letter which had been shown to Mitya, the possibility of his new rival's visit was very vaguely suggested. The letter was very indefinite, high-flown, and full of sentimentality. It must be noted that Grushenka had concealed from him the last lines of the letter, in which his return was alluded to more definitely. He had, besides, noticed at that moment, he remembered afterwards, a certain involuntary proud contempt for this missive from Siberia on Grushenka's face. Grushenka told him nothing of what had passed later between her and this rival; so that by degrees he had completely forgotten the officer's existence.

He felt that whatever might come later, whatever turn things might take, his final conflict with Fyodor Pavlovitch was close upon him, and must be decided before anything else. With a sinking heart he was expecting every moment Grushenka's decision, always believing that it would come suddenly, on the impulse of the moment. All of a sudden she would say to him: "Take me, I'm yours for ever," and it would all be over. He would seize her and bear her away at once to the ends of the earth. Oh, then he would bear her away at once, as far, far away as possible; to the farthest end of Russia, if not of the earth, then he would marry her, and settle down with her incognito, so that no one would know anything about them, there, here, or anywhere. Then, oh then, a new life would begin at once!

Of this different, reformed and "virtuous" life ("it must, it must be virtuous") he dreamed feverishly at every moment. He thirsted for that reformation and renewal. The filthy morass, in which he had sunk of his own free will, was too revolting to him, and, like very many men in such cases, he put faith above all in change of place. If only it were not for these people, if only it were not for these circumstances, if only he could fly away from this accursed place--he would be altogether regenerated, would enter on a new path. That was what he believed in, and what he was yearning for.

But all this could only be on condition of the first, the happy solution of the question. There was another possibility, a different and awful ending. Suddenly she might say to him: "Go away. I have just come to terms with Fyodor Pavlovitch. I am going to marry him and don't want you."--and then...but then...But Mitya did not know what would happen then. Up to the last hour he didn't know. That must be said to his credit. He had no definite intentions, had planned no crime. He was simply watching and spying in agony, while he prepared himself for the first, happy solution of his destiny. He drove away any other idea, in fact. But for that ending a quite different anxiety arose, a new, incidental, but yet fatal and insoluble difficulty presented itself.

If she were to say to him: "I'm yours; take me away," how could he take her away? Where had he the means, the money to do it? It was just at this time that all sources of revenue from Fyodor Pavlovitch, doles which had gone on without interruption for so many years, ceased. Grushenka had money, of course, but with regard to this Mitya suddenly evinced extraordinary pride; he wanted to carry her away and begin the new life with her himself, at his own expense, not at hers. He could not conceive of taking her money, and the very idea caused him a pang of intense repulsion. I won't enlarge on this fact or analyse it here, but confine myself to remarking that this was his attitude at the moment. All this may have arisen indirectly and unconsciously from the secret stings of his conscience for the money of Katerina Ivanovna that he had dishonestly appropriated. "I've been a scoundrel to one of them, and I shall be a scoundrel again to the other directly," was his feeling then, as he explained after: "and when Grushenka knows, she won't care for such a scoundrel."

Where then was he to get the means, where was he to get the fateful money? Without it, all would be lost and nothing could be done, "and only because I hadn't the money. Oh, the shame of it!"

To anticipate things: he did, perhaps, know where to get the money, knew, perhaps, where it lay at that moment. I will say no more of this here, as it will all be clear later. But his chief trouble, I must explain however obscurely, lay in the fact that to have that sum he knew of, to have the right to take it, he must first restore Katerina Ivanovna's three thousand--if not, "I'm a common pick-pocket, I'm a scoundrel, and I don't want to begin a new life as a scoundrel," Mitya decided. And so he made up his mind to move heaven and earth to return Katerina Ivanovna that three thousand, and that first of all. The final stage of this decision, so to say, had been reached only during the last hours, that is, after his last interview with Alyosha, two days before, on the high-road, on the evening when Grushenka had insulted Katerina Ivanovna, and Mitya, after hearing Alyosha's account of it, had admitted that he was a scoundrel, and told him to tell Katerina Ivanovna so, if it could be any comfort to her. After parting from his brother on that night, he had felt in his frenzy that it would be better "to murder and rob someone than fail to pay my debt to Katya. I'd rather everyone thought me a robber and a murderer; I'd rather go to Siberia than that Katya should have the right to say that I deceived her and stole her money, and used her money to run away with Grushenka and begin a new life! That I can't do!" So Mitya decided, grinding his teeth, and he might well fancy at times that his brain would give way. But meanwhile he went on struggling...

Strange to say, though one would have supposed there was nothing left for him but despair--for what chance had he, with nothing in the world, to raise such a sum?--yet to the very end he persisted in hoping that he would get that three thousand, that the money would somehow come to him of itself, as though it might drop from heaven. That is just how it is with people who, like Dmitri, have never had anything to do with money, except to squander what has come to them by inheritance without any effort of their own, and have no notion how money is obtained. A whirl of the most fantastic notions took possession of his brain immediately after he had parted with Alyosha two days before, and threw his thoughts into a tangle of confusion. This is how it was he pitched first on a perfectly wild enterprise. And perhaps to men of that kind in such circumstances the most impossible, fantastic schemes occur first, and seem most practical.

He suddenly determined to go to Samsonov, the merchant who was Grushenka's protector, and to propose a "scheme" to him, and by means of it to obtain from him at once the whole of the sum required. Of the commercial value of his scheme he had no doubt, not the slightest, and was only uncertain how Samsonov would look upon his freak, supposing he were to consider it from any but the commercial point of view. Though Mitya knew the merchant by sight, he was not acquainted with him and had never spoken a word to him. But for some unknown reason he had long entertained the conviction that the old reprobate, who was lying at death's door, would perhaps not at all object now to Grushenka's securing a respectable position, and marrying a man "to be depended upon." And he believed not only that he would not object, but that this was what he desired, and, if opportunity arose, that he would be ready to help. From some rumour, or perhaps from some stray word of Grushenka's, he had gathered further that the old man would perhaps prefer him to Fyodor Pavlovitch for Grushenka.

Possibly many of the readers of my novel will feel that in reckoning on such assistance, and being ready to take his bride, so to speak, from the hands of her protector, Dmitri showed great coarseness and want of delicacy. I will only observe that Mitya looked upon Grushenka's past as something completely over. He looked on that past with infinite pity and resolved with all the fervour of his passion that when once Grushenka told him she loved him and would marry him, it would mean the beginning of a new Grushenka and a new Dmitri, free from every vice. They would forgive one another and would begin their lives afresh. As for Kuzma Samsonov, Dmitri looked upon him as a man who had exercised a fateful influence in that remote past of Grushenka's, though she had never loved him, and who was now himself a thing of the past, completely done with, and, so to say, non-existent. Besides, Mitya hardly looked upon him as a man at all, for it was known to everyone in the town that he was only a shattered wreck, whose relations with Grushenka had changed their character and were now simply paternal, and that this had been so for a long time.

In any case there was much simplicity on Mitya's part in all this, for in spite of all his vices, he was a very simple-hearted man. It was an instance of this simplicity that Mitya was seriously persuaded that, being on the eve of his departure for the next world, old Kuzma must sincerely repent of his past relations with Grushenka, and that she had no more devoted friend and protector in the world than this, now harmless, old man.

After his conversation with Alyosha, at the cross-roads, he hardly slept all night, and at ten o'clock next morning, he was at the house of Samsonov and telling the servant to announce him. It was a very large and gloomy old house of two stories, with a lodge and outhouses. In the lower story lived Samsonov's two married sons with their families, his old sister, and his unmarried daughter. In the lodge lived two of his clerks, one of whom also had a large family. Both the lodge and the lower story were overcrowded, but the old man kept the upper floor to himself, and would not even let the daughter live there with him, though she waited upon him, and in spite of her asthma was obliged at certain fixed hours, and at any time he might call her, to run upstairs to him from below.

This upper floor contained a number of large rooms kept purely for show, furnished in the old-fashioned merchant style, with long monotonous rows of clumsy mahogany chairs along the walls, with glass chandeliers under shades, and gloomy mirrors on the walls. All these rooms were entirely empty and unused, for the old man kept to one room, a small, remote bedroom, where he was waited upon by an old servant with a kerchief on her head, and by a lad, who used to sit on the locker in the passage. Owing to his swollen legs, the old man could hardly walk at all, and was only rarely lifted from his leather armchair, when the old woman supporting him led him up and down the room once or twice. He was morose and taciturn even with this old woman.

When he was informed of the arrival of the "captain," he at once refused to see him. But Mitya persisted and sent his name up again. Samsonov questioned the lad minutely: What he looked like? Whether he was drunk? Was he going to make a row? The answer he received was: that he was sober, but wouldn't go away. The old man again refused to see him. Then Mitya, who had foreseen this, and purposely brought pencil and paper with him, wrote clearly on the piece of paper the words: "On most important business closely concerning Agrafena Alexandrovna," and sent it up to the old man.

After thinking a little Samsonov told the lad to take the visitor to the drawing-room, and sent the old woman downstairs with a summons to his younger son to come upstairs to him at once. This younger son, a man over six foot and of exceptional physical strength, who was closely-shaven and dressed in the European style, though his father still wore a kaftan and a beard, came at once without a comment. All the family trembled before the father. The old man had sent for this giant, not because he was afraid of the "captain" (he was by no means of a timorous temper), but in order to have a witness in case of any emergency. Supported by his son and the servant lad, he waddled at last into the drawing-room. It may be assumed that he felt considerable curiosity. The drawing-room in which Mitya was awaiting him was a vast, dreary room that laid a weight of depression on the heart. It had a double row of windows, a gallery, marbled walls, and three immense chandeliers with glass lustres covered with shades.

Mitya was sitting on a little chair at the entrance, awaiting his fate with nervous impatience. When the old man appeared at the opposite door, seventy feet away, Mitya jumped up at once, and with his long, military stride walked to meet him. Mitya was well dressed, in a frock-coat, buttoned up, with a round hat and black gloves in his hands, just as he had been three days before at the elder's, at the family meeting with his father and brothers. The old man waited for him, standing dignified and unbending, and Mitya felt at once that he had looked him through and through as he advanced. Mitya was greatly impressed, too, with Samsonov's immensely swollen face. His lower lip, which had always been thick, hung down now, looking like a bun. He bowed to his guest in dignified silence, motioned him to a low chair by the sofa, and, leaning on his son's arm he began lowering himself on to the sofa opposite, groaning painfully, so that Mitya, seeing his painful exertions, immediately felt remorseful and sensitively conscious of his insignificance in the presence of the dignified person he had ventured to disturb.

"What is it you want of me, sir?" said the old man, deliberately, distinctly, severely, but courteously, when he was at last seated.

Mitya started, leapt up, but sat down again. Then he began at once speaking with loud, nervous haste, gesticulating, and in a positive frenzy. He was unmistakably a man driven into a corner, on the brink of ruin, catching at the last straw, ready to sink if he failed. Old Samsonov probably grasped all this in an instant, though his face remained cold and immovable as a statue's.

"Most honoured sir, Kuzma Kuzmitch, you have no doubt heard more than once of my disputes with my father, Fyodor Pavlovitch Karamazov, who robbed me of my inheritance from my mother...seeing the whole town is gossiping about it...for here everyone's gossiping of what they shouldn't...and besides, it might have reached you through Grushenka...I beg your pardon, through Agrafena Alexandrovna...Agrafena Alexandrovna, the lady of whom I have the highest respect and esteem..."

So Mitya began, and broke down at the first sentence. We will not reproduce his speech word for word, but will only summarise the gist of it. Three months ago, he said, he had of express intention (Mitya purposely used these words instead of "intentionally") consulted a lawyer in the chief town of the province, "a distinguished lawyer, Kuzma Kuzmitch, Pavel Pavlovitch Korneplodov. You have perhaps heard of him? A man of vast intellect, the mind of a statesman...he knows you, too...spoke of you in the highest terms..." Mitya broke down again. But these breaks did not deter him. He leapt instantly over the gaps, and struggled on and on.

This Korneplodov, after questioning him minutely, and inspecting the documents he was able to bring him (Mitya alluded somewhat vaguely to these documents, and slurred over the subject with special haste), reported that they certainly might take proceedings concerning the village of Tchermashnya, which ought, he said, to have come to him, Mitya, from his mother, and so checkmate the old villain, his father..."because every door was not closed and justice might still find a loophole." In fact, he might reckon on an additional sum of six or even seven thousand roubles from Fyodor Pavlovitch, as Tchermashnya was worth, at least, twenty-five thousand, he might say twenty-eight thousand, in fact, "thirty, thirty, Kuzma Kuzmitch, and would you believe it, I didn't get seventeen from that heartless man!" So he, Mitya, had thrown the business up for the time, knowing nothing about the law, but on coming here was struck dumb by a cross--claim made upon him (here Mitya went adrift again and again took a flying leap forward), "so will not you, excellent and honoured Kuzma Kuzmitch, be willing to take up all my claims against that unnatural monster, and pay me a sum down of only three thousand?...You see, you cannot, in any case, lose over it. On my honour, my honour, I swear that. Quite the contrary, you may make six or seven thousand instead of three." Above all, he wanted this concluded that very day.

"I'll do the business with you at a notary's, or whatever it is...in fact, I'm ready to do anything...I'll hand over all the deeds...whatever you want, sign anything...and we could draw up the agreement at once...and if it were possible, if it were only possible, that very morning...You could pay me that three thousand, for there isn't a capitalist in this town to compare with you, and so would save me from...save me, in fact...for a good, I might say an honourable action...For I cherish the most honourable feelings for a certain person, whom you know well, and care for as a father. I would not have come, indeed, if it had not been as a father. And, indeed, it's a struggle of three in this business, for it's fate--that's a fearful thing, Kuzma Kuzmitch! A tragedy, Kuzma Kuzmitch, a tragedy! And as you've dropped out long ago, it's a tug-of-war between two. I'm expressing it awkwardly, perhaps, but I'm not a literary man. You see, I'm on the one side, and that monster on the other. So you must choose. It's either I or the monster. It all lies in your hands-.the fate of three lives, and the happiness of two... Excuse me, I'm making a mess of it, but you understand...I see from your venerable eyes that you understand...and if you don't understand, I'm done for...so you see!"

Mitya broke off his clumsy speech with that, "so you see!" and jumping up from his seat, awaited the answer to his foolish proposal. At the last phrase he had suddenly become hopelessly aware that it had all fallen flat, above all, that he had been talking utter nonsense.

"How strange it is! On the way here it seemed all right, and now it's nothing but nonsense." The idea suddenly dawned on his despairing mind. All the while he had been talking, the old man sat motionless, watching him with an icy expression in his eyes. After keeping him for a moment in suspense, Kuzma Kuzmitch pronounced at last in the most positive and chilling tone:

"Excuse me, we don't undertake such business."

Mitya suddenly felt his legs growing weak under him.

"What am I to do now, Kuzma Kuzmitch?" he muttered, with a pale smile. "I suppose it's all up with me--what do you think?"

"Excuse me..."

Mitya remained standing, staring motionless. He suddenly noticed a movement in the old man's face. He started.

"You see, sir, business of that sort's not in our line," said the old man slowly. "There's the court, and the lawyers--it's a perfect misery. But if you like, there is a man here you might apply to."

"Good heavens! Who is it? You're my salvation, Kuzma Kuzmitch," faltered Mitya.

"He doesn't live here, and he's not here just now. He is a peasant, he does business in timber. His name is Lyagavy. He's been haggling with Fyodor Pavlovitch for the last year, over your copse at Tchermashnya. They can't agree on the price, maybe you've heard? Now he's come back again and is staying with the priest at Ilyinskoe, about twelve versts from the Volovya station. He wrote to me, too, about the business of the copse, asking my advice. Fyodor Pavlovitch means to go and see him himself. So if you were to be beforehand with Fyodor Pavlovitch and to make Lyagavy the offer you've made me, he might possibly--"

"A brilliant idea!" Mitya interrupted ecstatically. "He's the very man, it would just suit him. He's haggling with him for it, being asked too much, and here he would have all the documents entitling him to the property itself. Ha ha ha!"

And Mitya suddenly went off into his short, wooden laugh, startling Samsonov.

"How can I thank you, Kuzma Kuzmitch?" cried Mitya effusively.

"Don't mention it," said Samsonov, inclining his head.

"But you don't know, you've saved me. Oh, it was a true presentiment brought me to you...So now to this priest!

"No need of thanks."

"I'll make haste and fly there. I'm afraid I've overtaxed your strength. I shall never forget it. It's a Russian says that, Kuzma Kuzmitch, a R-r-russian!"

"To be sure!" Mitya seized his hand to press it, but there was a malignant gleam in the old man's eye. Mitya drew back his hand, but at once blamed himself for his mistrustfulness. "It's because he's tired," he thought.

"For her sake! For her sake, Kuzma Kuzmitch! You understand that it's for her," he cried, his voice ringing through the room. He bowed, turned sharply round, and with the same long stride walked to the door without looking back. He was trembling with delight.

"Everything was on the verge of ruin and my guardian angel saved me," was the thought in his mind. And if such a business man as Samsonov (a most worthy old man, and what dignity!) had suggested this course, then...then success was assured. He would fly off immediately. "I will be back before night, I shall be back at night and the thing is done. Could the old man have been laughing at me?" exclaimed Mitya, as he strode towards his lodging. He could, of course, imagine nothing but that the advice was practical "from such a business man" with an understanding of the business, with an understanding of this Lyagavy (curious surname!). Or--the old man was laughing at him.

Alas! The second alternative was the correct one. Long afterwards, when the catastrophe had happened, old Samsonov himself confessed, laughing, that he had made a fool of the "captain." He was a cold, spiteful and sarcastic man, liable to violent antipathies. Whether it was the "captain's" excited face, or the foolish conviction of the "rake and spendthrift," that he, Samsonov, could be taken in by such a cock-and-bull story as his scheme, or his jealousy of Grushenka, in whose name this "scapegrace" had rushed in on him with such a tale to get money which worked on the old man, I can't tell. But at the instant when Mitya stood before him, feeling his legs grow weak under him, and frantically exclaiming that he was ruined, at that moment the old man looked at him with intense spite, and resolved to make a laughing-stock of him. When Mitya had gone, Kuzma Kuzmitch, white with rage, turned to his son and bade him see to it that that beggar be never seen again, and never admitted even into the yard, or else he'd--

He did not utter his threat. But even his son, who often saw him enraged, trembled with fear. For a whole hour afterwards, the old man was shaking with anger, and by evening he was worse, and sent for the doctor.

Chapter 2. Lyagavy

SO he must drive at full speed, and he had not the money for horses. He had forty copecks, and that was all, all that was left after so many years of prosperity! But he had at home an old silver watch which had long ceased to go. He snatched it up and carried it to a Jewish watch maker who had a shop in the market-place. The Jew gave him six roubles for it.

"And I didn't expect that cried Mitya, ecstatically. (He was still in a state of ecstasy.) He seized his six roubles and ran home. At home he borrowed three roubles from the people of the house, who loved him so much that they were pleased to give it him, though it was all they had. Mitya in his excitement told them on the spot that his fate would be decided that day, and he described, in desperate haste, the whole scheme he had put before Samsonov, the latter's decision, his own hopes for the future, and so on. These people had been told many of their lodger's secrets before, and so looked upon him as a gentleman who was not at all proud, and almost one of themselves. Having thus collected nine roubles Mitya sent for posting-horses to take him to the Volovya station. This was how the fact came to be remembered and established that "at midday, on the day before the event, Mitya had not a farthing, and that he had sold his watch to get money and had borrowed three roubles from his landlord, all in the presence of witnesses."

I note this fact, later on it will be apparent why I do so.

Though he was radiant with the joyful anticipation that he would at last solve all his difficulties, yet, as he drew near Volovya station, he trembled at the thought of what Grushenka might be doing in his absence. What if she made up her mind to-day to go to Fyodor Pavlovitch? This was why he had gone off without telling her and why he left orders with his landlady not to let out where he had gone, if anyone came to inquire for him.

"I must, I must get back to-night," he repeated, as he was jolted along in the cart, "and I dare say I shall have to bring this Lyagavy back here...to draw up the deed." So mused Mitya, with a throbbing heart, but alas! his dreams were not fated to be carried out.

To begin with, he was late, taking a short cut from Volovya station which turned out to be eighteen versts instead of twelve. Secondly, he did not find the priest at home at Ilyinskoe; he had gone off to a neighbouring village. While Mitya, setting off there with the same exhausted horses, was looking for him, it was almost dark.

The priest, a shy and amiable looking little man, informed him at once that though Lyagavy had been staying with him at first, he was now at Suhoy Possyolok, that he was staying the night in the forester's cottage, as he was buying timber there too. At Mitya's urgent request that he would take him to Lyagavy at once, and by so doing "save him, so to speak," the priest agreed, after some demur, to conduct him to Suhoy Possyolok; his curiosity was obviously aroused. But, unluckily, he advised their going on foot, as it would not be "much over" a verst. Mitya, of course, agreed, and marched off with his yard-long strides, so that the poor priest almost ran after him. He was a very cautious man, though not old.

Mitya at once began talking to him, too, of his plans, nervously and excitedly asking advice in regard to Lyagavy, and talking all the way. The priest listened attentively, but gave little advice. He turned off Mitya's questions with: "I don't know. Ah, I can't say. How can I tell?" and so on. When Mitya began to speak of his quarrel with his father over his inheritance, the priest was positively alarmed, as he was in some way dependent on Fyodor Pavlovitch. He inquired, however, with surprise, why he called the peasant-trader Gorstkin, Lyagavy, and obligingly explained to Mitya that, though the man's name really was Lyagavy, he was never called so, as he would be grievously offended at the name, and that he must be sure to call him Gorstkin, "or you'll do nothing with him; he won't even listen to you," said the priest in conclusion.

Mitya was somewhat surprised for a moment, and explained that that was what Samsonov had called him. On hearing this fact, the priest dropped the subject, though he would have done well to put into words his doubt whether, if Samsonov had sent him to that peasant, calling him Lyagavy, there was not something wrong about it and he was turning him into ridicule. But Mitya had no time to pause over such trifles. He hurried, striding along, and only when he reached Suhoy Possyolok did he realise that they had come not one verst, nor one and a half, but at least three. This annoyed him, but he controlled himself.

They went into the hut. The forester lived in one half of the hut, and Gorstkin was lodging in the other, the better room the other side of the passage. They went into that room and lighted a tallow candle. The hut was extremely overheated. On the table there was a samovar that had gone out, a tray with cups, an empty rum bottle, a bottle of vodka partly full, and some half-eaten crusts of wheaten bread. The visitor himself lay stretched at full length on the bench, with his coat crushed up under his head for a pillow, snoring heavily. Mitya stood in perplexity.

"Of course, I must wake him. My business is too important. I've come in such haste. I'm in a hurry to get back to-day," he said in great agitation. But the priest and the forester stood in silence, not giving their opinion. Mitya went up and began trying to wake him himself; he tried vigorously, but the sleeper did not wake.

"He's drunk," Mitya decided. "Good Lord! What am I to do? What am I to do?" And, terribly impatient, he began pulling him by the arms, by the legs, shaking his head, lifting him up and making him sit on the bench. Yet, after prolonged exertions, he could only succeed in getting the drunken man to utter absurd grunts, and violent, but inarticulate oaths.

"No, you'd better wait a little," the priest pronounced at last, "for he's obviously not in a fit state."

"He's been drinking the whole day," the forester chimed in.

"Good heavens!" cried Mitya. "If only you knew how important it is to me and how desperate I am!"

"No, you'd better wait till morning," the priest repeated.

"Till morning? Mercy! that's impossible!" And in his despair he was on the point of attacking the sleeping man again, but stopped short at once, realising the uselessness of his efforts. The priest said nothing, the sleepy forester looked gloomy.

"What terrible tragedies real life contrives for people," said Mitya, in complete despair. The perspiration was streaming down his face. The priest seized the moment to put before him, very reasonably, that, even if he succeeded in wakening the man, he would still be drunk and incapable of conversation. "And your business is important," he said, "so you'd certainly better put it off till morning." With a gesture of despair Mitya agreed.

"Father, I will stay here with a light, and seize the favourable moment. As soon as he wakes I'll begin. I'll pay you for the light," he said to the forester, "for the night's lodging, too; you'll remember Dmitri Karamazov. Only Father, I don't know what we're to do with you. Where will you sleep?"

"No, I'm going home. I'll take his horse and get home," he said, indicating the forester. "And now I'll say good-bye. I wish you all success."

So it was settled. The priest rode off on the forester's horse, delighted to escape, though he shook his head uneasily, wondering whether he ought not next day to inform his benefactor Fyodor Pavlovitch of this curious incident, "or he may in an unlucky hour hear of it, be angry, and withdraw his favour."

The forester, scratching himself, went back to his room without a word, and Mitya sat on the bench to "catch the favourable moment," as he expressed it. Profound dejection clung about his soul like a heavy mist. A profound, intense dejection! He sat thinking, but could reach no conclusion. The candle burnt dimly, a cricket chirped; it became insufferably close in the overheated room. He suddenly pictured the garden, the path behind the garden, the door of his father's house mysteriously opening and Grushenka running in. He leapt up from the bench.

"It's a tragedy!" he said, grinding his teeth. Mechanically he went up to the sleeping man and looked in his face. He was a lean, middle-aged peasant, with a very long face, flaxen curls, and a long, thin, reddish beard, wearing a blue cotton shirt and a black waistcoat, from the pocket of which peeped the chain of a silver watch. Mitya looked at his face with intense hatred, and for some unknown reason his curly hair particularly irritated him.

What was insufferably humiliating was that, after leaving things of such importance and making such sacrifices, he, Mitya, utterly worn out, should with business of such urgency be standing over this dolt on whom his whole fate depended, while he snored as though there were nothing the matter, as though he'd dropped from another planet.

"Oh, the irony of fate!" cried Mitya, and, quite losing his head, he fell again to rousing the tipsy peasant. He roused him with a sort of ferocity, pulled at him, pushed him, even beat him; but after five minutes of vain exertions, he returned to his bench in helpless despair, and sat down.

"Stupid! Stupid!" cried Mitya. "And how dishonourable it all is!" something made him add. His head began to ache horribly. "Should he fling it up and go away altogether?" he wondered. "No, wait till to-morrow now. I'll stay on purpose. What else did I come for? Besides, I've no means of going. How am I to get away from here now? Oh, the idiocy of it" But his head ached more and more. He sat without moving, and unconsciously dozed off and fell asleep as he sat. He seemed to have slept for two hours or more. He was waked up by his head aching so unbearably that he could have screamed. There was a hammering in his temples, and the top of his head ached. It was a long time before he could wake up fully and understand what had happened to him.

At last he realised that the room was full of charcoal fumes from the stove, and that he might die of suffocation. And the drunken peasant still lay snoring. The candle guttered and was about to go out. Mitya cried out, and ran staggering across the passage into the forester's room. The forester waked up at once, but hearing that the other room was full of fumes, to Mitya's surprise and annoyance, accepted the fact with strange unconcern, though he did go to see to it.

"But he's dead, he's dead! and...what am I to do then?" cried Mitya frantically.

They threw open the doors, opened a window and the chimney. Mitya brought a pail of water from the passage. First he wetted his own head, then, finding a rag of some sort, dipped it into the water, and put it on Lyagavy's head. The forester still treated the matter contemptuously, and when he opened the window said grumpily:

"It'll be all right, now."

He went back to sleep, leaving Mitya a lighted lantern. Mitya fussed about the drunken peasant for half an hour, wetting his head, and gravely resolved not to sleep all night. But he was so worn out that when he sat down for a moment to take breath, he closed his eyes, unconsciously stretched himself full length on the bench and slept like the dead.

It was dreadfully late when he waked. It was somewhere about nine o'clock. The sun was shining brightly in the two little windows of the hut. The curly-headed peasant was sitting on the bench and had his coat on. He had another samovar and another bottle in front of him. Yesterday's bottle had already been finished, and the new one was more than half empty. Mitya jumped up and saw at once that the cursed peasant was drunk again, hopelessly and incurably. He stared at him for a moment with wide opened eyes. The peasant was silently and slyly watching him, with insulting composure, and even a sort of contemptuous condescension, so Mitya fancied. He rushed up to him.

"Excuse me, you see...I...you've most likely heard from the forester here in the hut. I'm Lieutenant Dmitri Karamazov, the son of the old Karamazov whose copse you are buying."

"That's a lie!" said the peasant, calmly and confidently.

"A lie? You know Fyodor Pavlovitch?"

"I don't know any of your Fyodor Pavlovitches," said the peasant, speaking thickly.

"You're bargaining with him for the copse, for the copse. Do wake up, and collect yourself. Father Pavel of Ilyinskoe brought me here. You wrote to Samsonov, and he has sent me to you," Mitya gasped breathlessly.

"You're lying!" Lyagavy blurted out again. Mitya's legs went cold.

"For mercy's sake! It isn't a joke! You're drunk, perhaps. Yet you can speak and understand...or else...I understand nothing!"

"You're a painter!"

"For mercy's sake! I'm Karamazov, Dmitri Karamazov. I have an offer to make you, an advantageous offer...very advantageous offer, concerning the copse!"

The peasant stroked his beard importantly.

"No, you've contracted for the job and turned out a scamp. You're a scoundrel!"

"I assure you you're mistaken," cried Mitya, wringing his hands in despair. The peasant still stroked his beard, and suddenly screwed up his eyes cunningly.

"No, you show me this: you tell me the law that allows roguery. D'you hear? You're a scoundrel! Do you understand that?"

Mitya stepped back gloomily, and suddenly "something seemed to hit him on the head," as he said afterwards. In an instant a light seemed to dawn in his mind, "a light was kindled and I grasped it all." He stood, stupefied, wondering how he, after all a man of intelligence, could have yielded to such folly, have been led into such an adventure, and have kept it up for almost twenty-four hours, fussing round this Lyagavy, wetting his head.

"Why, the man's drunk, dead drunk, and he'll go on drinking now for a week; what's the use of waiting here? And what if Samsonov sent me here on purpose? What if she--? Oh God, what have I done?"

The peasant sat watching him and grinning. Another time Mitya might have killed the fool in a fury, but now he felt as weak as a child. He went quietly to the bench, took up his overcoat, put it on without a word, and went out of the hut. He did not find the forester in the next room; there was no one there. He took fifty copecks in small change out of his pocket and put them on the table for his night's lodging, the candle, and the trouble he had given. Coming out of the hut he saw nothing but forest all round. He walked at hazard, not knowing which way to turn out of the hut, to the right or to the left. Hurrying there the evening before with the priest, he had not noticed the road. He had no revengeful feeling for anybody, even for Samsonov, in his heart. He strode along a narrow forest path, aimless, dazed, without heeding where he was going. A child could have knocked him down, so weak was he in body and soul. He got out of the forest somehow, however, and a vista of fields, bare after the harvest, stretched as far as the eye could see.

"What despair! What death all round!" he repeated, striding on and on.

He was saved by meeting an old merchant who was being driven across country in a hired trap. When he overtook him, Mitya asked the way and it turned out that the old merchant, too, was going to Volovya. After some discussion Mitya got into the trap. Three hours later they arrived. At Volovya, Mitya at once ordered posting-horses to drive to the town, and suddenly realised that he was appallingly hungry. While the horses were being harnessed, an omelette was prepared for him. He ate it all in an instant, ate a huge hunk of bread, ate a sausage, and swallowed three glasses of vodka. After eating, his spirits and his heart grew lighter. He flew towards the town, urged on the driver, and suddenly made a new and "unalterable" plan to procure that "accursed money" before evening. "And to think, only to think that a man's life should be ruined for the sake of that paltry three thousand!" he cried, contemptuously. "I'll settle it to-day." And if it had not been for the thought of Grushenka and of what might have happened to her, which never left him, he would perhaps have become quite cheerful again...But the thought of her was stabbing him to the heart every moment, like a sharp knife.

At last they arrived, and Mitya at once ran to Grushenka.

Chapter 3. Gold Mines

THIS was the visit of Mitya of which Grushenka had spoken to Rakitin with such horror. She was just then expecting the "message," and was much relieved that Mitya had not been to see her that day or the day before. She hoped that "please God he won't come till I'm gone away," and he suddenly burst in on her. The rest we know already. To get him off her hands she suggested at once that he should walk with her to Samsonov's, where she said she absolutely must go "to settle his accounts," and when Mitya accompanied her at once, she said good-bye to him at the gate, making him promise to come at twelve o'clock to take her home again. Mitya, too, was delighted at this arrangement. If she was sitting at Samsonov's she could not be going to Fyodor Pavlovitch's, "if only she's not lying," he added at once. But he thought she was not lying from what he saw.

He was that sort of jealous man who, in the absence of the beloved woman, at once invents all sorts of awful fancies of what may be happening to her, and how she may be betraying him, but, when shaken, heartbroken, convinced of her faithlessness, he runs back to her, at the first glance at her face, her gay, laughing, affectionate face, he revives at once, lays aside all suspicion and with joyful shame abuses himself for his jealousy.

After leaving Grushenka at the gate he rushed home. Oh, he had so much still to do that day! But a load had been lifted from his heart, anyway.

"Now I must only make haste and find out from Smerdyakov whether anything happened there last night, whether, by any chance, she went to Fyodor Pavlovitch; ough!" floated through his mind.

Before he had time to reach his lodging, jealousy had surged up again in his restless heart.

Jealousy! "Othello was not jealous, he was trustful," observed Pushkin. And that remark alone is enough to show the deep insight of our great poet. Othello's soul was shattered and his whole outlook clouded simply because his ideal was destroyed. But Othello did not begin hiding, spying, peeping. He was trustful, on the contrary. He had to be led up, pushed on, excited with great difficulty before he could entertain the idea of deceit. The truly jealous man is not like that. It is impossible to picture to oneself the shame and moral degradation to which the jealous man can descend without a qualm of conscience. And yet it's not as though the jealous were all vulgar and base souls. On the contrary, a man of lofty feelings, whose love is pure and full of self-sacrifice, may yet hide under tables, bribe the vilest people, and be familiar with the lowest ignominy of spying and eavesdropping.

Othello was incapable of making up his mind to faithlessness--not incapable of forgiving it, but of making up his mind to it--though his soul was as innocent and free from malice as a babe's. It is not so with the really jealous man. It is hard to imagine what some jealous men can make up their mind to and overlook, and what they can forgive! The jealous are the readiest of all to forgive, and all women know it. The jealous man can forgive extraordinarily quickly (though, of course, after a violent scene), and he is able to forgive infidelity almost conclusively proved, the very kisses and embraces he has seen, if only he can somehow be convinced that it has all been "for the last time," and that his rival will vanish from that day forward, will depart to the ends of the earth, or that he himself will carry her away somewhere, where that dreaded rival will not get near her. Of course the reconciliation is only for an hour. For, even if the rival did disappear next day, he would invent another one and would be jealous of him. And one might wonder what there was in a love that had to be so watched over, what a love could be worth that needed such strenuous guarding. But that the jealous will never understand. And yet among them are men of noble hearts. It is remarkable, too, that those very men of noble hearts, standing hidden in some cupboard, listening and spying, never feel the stings of conscience at that moment, anyway, though they understand clearly enough with their "noble hearts" the shameful depths to which they have voluntarily sunk.

At the sight of Grushenka, Mitya's jealousy vanished, and, for an instant he became trustful and generous, and positively despised himself for his evil feelings. But it only proved that, in his love for the woman, there was an element of something far higher than he himself imagined, that it was not only a sensual passion, not only the "curve of her body," of which he had talked to Alyosha. But, as soon as Grushenka had gone, Mitya began to suspect her of all the low cunning of faithlessness, and he felt no sting of conscience at it.

And so jealousy surged up in him again. He had, in any case, to make haste. The first thing to be done was to get hold of at least a small, temporary loan of money. The nine roubles had almost all gone on his expedition. And, as we all know, one can't take a step without money. But he had thought over in the cart where he could get a loan. He had a brace of fine duelling pistols in a case, which he had not pawned till then because he prized them above all his possessions.

In the Metropolis tavern he had some time since made acquaintance with a young official and had learnt that this very opulent bachelor was passionately fond of weapons. He used to buy pistols, revolvers, daggers, hang them on his wall and show them to acquaintances. He prided himself on them, and was quite a specialist on the mechanism of the revolver. Mitya, without stopping to think, went straight to him, and offered to pawn his pistols to him for ten roubles. The official, delighted, began trying to persuade him to sell them outright. But Mitya would not consent, so the young man gave him ten roubles, protesting that nothing would induce him to take interest. They parted friends.

Mitya was in haste; he rushed towards Fyodor Pavlovitch's by the back way, to his arbour, to get hold of Smerdyakov as soon as possible. In this way the fact was established that three or four hours before a certain event, of which I shall speak later on, Mitya had not a farthing, and pawned for ten roubles a possession he valued, though, three hours later, he was in possession of thousands...But I am anticipating. From Marya Kondratyevna (the woman living near Fyodor Pavlovitch's) he learned the very disturbing fact of Smerdyakov's illness. He heard the story of his fall in the cellar, his fit, the doctor's visit, Fyodor Pavlovitch's anxiety; he heard with interest, too, that his brother Ivan had set off that morning for Moscow.

"Then he must have driven through Volovya before me," thought Dmitri, but he was terribly distressed about Smerdyakov. "What will happen now? Who'll keep watch for me? Who'll bring me word?" he thought. He began greedily questioning the women whether they had seen anything the evening before. They quite understood what he was trying to find out, and completely reassured him. No one had been there. Ivan Fyodorovitch had been there that night; everything had been perfectly as usual. Mitya grew thoughtful. He would certainly have to keep watch to-day, but where? Here or at Samsonov's gate? He decided that he must be on the lookout both here and there, and meanwhile...meanwhile...The difficulty was that he had to carry out the new plan that he had made on the journey back. He was sure of its success, but he must not delay acting upon it. Mitya resolved to sacrifice an hour to it: "In an hour I shall know everything, I shall settle everything, and then, then, then, first of all to Samsonov's. I'll inquire whether Grushenka's there and instantly be back here again, stay till eleven, and then to Samsonov's again to bring her home." This was what he decided.

He flew home, washed, combed his hair, brushed his clothes, dressed, and went to Madame Hohlakov's. Alas! he had built his hopes on her. He had resolved to borrow three thousand from that lady. And what was more, he felt suddenly convinced that she would not refuse to lend it to him. It may be wondered why, if he felt so certain, he had not gone to her at first, one of his own sort, so to speak, instead of to Samsonov, a man he did not know, who was not of his own class, and to whom he hardly knew how to speak.

But the fact was that he had never known Madame Hohlakov well, and had seen nothing of her for the last month, and that he knew she could not endure him. She had detested him from the first because he was engaged to Katerina Ivanovna, while she had, for some reason, suddenly conceived the desire that Katerina Ivanovna should throw him over, and marry the "charming, chivalrously refined Ivan, who had such excellent manners." Mitya's manners she detested. Mitya positively laughed at her, and had once said about her that she was just as lively and at her ease as she was uncultivated. But that morning in the cart a brilliant idea had struck him: "If she is so anxious I should not marry Katerina Ivanovna" (and he knew she was positively hysterical upon the subject) "why should she refuse me now that three thousand, just to enable me to leave Katya and get away from her for ever. These spoilt fine ladies, if they set their hearts on anything, will spare no expense to satisfy their caprice. Besides, she's so rich," Mitya argued.

As for his "plan" it was just the same as before; it consisted of the offer of his rights to Tchermashnya--but not with a commercial object, as it had been with Samsonov, not trying to allure the lady with the possibility of making a profit of six or seven thousand--but simply as a security for the debt. As he worked out this new idea, Mitya was enchanted with it, but so it always was with him in all his undertakings, in all his sudden decisions. He gave himself up to every new idea with passionate enthusiasm. Yet, when he mounted the steps of Madame Hohlakov's house he felt a shiver of fear run down his spine. At that moment he saw fully, as a mathematical certainty, that this was his last hope, that if this broke down, nothing else was left him in the world but to "rob and murder someone for the three thousand." It was half-past seven when he rang at the bell.

At first fortune seemed to smile upon him. As soon as he was announced he was received with extraordinary rapidity. "As though she were waiting for me," thought Mitya, and as soon as he had been led to the drawing-room, the lady of the house herself ran in, and declared at once that she was expecting him.

"I was expecting you! I was expecting you! Though I'd no reason to suppose you would come to see me, as you will admit yourself. Yet, I did expect you. You may marvel at my instinct, Dmitri Fyodorovitch, but I was convinced all the morning that you would come."

"That is certainly wonderful, madam," observed Mitya, sitting down limply, "but I have come to you on a matter of great importance...On a matter of supreme importance for me, that is, madam...for me alone...and I hasten--"

"I know you've come on most important business. Dmitri Fyodorovitch; it's not a case of presentiment, no reactionary harking back to the miraculous (have you heard about Father Zossima?). This is a case of mathematics: you couldn't help coming, after all that has passed with Katerina Ivanovna; you couldn't, you couldn't, that's a mathematical certainty."

"The realism of actual life, madam, that's what it is. But allow me to explain-"

"Realism indeed, Dmitri Fyodorovitch. I'm all for realism now. I've seen too much of miracles. You've heard that Father Zossima is dead?"

"No, madam, it's the first time I've heard of it." Mitya was a little surprised. The image of Alyosha rose to his mind.

"Last night, and only imagine-"

"Madam," said Mitya, "I can imagine nothing except that I'm in a desperate position, and that if you don't help me, everything will come to grief, and I first of all. Excuse me for the triviality of the expression, but I'm in a fever-"

"I know, I know that you're in a fever. You could hardly fail to be, and whatever you may say to me, I know beforehand. I have long been thinking over your destiny, Dmitri Fyodorovitch, I am watching over it and studying it...Oh, believe me, I'm an experienced doctor of the soul, Dmitri Fyodorovitch."

"Madam, if you are an experienced doctor, I'm certainly an experienced patient," said Mitya, with an effort to be polite, "and I feel that if you are watching over my destiny in this way, you will come to my help in my ruin, and so allow me, at least to explain to you the plan with which I have ventured to come to you...and what I am hoping of you...I have come, madam-"

"Don't explain it. It's of secondary importance. But as for help, you're not the first I have helped, Dmitri Fyodorovitch. You have most likely heard of my cousin, Madame Belmesov. Her husband was ruined, 'had come to grief,' as you characteristically express it, Dmitri Fyodorovitch. I recommended him to take to horse-breeding, and now he's doing well. Have you any idea of horse-breeding, Dmitri Fyodorovitch?"

"Not the faintest, madam; ah, madam, not the faintest!" cried Mitya, in nervous impatience, positively starting from his seat. "I simply implore you, madam, to listen to me. Only give me two minutes of free speech that I may just explain to you everything, the whole plan with which I have come. Besides, I am short of time. I'm in a fearful hurry," Mitya cried hysterically, feeling that she was just going to begin talking again, and hoping to cut her short. "I have come in despair...in the last gasp of despair, to beg you to lend me the sum of three thousand, a loan, but on safe, most safe security, madam, with the most trustworthy guarantees! Only let me explain-"

"You must tell me all that afterwards, afterwards!" Madame Hohlakov with a gesture demanded silence in her turn, "and whatever you may tell me, I know it all beforehand; I've told you so already. You ask for a certain sum, for three thousand, but I can give you more, immeasurably more; I will save you, Dmitri Fyodorovitch, but you must listen to me."

Mitya started from his seat again.

"Madam, will you really be so good!" he cried, with strong feeling. "Good God, you've saved me! You have saved a man from a violent death, from a bullet...My eternal gratitude "I will give you more, infinitely more than three thousand!" cried Madame Hohlakov, looking with a radiant smile at Mitya's ecstasy.

"Infinitely? But I don't need so much. I only need that fatal three thousand, and on my part I can give security for that sum with infinite gratitude, and I propose a plan which-"

"Enough, Dmitri Fyodorovitch, it's said and done." Madame Hohlakov cut him short, with the modest triumph of beneficence. "I have promised to save you, and I will save you. I will save you as I did Belmesov. What do you think of the gold mines, Dmitri Fyodorovitch?"

"Of the gold mines, madam? I have never thought anything about them."

"But I have thought of them for you. Thought of them over and over again. I have been watching you for the last month. I've watched you a hundred times as you've walked past, saying to myself: That's a man of energy who ought to be at the gold mines. I've studied your gait and come to the conclusion: that's a man who would find gold."

"From my gait, madam?" said Mitya, smiling.

"Yes, from your gait. You surely don't deny that character can be told from the gait, Dmitri Fyodorovitch? Science supports the idea. I'm all for science and realism now. After all this business with Father Zossima, which has so upset me, from this very day I'm a realist and I want to devote myself to practical usefulness. I'm cured. 'Enough!' as Turgeney says."

"But madam, the three thousand you so generously promised to lend me-"

"It is yours, Dmitri Fyodorovitch," Madame Hohlakov cut in at once. "The money is as good as in your pocket, not three thousand, but three million, Dmitri Fyodorovitch, in less than no time. I'll make you a present of the idea: you shall find gold mines, make millions, return and become a leading man, and wake us up and lead us to better things. Are we to leave it all to the Jews? You will found institutions and enterprises of all sorts. You will help the poor, and they will bless you. This is the age of railways, Dmitri Fyodorovitch. You'll become famous and indispensable to the Department of Finance, which is so badly off at present. The depreciation of the rouble keeps me awake at night, Dmitri Fyodorovitch; people don't know that side of me-"

"Madam, madam! Dmitri interrupted with an uneasy presentiment. "I shall indeed, perhaps, follow your advice, your wise advice, madam...I shall perhaps set off...to the gold mines...I'll come and see you again about it...many times, indeed...but now, that three thousand you so generously...oh, that would set me free, and if you could to-day...you see, I haven't a minute, a minute to lose to-day-"

"Enough, Dmitri Fyodorovitch, enough!" Madame Hohlakov interrupted emphatically. "The question is, will you go to the gold mines or not; have you quite made up your mind? Answer yes or no."

"I will go, madam, afterwards...I'll go where you like...but now-"

"Wait!" cried Madame Hohlakov. And jumping up and running to a handsome bureau with numerous little drawers, she began pulling out one drawer after another, looking for something with desperate haste.

"The three thousand," thought Mitya, his heart almost stopping, "and at the instant...without any papers or formalities...that's doing things in gentlemanly style! She's a splendid woman, if only she didn't talk so much!"

"Here!" cried Madame Hohlakov, running back joyfully to Mitya, "here is what I was looking for!"

It was a tiny silver ikon on a cord, such as is sometimes worn next the skin with a cross.

"This is from Kiev, Dmitri Fyodorovitch," she went on reverently, "from the relics of the Holy Martyr, Varvara. Let me put it on your neck myself, and with it dedicate you to a new life, to a new career."

And she actually put the cord round his neck, and began arranging it. In extreme embarrassment, Mitya bent down and helped her, and at last he got it under his neck-tie and collar through his shirt to his chest.

"Now you can set off," Madame Hohlakov pronounced, sitting down triumphantly in her place again.

"Madam, I am so touched. I don't know how to thank you, indeed...for such kindness, but...If only you knew how precious time is to me...That sum of money, for which I shall be indebted to your generosity...Oh, madam, since you are so kind, so touchingly generous to me," Mitya exclaimed impulsively, "then let me reveal to you...though, of course, you've known it a long time...that I love somebody here...I have been false to Katya...Katerina Ivanovna I should say...Oh, I've behaved inhumanly, dishonourably to her, but I fell in love here with another woman...a woman whom you, madam, perhaps, despise, for you know everything already, but whom I cannot leave on any account, and therefore that three thousand now-"

"Leave everything, Dmitri Fyodorovitch," Madame Hohlakov interrupted in the most decisive tone. "Leave everything, especially women. Gold mines are your goal, and there's no place for women there. Afterwards, when you come back rich and famous, you will find the girl of your heart in the highest society. That will be a modern girl, a girl of education and advanced ideas. By that time the dawning woman question will have gained ground, and the new woman will have appeared."

"Madam, that's not the point, not at all...Mitya clasped his hands in entreaty.

"Yes it is, Dmitri Fyodorovitch, just what you need; the very thing you're yearning for, though you don't realise it yourself. I am not at all opposed to the present woman movement, Dmitri Fyodorovitch. The development of woman, and even the political emancipation of woman in the near future--that's my ideal. I've a daughter myself, Dmitri Fyodorovitch, people don't know that side of me. I wrote a letter to the author, Shtchedrin, on that subject. He has taught me so much, so much about the vocation of woman. So last year I sent him an anonymous letter of two lines: 'I kiss and embrace you, my teacher, for the modern woman. Persevere.' And I signed myself, 'A Mother.' I thought of signing myself 'A contemporary Mother,' and hesitated, but I stuck to the simple 'Mother'; there's more moral beauty in that, Dmitri Fyodorovitch. And the word 'contemporary' might have reminded him of The Contemporary--a painful recollection owing to the censorship...Good Heavens, what is the matter!"

"Madam!" cried Mitya, jumping up at last, clasping his hands before her in helpless entreaty. "You will make me weep if you delay what you have so generously-"

"Oh, do weep, Dmitri Fyodorovitch, do weep! That's a noble feeling...such a path lies open before you! Tears will ease your heart, and later on you will return rejoicing. You will hasten to me from Siberia on purpose to share your joy with me-"

"But allow me, too!" Mitya cried suddenly.

"For the last time I entreat you, tell me, can I have the sum you promised me to-day, if not, when may I come for it?"

"What sum, Dmitri Fyodorovitch?"

"The three thousand you promised me...that you so generously-"

"Three thousand? Roubles? Oh, no, I haven't got three thousand," Madame Hohlakov announced with serene amazement. Mitya was stupefied.

"Why, you said just now you said...you said it was as good as in my hands-"

"Oh, no, you misunderstood me, Dmitri Fyodorovitch. In that case you misunderstood me. I was talking of the gold mines. It's true I promised you more, infinitely more than three thousand, I remember it all now, but I was referring to the gold mines."

"But the money? The three thousand?" Mitya exclaimed, awkwardly.

"Oh, if you meant money, I haven't any. I haven't a penny, Dmitri Fyodorovitch. I'm quarrelling with my steward about it, and I've just borrowed five hundred roubles from Miusov, myself. No, no, I've no money. And, do you know, Dmitri Fyodorovitch, if I had, I wouldn't give it to you. In the first place I never lend money. Lending money means losing friends. And I wouldn't give it to you particularly. I wouldn't give it you, because I like you and want to save you, for all you need is the gold mines, the gold mines, the gold mines!"

"Oh, the devil!" roared Mitya, and with all his might brought his fist down on the table.

"Aie! Aie!" cried Madame Hohlakov, alarmed, and she flew to the other end of the drawing-room.

Mitya spat on the ground, and strode rapidly out of the room, out of the house, into the street, into the darkness! He walked like one possessed, and beating himself on the breast, on the spot where he had struck himself two days previously, before Alyosha, the last time he saw him in the dark, on the road. What those blows upon his breast signified, on that spot, and what he meant by it--that was, for the time, a secret which was known to no one in the world, and had not been told even to Alyosha. But that secret meant for him more than disgrace; it meant ruin, suicide. So he had determined, if he did not get hold of the three thousand that would pay his debt to Katerina Ivanovna, and so remove from his breast, from that spot on his breast, the shame he carried upon it, that weighed on his conscience. All this will be fully explained to the reader later on, but now that his last hope had vanished, this man, so strong in appearance, burst out crying like a little child a few steps from the Hohlakovs' house. He walked on, and not knowing what he was doing, wiped away his tears with his fist. In this way he reached the square, and suddenly became aware that he had stumbled against something. He heard a piercing wail from an old woman whom he had almost knocked down.

"Good Lord, you've nearly killed me! Why don't you look where you're going, scapegrace?"

"Why, it's you!" cried Mitya, recognising the old woman in the dark. It was the old servant who waited on Samsonov, whom Mitya had particularly noticed the day before.

"And who are you, my good sir?" said the old woman in quite a different voice. "I don't know you in the dark."

"You live at Kuzma Kuzmitch's. You're the servant there?"

"Just so, sir, I was only running out to Prohoritch's...But I don't know you now."

"Tell me, my good woman, is Agrafena Alexandrovna there now?" said Mitya, beside himself with suspense. "I saw her to the house some time ago."

"She has been there, sir. She stayed a little while, and went off again."

"What? Went away?" cried Mitya. "When did she go?"

"Why, as soon as she came. She only stayed a minute. She only told Kuzma Kuzmitch a tale that made him laugh, and then she ran away."

"You're lying, damn you!" roared Mitya.

"Aie! Aie!" shrieked the old woman, but Mitya had vanished.

He ran with all his might to the house where Grushenka lived. At the moment he reached it, Grushenka was on her way to Mokroe. It was not more than a quarter of an hour after her departure.

Fenya was sitting with her grandmother, the old cook, Matryona, in the kitchen when "the captain" ran in. Fenya uttered a piercing shriek on seeing him.

"You scream?" roared Mitya, "where is she?"

But without giving the terror-stricken Fenya time to utter a word, he fell all of a heap at her feet.

"Fenya, for Christ's sake, tell me, where is she?"

"I don't know. Dmitri Fyodorovitch, my dear, I don't know. You may kill me but I can't tell you." Fenya swore and protested. "You went out with her yourself not long ago-"

"She came back!"

"Indeed she didn't. By God I swear she didn't come back."

"You're lying!" shouted Mitya. "From your terror I know where she is."

He rushed away. Fenya in her fright was glad she had got off so easily. But she knew very well that it was only that he was in such haste, or she might not have fared so well. But as he ran, he surprised both Fenya and old Matryona by an unexpected action. On the table stood a brass mortar, with a pestle in it, a small brass pestle, not much more than six inches long. Mitya already had opened the door with one hand when, with the other, he snatched up the pestle, and thrust it in his side-pocket.

"Oh Lord! He's going to murder someone!" cried Fenya, flinging up her hands.

Chapter 4. In the Dark

WHERE was he running? "Where could she be except at Fyodor Pavlovitch's? She must have run straight to him from Samsonov's, that was clear now. The whole intrigue, the whole deceit was evident."...It all rushed whirling through his mind. He did not run to Marya Kondratyevna's. "There was no need to go there...not the slightest need...he must raise no alarm...they would run and tell directly...Marya Kondratyevna was clearly in the plot, Smerdyakov too, he too, all had been bought over!"

He formed another plan of action: he ran a long way round Fyodor Pavlovitch's house, crossing the lane, running down Dmitrovsky Street, then over the little bridge, and so came straight to the deserted alley at the back, which was empty and uninhabited, with, on one side the hurdle fence of a neighbour's kitchen-garden, on the other the strong high fence that ran all round Fyodor Pavlovitch's garden. Here he chose a spot, apparently the very place, where according to the tradition, he knew Lizaveta had once climbed over it: "If she could climb over it," the thought, God knows why, occurred to him, "surely I can." He did in fact jump up, and instantly contrived to catch hold of the top of the fence. Then he vigorously pulled himself up and sat astride on it. Close by, in the garden stood the bathhouse, but from the fence he could see the lighted windows of the house too.

"Yes, the old man's bedroom is lighted up. She's there! and he leapt from the fence into the garden. Though he knew Grigory was ill and very likely Smerdyakov, too, and that there was no one to hear him, he instinctively hid himself, stood still, and began to listen. But there was dead silence on all sides and, as though of design, complete stillness, not the slightest breath of wind.

"And naught but the whispering silence," the line for some reason rose to his mind. "If only no one heard me jump over the fence! I think not." Standing still for a minute, he walked softly over the grass in the garden, avoiding the trees and shrubs. He walked slowly, creeping stealthily at every step, listening to his own footsteps. It took him five minutes to reach the lighted window. He remembered that just under the window there were several thick and high bushes of elder and whitebeam. The door from the house into the garden on the left-hand side was shut; he had carefully looked on purpose to see, in passing. At last he reached the bushes and hid behind them. He held his breath. "I must wait now," he thought, "to reassure them, in case they heard my footsteps and are listening...if only I don't cough or sneeze."

He waited two minutes. His heart was beating violently, and, at moments, he could scarcely breathe. "No, this throbbing at my heart won't stop," he thought. "I can't wait any longer." He was standing behind a bush in the shadow. The light of the window fell on the front part of the bush.

"How red the whitebeam berries are!" he murmured, not knowing why. Softly and noiselessly, step by step, he approached the window, and raised himself on tiptoe. All Fyodor Pavlovitch's bedroom lay open before him. It was not a large room, and was divided in two parts by a red screen, "Chinese," as Fyodor Pavlovitch used to call it. The word "Chinese" flashed into Mitya's mind, "and behind the screen, is Grushenka," thought Mitya. He began watching Fyodor Pavlovitch who was wearing his new striped-silk dressing-gown, which Mitya had never seen, and a silk cord with tassels round the waist. A clean, dandified shirt of fine linen with gold studs peeped out under the collar of the dressing-gown. On his head Fyodor Pavlovitch had the same red bandage which Alyosha had seen.

"He has got himself up," thought Mitya.

His father was standing near the window, apparently lost in thought. Suddenly he jerked up his head, listened a moment, and hearing nothing went up to the table, poured out half a glass of brandy from a decanter and drank it off. Then he uttered a deep sigh, again stood still a moment, walked carelessly up to the looking-glass on the wall, with his right hand raised the red bandage on his forehead a little, and began examining his bruises and scars, which had not yet disappeared.

"He's alone," thought Mitya, "in all probability he's alone."

Fyodor Pavlovitch moved away from the looking-glass, turned suddenly to the window and looked out. Mitya instantly slipped away into the shadow.

"She may be there behind the screen. Perhaps she's asleep by now," he thought, with a pang at his heart. Fyodor Pavlovitch moved away from the window. "He's looking for her out of the window, so she's not there. Why should he stare out into the dark? He's wild with impatience."...Mitya slipped back at once, and fell to gazing in at the window again. The old man was sitting down at the table, apparently disappointed. At last he put his elbow on the table, and laid his right cheek against his hand. Mitya watched him eagerly.

"He's alone, he's alone!" he repeated again. "If she were here, his face would be different."

Strange to say, a queer, irrational vexation rose up in his heart that she was not here. "It's not that she's not here," he explained to himself, immediately, "but that I can't tell for certain whether she is or not." Mitya remembered afterwards that his mind was at that moment exceptionally clear, that he took in everything to the slightest detail, and missed no point. But a feeling of misery, the misery of uncertainty and indecision, was growing in his heart with every instant. "Is she here or not?" The angry doubt filled his heart, and suddenly, making up his mind, he put out his hand and softly knocked on the window frame. He knocked the signal the old man had agreed upon with Smerdyakov, twice slowly and then three times more quickly, the signal that meant "Grushenka is here!"

The old man started, jerked up his head, and, jumping up quickly, ran to the window. Mitya slipped away into the shadow. Fyodor Pavlovitch opened the window and thrust his whole head out.

"Grushenka, is it you? Is it you?" he said, in a sort of trembling half-whisper. "Where are you, my angel, where are you?" He was fearfully agitated and breathless.

"He's alone," Mitya decided.

"Where are you?" cried the old man again; and he thrust his head out farther, thrust it out to the shoulders, gazing in all directions, right and left. "Come here, I've a little present for you. Come, I'll show you..."

"He means the three thousand," thought Mitya.

"But where are you? Are you at the door? I'll open it directly."

And the old man almost climbed out of the window, peering out to the right, where there was a door into the garden, trying to see into the darkness. In another second he would certainly have run out to open the door without waiting for Grushenka's answer.

Mitya looked at him from the side without stirring. The old man's profile that he loathed so, his pendent Adam's apple, his hooked nose, his lips that smiled in greedy expectation, were all brightly lighted up by the slanting lamplight falling on the left from the room. A horrible fury of hatred suddenly surged up in Mitya's heart: "There he was, his rival, the man who had tormented him, had ruined his life!" It was a rush of that sudden, furious, revengeful anger of which he had spoken, as though foreseeing it, to Alyosha, four days ago in the arbour, when, in answer to Alyosha's question, "How can you say you'll kill our father?" "I don't know, I don't know," he had said then. "Perhaps I shall not kill him, perhaps I shall. I'm afraid he'll suddenly be so loathsome to me at that moment. I hate his double chin, his nose, his eyes, his shameless grin. I feel a personal repulsion. That's what I'm afraid of, that's what may be too much for me."...This personal repulsion was growing unendurable. Mitya was beside himself, he suddenly pulled the brass pestle out of his pocket.

"God was watching over me then," Mitya himself said afterwards. At that very moment Grigory waked up on his bed of sickness. Earlier in the evening he had undergone the treatment which Smerdyakov had described to Ivan. He had rubbed himself all over with vodka mixed with a secret, very strong decoction, had drunk what was left of the mixture while his wife repeated a "certain prayer" over him, after which he had gone to bed. Marfa Ignatyevna had tasted the stuff, too, and, being unused to strong drink, slept like the dead beside her husband.

But Grigory waked up in the night, quite suddenly, and, after a moment's reflection, though he immediately felt a sharp pain in his back, he sat up in bed. Then he deliberated again, got up and dressed hurriedly. Perhaps his conscience was uneasy at the thought of sleeping while the house was unguarded "in such perilous times." Smerdyakov, exhausted by his fit, lay motionless in the next room. Marfa Ignatyevna did not stir. "The stuff's been too much for the woman," Grigory thought, glancing at her, and groaning, he went out on the steps. No doubt he only intended to look out from the steps, for he was hardly able to walk, the pain in his back and his right leg was intolerable. But he suddenly remembered that he had not locked the little gate into the garden that evening. He was the most punctual and precise of men, a man who adhered to an unchangeable routine, and habits that lasted for years. Limping and writhing with pain he went down the steps and towards the garden. Yes, the gate stood wide open. Mechanically he stepped into the garden. Perhaps he fancied something, perhaps caught some sound, and, glancing to the left he saw his master's window open. No one was looking out of it then.

"What's it open for? It's not summer now," thought Grigory, and suddenly, at that very instant he caught a glimpse of something extraordinary before him in the garden. Forty paces in front of him a man seemed to be running in the dark, a sort of shadow was moving very fast.

"Good Lord!" cried Grigory beside himself, and forgetting the pain in his back, he hurried to intercept the running figure. He took a short cut, evidently he knew the garden better; the flying figure went towards the bath-house, ran behind it and rushed to the garden fence. Grigory followed, not losing sight of him, and ran, forgetting everything. He reached the fence at the very moment the man was climbing over it. Grigory cried out, beside himself, pounced on him, and clutched his leg in his two hands.

Yes, his foreboding had not deceived him. He recognised him; it was he, the "monster," the "parricide."

"Parricide! the old man shouted so that the whole neighbourhood could hear, but he had not time to shout more, he fell at once, as though struck by lightning.

Mitya jumped back into the garden and bent over the fallen man. In Mitya's hands was a brass pestle, and he flung it mechanically in the grass. The pestle fell two paces from Grigory, not in the grass but on the path, in a most conspicuous place. For some seconds he examined the prostrate figure before him. The old man's head was covered with blood. Mitya put out his hand and began feeling it. He remembered afterwards clearly that he had been awfully anxious to make sure whether he had broken the old man's skull, or simply stunned him with the pestle. But the blood was flowing horribly; and in a moment Mitya's fingers were drenched with the hot stream. He remembered taking out of his pocket the clean white handkerchief with which he had provided himself for his visit to Madame Hohlakov, and putting it to the old man's head, senselessly trying to wipe the blood from his face and temples. But the handkerchief was instantly soaked with blood.

"Good heavens! What am I doing it for?" thought Mitya, suddenly pulling himself together. "If I have broken his skull, how can I find out now? And what difference does it make now?" he added, hopelessly. "If I've killed him, I've killed him...You've come to grief, old man, so there you must lie!" he said aloud. And suddenly turning to the fence, he vaulted over it into the lane and fell to running--the handkerchief soaked with blood he held, crushed up in his right fist, and as he ran he thrust it into the back pocket of his coat. He ran headlong, and the few passers-by who met him in the dark, in the streets, remembered afterwards that they had met a man running that night. He flew back again to the widow Morozov's house.

Immediately after he had left it that evening, Fenya had rushed to the chief porter, Nazar Ivanovitch, and besought him, for Christ's sake, "not to let the captain in again to-day or to-morrow." Nazar Ivanovitch promised, but went upstairs to his mistress who had suddenly sent for him, and meeting his nephew, a boy of twenty, who had recently come from the country, on the way up told him to take his place, but forgot to mention "the captain." Mitya, running up to the gate, knocked. The lad instantly recognised him, for Mitya had more than once tipped him. Opening the gate at once, he let him in, and hastened to inform him with a good-humoured smile that "Agrafena Alexandrovna is not at home now, you know."

"Where is she then, Prohor?" asked Mitya, stopping short.

"She set off this evening, some two hours ago, with Timofey, to Mokroe."

"What for?" cried Mitya.

"That I can't say. To see some officer. Someone invited her and horses were sent to fetch her."

Mitya left him, and ran like a madman to Fenya.

Chapter 5. A Sudden Resolution

SHE was sitting in the kitchen with her grandmother; they were both just going to bed. Relying on Nazar Ivanovitch, they had not locked themselves in. Mitya ran in, pounced on Fenya and seized her by the throat.

"Speak at once! Where is she? With whom is she now, at Mokroe?" he roared furiously.

Both the women squealed.

"Aie! I'll tell you. Aie! Dmitri Fyodorovitch, darling, I'll tell you everything directly, I won't hide anything," gabbled Fenya, frightened to death; "she's gone to Mokroe, to her officer."

"What officer?" roared Mitya.

"To her officer, the same one she used to know, the one who threw her over five years ago," cackled Fenya, as fast as she could speak.

Mitya withdrew the hands with which he was squeezing her throat. He stood facing her, pale as death, unable to utter a word, but his eyes showed that he realised it all, all, from the first word, and guessed the whole position. Poor Fenya was not in a condition at that moment to observe whether he understood or not. She remained sitting on the trunk as she had been when he ran into the room, trembling all over, holding her hands out before her as though trying to defend herself. She seemed to have grown rigid in that position. Her wide-opened, scared eyes were fixed immovably upon him. And to make matters worse, both his hands were smeared with blood. On the way, as he ran, he must have touched his forehead with them, wiping off the perspiration, so that on his forehead and his right cheek were bloodstained patches. Fenya was on the verge of hysterics. The old cook had jumped up and was staring at him like a mad woman, almost unconscious with terror.

Mitya stood for a moment, then mechanically sank on to a chair next to Fenya. He sat, not reflecting but, as it were, terror-stricken, benumbed. Yet everything was clear as day: that officer, he knew about him, he knew everything perfectly, he had known it from Grushenka herself, had known that a letter had come from him a month before. So that for a month, for a whole month, this had been going on, a secret from him, till the very arrival of this new man, and he had never thought of him! But how could he, how could he not have thought of him? Why was it he had forgotten this officer, like that, forgotten him as soon as he heard of him? That was the question that faced him like some monstrous thing. And he looked at this monstrous thing with horror, growing cold with horror.

But suddenly, as gently and mildly as a gentle and affectionate child, he began speaking to Fenya as though he had utterly forgotten how he had scared and hurt her just now. He fell to questioning Fenya with an extreme preciseness, astonishing in his position, and though the girl looked wildly at his blood-stained hands, she, too, with wonderful readiness and rapidity, answered every question as though eager to put the whole truth and nothing but the truth before him. Little by little, even with a sort of enjoyment, she began explaining every detail, not wanting to torment him, but, as it were, eager to be of the utmost service to him. She described the whole of that day, in great detail, the visit of Rakitin and Alyosha, how she, Fenya, had stood on the watch, how the mistress had set off, and how she had called out of the window to Alyosha to give him, Mitya, her greetings, and to tell him "to remember for ever how she had loved him for an hour."

Hearing of the message, Mitya suddenly smiled, and there was a flush of colour on his pale cheeks. At the same moment Fenya said to him, not a bit afraid now to be inquisitive:

"Look at your hands, Dmitri Fyodorovitch. They're all over blood!

"Yes," answered Mitya mechanically. He looked carelessly at his hands and at once forgot them and Fenya's question.

He sank into silence again. Twenty minutes had passed since he had run in. His first horror was over, but evidently some new fixed determination had taken possession of him. He suddenly stood up, smiling dreamily.

"What has happened to you, sir?" said Fenya, pointing to his hands again. She spoke compassionately, as though she felt very near to him now in his grief. Mitya looked at his hands again.

"That's blood, Fenya," he said, looking at her with a strange expression. "That's human blood, and my God! why was it shed? But...Fenya...there's a fence here" (he looked at her as though setting her a riddle), "a high fence, and terrible to look at. But at dawn to-morrow, when the sun rises, Mitya will leap over that fence...You don't understand what fence, Fenya, and, never mind...You'll hear to-morrow and understand...and now, good-bye. I won't stand in her way. I'll step aside, I know how to step aside. Live, my joy...You loved me for an hour, remember Mityenka Karamazov so for ever...She always used to call me Mityenka, do you remember?"

And with those words he went suddenly out of the kitchen. Fenya was almost more frightened at this sudden departure than she had been when he ran in and attacked her.

Just ten minutes later Dmitri went in to Pyotr Ilyitch Perhotin, the young official with whom he had pawned his pistols. It was by now half-past eight, and Pyotr Ilyitch had finished his evening tea, and had just put his coat on again to go to the Metropolis to play billiards. Mitya caught him coming out.

Seeing him with his face all smeared with blood, the young man uttered a cry of surprise.

"Good heavens! What is the matter?"

"I've come for my pistols," said Mitya, "and brought you the money. And thanks very much. I'm in a hurry, Pyotr Ilyitch, please make haste."

Pyotr Ilyitch grew more and more surprised; he suddenly caught sight of a bundle of banknotes in Mitya's hand, and what was more, he had walked in holding the notes as no one walks in and no one carries money: he had them in his right hand, and held them outstretched as if to show them. Perhotin's servant-boy, who met Mitya in the passage, said afterwards that he walked into the passage in the same way, with the money outstretched in his hand, so he must have been carrying them like that even in the streets. They were all rainbow-coloured hundred-rouble notes, and the fingers holding them were covered with blood.

When Pyotr Ilyitch was questioned later on as to the sum of money, he said that it was difficult to judge at a glance, but that it might have been two thousand, or perhaps three, but it was a big, "fat" bundle. "Dmitri Fyodorovitch," so he testified afterwards, "seemed unlike himself, too; not drunk, but, as it were, exalted, lost to everything, but at the same time, as it were, absorbed, as though pondering and searching for something and unable to come to a decision. He was in great haste, answered abruptly and very strangely, and at moments seemed not at all dejected but quite cheerful."

"But what is the matter with you? What's wrong?" cried Pyotr Ilyitch, looking wildly at his guest. "How is it that you're all covered with blood? Have you had a fall? Look at yourself!"

He took him by the elbow and led him to the glass.

Seeing his blood-stained face, Mitya started and scowled wrathfully.

"Damnation! That's the last straw," he muttered angrily, hurriedly changing the notes from his right hand to the left, and impulsively jerked the handkerchief out of his pocket. But the handkerchief turned out to be soaked with blood, too (it was the handkerchief he had used to wipe Grigory's face). There was scarcely a white spot on it, and it had not merely begun to dry, but had stiffened into a crumpled ball and could not be pulled apart. Mitya threw it angrily on the floor.

"Oh, damn it!" he said. "Haven't you a rag of some sort...to wipe my face?"

"So you're only stained, not wounded? You'd better wash," said Pyotr Ilyitch. "Here's a wash-stand. I'll pour you out some water."

"A wash-stand? That's all right...but where am I to put this?"

With the strangest perplexity he indicated his bundle of hundred-rouble notes, looking inquiringly at Pyotr Ilyitch as though it were for him to decide what he, Mitya, was to do with his own money.

"In your pocket, or on the table here. They won't be lost."

"In my pocket? Yes, in my pocket. All right...But, I say, that's all nonsense," he cried, as though suddenly coming out of his absorption. "Look here, let's first settle that business of the pistols. Give them back to me. Here's your money...because I am in great need of them...and I haven't a minute, a minute to spare."

And taking the topmost note from the bundle he held it out to Pyotr Ilyitch.

"But I shan't have change enough. Haven't you less?"

"No," said Mitya, looking again at the bundle, and as though not trusting his own words he turned over two or three of the topmost ones.

"No, they're all alike," he added, and again he looked inquiringly at Pyotr Ilyitch.

"How have you grown so rich?" the latter asked. "Wait, I'll send my boy to Plotnikov's, they close late--to see if they won't change it. Here, Misha!" he called into the passage.

"To Plotnikov's shop--first-rate!" cried Mitya, as though struck by an idea. "Misha," he turned to the boy as he came in, "look here, run to Plotnikov's and tell them that Dmitri Fyodorovitch sends his greetings, and will be there directly...But listen, listen, tell them to have champagne, three dozen bottles, ready before I come, and packed as it was to take to Mokroe. I took four dozen with me then," he added (suddenly addressing Pyotr Ilyitch); "they know all about it, don't you trouble, Misha," he turned again to the boy. "Stay, listen; tell them to put in cheese, Strasburg pies, smoked fish, ham, caviare, and everything, everything they've got, up to a hundred roubles, or a hundred and twenty as before...But wait: don't let them forget dessert, sweets, pears, watermelons, two or three or four--no, one melon's enough, and chocolate, candy, toffee, fondants; in fact, everything I took to Mokroe before, three hundred roubles' worth with the champagne...let it be just the same again. And remember, Misha, if you are called Misha--His name is Misha, isn't it?" He turned to Pyotr Ilyitch again.

"Wait a minute," Pyotr Ilyitch intervened listening and watching him uneasily, "you'd better go yourself and tell them. He'll muddle it."

"He will, I see he will! Eh, Misha! Why, I was going to kiss you for the commission...If you don't make a mistake, there's ten roubles for you, run along, make haste...Champagne's the chief thing, let them bring up champagne. And brandy, too, and red and white wine, and all I had then...They know what I had then."

"But listen!" Pyotr Ilyitch interrupted with some impatience. "I say, let him simply run and change the money and tell them not to close, and you go and tell them...Give him your note. Be off, Misha! Put your best leg forward!"

Pyotr Ilyitch seemed to hurry Misha off on purpose, because the boy remained standing with his mouth and eyes wide open, apparently understanding little of Mitya's orders, gazing up with amazement and terror at his bloodstained face and the trembling blood-stained fingers that held the notes.

"Well, now come and wash," said Pyotr Ilyitch sternly. "Put the money on the table or else in your pocket...That's right, come along. But take off your coat."

And beginning to help him off with his coat, he cried out again:

"Look, your coat's covered with blood, too!"

"That...it's not the coat. It's only a little here on the sleeve...And that's only here where the handkerchief lay. It must have soaked through. I must have sat on the handkerchief at Fenya's, and the blood's come through," Mitya explained at once with a child-like unconsciousness that was astounding. Pyotr Ilyitch listened, frowning.

"Well, you must have been up to something; you must have been fighting with someone," he muttered.

They began to wash. Pyotr Ilyitch held the jug and poured out the water. Mitya, in desperate haste, scarcely soaped his hands (they were trembling, and Pyotr Ilyitch remembered it afterwards). But the young official insisted on his soaping them thoroughly and rubbing them more. He seemed to exercise more and more sway over Mitya, as time went on. It may be noted in passing that he was a young man of sturdy character.

"Look, you haven't got your nails clean. Now rub your face; here, on your temples, by your ear...Will you go in that shirt? Where are you going? Look, all the cuff of your right sleeve is covered with blood."

"Yes, it's all bloody," observed Mitya, looking at the cuff of his shirt.

"Then change your shirt."

"I haven't time. You see I'll..." Mitya went on with the same confiding ingenuousness, drying his face and hands on the towel, and putting on his coat. "I'll turn it up at the wrist. It won't be seen under the coat...You see!"

"Tell me now, what game have you been up to? Have you been fighting with someone? In the tavern again, as before? Have you been beating that captain again?" Pyotr Ilyitch asked him reproachfully. "Whom have you been beating now...or killing, perhaps?"

"Nonsense!" said Mitya.

"Don't worry," said Mitya, and he suddenly laughed. "I smashed an old woman in the market-place just now."

"Smashed? An old woman?"

"An old man!" cried Mitya, looking Pyotr Ilyitch straight in the face, laughing, and shouting at him as though he were deaf.

"Confound it! An old woman, an old man...Have you killed someone?"

"We made it up. We had a row--and made it up. In a place I know of. We parted friends. A fool...He's forgiven me...He's sure to have forgiven me by now...if he had got up, he wouldn't have forgiven me"--Mitya suddenly winked--"only damn him, you know, I say, Pyotr Ilyitch, damn him! Don't worry about him! I don't want to just now!" Mitya snapped out, resolutely.

"Whatever do you want to go picking quarrels with everyone for?...Just as you did with that captain over some nonsense...You've been fighting and now you're rushing off on the spree--that's you all over! Three dozen champagne--what do you want all that for?"

"Bravo! Now give me the pistols. Upon my honour I've no time now. I should like to have a chat with you, my dear boy, but I haven't the time. And there's no need, it's too late for talking. Where's my money? Where have I put it?" he cried, thrusting his hands into his pockets.

"You put it on the table...yourself...Here it is. Had you forgotten? Money's like dirt or water to you, it seems. Here are your pistols. It's an odd thing, at six o'clock you pledged them for ten roubles, and now you've got thousands. Two or three I should say."

"Three, you bet," laughed Mitya, stuffing the notes into the side-pocket of his trousers.

"You'll lose it like that. Have you found a gold mine?"

"The mines? The gold mines?" Mitya shouted at the top of his voice and went off into a roar of laughter. "Would you like to go to the mines, Perhotin? There's a lady here who'll stump up three thousand for you, if only you'll go. She did it for me, she's so awfully fond of gold mines. Do you know Madame Hohlakov?"

"I don't know her, but I've heard of her and seen her. Did she really give you three thousand? Did she really?" said Pyotr Ilyitch, eyeing him dubiously.

"As soon as the sun rises to-morrow, as soon as Phoebus, ever young, flies upwards, praising and glorifying God, you go to her, this Madame Hohlakov, and ask her whether she did stump up that three thousand or not. Try and find out."

"I don't know on what terms you are...since you say it so positively, I suppose she did give it to you. You've got the money in your hand, but instead of going to Siberia you're spending it all...Where are you really off to now, eh?"

"To Mokroe."

"To Mokroe? But it's night!"

"Once the lad had all, now the lad has naught," cried Mitya suddenly.

"How 'naught'? You say that with all those thousands!"

"I'm not talking about thousands. Damn thousands! I'm talking of female character.

Fickle is the heart of woman

Treacherous and full of vice; I agree with Ulysses. That's what he says."

"I don't understand you!"

"Am I drunk?"

"Not drunk, but worse."

"I'm drunk in spirit, Pyotr Ilyitch, drunk in spirit! But that's enough!"

"What are you doing, loading the pistol?"

"I'm loading the pistol."

Unfastening the pistol-case, Mitya actually opened the powder horn, and carefully sprinkled and rammed in the charge. Then he took the bullet and, before inserting it, held it in two fingers in front of the candle.

"Why are you looking at the bullet?" asked Pyotr Ilyitch, watching him with uneasy curiosity.

"Oh, a fancy. Why, if you meant to put that bullet in your brain, would you look at it or not?"

"Why look at it?"

"It's going into my brain, so it's interesting to look and see what it's like. But that's foolishness, a moment's foolishness. Now that's done," he added, putting in the bullet and driving it home with the ramrod. "Pyotr Ilyitch, my dear fellow, that's nonsense, all nonsense, and if only you knew what nonsense! Give me a little piece of paper now."

"Here's some paper."

"No, a clean new piece, writing-paper. That's right."

And taking a pen from the table, Mitya rapidly wrote two lines, folded the paper in four, and thrust it in his waistcoat pocket. He put the pistols in the case, locked it up, and kept it in his hand. Then he looked at Pyotr Ilyitch with a slow, thoughtful smile.

"Now, let's go."

"Where are we going? No, wait a minute...Are you thinking of putting that bullet in your brain, perhaps?" Pyotr Ilyitch asked uneasily.

"I was fooling about the bullet! I want to live. I love life, You may be sure of that. I love golden-haired Phorbus and his warm light...Dear Pyotr Ilyitch, do you know how to step aside?"

"What do you mean by 'stepping aside'?"

"Making way. Making way for a dear creature, and for one I hate. And to let the one I hate become dear--that's what making way means! And to say to them: God bless you, go your way, pass on, while I-"

"While you-?"

"That's enough, let's go."

"Upon my word. I'll tell someone to prevent your going there," said Pyotr Ilyitch, looking at him. "What are you going to Mokroe for, now?"

"There's a woman there, a woman. That's enough for you. You shut up."

"Listen, though you're such a savage I've always liked you...I feel anxious."

"Thanks, old fellow. I'm a savage you say. Savages, savages! That's what I am always saying. Savages! Why, here's Misha! I was forgetting him."

Misha ran in, post-haste, with a handful of notes in change, and reported that everyone was in a bustle at the Plotnikovs'; "They're carrying down the bottles, and the fish, and the tea; it will all be ready directly." Mitya seized ten roubles and handed it to Pyotr Ilyitch, then tossed another ten-rouble note to Misha.

"Don't dare to do such a thing!" cried Pyotr Ilyitch. "I won't have it in my house, it's a bad, demoralising habit. Put your money away. Here, put it here, why waste it? It would come in handy to-morrow, and I dare say you'll be coming to me to borrow ten roubles again. Why do you keep putting the notes in your side pocket? Ah, you'll lose them!"

"I say, my dear fellow, let's go to Mokroe together."

"What should I go for?"

"I say, let's open a bottle at once, and drink to life! I want to drink, and especially to drink with you. I've never drunk with you, have I?"

"Very well, we can go to the Metropolis. I was just going there."

"I haven't time for that. Let's drink at the Plotnikovs', in the back room. Shall I ask you a riddle?"

"Ask away."

Mitya took the piece of paper out of his waistcoat pocket, unfolded it and showed it. In a large, distinct hand was written: "I punish myself for my whole life; my whole life I punish!"

"I will certainly speak to someone. I'll go at once," said Pyotr Ilyitch, after reading the paper.

"You won't have time, dear boy, come and have a drink. March!"

Plotnikov's shop was at the corner of the street, next door but one to Pyotr Ilyitch's. It was the largest grocery shop in our town, and by no means a bad one, belonging to some rich merchants. They kept everything that could be got in a Petersburg shop, grocery of all sort, wines "bottled by the brothers Eliseyev," fruits, cigars, tea, coffee, sugar, and so on. There were three shop-assistants and two errand boys always employed. Though our part of the country had grown poorer, the landowners had gone away, and trade had got worse, yet the grocery stores flourished as before, every year with increasing prosperity; there were plenty of purchasers for their goods.

They were awaiting Mitya with impatience in the shop. They had vivid recollections of how he had bought, three or four weeks ago, wine and goods of all sorts to the value of several hundred roubles, paid for in cash (they would never have let him have anything on credit, of course). They remembered that then, as now, he had had a bundle of hundred-rouble notes in his hand, and had scattered them at random, without bargaining, without reflecting, or caring to reflect what use so much wine and provisions would be to him. The story was told all over the town that, driving off then with Grushenka to Mokroe, he had "spent three thousand in one night and the following day, and had come back from the spree without a penny." He had picked up a whole troop of gypsies (encamped in our neighbourhood at the time), who for two days got money without stint out of him while he was drunk, and drank expensive wine without stint. People used to tell, laughing at Mitya, how he had given champagne to grimy-handed peasants, and feasted the village women and girls on sweets and Strasburg pies. Though to laugh at Mitya to his face was rather a risky proceeding, there was much laughter behind his back, especially in the tavern, at his own ingenuous public avowal that all he had got out of Grushenka by this "escapade" was "permission to kiss her foot, and that was the utmost she had allowed him."

By the time Mitya and Pyotr Ilyitch reached the shop, they found a cart with three horses harnessed abreast with bells, and with Andrey, the driver, ready waiting for Mitya at the entrance. In the shop they had almost entirely finished packing one box of provisions, and were only waiting for Mitya's arrival to nail it down and put it in the cart. Pyotr Ilyitch was astounded.

"Where did this cart come from in such a hurry?" he asked Mitya.

"I met Andrey as I ran to you, and told him to drive straight here to the shop. There's no time to lose. Last time I drove with Timofey, but Timofey now has gone on before me with the witch. Shall we be very late, Andrey?"

"They'll only get there an hour at most before us, not even that maybe. I got Timofey ready to start. I know how he'll go. Their pace won't be ours, Dmitri Fyodorovitch. How could it be? They won't get there an hour earlier!" Andrey, a lanky, red-haired, middle-aged driver, wearing a full-skirted coat, and with a kaftan on his arm, replied warmly.

"Fifty roubles for vodka if we're only an hour behind them."

"I warrant the time, Dmitri Fyodorovitch. Ech, they won't be half an hour before us, let alone an hour."

Though Mitya bustled about seeing after things, he gave his orders strangely, as it were, disconnectedly, and inconsecutively. He began a sentence and forgot the end of it. Pyotr Ilyitch found himself obliged to come to the rescue.

"Four hundred roubles' worth, not less than four hundred roubles' worth, just as it was then," commanded Mitya. "Four dozen champagne, not a bottle less."

"What do you want with so much? What's it for? Stay!" cried Pyotr Ilyitch. "What's this box? What's in it? Surely there isn't four hundred roubles' worth here?"

The officious shopmen began explaining with oily politeness that the first box contained only half a dozen bottles of champagne, and only "the most indispensable articles," such as savouries, sweets, toffee, etc. But the main part of the goods ordered would be packed and sent off, as on the previous occasion, in a special cart also with three horses travelling at full speed, so that it would arrive not more than an hour later than Dmitri Fyodorovitch himself.

"Not more than an hour! Not more than an hour! And put in more toffee and fondants. The girls there are so fond of it," Mitya insisted hotly.

"The fondants are all right. But what do you want with four dozen of champagne? One would be enough," said Pyotr Ilyitch, almost angry. He began bargaining, asking for a bill of the goods, and refused to be satisfied. But he only succeeded in saving a hundred roubles. In the end it was agreed that only three hundred roubles' worth should be sent.

"Well, you may go to the devil!" cried Pyotr Ilyitch, on second thoughts. "What's it to do with me? Throw away your money, since it's cost you nothing."

"This way, my economist, this way, don't be angry." Mitya drew him into a room at the back of the shop. "They'll give us a bottle here directly. We'll taste it. Ech, Pyotr Ilyitch, come along with me, for you're a nice fellow, the sort I like."

Mitya sat down on a wicker chair, before a little table, covered with a dirty dinner-napkin. Pyotr Ilyitch sat down opposite, and the champagne soon appeared, and oysters were suggested to the gentlemen. "First-class oysters, the last lot in."

"Hang the oysters. I don't eat them. And we don't need anything," cried Pyotr Ilyitch, almost angrily.

"There's no time for oysters," said Mitya. "And I'm not hungry. Do you know, friend," he said suddenly, with feeling, "I never have liked all this disorder."

"Who does like it? Three dozen of champagne for peasants, upon my word, that's enough to make anyone angry!"

"That's not what I mean. I'm talking of a higher order. There's no order in me, no higher order. But...that's all over. There's no need to grieve about it. It's too late, damn it! My whole life has been disorder, and one must set it in order. Is that a pun, eh?"

"You're raving, not making puns!

"Glory be to God in Heaven,
Glory be to God in me...

"That verse came from my heart once, it's not a verse, but a tear...I made it myself...not while I was pulling the captain's beard, though..."

"Why do you bring him in all of a sudden?"

"Why do I bring him in? Foolery! All things come to an end; all things are made equal. That's the long and short of it."

"You know, I keep thinking of your pistols."

"That's all foolery, too! Drink, and don't be fanciful. I love life. I've loved life too much, shamefully much. Enough! Let's drink to life, dear boy, I propose the toast. Why am I pleased with myself? I'm a scoundrel, but I'm satisfied with myself. And yet I'm tortured by the thought that I'm a scoundrel, but satisfied with myself. I bless the creation. I'm ready to bless God and His creation directly, but...I must kill one noxious insect for fear it should crawl and spoil life for others...Let us drink to life, dear brother. What can be more precious than life? Nothing! To life, and to one queen of queens!"

"Let's drink to life and to your queen, too, if you like."

They drank a glass each. Although Mitya was excited and expansive, yet he was melancholy, too. It was as though some heavy, overwhelming anxiety were weighing upon him.

"Misha...here's your Misha come! Misha, come here, my boy, drink this glass to Phoebus the golden-haired, of to-morrow morn..."

"What are you giving it him for?" cried Pyotr Ilyitch, irritably.

"Yes, yes, yes, let me! I want to!"

"E--ech!"

Misha emptied the glass, bowed, and ran out.

"He'll remember it afterwards," Mitya remarked. "Woman, I love woman! What is woman? The queen of creation! My heart is sad, my heart is sad, Pyotr Ilyitch. Do you remember Hamlet? 'I am very sorry, good Horatio! Alas, poor Yorick!' Perhaps that's me, Yorick? Yes, I'm Yorick now, and a skull afterwards."

Pyotr Ilyitch listened in silence. Mitya, too, was silent for a while.

"What dog's that you've got here?" he asked the shopman, casually, noticing a pretty little lap-dog with dark eyes, sitting in the corner.

"It belongs to Varvara Alexyevna, the mistress," answered the clerk. "She brought it and forgot it here. It must be taken back to her."

"I saw one like it...in the regiment..." murmured Mitya dreamily, "only that one had its hind leg broken...By the way, Pyotr Ilyitch, I wanted to ask you: have you ever stolen anything in your life?"

"What a question!"

"Oh, I didn't mean anything. From somebody's pocket, you know. I don't mean government money, everyone steals that, and no doubt you do, too..."

"You go to the devil."

"I'm talking of other people's money. Stealing straight out of a pocket? Out of a purse, eh?"

"I stole twenty copecks from my mother when I was nine years old. I took it off the table on the sly, and held it tight in my hand."

"Well, and what happened?"

"Oh, nothing. I kept it three days, then I felt ashamed, confessed, and gave it back."

"And what then?"

"Naturally I was whipped. But why do you ask? Have you stolen something?"

"I have," said Mitya, winking slyly.

"What have you stolen?" inquired Pyotr Ilyitch curiously.

"I stole twenty copecks from my mother when I was nine years old, and gave it back three days after."

As he said this, Mitya suddenly got up.

"Dmitri Fyodorovitch, won't you come now?" called Andrey from the door of the shop.

"Are you ready? We'll come!" Mitya started. "A few more last words and--Andrey, a glass of vodka at starting. Give him some brandy as well! That box" (the one with the pistols) "put under my seat. Good-bye, Pyotr Ilyitch, don't remember evil against me."

"But you're coming back to-morrow?"

"Will you settle the little bill now?" cried the clerk, springing forward.

"Oh yes, the bill. Of course."

He pulled the bundle of notes out of his pocket again, picked out three hundred roubles, threw them on the counter, and ran hurriedly out of the shop. Everyone followed him out, bowing and wishing him good luck. Andrey, coughing from the brandy he had just swallowed, jumped up on the box. But Mitya was only just taking his seat when suddenly to his surprise he saw Fenya before him. She ran up panting, clasped her hands before him with a cry, and plumped down at his feet.

"Dmitri Fyodorovitch, dear good Dmitri Fyodorovitch, don't harm my mistress. And it was I told you all about it...And don't murder him, he came first, he's hers! He'll marry Agrafena Alexandrovna now. That's why he's come back from Siberia. Dmitri Fyodorovitch, dear, don't take a fellow creature's life!"

"Tut-tut-tut! That's it, is it? So you're off there to make trouble!" muttered Pyotr Ilyitch. "Now, it's all clear, as clear as daylight. Dmitri Fyodorovitch, give me your pistols at once if you mean to behave like a man," he shouted aloud to Mitya. "Do you hear, Dmitri?"

"The pistols? Wait a bit, brother, I'll throw them into the pool on the road," answered Mitya. "Fenya, get up, don't kneel to me. Mitya won't hurt anyone, the silly fool won't hurt anyone again. But I say, Fenya," he shouted, after having taken his seat. "I hurt you just now, so forgive me and have pity on me, forgive a scoundrel...But it doesn't matter if you don't. It's all the same now. Now then, Andrey, look alive, fly along full speed!"

Andrey whipped up the horses, and the bells began ringing.

"Good-bye, Pyotr Ilyitch! My last tear is for you!..."

"He's not drunk, but he keeps babbling like a lunatic," Pyotr Ilyitch thought as he watched him go. He had half a mind to stay and see the cart packed with the remaining wines and provisions, knowing that they would deceive and defraud Mitya. But, suddenly feeling vexed with himself, he turned away with a curse and went to the tavern to play billiards.

"He's a fool, though he's a good fellow," he muttered as he went. "I've heard of that officer, Grushenka's former flame. Well, if he has turned up...Ech, those pistols! Damn it all! I'm not his nurse! Let them do what they like! Besides, it'll all come to nothing. They're a set of brawlers, that's all. They'll drink and fight, fight and make friends again. They are not men who do anything real. What does he mean by 'I'm stepping aside, I'm punishing myself'? It'll come to nothing! He's shouted such phrases a thousand times, drunk, in the taverns. But now he's not drunk. 'Drunk in spirit'--they're fond of fine phrases, the villains. Am I his nurse? He must have been fighting, his face was all over blood. With whom? I shall find out at the Metropolis. And his handkerchief was soaked in blood...It's still lying on my floor...Hang it!"

He reached the tavern in a bad humour and at once made up a game. The game cheered him. He played a second game, and suddenly began telling one of his partners that Dmitri Karamazov had come in for some cash again--something like three thousand roubles, and had gone to Mokroe again to spend it with Grushenka...This news roused singular interest in his listeners. They all spoke of it, not laughing, but with a strange gravity. They left off playing.

"Three thousand? But where can he have got three thousand?"

Questions were asked. The story of Madame Hohlakov's present was received with scepticism.

"Hasn't he robbed his old father?--that's the question."

"Three thousand! There's something odd about it."

"He boasted aloud that he would kill his father; we all heard him, here. And it was three thousand he talked about..."

Pyotr Ilyitch listened. All at once he became short and dry in his answers. He said not a word about the blood on Mitya's face and hands, though he had meant to speak of it at first.

They began a third game, and by degrees the talk about Mitya died away. But by the end of the third game, Pyotr Ilyitch felt no more desire for billiards; he laid down the cue, and without having supper as he had intended, he walked out of the tavern. When he reached the market-place he stood still in perplexity, wondering at himself. He realised that what he wanted was to go to Fyodor Pavlovitch's and find out if anything had happened there. "On account of some stupid nonsense as it's sure to turn out--am I going to wake up the household and make a scandal? Fooh! damn it, is it my business to look after them?"

In a very bad humour he went straight home, and suddenly remembered Fenya. "Damn it all! I ought to have questioned her just now," he thought with vexation, "I should have heard everything." And the desire to speak to her, and so find out, became so pressing and importunate that when he was halfway home he turned abruptly and went towards the house where Grushenka lodged. Going up to the gate he knocked. The sound of the knock in the silence of the night sobered him and made him feel annoyed. And no one answered him; everyone in the house was asleep.

"And I shall be making a fuss!" he thought, with a feeling of positive discomfort. But instead of going away altogether, he fell to knocking again with all his might, filling the street with clamour.

"Not coming? Well, I will knock them up, I will!" he muttered at each knock, fuming at himself, but at the same time he redoubled his knocks on the gate.

Chapter 6. "I Am Coming, Too!"

BUT Dmitri Fyodorovitch was speeding along the road. It was a little more than twenty versts to Mokroe, but Andrey's three horses galloped at such a pace that the distance might be covered in an hour and a quarter. The swift motion revived Mitya. The air was fresh and cool, there were big stars shining in the sky. It was the very night, and perhaps the very hour, in which Alyosha fell on the earth, and rapturously swore to love it for ever and ever.

All was confusion, confusion in Mitya's soul, but although many things were goading his heart, at that moment his whole being was yearning for her, his queen, to whom he was flying to look on her for the last time. One thing I can say for certain; his heart did not waver for one instant. I shall perhaps not be believed when I say that this jealous lover felt not the slightest jealousy of this new rival, who seemed to have sprung out of the earth. If any other had appeared on the scene, he would have been jealous at once, and would-perhaps have stained his fierce hands with blood again. But as he flew through the night, he felt no envy, no hostility even, for the man who had been her first lover...It is true he had not yet seen him.

"Here there was no room for dispute: it was her right and his; this was her first love which, after five years, she had not forgotten; so she had loved him only for those five years, and I, how do I come in? What right have I? Step aside, Mitya, and make way! What am I now? Now everything is over apart from the officer even if he had not appeared, everything would be over..."

These words would roughly have expressed his feelings, if he had been capable of reasoning. But he could not reason at that moment. His present plan of action had arisen without reasoning. At Fenya's first words, it had sprung from feeling, and been adopted in a flash, with all its consequences. And yet, in spite of his resolution, there was confusion in his soul, an agonising confusion: his resolution did not give him peace. There was so much behind that tortured him. And it seemed strange to him, at moments, to think that he had written his own sentence of death with pen and paper: "I punish myself," and the paper was lying there in his pocket, ready; the pistol was loaded; he had already resolved how, next morning, he would meet the first warm ray of "golden-haired Phoebus."

And yet he could not be quit of the past, of all that he had left behind and that tortured him. He felt that miserably, and the thought of it sank into his heart with despair. There was one moment when he felt an impulse to stop Andrey, to jump out of the cart, to pull out his loaded pistol, and to make an end of everything without waiting for the dawn. But that moment flew by like a spark. The horses galloped on, "devouring space," and as he drew near his goal, again the thought of her, of her alone, took more and more complete possession of his soul, chasing away the fearful images that had been haunting it. Oh, how he longed to look upon her, if only for a moment, if only from a distance!

"She's now with him," he thought, "now I shall see what she looks like with him, her first love, and that's all I want." Never had this woman, who was such a fateful influence in his life, aroused such love in his breast, such new and unknown feeling, surprising even to himself, a feeling tender to devoutness, to self-effacement before her! "I will efface myself!" he said, in a rush of almost hysterical ecstasy.

They had been galloping nearly an hour. Mitya was silent, and though Andrey was, as a rule, a talkative peasant, he did not utter a word, either. He seemed afraid to talk, he only whipped up smartly his three lean, but mettlesome, bay horses. Suddenly Mitya cried out in horrible anxiety:

"Andrey! What if they're asleep?"

This thought fell upon him like a blow. It had not occurred to him before.

"It may well be that they're gone to bed by now, Dmitri Fyodorovitch."

Mitya frowned as though in pain. Yes, indeed...he was rushing there...with such feelings...while they were asleep...she was asleep, perhaps, there too...An angry feeling surged up in his heart.

"Drive on, Andrey! Whip them up! Look alive!" he cried, beside himself.

"But maybe they're not in bed!" Andrey went on after a pause. "Timofey said they were a lot of them there-."

"At the station?"

"Not at the posting-station, but at Plastunov's, at the inn, where they let out horses, too."

"I know. So you say there are a lot of them? How's that? Who are they?" cried Mitya, greatly dismayed at this unexpected news.

"Well, Timofey was saying they're all gentlefolk. Two from our town--who they are I can't say--and there are two others, strangers, maybe more besides. I didn't ask particularly. They've set to playing cards, so Timofey said."

"Cards?"

"So, maybe they're not in bed if they're at cards. It's most likely not more than eleven."

"Quicker, Andrey! Quicker!" Mitya cried again, nervously.

"May I ask you something, sir?" said Andrey, after a pause. "Only I'm afraid of angering you, sir."

"What is it?"

"Why, Fenya threw herself at your feet just now, and begged you not to harm her mistress, and someone else, too...so you see, sir--It's I am taking you there...forgive me, sir, it's my conscience...maybe it's stupid of me to speak of it-."

Mitya suddenly seized him by the shoulders from behind.

"Are you a driver?" he asked frantically.

"Yes sir."

"Then you know that one has to make way. What would you say to a driver who wouldn't make way for anyone, but would just drive on and crush people? No, a driver mustn't run over people. One can't run over a man. One can't spoil people's lives. And if you have spoilt a life--punish yourself...If only you've spoilt, if only you've ruined anyone's life--punish yourself and go away."

These phrases burst from Mitya almost hysterically. Though Andrey was surprised at him, he kept up the conversation.

"That's right, Dmitri Fyodorovitch, you're quite right, one mustn't crush or torment a man, or any kind of creature, for every creature is created by God. Take a horse, for instance, for some folks, even among us drivers, drive anyhow. Nothing will restrain them, they just force it along."

"To hell?" Mitya interrupted, and went off into his abrupt, short laugh. "Andrey, simple soul," he seized him by the shoulders again, "tell me, will Dmitri Fyodorovitch Karamazov go to hell, or not, what do you think?"

"I don't know, darling, it depends on you, for you are...you see, sir, when the Son of God was nailed on the Cross and died, He went straight down to hell from the Cross, and set free all sinners that were in agony. And the devil groaned, because he thought that he would get no more sinners in hell. And God said to him, then, 'Don't groan, for you shall have all the mighty of the earth, the rulers, the chief judges, and the rich men, and shall be filled up as you have been in all the ages till I come again.' Those were His very words..."

"A peasant legend! Capital! Whip up the left, Andrey!"

"So you see, sir, who it is hell's for," said Andrey, whipping up the left horse, "but you're like a little child...that's how we look on you...and though you're hasty-tempered, sir, yet God will forgive you for your kind heart."

"And you, do you forgive me, Andrey?"

"What should I forgive you for, sir? You've never done me any harm."

"No, for everyone, for everyone, you here alone, on the road, will you forgive me for everyone? Speak, simple peasant heart!"

"Oh, sir! I feel afraid of driving you, your talk is so strange."

But Mitya did not hear. He was frantically praying and muttering to himself.

"Lord, receive me, with all my lawlessness, and do not condemn me. Let me pass by Thy judgment...do not condemn me, for I have condemned myself, do not condemn me, for I love Thee, O Lord. I am a wretch, but I love Thee. If Thou sendest me to hell, I shall love Thee there, and from there I shall cry out that I love Thee for ever and ever...But let me love to the end...Here and now for just five hours...till the first light of Thy day...for I love the queen of my soul...I love her and I cannot help loving her. Thou seest my whole heart...I shall gallop up, I shall fall before her and say, 'You are right to pass on and leave me. Farewell and forget your victim...never fret yourself about me!'"

"Mokroe!" cried Andrey, pointing ahead with his whip.

Through the pale darkness of the night loomed a solid black mass of buildings, flung down, as it were, in the vast plain. The village of Mokroe numbered two thousand inhabitants, but at that hour all were asleep, and only here and there a few lights still twinkled.

"Drive on, Andrey, I come!" Mitya exclaimed, feverishly.

"They're not asleep," said Andrey again, pointing with his whip to the Plastunovs' inn, which was at the entrance to the village. The six windows, looking on the street, were all brightly lighted up.

"They're not asleep," Mitya repeated joyously. "Quicker, Andrey! Gallop! Drive up with a dash! Set the bells ringing! Let all know that I have come. I'm coming! I'm coming, too!"

Andrey lashed his exhausted team into a gallop, drove with a dash and pulled up his steaming, panting horses at the high flight of steps.

Mitya jumped out of the cart just as the innkeeper, on his way to bed, peeped out from the steps curious to see who had arrived.

"Trifon Borissovitch, is that you?"

The innkeeper bent down, looked intently, ran down the steps, and rushed up to the guest with obsequious delight.

"Dmitri Fyodorovitch, your honour! Do I see you again?"

Trifon Borissovitch was a thick-set, healthy peasant, of middle height, with a rather fat face. His expression was severe and uncompromising, especially with the peasants of Mokroe, but he had the power of assuming the most obsequious countenance, when he had an inkling that it was to his interest. He dressed in Russian style, with a shirt buttoning down on one side, and a full-skirted coat. He had saved a good sum of money, but was for ever dreaming of improving his position. More than half the peasants were in his clutches, everyone in the neighbourhood was in debt to him. From the neighbouring landowners he bought and rented lands which were worked by the peasants, in payment of debts which they could never shake off. He was a widower, with four grown-up daughters. One of them was already a widow and lived in the inn with her two children, his grandchildren, and worked for him like a charwoman. Another of his daughters was married to a petty official, and in one of the rooms of the inn, on the wall could be seen, among the family photographs, a miniature photograph of this official in uniform and official epaulettes. The two younger daughters used to wear fashionable blue or green dresses, fitting tight at the back, and with trains a yard long, on Church holidays or when they went to pay visits. But next morning they would get up at dawn, as usual, sweep out the rooms with a birch-broom, empty the slops, and clean up after lodgers.

In spite of the thousands of roubles he had saved, Trifon Borissovitch was very fond of emptying the pockets of a drunken guest, and remembering that not a month ago he had, in twenty-four hours, made two if not three hundred roubles out of Dmitri, when he had come on his escapade with Grushenka, he met him now with eager welcome, scenting his prey the moment Mitya drove up to the steps.

"Dmitri Fyodorovitch, dear sir, we see you once more!"

"Stay, Trifon Borissovitch," began Mitya, "first and foremost, where is she?"

"Agrafena Alexandrovna?" The inn-keeper understood at once, looking sharply into Mitya's face. "She's here, too..."

"With whom? With whom?"

"Some strangers. One is an official gentleman, a Pole, to judge from his speech. He sent the horses for her from here; and there's another with him, a friend of his, or a fellow traveller, there's no telling. They're dressed like civilians."

"Well, are they feasting? Have they money?"

"Poor sort of a feast! Nothing to boast of, Dmitri Fyodorovitch."

"Nothing to boast of? And who are the others?"

"They're two gentlemen from the town...They've come back from Tcherny, and are putting up here. One's quite a young gentleman, a relative of Mr. Miusov he must be, but I've forgotten his name...and I expect you know the other, too, a gentleman called Maximov. He's been on a pilgrimage, so he says, to the monastery in the town. He's travelling with this young relation of Mr. Miusov."

"Is that all?"

"Stay, listen, Trifon Borissovitch. Tell me the chief thing: What of her? How is she?"

"Oh, she's only just come. She's sitting with them."

"Is she cheerful? Is she laughing?"

"No, I think she's not laughing much. She's sitting quite dull. She's combing the young gentleman's hair."

"The Pole--the officer?"

"He's not young, and he's not an officer, either. Not him, sir. It's the young gentleman that's Mr. Miusov's relation. I've forgotten his name."

"Kalganov?"

"That's it, Kalganov!"

"All right. I'll see for myself. Are they playing cards?"

"They have been playing, but they've left off. They've been drinking tea, the official gentleman asked for liqueurs."

"Stay, Trifon Borissovitch, stay, my good soul, I'll see for myself. Now answer one more question: are the gypsies here?"

"You can't have the gypsies now, Dmitri Fyodorovitch. The authorities have sent them away. But we've Jews that play the cymbals and the fiddle in the village, so one might send for them. They'd come."

"Send for them. Certainly send for them!" cried Mitya. "And you can get the girls together as you did then, Marya especially, Stepanida, too, and Arina. Two hundred roubles for a chorus!"

"Oh, for a sum like that I can get all the village together, though by now they're asleep. Are the peasants here worth such kindness, Dmitri Fyodorovitch, or the girls either? To spend a sum like that on such coarseness and rudeness! What's the good of giving a peasant a cigar to smoke, the stinking ruffian! And the girls are all lousy. Besides, I'll get my daughters up for nothing, let alone a sum like that. They've only just gone to bed, I'll give them a kick and set them singing for you. You gave the peasants champagne to drink the other day, e-ech!"

For all his pretended compassion for Mitya, Trifon Borissovitch had hidden half a dozen bottles of champagne on that last occasion, and had picked up a hundred-rouble note under the table, and it had remained in his clutches.

"Trifon Borissovitch, I sent more than one thousand flying last time I was here. Do you remember?"

"You did send it flying. I may well remember. You must have left three thousand behind you."

"Well, I've come to do the same again, do you see?"

And he pulled out his roll of notes, and held them up before the innkeeper's nose.

Now, listen and remember. In an hour's time the wine will arrive, savouries, pies, and sweets--bring them all up at once. That box Andrey has got is to be brought up at once, too. Open it, and hand champagne immediately. And the girls, we must have the girls, Marya especially."

He turned to the cart and pulled out the box of pistols.

"Here, Andrey, let's settle. Here's fifteen roubles for the drive, and fifty for vodka...for your readiness, for your love...Remember Karamazov!"

"I'm afraid, sir," Andrey. "Give me five roubles extra, but more I won't take. Trifon Borissovitch, bear witness. Forgive my foolish words..."

"What are you afraid of?" asked Mitya, scanning him. "Well, go to the devil, if that's it?" he cried, flinging him five roubles. "Now, Trifon Borissovitch, take me up quietly and let me first get a look at them, so that they don't see me. Where are they? In the blue room?"

Trifon Borissovitch looked apprehensively at Mitya, but at once obediently did his bidding. Leading him into the passage, he went himself into the first large room, adjoining that in which the visitors were sitting, and took the light away. Then he stealthily led Mitya in, and put him in a corner in the dark, whence he could freely watch the company without being seen. But Mitya did not look long, and, indeed, he could not see them; he saw her, his heart throbbed violently, and all was dark before his eyes.

She was sitting sideways to the table in a low chair, and beside her, on the sofa, was the pretty youth, Kalganov. She was holding his hand and seemed to be laughing, while he, seeming vexed and not looking at her, was saying something in a loud voice to Maximov, who sat the other side of the table, facing Grushenka. Maximov was laughing violently at something. On the sofa sat he, and on a chair by the sofa there was another stranger. The one on the sofa was lolling backwards, smoking a pipe, and Mitya had an impression of a stoutish, broad-faced, short little man, who was apparently angry about something. His friend, the other stranger, struck Mitya as extraordinarily tall, but he could make out nothing more. He caught his breath. He could not bear it for a minute, he put the pistol-case on a chest, and with a throbbing heart he walked, feeling cold all over, straight into the blue room to face the company.

"Aie!" shrieked Grushenka, the first to notice him.

WITH his long, rapid strides, Mitya walked straight up to the table.

"Gentlemen," he said in a loud voice, almost shouting, yet stammering at every word, "I...I'm all right! Don't be afraid!" he exclaimed, "I--there's nothing the matter," he turned suddenly to Grushenka, who had shrunk back in her chair towards Kalganov, and clasped his hand tightly. "I...I'm coming, too. I'm here till morning. Gentlemen, may I stay with you till morning? Only till morning, for the last time, in this same room?"

So he finished, turning to the fat little man, with the pipe, sitting on the sofa. The latter removed his pipe from his lips with dignity and observed severely:

"Panie,* we're here in private. There are other rooms."

* Pan and Panie mean Mr. in Polish. Pani means Mrs., Panovie, gentlemen.

"Why, it's you, Dmitri Fyodorovitch! What do you mean?" answered Kalgonov suddenly. "Sit down with us. How are you?"

"Delighted to see you, dear...and precious fellow, I always thought a lot of you." Mitya responded, joyfully and eagerly, at once holding out his hand across the table.

"Aie! How tight you squeeze! You've quite broken my fingers," laughed Kalganov.

"He always squeezes like that, always," Grushenka put in gaily, with a timid smile, seeming suddenly convinced from Mitya's face that he was not going to make a scene. She was watching him with intense curiosity and still some uneasiness. She was impressed by something about him, and indeed the last thing she expected of him was that he would come in and speak like this at such a moment.

"Good evening," Maximov ventured blandly on the left. Mitya rushed up to him, too.

"Good evening. You're here, too! How glad I am to find you here, too! Gentlemen, gentlemen, I--" (He addressed the Polish gentleman with the pipe again, evidently taking him for the most important person present.) "I flew here...I wanted to spend my last day, my last hour in this room, in this very room ...where I, too, adored...my queen...Forgive me, Panie," he cried wildly, "I flew here and vowed--Oh, don't be afraid, it's my last night! Let's drink to our good understanding. They'll bring the wine at once...I brought this with me." (Something made him pull out his bundle of notes.) "Allow me, panie! I want to have music, singing, a revel, as we had before. But the worm, the unnecessary worm, will crawl away, and there'll be no more of him. I will commemorate my day of joy on my last night."

He was almost choking. There was so much, so much he wanted to say, but strange exclamations were all that came from his lips. The Pole gazed fixedly at him, at the bundle of notes in his hand; looked at Grushenka, and was in evident perplexity.

"If my suverin lady is permitting--" he was beginning.

"What does 'suverin' mean? 'Sovereign,' I suppose?" interrupted Grushenka. "I can't help laughing at you, the way you talk. Sit down, Mitya, what are you talking about? Don't frighten us, please. You won't frighten us, will you? If you won't, I am glad to see you..."

"Me, me frighten you?" cried Mitya, flinging up his hands. "Oh, pass me by, go your way, I won't hinder you!..."

And suddenly he surprised them all, and no doubt himself as well, by flinging himself on a chair, and bursting into tears, turning his head away to the opposite wall, while his arms clasped the back of the chair tight, as though embracing it.

"Come, come, what a fellow you are!" cried Grushenka reproachfully. "That's just how he comes to see me-- he begins talking, and I can't make out what he means. He cried like that once before, and now he's crying again! It's shamefull Why are you crying? As though you had anything to cry for!" she added enigmatically, emphasising each word with some irritability.

"I...I'm not crying...Well, good evening!" He instantly turned round in his chair, and suddenly laughed, not his abrupt wooden laugh, but a long, quivering, inaudible nervous laugh.

"Well, there you are again...Come, cheer up, cheer up!" Grushenka said to him persuasively. "I'm very glad you've come, very glad, Mitya, do you hear, I'm very glad! I want him to stay here with us," she said peremptorily, addressing the whole company, though her words were obviously meant for the man sitting on the sofa. "I wish it, I wish it! And if he goes away I shall go, too!" she added with flashing eyes.

"What my queen commands is law!" pronounced the Pole, gallantly kissing Grushenka's hand. "I beg you, panie, to join our company," he added politely, addressing Mitya.

Mitya was jumping up with the obvious intention of delivering another tirade, but the words did not come.

"Let's drink, Panie," he blurted out instead of making a speech. Everyone laughed.

"Good heavens! I thought he was going to begin again!" Grushenka exclaimed nervously. "Do you hear, Mitya," she went on insistently, "don't prance about, but it's nice you've brought the champagne. I want some myself, and I can't bear liqueurs. And best of all, you've come yourself. We were fearfully dull here...You've come for a spree again, I suppose? But put your money in your pocket. Where did you get such a lot?"

Mitya had been, all this time, holding in his hand the crumpled bundle of notes on which the eyes of all, especially of the Poles, were fixed. In confusion he thrust them hurriedly into his pocket. He flushed. At that moment the innkeeper brought in an uncorked bottle of champagne, and glasses on a tray. Mitya snatched up the bottle, but he was so bewildered that he did not know what to do with it. Kalgonov took it from him and poured out the champagne.

"Another! Another bottle!" Mitya cried to the inn-keeper, and, forgetting to clink glasses with the Pole whom he had so solemnly invited to drink to their good understanding, he drank off his glass without waiting for anyone else. His whole countenance suddenly changed. The solemn and tragic expression with which he had entered vanished completely, and a look of something childlike came into his face. He seemed to have become suddenly gentle and subdued. He looked shyly and happily at everyone, with a continual nervous little laugh, and the blissful expression of a dog who has done wrong, been punished, and forgiven. He seemed to have forgotten everything, and was looking round at everyone with a childlike smile of delight. He looked at Grushenka, laughing continually, and bringing his chair close up to her. By degrees he had gained some idea of the two Poles, though he had formed no definite conception of them yet.

The Pole on the sofa struck him by his dignified demeanour and his Polish accent; and, above all, by his pipe. "Well, what of it? It's a good thing he's smoking a pipe," he reflected. The Pole's puffy, middle-aged face, with its tiny nose and two very thin, pointed, dyed and impudent-looking moustaches, had not so far roused the faintest doubts in Mitya. He was not even particularly struck by the Pole's absurd wig made in Siberia, with love-locks foolishly combed forward over the temples. "I suppose it's all right since he wears a wig," he went on, musing blissfully. The other, younger Pole, who was staring insolently and defiantly at the company and listening to the conversation with silent contempt, still only impressed Mitya by his great height, which was in striking contrast to the Pole on the sofa. "If he stood up he'd be six foot three." The thought flitted through Mitya's mind. It occurred to him, too, that this Pole must be the friend of the other, as it were, a "bodyguard," and no doubt the big Pole was at the disposal of the little Pole with the pipe. But this all seemed to Mitya perfectly right and not to be questioned. In his mood of doglike submissiveness all feeling of rivalry had died away.

Grushenka's mood and the enigmatic tone of some of her words he completely failed to grasp. All he understood, with thrilling heart, was that she was kind to him, that she had forgiven him, and made him sit by her. He was beside himself with delight, watching her sip her glass of champagne. The silence of the company seemed somehow to strike him, however, and he looked round at everyone with expectant eyes.

"Why are we sitting here though, gentlemen? Why don't you begin doing something?" his smiling eyes seemed to ask.

"He keeps talking nonsense, and we were all laughing," Kalgonov began suddenly, as though divining his thought, and pointing to Maximov.

Mitya immediately stared at Kalgonov and then at Maximov

"He's talking nonsense?" he laughed, his short, wooden laugh, seeming suddenly delighted at something--"ha ha!"

"Yes. Would you believe it, he will have it that all our cavalry officers in the twenties married Polish women. That's awful rot, isn't it?"

"Polish women?" repeated Mitya, perfectly ecstatic.

Kalgonov was well aware of Mitya's attitude to Grushenka, and he guessed about the Pole, too, but that did not so much interest him, perhaps did not interest him at all; what he was interested in was Maximov. He had come here with Maximov by chance, and he met the Poles here at the inn for the first time in his life. Grushenka he knew before, and had once been with someone to see her; but she had not taken to him. But here she looked at him very affectionately: before Mitya's arrival, she had been making much of him, but he seemed somehow to be unmoved by it. He was a boy, not over twenty, dressed like a dandy, with a very charming fair-skinned face, and splendid thick, fair hair. From his fair face looked out beautiful pale blue eyes, with an intelligent and sometimes even deep expression, beyond his age indeed, although the young man sometimes looked and talked quite like a child, and was not at all ashamed of it, even when he was aware of it himself. As a rule he was very wilful, even capricious, though always friendly. Sometimes there was something fixed and obstinate in his expression. He would look at you and listen, seeming all the while to be persistently dreaming over something else. Often he was listless and lazy; at other times he would grow excited, sometimes, apparently, over the most trivial matters.

"Only imagine, I've been taking him about with me for the last four days," he went on, indolently drawling his words, quite naturally though, without the slightest affectation. "Ever since your brother, do you remember, shoved him off the carriage and sent him flying. That made me take an interest in him at the time, and I took him into the country, but he keeps talking such rot I'm ashamed to be with him. I'm taking him back."

"The gentleman has not seen Polish ladies, and says what is impossible," the Pole with the pipe observed to Maximov.

He spoke Russian fairly well, much better, anyway, than he pretended. If he used Russian words, he always distorted them into a Polish form.

"But I was married to a Polish lady myself," tittered Maximov.

"But did you serve in the cavalry? You were talking about the cavalry. Were you a cavalry officer?" put in Kalgonov at once.

"Was he a cavalry officer indeed? Ha ha!" cried Mitya, listening eagerly, and turning his inquiring eyes to each as he spoke, as though there were no knowing what he might hear from each.

"No, you see," Maximov turned to him. "What I mean is that those pretty Polish ladies ...when they danced the mazurka with our Uhlans...when one of them dances a mazurka with a Uhlan she jumps on his knee like a kitten...a little white one...and the pan-father and pan-mother look on and allow it...They allow it...and next day the Uhlan comes and offers her his hand...That's how it is...offers her his hand, he he!" Maximov ended, tittering.

"The pan is a lajdak!"* the tall Pole on the chair growled suddenly and crossed one leg over the other. Mitya's eye was caught by his huge greased boot, with its thick, dirty sole. The dress of both the Poles looked rather greasy.

* Scoundrel.

"Well, now it's lajdak! What's he scolding about?" said Grushenka, suddenly vexed.

"Pani Agrippina, what the gentleman saw in Poland were servant girls, and not ladies of good birth," the Pole with the pipe observed to Grushenka.

"You can reckon on that," the tall Pole snapped contemptuously.

"What next! Let him talk! People talk, why hinder them? It makes it cheerful," Grushenka said crossly.

"I'm not hindering them, pani," said the Pole in the wig, with a long look at Grushenka, and relapsing into dignified silence he sucked his pipe again.

"No, no. The Polish gentleman spoke the truth." Kalgonov got excited again, as though it were a question of vast import. "He's never been in Poland, so how can he talk about it? I suppose you weren't married in Poland, were you?"

"No, in the Province of Smolensk. Only, a Uhlan had brought her to Russia before that, my future wife, with her mamma and her aunt, and another female relation with a grown-up son. He brought her straight from Poland and gave her up to me. He was a lieutenant in our regiment, a very nice young man. At first he meant to marry her himself. But he didn't marry her, because she turned out to be lame."

"So you married a lame woman?" cried Kalganov.

"Yes. They both deceived me a little bit at the time, and concealed it. I thought she was hopping; she kept hopping...I thought it was for fun."

"So pleased she was going to marry you!" yelled Kalganov, in a ringing, childish voice.

"Yes, so pleased. But it turned out to be quite a different cause. Afterwards, when we were married, after the wedding, that very evening, she confessed, and very touchingly asked forgiveness. 'I once jumped over a puddle when I was a child,' she said, 'and injured my leg.' He he!"

Kalgonov went off into the most childish laughter, almost falling on the sofa. Grushenka, too, laughed. Mitya was at the pinnacle of happiness.

"Do you know, that's the truth, he's not lying now," exclaimed Kalganov, turning to Mitya; "and do you know, he's been married twice; it's his first wife he's talking about. But his second wife, do you know, ran away, and is alive now."

"Is it possible?" said Mitya, turning quickly to Maximov with an expression of the utmost astonishment.

"Yes. She did run away. I've had that unpleasant experience," Maximov modestly assented, "with a monsieur. And what was worse, she'd had all my little property transferred to her beforehand. 'You're an educated man,' she said to me. 'You can always get your living.' She settled my business with that. A venerable bishop once said to me: 'One of your wives was lame, but the other was too light-footed.' He he!

"Listen, listen!" cried Kalganov, bubbling over, "if he's telling lies--and he often is--he's only doing it to amuse us all. There's no harm in that, is there? You know, I sometimes like him. He's awfully low, but it's natural to him, eh? Don't you think so? Some people are low from self-interest, but he's simply so, from nature. Only fancy, he claims (he was arguing about it all the way yesterday) that Gogol wrote Dead Souls about him. Do you remember, there's a landowner called Maximov in it, whom Nozdryov thrashed. He was charged, do you remember, 'for inflicting bodily injury with rods on the landowner Maximov in a drunken condition.' Would

198

you believe it, he claims that he was that Maximov and that he was beaten! Now can it be so? Tchitchikov made his journey, at the very latest, at the beginning of the twenties, so that the dates don't fit. He couldn't have been thrashed then, he couldn't, could he?"

It was diffcult to imagine what Kalgonov was excited about, but his excitement was genuine. Mitya followed his lead without protest.

"Well, but if they did thrash him!" he cried, laughing.

"It's not that they thrashed me exactly, but what I mean is--" put in Maximov.

"What do you mean? Either they thrashed you or they didn't."

"What o'clock is it, panie?" the Pole, with the pipe, asked his tall friend, with a bored expression. The other shrugged his shoulders in reply. Neither of them had a watch.

"Why not talk? Let other people talk. Mustn't other people talk because you're bored?" Grushenka flew at him with evident intention of finding fault. Something seemed for the first time to flash upon Mitya's mind. This time the Pole answered with unmistakable irritability.

"Pani, I didn't oppose it. I didn't say anything."

"All right then. Come, tell us your story," Grushenka cried to Maximov. "Why are you all silent?"

"There's nothing to tell, it's all so foolish," answered Maximov at once, with evident satisfaction, mincing a little. "Besides, all that's by way of allegory in Gogol, for he's made all the names have a meaning. Nozdryov was really called Nosov, and Kuvshinikov had quite a different name, he was called Shkvornev. Fenardi really was called Fenardi, only he wasn't an Italian but a Russian, and Mamsel Fenardi was a pretty girl with her pretty little legs in tights, and she had a little short skirt with spangles, and she kept turning round and round, only not for four hours but for four minutes only, and she bewitched everyone..."

"But what were you beaten for?" cried Kalganov.

"For Piron!" answered Maximov.

"What Piron?" cried Mitya.

"The famous French writer, Piron. We were all drinking then, a big party of us, in a tavern at that very fair. They'd invited me, and first of all I began quoting epigrams. 'Is that you, Boileau? What a funny get-up!' and Boileau answers that he's going to a masquerade, that is to the baths, he he! And they took it to themselves, so I made haste to repeat another, very sarcastic, well known to all educated people:

Yes, Sappho and Phaon are we!

But one grief is weighing on me.

You don't know your way to the sea!

"They were still more offended and began abusing me in the most unseemly way for it. And as ill-luck would have it, to set things right, I began telling a very cultivated anecdote about Piron, how he was not accepted into the French Academy, and to revenge himself wrote his own epitaph:

Ci-git Piron qui ne fut rien,

Pas meme academicien,*

* Here lies Piron, who was nothing, not even an Academician.

They seized me and thrashed me."

"But what for? What for?"

"For my education. People can thrash a man for anything," Maximov concluded, briefly and sententiously.

"Eh, that's enough! That's all stupid, I don't want to listen. I thought it would be amusing," Grushenka cut them short, suddenly.

Mitya started, and at once left off laughing. The tall Pole rose upon his feet, and with the haughty air of a man, bored and out of his element, began pacing from corner to corner of the room, his hands behind his back.

"Ah, he can't sit still," said Grushenka, looking at him contemptuously. Mitya began to feel anxious. He noticed besides, that the Pole on the sofa was looking at him with an irritable expression.

"Panie!" cried Mitya, "Let's drink! and the other pan, too! Let us drink."

In a flash he had pulled three glasses towards him, and filled them with champagne.

"To Poland, Panovie, I drink to your Poland!" cried Mitya.

"I shall be delighted, panie," said the Pole on the sofa, with dignity and affable condescension, and he took his glass.

"And the other pan, what's his name? Drink, most illustrious, take your glass!" Mitya urged.

"Pan Vrublevsky," put in the Pole on the sofa.

Pan Vrublevsky came up to the table, swaying as he walked.

"To Poland, Panovie!" cried Mitya, raisin, his glass. "Hurrah!"

All three drank. Mitya seized the bottle and again poured out three glasses.

"Now to Russia, Panovie, and let us be brothers!"

"Pour out some for us," said Grushenka; "I'll drink to Russia, too!"

"So will I," said Kalganov.

"And I would, too...to Russia, the old grandmother!" tittered Maximov.

"All! All!" cried Mitya. "Trifon Borissovitch, some more bottles!"

The other three bottles Mitya had brought with him were put on the table. Mitya filled the glasses.

"To Russia! Hurrah!" he shouted again. All drank the toast except the Poles, and Grushenka tossed off her whole glass at once. The Poles did not touch theirs.

"How's this, Panovie?" cried Mitya, "won't you drink it?"

Pan Vrublevsky took the glass, raised it and said with a resonant voice:

"To Russia as she was before 1772."

"Come, that's better!" cried the other Pole, and they both emptied their glasses at once.

"You're fools, you Panovie," broke suddenly from Mitya.

"Panie!" shouted both the Poles, menacingly, setting on Mitya like a couple of cocks. Pan Vrublevsky was specially furious.

"Can one help loving one's own country?" he shouted.

"Be silent! Don't quarrel! I won't have any quarrelling!" cried Grushenka imperiously, and she stamped her foot on the floor. Her face glowed, her eyes were shining. The effects of the glass she had just drunk were apparent. Mitya was terribly alarmed.

"Panovie, forgive me! It was my fault, I'm sorry. Vrublevsky, panie Vrublevsky, I'm sorry."

"Hold your tongue, you, anyway! Sit down, you stupid!". Grushenka scolded with angry annoyance.

Everyone sat down, all were silent, looking at one another.

"Gentlemen, I was the cause of it all," Mitya began again, unable to make anything of Grushenka's words. "Come, why are we sitting here? What shall we do...to amuse ourselves again?"

"Ach, it's certainly anything but amusing!" Kalgonov mumbled lazily.

"Let's play faro again, as we did just now," Maximov tittered suddenly.

"Faro? Splendid!" cried Mitya. "If only the panovie-"

"It's lite, panovie," the Pole on the sofa responded, as it were unwillingly.

"That's true," assented Pan Vrublevsky.

"Lite? What do you mean by 'lite'?" asked Grushenka.

"Late, pani! 'A late hour' I mean," the Pole on the sofa explained.

"It's always late with them. They can never do anything!" Grushenka almost shrieked in her anger. "They're dull themselves, so they want others to be dull. Before came, Mitya, they were just as silent and kept turning up their noses at me."

"My goddess!" cried the Pole on the sofa, "I see you're not well-disposed to me, that's why I'm gloomy. I'm ready, panie," added he, addressing Mitya.

"Begin, panie," Mitya assented, pulling his notes out of his pocket, and laying two hundred-rouble notes on the table. "I want to lose a lot to you. Take your cards. Make the bank."

"We'll have cards from the landlord, panie," said the little Pole, gravely and emphatically.

"That's much the best way," chimed in Pan Vrublevsky.

"From the landlord? Very good, I understand, let's get them from him. Cards!" Mitya shouted to the landlord.

The landlord brought in a new, unopened pack, and informed Mitya that the girls were getting ready, and that the Jews with the cymbals would most likely be here soon; but the cart with the provisions had not yet arrived. Mitya jumped up from the table and ran into the next room to give orders, but only three girls had arrived, and Marya was not there yet. And he did not know himself what orders to give and why he had run out. He only told them to take out of the box the presents for the girls, the sweets, the toffee and the fondants. "And vodka for Andrey, vodka for Andrey!" he cried in haste. "I was rude to Andrey!"

Suddenly Maximov, who had followed him out, touched him on the shoulder.

"Give me five roubles," he whispered to Mitya. "I'll stake something at faro, too, he he!"

"Capital! Splendid! Take ten, here!"

Again he took all the notes out of his pocket and picked out one for ten roubles. "And if you lose that, come again, come again."

"Very good," Maximov whispered joyfully, and he ran back again. Mitya, too, returned, apologising for having kept them waiting. The Poles had already sat down, and opened the pack. They looked much more amiable, almost cordial. The Pole on the sofa had lighted another pipe and was preparing to throw. He wore an air of solemnity.

"To your places, gentlemen," cried Pan Vrublevsky.

"No, I'm not going to play any more," observed Kalganov, "I've lost fifty roubles to them just now."

"The pan had no luck, perhaps he'll be lucky this time," the Pole on the sofa observed in his direction.

"How much in the bank? To correspond?" asked Mitya.

"That's according, panie, maybe a hundred, maybe two hundred, as much as you will stake." "A million!" laughed Mitya.

"The Pan Captain has heard of Pan Podvysotsky, perhaps?"

"What Podvysotsky?"

"In Warsaw there was a bank and anyone comes and stakes against it. Podvysotsky comes, sees a thousand gold pieces, stakes against the bank. The banker says, 'Panie Podvysotsky, are you laying down the gold, or must we trust to your honour?' 'To my honour, panie,' says Podvysotsky. 'So much the better.' The banker throws the dice. Podvysotsky wins. 'Take it, panie,' says the banker, and pulling out the drawer he gives him a million. 'Take it, panie, this is your gain.' There was a million in the bank. 'I didn't know that,' says Podvysotsky. 'Panie Podvysotsky,' said the banker, 'you pledged your honour and we pledged ours.' Podvysotsky took the million."

"That's not true," said Kalganov.

"Panie Kalganov, in gentlemanly society one doesn't say such things."

"As if a Polish gambler would give away a million!" cried Mitya, but checked himself at once. "Forgive me, panie, it's my fault again; he would, he would give away a million, for honour, for Polish honour. You see how I talk Polish, ha ha! Here, I stake ten roubles, the knave leads."

"And I put a rouble on the queen, the queen of hearts, the pretty little panienotchka* he! he!" laughed Maximov, pulling out his queen, and, as though trying to conceal it from everyone, he moved right up and crossed himself hurriedly under the table. Mitya won. The rouble won, too.

* Little miss.

"A corner!" cried Mitya.

"I'll bet another rouble, a 'single' stake," Maximov muttered gleefully, hugely delighted at having won a rouble.

"Lost!" shouted Mitya. "A 'double' on the seven!"

The seven too was trumped.

"Stop!" cried Kalganov suddenly.

"Double! Double!" Mitya doubled his stakes, and each time he doubled the stake, the card he doubled was trumped by the Poles. The rouble stakes kept winning.

"On the double!" shouted Mitya furiously.

"You've lost two hundred, panie. Will you stake another hundred?" the Pole on the sofa inquired.

"What? Lost two hundred already? Then another two hundred! All doubles!" And pulling his money out of his pocket, Mitya was about to fling two hundred roubles on the queen, but Kalgonov covered it with his hand.

"That's enough!" he shouted in his ringing voice.

"What's the matter?" Mitya stared at him.

"That's enough! I don't want you to play anymore. Don't!"

"Why?"

"Because I don't. Hang it, come away. That's why. I won't let you go on playing."

Mitya gazed at him in astonishment.

"Give it up, Mitya. He may be right. You've lost a lot as it is," said Grushenka, with a curious note in her voice. Both the Poles rose from their seats with a deeply offended air.

"Are you joking, panie?" said the short man, looking severely at Kalganov.

"How dare you!" Pan Vrublevsky, too, growled at Kalganov.

"Don't dare to shout like that," cried Grushenka. "Ah, you turkey-cocks!"

Mitya looked at each of them in turn. But something in Grushenka's face suddenly struck him, and at the same instant something new flashed into his mind--a strange new thought! "Pani Agrippina," the little Pole was beginning, crimson with anger, when Mitya suddenly went up to him and slapped him on the shoulder.

"Most illustrious, two words with you."cried Grushenka.

"What do you want?"

"In the next room, I've two words to say to you, something pleasant, very pleasant. You'll be glad to hear it."

The little pan was taken aback and looked apprehensively at Mitya. He agreed at once, however, on condition that Pan Vrublevsky went with them.

"The bodyguard? Let him come, and I want him, too. I must have him!" cried Mitya. "March, panovie!"

"Where are you going?" asked Grushenka, anxiously.

"We'll be back in one moment," answered Mitya.

There was a sort of boldness, a sudden confidence shining in his eyes. His face had looked very different when he entered the room an hour before.

He led the Poles, not into the large room where the chorus of girls was assembling and the table was being laid, but into the bedroom on the right, where the trunks and packages were kept, and there were two large beds, with pyramids of cotton pillows on each. There was a lighted candle on a small deal table in the corner. The small man and Mitya sat down to this table, facing each other, while the huge Vrublevsky stood beside them, his hands behind his back. The Poles looked severe but were evidently inquisitive.

"What can I do for you, panie?" lisped the little Pole.

"Well, look here, panie, I won't keep you long. There's money for you," he pulled out his notes. "Would you like three thousand? Take it and go your way."

The Pole gazed open-eyed at Mitya, with a searching look.

"Three thousand, panie?" He exchanged glances with Vrublevsky.

"Three, panovie, three! Listen, panie, I see you're a sensible man. Take three thousand and go to the devil, and Vrublevsky with you d'you hear? But, at once, this very minute, and for ever. You understand that, panie, for ever. Here's the door, you go out of it. What have you got there, a great-coat, a fur coat? I'll bring it out to you. They'll get the horses out directly, and then-good-bye, panie!"

Mitya awaited an answer with assurance. He had no doubts. An expression of extraordinary resolution passed over the Pole's face.

"And the money, panie?"

"The money, panie? Five hundred roubles I'll give you this moment for the journey, and as a first instalment, and two thousand five hundred to-morrow, in the town--I swear on my honour, I'll get it, I'll get it at any cost!" cried Mitya.

The Poles exchanged glances again. The short man's face looked more forbidding.

"Seven hundred, seven hundred, not five hundred, at once, this minute, cash down!" Mitya added, feeling something wrong. "What's the matter, panie? Don't you trust me? I can't give you the whole three thousand straight off. If I give it, you may come back to her to-morrow...Besides, I haven't the three thousand with me. I've got it at home in the town," faltered Mitya, his spirit sinking at every word he uttered. "Upon my word, the money's there, hidden."

In an instant an extraordinary sense of personal dignity showed itself in the little man's face.

"What next?" he asked ironically. "For shame!" and he spat on the floor. Pan Vrublevsky spat too.

"You do that, panie," said Mitya, recognising with despair that all was over, "because you hope to make more out of Grushenka? You're a couple of capons, that's what you are!"

"This is a mortal insult!" The little Pole turned as red as a crab, and he went out of the room, briskly, as though unwilling to hear another word. Vrublevsky swung out after him, and Mitya followed, confused and crestfallen. He was afraid of Grushenka, afraid that the Pan would at once raise an outcry. And so indeed he did. The Pole walked into the room and threw himself in a theatrical attitude before Grushenka.

"Pani Agrippina, I have received a mortal insult!" he exclaimed. But Grushenka suddenly lost all patience, as though they had wounded her in the tenderest spot.

"Speak Russian! Speak Russian!" she cried, "not another word of Polish! You used to talk Russian. You can't have forgotten it in five years."

She was red with passion.

"Pani Agrippina-"

"My name's Agrafena, Grushenka, speak Russian or I won't listen!"

The Pole gasped with offended dignity, and quickly and pompously delivered himself in broken Russian:

"Pani Agrafena, I came here to forget the past and forgive it, to forget all that has happened till to-day-"

"Forgive? Came here to forgive me?" Grushenka cut him short, jumping up from her seat.

"Just so, Pani, I'm not pusillanimous, I'm magnanimous. But I was astounded when I saw your lovers. Pan Mitya offered me three thousand, in the other room to depart. I spat in the pan's face."

"What? He offered you money for me?" cried Grushenka, hysterically. "Is it true, Mitya? How dare you? Am I for sale?"

"Panie, panie!" yelled Mitya, "she's pure and shining, and I have never been her lover! That's a lie..."

"How dare you defend me to him?" shrieked Grushenka. "It wasn't virtue kept me pure, and it wasn't that I was afraid of Kuzma, but that I might hold up my head when I met him, and tell him he's a scoundrel. And he did actually refuse the money?"

"He took it! He took it!" cried Mitya; "only he wanted to get the whole three thousand at once, and I could only give him seven hundred straight off."

"I see: he heard I had money, and came here to marry me!"

"Pani Agrippina!" cried the little Pole. "I'm--a knight, I'm--a nobleman, and not a lajdak. I came here to make you my wife and I find you a different woman, perverse and shameless."

"Oh, go back where you came from! I'll tell them to turn you out and you'll be turned out," cried Grushenka, furious. "I've been a fool, a fool, to have been miserable these five years! And it wasn't for his sake, it was my anger made me miserable. And this isn't he at all! Was he like this? It might be his father! Where did you get your wig from? He was a falcon, but this is a gander. He used to laugh and sing to me...And I've been crying for five years, damned fool, abject, shameless I was!

She sank back in her low chair and hid her face in her hands. At that instant the chorus of Mokroe began singing in the room on the left--a rollicking dance song.

"A regular Sodom!" Vrublevsky roared suddenly. "Landlord, send the shameless hussies away!"

The landlord, who had been for some time past inquisitively peeping in at the door, hearing shouts and guessing that his guests were quarrelling, at once entered the room.

"What are you shouting for? D'you want to split your throat?" he said, addressing Vrublevsky, with surprising rudeness.

"Animal!" bellowed Pan Vrublevsky.

"Animal? And what sort of cards were you playing with just now? I gave you a pack and you hid it. You played with marked cards! I could send you to Siberia for playing with false cards, d'you know that, for it's just the same as false banknotes...

And going up to the sofa he thrust his fingers between the sofa back and the cushion, and pulled out an unopened pack of cards.

"Here's my pack unopened!"

He held it up and showed it to all in the room. "From where I stood I saw him slip my pack away, and put his in place of it--you're a cheat and not a gentleman!"

"And I twice saw the pan change a card!" cried Kalganov.

"How shameful! How shameful!" exclaimed Grushenka, clasping her hands, and blushing for genuine shame. "Good Lord, he's come to that!"

"I thought so, too!" said Mitya. But before he had uttered the words, Vrublevsky, with a confused and infuriated face, shook his fist at Grushenka, shouting:

"You low harlot!"

Mitya flew at him at once, clutched him in both hands, lifted him in the air, and in one instant had carried him into the room on the right, from which they had just come.

"I've laid him on the floor, there," he announced, returning at once, gasping with excitement. "He's struggling, the scoundrel! But he won't come back, no fear of that!..."

He closed one half of the folding doors, and holding the other ajar called out to the little Pole:

"Most illustrious, will you please to retire as well?"

"My dear Dmitri Fyodorovitch," said Trifon Borissovitch, "make them give you back the money you lost. It's as good as stolen from you."

"I don't want my fifty roubles back," Kalgonov declared suddenly.

"I don't want my two hundred, either," cried Mitya, "I wouldn't take it for anything! Let him keep it as a consolation."

"Bravo, Mitya! You're a trump, Mitya!" cried Grushenka, and there was a note of fierce anger in the exclamation.

The little pan, crimson with fury but still mindful of his dignity, was making for the door, but he stopped short and said suddenly, addressing Grushenka:

"Pani, if you want to come with me, come. If not, good-bye."

And swelling with indignation and importance he went to the door. This was a man of character: he had so good an opinion of himself that after all that had passed, he still expected that she would marry him. Mitya slammed the door after him.

"Lock it," said Kalganov. But the key clicked on the other side, they had locked it from within.

"That's capital!" exclaimed Grushenka relentlessly. "Serve them right!"

Chapter 8. Delirium

WHAT followed was almost an orgy, a feast to which all were welcome. Grushenka was the first to call for wine.

"I want to drink. I want to be quite drunk, as we were before. Do you remember, Mitya, do you remember how we made friends here last time!"

Mitya himself was almost delirious, feeling that his happiness was at hand. But Grushenka was continually sending him away from her.

"Go and enjoy yourself. Tell them to dance, to make merry, 'let the stove and cottage dance'; as we had it last time," she kept exclaiming. She was tremendously excited. And Mitya hastened to obey her. The chorus were in the next room. The room in which they had been sitting till that moment was too small, and was divided in two by cotton curtains, behind which was a huge bed with a puffy feather mattress and a pyramid of cotton pillows. In the four rooms for visitors there were beds. Grushenka settled herself just at the door. Mitya set an easy chair for her. She had sat in the same place to watch the dancing and singing "the time before," when they had made merry there. All the girls who had come had been there then; the Jewish band with fiddles and zithers had come, too, and at last the long expected cart had arrived with the wines and provisions.

Mitya bustled about. All sorts of people began coming into the room to look on, peasants and their women, who had been roused from sleep and attracted by the hopes of another marvellous entertainment such as they had enjoyed a month before. Mitya remembered their faces, greeting and embracing everyone he knew. He uncorked bottles and poured out wine for everyone who presented himself. Only the girls were very eager for the champagne. The men preferred rum, brandy, and, above all, hot punch. Mitya had chocolate made for all the girls, and ordered that three samovars should be kept boiling all night to provide tea and punch for everyone to help himself.

An absurd chaotic confusion followed, but Mitya was in his natural element, and the more foolish it became, the more his spirits rose. If the peasants had asked him for money at that moment, he would have pulled out his notes and given them away right and left. This was probably why the landlord, Trifon Borissovitch, kept hovering about Mitya to protect him. He seemed to have given up all idea of going to bed that night; but he drank little, only one glass of punch, and kept a sharp look-out on Mitya's interests after his own fashion. He intervened in the nick of time, civilly and obsequiously persuading Mitya not to give away "cigars and Rhine wine," and, above all, money to the peasants as he had done before. He was very indignant, too, at the peasant girls drinking liqueur, and eating sweets.

"They're a lousy lot, Dmitri Fyodorovitch," he said. "I'd give them a kick, every one of them, and they'd take it as an honour- that's all they're worth!"

Mitya remembered Andrey again, and ordered punch to be sent out to him. "I was rude to him just now," he repeated with a sinking, softened voice. Kalgonov did to drink, and at first did not care for the girls singing; but after he had drunk a couple of glasses of champagne he became extraordinarily lively, strolling about the room, laughing and praising the music and the songs, admiring everyone and everything. Maximov, blissfully drunk, never left his side. Grushenka, too, was beginning to get drunk. Pointing to Kalganov, she said to Mitya:

"What a dear, charming boy he is!"

And Mitya, delighted, ran to kiss Kalgonov and Maximov. Oh, great were his hopes! She had said nothing yet, and seemed, indeed, purposely to refrain from speaking. But she looked at him from time to time with caressing and passionate eyes. At last she suddenly gripped his hand and drew him vigorously to her. She was sitting at the moment in the low chair by the door.

"How was it you came just now, eh? Have you walked in!...I was frightened. So you wanted to give me up to him, did you? Did you really want to?"

"I didn't want to spoil your happiness!" Mitya faltered blissfully. But she did not need his answer.

"Well, go and enjoy yourself..." she sent him away once more. "Don't cry, I'll call you back again."

He would run away and she listened to the singing and looked at the dancing, though her eyes followed him wherever he went. But in another quarter of an hour she would call him once more and again he would run back to her.

"Come, sit beside me, tell me, how did you hear about me, and my coming here yesterday? From whom did you first hear it?"

And Mitya began telling her all about it, disconnectedly, incoherently, feverishly. He spoke strangely, often frowning, and stopping abruptly.

"What are you frowning at?" she asked.

"Nothing...I left a man ill there. I'd give ten years of my life for him to get well, to know he was all right!"

"Well, never mind him, if he's ill. So you meant to shoot yourself to-morrow! What a silly boy! What for? I like such reckless fellows as you," she lisped, with a rather halting tongue. "So you would go any length for me, eh? Did you really mean to shoot yourself to-morrow, you stupid? No, wait a little. To-morrow I may have something to say to you...I won't say it to-day, but to-morrow. You'd like it to be to-day? No, I don't want to to-day. Come, go along now, go and amuse yourself."

Once, however, she called him, as it were, puzzled and uneasy.

"Why are you sad? I see you're sad...Yes, I see it," she added, looking intently into his eyes. "Though you keep kissing the peasants and shouting, I see something. No, be merry. I'm merry; you be merry, too...I love somebody here. Guess who it is. Ah, look, my boy has fallen asleep, poor dear, he's drunk."

She meant Kalganov. He was, in fact, drunk, and had dropped asleep for a moment, sitting on the sofa. But he was not merely drowsy from drink; he felt suddenly dejected, or, as he said, "bored." He was intensely depressed by the girls' songs, which, as the drinking went on, gradually became coarse and more reckless. And the dances were as bad. Two girls dressed up as bears, and a lively girl, called Stepanida, with a stick in her hand, acted the part of keeper, and began to "show them."

"Look alive, Marya, or you'll get the stick!

The bears rolled on the ground at last in the most unseemly fashion, amid roars of laughter from the closely-packed crowd of men and women.

"Well, let them! Let them!" said Grushenka sententiously, with an ecstatic expression on her face. "When they do get a day to enjoy themselves; why shouldn't folks be happy?"

Kalgonov looked as though he had been besmirched with dirt.

"It's swinish, all this peasant foolery," he murmured, moving away; "it's the game they play when it's light all night in summer."

He particularly disliked one "new" song to a jaunty dance-tune. It described how a gentleman came and tried his luck with the girls, to see whether they would love him:

The master came to try the girls:
Would they love him, would they not?
But the girls could not love the master:
He would beat me cruelly
And such love won't do for me.

Then a gypsy comes along and he, too, tries:
The gypsy came to try the girls:
Would they love him, would they not?
But they couldn't love the gypsy either:
He would be a thief, I fear,
And would cause me many a tear.

And many more men come to try their luck, among them a soldier:
The soldier came to try the girls:
Would they love him, would they not?

But the soldier is rejected with contempt, in two indecent lines, sung with absolute frankness and producing a furore in the audience. The song ends with a merchant:

The merchant came to try the girls:
Would they love him, would they not?
And it appears that he wins their love because:
The merchant will make gold for me
And his queen I'll gladly be.

Kalgonov was positively indignant.

"That's just a song of yesterday," he said aloud. "Who writes such things for them? They might just as well have had a railwayman or a Jew come to try his luck with the girls; they'd have carried all before them."

And, almost as though it were a personal affront, he declared, on the spot, that he was bored, sat down on the sofa and immediately fell asleep. His pretty little face looked rather pale, as it fell back on the sofa cushion.

"Look how pretty he is," said Grushenka, taking Mitya up to him. "I was combing his hair just now; his hair's like flax, and so thick..."

And, bending over him tenderly, she kissed his forehead. Kalgonov instantly opened his eyes, looked at her, stood up, and with the most anxious air inquired where was Maximov?

"So that's who it is you want." Grushenka laughed. "Stay with me a minute. Mitya, run and find his Maximov."

Maximov, it appeared, could not tear himself away from the girls, only running away from time to time to pour himself out a glass of liqueur. He had drunk two cups of chocolate. His face was red, and his nose was crimson; his eyes were moist, and mawkishly sweet.He ran up and announced that he was going to dance the "sabotiere."

"They taught me all those well-bred, aristocratic dances when I was little..."

"Go, go with him, Mitya, and I'll watch from here how he dances," said Grushenka.

"No, no, I'm coming to look on, too," exclaimed Kalganov, brushing aside in the most naive way Grushenka's offer to sit with him. They all went to look on. Maximov danced his dance. But it roused no great admiration in anyone but Mitya. It consisted of nothing but skipping and hopping, kicking the feet, and at every skip Maximov slapped the upturned sole of his foot. Kalgonov did not like it at all, but Mitya kissed the dancer.

"Thanks. You're tired perhaps? What are you looking for here? Would you like some sweets? A cigar, perhaps?"

"A cigarette."

"Don't you want a drink?"

"I'll just have a liqueur...Have you any chocolates?"

"Yes, there's a heap of them on the table there. Choose one, my dear soul!"

"I like one with vanilla...for old people. He he!

"No, brother, we've none of that special sort."

"I say," the old man bent down to whisper in Mitya's ear. "That girl there, little Marya, he he! How would it be if you were to help me make friends with her?"

"So that's what you're after! No, brother, that won't do!"

"I'd do no harm to anyone," Maximov muttered disconsolately.

"Oh, all right, all right. They only come here to dance and sing, you know, brother. But damn it all, wait a bit!...Eat and drink and be merry, meanwhile. Don't you want money?"

"Later on, perhaps," smiled Maximov.

"All right, all right..."

Mitya's head was burning. He went outside to the wooden balcony which ran round the whole building on the inner side, overlooking the courtyard. The fresh air revived him. He stood alone in a dark corner, and suddenly clutched his head in both hands. His scattered thoughts came together; his sensations blended into a whole and threw a sudden light into his mind. A fearful and terrible light! "If I'm to shoot myself, why not now?" passed through his mind. "Why not go for the pistols, bring them here, and here, in this dark dirty corner, make an end?" Almost a minute he undecided. A few hours earlier, when he had been dashing here, he was pursued by disgrace, by the theft he had committed, and that blood, that blood!...But yet it was easier for him then. Then everything was over: he had lost her, given her up. She was gone, for him--oh, then his death sentence had been easier for him; at least it had seemed necessary, inevitable, for what had he to stay on earth for?

But now? Was it the same as then? Now one phantom, one terror at least was at an end: that first, rightful lover, that fateful figure had vanished, leaving no trace. The terrible phantom had turned into something so small, so comic; it had been carried into the bedroom and locked in. It would never return. She was ashamed, and from her eyes he could see now whom she loved. Now he had everything to make life happy...but he could not go on living, he could not; oh, damnation! "O God! restore to life the man I knocked down at the fence! Let this fearful cup pass from me! Lord, thou hast wrought miracles for such sinners as me! But what, what if the old man's alive? Oh, then the shame of the other disgrace I would wipe away. I would restore the stolen money. I'd give it back; I'd get it somehow...No trace of that shame will remain except in my heart for ever! But no, no; oh, impossible cowardly dreams! Oh, damnation!"

Yet there was a ray of light and hope in his darkness. He jumped up and ran back to the room--to her, to her, his queen for ever! Was not one moment of her love worth all the rest of life, even in the agonies of disgrace? This wild question clutched at his heart. "To her, to her alone, to see her, to hear her, to think of nothing, to forget everything, if only for that night, for an hour, for a moment!" Just as he turned from the balcony into the passage, he came upon the landlord, Trifon Borissovitch. He thought he looked gloomy and worried, and fancied he had come to find him.

"What is it, Trifon Borissovitch? Are you looking for me?"

"No, sir," The landlord seemed disconcerted. "Why should I be looking for you? Where have you been?"

"Why do you look so glum? You're not angry, are you? Wait a bit, you shall soon get to bed...What's the time?"

"It'll be three o'clock. Past three, it must be."

"We'll leave off soon. We'll leave off."

"Don't mention it; it doesn't matter. Keep it up as long as you like..."

"What's the matter with him?" Mitya wondered for an instant, and he ran back to the room where the girls were dancing. But she was not there. She was not in the blue room either; there was no one but Kalgonov asleep on the sofa. Mitya peeped behind the curtain--she was there. She was sitting in the corner, on a trunk. Bent forward, with her head and arms on the bed close by, she was crying bitterly, doing her utmost to stifle her sobs that she might not be heard. Seeing Mitya, she beckoned him to her, and when he ran to her, she grasped his hand tightly.

"Mitya, Mitya, I loved him, you know. How I have loved him these five years, all that time! Did I love him or only my own anger? No, him, him! It's a lie that it was my anger I loved and not him. Mitya, I was only seventeen then; he was so kind to me, so merry; he used to sing to me...Or so it seemed to a silly girl like me...And now, O Lord, it's not the same man. Even his face is not the same; he's different altogether. I shouldn't have known him. I drove here with Timofey, and all the way I was thinking how I should meet him, what I should say to him, how we should look at one another. My soul was faint, and all of a sudden it was just as though he had emptied a pail of dirty water over me. He talked to me like a schoolmaster, all so grave and learned; he met me so solemnly that I was struck dumb. I couldn't get a word in. At first I thought he was ashamed to talk before his great big Pole. I sat staring at him and wondering why I couldn't say a word to him now. It must have been his wife that ruined him; you know he threw me up to get married. She must have changed him like that. Mitya, how shameful it is! Oh, Mitya, I'm ashamed, I'm ashamed for all my life. Curse it, curse it, curse those five years!"

And again she burst into tears, but clung tight to Mitya's hand and did not let it go.

"Mitya, darling, stay, don't go away. I want to say one word to you," she whispered, and suddenly raised her face to him. "Listen, tell me who it is I love? I love one man here. Who is that man? That's what you must tell me."

A smile lighted up her face that was swollen with weeping, and her eyes shone in the half darkness.

"A falcon flew in, and my heart sank. "Fool! that's the man you love!' That was what my heart whispered to me at once. You came in and all grew bright. What's he afraid of? I wondered. For you were frightened; you couldn't speak. It's not them he's afraid of--could you be frightened of anyone? It's me he's afraid of, I thought, only me. So Fenya told you, you little stupid, how I called to Alyosha out of the window that I'd loved Mityenka for one hour, and that I was going now to love...another. Mitya, Mitya, how could I be such a fool as to think I could love anyone after you? Do you forgive me, Mitya? Do you forgive me or not? Do you love me? Do you love me?" She jumped up and held him with both hands on his shoulders. Mitya, dumb with rapture, gazed into her eyes, at her face, at her smile, and suddenly clasped her tightly his arms and kissed her passionately.

"You will forgive me for having tormented you? It was through spite I tormented you all. It was for spite I drove the old man out of his mind...Do you remember how you drank at my house one day and broke the wine-glass? I remembered that and I broke a glass to-day and drank 'to my vile heart.' Mitya, my falcon, why don't you kiss me? He kissed me once, and now he draws back and looks and listens. Why listen to me? Kiss me, kiss me hard, that's right. if you love, well, then, love! I'll be your slave now, your slave for the rest of my life. It's sweet to be a slave. Kiss me! Beat me, ill-treat me, do what you will with me...And I do deserve to suffer. Stay, wait, afterwards, I won't have that..." she suddenly thrust him away. "Go along, Mitya, I'll come and have some wine, I want to be drunk, I'm going to get drunk and dance; I must, I must!" She tore herself away from him and disappeared behind the curtain. Mitya followed like a drunken man.

"Yes, come what may--whatever may happen now, for one minute I'd give the whole world," he thought. Grushenka did, in fact, toss off a whole glass of champagne at one gulp, and became at once very tipsy. She sat down in the same chair as before, with a blissful smile on her face. Her cheeks were glowing, her lips were burning, her flashing eyes were moist; there was passionate appeal in her eyes. Even Kalgonov felt a stir at the heart and went up to her.

"Did you feel how I kissed you when you were asleep just now?" she said thickly. "I'm drunk now, that's what it is...And aren't you drunk? And why isn't Mitya drinking? Why don't you drink, Mitya? I'm drunk, and you don't drink..."

"I am drunk! I'm drunk as it is...drunk with you...and now I'll be drunk with wine, too."

He drank off another glass, and--he thought it strange himself--that glass made him completely drunk. He was suddenly drunk, although till that moment he had been quite sober, he remembered that. From that moment everything whirled about him, as though he were delirious. He walked, laughed, talked to everybody, without knowing what he was doing. Only one persistent burning sensation made itself felt continually, "like a red-hot coal in his heart," he said afterwards. He went up to her, sat beside her, gazed at her, listened to her...She became very talkative, kept calling everyone to her, and beckoned to different girls out of the chorus. When the girl came up, she either kissed her, or made the sign of the cross over her. In another minute she might have cried. She was greatly amused by the "little old man," as she called Maximov. He ran up every minute to kiss her hands, each little finger," and finally he danced another dance to an old song, which he sang himself. He danced with special vigour to the refrain:

The little pig says--umph! umph! umph!
The little calf says--moo, moo, moo,
The little duck says--quack, quack, quack,
The little goose says--ga, ga, ga.

The hen goes strutting through the porch;

Troo-roo-roo-roo-roo, she'll say,

Troo-roo-roo-roo-roo, she'll say!

"Give him something, Mitya," said Grushenka. "Give him a present, he's poor, you know. Ah, the poor, the insulted!...Do you know, Mitya, I shall go into a nunnery. No, I really shall one day. Alyosha said something to me to-day that I shall remember all my life...Yes...But to-day let us dance. To-morrow to the nunnery, but to-day we'll dance. I want to play to-day, good people, and what of it? God will forgive us. If I were God, I'd forgive everyone: 'My dear sinners, from this day forth I forgive you.' I'm going to beg forgiveness: 'Forgive me, good people, a silly wench.' I'm a beast, that's what I am. But I want to pray. I gave a little onion. Wicked as I've been, I want to pray. Mitya, let them dance, don't stop them. Everyone in the world is good. Everyone--even the worst of them. The world's a nice place. Though we're bad the world's all right. We're good and bad, good and bad...Come, tell me, I've something to ask you: come here everyone, and I'll ask you: Why am I so good? You know I am good. I'm very good...Come, why am I so good?"

So Grushenka babbled on, getting more and more drunk. At last she announced that she was going to dance, too. She got up from her chair, staggering. "Mitya, don't give me any more wine--if I ask you, don't give it to me. Wine doesn't give peace. Everything's going round, the stove, and everything. I want to dance. Let everyone see how I dance...let them see how beautifully I dance..."

She really meant it. She pulled a white cambric handkerchief out of her pocket, and took it by one corner in her right hand, to wave it in the dance. Mitya ran to and fro, the girls were quiet, and got ready to break into a dancing song at the first signal. Maximov, hearing that Grushenka wanted to dance, squealed with delight, and ran skipping about in front of her, humming:

With legs so slim and sides so trim

And its little tail curled tight.

But Grushenka waved her handkerchief at him and drove him away.

"Sh-h! Mitya, why don't they come? Let everyone come...to look on. Call them in, too, that were locked in...Why did you lock them in? Tell them I'm going to dance. Let them look on, too..."

Mitya walked with a drunken swagger to the locked door, and began knocking to the Poles with his fist.

"Hi, you...Podvysotskis! Come, she's going to dance. She calls you."

"Lajdak!" one of the Poles shouted in reply.

"You're a lajdak yourself! You're a little scoundrel, that's what you are."

"Leave off laughing at Poland," said Kalganov sententiously. He too was drunk.

"Be quiet, boy! If I call him a scoundrel, it doesn't mean that I called all Poland so. One lajdak doesn't make a Poland. Be quiet, my pretty boy, eat a sweetmeat."

"Ach, what fellows! As though they were not men. Why won't they make friends?" said Grushenka, and went forward to dance. The chorus broke into "Ah, my porch, my new porch!" Grushenka flung back her head, half opened her lips, smiled, waved her handkerchief, and suddenly, with a violent lurch, stood still in the middle of the room, looking bewildered.

"I'm weak..." she said in an exhausted voice. "Forgive me...I'm weak, I can't...I'm sorry."

She bowed to the chorus, and then began bowing in all directions.

"I'm sorry...Forgive me..."

"The lady's been drinking. The pretty lady has been drinking," voices were heard saying.

"The lady's drunk too much," Maximov explained to the girls, giggling.

"Mitya, lead me away...take me," said Grushenka helplessly. Mitya pounced on her, snatched her up in his arms, and carried the precious burden through the curtains.

"Well, now I'll go," thought Kalganov, and walking out of the blue room, he closed the two halves of the door after him. But the orgy in the larger room went on and grew louder and louder. Mitya laid Grushenka on the bed and kissed her on the lips.

"Don't touch me..." she faltered, in an imploring voice. "Don't touch me, till I'm yours...I've told you I'm yours, but don't touch me...spare me...With them here, with them close, you mustn't. He's here. It's nasty here..."

"I'll obey you! I won't think of it...I worship you!" muttered Mitya. "Yes, it's nasty here, it's abominable."

And still holding her in his arms, he sank on his knees by the bedside.

"I know, though you're a brute, you're generous," Grushenka articulated with difficulty. "It must be honourable...it shall be honourable for the future...and let us be honest, let us be good, not brutes, but good...take me away, take me far away, do you hear? I don't want it to be here, but far, far away..."

"Oh, yes, yes, it must be!" said Mitya, pressing her in his arms. "I'll take you and we'll fly away...Oh, I'd give my whole life for one year only to know about that blood!"

"What blood?" asked Grushenka, bewildered.

"Nothing," muttered Mitya, through his teeth. "Grusha, you wanted to be honest, but I'm a thief. But I've stolen money from Katya...Disgrace, a disgrace!"

"From Katya, from that young lady? No, you didn't steal it. Give it back to her, take it from me...Why make a fuss? Now everything of mine is yours. What does money matter? We shall waste it anyway...Folks like us are bound to waste money. But we'd better go and work the land. I want to dig the earth with my own hands. We must work, do you hear? Alyosha said so. I won't be your mistress, I'll be faithful to you, I'll be your slave, I'll work for you. We'll go to the young lady and bow down to her together, so that she may forgive us, and then we'll go away. And if she won't forgive us, we'll go, anyway. Take her money and love me...Don't love her...Don't love her any more. If you love her, I shall strangle her...I'll put out both her eyes with a needle..."

"I love you. love only you. I'll love you in Siberia..."

"Why Siberia? Never mind, Siberia, if you like. I don't care...we'll work...there's snow in Siberia...I love driving in the snow...and must have bells...Do you hear, there's a bell ringing? Where is that bell ringing? There are people coming...Now it's stopped."

She closed her eyes, exhausted, and suddenly fell asleep for an instant. There had certainly been the sound of a bell in the distance, but the ringing had ceased. Mitya let his head sink on her breast. He did not notice that the bell had ceased ringing, nor did he notice that the songs had ceased, and that instead of singing and drunken clamour there was absolute stillness in the house. Grushenka opened her eyes.

"What's the matter? Was I asleep? Yes...a bell...I've been asleep and dreamt I was driving over the snow with bells, and I dozed. I was with someone I loved, with you. And far, far away. I was holding you and kissing you, nestling close to you. I was cold, and the snow glistened...You know how the snow glistens at night when the moon shines. It was as though I was not on earth. I woke up, and my dear one is close to me. How sweet that is!..."

"Close to you," murmured Mitya, kissing her dress, her bosom, her hands. And suddenly he had a strange fancy: it seemed to him that she was looking straight before her, not at him, not into his face, but over his head, with an intent, almost uncanny fixity. An expression of wonder, almost of alarm, came suddenly into her face.

"Mitya, who is that looking at us?" she whispered.

Mitya turned, and saw that someone had, in fact, parted the curtains and seemed to be watching them. And not one person alone, it seemed.

He jumped up and walked quickly to the intruder.

"Here, come to us, come here," said a voice, speaking not loudly, but firmly and peremptorily.

Mitya passed to the other side of the curtain and stood stock still. The room was filled with people, but not those who had been there before. An instantaneous shiver ran down his back, and he shuddered. He recognised all those people instantly. That tall, stout old man in the overcoat and forage-cap with a cockade--was the police captain, Mihail Makarovitch. And that "consumptive-looking" trim dandy,"who always has such polished boots"--that was the deputy prosecutor. "He has a chronometer worth four hundred roubles; he showed it to me." And that small young man in spectacles...Mitya forgot his surname though he knew him, had seen him: he was the "investigating lawyer," from the "school of jurisprudence," who had only lately come to the town. And this man--the inspector of police, Mavriky Mavrikyevitch, a man he knew well. And those fellows with the brass plates on, why are they here? And those other two...peasants...And there at the door Kalganov with Trifon Borissovitch...

"Gentlemen! What's this for, gentlemen?" began Mitya, but suddenly, as though beside himself, not knowing what he was doing, he cried aloud, at the top of his voice:

"I un-der-stand!"

The young man in spectacles moved forward suddenly, and stepping up to Mitya, began with dignity, though hurriedly:

"We have to make...in brief, I beg you to come this way, this way to the sofa...It is absolutely imperative that you should give an explanation."

"The old man!" cried Mitya frantically. "The old man and his blood!...I understand."

And he sank, almost fell, on a chair close by, as though he had been mown down by a scythe.

"You understand? He understands it! Monster and parricide! Your father's blood cries out against you!" the old captain of police roared suddenly, stepping up to Mitya.

He was beside himself, crimson in the face and quivering all over.

"This is impossible!" cried the small young man. "Mihail Makarovitch, Mihail Makarovitch, this won't do!...I beg you'll allow me to speak. I should never have expected such behaviour from you..."

"This is delirium, gentlemen, raving delirium," cried the captain of police; "look at him: drunk, at this time of night, in the company of a disreputable woman, with the blood of his father on his hands...It's delirium!..." "I beg you most earnestly, dear Mihail Makarovitch, to restrain your feelings," the prosecutor said in a rapid whisper to the old police captain, "or I shall be forced to resort to--"

But the little lawyer did not allow him to finish. He turned to Mitya, and delivered himself in a loud, firm, dignified voice:

"Ex-Lieutenant Karamazov, it is my duty to inform you that you are charged with the murder of your father, Fyodor Pavlovitch Karamazov, perpetrated this night..."

He said something more, and the prosecutor, too, put in something, but though Mitya heard them he did not understand them. He stared at them all with wild eyes.

Book IX. The Preliminary Investigation
Chapter 1. The Beginning of Perhotin's Official Career

PYOTR ILYITCH PERHOTIN, whom we left knocking at the strong locked gates of the widow Morozov's house, ended, of course, by making himself heard. Fenya, who was still excited by the fright she had had two hours before, and too much "upset" to go to bed, was almost frightened into hysterics on hearing the furious knocking at the gate. Though she had herself seen him drive away, she fancied that it must be Dmitri Fyodorovitch knocking again, no one else could knock so savagely. She ran to the house-porter, who had already waked up and gone out to the gate, and began imploring him not to open it. But having questioned Pyotr Ilyitch, and learned that he wanted to see Fenya on very "important business," the man made up his mind at last to open. Pyotr Ilyitch was admitted into Fenya's kitchen, but the girl begged him to allow the houseporter to be present, "because of her misgivings." He began questioning her and at once learnt the most vital fact, that is, that when Dmitri Fyodorovitch had run out to look for Grushenka, he had snatched up a pestle from the mortar, and that when he returned, the pestle was not with him and his hands were smeared with blood.

"And the blood was simply flowing, dripping from him, dripping!" Fenya kept exclaiming. This horrible detail was simply the product of her disordered imagination. But although not "dripping," Pyotr Ilyitch had himself seen those hands stained with blood, and had helped to wash them. Moreover, the question he had to decide was, not how soon the blood had dried, but where Dmitri Fyodorovitch had run with the pestle, or rather, whether it really was to Fyodor Pavlovitch's, and how he could satisfactorily ascertain. Pyotr Ilyitch persisted in returning to this point, and though he found out nothing conclusive, yet he carried away a conviction that Dmitri Fyodorovitch could have gone nowhere but to his father's house, and that, therefore, something must have happened there.

"And when he came back," Fenya added with excitement. "I told him the whole story, and then I began asking him, 'Why have you got blood on your hands, Dmitri Fyodorovitch?' and he answered that that was human blood, and that he had just killed someone. He confessed it all to me, and suddenly ran off like a madman. I sat down and began thinking, where's he run off to now like a madman? He'll go to Mokroe, I thought, and kill my mistress there. I ran out to beg him not to kill her. I was running to his lodgings, but I looked at Plotnikov's shop, and saw him just setting off, and there was no blood on his hands then." (Fenya had noticed this and remembered it.) Fenya's old grandmother confirmed her evidence as far as she was capable. After asking some further questions, Pyotr Ilyitch left the house, even more upset and uneasy than he had been when he entered it.

The most direct and the easiest thing for him to do would have been to go straight to Fyodor Pavlovitch's, to find out whether anything had happened there, and if so, what; and only to go to the police captain, as Pyotr Ilyitch firmly intended doing, when he had satisfied himself of the fact. But the night was dark, Fyodor Pavlovitch's gates were strong, and he would have to knock again. His acquaintance with Fyodor Pavlovitch was of the slightest, and what if, after he had been knocking, they opened to him, and nothing had happened? Fyodor Pavlovitch in his jeering way would go telling the story all over the town, how a stranger, called Perhotin, had broken in upon him at midnight to ask if anyone had killed him. It would make a scandal. And scandal was what Pyotr Ilyitch dreaded more than anything in the world.

Yet the feeling that possessed him was so strong, that though he stamped his foot angrily and swore at himself, he set off again, not to Fyodor Pavlovitch's but to Madame Hohlakov's. He decided that if she denied having just given Dmitri Fyodorovitch three thousand roubles, he would go straight to the police captain, but if she admitted having given him the money, he would go home and let the matter rest till next morning.

It is, of course, perfectly evident that there was even more likelihood of causing scandal by going at eleven o'clock at night to a fashionable lady, a complete stranger, and perhaps rousing her from her bed to ask her an amazing question, than by going to Fyodor Pavlovitch. But that is just how it is, sometimes, especially in cases like the present one, with the decisions of the most precise and phlegmatic people. Pyotr Ilyitch was by no means phlegmatic at that moment. He remembered all his life how a haunting uneasiness gradually gained possession of him, growing more and more painful and driving him on, against his will. Yet he kept cursing himself, of course, all the way for going to this lady, but "I will get to the bottom of it, I will!" he repeated for the tenth time, grinding his teeth, and he carried out his intention.

It was exactly eleven o'clock when he entered Madame Hohlakov's house. He was admitted into the yard pretty quickly, but, in response to his inquiry whether the lady was still up, the porter could give no answer, except that she was usually in bed by that time.

"Ask at the top of the stairs. If the lady wants to receive you, she'll receive you. If she won't, she won't."

Pyotr Ilyitch went up, but did not find things so easy here. The footman was unwilling to take in his name, but finally called a maid. Pyotr Ilyitch politely but insistently begged her to inform her lady that an official, living in the town, called Perhotin, had called on particular business, and that if it were not of the greatest importance he would not have ventured to come. "Tell her in those words, in those words exactly," he asked the girl.

She went away. He remained waiting in the entry. Madame Hohlakov herself was already in her bedroom, though not yet asleep. She had felt upset ever since Mitya's visit, and had a presentiment that she would not get through the night without the sick headache which always, with her, followed such excitement. She was surprised on hearing the announcement from the maid. She irritably declined to see him, however, though the unexpected visit at such an hour, of an "official living in the town," who was a total stranger, roused her feminine curiosity intensely. But this time Pyotr Ilyitch was as obstinate as a mule. He begged the maid most earnestly to take another message in these very words:

"That he had come on business of the greatest importance, and that Madame Hohlakov might have cause to regret it later, if she refused to see him now."

"I plunged headlong," he described it afterwards.

The maid, gazing at him in amazement, went to take his message again. Madame Hohlakov was impressed. She thought a little, asked what he looked like, and learned that he was "very well dressed, young, and so polite." We may note, parenthetically, that Pyotr Ilyitch was a rather good-looking young man, and well aware of the fact. Madame Hohlakov made up her mind to see him. She was in her dressing-gown and slippers, but she flung a black shawl over her shoulders. "The official" was asked to walk into the drawing-room, the very room in which Mitya had been received shortly before. The lady came to meet her visitor, with a sternly inquiring countenance, and, without asking him to sit down, began at once with the question:

"What do you want?"

"I have ventured to disturb you, madam, on a matter concerning our common acquaintance, Dmitri Fyodorovitch Karamazov," Perhotin began.

But he had hardly uttered the name, when the lady's face showed signs of acute irritation. She almost shrieked, and interrupted him in a fury:

"How much longer am I to be worried by that awful man?" she cried hysterically. "How dare you, sir, how could you venture to disturb a lady who is a stranger to you, in her own house at such an hour!...And to force yourself upon her to talk of a man who came here, to this very drawing-room, only three hours ago, to murder me, and went stamping out of the room, as no one would go out of a decent house. Let me tell you, sir, that I shall lodge a complaint against you, that I will not let it pass. Kindly leave me at once...I am a mother...I...I-"

"Murder! then he tried to murder you, too?"

"Why, has he killed somebody else?" Madame Hohlakov asked impulsively.

"If you would kindly listen, madam, for half a moment, I'll explain it all in a couple of words," answered Perhotin, firmly. "At five o'clock this afternoon Dmitri Fyodorovitch borrowed ten roubles from me, and I know for a fact he had no money. Yet at nine o'clock, he came to see me with a bundle of hundred-rouble notes in his hand, about two or three thousand roubles. His hands and face were all covered with blood, and he looked like a madman. When I asked him where he had got so much money, he answered that he had just received it from you, that you had given him a sum of three thousand to go to the gold mines..."

Madame Hohlakov's face assumed an expression of intense and painful excitement.

"Good God! He must have killed his old father!" she cried, clasping her hands. "I have never given him money, never! Oh, run, run!...Don't say another word Save the old man...run to his father...run!"

"Excuse me, madam, then you did not give him money? You remember for a fact that you did not give him any money?"

"No, I didn't, I didn't! I refused to give it him, for he could not appreciate it. He ran out in a fury, stamping. He rushed at me, but I slipped away...And let me tell you, as I wish to hide nothing from you now, that he positively spat at me. Can you fancy that! But why are we standing? Ah, sit down."

"Excuse me, I..."

"Or better run, run, you must run and save the poor old man from an awful death!"

"But if he has killed him already?"

"Ah, good heavens, yes! Then what are we to do now? What do you think we must do now?"

Meantime she had made Pyotr Ilyitch sit down and sat down herself, facing him briefly, but fairly clearly, Pyotr Ilyitch told her the history of the affair, that part of it at least which he had himself witnessed. He described, too, his visit to Fenya, and told her about the pestle. All these details produced an overwhelming effect on the distracted lady, who kept uttering shrieks, and covering her face with her hands...

"Would you believe it, I foresaw all this! I have that special faculty, whatever I imagine comes to pass. And how often I've looked at that awful man and always thought, that man will end by murdering me. And now it's happened...that is, if he hasn't murdered me, but only his own father, it's only because the finger of God preserved me, and what's more, he was ashamed to murder me because, in this very place, I put the holy ikon from the relics of the holy martyr, Saint Varvara, on his neck...And to think how near I was to death at that minute I went close up to him and he stretched out his neck to me!...Do you know, Pyotr Ilyitch (I think you said your name was Pyotr Ilyitch), I don't believe in miracles, but that ikon and this unmistakable miracle with me now--that shakes me, and I'm ready to believe in anything you like. Have you heard about Father Zossima?...But I don't know what I'm saying...and only fancy, with the ikon on his neck he spat at me...He only spat, it's true, he didn't murder me and...he dashed away! But what shall we do, what must we do now? What do you think?"

Pyotr Ilyitch got up, and announced that he was going straight to the police captain, to tell him all about it, and leave him to do what he thought fit.

"Oh, he's an excellent man, excellent! Mihail Makarovitch, I know him. Of course, he's the person to go to. How practical you are, Pyotr Ilyitch! How well you've thought of everything! I should never have thought of it in your place!"

"Especially as I know the police captain very well, too," observed Pyotr Ilyitch, who still continued to stand, and was obviously anxious to escape as quickly as possible from the impulsive lady, who would not let him say good-bye and go away.

"And be sure, be sure," she prattled on, "to come back and tell me what you see there, and what you find out...what comes to light...how they'll try him...and what he's condemned to...Tell me, we have no capital punishment, have we? But be sure to come, even if it's at three o'clock at night, at four, at half-past four...Tell them to wake me, to wake me, to shake me, if I don't get up...But, good heavens, I shan't sleep! But wait, hadn't I better come with you?"

"N-no. But if you would write three lines with your own hand, stating that you did not give Dmitri Fyodorovitch money, it might, perhaps, be of use...in case it's needed..."

"To be sure!" Madame Hohlakov skipped, delighted, to her bureau. "And you know I'm simply struck, amazed at your resourcefulness, your good sense in such affairs. Are you in the service here? I'm delighted to think that you're in the service here!"

And still speaking, she scribbled on half a sheet of notepaper the following lines:

I've never in my life lent to that unhappy man, Dmitri Fyodorovitch Karamazov (for, in spite of all, he is unhappy), three thousand roubles to-day. I've never given him money, never: That I swear by all thats holy!

K. Hohlakov

"Here's the note!" she turned quickly to Pyotr Ilyitch. "Go, save him. It's a noble deed on your part!"

And she made the sign of the cross three times over him. She ran out to accompany him to the passage.

"How grateful I am to you! You can't think how grateful I am to you for having come to me, first. How is it I haven't met you before? I shall feel flattered at seeing you at my house in the future. How delightful it is that you are living here!...Such precision! Such practical ability!...They must appreciate you, they must understand you. If there's anything I can do, believe me...oh, I love young people! I'm in love with young people! The younger generation are the one prop of our suffering country. Her one hope...Oh, go, go!..."

But Pyotr Ilyitch had already run away or she would not have let him go so soon. Yet Madame Hohlakov had made a rather agreeable impression on him, which had somewhat softened his anxiety at being drawn into such an unpleasant affair. Tastes differ, as we all know. "She's by no means so elderly," he thought, feeling pleased, "on the contrary I should have taken her for her daughter."

As for Madame Hohlakov, she was simply enchanted by the young man. "Such sence such exactness! in so young a man! in our day! and all that with such manners and appearance! People say the young people of to-day are no good for anything, but here's an example!" etc. So she simply forgot this "dreadful affair," and it was only as she was getting into bed, that, suddenly recalling "how near death she had been," she exclaimed: "Ah, it is awful, awful!"

But she fell at once into a sound, sweet sleep.

I would not, however, have dwelt on such trivial and irrelevant details, if this eccentric meeting of the young official with the by no means elderly widow had not subsequently turned out to be the foundation of the whole career of that practical and precise young man. His story is remembered to this day with amazement in our town, and I shall perhaps have something to say about it, when I have finished my long history of the Brothers Karamazov.

Chapter 2. The Alarm

OUR police captain, Mihail Makarovitch Makarov, a retired lieutenant-colonel, was a widower and an excellent man. He had only come to us three years previously, but had won general esteem, chiefly because he "knew how to keep society together." He was never without visitors, and could not have got on without them. Someone or other was always dining with him; he never sat down to table without guests. He gave regular dinners, too, on all sorts of occasions, sometimes most surprising ones. Though the fare was not recherche, it was abundant. The fish-pies were excellent, and the wine made up in quantity for what it lacked in quality.

The first room his guests entered was a well fitted billiard-room, with pictures of English race horses, in black frames on the walls, an essential decoration, as we all know, for a bachelor's billiard-room. There was card playing every evening at his house, if only at one table. But at frequent intervals, all the society of our town, with the mammas and young ladies, assembled at his house to dance. Mihail Makarovitch was a widower, he did not live alone. His widowed daughter lived with him, with her two unmarried daughters, grown-up girls, who had finished their education. They were of agreeable appearance and lively character, and though everyone knew they would have no dowry, they attracted all the young men of fashion to their grandfather's house.

Mihail Makarovitch was by no means very efficient in his work, though he performed his duties no worse than many others. To speak plainly, he was a man of rather narrow education. His understanding of the limits of his administrative power could not always be relied upon. It was not so much that he failed to grasp certain reforms enacted during the present reign, as that he made conspicuous blunders in his interpretation of them. This was not from any special lack of intelligence, but from carelessness, for he was always in to great a hurry to go into the subject.

"I have the heart of a soldier rather than of a civilian," he used to say of himself. He had not even formed a definite idea of the fundamental principles of the reforms connected with the emancipation of the serfs, and only picked it up, so to speak, from year to year, involuntarily increasing his knowledge by practice. And yet he was himself a landowner. Pyotr Ilyitch knew for certain that he would meet some of Mihail Makarovitch's visitors there that evening, but he didn't know which. As it happened, at that moment the prosecutor, and Varvinsky, our district doctor, a young man, who had only just come to us from Petersburg after taking a brilliant degree at the Academy of Medicine, were playing whist at the police captain's. Ippolit Kirillovitch, the prosecutor (he was really the deputy prosecutor, but we always called him the prosecutor), was rather a peculiar man, of about five and thirty, inclined to be consumptive, and married to a fat and childless woman. He was vain and irritable, though he had a good intellect, and even a kind heart. It seemed that all that was wrong with him was that he had a better opinion of himself than his ability warranted. And that made him seem constantly uneasy. He had, moreover, certain higher, even artistic, leanings, towards psychology, for instance, a special study of the human heart, a special knowledge of the criminal and his crime. He cherished a grievance on this ground, considering that he had been passed over in the service, and being firmly persuaded that in higher spheres he had not been properly appreciated, and had enemies. In gloomy moments he even threatened to give up his post, and practise as a barrister in criminal cases. The unexpected Karamazov case agitated him profoundly: "It was a case that might well be talked about all over Russia." But I am anticipating.

Nikolay Parfenovitch Nelyudov, the young investigating lawyer, who had only come from Petersburg two months before, was sitting in the next room with the young ladies. People talked about it afterwards and wondered that all the gentlemen should, as though intentionally, on the evening of "the crime" have been gathered together at the house of the executive authority. Yet it was perfectly simple and happened quite naturally.

Ippolit Kirillovitch's wife had had toothache for the last two days, and he was obliged to go out to escape from her groans. The doctor, from the very nature of his being, could not spend an evening except at cards. Nikolay Parfenovitch Nelyudov had been intending for three days past to drop in that evening at Mihail Makarovitch's, so to speak casually, so as slyly to startle the eldest granddaughter, Olga Mihailovna, by showing that he knew her secret, that he knew it was her birthday, and that she was trying to conceal it on purpose, so as not to be obliged to give a dance. He anticipated a great deal of merriment, many playful jests about her age, and her being afraid to reveal it, about his knowing her secret and telling everybody, and so on. The charming young man was a great adept at such teasing; the ladies had christened him "the naughty man," and he seemed to be delighted at the name. He was extremely well-bred, however, of good family, education and feelings, and, though leading a life of pleasure, his sallies were always innocent and in good taste. He was short, and delicate-looking. On his white, slender, little fingers he always wore a number of big, glittering rings. When he was engaged in his official duties, he always became extraordinarily grave, as though realising his position and the sanctity of the obligations laid upon him. He had a special gift for mystifying murderers and other criminals of the peasant class during interrogation, and if he did not win their respect, he certainly succeeded in arousing their wonder.

Pyotr Ilyitch was simply dumbfounded when he went into the police captain's. He saw instantly that everyone knew. They had positively thrown down their cards, all were standing up and talking. Even Nikolay Parfenovitch had left the young ladies and run in, looking strenuous and ready for action. Pyotr Ilyitch was met with the astounding news that old Fyodor Pavlovitch really had been murdered that evening in his own house, murdered and robbed. The news had only just reached them in the following manner:

Marfa Ignatyevna, the wife of old Grigory, who had been knocked senseless near the fence, was sleeping soundly in her bed and might well have slept till morning after the draught she had taken. But, all of a sudden she waked up, no doubt roused by a fearful epileptic scream from Smerdyakov, who was lying in the next room unconscious. That scream always preceded his fits, and always terrified and upset Marfa Ignatyevna. She could never get accustomed to it. She jumped up and ran half-awake to Smerdyakov's room. But it was dark there, and she could only hear the invalid beginning to gasp and struggle. Then Marfa Ignatyevna herself screamed out and was going to call her husband, but suddenly realised that when she had got up, he was not beside her in bed. She ran back to the bedstead and began groping with her hands, but the bed was really empty. Then he must have gone out where? She ran to the steps and timidly called him. She got no answer, of course, but she caught the sound of groans far away in the garden in the darkness. She listened. The groans were repeated, and it was evident they came from the garden.

"Good Lord! just as it was with Lizaveta Smerdyashtchaya!" she thought distractedly. She went timidly down the steps and saw that the gate into the garden was open.

"He must be out there, poor dear," she thought. She went up to the gate and all at once she distinctly heard Grigory calling her by name, Marfa! Marfa!" in a weak, moaning, dreadful voice.

"Lord, preserve us from harm!" Marfa Ignatyevna murmured, and ran towards the voice, and that was how she found Grigory. But she found him not by the fence where he had been knocked down, but about twenty paces off. It appeared later, that he had crawled away on coming to himself, and probably had been a long time getting so far, losing consciousness several times. She noticed at once that he was covered with blood, and screamed at the top of her voice. Grigory was muttering incoherently:

"He has murdered...his father murdered...Why scream, silly... run...fetch someone..."

But Marfa continued screaming, and seeing that her master's window was open and that there was a candle alight in the window, she ran there and began calling Fyodor Pavlovitch. But peeping in at the window, she saw a fearful sight. Her master was lying on his back, motionless, on the floor. His light-coloured dressing-gown and white shirt were soaked with blood. The candle on the table brightly lighted up the blood and the motionless dead face of Fyodor Pavlovitch.

Terror-stricken, Marfa rushed away from the window, ran out of the garden, drew the bolt of the big gate and ran headlong by the back way to the neighbour, Marya Konndratyevna. Both mother and daughter were asleep, but they waked up at Marfa's desperate and persistent screaming and knocking at the shutter. Marfa, shrieking and screaming incoherently, managed to tell them the main fact, and to beg for assistance. It happened that Foma had come back from his wanderings and was staying the night with them. They got him up immediately and all three ran to the scene of the crime. On the way, Marya Kondratyevna remembered that at about eight o'clock she heard a dreadful scream from their garden, and this was no doubt Grigory's scream, "Parricide!" uttered when he caught hold of Mitya's leg.

"Some one person screamed out and then was silent," Marya Kondratyevna explained as she ran. Running to the place where Grigory lay, the two women with the help of Foma carried him to the lodge. They lighted a candle and saw that Smerdyakov was no better, that he was writhing in convulsions, his eyes fixed in a squint, and that foam was flowing from his lips. They moistened Grigory's forehead with water mixed with vinager, and the water revived him at once. He asked immediately:

"Is the master murdered?"

Then Foma and both the women ran to the house and saw this time that not only the window, but also the door into the garden was wide open, though Fyodor Pavlovitch had for the last week locked himself in every night and did not allow even Grigory to come in on any pretext. Seeing that door open, they were afraid to go in to Fyodor Pavlovitch "for fear anything should happen afterwards." And when they returned to Grigory, the old man told them to go straight to the police captain. Marya Kondratyevna ran there and gave the alarm to the whole party at the police captain's. She arrived only five minutes before Pyotr Ilyitch, so that his story came, not as his own surmise and theory, but as the direct conformation by a witness, of the theory held by all, as to the identity of the criminal (a theory he had in the bottom of his heart refused to believe till that moment).

214

It was resolved to act with energy. The deputy police inspector of the town was commissioned to take four witnesses, to enter Fyodor Pavlovitch's house and there to open an inquiry on the spot, according to the regular forms, which I will not go into here. The district doctor, a zealous man, new to his work, almost insisted on accompanying the police captain, the prosecutor, and the investigating lawyer.

I will note briefly that Fyodor Pavlovitch was found to be quite dead, with his skull battered in. But with what? Most likely with the same weapon with which Grigory had been attacked. And immediately that weapon was found, Grigory, to whom all possible medical assistance was at once given, described in a weak and breaking voice how he had been knocked down. They began looking with a lantern by the fence and found the brass pestle dropped in a most conspicuous place on the garden path. There were no signs of disturbance in the room where Fyodor Pavlovitch was lying. But by the bed, behind the screen, they picked up from the floor a big and thick envelope with the inscription: "A present of three thousand roubles for my angel Grushenka, if she is willing to come." And below had been added by Fyodor Pavlovitch, "For my little chicken." There were three seals of red sealing-wax on the envelope, but it had been torn open and was empty: the money had been removed. They found also on the floor a piece of narrow pink ribbon, with which the envelope had been tied up.

One piece of Pyotr Ilyitch's evidence made a great impression on the prosecutor and the investigating magistrate, namely, his idea that Dmitri Fyodorovitch would shoot himself before daybreak, that he had resolved to do so, had spoken of it to Ilyitch, had taken the pistols, loaded them before him, written a letter, put it in his pocket, etc. When Pyotr Ilyitch, though still unwilling to believe in it, threatened to tell someone so as to prevent the suicide, Mitya had answered grinning: "You'll be too late." So they must make haste to Mokroe to find the criminal, before he really did shoot himself.

"That's clear, that's clear!" repeated the prosecutor in great excitement. "That's just the way with mad fellows like that: 'I shall kill myself to-morrow, so I'll make merry till I die!'"

The story of how he had bought the wine and provisions excited the prosecutor more than ever.

"Do you remember the fellow that murdered a merchant called Olsufyev, gentlemen? He stole fifteen hundred, went at once to have his hair curled, and then, without even hiding the money, carrying it almost in his hand in the same way, he went off to the girls."

All were delayed, however, by the inquiry, the search, and the formalities, etc., in the house of Fyodor Pavlovitch. It all took time and so, two hours before starting, they sent on ahead to Mokroe the officer of the rural police, Mavriky Mavrikyevitch Schmertsov, who had arrived in the town the morning before to get his pay. He was instructed to avoid raising the alarm when he reached Mokroe, but to keep constant watch over the "criminal" till the arrival of the proper authorities, to procure also witnesses for the arrest, police constables, and so on. Mavriky Mavrikyevitch did as he was told, preserving his incognito, and giving no one but his old acquaintance, Trifon Borissovitch, the slightest hint of his secret business. He had spoken to him just before Mitya met the landlord in the balcony, looking for him in the dark, and noticed at once a change in Trifon Borissovitch's face and voice. So neither Mitya nor anyone else knew that he was being watched. The box with the pistols had been carried off by Trifon Borissovitch and put in a suitable place. Only after four o'clock, almost at sunrise, all the officials, the police captain, the prosecutor, the investigating lawyer, drove up in two carriages, each drawn by three horses. The doctor remained at Fyodor Pavlovitch's to make a post-mortem next day on the body. But he was particularly interested in the condition of the servant, Smerdyakov.

"Such violent and protracted epileptic fits, recurring continually for twenty-four hours, are rarely to be met with, and are of interest to science," he declared enthusiastically to his companions, and as they left they laughingly congratulated him on his find. The prosecutor and the investigating lawyer distinctly remembered the doctor's saying that Smerdyakov could not outlive the night.

After these long, but I think necessary explanations, we will return to that moment of our tale at which we broke off.

Chapter 3. The Sufferings of a Soul. The First Ordeal

And so Mitya sat looking wildly at the people round him, not understanding what was said to him. Suddenly he got up, flung up his hands, and shouted aloud:

"I'm not guilty! I'm not guilty of that blood! I'm not guilty of my father's blood...I meant to kill him. But I'm not guilty. Not I."

But he had hardly said this, before Grushenka rushed from behind the curtain and flung herself at the police captain's feet.

"It was my fault! Mine! My wickedness!" she cried, in a heart-rending voice, bathed in tears, stretching out her clasped hands towards them. "He did it through me. I tortured him and drove him to it. I tortured that poor old man that's dead, too, in my wickedness, and brought him to this! It's my fault, mine first, mine most, my fault!"

"Yes, it's your fault! You're the chief criminal! You fury! You harlot! You're the most to blame!" shouted the police captain, threatening her with his hand. But he was quickly and resolutely suppressed. The prosecutor positively seized hold of him.

"This is absolutely irregular, Mihail Makarovitch!" he cried. "You are positively hindering the inquiry...You're ruining the case." he almost gasped.

"Follow the regular course! Follow the regular course!" cried Nikolay Parfenovitch, fearfully excited too, "otherwise it's absolutely impossible!..."

"Judge us together!" Grushenka cried frantically, still kneeling. "Punish us together. I will go with him now, if it's to death!"

"Grusha, my life, my blood, my holy one!" Mitya fell on his knees beside her and held her tight in his arms. "Don't believe her," he cried, "she's not guilty of anything, of any blood, of anything!"

He remembered afterwards that he was forcibly dragged away from her by several men, and that she was led out, and that when he recovered himself he was sitting at the table. Beside him and behind him stood the men with metal plates. Facing him on the other side of the table sat Nikolay Parfenovitch, the investigating lawyer. He kept persuading him to drink a little water out of a glass that stood on the table.

"That will refresh you, that will calm you. Be calm, don't be frightened," he added, extremely politely. Mitya (he remembered it afterwards) became suddenly intensely interested in his big rings, one with an amethyst, and another with a transparent bright yellow stone, of great brilliance. And long afterwards he remembered with wonder how those rings had riveted his attention through all those terrible hours of interrogation, so that he was utterly unable to tear himself away from them and dismiss them, as things that had nothing to do with his position. On Mitya's left side, in the place where Maximov had been sitting at the beginning of the evening, the prosecutor was now seated, and on Mitya's right hand, where Grushenka had been, was a rosy-cheeked young man in a sort of shabby hunting-jacket, with ink and paper before him. This was the secretary of the investigating lawyer, who had brought him with him. The police captain was now standing by the window at the other end of the room, beside Kalganov, who was sitting there.

"Drink some water," said the investigating lawyer softly, for the tenth time.

"I have drunk it, gentlemen, I have...but come gentlemen, crush me, punish me, decide my fate!" cried Mitya, staring with terribly fixed wide-open eyes at the investigating lawyer.

"So you positively declare that you are not guilty of the death of your father, Fyodor Pavlovitch?" asked the investigating lawyer, softly but insistently.

"I am not guilty. I am guilty of the blood of another old man, but not of my father's. And I weep for it! I killed, I killed the old man and knocked him down...But it's hard to have to answer for that murder with another, a terrible murder of which I am not guilty...It's a terrible accusation, gentlemen, a knockdown blow. But who has killed my father, who has killed him? Who can have killed him if I didn't? It's marvellous, extraordinary, impossible."

"Yes, who can have killed him?" the investigating lawyer was beginning, but Ippolit Kirillovitch, the prosecutor, glancing at him, addressed Mitya.

"You need not worry yourself about the old servant, Grigory Vasilyevitch. He is alive, he has recovered, and in spite of the terrible blows inflicted, according to his own and your evidence, by you, there seems no doubt that he will live, so the doctor says, at least."

"Alive? He's alive?" cried Mitya, flinging up his hands. His face beamed. "Lord, I thank Thee for the miracle Thou has wrought for me, a sinner and evildoer. That's an answer to my prayer. I've been praying all night." And he crossed himself three times. He was almost breathless.

"So from this Grigory we have received such important evidence concerning you, that-" The prosecutor would have continued, but Mitya suddenly jumped up from his chair.

"One minute, gentlemen, for God's sake, one minute; I will run to her-"

"Excuse me, at this moment it's quite impossible," Nikolay Parfenovitch almost shrieked. He, too, leapt to his feet. Mitya was seized by the men with the metal plates, but he sat down of his own accord...

"Gentlemen, what a pity! I wanted to see her for one minute only; I wanted to tell her that it has been washed away, it has gone, that blood that was weighing on my heart all night, and that I am not a murderer now! Gentlemen, she is my betrothed!" he said ecstatically and reverently, looking round at them all. "Oh, thank you, gentlemen! Oh, in one minute you have given me new life, new heart!...That old man used to carry me in his arms, gentlemen. He used to wash me in the tub when I was a baby three years old, abandoned by everyone, he was like a father to me!..."

"And so you-" the investigating lawyer began.

"Allow me, gentlemen, allow me one minute more," interposed Mitya, putting his elbows on the table and covering his face with his hands. "Let me have a moment to think, let me breathe, gentlemen. All this is horribly upsetting, horribly. A man is not a drum, gentlemen!"

"Drink a little more water," murmured Nikolay Parfenovitch. Mitya took his hands from his face and laughed. His eyes were confident. He seemed completely transformed in a moment. His whole bearing was changed; he was once more the equal of these men, with all of whom he was acquainted, as though they had all met the day before, when nothing had happened, at some social gathering. We may note in passing that, on his first arrival, Mitya had been made very welcome at the police captain's, but later, during the last month especially, Mitya had hardly called at all, and when the police captain met him, in the street, for instance, Mitya noticed that he frowned and only bowed out of politeness. His acquaintance with the prosecutor was less intimate, though he sometimes paid his wife, a nervous and fanciful lady, visits of politeness, without quite knowing why, and she always received him graciously and had, for some reason, taken an interest in him up to the last. He had not had time to get to know the investigating lawyer, though he had met him and talked to him twice, each time about the fair sex.

"You're a most skilful lawyer, I see, Nikolay Parfenovitch," cried Mitya, laughing gaily, "but I can help you now. Oh, gentlemen, I feel like a new man, and don't be offended at my addressing you so simply and directly. I'm rather drunk, too, I'll tell you that frankly. I believe I've had the honour and pleasure of meeting you, Nikolay Parfenovitch, at my kinsman Miusov's. Gentlemen, gentlemen, I don't pretend to be on equal terms with you. I understand, of course, in what character I am sitting before you. Oh, of course, there's a horrible suspicion...hanging over me...if Grigory has given evidence...A horrible suspicion! It's awful, awful, I understand that! But to business, gentlemen, I am ready, and we will make an end of it in one moment; for, listen, listen, gentlemen! Since I know I'm innocent, we can put an end to it in a minute. Can't we? Can't we?"

Mitya spoke much and quickly, nervously and effusively, as though he positively took his listeners to be his best friends.

"So, for the present, we will write that you absolutely deny the charge brought against you," said Nikolay Parfenovitch, impressively, and bending down to the secretary he dictated to him in an undertone what to write.

"Write it down? You want to write that down? Well, write it; I consent, I give my full consent, gentlemen, only...do you see?... Stay, stay, write this. Of disorderly conduct I am guilty, of violence on a poor old man I am guilty. And there is something else at the bottom of my heart, of which I am guilty, too but that you need not write down" (he turned suddenly to the secretary); "that's my personal life, gentlemen, that doesn't concern you, the bottom of my heart, that's to say...But of the murder of my old father I'm not guilty. That's a wild idea. It's quite a wild idea!...I will prove you that and you'll be convinced directly...You will laugh, gentlemen. You'll laugh yourselves at your suspicion!..."

"Be calm, Dmitri Fyodorovitch," said the investigating lawyer evidently trying to allay Mitya's excitement by his own composure. "Before we go on with our inquiry, I should like, if you will consent to answer, to hear you confirm the statement that you disliked your father, Fyodor Pavlovitch, that you were involved in continual disputes with him. Here at least, a quarter of an hour ago, you exclaimed that you wanted to kill him: 'I didn't kill him,' you said,'but I wanted to kill him.'"

"Did I exclaim that? Ach, that may be so, gentlemen! Yes, unhappily, I did want to kill him...many times I wanted to... unhappily, unhappily!"

"You wanted to. Would you consent to explain what motives precisely led you to such a sentiment of hatred for your parent?"

"What is there to explain, gentlemen?" Mitya shrugged his shoulders sullenly, looking down. "I have never concealed my feelings. All the town knows about it--everyone knows in the tavern. Only lately I declared them in Father Zossima's cell. And the very same day, in the evening I beat my father. I nearly killed him, and I swore I'd come again and kill him, before witnesses...Oh, a thousand witnesses! I've been shouting it aloud for the last month, anyone can tell you that!...The fact stares you in the face, it speaks for itself, it cries aloud, but feelings, gentlemen, feelings are another matter. You see, gentlemen"--Mitya frowned--"it seemed to me that about feelings you've no right to question me. I know that you are bound by your office, I quite understand that, but that's my affair, my private, intimate affair, yet...since I haven't concealed my feelings in the past...in the tavern, for instance, I've talked to everyone, so...so I won't make a secret of it now. You see, I understand, gentlemen, that there are terrible facts against me in this business. I told everyone that I'd kill him, and now, all of a sudden, he's been killed. So it must have been me! Ha ha! I can make allowances for you, gentlemen, I can quite make allowances. I'm struck all of a heap myself, for who can have murdered him, if not I? That's what it comes to, isn't it? If not I, who can it be, who? Gentlemen, I want to know, I insist on knowing!" he exclaimed suddenly. "Where was he murdered? How was he murdered? How, and with what? Tell me," he asked quickly, looking at the two lawyers.

"We found him in his study, lying on his back on the floor, with his head battered in," said the prosecutor.

"That's horrible!" Mitya shuddered and, putting his elbows on the table, hid his face in his right hand.

"We will continue," interposed Nikolay Parfenovitch. "So what was it that impelled you to this sentiment of hatred? You have asserted in public, I believe, that it was based upon jealousy?"

"Well, yes, jealousy. not only jealousy."

"Disputes about money?"

"Yes, about money, too."

"There was a dispute about three thousand roubles, I think, which you claimed as part of your inheritance?"

"Three thousand! More, more," cried Mitya hotly; "more than six thousand, more than ten, perhaps. I told everyone so, shouted it at them. But I made up my mind to let it go at three thousand. I was desperately in need of that three thousand...so the bundle of notes for three thousand that I knew he kept under his pillow, ready for Grushenka, I considered as simply stolen from me. Yes, gentlemen, I looked upon it as mine, as my own property..."

The prosecutor looked significantly at the investigating lawyer, and had time to wink at him on the sly.

"We will return to that subject later," said the lawyer promptly. "You will allow us to note that point and write it down; that you looked upon that money as your own property?"

"Write it down, by all means. I know that's another fact that tells against me, but I'm not afraid of facts and I tell them against myself. Do you hear? Do you know, gentlemen, you take me for a different sort of man from what I am," he added, suddenly gloomy and dejected. "You have to deal with a man of honour, a man of the highest honour; above all don't lose sight of it--a man who's done a lot of nasty things, but has always been, and still is, honourable at bottom, in his inner being. I don't know how to express it. That's just what's made me wretched all my life, that I yearned to be honourable, that I was, so to say, a martyr to a sense of honour, seeking for it with a lantern, with the lantern of Diogenes, and yet all my life I've been doing filthy things like all of us, gentlemen...that is like me alone. That was a mistake, like me alone, me alone!...Gentlemen, my head aches..." His brows contracted with pain. "You see, gentlemen, I couldn't bear the look of him, there was something in him ignoble, impudent, trampling on everything sacred, something sneering and irreverent, loathsome, loathsome. But now that he's dead, I feel differently."

"How do you mean?"

"I don't feel differently, but I wish I hadn't hated him so."

"You feel penitent?"

"No, not penitent, don't write that. I'm not much good myself; I'm not very beautiful, so I had no right to consider him repulsive. That's what I mean. Write that down, if you like."

Saying this Mitya became very mournful. He had grown more and more gloomy as the inquiry continued.

At that moment another unexpected scene followed. Though Grushenka had been removed, she had not been taken far away, only into the room next but one from the blue room, in which the examination was proceeding. It was a little room with one window, next beyond the large room in which they had danced and feasted so lavishly. She was sitting there with no one by her but Maximov, who was terribly depressed, terribly scared, and clung to her side, as though for security. At their door stood one of the peasants with a metal plate on his breast. Grushenka was crying, and suddenly her grief was too much for her, she jumped up, flung up her arms and, with a loud wail of sorrow, rushed out of the room to him, to her Mitya, and so unexpectedly that they had not time to stop her. Mitya, hearing her cry, trembled, jumped up, and with a yell rushed impetuously to meet her, not knowing what he was doing. But they were not allowed to come together, though they saw one another. He was seized by the arms. He struggled, and tried to tear himself away. It took three or four men to hold him. She was seized too, and he saw her stretching out her arms to him, crying aloud as they carried her away. When the scene was over, he came to himself again, sitting in the same place as before, opposite the investigating lawyer, and crying out to them:

"What do you want with her? Why do you torment her? She's done nothing, nothing!

The lawyers tried to soothe him. About ten minutes passed like this. At last Mihail Makarovitch, who had been absent, came hurriedly into the room, and said in a loud and excited voice to the prosecutor:

"She's been removed, she's downstairs. Will you allow me to say one word to this unhappy man, gentlemen? In your presence, gentlemen, in your presence."

"By all means, Mihail Makarovitch," answered the investigating lawyer. "In the present case we have nothing against it."

"Listen, Dmitri Fyodorovitch, my dear fellow," began the police captain, and there was a look of warm, almost fatherly, feeling for the luckless prisoner on his excited face. "I took your Agrafena Alexandrovna downstairs myself, and confided her to the care of the landlord's daughters, and that old fellow Maximov is with her all the time. And I soothed her, do you hear? I soothed and calmed her. I impressed on her that you have to clear yourself, so she mustn't hinder you, must not depress you, or you may lose your head and say the wrong thing in your evidence. In fact, I talked to her and she understood. She's a sensible girl, my boy, a good-hearted girl, she would have kissed my old hands, begging help for you. She sent me herself, to tell you not to worry about her. And I must go, my dear fellow, I must go and tell her that you are calm and comforted about her. And so you must be calm, do you understand? I was unfair to her; she is a Christian soul, gentlemen, yes, I tell you, she's a gentle soul, and not to blame for anything. So what am I to tell her, Dmitri Fyodorovitch? Will you sit quiet or not?"

The good-natured police captain said a great deal that was irregular, but Grushenka's suffering, a fellow creature's suffering, touched his good-natured heart, and tears stood in his eyes. Mitya jumped up and rushed towards him.

"Forgive me, gentlemen, oh, allow me, allow me!" he cried. "You've the heart of an angel, an angel, Mihail Makarovitch, I thank you for her. I will, I will be calm, cheerful, in fact. Tell her, in the kindness of your heart, that I am cheerful, quite cheerful, that I shall be laughing in a minute, knowing that she has a guardian angel like you. I shall have done with all this directly, and as soon as I'm free, I'll be with her, she'll see, let her wait. Gentlemen," he said, turning to the two lawyers, now I'll open my whole soul to you; I'll pour out everything. We'll finish this off directly, finish it off gaily. We shall laugh at it in the end, shan't we? But gentlemen, that woman is the queen of my heart. Oh, let me tell you that. That one thing I'll tell you now...I see I'm with honourable men. She is my light, she is my holy one, and if only you knew! Did you hear her cry, 'I'll go to death with you'? And what have I, a penniless beggar, done for her? Why such love for me? How can a clumsy, ugly brute like me, with my ugly face, deserve such love, that she is ready to go to exile with me? And how she fell down at your feet for my sake, just now!...and yet she's proud and has done nothing! How can I help adoring her, how can I help crying out and rushing to her as I did just now? Gentlemen, forgive me! But now, now I am comforted."

And he sank back in his chair and, covering his face with his hands, burst into tears. But they were happy tears. He recovered himself instantly. The old police captain seemed much pleased, and the lawyers also. They felt that the examination was passing into a new phase. When the police captain went out, Mitya was positively gay.

"Now, gentlemen, I am at your disposal, entirely at your disposal. And if it were not for all these trivial details, we should understand one another in a minute. I'm at those details again. I'm at your disposal, gentlemen, but I declare that we must have mutual confidence, you in me and I in you, or there'll be no end to it. I speak in your interests. To business, gentlemen, to business, and don't rummage in my soul; don't tease me with trifles, but only ask me about facts and what matters, and I will satisfy you at once. And damn the details!"

So spoke Mitya. The interrogation began again.

Chapter 4. The Second Ordeal

"YOU don't know how you encourage us, Dmitri Fyodorovitch, by your readiness to answer," said Nikolay Parfenovitch, with an animated air, and obvious satisfaction beaming in his very prominent, short-sighted, light grey eyes, from which he had removed his spectacles a moment before. "And you have made a very just remark about the mutual confidence, without which it is sometimes positively impossible to get on in cases of such importance, if the suspected party really hopes and desires to defend himself and is in a position to do so. We on our side, will do everything in our power, and you can see for yourself how we are conducting the case. You approve, Ippolit Kirillovitch?" He turned to the prosecutor.

"Oh, undoubtedly," replied the prosecutor. His tone was somewhat cold, compared with Nikolay Parfenovitch's impulsiveness.

I will note once for all that Nikolay Parfenovitch, who had but lately arrived among us, had from the first felt marked respect for Ippolit Kirillovitch, our prosecutor, and had become almost his bosom friend. He was almost the only person who put implicit faith in Ippolit Kirillovitch's extraordinary talents as a psychologist and orator and in the justice of his grievance. He had heard of him in Petersburg. On the other hand, young Nikolay Parfenovitch was the only person in the whole world whom our "unappreciated" prosecutor genuinely liked. On their way to Mokroe they had time to come to an understanding about the present case. And now as they sat at the table, the sharp-witted junior caught and interpreted every indication on his senior colleague's face--half a word, a glance, or a wink.

"Gentlemen, only let me tell my own story and don't interrupt me with trivial questions and I'll tell you everything in a moment," said Mitya excitedly.

"Excellent! Thank you. But before we proceed to listen to your communication, will you allow me to inquire as to another little fact of great interest to us? I mean the ten roubles you borrowed yesterday at about five o'clock on the security of your pistols, from your friend, Pyotr Ilyitch Perhotin."

"I pledged them, gentlemen. I pledged them for ten roubles. What more? That's all about it. As soon as I got back to town I pledged them."

"You got back to town? Then you had been out of town?"

"Yes, I went a journey of forty versts into the country. Didn't you know?"

The prosecutor and Nikolay Parfenovitch exchanged glances.

"Well, how would it be if you began your story with a systematic description of all you did yesterday, from the morning onwards? Allow us, for instance, to inquire why you were absent from the town, and just when you left and when you came back--all those facts."

"You should have asked me like that from the beginning," cried Mitya, laughing aloud, "and, if you like, we won't begin from yesterday, but from the morning of the day before; then you'll understand how, why, and where I went. I went the day before yesterday, gentlemen, to a merchant of the town, called Samsonov, to borrow three thousand roubles from him on safe security. It was a pressing matter, gentlemen, it was a sudden necessity."

"Allow me to interrupt you," the prosecutor put in politely. "Why were you in such pressing need for just that sum, three thousand?"

"Oh, gentlemen, you needn't go into details, how, when and why, and why just so much money, and not so much, and all that rigmarole. Why, it'll run to three volumes, and then you'll want an epilogue!" Mitya said all this with the good-natured but impatient familiarity of a man who is anxious to tell the whole truth and is full of the best intentions.

"Gentlemen!"--he corrected himself hurriedly--"don't be vexed with me for my restiveness, I beg you again. Believe me once more, I feel the greatest respect for you and understand the true position of affairs. Don't think I'm drunk. I'm quite sober now. And, besides, being drunk would be no hindrance. It's with me, you know, like the saying: 'When he is sober, he is a fool; when he is drunk, he is a wise man.' Ha ha! But I see, gentlemen, it's not the proper thing to make jokes to you, till we've had our explanation, I mean. And I've my own dignity to keep up, too. I quite understand the difference for the moment. I am, after all, in the position of a criminal, and so, far from being on equal terms with you. And it's your business to watch me. I can't expect you to pat me on the head for what I did to Grigory, for one can't break old men's heads with impunity. I suppose you'll put me away for him for six months, or a year perhaps, in a house of correction. I don't know what the punishment is-- but it will be without loss of the rights of my rank, without loss of my rank, won't it? So you see, gentlemen, I understand the distinction between us...But you must see that you could puzzle God Himself with such questions. 'How did you step? Where did you step? When did you step? And on what did you step?' I shall get mixed up, if you go on like this, and you will put it all down against me. And what will that lead to? To nothing! And even if it's nonsense I'm talking now, let me finish, and you, gentlemen, being men of honour and refinement, will forgive me! I'll finish by asking you, gentlemen, to drop that conventional method of questioning. I mean, beginning from some miserable trifle, how I got up, what I had for breakfast, how I spat, and where I spat, and so distracting the attention of the criminal, suddenly stun him with an overwhelming question, 'Whom did you murder? Whom did you rob?' Ha-ha! That's your regulation method, that's where all your cunning comes in. You can put peasants off their guard like that, but not me. I know the tricks. I've been in the service, too. Ha ha ha! You're not angry, gentlemen? You forgive my impertinence?" he cried, looking at them with a good-nature that was almost surprising. "It's only Mitya Karamazov, you know, so you can overlook it. It would be inexcusable in a sensible man; but you can forgive it in Mitya. Ha ha!"

Nikolay Parfenovitch listened, and laughed too. Though the prosecutor did not laugh, he kept his eyes fixed keenly on Mitya, as though anxious not to miss the least syllable, the slightest movement, the smallest twitch of any feature of his face.

"That's how we have treated you from the beginning," said Nikolay Parfenovitch, still laughing. "We haven't tried to put you out by asking how you got up in the morning and what you had for breakfast. We began, indeed, with questions of the greatest importance."

"I understand. I saw it and appreciated it, and I appreciate still more your present kindness to me, an unprecedented kindness, worthy of your noble hearts. We three here are gentlemen and let everything be on the footing of mutual confidence between educated, well-bred people, who have the common bond of noble birth and honour. In any case, allow me to look upon you as my best friends at this moment of my life, at this moment when my honour is assailed. That's no offence to you, gentlemen, is it?"

On the contrary. You've expressed all that so well, Dmitri Fyodorovitch," Nikolay Parfenovitch answered with dignified approbation.

"And enough of those trivial questions, gentlemen, all those tricky questions! cried Mitya enthusiastically. "Or there's simply no knowing where we shall get to! Is there?"

"I will follow your sensible advice entirely," the prosecutor interposed, addressing Mitya. "I don't withdraw my question, however. It is now vitally important for us to know exactly why you needed that sum, I mean precisely three thousand."

"Why I needed it?...Oh, for one thing and another...Well, it was to pay a debt."

"A debt to whom?"

"That I absolutely refuse to answer, gentlemen. Not because I couldn't, or because I shouldn't dare, or because it would be damaging, for it's all a paltry matter and absolutely trifling, but--I won't, because it's a matter of principle: that's my private life, and I won't allow any intrusion into my private life. That's my principle. Your question has no bearing on the case, and whatever has nothing to do with the case is my private affair. I wanted to pay a debt. I wanted to pay a debt of honour but to whom I won't say."

"Allow me to make a note of that," said the prosecutor.

"By all means. Write down that I won't say, that I won't. Write that I should think it dishonourable to say. Ech! you can write it; you've nothing else to do with your time."

"Allow me to caution you, sir, and to remind you once more, if you are unaware of it," the prosecutor began, with a peculiar and stern impressiveness, "that you have a perfect right not to answer the questions put to you now, and we on our side have no right to extort an answer from you, if you decline to give it for one reason or another. That is entirely a matter for your personal decision. But it is our duty, on the other hand, in such cases as the present, to explain and set before you the degree of injury you will be doing yourself by refusing to give this or that piece of evidence. After which I will beg you to continue."

"Gentlemen, I'm not angry...I..."Mitya muttered in a rather disconcerted tone. "Well, gentlemen, you see, that Samsonov to whom I went then..."

We will, of course, not reproduce his account of what is known to the reader already. Mitya was impatiently anxious not to omit the slightest detail. At the same time he was in a hurry to get it over. But as he gave his evidence it was written down, and therefore they had continually to pull him up. Mitya disliked this, but submitted; got angry, though still good-humouredly. He did, it is true, exclaim, from time to time, "Gentlemen, that's enough to make an angel out of patience!" Or, "Gentlemen, it's no good your irritating me."

But even though he exclaimed he still preserved for a time his genially expansive mood. So he told them how Samsonov had made a fool of him two days before. (He had completely realised by now that he had been fooled.) The sale of his watch for six roubles to obtain money for the journey was something new to the lawyers. They were at once greatly interested, and even, to Mitya's intense indignation, thought it necessary to write the fact down as a secondary confirmation of the circumstance that he had hardly a farthing in his pocket at the time. Little by little Mitya began to grow surly. Then, after describing his journey to see Lyagavy, the night spent in the stifling hut, and so on, he came to his return to the town. Here he began, without being particularly urged, to give a minute account of the agonies of jealousy he endured on Grushenka's account.

He was heard with silent attention. They inquired particularly into the circumstance of his having a place of ambush in Marya Kondratyevna's house at the back of Fyodor Pavlovitch's garden to keep watch on Grushenka, and of Smerdyakov's bringing him information. They laid particular stress on this, and noted it down. Of his jealousy he spoke warmly and at length, and though inwardly ashamed at exposing his most intimate feelings to "public ignominy," so to speak, he evidently overcame his shame in order to tell the truth. The frigid severity with which the investigating lawyer, and still more the prosecutor, stared intently at him as he told his story, disconcerted him at last considerably.

"That boy, Nikolay Parfenovitch, to whom I was talking nonsense about women only a few days ago, and that sickly prosecutor are not worth my telling this to," he reflected mournfully. "It's ignominious. 'Be patient, humble, hold thy peace.'" He wound up his reflections with that line. But he pulled himself together to go on again. When he came to telling of his visit to Madame Hohlakov, he regained his spirits and even wished to tell a little anecdote of that lady which had nothing to do with the case. But the investigating lawyer stopped him, and civilly suggested that he should pass on to "more essential matters." At last, when he described his despair and told them how, when he left Madame Hohlakov's, he thought that he'd "get three thousand if he had to murder someone to do it," they stopped him again and noted down that he had "meant to murder someone." Mitya let them write it without protest. At last he reached the point in his story when he learned that Grushenka had deceived him and had returned from Samsonov's as soon as he left her there, though she had said that she would stay there till midnight.

"If I didn't kill Fenya then, gentlemen, it was only because I hadn't time," broke from him suddenly at that point in his story. That, too, was carefully written down. Mitya waited gloomily, and was beginning to tell how he ran into his father's garden when the investigating lawyer suddenly stopped him, and opening the big portfolio that lay on the sofa beside him he brought out the brass pestle.

"Do you recognise this object?" he asked, showing it to Mitya.

"Oh, yes," he laughed gloomily. "Of course, I recognise it. Let me have a look at it...Damn it, never mind!"

"You have forgotten to mention it," observed the investigating lawyer.

"Hang it all, I shouldn't have concealed it from you. Do you suppose I could have managed without it? It simply escaped my memory."

"Be so good as to tell us precisely how you came to arm yourself with it."

"Certainly I will be so good, gentlemen."

And Mitya described how he took the pestle and ran.

"But what object had you in view in arming yourself with such a weapon?"

"What object? No object. I just picked it up and ran off."

"What for, if you had no object?"

Mitya's wrath flared up. He looked intently at "the boy" and smiled gloomily and malignantly. He was feeling more and more ashamed at having told "such people" the story of his jealousy so sincerely and spontaneously.

"Bother the pestle!" broke from him suddenly.

"But still-"

"Oh, to keep off dogs...Oh, because it was dark...In case anything turned up."

"But have you ever on previous occasions taken a weapon with you when you went out, since you're afraid of the dark?"

"Ugh! damn it all, gentlemen! There's positively no talking to you!" cried Mitya, exasperated beyond endurance, and turning to the secretary, crimson with anger, he said quickly, with a note of fury in his voice:

"Write down at once...at once...'that I snatched up the pestle to go and kill my father...Fyodor Pavlovitch...by hitting him on the head with it!' Well, now are you satisfied, gentlemen? Are your minds relieved?" he said, glaring defiantly at the lawyers.

"We quite understand that you made that statement just now through exasperation with us and the questions we put to you, which you consider trivial, though they are, in fact, essential," the prosecutor remarked drily in reply.

"Well, upon my word, gentlemen! Yes, I took the pestle...What does one pick things up for at such moments? I don't know what for. I snatched it up and ran--that's all. For to me, gentlemen, passons, or I declare I won't tell you any more."

He sat with his elbows on the table and his head in his hand. He sat sideways to them and gazed at the wall, struggling against a feeling of nausea. He had, in fact, an awful inclination to get up and declare that he wouldn't say another word, "not if you hang me for it."

"You see, gentlemen," he said at last, with difficulty controlling himself, "you see. I listen to you and am haunted by a dream...It's a dream I have sometimes, you know...I often dream it--it's always the same...that someone is hunting me, someone I'm awfully afraid of...that he's hunting me in the dark, in the night...tracking me, and I hide somewhere from him, behind a door or cupboard, hide in a degrading way, and the worst of it is, he always knows where I am, but he pretends not to know where I am on purpose, to prolong my agony, to enjoy my terror...That's just what you're doing now. It's just like that!"

"Is that the sort of thing you dream about?" inquired the prosecutor.

"Yes, it is. Don't you want to write it down?" said Mitya, with a distorted smile.

"No; no need to write it down. But still you do have curious dreams."

"It's not a question of dreams now, gentlemen--this is realism, this is real life! I'm a wolf and you're the hunters. Well, hunt him down!"

"You are wrong to make such comparisons." began Nikolay Parfenovitch, with extraordinary softness.

"No, I'm not wrong, at all!" Mitya flared up again, though his outburst of wrath had obviously relieved his heart. He grew more good humoured at every word. "You may not trust a criminal or a man on trial tortured by your questions, but an honourable man, the honourable impulses of the heart (I say that boldly!)--no! That you must believe you have no right indeed...but--

Be   silent,   heart,
Be patient, humble, hold thy peace.

Well, shall I go on?" he broke off gloomily.

"If you'll be so kind," answered Nikolay Parfenovitch.

THOUGH Mitya spoke sullenly, it was evident that he was trying more than ever not to forget or miss a single detail of his story. He told them how he had leapt over the fence into his father's garden; how he had gone up to the window; told them all that had passed under the window. Clearly, precisely, distinctly, he described the feelings that troubled him during those moments in the garden when he longed so terribly to know whether Grushenka was with his father or not. But, strange to say, both the lawyers listened now with a sort of awful reserve, looked coldly at him, asked few questions. Mitya could gather nothing from their faces.

"They're angry and offended," he thought. "Well, bother them!"

When he described how he made up his mind at last to make the "signal" to his father that Grushenka had come, so that he should open the window, the lawyers paid no attention to the word "signal," as though they entirely failed to grasp the meaning of the word in this connection: so much so, that Mitya noticed it. Coming at last to the moment when, seeing his father peering out of the window, his hatred flared up and he pulled the pestle out of his pocket, he suddenly, as though of design, stopped short. He sat gazing at the wall and was aware that their eyes were fixed upon him.

"Well?" said the investigating lawyer. "You pulled out the weapon and...and what happened then?"

"Then? Why, then I murdered him...hit him on the head and cracked his skull...I suppose that's your story. That's it!"

His eyes suddenly flashed. All his smothered wrath suddenly flamed up with extraordinary violence in his soul.

"Our story?" repeated Nikolay Parfenovitch.

Mitya dropped his eyes and was a long time silent.

"My story, gentlemen? Well, was like this," he began softly. "Whether it was like this," he began softly. "Whether it was someone's tears, or my mother prayed to God, or a good angel kissed me at that instant, I don't know. But the devil was conquered. I rushed from the window and ran to the fence. My father was alarmed and, for the first time, he saw me then, cried out, and sprang back from the window. I remember that very well. I ran across the garden to the fence...and there Grigory caught me, when I was sitting on the fence."

At that point he raised his eyes at last and looked at his listeners. They seemed to be staring at him with perfectly unruffled attention. A sort of paroxysm of indignation seized on Mitya's soul.

"Why, you're laughing at me at this moment, gentlemen!" he broke off suddenly.

"What makes you think that?" observed Nikolay Parfenovitch.

"You don't believe one word--that's why! I understand, of course, that I have come to the vital point. The old man's lying there now with his skull broken, while I--after dramatically describing how I wanted to kill him, and how I snatched up the pestle--I suddenly run away from the window. A romance! Poetry! As though one could believe a fellow on his word. Ha ha! You are scoffers, gentlemen!"

And he swung round on his chair so that it creaked.

"And did you notice," asked the prosecutor suddenly, as though not observing Mitya's excitement, "did you notice when you ran away from the window, whether the door into the garden was open?"

"No, it was not open."

"It was not?"

"It was shut. And who could open it? Bah! the door. Wait a bit!" he seemed suddenly to bethink himself, and almost with a start:

"Why, did you find the door open?"

"Yes, it was open."

"Why, who could have opened it if you did not open it yourselves?" cried Mitya, greatly astonished.

"The door stood open, and your father's murderer undoubtedly went in at that door, and, having accomplished the crime, went out again by the same door," the prosecutor pronounced deliberately, as though chiselling out each word separately. "That is perfectly clear. The murder was committed in the room and not through the window; that is absolutely certain from the examination that has been made, from the position of the body and everything. There can be no doubt of that circumstance."

Mitya was absolutely dumbfounded.

"But that's utterly impossible!" he cried, completely at a loss. "I...I didn't go in...I tell you positively, definitely, the door was shut the whole time I was in the garden, and when I ran out of the garden. I only stood at the window and saw him through the window. That's all, that's all...I remember to the last minute. And if I didn't remember, it would be just the same. I know it, for no one knew the signals except Smerdyakov, and me, and the dead man. And he wouldn't have opened the door to anyone in the world without the signals."

"Signals? What signals?" asked the prosecutor, with greedy, almost hysterical, curiosity. He instantly lost all trace of his reserve and dignity. He asked the question with a sort of cringing timidity. He scented an important fact of which he had known nothing, and was already filled with dread that Mitya might be unwilling to disclose it.

"So you didn't know!" Mitya winked at him with a malicious and mocking smile. "What if I won't tell you? From whom could you find out? No one knew about the signals except my father, Smerdyakov, and me: that was all. Heaven knew, too, but it won't tell you. But it's an interesting fact. There's no knowing what you might build on it. Ha ha! Take comfort, gentlemen, I'll reveal it. You've some foolish idea in your hearts. You don't know the man you have to deal with! You have to do with a prisoner who gives evidence against himself, to his own damage! Yes, for I'm a man of honour and you--are not."

The prosecutor swallowed this without a murmur. He was trembling with impatience to hear the new fact. Minutely and diffusely Mitya told them everything about the signals invented by Fyodor Pavlovitch for Smerdyakov. He told them exactly what every tap on the window meant, tapped the signals on the table, and when Nikolay Parfenovitch said that he supposed he, Mitya, had tapped the signal "Grushenka has come," when he tapped to his father, he answered precisely that he had tapped that signal, that "Grushenka had come."

"So now you can build up your tower," Mitya broke off, and again turned away from them contemptuously.

"So no one knew of the signals but your dead father, you, and the valet Smerdyakov? And no one else?" Nikolay Parfenovitch inquired once more.

"Yes. The valet Smerdyakov, and Heaven. Write down about Heaven. That may be of use. Besides, you will need God yourselves."

And they had already of course, begun writing it down. But while they wrote, the prosecutor said suddenly, as though pitching on a new idea:

"But if Smerdyakov also knew of these signals and you absolutely deny all responsibility for the death of your father, was it not he, perhaps, who knocked the signal agreed upon, induced your father to open to him, and then...committed the crime?"

Mitya turned upon him a look of profound irony and intense hatred. His silent stare lasted so long that it made the prosecutor blink.

"You've caught the fox again," commented Mitya at last; "you've got the beast by the tail. Ha ha! I see through you, Mr. Prosecutor. You thought, of course, that I should jump at that, catch at your prompting, and shout with all my might, 'Aie! it's Smerdyakov; he's the murderer.' Confess that's what you thought. Confess, and I'll go on."

But the prosecutor did not confess. He held his tongue and waited.

"You're mistaken. I'm not going to shout, 'It's Smerdyakov,'" said Mitya.

"And you don't even suspect him?"

"Why, do you suspect him?"

"He is suspected, too."

Mitya fixed his eyes on the floor.

"Joking apart," he brought out gloomily. "Listen. From the very beginning, almost from the moment when I ran out to you from behind the curtain, I've had the thought of Smerdyakov in my mind. I've been sitting here, shouting that I'm innocent and thinking all the time 'Smerdyakov!' I can't get Smerdyakov out of my head. In fact, I, too, thought of Smerdyakov just now; but only for a second. Almost at once I thought, 'No, it's not Smerdyakov.' It's not his doing, gentlemen."

"In that case is there anybody else you suspect?" Nikolay Parfenovitch inquired cautiously.

"I don't know anyone it could be, whether it's the hand of Heaven or of Satan, but...not Smerdyakov," Mitya jerked out with decision.

"But what makes you affirm so confidently and emphatically that it's not he?"

"From my conviction--my impression. Because Smerdyakov is a man of the most abject character and a coward. He's not a coward, he's the epitome of all the cowardice in the world walking on two legs. He has the heart of a chicken. When he talked to me, he was always trembling for fear I should kill him, though I never raised my hand against him. He fell at my feet and blubbered; he has kissed these very boots, literally, beseeching me 'not to frighten him.' Do you hear? 'Not to frighten him.' What a thing to say! Why, I offered him money. He's a puling chicken--sickly, epileptic, weak-minded--a child of eight could thrash him. He has no character worth talking about. It's not Smerdyakov, gentlemen. He doesn't care for money; he wouldn't take my presents. Besides, what motive had he for murdering the old man? Why, he's very likely his son, you know--his natural son. Do you know that?"

"We have heard that legend. But you are your father's son, too, you know; yet you yourself told everyone you meant to murder him."

"That's a thrust! And a nasty, mean one, too! I'm not afraid! Oh, gentlemen, isn't it too base of you to say that to my face? It's base, because I told you that myself. I not only wanted to murder him, but I might have done it. And, what's more, I went out of my way to tell you of my own accord that I nearly murdered him. But, you see, I didn't murder him; you see, my guardian angel saved me--that's what you've not taken into account. And that's why it's so base of you. For I didn't kill him, I didn't kill him! Do you hear, I did not kill him."

He was almost choking. He had not been so moved before during the whole interrogation.

"And what has he told you, gentlemen--Smerdyakov, I mean?" he added suddenly, after a pause. "May I ask that question?"

"You may ask any question," the prosecutor replied with frigid severity, "any question relating to the facts of the case, and we are, I repeat, bound to answer every inquiry you make. We found the servant Smerdyakov, concerning whom you inquire, lying unconscious in his bed, in an epileptic fit of extreme severity, that had recurred, possibly, ten times. The doctor who was with us told us, after seeing him, that he may possibly not outlive the night."

"Well, if that's so, the devil must have killed him," broke suddenly from Mitya, as though until that moment had been asking himself: "Was it Smerdyakov or not?"

"We will come back to this later," Nikolay Parfenovitch decided. "Now wouldn't you like to continue your statement?"

Mitya asked for a rest. His request was courteously granted. After resting, he went on with his story. But he was evidently depressed. He was exhausted, mortified, and morally shaken. To make things worse the prosecutor exasperated him, as though intentionally, by vexatious interruptions about "trifling points." Scarcely had Mitya described how, sitting on the wall, he had struck Grigory on the head with the pestle, while the old man had hold of his left leg, and how he then jumped down to look at him, when the prosecutor stopped him to ask him to describe exactly how he was sitting on the wall. Mitya was surprised.

"Oh, I was sitting like this, astride, one leg on one side of the wall and one on the other."

"And the pestle?"

"The pestle was in my hand."

"Not in your pocket? Do you remember that precisely? Was it a violent blow you gave him?"

"It must have been a violent one. But why do you ask?"

"Would you mind sitting on the chair just as you sat on the wall then and showing us just how you moved your arm, and in what direction?"

"You're making fun of me, aren't you?" asked Mitya, looking haughtily at the speaker; but the latter did not flinch.

Mitya turned abruptly, sat astride on his chair, and swung his arm.

"This was how I struck him! That's how I knocked him down! What more do you want?"

"Thank you. May I trouble you now to explain why you jumped down, with what object, and what you had in view?"

"Oh, hang it!...I jumped down to look at the man I'd hurt...I don't know what for!"

"Though you were so excited and were running away?"

"Yes, though I was excited and running away."

"You wanted to help him?"

"Help!...Yes, perhaps I did want to help him...I don't remember."

"You don't remember? Then you didn't quite know what you were doing?"

"Not at all. I remember everything--every detail. I jumped down to look at him, and wiped his face with my handkerchief."

"We have seen your handkerchief. Did you hope to restore him to consciousness?"

"I don't know whether I hoped it. I simply wanted to make sure whether he was alive or not."

"Ah! You wanted to be sure? Well, what then?"

"I'm not a doctor. I couldn't decide. I ran away thinking I'd killed him. And now he's recovered."

"Excellent," commented the prosecutor. "Thank you. That's all I wanted. Kindly proceed."

Alas! it never entered Mitya's head to tell them, though he remembered it, that he had jumped back from pity, and standing over the prostrate figure had even uttered some words of regret: "You've come to grief, old man--there's no help for it. Well, there you must lie."

The prosecutor could only draw one conclusion: that the man had jumped back "at such a moment and in such excitement simply with the object of ascertaining whether the only witness of his crime were dead; that he must therefore have been a man of great strength, coolness, decision, and foresight even at such a moment,"...and so on. The prosecutor was satisfied: "I've provoked the nervous fellow by 'trifles' and he has said more than he meant With painful effort Mitya went on. But this time he was pulled up immediately by Nikolay Parfenovitch.

"How came you to run to the servant, Fedosya Markovna, with your hands so covered with blood, and, as it appears, your face, too?"

"Why, I didn't notice the blood at all at the time," answered Mitya.

"That's quite likely. It does happen sometimes." The prosecutor exchanged glances with Nikolay Parfenovitch.

"I simply didn't notice. You're quite right there, prosecutor," Mitya assented suddenly.

Next came the account of Mitya's sudden determination to "step aside" and make way for their happiness. But he could not make up his mind to open his heart to them as before, and tell them about "the queen of his soul." He disliked speaking of her before these chilly persons "who were fastening on him like bugs." And so in response to their reiterated questions he answered briefly and abruptly:

"Well, I made up my mind to kill myself. What had I left to live for? That question stared me in the face. Her first rightful lover had come back, the man who wronged her but who'd hurried back to offer his love, after five years, and atone for the wrong with marriage...So I knew it was all over for me...And behind me disgrace, and that blood--Grigory's...What had I to live for? So I went to redeem the pistols I had pledged, to load them and put a bullet in my brain to-morrow."

"And a grand feast the night before?"

"Yes, a grand feast the night before. Damn it all, gentlemen! Do make haste and finish it. I meant to shoot myself not far from here, beyond the village, and I'd planned to do it at five o'clock in the morning. And I had a note in my pocket already. I wrote it at Perhotin's when I loaded my pistols. Here's the letter. Read it! It's not for you I tell it," he added contemptuously. He took it from his waistcoat pocket and flung it on the table. The lawyers read it with curiosity, and, as is usual, added it to the papers connected with the case.

"And you didn't even think of washing your hands at Perhotin's? You were not afraid then of arousing suspicion?"

"What suspicion? Suspicion or not, I should have galloped here just the same, and shot myself at five o'clock, and you wouldn't have been in time to do anything. If it hadn't been for what's happened to my father, you would have known nothing about it, and wouldn't have come here. Oh, it's the devil's doing. It was the devil murdered father, it was through the devil that you found it out so soon. How did you manage to get here so quick? It's marvellous, a dream!"

"Mr. Perhotin informed us that when you came to him, you held in your hands...your blood-stained hands...your money...a lot of money...a bundle of hundred-rouble notes, and that his servant-boy saw it too."

"That's true, gentlemen. I remember it was so."

"Now, there's one little point presents itself. Can you inform us," Nikolay Parfenovitch began, with extreme gentleness, "where did you get so much money all of a sudden, when it appears from the facts, from the reckoning of time, that you had not been home?"

The prosecutor's brows contracted at the question being asked so plainly, but he did not interrupt Nikolay Parfenovitch.

"No, I didn't go home," answered Mitya, apparently perfectly composed, but looking at the floor.

"Allow me then to repeat my question," Nikolay Parfenovitch went on as though creeping up to the subject. "Where were you able to procure such a sum all at once, when by your own confession, at five o'clock the same day you-"

"I was in want of ten roubles and pledged my pistols with Perhotin, and then went to Madame Hohlakov to borrow three thousand which she wouldn't give me, and so on, and all the rest of it," Mitya interrupted sharply. "Yes, gentlemen, I was in want of it, and suddenly thousands turned up, eh? Do you know, gentlemen, you're both afraid now 'what if he won't tell us where he got it?' That's just how it is. I'm not going to tell you, gentlemen. You've guessed right. You'll never know," said Mitya, chipping out each word with extraordinary determination. The lawyers were silent for a moment.

"You must understand, Mr. Karamazov, that it is of vital importance for us to know," said Nikolay Parfenovitch, softly and suavely.

"I understand; but still I won't tell you."

The prosecutor, too, intervened, and again reminded the prisoner that he was at liberty to refuse to answer questions, if he thought it to his interest, and so on. But in view of the damage he might do himself by his silence, especially in a case of such importance as--

"And so on, gentlemen, and so on. Enough! I've heard that rigmarole before," Mitya interrupted again. "I can see for myself how important it is, and that this is the vital point, and still I won't say."

"What is it to us? It's not our business, but yours...You are doing yourself harm," observed Nikolay Parfenovitch nervously.

"You see, gentlemen, joking apart"--Mitya lifted his eyes and looked firmly at them both--"I had an inkling from the first that we should come to loggerheads at this point. But at first when I began to give my evidence, it was all still far away and misty; it was all floating, and I was so simple that I began with the supposition of mutual confidence existing between us. Now I can see for myself that such confidence is out of the question, for in any case we were bound to come to this cursed stumbling-block. And now we've come to it! It's impossible and there's an end of it! But I don't blame you. You can't believe it all simply on my word. I understand that, of course."

He relapsed into gloomy silence.

"Couldn't you, without abandoning your resolution to be silent about the chief point, could you not, at the same time, give us some slight hint as to the nature of the motives which are strong enough to induce you to refuse to answer, at a crisis so full of danger to you?"

Mitya smiled mournfully, almost dreamily.

"I'm much more good-natured than you think, gentlemen. I'll tell you the reason why and give you that hint, though you don't deserve it. I won't speak of that, gentlemen, because it would be a stain on my honour. The answer to the question where I got the money would expose me to far greater disgrace than the murder and robbing of my father, if I had murdered and robbed him. That's why I can't tell you. I can't for fear of disgrace. What, gentlemen, are you going to write that down?"

"Yes, we'll write it down," lisped Nikolay Parfenovitch.

"You ought not to write that down about 'disgrace.' I only told you that in the goodness of my heart. I needn't have told you. I made you a present of it, so to speak, and you pounce upon it at once. Oh, well, write--write what you like," he concluded, with scornful disgust. "I'm not afraid of you and I can still hold up my head before you."

"And can't you tell us the nature of that disgrace?" Nikolay Parfenovitch hazarded.

The prosecutor frowned darkly.

"No, no, c'est fini, don't trouble yourselves. It's not worth while soiling one's hands. I have soiled myself enough through you as it is. You're not worth it--no one is. Enough, gentlemen. I'm not going on."

This was said too peremptorily. Nikolay Parfenovitch did not insist further, but from Ippolit Kirillovitch's eyes he saw that he had not given up hope.

"Can you not, at least, tell us what sum you had in your hands when you went into Mr. Perhotin's--how many roubles exactly?"

"I can't tell you that."

"You spoke to Mr. Perhotin, I believe, of having received three thousand from Madame Hohlakov."

"Perhaps I did. Enough, gentlemen. I won't say how much I had."

"Will you be so good then as to tell us how you came here and what you have done since you arrived?"

"Oh! you might ask the people here about that. But I'll tell you if you like."

He proceeded to do so, but we won't repeat his story. He told it dryly and curtly. Of the raptures of his love he said nothing, but told them that he abandoned his determination to shoot himself, owing to "new factors in the case." He told the story without going into motives or details. And this time the lawyers did not worry him much. It was obvious that there was no essential point of interest to them here.

"We shall verify all that. We will come back to it during the examination of the witnesses, which will, of course, take place in your presence," said Nikolay Parfenovitch in conclusion. "And now allow me to request you to lay on the table everything in your possession, especially all the money you still have about you."

"My money, gentlemen? Certainly. I understand that that is necessary. I'm surprised, indeed, that you haven't inquired about it before. It's true I couldn't get away anywhere. I'm sitting here where I can be seen. But here's my money--count it--take it. That's all, I think."

He turned it all out of his pockets; even the small change--two pieces of twenty copecks--he pulled out of his waistcoat pocket. They counted the money, which amounted to eight hundred and thirty-six roubles, and forty copecks.

"And is that all?" asked the investigating lawyer.

"You stated just now in your evidence that you spent three hundred roubles at Plotnikovs'. You gave Perhotin ten, your driver twenty, here you lost two hundred, then..."

Nikolay Parfenovitch reckoned it all up. Mitya helped him readily. They recollected every farthing and included it in the reckoning. Nikolay Parfenovitch hurriedly added up the total. "With this eight hundred you must have had about fifteen hundred at first?"

"I suppose so," snapped Mitya.

"How is it they all assert there was much more?"

"Let them assert it."

"But you asserted it yourself."

"Yes, I did, too."

"We will compare all this with the evidence of other persons not yet examined. Don't be anxious about your money. It will be properly taken care of and be at your disposal at the conclusion of...what is beginning...if it appears, or, so to speak, is proved that you have undisputed right to it. Well, and now..."

Nikolay Parfenovitch suddenly got up, and informed Mitya firmly that it was his duty and obligation to conduct a minute and thorough search "of your clothes and everything else..."

"By all means, gentlemen. I'll turn out all my pockets, if you like."

And he did, in fact, begin turning out his pockets.

"It will be necessary to take off your clothes, too."

"What! Undress? Ugh! Damn it! Won't you search me as I am? Can't you?"

"It's utterly impossible, Dmitri Fyodorovitch. You must take off your clothes."

"As you like," Mitya submitted gloomily; "only, please, not here, but behind the curtains. Who will search them?"

"Behind the curtains, of course."

Nikolay Parfenovitch bent his head in assent. His small face wore an expression of peculiar solemnity.

Chapter 6. The Prosecutor Catches Mitya

SOMETHING utterly unexpected and amazing to Mitya followed. He could never, even a minute before, have conceived that anyone could behave like that to him, Mitya Karamazov. What was worst of all, there was something humiliating in it, and on their side something "supercilious and scornful." It was nothing to take off his coat, but he was asked to undress further, or rather not asked but "commanded," he quite understood that. From pride and contempt he submitted without a word. Several peasants accompanied the lawyers and remained on the same side of the curtain. "To be ready if force is required," thought Mitya, "and perhaps for some other reason, too."

"Well, must I take off my shirt, too?" he asked sharply, but Nikolay Parfenovitch did not answer. He was busily engaged with the prosecutor in examining the coat, the trousers, the waistcoat and the cap; and it was evident that they were both much interested in the scrutiny. "They make no bones about it," thought Mitya, "they don't keep up the most elementary politeness."

"I ask you for the second time--need I take off my shirt or not?" he said, still more sharply and irritably.

"Don't trouble yourself. We will tell you what to do," Nikolay Parfenovitch said, and his voice was positively peremptory, or so it seemed to Mitya.

Meantime a consultation was going on in undertones between the lawyers. There turned out to be on the coat, especially on the left side at the back, a huge patch of blood, dry, and still stiff. There were bloodstains on the trousers, too. Nikolay Parfenovitch, moreover, in the presence of the peasant witnesses, passed his fingers along the collar, the cuffs, and all the seams of the coat and trousers, obviously looking for something--money, of course. He didn't even hide from Mitya his suspicion that he was capable of sewing money up in his clothes.

"He treats me not as an officer but as a thief," Mitya muttered to himself. They communicated their ideas to one another with amazing frankness. The secretary, for instance, who was also behind the curtain, fussing about and listening, called Nikolay Parfenovitch's attention to the cap, which they were also fingering.

"You remember Gridyenko, the copying clerk," observed the secretary. "Last summer he received the wages of the whole office, and pretended to have lost the money when he was drunk. And where was it found? Why, in just such pipings in his cap. The hundred-rouble notes were screwed up in little rolls and sewed in the piping."

Both the lawyers remembered Gridyenko's case perfectly, and so laid aside Mitya's cap, and decided that all his clothes must be more thoroughly examined later.

"Excuse me," cried Nikolay Parfenovitch, suddenly, noticing that the right cuff of Mitya's shirt was turned in, and covered with blood, "excuse me, what's that, blood?"

"Yes," Mitya jerked out.

"That is, what blood?...and why is the cuff turned in?"

Mitya told him how he had got the sleeve stained with blood looking after Grigory, and had turned it inside when he was washing his hands at Perhotin's.

"You must take off your shirt, too. That's very important as material evidence."

Mitya flushed red and flew into a rage.

"What, am I to stay naked?" he shouted.

"Don't disturb yourself. We will arrange something. And meanwhile take off your socks."

"You're not joking? Is that really necessary?"

Mitya's eyes flashed.

"We are in no mood for joking," answered Nikolay Parfenovitch sternly.

"Well, if I must-" muttered Mitya, and sitting down on the bed, he took off his socks. He felt unbearably awkward. All were clothed, while he was naked, and strange to say, when he was undressed he felt somehow guilty in their presence, and was almost ready to believe himself that he was inferior to them, and that now they had a perfect right to despise him.

"When all are undressed, one is somehow not ashamed, but when one's the only one undressed and everybody is looking, it's degrading," he kept repeating to himself, again and again. "It's like a dream; I've sometimes dreamed of being in such degrading positions." It was a misery to him to take off his socks. They were very dirty, and so were his underclothes, and now everyone could see it. And what was worse, he disliked his feet. All his life he had thought both his big toes hideous. He particularly loathed the coarse, flat, crooked nail on the right one, and now they would all see it. Feeling intolerably ashamed made him, at once and intentionally, rougher. He pulled off his shirt, himself.

"Would you like to look anywhere else if you're not ashamed to?"

"No, there's no need to, at present."

"Well, am I to stay naked like this?" he added savagely.

"Yes, that can't be helped for the time...Kindly sit down here for a while. You can wrap yourself in a quilt from the bed, and I...I'll see to all this."

All the things were shown to the witnesses. The report of the search was drawn up, and at last Nikolay Parfenovitch went out, and the clothes were carried out after him. Ippolit Kirillovitch went out, too. Mitya was left alone with the peasants, who stood in silence, never taking their eyes off him. Mitya wrapped himself up in the quilt. He felt cold. His bare feet stuck out, and he couldn't pull the quilt over so as to cover them. Nikolay Parfenovitch seemed to be gone a long time, "an insufferable time."

"He thinks of me as a puppy," thought Mitya, gnashing his teeth. "That rotten prosecutor has gone, too, contemptuous no doubt, it disgusts him to see me naked!"

Mitya imagined, however, that his clothes would be examined and returned to him. But what was his indignation when Nikolay Parfenovitch came back with quite different clothes, brought in behind him by a peasant.

"Here are clothes for you," he observed airily, seeming well satisfied with the success of his mission. "Mr. Kalganov has kindly provided these for this unusual emergency, as well as a clean shirt. Luckily he had them all in his trunk. You can keep your own socks and underclothes."

Mitya flew into a passion.

"I won't have other people's clothes!" he shouted menacingly, "give me my own!"

"It's impossible!"

"Give me my own. Damn Kalganov and his clothes, too!"

It was a long time before they could persuade him. But they succeeded somehow in quieting him down. They impressed upon him that his clothes, being stained with blood, must be "included with the other material evidence," and that they "had not even the right to let him have them now...taking into consideration the possible outcome of the case." Mitya at last understood this. He subsided into gloomy silence and hurriedly dressed himself. He merely observed, as he put them on, that the clothes were much better than his old ones, and that he disliked "gaining by the change." The coat was, besides, "ridiculously tight. Am I to be dressed up like a fool...for your amusement?"

They urged upon him again that he was exaggerating, that Kalganov was only a little taller, so that only the trousers might be a little too long. But the coat turned out to be really tight in the shoulders.

"Damn it all! I can hardly button it," Mitya grumbled. "Be so good as to tell Mr. Kalganov from me that I didn't ask for his clothes, and it's not my doing that they've dressed me up like a clown."

"He understands that, and is sorry...I mean, not sorry to lend you his clothes, but sorry about all this business," mumbled Nikolay Parfenovitch.

"Confound his sorrow! Well, where now? Am I to go on sitting here?"

He was asked to go back to the "other room." Mitya went in, scowling with anger, and trying to avoid looking at anyone. Dressed in another man's clothes he felt himself disgraced, even in the eyes of the peasants, and of Trifon Borissovitch, whose face appeared, for some reason, in the doorway, and vanished immediately. "He's come to look at me dressed up," thought Mitya. He sat down on the same chair as before. He had an absurd nightmarish feeling, as though he were out of his mind.

"Well, what now? Are you going to flog me? That's all that's left for you," he said, clenching his teeth and addressing the prosecutor. He would not turn to Nikolay Parfenovitch, as though he disdained to speak to him.

"He looked too closely at my socks, and turned them inside out on purpose to show everyone how dirty they were--the scoundrel!"

"Well, now we must proceed to the examination of witnesses," observed Nikolay Parfenovitch, as though in reply to Mitya's question.

"Yes," said the prosecutor thoughtfully, as though reflecting on something.

"We've done what we could in your interest, Dmitri Fyodorovitch," Nikolay Parfenovitch went on, "but having received from you such an uncompromising refusal to explain to us the source from which you obtained the money found upon you, we are, at the present moment-"

"What is the stone in your ring?" Mitya interrupted suddenly, as though awakening from a reverie. He pointed to one of the three large rings adorning Nikolay Parfenovitch's right hand.

"Ring?" repeated Nikolay Parfenovitch with surprise.

"Yes, that one...on your middle finger, with the little veins in it, what stone is that?" Mitya persisted, like a peevish child.

"That's a smoky topaz," said Nikolay Parfenovitch, smiling. "Would you like to look at it? I'll take it off..."

"No, don't take it off," cried Mitya furiously, suddenly waking up, and angry with himself. "Don't take it off...there's no need...Damn it!...Gentlemen, you've sullied my heart! Can you suppose that I would conceal it from you, if I had really killed my father, that I would shuffle, lie, and hide myself? No, that's not like Dmitri Karamazov, that he couldn't do, and if I were guilty, I swear I shouldn't have waited for your coming, or for the sunrise as I meant at first, but should have killed myself before this, without waiting for the dawn! I know that about myself now. I couldn't have learnt so much in twenty years as I've found out in this accursed night!...And should I have been like this on this night, and at this moment, sitting with you, could I have talked like this, could I have moved like this, could I have looked at you and at the world like this, if I had really been the murderer of my father, when the very thought of having accidentally killed Grigory gave me no peace all night-- not from fear--oh, not simply from fear of your punishment! The disgrace of it! And you expect me to be open with such scoffers as you, who see nothing and believe in nothing, blind moles and scoffers, and to tell you another nasty thing I've done, another disgrace, even if that would save me from your accusation! No, better Siberia! The man who opened the door to my father and went in at that door, he killed him, he robbed him. Who was he? I'm racking my brains and can't think who. But I can tell you it was not Dmitri Karamazov, and that's all I can tell you, and that's enough, enough, leave me alone...Exile me, punish me, but don't bother me any more. I'll say no more. Call your witnesses!"

Mitya uttered his sudden monologue as though he were determined to be absolutely silent for the future. The prosecutor watched him the whole time and only when he had ceased speaking, observed, as though it were the most ordinary thing, with the most frigid and composed air:

"Oh, about the open door of which you spoke just now, we may as well inform you, by the way, now, of a very interesting piece of evidence of the greatest importance both to you and to us, that has been given us by Grigory, the old man you wounded. On his recovery, he clearly and emphatically stated, in reply to our questions, that when, on coming out to the steps, and hearing a noise in the garden, he made up his mind to go into it through the little gate which stood open, before he noticed you running, as you have told us already, in the dark from the open window where you saw your father, he, Grigory, glanced to the left, and, while noticing the open window, observed at the same time, much nearer to him, the door, standing wide open--that door which you have stated to have been shut the whole time you were in the garden. I will not conceal from you that Grigory himself confidently affirms and bears witness that you must have run from that door, though, of course, he did not see you do so with his own eyes, since he only noticed you first some distance away in the garden, running towards the fence."

Mitya had leapt up from his chair half-way through this speech.

"Nonsense!" he yelled, in a sudden frenzy, "it's a barefaced lie. He couldn't have seen the door open because it was shut. He's lying!"

"I consider it my duty to repeat that he is firm in his statement. He does not waver. He adheres to it. We've cross-examined him several times."

"Precisely. I have cross-examined him several times," Nikolay Parfenovitch confirmed warmly.

"It's false, false! It's either an attempt to slander me, or the hallucination of a madman," Mitya still shouted. "He's simply raving, from loss of blood, from the wound. He must have fancied it when he came to...He's raving."

"Yes, but he noticed the open door, not when he came to after his injuries, but before that, as soon as he went into the garden from the lodge."

"But it's false, it's false! It can't be so! He's slandering me from spite...He couldn't have seen it...I didn't come from the door," gasped Mitya.

The prosecutor turned to Nikolay Parfenovitch and said to him impressively:

"Confront him with it."

"Do you recognise this object?"

Nikolay Parfenovitch laid upon the table a large and thick official envelope, on which three seals still remained intact. The envelope was empty, and slit open at one end. Mitya stared at it with open eyes.

"It...it must be that envelope of my father's, the envelope that contained the three thousand roubles...and if there's inscribed on it, allow me, 'For my little chicken'...yes--three thousand!" he shouted, "do you see, three thousand, do you see?"

"Of course, we see. But we didn't find the money in it. It was empty, and lying on the floor by the bed, behind the screen."

For some seconds Mitya stood as though thunderstruck.

"Gentlemen, it's Smerdyakov!" he shouted suddenly, at the top of his voice. "It's he who's murdered him! He's robbed him! No one else knew where the old man hid the envelope. It's Smerdyakov, that's clear, now!"

"But you, too, knew of the envelope and that it was under the pillow."

"I never knew it. I've never seen it. This is the first time I've looked at it. I'd only heard of it from Smerdyakov...He was the only one who knew where the old man kept it hidden, I didn't know..." Mitya was completely breathless.

"But you told us yourself that the envelope was under your deceased father's pillow. You especially stated that it was under the pillow, so you must have known it."

"We've got it written down," confirmed Nikolay Parfenovitch.

"Nonsense! It's absurd! I'd no idea it was under the pillow. And perhaps it wasn't under the pillow at all...It was just a chance guess that it was under the pillow. What does Smerdyakov say? Have you asked him where it was? What does Smerdyakov say? That's the chief point...And I went out of my way to tell lies against myself...I told you without thinking that it was under the pillow, and now you--Oh, you know how one says the wrong thing, without meaning it. No one knew but Smerdyakov, only Smerdyakov, and no one else...He didn't even tell me where it was! But it's his doing, his doing; there's no doubt about it, he murdered him, that's as clear as daylight now," Mitya exclaimed more and more frantically, repeating himself incoherently, and growing more and more exasperated and excited. "You must understand that, and arrest him at once...He must have killed him while I was running away and while Grigory was unconscious, that's clear now...He gave the signal and father opened to him...for no one but he knew the signal, and without the signal father would never have opened the door..."

"But you're again forgetting the circumstance," the prosecutor observed, still speaking with the same restraint, though with a note of triumph, "that there was no need to give the signal if the door already stood open when you were there, while you were in the garden..."

"The door, the door," muttered Mitya, and he stared speechless at the prosecutor. He sank back helpless in his chair. All were silent.

"Yes, the door!...It's a nightmare! God is against me!" he exclaimed, staring before him in complete stupefaction.

"Come, you see," the prosecutor went on with dignity, "and you can judge for yourself, Dmitri Fyodorovitch. On the one hand, we have the evidence of the open door from which you ran out, a fact which overwhelms you and us. On the other side, your incomprehensible, persistent, and, so to speak, obdurate silence with regard to the source from which you obtained the money which was so suddenly seen in your hands, when only three hours earlier, on your own showing, you pledged your pistols for the sake of ten roubles! In view of all these facts, judge for yourself. What are we to believe, and what can we depend upon? And don't accuse us of being 'frigid, cynical, scoffing people,' who are incapable of believing in the generous impulses of your heart...Try to enter into our position..."

Mitya was indescribably agitated. He turned pale.

"Very well!" he exclaimed suddenly, "I will tell you my secret. I'll tell you where I got the money!...I'll reveal my shame, that I may not have to blame myself or you hereafter."

"And believe me, Dmitri Fyodorovitch," put in Nikolay Parfenovitch, in a voice of almost pathetic delight, "that every sincere and complete confession on your part at this moment may, later on, have an immense influence in your favour, and may, indeed, moreover-"

But the prosecutor gave him a slight shove under the table, and he checked himself in time. Mitya, it is true, had not heard him.

Chapter 7. Mitya's Great Secret Received with Hisses

"GENTLEMEN," he began, still in the same agitation, "I want to make a full confession: that money was my own."

The lawyer's faces lengthened. That was not at all what they expected.

"How do you mean?" faltered Nikolay Parfenovitch, "when at five o'clock on the same day, from your own confession-"

"Damn five o'clock on the same day and my own confession! That's nothing to do with it now! That money was my own, my own, that is, stolen by me...not mine, I mean, but stolen by me, and it was fifteen hundred roubles, and I had it on me all the time, all the time..."

"But where did you get it?"

"I took it off my neck, gentlemen, off this very neck...it was here, round my neck, sewn up in a rag, and I'd had it round my neck a long time, it's a month since I put it round my neck...to my shame and disgrace!"

"And from whom did you...appropriate it?"

"You mean, 'steal it'? Speak out plainly now. Yes, I consider that I practically stole it, but, if you prefer, I 'appropriated it.' I consider I stole it. And last night I stole it finally."

"Last night? But you said that it's a month since you...obtained it?..."

"Yes. But not from my father. Not from my father, don't be uneasy. I didn't steal it from my father, but from her. Let me tell you without interrupting. It's hard to do, you know. You see, a month ago, I was sent for by Katerina Ivanovna, formerly my betrothed. Do you know her?"

"Yes, of course."

"I know you know her. She's a noble creature, noblest of the noble. But she has hated me ever so long, oh, ever so long...and hated me with good reason, good reason!"

"Katerina Ivanovna!" Nikolay Parfenovitch exclaimed with wonder. The prosecutor, too, stared.

"Oh, don't take her name in vain! I'm a scoundrel to bring her into it. Yes, I've seen that she hated me...a long while...From the very first, even that evening at my lodging...but enough, enough. You're unworthy even to know of that. No need of that at all...I need only tell you that she sent for me a month ago, gave me three thousand roubles to send off to her sister and another relation in Moscow (as though she couldn't have sent it off herself!) and I...it was just at that fatal moment in my life when I...well, in fact, when I'd just come to love another, her, she's sitting down below now, Grushenka. I carried her off here to Mokroe then, and wasted here in two days half that damned three thousand, but the other half I kept on me. Well, I've kept that other half, that fifteen hundred, like a locket round my neck, but yesterday I undid it, and spent it. What's left of it, eight hundred roubles, is in your hands now, Nikolay Parfenovitch. That's the change out of the fifteen hundred I had yesterday."

"Excuse me. How's that? Why, when you were here a month ago you spent three thousand, not fifteen hundred, everybody knows that."

"Who knows it? Who counted the money? Did I let anyone count it?"

"Why, you told everyone yourself that you'd spent exactly three thousand."

"It's true, I did. I told the whole town so, and the whole town said so. And here, at Mokroe, too, everyone reckoned it was three thousand. Yet I didn't spend three thousand, but fifteen hundred. And the other fifteen hundred I sewed into a little bag. That's how it was, gentlemen. That's where I got that money yesterday..."

"This is almost miraculous," murmured Nikolay Parfenovitch.

"Allow me to inquire," observed the prosecutor at last, "have you informed anyone whatever of this circumstance before; I mean that you had fifteen hundred left about you a month ago?"

"I told no one."

"That's strange. Do you mean absolutely no one?"

"Absolutely no one. No one and nobody."

"What was your reason for this reticence? What was your motive for making such a secret of it? To be more precise: You have told us at last your secret, in your words, so 'disgraceful,' though in reality--that is, of course, comparatively speaking--this action, that is, the appropriation of three thousand roubles belonging to someone else, and, of course, only for a time is, in my view at least, only an act of the greatest recklessness and not so disgraceful, when one takes into consideration your character...Even admitting that it was an action in the highest degree discreditable, still, discreditable is not 'disgraceful.'...Many people have already guessed, during this last month, about the three thousand of Katerina Ivanovna's that you have spent, and I heard the legend myself, apart from your confession...Mihail Makarovitch, for instance, had heard it, too, so that indeed, it was scarcely a legend, but the gossip of the whole town. There are indications, too, if I am not mistaken, that you confessed this yourself to someone, I mean that the money was Katerina Ivanovna's, and so, it's extremely surprising to me that hitherto, that is, up to the present moment, you have made such an extraordinary secret of the fifteen hundred you say you put by, apparently connecting a feeling of positive horror with that secret...It's not easy to believe that it could cost you such distress to confess such a secret...You cried out, just now, that Siberia would be better than confessing it..."

The prosecutor ceased speaking. He was provoked. He did not conceal his vexation, which was almost anger, and gave vent to all his accumulated spleen, disconnectedly and incoherently, without choosing words.

"It's not the fifteen hundred that's the disgrace, but that I put it apart from the rest of the three thousand," said Mitya firmly.

"Why?" smiled the prosecutor irritably. "What is there disgraceful, to your thinking, in your having set aside half of the three thousand you had discreditably, if you prefer, 'disgracefully,' appropriated? Your taking the three thousand is more important than what you did with it. And by the way, why did you do that--why did you set apart that half, for what purpose, for what object did you do it? Can you explain that to us?"

"Oh, gentlemen, the purpose is the whole point!" cried Mitya. "I put it aside because I was vile, that is, because I was calculating, and to be calculating in such a case is vile...and that vileness has been going on a whole month."

"It's incomprehensible."

"I wonder at you. But I'll make it clearer. Perhaps it really is incomprehensible. You see, attend to what I say. I appropriate three thousand entrusted to my honour; I spend it on a spree, say I spend it all, and next morning I go to her and say, 'Katya, I've done wrong, I've squandered your three thousand'; well, is that right? No, it's not right--it's dishonest and cowardly; I'm a beast, with no more self-control than a beast, that's so, isn't it? But still I'm not a thief? Not a downright thief, you'll admit! I squandered it, but I didn't steal it. Now a second, rather more favourable alternative: follow me carefully, or I may get confused again--my head's going round--and so, for the second alternative: I spend here only fifteen hundred out of the three thousand, that is, only half. Next day I go and take that half to her: 'Katya, take this fifteen hundred from me, I'm a low beast, and an untrustworthy scoundrel, for I've wasted half the money, and I shall waste this, too, so keep me from temptation!' Well, what of that alternative? I should be a beast and a scoundrel, and whatever you like; but not a thief, not altogether a thief, or I should not have brought back what was left, but have kept that, too. She would see at once that since I brought back half, I should pay back what I'd spent, that I should never give up trying to, that I should work to get it and pay it back. So in that case I should be a scoundrel, but not a thief, you may say what you like, not a thief!"

"I admit that there is a certain distinction," said the prosecutor, with a cold smile. "But it's strange that you see such a vital difference."

"Yes, I see a vital difference. Every man may be a scoundrel, and perhaps every man is a scoundrel, but not everyone can be a thief; it takes an arch-scoundrel to be that. Oh, of course, I don't know how to make these fine distinctions...but a thief is lower than a scoundrel, that's my conviction. Listen, I carry the money about me a whole month; I may make up my mind to give it back to-morrow, and I'm a scoundrel no longer; but I cannot make up my mind, you see, though I'm making up my mind every day, and every day spurring myself on to do it, and yet for a whole month I can't bring myself to it, you see. Is that right to your thinking, is that right?"

"Certainly, that's not right; that I can quite understand, and that I don't dispute," answered the prosecutor with reserve. "And let us give up all discussion of these subtleties and distinctions, and, if you will be so kind, get back to the point. And the point is, that you have still not told us, although we've asked you, why, in the first place, you halved the money, squandering one half and hiding the other? For what purpose exactly did you hide it, what did you mean to do with that fifteen hundred? I insist upon that question, Dmitri Fyodorovitch."

"Yes, of course!" cried Mitya, striking himself on the forehead; "forgive me, I'm worrying you, and am not explaining the chief point, or you'd understand in a minute, for it's just the motive of it that's the disgrace! You see, it was all to do with the old man, my dead father. He was always pestering Agrafena and I was jealous; I thought then that she was hesitating between me and him. So I kept thinking everyday, suppose she were to make up her mind all of a sudden, suppose she were to leave off tormenting me, and were suddenly to say to me, 'I love you, not him; take me to the other end of the world.' And I'd only forty copecks; how could I take her away, what could I do? Why, I'd be lost. You see, I didn't know her then, I didn't understand her, I thought she wanted money, and that she wouldn't forgive my poverty. And so I fiendishly counted out the half of that three thousand, sewed it up, calculating on it, sewed it up before I was drunk, and after I had sewn it up, I went off to get drunk on the rest. Yes, that was base. Do you understand now?"

Both the lawyers laughed aloud.

"I should have called it sensible and moral on your part not to have squandered it all," chuckled Nikolay Parfenovitch, "for after all what does it amount to?"

"Why, that I stole it, that's what it amounts to! Oh, God, you horrify me by not understanding! Every day that I had that fifteen hundred sewn up round my neck, every day and every hour I said to myself, 'You're a thief! you're a thief!' Yes, that's why I've been so savage all this month, that's why I fought in the tavern, that's why I attacked my father, it was because I felt I was a thief. I couldn't make up my mind; I didn't dare even to tell Alyosha, my brother, about that fifteen hundred: I felt I was such a scoundrel and such a pickpocket. But, do you know, while I carried it I said to myself at the same time every hour: 'No, Dmitri Fyodorovitch, you may yet not be a thief.' Why? Because I might go next day and pay back that fifteen hundred to Katya. And only yesterday I made up my mind to tear my amulet off my neck, on my way from Fenya's to Perhotin. I hadn't been able till that moment to bring myself to it. And it was only when I tore it off that I became a downright thief, a thief and a dishonest man for the rest of my life. Why? Because, with that I destroyed, too, my dream of going to Katya and saying, 'I'm a scoundrel, but not a thief! Do you understand now? Do you understand?"

"What was it made you decide to do it yesterday?" Nikolay Parfenovitch interrupted.

"Why? It's absurd to ask. Because I had condemned myself to die at five o'clock this morning, here, at dawn. I thought it made no difference whether I died a thief or a man of honour. But I see it's not so, it turns out that it does make a difference. Believe me, gentlemen, what has tortured me most during this night has not been the thought that I'd killed the old servant, and that I was in danger of Siberia just when my love was being rewarded, and Heaven was open to me again. Oh, that did torture me, but not in the same way; not so much as the damned consciousness that I had torn that damned money off my breast at last and spent it, and had become a downright thief! Oh, gentlemen, I tell you again, with a bleeding heart, I have learnt a great deal this night. I have learnt that it's not only impossible to live a scoundrel, but impossible to die a scoundrel...No, gentlemen, one must die honest..."

Mitya was pale. His face had a haggard and exhausted look, in spite of his being intensely excited.

"I am beginning to understand you, Dmitri Fyodorovitch," the prosecutor said slowly, a soft and almost compassionate tone. "But all this, if you'll excuse my saying so, is a matter of nerves, in my opinion...your overwrought nerves, that's what it is. And why, for instance, should you not have saved yourself such misery for almost a month, by going and returning that fifteen hundred to the lady who had entrusted it to you? And why could you not have explained things to her, and in view of your position, which you describe as being so awful, why could you not have had recourse to the plan which would so naturally have occurred to one's mind, that is, after honourably confessing your errors to her, why could you not have asked her to lend you the sum needed for your expenses, which, with her generous heart, she would certainly not have refused you in your distress, especially if it had been with some guarantee, or even on the security you offered to the merchant Samsonov, and to Madame Hohlakov? I suppose you still regard that security as of value?"

Mitya suddenly crimsoned.

"Surely you don't think me such an out and out scoundrel as that? You can't be speaking in earnest?" he said, with indignation, looking the prosecutor straight in the face, and seeming unable to believe his ears.

"I assure you I'm in earnest...Why do you imagine I'm not serious?" It was the prosecutor's turn to be surprised.

"Oh, how base that would have been! Gentlemen, do you know, you are torturing me! Let me tell you everything, so be it. I'll confess all my infernal wickedness, but to put you to shame, and you'll be surprised yourselves at the depth of ignominy to which a medley of human passions can sink. You must know that I already had that plan myself, that plan you spoke of, just now, prosecutor! Yes, gentlemen, I, too, have had that thought in my mind all this current month, so that I was on the point of deciding to go to Katya--I was mean enough for that. But to go to her, to tell her of my treachery, and for that very treachery, to carry it out, for the expenses of that treachery, to beg for money from her, Katya (to beg, do you hear, to beg), and go straight from her to run away with the other, the rival, who hated and insulted her--to think of it! You must be mad, prosecutor!"

"Mad I am not, but I did speak in haste, without thinking...of that feminine jealousy...if there could be jealousy in this case, as you assert...yes, perhaps there is something of the kind," said the prosecutor, smiling.

"But that would have been so infamous!" Mitya brought his fist down on the table fiercely. "That would have been filthy beyond everything! Yes, do you know that she might have given me that money, yes, and she would have given it, too; she'd have been certain to give it, to be revenged on me, she'd have given it to satisfy her vengeance, to show her contempt for me, for hers is an infernal nature, too, and she's a woman of great wrath. I'd have taken the money, too, oh, I should have taken it; I should have taken it, and then, for the rest of my life...oh, God! Forgive me, gentlemen, I'm making such an outcry because I've had that thought in my mind so lately, only the day before yesterday, that night when I was having all that bother with Lyagavy, and afterwards yesterday, all day yesterday, I remember, till that happened..."

"Till what happened?" put in Nikolay Parfenovitch inquisitively, but Mitya did not hear it.

"I have made you an awful confession," Mitya said gloomily in conclusion. "You must appreciate it, and what's more, you must respect it, for if not, if that leaves your souls untouched, then you've simply no respect for me, gentlemen, I tell you that, and I shall die of shame at having confessed it to men like you! Oh, I shall shoot myself! Yes, I see, I see already that you don't believe me. What, you want to write that down, too?" he cried in dismay.

"Yes, what you said just now," said Nikolay Parfenovitch, looking at him surprise, "that is, that up to the last hour you were still contemplating going to Katerina Ivanovna to beg that sum from her...I assure you, that's a very important piece of evidence for us, Dmitri Fyodorovitch, I mean for the whole case...and particularly for you, particularly important for you."

"Have mercy, gentlemen!" Mitya flung up his hands. "Don't write that, anyway; have some shame. Here I've torn my heart asunder before you, and you seize the opportunity and are fingering the wounds in both halves...Oh, my God!"

In despair he hid his face in his hands.

"Don't worry yourself so, Dmitri Fyodorovitch," observed the prosecutor, "everything that is written down will be read over to you afterwards, and what you don't agree to we'll alter as you like. But now I'll ask you one little question for the second time. Has no one, absolutely no one, heard from you of that money you sewed up? That, I must tell you, is almost impossible to believe."

"No one, no one, I told you so before, or you've not understood anything! Let me alone!"

"Very well, this matter is bound to be explained, and there's plenty of time for it, but meantime, consider; we have perhaps a dozen witnesses that you yourself spread it abroad, and even shouted almost everywhere about the three thousand you'd spent here; three thousand, not fifteen hundred. And now, too, when you got hold of the money you had yesterday, you gave many people to understand that you had brought three thousand with you."

"You've got not dozens, but hundreds of witnesses, two hundred witnesses, two hundred have heard it, thousands have heard it!" cried Mitya.

"Well, you see, all bear witness to it. And the word all means something."

"It means nothing. I talked rot, and everyone began repeating it."

"But what need had you to 'talk rot,' as you call it?"

"The devil knows. From bravado perhaps...at having wasted so much money...To try and forget that money I had sewn up, perhaps...yes, that was why...damn it...how often will you ask me that question? Well, I told a fib, and that was the end of it; once I'd said it, I didn't care to correct it. What does a man tell lies for sometimes?"

"That's very difficult to decide, Dmitri Fyodorovitch, what makes a man tell lies," observed the prosecutor impressively. "Tell me, though, was that 'amulet,' as you call it, on your neck, a big thing?"

"No, not big."

"How big, for instance?"

"If you fold a hundred-rouble note in half, that would be the size."

"You'd better show us the remains of it. You must have them somewhere."

"Damnation, what nonsense! I don't know where they are."

"But excuse me: where and when did you take it off your neck? According to your own evidence you didn't go home."

"When I was going from Fenya's to Perhotin's, on the way I tore it off my neck and took out the money."

"In the dark?"

"What should I want a light for? I did it with my fingers in one minute."

"Without scissors, in the street?"

"In the market-place I think it was. Why scissors? It was an old rag. It was torn in a minute."

"Where did you put it afterwards?"

"I dropped it there."

"Where was it, exactly?"

"In the market-place, in the market-place! The devil knows whereabouts. What do you want to know for?"

"That's extremely important, Dmitri Fyodorovitch. It would be material evidence in your favour. How is it you don't understand that? Who helped you to sew it up a month ago?"

"No one helped me. I did it myself."

"Can you sew?"

"A soldier has to know how to sew. No knowledge was needed to do that."

"Where did you get the material, that is, the rag in which you sewed the money?"

"Are you laughing at me?"

"Not at all. And we are in no mood for laughing, Dmitri Fyodorovitch."

"I don't know where I got the rag from--somewhere, I suppose."

"I should have thought you couldn't have forgotten it?"

"Upon my word, I don't remember. I might have torn a bit off my linen."

"That's very interesting. We might find in your lodgings to-morrow the shirt or whatever it is from which you tore the rag. What sort of rag was it, cloth or linen?"

"Goodness only knows what it was. Wait a bit...I believe I didn't tear it off anything. It was a bit of calico...I believe I sewed it up in a cap of my landlady's."

"In your landlady's cap?"

"Yes. I took it from her."

"How did you get it?"

"You see, I remember once taking a cap for a rag, perhaps to wipe my pen on. I took it without asking, because it was a worthless rag. I tore it up, and I took the notes and sewed them up in it. I believe it was in that very rag I sewed them. An old piece of calico, washed a thousand times."

"And you remember that for certain now?"

"I don't know whether for certain. I think it was in the cap. But, hang it, what does it matter?"

"In that case your landlady will remember that the thing was lost?"

"No, she won't, she didn't miss it. It was an old rag, I tell you, an old rag not worth a farthing."

"And where did you get the needle and thread?"

"I'll stop now. I won't say any more. Enough of it!" said Mitya, losing his temper at last.

"It's strange that you should have so completely forgotten where you threw the pieces in the market-place."

"Give orders for the market-place to be swept to-morrow, and perhaps you'll find it," said Mitya sneering. "Enough, gentlemen, enough!" he decided, in an exhausted voice. "I see you don't believe me! Not for a moment! It's my fault, not yours. I ought not to have been so ready. Why, why did I degrade myself by confessing my secret to you? it's a joke to you. I see that from your eyes. You led me on to it, prosecutor! Sing a hymn of triumph if you can...Damn you, you torturers!"

He bent his head, and hid his face in his hands. The lawyers were silent. A minute later he raised his head and looked at them almost vacantly. His face now expressed complete, hopeless despair, and he sat mute and passive as though hardly conscious of what was happening. In the meantime they had to finish what they were about. They had immediately to begin examining the witnesses. It was by now eight o'clock in the morning. The lights had been extinguished long ago. Mihail Makarovitch and Kalganov, who had been continually in and out of the room all the while the interrogation had been going on, had now both gone out again. The lawyers, too, looked very tired. It was a wretched morning, the whole sky was overcast, and the rain streamed down in bucketfuls. Mitya gazed blankly out of window.

"May I look out of window?" he asked Nikolay Parfenovitch, suddenly.

"Oh, as much as you like," the latter replied.

Mitya got up and went to the window...The rain lashed against its little greenish panes. He could see the muddy road just below the house, and farther away, in the rain and mist, a row of poor, black, dismal huts, looking even blacker and poorer in the rain. Mitya thought of "Phoebus the golden-haired, and how he had meant to shoot himself at his first ray. "Perhaps it would be even better on a morning like this," he thought with a smile, and suddenly, flinging his hand downwards, he turned to his "torturers."

"Gentlemen," he cried, "I see that I am lost! But she? Tell me about her, I beseech you. Surely she need not be ruined with me? She's innocent, you know, she was out of her mind when she cried last night 'It's all my fault!' She's done nothing, nothing! I've been grieving over her all night as I sat with you...Can't you, won't you tell me what you are going to do with her now?"

"You can set your mind quite at rest on that score, Dmitri Fyodorovitch," the prosecutor answered at once, with evident alacrity. "We have, so far, no grounds for interfering with the lady in whom you are so interested. I trust that it may be the same in the later development of the case...On the contrary, we'll do everything that lies in our power in that matter. Set your mind completely at rest."

"Gentlemen, I thank you. I knew that you were honest, straightforward people in spite of everything. You've taken a load off my heart...Well, what are we to do now? I'm ready."

"Well, we ought to make haste. We must pass to examining the witnesses without delay. That must be done in your presence and therefore-"

"Shouldn't we have some tea first?" interposed Nikolay Parfenovitch, "I think we've deserved it!"

They decided that if tea were ready downstairs (Mihail Makarovitch had, no doubt, gone down to get some) they would have a glass and then "go on and on," putting off their proper breakfast until a more favourable opportunity. Tea really was ready below, and was soon brought up. Mitya at first refused the glass that Nikolay Parfenovitch politely offered him, but afterwards he asked for it himself and drank it greedily. He looked surprisingly exhausted. It might have been supposed from his Herculean strength that one night of carousing, even accompanied by the most violent emotions, could have had little effect on him. But he felt that he could hardly hold his head up, and from time to time all the objects about him seemed heaving and dancing before his eyes. "A little more and I shall begin raving," he said to himself.

THE examination of the witnesses began. But we will not continue our story in such detail as before. And so we will not dwell on how Nikolay Parfenovitch impressed on every witness called that he must give his evidence in accordance with truth and conscience, and that he would afterwards have to repeat his evidence on oath, how every witness was called upon to sign the protocol of his evidence, and so on. We will only note that the point principally insisted upon in the examination was the question of the three thousand roubles; that is, was the sum spent here, at Mokroe, by Mitya on the first occasion, a month before, three thousand or fifteen hundred? And again had he spent three thousand or fifteen hundred yesterday? Alas, all the evidence given by everyone turned out to be against Mitya. There was not one in his favour, and some witnesses introduced new, almost crushing facts, in contradiction of his, Mitya's, story.

The first witness examined was Trifon Borissovitch. He was not in the least abashed as he stood before the lawyers. He had, on the contrary, an air of stern and severe indignation with the accused, which gave him an appearance of truthfulness and personal dignity. He spoke little, and with reserve, waited to be questioned, answered precisely and deliberately. Firmly and unhesitatingly he bore witness that the sum spent a month before could not have been less than three thousand, that all the peasants about here would testify that they had heard the sum of three thousand mentioned by Dmitri Fyodorovitch himself. "What a lot of money he flung away on the Gypsy girls alone! He wasted a thousand, I daresay, on them alone."

"I don't believe I gave them five hundred," was Mitya's gloomy comment on this. "It's a pity I didn't count the money at the time, but I was drunk..."

Mitya was sitting sideways with his back to the curtains. He listened gloomily, with a melancholy and exhausted air, as though he would say:

"Oh, say what you like. It makes no difference now."

"More than a thousand went on them, Dmitri Fyodorovitch," retorted Trifon Borissovitch firmly. "You flung it about at random and they picked it up. They were a rascally, thievish lot, horse-stealers, they've been driven away from here, or maybe they'd bear witness themselves how much they got from you. I saw the sum in your hands, myself--count it I didn't, you didn't let me, that's true enough--but by the look of it I should say it was far more than fifteen hundred...fifteen hundred, indeed! We've seen money too. We can judge of amounts..."

As for the sum spent yesterday he asserted that Dmitri Fyodorovitch had told him, as soon as he arrived, that he had brought three thousand with him.

"Come now, is that so, Trifon Borissovitch?" replied Mitya. "Surely I didn't declare so positively that I'd brought three thousand?"

"You did say so, Dmitri Fyodorovitch. You said it before Andrey. Andrey himself is still here. Send for him. And in the hall, when you were treating the chorus, you shouted straight out that you would leave your sixth thousand here--that is, with what you spent before, we must understand. Stepan and Semyon heard it, and Pyotr Fomitch Kalganov, too, was standing beside you at the time. Maybe he'd remember it..."

The evidence as to the "sixth" thousand made an extraordinary impression on the two lawyers. They were delighted with this new mode of reckoning; three and three made six, three thousand then and three now made six, that was clear.

They questioned all the peasants suggested by Trifon Borissovitch, Stepan and Semyon, the driver Andrey, and Kalganov. The peasants and the driver unhesitatingly confirmed Trifon Borissovitch's evidence. They noted down, with particular care, Andrey's account of the conversation he had had with Mitya on the road: "'Where,' says he, 'am I, Dmitri Fyodorovitch, going, to heaven or to hell, and shall I be forgiven in the next world or not?'" The psychological Ippolit Kirillovitch heard this with a subtle smile, and ended by recommending that these remarks as to where Dmitri Fyodorovitch would go should be "included in the case."

Kalganov, when called, came in reluctantly, frowning and ill-humoured, and he spoke to the lawyers as though he had never met them before in his life, though they were acquaintances whom he had been meeting every day for a long time past. He began by saying that "he knew nothing about it and didn't want to." But it appeared that he had heard of the" sixth" thousand, and he admitted that he had been standing close by at the moment. As far as he could see he "didn't know" how much money Mitya had in his hands. He affirmed that the Poles had cheated at cards. In reply to reiterated questions he stated that, after the Poles had been turned out, Mitya's position with Agrafena Alexandrovna had certainly improved, and that she had said that she loved him. He spoke of Agrafena Alexandrovna with reserve and respect, as though she had been a lady of the best society, and did not once allow himself to call her Grushenka. In spite of the young man's obvious repugnance at giving evidence, Ippolit Kirillovitch examined him at great length, and only from him learnt all the details of what made up Mitya's "romance," so to say, on that night. Mitya did not once pull Kalganov up. At last they let the young man go, and he left the room with unconcealed indignation.

The Poles, too, were examined. Though they had gone to bed in their room, they had not slept all night, and on the arrival of the police officers they hastily dressed and got ready, realising that they would certainly be sent for. They gave their evidence with dignity, though not without some uneasiness. The little Pole turned out to be a retired official of the twelfth class, who had served in Siberia as a veterinary surgeon. His name was Mussyalovitch. Pan Vrubelvsky turned out to be an uncertificated dentist. Although Nikolay Parfenovitch asked them questions on entering the room they both addressed their answers to Mihail Makarovitch, who was standing on one side, taking him in their ignorance for the most important person and in command, and addressed him at every word as "Pan Colonel." Only after several reproofs from Mihail Makarovitch himself, they grasped that they had to address their answers to Nikolay Parfenovitch only. It turned out that they could speak Russian quite correctly except for their accent in some words. Of his relations with Grushenka, past and present, Pan Mussyalovitch spoke proudly and warmly, so that Mitya was roused at once and declared that he would not allow the "scoundrel" to speak like that in his presence! Pan Mussyalovitch at once called attention to the word "scoundrel," and begged that it should be put down in the protocol. Mitya fumed with rage.

"He's a scoundrel! A scoundrel! You can put that down. And put down, too, that, in spite of the protocol I still declare that he's a scoundrel!" he cried.

Though Nikolay Parfenovitch did insert this in the protocol, he showed the most praiseworthy tact and management. After sternly reprimanding Mitya, he cut short all further inquiry into the romantic aspect of the case, and hastened to pass to what was essential. One piece of evidence given by the Poles roused special interest in the lawyers: that was how, in that very room, Mitya had tried to buy off Pan Mussyalovitch, and had offered him three thousand roubles to resign his claims, seven hundred roubles down, and the remaining two thousand three hundred "to be paid next day in the town." He had sworn at the time that he had not the whole sum with him at Mokroe, but that his money was in the town. Mitya observed hotly that he had not said that he would be sure to pay him the remainder next day in the town. But Pan Vrublevsky confirmed the statement, and Mitya, after thinking for a moment admitted, frowning, that it must have been as the Poles stated, that he had been excited at the time, and might indeed have said so.

The prosecutor positively pounced on this piece of evidence. It seemed to establish for the prosecution (and they did, in fact, base this deduction on it) that half, or a part of, the three thousand that had come into Mitya's hands might really have been left somewhere hidden in the town, or even, perhaps, somewhere here, in Mokroe. This would explain the circumstance, so baffling for the prosecution, that only eight hundred roubles were to be found in Mitya's hands. This circumstance had been the one piece of evidence which, insignificant as it was, had hitherto told, to some extent, in Mitya's favour. Now this one piece of evidence in his favour had broken down. In answer to the prosecutor's inquiry, where he would have got the remaining two thousand three hundred roubles, since he himself had denied having more than fifteen hundred, Mitya confidently replied that he had meant to offer the "little chap," not money, but a formal deed of conveyance of his rights to the village of Tchermashnya, those rights which he had already offered to Samsonov and Madame Hohlakov. The prosecutor positively smiled at the "innocence of this subterfuge."

"And you imagine he would have accepted such a deed as a substitute for two thousand three hundred roubles in cash?"

"He certainly would have accepted it," Mitya declared warmly. "Why, look here, he might have grabbed not two thousand, but four or six, for it. He would have put his lawyers, Poles and Jews, on to the job, and might have got, not three thousand, but the whole property out of the old man."

The evidence of Pan Mussyalovitch was, of course, entered in the protocol in the fullest detail. Then they let the Poles go. The incident of the cheating at cards was hardly touched upon. Nikolay Parfenovitch was too well pleased with them, as it was, and did not want to worry them with trifles, moreover, it was nothing but a foolish, drunken quarrel over cards. There had been drinking and disorder enough, that night...So the two hundred roubles remained in the pockets of the Poles.

Then old Maximov was summoned. He came in timidly, approached with little steps, looking very dishevelled and depressed. He had, all this time, taken refuge below with Grushenka, sitting dumbly beside her, and "now and then he'd begin blubbering over her and wiping his eyes with a blue check handkerchief," as Mihail Makarovitch described afterwards. So that she herself began trying to pacify and comfort him. The old man at once confessed that he had done wrong, that he had borrowed "ten roubles in my poverty," from Dmitri Fyodorovitch, and that he was ready to pay it back. To Nikolay Parfenovitch's direct question, had he noticed how much money Dmitri Fyodorovitch held in his hand, as he must have been able to see the sum better than anyone when he took the note from him, Maximov, in the most positive manner, declared that there was twenty thousand.

"Have you ever seen so much as twenty thousand before, then?" inquired Nikolay Parfenovitch, with a smile.

"To be sure I have, not twenty, but seven, when my wife mortgaged my little property. She'd only let me look at it from a distance, boasting of it to me. It was a very thick bundle, all rainbow-coloured notes. And Dmitri Fyodorovitch's were all rainbow-coloured..."

He was not kept long. At last it was Grushenka's turn. Nikolay Parfenovitch was obviously apprehensive of the effect her appearance might have on Mitya, and he muttered a few words of admonition to him, but Mitya bowed his head in silence, giving him to understand "that he would not make a scene." Mihail Makarovitch himself led Grushenka in. She entered with a stern and gloomy face, that looked almost composed, and sat down quietly on the chair offered her by Nikolay Parfenovitch. She was very pale, she seemed to be cold, and wrapped herself closely in her magnificent black shawl. She was suffering from a slight feverish chill--the first symptom of the long illness which followed that night. Her grave air, her direct earnest look and quiet manner made a very favourable impression on everyone. Nikolay Parfenovitch was even a little bit "fascinated." He admitted himself, when talking about it afterwards, that only then had he seen "how handsome the woman was," for, though he had seen her several times he had always looked upon her as something of a "provincial hetaira." "She has the manners of the best society," he said enthusiastically, gossiping about her in a circle of ladies. But this was received with positive indignation by the ladies, who immediately called him a "naughty man," to his great satisfaction.

As she entered the room, Grushenka only glanced for an instant at Mitya, who looked at her uneasily. But her face reassured him at once. After the first inevitable inquiries and warnings, Nikolay Parfenovitch asked her, hesitating a little, but preserving the most courteous manner, on what terms she was with the retired lieutenant, Dmitri Fyodorovitch Karamazov. To this Grushenka firmly and quietly replied:

"He was an acquaintance. He came to see me as an acquaintance during the last month." To further inquisitive questions she answered plainly and with complete frankness, that, though "at times" she had thought him attractive, she had not loved him, but had won his heart as well as his old father's "in my nasty spite," that she had seen that Mitya was very jealous of Fyodor Pavlovitch and everyone else; but that had only amused her. She had never meant to go to Fyodor Pavlovitch, she had simply been laughing at him. "I had no thoughts for either of them all this last month. I was expecting another man who had wronged me. But I think," she said in conclusion, "that there's no need for you to inquire about that, nor for me to answer you, for that's my own affair."

Nikolay Parfenovitch immediately acted upon this hint. He again dismissed the "romantic" aspect of the case and passed to the serious one, that is, to the question of most importance, concerning the three thousand roubles. Grushenka confirmed the statement that three thousand roubles had certainly been spent on the first carousal at Mokroe, and, though she had not counted the money herself, she had heard that it was three thousand from Dmitri Fyodorovitch's own lips.

"Did he tell you that alone, or before someone else, or did you only hear him speak of it to others in your presence?" the prosecutor inquired immediately.

To which Grushenka replied that she had heard him say so before other people, and had heard him say so when they were alone.

"Did he say it to you alone once, or several times?" inquired the prosecutor, and learned that he had told Grushenka so several times.

Ippolit Kirillovitch was very well satisfied with this piece of evidence. Further examination elicited that Grushenka knew, too, where that money had come from, and that Dmitri Fyodorovitch had got it from Katerina Ivanovna.

"And did you never, once, hear that the money spent a month ago was not three thousand, but less, and that Dmitri Fyodorovitch had saved half that sum for his own use?"

"No, I never heard that," answered Grushenka.

It was explained further that Mitya had, on the contrary, often told her that he hadn't a farthing.

"He was always expecting to get some from his father," said Grushenka in conclusion.

"Did he never say before you...casually, or in a moment of irritation," Nikolay Parfenovitch put in suddenly, "that he intended to make an attempt on his father's life?"

"Ach, he did say so," sighed Grushenka.

"Once or several times?"

"He mentioned it several times, always in anger."

"And did you believe he would do it?"

"No, I never believed it," she answered firmly. "I had faith in his noble heart."

"Gentlemen, allow me," cried Mitya suddenly, "allow me to say one word to Agrafena Alexandrovna, in your presence."

"You can speak," Nikolay Parfenovitch assented.

"Agrafena Alexandrovna!" Mitya got up from his chair, "have faith in God and in me. I am not guilty of my father's murder!"

Having uttered these words Mitya sat down again on his chair. Grushenka stood up and crossed herself devoutly before the ikon.

"Thanks be to Thee, O Lord," she said, in a voice thrilled with emotion, and still standing, she turned to Nikolay Parfenovitch and added:

"As he has spoken now, believe it! I know him. He'll say anything as a joke or from obstinacy, but he'll never deceive you against his conscience. He's telling the whole truth, you may believe it."

"Thanks, Agrafena Alexandrovna, you've given me fresh courage," Mitya responded in a quivering voice.

As to the money spent the previous day, she declared that she did not know what sum it was, but had heard him tell several people that he had three thousand with him. And to the question where he got the money, she said that he had told her that he had "stolen" it from Katerina Ivanovna, and that she had replied to that that he hadn't stolen it, and that he must pay the money back next day. On the prosecutor's asking her emphatically whether the money he said he had stolen from Katerina Ivanovna was what he had spent yesterday, or what he had squandered here a month ago, she declared that he meant the money spent a month ago, and that that was how she understood him.

Grushenka was at last released, and Nikolay Parfenovitch informed her impulsively that she might at once return to the town and that if he could be of any assistance to her, with horses for example, or if she would care for an escort, he...would be--

"I thank you sincerely," said Grushenka, bowing to him, "I'm going with this old gentleman; I am driving him back to town with me, and meanwhile, if you'll allow me, I'll wait below to hear what you decide about Dmitri Fyodorovitch."

She went out. Mitya was calm, and even looked more cheerful, but only for a moment. He felt more and more oppressed by a strange physical weakness. His eyes were closing with fatigue. The examination of the witnesses was, at last, over. They procceded to a revision of the protocol. Mitya got up, moved from his chair to the corner by the curtain, lay down on a large chest covered with a rug, and instantly fell asleep.

He had a strange dream, utterly out of keeping with the place and the time.

He was driving somewhere in the steppes, where he had been stationed long ago, and a peasant was driving him in a cart with a pair of horses, through snow and sleet. He was cold, it was early in November, and the snow was falling in big wet flakes, melting as soon as it touched the earth. And the peasant drove him smartly, he had a fair, long beard. He was not an old man, somewhere about fifty, and he had on a grey peasant's smock. Not far off was a village, he could see the black huts, and half the huts were burnt down, there were only the charred beams sticking up. And as they drove in, there were peasant women drawn up along the road, a lot of women, a whole row, all thin and wan, with their faces a sort of brownish colour, especially one at the edge, a tall, bony woman, who looked forty, but might have been only twenty, with a long thin face. And in her arms was a little baby crying. And her breasts seemed so dried up that there was not a drop of milk in them. And the child cried and cried, and held out its little bare arms, with its little fists blue from cold.

"Why are they crying? Why are they crying?" Mitya asked, as they dashed gaily by.

"It's the babe," answered the driver, "the babe weeping."

And Mitya was struck by his saying, in his peasant way, "the babe," and he liked the peasant's calling it a "babe." There seemed more pity in it.

"But why is it weeping?" Mitya persisted stupidly, "why are its little arms bare? Why don't they wrap it up?"

"The babe's cold, its little clothes are frozen and don't warm it."

"But why is it? Why?" foolish Mitya still persisted.

"Why, they're poor people, burnt out. They've no bread. They're begging because they've been burnt out."

"No, no," Mitya, as it were, still did not understand. "Tell me why it is those poor mothers stand there? Why are people poor? Why is the babe poor? Why is the steppe barren? Why don't they hug each other and kiss? Why don't they sing songs of joy? Why are they so dark from black misery? Why don't they feed the babe?"

And he felt that, though his questions were unreasonable and senseless, yet he wanted to ask just that, and he had to ask it just in that way. And he felt that a passion of pity, such as he had never known before, was rising in his heart, that he wanted to cry, that he wanted to do something for them all, so that the babe should weep no more, so that the dark-faced, dried-up mother should not weep, that no one should shed tears again from that moment, and he wanted to do it at once, at once, regardless of all obstacles, with all the recklessness of the Karamazovs.

"And I'm coming with you. I won't leave you now for the rest of my life, I'm coming with you", he heard close beside him Grushenka's tender voice, thrilling with emotion. And his heart glowed, and he struggled forward towards the light, and he longed to live, to live, to go on and on, towards the new, beckoning light, and to hasten, hasten, now, at once! "What! Where?" he exclaimed opening his eyes, and sitting up on the chest, as though he had revived from a swoon, smiling brightly. Nikolay Parfenovitch was standing over him, suggesting that he should hear the protocol read aloud and sign it. Mitya guessed that he had been asleep an hour or more, but he did not hear Nikolay Parfenovitch. He was suddenly struck by the fact that there was a pillow under his head, which hadn't been there when he had leant back, exhausted, on the chest.

"Who put that pillow under my head? Who was so kind?" he cried, with a sort of ecstatic gratitude, and tears in his voice, as though some great kindness had been shown him.

He never found out who this kind man was; perhaps one of the peasant witnesses, or Nikolay Parfenovitch's little secretary, had compassionately thought to put a pillow under his head; but his whole soul was quivering with tears. He went to the table and said that he would sign whatever they liked.

"I've had a good dream, gentlemen," he said in a strange voice, with a new light, as of joy, in his face.

Chapter 9. They Carry Mitya Away

WHEN the protocol had been signed, Nikolay Parfenovitch turned solemnly to the prisoner and read him the "Committal," setting forth, that in such a year, on such a day, in such a place, the investigating lawyer of such-and-such a district court, having examined so-and-so (to wit, Mitya) accused of this and of that (all the charges were carefully written out) and having considered that the accused, not pleading guilty to the charges made against him, had brought forward nothing in his defence, while the witnesses, so-and-so, and so-and-so, and the circumstances such-and-such testify against him, acting in accordance with such-and-such articles of the Statute Book, and so on, has ruled, that, in order to preclude so-and-so (Mitya) from all means of evading pursuit and judgment, he be detained in such-and-such a prison, which he hereby notifies to the accused and communicates a copy of this same "Committal" to the deputy prosecutor, and so on, and so on.

In brief, Mitya was informed that he was, from that moment, a prisoner, and that he would be driven at once to the town, and there shut up in a very unpleasant place. Mitya listened attentively, and only shrugged his shoulders.

"Well, gentlemen, I don't blame you. I'm ready...I understand that there's nothing else for you to do."

Nikolay Parfenovitch informed him gently that he would be escorted at once by the rural police officer, Mavriky Mavrikyevitch, who happened to be on the spot...

"Stay," Mitya interrupted, suddenly, and impelled by uncontrollable feeling he pronounced, addressing all in the room:

"Gentlemen, we're all cruel, we're all monsters, we all make men weep, and mothers, and babes at the breast, but of all, let it be settled here, now, of all I am the lowest reptile! I've sworn to amend, and every day I've done the same filthy things. I understand now that such men as I need a blow, a blow of destiny to catch them as with a noose, and bind them by a force from without. Never, never should I have risen of myself! But the thunderbolt has fallen. I accept the torture of accusation, and my public shame; I want to suffer and by suffering I shall be purified. Perhaps I shall be purified, gentlemen? But listen, for the last time, I am not guilty of my father's blood. I accept my punishment, not because I killed him, but because I meant to kill him, and perhaps I really might have killed him. Still I mean to fight it out with you. I warn you of that. I'll fight it out with you to the end, and then God will decide. Good-bye, gentlemen, don't be vexed with me for having shouted at you during the examination. Oh, I was still such a fool then...In another minute I shall be a prisoner, but now, for the last time, as a free man, Dmitri Karamazov offers you his hand. Saying good-bye to you, I say it to all men."

His voice quivered and he stretched out his hand, but Nikolay Parfenovitch, who happened to stand nearest to him, with a sudden, almost nervous movement, hid his hands behind his back. Mitya instantly noticed this, and started. He let his outstretched hand fall at once.

"The preliminary inquiry is not yet over," Nikolay Parfenovitch faltered, somewhat embarrassed. "We will continue it in the town, and I, for my part, of course, am ready to wish you all success...in your defence...As a matter of fact, Dmitri Fyodorovitch, I've always been disposed to regard you as, so to speak, more unfortunate than guilty. All of us here, if I may make bold to speak for all, we are all ready to recognise that you are, at bottom, a young man of honour, but, alas, one who has been carried away by certain passions to a somewhat excessive degree..."

Nikolay Parfenovitch's little figure was positively majestic by the time he had finished speaking. It struck Mitya that in another minute this "boy" would take his arm, lead him to another corner, and renew their conversation about "girls." But many quite irrelevant and inappropriate thoughts sometimes occur even to a prisoner when he is being led out to execution.

"Gentlemen, you are good, you are humane, may I see her to say 'good-bye' for the last time?" asked Mitya.

"Certainly, but considering...in fact, now it's impossible except in the presence of-"

"Oh, well, if it must be so, it must!"

Grushenka was brought in, but the farewell was brief, and of few words, and did not at all satisfy Nikolay Parfenovitch. Grushenka made a deep bow to Mitya.

"I have told you I am yours, and I will be yours. I will follow you for ever, wherever they may send you. Farewell; you are guiltless, though you've been your own undoing."

Her lips quivered, tears flowed from her eyes.

"Forgive me, Grusha, for my love, for ruining you, too, with my love."

Mitya would have said something more, but he broke off and went out. He was at once surrounded by men who kept a constant watch on him. At the bottom of the steps to which he had driven up with such a dash the day before with Andrey's three horses, two carts stood in readiness. Mavriky Mavrikyevitch, a sturdy, thick-set man with a wrinkled face, was annoyed about something, some sudden irregularity. He was shouting angrily. He asked Mitya to get into the cart with somewhat excessive surliness.

"When I stood him drinks in the tavern, the man had quite a different face," thought Mitya, as he got in. At the gates there was a crowd of people, peasants, women, and drivers. Trifon Borissovitch came down the steps too. All stared at Mitya.

"Forgive me at parting, good people!" Mitya shouted suddenly from the cart.

"Forgive us too!" he heard two or three voices.

"Good-bye to you, too, Trifon Borissovitch!"

But Trifon Borissovitch did not even turn round. He was, perhaps, too busy. He, too, was shouting and fussing about something. It appeared that everything was not yet ready in the second cart, in which two constables were to accompany Mavriky Mavrikyevitch. The peasant who had been ordered to drive the second cart was pulling on his smock, stoutly maintaining that it was not his turn to go, but Akim's. But Akim was not to be seen. They ran to look for him. The peasant persisted and besought them to wait.

"You see what our peasants are, Mavriky Mavrikyevitch. They've no shame!" exclaimed Trifon Borissovitch. "Akim gave you twenty-five copecks the day before yesterday. You've drunk it all and now you cry out. I'm simply surprised at your good-nature, with our low peasants, Mavriky Mavrikyevitch, that's all I can say."

"But what do we want a second cart for?" Mitya put in. "Let's start with the one, Mavriky Mavrikyevitch. I won't be unruly, I won't run away from you, old fellow. What do we want an escort for?"

"I'll trouble you, sir, to learn how to speak to me if you've never been taught. I'm not 'old fellow' to you, and you can keep your advice for another time!" Mavriky Mavrikyevitch snapped out savagely, as though glad to vent his wrath.

Mitya was reduced to silence. He flushed all over. A moment later he felt suddenly very cold. The rain had ceased, but the dull sky was still overcast with clouds, and a keen wind was blowing straight in his face.

"I've taken a chill," thought Mitya, twitching his shoulders.

At last Mavriky Mavrikyevitch, too, got into the cart, sat down heavily, and, as though without noticing it, squeezed Mitya into the corner. It is true that he was out of humour and greatly disliked the task that had been laid upon him.

"Good-bye, Trifon Borissovitch!" Mitya shouted again, and felt himself, that he had not called out this time from good-nature, but involuntarily, from resentment.

But Trifon Borissovitch stood proudly, with both hands behind his back, and staring straight at Mitya with a stern and angry face, he made no reply.

"Good-bye, Dmitri Fyodorovitch, good-bye!" he heard all at once the voice of Kalganov, who had suddenly darted out. Running up to the cart he held out his hand to Mitya. He had no cap on.

Mitya had time to seize and press his hand.

"Good-bye, dear fellow! I shan't forget your generosity," he cried warmly.

But the cart moved and their hands parted. The bell began ringing and Mitya was driven off.

Kalganov ran back, sat down in a corner, bent his head, hid his face in his hands, and burst out crying. For a long while he sat like that, crying as though he were a little boy instead of a young man of twenty. Oh, he believed almost without doubt in Mitya's guilt.

"What are these people? What can men be after this?" he exclaimed incoherently, in bitter despondency, almost despair. At that moment he had no desire to live.

"Is it worth it? Is it worth it?" exclaimed the boy in his grief.

PART IV

Book X. The Boys
Chapter 1. Kolya Krassotkin

IT was the beginning of November. There had been a hard frost, eleven degrees Reaumur, without snow, but a little dry snow had fallen on the frozen ground during the night, and a keen dry wind was lifting and blowing it along the dreary streets of our town, especially about the market-place. It was a dull morning, but the snow had ceased.

Not far from the market-place, close to Plotnikov's shop, there stood a small house, very clean both without and within. It belonged to Madame Krassotkin, the widow of a former provincial secretary, who had been dead for fourteen years. His widow, still a nice-looking woman of thirty-two, was living in her neat little house on her private means. She lived in respectable seclusion; she was of a soft but fairly cheerful disposition. She was about eighteen at the time of her husband's death; she had been married only a year and had just borne him a son. From the day of his death she had devoted herself heart and soul to the bringing up of her precious treasure, her boy Kolya. Though she had loved him passionately those fourteen years, he had caused her far more suffering than happiness. She had been trembling and fainting with terror almost every day, afraid he would fall ill, would catch cold, do something naughty, climb on a chair and fall off it, and so on and so on. When Kolya began going to school, the mother devoted herself to studying all the sciences with him so as to help him, and go through his lessons with him. She hastened to make the acquaintance of the teachers and their wives, even made up to Kolya's schoolfellows, and fawned upon them in the hope of thus saving Kolya from being teased, laughed at, or beaten by them. She went so far that the boys actually began to mock at him on her account and taunt him with being a "mother's darling."

But the boy could take his own part. He was a resolute boy, "tremendously strong," as was rumoured in his class, and soon proved to be the fact; he was agile, strong-willed, and of an audacious and enterprising temper. He was good at lessons, and there was a rumour in the school that he could beat the teacher, Dardanelov, at arithmetic and universal history. Though he looked down upon everyone, he was a good comrade and not supercilious. He accepted his schoolfellows' respect as his due, but was friendly with them. Above all, he knew where to draw the line. He could restrain himself on occasion, and in his relations with the teachers he never overstepped that last mystic limit beyond which a prank becomes an unpardonable breach of discipline. But he was as fond of mischief on every possible occasion as the smallest boy in the school, and not so much for the sake of mischief as for creating a sensation, inventing something, something effective and conspicuous. He was extremely vain. He knew how to make even his mother give way to him; he was almost despotic in his control of her. She gave way to him, oh, she had given way to him for years. The one thought unendurable to her was that her boy had no great love for her. She was always fancying that Kolya was "unfeeling" to her, and at times, dissolving into hysterical tears, she used to reproach him with his coldness. The boy disliked this, and the more demonstrations of feeling were demanded of him, the more he seemed intentionally to avoid them. Yet it was not intentional on his part but instinctive--it was his character. His mother was mistaken; he was very fond of her. He only disliked "sheepish sentimentality," as he expressed it in his schoolboy language.

There was a bookcase in the house containing a few books that had been his father's. Kolya was fond of reading, and had read several of them by himself. His mother did not mind that and only wondered sometimes at seeing the boy stand for hours by the bookcase poring over a book instead of going to play. And in that way Kolya read some things unsuitable for his age.

Though the boy, as a rule, knew where to draw the line in his mischief, he had of late begun to play pranks that caused his mother serious alarm. It is true there was nothing vicious in what he did, but a wild mad recklessness.

It happened that July, during the summer holidays, that the mother and son went to another district, forty-five miles away, to spend a week with a distant relation, whose husband was an official at the railway station (the very station, the nearest one to our town, from which a month later Ivan Fyodorovitch Karamazov set off for Moscow). There Kolya began by carefully investigating every detail connected with the railways, knowing that he could impress his schoolfellows when he got home with his newly acquired knowledge. But there happened to be some other boys in the place with whom he soon made friends. Some of them were living at the station, others in the neighbourhood; there were six or seven of them, all between twelve and fifteen, and two of them came from our town. The boys played together, and on the fourth or fifth day of Kolya's stay at the station, a mad bet was made by the foolish boys. Kolya, who was almost the youngest of the party and rather looked down upon by the others in consequence, was moved by vanity or by reckless bravado to bet them two roubles that he would lie down between the rails at night when the eleven o'clock train was due, and would lie there without moving while the train rolled over him at full speed. It is true they made a preliminary investigation, from which it appeared that it was possible to lie so flat between the rails that the train could pass over without touching, but to lie there was no joke! Kolya maintained stoutly that he would. At first they laughed at him, called him a little liar, a braggart, but that only egged him on. What piqued him most was that these boys of fifteen turned up their noses at him too superciliously, and were at first disposed to treat him as "a small boy," not fit to associate with them, and that was an unendurable insult. And so it was resolved to go in the evening, half a mile from the station, so that the train might have time to get up full speed after leaving the station The boys assembled. It was a pitch-dark night without a moon. At the time fixed, Kolya lay down between the rails. The five others who had taken the bet waited among the bushes below the embankment, their hearts beating with suspense, which was followed by alarm and remorse. At last they heard in the distance the rumble of the train leaving the station. Two red lights gleamed out of the darkness; the monster roared as it approached.

"Run, run away from the rails," the boys cried to Kolya from the bushes, breathless with terror. But it was too late: the train darted up and flew past. The boys rushed to Kolya. He lay without moving. They began pulling at him, lifting him up. He suddenly got up and walked away without a word. Then he explained that he had lain there as though he were insensible to frighten them, but the fact was that he really had lost consciousness, as he confessed long after to his mother. In this way his reputation as "a desperate character," was established for ever. He returned home to the station as white as a sheet. Next day he had a slight attack of nervous fever, but he was in high spirits and well pleased with himself. The incident did not become known at once, but when they came back to the town it penetrated to the school and even reached the ears of the masters. But then Kolya's mother hastened to entreat the masters on her boy's behalf, and in the end Dardanelov, a respected and influential teacher, exerted himself in his favour, and the affair was ignored.

Dardanelov was a middle-aged bachelor, who had been passionately in love with Madame Krassotkin for many years past, and had once already, about a year previously, ventured, trembling with fear and the delicacy of his sentiments, to offer her most respectfully his hand in marriage. But she refused him resolutely, feeling that to accept him would be an act of treachery to her son, though Dardanelov had, to judge from certain mysterious symptoms, reason for believing that he was not an object of aversion to the charming but too chaste and tender-hearted widow. Kolya's mad prank seemed to have broken the ice, and Dardanelov was rewarded for his intercession by a suggestion of hope. The suggestion, it is true, was a faint one, but then Dardanelov was such a paragon of purity and delicacy that it was enough for the time being to make him perfectly happy. He was fond of the boy, though he would have felt it beneath him to try and win him over, and was severe and strict with him in class. Kolya, too, kept him at a respectful distance. He learned his lessons perfectly; he was second in his class, was reserved with Dardanelov, and the whole class firmly believed that Kolya was so good at universal history that he could "beat" even Dardanelov. Kolya did indeed ask him the question, "Who founded Troy?" to which Dardanelov had made a very vague reply, referring to the movements and migrations of races, to the remoteness of the period, to the mythical legends. But the question, "Who had founded Troy?" that is, what individuals, he could not answer, and even for some reason regarded the question as idle and frivolous. But the boys remained convinced that Dardanelov did not know who founded Troy. Kolya had read of the founders of Troy in Smaragdov, whose history was among the books in his father's bookcase. In the end all the boys became interested in the question, who it was that had founded Troy, but Krassotkin would not tell his secret, and his reputation for knowledge remained unshaken.

After the incident on the railway a certain change came over Kolya's attitude to his mother. When Anna Fyodorovna (Madame Krassotkin) heard of her son's exploit, she almost went out of her mind with horror. She had such terrible attacks of hysterics, lasting with intervals for several days, that Kolya, seriously alarmed at last, promised on his honour that such pranks should never be repeated. He swore on his knees before the holy image, and swore by the memory of his father, at Madame Krassotkin's instance, and the "manly" Kolya burst into tears like a boy of six. And all that day the mother and son were constantly rushing into each other's arms sobbing. Next day Kolya woke up as "unfeeling" as before, but he had become more silent, more modest, sterner, and more thoughtful.

Six weeks later, it is true, he got into another scrape, which even brought his name to the ears of our Justice of the Peace, but it was a scrape of quite another kind, amusing, foolish, and he did not, as it turned out, take the leading part in it, but was only implicated in it. But of this later. His mother still fretted and trembled, but the more uneasy she became, the greater were the hopes of Dardanelov. It must be noted that Kolya understood and divined what was in Dardanelov's heart and, of course, despised him profoundly for his "feelings"; he had in the past been so tactless as to show this contempt before his mother, hinting vaguely that he knew what Dardanelov was after. But from the time of the railway incident his behaviour in this respect also was changed; he did not allow himself the remotest allusion to the subject and began to speak more respectfully of Dardanelov before his mother, which the sensitive woman at once appreciated with boundless gratitude. But at the slightest mention of

Dardanelov by a visitor in Kolya's presence, she would flush as pink as a rose. At such moments Kolya would either stare out of the window scowling, or would investigate the state of his boots, or would shout angrily for "Perezvon," the big, shaggy, mangy dog, which he had picked up a month before, brought home, and kept for some reason secretly indoors, not showing him to any of his schoolfellows. He bullied him frightfully, teaching him all sorts of tricks, so that the poor dog howled for him whenever he was absent at school, and when he came in, whined with delight, rushed about as if he were crazy, begged, lay down on the ground pretending to be dead, and so on; in fact, showed all the tricks he had taught him, not at the word of command, but simply from the zeal of his excited and grateful heart.

I have forgotten, by the way, to mention that Kolya Krassotkin was the boy stabbed with a penknife by the boy already known to the reader as the son of Captain Snegiryov. Ilusha had been defending his father when the schoolboys jeered at him, shouting the nickname "wisp of tow."

Chapter 2. Children

AND so on that frosty, snowy, and windy day in November, Kolya Krassotkin was sitting at home. It was Sunday and there was no school. It had just struck eleven, and he particularly wanted to go out "on very urgent business," but he was left alone in charge of the house, for it so happened that all its elder inmates were absent owing to a sudden and singular event. Madame Krassotkin had let two little rooms, separated from the rest of the house by a passage, to a doctor's wife with her two small children. This lady was the same age as Anna Fyodorovna, and a great friend of hers. Her husband, the doctor, had taken his departure twelve months before, going first to Orenburg and then to Tashkend, and for the last six months she had not heard a word from him. Had it not been for her friendship with Madame Krassotkin, which was some consolation to the forsaken lady, she would certainly have completely dissolved away in tears. And now, to add to her misfortunes, Katerina, her only servant, was suddenly moved the evening before to announce, to her mistress's amazement, that she proposed to bring a child into the world before morning. It seemed almost miraculous to everyone that no one had noticed the probability of it before. The astounded doctor's wife decided to move Katerina while there was still time to an establishment in the town kept by a midwife for such emergencies. As she set great store by her servant, she promptly carried out this plan and remained there looking after her. By the morning all Madame Krassotkin's friendly sympathy and energy were called upon to render assistance and appeal to someone for help in the case.

So both the ladies were absent from home, the Krassotkins' servant, Agafya, had gone out to the market, and Kolya was thus left for a time to protect and look after "the kids," that is, the son and daughter of the doctor's wife, who were left alone. Kolya was not afraid of taking care of the house, besides he had Perezvon, who had been told to lie flat, without moving, under the bench in the hall. Every time Kolya, walking to and fro through the rooms, came into the hall, the dog shook his head and gave two loud and insinuating taps on the floor with his tail, but alas! the whistle did not sound to release him. Kolya looked sternly at the luckless dog, who relapsed again into obedient rigidity. The one thing that troubled Kolya was "the kids." He looked, of course, with the utmost scorn on Katerina's unexpected adventure, but he was very fond of the bereaved "kiddies," and had already taken them a picture-book. Nastya, the elder, a girl of eight, could read, and Kostya, the boy, aged seven, was very fond of being read to by her. Krassotkin could, of course, have provided more diverting entertainment for them. He could have made them stand side by side and played soldiers with them, or sent them hiding all over the house. He had done so more than once before and was not above doing it, so much so that a report once spread at school that Krassotkin played horses with the little lodgers at home, prancing with his head on one side like a trace-horse. But Krassotkin haughtily parried this thrust, pointing out that to play horses with boys of one's own age, boys of thirteen, would certainly be disgraceful "at this date," but that he did it for the sake of "the kids" because he liked them, and no one had a right to call him to account for his feelings. The two "kids" adored him.

But on this occasion he was in no mood for games. He had very important business of his own before him, something almost mysterious. Meanwhile time was passing and Agafya, with whom he could have left the children, would not come back from market. He had several times already crossed the passage, opened the door of the lodgers' room and looked anxiously at "the kids" who were sitting over the book, as he had bidden them. Every time he opened the door they grinned at him, hoping he would come in and would do something delightful and amusing. But Kolya was bothered and did not go in.

At last it struck eleven and he made up his mind, once for all, that if that "damned" Agafya did not come back within ten minutes he should go out without waiting for her, making "the kids" promise, of course, to be brave when he was away, not to be naughty, not to cry from fright. With this idea he put on his wadded winter overcoat with its catskin fur collar, slung his satchel round his shoulder, and, regardless of his mother's constantly reiterated entreaties that he would always put on goloshes in such cold weather, he looked at them contemptuously as he crossed the hall and went out with only his boots on. Perezvon, seeing him in his outdoor clothes, began tapping nervously, yet vigorously, on the floor with his tail. Twitching all over, he even uttered a plaintive whine. But Kolya, seeing his dog's passionate excitement, decided that it was a breach of discipline, kept him for another minute under the bench, and only when he had opened the door into the passage, whistled for him. The dog leapt up like a mad creature and rushed bounding before him rapturously.

Kolya opened the door to peep at "the kids." They were both sitting as before at the table, not reading but warmly disputing about something. The children often argued together about various exciting problems of life, and Nastya, being the elder, always got the best of it. If Kostya did not agree with her, he almost always appealed to Kolya Krassotkin, and his verdict was regarded as infallible by both of them. This time the "kids'" discussion rather interested Krassotkin, and he stood still in the passage to listen. The children saw he was listening and that made them dispute with even greater energy.

"I shall never, never believe," Nastya prattled, "that the old women find babies among the cabbages in the kitchen garden. It's winter now and there are no cabbages, and so the old woman couldn't have taken Katerina a daughter."

Kolya whistled to himself.

"Or perhaps they do bring babies from somewhere, but only to those who are married."

Kostya stared at Nastya and listened, pondering profoundly.

"Nastya, how silly you are!" he said at last, firmly and calmly. "How can Katerina have a baby when she isn't married?"

Nastya was exasperated.

"You know nothing about it," she snapped irritably. "Perhaps she has a husband, only he is in prison, so now she's got a baby."

"But is her husband in prison?" the matter-of-fact Kostya inquired gravely.

"Or, I tell you what," Nastya interrupted impulsively, completely rejecting and forgetting her first hypothesis. "She hasn't a husband, you are right there, but she wants to be married, and so she's been thinking of getting married, and thinking and thinking of it till now she's got it, that is, not a husband but a baby."

"Well, perhaps so," Kostya agreed, entirely vanquished. "But you didn't say so before. So how could I tell?"

"Come, kiddies," said Kolya, stepping into the room. "You're terrible people, I see."

"And Perezvon with you!" grinned Kostya, and began snapping his fingers and calling Perezvon.

"I am in a difficulty, kids," Krassotkin began solemnly, "and you must help me. Agafya must have broken her leg, since she has not turned up till now, that's certain. I must go out. Will you let me go?"

The children looked anxiously at one another. Their smiling faces showed signs of uneasiness, but they did not yet fully grasp what was expected of them.

"You won't be naughty while I am gone? You won't climb on the cupboard and break your legs? You won't be frightened alone and cry?"

A look of profound despondency came into the children's faces.

"And I could show you something as a reward, a little copper cannon which can be fired with real gunpowder."

The children's faces instantly brightened. "Show us the cannon," said Kostya, beaming all over.

Krassotkin put his hand in his satchel, and pulling out a little bronze cannon stood it on the table.

"Ah, you are bound to ask that! Look, it's on wheels." He rolled the toy on along the table. "And it can be fired off, too. It can be loaded with shot and fired off."

"And it could kill anyone?"

"It can kill anyone; you've only got to aim at anybody," and Krassotkin explained where the powder had to be put, where the shot should be rolled in, showing a tiny hole like a touch-hole, and told them that it kicked when it was fired.

The children listened with intense interest. What particularly struck their imagination was that the cannon kicked.

"And have you got any powder?" Nastya inquired.

"Yes."

"Show us the powder, too," she drawled with a smile of entreaty.

Krassotkin dived again into his satchel and pulled out a small flask containing a little real gunpowder. He had some shot, too, in a screw of paper. He even uncorked the flask and shook a little powder into the palm of his hand.

"One has to be careful there's no fire about, or it would blow up and kill us all," Krassotkin warned them sensationally.

The children gazed at the powder with an awe-stricken alarm that only intensified their enjoyment. But Kostya liked the shot better.

"And does the shot burn?" he inquired.

"No, it doesn't."

"Give me a little shot," he asked in an imploring voice.

"I'll give you a little shot; here, take it, but don't show it to your mother till I come back, or she'll be sure to think it's gunpowder, and will die of fright and give you a thrashing."

"Mother never does whip us," Nastya observed at once.

"I know, I only said it to finish the sentence. And don't you ever deceive your mother except just this once, until I come back. And so, kiddies, can I go out? You won't be frightened and cry when I'm gone?"

"We sha-all cry," drawled Kostya, on the verge of tears already.

"We shall cry, we shall be sure to cry," Nastya chimed in with timid haste.

"Oh, children, children, how fraught with peril are your years! There's no help for it, chickens; I shall have to stay with you I don't know how long. And time is passing, time is passing, oogh!"

"Tell Perezvon to pretend to be dead!" Kostya begged.

"There's no help for it, we must have recourse to Perezvon. Ici, Perezvon." And Kolya began giving orders to the dog, who performed all his tricks.

He was a rough-haired dog, of medium size, with a coat of a sort of lilac-grey colour. He was blind in his right eye, and his left ear was torn. He whined and jumped, stood and walked on his hind legs, lay on his back with his paws in the air, rigid as though he were dead. While this last performance was going on, the door opened and Agafya, Madame Krassotkin's servant, a stout woman of forty, marked with small-pox, appeared in the doorway. She had come back from market and had a bag full of provisions in her hand. Holding up the bag of provisions in her left hand she stood still to watch the dog. Though Kolya had been so anxious for her return, he did not cut short the performance, and after keeping Perezvon dead for the usual time, at last he whistled to him. The dog jumped up and began bounding about in his joy at having done his duty.

"Only think, a dog!" Agafya observed sententiously.

"Why are you late, female?" asked Krassotkin sternly.

"Female, indeed! Go on with you, you brat."

"Brat?"

"Yes, a brat. What is it to you if I'm late; if I'm late, you may be sure I have good reason," muttered Agafya, busying herself about the stove, without a trace of anger or displeasure in her voice. She seemed quite pleased, in fact, to enjoy a skirmish with her merry young master.

"Listen, you frivolous young woman," Krassotkin began, getting up from the sofa, "can you swear by all you hold sacred in the world and something else besides, that you will watch vigilantly over the kids in my absence? I am going out."

"And what am I going to swear for?" laughed Agafya. "I shall look after them without that."

"No, you must swear on your eternal salvation. Else I shan't go."

"Well, don't then. What does it matter to me? It's cold out; stay at home."

"Kids," Kolya turned to the children, "this woman will stay with you till I come back or till your mother comes, for she ought to have been back long ago. She will give you some lunch, too. You'll give them something, Agafya, won't you?"

"That I can do."

"Good-bye, chickens, I go with my heart at rest. And you, granny," he added gravely, in an undertone, as he passed Agafya, "I hope you'll spare their tender years and not tell them any of your old woman's nonsense about Katerina. Ici, Perezvon!"

"Get along with you!" retorted Agafya, really angry this time. "Ridiculous boy! You want a whipping for saying such things, that's what you want!"

Chapter 3. The Schoolboy

BUT Kolya did not hear her. At last he could go out. As he went out at the gate he looked round him, shrugged up his shoulders, and saying "It is freezing," went straight along the street and turned off to the right towards the market-place. When he reached the last house but one before the market-place he stopped at the gate, pulled a whistle out of his pocket, and whistled with all his might as though giving a signal. He had not to wait more than a minute before a rosy-cheeked boy of about eleven, wearing a warm, neat and even stylish coat, darted out to meet him. This was Smurov, a boy in the preparatory class (two classes below Kolya Krassotkin), son of a well-to-do official. Apparently he was forbidden by his parents to associate with Krassotkin, who was well known to be a desperately naughty boy, so Smurov was obviously slipping out on the sly. He was--if the reader has not forgotten one of the group of boys who two months before had thrown stones at Ilusha. He was the one who told Alyosha about Ilusha.

"I've been waiting for you for the last hour, Krassotkin," said Smurov stolidly, and the boys strode towards the market-place.

"I am late," answered Krassotkin. "I was detained by circumstances. You won't be thrashed for coming with me?"

"Come, I say, I'm never thrashed! And you've got Perezvon with you?"

"Yes."

"You're taking him, too?"

"Yes."

"Ah! if it were only Zhutchka!"

"That's impossible. Zhutchka's non-existent. Zhutchka is lost in the mists of obscurity."

"Ah! couldn't we do this?" Smurov suddenly stood still. "You see Ilusha says that Zhutchka was a shaggy, greyish, smoky-looking dog like Perezvon. Couldn't you tell him this is Zhutchka, and he might believe you?"

"Boy, shun a lie, that's one thing; even with a good object- that's another. Above all, I hope you've not told them anything about my coming."

"Heaven forbid! I know what I am about. But you won't comfort him with Perezvon," said Smurov, with a sigh. "You know his father, the captain, 'the wisp of tow,' told us that he was going to bring him a real mastiff pup, with a black nose, to-day. He thinks that would comfort Ilusha; but I doubt it."

"And how is Ilusha?"

"Ah, he is bad, very bad! I believe he's in consumption: he is quite conscious, but his breathing! His breathing's gone wrong. The other day he asked to have his boots on to be led round the room. He tried to walk, but he couldn't stand. 'Ah, I told you before, father,' he said, 'that those boots were no good. I could never walk properly in them.' He fancied it was his boots that made him stagger, but it was simply weakness, really. He won't live another week. Herzenstube is looking after him. Now they are rich again--they've got heaps of money.

"They are rogues."

"Who are rogues?"

"Doctors and the whole crew of quacks collectively, and also, of course, individually. I don't believe in medicine. It's a useless institution. I mean to go into all that. But what's that sentimentality you've got up there? The whole class seems to be there every day."

"Not the whole class: it's only ten of our fellows who go to see him every day. There's nothing in that."

"What I don't understand in all this is the part that Alexey Karamazov is taking in it. His brother's going to be tried to-morrow or next day for such a crime, and yet he has so much time to spend on sentimentality with boys."

"There's no sentimentality about it. You are going yourself now to make it up with Ilusha."

"Make it up with him? What an absurd expression! But I allow no one to analyse my actions."

"And how pleased Ilusha will be to see you! He has no idea that you are coming. Why was it, why was it you wouldn't come all this time?" Smurov cried with sudden warmth.

"My dear boy, that's my business, not yours.

I am going of myself because I choose to, but you've all been hauled there by Alexey Karamazov--there's a difference, you know. And how do you know? I may not be going to make it up at all. It's a stupid expression."

"It's not Karamazov at all; it's not his doing. Our fellows began going there of themselves. Of course, they went with Karamazov at first. And there's been nothing of that sort of silliness. First one went, and then another. His father was awfully pleased to see us. You know he will simply go out of his mind if Ilusha dies. He sees that Ilusha's dying. And he seems so glad we've made it up with Ilusha. Ilusha asked after you, that was all. He just asks and says no more. His father will go out of his mind or hang himself. He behaved like a madman before. You know he is a very decent man. We made a mistake then. It's all the fault of that murderer who beat him then."

"Karamazov's a riddle to me all the same. I might have made his acquaintance long ago, but I like to have a proper pride in some cases. Besides, I have a theory about him which I must work out and verify."

Kolya subsided into dignified silence. Smurov, too, was silent. Smurov, of course, worshipped Krassotkin and never dreamed of putting himself on a level with him. Now he was tremendously interested at Kolya's saying that he was "going of himself" to see Ilusha. He felt that there must be some mystery in Kolya's suddenly taking it into his head to go to him that day. They crossed the market-place, in which at that hour were many loaded wagons from the country and a great number of live fowls. The market women were selling rolls, cottons and threads, etc., in their booths. These Sunday markets were naively called "fairs" in the town, and there were many such fairs in the year.

Perezvon ran about in the wildest spirits, sniffing about first one side, then the other. When he met other dogs they zealously smelt each other over according to the rules of canine etiquette.

"I like to watch such realistic scenes, Smurov," said Kolya suddenly. "Have you noticed how dogs sniff at one another when they meet? It seems to be a law of their nature."

"Yes; it's a funny habit."

"No, it's not funny; you are wrong there. There's nothing funny in nature, however funny it may seem to man with his prejudices. If dogs could reason and criticise us they'd be sure to find just as much that would be funny to them, if not far more, in the social relations of men, their masters--far more, indeed. I repeat that, because I am convinced that there is far more foolishness among us. That's Rakitin's idea--a remarkable idea. I am a Socialist, Smurov."

"And what is a Socialist?" asked Smurov.

"That's when all are equal and all have property in common, there are no marriages, and everyone has any religion and laws he likes best, and all the rest of it. You are not old enough to understand that yet. It's cold, though."

"Yes, twelve degrees of frost. Father looked at the thermometer just now."

"Have you noticed, Smurov, that in the middle of winter we don't feel so cold even when there are fifteen or eighteen degrees of frost as we do now, in the beginning of winter, when there is a sudden frost of twelve degrees, especially when there is not much snow. It's because people are not used to it. Everything is habit with men, everything even in their social and political relations. Habit is the great motive-power. What a funny-looking peasant!"

Kolya pointed to a tall peasant, with a good-natured countenance in a long sheepskin coat, who was standing by his wagon, clapping together his hands, in their shapeless leather gloves, to warm them. His long fair beard was all white with frost.

"That peasant's beard's frozen," Kolya cried in a loud provocative voice as he passed him.

"Lots of people's beards are frozen," the peasant replied, calmly and sententiously.

"Don't provoke him," observed Smurov.

"It's all right; he won't be cross; he's a nice fellow. Good-bye, Matvey."

"Good-bye."

"Is your name Matvey?"

"Yes. Didn't you know?"

"No, I didn't. It was a guess."

"You don't say so! You are a schoolboy, I suppose?"

"Yes."

"You get whipped, I expect?"

"Nothing to speak of--sometimes."

"Does it hurt?"

"Well, yes, it does."

"Ech, what a life!" The peasant heaved a sigh from the bottom of his heart.

"Good-bye, Matvey."

"Good-bye. You are a nice chap, that you are."

The boys went on.

"That was a nice peasant," Kolya observed to Smurov. "I like talking to the peasants, and am always glad to do them justice."

"Why did you tell a lie, pretending we are thrashed?" asked Smurov.

"I had to say that to please him."

"How do you mean?"

"You know, Smurov, I don't like being asked the same thing twice. I like people to understand at the first word. Some things can't be explained. According to a peasant's notions, schoolboys are whipped, and must be whipped. What would a schoolboy be if he were not whipped? And if I were to tell him we are not, he'd be disappointed. But you don't understand that. One has to know how to talk to the peasants."

"Only don't tease them, please, or you'll get into another scrape as you did about that goose."

"So you're afraid?"

"Don't laugh, Kolya. Of course I'm afraid. My father would be awfully cross. I am strictly forbidden to go out with you."

"Don't be uneasy, nothing will happen this time. Hallo, Natasha!" he shouted to a market woman in one of the booths.

"Call me Natasha! What next! My name is Marya," the middle-aged marketwoman shouted at him.

"I am so glad it's Marya. Good-bye!"

"Ah, you young rascal! A brat like you to carry on so!"

"I'm in a hurry. I can't stay now. You shall tell me next Sunday." Kolya waved his hand at her, as though she had attacked him and not he her.

"I've nothing to tell you next Sunday. You set upon me, you impudent young monkey. I didn't say anything," bawled Marya. "You want a whipping, that's what you want, you saucy jackanapes!"

There was a roar of laughter among the other market women round her. Suddenly a man in a violent rage darted out from the arcade of shops close by. He was a young man, not a native of the town, with dark, curly hair and a long, pale face, marked with smallpox. He wore a long blue coat and a peaked cap, and looked like a merchant's clerk. He was in a state of stupid excitement and brandished his fist at Kolya.

"I know you!" he cried angrily, "I know you!"

Kolya stared at him. He could not recall when he could have had a row with the man. But he had been in so many rows in the street that he could hardly remember them all.

"Do you?" he asked sarcastically.

"I know you! I know you!" the man repeated idiotically.

So much the better for you. Well, it's time I was going. Good-bye!"

"You are at your saucy pranks again?" cried the man. "You are at your saucy pranks again? I know, you are at it again!"

"It's not your business, brother, if I am at my saucy pranks again," said Kolya, standing still and scanning him.

"Not my business?"

"No; it's not your business."

"Whose then? Whose then? Whose then?"

"It's Trifon Nikititch's business, not yours."

"What Trifon Nikititch?" asked the youth, staring with loutish amazement at Kolya, but still as angry as ever. Kolya scanned him gravely.

"Have you been to the Church of the Ascension?" he suddenly asked him, with stern emphasis.

"What Church of Ascension? What for? No, I haven't," said the young man, somewhat taken aback.

"Do you know Sabaneyev?" Kolya went on even more emphatically and even more severely.

"What Sabaneyev? No, I don't know him."

"Well then you can go to the devil," said Kolya, cutting short the conversation; and turning sharply to the right he strode quickly on his way as though he disdained further conversation with a dolt who did not even know Sabaneyev.

"Stop, heigh! What Sabaneyev?" the young man recovered from his momentary stupefaction and was as excited as before. "What did he say?" He turned to the market women with a silly stare.

The women laughed.

"You can never tell what he's after," said one of them.

"What Sabaneyev is it he's talking about?" the young man repeated, still furious and brandishing his right arm.

"It must be a Sabaneyev who worked for the Kuzmitchovs, that's who it must be," one of the women suggested.

The young man stared at her wildly.

"For the Kuzmitchovs?" repeated another woman. "But his name wasn't Trifon. His name's Kuzma, not Trifon; but the boy said Trifon Nikititch, so it can't be the same."

"His name is not Trifon and not Sabaneyev, it's Tchizhov," put in suddenly a third woman, who had hitherto been silent, listening gravely. "Alexey Ivanitch is his name. Tchizhov, Alexey Ivanitch."

"Not a doubt about it, it's Tchizhov," a fourth woman emphatically confirmed the statement.

The bewildered youth gazed from one to another.

"But what did he ask for, what did he ask for, good people?" he cried almost in desperation." 'Do you know Sabaneyev?' says he. And who the devil's to know who is Sabaneyev?"

"You're a senseless fellow. I tell you it's not Sabaneyev, but Tchizhov, Alexey Ivanitch Tchizhov, that's who it is!" one of the women shouted at him impressively.

"What Tchizhov? Who is he? Tell me, if you know."

"That tall, snivelling fellow who used to sit in the market in the summer."

"And what's your Tchizhov to do with me, good people, eh?"

"How can I tell what he's to do with you?" put in another. "You ought to know yourself what you want with him, if you make such a clamour about him. He spoke to you, he did not speak to us, you stupid. Don't you really know him?"

"Know whom?"

"Tchizhov."

"The devil take Tchizhov and you with him. I'll give him a hiding, that I will. He was laughing at me!"

"Will give Tchizhov a hiding! More likely he will give you one. You are a fool, that's what you are!"

"Not Tchizhov, not Tchizhov, you spiteful, mischievous woman. I'll give the boy a hiding. Catch him, catch him, he was laughing at me

The woman guffawed. But Kolya was by now a long way off, marching along with a triumphant air. Smurov walked beside him, looking round at the shouting group far behind. He too was in high spirits, though he was still afraid of getting into some scrape in Kolya's company.

"What Sabaneyev did you mean?" he asked Kolya, foreseeing what his answer would be.

"How do I know? Now there'll be a hubbub among them all day. I like to stir up fools in every class of society. There's another blockhead, that peasant there. You know, they say 'there's no one stupider than a stupid Frenchman,' but a stupid Russian shows it in his face just as much. Can't you see it all over his face that he is a fool, that peasant, eh?"

"Let him alone, Kolya. Let's go on."

"Nothing could stop me, now I am once off. Hey, good morning, peasant!"

A sturdy-looking peasant, with a round, simple face and grizzled beard, who was walking by, raised his head and looked at the boy. He seemed not quite sober.

"Good morning, if you are not laughing at me," he said deliberately in reply.

"And if I am?" laughed Kolya.

"Well, a joke's a joke. Laugh away. I don't mind. There's no harm in a joke."

"I beg your pardon, brother, it was a joke."

"Well, God forgive you!"

"Do you forgive me, too?"

"I quite forgive you. Go along."

"I say, you seem a clever peasant."

"Cleverer than you," the peasant answered unexpectedly, with the same gravity.

"I doubt it," said Kolya, somewhat taken aback.

"It's true, though."

"Perhaps it is."

"It is, brother."

"Good-bye, peasant!"

"Good-bye!"

"There are all sorts of peasants," Kolya observed to Smurov after a brief silence. "How could I tell I had hit on a clever one? I am always ready to recognise intelligence in the peasantry."

In the distance the cathedral clock struck half-past eleven. The boys made haste and they walked as far as Captain Snegiryov's lodging, a considerable distance, quickly and almost in silence. Twenty paces from the house Kolya stopped and told Smurov to go on ahead and ask Karamazov to come out to him.

"One must sniff round a bit first," he observed to Smurov.

"Why ask him to come out?" Smurov protested. "You go in; they will be awfully glad to see you. What's the sense of making friends in the frost out here?"

"I know why I want to see him out here in the frost," Kolya cut him short in the despotic tone he was fond of adopting with "small boys," and Smurov ran to do his bidding.

Chapter 4. The Lost Dog

KOLYA leaned against the fence with an air of dignity, waiting for Alyosha to appear. Yes, he had long wanted to meet him. He had heard a great deal about him from the boys, but hitherto he had always maintained an appearance of disdainful indifference when he was mentioned, and he had even "criticised" what he heard about Alyosha. But secretely he had a great longing to make his acquaintance; there was something sympathetic and attractive in all he was told about Alyosha. So the present moment was important: to begin with, he had to show himself at his best, to show his independence. "Or he'll think of me as thirteen and take me for a boy, like the rest of them. And what are these boys to him? I shall ask him when I get to know him. It's a pity I am so short, though. Tuzikov is younger than I am, yet he is half a head taller. But I have a clever face. I am not good-looking. I know I'm hideous, but I've a clever face. I mustn't talk too freely; if I fall into his arms all at once, he may think--Tfoo! how horrible if he should think--!"

Such were the thoughts that excited Kolya while he was doing his utmost to assume the most independent air. What distressed him most was his being so short; he did not mind so much his "hideous" face, as being so short. On the wall in a corner at home he had the year before made a pencil-mark to show his height, and every two months since he anxiously measured himself against it to see how much he had gained. But alas! he grew very slowly, and this sometimes reduced him almost to despair. His face was in reality by no means "hideous"; on the contrary, it was rather attractive, with a fair, pale skin, freckled. His small, lively grey eyes had a fearless look, and often glowed with feeling. He had rather high cheekbones; small, very red, but not very thick, lips; his nose was small and unmistakably turned up. "I've a regular pug nose, a regular pug nose," Kolya used to mutter to himself when he looked in the looking-glass, and he always left it with indignation. "But perhaps I haven't got a clever face?" he sometimes thought, doubtful even of that. But it must not be supposed that his mind was preoccupied with his face and his height. On the contrary, however bitter the moments before the looking-glass were to him, he quickly forgot them, and forgot them for a long time, "abandoning himself entirely to ideas and to real life," as he formulated it to himself.

Alyosha came out quickly and hastened up to Kolya. Before he reached him, Kolya could see that he looked delighted. "Can he be so glad to see me?" Kolya wondered, feeling pleased. We may note here, in passing, that Alyosha's appearance had undergone a complete change since we saw him last. He had abandoned his cassock and was wearing now a wellcut coat, a soft, round hat, and his hair had been cropped short. All this was very becoming to him, and he looked quite handsome. His charming face always had a good-humoured expression; but there was a gentleness and serenity in his good-humour. To Kolya's surprise, Alyosha came out to him just as he was, without an overcoat. He had evidently come in haste. He held out his hand to Kolya at once.

"Here you are at last! How anxious we've been to see you!"

"There were reasons which you shall know directly. Anyway, I am glad to make your acquaintance. I've long been hoping for an opportunity, and have heard a great deal about you," Kolya muttered, a little breathless.

"We should have met anyway. I've heard a great deal about you, too; but you've been a long time coming here."

"Tell me, how are things going?"

"Ilusha is very ill. He is certainly dying."

"How awful! You must admit that medicine is a fraud, Karamazov," cried Kolya warmly.

"Ilusha has mentioned you often, very often, even in his sleep, in delirium, you know. One can see that you used to be very, very dear to him...before the incident...with the knife...Then there's another reason...Tell me, is that your dog?"

"Yes Perezvon."

"Not Zhutchka?" Alyosha looked at Kolya with eyes full of pity. "Is she lost for ever?"

"I know you would all like it to be Zhutchka. I've heard all about it." Kolya smiled mysteriously. "Listen, Karamazov, I'll tell you all about it. That's what I came for; that's what I asked you to come out here for, to explain the whole episode to you before we go in," he began with animation. "You see, Karamazov, Ilusha came into the preparatory class last spring. Well, you know what our preparatory class is--a lot of small boys. They began teasing Ilusha at once. I am two classes higher up, and, of course, I only look on at them from a distance. I saw the boy was weak and small, but he wouldn't give in to them; he fought with them. I saw he was proud, and his eyes were full of fire. I like children like that. And they teased him all the more. The worst of it was he was horribly dressed at the time, his breeches were too small for him, and there were holes in his boots. They worried him about it; they jeered at him. That I can't stand. I stood up for him at once, and gave it to them hot. I beat them, but they adore me, do you know, Karamazov?" Kolya boasted impulsively; "but I am always fond of children. I've two chickens in my hands at home now--that's what detained me to-day. So they left off beating Ilusha and I took him under my protection. I saw the boy was proud. I tell you that, the boy was proud; but in the end he became slavishly devoted to me: he did my slightest bidding, obeyed me as though I were God, tried to copy me. In the intervals between the classes he used to run to me at once' and I'd go about with him. On Sundays, too. They always laugh when an older boy makes friends with a younger one like that; but that's a prejudice. If it's my fancy, that's enough. I am teaching him, developing him. Why shouldn't I develop him if I like him? Here you, Karamazov, have taken up with all these nestlings. I see you want to influence the younger generation--to develop them, to be of use to them, and I assure you this trait in your character, which I knew by hearsay, attracted me more than anything. Let us get to the point, though. I noticed that there was a sort of softness and sentimentality coming over the boy, and you know I have a positive hatred of this sheepish sentimentality, and I have had it from a baby. There were contradictions in him, too: he was proud, but he was slavishly devoted to me, and yet all at once his eyes would flash and he'd refuse to agree with me; he'd argue, fly into a rage. I used sometimes to propound certain ideas; I could see that it was not so much that he disagreed with the ideas, but that he was simply rebelling against me, because I was cool in responding to his endearments. And so, in order to train him properly, the tenderer he was, the colder I became. I did it on purpose: that was my idea. My object was to form his character, to lick him into shape, to make a man of him...and besides...no doubt, you understand me at a word. Suddenly I noticed for three days in succession he was downcast and dejected, not because of my coldness, but for something else, something more important. I wondered what the tragedy was. I have pumped him and found out that he had somehow got to know Smerdyakov, who was footman to your late father--it was before his death, of course--and he taught the little fool a silly trick--that is, a brutal, nasty trick. He told him to take a piece of bread, to stick a pin in it, and throw it to one of those hungry dogs who snap up anything without biting it, and then to watch and see what would happen. So they prepared a piece of bread like that and threw it to Zhutchka, that shaggy dog there's been such a fuss about. The people of the house it belonged to never fed it at all, though it barked all day. (Do you like that stupid barking, Karamazov? I can't stand it.) So it rushed at the bread, swallowed it, and began to squeal; it turned round and round and ran away, squealing as it ran out of sight. That was Ilusha's own account of it. He confessed it to me, and cried bitterly. He hugged me, shaking all over. He kept on repeating 'He ran away squealing': the sight of that haunted him. He was tormented by remorse, I could see that. I took it seriously. I determined to give him a lesson for other things as well. So I must confess I wasn't quite straightforward, and pretended to be more indignant perhaps than I was. 'You've done a nasty thing,' I said, 'you are a scoundrel. I won't tell of it, of course, but I shall have nothing more to do with you for a time. I'll think it over and let you know through Smurov'--that's the boy who's just come with me; he's always ready to do anything for me-- 'whether I will have anything to do with you in the future or whether I give you up for good as a scoundrel.' He was tremendously upset. I must own I felt I'd gone too far as I spoke, but there was no help for it. I did what I thought best at the time. A day or two after, I sent Smurov to tell him that I would not speak to him again. That's what we call it when two schoolfellows refuse to have anything more to do with one another. Secretly I only meant to send him to Coventry for a few days and then, if I saw signs of repentance, to hold out my hand to him again. That was my intention. But what do you think happened? He heard Smurov's message, his eyes flashed. 'Tell Krassotkin for me,' he cried, 'that I will throw bread with pins to all the dogs--all--all of them!' 'So he's going in for a little temper. We must smoke it out of him.' And I began to treat him with contempt; whenever I met him I turned away or smiled sarcastically. And just then that affair with his father happened. You remember? You must realise that he was fearfully worked up by what had happened already. The boys, seeing I'd given him up, set on him and taunted him, shouting, 'Wisp of tow, wisp of tow!' And he had soon regular skirmishes with them, which I am very sorry for. They seem to have given him one very bad beating. One day he flew at them all as they were coming out of school. I stood a few yards off, looking on. And, I swear, I don't remember that I laughed; it was quite the other way, I felt awfully sorry for him; in another minute I would have run up to take his part. But he suddenly met my eyes. I don't know what he fancied; but he pulled out a penknife, rushed at me, and struck at my thigh, here in my right leg. I didn't move. I don't mind owning I am plucky sometimes, Karamazov. I simply looked at him contemptuously, as though to say, 'This is how you repay all my kindness! Do it again if you like, I'm at your service.' But he didn't stab me again; he broke down; he was frightened at what he had done; he threw away the knife, burst out crying, and ran away. I did not sneak on him, of course, and I made them all keep quiet, so it shouldn't come to the ears of the masters. I didn't even tell my mother till it had healed up. And the wound was a mere scratch. And then I heard that the same day he'd been throwing stones and had bitten your finger--but you understand now what a state he was in! Well, it can't be helped: it was stupid of me not to come and forgive him--that is, to make it up with him--when he was taken ill. I am sorry for it now. But I had a special reason. So now I've told you all about it...but I'm afraid it was stupid of me."

"Oh, what a pity," exclaimed Alyosha, with feeling, "that I didn't know before what terms you were on with him, or I'd have come to you long ago to beg you to go to him with me. Would you believe it, when he was feverish he talked about you in delirium. I didn't know how much you were to him! And you've really not succeeded in finding that dog? His father and the boys have been hunting all over the town for it. Would you believe it, since he's been ill, I've three times heard him repeat with tears, 'It's because I killed Zhutchka, father, that I am ill now. God is punishing me for it.' He can't get that idea out of his head. And if the dog were found and proved to be alive, one might almost fancy the joy would cure him. We have all rested our hopes on you."

"Tell me, what made you hope that I should be the one to find him?" Kolya asked, with great curiosity. "Why did you reckon on me rather than anyone else?"

"There was a report that you were looking for the dog, and that you would bring it when you'd found it. Smurov said something of the sort. We've all been trying to persuade Ilusha that the dog is alive, that it's been seen. The boys brought him a live hare: he just looked at it, with a faint smile, and asked them to set it free in

253

the fields. And so we did. His father has just this moment come back, bringing him a mastiff pup, hoping to comfort him with that; but I think it only makes it worse."

"Tell me, Karamazov, what sort of man is the father? I know him, but what do you make of him--a mountebank, a buffoon?"

"Oh no; there are people of deep feeling who have been somehow crushed. Buffoonery in them is a form of resentful irony against those to whom they daren't speak the truth, from having been for years humiliated and intimidated by them. Believe me, Krassotkin, that sort of buffoonery is sometimes tragic in the extreme. His whole life now is centred in Ilusha, and if Ilusha dies, he will either go mad with grief or kill himself. I feel almost certain of that when I look at him now."

"I understand you, Karamazov. I see you understand human nature," Kolya added, with feeling.

"And as soon as I saw you with a dog, I thought it was Zhutchka you were bringing."

"Wait a bit, Karamazov, perhaps we shall find it yet; but this is Perezvon. I'll let him go in now and perhaps it will amuse Ilusha more than the mastiff pup. Wait a bit, Karamazov, you will know something in a minute. But, I say, I am keeping you here!" Kolya cried suddenly. "You've no overcoat on in this bitter cold. You see what an egoist I am. Oh, we are all egoists, Karamazov!"

"Don't trouble; it is cold, but I don't often catch cold. Let us go in, though, and, by the way, what is your name? I know you are called Kolya, but what else?"

"Nikolay--Nikolay Ivanovitch Krassotkin, or, as they say in official documents, 'Krassotkin son.'" Kolya laughed for some reason, but added suddenly, "Of course I hate my name Nikolay."

"Why so?"

"It's so trivial, so ordinary."

"You are thirteen?" asked Alyosha.

"No, fourteen--that is, I shall be fourteen very soon, in a fortnight. I'll confess one weakness of mine, Karamazov, just to you, since it's our first meeting, so that you may understand my character at once. I hate being asked my age, more than that...and in fact...there's a libellous story going about me, that last week I played robbers with the preparatory boys. It's a fact that I did play with them, but it's a perfect libel to say I did it for my own amusement. I have reasons for believing that you've heard the story; but I wasn't playing for my own amusement, it was for the sake of the children, because they couldn't think of anything to do by themselves. But they've always got some silly tale. This is an awful town for gossip, I can tell you."

"But what if you had been playing for your own amusement, what's the harm?"

"Come, I say, for my own amusement! You don't play horses, do you?"

"But you must look at it like this," said Alyosha, smiling. "Grown-up people go to the theatre and there the adventures of all sorts of heroes are represented--sometimes there are robbers and battles, too--and isn't that just the same thing, in a different form, of course? And young people's games of soldiers or robbers in their playtime are also art in its first stage. You know, they spring from the growing artistic instincts of the young. And sometimes these games are much better than performances in the theatre; the only difference is that people go there to look at the actors, while in these games the young people are the actors themselves. But that's only natural."

"You think so? Is that your idea?" Kolya looked at him intently. "Oh, you know, that's rather an interesting view. When I go home, I'll think it over. I'll admit I thought I might learn something from you. I've come to learn of you, Karamazov," Kolya concluded, in a voice full of spontaneous feeling.

"And I of you," said Alyosha, smiling and pressing his hand.

Kolya was much pleased with Alyosha. What struck him most was that he treated him exactly like an equal and that he talked to him just as if he were "quite grown up."

"I'll show you something directly, Karamazov; it's a theatrical performance, too," he said, laughing nervously. "That's why I've come."

"Let us go first to the people of the house, on the left. All the boys leave their coats in there, because the room is small and hot."

"Oh, I'm only coming in for a minute. I'll keep on my overcoat. Perezvon will stay here in the passage and be dead. Ici, Perezvon, lie down and be dead! You see how he's dead. I'll go in first and explore, then I'll whistle to him when I think fit, and you'll see, he'll dash in like mad. Only Smurov must not forget to open the door at the moment. I'll arrange it all and you'll see something."

Chapter 5. By Ilusha's Bedside

THE room inhabited by the family of the retired captain Snegiryov is already familiar to the reader. It was close and crowded at that moment with a number of visitors. Several boys were sitting with Ilusha, and though all of them, like Smurov, were prepared to deny that it was Alyosha who had brought them and reconciled them with Ilusha, it was really the fact. All the art he had used had been to take them, one by one, to Ilusha, without "sheepish sentimentality," appearing to do so casually and without design. It was a great consolation to Ilusha in his suffering. He was greatly touched by seeing the almost tender affection and sympathy shown him by these boys, who had been his enemies. Krassotkin was the only one missing and his absence was a heavy load on Ilusha's heart. Perhaps the bitterest of all his bitter memories was his stabbing Krassotkin, who had been his one friend and protector. Clever little Smurov, who was the first to make it up with Ilusha, thought it was so. But when Smurov hinted to Krassotkin that Alyosha wanted to come and see him about something, the latter cut him short, bidding Smurov tell "Karamazov" at once that he knew best what to do, that he wanted no one's advice, and that, if he went to see Ilusha, he would choose his own time for he had "his own reasons."

That was a fortnight before this Sunday. That was why Alyosha had not been to see him, as he had meant to. But though he waited he sent Smurov to him twice again. Both times Krassotkin met him with a curt, impatient refusal, sending Alyosha a message not to bother him any more, that if he came himself, he, Krassotkin, would not go to Ilusha at all. Up to the very last day, Smurov did not know that Kolya meant to go to Ilusha that morning, and only the evening before, as he parted from Smurov, Kolya abruptly told him to wait at home for him next morning, for he would go with him to the Snegiryovs, but warned him on no account to say he was coming, as he wanted to drop in casually. Smurov obeyed. Smurov's fancy that Kolya would bring back the lost dog was based on the words Kolya had dropped that "they must be asses not to find the dog, if it was alive." When Smurov, waiting for an opportunity, timidly hinted at his guess about the dog, Krassotkin flew into a violent rage. "I'm not such an ass as to go hunting about the town for other people's dogs when I've got a dog of my own! And how can you imagine a dog could be alive after swallowing a pin? Sheepish sentimentality, thats what it is!

For the last fortnight Ilusha had not left his little bed under the ikons in the corner. He had not been to school since the day he met Alyosha and bit his finger. He was taken ill the same day, though for a month afterwards he was sometimes able to get up and walk about the room and passage. But latterly he had become so weak that he could not move without help from his father. His father was terribly concerned about him. He even gave up drinking and was almost crazy with terror that his boy would die. And often, especially after leading him round the room on his arm and putting him back to bed, he would run to a dark corner in the passage and, leaning his head against the wall, he would break into paroxysms of violent weeping, stifling his sobs that they might not be heard by Ilusha.

Returning to the room, he would usually begin doing something to amuse and comfort his precious boy: he would tell him stories, funny anecdotes, or would mimic comic people he had happened to meet, even imitate the howls and cries of animals. But Ilusha could not bear to see his father fooling and playing the buffoon. Though the boy tried not to show how he disliked it, he saw with an aching heart that his father was an object of contempt, and he was continually haunted by the memory of the "wisp of tow" and that "terrible day."

Nina, Ilusha's gentle, crippled sister, did not like her father's buffoonery either (Varvara had been gone for some time past to Petersburg to study at the university). But the half-imbecile mother was greatly diverted and laughed heartily when her husband began capering about or performing something. It was the only way she could be amused; all the rest of the time she was grumbling and complaining that now everyone had forgotten her, that no one treated her with respect, that she was slighted, and so on. But during the last few days she had completely changed. She began looking constantly at Ilusha's bed in the corner and seemed lost in thought. She was more silent, quieter, and, if she cried, she cried quietly so as not to be heard. The captain noticed the change in her with mournful perplexity. The boys' visits at first only angered her, but later on their merry shouts and stories began to divert her, and at last she liked them so much that, if the boys had given up coming, she would have felt dreary without them. When the children told some story or played a game, she laughed and clapped her hands. She called some of them to her and kissed them. She was particularly fond of Smurov.

As for the captain, the presence in his room of the children, who came to cheer up Ilusha, filled his heart from the first with ecstatic joy. He even hoped that Ilusha would now get over his depression and that that would hasten his recovery. In spite of his alarm about Ilusha, he had not, till lately, felt one minute's doubt of his boy's ultimate recovery.

He met his little visitors with homage, waited upon them hand and foot; he was ready to be their horse and even began letting them ride on his back, but Ilusha did not like the game and it was given up. He began buying little things for them, gingerbread and nuts, gave them tea and cut them sandwiches. It must be noted that all this time he had plenty of money. He had taken the two hundred roubles from Katerina Ivanovna just as Alyosha had predicted he would. And afterwards Katerina Ivanovna, learning more about their circumstances and Ilusha's illness, visited them herself, made the acquaintance of the family, and succeeded in fascinating the half-imbecile mother. Since then she had been lavish in helping them, and the captain, terror-stricken at the thought that his boy might be dying, forgot his pride and humbly accepted her assistance.

All this time Doctor Herzenstube, who was called in by Katerina Ivanovna, came punctually every other day, but little was gained by his visits and he dosed the invalid mercilessly. But on that Sunday morning a new doctor was expected, who had come from Moscow, where he had a great reputation. Katerina Ivanovna had sent for him from Moscow at great expense, not expressly for Ilusha, but for another object of which more will be said in its place hereafter. But, as he had come, she had asked him to see Ilusha as well, and the captain had been told to expect him. He hadn't the slightest idea that Kolya Krassotkin was coming, though he had long wished for a visit from the boy for whom Ilusha was fretting.

At the moment when Krassotkin opened the door and came into the room, the captain and all the boys were round Ilusha's bed, looking at a tiny mastiff pup, which had only been born the day before, though the captain had bespoken it a week ago to comfort and amuse Ilusha, who was still fretting over the lost and probably dead Zhutchka. Ilusha, who had heard three days before that he was to be presented with a puppy, not an ordinary puppy, but a pedigree mastiff (a very important point, of course), tried from delicacy of feeling to pretend that he was pleased. But his father and the boys could not help seeing that the puppy only served to recall to his little heart the thought of the unhappy dog he had killed. The puppy lay beside him feebly moving and he, smiling sadly, stroked it with his thin, pale, wasted hand. Clearly he liked the puppy, but...it wasn't Zhutchka; if he could have had Zhutchka and the puppy, too, then he would have been completely happy.

"Krassotkin!" cried one of the boys suddenly. He was the first to see him come in.

Krassotkin's entrance made a general sensation; the boys moved away and stood on each side of the bed, so that he could get a full view of Ilusha. The captain ran eagerly to meet Kolya.

"Please come in...you are welcome!" he said hurriedly. "Ilusha, Mr. Krassotkin has come to see you!"

But Krassotkin, shaking hands with him hurriedly, instantly showed his complete knowledge of the manners of good society. He turned first to the captain's wife sitting in her armchair, who was very ill-humoured at the moment, and was grumbling that the boys stood between her and Ilusha's bed and did not let her see the new puppy. With the greatest courtesy he made her a bow, scraping his foot, and turning to Nina, he made her, as the only other lady present, a similar bow. This polite behaviour made an extremely favourable impression on the deranged lady.

"There,.you can see at once he is a young man that has been well brought up," she commented aloud, throwing up her hands; "But as for our other visitors they come in one on the top of another."

"How do you mean, mamma, one on the top of another, how is that?" muttered the captain affectionately, though a little anxious on her account.

"That's how they ride in. They get on each other's shoulders in the passage and prance in like that on a respectable family. Strange sort of visitors!"

"But who's come in like that, mamma?"

"Why, that boy came in riding on that one's back and this one on that one's."

Kolya was already by Ilusha's bedside. The sick boy turned visibly paler. He raised himself in the bed and looked intently at Kolya. Kolya had not seen his little friend for two months, and he was overwhelmed at the sight of him. He had never imagined that he would see such a wasted, yellow face, such enormous, feverishly glowing eyes and such thin little hands. He saw, with grieved surprise, Ilusha's rapid, hard breathing and dry lips. He stepped close to him, held out his hand, and almost overwhelmed, he said:

"Well, old man...how are you?" But his voice failed him, he couldn't achieve an appearance of ease; his face suddenly twitched and the corners of his mouth quivered. Ilusha smiled a pitiful little smile, still unable to utter a word. Something moved Kolya to raise his hand and pass it over Ilusha's hair.

"Never mind!" he murmured softly to him to cheer him up, or perhaps not knowing why he said it. For a minute they were silent again.

"Hallo, so you've got a new puppy?" Kolya said suddenly, in a most callous voice.

"Ye-es," answered Ilusha in a long whisper, gasping for breath.

"A black nose, that means he'll be fierce, a good house-dog," Kolya observed gravely and stolidly, as if the only thing he cared about was the puppy and its black nose. But in reality he still had to do his utmost to control his feelings not to burst out crying like a child, and do what he would he could not control it. "When it grows up, you'll have to keep it on the chain, I'm sure."

"He'll be a huge dog!" cried one of the boys.

"Of course he will," "a mastiff," "large," "like this," "as big as a calf," shouted several voices.

"As big as a calf, as a real calf," chimed in the captain. "I got one like that on purpose, one of the fiercest breed, and his parents are huge and very fierce, they stand as high as this from the floor...Sit down here, on

Ilusha's bed, or here on the bench. You are welcome, we've been hoping to see you a long time...You were so kind as to come with Alexey Fyodorovitch?"

Krassotkin sat on the edge of the bed, at Ilusha's feet. Though he had perhaps prepared a free-and-easy opening for the conversation on his way, now he completely lost the thread of it.

"No...I came with Perezvon. I've got a dog now, called Perezvon. A Slavonic name. He's out there...if I whistle, he'll run in. I've brought a dog, too," he said, addressing Ilusha all at once. "Do you remember Zhutchka, old man?" he suddenly fired the question at him.

Ilusha's little face quivered. He looked with an agonised expression at Kolya. Alyosha, standing at the door, frowned and signed to Kolya not to speak of Zhutchka, but he did not or would not notice.

"Where...is Zhutchka?" Ilusha asked in a broken voice.

"Oh well, my boy, your Zhutchka's lost and done for!"

Ilusha did not speak, but he fixed an intent gaze once more on Kolya. Alyosha, catching Kolya's eye, signed to him vigourously again, but he turned away his eyes pretending not to have noticed.

"It must have run away and died somewhere. It must have died after a meal like that," Kolya pronounced pitilessly, though he seemed a little breathless. "But I've got a dog, Perezvon...A Slavonic name...I've brought him to show you."

"I don't want him!" said Ilusha suddenly.

"No, no, you really must see him...it will amuse you. I brought him on purpose...He's the same sort of shaggy dog...You allow me to call in my dog, madam?" He suddenly addressed Madame Snegiryov, with inexplicable excitement in his manner.

"I don't want him, I don't want him!" cried Ilusha, with a mournful break in his voice. There was a reproachful light in his eyes.

"You'd better," the captain started up from the chest by the wall on which he had just sat down, "you'd better...another time," he muttered, but Kolya could not be restrained. He hurriedly shouted to Smurov, "Open the door," and as soon as it was open, he blew his whistle. Perezvon dashed headlong into the room.

"Jump, Perezvon, beg! Beg!" shouted Kolya, jumping up, and the dog stood erect on its hind-legs by Ilusha's bedside. What followed was a surprise to everyone: Ilusha started, lurched violently forward, bent over Perezvon and gazed at him, faint with suspense.

"It's...Zhutchka!" he cried suddenly, in a voice breaking with joy and suffering.

"And who did you think it was?" Krassotkin shouted with all his might, in a ringing, happy voice, and bending down he seized the dog and lifted him up to Ilusha.

"Look, old man, you see, blind of one eye and the left ear is torn, just the marks you described to me. It was by that I found him. I found him directly. He did not belong to anyone!" he explained, to the captain, to his wife, to Alyosha and then again to Ilusha. "He used to live in the Fedotovs' backyard. Though he made his home there, they did not feed him. He was a stray dog that had run away from the village...I found him...You see, old man, he couldn't have swallowed what you gave him. If he had, he must have died, he must have! So he must have spat it out, since he is alive. You did not see him do it. But the pin pricked his tongue, that is why he squealed. He ran away squealing and you thought he'd swallowed it. He might well squeal, because the skin of dogs' mouths is so tender...tenderer than in men, much tenderer!" Kolya cried impetuously, his face glowing and radiant with delight. Ilusha could not speak. White as a sheet, he gazed open-mouthed at Kolya, with his great eyes almost starting out of his head. And if Krassotkin, who had no suspicion of it, had known what a disastrous and fatal effect such a moment might have on the sick child's health, nothing would have induced him to play such a trick on him. But Alyosha was perhaps the only person in the room who realised it. As for the captain he behaved like a small child.

"Zhutchka! It's Zhutchka!" he cried in a blissful voice, "Ilusha, this is Zhutchka, your Zhutchka! Mamma, this is Zhutchka!" He was almost weeping.

"And I never guessed!" cried Smurov regretfully. "Bravo, Krassotkin! I said he'd find the dog and here he's found him."

"Here he's found him!" another boy repeated gleefully.

"Krassotkin's a brick! cried a third voice.

"He's a brick, he's a brick!" cried the other boys, and they began clapping.

"Wait, wait," Krassotkin did his utmost to shout above them all. "I'll tell you how it happened, that's the whole point. I found him, I took him home and hid him at once. I kept him locked up at home and did not show him to anyone till to-day. Only Smurov has known for the last fortnight, but I assured him this dog was called Perezvon and he did not guess. And meanwhile I taught the dog all sorts of tricks. You should only see all the things he can do! I trained him so as to bring you a well trained dog, in good condition, old man, so as to be able to say to you, 'See, old man, what a fine dog your Zhutchka is now!' Haven't you a bit of meat? He'll show you a trick that will make you die with laughing. A piece of meat, haven't you got any?"

The captain ran across the passage to the landlady, where their cooking was done. Not to lose precious time, Kolya, in desperate haste, shouted to Perezvon, "Dead!" And the dog immediately turned round and lay on his back with its four paws in the air. The boys laughed, Ilusha looked on with the same suffering smile, but the person most delighted with the dog's performance was "mamma." She laughed at the dog and began snapping her fingers and calling it, "Perezvon, Perezvon!"

"Nothing will make him get up, nothing!" Kolya cried triumphantly, proud of his success. "He won't move for all the shouting in the world, but if I call to him, he'll jump up in a minute. Ici, Perezvon!" The dog leapt up and bounded about, whining with delight. The captain ran back with a piece of cooked beef.

"Is it hot?" Kolya inquired hurriedly, with a business-like air, taking the meat. "Dogs don't like hot things. No, it's all right. Look, everybody, look, Ilusha, look, old man; why aren't you looking? He does not look at him, now I've brought him."

The new trick consisted in making the dog stand motionless with his nose out and putting a tempting morsel of meat just on his nose. The luckless dog had to stand without moving, with the meat on his nose, as long as his master chose to keep him, without a movement, perhaps for half an hour. But he kept Perezvon only for a brief moment.

"Paid for!" cried Kolya, and the meat passed in a flash from the dog's nose to his mouth. The audience, of course, expressed enthusiasm and surprise.

"Can you really have put off coming all this time simply to train the dog?" exclaimed Alyosha, with an involuntary note of reproach in his voice.

"Simply for that!" answered Kolya, with perfect simplicity. "I wanted to show him in all his glory."

"Perezvon! Perezvon," called Ilusha suddenly, snapping his thin fingers and beckoning to the dog.

"What is it? Let him jump up on the bed! Ici, Perezvon!" Kolya slapped the bed and Perezvon darted up by Ilusha. The boy threw both arms round his head and Perezvon instantly licked his cheek. Ilusha crept close to him, stretched himself out in bed and hid his face in the dog's shaggy coat.

"Dear, dear!" kept exclaiming the captain. Kolya sat down again on the edge of the bed.

"Ilusha, I can show you another trick. I've brought you a little cannon. You remember, I told you about it before and you said how much you'd like to see it. Well, here, I've brought it to you."

And Kolya hurriedly pulled out of his satchel the little bronze cannon. He hurried, because he was happy himself. Another time he would have waited till the sensation made by Perezvon had passed off, now he hurried on, regardless of all consideration. "You are all happy now," he felt, "so here's something to make you happier!" He was perfectly enchanted himself.

"I've been coveting this thing for a long while; it's for you, old man, it's for you. It belonged to Morozov, it was no use to him, he had it from his brother. I swopped a book from father's book-case for it, A Kinsman of Mahomet, or Salutary Folly, a scandalous book published in Moscow a hundred years ago, before they had any censorship. And Morozov has a taste for such things. He was grateful to me, too..."

Kolya held the cannon in his hand so that all could see and admire it. Ilusha raised himself, and, with his right arm still round the dog, he gazed enchanted at the toy. The sensation was even greater when Kolya announced that he had gunpowder too, and that it could be fired off at once "if it won't alarm the ladies." "Mamma" immediately asked to look at the toy closer and her request was granted. She was much pleased with the little bronze cannon on wheels and began rolling it to and fro on her lap. She readily gave permission for the cannon to be fired, without any idea of what she had been asked. Kolya showed the powder and the shot. The captain, as a military man, undertook to load it, putting in a minute quantity of powder. He asked that the shot might be put off till another time. The cannon was put on the floor, aiming towards an empty part of the room, three grains of powder were thrust into the touchhole and a match was put to it. A magnificent explosion followed. Mamma was startled, but at once laughed with delight. The boys gazed in speechless triumph. But the captain, looking at Ilusha, was more enchanted than any of them. Kolya picked up the cannon and immediately presented it to Ilusha, together with the powder and the shot.

"I got it for you, for you! I've been keeping it for you a long time," he repeated once more in his delight.

"Oh, give it to me! No, give me the cannon!" mamma began begging like a little child. Her face showed a piteous fear that she would not get it. Kolya was disconcerted. The captain fidgeted uneasily.

"Mamma, mamma," he ran to her, "the cannon's yours, of course, but let Ilusha have it, because it's a present to him, but it's just as good as yours. Ilusha will always let you play with it; it shall belong to both of you, both of you."

"No, I don't want it to belong to both of us; I want it to be mine altogether, not Ilusha's," persisted mamma, on the point of tears.

"Take it, mother, here, keep it!" Ilusha cried. "Krassotkin, may I give it to my mother?" he turned to Krassotkin with an imploring face, as though he were afraid he might be offended at his giving his present to someone else.

"Of course you may," Krassotkin assented heartily, and, taking the cannon from Ilusha, he handed it himself to mamma with a polite bow. She was so touched that she cried.

"Ilusha, darling, he's the one who loves his mammal" she said tenderly, and at once began wheeling the cannon to and fro on her lap again.

"Mamma, let me kiss your hand." The captain darted up to her at once and did so.

"And I never saw such a charming fellow as this nice boy," said the grateful lady, pointing to Krassotkin.

"And I'll bring you as much powder as you like, Ilusha. We make the powder ourselves now. Borovikov found out how it's made- twenty-four parts of saltpetre, ten of sulphur and six of birchwood charcoal. It's all pounded together, mixed into a paste with water and rubbed through a tammy sieve-that's how it's done."

"Smurov told me about your powder, only father says it's not real gunpowder," responded Ilusha.

"Not real?" Kolya flushed. "It burns. I don't know, of course."

"No, I didn't mean that," put in the captain with a guilty face. "I only said that real powder is not made like that, but that's nothing, it can be made so."

"I don't know, you know best. We lighted some in a pomatum pot, it burned splendidly, it all burnt away leaving only a tiny ash. But that was only the paste, and if you rub it through...but of course you know best, I don't know...And Bulkin's father thrashed him on account of our powder, did you hear?" he turned to Ilusha.

"We had prepared a whole bottle of it and he used to keep it under his bed. His father saw it. He said it might explode, and thrashed him on the spot. He was going to make a complaint against me to the masters. He is not allowed to go about with me now, no one is allowed to go about with me now. Smurov is not allowed to either; I've got a bad name with everyone. They say I'm a 'desperate character,'" Kolya smiled scornfully. "It all began from what happened on the railway."

"Ah, we've heard of that exploit of yours, too," cried the captain. "How could you lie still on the line? Is it possible you weren't the least afraid, lying there under the train? Weren't you frightened?"

The captain was abject in his flattery of Kolya.

"N--not particularly," answered Kolya carelessly. "What's blasted my reputation more than anything here was that cursed goose," he said, turning again to Ilusha--but though he assumed an unconcerned air as he talked, he still could not control himself and was continually missing the note he tried to keep up.

"Ah! I heard about the goose!" Ilusha laughed, beaming all over. "They told me, but I didn't understand. Did they really take you to the court?"

"The most stupid, trivial affair, they made a mountain of a mole-hill as they always do," Kolya began carelessly. "I was walking through the market-place here one day, just when they'd driven in the geese. I stopped and looked at them. All at once a fellow, who is an errand-boy at Plotnikov's now, looked at me and said, 'What are you looking at the geese for?' I looked at him; he was a stupid, moon-faced fellow of twenty. I am always on the side of the peasantry, you know. I like talking to the peasants...We've dropped behind the peasants that's an axiom. I believe you are laughing, Karamazov?"

"No, Heaven forbid, I am listening," said Alyosha with a most good-natured air, and the sensitive Kolya was immediately reassured."

"My theory, Karamazov, is clear and simple," he hurried on again, looking pleased. "I believe in the people and am always glad to give them their due, but I am not for spoiling them, that is a sine qua non...But I was telling you about the goose. So I turned to the fool and answered, 'I am wondering what the goose thinks about.' He looked at me quite stupidly, 'And what does the goose think about?' he asked. 'Do you see that cart full of oats?'I said. 'The oats are dropping out of the sack, and the goose has put its neck right under the wheel to gobble them up--do you see?' 'I see that quite well,' he said. 'Well,' said I, 'if that cart were to move on a little, would it break the goose's neck or not?' 'It'd be sure to break it,' and he grinned all over his face, highly delighted. 'Come on, then,' said I, 'let's try.' 'Let's,' he said. And it did not take us long to arrange: he stood at the bridle without being noticed, and I stood on one side to direct the goose. And the owner wasn't looking, he was talking to someone, so I had nothing to do, the goose thrust its head in after the oats of itself, under the cart, just under the wheel. I winked at the lad, he tugged at the bridle, and crack. The goose's neck was broken in half. And, as luck would have it, all the peasants saw us at that moment and they kicked up a shindy at once. 'You did that on purpose!' 'No, not on purpose.' 'Yes, you did, on purpose!' Well, they shouted, 'Take him to the justice of the peace!' They took me, too. 'You were there, too,' they said, 'you helped, you're known all over the market!' And, for some reason, I really am known all over the market," Kolya added conceitedly. "We all went off to the justice's, they brought the goose, too. The fellow was crying in a great funk, simply blubbering like a woman. And the farmer kept shouting that you could kill any number of geese like that. Well, of course, there were witnesses. The justice of the peace settled it in a minute, that the farmer was to be paid a rouble for the goose, and the fellow to have the goose. And he was warned not to play such pranks again. And the fellow kept blubbering like a woman. 'It wasn't me,' he said, 'it was he egged me on,' and he pointed to me. I answered with the utmost composure that I hadn't egged him on, that I simply stated the general proposition, had spoken hypothetically. The justice of the peace smiled and was vexed with himself once for having smiled. 'I'll complain to your masters of you, so that for the future you mayn't waste your time on such general propositions, instead of sitting at your books and learning your lessons.' He didn't complain to the masters, that was a joke, but the matter noised abroad and came to the ears of the masters. Their ears are long, you know! The classical master, Kolbasnikov, was particularly shocked about it, but Dardanelov got me off again. But Kolbasnikov is savage with everyone now like a green ass. Did you know, Ilusha, he is just married, got a dowry of a thousand roubles, and his bride's a regular fright of the first rank and the last degree. The third-class fellows wrote an epigram on it:

Astounding news has reached the class,

Kolbasnikov has been an ass.

And so on, awfully funny, I'll bring it to you later on. I say nothing against Dardanelov, he is a learned man, there's no doubt about it. I respect men like that and it's not because he stood up for me."

"But you took him down about the founders of Troy!" Smurov put in suddenly, proud of Krassotkin at such a moment. He was particularly pleased with the story of the goose.

"Did you really take him down?" the captain inquired, in a flattering way. "On the question who founded Troy? We heard of it, Ilusha told me about it at the time."

"He knows everything, father, he knows more than any of us!" put in Ilusha; "he only pretends to be like that, but really he is top in every subject..."

Ilusha looked at Kolya with infinite happiness.

"Oh, that's all nonsense about Troy, a trivial matter. I consider this an unimportant question," said Kolya with haughty humility. He had by now completely recovered his dignity, though he was still a little uneasy. He felt that he was greatly excited and that he had talked about the goose, for instance, with too little reserve, while Alyosha had looked serious and had not said a word all the time. And the vain boy began by degrees to have a rankling fear that Alyosha was silent because he despised him, and thought he was showing off before him. If he dared to think anything like that, Kolya would--

"I regard the question as quite a trivial one," he rapped out again, proudly.

"And I know who founded Troy," a boy, who had not spoken before, said suddenly, to the surprise of everyone. He was silent and seemed to be shy. He was a pretty boy of about eleven, called Kartashov. He was sitting near the door. Kolya looked at him with dignified amazement.

The fact was that the identity of the founders of Troy had become a secret for the whole school, a secret which could only be discovered by reading Smaragdov, and no one had Smaragdov but Kolya. One day, when Kolya's back was turned, Kartashov hastily opened Smaragdov, which lay among Kolya's books, and immediately lighted on the passage relating to the foundation of Troy. This was a good time ago, but he felt uneasy and could not bring himself to announce publicly that he too knew who had founded Troy, afraid of what might happen and of Krassotkin's somehow putting him to shame over it. But now he couldn't resist saying it. For weeks he had been longing to.

"Well, who did found it?" Kolya, turning to him with haughty superciliousness. He saw from his face that he really did know and at once made up his mind how to take it. There was so to speak, a discordant note in the general harmony.

"Troy was founded by Teucer, Dardanus, Ilius and Tros," the boy rapped out at once, and in the same instant he blushed, blushed so, that it was painful to look at him. But the boys stared at him, stared at him for a whole minute, and then all the staring eyes turned at once and were fastened upon Kolya, who was still scanning the audacious boy with disdainful composure.

"In what sense did they found it?" he deigned to comment at last. "And what is meant by founding a city or a state? What do they do? Did they go and each lay a brick, do you suppose?"

There was laughter. The offending boy turned from pink to crimson. He was silent and on the point of tears. Kolya held him so for a minute.

"Before you talk of a historical event like the foundation of a nationality, you must first understand what you mean by it," he admonished him in stern, incisive tones. "But I attach no consequence to these old wives' tales and I don't think much of universal history in general," he added carelessly, addressing the company generally.

"Universal history?" the captain inquired, looking almost scared.

"Yes, universal history! It's the study of the successive follies of mankind and nothing more. The only subjects I respect are mathematics and natural science," said Kolya. He was showing off and he stole a glance at

Alyosha; his was the only opinion he was afraid of there. But Alyosha was still silent and still serious as before. If Alyosha had said a word it would have stopped him, but Alyosha was silent and "it might be the silence of contempt," and that finally irritated Kolya.

"The classical languages, too...they are simply madness, nothing more. You seem to disagree with me again, Karamazov?"

"I don't agree," said Alyosha, with a faint smile.

"The study of the classics, if you ask my opinion, is simply a police measure, that's simply why it has been introduced into our schools." By degrees Kolya began to get breathless again. "Latin and Greek were introduced because they are a bore and because they stupefy the intellect. It was dull before, so what could they do to make things duller? It was senseless enough before, so what could they do to make it more senseless? So they thought of Greek and Latin. That's my opinion, I hope I shall never change it," Kolya finished abruptly. His cheeks were flushed.

"That's true," assented Smurov suddenly, in a ringing tone of conviction. He had listened attentively.

"And yet he is first in Latin himself," cried one of the group of boys suddenly.

"Yes, father, he says that and yet he is first in Latin," echoed Ilusha.

"What of it?" Kolya thought fit to defend himself, though the praise was very sweet to him. "I am fagging away at Latin because I have to, because I promised my mother to pass my examination, and I think that whatever you do, it's worth doing it well. But in my soul I have a profound contempt for the classics and all that fraud...You don't agree, Karamazov?"

"Why 'fraud'?" Alyosha smiled again.

"Well, all the classical authors have been translated into all languages, so it was not for the sake of studying the classics they introduced Latin, but solely as a police measure, to stupefy the intelligence. So what can one call it but a fraud?"

"Why, who taught you all this?" cried Alyosha, surprised at last.

"In the first place I am capable of thinking for myself without being taught. Besides, what I said just now about the classics being translated our teacher Kolbasnikov has said to the whole of the third class."

"The doctor has come!" cried Nina, who had been silent till then.

A carriage belonging to Madame Hohlakov drove up to the gate. The captain, who had been expecting the doctor all the morning, rushed headlong out to meet him. "Mamma" pulled herself together and assumed a dignified air. Alyosha went up to Ilusha and began setting his pillows straight. Nina, from her invalid chair, anxiously watched him putting the bed tidy. The boys hurriedly took leave. Some of them promised to come again in the evening. Kolya called Perezvon and the dog jumped off the bed.

"I won't go away, I won't go away," Kolya said hastily to Ilusha. "I'll wait in the passage and come back when the doctor's gone, I'll come back with Perezvon."

But by now the doctor had entered, an important-looking person with long, dark whiskers and a shiny, shaven chin, wearing a bearskin coat. As he crossed the threshold he stopped, taken aback; he probably fancied he had come to the wrong place. "How is this? Where am I?" he muttered, not removing his coat nor his peaked sealskin cap. The crowd, the poverty of the room, the washing hanging on a line in the corner, puzzled him. The captain, bent double, was bowing low before him.

"It's here, sir, here, sir," he muttered cringingly; "it's here, you've come right, you were coming to us..."

"Sne-gi-ryov?" the doctor said loudly and pompously. "Mr. Snegiryov--is that you?"

"That's me, sir!"

"Ah!"

The doctor looked round the room with a squeamish air once more and threw off his coat, displaying to all eyes the grand decoration at his neck. The captain caught the fur coat in the air, and the doctor took off his cap.

"Where is the patient?" he asked emphatically.

Chapter 6. Precocity

"WHAT do you think the doctor will say to him?" Kolya asked quickly. "What a repulsive mug, though, hasn't he? I can't endure medicine!"

"Ilusha is dying. I think that's certain," answered Alyosha, mournfully.

"They are rogues! Medicine's a fraud! I am glad to have made your acquaintance, though, Karamazov. I wanted to know you for a long time. I am only sorry we meet in such sad circumstances."

Kolya had a great inclination to say something even warmer and more demonstrative, but he felt ill at ease. Alyosha noticed this, smiled, and pressed his hand.

"I've long learned to respect you as a rare person," Kolya muttered again, faltering and uncertain. "I have heard you are a mystic and have been in the monastery. I know you are a mystic, but...that hasn't put me off. Contact with real life will cure you...It's always so with characters like yours."

"What do you mean by mystic? Cure me of what?" Alyosha was rather astonished.

"Oh, God and all the rest of it."

"What, don't you believe in God?"

"Oh, I've nothing against God. Of course, God is only a hypothesis, but...I admit that He is needed...for the order of the universe and all that...and that if there were no God He would have to be invented," added Kolya, beginning to blush. He suddenly fancied that Alyosha might think he was trying to show off his knowledge and to prove that he was "grown up." "I haven't the slightest desire to show off my knowledge to him," Kolya thought indignantly. And all of a sudden he felt horribly annoyed.

"I must confess I can't endure entering on such discussions," he said with a final air. "It's possible for one who doesn't believe in God to love mankind, don't you think so? Voltaire didn't believe in God and loved mankind?" ("I am at it again," he thought to himself.)

"Voltaire believed in God, though not very much, I think, and I don't think he loved mankind very much either," said Alyosha quietly, gently, and quite naturally, as though he were talking to someone of his own age, or even older. Kolya was particularly struck by Alyosha's apparent diffidence about his opinion of Voltaire. He seemed to be leaving the question for him, little Kolya, to settle.

"Have you read Voltaire?" Alyosha finished.

"No, not to say read...But I've read Candide in the Russian translation...in an absurd, grotesque, old translation.. (At it again! again!)"

"And did you understand it?"

"Oh, yes, everything...That is...Why do you suppose I shouldn't understand it? There's a lot of nastiness in it, of course...Of course I can understand that it's a philosophical novel and written to advocate an idea..." Kolya was getting mixed by now. "I am a Socialist, Karamazov, I am an incurable Socialist," he announced suddenly, apropos of nothing.

"A Socialist?" laughed Alyosha. "But when have you had time to become one? Why, I thought you were only thirteen?"

Kolya winced.

"In the first place I am not thirteen, but fourteen, fourteen in a fortnight," he flushed angrily, "and in the second place I am at a complete loss to understand what my age has to do with it? The question is what are my convictions, not what is my age, isn't it?"

"When you are older, you'll understand for yourself the influence of age on convictions. I fancied, too, that you were not expressing your own ideas," Alyosha answered serenely and modestly, but Kolya interrupted him hotly:

"Come, you want obedience and mysticism. You must admit that the Christian religion, for instance, has only been of use to the rich and the powerful to keep the lower classes in slavery. That's so, isn't it?"

"Ah, I know where you read that, and I am sure someone told you so!" cried Alyosha.

"I say, what makes you think I read it? And certainly no one told so. I can think for myself...I am not opposed to Christ, if you like. He was a most humane person, and if He were alive to-day, He would be found in the ranks of the revolutionists, and would perhaps play a conspicuous part...There's no doubt about that."

"Oh, where, where did you get that from? What fool have you made friends with?" exclaimed Alyosha.

"Come, the truth will out! It has so chanced that I have often talked to Mr. Rakitin, of course, but...old Byelinsky said that, too, so they say."

"Byelinsky? I don't remember. He hasn't written that anywhere."

"If he didn't write it, they say he said it. I heard that from a...but never mind."

"And have you read Byelinsky?"

"Well, no...I haven't read all of him, but...I read the passage about Tatyana, why she didn't go off with Onyegin."

"Didn't go off with Onyegin? Surely you don't...understand that already?"

"Why, you seem to take me for little Smurov," said Kolya, with a grin of irritation. "But please don't suppose I am such a revolutionist. I often disagree with Mr. Rakitin. Though I mention Tatyana, I am not at all for the emancipation of women. I acknowledge that women are a subject race and must obey. Les femmes tricottent,* Napoleon said." Kolya, for some reason, smiled, "And on that question at least I am quite of one mind with that pseudo-great man. I think, too, that to leave one's own country and fly to America is mean, worse than mean-- silly. Why go to America when one may be of great service to humanity here? Now especially. There's a perfect mass of fruitful activity open to us. That's what I answered."

* Let the women knit.

"What do you mean? Answered whom? Has someone suggested your going to America already?"

"I must own, they've been at me to go, but I declined. That's between ourselves, of course, Karamazov; do you hear, not a word to anyone. I say this only to you. I am not at all anxious to fall into the clutches of the secret police and take lessons at the Chain bridge.

Long will you remember

The house at the Chain bridge.

Do you remember? It's splendid. Why are you laughing? You don't suppose I am fibbing, do you?" ("What if he should find out that I've only that one number of The Bell in father's book case, and haven't read any more of it?" Kolya thought with a shudder.)

"Oh no, I am not laughing and don't suppose for a moment that you are lying. No, indeed, I can't suppose so, for all this, alas! is perfectly true. But tell me, have you read Pushkin--Onyegin, for instance?...You spoke just now of Tatyana."

"No, I haven't read it yet, but I want to read it. I have no prejudices, Karamazov; I want to hear both sides. What makes you ask?"

"Oh, nothing."

"Tell me, Karamazov, have you an awful contempt for me?" Kolya rapped out suddenly and drew himself up before Alyosha, as though he were on drill. "Be so kind as to tell me, without beating about the bush."

"I have a contempt for you?" Alyosha looked at him wondering. "What for? I am only sad that a charming nature such as yours should be perverted by all this crude nonsense before you have begun life."

"Don't be anxious about my nature," Kolya interrupted, not without complacency. "But it's true that I am stupidly sensitive, crudely sensitive. You smiled just now, and I fancied you seemed to-"

"Oh, my smile meant something quite different. I'll tell you why I smiled. Not long ago I read the criticism made by a German who had lived in Russia, on our students and schoolboys of to-day. 'Show a Russian schoolboy,' he writes, 'a map of the stars, which he knows nothing about, and he will give you back the map next day with corrections on it.' No knowledge and unbounded conceit--that's what the German meant to say about the Russian schoolboy."

"Yes, that's perfectly right," Kolya laughed suddenly, "exactly so! Bravo the German! But he did not see the good side, what do you think? Conceit may be, that comes from youth, that will be corrected if need be, but, on the other hand, there is an independent spirit almost from childhood, boldness of thought and conviction, and not the spirit of these sausage makers, grovelling before authority...But the German was right all the same. Bravo the German! But Germans want strangling all the same. Though they are so good at science and learning they must be strangled."

"Strangled, what for?" smiled Alyosha.

"Well, perhaps I am talking nonsense, I agree. I am awfully childish sometimes, and when I am pleased about anything I can't restrain myself and am ready to talk any stuff. But, I say, we are chattering away here about nothing, and that doctor has been a long time in there. But perhaps he's examining the mamma and that poor crippled Nina. I liked that Nina, you know. She whispered to me suddenly as I was coming away, 'Why didn't you come before?' And in such a voice, so reproachfully! I think she is awfully nice and pathetic."

"Yes, yes! Well, you'll be coming often, you will see what she is like. It would do you a great deal of good to know people like that, to learn to value a great deal which you will find out from knowing these people," Alyosha observed warmly. "That would have more effect on you than anything."

"Oh, how I regret and blame myself for not having come sooner!" Kolya exclaimed, with bitter feeling.

"Yes, it's a great pity. You saw for yourself how delighted the poor child was to see you. And how he fretted for you to come!"

"Don't tell me! You make it worse! But it serves me right. What kept me from coming was my conceit, my egoistic vanity, and the beastly wilfulness, which I never can get rid of, though I've been struggling with it all my life. I see that now. I am a beast in lots of ways, Karamazov!"

"No, you have a charming nature, though it's been distorted, and I quite understand why you have had such an influence on this generous, morbidly sensitive boy," Alyosha answered warmly.

"And you say that to me!" cried Kolya; "and would you believe it, I thought--I've thought several times since I've been here--that you despised me! If only you knew how I prize your opinion!"

"But are you really so sensitive? At your age! Would you believe it, just now, when you were telling your story, I thought, as I watched you, that you must be very sensitive!"

"You thought so? What an eye you've got, I say! I bet that was when I was talking about the goose. That was just when I was fancying you had a great contempt for me for being in such a hurry to show off, and for a moment I quite hated you for it, and began talking like a fool. Then I fancied--just now, here--when I said that if there were no God He would have to be invented, that I was in too great a hurry to display my knowledge, especially as I got that phrase out of a book. But I swear I wasn't showing off out of vanity, though I really don't know why. Because I was so pleased? Yes, I believe it was because I was so pleased...though it's perfectly disgraceful for anyone to be gushing directly they are pleased, I know that. But I am convinced now that you don't despise me; it was all my imagination. Oh, Karamazov, I am profoundly unhappy. I sometimes fancy all sorts of things, that everyone is laughing at me, the whole world, and then I feel ready to overturn the whole order of things."

"And you worry everyone about you," smiled Alyosha.

"Yes, I worry everyone about me, especially my mother. Karamazov, tell me, am I very ridiculous now?"

"Don't think about that, don't think of it at all!" cried Alyosha. "And what does ridiculous mean? Isn't everyone constantly being or seeming ridiculous? Besides, nearly all clever people now are fearfully afraid of being ridiculous, and that makes them unhappy. All I am surprised at is that you should be feeling that so early, though I've observed it for some time past,, not only in you. Nowadays the very children have begun to suffer from it. It's almost a sort of insanity. The devil has taken the form of that vanity and entered into the whole generation; it's simply the devil," added Alyosha, without a trace of the smile that Kolya, staring at him, expected to see. "You are like everyone else," said Alyosha, in conclusion, "that is, like very many others. Only you must not be like everybody else, that's all."

"Even if everyone is like that?"

"Yes, even if everyone is like that. You be the only one not like it. You really are not like everyone else, here you are not ashamed to confess to something bad and even ridiculous. And who will admit so much in these days? No one. And people have even ceased to feel the impulse to self-criticism. Don't be like everyone else, even if you are the only one."

"Splendid! I was not mistaken in you. You know how to console one. Oh, how I have longed to know you, Karamazov! I've long been eager for this meeting. Can you really have thought about me, too? You said just now that you thought of me, too?"

"Yes, I'd heard of you and had thought of you, too...and if it's partly vanity that makes you ask, it doesn't matter."

"Do you know, Karamazov, our talk has been like a declaration of love," said Kolya, in a bashful and melting voice. "That's not ridiculous, is it?"

"Not at all ridiculous, and if it were, it wouldn't matter, because it's been a good thing." Alyosha smiled brightly.

"But do you know, Karamazov, you must admit that you are a little ashamed yourself, now...I see it by your eyes." Kolya smiled with a sort of sly happiness.

"Why ashamed?"

"Well, why are you blushing?"

"It was you made me blush," laughed Alyosha, and he really did blush. "Oh, well, I am a little, goodness knows why, I don't know..." he muttered, almost embarrassed.

"Oh, how I love you and admire you at this moment just because you are rather ashamed! Because you are just like me," cried Kolya, in positive ecstasy. His cheeks glowed, his eyes beamed.

"You know, Kolya, you will be very unhappy in your life," something made Alyosha say suddenly.

"I know, I know. How you know it all before hand!" Kolya agreed at once.

"But you will bless life on the whole, all the same."

"Just so, hurrah! You are a prophet. Oh, we shall get on together, Karamazov! Do you know, what delights me most, is that you treat me quite like an equal. But we are not equals, no, we are not, you are better! But we shall get on. Do you know, all this last month, I've been saying to myself, 'Either we shall be friends at once, for ever, or we shall part enemies to the grave!'"

"And saying that, of course, you loved me," Alyosha laughed gaily.

"I did. I loved you awfully. I've been loving and dreaming of you. And how do you know it all beforehand? Ah, here's the doctor. Goodness! What will he tell us? Look at his face!"

Chapter 7. Ilusha

THE doctor came out of the room again, muffled in his fur coat and with his cap on his head. His face looked almost angry and disgusted, as though he were afraid of getting dirty. He cast a cursory glance round the passage, looking sternly at Alyosha and Kolya as he did so. Alyosha waved from the door to the coachman, and the carriage that had brought the doctor drove up. The captain darted out after the doctor, and, bowing apologetically, stopped him to get the last word. The poor fellow looked utterly crushed; there was a scared look in his eyes.

"Your Excellency, your Excellency...is it possible?" he began, but could not go on and clasped his hands in despair. Yet he still gazed imploringly at the doctor, as though a word from him might still change the poor boy's fate.

"I can't help it, I am not God!" the doctor answered offhand, though with the customary impressiveness.

"Doctor...your Excellency...and will it be soon, soon?"

"You must be prepared for anything," said the doctor in emphatic and incisive tones, and dropping his eyes, he was about to step out to the coach.

"Your Excellency, for Christ's sake!" the terror-stricken captain stopped him again. "Your Excellency! But can nothing, absolutely nothing save him now?"

"It's not in my hands now," said the doctor impatiently, "but h'm!..." he stopped suddenly. "If you could, for instance...send...your patient...at once, without delay" (the words "at once, without delay," the doctor uttered with an almost wrathful sternness that made the captain start) "to Syracuse, the change to the new be-ne-ficial

"To Syracuse!" cried the captain, unable to grasp what was said.

"Syracuse is in Sicily," Kolya jerked out suddenly in explanation. The doctor looked at him.

"Sicily! Your Excellency," faltered the captain, "but you've seen"--he spread out his hands, indicating his surroundings--"mamma and my family?"

"N-no, Sicily is not the place for the family, the family should go to Caucasus in the early spring...your daughter must go to the Caucasus, and your wife...after a course of the waters in the Caucasus for her rheumatism...must be sent straight to Paris to the mental specialist Lepelletier; I could give you a note to him, and then...there might be a change-"

"Doctor, doctor! But you see!" The captain flung wide his hands again despairingly, indicating the bare wooden walls of the passage.

"Well, that's not my business," grinned the doctor. "I have only told you the answer of medical science to your question as to possible

"Don't be afraid, apothecary, my dog won't bite you," Kolya rapped out loudly, noticing the doctor's rather uneasy glance at Perezvon, who was standing in the doorway. There was a wrathful note in Kolya's voice. He used the word apothecary instead of doctor on purpose, and, as he explained afterwards, used it "to insult him."

"What's that?" The doctor flung up his head, staring with surprise at Kolya. "Who's this?" he addressed Alyosha, as though asking him to explain.

"It's Perezvon's master, don't worry about me," Kolya said incisively again.

"Perezvon?"* repeated the doctor, perplexed.

* i.e. a chime of bells.

"He hears the bell, but where it is he cannot tell. Good-bye, we shall meet in Syracuse."

"Who's this? Who's this?" The doctor flew into a terrible rage.

"He is a schoolboy, doctor, he is a mischievous boy; take no notice of him," said Alyosha, frowning and speaking quickly. "Kolya, hold your tongue!" he cried to Krassotkin. "Take no notice of him, doctor," he repeated, rather impatiently.

"He wants a thrashing, a good thrashing!" The doctor stamped in a perfect fury.

"And you know, apothecary, my Perezvon might bite!" said Kolya, turning pale, with quivering voice and flashing eyes. "Ici, Perezvon!"

"Kolya, if you say another word, I'll have nothing more to do with you," Alyosha cried peremptorily.

"There is only one man in the world who can command Nikolay Krassotkin--this is the man," Kolya pointed to Alyosha. "I obey him, good-bye!"

He stepped forward, opened the door, and quickly went into the inner room. Perezvon flew after him. The doctor stood still for five seconds in amazement, looking at Alyosha; then, with a curse, he went out quickly to the carriage, repeating aloud, "This is...this is...I don't know what it is!" The captain darted forward to help him into the carriage. Alyosha followed Kolya into the room. He was already by Ilusha's bedside. The sick boy was holding his hand and calling for his father. A minute later the captain, too, came back.

"Father, father, come...we..." Ilusha faltered in violent excitement, but apparently unable to go on, he flung his wasted arms, found his father and Kolya, uniting them in one embrace, and hugging them as tightly as he could. The captain suddenly began to shake with dumb sobs, and Kolya's lips and chin twitched.

"Father, father! How sorry I am for you!" Ilusha moaned bitterly.

"Ilusha...darling...the doctor said...you would be all right...we shall be happy...the doctor..." the captain began.

"Ah, father! I know what the new doctor said to you about me...I saw!" cried Ilusha, and again he hugged them both with all his strength, hiding his face on his father's shoulder.

"Father, don't cry, and when I die get a good boy, another one...choose one of them all, a good one, call him Ilusha and love him instead of me..."

"Hush, old man, you'll get well," Krassotkin cried suddenly, in a voice that sounded angry.

"But don't ever forget me, father," Ilusha went on, "come to my grave...and father, bury me by our big stone, where we used to go for our walk, and come to me there with Krassotkin in the evening...and Perezvon...I shall expect you...Father, father!"

His voice broke. They were all three silent, still embracing. Nina was crying, quietly in her chair, and at last seeing them all crying, "mamma," too, burst into tears.

"Ilusha! Ilusha!" she exclaimed.

Krassotkin suddenly released himself from Ilusha's embrace.

"Good-bye, old man, mother expects me back to dinner," he said quickly. "What a pity I did not tell her! She will be dreadfully anxious...But after dinner I'll come back to you for the whole day, for the whole evening, and I'll tell you all sorts of things, all sorts of things. And I'll bring Perezvon, but now I will take him with me, because he will begin to howl when I am away and bother you. Good-bye!

And he ran out into the passage. He didn't want to cry, but in the passage he burst into tears. Alyosha found him crying.

"Kolya, you must be sure to keep your word and come, or he will be terribly disappointed," Alyosha said emphatically.

"I will! Oh, how I curse myself for not having come before" muttered Kolya, crying, and no longer ashamed of it.

At that moment the captain flew out of the room, and at once closed the door behind him. His face looked frenzied, his lips were trembling. He stood before the two and flung up his arms.

"I don't want a good boy! I don't want another boy!" he muttered in a wild whisper, clenching his teeth. "If I forget thee, knees before the wooden bench. Pressing his fists against his head, he began sobbing with absurd whimpering cries, doing his utmost that his cries should not be heard in the room.

Kolya ran out into the street.

"Good-bye, Karamazov? Will you come yourself?" he cried sharply and angrily to Alyosha.

"I will certainly come in the evening."

"What was that he said about Jerusalem?...What did he mean by that?"

"It's from the Bible. 'If I forget thee, Jerusalem,' that is, if I forget all that is most precious to me, if I let anything take its place, then may-"

"I understand, that's enough! Mind you come! Ici, Perezvon!" he cried with positive ferocity to the dog, and with rapid strides he went home.

Book XI. Ivan

Chapter 1. At Grushenka's

ALYOSHA went towards the cathedral square to the widow Morozov's house to see Grushenka, who had sent Fenya to him early in the morning with an urgent message begging him to come. Questioning Fenya, Alyosha learned that her mistress had been particularly distressed since the previous day. During the two months that had passed since Mitya's arrest, Alyosha had called frequently at the widow Morozov's house, both from his own inclination and to take messages for Mitya. Three days after Mitya's arrest, Grushenka was taken very ill and was ill for nearly five weeks. For one whole week she was unconscious. She was very much changed--thinner and a little sallow, though she had for the past fortnight been well enough to go out. But to Alyosha her face was even more attractive than before, and he liked to meet her eyes when he went in to her. A look of firmness and intelligent purpose had developed in her face. There were signs of a spiritual transformation in her, and a steadfast, fine and humble determination that nothing could shake could be discerned in her. There was a small vertical line between her brows which gave her charming face a look of concentrated thought, almost austere at the first glance. There was scarcely a trace of her former frivolity.

It seemed strange to Alyosha, too, that in spite of the calamity that had overtaken the poor girl, betrothed to a man who had been arrested for a terrible crime, almost at the instant of their betrothal, in spite of her illness and the almost inevitable sentence hanging over Mitya, Grushenka had not yet lost her youthful cheerfulness. There was a soft light in the once proud eyes, though at times they gleamed with the old vindictive fire when she was visited by one disturbing thought stronger than ever in her heart. The object of that uneasiness was the same as ever--Katerina Ivanovna, of whom Grushenka had even raved when she lay in delirium. Alyosha knew that she was fearfully jealous of her. Yet Katerina Ivanovna had not once visited Mitya in his prison, though she might have done it whenever she liked. All this made a difficult problem for Alyosha, for he was the only person to whom Grushenka opened her heart and from whom she was continually asking advice. Sometimes he was unable to say anything.

Full of anxiety he entered her lodging. She was at home. She had returned from seeing Mitya half an hour before, and from the rapid movement with which she leapt up from her chair to meet him he saw that she had been expecting him with great impatience. A pack of cards dealt for a game of "fools" lay on the table. A bed had been made up on the leather sofa on the other side and Maximov lay, half reclining, on it. He wore a dressing-gown and a cotton nightcap, and was evidently ill and weak, though he was smiling blissfully. When the homeless old man returned with Grushenka from Mokroe two months before, he had simply stayed on and was still staying with her. He arrived with her in rain and sleet, sat down on the sofa, drenched and scared, and gazed mutely at her with a timid, appealing smile. Grushenka, who was in terrible grief and in the first stage of fever, almost forgot his existence in all she had to do the first half hour after her arrival. Suddenly she chanced to look at him intently: he laughed a pitiful, helpless little laugh. She called Fenya and told her to give him something to eat. All that day he sat in the same place, almost without stirring. When it got dark and the shutters were closed, Fenya asked her mistress:

"Is the gentleman going to stay the night, mistress?"

"Yes; make him a bed on the sofa," answered Grushenka.

Questioning him more in detail, Grushenka learned from him that he had literally nowhere to go, and that "Mr. Kalganov, my benefactor, told me straight that he wouldn't receive me again and gave me five roubles."

"Well, God bless you, you'd better stay, then," Grushenka decided in her grief, smiling compassionately at him. Her smile wrung the old man's heart and his lips twitched with grateful tears. And so the destitute wanderer had stayed with her ever since. He did not leave the house even when she was ill. Fenya and her grandmother, the cook, did not turn him out, but went on serving him meals and making up his bed on the sofa. Grushenka had grown used to him, and coming back from seeing Mitya (whom she had begun to visit in prison before she was really well) she would sit down and begin talking to "Maximushka" about trifling matters, to keep her from thinking of her sorrow. The old man turned out to be a good story-teller on occasions, so that at last he became necessary to her. Grushenka saw scarcely anyone else beside Alyosha, who did not come every day and never stayed long. Her old merchant lay seriously ill at this time, "at his last gasp" as they said in the town, and he did, in fact, die a week after Mitya's trial. Three weeks before his death, feeling the end approaching, he made his sons, their wives and children, come upstairs to him at last and bade them not leave him again. From that moment he gave strict orders to his servants not to admit Grushenka and to tell her if she came, "The master wishes you long life and happiness and tells you to forget him." But Grushenka sent almost every day to inquire after him.

"You've come at last!" she cried, flinging down the cards and joyfully greeting Alyosha, "and Maximushka's been scaring me that perhaps you wouldn't come. Ah, how I need you! Sit down to the table. What will you have coffee?"

"Yes, please," said Alyosha, sitting down at the table. "I am very hungry."

"That's right. Fenya, Fenya, coffee," cried Grushenka. "It's been made a long time ready for you. And bring some little pies, and mind they are hot. Do you know, we've had a storm over those pies to-day. I took them to the prison for him, and would you believe it, he threw them back to me: he would not eat them. He flung one of them on the floor and stamped on it. So I said to him: 'I shall leave them with the warder; if you don't eat them before evening, it will be that your venomous spite is enough for you!' With that I went away. We quarrelled again, would you believe it? Whenever I go we quarrel."

Grushenka said all this in one breath in her agitation. Maximov, feeling nervous, at once smiled and looked on the floor.

"What did you quarrel about this time?" asked Alyosha.

"I didn't expect it in the least. Only fancy, he is jealous of the Pole. 'Why are you keeping him?' he said. 'So you've begun keeping him.' He is jealous, jealous of me all the time, jealous eating and sleeping! He even took into his head to be jealous of Kuzma last week."

"But he knew about the Pole before?"

"Yes, but there it is. He has known about him from the very beginning but to-day he suddenly got up and began scolding about him. I am ashamed to repeat what he said. Silly fellow! Rakitin went in as I came out. Perhaps Rakitin is egging him on. What do you think?" she added carelessly.

"He loves you, that's what it is; he loves you so much. And now he is particularly worried."

"I should think he might be, with the trial to-morrow. And I went to him to say something about to-morrow, for I dread to think what's going to happen then. You say that he is worried, but how worried I am! And he talks about the Pole! He's too silly! He is not jealous of Maximushka yet, anyway."

"My wife was dreadfully jealous over me, too," Maximov put in his word.

"Jealous of you?" Grushenka laughed in spite of herself. "Of whom could she have been jealous?"

"Of the servant girls."

"Hold your tongue, Maximushka, I am in no laughing mood now; I feel angry. Don't ogle the pies. I shan't give you any; they are not good for you, and I won't give you any vodka either. I have to look after him, too, just as though I kept an almshouse," she laughed.

"I don't deserve your kindness. I am a worthless creature," said Maximov, with tears in his voice. "You would do better to spend your kindness on people of more use than me."

"Ech, everyone is of use, Maximushka, and how can we tell who's of most use? If only that Pole didn't exist, Alyosha. He's taken it into his head to fall ill, too, to-day. I've been to see him also. And I shall send him some pies, too, on purpose. I hadn't sent him any, but Mitya accused me of it, so now I shall send some! Ah, here's Fenya with a letter! Yes, it's from the Poles--begging again!"

Pan Mussyalovitch had indeed sent an extremely long and characteristically eloquent letter in which he begged her to lend him three roubles. In the letter was enclosed a receipt for the sum, with a promise to repay it within three months, signed by Pan Vrublevsky as well. Grushenka had received many such letters, accompanied by such receipts, from her former lover during the fortnight of her convalescence. But she knew that the two Poles had been to ask after her health during her illness. The first letter Grushenka got from them was a long one, written on large notepaper and with a big family crest on the seal. It was so obscure and rhetorical that Grushenka put it down before she had read half, unable to make head or tail of it. She could not attend to letters then. The first letter was followed next day by another in which Pan Mussyalovitch begged her for a loan of two thousand roubles for a very short period. Grushenka left that letter, too, unanswered. A whole series of letters had followed--one every day--all as pompous and rhetorical, but the loan asked for, gradually diminishing, dropped to a hundred roubles, than to twenty-five, to ten, and finally Grushenka received a letter in which both the Poles begged her for only one rouble and included a receipt signed by both.

Then Grushenka suddenly felt sorry for them, and at dusk she went round herself to their lodging. She found the two Poles in great poverty, almost destitution, without food or fuel, without cigarettes, in debt to their landlady. The two hundred roubles they had carried off from Mitya at Mokroe had soon disappeared. But Grushenka was surprised at their meeting her with arrogant dignity and self-assertion, with the greatest punctilio and pompous speeches. Grushenka simply laughed, and gave her former admirer ten roubles. Then, laughing, she told Mitya of it and he was not in the least jealous. But ever since, the Poles had attached themselves to Grushenka and bombarded her daily with requests for money and she had always sent them small sums. And now that day Mitya had taken it into his head to be fearfully jealous.

"Like a fool, I went round to him just for a minute, on the way to see Mitya, for he is ill, too, my Pole," Grushenka began again with nervous haste. "I was laughing, telling Mitya about it. 'Fancy,' I said, 'my Pole had the happy thought to sing his old songs to me to the guitar. He thought I would be touched and marry him!' Mitya leapt up swearing...So, there, I'll send them the pies! Fenya, is it that little girl they've sent? Here, give her three roubles and pack up a dozen pies in a paper and tell her to take them. And you, Alyosha, be sure to tell Mitya that I did send them the pies."

"I wouldn't tell him for anything," said Alyosha, smiling.

"Ech! You think he is unhappy about it. Why, he's jealous on purpose. He doesn't care," said Grushenka bitterly.

"On purpose?" queried Alyosha.

"I tell you you are silly, Alyosha. You know nothing about it, with all your cleverness. I am not offended that he is jealous of a girl like me. I would be offended if he were not jealous. I am like that. I am not offended at jealousy. I have a fierce heart, too. I can be jealous myself. Only what offends me is that he doesn't love me at all. I tell you he is jealous now on purpose. Am I blind? Don't I see? He began talking to me just now of that woman, of Katerina, saying she was this and that, how she had ordered a doctor from Moscow for him, to try and save him; how she had ordered the best counsel, the most learned one, too. So he loves her, if he'll praise her to my face, more shame to him! He's treated me badly himself, so he attacked me, to make out I am in fault first and to throw it all on me. 'You were with your Pole before me, so I can't be blamed for Katerina,' that's what it amounts to. He wants to throw the whole blame on me. He attacked me on purpose, on purpose, I tell you, but I'll-"

Grushenka could not finish saying what she would do. She hid her eyes in her handkerchief and sobbed violently.

"He doesn't love Katerina Ivanovna," said Alyosha firmly.

"Well, whether he loves her or not, I'll soon find out for myself," said Grushenka, with a menacing note in her voice, taking the handkerchief from her eyes. Her face was distorted. Alyosha saw sorrowfully that from being mild and serene, it had become sullen and spiteful.

"Enough of this foolishness," she said suddenly; "it's not for that I sent for you. Alyosha, darling, to-morrow--what will happen to-morrow? That's what worries me! And it's only me it worries! I look at everyone and no one is thinking of it. No one cares about it. Are you thinking about it even? To-morrow he'll be tried, you know. Tell me, how will he be tried? You know it's the valet, the valet killed him! Good heavens! Can they condemn him in place of the valet and will no one stand up for him? They haven't troubled the valet at all, have they?"

"He's been severely cross-examined," observed Alyosha thoughtfully; "but everyone came to the conclusion it was not he. Now he is lying very ill. He has been ill ever since that attack. Really ill," added Alyosha.

"Oh, dear! couldn't you go to that counsel yourself and tell him the whole thing by yourself? He's been brought from Petersburg for three thousand roubles, they say."

"We gave these three thousand together--Ivan, Katerina Ivanovna and I--but she paid two thousand for the doctor from Moscow herself. The counsel Fetyukovitch would have charged more, but the case has become known all over Russia; it's talked of in all the papers and journals. Fetyukovitch agreed to come more for the glory of the thing, because the case has become so notorious. I saw him yesterday."

"Well? Did you talk to him?" Grushenka put in eagerly.

"He listened and said nothing. He told me that he had already formed his opinion. But he promised to give my words consideration."

"Consideration! Ah, they are swindlers! They'll ruin him. And why did she send for the doctor?"

"As an expert. They want to prove that Mitya's mad and committed the murder when he didn't know what he was doing," Alyosha smiled gently, "but Mitya won't agree to that."

"Yes; but that would be the truth if he had killed him!" cried Grushenka. "He was mad then, perfectly mad, and that was my fault, wretch that I am! But, of course, he didn't do it, he didn't do it! And they are all against him, the whole town. Even Fenya's evidence went to prove he had done it. And the people at the shop, and that official, and at the tavern, too, before, people had heard him say so! They are all, all against him, all crying out against him."

"Yes, there's a fearful accumulation of evidence," Alyosha observed grimly.

"And Grigory--Grigory Vassilyevitch--sticks to his story that the door was open, persists that he saw it--there's no shaking him. I went and talked to him myself. He's rude about it, too."

"Yes, that's perhaps the strongest evidence against him," said Alyosha.

"And as for Mitya's being mad, he certainly seems like it now," Grushenka began with a peculiarly anxious and mysterious air. "Do you know, Alyosha, I've been wanting to talk to you about it for a long time. I go to him every day and simply wonder at him. Tell me, now, what do you suppose he's always talking about? He talks and talks and I can make nothing of it. I fancied he was talking of something intellectual that I couldn't understand in my foolishness. Only he suddenly began talking to me about a babe--that is, about some child. 'Why is the babe poor?' he said. 'It's for that babe I am going to Siberia now. I am not a murderer, but I must go to Siberia!' What that meant, what babe, I couldn't tell for the life of me. Only I cried when he said it, because he said it so nicely. He cried himself, and I cried, too. He suddenly kissed me and made the sign of the cross over me. What did it mean, Alyosha, tell me? What is this babe?"

"It must be Rakitin, who's been going to see him lately," smiled Alyosha, "though...that's not Rakitin's doing. I didn't see Mitya yesterday. I'll see him to-day."

"No, it's not Rakitin; it's his brother Ivan Fyodorovitch upsetting him. It's his going to see him, that's what it is," Grushenka began, and suddenly broke off. Alyosha gazed at her in amazement.

"Ivan's going? Has he been to see him? Mitya told me himself that Ivan hasn't been once."

"There...there! What a girl I am! Blurting things out!" exclaimed Grushenka, confused and suddenly blushing. "Stay, Alyosha, hush! Since I've said so much I'll tell the whole truth--he's been to see him twice, the first directly he arrived. He galloped here from Moscow at once, of course, before I was taken ill; and the second time was a week ago. He told Mitya not to tell you about it, under any circumstances; and not to tell anyone, in fact. He came secretly."

Alyosha sat plunged in thought, considering something. The news evidently impressed him.

"Ivan doesn't talk to me of Mitya's case," he said slowly. "He's said very little to me these last two months. And whenever I go to see him, he seems vexed at my coming, so I've not been to him for the last three weeks. H'm!...if he was there a week ago...there certainly has been a change in Mitya this week."

"There has been a change," Grushenka assented quickly. "They have a secret, they have a secret! Mitya told me himself there was a secret, and such a secret that Mitya can't rest. Before then, he was cheerful--and, indeed, he is cheerful now--but when he shakes his head like that, you know, and strides about the room and keeps pulling at the hair on his right temple with his right hand, I know there is something on his mind worrying him...I know! He was cheerful before, though, indeed, he is cheerful to-day."

"But you said he was worried."

"Yes, he is worried and yet cheerful. He keeps on being irritable for a minute and then cheerful and then irritable again. And you know, Alyosha, I am constantly wondering at him--with this awful thing hanging over him, he sometimes laughs at such trifles as though he were a baby himself."

"And did he really tell you not to tell me about Ivan? Did he say, 'Don't tell him'?"

"Yes, he told me, 'Don't tell him.' It's you that Mitya's most afraid of. Because it's a secret: he said himself it was a secret. Alyosha, darling, go to him and find out what their secret is and come and tell me," Grushenka besought him with sudden eagerness. "Set my mind at rest that I may know the worst that's in store for me. That's why I sent for you."

"You think it's something to do with you? If it were, he wouldn't have told you there was a secret."

"I don't know. Perhaps he wants to tell me, but doesn't dare to. He warns me. There is a secret, he tells me, but he won't tell me what it is."

"What do you think yourself?"

"What do I think? It's the end for me, that's what I think. They all three have been plotting my end, for Katerina's in it. It's all Katerina, it all comes from her. She is this and that, and that means that I am not. He tells me that beforehand--warns me. He is planning to throw me over, that's the whole secret. They've planned it together, the three of them--Mitya, Katerina, and Ivan Fyodorovitch. Alyosha, I've been wanting to ask you a long time. A week ago he suddenly told me that Ivan was in love with Katerina, because he often goes to see her. Did he tell me the truth or not? Tell me, on your conscience, tell me the worst."

"I won't tell you a lie. Ivan is not in love with Katerina Ivanovna, I think."

"Oh, that's what I thought! He is lying to me, shameless deceiver, that's what it is! And he was jealous of me just now, so as to put the blame on me afterwards. He is stupid, he can't disguise what he is doing; he is so open, you know...But I'll give it to him, I'll give it to him! 'You believe I did it,' he said. He said that to me, to me. He reproached me with that! God forgive him! You wait, I'll make it hot for Katerina at the trial! I'll just say a word then...I'll tell everything then!" And again she cried bitterly.

"This I can tell you for certain, Grushenka," Alyosha said, getting up. "First, that he loves you, loves you more than anyone in the world, and you only, believe me. I know. I do know. The second thing is that I don't want to worm his secret out of him, but if he'll tell me of himself to-day, I shall tell him straight out that I have promised to tell you. Then I'll come to you to-day and tell you. Only...I fancy...Katerina Ivanovna has nothing to do with it, and that the secret is about something else. That's certain. It isn't likely it's about Katerina Ivanovna, it seems to me. Good-bye for now."

Alyosha shook hands with her. Grushenka was still crying. He saw that she put little faith in his consolation, but she was better for having had her sorrow out, for having spoken of it. He was sorry to leave her in such a state of mind, but he was in haste. He had a great many things to do still.

Chapter 2. The Injured Foot

THE first of these things was at the house of Madame Hohlakov, and he hurried there to get it over as quickly as possible and not be too late for Mitya. Madame Hohlakov had been slightly ailing for the last three weeks: her foot had for some reason swollen up, and though she was not in bed, she lay all day half-reclining on the couch in her boudoir, in a fascinating but decorous deshabille. Alyosha had once noted with innocent amusement that, in spite of her illness, Madame Hohlakov had begun to be rather dressy--topknots, ribbons, loose wrappers had made their appearance, and he had an inkling of the reason, though he dismissed such ideas from his mind as frivolous. During the last two months the young official, Perhotin, had become a regular visitor at the house.

Alyosha had not called for four days and he was in haste to go straight to Lise, as it was with her he had to speak, for Lise had sent a maid to him the previous day specially asking him to come to her "about something very important," a request which, for certain reasons, had interest for Alyosha. But while the maid went to take his name in to Lise, Madame Hohlakov heard of his arrival from someone, and immediately sent to beg him to come to her "just for one minute." Alyosha reflected that it was better to accede to the mamma's request, or else she would be sending down to Lise's room every minute that he was there. Madame Hohlakov was lying on a couch. She was particularly smartly dressed and was evidently in a state of extreme nervous excitement. She greeted Alyosha with cries of rapture.

"It's ages, ages, perfect ages since I've seen you! It's a whole week--only think of it! Ah, but you were here only four days ago, on Wednesday. You have come to see Lise. I'm sure you meant to slip into her room on tiptoe, without my hearing you. My dear, dear Alexey Fyodorovitch, if you only knew how worried I am about her! But of that later, though that's the most important thing, of that later. Dear Alexey Fyodorovitch, I trust you implicitly with my Lise. Since the death of Father Zossima--God rest his soul!" (she crossed herself)--"I look upon you as a monk, though you look charming in your new suit. Where did you find such a tailor in these parts? No, no, that's not the chief thing--of that later. Forgive me for sometimes calling you Alyosha; an old woman like me may take liberties," she smiled coquettishly; "but that will do later, too. The important thing is that I shouldn't forget what is important. Please remind me of it yourself. As soon as my tongue runs away with me, you just say 'the important thing?' Ach! how do I know now what is of most importance? Ever since Lise took back her promise--her childish promise, Alexey Fyodorovitch--to marry you, you've realised, of course, that it was only the playful fancy of a sick child who had been so long confined to her chair--thank God, she can walk now!...that-new doctor Katya sent for from Moscow for your unhappy brother, who will to-morrow--but why speak of to-morrow? I am ready to die at the very thought of to-morrow. Ready to die of curiosity...That doctor was with us yesterday and saw Lise...I paid him fifty roubles for the visit. But that's not the point, that's not the point again. You see, I'm mixing everything up. I am in such a hurry. Why am I in a hurry? I don't understand. It's awful how I seem growing unable to understand anything. Everything seems mixed up in a sort of tangle. I am afraid you are so bored you will jump up and run away, and that will be all I shall see of you. Goodness! Why are we sitting here and no coffee? Yulia, Glafira, coffee!"

Alyosha made haste to thank her, and said that he had only just had coffee.

"Where?"

"At Agrfena Alexandrovna's."

"At...at that woman's? Ah, it's she has brought ruin on everyone. I know nothing about it though. They say she has become a saint, though it's rather late in the day. She had better have done it before. What use is it now? Hush, hush, Alexey Fyodorovitch, for I have so much to say to you that I am afraid I shall tell you nothing. This awful trial...I shall certainly go, I am making arrangements. I shall be carried there in my chair; besides I can sit up. I shall have people with me. And, you know, I am a witness. How shall I speak, how shall I speak? I don't know what I shall say. One has to take an oath, hasn't one?"

"Yes; but I don't think you will be able to go."

"I can sit up. Ah, you put me out! Ah! this trial, this savage act, and then they are all going to Siberia, some are getting married, and all this so quickly, so quickly, everything's changing, and at last--nothing. All grow old and have death to look forward to. Well, so be it! I am weary. This Katya, cette charmante personne, has disappointed all my hopes. Now she is going to follow one of your brothers to Siberia, and your other brother is going to follow her, and will live in the nearest town, and they will all torment one another. It drives me out of my mind. Worst of all--the publicity. The story has been told a million times over in all the papers in Moscow and Petersburg. Ah! yes, would you believe it, there's a paragraph that I was 'a dear friend' of your brother's--, I can't repeat the horrid word. just fancy, just fancy!"

"Impossible! Where was the paragraph? What did it say?"

"I'll show you directly. I got the paper and read it yesterday. Here, in the Petersburg paper Gossip. The paper began coming out this year. I am awfully fond of gossip, and I take it in, and now it pays me out--this is what gossip comes to! Here it is, here, this passage. Read it."

And she handed Alyosha a sheet of newspaper which had been under her pillow.

It was not exactly that she was upset, she seemed overwhelmed and perhaps everything really was mixed up in a tangle in her head. The paragraph was very typical, and must have been a great shock to her, but, fortunately perhaps, she was unable to keep her mind fixed on any one subject at that moment, and so might race off in a minute to something else and quite forget the newspaper.

Alyosha was well aware that the story of the terrible case had spread all over Russia. And, good heavens! what wild rumours about his brother, about the Karamazovs, and about himself he had read in the course of those two months, among other equally credible items! One paper had even stated that he had gone into a monastery and become a monk, in horror at his brother's crime. Another contradicted this, and stated that he and his elder, Father Zossima, had broken into the monastery chest and "made tracks from the monastery." The present paragraph in the paper Gossip was under the heading, "The Karamazov Case at Skotoprigonyevsk." (That, alas! was the name of our little town. I had hitherto kept it concealed.) It was brief, and Madame Hohlakov was not directly mentioned in it. No names appeared, in fact. It was merely stated that the criminal, whose approaching trial was making such a sensation--retired army captain, an idle swaggerer, and reactionary bully--was continually involved in amorous intrigues, and particularly popular with certain ladies "who were pining in solitude." One such lady, a pining widow, who tried to seem young though she had a grown-up daughter, was so fascinated by him that only two hours before the crime she offered him three thousand roubles, on condition that he would elope with her to the gold mines. But the criminal, counting on escaping punishment, had preferred to murder his father to get the three thousand rather than go off to Siberia with the middle-aged charms of his pining lady. This playful paragraph finished, of course, with an outburst of generous indignation at the wickedness of parricide and at the lately abolished institution of serfdom. Reading it with curiosity, Alyosha folded up the paper and handed it back to Madame Hohlakov.

"Well, that must be me," she hurried on again. "Of course I am meant. Scarcely more than an hour before, I suggested gold mines to him, and here they talk of 'middle-aged charms' as though that were my motive! He writes that out of spite! God Almighty forgive him for the middle-aged charms, as I forgive him! You know it's Do you know who it is? It's your friend Rakitin."

"Perhaps," said Alyosha, "though I've heard nothing about it."

"It's he, it's he! No 'perhaps' about it. You know I turned him out of the house...You know all that story, don't you?"

"I know that you asked him not to visit you for the future, but why it was, I haven't heard...from you, at least."

"Ah, then you've heard it from him! He abuses me, I suppose, abuses me dreadfully?"

"Yes, he does; but then he abuses everyone. But why you've given him up I, haven't heard from him either. I meet him very seldom now, indeed. We are not friends."

"Well, then, I'll tell you all about it. There's no help for it, I'll confess, for there is one point in which I was perhaps to blame. Only a little, little point, so little that perhaps it doesn't count. You see, my dear boy"-- Madame Hohlakov suddenly looked arch and a charming, though enigmatic, smile played about her lips--"you see, I suspect...You must forgive me, Alyosha. I am like a mother to you...No, no; quite the contrary. I speak to you now as though you were my father--mother's quite out of place. Well, it's as though I were confessing to Father Zossima, that's just it. I called you a monk just now. Well, that poor young man, your friend, Rakitin (Mercy on us! I can't be angry with him. I feel cross, but not very), that frivolous young man, would you believe it, seems to have taken it into his head to fall in love with me. I only noticed it later. At first--a month ago--he only began to come oftener to see me, almost every day; though, of course, we were acquainted before. I knew nothing about it...and suddenly it dawned upon me, and I began to notice things with surprise. You know, two months ago, that modest, charming, excellent young man, Ilyitch Perhotin, who's in the service here, began to be a regular visitor at the house. You met him here ever so many times yourself. And he is an excellent, earnest young man, isn't he? He comes once every three days, not every day (though I should be glad to see him every day), and always so well dressed. Altogether, I love young people, Alyosha, talented, modest, like you, and he has almost the mind of a statesman, he talks so charmingly, and I shall certainly, certainly try and get promotion for him. He is a future diplomat. On that awful day he almost saved me from death by coming in the night. And your friend Rakitin comes in such boots, and always stretches them out on the carpet...He began hinting at his feelings, in fact, and one day, as he was going, he squeezed my hand terribly hard. My foot began to swell directly after he pressed my hand like that. He had met Pyotr Ilyitch here before, and would you believe it, he is always gibing at him, growling at him, for some reason. I simply looked at the way they went on together and laughed inwardly. So I was sitting here alone--no, I was laid up then. Well, I was lying here alone and suddenly Rakitin comes in, and only fancy! brought me some verses of his own composition--a short poem, on my bad foot: that is, he described my foot in a poem. Wait a minute--how did it go?

A captivating little foot.

It began somehow like that. I can never remember poetry. I've got it here. I'll show it to you later. But it's a charming thing--charming; and, you know, it's not only about the foot, it had a good moral, too, a charming idea, only I've forgotten it; in fact, it was just the thing for an album. So, of course, I thanked him, and he was evidently flattered. I'd hardly had time to thank him when in comes Pyotr Ilyitch, and Rakitin suddenly looked as black as night. I could see that Pyotr Ilyitch was in the way, for Rakitin certainly wanted to say something after giving me the verses. I had a presentiment of it; but Pyotr Ilyitch came in. I showed Pyotr Ilyitch the verses and didn't say who was the author. But I am convinced that he guessed, though he won't own it to this day, and declares he had no idea. But he says that on purpose. Pyotr Ilyitch began to laugh at once, and fell to criticising it. 'Wretched doggerel,' he said they were, 'some divinity student must have written them,' and with such vehemence, such vehemence! Then, instead of laughing, your friend flew into a rage. 'Good gracious!' I thought, 'they'll fly at each other.' 'It was I who wrote them,' said he. 'I wrote them as a joke,' he said, 'for I think it degrading to write verses...But they are good poetry. They want to put a monument to your Pushkin for writing about women's feet, while I wrote with a moral purpose, and you,' said he, 'are an advocate of serfdom. You've no humane ideas,' said he. 'You have no modern enlightened feelings, you are uninfluenced by progress, you are a mere official,' he said, 'and you take bribes.' Then I began screaming and imploring them. And, you know, Pyotr Ilyitch is anything but a coward. He at once took up the most gentlemanly tone, looked at him sarcastically, listened, and apologised. 'I'd no idea,' said he. 'I shouldn't have said it, if I had known. I should have praised it. Poets are all so irritable,' he said. In short, he laughed at him under cover of the most gentlemanly tone. He explained to me afterwards that it was all sarcastic. I thought he was in earnest. Only as I lay there, just as before you now, I thought, 'Would it, or would it not, be the proper thing for me to turn Rakitin out for shouting so rudely at a visitor in my house?' And, would you believe it, I lay here, shut my eyes, and wondered, would it be the proper thing or not. I kept worrying and worrying, and my heart began to beat, and I couldn't make up my mind whether to make an outcry or not. One voice seemed to be telling me, 'Speak,' and the other 'No, don't speak.' And no sooner had the second voice said that than I cried out, and fainted. Of course, there was a fuss. I got up suddenly and said to Rakitin, 'It's painful for me to say it, but I don't wish to see you in my house again.' So I turned him out. Ah! Alexey Fyodorovitch, I know myself I did wrong. I was putting it on. I wasn't angry with him at all, really; but I suddenly fancied--that was what did it--that it would be such a fine scene...And yet, believe me, it was quite natural, for I really shed tears and cried for several days afterwards, and then suddenly, one afternoon, I forgot all about it. So it's a fortnight since he's been here, and I kept wondering whether he would come again. I wondered even yesterday, then suddenly last night came this Gossip. I read it and gasped. Who could have written it? He must have written it. He went home, sat down, wrote it on the spot, sent it, and they put it in. It was a fortnight ago, you see. But, Alyosha, it's awful how I keep talking and don't say what I want to say. the words come of themselves!"

"It's very important for me to be in time to see my brother to-day," Alyosha faltered.

"To be sure, to be sure! You bring it all back to me. Listen, what is an aberration?"

"What aberration?" asked Alyosha, wondering.

"In the legal sense. An aberration in which everything is pardonable. Whatever you do, you will be acquitted at once."

"What do you mean?"

"I'll tell you. This Katya...Ah! she is a charming, charming creature, only I never can make out who it is she is in love with. She was with me some time ago and I couldn't get anything out of her. Especially as she won't talk to me except on the surface now. She is always talking about my health and nothing else, and she takes up such a tone with me, too. I simply said to myself, 'Well so be it. I don't care'...Oh, yes. I was talking of aberration. This doctor has come. You know a doctor has come? Of course, you know it--the one who discovers madmen. You wrote for him. No, it wasn't you, but Katya. It's all Katya's doing. Well, you see, a man may be sitting perfectly sane and suddenly have an aberration. He may be conscious and know what he is doing and yet be in a state of aberration. And there's no doubt that Dmitri Fyodorovitch was suffering from aberration. They found out about aberration as soon as the law courts were reformed. It's all the good effect of the reformed law courts. The doctor has been here and questioned me about that evening, about the gold mines. 'How did he seem then?' he asked me. He must have been in a state of aberration. He came in shouting, 'Money, money, three thousand! Give me three thousand!' and then went away and immediately did the murder. 'I don't want to murder him,' he said, and he suddenly went and murdered him. That's why they'll acquit him, because he struggled against it and yet he murdered him."

"But he didn't murder him," Alyosha interrupted rather sharply. He felt more and more sick with anxiety and impatience.

"Yes, I know it was that old man Grigory murdered him."

"Grigory?" cried Alyosha.

"Yes, yes; it was Grigory. He lay as Dmitri Fyodorovitch struck him down, and then got up, saw the door open, went in and killed Fyodor Pavlovitch."

"But why, why?"

"Suffering from aberration. When he recovered from the blow Dmitri Fyodorovitch gave him on the head, he was suffering from aberration: he went and committed the murder. As for his saying he didn't, he very likely doesn't remember. Only, you know, it'll be better, ever so much better, if Dmitri Fyodorovitch murdered him. And that's how it must have been, though I say it was Grigory. It certainly was Dmitri Fyodorovitch, and that's better, ever so much better! Oh! not better that a son should have killed his father, I don't defend that. Children ought to honour their parents, and yet it would be better if it were he, as you'd have nothing to cry over then, for he did it when he was unconscious or rather when he was conscious, but did not know what he was doing. Let them acquit him--that's so humane, and would show what a blessing reformed law courts are. I knew nothing about it, but they say they have been so a long time. And when I heard it yesterday, I was so struck by it that I wanted to send for you at once. And if he is acquitted, make him come straight from the law courts to dinner with me, and I'll have a party of friends, and we'll drink to the reformed law courts. I don't believe he'd be dangerous; besides, I'll invite a great many friends, so that he could always be led out if he did anything. And then he might be made a justice of the peace or something in another town, for those who have been in trouble themselves make the best judges. And, besides, who isn't suffering from aberration nowadays?--you, I, all of us, are in a state of aberration, and there are ever so many examples of it: a man sits singing a song, suddenly something annoys him, he takes a pistol and shoots the first person he comes across, and no one blames him for it. I read that lately, and all the doctors confirm it. The doctors are always confirming; they confirm,--anything.

Why, my Lise is in a state of aberration. She made me cry again yesterday, and the day before, too, and to-day I suddenly realised that it's all due to aberration. Oh, Lise grieves me so! I believe she's quite mad. Why did she send for you? Did she send for you or did you come of yourself?"

"Yes, she sent for me, and I am just going to her." Alyosha got up resolutely.

"Oh, my dear, dear Alexey Fyodorovitch, perhaps that's what's most important," Madame Hohlakov cried, suddenly bursting into tears. "God knows I trust Lise to you with all my heart, and it's no matter her sending for you on the sly, without telling her mother. But forgive me, I can't trust my daughter so easily to your brother Ivan Fyodorovitch, though I still consider him the most chivalrous young man. But only fancy, he's been to see Lise and I knew nothing about it!"

"How? What? When?" Alyosha was exceedingly surprised. He had not sat down again and listened standing.

"I will tell you; that's perhaps why I asked you to come, for I don't know now why I did ask you to come. Well, Ivan Fyodorovitch has been to see me twice, since he came back from Moscow. First time he came as a friend to call on me, and the second time Katya was here and he came because he heard she was here. I didn't, of course, expect him to come often, knowing what a lot he has to do as it is, vous comprenez, cette affaire et la mort terrible de votre papa. (You know, this affair and your father's terrible death.) But I suddenly heard he'd been here again, not to see me but to see Lise. That's six days ago now. He came, stayed five minutes, and went away. And I didn't hear of it till three days afterwards, from Glafira, so it was a great shock to me. I sent for Lise directly. She laughed. 'He thought you were asleep,' she said, 'and came in to me to ask after your health.' Of course, that's how it happened. But Lise, Lise, mercy on us, how she distresses me! Would you believe it, one night, four days ago, just after you saw her last time, and had gone away, she suddenly had a fit, screaming, shrieking, hysterics! Why is it I never have hysterics? Then, next day another fit, and the same thing on the third, and yesterday too, and then yesterday that aberration. She suddenly screamed out, 'I hate Ivan Fyodorovitch. I insist on your never letting him come to the house again.' I was struck dumb at these amazing words, and answered, 'On what grounds could I refuse to see such an excellent young man, a young man of such learning too, and so unfortunate?'--for all this business is a misfortune, isn't it?' She suddenly burst out laughing at my words, and so rudely, you know. Well, I was pleased; I thought I had amused her and the fits would pass off, especially as I wanted to refuse to see Ivan Fyodorovitch anyway on account of his strange visits without my knowledge, and meant to ask him for an explanation. But early this morning Lise waked up and flew into a passion with Yulia, and, would you believe it, slapped her in the face. That's monstrous; I am always polite to my servants. And an hour later she was hugging Yulia's feet and kissing them. She sent a message to me that she wasn't coming to me at all, and would never come and see me again, and when I dragged myself down to her, she rushed to kiss me, crying, and as she kissed me, she pushed me out of the room without saying a word, so I couldn't find out what was the matter. Now, dear Alexey Fyodorovitch, I rest all my hopes on you, and, of course, my whole life is in your hands. I simply beg you to go to Lise and find out everything from her, as you alone can, and come back and tell--me, her mother, for you understand it will be the death of me, simply the death of me, if this goes on, or else I shall run away. I can stand no more. I have patience; but I may lose patience, and then...then something awful will happen. Ah, dear me! At last, Pyotr Ilyitch!" cried Madame Hohlakov, beaming all over as she saw Perhotin enter the room. "You are late, you are late! Well, sit down, speak, put us out of suspense. What does the counsel say. Where are you off to, Alexey Fyodorovitch?"

"To Lise."

"Oh, yes. You won't forget, you won't forget what I asked you? It's a question of life and death!

"Of course, I won't forget, if I can...but I am so late," muttered Alyosha, beating a hasty retreat.

"No, be sure, be sure to come in; don't say 'If you can.' I shall die if you don't," Madame Hohlakov called after him, but Alyosha had already left the room.

Chapter 3. A Little Demon

GOING in to Lise, he found her half reclining in the invalid-chair, in which she had been wheeled when she was unable to walk. She did not move to meet him, but her sharp, keen eyes were simply riveted on his face. There was a feverish look in her eyes, her face was pale and yellow. Alyosha was amazed at the change that had taken place in her in three days. She was positively thinner. She did not hold out her hand to him. He touched the thin, long fingers which lay motionless on her dress, then he sat down facing her, without a word.

"I know you are in a hurry to get to the prison," Lise said curtly, "and mamma's kept you there for hours; she's just been telling you about me and Yulia."

"How do you know?" asked Alyosha.

"I've been listening. Why do you stare at me? I want to listen and I do listen, there's no harm in that. I don't apologise."

"You are upset about something?"

"On the contrary, I am very happy. I've only just been reflecting for the thirtieth time what a good thing it is I refused you and shall not be your wife. You are not fit to be a husband. If I were to marry you and give you a note to take to the man I loved after you, you'd take it and be sure to give it to him and bring an answer back, too. If you were forty, you would still go on taking my love-letters for me."

She suddenly laughed.

"There is something spiteful and yet open-hearted about you," Alyosha smiled to her.

"The open-heartedness consists in my not being ashamed of myself with you. What's more, I don't want to feel ashamed with you, just with you. Alyosha, why is it I don't respect you? I am very fond of you, but I don't respect you. If I respected you, I shouldn't talk to you without shame, should I?"

"No."

"But do you believe that I am not ashamed with you?"

"No, I don't believe it."

Lise laughed nervously again; she spoke rapidly.

"I sent your brother, Dmitri Fyodorovitch, some sweets in prison. Alyosha, you know, you are quite pretty! I shall love you awfully for having so quickly allowed me not to love you."

"Why did you send for me to-day, Lise?"

"I wanted to tell you of a longing I have. I should like some one to torture me, marry me and then torture me, deceive me and go away. I don't want to be happy."

"You are in love with disorder?"

"Yes, I want disorder. I keep wanting to set fire to the house. I keep imagining how I'll creep up and set fire to the house on the sly; it must be on the sly. They'll try to put it out, but it'll go on burning. And I shall know and say nothing. Ah, what silliness! And how bored I am!"

She waved her hand with a look of repulsion.

"It's your luxurious life," said Alyosha, softly"

"Is it better, then, to be poor?"

"Yes, it is better."

"That's what your monk taught you. That's not true. Let me be rich and all the rest poor, I'll eat sweets and drink cream and not give any to anyone else. Ach, don't speak, don't say anything"; she shook her hand at him, though Alyosha had not opened his mouth. "You've told me all that before, I know it all by heart. It bores me. If I am ever poor, I shall murder somebody, and even if I am rich, I may murder someone, perhaps--why do nothing! But do you know, I should like to reap, cut the rye? I'll marry you, and you shall become a peasant, a real peasant; we'll keep a colt, shall we? Do you know Kalganov?"

"Yes."

"He is always wandering about, dreaming. He says, 'Why live in real life? It's better to dream. One can dream the most delightful things, but real life is a bore.' But he'll be married soon for all that; he's been making love to me already. Can you spin tops?"

"Yes."

"Well, he's just like a top: he wants to be wound up and set spinning and then to be lashed, lashed, lashed with a whip. If I marry him, I'll keep him spinning all his life. You are not ashamed to be with me?"

"No."

"You are awfully cross, because I don't talk about holy things. I don't want to be holy. What will they do to one in the next world for the greatest sin? You must know all about that."

"God will censure you." Alyosha was watching her steadily.

"That's just what I should like. I would go up and they would censure me, and I would burst out laughing in their faces. I should dreadfully like to set fire to the house, Alyosha, to our house; you still don't believe me?"

"Why? There are children of twelve years old, who have a longing to set fire to something and they do set things on fire, too. It's a sort of disease."

"That's not true, that's not true; there may be children, but that's not what I mean."

"You take evil for good; it's a passing crisis; it's the result of your illness, perhaps."

"You do despise me, though! It's simply that I don't want to do good, I want to do evil, and it has nothing to do with illness."

"Why do evil?"

"So that everything might be destroyed. Ah, how nice it would be if everything were destroyed! You know, Alyosha, I sometimes think of doing a fearful lot of harm and everything bad, and I should do it for a long while on the sly and suddenly everyone would find it out. Everyone will stand round and point their fingers at me and I would look at them all. That would be awfully nice. Why would it be so nice, Alyosha?"

"I don't know. It's a craving to destroy something good or, as you say, to set fire to something. It happens sometimes."

"I not only say it, I shall do it."

"I believe you."

"Ah, how I love you for saying you believe me. And you are not lying one little bit. But perhaps you think that I am saying all this on purpose to annoy you?"

"No, I don't think that...though perhaps there is a little desire to do that in it, too."

"There is a little. I never can tell lies to you," she declared, with a strange fire in her eyes.

What struck Alyosha above everything was her earnestness. There was not a trace of humour or jesting in her face now, though, in old days, fun and gaiety never deserted her even at her most "earnest" moments.

"There are moments when people love crime," said Alyosha thoughtfully.

"Yes, yes! You have uttered my thought; they love crime, everyone loves crime, they love it always, not at some 'moments.' You know, it's as though people have made an agreement to lie about it and have lied about it ever since. They all declare that they hate evil, but secretly they all love it."

"And are you still reading nasty books?"

"Yes, I am. Mamma reads them and hides them under her pillow and I steal them."

"Aren't you ashamed to destroy yourself?"

"I want to destroy myself. There's a boy here, who lay down between the railway lines when the train was passing. Lucky fellow! Listen, your brother is being tried now for murdering his father and everyone loves his having killed his father."

"Loves his having killed his father?"

"Yes, loves it; everyone loves it! Everybody says it's so awful, but secretly they simply love it. I for one love it."

"There is some truth in what you say about everyone," said Alyosha softly.

"Oh, what ideas you have!" Lise shrieked in delight. "And you a monk, too! You wouldn't believe how I respect you, Alyosha, for never telling lies. Oh, I must tell you a funny dream of mine. I sometimes dream of devils. It's night; I am in my room with a candle and suddenly there are devils all over the place, in all the corners, under the table, and they open the doors; there's a crowd of them behind the doors and they want to come and seize me. And they are just coming, just seizing me. But I suddenly cross myself and they all draw back, though they don't go away altogether, they stand at the doors and in the corners, waiting. And suddenly I have a frightful longing to revile God aloud, and so I begin, and then they come crowding back to me, delighted, and seize me again and I cross myself again and they all draw back. It's awful fun, it takes one's breath away."

"I've had the same dream, too," said Alyosha suddenly.

"Really?" cried Lise, surprised. "I say, Alyosha, don't laugh, that's awfully important. Could two different people have the same dream?"

"It seems they can."

"Alyosha, I tell you, it's awfully important," Lise went on, with really excessive amazement. "It's not the dream that's important, but your having the same dream as me. You never lie to me, don't lie now; is it true? You are not laughing?"

"It's true."

Lise seemed extraordinarily impressed and for half a minute she was silent.

"Alyosha, come and see me, come and see me more often," she said suddenly, in a supplicating voice.

"I'll always come to see you, all my life," answered Alyosha firmly.

"You are the only person I can talk to, you know," Lise began again. "I talk to no one but myself and you. Only you in the whole world. And to you more readily than to myself. And I am not a bit ashamed with you, not a bit. Alyosha, why am I not ashamed with you, not a bit? Alyosha, is it true that at Easter the Jews steal a child and kill it?"

"I don't know."

"There's a book here in which I read about the trial of a Jew, who took a child of four years old and cut off the fingers from both hands, and then crucified him on the wall, hammered nails into him and crucified him, and afterwards, when he was tried, he said that the child died soon, within four hours. That was 'soon'! He said the child moaned, kept on moaning and he stood admiring it. That's nice!"

"Nice?"

"Nice; I sometimes imagine that it was I who crucified him. He would hang there moaning and I would sit opposite him eating pineapple compote. I am awfully fond of pineapple compote. Do you like it?"

Alyosha looked at her in silence. Her pale, sallow face was suddenly contorted, her eyes burned.

276

"You know, when I read about that Jew I shook with sobs all night. I kept fancying how the little thing cried and moaned (a child of four years old understands, you know), and all the while the thought of pineapple compote haunted me. In the morning I wrote a letter to a certain person, begging him particularly to come and see me. He came and I suddenly told him all about the child and the pineapple compote. All about it, all, and said that it was nice. He laughed and said it really was nice. Then he got up and went away. He was only here five minutes. Did he despise me? Did he despise me? Tell me, tell me, Alyosha, did he despise me or not?" She sat up on the couch, with flashing eyes.

"Tell me," Alyosha asked anxiously, "did you send for that person?"

"Yes, I did."

"Did you send him a letter?"

"Yes."

"Simply to ask about that, about that child?"

"No, not about that at all. But when he came, I asked him about that at once. He answered, laughed, got up and went away."

"That person behaved honourably," Alyosha murmured.

"And did he despise me? Did he laugh at me?"

"No, for perhaps he believes in the pineapple compote himself. He is very ill now, too, Lise."

"Yes, he does believe in it," said Lise, with flashing eyes.

"He doesn't despise anyone," Alyosha went on. "Only he does not believe anyone. If he doesn't believe in people, of course, he does despise them."

"Then he despises me, me?"

"You, too."

"Good." Lise seemed to grind her teeth. "When he went out laughing, I felt that it was nice to be despised. The child with fingers cut off is nice, and to be despised is nice..."

And she laughed in Alyosha's face, a feverish malicious laugh.

"Do you know, Alyosha, do you know, I should like--Alyosha, save me!" She suddenly jumped from the couch, rushed to him and seized him with both hands. "Save me!" she almost groaned. "Is there anyone in the world I could tell what I've told you? I've told you the truth, the truth. I shall kill myself, because I loathe everything! I don't want to live, because I loathe everything! I loathe everything, everything. Alyosha, why don't you love me in the least?" she finished in a frenzy.

"But I do love you!" answered Alyosha warmly.

"And will you weep over me, will you?"

"Yes."

"Not because I won't be your wife, but simply weep for me?"

"Yes."

"Thank you! It's only your tears I want. Everyone else may punish me and trample me under foot, everyone, everyone, not excepting anyone. For I don't love anyone. Do you hear, not anyone! On the contrary, I hate him! Go, Alyosha; it's time you went to your brother"; she tore herself away from him suddenly.

"How can I leave you like this?" said Alyosha, almost in alarm.

"Go to your brother, the prison will be shut; go, here's your hat. Give my love to Mitya, go, go!"

And she almost forcibly pushed Alyosha out of the door. He looked at her with pained surprise, when he was suddenly aware of a letter in his right hand, a tiny letter folded up tight and sealed. He glanced at it and instantly read the address, "To Ivan Fyodorovitch Karamazov." He looked quickly at Lise. Her face had become almost menacing.

"Give it to him, you must give it to him!" she ordered him, trembling and beside herself. "To-day, at once, or I'll poison myself! That's why I sent for you."

And she slammed the door quickly. The bolt clicked. Alyosha put the note in his pocket and went straight downstairs, without going back to Madame Hohlakov; forgetting her, in fact. As soon as Alyosha had gone, Lise unbolted the door, opened it a little, put her finger in the crack and slammed the door with all her might, pinching her finger. Ten seconds after, releasing her finger, she walked softly, slowly to her chair, sat up straight in it and looked intently at her blackened finger and at the blood that oozed from under the nail. Her lips were quivering and she kept whispering rapidly to herself:

"I am a wretch, wretch, wretch, wretch!"

IT was quite late (days are short in November) when Alyosha rang at the prison gate. It was beginning to get dusk. But Alyosha knew that he would be admitted without difficulty. Things were managed in our little town, as everywhere else. At first, of course, on the conclusion of the preliminary inquiry, relations and a few other persons could only obtain interviews with Mitya by going through certain inevitable formalities. But later, though the formalities were not relaxed, exceptions were made for some, at least, of Mitya's visitors. So much so, that sometimes the interviews with the prisoner in the room set aside for the purpose were practically tete-a-tete.

These exceptions, however, were few in number; only Grushenka, Alyosha and Rakitin were treated like this. But the captain of the police, Mihail Mihailovitch, was very favourably disposed to Grushenka. His abuse of her at Mokroe weighed on the old man's conscience, and when he learned the whole story, he completely changed his view of her. And strange to say, though he was firmly persuaded of his guilt, yet after Mitya was once in prison, the old man came to take a more and more lenient view of him. "He was a man of good heart, perhaps," he thought, "who had come to grief from drinking and dissipation." His first horror had been succeeded by pity. As for Alyosha, the police captain was very fond of him and had known him for a long time. Rakitin, who had of late taken to coming very often to see the prisoner, was one of the most intimate acquaintances of the "police captain's young ladies," as he called them, and was always hanging about their house. He gave lessons in the house of the prison superintendent, too, who, though scrupulous in the performance of his duties, was a kindhearted old man. Alyosha, again, had an intimate acquaintance of long standing with the superintendent, who was fond of talking to him, generally on sacred subjects. He respected Ivan Fyodorovitch, and stood in awe of his opinion, though he was a great philosopher himself; "self-taught," of course. But Alyosha had an irresistible attraction for him. During the last year the old man had taken to studying the Apocryphal Gospels, and constantly talked over his impressions with his young friend. He used to come and see him in the monastery and discussed for hours together with him and with the monks. So even if Alyosha were late at the prison, he had only to go to the superintendent and everything was made easy. Besides, everyone in the prison, down to the humblest warder, had grown used to Alyosha. The sentry, of course, did not trouble him so long as the authorities were satisfied.

When Mitya was summoned from his cell, he always went downstairs, to the place set aside for interviews. As Alyosha entered the room he came upon Rakitin, who was just taking leave of Mitya. They were both talking loudly. Mitya was laughing heartily as he saw him out, while Rakitin seemed grumbling. Rakitin did not like meeting Alyosha, especially of late. He scarcely spoke to him, and bowed to him stiffly. Seeing Alyosha enter now, he frowned and looked away, as though he were entirely absorbed in buttoning his big, warm, fur-trimmed overcoat. Then he began looking at once for his umbrella.

"I must mind not to forget my belongings," he muttered, simply to say something.

"Mind you don't forget other people's belongings," said Mitya, as a joke, and laughed at once at his own wit. Rakitin fired up instantly.

"You'd better give that advice to your own family, who've always been a slave-driving lot, and not to Rakitin," he cried, suddenly trembling with anger.

"What's the matter? I was joking," cried Mitya. "Damn it all! They are all like that." He turned to Alyosha, nodding towards Rakitin's hurriedly retreating figure. "He was sitting here, laughing and cheerful, and all at once he boils up like that. He didn't even nod to you. Have you broken with him completely? Why are you so late? I've not been simply waiting, but thirsting for you the whole morning. But never mind. We'll make up for it now."

"Why does he come here so often? Surely you are not such great friends?" asked Alyosha. He, too, nodded at the door through which Rakitin had disappeared.

"Great friends with Rakitin? No, not as much as that. Is it likely--a pig like that? He considers I am...a blackguard. They can't understand a joke either, that's the worst of such people. They never understand a joke, and their souls are dry, dry and flat; they remind me of prison walls when I was first brought here. But he is a clever fellow, very clever. Well, Alexey, it's all over with me now."

He sat down on the bench and made Alyosha sit down beside him.

"Yes, the trial's to-morrow. Are you so hopeless, brother?" Alyosha said, with an apprehensive feeling.

"What are you talking about?" said Mitya, looking at him rather uncertainly. "Oh, you mean the trial! Damn it all! Till now we've been talking of things that don't matter, about this trial, but I haven't said a word to you about the chief thing. Yes, the trial is to-morrow; but it wasn't the trial I meant, when I said it was all over with me. Why do you look at me so critically?"

"What do you mean, Mitya?"

"Ideas, ideas, that's all! Ethics! What is ethics?"

"Ethics?" asked Alyosha, wondering.

"Yes; is it a science?"

"Yes, there is such a science...but...I confess I can't explain to you what sort of science it is."

"Rakitin knows. Rakitin knows a lot, damn him! He's not going to be a monk. He means to go to Petersburg. There he'll go in for criticism of an elevating tendency. Who knows, he may be of use and make his own career, too. Ough! they are first-rate, these people, at making a career! Damn ethics, I am done for, Alexey, I am, you man of God! I love you more than anyone. It makes my heart yearn to look at you. Who was Karl Bernard?"

"Karl Bernard?" Alyosha was surprised again.

"No, not Karl. Stay, I made a mistake. Claude Bernard. What was he? Chemist or what?"

"He must be a savant," answered Alyosha; "but I confess I can't tell you much about him, either. I've heard of him as a savant, but what sort I don't know."

"Well, damn him, then! I don't know either," swore Mitya. "A scoundrel of some sort, most likely. They are all scoundrels. And Rakitin will make his way. Rakitin will get on anywhere; he is another Bernard. Ugh, these Bernards! They are all over the place."

"But what is the matter?" Alyosha asked insistently.

"He wants to write an article about me, about my case, and so begin his literary career. That's what he comes for; he said so himself. He wants to prove some theory. He wants to say 'he couldn't help murdering his father, he was corrupted by his environment,' and so on. He explained it all to me. He is going to put in a tinge of Socialism, he says. But there, damn the fellow, he can put in a tinge if he likes, I don't care. He can't bear Ivan, he hates him. He's not fond of you, either. But I don't turn him out, for he is a clever fellow. Awfully conceited, though. I said to him just now,' The Karamazovs are not blackguards, but philosophers; for all true Russians are philosophers, and though you've studied, you are not a philosopher--you are a low fellow.' He laughed, so maliciously. And I said to him, 'De ideabus non est disputandum.'* Isn't that rather good? I can set up for being a classic, you see!" Mitya laughed suddenly.

* There's no disputing ideas.

"Why is it all over with you? You said so just now," Alyosha interposed.

"Why is it all over with me? H'm!...The fact of it is...if you take it as a whole, I am sorry to lose God--that's why it is."

"What do you mean by 'sorry to lose God'?"

"Imagine: inside, in the nerves, in the head--that is, these nerves are there in the brain...(damn them!) there are sort of little tails, the little tails of those nerves, and as soon as they begin quivering...that is, you see, I look at something with my eyes and then they begin quivering, those little tails...and when they quiver, then an image appears...it doesn't appear at once, but an instant, a second, passes...and then something like a moment appears; that is, not a moment--devil take the moment!--but an image; that is, an object, or an action, damn it! That's why I see and then think, because of those tails, not at all because I've got a soul, and that I am some sort of image and likeness. All that is nonsense! Rakitin explained it all to me yesterday, brother, and it simply bowled me over. It's magnificent, Alyosha, this science! A new man's arising--that I understand...And yet I am sorry to lose God!"

"Well, that's a good thing, anyway," said Alyosha.

"That I am sorry to lose God? It's chemistry, brother, chemistry! There's no help for it, your reverence, you must make way for chemistry. And Rakitin does dislike God. Ough! doesn't he dislike Him! That's the sore point with all of them. But they conceal it. They tell lies. They pretend. 'Will you preach this in your reviews?' I asked him. 'Oh, well, if I did it openly, they won't let it through, 'he said. He laughed. 'But what will become of men then?' I asked him, 'without God and immortal life? All things are lawful then, they can do what they like?' 'Didn't you know?' he said laughing, 'a clever man can do what he likes,' he said. 'A clever man knows his way about, but you've put your foot in it, committing a murder, and now you are rotting in prison.' He says that to my face! A regular pig! I used to kick such people out, but now I listen to them. He talks a lot of sense, too. Writes well. He began reading me an article last week. I copied out three lines of it. Wait a minute. Here it is."

Mitya hurriedly pulled out a piece of paper from his pocket and read:

"'In order to determine this question, it is above all essential to put one's personality in contradiction to one's reality.' Do you understand that?"

"No, I don't," said Alyosha. He looked at Mitya and listened to him with curiosity.

"I don't understand either. It's dark and obscure, but intellectual. 'Everyone writes like that now,' he says, 'it's the effect of their environment.' They are afraid of the environment. He writes poetry, too, the rascal. He's written in honour of Madame Hohlakov's foot. Ha ha ha!"

"I've heard about it," said Alyosha.

"Have you? And have you heard the poem?"

"No."

"I've got it. Here it is. I'll read it to you. You don't know--I haven't told you--there's quite a story about it. He's a rascal! Three weeks ago he began to tease me. 'You've got yourself into a mess, like a fool, for the sake of three thousand, but I'm going to collar a hundred and fifty thousand. I am going to marry a widow and buy a house in Petersburg.' And he told me he was courting Madame Hohlakov. She hadn't much brains in her youth, and now at forty she has lost what she had. 'But she's awfully sentimental,' he says; 'that's how I shall get hold of her. When I marry her, I shall take her to Petersburg and there I shall start a newspaper.' And his mouth was simply watering, the beast, not for the widow, but for the hundred and fifty thousand. And he made me believe it. He came to see me every day. 'She is coming round,' he declared. He was beaming with delight. And then, all of a sudden, he was turned out of the house. Perhotin's carrying everything before him, bravo! I could kiss the silly old noodle for turning him out of the house. And he had written this doggerel. 'It's the first time I've soiled my hands with writing poetry,' he said. 'It's to win her heart, so it's in a good cause. When I get hold of the silly woman's fortune, I can be of great social utility.' They have this social justification for every nasty thing they do! 'Anyway it's better than your Pushkin's poetry,' he said, 'for I've managed to advocate enlightenment even in that.' I understand what he means about Pushkin, I quite see that, if he really was a man of talent and only wrote about women's feet. But wasn't Rakitin stuck up about his doggerel! The vanity of these fellows! 'On the convalescence of the swollen foot of the object of my affections'--he thought of that for a title. He's a waggish fellow.

A captivating little foot,
Though swollen and red and tender!
The doctors come and plasters put,
But still they cannot mend her.
Yet, 'tis not for her foot I dread--
A theme for Pushkin's muse more fit--
It's not her foot, it is her head:
I tremble for her loss of wit!
For as her foot swells, strange to say,
Her intellect is on the wane--
Oh, for some remedy I pray

That may restore both foot and brain! He is a pig, a regular pig, but he's very arch, the rascal! And he really has put in a progressive idea. And wasn't he angry when she kicked him out! He was gnashing his teeth!"

"He's taken his revenge already," said Alyosha. "He's written a paragraph about Madame Hohlakov."

And Alyosha told him briefly about the paragraph in Gossip.

"That's his doing, that's his doing!" Mitya assented, frowning. "That's him! These paragraphs...I know...the insulting things that have been written about Grushenka, for instance...And about Katya, too...H'm!"

He walked across the room with a harassed air.

"Brother, I cannot stay long," Alyosha said, after a pause. "To-morrow will be a great and awful day for you, the judgment of God will be accomplished...I am amazed at you, you walk about here, talking of I don't know what..."

"No, don't be amazed at me," Mitya broke in warmly. "Am I to talk of that stinking dog? Of the murderer? We've talked enough of him. I don't want to say more of the stinking son of Stinking Lizaveta! God will kill him, you will see. Hush!"

He went up to Alyosha excitedly and kissed him. His eyes glowed.

"Rakitin wouldn't understand it," he began in a sort of exaltation; "but you, you'll understand it all. That's why I was thirsting for you. You see, there's so much I've been wanting to tell you for ever so long, here, within these peeling walls, but I haven't said a word about what matters most; the moment never seems to have come. Now I can wait no longer. I must pour out my heart to you. Brother, these last two months I've found in myself a new man. A new man has risen up in me. He was hidden in me, but would never have come to the surface, if it hadn't been for this blow from heaven. I am afraid! And what do I care if I spend twenty years in the mines, breaking ore with a hammer? I am not a bit afraid of that--it's something else I am afraid of now: that that new man may leave me. Even there, in the mines, underground, I may find a human heart in another convict and murderer by my side, and I may make friends with him, for even there one may live and love and suffer. One may thaw and revive a frozen heart in that convict, one may wait upon him for years, and at last bring up from the dark depths a lofty soul, a feeling, suffering creature; one may bring forth an angel, create a hero! There are so many of them, hundreds of them, and we are all to blame for them. Why was it I dreamed of that 'babe' at such a moment? 'Why is the babe so poor?' That was a sign to me at that moment. It's for the babe I'm going. Because we are all responsible for all. For all the 'babes,' for there are big children as well as little children All are 'babes.' I go for all, because someone must go for all. I didn't kill father, but I've got to go. I accept it. It's all come to me here, here, within these peeling walls. There are numbers of them there, hundreds of them underground, with hammers in their hands. Oh, yes, we shall be in chains and there will be no freedom, but then, in our great sorrow, we shall rise again to joy, without which man cannot live nor God exist, for God gives joy: it's His privilege--a grand one. Ah, man should be dissolved in prayer! What should I be underground there without God? Rakitin's laughing! If they drive God from the earth, we shall shelter Him underground. One cannot exist in prison without God; it's even more impossible than out of prison. And then we men underground will sing from the bowels of the earth a glorious hymn to God, with Whom is joy. Hail to God and His joy! I love Him!"

Mitya was almost gasping for breath as he uttered his wild speech. He turned pale, his lips quivered, and tears rolled down his cheeks.

"Yes, life is full, there is life even underground," he began again. "You wouldn't believe, Alexey, how I want to live now, what a thirst for existence and consciousness has sprung up in me within these peeling walls. Rakitin doesn't understand that; all he cares about is building a house and letting flats. But I've been longing for you. And what is suffering? I am not afraid of it, even if it were beyond reckoning. I am not afraid of it now. I was afraid of it before. Do you know, perhaps I won't answer at the trial at all...And I seem to have such strength in me now, that I think I could stand anything, any suffering, only to be able to say and to repeat to myself every moment, 'I exist.' In thousands of agonies--I exist. I'm tormented on the rack--but I exist! Though I sit alone on a pillar--I exist! I see the sun, and if I don't see the sun, I know it's there. And there's a whole life in that, in knowing that the sun is there. Alyosha, my angel, all these philosophies are the death of me. Damn them! Brother Ivan-"

"What of brother Ivan?" interrupted Alyosha, but Mitya did not hear.

"You see, I never had any of these doubts before, but it was all hidden away in me. It was perhaps just because ideas I did not understand were surging up in me, that I used to drink and fight and rage. It was to stifle them in myself, to still them, to smother them. Ivan is not Rakitin, there is an idea in him. Ivan is a sphinx and is silent; he is always silent. It's God that's worrying me. That's the only thing that's worrying me. What if He doesn't exist? What if Rakitin's right--that it's an idea made up by men? Then if He doesn't exist, man is the chief of the earth, of the universe. Magnificent! Only how is he going to be good without God? That's the question. I always come back to that. For whom is man going to love then? To whom will he be thankful? To whom will he sing the hymn? Rakitin laughs. Rakitin says that one can love humanity without God. Well, only a snivelling idiot can maintain that. I can't understand it. Life's easy for Rakitin. 'You'd better think about the extension of civic rights, or even of keeping down the price of meat. You will show your love for humanity more simply and directly by that, than by philosophy.' I answered him, 'Well, but you, without a God, are more likely to raise the price of meat, if it suits you, and make a rouble on every copeck.' He lost his temper. But after all, what is goodness? Answer me that, Alexey. Goodness is one thing with me and another with a Chinaman, so it's a relative thing. Or isn't it? Is it not relative? A treacherous question! You won't laugh if I tell you it's kept me awake two nights. I only wonder now how people can live and think nothing about it. Vanity! Ivan has no God. He has an idea. It's beyond me. But he is silent. I believe he is a Freemason. I asked him, but he is silent. I wanted to drink from the springs of his soul--he was silent. But once he did drop a word."

"What did he say?" Alyosha took it up quickly.

"I said to him, 'Then everything is lawful, if it is so?' He frowned. 'Fyodor Pavlovitch, our papa,' he said, 'was a pig, but his ideas were right enough.' That was what he dropped. That was all he said. That was going one better than Rakitin."

"Yes," Alyosha assented bitterly. "When was he with you?"

"Of that later; now I must speak of something else. I have said nothing about Ivan to you before. I put it off to the last. When my business here is over and the verdict has been given, then I'll tell you something. I'll tell you everything. We've something tremendous on hand...And you shall be my judge in it. But don't begin about that now; be silent. You talk of to-morrow, of the trial; but, would you believe it, I know nothing about it."

"Have you talked to the counsel?"

"What's the use of the counsel? I told him all about it. He's a soft, city-bred rogue--a Bernard! But he doesn't believe me--not a bit of it. Only imagine, he believes I did it. I see it. 'In that case,' I asked him, 'why have you come to defend me?' Hang them all! They've got a doctor down, too, want to prove I'm mad. I won't have that! Katerina Ivanovna wants to do her 'duty' to the end, whatever the strain!" Mitya smiled bitterly. "The cat! Hard-hearted creature! She knows that I said of her at Mokroe that she was a woman of 'great wrath.' They repeated it.

Yes, the facts against me have grown numerous as the sands of the sea. Grigory sticks to his point. Grigory's honest, but a fool. Many people are honest because they are fools: that's Rakitin's idea. Grigory's my enemy. And there are some people who are better as foes than friends. I mean Katerina Ivanovna. I am afraid, oh, I am afraid she will tell how she bowed to the ground after that four thousand. She'll pay it back to the last farthing. I don't want her sacrifice; they'll put me to shame at the trial. I wonder how I can stand it. Go to her, Alyosha, ask her not to speak of that in the court, can't you? But damn it all, it doesn't matter! I shall get through somehow. I don't pity her. It's her own doing. She deserves what she gets. I shall have my own story to tell, Alexey." He smiled bitterly again. "Only...only Grusha, Grusha! Good Lord! Why should she have such suffering to bear?" he exclaimed suddenly, with tears. "Grusha's killing me; the thought of her's killing me, killing me. She was with me just now..."

"She told me she was very much grieved by you to-day."

"I know. Confound my temper! It was jealousy. I was sorry, I kissed her as she was going. I didn't ask her forgiveness."

"Why didn't you?" exclaimed Alyosha.

Suddenly Mitya laughed almost mirthfully.

"God preserve you, my dear boy, from ever asking forgiveness for a fault from a woman you love. From one you love especially, however greatly you may have been in fault. For a woman--devil only knows what to make of a woman! I know something about them, anyway. But try acknowledging you are in fault to a woman. Say, 'I am sorry, forgive me,' and a shower of reproaches will follow! Nothing will make her forgive you simply and directly, she'll humble you to the dust, bring forward things that have never happened, recall everything, forget nothing, add something of her own, and only then forgive you. And even the best, the best of them do it. She'll scrape up all the scrapings and load them on your head. They are ready to flay you alive, I tell you, every one of them, all these angels without whom we cannot live! I tell you plainly and openly, dear boy, every decent man ought to be under some woman's thumb. That's my conviction--not conviction, but feeling. A man ought to be magnanimous, and it's no disgrace to a man! No disgrace to a hero, not even a Caesar! But don't ever beg her pardon all the same for anything. Remember that rule given you by your brother Mitya, who's come to ruin through women. No, I'd better make it up to Grusha somehow, without begging pardon. I worship her, Alexey, worship her. Only she doesn't see it. No, she still thinks I don't love her enough. And she tortures me, tortures me with her love. The past was nothing! In the past it was only those infernal curves of hers that tortured me, but now I've taken all her soul into my soul and through her I've become a man myself. Will they marry us? If they don't, I shall die of jealousy. I imagine something every day...What did she say to you about me?"

Alyosha repeated all Grushenka had said to him that day. Mitya listened, made him repeat things, and seemed pleased.

"Then she is not angry at my being jealous?" he exclaimed. "She is a regular woman! 'I've a fierce heart myself!' Ah, I love such fierce hearts, though I can't bear anyone's being jealous of me. I can't endure it. We shall fight. But I shall love her, I shall love her infinitely. Will they marry us? Do they let convicts marry? That's the question. And without her I can't exist..."

Mitya walked frowning across the room. It was almost dark. He suddenly seemed terribly worried.

"So there's a secret, she says, a secret? We have got up a plot against her, and Katya is mixed up in it, she thinks. No, my good Grushenka, that's not it. You are very wide of the mark, in your foolish feminine way. Alyosha, darling, well, here goes! I'll tell you our secret!"

He looked round, went close up quickly to Alyosha, who was standing before him, and whispered to him with an air of mystery, though in reality no one could hear them: the old warder was dozing in the corner, and not a word could reach the ears of the soldiers on guard.

"I will tell you all our secret," Mitya whispered hurriedly. "I meant to tell you later, for how could I decide on anything without you? You are everything to me. Though I say that Ivan is superior to us, you are my angel. It's your decision will decide it. Perhaps it's you that is superior and not Ivan. You see, it's a question of conscience, question of the higher conscience--the secret is so important that I can't settle it myself, and I've put it off till I could speak to you. But anyway it's too early to decide now, for we must wait for the verdict. As soon as the verdict is given, you shall decide my fate. Don't decide it now. I'll tell you now. You listen, but don't decide. Stand and keep quiet. I won't tell you everything. I'll only tell you the idea, without details, and you keep quiet. Not a question, not a movement. You agree? But, goodness, what shall I do with your eyes? I'm afraid your eyes will tell me your decision, even if you don't speak. Oo! I'm afraid! Alyosha, listen! Ivan suggests my escaping. I won't tell you the details: it's all been thought out: it can all be arranged. Hush, don't decide. I should go to America with Grusha. You know I can't live without Grusha! What if they won't let her follow me to Siberia? Do they let convicts get married? Ivan thinks not. And without Grusha what should I do there underground with a hammer? I should only smash my skull with the hammer! But, on the other hand, my conscience? I should have run away from suffering. A sign has come, I reject the sign. I have a way of salvation and I turn my back on it. Ivan says that in America, 'with the goodwill,' I can be of more use than underground. But what becomes of our hymn from underground? What's America? America is vanity again! And there's a lot of swindling in America, too, I expect. I should have run away from crucifixion! I tell you, you know, Alexey, because you are the only person who can understand this. There's no one else. It's folly, madness to others, all I've told you of the hymn. They'll say I'm out of my mind or a fool. I am not out of my mind and I am not a fool. Ivan understands about the hymn, too. He understands, only he doesn't answer--he doesn't speak. He doesn't believe in the hymn. Don't speak, don't speak. I see how you look! You have already decided. Don't decide, spare me! I can't live without Grusha. Wait till after the trial!"

Mitya ended beside himself. He held Alyosha with both hands on his shoulders, and his yearning, feverish eyes were fixed on his brother's.

"They don't let convicts marry, do they?" he repeated for the third time in a supplicating voice.

Alyosha listened with extreme surprise and was deeply moved.

"Tell me one thing," he said. "Is Ivan very keen on it, and whose idea was it?"

"His, his, and he is very keen on it. He didn't come to see me at first, then he suddenly came a week ago and he began about it straight away. He is awfully keen on it. He doesn't ask me, but orders me to escape. He doesn't doubt of my obeying him, though I showed him all my heart as I have to you, and told him about the hymn, too. He told me he'd arrange it; he's found out about everything. But of that later. He's simply set on it. It's all a matter of money: he'll pay ten thousand for escape and give me twenty thousand for America. And he says we can arrange a magnificent escape for ten thousand."

"And he told you on no account to tell me?" Alyosha asked again.

"To tell no one, and especially not you; on no account to tell you. He is afraid, no doubt, that you'll stand before me as my conscience. Don't tell him I told you. Don't tell him, for anything."

"You are right," Alyosha pronounced; "it's impossible to decide anything before the trial is over. After the trial you'll decide of yourself. Then you'll find that new man in yourself and he will decide."

"A new man, or a Bernard who'll decide a la Bernard, for I believe I'm a contemptible Bernard myself," said Mitya, with a bitter grin.

"But, brother, have you no hope then of being acquitted?"

Mitya shrugged his shoulders nervously and shook his head.

"Alyosha, darling, it's time you were going," he said, with a sudden haste. "There's the superintendent shouting in the yard. He'll be here directly. We are late; it's irregular. Embrace me quickly. Kiss me! Sign me with the cross, darling, for the cross I have to bear to-morrow."

They embraced and kissed.

"Ivan," said Mitya suddenly, "suggests my escaping; but, of course, he believes I did it."

A mournful smile came on to his lips.

"Have you asked him whether he believes it?" asked Alyosha.

"No, I haven't. I wanted to, but I couldn't. I hadn't the courage. But I saw it from his eyes. Well, good-bye!"

Once more they kissed hurriedly, and Alyosha was just going out, when Mitya suddenly called him back.

"Stand facing me! That's right!" And again he seized Alyosha, putting both hands on his shoulders. His face became suddenly quite pale, so that it was dreadfully apparent, even through the gathering darkness. His lips twitched, his eyes fastened upon Alyosha.

"Alyosha, tell me the whole truth, as you would before God. Do you believe I did it? Do you, do you in yourself, believe it? The whole truth, don't lie!" he cried desperately.

Everything seemed heaving before Alyosha, and he felt something like a stab at his heart.

"Hush! What do you mean?" he faltered helplessly.

"The whole truth, the whole, don't lie!" repeated Mitya.

"I've never for one instant believed that you were the murderer!" broke in a shaking voice from Alyosha's breast, and he raised his right hand in the air, as though calling God to witness his words.

Mitya's whole face was lighted up with bliss.

"Thank you!" he articulated slowly, as though letting a sigh escape him after fainting. "Now you have given me new life. Would you believe it, till this moment I've been afraid to ask you, you, even you. Well, go! You've given me strength for to-morrow. God bless you! Come, go along! Love Ivan!" was Mitya's last word.

Alyosha went out in tears. Such distrustfulness in Mitya, such lack of confidence even to him, to Alyosha--all this suddenly opened before Alyosha an unsuspected depth of hopeless grief and despair in the soul of his unhappy brother. Intense, infinite compassion overwhelmed him instantly. There was a poignant ache in his torn heart. "Love Ivan"--he suddenly recalled Mitya's words. And he was going to Ivan. He badly wanted to see Ivan all day. He was as much worried about Ivan as about Mitya, and more than ever now.

ON the way to Ivan he had to pass the house where Katerina Ivanovna was living. There was light in the windows. He suddenly stopped and resolved to go in. He had not seen Katerina Ivanovna for more than a week. But now it struck him that Ivan might be with her, especially on the eve of the terrible day. Ringing, and mounting the staircase, which was dimly lighted by a Chinese lantern, he saw a man coming down, and as they met, he recognised him as his brother. So he was just coming from Katerina Ivanovna.

"Ah, it's only you," said Ivan dryly. "Well, good-bye! You are going to her?"

"Yes."

"I don't advise you to; she's upset and you'll upset her more."

A door was instantly flung open above, and a voice cried suddenly:

"No, no! Alexey Fyodorovitch, have you come from him?"

"Yes, I have been with him."

"Has he sent me any message? Come up, Alyosha, and you, Ivan Fyodorovitch, you must come back, you must. Do you hear?"

There was such a peremptory note in Katya's voice that Ivan, after a moment's hesitation, made up his mind to go back with Alyosha.

"She was listening," he murmured angrily to himself, but Alyosha heard it.

"Excuse my keeping my greatcoat on," said Ivan, going into the drawing-room. "I won't sit down. I won't stay more than a minute."

"Sit down, Alexey Fyodorovitch," said Katerina Ivanovna, though she remained standing. She had changed very little during this time, but there was an ominous gleam in her dark eyes. Alyosha remembered afterwards that she had struck him as particularly handsome at that moment.

"What did he ask you to tell me?"

"Only one thing," said Alyosha, looking her straight in the face, "that you would spare yourself and say nothing at the trial of what" (he was a little confused) "...passed between you...at the time of your first acquaintance...in that town."

"Ah! that I bowed down to the ground for that money!" She broke into a bitter laugh. "Why, is he afraid for me or for himself? He asks me to spare--whom? Him or myself? Tell me, Alexey Fyodorovitch!"

Alyosha watched her intently, trying to understand her.

"Both yourself and him," he answered softly.

"I am glad to hear it," she snapped out maliciously, and she suddenly blushed.

"You don't know me yet, Alexey Fyodorovitch," she said menacingly. "And I don't know myself yet. Perhaps you'll want to trample me under foot after my examination to-morrow."

"You will give your evidence honourably," said Alyosha; "that's all that's wanted."

"Women are often dishonourable," she snarled. "Only an hour ago I was thinking I felt afraid to touch that monster...as though he were a reptile...but no, he is still a human being to me! But did he do it? Is he the murderer?" she cried, all of a sudden, hysterically, turning quickly to Ivan. Alyosha saw at once that she had asked Ivan that question before, perhaps only a moment before he came in, and not for the first time, but for the hundredth, and that they had ended by quarrelling.

"I've been to see Smerdyakov...It was you, you who persuaded me that he murdered his father. It's only you I believed" she continued, still addressing Ivan. He gave her a sort of strained smile. Alyosha started at her tone. He had not suspected such familiar intimacy between them.

"Well, that's enough, anyway," Ivan cut short the conversation. "I am going. I'll come to-morrow." And turning at once, he walked out of the room and went straight downstairs.

With an imperious gesture, Katerina Ivanovna seized Alyosha by both hands.

"Follow him! Overtake him! Don't leave him alone for a minute!" she said, in a hurried whisper. "He's mad! Don't you know that he's mad? He is in a fever, nervous fever. The doctor told me so. Go, run after him..."

Alyosha jumped up and ran after Ivan, who was not fifty paces ahead of him.

"What do you want?" He turned quickly on Alyosha, seeing that he was running after him. "She told you to catch me up, because I'm mad. I know it all by heart," he added irritably.

"She is mistaken, of course; but she is right that you are ill," said Alyosha. "I was looking at your face just now. You look very ill, Ivan."

Ivan walked on without stopping. Alyosha followed him.

"And do you know, Alexey Fyodorovitch, how people do go out of their minds?" Ivan asked in a a voice suddenly quiet, without a trace of irritation, with a note of the simplest curiosity.

"No, I don't. I suppose there are all kinds of insanity."

"And can one observe that one's going mad oneself?"

"I imagine one can't see oneself clearly in such circumstances," Alyosha answered with surprise.

Ivan paused for half a minute.

"If you want to talk to me, please change the subject," he said suddenly.

"Oh, while I think of it, I have a letter for you," said Alyosha timidly, and he took Lise's note from his pocket and held it out to Ivan. They were just under a lamp-post. Ivan recognised the handwriting at once.

"Ah, from that little demon!" he laughed maliciously, and, without opening the envelope, he tore it into bits and threw it in the air. The bits were scattered by the wind.

"She's not sixteen yet, I believe, and already offering herself," he said contemptuously, striding along the street again.

"How do you mean, offering herself?" exclaimed Alyosha.

"As wanton women offer themselves, to be sure."

"How can you, Ivan, how can you?" Alyosha cried warmly, in a grieved voice. "She is a child; you are insulting a child! She is ill; she is very ill, too. She is on the verge of insanity, too, perhaps...I had hoped to hear something from you...that would save her."

"You'll hear nothing from me. If she is a child, I am not her nurse. Be quiet, Alexey. Don't go on about her. I am not even thinking about it."

They were silent again for a moment.

"She will be praying all night now to the Mother of God to show her how to act to-morrow at the trial," he said sharply and angrily again.

"You...you mean Katerina Ivanovna?"

"Yes. Whether she's to save Mitya or ruin him. She'll pray for light from above. She can't make up her mind for herself, you see. She has not had time to decide yet. She takes me for her nurse, too. She wants me to sing lullabies to her."

"Katerina Ivanovna loves you, brother," said Alyosha sadly.

"Perhaps; but I am not very keen on her."

"She is suffering. Why do you...sometimes say things to her that give her hope?" Alyosha went on, with timid reproach. "I know that you've given her hope. Forgive me for speaking to you like this," he added.

"I can't behave to her as I ought--break off altogether and tell her so straight out," said Ivan, irritably. "I must wait till sentence is passed on the murderer. If I break off with her now, she will avenge herself on me by ruining that scoundrel to-morrow at the trial, for she hates him and knows she hates him. It's all a lie--lie upon lie! As long as I don't break off with her, she goes on hoping, and she won't ruin that monster, knowing how I want to get him out of trouble. If only that damned verdict would come!"

The words "murderer" and "monster" echoed painfully in Alyosha's heart.

"But how can she ruin Mitya?" he asked, pondering on Ivan's words. "What evidence can she give that would ruin Mitya?"

"You don't know that yet. She's got a document in her hands, in Mitya's own writing, that proves conclusively that he did murder Fyodor Pavlovitch."

"That's impossible!" cried Alyosha.

"Why is it impossible? I've read it myself."

"There can't be such a document!" Alyosha repeated warmly. "There can't be, because he's not the murderer. It's not he murdered father, not he!"

Ivan suddenly stopped.

"Who is the murderer then, according to you?" he asked, with apparent coldness. There was even a supercilious note in his voice.

"You know who," Alyosha pronounced in a low, penetrating voice.

"Who? You mean the myth about that crazy idiot, the epileptic, Smerdyakov?"

Alyosha suddenly felt himself trembling all over.

"You know who," broke helplessly from him. He could scarcely breathe.

"Who? Who?" Ivan cried almost fiercely. All his restraint suddenly vanished.

"I only know one thing," Alyosha went on, still almost in a whisper, "it wasn't you killed father."

"'Not you'! What do you mean by 'not you'?" Ivan was thunderstruck.

"It was not you killed father, not you! Alyosha repeated firmly.

The silence lasted for half a minute.

"I know I didn't. Are you raving?" said Ivan, with a pale, distorted smile. His eyes were riveted on Alyosha. They were standing again under a lamp-post.

"No, Ivan. You've told yourself several times that you are the murderer."

"When did I say so? I was in Moscow...When have I said so?" Ivan faltered helplessly.

"You've said so to yourself many times, when you've been alone during these two dreadful months," Alyosha went on softly and distinctly as before. Yet he was speaking now, as it were, not of himself, not of his own will, but obeying some irresistible command. "You have accused yourself and have confessed to yourself that you are the murderer and no one else. But you didn't do it: you are mistaken: you are not the murderer. Do you hear? It was not you! God has sent me to tell you so."

They were both silent. The silence lasted a whole long minute. They were both standing still, gazing into each other's eyes. They were both pale. Suddenly Ivan began trembling all over, and clutched Alyosha's shoulder.

"You've been in my room!" he whispered hoarsely. "You've been there at night, when he came...Confess...have you seen him, have you seen him?"

"Whom do you mean--Mitya?" Alyosha asked, bewildered.

"Not him, damn the monster!" Ivan shouted, in a frenzy, "Do you know that he visits me? How did you find out? Speak!"

"Who is he? I don't know whom you are talking about," Alyosha faltered, beginning to be alarmed.

"Yes, you do know. or how could you--? It's impossible that you don't know."

Suddenly he seemed to check himself. He stood still and seemed to reflect. A strange grin contorted his lips.

"Brother," Alyosha began again, in a shaking voice, "I have said this to you, because you'll believe my word, I know that. I tell you once and for all, it's not you. You hear, once for all! God has put it into my heart to say this to you, even though it may make you hate me from this hour."

But by now Ivan had apparently regained his self-control.

"Alexey Fyodorovitch," he said, with a cold smile, "I can't endure prophets and epileptics--messengers from God especially--and you know that only too well. I break off all relations with you from this moment and probably for ever. I beg you to leave me at this turning. It's the way to your lodgings, too. You'd better be particularly careful not to come to me to-day! Do you hear?"

He turned and walked on with a firm step, not looking back.

"Brother," Alyosha called after him, "if anything happens to you to-day, turn to me before anyone!"

But Ivan made no reply. Alyosha stood under the lamp-post at the cross roads, till Ivan had vanished into the darkness. Then he turned and walked slowly homewards. Both Alyosha and Ivan were living in lodgings; neither of them was willing to live in Fyodor Pavlovitch's empty house. Alyosha had a furnished room in the house of some working people. Ivan lived some distance from him. He had taken a roomy and fairly comfortable lodge attached to a fine house that belonged to a well-to-do lady, the widow of an official. But his only attendant was a deaf and rheumatic old crone who went to bed at six o'clock every evening and got up at six in the morning. Ivan had become remarkably indifferent to his comforts of late, and very fond of being alone. He did everything for himself in the one room he lived in, and rarely entered any of the other rooms in his abode.

He reached the gate of the house and had his hand on the bell, when he suddenly stopped. He felt that he was trembling all over with anger. Suddenly he let go of the bell, turned back with a curse, and walked with rapid steps in the opposite direction. He walked a mile and a half to a tiny, slanting, wooden house, almost a hut, where Marya Kondratyevna, the neighbour who used to come to Fyodor Pavlovitch's kitchen for soup and to whom Smerdyakov had once sung his songs and played on the guitar, was now lodging. She had sold their little house, and was now living here with her mother. Smerdyakov, who was ill--almost dying-had been with them ever since Fyodor Pavlovitch's death. It was to him Ivan was going now, drawn by a sudden and irresistible prompting.

Chapter 6. The First Interview with Smerdyakov

THIS was the third time that Ivan had been to see Smerdyakov since his return from Moscow. The first time he had seen him and talked to him was on the first day of his arrival, then he had visited him once more, a fortnight later. But his visits had ended with that second one, so that it was now over a month since he had seen him. And he had scarcely heard anything of him.

Ivan had only returned five days after his father's death, so that he was not present at the funeral, which took place the day before he came back. The cause of his delay was that Alyosha, not knowing his Moscow address, had to apply to Katerina Ivanovna to telegraph to him, and she, not knowing his address either, telegraphed to her sister and aunt, reckoning on Ivan's going to see them as soon as he arrived in Moscow. But he did not go to them till four days after his arrival. When he got the telegram, he had, of course, set off post-haste to our town. The first to meet him was Alyosha, and Ivan was greatly surprised to find that, in opposition to the general opinion of the town, he refused to entertain a suspicion against Mitya, and spoke openly of Smerdyakov as the murderer. Later on, after seeing the police captain and the prosecutor, and hearing the details of the charge and the arrest, he was still more surprised at Alyosha, and ascribed his opinion only to his exaggerated brotherly feeling and sympathy with Mitya, of whom Alyosha, as Ivan knew, was very fond.

By the way, let us say a word or two of Ivan's feeling to his brother Dmitri. He positively disliked him; at most, felt sometimes a compassion for him, and even that was mixed with great contempt, almost repugnance. Mitya's whole personality, even his appearance, was extremely unattractive to him. Ivan looked with indignation on Katerina Ivanovna's love for his brother. Yet he went to see Mitya on the first day of his arrival, and that interview, far from shaking Ivan's belief in his guilt, positively strengthened it. He found his brother agitated, nervously excited. Mitya had been talkative, but very absent-minded and incoherent. He used violent language, accused Smerdyakov, and was fearfully muddled. He talked principally about the three thousand roubles, which he said had been "stolen" from him by his father.

"The money was mine, it was my money," Mitya kept repeating. "Even if I had stolen it, I should have had the right."

He hardly contested the evidence against him, and if he tried to turn a fact to his advantage, it was in an absurd and incoherent way. He hardly seemed to wish to defend himself to Ivan or anyone else. Quite the contrary, he was angry and proudly scornful of the charges against him; he was continually firing up and abusing everyone. He only laughed contemptuously at Grigory's evidence about the open door, and declared that it was "the devil that opened it." But he could not bring forward any coherent explanation of the fact. He even succeeded in insulting Ivan during their first interview, telling him sharply that it was not for people who declared that "everything was lawful," to suspect and question him. Altogether he was anything but friendly with Ivan on that occasion. Immediately after that interview with Mitya, Ivan went for the first time to see Smerdyakov.

In the railway train on his way from Moscow, he kept thinking of Smerdyakov and of his last conversation with him on the evening before he went away. Many things seemed to him puzzling and suspicious. when he gave his evidence to the investigating lawyer Ivan said nothing, for the time, of that conversation. He put that off till he had seen Smerdyakov, who was at that time in the hospital.

Doctor Herzenstube and Varvinsky, the doctor he met in the hospital, confidently asserted in reply to Ivan's persistent questions, that Smerdyakov's epileptic attack was unmistakably genuine, and were surprised indeed at Ivan asking whether he might not have been shamming on the day of the catastrophe. They gave him to understand that the attack was an exceptional one, the fits persisting and recurring several times, so that the patient's life was positively in danger, and it was only now, after they had applied remedies, that they could assert with confidence that the patient would survive. "Though it might well be," added Doctor Herzenstube, "that his reason would be impaired for a considerable period, if not permanently." On Ivan's asking impatiently whether that meant that he was now mad, they told him that this was not yet the case, in the full sense of the word, but that certain abnormalities were perceptible. Ivan decided to find out for himself what those abnormalities were.

At the hospital he was at once allowed to see the patient. Smerdyakov was lying on a truckle-bed in a separate ward. There was only one other bed in the room, and in it lay a tradesman of the town, swollen with dropsy, who was obviously almost dying; he could be no hindrance to their conversation. Smerdyakov grinned uncertainly on seeing Ivan, and for the first instant seemed nervous. So at least Ivan fancied. But that was only momentary. For the rest of the time he was struck, on the contrary, by Smerdyakov's composure. From the first glance Ivan had no doubt that he was very ill. He was very weak; he spoke slowly, seeming to move his tongue with difficulty; he was much thinner and sallower.Throughout the interview, which lasted twenty minutes, he kept complaining of headache and of pain in all his limbs. His thin emasculate face seemed to have become so tiny; his hair was ruffled, and his crest of curls in front stood up in a thin tuft. But in the left eye, which was screwed up and seemed to be insinuating something, Smerdyakov showed himself unchanged. "It's always worth while speaking to a clever man." Ivan was reminded of that at once. He sat down on the stool at his feet. Smerdyakov, with painful effort, shifted his position in bed, but he was not the first to speak. He remained dumb, and did not even look much interested.

"Can you. talk to me?" asked Ivan. "I won't tire you much."

"Certainly I can," mumbled Smerdyakov, in a faint voice. "Has your honour been back long?" he added patronisingly, as though encouraging a nervous visitor.

"I only arrived to-day...To see the mess you are in here."

Smerdyakov sighed.

"Why do you sigh? You knew of it all along," Ivan blurted out.

Smerdyakov was stolidly silent for a while.

"How could I help knowing? It was clear beforehand. But how could I tell it would turn out like that?"

"What would turn out? Don't prevaricate! You've foretold you'd have a fit; on the way down to the cellar, you know. You mentioned the very spot."

"Have you said so at the examination yet?" Smerdyakov queried with composure.

Ivan felt suddenly angry.

"No, I haven't yet, but I certainly shall. You must explain a great deal to me, my man; and let me tell you, I am not going to let you play with me!"

"Why should I play with you, when I put my whole trust in you, as in God Almighty?" said Smerdyakov, with the same composure, only for a moment closing his eyes.

"In the first place," began Ivan, "I know that epileptic fits can't be told beforehand. I've inquired; don't try and take me in. You can't foretell the day and the hour. How was it you told me the day and the hour beforehand, and about the cellar, too? How could you tell that you would fall down the cellar stairs in a fit, if you didn't sham a fit on purpose?"

"I had to go to the cellar anyway, several times a day, indeed," Smerdyakov drawled deliberately. "I fell from the garret just in the same way a year ago. It's quite true you can't tell the day and hour of a fit beforehand, but you can always have a presentiment of it."

"But you did foretell the day and the hour!"

"In regard to my epilepsy, sir, you had much better inquire of the doctors here. You can ask them whether it was a real fit or a sham; it's no use my saying any more about it."

"And the cellar? How could you know beforehand of the cellar?"

"You don't seem able to get over that cellar! As I was going down to the cellar, I was in terrible dread and doubt. What frightened me most was losing you and being left without defence in all the world. So I went down into the cellar thinking, 'Here, it'll come on directly, it'll strike me down directly, shall I fall?' And it was through this fear that I suddenly felt the spasm that always comes...and so I went flying. All that and all my previous conversation with you at the gate the evening before, when I told you how frightened I was and spoke of the cellar, I told all that to Doctor Herzenstube and Nikolay Parfenovitch, the investigating lawyer, and it's all been written down in the protocol. And the doctor here, Mr. Varvinsky, maintained to all of them that it was just the thought of it brought it on, the apprehension that I might fall. It was just then that the fit seized me. And so they've written it down, that it's just how it must have happened, simply from my fear."

As he finished, Smerdyakov. drew a deep breath, as though exhausted.

"Then you have said all that in your evidence?" said Ivan, somewhat taken aback. He had meant to frighten him with the threat of repeating their conversation, and it appeared that Smerdyakov had already reported it all himself.

"What have I to be afraid of? Let them write down the whole truth," Smerdyakov pronounced firmly.

"And have you told them every word of our conversation at the gate?"

"No, not to say every word."

"And did you tell them that you can sham fits, as you boasted then?"

"No, I didn't tell them that either."

"Tell me now, why did you send me then to Tchermashnya?"

"I was afraid you'd go away to Moscow; Tchermashnya is nearer, anyway."

"You are lying; you suggested my going away yourself; you told me to get out of the way of trouble."

"That was simply out of affection and my sincere devotion to you, foreseeing trouble in the house, to spare you. Only I wanted to spare myself even more. That's why I told you to get out of harm's way, that you might understand that there would be trouble in the house, and would remain at home to protect your father."

"You might have said it more directly, you blockhead!" Ivan suddenly fired up.

"How could I have said it more directly then? It was simply my fear that made me speak, and you might have been angry, too. I might well have been apprehensive that Dmitri Fyodorovitch would make a scene and carry away that money, for he considered it as good as his own; but who could tell that it would end in a murder like this? I thought that he would only carry off the three thousand that lay under the master's mattress in the envelope, and you see, he's murdered him. How could you guess it either, sir?"

"But if you say yourself that it couldn't be guessed, how could I have guessed and stayed at home? You contradict yourself!" said Ivan, pondering.

"You might have guessed from my sending you to Tchermashnya and not to Moscow."

"How could I guess it from that?"

Smerdyakov seemed much exhausted, and again he was silent for a minute.

"You might have guessed from the fact of my asking you not to go to Moscow, but to Tchermashnya, that I wanted to have you nearer, for Moscow's a long way off, and Dmitri Fyodorovitch, knowing you are not far off, would not be so bold. And if anything had happened, you might have come to protect me, too, for I warned you of Grigory Vassilyevitch's illness, and that I was afraid of having a fit. And when I explained those knocks to you, by means of which one could go in to the deceased, and that Dmitri Fyodorovitch knew them all through me, I thought that you would guess yourself that he would be sure to do something, and so wouldn't go to Tchermashnya even, but would stay."

"He talks very coherently," thought Ivan, "though he does mumble; what's the derangement of his faculties that Herzenstube talked of?"

"You are cunning with me, damn you!" he exclaimed, getting angry.

"But I thought at the time that you quite guessed," Smerdyakov parried with the simplest air.

"If I'd guessed, I should have stayed," cried Ivan.

"Why, I thought that it was because you guessed, that you went away in such a hurry, only to get out of trouble, only to run away and save yourself in your fright."

"You think that everyone is as great a coward as yourself?"

"Forgive me, I thought you were like me."

"Of course, I ought to have guessed," Ivan said in agitation; "and I did guess there was some mischief brewing on your part...only you are lying, you are lying again," he cried, suddenly recollecting. "Do you remember how you went up to the carriage and said to me, 'It's always worth while speaking to a clever man'? So you were glad I went away, since you praised me?"

Smerdyakov sighed again and again. A trace of colour came into his face.

"If I was pleased," he articulated rather breathlessly, "it was simply because you agreed not to go to Moscow, but to Tchermashnya. For it was nearer, anyway. Only when I said these words to you, it was not by way of praise, but of reproach. You didn't understand it."

"What reproach?"

"Why, that foreseeing such a calamity you deserted your own father, and would not protect us, for I might have been taken up any time for stealing that three thousand."

"Damn you!" Ivan swore again. "Stay, did you tell the prosecutor and the investigating lawyer about those knocks?"

"I told them everything just as it was."

Ivan wondered inwardly again.

"If I thought of anything then," he began again, "it was solely of some wickedness on your part. Dmitri might kill him, but that he would steal--I did not believe that then...But I was prepared for any wickedness from you. You told me yourself you could sham a fit. What did you say that for?"

"It was just through my simplicity, and I never have shammed a fit on purpose in my life. And I only said so then to boast to you. It was just foolishness. I liked you so much then, and was open-hearted with you."

"My brother directly accuses you of the murder and theft."

"What else is left for him to do?" said Smerdyakov, with a bitter grin. "And who will believe him with all the proofs against him? Grigory Vassilyevitch saw the door open. What can he say after that? But never mind him! He is trembling to save himself."

He slowly ceased speaking; then suddenly, as though on reflection, added:

"And look here again. He wants to throw it on me and make out that it is the work of my hands--I've heard that already. But as to my being clever at shamming a fit: should I have told you beforehand that I could sham one, if I really had had such a design against your father? If I had been planning such a murder could I have been such a fool as to give such evidence against myself beforehand? And to his son, too! Upon my word! Is that likely? As if that could be; such a thing has never happened. No one hears this talk of ours now, except Providence itself, and if you were to tell of it to the prosecutor and Nikolay Parfenovitch you might defend me completely by doing so, for who would be likely to be such a criminal, if he is so open-hearted beforehand? Anyone can see that."

"Well," and Ivan got up to cut short the conversation, struck by Smerdyakov's last argument. "I don't suspect you at all, and I think it's absurd, indeed, to suspect you. On the contrary, I am grateful to you for setting my mind at rest. Now I am going, but I'll come again. Meanwhile, good-bye. Get well. Is there anything you want?"

"I am very thankful for everything. Marfa Ignatyevna does not forget me, and provides me anything I want, according to her kindness. Good people visit me every day."

"Good-bye. But I shan't say anything of your being able to sham a fit, and I don't advise you to, either," something made Ivan say suddenly.

"I quite understand. And if you don't speak of that, I shall say nothing of that conversation of ours at the gate."

Then it happened that Ivan went out, and only when he had gone a dozen steps along the corridor, he suddenly felt that there was an insulting significance in Smerdyakov's last words. He was almost on the point of turning back, but it was only a passing impulse, and muttering, "Nonsense!" he went out of the hospital.

His chief feeling was one of relief at the fact that it was not Smerdyakov, but Mitya, who had committed the murder, though he might have been expected to feel the opposite. He did not want to analyse the reason for this feeling, and even felt a positive repugnance at prying into his sensations. He felt as though he wanted to make haste to forget something. In the following days he became convinced of Mitya's guilt, as he got to know all the weight of evidence against him. There was evidence of people of no importance, Fenya and her mother, for instance, but the effect of it was almost overpowering. As to Perhotin, the people at the tavern, and at Plotnikov's shop, as well as the witnesses at Mokroe, their evidence seemed conclusive. It was the details that were so damning. The secret of the knocks impressed the lawyers almost as much as Grigory's evidence as to the open door. Grigory's wife, Marfa, in answer to Ivan's questions, declared that Smerdyakov had been lying all night the other side of the partition wall, "He was not three paces from our bed," and that although she was a sound sleeper she waked several times and heard him moaning, "He was moaning the whole time, moaning continually."

Talking to Herzenstube, and giving it as his opinion that Smerdyakov was not mad, but only rather weak, Ivan only evoked from the old man a subtle smile.

"Do you know how he spends his time now?" he asked; "learning lists of French words by heart. He has an exercise-book under his pillow with the French words written out in Russian letters for him by someone, he he he!"

Ivan ended by dismissing all doubts. He could not think of Dmitri without repulsion. Only one thing was strange, however. Alyosha persisted that Dmitri was not the murderer, and that "in all probability" Smerdyakov was. Ivan always felt that Alyosha's opinion meant a great deal to him, and so he was astonished at it now. Another thing that was strange was that Alyosha did not make any attempt to talk about Mitya with Ivan, that he never began on the subject and only answered his questions. This, too, struck Ivan particularly.

But he was very much preoccupied at that time with something quite apart from that. On his return from Moscow, he abandoned himself hopelessly to his mad and consuming passion for Katerina Ivanovna. This is not the time to begin to speak of this new passion of Ivan's, which left its mark on all the rest of his life: this would furnish the subject for another novel, which I may perhaps never write. But I cannot omit to mention here that when Ivan, on leaving Katerina Ivanovna with Alyosha, as I've related already, told him, "I am not keen on her," it was an absolute lie: he loved her madly, though at times he hated her so that he might have murdered her. Many causes helped to bring about this feeling. Shattered by what had happened with Mitya, she rushed on Ivan's return to meet him as her one salvation. She was hurt, insulted and humiliated in her feelings. And here the man had come back to her, who had loved her so ardently before (oh! she knew that very well), and whose heart and intellect she considered so superior to her own. But the sternly virtuous girl did not abandon herself altogether to the man she loved, in spite of the Karamazov violence of his passions and the great fascination he had for her. She was continually tormented at the same time by remorse for having deserted Mitya, and in moments of discord and violent anger (and they were numerous) she told Ivan so plainly. This was what he had called to Alyosha "lies upon lies." There was, of course, much that was false in it, and that angered Ivan more than anything...But of all this later.

He did, in fact, for a time almost forget Smerdyakov's existence, and yet, a fortnight after his first visit to him, he began to be haunted by the same strange thoughts as before. It's enough to say that he was continually asking himself, why was it that on that last night in Fyodor Pavlovitch's house he had crept out on to the stairs like a thief and listened to hear what his father was doing below? Why had he recalled that afterwards with repulsion? Why next morning, had he been suddenly so depressed on the journey? Why, as he reached Moscow, had he said to himself, "I am a scoundrel"? And now he almost fancied that these tormenting thoughts would make him even forget Katerina Ivanovna, so completely did they take possession of him again. It was just after fancying this, that he met Alyosha in the street. He stopped him at once, and put a question to him:

"Do you remember when Dmitri burst in after dinner and beat father, and afterwards I told you in the yard that I reserved 'the right to desire'?...Tell me, did you think then that I desired father's death or not?"

"I did think so," answered Alyosha, softly.

"It was so, too; it was not a matter of guessing. But didn't you fancy then that what I wished was just that one reptile should devour another'; that is, just that Dmitri should kill father, and as soon as possible...and that I myself was even prepared to help to bring that about?"

Alyosha turned rather pale, and looked silently into his brother's face.

"Speak!" cried Ivan, "I want above everything to know what you thought then. I want the truth, the truth!"

He drew a deep breath, looking angrily at Alyosha before his answer came.

"Forgive me, I did think that, too, at the time," whispered Alyosha, and he did not add one softening phrase.

"Thanks," snapped Ivan, and, leaving Alyosha, he went quickly on his way. From that time Alyosha noticed that Ivan began obviously to avoid him and seemed even to have taken a dislike to him, so much so that

Alyosha gave up going to see him. Immediately after that meeting with him, Ivan had not gone home, but went straight to Smerdyakov again.

Chapter 7. The Second Visit to Smerdyakov

BY that time Smerdyakov had been discharged from the hospital. Ivan knew his new lodging, the dilapidated little wooden house, divided in two by a passage, on one side of which lived Marya Kondratyevna and her mother, and on the other, Smerdyakov. No one knew on what terms he lived with them, whether as a friend or as a lodger. It was supposed afterwards that he had come to stay with them as Marya Kondratyevna's betrothed, and was living there for a time without paying for board or lodging. Both mother and daughter had the greatest respect for him and looked upon him as greatly superior to themselves.

Ivan knocked, and, on the door being opened, went straight into the passage. By Marya Kondratyevna's directions he went straight to the better room on the left, occupied by Smerdyakov. There was a tiled stove in the room and it was extremely hot. The walls were gay with blue paper, which was a good deal used however, and in the cracks under it cockroaches swarmed in amazing numbers, so that there was a continual rustling from them. The furniture was very scanty: two benches against each wall and two chairs by the table. The table of plain wood was covered with a cloth with pink patterns on it. There was a pot of geranium on each of the two little windows. In the corner there was a case of ikons. On the table stood a little copper samovar with many dents in it, and a tray with two cups. But Smerdyakov had finished tea and the samovar was out. He was sitting at the table on a bench. He was looking at an exercise-book and slowly writing with a pen. There was a bottle of ink by him and a flat iron candlestick, but with a composite candle. Ivan saw at once from Smerdyakov's face that he had completely recovered from his illness. His face was fresher, fuller, his hair stood up jauntily in front, and was plastered down at the sides. He was sitting in a parti-coloured, wadded dressing-gown, rather dirty and frayed, however. He had spectacles on his nose, which Ivan had never seen him wearing before. This trifling circumstance suddenly redoubled Ivan's anger: "A creature like that and wearing spectacles!"

Smerdyakov slowly raised his head and looked intently at his visitor through his spectacles; then he slowly took them off and rose from the bench, but by no means respectfully, almost lazily, doing the least possible required by common civility. All this struck Ivan instantly; he took it all in and noted it at once--most of all the look in Smerdyakov's eyes, positively malicious, churlish and haughty. "What do you want to intrude for?" it seemed to say; "we settled everything then; why have you come again?" Ivan could scarcely control himself.

"It's hot here," he said, still standing, and unbuttoned his overcoat.

"Take off your coat," Smerdyakov conceded.

Ivan took off his coat and threw it on a bench with trembling hands. He took a chair, moved it quickly to the table and sat down. Smerdyakov managed to sit down on his bench before him.

"To begin with, are we alone?" Ivan asked sternly and impulsively. "Can they overhear us in there?"

"No one can hear anything. You've seen for yourself: there's a passage."

"Listen, my good fellow; what was that you babbled, as I was leaving the hospital, that if I said nothing about your faculty of shamming fits, you wouldn't tell the investigating lawyer all our conversation at the gate? What do you mean by all? What could you mean by it? Were you threatening me? Have I entered into some sort of compact with you? Do you suppose I am afraid of you?"

Ivan said this in a perfect fury, giving him to understand with obvious intention that he scorned any subterfuge or indirectness and meant to show his cards. Smerdyakov's eyes gleamed resentfully, his left eye winked, and he at once gave his answer, with his habitual composure and deliberation. "You want to have everything above-board; very well, you shall have it," he seemed to say.

"This is what I meant then, and this is why I said that, that you, knowing beforehand of this murder of your own parent, left him to his fate, and that people mightn't after that conclude any evil about your feelings and perhaps of something else, too--that's what I promised not to tell the authorities."

Though Smerdyakov spoke without haste and obviously controlling himself, yet there was something in his voice, determined and emphatic, resentful and insolently defiant. He stared impudently at Ivan. A mist passed before Ivan's eyes for the first moment.

"How? What? Are you out of your mind?"

"I'm perfectly in possession of all my faculties."

"Do you suppose I knew of the murder?" Ivan cried at last, and he brought his fist violently on the table. "What do you mean by 'something else, too'? Speak, scoundrel!"

Smerdyakov was silent and still scanned Ivan with the same insolent stare.

"Speak, you stinking rogue, what is that 'something else, too'?"

"The 'something else' I meant was that you probably, too, were very desirous of your parent's death."

Ivan jumped up and struck him with all his might on the shoulder, so that he fell back against the wall. In an instant his face was bathed in tears. Saying, "It's a shame, sir, to strike a sick man," he dried his eyes with a very dirty blue check handkerchief and sank into quiet weeping. A minute passed.

"That's enough! Leave off," Ivan said peremptorily, sitting down again. "Don't put me out of all patience."

Smerdyakov took the rag from his eyes. Every line of his puckered face reflected the insult he had just received.

"So you thought then, you scoundrel, that together with Dmitri I meant to kill my father?"

"I didn't know what thoughts were in your mind then," said Smerdyakov resentfully; "and so I stopped you then at the gate to sound you on that very point."

"To sound what, what?"

"Why, that very circumstance, whether you wanted your father to be murdered or not."

What infuriated Ivan more than anything was the aggressive, insolent tone to which Smerdyakov persistently adhered.

"It was you murdered him?" he cried suddenly.

Smerdyakov smiled contemptuously.

"You know of yourself, for a fact, that it wasn't I murdered him. And I should have thought that there was no need for a sensible man to speak of it again."

"But why, why had you such a suspicion about me at the time?"

"As you know already, it was simply from fear. For I was in such a position, shaking with fear, that I suspected everyone. I resolved to sound you, too, for I thought if you wanted the same as your brother, then the business was as good as settled and I should be crushed like a fly, too."

"Look here, you didn't say that a fortnight ago."

"I meant the same when I talked to you in the hospital, only I thought you'd understand without wasting words, and that being such a sensible man you wouldn't care to talk of it openly."

"What next! Come answer, answer, I insist: what was it...what could I have done to put such a degrading suspicion into your mean soul?"

"As for the murder, you couldn't have done that and didn't want to, but as for wanting someone else to do it, that was just what you did want."

"And how coolly, how coolly he speakst But why should I have wanted it; what grounds had I for wanting it?"

"What grounds had you? What about the inheritance?" said Smerdyakov sarcastically, and, as it were, vindictively. "Why, after your parent's death there was at least forty thousand to come to each of you, and very likely more, but if Fyodor Pavlovitch got married then to that lady, Agrafena Alexandrovna, she would have had all his capital made over to her directly after the wedding, for she's plenty of sense, so that your parent would not have left you two roubles between the three of you. And were they far from a wedding, either? Not a hair's-breadth: that lady had only to lift her little finger and he would have run after her to church, with his tongue out."

Ivan restrained himself with painful effort.

"Very good," he commented at last. "You see, I haven't jumped up, I haven't knocked you down, I haven't killed you. Speak on. So, according to you, I had fixed on Dmitri to do it; I was reckoning on him?"

"How could you help reckoning on him? If he killed him, then he would lose all the rights of a nobleman, his rank and property, and would go off to exile; so his share of the inheritance would come to you and your brother Alexey Fyodorovitch in equal parts; so you'd each have not forty, but sixty thousand each. There's not a doubt you did reckon on Dmitri Fyodorovitch."

"What I put up with from you! Listen, scoundrel, if I had reckoned on anyone then, it would have been on you, not on Dmitri, and I swear I did expect some wickedness from you...at the time...I remember my impression!"

"I thought, too, for a minute, at the time, that you were reckoning on me as well," said Smerdyakov, with a sarcastic grin. "So that it was just by that more than anything you showed me what was in your mind. For if you had a foreboding about me and yet went away, you as good as said to me, 'You can murder my parent, I won't hinder you!'"

"You scoundrel! So that's how you understood it!"

"It was all that going to Tchermashnya. Why! You were meaning to go to Moscow and refused all your father's entreaties to go to Tchermashnya--and simply at a foolish word from me you consented at once! What reason had you to consent to Tchermashnya? Since you went to Tchermashnya with no reason, simply at my word, it shows that you must have expected something from me."

No, I swear I didn't!" shouted Ivan, grinding his teeth.

"You didn't? Then you ought, as your father's son, to have had me taken to the lock-up and thrashed at once for my words then...or at least, to have given me a punch in the face on the spot, but you were not a bit angry, if you please, and at once in a friendly way acted on my foolish word and went away, which was utterly absurd, for you ought to have stayed to save your parent's life. How could I help drawing my conclusions?"

Ivan sat scowling, both his fists convulsively pressed on his knees.

"Yes, I am sorry I didn't punch you in the face," he said with a bitter smile. "I couldn't have taken you to the lock-up just then. Who would have believed me and what charge could I bring against you? But the punch in the face...oh, I'm sorry I didn't think of it. Though blows are forbidden, I should have pounded your ugly face to a jelly."

Smerdyakov looked at him almost with relish.

"In the ordinary occasions of life," he said in the same complacent and sententious tone in which he had taunted Grigory and argued with him about religion at Fyodor Pavlovitch's table, "in the ordinary occasions of life, blows on the face are forbidden nowadays by law, and people have given them up, but in exceptional occasions of life people still fly to blows, not only among us but all over the world, be it even the fullest republic of France, just as in the time of Adam and Eve, and they never will leave off, but you, even in an exceptional case, did not dare."

"What are you learning French words for?" Ivan nodded towards the exercise-book lying on the table.

"Why shouldn't I learn them so as to improve my education, supposing that I may myself chance to go some day to those happy parts of Europe?"

"Listen, monster." Ivan's eyes flashed and he trembled all over. "I am not afraid of your accusations; you can say what you like about me, and if I don't beat you to death, it's simply because I suspect you of that crime and I'll drag you to justice. I'll unmask you."

"To my thinking, you'd better keep quiet, for what can you accuse me of, considering my absolute innocence? And who would believe you? Only if you begin, I shall tell everything, too, for I must defend myself."

"Do you think I am afraid of you now?"

"If the court doesn't believe all I've said to you just now, the public will, and you will be ashamed."

"That's as much as to say, 'It's always worth while speaking to a sensible man,' eh?" snarled Ivan.

"You hit the mark, indeed. And you'd better be sensible."

Ivan got up, shaking all over with indignation, put on his coat, and without replying further to Smerdyakov, without even looking at him, walked quickly out of the cottage. The cool evening air refreshed him. There was a bright moon in the sky. A nightmare of ideas and sensations filled his soul. "Shall I go at once and give information against Smerdyakov? But what information can I give? He is not guilty, anyway. On the contrary, he'll accuse me. And in fact, why did I set off for Tchermashnya then? What for? What for?" Ivan asked himself. "Yes, of course, I was expecting something and he is right..." And he remembered for the hundredth time how, on the last night in his father's house, he had listened on the stairs. But he remembered it now with such anguish that he stood still on the spot as though he had been stabbed. "Yes, I expected it then, that's true! I wanted the murder, I did want the murder! Did I want the murder? Did I want it? I must kill Smerdyakov! If I don't dare kill Smerdyakov now, life is not worth living!"

Ivan did not go home, but went straight to Katerina Ivanovna and alarmed her by his appearance. He was like a madman. He repeated all his conversation with Smerdyakov, every syllable of it. He couldn't be calmed, however much she tried to soothe him: he kept walking about the room, speaking strangely, disconnectedly. At last he sat down, put his elbows on the table, leaned his head on his hands and pronounced this strange sentence: "If it's not Dmitri, but Smerdyakov who's the murderer, I share his guilt, for I put him up to it. Whether I did, I don't know yet. But if he is the murderer, and not Dmitri, then, of course, I am the murderer, too."

When Katerina Ivanovna heard that, she got up from her seat without a word, went to her writing-table, opened a box standing on it, took out a sheet of paper and laid it before Ivan. This was the document of which Ivan spoke to Alyosha later on as a "conclusive proof" that Dmitri had killed his father. It was the letter written by Mitya to Katerina Ivanovna when he was drunk, on the very evening he met Alyosha at the crossroads on the way to the monastery, after the scene at Katerina Ivanovna's, when Grushenka had insulted her. Then, parting from Alyosha, Mitya had rushed to Grushenka. I don't know whether he saw her, but in the evening he was at the Metropolis, where he got thoroughly drunk. Then he asked for pen and paper and wrote a document of weighty consequences to himself. It was a wordy, disconnected, frantic letter, a drunken letter, in fact. It was like the talk of a drunken man, who, on his return home, begins with extraordinary heat telling his wife or one of his household how he has just been insulted, what a rascal had just insulted him, what a fine fellow he is on the other hand, and how he will pay that scoundrel out; and all that at great length, with great excitement and incoherence, with drunken tears and blows on the table. The letter was written on a dirty piece of ordinary paper of the cheapest kind. It had been provided by the tavern and there were figures scrawled on the back of it. There was evidently not space enough for his drunken verbosity and Mitya not only filled the margins but had written the last line right across the rest. The letter ran as follows:

FATAL KATYA: To-morrow I will get the money and repay your three thousand and farewell, woman of great wrath, but farewell, too, my love! Let us make an end! To-morrow I shall try and get it from everyone, and if I can't borrow it, I give you my word of honour I shall go to my father and break his skull and take the money from under the pillow, if only Ivan has gone. It I have to go to Siberia for it, I'll give you back your three thousand. And farewell. I bow down to the ground before you, for I've been a scoundrel to you. Forgive me! No, better not forgive me, you'll be happier and so shall I! Better Siberia than your love, for I love another woman and you got to know her too well to-day, so how can you forgive? I will murder the man who's robbed me! I'll leave you all and go to the East so as to see no one again. Not her either, for you are not my only tormentress; she is too. Farewel!

P.S.--I write my curse, but I adore you! I hear it in my heart. One string is left, and it vibrates. Better tear my heart in two! I shall kill myself, but first of all that cur. I shall tear three thousand from him and fling it to you. Though I've been a scoundrel to you, I am not a thief! You can expect three thousand. The cur keeps it under his mattress, in pink ribbon. I am not a thief, but I'll murder my thief. Katya, don't look disdainful. Dmitri is not a thief! but a murderer! He has murdered his father and ruined himself to hold his ground, rather than endure your pride. And he doesn't love you.

P.P.S.--I kiss your feet, farewell!

P.P.P.S.--Katya, pray to God that someone'll give me the money. Then I shall not be steeped in gore, and if no one does--I shall! Kill me!

Your slave and enemy,

D. KARAMAZOV

When Ivan read this "document" he was convinced. So then it was his brother, not Smerdyakov. And if not Smerdyakov, then not he, Ivan. This letter at once assumed in his eyes the aspect of a logical proof. There could be no longer the slightest doubt of Mitya's guilt. The suspicion never occurred to Ivan, by the way, that Mitya might have committed the murder in conjunction with Smerdyakov, and, indeed, such a theory did not fit in with the facts. Ivan was completely reassured. The next morning he only thought of Smerdyakov and his gibes with contempt. A few days later he positively wondered how he could have been so horribly distressed at his suspicions. He resolved to dismiss him with contempt and forget him. So passed a month. He made no further inquiry about Smerdyakov, but twice he happened to hear that he was very ill and out of his mind.

"He'll end in madness," the young doctor Varvinsky observed about him, and Ivan remembered this. During the last week of that month Ivan himself began to feel very ill. He went to consult the Moscow doctor who had been sent for by Katerina Ivanovna just before the trial. And just at that time his relations with Katerina Ivanovna became acutely strained. They were like two enemies in love with one another. Katerina Ivanovna's "returns" to Mitya, that is, her brief but violent revulsions of feeling in his favour, drove Ivan to perfect frenzy. Strange to say, until that last scene described above, when Alyosha came from Mitya to Katerina Ivanovna, Ivan had never once, during that month, heard her express a doubt of Mitya's guilt, in spite of those "returns" that were so hateful to him. It is remarkable, too, that while he felt that he hated Mitya more and more every day, he realised that it was not on account of Katya's "returns" that he hated him, but just because he was the murderer of his father. He was conscious of this and fully recognised it to himself.

Nevertheless, he went to see Mitya ten days before the trial and proposed to him a plan of escape--a plan he had obviously thought over a long time. He was partly impelled to do this by a sore place still left in his heart from a phrase of Smerdyakov's, that it was to his, Ivan's, advantage that his brother should be convicted, as that would increase his inheritance and Alyosha's from forty to sixty thousand roubles. He determined to sacrifice thirty thousand on arranging Mitya's escape. On his return from seeing him, he was very mournful and dispirited; he suddenly began to feel that he was anxious for Mitya's escape, not only to heal that sore place by sacrificing thirty thousand, but for another reason. "Is it because I am as much a murderer at heart?" he asked himself. Something very deep down seemed burning and rankling in his soul. His pride above all suffered cruelly all that month. But of that later...

When, after his conversation with Alyosha, Ivan suddenly decided with his hand on the bell of his lodging to go to Smerdyakov, he obeyed a sudden and peculiar impulse of indignation. He suddenly remembered how Katerina Ivanovna had only just cried out to him in Alyosha's presence: "It was you, you, persuaded me of his" (that is, Mitya's) "guilt!" Ivan was thunderstruck when he recalled it. He had never once tried to persuade her that Mitya was the murderer; on the contrary, he had suspected himself in her presence, that time when he came back from Smerdyakov. It was she, she, who had produced that "document" and proved his brother's guilt. And now she suddenly exclaimed: "I've been at Smerdyakov's myself!" When had she been there? Ivan had known nothing of it. So she was not at all so sure of Mitya's guilt! And what could Smerdyakov have told her? What,

what, had he said to her? His heart burned with violent anger. He could not understand how he could, half an hour before, have let those words pass and not have cried out at the moment. He let go of the bell and rushed off to Smerdyakov. "I shall kill him, perhaps, this time," he thought on the way.

Chapter 8. The Third and Last Interview with Smerdyakov

WHEN he was half-way there, the keen dry wind that had been blowing early that morning rose again, and a fine dry snow began falling thickly. It did not lie on the ground, but was whirled about by the wind, and soon there was a regular snowstorm. There were scarcely any lamp-posts in the part of the town where Smerdyakov lived. Ivan strode alone in the darkness, unconscious of the storm, instinctively picking out his way. His head ached and there was a painful throbbing in his temples. He felt that his hands were twitching convulsively. Not far from Marya Kondratyevna's cottage, Ivan suddenly came upon a solitary drunken little peasant. He was wearing a coarse and patched coat, and was walking in zigzags, grumbling and swearing to himself. Then suddenly he would begin singing in a husky drunken voice:

Ach, Vanka's gone to Petersburg;

I won't wait till he comes back.

But he broke off every time at the second line and began swearing again; then he would begin the same song again. Ivan felt an intense hatred for him before he had thought about him at all. Suddenly he realised his presence and felt an irresistible impulse to knock him down. At that moment they met, and the peasant with a violent lurch fell full tilt against Ivan, who pushed him back furiously. The peasant went flying backwards and fell like a log on the frozen ground. He uttered one plaintive "O--oh!" and then was silent. Ivan stepped up to him. He was lying on his back, without movement or consciousness. "He will be frozen," thought Ivan, and he went on his way to Smerdyakov's.

In the passage, Marya Kondratyevna, who ran out to open the door with a candle in her hand, whispered that Smerdyakov was very ill; "It's not that he's laid up, but he seems not himself, and he even told us to take the tea away; he wouldn't have any."

"Why, does he make a row?" asked Ivan coarsely.

"Oh dear no, quite the contrary, he's very quiet. Only please don't talk to him too long," Marya Kondratyevna begged him. Ivan opened the door and stepped into the room.

It was over-heated as before, but there were changes in the room. One of the benches at the side had been removed, and in its place had been put a large old mahogany leather sofa, on which a bed had been made up, with fairly clean white pillows. Smerdyakov was sitting on the sofa, wearing the same dressing-gown. The table had been brought out in front of the sofa, so that there was hardly room to move. On the table lay a thick book in yellow cover, but Smerdyakov was not reading it. He seemed to be sitting doing nothing. He met Ivan with a slow silent gaze, and was apparently not at all surprised at his coming. There was a great change in his face; he was much thinner and sallower. His eyes were sunken and there were blue marks under them.

"Why, you really are ill?" Ivan stopped short. "I won't keep you long, I wont even take off my coat. Where can one sit down?"

He went to the other end of the table, moved up a chair and sat down on it.

"Why do you look at me without speaking? We only come with one question, and I swear I won't go without an answer. Has the young lady, Katerina Ivanovna, been with you?"

Smerdyakov still remained silent, looking quietly at Ivan as before. Suddenly, with a motion of his hand, he turned his face away.

"What's the matter with you?" cried Ivan.

"Nothing."

"What do you mean by 'nothing'?"

"Yes, she has. It's no matter to you. Let me alone."

"No, I won't let you alone. Tell me, when was she here?"

"Why, I'd quite forgotten about her," said Smerdyakov, with a scornful smile, and turning his face to Ivan again, he stared at him with a look of frenzied hatred, the same look that he had fixed on him at their last interview, a month before.

"You seem very ill yourself, your face is sunken; you don't look like yourself," he said to Ivan.

"Never mind my health, tell me what I ask you."

"But why are your eyes so yellow? The whites are quite yellow. Are you so worried?" He smiled contemptuously and suddenly laughed outright.

"Listen; I've told you I won't go away without an answer!" Ivan cried, intensely irritated.

"Why do you keep pestering me? Why do you torment me?" said Smerdyakov, with a look of suffering.

"Damn it! I've nothing to do with you. Just answer my question and I'll go away."

"I've no answer to give you," said Smerdyakov, looking down again.

"You may be sure I'll make you answer!"

"Why are you so uneasy?" Smerdyakov stared at him, not simply with contempt, but almost with repulsion. "Is this because the trial begins to-morrow? Nothing will happen to you; can't you believe that at last? Go home, go to bed and sleep in peace, don't be afraid of anything."

"I don't understand you...What have I to be afraid of to-morrow?" Ivan articulated in astonishment, and suddenly a chill breath of fear did in fact pass over his soul. Smerdyakov measured him with his eyes.

"You don't understand?" he drawled reproachfully. "It's a strange thing a sensible man should care to play such a farce!"

Ivan looked at him speechless. The startling, incredibly supercilious tone of this man who had once been his valet, was extraordinary in itself. He had not taken such a tone even at their last interview.

"I tell you, you've nothing to be afraid of. I won't say anything about you; there's no proof against you. I say, how your hands are trembling! Why are your fingers moving like that? Go home, you did not murder him."

Ivan started. He remembered Alyosha.

"I know it was not I," he faltered.

"Do you?" Smerdyakov caught him up again.

Ivan jumped up and seized him by the shoulder.

"Tell me everything, you viper! Tell me everything!"

Smerdyakov was not in the least scared. He only riveted his eyes on Ivan with insane hatred.

"Well, it was you who murdered him, if that's it," he whispered furiously.

Ivan sank back on his chair, as though pondering something. He laughed malignantly.

"You mean my going away. What you talked about last time?"

"You stood before me last time and understood it all, and you understand it now."

"All I understand is that you are mad."

"Aren't you tired of it? Here we are face to face; what's the use of going on keeping up a farce to each other? Are you still trying to throw it all on me, to my face? You murdered him; you are the real murderer, I was only your instrument, your faithful servant, and it was following your words I did it."

"Did it? Why, did you murder him?" Ivan turned cold.

Something seemed to give way in his brain, and he shuddered all over with a cold shiver. Then Smerdyakov himself looked at him wonderingly; probably the genuineness of Ivan's horror struck him.

"You don't mean to say you really did not know?" he faltered mistrustfully, looking with a forced smile into his eyes. Ivan still gazed at him, and seemed unable to speak.

Ach, Vanka's gone to Petersburg;

I won't wait till he comes back, suddenly echoed in his head.

"Do you know, I am afraid that you are a dream, a phantom sitting before me," he muttered.

"There's no phantom here, but only us two and one other. No doubt he is here, that third, between us."

"Who is he? Who is here? What third person?" Ivan cried in alarm, looking about him, his eyes hastily searching in every corner.

"That third is God Himself--Providence. He is the third beside us now. Only don't look for Him, you won't find him."

"It's a lie that you killed him!" Ivan cried madly. "You are mad, or teasing me again!"

Smerdyakov, as before, watched him curiously, with no sign of fear. He could still scarcely get over his incredulity; he still fancied that Ivan knew everything and was trying to "throw it all on him to his face."

"Wait a minute," he said at last in a weak voice, and suddenly bringing up his left leg from under the table, he began turning up his trouser leg. He was wearing long white stockings and slippers. Slowly he took off his garter and fumbled to the bottom of his stocking. Ivan gazed at him, and suddenly shuddered in a paroxysm of terror.

"He's mad!" he cried, and rapidly jumping up, he drew back, so that he knocked his back against the wall and stood up against it, stiff and straight. He looked with insane terror at Smerdyakov, who, entirely unaffected by his terror, continued fumbling in his stocking, as though he were making an effort to get hold of something with his fingers and pull it out. At last he got hold of it and began pulling it out. Ivan saw that it was a piece of paper, or perhaps a roll of papers. Smerdyakov pulled it out and laid it on the table.

"Here," he said quietly.

"What is it?" asked Ivan, trembling.

"Kindly look at it," Smerdyakov answered, still in the same low tone.

Ivan stepped up to the table, took up the roll of paper and began unfolding it, but suddenly drew back his fingers, as though from contact with a loathsome reptile.

"Your hands keep twitching," observed Smerdyakov, and he deliberately unfolded the bundle himself. Under the wrapper were three packets of hundred-rouble notes.

"They are all here, all the three thousand roubles; you need not count them. Take them," Smerdyakov suggested to Ivan, nodding at the notes. Ivan sank back in his chair. He was as white as a handkerchief.

"You frightened me...with your stocking," he said, with a strange grin.

"Can you really not have known till now?" Smerdyakov asked once more.

"No, I did not know. I kept thinking of Dmitri. Brother, brother! Ach!" He suddenly clutched his head in both hands.

"Listen. Did you kill him alone? With my brother's help or without?"

"It was only with you, with your help, I killed him, and Dmitri Fyodorovitch is quite innocent."

"All right, all right. Talk about me later. Why do I keep on trembling? I can't speak properly."

"You were bold enough then. You said 'everything was lawful,' and how frightened you are now," Smerdyakov muttered in surprise. "Won't you have some lemonade? I'll ask for some at once. It's very refreshing. Only I must hide this first."

And again he motioned at the notes. He was just going to get up and call at the door to Marya Kondratyevna to make some lemonade and bring it them, but, looking for something to cover up the notes that she might not see them, he first took out his handkerchief, and as it turned out to be very dirty, took up the big yellow book that Ivan had noticed at first lying on the table, and put it over the notes. The book was The Sayings of the Holy Father Isaac the Syrian. Ivan read it mechanically.

"I won't have any lemonade," he said. "Talk of me later. Sit down and tell me how you did it. Tell me all about it."

"You'd better take off your greatcoat, or you'll be too hot." Ivan, as though he'd only just thought of it, took off his coat, and, without getting up from his chair, threw it on the bench.

"Speak, please, speak."

He seemed calmer. He waited, feeling sure that Smerdyakov would tell him all about it.

"How it was done?" sighed Smerdyakov. "It was done in a most natural way, following your very words."

"Of my words later," Ivan broke in again, apparently with complete self-possession, firmly uttering his words, and not shouting as before. "Only tell me in detail how you did it. Everything, as it happened. Don't forget anything. The details, above everything, the details, I beg you."

"You'd gone away, then I fell into the cellar."

"In a fit or in a sham one?"

"A sham one, naturally. I shammed it all. I went quietly down the steps to the very bottom and lay down quietly, and as I lay down I gave a scream, and struggled, till they carried me out."

"Stay! And were you shamming all along, afterwards, and in the hospital?"

"No, not at all. Next day, in the morning, before they took me to the hospital, I had a real attack and a more violent one than I've had for years. For two days I was quite unconscious."

"All right, all right. Go on."

"They laid me on the bed. I knew I'd be the other side of the partition, for whenever I was ill, Marfa Ignatyevna used to put me there, near them. She's always been very kind to me, from my birth up. At night I moaned, but quietly. I kept expecting Dmitri Fyodorovitch to come."

"Expecting him? To come to you?"

"Not to me. I expected him to come into the house, for I'd no doubt that he'd come that night, for being without me and getting no news, he'd be sure to come and climb over the fence, as he used to, and do something."

"And if he hadn't come?"

"Then nothing would have happened. I should never have brought myself to it without him."

"All right, all right. speak more intelligibly, don't hurry; above all, don't leave anything out!"

"I expected him to kill Fyodor Pavlovitch. I thought that was certain, for I had prepared him for it...during the last few days...He knew about the knocks, that was the chief thing. With his suspiciousness and the fury which had been growing in him all those days, he was bound to get into the house by means of those taps. That was inevitable, so I was expecting him."

"Stay," Ivan interrupted; "if he had killed him, he would have taken the money and carried it away; you must have considered that. What would you have got by it afterwards? I don't see." "But he would never have found the money. That was only what I told him, that the money was under the mattress. But that wasn't true. It had been lying in a box. And afterwards I suggested to Fyodor Pavlovitch, as I was the only person he trusted, to hide the envelope with the notes in the corner behind the ikons, for no one would have guessed that place, especially if they came in a hurry. So that's where the envelope lay, in the corner behind the ikons. It would have been absurd to keep it under the mattress; the box, anyway, could be locked. But all believe it was under the mattress. A stupid thing to believe. So if Dmitri Fyodorovitch had committed the murder, finding nothing, he would either have run away in a hurry, afraid of every sound, as always happens with murderers, or he would have been arrested. So I could always have clambered up to the ikons and have taken away the money next morning or even that night, and it would have all been put down to Dmitri Fyodorovitch. I could reckon upon that."

"But what if he did not kill him, but only knocked him down?"

"If he did not kill him, of course, I would not have ventured to take the money, and nothing would have happened. But I calculated that he would beat him senseless, and I should have time to take it then, and then I'd make out to Fyodor Pavlovitch that it was no one but Dmitri Fyodorovitch who had taken the money after beating him."

"Stop...I am getting mixed. Then it was Dmitri after all who killed him; you only took the money?"

"No, he didn't kill him. Well, I might as well have told you now that he was the murderer...But I don't want to lie to you now because...because if you really haven't understood till now, as I see for myself, and are not pretending, so as to throw your guilt on me to my very face, you are still responsible for it all, since you knew of the murder and charged me to do it, and went away knowing all about it. And so I want to prove to your face this evening that you are the only real murderer in the whole affair, and I am not the real murderer, though I did kill him. You are the rightful murderer."

"Why, why, am I a murderer? Oh, God!" Ivan cried, unable to restrain himself at last, and forgetting that he had put off discussing himself till the end of the conversation. "You still mean that Tchermashnya? Stay, tell me, why did you want my consent, if you really took Tchermashnya for consent? How will you explain that now?"

"Assured of your consent, I should have known that you wouldn't have made an outcry over those three thousand being lost, even if I'd been suspected, instead of Dmitri Fyodorovitch, or as his accomplice; on the contrary, you would have protected me from others...And when you got your inheritance you would have rewarded me when you were able, all the rest of your life. For you'd have received your inheritance through me, seeing that if he had married Agrafena Alexandrovna, you wouldn't have had a farthing."

"Ah! Then you intended to worry me all my life afterwards," snarled Ivan. "And what if I hadn't gone away then, but had informed against you?"

"What could you have informed? That I persuaded you to go to Tcherinashnya? That's all nonsense. Besides, after our conversation you would either have gone away or have stayed. If you had stayed, nothing would have happened. I should have known that you didn't want it done, and should have attempted nothing. As you went away, it meant you assured me that you wouldn't dare to inform against me at the trial, and that you'd overlook my having the three thousand. And, indeed, you couldn't have prosecuted me afterwards, because then I should have told it all in the court; that is, not that I had stolen the money or killed him--I shouldn't have said that--but that you'd put me up to the theft and the murder, though I didn't consent to it. That's why I needed your consent, so that you couldn't have cornered me afterwards, for what proof could you have had? I could always have cornered you, revealing your eagerness for your father's death, and I tell you the public would have believed it all, and you would have been ashamed for the rest of your life."

"Was I then so eager, was I?" Ivan snarled again.

"To be sure you were, and by your consent you silently sanctioned my doing it." Smerdyakov looked resolutely at Ivan. He was very weak and spoke slowly and wearily, but some hidden inner force urged him on. He evidently had some design. Ivan felt that.

"Go on," he said. "Tell me what happened that night."

"What more is there to tell! I lay there and I thought I heard the master shout. And before that Grigory Vassilyevitch had suddenly got up and came out, and he suddenly gave a scream, and then all was silence and darkness. I lay there waiting, my heart beating; I couldn't bear it. I got up at last, went out. I saw the window open on the left into the garden, and I stepped to the left to listen whether he was sitting there alive, and I heard the master moving about, sighing, so I knew he was alive. 'Ech!' I thought. I went to the window and shouted to the master, 'It's I.' And he shouted to me, 'He's been, he's been; he's run away.' He meant Dmitri Fyodorovitch had been. 'He's killed Grigory!' "Where?' I whispered. 'There, in the corner,' he pointed. He was whispering, too. 'Wait a bit," I said. I went to the corner of the garden to look, and there I came upon Grigory Vassilyevitch lying by the wall, covered with blood, senseless. So it's true that Dmitri Fyodorovitch has been here, was the thought that came into my head, and I determined on the spot to make an end of it, as Grigory Vassilyevitch, even if he were alive, would see nothing of it, as he lay there senseless. The only risk was that Marfa Ignatyevna might wake up. I felt that at the moment, but the longing to get it done came over me, till I could scarcely breathe. I went back to the window to the master and said, 'She's here, she's come; Agrafena Alexandrovna has come, wants to be let in.' And he started like a baby. 'Where is she?' he fairly gasped, but couldn't believe it. 'She's standing there,' said I. 'Open.' He looked out of the window at me, half believing and half distrustful, but afraid to open. 'Why, he is afraid of me now,' I thought. And it was funny. I bethought me to knock on the window-frame those taps we'd agreed upon as a signal that Grushenka had come, in his presence, before his eyes. He didn't seem to believe my word, but as soon as he heard the taps, he ran at once to open the door. He opened it. I would have gone in, but he stood in the way to prevent me passing. 'Where is she? Where is she?' He looked at me, all of a tremble. 'Well,' thought I, 'if he's so frightened of me as all that, it's a bad lookout!' And my legs went weak with fright that he wouldn't let me in or would call out, or Marfa Ignatyevna would run up, or something else might happen. I don't remember now, but I must have stood pale, facing him. I whispered to him, 'Why, she's there, there, under the window; how is it you don't see her?' I said. 'Bring her then, bring her.' 'She's afraid,' said I; 'she was frightened at the noise, she's hidden in the bushes; go and call to her yourself from the study.' He ran to the window, put the candle in the window. 'Grushenka,' he cried, 'Grushenka, are you here?' Though he cried that, he didn't want to lean out of the window, he didn't want to move away from me, for he was panic-stricken; he was so frightened he didn't dare to turn his back on me. 'Why, here she is,' said I. I went up to the window and leaned right out of it. 'Here she is; she's in the bush, laughing at you, don't you see her?' He suddenly believed it; he was all of a shake--he was awfully crazy about her--and he leaned right out of the window. I snatched up that iron paper-weight from his table; do you remember, weighing about three pounds? I swung it and hit him on the top of the skull with the corner of it. He didn't even cry out. He only sank down suddenly, and I hit him again and a third time. And the third time I knew I'd broken his skull. He suddenly rolled on his back, face upwards, covered with blood. I looked round. There was no blood on me, not a spot. I wiped the paper-weight, put it back, went up to the ikons, took the money out of the envelope, and flung the envelope on the floor and the pink ribbon beside it. I went out into the garden all of a tremble, straight to the apple-tree with a hollow in it--you know that hollow. I'd marked it long before and put a rag and a piece of paper ready in it. I wrapped all the notes in the rag and stuffed it deep down in the hole. And there it stayed for over a fortnight. I took it out later, when I came out of the hospital. I went back to my bed, lay down and thought, 'If Grigory Vassilyevitch has been killed outright it may be a bad job for me, but if he is not killed and recovers, it will be first-rate, for then he'll bear witness that Dmitri Fyodorovitch has been here, and so he must have killed him and taken the money.' Then I began groaning with suspense and impatience, so as to wake Marfa Ignatyevna as soon as possible. At last she got up and she rushed to me, but when she saw Grigory Vassilyevitch was not there, she ran out, and I heard her scream in the garden. And that set it all going and set my mind at rest."

He stopped. Ivan had listened all the time in dead silence without stirring or taking his eyes off him. As he told his story Smerdyakov glanced at him from time to time, but for the most part kept his eyes averted. When he had finished he was evidently agitated and was breathing hard. The perspiration stood out on his face. But it was impossible to tell whether it was remorse he was feeling, or what.

"Stay," cried Ivan pondering. "What about the door? If he only opened the door to you, how could Grigory have seen it open before? For Grigory saw it before you went."

It was remarkable that Ivan spoke quite amicably, in a different tone, not angry as before, so if anyone had opened the door at that moment and peeped in at them, he would certainly have concluded that they were talking peaceably about some ordinary, though interesting, subject.

"As for that door and having seen it open, that's only his fancy," said Smerdyakov, with a wry smile. "He is not a man, I assure you, but an obstinate mule. He didn't see it, but fancied he had seen it, and there's no shaking him. It's just our luck he took that notion into his head, for they can't fail to convict Dmitri Fyodorovitch after that."

"Listen..." said Ivan, beginning to seem bewildered again and making an effort to grasp something. "Listen. There are a lot of questions I want to ask you, but I forget them...I keep forgetting and getting mixed up. Yes. Tell me this at least, why did you open the envelope and leave it there on the floor? Why didn't you simply carry off the envelope?...When you were telling me, I thought you spoke about it as though it were the right thing to do...but why, I can't understand..."

"I did that for a good reason. For if a man had known all about it, as I did for instance, if he'd seen those notes before, and perhaps had put them in that envelope himself, and had seen the envelope sealed up and addressed, with his own eyes, if such a man had done the murder, what should have made him tear open the envelope afterwards, especially in such desperate haste, since he'd know for certain the notes must be in the envelope? No, if the robber had been someone like me, he'd simply have put the envelope straight in his pocket and got away with it as fast as he could. But it'd be quite different with Dmitri Fyodorovitch. He only knew about the envelope by hearsay; he had never seen it, and if he'd found it, for instance, under the mattress, he'd have torn it open as quickly as possible to make sure the notes were in it. And he'd have thrown the envelope down, without having time to think that it would be evidence against him. Because he was not an habitual thief and had never directly stolen anything before, for he is a gentleman born, and if he did bring himself to steal, it would not be regular stealing, but simply taking what was his own, for he'd told the whole town he meant to before, and had even bragged aloud before everyone that he'd go and take his property from Fyodor Pavlovitch. I didn't say that openly to the prosecutor when I was being examined, but quite the contrary, I brought him to it by a hint, as though I didn't see it myself, and as though he'd thought of it himself and I hadn't prompted him; so that Mr. Prosecutor's mouth positively watered at my suggestion."

"But can you possibly have thought of all that on the spot?" cried Ivan, overcome with astonishment. He looked at Smerdyakov again with alarm.

"Mercy on us! Could anyone think of it all in such a desperate hurry? It was all thought out beforehand."

"Well...well, it was the devil helped you!" Ivan cried again. "No, you are not a fool, you are far cleverer than I thought..."

He got up, obviously intending to walk across the room. He was in terrible distress. But as the table blocked his way, and there was hardly room to pass between the table and the wall, he only turned round where he stood and sat down again. Perhaps the impossibility of moving irritated him, as he suddenly cried out almost as furiously as before.

"Listen, you miserable, contemptible creature! Don't you understand that if I haven't killed you, it's simply because I am keeping you to answer to-morrow at the trial. God sees," Ivan raised his hand, "perhaps I, too, was guilty; perhaps I really had a secret desire for my father's...death, but I swear I was not as guilty as you think, and perhaps I didn't urge you on at all. No, no, I didn't urge you on! But no matter, I will give evidence against myself to-morrow at the trial. I'm determined to! I shall tell everything, everything. But we'll make our appearance together. And whatever you may say against me at the trial, whatever evidence you give, I'll face it; I am not afraid of you. I'll confirm it all myself! But you must confess, too! You must, you must; we'll go together. That's how it shall be!"

Ivan said this solemnly and resolutely and from his flashing eyes alone it could be seen that it would be so.

"You are ill, I see; you are quite ill. Your eyes are yellow," Smerdyakov commented, without the least irony, with apparent sympathy in fact.

"We'll go together," Ivan repeated. "And if you won't go, no matter, I'll go alone."

Smerdyakov paused as though pondering.

"There'll be nothing of the sort, and you won't go," he concluded at last positively.

"You don't understand me," Ivan exclaimed reproachfully.

"You'll be too much ashamed, if you confess it all. And, what's more, it will be no use at all, for I shall say straight out that I never said anything of the sort to you, and that you are either ill (and it looks like it, too), or that you're so sorry for your brother that you are sacrificing yourself to save him and have invented it all against me, for you've always thought no more of me than if I'd been a fly. And who will believe you, and what single proof have you got?"

"Listen, you showed me those notes just now to convince me."

Smerdyakov lifted the book off the notes and laid it on one side.

"Take that money away with you," Smerdyakov sighed.

"Of course, I shall take it. But why do you give it to me, if you committed the murder for the sake of it?" Ivan looked at him with great surprise.

"I don't want it," Smerdyakov articulated in a shaking voice, with a gesture of refusal. "I did have an idea of beginning a new life with that money in Moscow or, better still, abroad. I did dream of it, chiefly because 'all things are lawful.' That was quite right what you taught me, for you talked a lot to me about that. For if there's no everlasting God, there's no such thing as virtue, and there's no need of it. You were right there. So that's how I looked at it."

"Did you come to that of yourself?" asked Ivan, with a wry smile.

"With your guidance."

"And now, I suppose, you believe in God, since you are giving back the money?"

"No, I don't believe," whispered Smerdyakov.

"Then why are you giving it back?"

"Leave off...that's enough!" Smerdyakov waved his hand again. "You used to say yourself that everything was lawful, so now why are you so upset, too? You even want to go and give evidence against yourself...Only there'll be nothing of the sort! You won't go to give evidence," Smerdyakov decided with conviction.

"You'll see," said Ivan.

"It isn't possible. You are very clever. You are fond of money, I know that. You like to be respected, too, for you're very proud; you are far too fond of female charms, too, and you mind most of all about living in undisturbed comfort, without having to depend on anyone--that's what you care most about. You won't want to spoil your life for ever by taking such a disgrace on yourself. You are like Fyodor Pavlovitch, you are more like him than any of his children; you've the same soul as he had."

"You are not a fool," said Ivan, seeming struck. The blood rushed to his face. "You are serious now!" he observed, looking suddenly at Smerdyakov with a different expression.

"It was your pride made you think I was a fool. Take the money."

Ivan took the three rolls of notes and put them in his pocket without wrapping them in anything.

"I shall show them at the court to-morrow," he said.

"Nobody will believe you, as you've plenty of money of your own; you may simply have taken it out of your cash-box and brought it to the court."

Ivan rose from his seat.

"I repeat," he said, "the only reason I haven't killed you is that I need you for to-morrow, remember that, don't forget it!"

"Well, kill me. Kill me now," Smerdyakov said, all at once looking strangely at Ivan. "You won't dare do that even!" he added, with a bitter smile. "You won't dare to do anything, you, who used to be so bold!"

"Till to-morrow," cried Ivan, and moved to go out.

"Stay a moment...Show me those notes again."

Ivan took out the notes and showed them to him. Smerdyakov looked at them for ten seconds.

"Well, you can go," he said, with a wave of his hand. "Ivan Fyodorovitch!" he called after him again.

"What do you want?" Ivan turned without stopping.

"Good-bye!"

"Till to-morrow!" Ivan cried again, and he walked out of the cottage.

The snowstorm was still raging. He walked the first few steps boldly, but suddenly began staggering. "It's something physical," he thought with a grin. Something like joy was springing up in his heart. He was conscious of unbounded resolution; he would make an end of the wavering that had so tortured him of late. His determination was taken, "and now it will not be changed," he thought with relief. At that moment he stumbled against something and almost fell down. Stopping short, he made out at his feet the peasant he had knocked down, still lying senseless and motionless. The snow had almost covered his face. Ivan seized him and lifted him in his arms. Seeing a light in the little house to the right he went up, knocked at the shutters, and asked the man to whom the house belonged to help him carry the peasant to the police station, promising him three roubles. The man got ready and came out. I won't describe in detail how Ivan succeeded in his object, bringing the peasant to the police-station and arranging for a doctor to see him at once, providing with a liberal hand for the expenses. I will only say that this business took a whole hour, but Ivan was well content with it. His mind wandered and worked incessantly.

"If I had not taken my decision so firmly for to-morrow," he reflected with satisfaction, "I should not have stayed a whole hour to look after the peasant, but should have passed by, without caring about his being frozen. I am quite capable of watching myself, by the way," he thought at the same instant, with still greater satisfaction, "although they have decided that I am going out of my mind!"

Just as he reached his own house he stopped short, asking himself suddenly hadn't he better go at once to the prosecutor and tell him everything. He decided the question by turning back to the house. "Everything together to-morrow!" he whispered to himself, and, strange to say, almost all his gladness and selfsatisfaction passed in one instant.

As he entered his own room he felt something like a touch of ice on his heart, like a recollection or, more exactly, a reminder, of something agonising and revolting that was in that room now, at that moment, and had been there before. He sank wearily on his sofa. The old woman brought him a samovar; he made tea, but did not touch it. He sat on the sofa and felt giddy. He felt that he was ill and helpless. He was beginning to drop asleep, but got up uneasily and walked across the room to shake off his drowsiness. At moments he fancied he was delirious, but it was not illness that he thought of most. Sitting down again, he began looking round, as though searching for something. This happened several times. At last his eyes were fastened intently on one point. Ivan smiled, but an angry flush suffused his face. He sat a long time in his place, his head propped on both arms, though he looked sideways at the same point, at the sofa that stood against the opposite wall. There was evidently something, some object, that irritated him there, worried him and tormented him.

I AM NOT a doctor, but yet I feel that the moment has come when I must inevitably give the reader some account of the nature of Ivan's illness. Anticipating events I can say at least one thing: he was at that moment on the very eve of an attack of brain fever. Though his health had long been affected, it had offered a stubborn resistance to the fever which in the end gained complete mastery over it. Though I know nothing of medicine, I venture to hazard the suggestion that he really had perhaps, by a terrible effort of will, succeeded in delaying the attack for a time, hoping, of course, to check it completely. He knew that he was unwell, but he loathed the thought of being ill at that fatal time, at the approaching crisis in his life, when he needed to have all his wits about him, to say what he had to say boldly and resolutely and "to justify himself to himself."

He had, however, consulted the new doctor, who had been brought from Moscow by a fantastic notion of Katerina Ivanovna's to which I have referred already. After listening to him and examining him the doctor came to the conclusion that he was actually suffering from some disorder of the brain, and was not at all surprised by an admission which Ivan had reluctantly made him. "Hallucinations are quite likely in your condition," the doctor opined, 'though it would be better to verify them...you must take steps at once, without a moment's delay, or things will go badly with you." But Ivan did not follow this judicious advice and did not take to his bed to be nursed. "I am walking about, so I am strong enough, if I drop, it'll be different then, anyone may nurse me who likes," he decided, dismissing the subject.

And so he was sitting almost conscious himself of his delirium and, as I have said already, looking persistently at some object on the sofa against the opposite wall. Someone appeared to be sitting there, though goodness knows how he had come in, for he had not been in the room when Ivan came into it, on his return from Smerdyakov. This was a person or, more accurately speaking, a Russian gentleman of a particular kind, no longer young, qui faisait la cinquantaine,* as the French say, with rather long, still thick, dark hair, slightly streaked with grey and a small pointed beard. He was wearing a brownish reefer jacket, rather shabby, evidently made by a good tailor though, and of a fashion at least three years old, that had been discarded by smart and well-to-do people for the last two years. His linen and his long scarf-like neck-tie were all such as are worn by people who aim at being stylish, but on closer inspection his linen was not overclean and his wide scarf was very threadbare. The visitor's check trousers were of excellent cut, but were too light in colour and too tight for the present fashion. His soft fluffy white hat was out of keeping with the season.

* Fiftyish.

In brief there was every appearance of gentility on straitened means. It looked as though the gentleman belonged to that class of idle landowners who used to flourish in the times of serfdom. He had unmistakably been, at some time, in good and fashionable society, had once had good connections, had possibly preserved them indeed, but, after a gay youth, becoming gradually impoverished on the abolition of serfdom, he had sunk into the position of a poor relation of the best class, wandering from one good old friend to another and received by them for his companionable and accommodating disposition and as being, after all, a gentleman who could be asked to sit down with anyone, though, of course, not in a place of honour. Such gentlemen of accommodating temper and dependent position, who can tell a story, take a hand at cards, and who have a distinct aversion for any duties that may be forced upon them, are usually solitary creatures, either bachelors or widowers. Sometimes they have children, but if so, the children are always being brought up at a distance, at some aunt's, to whom these gentlemen never allude in good society, seeming ashamed of the relationship. They gradually lose sight of their children altogether, though at intervals they receive a birthday or Christmas letter from them and sometimes even answer it.

The countenance of the unexpected visitor was not so much good-natured, as accommodating and ready to assume any amiable expression as occasion might arise. He had no watch, but he had a tortoise-shell lorgnette on a black ribbon. On the middle finger of his right hand was a massive gold ring with a cheap opal stone in it.

Ivan was angrily silent and would not begin the conversation. The visitor waited and sat exactly like a poor relation who had come down from his room to keep his host company at tea, and was discreetly silent, seeing that his host was frowning and preoccupied. But he was ready for any affable conversation as soon as his host should begin it. All at once his face expressed a sudden solicitude.

"I say," he began to Ivan, "excuse me, I only mention it to remind you. You went to Smerdyakov's to find out about Katerina Ivanovna, but you came away without finding out anything about her, you probably forgot-"

"Ah, yes." broke from Ivan and his face grew gloomy with uneasiness. "Yes, I'd forgotten...but it doesn't matter now, never mind, till to-morrow," he muttered to himself, "and you," he added, addressing his visitor, "I should have remembered that myself in a minute, for that was just what was tormenting me! Why do you interfere, as if I should believe that you prompted me, and that I didn't remember it of myself?"

"Don't believe it then," said the gentleman, smiling amicably, "what's the good of believing against your will? Besides, proofs are no help to believing, especially material proofs. Thomas believed, not because he saw Christ risen, but because he wanted to believe, before he saw. Look at the spiritualists, for instance...I am very fond of them...only fancy, they imagine that they are serving the cause of religion, because the devils show them their horns from the other world. That, they say, is a material proof, so to speak, of the existence of another world. The other world and material proofs, what next! And if you come to that, does proving there's a devil prove that there's a God? I want to join an idealist society, I'll lead the opposition in it, I'll say I am a realist, but not a materialist, he he!"

"Listen," Ivan suddenly got up from the table. "I seem to be delirious...I am delirious, in fact, talk any nonsense you like, I don't care! You won't drive me to fury, as you did last time. But I feel somehow ashamed...I want to walk about the room...I sometimes don't see you and don't even hear your voice as I did last time, but I always guess what you are prating, for it's I, I myself speaking, not you. Only I don't know whether I was dreaming last time or whether I really saw you. I'll wet a towel and put it on my head and perhaps you'll vanish into air."

Ivan went into the corner, took a towel, and did as he said, and with a wet towel on his head began walking up and down the room.

"I am so glad you treat me so familiarly," the visitor began.

"Fool," laughed Ivan, "do you suppose I should stand on ceremony with you? I am in good spirits now, though I've a pain in my forehead...and in the top of my head...only please don't talk philosophy, as you did last time. If you can't take yourself off, talk of something amusing. Talk gossip, you are a poor relation, you ought to talk gossip. What a nightmare to have! But I am not afraid of you. I'll get the better of you. I won't be taken to a mad-house!"

"C'est charmant, poor relation. Yes, I am in my natural shape. For what am I on earth but a poor relation? By the way, I am listening to you and am rather surprised to find you are actually beginning to take me for something real, not simply your fancy, as you persisted in declaring last time-"

"Never for one minute have I taken you for reality," Ivan cried with a sort of fury. "You are a lie, you are my illness, you are a phantom. It's only that I don't know how to destroy you and I see I must suffer for a time. You are my hallucination. You are the incarnation of myself, but only of one side of me...of my thoughts and feelings, but only the nastiest and stupidest of them. From that point of view you might be of interest to me, if only I had time to waste on you-"

"Excuse me, excuse me, I'll catch you. When you flew out at Alyosha under the lamp-post this evening and shouted to him, 'You learnt it from him! How do you know that he visits me?' You were thinking of me then. So for one brief moment you did believe that I really exist," the gentleman laughed blandly.

"Yes, that was a moment of weakness...but I couldn't believe in you. I don't know whether I was asleep or awake last time. Perhaps I was only dreaming then and didn't see you really at all-"

"And why were you so surly with Alyosha just now? He is a dear; I've treated him badly over Father Zossima."

"Don't talk of Alyosha! How dare you, you flunkey!" Ivan laughed again.

"You scold me, but you laugh--that's a good sign. But you are ever so much more polite than you were last time and I know why: that great resolution of yours-"

"Don't speak of my resolution," cried Ivan, savagely.

"I understand, I understand, c'est noble, c'est charmant, you are going to defend your brother and to sacrifice yourself...C'est chevaleresque."

"Hold your tongue, I'll kick you!"

"I shan't be altogether sorry, for then my object will be attained. If you kick me, you must believe in my reality, for people don't kick ghosts. Joking apart, it doesn't matter to me, scold if you like, though it's better to be a trifle more polite even to me. 'Fool, flunkey!' what words!"

"Scolding you, I scold myself," Ivan laughed again, "you are myself, myself, only with a different face. You just say what I am thinking...and are incapable of saying anything new!"

"If I am like you in my way of thinking, it's all to my credit," the gentleman declared, with delicacy and dignity.

"You choose out only my worst thoughts, and what's more, the stupid ones. You are stupid and vulgar. You are awfully stupid. No, I can't put up with you! What am I to do, what am I to do?" Ivan said through his clenched teeth.

"My dear friend, above all things I want to behave like a gentleman and to be recognised as such," the visitor began in an access of deprecating and simple-hearted pride, typical of a poor relation. "I am poor, but...I won't say very honest, but...it's an axiom generally accepted in society that I am a fallen angel. I certainly can't conceive how I can ever have been an angel. If I ever was, it must have been so long ago that there's no harm in forgetting it. Now I only prize the reputation of being a gentlemanly person and live as I can, trying to make myself agreeable. I love men genuinely, I've been greatly calumniated! Here when I stay with you from time to time, my life gains a kind of reality and that's what I like most of all. You see, like you, I suffer from the fantastic and so I love the realism of earth. Here, with you, everything is circumscribed, here all is formulated and geometrical, while we have nothing but indeterminate equations! I wander about here dreaming. I like dreaming. Besides, on earth I become superstitious. Please don't laugh, that's just what I like, to become superstitious. I adopt all your habits here: I've grown fond of going to the public baths, would you believe it? and I go and steam myself with merchants and priests. What I dream of is becoming incarnate once for all and irrevocably in the form of some merchant's wife weighing eighteen stone, and of believing all she believes. My ideal is to go to church and offer a candle in simple-hearted faith, upon my word it is. Then there would be an end to my sufferings. I like being doctored too; in the spring there was an outbreak of smallpox and I went and was vaccinated in a foundling hospital--if only you knew how I enjoyed myself that day. I subscribed ten roubles in the cause of the Slavs!...But you are not listening. Do you know, you are not at all well this evening? I know you went yesterday to that doctor...well, what about your health? What did the doctor say?"

"Fool!" Ivan snapped out.

"But you are clever, anyway. You are scolding again? I didn't ask out of sympathy. You needn't answer. Now rheumatism has come in again-"

"Fool!" repeated Ivan.

"You keep saying the same thing; but I had such an attack of rheumatism last year that I remember it to this day."

"The devil have rheumatism!"

"Why not, if I sometimes put on fleshly form? I put on fleshly form and I take the consequences. Satan sum et nihil humanum a me alienum puto."*

* I am Satan, and deem nothing human alien to me.

"What, what, Satan sum et nihil humanum...that's not bad for the devil!"

"I am glad I've pleased you at last."

"But you didn't get that from me." Ivan stopped suddenly, seeming struck. "That never entered my head, that's strange."

"C'est du nouveau, n'est-ce pas?"* This time I'll act honestly and explain to you. Listen, in dreams and especially in nightmares, from indigestion or anything, a man sees sometimes such artistic visions, such complex and real actuality, such events, even a whole world of events, woven into such a plot, with such unexpected details from the most exalted matters to the last button on a cuff, as I swear Leo Tolstoy has never invented. Yet such dreams are sometimes seen not by writers, but by the most ordinary people, officials, journalists, priests...The subject is a complete enigma. A statesman confessed to me, indeed, that all his best ideas came to him when he was asleep. Well, that's how it is now, though I am your hallucination, yet just as in a nightmare, I say original things which had not entered your head before. So I don't repeat your ideas, yet I am only your nightmare, nothing more."

* It's new, isn't it?

"You are lying, your aim is to convince me you exist apart and are not my nightmare, and now you are asserting you are a dream."

"My dear fellow, I've adopted a special method to-day, I'll explain it to you afterwards. Stay, where did I break off? Oh, yes! I caught cold then, only not here but yonder."

"Where is yonder? Tell me, will you be here long. Can't you go away?" Ivan exclaimed almost in despair. He ceased walking to and fro, sat down on the sofa, leaned his elbows on the table again and held his head tight in both hands. He pulled the wet towel off and flung it away in vexation. It was evidently of no use.

"Your nerves are out of order," observed the gentleman, with a carelessly easy, though perfectly polite, air. "You are angry with me even for being able to catch cold, though it happened in a most natural way. I was hurrying then to a diplomatic soiree at the house of a lady of high rank in Petersburg, who was aiming at influence in the Ministry. Well, an evening suit, white tie, gloves, though I was God knows where and had to fly through space to reach your earth...Of course, it took only an instant, but you know a ray of light from the sun takes full eight minutes, and fancy in an evening suit and open waistcoat. Spirits don't freeze, but when one's in fleshly form, well...in brief, I didn't think, and set off, and you know in those ethereal spaces, in the water that is above the firmament, there's such a frost...at least one can't call it frost, you fancy, 150 degrees below zero! You know the game the village girls play--they invite the unwary to lick an axe in thirty degrees of frost, the tongue instantly freezes to it and the dupe tears the skin off, so it bleeds. But that's only in 30 degrees, in 150 degrees I imagine it would be enough to put your finger on the axe and it would be the end of it...if only there could be an axe there."

"And can there be an axe there?" Ivan interrupted, carelessly and disdainfully. He was exerting himself to the utmost not to believe in the delusion and not to sink into complete insanity.

"An axe?" the guest interrupted in surprise.

"Yes, what would become of an axe there?" Ivan cried suddenly, with a sort of savage and insistent obstinacy.

"What would become of an axe in space? Quelle idee! If it were to fall to any distance, it would begin, I think, flying round the earth without knowing why, like a satellite. The astronomers would calculate the rising and the setting of the axe; Gatzuk would put it in his calendar, that's all."

"You are stupid, awfully stupid," said Ivan peevishly. "Fib more cleverly or I won't listen. You want to get the better of me by realism, to convince me that you exist, but I don't want to believe you exist! I won't believe it!"

"But I am not fibbing, it's all the truth; the truth is unhappily hardly ever amusing. I see you persist in expecting something big of me, and perhaps something fine. That's a great pity, for I only give what I can-"

"Don't talk philosophy, you ass!"

"Philosophy, indeed, when all my right side is numb and I am moaning and groaning. I've tried all the medical faculty: they can diagnose beautifully, they have the whole of your disease at their finger-tips, but they've no idea how to cure you. There was an enthusiastic little student here, 'You may die,' said he, 'but you'll know perfectly what disease you are dying of!' And then what a way they have of sending people to specialists! 'We only diagnose,' they say, 'but go to such-and-such a specialist, he'll cure you.' The old doctor who used to cure all sorts of disease has completely disappeared, I assure you, now there are only specialists and they all advertise in the newspapers. If anything is wrong with your nose, they send you to Paris: there, they say, is a European specialist who cures noses. If you go to Paris, he'll look at your nose; I can only cure your right nostril, he'll tell you, for I don't cure the left nostril, that's not my speciality, but go to Vienna, there there's a specialist who will cure your left nostril. What are you to do? I fell back on popular remedies, a German doctor advised me to rub myself with honey and salt in the bath-house. Solely to get an extra bath I went, smeared myself all over and it did me no good at all. In despair I wrote to Count Mattei in Milan. He sent me a book and some drops, bless him, and, only fancy, Hoff's malt extract cured me! I bought it by accident, drank a bottle and a half of it, and I was ready to dance, it took it away completely. I made up my mind to write to the papers to thank him, I was prompted by a feeling of gratitude, and only fancy, it led to no end of a bother: not a single paper would take my letter. 'It would be very reactionary,' they said, 'none will believe it. Le diable n'existe point.* You'd better remain anonymous,' they advised me. What use is a letter of thanks if it's anonymous? I laughed with the men at the newspaper office; 'It's reactionary to believe in God in our days,' I said, 'but I am the devil, so I may be believed in.' 'We quite understand that,' they said. 'Who doesn't believe in the devil? Yet it won't do, it might injure our reputation. As a joke, if you like.' But I thought as a joke it wouldn't be very witty. So it wasn't printed. And do you know, I have felt sore about it to this day. My best feelings, gratitude, for instance, are literally denied me simply from my social position."

* The devil does not exist.

"Philosophical reflections again?" Ivan snarled malignantly.

"God preserve me from it, but one can't help complaining sometimes. I am a slandered man. You upbraid me every moment with being stupid. One can see you are young. My dear fellow, intelligence isn't the only thing! I have naturally a kind and merry heart. 'I also write vaudevilles of all sorts.' You seem to take me for Hlestakov grown old, but my fate is a far more serious one. Before time was, by some decree which I could never make out, I was predestined 'to deny' and yet I am genuinely good-hearted and not at all inclined to negation. 'No, you must go and deny, without denial there's no criticism and what would a journal be without a column of criticism?' Without criticism it would be nothing but one 'hosannah.' But nothing but hosannah is not enough for life, the hosannah must be tried in the crucible of doubt and so on, in the same style. But I don't meddle in that, I didn't create it, I am not answerable for it. Well, they've chosen their scapegoat, they've made me write the column of criticism and so life was made possible. We understand that comedy; I, for instance, simply ask for annihilation. No, live, I am told, for there'd be nothing without you. If everything in the universe were sensible, nothing would happen. There would be no events without you, and there must be events. So against the grain I serve to produce events and do what's irrational because I am commanded to. For all their indisputable intelligence, men take this farce as something serious, and that is their tragedy. They suffer, of course...but then they live, they live a real life, not a fantastic one, for suffering is life. Without suffering what would be the pleasure of it? It would be transformed into an endless church service; it would be holy, but tedious. But what about me? I suffer, but still, I don't live. I am x in an indeterminate equation. I am a sort of phantom in life who has lost all beginning and end, and who has even forgotten his own name. You are laughing--no, you are not laughing, you are angry again. You are for ever angry, all you care about is intelligence, but I repeat again that I would give away all this superstellar life, all the ranks and honours, simply to be transformed into the soul of a merchant's wife weighing eighteen stone and set candles at God's shrine."

"Then even you don't believe in God?" said Ivan, with a smile of hatred.

"What can I say?--that is, if you are in earnest-"

"Is there a God or not?" Ivan cried with the same savage intensity.

"Ah, then you are in earnest! My dear fellow, upon my word I don't know. There! I've said it now!"

"You don't know, but you see God? No, you are not someone apart, you are myself, you are I and nothing more! You are rubbish, you are my fancy!"

"Well, if you like, I have the same philosophy as you, that would be true. Je pense, donc je suis,* I know that for a fact; all the rest, all these worlds, God and even Satan--all that is not proved, to my mind. Does all that exist of itself, or is it only an emanation of myself, a logical development of my ego which alone has existed for ever: but I make haste to stop, for I believe you will be jumping up to beat me directly."

* I think, therefore I am.

"You'd better tell me some anecdote!" said Ivan miserably.

"There is an anecdote precisely on our subject, or rather a legend, not an anecdote. You reproach me with unbelief; you see, you say, yet you don't believe. But, my dear fellow, I am not the only one like that. We are all in a muddle over there now and all through your science. Once there used to be atoms, five senses, four elements, and then everything hung together somehow. There were atoms in the ancient world even, but since we've learned that you've discovered the chemical molecule and protoplasm and the devil knows what, we had to lower our crest. There's a regular muddle, and, above all, superstition, scandal; there's as much scandal among us as among you, you know; a little more in fact, and spying, indeed, for we have our secret police department where private information is received. Well, this wild legend belongs to our middle ages--not yours, but ours-- and no one believes it even among us, except the old ladies of eighteen stone, not your old ladies I mean, but ours. We've everything you have, I am revealing one of our secrets out of friendship for you; though it's forbidden. This legend is about Paradise. There was, they say, here on earth a thinker and philosopher. He rejected everything, 'laws, conscience, faith,' and, above all, the future life. He died; he expected to go straight to darkness and death and he found a future life before him. He was astounded and indignant. 'This is against my principles!' he said. And he was punished for that...that is, you must excuse me, I am just repeating what I heard myself, it's only a legend...he was sentenced to walk a quadrillion kilometres in the dark (we've adopted the metric system, you know): and when he has finished that quadrillion, the gates of heaven would be opened to him and he'll be forgiven-"

"And what tortures have you in the other world besides the quadrillion kilometres?" asked Ivan, with a strange eagerness.

"What tortures? Ah, don't ask. In old days we had all sorts, but now they have taken chiefly to moral punishments--'the stings of conscience' and all that nonsense. We got that, too, from you, from the softening of your manners. And who's the better for it? Only those who have got no conscience, for how can they be tortured by conscience when they have none? But decent people who have conscience and a sense of honour suffer for it. Reforms, when the ground has not been prepared for them, especially if they are institutions copied from abroad, do nothing but mischief! The ancient fire was better. Well, this man, who was condemned to the quadrillion kilometres, stood still, looked round and lay down across the road. 'I won't go, I refuse on principle!' Take the soul of an enlightened Russian atheist and mix it with the soul of the prophet Jonah, who sulked for three days and nights in the belly of the whale, and you get the character of that thinker who lay across the road."

"What did he lie on there?"

"Well, I suppose there was something to lie on. You are not laughing?"

"Bravo!" cried Ivan, still with the same strange eagerness. Now he was listening with an unexpected curiosity. "Well, is he lying there now?"

"That's the point, that he isn't. He lay there almost a thousand years and then he got up and went on."

"What an ass!" cried Ivan, laughing nervously and still seeming to be pondering something intently. "Does it make any difference whether he lies there for ever or walks the quadrillion kilometres? It would take a billion years to walk it?"

"Much more than that. I haven't got a pencil and paper or I could work it out. But he got there long ago, and that's where the story begins."

"What, he got there? But how did he get the billion years to do it?"

"Why, you keep thinking of our present earth! But our present earth may have been repeated a billion times. Why, it's become extinct, been frozen; cracked, broken to bits, disintegrated into its elements, again 'the water above the firmament,' then again a comet, again a sun, again from the sun it becomes earth--and the same sequence may have been repeated endlessly and exactly the same to every detail, most unseemly and insufferably tedious-"

"Well, well, what happened when he arrived?"

"Why, the moment the gates of Paradise were open and he walked in; before he had been there two seconds, by his watch (though to my thinking his watch must have long dissolved into its elements on the way), he cried out that those two seconds were worth walking not a quadrillion kilometres but a quadrillion of quadrillions, raised to the quadrillionth power! In fact, he sang 'hosannah' and overdid it so, that some persons there of lofty ideas wouldn't shake hands with him at first--he'd become too rapidly reactionary, they said. The Russian temperament. I repeat, it's a legend. I give it for what it's worth, so that's the sort of ideas we have on such subjects even now."

"I've caught you!" Ivan cried, with an almost childish delight, as though he had succeeded in remembering something at last. "That anecdote about the quadrillion years, I made up myself! I was seventeen then, I was at the high school. I made up that anecdote and told it to a schoolfellow called Korovkin, it was at Moscow...The anecdote is so characteristic that I couldn't have taken it from anywhere. I thought I'd forgotten it...but I've unconsciously recalled it--I recalled it myself--it was not you telling it! Thousands of things are unconsciously remembered like that even when people are being taken to execution...it's come back to me in a dream. You are that dream! You are a dream, not a living creature!"

"From the vehemence with which you deny my existence," laughed the gentleman, "I am convinced that you believe in me."

"Not in the slightest! I haven't a hundredth part of a grain of faith in you!"

"But you have the thousandth of a grain. Homeopathic doses perhaps are the strongest. Confess that you have faith even to the ten-thousandth of a grain."

"Not for one minute," cried Ivan furiously. "But I should like to believe in you," he added strangely.

"Aha! There's an admission! But I am good-natured. I'll come to your assistance again. Listen, it was I caught you, not you me. I told you your anecdote you'd forgotten, on purpose, so as to destroy your faith in me completely."

"You are lying. The object of your visit is to convince me of your existence!"

"Just so. But hesitation, suspense, conflict between belief and disbelief--is sometimes such torture to a conscientious man, such as you are, that it's better to hang oneself at once. Knowing that you are inclined to believe in me, I administered some disbelief by telling you that anecdote. I lead you to belief and disbelief by turns, and I have my motive in it. It's the new method. As soon as you disbelieve in me completely, you'll begin assuring me to my face that I am not a dream but a reality. I know you. Then I shall have attained my object, which is an honourable one. I shall sow in you only a tiny grain of faith and it will grow into an oak-tree--and such an oak-tree that, sitting on it, you will long to enter the ranks of 'the hermits in the wilderness and the saintly women,' for that is what you are secretly longing for. You'll dine on locusts, you'll wander into the wilderness to save your soul!"

"Then it's for the salvation of my soul you are working, is it, you scoundrel?"

"One must do a good work sometimes. How ill-humoured you are!"

"Fool! did you ever tempt those holy men who ate locusts and prayed seventeen years in the wilderness till they were overgrown with moss?"

"My dear fellow, I've done nothing else. One forgets the whole world and all the worlds, and sticks to one such saint, because he is a very precious diamond. One such soul, you know, is sometimes worth a whole constellation. We have our system of reckoning, you know. The conquest is priceless! And some of them, on my word, are not inferior to you in culture, though you won't believe it. They can contemplate such depths of belief and disbelief at the same moment that sometimes it really seems that they are within a hair's-breadth of being 'turned upside down,' as the actor Gorbunov says."

"Well, did you get your nose pulled?"

"My dear fellow," observed the visitor sententiously, "it's better to get off with your nose pulled than without a nose at all. As an afflicted marquis observed not long ago (he must have been treated by a specialist) in confession to his spiritual father--a Jesuit. I was present, it was simply charming. 'Give me back my nose!' he said, and he beat his breast. 'My son,' said the priest evasively, 'all things are accomplished in accordance with the inscrutable decrees of Providence, and what seems a misfortune sometimes leads to extraordinary, though unapparent, benefits. If stern destiny has deprived you of your nose, it's to your advantage that no one can ever pull you by your nose.' 'Holy father, that's no comfort,' cried the despairing marquis. 'I'd be delighted to have my nose pulled every day of my life, if it were only in its proper place.' 'My son,' sighs the priest, 'you can't expect every blessing at once. This is murmuring against Providence, who even in this has not forgotten you, for if you repine as you repined just now, declaring you'd be glad to have your nose pulled for the rest of your life, your desire has already been fulfilled indirectly, for when you lost your nose, you were led by the nose.'

"Fool, how stupid!" cried Ivan.

"My dear friend, I only wanted to amuse you. But I swear that's the genuine Jesuit casuistry and I swear that it all happened word for word as I've told you. It happened lately and gave me a great deal of trouble. The unhappy young man shot himself that very night when he got home. I was by his side till the very last moment. Those Jesuit confessionals are really my most delightful diversion at melancholy moments. Here's another incident that happened only the other day. A little blonde Norman girl of twenty--a buxom, unsophisticated beauty that would make your mouth water--comes to an old priest. She bends down and whispers her sin into the grating. 'Why, my daughter, have you fallen again already?' cries the priest: 'O Sancta Maria, what do I hear! Not the same man this time, how long is this going on? Aren't you ashamed!' 'Ah, mon pere,' answers the sinner with tears of penitence, 'Ca lui fait tant de plaisir, et a moi si peu de peine!'* Fancy, such an answer! I drew back. It was the cry of nature, better than innocence itself, if you like. I absolved her sin on the spot and was turning to go, but I was forced to turn back. I heard the priest at the grating making an appointment with her for the evening--though he was an old man hard as flint, he fell in an instant! It was nature, the truth of nature asserted its rights! What, you are turning up your nose again? Angry again? I don't know how to please you-"

* Ah, my father, this gives him so much pleasure, and me so little pain!

"Leave me alone, you are beating on my brain like a haunting nightmare," Ivan moaned miserably, helpless before his apparition. "I am bored with you, agonisingly and insufferably. I would give anything to be able to shake you off!"

"I repeat, moderate your expectations, don't demand of me 'everything great and noble,' and you'll see how well we shall get on," said the gentleman impressively. "You are really angry with me for not having appeared to you in a red glow, with thunder and lightning, with scorched wings, but have shown myself in such a modest form. You are wounded, in the first place, in your asthetic feelings, and, secondly, in your pride. How could such a vulgar devil visit such a great man as you! Yes, there is that romantic strain in you, that was so derided by Byelinsky. I can't help it, young man, as I got ready to come to you I did think as a joke of appearing in the figure of a retired general who had served in the Caucasus, with a star of the Lion and the Sun on my coat. But I was positively afraid of doing it, for you'd have thrashed me for daring to pin the Lion and the Sun on my coat, instead of, at least, the Polar Star or the Sirius. And you keep on saying I am stupid, but, mercy on us! I make no claim to be equal to you in intelligence. Mephistopheles declared to Faust that he desired evil, but did only good. Well, he can say what he likes, it's quite the opposite with me. I am perhaps the one man in all creation who loves the truth and genuinely desires good. I was there when the Word, Who died on the Cross, rose up into heaven bearing on His bosom the soul of the penitent thief. I heard the glad shrieks of the cherubim singing and shouting hosannah and the thunderous rapture of the seraphim which shook heaven and all creation, and I swear to you by all that's sacred, I longed to join the choir and shout hosannah with them all. The word had almost escaped me, had almost broken from my lips...you know how susceptible and aesthetically impressionable I am. But common sense--oh, a most unhappy trait in my character--kept me in due bounds and I let the moment pass! For what would have happened, I reflected, what would have happened after my hosannah? Everything on earth would have been extinguished at once and no events could have occurred. And so, solely from a sense of duty and my social position, was forced to suppress the good moment and to stick to my nasty task. Somebody takes all the credit of what's good for Himself, and nothing but nastiness is left for me. But I don't envy the honour of a life of idle imposture, I am not ambitious. Why am I, of all creatures in the world, doomed to be cursed by all decent people and even to be kicked, for if I put on mortal form I am bound to take such consequences sometimes? I know, of course, there's a secret in it, but they won't tell me the secret for anything, for then perhaps, seeing the meaning of it, I might bawl hosannah, and the indispensable minus would disappear at once, and good sense would reign supreme throughout the whole world. And that, of course, would mean the end of everything, even of magazines and newspapers, for who would take them in? I know that at the end of all things I shall be reconciled. I, too, shall walk my quadrillion and learn the secret. But till that happens I am sulking and fulfil my destiny though it's against the grain--that is, to ruin thousands for the sake of saving one. How many souls have had to be ruined and how many honourable reputations destroyed for the sake of that one righteous man, Job, over whom they made such a fool of me in old days! Yes, till the secret is revealed, there are two sorts of truths for me--one, their truth, yonder, which I know nothing about so far, and the other my own. And there's no knowing which will turn out the better...Are you asleep?"

"I might well be," Ivan groaned angrily. "All my stupid ideas-- outgrown, thrashed out long ago, and flung aside like a dead carcass you present to me as something new!"

"There's no pleasing you! And I thought I should fascinate you by my literary style. That hosannah in the skies really wasn't bad, was it? And then that ironical tone a la Heine, eh?"

"No, I was never such a flunkey! How then could my soul beget a flunkey like you?"

"My dear fellow, I know a most charming and attractive young Russian gentleman, a young thinker and a great lover of literature and art, the author of a promising poem entitled The Grand Inquisitor. I was only thinking of him!"

"I forbid you to speak of The Grand Inquisitor," cried Ivan, crimson with shame.

"And the Geological Cataclysm. Do you remember? That was a poem, now!"

"Hold your tongue, or I'll kill you!"

"You'll kill me? No, excuse me, I will speak. I came to treat myself to that pleasure. Oh, I love the dreams of my ardent young friends, quivering with eagerness for life! 'There are new men,' you decided last spring, when you were meaning to come here, 'they propose to destroy everything and begin with cannibalism. Stupid fellows! they didn't ask my advice! I maintain that nothing need be destroyed, that we only need to destroy the idea of God in man, that's how we have to set to work. It's that, that we must begin with. Oh, blind race of men who have no understanding! As soon as men have all of them denied God--and I believe that period, analogous with geological periods, will come to pass--the old conception of the universe will fall of itself without cannibalism, and, what's more, the old morality, and everything will begin anew. Men will unite to take from life all it can give, but only for joy and happiness in the present world. Man will be lifted up with a spirit of divine Titanic pride and the man-god will appear. From hour to hour extending his conquest of nature infinitely by his will and his science, man will feel such lofty joy from hour to hour in doing it that it will make up for all his old dreams of the joys of heaven. Everyone will know that he is mortal and will accept death proudly and serenely like a god. His pride will teach him that it's useless for him to repine at life's being a moment, and he will love his brother without need of reward. Love will be sufficient only for a moment of life, but the very consciousness of its momentariness will intensify its fire, which now is dissipated in dreams of eternal love beyond the grave'...and so on and so on in the same style. Charming!"

Ivan sat with his eyes on the floor, and his hands pressed to his ears, but he began trembling all over. The voice continued.

"The question now is, my young thinker reflected, is it possible that such a period will ever come? If it does, everything is determined and humanity is settled for ever. But as, owing to man's inveterate stupidity, this cannot come about for at least a thousand years, everyone who recognises the truth even now may legitimately order his life as he pleases, on the new principles. In that sense, 'all things are lawful' for him. What's more, even if this period never comes to pass, since there is anyway no God and no immortality, the new man may well become the man-god, even if he is the only one in the whole world, and promoted to his new position, he may lightheartedly overstep all the barriers of the old morality of the old slaveman, if necessary. There is no law for God. Where God stands, the place is holy. Where I stand will be at once the foremost place...'all things are lawful' and that's the end of it! That's all very charming; but if you want to swindle why do you want a moral sanction for doing it? But that's our modern Russian all over. He can't bring himself to swindle without a moral sanction. He is so in love with truth-"

The visitor talked, obviously carried away by his own eloquence, speaking louder and louder and looking ironically at his host. But he did not succeed in finishing; Ivan suddenly snatched a glass from the table and flung it at the orator.

"Ah, mais c'est bete enfin,"* cried the latter, jumping up from the sofa and shaking the drops of tea off himself. "He remembers Luther's inkstand! He takes me for a dream and throws glasses at a dream! It's like a woman! I suspected you were only pretending to stop up your ears."

* But after all, that's stupid.

A loud, persistent knocking was suddenly heard at the window. Ivan jumped up from the sofa.

"Do you hear? You'd better open," cried the visitor; "it's your brother Alyosha with the most interesting and surprising news, I'll be bound!"

"Be silent, deceiver, I knew it was Alyosha, I felt he was coming, and of course he has not come for nothing; of course he brings 'news,'" Ivan exclaimed frantically.

"Open, open to him. There's a snowstorm and he is your brother. Monsieur sait-il le temps qu'il fait? C'est a ne pas mettre un chien dehors."*

* Does the gentleman know the weather he's making? It's not weather for a dog.

The knocking continued. Ivan wanted to rush to the window, but something seemed to fetter his arms and legs. He strained every effort to break his chains, but in vain. The knocking at the window grew louder and louder. At last the chains were broken and Ivan leapt up from the sofa. He looked round him wildly. Both candles had almost burnt out, the glass he had just thrown at his visitor stood before him on the table, and there was no one on the sofa opposite. The knocking on the window frame went on persistently, but it was by no means so loud as it had seemed in his dream; on the contrary, it was quite subdued.

"It was not a dream! No, I swear it was not a dream, it all happened just now!" cried Ivan. He rushed to the window and opened the movable pane.

"Alyosha, I told you not to come," he cried fiercely to his brother. "In two words, what do you want? In two words, do you hear?"

"An hour ago Smerdyakov hanged himself," Alyosha answered from the yard.

"Come round to the steps, I'll open at once," said Ivan, going to open the door to Alyosha.

Chapter 10. "It Was He Who Said That"

ALYOSHA coming in told Ivan that a little over an hour ago Marya Kondratyevna had run to his rooms and informed him Smerdyakov had taken his own life. "I went in to clear away the samovar and he was hanging on a nail in the wall." On Alyosha's inquiring whether she had informed the police, she answered that she had told no one, "but I flew straight to you, I've run all the way." She seemed perfectly crazy, Alyosha reported, and was shaking like a leaf. When Alyosha ran with her to the cottage, he found Smerdyakov still hanging. On the table lay a note: "I destroy my life of my own will and desire, so as to throw no blame on anyone." Alyosha left the note on the table and went straight to the police captain and told him all about it. "And from him I've come straight to you," said Alyosha, in conclusion, looking intently into Ivan's face. He had not taken his eyes off him while he told his story, as though struck by something in his expression.

"Brother," he cried suddenly, "you must be terribly ill. You look and don't seem to understand what I tell you."

"It's a good thing you came," said Ivan, as though brooding, and not hearing Alyosha's exclamation. "I knew he had hanged himself."

"From whom?"

"I don't know. But I knew. Did I know? Yes, he told me. He told me so just now."

Ivan stood in the middle of the room, and still spoke in the same brooding tone, looking at the ground.

"Who is he?" asked Alyosha, involuntarily looking round.

"He's slipped away."

Ivan raised his head and smiled softly.

"He was afraid of you, of a dove like you. You are a 'pure cherub.' Dmitri calls you a cherub. Cherub!...the thunderous rapture of the seraphim. What are seraphim? Perhaps a whole constellation. But perhaps that constellation is only a chemical molecule. There's a constellation of the Lion and the Sun. Don't you know it?"

"Brother, sit down," said Alyosha in alarm. "For goodness' sake, sit down on the sofa! You are delirious; put your head on the pillow, that's right. Would you like a wet towel on your head? Perhaps it will do you good."

"Give me the towel: it's here on the chair. I just threw it down there."

"It's not here. Don't worry yourself. I know where it is--here," said Alyosha, finding a clean towel, folded up and unused, by Ivan's dressing-table in the other corner of the room. Ivan looked strangely at the towel: recollection seemed to come back to him for an instant.

"Stay"--he got up from the sofa--"an hour ago I took that new towel from there and wetted it. I wrapped it round my head and threw it down here...How is it it's dry? There was no other."

"You put that towel on your head?" asked Alyosha.

"Yes, and walked up and down the room an hour ago...Why have the candles burnt down so? What's the time?"

"Nearly twelve"

"No, no, no!" Ivan cried suddenly. "It was not a dream. He was here; he was sitting here, on that sofa. When you knocked at the window, I threw a glass at him...this one. Wait a minute. I was asleep last time, but this dream was not a dream. It has happened before. I have dreams now, Alyosha...yet they are not dreams, but reality. I walk about, talk and see...though I am asleep. But he was sitting here, on that sofa there...He is frightfully stupid, Alyosha, frightfully stupid." Ivan laughed suddenly and began pacing about the room.

"Who is stupid? Of whom are you talking, brother?" Alyosha asked anxiously again.

"The devil! He's taken to visiting me. He's been here twice, almost three times. He taunted me with being angry at his being a simple devil and not Satan, with scorched wings, in thunder and lightning. But he is not Satan: that's a lie. He is an impostor. He is simply a devil--a paltry, trivial devil. He goes to the baths. If you undressed him, you'd be sure to find he had a tail, long and smooth like a Danish dog's, a yard long, dun colour...Alyosha, you are cold. You've been in the snow. Would you like some tea? What? Is it cold? Shall I tell her to bring some? C'est a ne pas mettre un chien dehors..."

Alyosha ran to the washing-stand, wetted the towel, persuaded Ivan to sit down again, and put the wet towel round his head. He sat down beside him.

"What were you telling me just now about Lise?" Ivan began again. (He was becoming very talkative.) "I like Lise. I said something nasty about her. It was a lie. I like her...I am afraid for Katya to-morrow. I am more afraid of her than of anything. On account of the future. She will cast me off to-morrow and trample me under foot. She thinks that I am ruining Mitya from jealousy on her account! Yes, she thinks that! But it's not so. To-morrow the cross, but not the gallows. No, I shan't hang myself. Do you know, I can never commit suicide, Alyosha. Is it because I am base? I am not a coward. Is it from love of life? How did I know that Smerdyakov had hanged himself? Yes, it was he told me so."

"And you are quite convinced that there has been someone here?" asked Alyosha.

"Yes, on that sofa in the corner. You would have driven him away. You did drive him away: he disappeared when you arrived. I love your face, Alyosha. Did you know that I loved your face? And he is myself, Alyosha. All that's base in me, all that's mean and contemptible. Yes, I am a romantic. He guessed it...though it's a libel. He is frightfully stupid; but it's to his advantage. He has cunning, animal cunning--he knew how to infuriate me. He kept taunting me with believing in him, and that was how he made me listen to him. He fooled me like a boy. He told me a great deal that was true about myself, though. I should never have owned it to myself. Do you know, Alyosha," Ivan added in an intensely earnest and confidential tone, "I should be awfully glad to think that it was he and not I."

"He has worn you out," said Alyosha, looking compassionately at his brother.

"He's been teasing me. And you know he does it so cleverly, so cleverly. 'Conscience! What is conscience? I make it up for myself. Why am I tormented by it? From habit. From the universal habit of mankind for the seven thousand years. So let us give it up, and we shall be gods.' It was he said that, it was he said that!"

"And not you, not you?" Alyosha could not help crying, looking frankly at his brother. "Never mind him, anyway; have done with him and forget him. And let him take with him all that you curse now, and never come back!"

"Yes, but he is spiteful. He laughed at me. He was impudent, Alyosha," Ivan said, with a shudder of offence. "But he was unfair to me, unfair to me about lots of things. He told lies about me to my face. 'Oh, you are going to perform an act of heroic virtue: to confess you murdered your father, that the valet murdered him at your instigation.'"

"Brother," Alyosha interposed, "restrain yourself. It was not you murdered him. It's not true!"

"That's what he says, he, and he knows it. 'You are going to perform an act of heroic virtue, and you don't believe in virtue; that's what tortures you and makes you angry, that's why you are so vindictive.' He said that to me about me and he knows what he says."

"It's you say that, not he," exclaimed Alyosha mournfully, "and you say it because you are ill and delirious, tormenting yourself."

"No, he knows what he says. 'You are going from pride,' he says. 'You'll stand up and say it was I killed him, and why do you writhe with horror? You are lying! I despise your opinion, I despise your horror!' He said that about me. 'And do you know you are longing for their praise--"he is a criminal, a murderer, but what a generous soul; he wanted to save his brother and he confessed." That's a lie Alyosha!" Ivan cried suddenly, with flashing eyes. "I don't want the low rabble to praise me, I swear I don't! That's a lie! That's why I threw the glass at him and it broke against his ugly face."

"Brother, calm yourself, stop!" Alyosha entreated him.

"Yes, he knows how to torment one. He's cruel," Ivan went on, unheeding. "I had an inkling from the first what he came for. 'Granting that you go through pride, still you had a hope that Smerdyakov might be convicted and sent to Siberia, and Mitya would be acquitted, while you would only be punished, with moral condemnation' ('Do you hear?' he laughed then)--'and some people will praise you. But now Smerdyakov's dead, he has hanged himself, and who'll believe you alone? But yet you are going, you are going, you'll go all the same, you've decided to go. What are you going for now?' That's awful, Alyosha. I can't endure such questions. Who dare ask me such questions?"

"Brother," interposed Alyosha--his heart sank with terror, but he still seemed to hope to bring Ivan to reason-- "how could he have told you of Smerdyakov's death before I came, when no one knew of it and there was no time for anyone to know of it?"

"He told me," said Ivan firmly, refusing to admit a doubt. "It was all he did talk about, if you come to that. 'And it would be all right if you believed in virtue,' he said. 'No matter if they disbelieve you, you are going for the sake of principle. But you are a little pig like Fyodor Pavlovitch, and what do you want with virtue? Why do you want to go meddling if your sacrifice is of no use to anyone? Because you don't know yourself why you go! Oh, you'd give a great deal to know yourself why you go! And can you have made up your mind? You've not made up your mind. You'll sit all night deliberating whether to go or not. But you will go; you know you'll go. You know that whichever way you decide, the decision does not depend on you. You'll go because you won't

311

dare not to go. Why won't you dare? You must guess that for yourself. That's a riddle for you!' He got up and went away. You came and he went. He called me a coward, Alyosha! Le mot de l'enigme is that I am a coward. 'It is not for such eagles to soar above the earth.'It was he added that--he! And Smerdyakov said the same. He must be killed! Katya despises me. I've seen that for a month past. Even Lise will begin to despise me! 'You are going in order to be praised.' That's a brutal lie! And you despise me too, Alyosha. Now I am going to hate you again! And I hate the monster, too! I hate the monster! I don't want to save the monster. Let him rot in Siberia! He's begun singing a hymn! Oh, to-morrow I'll go, stand before them, and spit in their faces!"

He jumped up in a frenzy, flung off the towel, and fell to pacing up and down the room again. Alyosha recalled what he had just said. "I seem to be sleeping awake...I walk, I speak, I see, but I am asleep." It seemed to be just like that now. Alyosha did not leave him. The thought passed through his mind to run for a doctor, but he was afraid to leave his brother alone: there was no one to whom he could leave him. By degrees Ivan lost consciousness completely at last. He still went on talking, talking incessantly, but quite incoherently, and even articulated his words with difficulty. Suddenly he staggered violently; but Alyosha was in time to support him. Ivan let him lead him to his bed. Alyosha undressed him somehow and put him to bed. He sat watching over him for another two hours. The sick man slept soundly, without stirring, breathing softly and evenly. Alyosha took a pillow and lay down on the sofa, without undressing.

As he fell asleep he prayed for Mitya and Ivan. He began to understand Ivan's illness. "The anguish of a proud determination. An earnest conscience!" God, in Whom he disbelieved, and His truth were gaining mastery over his heart, which still refused to submit. "Yes," the thought floated through Alyosha's head as it lay on the pillow, "yes, if Smerdyakov is dead, no one will believe Ivan's evidence; but he will go and give it." Alyosha smiled softly. "God will conquer!" he thought. "He will either rise up in the light of truth, or...he'll perish in hate, revenging on himself and on everyone his having served the cause he does not believe in," Alyosha added bitterly, and again he prayed for Ivan.

Book XII. A Judicial Error
Chapter 1. The Fatal Day

AT ten o'clock in the morning of the day following the events I have described, the trial of Dmitri Karamazov began in our district court.

I hasten to emphasise the fact that I am far from esteeming myself capable of reporting all that took place at the trial in full detail, or even in the actual order of events. I imagine that to mention everything with full explanation would fill a volume, even a very large one. And so I trust I may not be reproached, for confining myself to what struck me. I may have selected as of most interest what was of secondary importance, and may have omitted the most prominent and essential details. But I see I shall do better not to apologise. I will do my best and the reader will see for himself that I have done all I can.

And, to begin with, before entering the court, I will mention what surprised me most on that day. Indeed, as it appeared later, everyone was surprised at it, too. We all knew that the affair had aroused great interest, that everyone was burning with impatience for the trial to begin, that it had been a subject of talk, conjecture, exclamation and surmise for the last two months in local society. Everyone knew, too, that the case had become known throughout Russia, but yet we had not imagined that it had aroused such burning, such intense, interest in everyone, not only among ourselves, but all over Russia. This became evident at the trial this day.

Visitors had arrived not only from the chief town of our province, but from several other Russian towns, as well as from Moscow and Petersburg. Among them were lawyers, ladies, and even several distinguished personages. Every ticket of admission had been snatched up. A special place behind the table at which the three judges sat was set apart for the most distinguished and important of the men visitors; a row of arm-chairs had been placed there--something exceptional, which had never been allowed before. A large proportion not less than half of the public--were ladies. There was such a large number of lawyers from all parts that they did not know where to seat them, for every ticket had long since been eagerly sought for and distributed. I saw at the end of the room, behind the platform, a special partition hurriedly put up, behind which all these lawyers were admitted, and they thought themselves lucky to have standing room there, for all chairs had been removed for the sake of space, and the crowd behind the partition stood throughout the case closely packed, shoulder to shoulder.

Some of the ladies, especially those who came from a distance, made their appearance in the gallery very smartly dressed, but the majority of the ladies were oblivious even of dress. Their faces betrayed hysterical, intense, almost morbid, curiosity. A peculiar fact--established afterwards by many observations--was that almost all the ladies, or, at least the vast majority of them, were on Mitya's side and in favour of his being acquitted. This was perhaps chiefly owing to his reputation as a conqueror of female hearts. It was known that two women rivals were to appear in the case. One of them--Katerina Ivanovna--was an object of general interest. All sorts of extraordinary tales were told about her, amazing anecdotes of her passion for Mitya, in spite of his crime. Her pride and "aristocratic connections" were particularly insisted upon (she had called upon scarcely anyone in the town). People said she intended to petition the Government for leave to accompany the criminal to Siberia and to be married to him somewhere in the mines. The appearance of Grushenka in court was awaited with no less impatience. The public was looking forward with anxious curiosity to the meeting of the two rivals--the proud aristocratic girl and "the hetaira." But Grushenka was a more familiar figure to the ladies of the district than Katerina Ivanovna. They had already seen "the woman who had ruined Fyodor Pavlovitch and his unhappy son," and all, almost without exception, wondered how father and son could be so in love with "such a very common, ordinary Russian girl, who was not even pretty."

In brief, there was a great deal of talk. I know for a fact that there were several serious family quarrels on Mitya's account in our town. Many ladies quarrelled violently with their husbands over differences of opinion about the dreadful case, and it was that the husbands of these ladies, far from being favourably disposed to the prisoner, should enter the court bitterly prejudiced against him. In fact, one may say pretty certainly that the masculine, as distinguished from the feminine, part of the audience was biased against the prisoner. There were numbers of severe, frowning, even vindictive faces. Mitya, indeed, had managed to offend many people during his stay in the town. Some of the visitors were, of course, in excellent spirits and quite unconcerned as to the fate of Mitya personally. But all were interested in the trial, and the majority of the men were certainly hoping for the conviction of the criminal, except perhaps the lawyers, who were more interested in the legal than in the moral aspect of the case.

Everybody was excited at the presence of the celebrated lawyer, Fetyukovitch. His talent was well known, and this was not the first time he had defended notorious criminal cases in the provinces. And if he defended them, such cases became celebrated and long remembered all over Russia. There were stories, too, about our prosecutor and about the President of the Court. It was said that Ippolit Kirillovitch was in a tremor at meeting Fetyukovitch, and that they had been enemies from the beginning of their careers in Petersburg, that though our sensitive prosecutor, who always considered that he had been aggrieved by someone in Petersburg because his talents had not been properly appreciated, was keenly excited over the Karamazov case, and was even dreaming of rebuilding his flagging fortunes by means of it, Fetyukovitch, they said, was his one anxiety. But these rumours were not quite just. Our prosecutor was not one of those men who lose heart in face of danger. On the contrary, his self-confidence increased with the increase of danger. It must be noted that our prosecutor was in general too hasty and morbidly impressionable. He would put his whole soul into some case and work at it as though his whole fate and his whole fortune depended on its result. This was the subject of some ridicule in the legal world, for just by this characteristic our prosecutor had gained a wider notoriety than could have been expected from his modest position. People laughed particularly at his passion for psychology. In my opinion, they were wrong, and our prosecutor was, I believe, a character of greater depth than was generally supposed. But with his delicate health he had failed to make his mark at the outset of his career and had never made up for it later.

As for the President of our Court, I can only say that he was a humane and cultured man, who had a practical knowledge of his work and progressive views. He was rather ambitious, but did not concern himself greatly about his future career. The great aim of his life was to be a man of advanced ideas. He was, too, a man of connections and property. He felt, as we learnt afterwards, rather strongly about the Karamazov case, but from a social, not from a personal standpoint. He was interested in it as a social phenomenon, in its classification and its character as a product of our social conditions, as typical of the national character, and so on, and so on. His attitude to the personal aspect of the case, to its tragic significance and the persons involved in it, including the prisoner, was rather indifferent and abstract, as was perhaps fitting, indeed.

The court was packed and overflowing long before the judges made their appearance. Our court is the best hall in the town--spacious, lofty, and good for sound. On the right of the judges, who were on a raised platform, a table and two rows of chairs had been put ready for the jury. On the left was the place for the prisoner and the counsel for the defence. In the middle of the court, near the judges, was a table with the "material proofs." On it lay Fyodor Pavlovitch's white silk dressing-gown, stained with blood; the fatal brass pestle with which the supposed murder had been committed; Mitya's shirt, with a blood-stained sleeve; his coat, stained with blood in patches over the pocket in which he had put his handkerchief; the handkerchief itself, stiff with blood and by now quite yellow; the pistol loaded by Mitya at Perhotin's with a view to suicide, and taken from him on the sly at Mokroe by Trifon Borrissovitch; the envelope in which the three thousand roubles had been put ready for Grushenka, the narrow pink ribbon with which it had been tied, and many other articles I don't remember. In the body of the hall, at some distance, came the seats for the public. But in front of the balustrade a few chairs had been placed for witnesses who remained in the court after giving their evidence.

At ten o'clock the three judges arrived--the President, one honorary justice of the peace, and one other. The prosecutor, of course, entered immediately after. The President was a short, stout, thick-set man of fifty, with a dyspeptic complexion, dark hair turning grey and cut short, and a red ribbon, of what Order I don't remember. The prosecutor struck me and the others, too, as looking particularly pale, almost green. His face seemed to have grown suddenly thinner, perhaps in a single night, for I had seen him looking as usual only two days before. The President began with asking the court whether all the jury were present.

But I see I can't go on like this, partly because some things I did not hear, others I did not notice, and others I have forgotten, but most of all because, as I have said before, I have literally no time or space to mention everything that was said and done. I only know that neither side objected to very many of the jurymen. I remember the twelve jurymen--four were petty officials of the town, two were merchants, and six peasants and artisans of the town. I remember, long before the trial, questions were continually asked with some surprise, especially by ladies: "Can such a delicate, complex and psychological case be submitted for decision to petty officials and even peasants?" and "What can an official, still more a peasant, understand in such an affair?" All the four officials in the jury were, in fact, men of no consequence and of low rank. Except one who was rather younger, they were grey-headed men, little known in society, who had vegetated on a pitiful salary, and who probably had elderly, unpresentable wives and crowds of children, perhaps even without shoes and stockings. At most, they spent their leisure over cards and, of course, had never read a single book. The two merchants looked respectable, but were strangely silent and stolid. One of them was close-shaven, and was dressed in European style; the other had a small, grey beard, and wore a red ribbon with some sort of a medal upon it on his neck. There is no need to speak of the artisans and the peasants. The artisans of Skotoprigonyevsk are almost peasants, and even work on the land. Two of them also wore European dress, and, perhaps for that reason, were dirtier and more uninviting-looking than the others. So that one might well wonder, as I did as soon as I had looked at them, "what men like that could possibly make of such a case?" Yet their faces made a strangely imposing, almost menacing, impression; they were stern and frowning.

At last the President opened the case of the murder of Fyodor Pavlovitch Karamazov. I don't quite remember how he described him. The court usher was told to bring in the prisoner, and Mitya made his appearance. There was a hush through the court. One could have heard a fly. I don't know how it was with others, but Mitya made a most unfavourable impression on me. He looked an awful dandy in a brand-new frock-coat. I heard afterwards that he had ordered it in Moscow expressly for the occasion from his own tailor, who had his measure. He wore immaculate black kid gloves and exquisite linen. He walked in with his yard-long strides, looking stiffly straight in front of him, and sat down in his place with a most unperturbed air.

At the same moment the counsel for defence, the celebrated Fetyukovitch, entered, and a sort of subdued hum passed through the court. He was a tall, spare man, with long thin legs, with extremely long, thin, pale fingers, clean-shaven face, demurely brushed, rather short hair, and thin lips that were at times curved into something between a sneer and a smile. He looked about forty. His face would have been pleasant, if it had not been for his eyes, which, in themselves small and inexpressive, were set remarkably close together, with only the thin, long nose as a dividing line between them. In fact, there was something strikingly birdlike about his face. He was in evening dress and white tie.

I remember the President's first questions to Mitya, about his name, his calling, and so on. Mitya answered sharply, and his voice was so unexpectedly loud that it made the President start and look at the prisoner with surprise. Then followed a list of persons who were to take part in the proceedings--that is, of the witnesses and experts. It was a long list. Four of the witnesses were not present--Miusov, who had given evidence at the preliminary inquiry, but was now in Paris; Madame Hohlakov and Maximov, who were absent through illness; and Smerdyakov, through his sudden death, of which an official statement from the police was presented. The news of Smerdyakov's death produced a sudden stir and whisper in the court. Many of the audience, of course, had not heard of the sudden suicide. What struck people most was Mitya's sudden outburst. As soon as the statement of Smerdyakov's death was made, he cried out aloud from his place:

"He was a dog and died like a dog!"

I remember how his counsel rushed to him, and how the President addressed him, threatening to take stern measures, if such an irregularity were repeated. Mitya nodded and in a subdued voice repeated several times abruptly to his counsel, with no show of regret:

"I won't again, I won't. It escaped me. I won't do it again."

And, of course, this brief episode did him no good with the jury or the public. His character was displayed, and it spoke for itself. It was under the influence of this incident that the opening statement was read. It was rather short, but circumstantial. It only stated the chief reasons why he had been arrested, why he must be tried, and so on. Yet it made a great impression on me. The clerk read it loudly and distinctly. The whole tragedy was suddenly unfolded before us, concentrated, in bold relief, in a fatal and pitiless light. I remember how, immediately after it had been read, the President asked Mitya in a loud impressive voice:

"Prisoner, do you plead guilty?"

Mitya suddenly rose from his seat.

"I plead guilty to drunkenness and dissipation," he exclaimed, again in a startling, almost frenzied, voice, "to idleness and debauchery. I meant to become an honest man for good, just at the moment when I was struck down by fate. But I am not guilty of the death of that old man, my enemy and my father. No, no, I am not guilty of robbing him! I could not be. Dmitri Karamazov is a scoundrel, but not a thief."

He sat down again, visibly trembling all over. The President again briefly, but impressively, admonished him to answer only what was asked, and not to go off into irrelevant exclamations. Then he ordered the case to proceed. All the witnesses were led up to take the oath. Then I saw them all together. The brothers of the prisoner were, however, allowed to give evidence without taking the oath. After an exhortation from the priest and the President, the witnesses were led away and were made to sit as far as possible apart from one another. Then they began calling them up one by one.

Chapter 2. Dangerous Witnesses

I DO NOT know whether the witnesses for the defence and for the prosecution were separated into groups by the President, and whether it was arranged to call them in a certain order. But no doubt it was so. I only know that the witnesses for the prosecution were called first. I repeat I don't intend to describe all the questions step by step. Besides, my account would be to some extent superfluous, because in the speeches for the prosecution and for the defence the whole course of the evidence was brought together and set in a strong and significant light, and I took down parts of those two remarkable speeches in full, and will quote them in due course, together with one extraordinary and quite unexpected episode, which occurred before the final speeches, and undoubtedly influenced the sinister and fatal outcome of the trial.

I will only observe that from the first moments of the trial one peculiar characteristic of the case was conspicuous and observed by all, that is, the overwhelming strength of the prosecution as compared with the arguments the defence had to rely upon. Everyone realised it from the first moment that the facts began to group themselves round a single point, and the whole horrible and bloody crime was gradually revealed. Everyone, perhaps, felt from the first that the case was beyond dispute, that there was no doubt about it, that there could be really no discussion, and that the defence was only a matter of form, and that the prisoner was guilty, obviously and conclusively guilty. I imagine that even the ladies, who were so impatiently longing for the acquittal of the interesting prisoner, were at the same time, without exception, convinced of his guilt. What's more, I believe they would have been mortified if his guilt had not been so firmly established, as that would have lessened the effect of the closing scene of the criminal's acquittal. That he would be acquitted, all the ladies, strange to say, were firmly persuaded up to the very last moment. "He is guilty, but he will be acquitted, from motives of humanity, in accordance with the new ideas, the new sentiments that had come into fashion," and so on, and so on. And that was why they had crowded into the court so impatiently. The men were more interested in the contest between the prosecutor and the famous Fetyukovitch. All were wondering and asking themselves what could even a talent like Fetyukovitch's make of such a desperate case; and so they followed his achievements, step by step, with concentrated attention.

But Fetyukovitch remained an enigma to all up to the very end, up to his speech. Persons of experience suspected that he had some design, that he was working towards some object, but it was almost impossible to guess what it was. His confidence and self-reliance were unmistakable, however. Everyone noticed with pleasure, moreover, that he, after so short a stay, not more than three days, perhaps, among us, had so wonderfully succeeded in mastering the case and "had studied it to a nicety." People described with relish, afterwards, how cleverly he had "taken down" all the witnesses for the prosecution, and as far as possible perplexed them and, what's more, had aspersed their reputation and so depreciated the value of their evidence. But it was supposed that he did this rather by way of sport, so to speak, for professional glory, to show nothing had been omitted of the accepted methods, for all were convinced that he could do no real good by such disparagement of the witnesses, and probably was more aware of this than anyone, having some idea of his own in the background, some concealed weapon of defence, which he would suddenly reveal when the time came. But meanwhile, conscious of his strength, he seemed to be diverting himself.

So, for instance, when Grigory, Fyodor Pavlovitch's old servant, who had given the most damning piece of evidence about the open door, was examined, the counsel for the defence positively fastened upon him when his turn came to question him. It must be noted that Grigory entered the trial with a composed and almost stately air, not the least disconcerted by the majesty of the court or the vast audience listening to him. He gave evidence with as much confidence as though he had been talking with his Marfa, only perhaps more respectfully. It was impossible to make him contradict himself. The prosecutor questioned him first in detail about the family life of the Karamazovs. The family picture stood out in lurid colours. It was plain to ear and eye that the witness was guileless and impartial. In spite of his profound reverence for the memory of his deceased master, he yet bore witness that he had been unjust to Mitya and "hadn't brought up his children as he should. He'd have been devoured by lice when he was little, if it hadn't been for me," he added, describing Mitya's early childhood. "It wasn't fair either of the father to wrong his son over his mother's property, which was by right his."

In reply to the prosecutor's question what grounds he had for asserting that Fyodor Pavlovitch had wronged his son in their money relations, Grigory, to the surprise of everyone, had no proof at all to bring forward, but he still persisted that the arrangement with the son was "unfair," and that he ought "to have paid him several thousand roubles more." I must note, by the way, that the prosecutor asked this question (whether Fyodor Pavlovitch had really kept back part of Mitya's inheritance) with marked persistence of all the witnesses who could be asked it, not excepting Alyosha and Ivan, but he obtained no exact information from anyone; all alleged that it was so, but were unable to bring forward any distinct proof. Grigory's description of the scene at the dinner-table, when Dmitri had burst in and beaten his father, threatening to come back to kill him, made a sinister impression on the court, especially as the old servant's composure in telling it, his parsimony of words, and peculiar phraseology were as effective as eloquence. He observed that he was not angry with Mitya for having knocked him down and struck him on the face; he had forgiven him long ago, he said. Of the deceased Smerdyakov he observed, crossing himself, that he was a lad of ability, but stupid and afflicted, and, worse still, an infidel, and that it was Fyodor Pavlovitch and his elder son who had taught him to be so. But he defended Smerdyakov's honesty almost with warmth, and related how Smerdyakov had once found the master's money in the yard, and, instead of concealing it, had taken it to his master, who had rewarded him with a "gold piece" for it, and trusted him implicitly from that time forward. He maintained obstinately that the door into the garden had been open. But he was asked so many questions that I can't recall them all.

At last the counsel for the defence began to cross-examine him, and the first question he asked was about the envelope in which Fyodor Pavlovitch was supposed to have put three thousand roubles for "a certain person." "Have you ever seen it, you, who were for so many years in close attendance on your master?" Grigory answered that he had not seen it and had never heard of the money from anyone "till everybody was talking about it." This question about the envelope Fetyukovitch put to everyone who could conceivably have known of it, as persistently as the prosecutor asked his question about Dmitri's inheritance, and got the same answer from all, that no one had seen the envelope, though many had heard of it. From the beginning everyone noticed Fetyukovitch's persistence on this subject.

"Now, with your permission I'll ask you a question," Fetyukovitch said, suddenly and unexpectedly. "Of what was that balsam, or, rather, decoction, made, which, as we learn from the preliminary inquiry, you used on that evening to rub your lumbago, in the hope of curing it?"

Grigory looked blankly at the questioner, and after a brief silence muttered, "There was saffron in it."

"Nothing but saffron? Don't you remember any other ingredient?"

"There was milfoil in it, too."

"And pepper perhaps?" Fetyukovitch queried.

"Yes, there was pepper, too."

"Etcetera. And all dissolved in vodka?"

"In spirit."

There was a faint sound of laughter in the court.

"You see, in spirit. After rubbing your back, I believe, you drank what was left in the bottle with a certain pious prayer, only known to your wife?"

"I did."

"Did you drink much? Roughly speaking, a wine-glass or two?"

"It might have been a tumbler-full."

"A tumbler-full, even. Perhaps a tumbler and a half?"

Grigory did not answer. He seemed to see what was meant.

"A glass and a half of neat spirit--is not at all bad, don't you think? You might see the gates of heaven open, not only the door into the garden?"

Grigory remained silent. There was another laugh in the court. The President made a movement.

"Do you know for a fact," Fetyukovitch persisted, "whether you were awake or not when you saw the open door?"

"I was on my legs."

"That's not a proof that you were awake." (There was again laughter in the court.) "Could you have answered at that moment, if anyone had asked you a question--for instance, what year it is?"

"I don't know."

"And what year is it, Anno Domini, do you know?"

Grigory stood with a perplexed face, looking straight at his tormentor. Strange to say, it appeared he really did not know what year it was.

"But perhaps you can tell me how many fingers you have on your hands?"

"I am a servant," Grigory said suddenly, in a loud and distinct voice. "If my betters think fit to make game of me, it is my duty to suffer it."

Fetyukovitch was a little taken aback, and the President intervened, reminding him that he must ask more relevant questions. Fetyukovitch bowed with dignity and said that he had no more questions to ask of the witness. The public and the jury, of course, were left with a grain of doubt in their minds as to the evidence of a man who might, while undergoing a certain cure, have seen "the gates of heaven," and who did not even know what year he was living in. But before Grigory left the box another episode occurred. The President, turning to the prisoner, asked him whether he had any comment to make on the evidence of the last witness.

"Except about the door, all he has said is true," cried Mitya, in a loud voice. "For combing the lice off me, I thank him; for forgiving my blows, I thank him. The old man has been honest all his life and as faithful to my father as seven hundred poodles."

"Prisoner, be careful in your language," the President admonished him.

"I am not a poodle," Grigory muttered.

"All right, it's I am a poodle myself," cried Mitya. "If it's an insult, I take it to myself and I beg his pardon. I was a beast and cruel to him. I was cruel to Aesop too."

"What Aesop?" the President asked sternly again.

"Oh, Pierrot...my father, Fyodor Pavlovitch."

The President again and again warned Mitya impressively and very sternly to be more careful in his language.

"You are injuring yourself in the opinion of your judges."

The counsel for the defence was equally clever in dealing with the evidence of Rakitin. I may remark that Rakitin was one of the leading witnesses and one to whom the prosecutor attached great significance. It appeared that he knew everything; his knowledge was amazing, he had been everywhere, seen everything, talked to everybody, knew every detail of the biography of Fyodor Pavlovitch and all the Karamazovs. Of the envelope, it is true, he had only heard from Mitya himself. But he described minutely Mitya's exploits in the Metropolis, all his compromising doings and sayings, and told the story of Captain Snegiryov's "wisp of tow." But even Rakitin could say nothing positive about Mitya's inheritance, and confined himself to contemptuous generalities.

"Who could tell which of them was to blame, and which was in debt to the other, with their crazy Karamazov way of muddling things so that no one could make head or tail of it?" He attributed the tragic crime to the habits that had become ingrained by ages of serfdom and the distressed condition of Russia, due to the lack of appropriate institutions. He was, in fact, allowed some latitude of speech. This was the first occasion on which Rakitin showed what he could do, and attracted notice. The prosecutor knew that the witness was preparing a magazine article on the case, and afterwards in his speech, as we shall see later, quoted some ideas from the article, showing that he had seen it already. The picture drawn by the witness was a gloomy and sinister one, and greatly strengthened the case for the prosecution. Altogether, Rakatin's discourse fascinated the public by its independence and the extraordinary nobility of its ideas. There were even two or three outbreaks of applause when he spoke of serfdom and the distressed condition of Russia.

But Rakitin, in his youthful ardour, made a slight blunder, of which the counsel for the defence at once adroitly took advantage. Answering certain questions about Grushenka and carried away by the loftiness of his own sentiments and his success, of which he was, of course, conscious, he went so far as to speak somewhat contemptuously of Agrafena Alexandrovna as "the kept mistress of Samsonov." He would have given a good deal to take back his words afterwards, for Fetyukovitch caught him out over it at once. And it was all because Rakitin had not reckoned on the lawyer having been able to become so intimately acquainted with every detail in so short a time.

"Allow me to ask," began the counsel for the defence, with the most affable and even respectful smile, "you are, of course, the same Mr. Rakitin whose pamphlet, The Life of the Deceased Elder, Father Zossima, published by the diocesan authorities, full of profound and religious reflections and preceded by an excellent and devout dedication to the bishop, I have just read with such pleasure?"

"I did not write it for publication...it was published afterwards," muttered Rakitin, for some reason fearfully disconcerted and almost ashamed.

"Oh, that's excellent! A thinker like you can, and indeed ought to, take the widest view of every social question. Your most instructive pamphlet has been widely circulated through the patronage of the bishop, and has been of appreciable service...But this is the chief thing I should like to learn from you. You stated just now that you were very intimately acquainted with Madame Svyetlov." (It must be noted that Grushenka's surname was Svyetlov. I heard it for the first time that day, during the case.)

"I cannot answer for all my acquaintances...I am a young man...and who can be responsible for everyone he meets?" cried Rakitin, flushing all over.

"I understand, I quite understand," cried Fetyukovitch; as though he, too, were embarrassed and in haste to excuse himself. "You, like any other, might well be interested in an acquaintance with a young and beautiful woman who would readily entertain the elite of the youth of the neighbourhood, but...I only wanted to know...It has come to my knowledge, that Madame Svyetlov was particularly anxious a couple of months ago to make the acquaintance of the younger Karamazov, Alexey Fyodorovitch, and promised you twenty-five roubles, if you would bring him to her in his monastic dress. And that actually took place on the evening of the day on which the terrible crime, which is the subject of the present investigation, was committed. You brought Alexey Karamazov to Madame Svyetlov, and did you receive the twenty-five roubles from Madame Svyetlov as a reward, that's what I wanted to hear from you?"

"It was a joke...I don't, see of what interest that can be to you...I took it for a joke...meaning to give it back later..."

"Then you did take--but you have not given it back yet...or have you?"

"That's of no consequence," muttered Rakitin, "I refuse to answer such questions...Of course, I shall give it back."

The President intervened, but Fetyukovitch declared he had no more questions to ask of the witness. Mr. Rakitin left the witness-box not absolutely without a stain upon his character. The effect left by the lofty idealism of his speech was somewhat marred, and Fetyukovitch's expression, as he watched him walk away, seemed to suggest to the public "this is a specimen of the lofty-minded persons who accuse him." I remember that this incident, too, did not pass off without an outbreak from Mitya. Enraged by the tone in which Rakitin had referred to Grushenka, he suddenly shouted "Bernard!" When, after Rakitin's cross-examination, the President asked the prisoner if he had anything to say, Mitya cried loudly:

"Since I've been arrested, he has borrowed money from me! He is a contemptible Bernard and opportunist, and he doesn't believe in God; he took the bishop in!"

Mitya of course, was pulled up again for the intemperance of his language, but Rakitin was done for. Captain Snegiryov's evidence was a failure, too, but from quite a different reason. He appeared in ragged and dirty clothes, muddy boots, and in spite of the vigilance and expert observation of the police officers, he turned out to be hopelessly drunk. On being asked about Mitya's attack upon him, he refused to answer.

"God bless him. Ilusha told me not to. God will make it up to me yonder."

"Who told you not to tell? Of whom are you talking?"

"Ilusha, my little son. 'Father, father, how he insulted you!' He said that at the stone. Now he is dying..."

The captain suddenly began sobbing, and plumped down on His knees before the President. He was hurriedly led away amidst the laughter of the public. The effect prepared by the prosecutor did not come off at all.

Fetyukovitch went on making the most of every opportunity, and amazed people more and more by his minute knowledge of the case. Thus, for example, Trifon Borissovitch made a great impression, of course, very prejudicial to Mitya. He calculated almost on his fingers that on his first visit to Mokroe, Mitya must have spent three thousand roubles, "or very little less. Just think what he squandered on those gypsy girls alone! And as for our lousy peasants, it wasn't a case of flinging half a rouble in the street, he made them presents of twenty-five roubles each, at least, he didn't give them less. And what a lot of money was simply stolen from him! And if anyone did steal, he did not leave a receipt. How could one catch the thief when he was flinging his money away all the time? Our peasants are robbers, you know; they have no care for their souls. And the way he went on with the girls, our village girls! They're completely set up since then, I tell you, they used to be poor." He recalled, in fact, every item of expense and added it all up. So the theory that only fifteen hundred had been spent and the rest had been put aside in a little bag seemed inconceivable.

"I saw three thousand as clear as a penny in his hands, I saw it with my own eyes; I should think I ought to know how to reckon money," cried Trifon Borissovitch, doing his best to satisfy "his betters."

When Fetyukovitch had to cross-examine him, he scarcely tried to refute his evidence, but began asking him about an incident at the first carousal at Mokroe, a month before the arrest, when Timofey and another peasant called Akim had picked up on the floor in the passage a hundred roubles dropped by Mitya when he was drunk, and had given them to Trifon Borissovitch and received a rouble each from him for doing so. "Well," asked the lawyer," did you give that hundred roubles back to Mr. Karamazov?" Trifon Borissovitch shuffled in vain...He was obliged, after the peasants had been examined, to admit the finding of the hundred roubles, only adding that he had religiously returned it all to Dmitri Fyodorovitch "in perfect honesty, and it's only because his honour was in liquor at the time, he wouldn't remember it." But, as he had denied the incident of the hundred roubles till the peasants had been called to prove it, his evidence as to returning the money to Mitya was naturally regarded with great suspicion. So one of the most dangerous witnesses brought forward by the prosecution was again discredited.

The same thing happened with the Poles. They took up an attitude of pride and independence; they vociferated loudly that they had both been in the service of the Crown, and that "Pan Mitya" had offered them three thousand "to buy their honour," and that they had seen a large sum of money in his hands. Pan Mussyalovitch introduced a terrible number of Polish words into his sentences, and seeing that this only increased his consequence in the eyes of the President and the prosecutor, grew more and more pompous, and ended by talking in Polish altogether. But Fetyukovitch caught them, too, in his snares. Trifon Borissovitch, recalled, was forced, in spite of his evasions, to admit that Pan Vrublevsky had substituted another pack of cards for the one he had provided, and that Pan Mussyalovitch had cheated during the game. Kalgonov confirmed this, and both the Poles left the witness-box with damaged reputations, amidst laughter from the public.

Then exactly the same thing happened with almost all the most dangerous witnesses. Fetyukovitch succeeded in casting a slur on all of them, and dismissing them with a certain derision. The lawyers and experts were lost in admiration, and were only at a loss to understand what good purpose could be served by it, for all, I repeat, felt that the case for the prosecution could not be refuted, but was growing more and more tragically overwhelming. But from the confidence of the "great magician" they saw that he was serene, and they waited, feeling that "such a man" had not come from Petersburg for nothing, and that he was not a man to return unsuccessful.

Chapter 3. The Medical Experts and a Pound of Nuts

THE evidence of the medical experts, too, was of little use to the prisoner. And it appeared later that Fetyukovitch had not reckoned much upon it. The medical line of defence had only been taken up through the insistence of Katerina Ivanovna, who had sent for a celebrated doctor from Moscow on purpose. The case for the defence could, of course, lose nothing by it and might, with luck, gain something from it. There was, however, an element of comedy about it, through the difference of opinion of the doctors. The medical experts were the famous doctor from Moscow, our doctor, Herzenstube, and the young doctor, Varvinsky. The two latter appeared also as witnesses for the prosecution.

The first to be called in the capacity of expert was Doctor Herzenstube. He was a grey and bald old man of seventy, of middle height and sturdy build. He was much esteemed and respected by everyone in the town. He was a conscientious doctor and an excellent and pious man, a Hernguter or Moravian brother, I am not quite sure which. He had been living amongst us for many years and behaved with wonderful dignity. He was a kind-hearted and humane man. He treated the sick poor and peasants for nothing, visited them in their slums and huts, and left money for medicine, but he was as obstinate as a mule. If once he had taken an idea into his head, there was no shaking it. Almost everyone in the town was aware, by the way, that the famous doctor had, within the first two or three days of his presence among us, uttered some extremely offensive allusions to Doctor Herzenstube's qualifications. Though the Moscow doctor asked twenty-five roubles for a visit, several people in the town were glad to take advantage of his arrival, and rushed to consult him regardless of expense. All these had, of course, been previously patients of Doctor Herzenstube, and the celebrated doctor had criticised his treatment with extreme harshness. Finally, he had asked the patients as soon as he saw them, "Well, who has been cramming you with nostrums? Herzenstube? He he!" Doctor Herzenstube, of course, heard all this, and now all the three doctors made their appearance, one after another, to be examined.

Doctor Herzenstube roundly declared that the abnormality of the prisoner's mental faculties was self-evident. Then giving his grounds for this opinion, which I omit here, he added that the abnormality was not only evident in many of the prisoner's actions in the past, but was apparent even now at this very moment. When he was asked to explain how it was apparent now at this moment, the old doctor, with simple-hearted directness, pointed out that the prisoner had "an extraordinary air, remarkable in the circumstances"; that he had "marched in like a soldier, looking straight before him, though it would have been more natural for him to look to the left where, among the public, the ladies were sitting, seeing that he was a great admirer of the fair sex and must be thinking much of what the ladies are saying of him now," the old man concluded in his peculiar language.

I must add that he spoke Russian readily, but every phrase was formed in German style, which did not, however, trouble him, for it had always been a weakness of his to believe that he spoke Russian perfectly, better indeed than Russians. And he was very fond of using Russian proverbs, always declaring that the Russian proverbs were the best and most expressive sayings in the whole world. I may remark, too, that in conversation, through absent-mindedness he often forgot the most ordinary words, which sometimes went out of his head, though he knew them perfectly. The same thing happened, though, when he spoke German, and at such times he always waved his hand before his face as though trying to catch the lost word, and no one could induce him to go on speaking till he had found the missing word. His remark that the prisoner ought to have looked at the ladies on entering roused a whisper of amusement in the audience. All our ladies were very fond of our old doctor; they knew, too, that having been all his life a bachelor and a religious man of exemplary conduct, he looked upon women as lofty creatures. And so his unexpected observation struck everyone as very queer.

The Moscow doctor, being questioned in his turn, definitely and emphatically repeated that he considered the prisoner's mental condition abnormal in the highest degree. He talked at length and with erudition of "aberration" and "mania," and argued that, from all the facts collected, the prisoner had undoubtedly been in a condition of aberration for several days before his arrest, and, if the crime had been committed by him, it must, even if he were conscious of it, have been almost involuntary, as he had not the power to control the morbid impulse that possessed him.

But apart from temporary aberration, the doctor diagnosed mania, which promised, in his words, to lead to complete insanity in the future. (It must be noted that I report this in my own words, the doctor made use of very learned and professional language.) "All his actions are in contravention of common sense and logic," he continued. "Not to refer to what I have not seen, that is, the crime itself and the whole catastrophe, the day before yesterday, while he was talking to me, he had an unaccountably fixed look in his eye. He laughed unexpectedly when there was nothing to laugh at. He showed continual and inexplicable irritability, using strange words, 'Bernard!' 'Ethics!' and others equally inappropriate." But the doctor detected mania, above all, in the fact that the prisoner could not even speak of the three thousand roubles, of which he considered himself to have been cheated, without extraordinary irritation, though he could speak comparatively lightly of other misfortunes and grievances. According to all accounts, he had even in the past, whenever the subject of the three thousand roubles was touched on, flown into a perfect frenzy, and yet he was reported to be a disinterested and not grasping man.

"As to the opinion of my learned colleague," the Moscow doctor added ironically in conclusion "that the prisoner would, entering the court, have naturally looked at the ladies and not straight before him, I will only say that, apart from the playfulness of this theory, it is radically unsound. For though I fully agree that the prisoner, on entering the court where his fate will be decided, would not naturally look straight before him in that fixed way, and that that may really be a sign of his abnormal mental condition, at the same time I maintain that he would naturally not look to the left at the ladies, but, on the contrary, to the right to find his legal adviser, on whose help all his hopes rest and on whose defence all his future depends." The doctor expressed his opinion positively and emphatically.

But the unexpected pronouncement of Doctor Varvinsky gave the last touch of comedy to the difference of opinion between the experts. In his opinion the prisoner was now, and had been all along, in a perfectly normal condition, and, although he certainly must have been in a nervous and exceedingly excited state before his arrest, this might have been due to several perfectly obvious causes, jealousy, anger, continual drunkenness, and so on. But this nervous condition would not involve the mental abberation of which mention had just been made. As to the question whether the prisoner should have looked to the left or to the right on entering the court, "in his modest opinion," the prisoner would naturally look straight before him on entering the court, as he had in fact done, as that was where the judges, on whom his fate depended, were sitting. So that it was just by looking straight before him that he showed his perfectly normal state of mind at the present. The young doctor concluded his "modest" testimony with some heat.

"Bravo, doctor!" cried Mitya, from his seat, "just so!"

Mitya, of course, was checked, but the young doctor's opinion had a decisive influence on the judges and on the public, and, as appeared afterwards, everyone agreed with him. But Doctor Herzenstube, when called as a witness, was quite unexpectedly of use to Mitya. As an old resident in the town, who had known the Karamazov family for years, he furnished some facts of great value for the prosecution, and suddenly, as though recalling something, he added:

"But the poor young man might have had a very different life, for he had a good heart both in childhood and after childhood, that I know. But the Russian proverb says, 'If a man has one head, it's good, but if another clever man comes to visit him, it would be better still, for then there will be two heads and not only one.'"

"One head is good, but two are better," the prosecutor put in impatiently. He knew the old man's habit of talking slowly and deliberately, regardless of the impression he was making and of the delay he was causing, and highly prizing his flat, dull and always gleefully complacent German wit. The old man was fond of making jokes.

"Oh, yes, that's what I say," he went on stubbornly. "One head is good, but two are much better, but he did not meet another head with wits, and his wits went. Where did they go? I've forgotten the word." He went on, passing his hand before his eyes, "Oh, yes, spazieren."*

* Promenading.

"Wandering?"

"Oh, yes, wandering, that's what I say. Well, his wits went wandering and fell in such a deep hole that he lost himself. And yet he was a grateful and sensitive boy. Oh, I remember him very well, a little chap so high, left neglected by his father in the back yard, when he ran about without boots on his feet, and his little breeches hanging by one button."

A note of feeling and tenderness suddenly came into the honest old man's voice. Fetyukovitch positively started, as though scenting something, and caught at it instantly.

"Oh, yes, I was a young man then...I was...well, I was forty-five then, and had only just come here. And I was so sorry for the boy then; I asked myself why shouldn't I buy him a pound of...a pound of what? I've forgotten what it's called. A pound of what children are very fond of, what is it, what is it?" The doctor began waving his hands again. "It grows on a tree and is gathered and given to everyone..."

"Apples?"

"Oh, no, no. You have a dozen of apples, not a pound...No, there are a lot of them, and call little. You put them in the mouth and crack."

"Quite so, nuts, I say so." The doctor repeated in the calmest way as though he had been at no loss for a word. "And I bought him a pound of nuts, for no one had ever bought the boy a pound of nuts before. And I lifted my finger and said to him, 'Boy, Gott der Vater.' He laughed and said, 'Gott der Vater'...'Gott der Sohn.' He laughed again and lisped 'Gott der Sohn.' 'Gott der heilige Geist.' Then he laughed and said as best he could, 'Gott der heilige Geist.' I went away, and two days after I happened to be passing, and he shouted to me of himself, 'Uncle, Gott der Vater, Gott der Sohn,' and he had only forgotten 'Gott der heilige Geist.' But I reminded him of it and I felt very sorry for him again. But he was taken away, and I did not see him again. Twenty-three years passed. I am sitting one morning in my study, a white-haired old man, when there walks into the room a blooming young man, whom I should never have recognised, but he held up his finger and said, laughing, 'Gott der Vater, Gott der Sohn, and Gott der heilige Geist. I have just arrived and have come to thank you for that pound of nuts, for no one else ever bought me a pound of nuts; you are the only one that ever did.' then I remembered my happy youth and the poor child in the yard, without boots on his feet, and my heart was touched and I said, 'You are a grateful young man, for you have remembered all your life the pound of nuts I bought you in your childhood.' And I embraced him and blessed him. And I shed tears. He laughed, but he shed tears, too...for the Russian often laughs when he ought to be weeping. But he did weep; I saw it. And now, alas!..."

"And I am weeping now, German, I am weeping now, too, you saintly man," Mitya cried suddenly.

In any case the anecdote made a certain favourable impression on the public. But the chief sensation in Mitya's favour was created by the evidence of Katerina Ivanovna, which I will describe directly. Indeed, when the witnesses a decharge, that is, called the defence, began giving evidence, fortune seemed all at once markedly more favourable to Mitya, and what was particularly striking, this was a surprise even to the counsel for the defence. But before Katerina Ivanovna was called, Alyosha was examined, and he recalled a fact which seemed to furnish positive evidence against one important point made by the prosecution.

Chapter 4. Fortune Smiles on Mitya

IT came quite as a surprise even to Alyosha himself. He was not required to take the oath, and I remember that both sides addressed him very gently and sympathetically. It was evident that his reputation for goodness had preceded him. Alyosha gave his evidence modestly and with restraint, but his warm sympathy for his unhappy brother was unmistakable. In answer to one question, he sketched his brother's character as that of a man, violent-tempered perhaps and carried away by his passions, but at the same time honourable, proud and generous, capable of self-sacrifice, if necessary. He admitted, however, that, through his passion for Grushenka and his rivalry with his father, his brother had been of late in an intolerable position. But he repelled with indignation the suggestion that his brother might have committed a murder for the sake of gain, though he recognised that the three thousand roubles had become almost an obsession with Mitya; that upon them as part of the inheritance he had been cheated of by his father, and that, indifferent as he was to money as a rule, he could not even speak of that three thousand without fury. As for the rivalry of the two "ladies," as the prosecutor expressed it--that is, of Grushenka and Katya--he answered evasively and was even unwilling to answer one or two questions altogether.

"Did your brother tell you, anyway, that he intended to kill your father?" asked the prosecutor. "You can refuse to answer if you think necessary," he added.

"He did not tell me so directly," answered Alyosha.

"How so? Did he indirectly?"

"He spoke to me once of his hatred for our father and his fear that at an extreme moment...at a moment of fury, he might perhaps murder him."

"And you believed him?"

"I am afraid to say that I did. But I never doubted that some higher feeling would always save him at that fatal moment, as it has indeed saved him, for it was not he killed my father," Alyosha said firmly, in a loud voice that was heard throughout the court.

The prosecutor started like a war-horse at the sound of a trumpet.

"Let me assure you that I fully believe in the complete sincerity of your conviction and do not explain it by or identify it with your affection for your unhappy brother. Your peculiar view of the whole tragic episode is known to us already from the preliminary investigation. I won't attempt to conceal from you that it is highly individual and contradicts all the other evidence collected by the prosecution. And so I think it essential to press you to tell me what facts have led you to this conviction of your brother's innocence and of the guilt of another person against whom you gave evidence at the preliminary inquiry?"

"I only answered the questions asked me at the preliminary inquiry," replied Alyosha, slowly and calmly. "I made no accusation against Smerdyakov of myself."

"Yet you gave evidence against him?"

"I was led to do so by my brother Dmitri's words. I was told what took place at his arrest and how he had pointed to Smerdyakov before I was examined. I believe absolutely that my brother is innocent, and if he didn't commit the murder, then-"

"Then Smerdyakov? Why Smerdyakov? And why are you so completely persuaded of your brother's innocence?"

"I cannot help believing my brother. I know he wouldn't lie to me. I saw from his face he wasn't lying."

"Only from his face? Is that all the proof you have?"

"I have no other proof."

"And of Smerdyakov's guilt you have no proof whatever but your brother's word and the expression of his face?"

"No, I have no other proof."

The prosecutor dropped the examination at this point. The impression left by Alyosha's evidence on the public was most disappointing. There had been talk about Smerdyakov before the trial; someone had heard something, someone had pointed out something else, it was said that Alyosha had gathered together some extraordinary proofs of his brother's innocence and Smerdyakov's guilt, and after all there was nothing, no evidence except certain moral convictions so natural in a brother.

But Fetyukovitch began his cross-examination. On his asking Alyosha when it was that the prisoner had told him of his hatred for his father and that he might kill him, and whether he had heard it, for instance, at their last meeting before the catastrophe, Alyosha started as he answered, as though only just recollecting and understanding something.

"I remember one circumstance now which I'd quite forgotten myself. It wasn't clear to me at the time, but now-"

And, obviously only now for the first time struck by an idea, he recounted eagerly how, at his last interview with Mitya that evening under the tree, on the road to the monastery, Mitya had struck himself on the breast, "the upper part of the breast," and had repeated several times that he had a means of regaining his honour, that that means was here, here on his breast. "I thought, when he struck himself on the breast, he meant that it was in his heart," Alyosha continued, "that he might find in his heart strength to save himself from some awful disgrace which was awaiting him and which he did not dare confess even to me. I must confess I did think at the time that he was speaking of our father, and that the disgrace he was shuddering at was the thought of going to our father and doing some violence to him. Yet it was just then that he pointed to something on his breast, so that I remember the idea struck me at the time that the heart is not on that part of the breast, but below, and that he struck himself much too high, just below the neck, and kept pointing to that place. My idea seemed silly to me at the time, but he was perhaps pointing then to that little bag in which he had fifteen hundred roubles!"

"Just so, Mitya cried from his place. "That's right, Alyosha, it was the little bag I struck with my fist."

Fetyukovitch flew to him in hot haste entreating him to keep quiet, and at the same instant pounced on Alyosha. Alyosha, carried away himself by his recollection, warmly expressed his theory that this disgrace was probably just that fifteen hundred roubles on him, which he might have returned to Katerina Ivanovna as half of what he owed her, but which he had yet determined not to repay her and to use for another purpose--namely, to enable him to elope with Grushenka, if she consented.

"It is so, it must be so," exclaimed Alyosha, in sudden excitement. "My brother cried several times that half of the disgrace, half of it (he said half several times) he could free himself from at once, but that he was so unhappy in his weakness of will that he wouldn't do it...that he knew beforehand he was incapable of doing it!"

"And you clearly, confidently remember that he struck himself just on this part of the breast?" Fetyukovitch asked eagerly.

"Clearly and confidently, for I thought at the time, 'Why does he strike himself up there when the heart is lower down?' and the thought seemed stupid to me at the time...I remember its seeming stupid...it flashed through my mind. That's what brought it back to me just now. How could I have forgotten it till now? It was that little bag he meant when he said he had the means but wouldn't give back that fifteen hundred. And when he was arrested at Mokroe he cried out--I know, I was told it--that he considered it the most disgraceful act of his life that when he had the means of repaying Katerina Ivanovna half (half, note!) what he owed her, he yet could not bring himself to repay the money and preferred to remain a thief in her eyes rather than part with it. And what torture, what torture that debt has been to him!" Alyosha exclaimed in conclusion.

The prosecutor, of course, intervened. He asked Alyosha to describe once more how it had all happened, and several times insisted on the question, "Had the prisoner seemed to point to anything? Perhaps he had simply struck himself with his fist on the breast?"

"But it was not with his fist," cried Alyosha; "he pointed with his fingers and pointed here, very high up...How could I have so completely forgotten it till this moment?"

The President asked Mitya what he had to say to the last witness's evidence. Mitya confirmed it, saying that he had been pointing to the fifteen hundred roubles which were on his breast, just below the neck, and that that was, of course, the disgrace, "A disgrace I cannot deny, the most shameful act of my whole life," cried Mitya. "I might have repaid it and didn't repay it. I preferred to remain a thief in her eyes rather than give it back. And the most shameful part of it was that I knew beforehand I shouldn't give it back! You are right, Alyosha! Thanks, Alyosha!"

So Alyosha's cross-examination ended. What was important and striking about it was that one fact at least had been found, and even though this were only one tiny bit of evidence, a mere hint at evidence, it did go some little way towards proving that the bag had existed and had contained fifteen hundred roubles and that the prisoner had not been lying at the preliminary inquiry when he alleged at Mokroe that those fifteen hundred roubles were "his own." Alyosha was glad. With a flushed face he moved away to the seat assigned to him. He kept repeating to himself: "How was it I forgot? How could I have forgotten it? And what made it come back to me now?"

Katerina Ivanovna was called to the witness-box. As she entered something extraordinary happened in the court. The ladies clutched their lorgnettes and opera-glasses. There was a stir among the men: some stood up to get a better view. Everybody alleged afterwards that Mitya had turned "white as a sheet" on her entrance. All in black, she advanced modestly, almost timidly. It was impossible to tell from her face that she was agitated; but there was a resolute gleam in her dark and gloomy eyes. I may remark that many people mentioned that she looked particularly handsome at that moment. She spoke softly but clearly, so that she was heard all over the court. She expressed herself with composure, or at least tried to appear composed. The President began his examination discreetly and very respectfully, as though afraid to touch on "certain chords," and showing consideration for her great unhappiness. But in answer to one of the first questions Katerina Ivanovna replied firmly that she had been formerly betrothed to the prisoner, "until he left me of his own accord..." she added quietly. When they asked her about the three thousand she had entrusted to Mitya to post to her relations, she said firmly, "I didn't give him the money simply to send it off. I felt at the time that he was in great need of money...I gave him the three thousand on the understanding that he should post it within the month if he cared to. There was no need for him to worry himself about that debt afterwards."

I will not repeat all the questions asked her and all her answers in detail. I will only give the substance of her evidence.

"I was firmly convinced that he would send off that sum as soon as he got money from his father," she went on. "I have never doubted his disinterestedness and his honesty...his scrupulous honesty...in money matters. He felt quite certain that he would receive the money from his father, and spoke to me several times about it. I knew he had a feud with his father and have always believed that he had been unfairly treated by his father. I don't remember any threat uttered by him against his father. He certainly never uttered any such threat before me. If he had come to me at that time, I should have at once relieved his anxiety about that unlucky three thousand roubles, but he had given up coming to see me...and I myself was put in such a position...that I could not invite him...And I had no right, indeed, to be exacting as to that money, she added suddenly, and there was a ring of resolution in her voice. "I was once indebted to him for assistance in money for more than three thousand, and I took it, although I could not at that time foresee that I should ever be in a position to repay my debt."

There was a note of defiance in her voice. It was then Fetyukovitch began his cross-examination.

"Did that take place not here, but at the beginning of your acquaintance?" Fetyukovitch suggested cautiously, feeling his way, instantly scenting something favourable. I must mention in parenthesis that, though Fetyukovitch had been brought from Petersburg partly at the instance of Katerina Ivanovna herself, he knew nothing about the episode of the four thousand roubles given her by Mitya, and of her "bowing to the ground to him." She concealed this from him and said nothing about it, and that was strange. It may be pretty certainly assumed that she herself did not know till the very last minute whether she would speak of that episode in the court, and waited for the inspiration of the moment.

No, I can never forget those moments. She began telling her story. She told everything, the whole episode that Mitya had told Alyosha, and her bowing to the ground, and her reason. She told about her father and her going to Mitya, and did not in one word, in a single hint, suggest that Mitya had himself, through her sister, proposed they should "send him Katerina Ivanovna" to fetch the money. She generously concealed that and was not ashamed to make it appear as though she had of her own impulse run to the young officer, relying on something...to beg him for the money. It was something tremendous! I turned cold and trembled as I listened. The court was hushed, trying to catch each word. It was something unexampled. Even from such a self-willed and contemptuously proud girl as she was, such an extremely frank avowal, such sacrifice, such self-immolation, seemed incredible. And for what, for whom? To save the man who had deceived and insulted her and to help, in however small a degree, in saving him, by creating a strong impression in his favour. And, indeed, the figure of the young officer who, with a respectful bow to the innocent girl, handed her his last four thousand roubles--all he had in the world--was thrown into a very sympathetic and attractive light, but...I had a painful misgiving at heart! I felt that calumny might come of it later (and it did, in fact, it did). It was repeated all over the town afterwards with spiteful laughter that was perhaps not quite complete--that is, in the statement that the officer had let the young lady depart "with nothing but a respectful bow." It was hinted that something was here omitted.

"And even if nothing had been omitted, if this were the whole story," the most highly respected of our ladies maintained, "even then it's very doubtful whether it was creditable for a young girl to behave in that way, even for the sake of saving her father."

And can Katerina Ivanovna, with her intelligence, her morbid sensitiveness, have failed to understand that people would talk like that? She must have understood it, yet she made up her mind to tell everything. Of course, all these nasty little suspicions as to the truth of her story only arose afterwards and at the first moment all were deeply impressed by it. As for the judges and the lawyers, they listened in reverent, almost shamefaced silence to Katerina Ivanovna. The prosecutor did not venture upon even one question on the subject. Fetyukovitch made a low bow to her. Oh, he was almost triumphant! Much ground had been gained. For a man to give his last four thousand on a generous impulse and then for the same man to murder his father for the sake of robbing him of three thousand--the idea seemed too incongruous. Fetyukovitch felt that now the charge of theft, at least, was as good as disproved. "The case" was thrown into quite a different light. There was a wave of sympathy for Mitya. As for him...I was told that once or twice, while Katerina Ivanovna was giving her evidence, he jumped up from his seat, sank back again, and hid his face in his hands. But when she had finished, he suddenly cried in a sobbing voice:

"Katya, why have you ruined me?" and his sobs were audible all over the court. But he instantly restrained himself, and cried again:

"Now I am condemned!"

Then he sat rigid in his place, with his teeth clenched and his arms across his chest. Katerina Ivanovna remained in the court and sat down in her place. She was pale and sat with her eyes cast down. Those who were sitting near her declared that for a long time she shivered all over as though in a fever. Grushenka was called.

I am approaching the sudden catastrophe which was perhaps the final cause of Mitya's ruin. For I am convinced, so is everyone--all the lawyers said the same afterwards--that if the episode had not occurred, the prisoner would at least have been recommended to mercy. But of that later. A few words first about Grushenka.

She, too, was dressed entirely in black, with her magnificent black shawl on her shoulders. She walked to the witness-box with her smooth, noiseless tread, with the slightly swaying gait common in women of full figure. She looked steadily at the President, turning her eyes neither to the right nor to the left. To my thinking she looked very handsome at that moment, and not at all pale, as the ladies alleged afterwards. They declared, too, that she had a concentrated and spiteful expression. I believe that she was simply irritated and painfully conscious of the contemptuous and inquisitive eyes of our scandal-loving public. She was proud and could not stand contempt. She was one of those people who flare up, angry and eager to retaliate, at the mere suggestion of contempt. There was an element of timidity, too, of course, and inward shame at her own timidity, so it was not strange that her tone kept changing. At one moment it was angry, contemptuous and rough, and at another there was a sincere note of self-condemnation. Sometimes she spoke as though she were taking a desperate plunge; as though she felt, "I don't care what happens, I'll say it..." Apropos of her acquaintance with Fyodor Pavlovitch, she remarked curtly, "That's all nonsense, and was it my fault that he would pester me?" But a minute later she added, "It was all my fault. I was laughing at them both--at the old man and at him, too--and I brought both of them to this. It was all on account of me it happened."

Samsonov's name came up somehow. "That's nobody's business," she snapped at once, with a sort of insolent defiance. "He was my benefactor; he took me when I hadn't a shoe to my foot, when my family had turned me out." The President reminded her, though very politely, that she must answer the questions directly, without going off into irrelevant details. Grushenka crimsoned and her eyes flashed.

The envelope with the notes in it she had not seen, but had only heard from "that wicked wretch" that Fyodor Pavlovitch had an envelope with notes for three thousand in it. "But that was all foolishness. I was only laughing. I wouldn't have gone to him for anything."

"To whom are you referring as 'that wicked wretch'?" inquired the prosecutor.

"The lackey, Smerdyakov, who murdered his master and hanged himself last night."

She was, of course, at once asked what ground she had for such a definite accusation; but it appeared that she, too, had no grounds for it.

"Dmitri Fyodorovitch told me so himself; you can believe him. The woman who came between us has ruined him; she is the cause of it all, let me tell you," Grushenka added. She seemed to be quivering with hatred, and there was a vindictive note in her voice.

She was again asked to whom she was referring.

"The young lady, Katerina Ivanovna there. She sent for me, offered me chocolate, tried to fascinate me. There's not much true shame about her, I can tell you that..."

At this point the President checked her sternly, begging her to moderate her language. But the jealous woman's heart was burning, and she did not care what she did.

"When the prisoner was arrested at Mokroe," the prosecutor asked, "everyone saw and heard you run out of the next room and cry out: 'It's all my fault. We'll go to Siberia together!' So you already believed him to have murdered his father?"

"I don't remember what I felt at the time," answered Grushenka. "Everyone was crying out that he had killed his father, and I felt that it was my fault, that it was on my account he had murdered him. But when he said he wasn't guilty, I believed him at once, and I believe him now and always shall believe him. He is not the man to tell a lie."

Fetyukovitch began his cross-examination. I remember that among other things he asked about Rakitin and the twenty-five roubles "you paid him for bringing Alexey Fyodorovitch Karamazov to see you."

"There was nothing strange about his taking the money," sneered Grushenka, with angry contempt. "He was always coming to me for money: he used to get thirty roubles a month at least out of me, chiefly for luxuries: he had enough to keep him without my help."

"What led you to be so liberal to Mr. Rakitin?" Fetyukovitch asked, in spite of an uneasy movement on the part of the President.

"Why, he is my cousin. His mother was my mother's sister. But he's always besought me not to tell anyone here of it, he is so dreadfully ashamed of me."

This fact was a complete surprise to everyone; no one in the town nor in the monastery, not even Mitya, knew of it. I was told that Rakitin turned purple with shame where he sat. Grushenka had somehow heard before she came into the court that he had given evidence against Mitya, and so she was angry. The whole effect on the public, of Rakitin's speech, of his noble sentiments, of his attacks upon serfdom and the political disorder of Russia, was this time finally ruined. Fetyukovitch was satisfied: it was another godsend. Grushenka's cross-examination did not last long and, of course, there could be nothing particularly new in her evidence. She left a very disagreeable impression on the public; hundreds of contemptuous eyes were fixed upon her, as she finished giving her evidence and sat down again in the court, at a good distance from Katerina Ivanovna. Mitya was silent throughout her evidence. He sat as though turned to stone, with his eyes fixed on the ground.

Ivan was called to give evidence.

I MAY note that he had been called before Alyosha. But the usher of the court announced to the President that, owing to an attack of illness or some sort of fit, the witness could not appear at the moment, but was ready to give his evidence as soon as he recovered. But no one seemed to have heard it and it only came out later.

His entrance was for the first moment almost unnoticed. The principal witnesses, especially the two rival ladies, had already been questioned. Curiosity was satisfied for the time; the public was feeling almost fatigued. Several more witnesses were still to be heard, who probably had little information to give after all that had been given. Time was passing. Ivan walked up with extraordinary slowness, looking at no one, and with his head bowed, as though plunged in gloomy thought. He was irreproachably dressed, but his face made a painful impression, on me at least: there was an earthy look in it, a look like a dying man's. His eyes were lustreless; he raised them and looked slowly round the court. Alyosha jumped up from his seat and moaned "Ah!" I remember that, but it was hardly noticed.

The President began by informing him that he was a witness not on oath, that he might answer or refuse to answer, but that, of course, he must bear witness according to his conscience, and so on, and so on. Ivan listened and looked at him blankly, but his face gradually relaxed into a smile, and as soon as the President, looking at him in astonishment, finished, he laughed outright.

"Well, and what else?" he asked in a loud voice.

There was a hush in the court; there was a feeling of something strange. The President showed signs of uneasiness.

"You...are perhaps still unwell?" he began, looking everywhere for the usher.

"Don't trouble yourself, your excellency, I am well enough and can tell you something interesting," Ivan answered with sudden calmness and respectfulness.

"You have some special communication to make?" the President went on, still mistrustfully.

Ivan looked down, waited a few seconds and, raising his head, answered, almost stammering:

"No...I haven't. I have nothing particular."

They began asking him questions. He answered, as it were, reluctantly, with extreme brevity, with a sort of disgust which grew more and more marked, though he answered rationally. To many questions he answered that he did not know. He knew nothing of his father's money relations with Dmitri. "I wasn't interested in the subject," he added. Threats to murder his father he had heard from the prisoner. Of the money in the envelope he had heard from Smerdyakov.

"The same thing over and over again," he interrupted suddenly, with a look of weariness. "I have nothing particular to tell the court."

"I see you are unwell and understand your feelings," the President began.

He turned to the prosecutor and the counsel for the defence to invite them to examine the witness, if necessary, when Ivan suddenly asked in an exhausted voice:

"Let me go, your excellency, I feel very ill."

And with these words, without waiting for permission, he turned to walk out of the court. But after taking four steps he stood still, as though he had reached a decision, smiled slowly, and went back.

"I am like the peasant girl, your excellency...you know. How does it go? 'I'll stand up if I like, and I won't if I don't.' They were trying to put on her sarafan to take her to church to be married, and she said, 'I'll stand up if I like, and I won't if I don't.'...It's in some book about the peasantry."

"What do you mean by that?" the President asked severely.

"Why, this," Ivan suddenly pulled out a roll of notes. "Here's the money...the notes that lay in that envelope" (he nodded towards the table on which lay the material evidence), "for the sake of which our father was murdered. Where shall I put them? Mr. Superintendent, take them."

The usher of the court took the whole roll and handed it to the President.

"How could this money have come into your possession if it is the same money?" the President asked wonderingly.

"I got them from Smerdyakov, from the murderer, yesterday...I was with him just before he hanged himself. It was he, not my brother, killed our father. He murdered him and I incited him to do it...Who doesn't desire his father's death?"

"Are you in your right mind?" broke involuntarily from the President.

"I should think I am in my right mind...in the same nasty mind as all of you...as all these...ugly faces." He turned suddenly to the audience. "My father has been murdered and they pretend they are horrified," he snarled, with furious contempt. "They keep up the sham with one another. Liars! They all desire the death of their fathers. One reptile devours another...If there hadn't been a murder, they'd have been angry and gone home ill-humoured. It's a spectacle they want! Panem et circenses.* Though I am one to talk! Have you any water? Give me a drink for Christ's sake!" He suddenly clutched his head.

* Bread and circuses.

The usher at once approached him. Alyosha jumped up and cried, "He is ill. Don't believe him: he has brain fever." Katerina Ivanovna rose impulsively from her seat and, rigid with horror, gazed at Ivan. Mitya stood up and greedily looked at his brother and listened to him with a wild, strange smile.

"Don't disturb yourselves. I am not mad, I am only a murderer," Ivan began again. "You can't expect eloquence from a murderer," he added suddenly for some reason and laughed a queer laugh.

The prosecutor bent over to the President in obvious dismay. The two other judges communicated in agitated whispers. Fetyukovitch pricked up his ears as he listened: the hall was hushed in expectation. The President seemed suddenly to recollect himself.

"Witness, your words are incomprehensible and impossible here. Calm yourself, if you can, and tell your story...if you really have something to tell. How can you confirm your statement...if indeed you are not delirious?"

"That's just it. I have no proof. That cur Smerdyakov won't send you proofs from the other world...in an envelope. You think of nothing but envelopes--one is enough. I've no witnesses...except one, perhaps," he smiled thoughtfully.

"Who is your witness?"

"He has a tail, your excellency, and that would be irregular! Le diable n'existe point! Don't pay attention: he is a paltry, pitiful devil," he added suddenly. He ceased laughing and spoke as it were, confidentially. "He is here somewhere, no doubt--under that table with the material evidence on it, perhaps. Where should he sit if not there? You see, listen to me. I told him I don't want to keep quiet, and he talked about the geological cataclysm...idiocy! Come, release the monster...he's been singing a hymn. That's because his heart is light! It's like a drunken man in the street bawling how 'Vanka went to Petersburg,' and I would give a quadrillion quadrillions for two seconds of joy. You don't know me! Oh, how stupid all this business is! Come, take me instead of him! I didn't come for nothing...Why, why is everything so stupid?..."

And he began slowly, and as it were reflectively, looking round him again. But the court was all excitement by now. Alyosha rushed towards him, but the court usher had already seized Ivan by the arm.

"What are you about?" he cried, staring into the man's face, and suddenly seizing him by the shoulders, he flung him violently to the floor. But the police were on the spot and he was seized. He screamed furiously. And all the time he was being removed, he yelled and screamed something incoherent.

The whole court was thrown into confusion. I don't remember everything as it happened. I was excited myself and could not follow. I only know that afterwards, when everything was quiet again and everyone understood what had happened, the court usher came in for a reprimand, though he very reasonably explained that the witness had been quite well, that the doctor had seen him an hour ago, when he had a slight attack of giddiness, but that, until he had come into the court, he had talked quite consecutively, so that nothing could have been foreseen--that he had, in fact, insisted on giving evidence. But before everyone had completely regained their composure and recovered from this scene, it was followed by another. Katerina Ivanovna had an attack of hysterics. She sobbed, shrieking loudly, but refused to leave the court, struggled, and besought them not to remove her. Suddenly she cried to the President:

"There is more evidence I must give at once ...at once! Here is a document, a letter...take it, read it quickly, quickly! It's a letter from that monster...that man there, there!" she pointed to Mitya. "It was he killed his father, you will see that directly. He wrote to me how he would kill his father! But the other one is ill, he is ill, he is delirious!" she kept crying out, beside herself.

The court usher took the document she held out to the President, and she, dropping into her chair, hiding her face in her hands, began convulsively and noiselessly sobbing, shaking all over, and stifling every sound for fear she should be ejected from the court. The document she had handed up was that letter Mitya had written at the Metropolis tavern, which Ivan had spoken of as a "mathematical proof." Alas! its mathematical conclusiveness was recognised, and had it not been for that letter, Mitya might have escaped his doom or, at least, that doom would have been less terrible. It was, I repeat, difficult to notice every detail. What followed is still confused to my mind. The President must, I suppose, have at once passed on the document to the judges, the jury, and the lawyers on both sides. I only remember how they began examining the witness. On being gently asked by the President whether she had recovered sufficiently, Katerina Ivanovna exclaimed impetuously:

"I am ready, I am ready! I am quite equal to answering you," she added, evidently still afraid that she would somehow be prevented from giving evidence. She was asked to explain in detail what this letter was and under what circumstances she received it.

"I received it the day before the crime was committed, but he wrote it the day before that, at the tavern--that is, two days before he committed the crime. Look, it is written on some sort of bill!" she cried breathlessly. "He hated me at that time, because he had behaved contemptibly and was running after that creature ...and because he owed me that three thousand...Oh! he was humiliated by that three thousand on account of his own meanness! This is how it happened about that three thousand. I beg you, I beseech you, to hear me. Three weeks before he murdered his father, he came to me one morning. I knew he was in want of money, and what he wanted it for. Yes, yes--to win that creature and carry her off. I knew then that he had been false to me and meant to abandon me, and it was I, I, who gave him that money, who offered it to him on the pretext of his sending it to my sister in Moscow. And as I gave it him, I looked him in the face and said that he could send it when he liked, 'in a month's time would do.' How, how could he have failed to understand that I was practically telling him to his face, 'You want money to be false to me with your creature, so here's the money for you. I give it to you myself. Take it, if you have so little honour as to take it!' I wanted to prove what he was, and what happened? He took it, he took it, and squandered it with that creature in one night...But he knew, he knew that I knew all about it. I assure you he understood, too, that I gave him that money to test him, to see whether he was so lost to all sense of honour as to take it from me. I looked into his eyes and he looked into mine, and he understood it all and he took it--he carried off my money!"

"That's true, Katya," Mitya roared suddenly, "I looked into your eyes and I knew that you were dishonouring me, and yet I took your money. Despise me as a scoundrel, despise me, all of you! I've deserved it!"

"Prisoner," cried the President, "another word and I will order you to be removed."

"That money was a torment to him," Katya went on with impulsive haste. "He wanted to repay it me. He wanted to, that's true; but he needed money for that creature, too. So he murdered his father, but he didn't repay me, and went off with her to that village where he was arrested. There, again, he squandered the money he had stolen after the murder of his father. And a day before the murder he wrote me this letter. He was drunk when he wrote it. I saw it at once, at the time. He wrote it from spite, and feeling certain, positively certain, that I should never show it to anyone, even if he did kill him, or else he wouldn't have written it. For he knew I shouldn't want to revenge myself and ruin him! But read it, read it attentively--more attentively, please--and you will see that he had described it all in his letter, all beforehand, how he would kill his father and where his money was kept. Look, please, don't overlook that, there's one phrase there, 'I shall kill him as soon as Ivan has gone away.' he thought it all out beforehand how he would kill him," Katerina Ivanovna pointed out to the court with venomous and malignant triumph. Oh! it was clear she had studied every line of that letter and detected every meaning underlining it. "If he hadn't been drunk, he wouldn't have written to me; but, look, everything is written there beforehand, just as he committed the murder after. A complete programme of it!" she exclaimed frantically.

She was reckless now of all consequences to herself, though, no doubt, she had foreseen them even a month ago, for even then, perhaps, shaking with anger, she had pondered whether to show it at the trial or not. Now she had taken the fatal plunge. I remember that the letter was read aloud by the clerk, directly afterwards, I believe. It made an overwhelming impression. They asked Mitya whether he admitted having written the letter.

"It's mine, mine!" cried Mitya. "I shouldn't have written it if I hadn't been drunk!...We've hated each other for many things, Katya, but I swear, I swear I loved you even while I hated you, and you didn't love me!"

He sank back on his seat, wringing his hands in despair. The prosecutor and counsel for the defence began cross-examining her, chiefly to ascertain what had induced her to conceal such a document and to give her evidence in quite a different tone and spirit just before.

"Yes, yes. I was telling lies just now. I was lying against my honour and my conscience, but I wanted to save him, for he has hated and despised me so!" Katya cried madly. "Oh, he has despised me horribly, he has always despised me, and do you know, he has despised me from the very moment that I bowed down to him for that money. I saw that...I felt it at once at the time, but for a long time I wouldn't believe it. How often I have read it in his eyes, 'You came of yourself, though.' Oh, he didn't understand, he had no idea why I ran to him, he can suspect nothing but baseness, he judged me by himself, he thought everyone was like himself!" Katya hissed furiously, in a perfect frenzy. "And he only wanted to marry me, because I'd inherited a fortune, because of that, because of that! I always suspected it was because of that! Oh, he is a brute! He was always convinced that I should be trembling with shame all my life before him, because I went to him then, and that he had a right to despise me forever for it, and so to be superior to me--that's why he wanted to marry me! That's so, that's all so! I tried to conquer him by my love--a love that knew no bounds. I even tried to forgive his faithlessness; but he understood nothing, nothing! How could he understand indeed? He is a monster! I only received that letter the next evening: it was brought me from the tavern--and only that morning, only that morning I wanted to forgive him everything, everything--even his treachery!"

The President and the prosecutor, of course, tried to calm her. I can't help thinking that they felt ashamed of taking advantage of her hysteria and of listening to such avowals. I remember hearing them say to her, "We understand how hard it is for you; be sure we are able to feel for you," and so on, and so on. And yet they dragged the evidence out of the raving, hysterical woman. She described at last with extraordinary clearness, which is so often seen, though only for a moment, in such overwrought states, how Ivan had been nearly driven out of his mind during the last two months trying to save "the monster and murderer," his brother.

"He tortured himself," she exclaimed, "he was always trying to minimise his brother's guilt and confessing to me that he, too, had never loved his father, and perhaps desired his death himself. Oh, he has a tender, over-tender conscience! He tormented himself with his conscience! He told me everything, everything! He came every day and talked to me as his only friend. I have the honour to be his only friend!" she cried suddenly with a sort of defiance, and her eyes flashed. "He had been twice to see Smerdyakov. One day he came to me and said, 'If it was not my brother, but Smerdyakov committed the murder' (for the legend was circulating everywhere that Smerdyakov had done it), 'perhaps I too am guilty, for Smerdyakov knew I didn't like my father and perhaps believed that I desired my father's death.' Then I brought out that letter and showed it him. He was entirely convinced that his brother had done it, and he was overwhelmed by it. He couldn't endure the thought that his own brother was a parricide! Only a week ago I saw that it was making him ill. During the last few days he has talked incoherently in my presence. I saw his mind was giving way. He walked about, raving; he was seen muttering in the streets. The doctor from Moscow, at my request, examined him the day before yesterday and told me that he was on the eve of brain fever--and all on his account, on account of this monster! And last night he learnt that Smerdyakov was dead! It was such a shock that it drove him out of his mind...and all through this monster, all for the sake of saving the monster!"

Oh, of course, such an outpouring, such an avowal is only possible once in a lifetime--at the hour of death, for instance, on the way to the scaffold! But it was in Katya's character, and it was such a moment in her life. It was the same impetuous Katya who had thrown herself on the mercy of a young profligate to save her father; the same Katya who had just before, in her pride and chastity, sacrificed herself and her maidenly modesty before all these people, telling of Mitya's generous conduct, in the hope of softening his fate a little. And now, again, she sacrificed herself; but this time it was for another, and perhaps only now--perhaps only at this moment--she felt and knew how dear that other was to her! She had sacrificed herself in terror for him; conceiving all of a sudden that he had ruined himself by his confession that it was he who had committed the murder, not his brother, she had sacrificed herself to save him, to save his good name, his reputation!

And yet one terrible doubt occurred to one--was she lying in her description of her former relations with Mitya?--that was the question. No, she had not intentionally slandered him when she cried that Mitya despised her for her bowing down to him! She believed it herself. She had been firmly convinced, perhaps ever since that bow, that the simplehearted Mitya, who even then adored her, was laughing at her and despising her. She had loved him with an hysterical, "lacerated" love only from pride, from wounded pride, and that love was not like love, but more like revenge. Oh! perhaps that lacerated love would have grown into real love, perhaps Katya longed for nothing more than that, but Mitya's faithlessness had wounded her to the bottom of her heart, and her heart could not forgive him. The moment of revenge had come upon her suddenly, and all that had been accumulating so long and so painfully in the offended woman's breast burst out all at once and unexpectedly. She betrayed Mitya, but she betrayed herself, too. And no sooner had she given full expression to her feelings than the tension of course was over and she was overwhelmed with shame. Hysterics began again: she fell on the floor, sobbing and screaming. She was carried out. At that moment Grushenka, with a wail, rushed towards Mitya before they had time to prevent her.

"Mitya," she wailed, "your serpent has destroyed you! There, she has shown you what she is!" she shouted to the judges, shaking with anger. At a signal from the President they seized her and tried to remove her from the court. She wouldn't allow it. She fought and struggled to get back to Mitya. Mitya uttered a cry and struggled to get to her. He was overpowered.

Yes, I think the ladies who came to see the spectacle must have been satisfied--the show had been a varied one. Then I remember the Moscow doctor appeared on the scene. I believe the President had previously sent the court usher to arrange for medical aid for Ivan. The doctor announced to the court that the sick man was suffering from a dangerous attack of brain fever, and that he must be at once removed. In answer to questions from the prosecutor and the counsel for the defence he said that the patient had come to him of his own accord the day before yesterday and that he had warned him that he had such an attack coming on, but he had not consented to be looked after. "He was certainly not in a normal state of mind: he told me himself that he saw visions when he was awake, that he met several persons in the street, who were dead, and that Satan visited him every evening," said the doctor, in conclusion. Having given his evidence, the celebrated doctor withdrew. The letter produced by Katerina Ivanovna was added to the material proofs. After some deliberation, the judges decided to proceed with the trial and to enter both the unexpected pieces of evidence (given by Ivan and Katerina Ivanovna) on the protocol.

But I will not detail the evidence of the other witnesses, who only repeated and confirmed what had been said before, though all with their characteristic peculiarities. I repeat, all was brought together in the prosecutor's speech, which I shall quote immediately. Everyone was excited, everyone was electrified by the late catastrophe, and all were awaiting the speeches for the prosecution and the defence with intense impatience. Fetyukovitch was obviously shaken by Katerina Ivanovna's evidence. But the prosecutor was triumphant. When all the evidence had been taken, the court was adjourned for almost an hour. I believe it was just eight o'clock when the President returned to his seat and our prosecutor, Ippolit Kirillovitch, began his speech.

Chapter 6. The Prosecutor's Speech. Sketches of Character

IPPOLIT KIRILLOVITCH began his speech, trembling with nervousness, with cold sweat on his forehead, feeling hot and cold all over by turns. He described this himself afterwards. He regarded this speech as his chef-d'oeuvre, the chef-d'oeuvre of his whole life, as his swan-song. He died, it is true, nine months later of rapid consumption, so that he had the right, as it turned out, to compare himself to a swan singing his last song. He had put his whole heart and all the brain he had into that speech. And poor Ippolit Kirillovitch unexpectedly revealed that at least some feeling for the public welfare and "the eternal question" lay concealed in him. Where his speech really excelled was in its sincerity. He genuinely believed in the prisoner's guilt; he was accusing him not as an official duty only, and in calling for vengeance he quivered with a genuine passion "for the security of society." Even the ladies in thee audience, though they remained hostile to Ippolit Kirillovitch, admitted that he made an extraordinary impression on them. He began in a breaking voice, but it soon gained strength and filled the court to the end of his speech. But as soon as he had finished, he almost fainted.

"Gentlemen of the jury," began the prosecutor, "this case has made a stir throughout Russia. But what is there to wonder at, what is there so peculiarly horrifying in it for us? We are so accustomed to such crimes! That's what's so horrible, that such dark deeds have ceased to horrify us. What ought to horrify us is that we are so accustomed to it, and not this or that isolated crime. What are the causes of our indifference, our lukewarm attitude to such deeds, to such signs of the times, ominous of an unenviable future? Is it our cynicism, is it the premature exhaustion of intellect and imagination in a society that is sinking into decay, in spite of its youth? Is it that our moral principles are shattered to their foundations, or is it, perhaps, a complete lack of such principles among us? I cannot answer such questions; nevertheless they are disturbing, and every citizen not only must, but ought to be harassed by them. Our newborn and still timid press has done good service to the public already, for without it we should never have heard of the horrors of unbridled violence and moral degradation which are continually made known by the press, not merely to those who attend the new jury courts established in the present reign, but to everyone. And what do we read almost daily? Of things beside which the present case grows pale, and seems almost commonplace. But what is most important is that the majority of our national crimes of violence bear witness to a widespread evil, now so general among us that it is difficult to contend against it.

"One day we see a brilliant young officer of high society, at the very outset of his career, in a cowardly underhand way, without a pang of conscience, murdering an official who had once been his benefactor, and the servant girl, to steal his own I O U and what ready money he could find on him; 'it will come in handy for my pleasures in the fashionable world and for my career in the future.' After murdering them, he puts pillows under the head of each of his victims; he goes away. Next, a young hero 'decorated for bravery' kills the mother of his chief and benefactor, like a highwayman, and to urge his companions to join him he asserts that 'she loves him like a son, and so will follow all his directions and take no precautions.' Granted that he is a monster, yet I dare not say in these days that he is unique. Another man will not commit the murder, but will feel and think like him, and is as dishonourable in soul. In silence, alone with his conscience, he asks himself perhaps, 'What is honour, and isn't the condemnation of bloodshed a prejudice?'

"Perhaps people will cry out against me that I am morbid, hysterical, that it is a monstrous slander, that I am exaggerating. Let them say so--and heavens! I should be the first to rejoice if it were so! Oh, don't believe me, think of me as morbid, but remember my words; if only a tenth, if only a twentieth part of what I say is true-- even so it's awful! Look how our young people commit suicide, without asking themselves Hamlet's question what there is beyond, without a sign of such a question, as though all that relates to the soul and to what awaits us beyond the grave had long been erased in their minds and buried under the sands. Look at our vice, at our profligates. Fyodor Pavlovitch, the luckless victim in the present case, was almost an innocent babe compared with many of them. And yet we all knew him, 'he lived among us!'...

"Yes, one day perhaps the leading intellects of Russia and of Europe will study the psychology of Russian crime, for the subject is worth it. But this study will come later, at leisure, when all the tragic topsy-turvydom of to-day is farther behind us, so that it's possible to examine it with more insight and more impartiality than I can do. Now we are either horrified or pretend to be horrified, though we really gloat over the spectacle, and love strong and eccentric sensations which tickle our cynical, pampered idleness. Or, like little children, we brush the dreadful ghosts away and hide our heads in the pillow so as to return to our sports and merriment as soon as they have vanished. But we must one day begin life in sober earnest, we must look at ourselves as a society; it's time we tried to grasp something of our social position, or at least to make a beginning in that direction.

"A great writer* of the last epoch, comparing Russia to a swift troika galloping to an unknown goal, exclaims, 'Oh, troika, birdlike troika, who invented thee!' and adds, in proud ecstasy, that all the peoples of the world stand aside respectfully to make way for the recklessly galloping troika to pass. That may be, they may stand aside, respectfully or no, but in my poor opinion the great writer ended his book in this way either in an excess of childish and naive optimism, or simply in fear of the censorship of the day. For if the troika were drawn by his heroes, Sobakevitch, Nozdryov, Tchitchikov, it could reach no rational goal, whoever might be driving it. And those were the heroes of an older generation, ours are worse specimens still..."

* Gogol.

At this point Ippolit Kirillovitch's speech was interrupted by applause. The liberal significance of this simile was appreciated. The applause was, it's true, of brief duration, so that the President did not think it necessary to caution the public, and only looked severely in the direction of the offenders. But Ippolit Kirillovitch was encouraged; he had never been applauded before! He had been all his life unable to get a hearing, and now he suddenly had an opportunity of securing the ear of all Russia.

"What, after all, is this Karamazov family, which has gained such an unenviable notoriety throughout Russia?" he continued. "Perhaps I am exaggerating, but it seems to me that certain fundamental features of the educated class of to-day are reflected in this family picture--only, of course, in miniature, 'like the sun in a drop of water.' Think of that unhappy, vicious, unbridled old man, who has met with such a melancholy end, the head of a family! Beginning life of noble birth, but in a poor dependent position, through an unexpected marriage he came into a small fortune. A petty knave, a toady and buffoon, of fairly good, though undeveloped, intelligence, he was, above all, a moneylender, who grew bolder with growing prosperity. His abject and servile characteristics disappeared, his, malicious and sarcastic cynicism was all that remained. On the spiritual side he was undeveloped, while his vitality was excessive. He saw nothing in life but sensual pleasure, and he brought his children up to be the same. He had no feelings for his duties as a father. He ridiculed those duties. He left his little children to the servants, and was glad to be rid of them, forgot about them completely. The old man's maxim was Apres moi le deluge.* He was an example of everything that is opposed to civic duty, of the most complete and malignant individualism. 'The world may burn for aught I care, so long as I am all right,' and he was all right; he was content, he was eager to go on living in the same way for another twenty or thirty years. He swindled his own son and spent his money, his maternal inheritance, on trying to get his mistress from him. No, I don't intend to leave the prisoner's defence altogether to my talented colleague from Petersburg. I will speak the truth myself, I can well understand what resentment he had heaped up in his son's heart against him.

* After me, the deluge.

"But enough, enough of that unhappy old man; he has paid the penalty. Let us remember, however, that he was a father, and one of the typical fathers of to-day. Am I unjust, indeed, in saying that he is typical of many modern fathers? Alas! many of them only differ in not openly professing such cynicism, for they are better educated, more cultured, but their philosophy is essentially the same as his. Perhaps I am a pessimist, but you have agreed to forgive me. Let us agree beforehand, you need not believe me, but let me speak. Let me say what I have to say, and remember something of my words.

"Now for the children of this father, this head of a family. One of them is the prisoner before us, all the rest of my speech will deal with him. Of the other two I will speak only cursorily.

"The elder is one of those modern young men of brilliant education and vigorous intellect, who has lost all faith in everything. He has denied and rejected much already, like his father. We have all heard him, he was a welcome guest in local society. He never concealed his opinions, quite the contrary in fact, which justifies me in speaking rather openly of him now, of course, not as an individual, but as a member of the Karamazov family. Another personage closely connected with the case died here by his own hand last night. I mean an afflicted idiot, formerly the servant, and possibly the illegitimate son, of Fyodor Pavlovitch, Smerdyakov. At the preliminary inquiry, he told me with hysterical tears how the young Ivan Karamazov had horrified him by his spiritual audacity. 'Everything in the world is lawful according to him, and nothing must be forbidden in the future--that is what he always taught me.' I believe that idiot was driven out of his mind by this theory, though, of course, the epileptic attacks from which he suffered, and this terrible catastrophe, have helped to unhinge his faculties. But he dropped one very interesting observation, which would have done credit to a more intelligent observer, and that is, indeed, why I've mentioned it: 'If there is one of the sons that is like Fyodor Pavlovitch in character, it is Ivan Fyodorovitch.'

"With that remark I conclude my sketch of his character, feeling it indelicate to continue further. Oh, I don't want to draw any further conclusions and croak like a raven over the young man's future. We've seen to-day in this court that there are still good impulses in his young heart, that family feeling has not been destroyed in him by lack of faith and cynicism, which have come to him rather by inheritance than by the exercise of independent thought.

"Then the third son. Oh, he is a devout and modest youth, who does not share his elder brother's gloomy and destructive theory of life. He has sought to cling to the 'ideas of the people,' or to what goes by that name in some circles of our intellectual classes. He clung to the monastery, and was within an ace of becoming a monk. He seems to me to have betrayed unconsciously, and so early, that timid despair which leads so many in our unhappy society, who dread cynicism and its corrupting influences, and mistakenly attribute all the mischief to European enlightenment, to return to their 'native soil,' as they say, to the bosom, so to speak, of their mother earth, like frightened children, yearning to fall asleep on the withered bosom of their decrepit mother, and to sleep there for ever, only to escape the horrors that terrify them.

"For my part I wish the excellent and gifted young man every success; I trust that youthful idealism and impulse towards the ideas of the people may never degenerate, as often happens, on the moral side into gloomy mysticism, and on the political into blind chauvinism--two elements which are even a greater menace to Russia than the premature decay, due to misunderstanding and gratuitous adoption of European ideas, from which his elder brother is suffering."

Two or three people clapped their hands at the mention of chauvinism and mysticism. Ippolit Kirillovitch had been, indeed, carried away by his own eloquence. All this had little to do with the case in hand, to say nothing of the fact of its being somewhat vague, but the sickly and consumptive man was overcome by the desire to express himself once in his life. People said afterwards that he was actuated by unworthy motives in his criticism of Ivan, because the latter had on one or two occasions got the better of him in argument, and Ippolit Kirillovitch, remembering it, tried now to take his revenge. But I don't know whether it was true. All this was only introductory, however, and the speech passed to more direct consideration of the case.

"But to return to the eldest son," Ippolit Kirillovitch went on. "He is the prisoner before us. We have his life and his actions, too, before us; the fatal day has come and all has been brought to the surface. While his brothers seem to stand for 'Europeanism' and 'the principles of the people,' he seems to represent Russia as she is. Oh, not all Russia, not all! God preserve us, if it were! Yet, here we have her, our mother Russia, the very scent and sound of her. Oh, he is spontaneous, he is a marvellous mingling of good and evil, he is a lover of culture and Schiller, yet he brawls in taverns and plucks out the beards of his boon companions. Oh, he, too, can be good and noble, but only when all goes well with him. What is more, he can be carried off his feet, positively carried off his feet by noble ideals, but only if they come of themselves, if they fall from heaven for him, if they need not be paid for. He dislikes paying for anything, but is very fond of receiving, and that's so with him in everything. Oh, give him every possible good in life (he couldn't be content with less), and put no obstacle in his way, and he will show that he, too, can be noble. He is not greedy, no, but he must have money, a great deal of money, and you will see how generously, with what scorn of filthy lucre, he will fling it all away in the reckless dissipation of one night. But if he has not money, he will show what he is ready to do to get it when he is in great need of it. But all this later, let us take events in their chronological order.

"First, we have before us a poor abandoned child, running about the back-yard 'without boots on his feet,' as our worthy and esteemed fellow citizen, of foreign origin, alas! expressed it just now. I repeat it again, I yield to no one the defence of the criminal. I am here to accuse him, but to defend him also. Yes, I, too, am human; I, too, can weigh the influence of home and childhood on the character. But the boy grows up and becomes an officer; for a duel and other reckless conduct he is exiled to one of the remote frontier towns of Russia. There he led a wild life as an officer. And, of course, he needed money, money before all things, and so after prolonged disputes he came to a settlement with his father, and the last six thousand was sent him. A letter is in existence in which he practically gives up his claim to the rest and settles his conflict with his father over the inheritance on the payment of this six thousand.

"Then came his meeting with a young girl of lofty character and brilliant education. Oh, I do not venture to repeat the details; you have only just heard them. Honour, self-sacrifice were shown there, and I will be silent. The figure of the young officer, frivolous and profligate, doing homage to true nobility and a lofty ideal, was shown in a very sympathetic light before us. But the other side of the medal was unexpectedly turned to us immediately after in this very court. Again I will not venture to conjecture why it happened so, but there were causes. The same lady, bathed in tears of long-concealed indignation, alleged that he, he of all men, had despised her for her action, which, though incautious, reckless perhaps, was still dictated by lofty and generous motives. He, he, the girl's betrothed, looked at her with that smile of mockery, which was more insufferable from him than from anyone. And knowing that he had already deceived her (he had deceived her, believing that she was bound to endure everything from him, even treachery), she intentionally offered him three thousand roubles, and clearly, too clearly, let him understand that she was offering him money to deceive her. 'Well, will you take it or not, are you so lost to shame?' was the dumb question in her scrutinising eyes. He looked at her, saw clearly what was in her mind (he's admitted here before you that he understood it all), appropriated that three thousand unconditionally, and squandered it in two days with the new object of his affections.

"What are we to believe then? The first legend of the young officer sacrificing his last farthing in a noble impulse of generosity and doing reverence to virtue, or this other revolting picture? As a rule, between two extremes one has to find the mean, but in the present case this is not true. The probability is that in the first case he was genuinely noble, and in the second as genuinely base. And why? Because he was of the broad Karamazov character--that's just what I am leading up to--capable of combining the most incongruous contradictions, and capable of the greatest heights and of the greatest depths. Remember the brilliant remark made by a young observer who has seen the Karamazov family at close quarters--Mr. Rakitin: 'The sense of their own degradation is as essential to those reckless, unbridled natures as the sense of their lofty generosity.' And that's true, they need continually this unnatural mixture. Two extremes at the same moment, or they are miserable and dissatisfied and their existence is incomplete. They are wide, wide as mother Russia; they include everything and put up with everything.

"By the way, gentlemen of the jury, we've just touched upon that three thousand roubles, and I will venture to anticipate things a little. Can you conceive that a man like that, on receiving that sum and in such a way, at the price of such shame, such disgrace, such utter degradation, could have been capable that very day of setting apart half that sum, that very day, and sewing it up in a little bag, and would have had the firmness of character to carry it about with him for a whole month afterwards, in spite of every temptation and his extreme need of it! Neither in drunken debauchery in taverns, nor when he was flying into the country, trying to get from God knows whom, the money so essential to him to remove the object of his affections from being tempted by his father, did he bring himself to touch that little bag! Why, if only to avoid abandoning his mistress to the rival of whom he was so jealous, he would have been certain to have opened that bag and to have stayed at home to keep watch over her, and to await the moment when she would say to him at last 'I am yours,' and to fly with her far from their fatal surroundings.

"But no, he did not touch his talisman, and what is the reason he gives for it? The chief reason, as I have just said, was that when she would say' I am yours, take me where you will,' he might have the wherewithal to take her. But that first reason, in the prisoner's own words, was of little weight beside the second. While I have that money on me, he said, I am a scoundrel, not a thief, for I can always go to my insulted betrothed, and, laying down half the sum I have fraudulently appropriated, I can always say to her, 'You see, I've squandered half your money, and shown I am a weak and immoral man, and, if you like, a scoundrel' (I use the prisoner's own expressions), 'but though I am a scoundrel, I am not a thief, for if I had been a thief, I shouldn't have brought you back this half of the money, but should have taken it as I did the other half!' A marvellous explanation! This frantic, but weak man, who could not resist the temptation of accepting the three thousand roubles at the price of such disgrace, this very man suddenly develops the most stoical firmness, and carries about a thousand roubles without daring to touch it. Does that fit in at all with the character we have analysed? No, and I venture to tell you how the real Dmitri Karamazov would have behaved in such circumstances, if he really had brought himself to put away the money.

"At the first temptation--for instance, to entertain the woman with whom he had already squandered half the money--he would have unpicked his little bag and have taken out some hundred roubles, for why should he have taken back precisely half the money, that is, fifteen hundred roubles? Why not fourteen hundred? He could just as well have said then that he was not a thief, because he brought back fourteen hundred roubles. Then another time he would have unpicked it again and taken out another hundred, and then a third, and then a fourth, and before the end of the month he would have taken the last note but one, feeling that if he took back only a hundred it would answer the purpose, for a thief would have stolen it all. And then he would have looked at this last note, and have said to himself, 'It's really not worth while to give back one hundred; let's spend that, too!' That's how the real Dmitri Karamazov, as we know him, would have behaved. One cannot imagine anything more incongruous with the actual fact than this legend of the little bag. Nothing could be more inconceivable. But we shall return to that later."

After touching upon what had come out in the proceedings concerning the financial relations of father and son, and arguing again and again that it was utterly impossible, from the facts known, to determine which was in the wrong, Ippolit Kirillovitch passed to the evidence of the medical experts in reference to Mitya's fixed idea about the three thousand owing him.

Chapter 7. An Historical Survey

"THE medical experts have striven to convince us that the prisoner is out of his mind and, in fact, a maniac. I maintain that he is in his right mind, and that if he had not been, he would have behaved more cleverly. As for his being a maniac, that I would agree with, but only in one point, that is, his fixed idea about the three thousand. Yet I think one might find a much simpler cause than his tendency to insanity. For my part I agree thoroughly with the young doctor who maintained that the prisoner's mental faculties have always been normal, and that he has only been irritable and exasperated. The object of the prisoner's continual and violent anger was not the sum itself; there was a special motive at the bottom of it. That motive is jealousy!"

Here Ippolit Kirillovitch described at length the prisoner's fatal passion for Grushenka. He began from the moment when the prisoner went to the "young person's" lodgings "to beat her"--"I use his own expression," the prosecutor explained--"but instead of beating her, he remained there, at her feet. That was the beginning of the passion. At the same time the prisoner's father was captivated by the same young person--a strange and fatal coincidence, for they both lost their hearts to her simultaneously, though both had known her before. And she inspired in both of them the most violent, characteristically Karamazov passion. We have her own confession: 'I was laughing at both of them.' Yes, the sudden desire to make a jest of them came over her, and she conquered both of them at once. The old man, who worshipped money, at once set aside three thousand roubles as a reward for one visit from her, but soon after that, he would have been happy to lay his property and his name at her feet, if only she would become his lawful wife. We have good evidence of this. As for the prisoner, the tragedy of his fate is evident; it is before us. But such was the young person's 'game.' The enchantress gave the unhappy young man no hope until the last moment, when he knelt before her, stretching out hands that were already stained with the blood of his father and rival. It was in that position that he was arrested. 'Send me to Siberia with him, I have brought him to this, I am most to blame,' the woman herself cried, in genuine remorse at the moment of his arrest.

"The talented young man, to whom I have referred already, Mr. Rakitin, characterised this heroine in brief and impressive terms: 'She was disillusioned early in life, deceived and ruined by a betrothed, who seduced and abandoned her. She was left in poverty, cursed by her respectable family and taken under the protection of a wealthy old man, whom she still, however, considers as her benefactor. There was perhaps much that was good in her young heart, but it was embittered too early. She became prudent and saved money. She grew sarcastic and resentful against society.' After this sketch of her character it may well be understood that she might laugh at both of them simply from mischief, from malice.

"After a month of hopeless love and moral degradation, during which he betrayed his betrothed and appropriated money entrusted to his honour, the prisoner was driven almost to frenzy, almost to madness by continual jealousy--and of whom? His father! And the worst of it was that the crazy old man was alluring and enticing the object of his affection by means of that very three thousand roubles, which the son looked upon as his own property, part of his inheritance from his mother, of which his father was cheating him. Yes, I admit it was hard to bear! It might well drive a man to madness. It was not the money, but the fact that this money was used with such revolting cynicism to ruin his happiness!"

Then the prosecutor went on to describe how the idea of murdering his father had entered the prisoner's head, and illustrated his theory with facts.

"At first he only talked about it in taverns--he was talking about it all that month. Ah, he likes being always surrounded with company, and he likes to tell his companions everything, even his most diabolical and dangerous ideas; he likes to share every thought with others, and expects, for some reason, that those he confides in will meet him with perfect sympathy, enter into all his troubles and anxieties, take his part and not oppose him in anything. If not, he flies into a rage and smashes up everything in the tavern. (Then followed the anecdote about Captain Snegiryov.) Those who heard the prisoner began to think at last that he might mean more than threats, and that such a frenzy might turn threats into actions."

Here the prosecutor described the meeting of the family at the monastery, the conversations with Alyosha, and the horrible scene of violence when the prisoner had rushed into his father's house just after dinner.

"I cannot positively assert," the prosecutor continued, "that the prisoner fully intended to murder his father before that incident. Yet the idea had several times presented itself to him, and he had deliberated on it--for that we have facts, witnesses, and his own words. I confess, gentlemen of the jury," he added, "that till to-day I have been uncertain whether to attribute to the prisoner conscious premeditation. I was firmly convinced that he had pictured the fatal moment beforehand, but had only pictured it, contemplating it as a possibility. He had not definitely considered when and how he might commit the crime.

"But I was only uncertain till to-day, till that fatal document was presented to the court just now. You yourselves heard that young lady's exclamation, 'It is the plan, the programme of the murder!' That is how she defined that miserable, drunken letter of the unhappy prisoner. And, in fact, from that letter we see that the whole fact of the murder was premeditated. It was written two days before, and so we know now for a fact that, forty-eight hours before the perpetration of his terrible design, the prisoner swore that, if he could not get money next day, he would murder his father in order to take the envelope with the notes from under his pillow, as soon as Ivan had left. 'As soon as Ivan had gone away'--you hear that; so he had thought everything out, weighing every circumstance, and he carried it all out just as he had written it. The proof of premeditation is conclusive; the crime must have been committed for the sake of the money, that is stated clearly, that is written and signed. The prisoner does not deny his signature.

"I shall be told he was drunk when he wrote it. But that does not diminish the value of the letter, quite the contrary; he wrote when drunk what he had planned when sober. Had he not planned it when sober, he would not have written it when drunk. I shall be asked: Then why did he talk about it in taverns? A man who premeditates such a crime is silent and keeps it to himself. Yes, but he talked about it before he had formed a plan, when he had only the desire, only the impulse to it. Afterwards he talked less about it. On the evening he wrote that letter at the Metropolis tavern, contrary to his custom he was silent, though he had been drinking. He did not play billiards, he sat in a corner, talked to no one. He did indeed turn a shopman out of his seat, but that was done almost unconsciously, because he could never enter a tavern without making a disturbance. It is true that after he had taken the final decision, he must have felt apprehensive that he had talked too much about his design beforehand, and that this might lead to his arrest and prosecution afterwards. But there was nothing for it; he could not take his words back, but his luck had served him before, it would serve him again. He believed in his star, you know! I must confess, too, that he did a great deal to avoid the fatal catastrophe. 'To-morrow I shall try and borrow the money from everyone,' as he writes in his peculiar language,' and if they won't give it to me, there will be bloodshed.'"

Here Ippolit Kirillovitch passed to a detailed description of all Mitya's efforts to borrow the money. He described his visit to Samsonov, his journey to Lyagavy. "Harassed, jeered at, hungry, after selling his watch to pay for the journey (though he tells us he had fifteen hundred roubles on him--a likely story), tortured by jealousy at having left the object of his affections in the town, suspecting that she would go to Fyodor Pavlovitch in his absense, he returned at last to the town, to find, to his joy, that she had not been near his father. He accompanied her himself to her protector. (Strange to say, he doesn't seem to have been jealous of Samsonov, which is psychologically interesting.) Then he hastens back to his ambush in the back gardens, and then learns that Smerdyakov is in a fit, that the other servant is ill--the coast is clear and he knows the 'signals'-- what a temptation! Still he resists it; he goes off to a lady who has for some time been residing in the town, and who is highly esteemed among us, Madame Hohlakov. That lady, who had long watched his career with compassion, gave him the most judicious advice, to give up his dissipated life, his unseemly love-affair, the waste of his youth and vigour in pot-house debauchery, and to set off to Siberia to the gold mines: 'that would be an outlet for your turbulent energies, your romantic character, your thirst for adventure.'"

After describing the result of this conversation and the moment when the prisoner learnt that Grushenka had not remained at Samsonov's, the sudden frenzy of the luckless man worn out with jealousy and nervous exhaustion, at the thought that she had deceived him and was now with his father, Ippolit Kirillovitch concluded by dwelling upon the fatal influence of chance. "Had the maid told him that her mistress was at Mokroe with her former lover, nothing would have happened. But she lost her head, she could only swear and protest her ignorance, and if the prisoner did not kill her on the spot, it was only because he flew in pursuit of his false mistress.

"But note, frantic as he was, he took with him a brass pestle. Why that? Why not some other weapon? But since he had been contemplating his plan and preparing himself for it for a whole month, he would snatch up anything like a weapon that caught his eye. He had realised for a month past that any object of the kind would serve as a weapon, so he instantly, without hesitation, recognised that it would serve his purpose. So it was by no means unconsciously, by no means involuntarily, that he snatched up that fatal pestle. And then we find him in his father's garden--the coast is clear, there are no witnesses, darkness and jealousy. The suspicion that she was there, with him, with his rival, in his arms, and perhaps laughing at him at that moment--took his breath away. And it was not mere suspicion, the deception was open, obvious. She must be there, in that lighted room, she must be behind the screen; and the unhappy man would have us believe that he stole up to the window, peeped respectfully in, and discreetly withdrew, for fear something terrible and immoral should happen. And he tries to persuade us of that, us, who understand his character, who know his state of mind at the moment, and that he knew the signals by which he could at once enter the house." At this point Ippolit Kirillovitch broke off to discuss exhaustively the suspected connection of Smerdyakov with the murder. He did this very circumstantially, and everyone realised that, although he professed to despise that suspicion, he thought the subject of great importance.

Chapter 8. A Treatise on Smerdyakov

"TO begin with, what was the source of this suspicion?" (Ippolit Kirillovitch began). "The first person who cried out that Smerdyakov had committed the murder was the prisoner himself at the moment of his arrest, yet from that time to this he had not brought forward a single fact to confirm the charge, nor the faintest suggestion of a fact. The charge is confirmed by three persons only--the two brothers of the prisoner and Madame Svyetlov. The elder of these brothers expressed his suspicions only to-day, when he was undoubtedly suffering from brain fever. But we know that for the last two months he has completely shared our conviction of his brother's guilt and did not attempt to combat that idea. But of that later. The younger brother has admitted that he has not the slightest fact to support his notion of Smerdyakov's guilt, and has only been led to that conclusion from the prisoner's own words and the expression of his face. Yes, that astounding piece of evidence has been brought forward twice to-day by him. Madame Svyetslov was even more astounding. 'What the prisoner tells you, you must believe; he is not a man to tell a lie.' That is all the evidence against Smerdyakov produced by these three persons. who are all deeply concerned in the prisoner's fate. And yet the theory of Smerdyakov's guilt has been noised about, has been and is still maintained. Is it credible? Is it conceivable?"

Here Ippolit Kirillovitch thought it necessary to describe the personality of Smerdyakov, "who had cut short his life in a fit of insanity." He depicted him as a man of weak intellect, with a smattering of education, who had been thrown off his balance by philosophical ideas above his level and certain modern theories of duty, which he learnt in practice from the reckless life of his master, who was also perhaps his father--Fyodor Pavlovitch; and, theoretically, from various strange philosophical conversations with his master's elder son, Ivan Fyodorovitch, who readily indulged in this diversion, probably feeling dull or wishing to amuse himself at the valet's expense. "He spoke to me himself of his spiritual condition during the last few days at his father's house," Ippolit Kirillovitch explained; "but others too have borne witness to it--the prisoner himself, his brother, and the servant Grigory--that is, all who knew him well.

"Moreover, Smerdyakov, whose health was shaken by his attacks of epilepsy, had not the courage of a chicken. 'He fell at my feet and kissed them,' the prisoner himself has told us, before he realised how damaging such a statement was to himself. 'He is an epileptic chicken,' he declared about him in his characteristic language. And the prisoner chose him for his confidant (we have his own word for it) and he frightened him into consenting at last to act as a spy for him. In that capacity he deceived his master, revealing to the prisoner the existence of the envelope with the notes in it and the signals by means of which he could get into the house. How could he help telling him, indeed? 'He would have killed me, I could see that he would have killed me,' he said at the inquiry, trembling and shaking even before us, though his tormentor was by that time arrested and could do him no harm. 'He suspected me at every instant. In fear and trembling I hastened to tell him every secret to pacify him, that he might see that I had not deceived him and let me off alive.' Those are his own words. I wrote them down and I remember them. 'When he began shouting at me, I would fall on my knees.'

"He was naturally very honest and enjoyed the complete confidence of his master, ever since he had restored him some money he had lost. So it may be supposed that the poor fellow suffered pangs of remorse at having deceived his master, whom he loved as his benefactor. Persons severely afflicted with epilepsy are, so the most skilful doctors tell us, always prone to continual and morbid self-reproach. They worry over their 'wickedness,' they are tormented by pangs of conscience, often entirely without cause; they exaggerate and often invent all sorts of faults and crimes. And here we have a man of that type who had really been driven to wrongdoing by terror and intimidation.

"He had, besides, a strong presentiment that something terrible would be the outcome of the situation that was developing before his eyes. When Ivan Fyodorovitch was leaving for Moscow, just before the catastrophe, Smerdyakov besought him to remain, though he was too timid to tell him plainly what he feared. He confined himself to hints, but his hints were not understood.

"It must be observed that he looked on Ivan Fyodorovitch as a protector, whose presence in the house was a guarantee that no harm would come to pass. Remember the phrase in Dmitri Karamazov's drunken letter, 'I shall kill the old man, if only Ivan goes away.' So Ivan Fyodorovitch's presence seemed to everyone a guarantee of peace and order in the house.

"But he went away, and within an hour of his young master's departure Smerdyakov was taken with an epileptic fit. But that's perfectly intelligible. Here I must mention that Smerdyakov, oppressed by terror and despair of a sort, had felt during those last few days that one of the fits from which he had suffered before at moments of strain, might be coming upon him again. The day and hour of such an attack cannot, of course, be foreseen, but every epileptic can feel beforehand that he is likely to have one. So the doctors tell us. And so, as soon as Ivan Fyodorovitch had driven out of the yard, Smerdyakov, depressed by his lonely and unprotected position, went to the cellar. He went down the stairs wondering if he would have a fit or not, and what if it were to come upon him at once. And that very apprehension, that very wonder, brought on the spasm in his throat that always precedes such attacks, and he fell unconscious into the cellar. And in this perfectly natural occurrence people try to detect a suspicion, a hint that he was shamming an attack on purpose. But, if it were on purpose, the question arises at once, what was his motive? What was he reckoning on? What was he aiming at? I say nothing about medicine: science, I am told, may go astray: the doctors were not able to discriminate between the counterfeit and the real. That may be so, but answer me one question: what motive had he for such a counterfeit? Could he, had he been plotting the murder, have desired to attract the attention of the household by having a fit just before?

"You see, gentlemen of the jury, on the night of the murder, there were five persons in Fyodor Pavlovitch's-- Fyodor Pavlovitch himself (but he did not kill himself, that's evident); then his servant, Grigory, but he was almost killed himself; the third person was Grigory's wife, Marfa Ignatyevna, but it would be simply shameful to imagine her murdering her master. Two persons are left--the prisoner and Smerdyakov. But, if we are to believe the prisoner's statement that he is not the murderer, then Smerdyakov must have been, for there is no other alternative, no one else can be found. That is what accounts for the artful, astounding accusation against the unhappy idiot who committed suicide yesterday. Had a shadow of suspicion rested on anyone else, had there been any sixth person, I am persuaded that even the prisoner would have been ashamed to accuse Smerdyakov, and would have accused that sixth person, for to charge Smerdyakov with that murder is perfectly absurd.

"Gentlemen, let us lay aside psychology, let us lay aside medicine, let us even lay aside logic, let us turn only to the facts and see what the facts tell us. If Smerdyakov killed him, how did he do it? Alone or with the assistance of the prisoner? Let us consider the first alternative--that he did it alone. If he had killed him it must have been with some object, for some advantage to himself. But not having a shadow of the motive that the prisoner had for the murder--hatred, jealousy, and so on--Smerdyakov could only have murdered him for the sake of gain, in order to appropriate the three thousand roubles he had seen his master put in the envelope. And yet he tells another person--and a person most closely interested, that is, the prisoner--everything about the money and the signals, where the envelope lay, what was written on it, what it was tied up with, and, above all, told him of those signals by which he could enter the house. Did he do this simply to betray himself, or to invite to the same enterprise one who would be anxious to get that envelope for himself? 'Yes,' I shall be told, 'but he betrayed it from fear.' But how do you explain this? A man who could conceive such an audacious, savage act, and carry it out, tells facts which are known to no one else in the world, and which, if he held his tongue, no one would ever have guessed!

"No, however cowardly he might be, if he had plotted such a crime, nothing would have induced him to tell anyone about the envelope and the signals, for that was as good as betraying himself beforehand. He would have invented something, he would have told some lie if he had been forced to give information, but he would have been silent about that. For, on the other hand, if he had said nothing about the money, but had committed the murder and stolen the money, no one in the world could have charged him with murder for the sake of robbery, since no one but he had seen the money, no one but he knew of its existence in the house. Even if he had been accused of the murder, it could only have been thought that he had committed it from some other motive. But since no one had observed any such motive in him beforehand, and everyone saw, on the contrary, that his master was fond of him and honoured him with his confidence, he would, of course, have been the last to be suspected. People would have suspected first the man who had a motive, a man who had himself declared he had such motives, who had made no secret of it; they would, in fact, have suspected the son of the murdered man, Dmitri Fyodorovitch. Had Smerdyakov killed and robbed him, and the son been accused of it, that would, of course, have suited Smerdyakov. Yet are we to believe that, though plotting the murder, he told that son, Dmitri, about the money, the envelope, and the signals? Is that logical? Is that clear?

"When the day of the murder planned by Smerdyakov came, we have him falling downstairs in a feigned fit-- with what object? In the first place that Grigory, who had been intending to take his medicine, might put it off and remain on guard, seeing there was no one to look after the house, and, in the second place, I suppose, that his master seeing that there was no one to guard him, and in terror of a visit from his son, might redouble his vigilance and precaution. And, most of all, I suppose that he, Smerdyakov, disabled by the fit, might be carried from the kitchen, where he always slept, apart from all the rest, and where he could go in and out as he liked, to Grigory's room at the other end of the lodge, where he was always put, shut off by a screen three paces from their own bed. This was the immemorial custom established by his master and the kindhearted Marfa

Ignatyevna, whenever he had a fit. There, lying behind the screen, he would most likely, to keep up the sham, have begun groaning, and so keeping them awake all night (as Grigory and his wife testified). And all this, we are to believe, that he might more conveniently get up and murder his master!

"But I shall be told that he shammed illness on purpose that he might not be suspected and that he told the prisoner of the money and the signals to tempt him to commit the murder, and when he had murdered him and had gone away with the money, making a noise, most likely, and waking people, Smerdyakov got up, am I to believe, and went in--what for? To murder his master a second time and carry off the money that had already been stolen? Gentlemen, are you laughing? I am ashamed to put forward such suggestions, but, incredible as it seems, that's just what the prisoner alleges. When he had left the house, had knocked Grigory down and raised an alarm, he tells us Smerdyakov got up, went in and murdered his master and stole the money! I won't press the point that Smerdyakov could hardly have reckoned on this beforehand, and have foreseen that the furious and exasperated son would simply come to peep in respectfully, though he knew the signals, and beat a retreat, leaving Smerdyakov his booty. Gentlemen of the jury, I put this question to you in earnest: when was the moment when Smerdyakov could have committed his crime? Name that moment, or you can't accuse him.

"But, perhaps, the fit was a real one, the sick man suddenly recovered, heard a shout, and went out. Well-- what then? He looked about him and said, 'Why not go and kill the master?' And how did he know what had happened, since he had been lying unconscious till that moment? But there's a limit to these flights of fancy.

"'Quite so,' some astute people will tell me, 'but what if they were in agreement? What if they murdered him together and shared the money--what then?' A weighty question, truly! And the facts to confirm it are astounding. One commits the murder and takes all the trouble while his accomplice lies on one side shamming a fit, apparently to arouse suspicion in everyone, alarm in his master and alarm in Grigory. It would be interesting to know what motives could have induced the two accomplices to form such an insane plan.

"But perhaps it was not a case of active complicity on Smerdyakov's part, but only of passive acquiescence; perhaps Smerdyakov was intimidated and agreed not to prevent the murder, and foreseeing that he would be blamed for letting his master be murdered, without screaming for help or resisting, he may have obtained permission from Dmitri Karamazov to get out of the way by shamming a fit--'you may murder him as you like; it's nothing to me.' But as this attack of Smerdyakov's was bound to throw the household into confusion, Dmitri Karamazov could never have agreed to such a plan. I will waive that point however. Supposing that he did agree, it would still follow that Dmitri Karamazov is the murderer and the instigator, and Smerdyakov is only a passive accomplice, and not even an accomplice, but merely acquiesced against his will through terror.

"But what do we see? As soon as he is arrested the prisoner instantly throws all the blame on Smerdyakov, not accusing him of being his accomplice, but of being himself the murderer. 'He did it alone,' he says. 'He murdered and robbed him. It was the work of his hands.' Strange sort of accomplices who begin to accuse one another at once! And think of the risk for Karamazov. After committing the murder while his accomplice lay in bed, he throws the blame on the invalid, who might well have resented it and in self-preservation might well have confessed the truth. For he might well have seen that the court would at once judge how far he was responsible, and so he might well have reckoned that if he were punished, it would be far less severely than the real murderer. But in that case he would have been certain to make a confession, yet he has not done so. Smerdyakov never hinted at their complicity, though the actual murderer persisted in accusing him and declaring that he had committed the crime alone.

"What's more, Smerdyakov at the inquiry volunteered the statement that it was he who had told the prisoner of the envelope of notes and of the signals, and that, but for him, he would have known nothing about them. If he had really been a guilty accomplice, would he so readily have made this statement at the inquiry? On the contrary, he would have tried to conceal it, to distort the facts or minimise them. But he was far from distorting or minimising them. No one but an innocent man, who had no fear of being charged with complicity, could have acted as he did. And in a fit of melancholy arising from his disease and this catastrophe he hanged himself yesterday. He left a note written in his peculiar language, 'I destroy myself of my own will and inclination so as to throw no blame on anyone.' What would it have cost him to add: 'I am the murderer, not Karamazov'? But that he did not add. Did his conscience lead him to suicide and not to avowing his guilt?

"And what followed? Notes for three thousand roubles were brought into the court just now, and we were told that they were the same that lay in the envelope now on the table before us, and that the witness had received them from Smerdyakov the day before. But I need not recall the painful scene, though I will make one or two comments, selecting such trivial ones as might not be obvious at first sight to everyone, and so may be overlooked. In the first place, Smerdyakov must have given back the money and hanged himself yesterday from remorse. And only yesterday he confessed his guilt to Ivan Karamazov, as the latter informs us. If it were not so, indeed, why should Ivan Fyodorovitch have kept silence till now? And so, if he has confessed, then why, I ask again, did he not avow the whole truth in the last letter he left behind, knowing that the innocent prisoner had to face this terrible ordeal the next day?

"The money alone is no proof. A week ago, quite by chance, the fact came to the knowledge of myself and two other persons in this court that Ivan Fyodorovitch had sent two five per cent coupons of five thousand each--that is, ten thousand in all--to the chief town of the province to be changed. I only mention this to point out that anyone may have money, and that it can't be proved that these notes are the same as were in Fyodor Pavlovitch's envelope.

"Ivan Karamazov, after receiving yesterday a communication of such importance from the real murderer, did not stir. Why didn't he report it at once? Why did he put it all off till morning? I think I have a right to conjecture why. His health had been giving way for a week past: he had admitted to a doctor and to his most intimate friends that he was suffering from hallucinations and seeing phantoms of the dead: he was on the eve of the attack of brain fever by which he has been stricken down to-day. In this condition he suddenly heard of Smerdyakov's death, and at once reflected, 'The man is dead, I can throw the blame on him and save my brother. I have money. I will take a roll of notes and say that Smerdyakov gave them me before his death.' You will say that was dishonourable: it's dishonourable to slander even the dead, and even to save a brother. True, but what if he slandered him unconsciously? What if, finally unhinged by the sudden news of the valet's death, he imagined it really was so? You saw the recent scene: you have seen the witness's condition. He was standing up and was speaking, but where was his mind?

"Then followed the document, the prisoner's letter written two days before the crime, and containing a complete programme of the murder. Why, then, are we looking for any other programme? The crime was committed precisely according to this programme, and by no other than the writer of it. Yes, gentlemen of the jury, it went off without a hitch! He did not run respectfully and timidly away from his father's window, though he was firmly convinced that the object of his affections was with him. No, that is absurd and unlikely! He went in and murdered him. Most likely he killed him in anger, burning with resentment, as soon as he looked on his hated rival. But having killed him, probably with one blow of the brass pestle, and having convinced himself, after careful search, that she was not there, he did not, however, forget to put his hand under the pillow and take out the envelope, the torn cover of which lies now on the table before us.

"I mention this fact that you may note one, to my thinking, very characteristic circumstance. Had he been an experienced murderer and had he committed the murder for the sake of gain only, would he have left the torn envelope on the floor as it was found, beside the corpse? Had it been Smerdyakov, for instance, murdering his master to rob him, he would have simply carried away the envelope with him, without troubling himself to open it over his victim's corpse, for he would have known for certain that the notes were in the envelope--they had been put in and sealed up in his presence--and had he taken the envelope with him, no one would ever have known of the robbery. I ask you, gentlemen, would Smerdyakov have behaved in that way? Would he have left the envelope on the floor?

"No, this was the action of a frantic murderer, a murderer who was not a thief and had never stolen before that day, who snatched the notes from under the pillow, not like a thief stealing them, but as though seizing his own property from the thief who had stolen it. For that was the idea which had become almost an insane obsession in Dmitri Karamazov in regard to that money. And pouncing upon the envelope, which he had never seen before, he tore it open to make sure whether the money was in it, and ran away with the money in his pocket, even forgetting to consider that he had left an astounding piece of evidence against himself in that torn envelope on the floor. All because it was Karamazov, not Smerdyakov, he didn't think, he didn't reflect, and how should he? He ran away; he heard behind him the servant cry out; the old man caught him, stopped him and was felled to the ground by the brass pestle.

"The prisoner, moved by pity, leapt down to look at him. Would you believe it, he tells us that he leapt down out of pity, out of compassion, to see whether he could do anything for him. Was that a moment to show compassion? No; he jumped down simply to make certain whether the only witness of his crime were dead or alive. Any other feeling, any other motive would be unnatural. Note that he took trouble over Grigory, wiped his head with his handkerchief and, convincing himself he was dead, he ran to the house of his mistress, dazed and covered with blood. How was it he never thought that he was covered with blood and would be at once detected? But the prisoner himself assures us that he did not even notice that he was covered with blood. That may be believed, that is very possible, that always happens at such moments with criminals. On one point they will show diabolical cunning, while another will escape them altogether. But he was thinking at that moment of one thing only--where was she? He wanted to find out at once where she was, so he ran to her lodging and learnt an unexpected and astounding piece of news--she had gone off to Mokroe to meet her first lover."

IPPOLIT KIRILLOVITCH had chosen the historial method of exposition, beloved by all nervous orators, who find in its limitation a check on their own eager rhetoric. At this moment in his speech he went off into a dissertation on Grushenka's "first lover," and brought forward several interesting thoughts on this theme.

"Karamazov, who had been frantically jealous of everyone, collapsed, so to speak, and effaced himself at once before this first lover. What makes it all the more strange is that he seems to have hardly thought of this formidable rival. But he had looked upon him as a remote danger, and Karamazov always lives in the present. Possibly he regarded him as a fiction. But his wounded heart grasped instantly that the woman had been concealing this new rival and deceiving him, because he was anything but a fiction to her, because he was the one hope of her life. Grasping this instantly, he resigned himself.

"Gentlemen of the jury, I cannot help dwelling on this unexpected trait in the prisoner's character. He suddenly evinces an irresistible desire for justice, a respect for woman and a recognition of her right to love. And all this at the very moment when he had stained his hands with his father's blood for her sake! It is true that the blood he had shed was already crying out for vengeance, for, after having ruined his soul and his life in this world, he was forced to ask himself at that same instant what he was and what he could be now to her, to that being, dearer to him than his own soul, in comparison with that former lover who had returned penitent, with new love, to the woman he had once betrayed, with honourable offers, with the promise of a reformed and happy life. And he, luckless man, what could he give her now, what could he offer her?

"Karamazov felt all this, knew that all ways were barred to him by his crime and that he was a criminal under sentence, and not a man with life before him! This thought crushed him. And so he instantly flew to one frantic plan, which, to a man of Karamazov's character, must have appeared the one inevitable way out of his terrible position. That way out was suicide. He ran for the pistols he had left in pledge with his friend Perhotin and on the way, as he ran, he pulled out of his pocket the money, for the sake of which he had stained his hands with his father's gore. Oh, now he needed money more than ever. Karamazov would die, Karamazov would shoot himself and it should be remembered! To be sure, he was a poet and had burnt the candle at both ends all his life. 'To her, to her! and there, oh, there I will give a feast to the whole world, such as never was before, that will be remembered and talked of long after! In the midst of shouts of wild merriment, reckless gypsy songs and dances I shall raise the glass and drink to the woman I adore and her new-found happiness! And then, on the spot, at her feet, I shall dash out my brains before her and punish myself! She will remember Mitya Karamazov sometimes, she will see how Mitya loved her, she will feel for Mitya!'

"Here we see in excess a love of effect, a romantic despair and sentimentality, and the wild recklessness of the Karamazovs. Yes, but there is something else, gentlemen of the jury, something that cries out in the soul, throbs incessantly in the mind, and poisons the heart unto death--that something is conscience, gentlemen of the jury, its judgment, its terrible torments! The pistol will settle everything, the pistol is the only way out! But beyond--I don't know whether Karamazov wondered at that moment 'What lies beyond,' whether Karamazov could, like Hamlet, wonder 'What lies beyond.' No, gentlemen of the jury, they have their Hamlets, but we still have our Karamazovs!"

Here Ippolit Kirillovitch drew a minute picture of Mitya's preparations, the scene at Perhotin's, at the shop, with the drivers. He quoted numerous words and actions, confirmed by witnesses, and the picture made a terrible impression on the audience. The guilt of this harassed and desperate man stood out clear and convincing, when the facts were brought together.

"What need had he of precaution? Two or three times he almost confessed, hinted at it, all but spoke out." (Then followed the evidence given by witnesses.) "He even cried out to the peasant who drove him, 'Do you know, you are driving a murderer!' But it was impossible for him to speak out, he had to get to Mokroe and there to finish his romance. But what was awaiting the luckless man? Almost from the first minute at Mokroe he saw that his invincible rival was perhaps by no means so invincible, that the toast to their new-found happiness was not desired and would not be acceptable. But you know the facts, gentlemen of the jury, from the preliminary inquiry. Karamazov's triumph over his rival was complete and his soul passed into quite a new phase, perhaps the most terrible phase through which his soul has passed or will pass.

"One may say with certainty, gentlemen of the jury," the prosecutor continued, "that outraged nature and the criminal heart bring their own vengeance more completely than any earthly justice. What's more, justice and punishment on earth positively alleviate the punishment of nature and are, indeed, essential to the soul of the criminal at such moments, as its salvation from despair. For I cannot imagine the horror and moral suffering of Karamazov when he learnt that she loved him, that for his sake she had rejected her first lover, that she was summoning him, Mitya, to a new life, that she was promising him happiness--and when? When everything was over for him and nothing was possible!

"By the way, I will note in parenthesis a point of importance for the light it throws on the prisoner's position at the moment. This woman, this love of his, had been till the last moment, till the very instant of his arrest, a being unattainable, passionately desired by him but unattainable. Yet why did he not shoot himself then, why did he relinquish his design and even forget where his pistol was? It was just that passionate desire for love and the hope of satisfying it that restrained him. Throughout their revels he kept close to his adored mistress, who was at the banquet with him and was more charming and fascinating to him than ever--he did not leave her side, abasing himself in his homage before her.

"His passion might well, for a moment, stifle not only the fear of arrest, but even the torments of conscience. For a moment, oh, only for a moment! I can picture the state of mind of the criminal hopelessly enslaved by these influences--first, the influence of drink, of noise and excitement, of the thud of the dance and the scream of the song, and of her, flushed with wine, singing and dancing and laughing to him! Secondly, the hope in the background that the fatal end might still be far off, that not till next morning, at least, they would come and take him. So he had a few hours and that's much, very much! In a few hours one can think of many things. I imagine that he felt something like what criminals feel when they are being taken to the scaffold. They have another long, long street to pass down and at walking pace, past thousands of people. Then there will be a turning into another street and only at the end of that street the dread place of execution! I fancy that at the beginning of the journey the condemned man, sitting on his shameful cart, must feel that he has infinite life still before him. The houses recede, the cart moves on--oh, that's nothing, it's still far to the turning into the second street and he still looks boldly to right and to left at those thousands of callously curious people with their eyes fixed on him, and he still fancies that he is just such a man as they. But now the turning comes to the next street. Oh, that's nothing, nothing, there's still a whole street before him, and however many houses have been passed, he will still think there are many left. And so to the very end, to the very scaffold.

"This I imagine is how it was with Karamazov then. 'They've not had time yet,' he must have thought, 'I may still find some way out, oh, there's still time to make some plan of defence, and now, now--she is so fascinating!'

"His soul was full of confusion and dread, but he managed, however, to put aside half his money and hide it somewhere--I cannot otherwise explain the disappearance of quite half of the three thousand he had just taken from his father's pillow. He had been in Mokroe more than once before, he had caroused there for two days together already, he knew the old big house with all its passages and outbuildings. I imagine that part of the money was hidden in that house, not long before the arrest, in some crevice, under some floor, in some corner, under the roof. With what object? I shall be asked. Why, the catastrophe may take place at once, of course; he hadn't yet considered how to meet it, he hadn't the time, his head was throbbing and his heart was with her, but money--money was indispensable in any case! With money a man is always a man. Perhaps such foresight at such a moment may strike you as unnatural? But he assures us himself that a month before, at a critical and exciting moment, he had halved his money and sewn it up in a little bag. And though that was not true, as we shall prove directly, it shows the idea was a familiar one to Karamazov, he had contemplated it. What's more, when he declared at the inquiry that he had put fifteen hundred roubles in a bag (which never existed) he may have invented that little bag on the inspiration of the moment, because he had two hours before divided his money and hidden half of it at Mokroe till morning, in case of emergency, simply not to have it on himself. Two extremes, gentlemen of the jury, remember that Karamazov can contemplate two extremes and both at once.

"We have looked in the house, but we haven't found the money. It may still be there or it may have disappeared next day and be in the prisoner's hands now. In any case he was at her side, on his knees before her, she was lying on the bed, he had his hands stretched out to her and he had so entirely forgotten everything that he did not even hear the men coming to arrest him. He hadn't time to prepare any line of defence in his mind. He was caught unawares and confronted with his judges, the arbiters of his destiny.

"Gentlemen of the jury, there are moments in the execution of our duties when it is terrible for us to face a man, terrible on his account, too! The moments of contemplating that animal fear, when the criminal sees that all is lost, but still struggles, still means to struggle, the moments when every instinct of self-preservation rises up in him at once and he looks at you with questioning and suffering eyes, studies you, your face, your thoughts, uncertain on which side you will strike, and his distracted mind frames thousands of plans in an instant, but he is still afraid to speak, afraid of giving himself away! This purgatory of the spirit, this animal thirst for self-preservation, these humiliating moments of the human soul, are awful, and sometimes arouse horror and compassion for the criminal even in the lawyer. And this was what we all witnessed then.

"At first he was thunderstruck and in his terror dropped some very compromising phrases. 'Blood! I've deserved it!' But he quickly restrained himself. He had not prepared what he was to say, what answer he was to make, he had nothing but a bare denial ready. 'I am not guilty of my father's death.' That was his fence for the moment and behind it he hoped to throw up a barricade of some sort. His first compromising exclamations he hastened to explain by declaring that he was responsible for the death of the servant Grigory only. 'Of that bloodshed I am guilty, but who has killed my father, gentlemen, who has killed him? Who can have killed him, if not I?' Do you hear, he asked us that, us, who had come to ask him that question! Do you hear that uttered with such premature haste--'if not I'--the animal cunning, the naivete the Karamazov impatience of it? 'I didn't kill him and you mustn't think I did! I wanted to kill him, gentlemen, I wanted to kill him,' he hastens to admit (he was in a hurry, in a terrible hurry), 'but still I am not guilty, it is not I murdered him.' He concedes to us that he wanted to murder him, as though to say, you can see for yourselves how truthful I am, so you'll believe all the sooner that I didn't murder him. Oh, in such cases the criminal is often amazingly shallow and credulous.

"At that point one of the lawyers asked him, as it were incidentally, the most simple question, 'Wasn't it Smerdyakov killed him?' Then, as we expected, he was horribly angry at our having anticipated him and caught him unawares, before he had time to pave the way to choose and snatch the moment when it would be most natural to bring in Smerdyakov's name. He rushed at once to the other extreme, as he always does, and began to assure us that Smerdyakov could not have killed him, was not capable of it. But don't believe him, that was only his cunning; he didn't really give up the idea of Smerdyakov; on the contrary, he meant to bring him forward again; for, indeed, he had no one else to bring forward, but he would do that later, because for the moment that line was spoiled for him. He would bring him forward perhaps next day, or even a few days later, choosing an opportunity to cry out to us, 'You know I was more sceptical about Smerdyakov than you, you remember that yourselves, but now I am convinced. He killed him, he must have done!' And for the present he falls back upon a gloomy and irritable denial. Impatience and anger prompted him, however, to the most inept and incredible explanation of how he looked into his father's window and how he respectfully withdrew. The worst of it was that he was unaware of the position of affairs, of the evidence given by Grigory.

"We proceeded to search him. The search angered, but encouraged him, the whole three thousand had not been found on him, only half of it. And no doubt only at that moment of angry silence, the fiction of the little bag first occurred to him. No doubt he was conscious himself of the improbability of the story and strove painfully to make it sound more likely, to weave it into a romance that would sound plausible. In such cases the first duty, the chief task of the investigating lawyers, is to prevent the criminal being prepared, to pounce upon him unexpectedly so that he may blurt out his cherished ideas in all their simplicity, improbability and inconsistency. The criminal can only be made to speak by the sudden and apparently incidental communication of some new fact, of some circumstance of great importance in the case, of which he had no previous idea and could not have foreseen. We had such a fact in readiness--that was Grigory's evidence about the open door through which the prisoner had run out. He had completely forgotten about that door and had not even suspected that Grigory could have seen it.

"The effect of it was amazing. He leapt up and shouted to us, 'Then Smerdyakov murdered him, it was Smerdyakov!' and so betrayed the basis of the defence he was keeping back, and betrayed it in its most improbable shape, for Smerdyakov could only have committed the murder after he had knocked Grigory down and run away. When we told him that Grigory saw the door was open before he fell down, and had heard Smerdyakov behind the screen as he came out of his bedroom--Karamazov was positively crushed. My esteemed and witty colleague, Nikolay Parfenovitch, told me afterwards that he was almost moved to tears at the sight of him. And to improve matters, the prisoner hastened to tell us about the much-talked-of little bag--so be it, you shall hear this romance!

"Gentlemen of the jury, I have told you already why I consider this romance not only an absurdity, but the most improbable invention that could have been brought forward in the circumstances. If one tried for a bet to invent the most unlikely story, one could hardly find anything more incredible. The worst of such stories is that the triumphant romancers can always be put to confusion and crushed by the very details in which real life is so rich and which these unhappy and involuntary storytellers neglect as insignificant trifles. Oh, they have no thought to spare for such details, their minds are concentrated on their grand invention as a whole, and fancy anyone daring to pull them up for a trifle! But that's how they are caught. The prisoner was asked the question, 'Where did you get the stuff for your little bag and who made it for you?' 'I made it myself.' 'And where did you get the linen?' The prisoner was positively offended, he thought it almost insulting to ask him such a trivial question, and would you believe it, his resentment was genuine! But they are all like that. 'I tore it off my shirt.' "Then we shall find that shirt among your linen to-morrow, with a piece torn off.' And only fancy, gentlemen of the jury, if we really had found that torn shirt (and how could we have failed to find it in his chest of drawers or trunk?) that would have been a fact, a material fact in support of his statement! But he was incapable of that reflection. 'I don't remember, it may not have been off my shirt, I sewed it up in one of my landlady's caps.' 'What sort of a cap?' 'It was an old cotton rag of hers lying about.' 'And do you remember that clearly?' 'No, I don't.' And he was angry, very angry, and yet imagine not remembering it! At the most terrible moments of man's life, for instance when he is being led to execution, he remembers just such trifles. He will forget anything but some green roof that has flashed past him on the road, or a jackdaw on a cross--that he will remember. He concealed the making of that little bag from his household, he must have remembered his humiliating fear that someone might come in and find him needle in hand, how at the slightest sound he slipped behind the screen (there is a screen in his lodgings).

"But, gentlemen of the jury, why do I tell you all this, all these details, trifles?" cried Ippolit Kirillovitch suddenly. "Just because the prisoner still persists in these absurdities to this moment. He has not explained anything since that fatal night two months ago, he has not added one actual illuminating fact to his former fantastic statements; all those are trivialities. 'You must believe it on my honour.' Oh, we are glad to believe it, we are eager to believe it, even if only on his word of honour! Are we jackals thirsting for human blood? Show us a single fact in the prisoner's favour and we shall rejoice; but let it be a substantial, real fact, and not a conclusion drawn from the prisoner's expression by his own brother, or that when he beat himself on the breast he must have meant to point to the little bag, in the darkness, too. We shall rejoice at the new fact, we shall be the first to repudiate our charge, we shall hasten to repudiate it. But now justice cries out and we persist, we cannot repudiate anything."

Ippolit Kirillovitch passed to his final peroration. He looked as though he was in a fever, he spoke of the blood that cried for vengeance, the blood of the father murdered by his son, with the base motive of robbery! He pointed to the tragic and glaring consistency of the facts.

"And whatever you may hear from the talented and celebrated counsel for the defence," Ippolit Kirillovitch could not resist adding, "whatever eloquent and touching appeals may be made to your sensibilities, remember that at this moment you are in a temple of justice. Remember that you are the champions of our justice, the champions of our holy Russia, of her principles, her family, everything that she holds sacred! Yes, you represent Russia here at this moment, and your verdict will be heard not in this hall only but will re-echo throughout the whole of Russia, and all Russia will hear you, as her champions and her judges, and she will be encouraged or disheartened by your verdict. Do not disappoint Russia and her expectations. Our fatal troika dashes on in her headlong flight perhaps to destruction and in all Russia for long past men have stretched out imploring hands and called a halt to its furious reckless course. And if other nations stand aside from that troika that may be, not from respect, as the poet would fain believe, but simply from horror. From horror, perhaps from disgust. And well it is that they stand aside, but maybe they will cease one day to do so and will form a firm wall confronting the hurrying apparition and will check the frenzied rush of our lawlessness, for the sake of their own safety, enlightenment and civilisation. Already we have heard voices of alarm from Europe, they already begin to sound. Do not tempt them! Do not heap up their growing hatred by a sentence justifying the murder of a father by his son."

Though Ippolit Kirillovitch was genuinely moved, he wound up his speech with this rhetorical appeal--and the effect produced by him was extraordinary. When he had finished his speech, he went out hurriedly and, as I have mentioned before, almost fainted in the adjoining room. There was no applause in the court, but serious persons were pleased. The ladies were not so well satisfied, though even they were pleased with his eloquence, especially as they had no apprehensions as to the upshot of the trial and had full trust in Fetyukovitch. "He will speak at last and of course carry all before him."

Everyone looked at Mitya; he sat silent through the whole of the prosecutor's speech, clenching his teeth, with his hands clasped, and his head bowed. Only from time to time he raised his head and listened, especially when Grushenka was spoken of. When the prosecutor mentioned Rakitin's opinion of her, a smile of contempt and anger passed over his face and he murmured rather audibly, "The Bernards!" When Ippolit Kirillovitch described how he had questioned and tortured him at Mokroe, Mitya raised his head and listened with intense curiosity. At one point he seemed about to jump up and cry out, but controlled himself and only shrugged his shoulders disdainfully. People talked afterwards of the end of the speech, of the prosecutor's feat in examining the prisoner at Mokroe, and jeered at Ippolit Kirillovitch. "The man could not resist boasting of his cleverness," they said.

The court was adjourned, but only for a short interval, a quarter of an hour or twenty minutes at most. There was a hum of conversation and exclamations in the audience. I remember some of them.

"A weighty speech," a gentleman in one group observed gravely.

"He brought in too much psychology," said another voice.

"But it was all true, the absolute truth!"

"Yes, he is first rate at it."

"He summed it all up."

"Yes, he summed us up, too," chimed in another voice, "Do you remember, at the beginning of his speech, making out we were all like Fyodor Pavlovitch?"

"And at the end, too. But that was all rot."

"And obscure too."

"He was a little too much carried away."

"It's unjust, it's unjust."

"No, it was smartly done, anyway. He's had long to wait, but he's had his say, ha ha!"

"What will the counsel for the defence say?"

In another group I heard:

"He had no business to make a thrust at the Petersburg man like that; 'appealing to your sensibilities'--do you remember?"

"Yes, that was awkward of him."

"He was in too great a hurry."

"He is a nervous man."

"We laugh, but what must the prisoner be feeling?"

"Yes, what must it be for Mitya?"

In a third group:

"What lady is that, the fat one, with the lorgnette, sitting at the end?"

"She is a general's wife, divorced, I know her."

"That's why she has the lorgnette."

"She is not good for much."

"Oh no, she is a piquante little woman."

"Two places beyond her there is a little fair woman, she is prettier."

"They caught him smartly at Mokroe, didn't they, eh?"

"Oh, it was smart enough. We've heard it before, how often he has told the story at people's houses!"

"And he couldn't resist doing it now. That's vanity."

"He is a man with a grievance, he he!"

"Yes, and quick to take offence. And there was too much rhetoric, such long sentences."

"Yes, he tries to alarm us, he kept trying to alarm us. Do you remember about the troika? Something about 'They have Hamlets, but we have, so far, only Karamazovs!' That was cleverly said!"

"That was to propitiate the liberals. He is afraid of them."

"Yes, and he is afraid of the lawyer, too."

"Yes, what will Fetyukovitch say?"

"Whatever he says, he won't get round our peasants."

"Don't you think so?"

A fourth group:

"What he said about the troika was good, that piece about the other nations."

"And that was true what he said about other nations not standing it."

"What do you mean?"

"Why, in the English Parliment a Member got up last week and speaking about the Nihilists asked the Ministry whether it was not high time to intervene, to educate this barbarous people. Ippolit was thinking of him, I know he was. He was talking about that last week."

"Not an easy job."

"Not an easy job? Why not?"

"Why, we'd shut up Kronstadt and not let them have any corn. Where would they get it?"

"In America. They get it from America now."

"Nonsense!"

But the bell rang, all rushed to their places. Fetyukovitch mounted the tribune.

Chapter 10. The Speech for the Defence. An Argument that Cuts Both Ways

ALL was hushed as the first words of the famous orator rang out. The eyes of the audience were fastened upon him. He began very simply and directly, with an air of conviction, but not the slightest trace of conceit. He made no attempt at eloquence, at pathos, or emotional phrases. He was like a man speaking in a circle of intimate and sympathetic friends. His voice was a fine one, sonorous and sympathetic, and there was something genuine and simple in the very sound of it. But everyone realised at once that the speaker might suddenly rise to genuine pathos and "pierce the heart with untold power." His language was perhaps more irregular than Ippolit Kirillovitch's, but he spoke without long phrases, and indeed, with more precision. One thing did not please the ladies: he kept bending forward, especially at the beginning of his speech, not exactly bowing, but as though he were about to dart at his listeners, bending his long spine in half, as though there were a spring in the middle that enabled him to bend almost at right angles.

At the beginning of his speech he spoke rather disconnectedly, without system, one may say, dealing with facts separately, though, at the end, these facts formed a whole. His speech might be divided into two parts, the first consisting of criticism in refutation of the charge, sometimes malicious and sarcastic. But in the second half he suddenly changed his tone, and even his manner, and at once rose to pathos. The audience seemed on the lookout for it, and quivered with enthusiasm.

He went straight to the point, and began by saying that although he practised in Petersburg, he had more than once visited provincial towns to defend prisoners, of whose innocence he had a conviction or at least a preconceived idea. "That is what has happened to me in the present case," he explained. "From the very first accounts in the newspapers I was struck by something which strongly prepossessed me in the prisoner's favour. What interested me most was a fact which often occurs in legal practice, but rarely, I think, in such an extreme and peculiar form as in the present case. I ought to formulate that peculiarity only at the end of my speech, but I will do so at the very beginning, for it is my weakness to go to work directly, not keeping my effects in reserve and economising my material. That may be imprudent on my part, but at least it's sincere. What I have in my mind is this: there is an overwhelming chain of evidence against the prisoner, and at the same time not one fact that will stand criticism, if it is examined separately. As I followed the case more closely in the papers my idea was more and more confirmed, and I suddenly received from the prisoner's relatives a request to undertake his defence. I at once hurried here, and here I became completely convinced. It was to break down this terrible chain of facts, and to show that each piece of evidence taken separately was unproved and fantastic, that I undertook the case."

So Fetyukovitch began.

"Gentlemen of the jury," he suddenly protested, "I am new to this district. I have no preconceived ideas. The prisoner, a man of turbulent and unbridled temper, has not insulted me. But he has insulted perhaps hundreds of persons in this town, and so prejudiced many people against him beforehand. Of course I recognise that the moral sentiment of local society is justly excited against him. The prisoner is of turbulent and violent temper. Yet he was received in society here; he was even welcome in the family of my talented friend, the prosecutor."

(N.B. At these words there were two or three laughs in the audience, quickly suppressed, but noticed by all. All of us knew that the prosecutor received Mitya against his will, solely because he had somehow interested his wife--a lady of the highest virtue and moral worth, but fanciful, capricious, and fond of opposing her husband, especially in trifles. Mitya's visits, however, had not been frequent.)

"Nevertheless I venture to suggest," Fetyukovitch continued, "that in spite of his independent mind and just character, my opponent may have formed a mistaken prejudice against my unfortunate client. Oh, that is so natural; the unfortunate man has only too well deserved such prejudice. Outraged morality, and still more outraged taste, is often relentless. We have, in the talented prosecutor's speech, heard a stern analysis of the prisoner's character and conduct, and his severe critical attitude to the case was evident. And, what's more, he went into psychological subtleties into which he could not have entered, if he had the least conscious and malicious prejudice against the prisoner. But there are things which are even worse, even more fatal in such cases, than the most malicious and consciously unfair attitude. It is worse if we are carried away by the artistic instinct, by the desire to create, so to speak, a romance, especially if God has endowed us with psychological insight. Before I started on my way here, I was warned in Petersburg, and was myself aware, that I should find here a talented opponent whose psychological insight and subtlety had gained him peculiar renown in legal circles of recent years. But profound as psychology is, it's a knife that cuts both ways." (Laughter among the public.) "You will, of course, forgive me my comparison; I can't boast of eloquence. But I will take as an example any point in the prosecutor's speech.

"The prisoner, running away in the garden in the dark, climbed over the fence, was seized by the servant, and knocked him down with a brass pestle. Then he jumped back into the garden and spent five minutes over the man, trying to discover whether he had killed him or not. And the prosecutor refuses to believe the prisoner's statement that he ran to old Grigory out of pity. 'No,' he says, 'such sensibility is impossible at such a moment, that's unnatural; he ran to find out whether the only witness of his crime was dead or alive, and so showed that he had committed the murder, since he would not have run back for any other reason.'

"Here you have psychology; but let us take the same method and apply it to the case the other way round, and our result will be no less probable. The murderer, we are told, leapt down to find out, as a precaution, whether the witness was alive or not, yet he had left in his murdered father's study, as the prosecutor himself argues, an amazing piece of evidence in the shape of a torn envelope, with an inscription that there had been three thousand roubles in it. 'If he had carried that envelope away with him, no one in the world would have known of that envelope and of the notes in it, and that the money had been stolen by the prisoner.' Those are the prosecutor's own words. So on one side you see a complete absence of precaution, a man who has lost his head and run away in a fright, leaving that clue on the floor, and two minutes later, when he has killed another man, we are entitled to assume the most heartless and calculating foresight in him. But even admitting this was so, it is psychological subtlety, I suppose, that discerns that under certain circumstances I become as bloodthirsty and keen-sighted as a Caucasian eagle, while at the next I am as timid and blind as a mole. But if I am so bloodthirsty and cruelly calculating that when I kill a man I only run back to find out whether he is alive to witness against me, why should I spend five minutes looking after my victim at the risk of encountering other witnesses? Why soak my handkerchief, wiping the blood off his head so that it may be evidence against me later? If he were so cold-hearted and calculating, why not hit the servant on the head again and again with the same pestle so as to kill him outright and relieve himself of all anxiety about the witness?

"Again, though he ran to see whether the witness was alive, he left another witness on the path, that brass pestle which he had taken from the two women, and which they could always recognise afterwards as theirs, and prove that he had taken it from them. And it is not as though he had forgotten it on the path, dropped it through carelessness or haste, no, he had flung away his weapon, for it was found fifteen paces from where Grigory lay. Why did he do so? just because he was grieved at having killed a man, an old servant; and he flung away the pestle with a curse, as a murderous weapon. That's how it must have been, what other reason could he have had for throwing it so far? And if he was capable of feeling grief and pity at having killed a man, it shows that he was innocent of his father's murder. Had he murdered him, he would never have run to another victim out of pity; then he would have felt differently; his thoughts would have been centred on self-preservation. He would have had none to spare for pity, that is beyond doubt. On the contrary, he would have broken his skull instead of spending five minutes looking after him. There was room for pity and good-feeling just because his conscience had been clear till then. Here we have a different psychology. I have purposely resorted to this method, gentlemen of the jury, to show that you can prove anything by it. It all depends on who makes use of it. Psychology lures even most serious people into romancing, and quite unconsciously. I am speaking of the abuse of psychology, gentlemen."

Sounds of approval and laughter, at the expense of the prosecutor, were again audible in the court. I will not repeat the speech in detail; I will only quote some passages from it, some leading points.

Chapter 11. There Was No Money. There Was No Robbery

THERE was one point that struck everyone in Fetyukovitch's speech. He flatly denied the existence of the fatal three thousand roubles, and consequently, the possibility of their having been stolen.

"Gentlemen of the jury," he began. "Every new and unprejudiced observer must be struck by a characteristic peculiarity in the present case, namely, the charge of robbery, and the complete impossibility of proving that there was anything to be stolen. We are told that money was stolen--three thousand roubles but whether those roubles ever existed, nobody knows. Consider, how have we heard of that sum, and who has seen the notes? The only person who saw them, and stated that they had been put in the envelope, was the servant, Smerdyakov. He had spoken of it to the prisoner and his brother, Ivan Fyodorovitch, before the catastrophe. Madame Svyetlov, too, had been told of it. But not one of these three persons had actually seen the notes, no one but Smerdyakov had seen them.

"Here the question arises, if it's true that they did exist, and that Smerdyakov had seen them, when did he see them for the last time? What if his master had taken the notes from under his bed and put them back in his cash-box without telling him? Note, that according to Smerdyakov's story the notes were kept under the mattress; the prisoner must have pulled them out, and yet the bed was absolutely unrumpled; that is carefully recorded in the protocol. How could the prisoner have found the notes without disturbing the bed? How could he have helped soiling with his blood-stained hands the fine and spotless linen with which the bed had been purposely made?

"But I shall be asked: What about the envelope on the floor? Yes, it's worth saying a word or two about that envelope. I was somewhat surprised just now to hear the highly talented prosecutor declare of himself--of himself, observe--that but for that envelope, but for its being left on the floor, no one in the world would have known of the existence of that envelope and the notes in it, and therefore of the prisoner's having stolen it. And so that torn scrap of paper is, by the prosecutor's own admission, the sole proof on which the charge of robbery rests, 'otherwise no one would have known of the robbery, nor perhaps even of the money.' But is the mere fact that that scrap of paper was lying on the floor a proof that there was money in it, and that that money had been stolen? Yet, it will be objected, Smerdyakov had seen the money in the envelope. But when, when had he seen it for the last time, I ask you that? I talked to Smerdyakov, and he told me that he had seen the notes two days before the catastrophe. Then why not imagine that old Fyodor Pavlovitch, locked up alone in impatient and hysterical expectation of the object of his adoration, may have whiled away the time by breaking open the envelope and taking out the notes. 'What's the use of the envelope?' he may have asked himself. 'She won't believe the notes are there, but when I show her the thirty rainbow-coloured notes in one roll, it will make more impression, you may be sure, it will make her mouth water.' And so he tears open the envelope, takes out the money, and flings the envelope on the floor, conscious of being the owner and untroubled by any fears of leaving evidence.

"Listen, gentlemen, could anything be more likely than this theory and such an action? Why is it out of the question? But if anything of the sort could have taken place, the charge of robbery falls to the ground; if there was no money, there was no theft of it. If the envelope on the floor may be taken as evidence that there had been money in it, why may I not maintain the opposite, that the envelope was on the floor because the money had been taken from it by its owner?

"But I shall be asked what became of the money if Fyodor Pavlovitch took it out of the envelope since it was not found when the police searched the house? In the first place, part of the money was found in the cash-box, and secondly, he might have taken it out that morning or the evening before to make some other use of it, to give or send it away; he may have changed his idea, his plan of action completely, without thinking it necessary to announce the fact to Smerdyakov beforehand. And if there is the barest possibility of such an explanation, how can the prisoner be so positively accused of having committed murder for the sake of robbery, and of having actually carried out that robbery? This is encroaching on the domain of romance. If it is maintained that something has been stolen, the thing must be produced, or at least its existence must be proved beyond doubt. Yet no one had ever seen these notes.

"Not long ago in Petersburg a young man of eighteen, hardly more than a boy, who carried on a small business as a costermonger, went in broad daylight into a moneychanger's shop with an axe, and with extraordinary, typical audacity killed the master of the shop and carried off fifteen hundred roubles. Five hours later he was arrested, and, except fifteen roubles he had already managed to spend, the whole sum was found on him. Moreover, the shopman, on his return to the shop after the murder, informed the police not only of the exact sum stolen, but even of the notes and gold coins of which that sum was made up, and those very notes and coins were found on the criminal. This was followed by a full and genuine confession on the part of the murderer. That's what I call evidence, gentlemen of the jury! In that case I know, I see, I touch the money, and cannot deny its existence. Is it the same in the present case? And yet it is a question of life and death.

"Yes, I shall be told, but he was carousing that night, squandering money; he was shown to have had fifteen hundred roubles--where did he get the money? But the very fact that only fifteen hundred could be found, and the other half of the sum could nowhere be discovered, shows that that money was not the same, and had never been in any envelope. By strict calculation of time it was proved at the preliminary inquiry that the prisoner ran straight from those women servants to Perhotin's without going home, and that he had been nowhere. So he had been all the time in company and therefore could not have divided the three thousand in half and hidden half in the town. It's just this consideration that has led the prosecutor to assume that the money is hidden in some crevice at Mokroe. Why not in the dungeons of the castle of Udolpho, gentlemen? Isn't this supposition really too fantastic and too romantic? And observe, if that supposition breaks down, the whole charge of robbery is scattered to the winds, for in that case what could have become of the other fifteen hundred roubles? By what miracle could they have disappeared, since it's proved the prisoner went nowhere else? And we are ready to ruin a man's life with such tales!

"I shall be told that he could not explain where he got the fifteen hundred that he had. and everyone knew that he was without money before that night. Who knew it, pray? The prisoner has made a clear and unflinching statement of the source of that money, and if you will have it so, gentlemen of the jury, nothing can be more probable than that statement, and more consistent with the temper and spirit of the prisoner. The prosecutor is charmed with his own romance. A man of weak will, who had brought himself to take the three thousand so insultingly offered by his betrothed, could not, we are told, have set aside half and sewn it up, but would, even if he had done so, have unpicked it every two days and taken out a hundred, and so would have spent it all in a month. All this, you will remember, was put forward in a tone what brooked no contradiction. But what if the thing happened quite differently? What if you've been weaving a romance, and about quite a different kind of man? That's just it, you have invented quite a different man!

"I shall be told, perhaps, there are witnesses that he spent on one day all that three thousand given him by his betrothed a month before the catastrophe, so he could not have divided the sum in half. But who are these witnesses? The value of their evidence has been shown in court already. Besides, in another man's hand a crust always seems larger, and no one of these witnesses counted that money; they all judged simply at sight. And the witness Maximov has testified that the prisoner had twenty thousand in his hand. You see, gentlemen of the jury, psychology is a two edged weapon. Let me turn the other edge now and see what comes of it.

"A month before the catastrophe the prisoner was entrusted by Katerina Ivanovna with three thousand roubles to send off by post. But the question is: is it true that they were entrusted to him in such an insulting and degrading way as was proclaimed just now? The first statement made by the young lady on the subject was different, perfectly different. In the second statement we heard only cries of resentment and revenge, cries of long-concealed hatred. And the very fact that the witness gave her first evidence incorrectly gives us a right to conclude that her second piece of evidence may have been incorrect also. The prosecutor will not, dare not (his own words) touch on that story. So be it. I will not touch on it either, but will only venture to observe that if a lofty and high-principled person, such as that highly respected young lady unquestionably is, if such a person, I say, allows herself suddenly in court to contradict her first statement, with the obvious motive of ruining the prisoner, it is clear that this evidence has been given not impartially, not coolly. Have not we the right to assume that a revengeful woman might have exaggerated much? Yes, she may well have exaggerated, in particular, the insult and humiliation of her offering him the money. No, it was offered in such a way that it was possible to take it, especially for a man so easygoing as the prisoner, above all, as he expected to receive shortly from his father the three thousand roubles that he reckoned was owing to him. It was unreflecting of him, but it was just his irresponsible want of reflection that made him so confident that his father would give him the money, that he would get it, and so could always dispatch the money entrusted to him and repay the debt.

"But the prosecutor refuses to allow that he could the same day have set aside half the money and sewn it up in a little bag. That's not his character, he tells us, he couldn't have had such feelings. But yet he talked himself of the broad Karamazov nature; he cried out about the two extremes which a Karamazov can contemplate at once. Karamazov is just such a two-sided nature, fluctuating between two extremes, that even when moved by the most violent craving for riotous gaiety, he can pull himself up, if something strikes him on the other side. And on the other side is love that new love which had flamed up in his heart, and for that love he needed money; oh, far more than for carousing with his mistress. If she were to say to him, 'I am yours, I won't have Fyodor Pavlovitch,' then he must have money to take her away. That was more important than carousing. Could a Karamazov fail to understand it? That anxiety was just what he was suffering from--what is there improbable in his laying aside that money and concealing it in case of emergency?

"But time passed, and Fyodor Pavlovitch did not give the prisoner the expected three thousand; on the contrary, the latter heard that he meant to use this sum to seduce the woman he, the prisoner, loved. 'If Fyodor Pavlovitch doesn't give the money,' he thought, 'I shall be put in the position of a thief before Katerina Ivanovna.' And then the idea presented itself to him that he would go to Katerina Ivanovna, lay before her the fifteen hundred roubles he still carried round his neck, and say, 'I am a scoundrel, but not a thief.' So here we have already a twofold reason why he should guard that sum of money as the apple of his eye, why he shouldn't unpick the little bag, and spend it a hundred at a time. Why should you deny the prisoner a sense of honour? Yes, he has a sense of honour, granted that it's misplaced, granted it's often mistaken, yet it exists and amounts to a passion, and he has proved that.

"But now the affair becomes even more complex; his jealous torments reach a climax, and those same two questions torture his fevered brain more and more: 'If I repay Katerina Ivanovna, where can I find the means to go off with Grushenka?' If he behaved wildly, drank, and made disturbances in the taverns in the course of that month, it was perhaps because he was wretched and strained beyond his powers of endurance. These two questions became so acute that they drove him at last to despair. He sent his younger brother to beg for the last time for the three thousand roubles, but without waiting for a reply, burst in himself and ended by beating the old man in the presence of witnesses. After that he had no prospect of getting it from anyone; his father would not give it him after that beating.

"The same evening he struck himself on the breast, just on the upper part of the breast where the little bag was, and swore to his brother that he had the means of not being a scoundrel, but that still he would remain a scoundrel, for he foresaw that he would not use that means, that he wouldn't have the character, that he wouldn't have the will-power to do it. Why, why does the prosecutor refuse to believe the evidence of Alexey Karamazov, given so genuinely and sincerely, so spontaneously and convincingly? And why, on the contrary, does he force me to believe in money hidden in a crevice, in the dungeons of the castle of Udolpho?

"The same evening, after his talk with his brother, the prisoner wrote that fatal letter, and that letter is the chief, the most stupendous proof of the prisoner having committed robbery! 'I shall beg from everyone, and if I don't get it I shall murder my father and shall take the envelope with the pink ribbon on it from under his mattress as soon as Ivan has gone.' A full programme of the murder, we are told, so it must have been he. 'It has all been done as he wrote,' cries the prosecutor.

"But in the first place, it's the letter of a drunken man and written in great irritation; secondly, he writes of the envelope from what he has heard from Smerdyakov again, for he has not seen the envelope himself; and thirdly, he wrote it indeed, but how can you prove that he did it? Did the prisoner take the envelope from under the pillow, did he find the money, did that money exist indeed? And was it to get money that the prisoner ran off, if you remember? He ran off post-haste not to steal, but to find out where she was, the woman who had crushed him. He was not running to carry out a programme, to carry out what he had written, that is, not for an act of premeditated robbery, but he ran suddenly, spontaneously, in a jealous fury. Yes! I shall be told, but when he got there and murdered him he seized the money, too. But did he murder him after all? The charge of robbery I repudiate with indignation. A man cannot be accused of robbery, if it's impossible to state accurately what he has stolen; that's an axiom. But did he murder him without robbery, did he murder him at all? Is that proved? Isn't that, too, a romance?"

Chapter 12. And There Was No Murder Either

"ALLOW me, gentlemen of the jury, to remind you that a man's life is at stake and that you must be careful. We have heard the prosecutor himself admit that until to-day he hesitated to accuse the prisoner of a full and conscious premeditation of the crime; he hesitated till he saw that fatal drunken letter which was produced in court to-day. 'All was done as written.' But, I repeat again, he was running to her, to seek her, solely to find out where she was. That's a fact that can't be disputed. Had she been at home, he would not have run away, but would have remained at her side, and so would not have done what he promised in the letter. He ran unexpectedly and accidentally, and by that time very likely he did not even remember his drunken letter. 'He snatched up the pestle,' they say, and you will remember how a whole edifice of psychology was built on that pestle--why he was bound to look at that pestle as a weapon, to snatch it up, and so on, and so on. A very commonplace idea occurs to me at this point: What if that pestle had not been in sight, had not been lying on the shelf from which it was snatched by the prisoner, but had been put away in a cupboard? It would not have caught the prisoner's eye, and he would have run away without a weapon, with empty hands, and then he would certainly not have killed anyone. How then can I look upon the pestle as a proof of premeditation?

"Yes, but he talked in the taverns of murdering his father, and two days before, on the evening when he wrote his drunken letter, he was quiet and only quarrelled with a shopman in the tavern, because a Karamazov could not help quarrelling, forsooth! But my answer to that is, that, if he was planning such a murder in accordance with his letter, he certainly would not have quarrelled even with a shopman, and probably would not have gone into the tavern at all, because a person plotting such a crime seeks quiet and retirement, seeks to efface himself, to avoid being seen and heard, and that not from calculation, but from instinct. Gentlemen of the jury, the psychological method is a two-edged weapon, and we, too, can use it. As for all this shouting in taverns throughout the month, don't we often hear children, or drunkards coming out of taverns shout, 'I'll kill you'? but they don't murder anyone. And that fatal letter--isn't that simply drunken irritability, too? Isn't that simply the shout of the brawler outside the tavern, 'I'll kill you! I'll kill the lot of you!' Why not, why could it not be that? What reason have we to call that letter 'fatal' rather than absurd? Because his father has been found murdered, because a witness saw the prisoner running out of the garden with a weapon in his hand, and was knocked down by him: therefore, we are told, everything was done as he had planned in writing, and the letter was not 'absurd,' but 'fatal.'

"Now, thank God! we've come to the real point: 'since he was in the garden, he must have murdered him.' In those few words: 'since he was, then he must' lies the whole case for the prosecution. He was there, so he must have. And what if there is no must about it, even if he was there? Oh, I admit that the chain of evidence--the coincidences--are really suggestive. But examine all these facts separately, regardless of their connection. Why, for instance, does the prosecution refuse to admit the truth of the prisoner's statement that he ran away from his father's window? Remember the sarcasms in which the prosecutor indulged at the expense of the respectful and 'pious' sentiments which suddenly came over the murderer. But what if there were something of the sort, a feeling of religious awe, if not of filial respect? 'My mother must have been praying for me at that moment,' were the prisoner's words at the preliminary inquiry, and so he ran away as soon as he convinced himself that Madame Svyetlov was not in his father's house. 'But he could not convince himself by looking through the window,' the prosecutor objects. But why couldn't he? Why? The window opened at the signals given by the prisoner. Some word might have been uttered by Fyodor Pavlovitch, some exclamation which showed the prisoner that she was not there. Why should we assume everything as we imagine it, as we make up our minds to imagine it? A thousand things may happen in reality which elude the subtlest imagination.

"'Yes, but Grigory saw the door open and so the prisoner certainly was in the house, therefore he killed him.' Now about that door, gentlemen of the jury...Observe that we have only the statement of one witness as to that door, and he was at the time in such a condition, that--but supposing the door was open; supposing the prisoner has lied in denying it, from an instinct of self-defence, natural in his position; supposing he did go into the house--well, what then? How does it follow that because he was there he committed the murder? He might have dashed in, run through the rooms; might have pushed his father away; might have struck him; but as soon as he had made sure Madame Svyetlov was not there, he may have run away rejoicing that she was not there and that he had not killed his father. And it was perhaps just because he had escaped from the temptation to kill his father, because he had a clear conscience and was rejoicing at not having killed him, that he was capable of a pure feeling, the feeling of pity and compassion, and leapt off the fence a minute later to the assistance of Grigory after he had, in his excitement, knocked him down.

"With terrible eloquence the prosecutor has described to us the dreadful state of the prisoner's mind at Mokroe when love again lay before him calling him to new life, while love was impossible for him because he had his father's bloodstained corpse behind him and beyond that corpse--retribution. And yet the prosecutor allowed him love, which he explained, according to his method, talking about this drunken condition, about a criminal being taken to execution, about it being still far off, and so on and so on. But again I ask, Mr. Prosecutor, have you not invented a new personality? Is the prisoner so coarse and heartless as to be able to think at that moment of love and of dodges to escape punishment, if his hands were really stained with his father's blood? No, no, no! As soon as it was made plain to him that she loved him and called him to her side, promising him new happiness, oh! then, I protest he must have felt the impulse to suicide doubled, trebled, and must have killed himself, if he had his father's murder on his conscience. Oh, no! he would not have forgotten where his pistols lay! I know the prisoner: the savage, stony heartlessness ascribed to him by the prosecutor is inconsistent with his character. He would have killed himself, that's certain. He did not kill himself just because 'his mother's prayers had saved him,' and he was innocent of his father's blood. He was troubled, he was grieving that night at Mokroe only about old Grigory and praying to God that the old man would recover, that his blow had not been fatal, and that he would not have to suffer for it. Why not accept such an interpretation of the facts? What trustworthy proof have we that the prisoner is lying?

"But we shall be told at once again, 'There is his father's corpse! If he ran away without murdering him, who did murder him?' Here, I repeat, you have the whole logic of the prosecution. Who murdered him, if not he? There's no one to put in his place.

"Gentlemen of the jury, is that really so? Is it positively, actually true that there is no one else at all? We've heard the prosecutor count on his fingers all the persons who were in that house that night. They were five in number; three of them, I agree, could not have been responsible--the murdered man himself, old Grigory, and his wife. There are left then the prisoner and Smerdyakov, and the prosecutor dramatically exclaims that the prisoner pointed to Smerdyakov because he had no one else to fix on, that had there been a sixth person, even a phantom of a sixth person, he would have abandoned the charge against Smerdyakov at once in shame and have accused that other. But, gentlemen of the jury, why may I not draw the very opposite conclusion? There are two persons--the prisoner and Smerdyakov. Why can I not say that you accuse my client, simply because you have no one else to accuse? And you have no one else only because you have determined to exclude Smerdyakov from all suspicion.

"It's true, indeed, Smerdyakov is accused only by the prisoner, his two brothers, and Madame Svyetlov. But there are others who accuse him: there are vague rumours of a question, of a suspicion, an obscure report, a feeling of expectation. Finally, we have the evidence of a combination of facts very suggestive, though, I admit, inconclusive. In the first place we have precisely on the day of the catastrophe that fit, for the genuineness of which the prosecutor, for some reason, has felt obliged to make a careful defence. Then Smerdyakov's sudden suicide on the eve of the trial. Then the equally startling evidence given in court to-day by the elder of the prisoner's brothers, who had believed in his guilt, but has to-day produced a bundle of notes and proclaimed Smerdyakov as the murderer. Oh, I fully share the court's and the prosecutor's conviction that Ivan Karamazov is suffering from brain fever, that his statement may really be a desperate effort, planned in delirium, to save his brother by throwing the guilt on the dead man. But again Smerdyakov's name is pronounced, again there is a suggestion of mystery. There is something unexplained, incomplete. And perhaps it may one day be explained. But we won't go into that now. Of that later.

"The court has resolved to go on with the trial, but, meantime, I might make a few remarks about the character-sketch of Smerdyakov drawn with subtlety and talent by the prosecutor. But while I admire his talent I cannot agree with him. I have visited Smerdyakov, I have seen him and talked to him, and he made a very different impression on me. He was weak in health, it is true; but in character, in spirit, he was by no means the weak man the prosecutor has made him out to be. I found in him no trace of the timidity on which the prosecutor so insisted. There was no simplicity about him, either. I found in him, on the contrary, an extreme mistrustfulness concealed under a mask of naivete, and an intelligence of considerable range. The prosecutor was too simple in taking him for weak-minded. He made a very definite impression on me: I left him with the conviction that he was a distinctly spiteful creature, excessively ambitious, vindictive, and intensely envious. I made some inquiries: he resented his parentage, was ashamed of it, and would clench his teeth when he remembered that he was the son of 'stinking Lizaveta.' He was disrespectful to the servant Grigory and his wife, who had cared for him in his childhood. He cursed and jeered at Russia. He dreamed of going to France and becoming a Frenchman. He used often to say that he hadn't the means to do so. I fancy he loved no one but himself and had a strangely high opinion of himself. His conception of culture was limited to good clothes, clean shirt-fronts and polished boots. Believing himself to be the illegitimate son of Fyodor Pavlovitch (there is evidence of this), he might well have resented his position, compared with that of his master's legitimate sons. They had everything, he nothing. They had all the rights, they had the inheritance, while he was only the cook. He told me himself that he had helped Fyodor Pavlovitch to put the notes in the envelope. The destination of that sum--a sum which would have made his career--must have been hateful to him. Moreover, he saw three thousand roubles in new rainbow-coloured notes. (I asked him about that on purpose.) Oh, beware of showing an ambitious and envious man a large sum of money at once! And it was the first time he had seen so much money in the hands of one man. The sight of the rainbow-coloured notes may have made a morbid impression on his imagination, but with no immediate results.

"The talented prosecutor, with extraordinary subtlety, sketched for us all the arguments for and against the hypothesis of Smerdyakov's guilt, and asked us in particular what motive he had in feigning a fit. But he may not have been feigning at all, the fit may have happened quite naturally, but it may have passed off quite naturally, and the sick man may have recovered, not completely perhaps, but still regaining consciousness, as happens with epileptics.

"The prosecutor asks at what moment could Smerdyakov have committed the murder. But it is very easy to point out that moment. He might have waked up from deep sleep (for he was only asleep--an epileptic fit is always followed by a deep sleep) at that moment when the old Grigory shouted at the top of his voice 'Parricide!' That shout in the dark and stillness may have waked Smerdyakov whose sleep may have been less sound at the moment: he might naturally have waked up an hour before.

"Getting out of bed, he goes almost unconsciously and with no definite motive towards the sound to see what's the matter. His head is still clouded with his attack, his faculties are half asleep; but, once in the garden, he walks to the lighted windows and he hears terrible news from his master, who would be, of course, glad to see him. His mind sets to work at once. He hears all the details from his frightened master, and gradually in his disordered brain there shapes itself an idea--terrible, but seductive and irresistibly logical. To kill the old man, take the three thousand, and throw all the blame on to his young master. A terrible lust of money, of booty, might seize upon him as he realised his security from detection. Oh! these sudden and irresistible impulses come so often when there is a favourable opportunity, and especially with murderers who have had no idea of committing a murder beforehand. And Smerdyakov may have gone in and carried out his plan. With what weapon? Why, with any stone picked up in the garden. But what for, with what object? Why, the three thousand which means a career for him. Oh, I am not contradicting myself--the money may have existed. And perhaps Smerdyakov alone knew where to find it, where his master kept it. And the covering of the money--the torn envelope on the floor?

"Just now, when the prosecutor was explaining his subtle theory that only an inexperienced thief like Karamazov would have left the envelope on the floor, and not one like Smerdyakov, who would have avoided leaving a piece of evidence against himself, I thought as I listened that I was hearing something very familiar, and, would you believe it, I have heard that very argument, that very conjecture, of how Karamazov would have behaved, precisely two days before, from Smerdyakov himself. What's more, it struck me at the time. I fancied that there was an artificial simplicity about him; that he was in a hurry to suggest this idea to me that I might fancy it was my own. He insinuated it, as it were. Did he not insinuate the same idea at the inquiry and suggest it to the talented prosecutor?

"I shall be asked, 'What about the old woman, Grigory's wife? She heard the sick man moaning close by, all night.' Yes, she heard it, but that evidence is extremely unreliable. I knew a lady who complained bitterly that she had been kept awake all night by a dog in the yard. Yet the poor beast, it appeared, had only yelped once or twice in the night. And that's natural. If anyone is asleep and hears a groan he wakes up, annoyed at being waked, but instantly falls asleep again. Two hours later, again a groan, he wakes up and falls asleep again; and the same thing again two hours later--three times altogether in the night. Next morning the sleeper wakes up and complains that someone has been groaning all night and keeping him awake. And it is bound to seem so to him: the intervals of two hours of sleep he does not remember, he only remembers the moments of waking, so he feels he has been waked up all night.

"But why, why, asks the prosecutor, did not Smerdyakov confess in his last letter? Why did his conscience prompt him to one step and not to both? But, excuse me, conscience implies penitence, and the suicide may not have felt penitence, but only despair. Despair and penitence are two very different things. Despair may be vindictive and irreconcilable, and the suicide, laying his hands on himself, may well have felt redoubled hatred for those whom he had envied all his life.

"Gentlemen of the jury, beware of a miscarriage of justice! What is there unlikely in all I have put before you just now? Find the error in my reasoning; find the impossibility, the absurdity. And if there is but a shade of possibility, but a shade of probability in my propositions, do not condemn him. And is there only a shade? I swear by all that is sacred, I fully believe in the explanation of the murder I have just put forward. What troubles me and makes me indignant is that of all the mass of facts heaped up by the prosecution against the prisoner, there is not a single one certain and irrefutable. And yet the unhappy man is to be ruined by the accumulation of these facts. Yes, the accumulated effect is awful: the blood, the blood dripping from his fingers, the bloodstained shirt, the dark night resounding with the shout 'Parricide!' and the old man falling with a broken head. And then the mass of phrases, statements, gestures, shouts! Oh! this has so much influence, it can so bias the mind; but, gentlemen of the jury, can it bias your minds? Remember, you have been given absolute power to bind and to loose, but the greater the power, the more terrible its responsibility.

"I do not draw back one iota from what I have said just now, but suppose for one moment I agreed with the prosecution that my luckless client had stained his hands with his father's blood. This is only hypothesis, I repeat; I never for one instant doubt of his innocence. But, so be it, I assume that my client is guilty of parricide. Even so, hear what I have to say. I have it in my heart to say something more to you, for I feel that there must be a great conflict in your hearts and minds...Forgive my referring to your hearts and minds, gentlemen of the jury, but I want to be truthful and sincere to the end. Let us all be sincere!"

At this point the speech was interrupted by rather loud applause. The last words, indeed, were pronounced with a note of such sincerity that everyone felt that he really might have something to say, and that what he was about to say would be of the greatest consequence. But the President, hearing the applause, in a loud voice threatened to clear the court if such an incident were repeated. Every sound was hushed and Fetyukovitch began in a voice full of feeling quite unlike the tone he had used hitherto.

Chapter 13. A Corrupter of Thought

"IT'S not only the accumulation of facts that threatens my client with ruin, gentlemen of the jury," he began, "what is really damning for my client is one fact--the dead body of his father. Had it been an ordinary case of murder you would have rejected the charge in view of the triviality, the incompleteness, and the fantastic character of the evidence, if you examine each part of it separately; or, at least, you would have hesitated to ruin a man's life simply from the prejudice against him which he has, alas! only too well deserved. But it's not an ordinary case of murder, it's a case of parricide. That impresses men's minds, and to such a degree that the very triviality and incompleteness of the evidence becomes less trivial and less incomplete even to an unprejudiced mind. How can such a prisoner be acquitted? What if he committed the murder and gets off unpunished? That is what everyone, almost involuntarily, instinctively, feels at heart.

"Yes, it's a fearful thing to shed a father's blood--the father who has begotten me, loved me, not spared his life for me, grieved over my illnesses from childhood up, troubled all his life for my happiness, and has lived in my joys, in my successes. To murder such a father--that's inconceivable. Gentlemen of the jury, what is a father--a real father? What is the meaning of that great word? What is the great idea in that name? We have just indicated in part what a true father is and what he ought to be. In the case in which we are now so deeply occupied and over which our hearts are aching--in the present case, the father, Fyodor Pavlovitch Karamazov, did not correspond to that conception of a father to which we have just referred. That's the misfortune. And indeed some fathers are a misfortune. Let us examine this misfortune rather more closely: we must shrink from nothing, gentlemen of the jury, considering the importance of the decision you have to make. It's our particular duty not to shrink from any idea, like children or frightened women, as the talented prosecutor happily expresses it.

"But in the course of his heated speech my esteemed opponent (and he was my opponent before I opened my lips) exclaimed several times, 'Oh, I will not yield the defence of the prisoner to the lawyer who has come down from Petersburg. I accuse, but I defend also!' He exclaimed that several times, but forgot to mention that if this terrible prisoner was for twenty-three years so grateful for a mere pound of nuts given him by the only man who had been kind to him, as a child in his father's house, might not such a man well have remembered for twenty-three years how he ran in his father's back-yard, without boots on his feet and with his little trousers hanging by one button'--to use the expression of the kindhearted doctor, Herzenstube?

"Oh, gentlemen of the jury, why need we look more closely at this misfortune, why repeat what we all know already? What did my client meet with when he arrived here, at his father's house, and why depict my client as a heartless egoist and monster? He is uncontrolled, he is wild and unruly--we are trying him now for that--but who is responsible for his life? Who is responsible for his having received such an unseemly bringing up, in spite of his excellent disposition and his grateful and sensitive heart? Did anyone train him to be reasonable? Was he enlightened by study? Did anyone love him ever so little in his childhood? My client was left to the care of Providence like a beast of the field. He thirsted perhaps to see his father after long years of separation. A thousand times perhaps he may, recalling his childhood, have driven away the loathsome phantoms that haunted his childish dreams and with all his heart he may have longed to embrace and to forgive his father! And what awaited him? He was met by cynical taunts, suspicions and wrangling about money. He heard nothing but revolting talk and vicious precepts uttered daily over the brandy, and at last he saw his father seducing his mistress from him with his own money. Oh, gentlemen of the jury, that was cruel and revolting! And that old man was always complaining of the disrespect and cruelty of his son. He slandered him in society, injured him, calumniated him, bought up his unpaid debts to get him thrown into prison.

"Gentlemen of the jury, people like my client, who are fierce, unruly, and uncontrolled on the surface, are sometimes, most frequently indeed, exceedingly tender-hearted, only they don't express it. Don't laugh, don't laugh at my idea! The talented prosecutor laughed mercilessly just now at my client for loving Schiller--loving the sublime and beautiful! I should not have laughed at that in his place. Yes, such natures--oh, let me speak in defence of such natures, so often and so cruelly misunderstood--these natures often thirst for tenderness, goodness, and justice, as it were, in contrast to themselves, their unruliness, their ferocity--they thirst for it unconsciously. Passionate and fierce on the surface, they are painfully capable of loving woman, for instance, and with a spiritual and elevated love. Again do not laugh at me, this is very often the case in such natures. But they cannot hide their passions--sometimes very coarse--and that is conspicuous and is noticed, but the inner man is unseen. Their passions are quickly exhausted; but, by the side of a noble and lofty creature that seemingly coarse and rough man seeks a new life, seeks to correct himself, to be better, to become noble and honourable, 'sublime and beautiful,' however much the expression has been ridiculed.

"I said just now that I would not venture to touch upon my client's engagement. But I may say half a word. What we heard just now was not evidence, but only the scream of a frenzied and revengeful woman, and it was not for her--oh, not for her!--to reproach him with treachery, for she has betrayed him! If she had had but a little time for reflection she would not have given such evidence. Oh, do not believe her! No, my client is not a monster, as she called him!

"The Lover of Mankind on the eve of His Crucifixion said: 'I am the Good Shepherd. The good shepherd lays down his life for his sheep, so that not one of them might be lost.' Let not a man's soul be lost through us!

"I asked just now what does 'father' mean, and exclaimed that it was a great word, a precious name. But one must use words honestly, gentlemen, and I venture to call things by their right names: such a father as old Karamazov cannot be called a father and does not deserve to be. Filial love for an unworthy father is an absurdity, an impossibility. Love cannot be created from nothing: only God can create something from nothing.

"'Fathers, provoke not your children to wrath,' the apostle writes, from a heart glowing with love. It's not for the sake of my client that I quote these sacred words, I mention them for all fathers. Who has authorised me to preach to fathers? No one. But as a man and a citizen I make my appeal--vivos voco! We are not long on earth, we do many evil deeds and say many evil words. So let us all catch a favourable moment when we are all together to say a good word to each other. That's what I am doing: while I am in this place I take advantage of my opportunity. Not for nothing is this tribune given us by the highest authority--all Russia hears us! I am not speaking only for the fathers here present, I cry aloud to all fathers: 'Fathers, provoke not your children to wrath.' Yes, let us first fulfil Christ's injunction ourselves and only then venture to expect it of our children. Otherwise we are not fathers, but enemies of our children, and they are not our children, but our enemies, and we have made them our enemies ourselves. 'What measure ye mete it shall be measured unto you again'--it's not I who say that, it's the Gospel precept, measure to others according as they measure to you. How can we blame children if they measure us according to our measure?

"Not long ago a servant girl in Finland was suspected of having secretly given birth to a child. She was watched, and a box of which no one knew anything was found in the corner of the loft, behind some bricks. It was opened and inside was found the body of a new-born child which she had killed. In the same box were found the skeletons of two other babies which, according to her own confession, she had killed at the moment of their birth.

"Gentlemen of the jury, was she a mother to her children? She gave birth to them, indeed; but was she a mother to them? Would anyone venture to give her the sacred name of mother? Let us be bold, gentlemen, let us be audacious even: it's our duty to be so at this moment and not to be afraid of certain words and ideas like the Moscow women in Ostrovsky's play, who are scared at the sound of certain words. No, let us prove that the progress of the last few years has touched even us, and let us say plainly, the father is not merely he who begets the child, but he who begets it and does his duty by it.

"Oh, of course, there is the other meaning, there is the other interpretation of the word 'father,' which insists that any father, even though he be a monster, even though he be the enemy of his children, still remains my father simply because he begot me. But this is, so to say, the mystical meaning which I cannot comprehend with my intellect, but can only accept by faith, or, better to say, on faith, like many other things which I do not understand, but which religion bids me believe. But in that case let it be kept outside the sphere of actual life. In the sphere of actual life, which has, indeed, its own rights, but also lays upon us great duties and obligations, in that sphere, if we want to be humane--Christian, in fact--we must, or ought to, act only upon convictions justified by reason and experience, which have been passed through the crucible of analysis; in a word, we must act rationally, and not as though in dream and delirium, that we may not do harm, that we may not ill-treat and ruin a man. Then it will be real Christian work, not only mystic, but rational and philanthropic..."

There was violent applause at this passage from many parts of the court, but Fetyukovitch waved his hands as though imploring them to let him finish without interruption. The court relapsed into silence at once. The orator went on.

"Do you suppose, gentlemen, that our children as they grow up and begin to reason can avoid such questions? No, they cannot, and we will not impose on them an impossible restriction. The sight of an unworthy father involuntarily suggests tormenting questions to a young creature, especially when he compares him with the excellent fathers of his companions. The conventional answer to this question is: 'He begot you, and you are his flesh and blood, and therefore you are bound to love him.' The youth involuntarily reflects: 'But did he love me when he begot me?' he asks, wondering more and more. 'Was it for my sake he begot me? He did not know me, not even my sex, at that moment, at the moment of passion, perhaps, inflamed by wine, and he has only transmitted to me a propensity to drunkenness--that's all he's done for me...Why am I bound to love him simply for begetting me when he has cared nothing for me all my life after?'

"Oh, perhaps those questions strike you as coarse and cruel, but do not expect an impossible restraint from a young mind. 'Drive nature out of the door and it will fly in at the window,' and, above all, let us not be afraid of words, but decide the question according to the dictates of reason and humanity and not of mystic ideas. How shall it be decided? Why, like this. Let the son stand before his father and ask him, 'Father, tell me, why must I love you? Father, show me that I must love you,' and if that father is able to answer him and show him good reason, we have a real, normal, parental relation, not resting on mystical prejudice, but on a rational, responsible and strictly humanitarian basis. But if he does not, there's an end to the family tie. He is not a father to him, and the son has a right to look upon him as a stranger, and even an enemy. Our tribune, gentlemen of the jury, ought to be a school of true and sound ideas."

(Here the orator was interrupted by irrepressible and almost frantic applause. Of course, it was not the whole audience, but a good half of it applauded. The fathers and mothers present applauded. Shrieks and exclamations were heard from the gallery, where the ladies were sitting. Handkerchiefs were waved. The President began ringing his bell with all his might. He was obviously irritated by the behaviour of the audience, but did not venture to clear the court as he had threatened. Even persons of high position, old men with stars on their breasts, sitting on specially reserved seats behind the judges, applauded the orator and waved their handkerchiefs. So that when the noise died down, the President confined himself to repeating his stern threat to clear the court, and Fetyukovitch, excited and triumphant, continued his speech.)

"Gentlemen of the jury, you remember that awful night of which so much has been said to-day, when the son got over the fence and stood face to face with the enemy and persecutor who had begotten him. I insist most emphatically it was not for money he ran to his father's house: the charge of robbery is an absurdity, as I proved before. And it was not to murder him he broke into the house, oh, no! If he had had that design he would, at least, have taken the precaution of arming himself beforehand. The brass pestle he caught up instinctively without knowing why he did it. Granted that he deceived his father by tapping at the window, granted that he made his way in--I've said already that I do not for a moment believe that legend, but let it be so, let us suppose it for a moment. Gentlemen, I swear to you by all that's holy, if it had not been his father, but an ordinary enemy, he would, after running through the rooms and satisfying himself that the woman was not there, have made off, post-haste, without doing any harm to his rival. He would have struck him, pushed him away perhaps, nothing more, for he had no thought and no time to spare for that. What he wanted to know was where she was. But his father, his father! The mere sight of the father who had hated him from his childhood, had been his enemy, his persecutor, and now his unnatural rival, was enough! A feeling of hatred came over him involuntarily, irresistibly, clouding his reason. It all surged up in one moment! It was an impulse of madness and insanity, but also an impulse of nature, irresistibly and unconsciously (like everything in nature) avenging the violation of its eternal laws.

"But the prisoner even then did not murder him--I maintain that, I cry that aloud!--no, he only brandished the pestle in a burst of indignant disgust, not meaning to kill him, not knowing that he would kill him. Had he not had this fatal pestle in his hand, he would have only knocked his father down perhaps, but would not have killed him. As he ran away, he did not know whether he had killed the old man. Such a murder is not a murder. Such a murder is not a parricide. No, the murder of such a father cannot be called parricide. Such a murder can only be reckoned parricide by prejudice.

"But I appeal to you again and again from the depths of my soul; did this murder actually take place? Gentlemen of the jury, if we convict and punish him, he will say to himself: 'These people have done nothing for my bringing up, for my education, nothing to improve my lot, nothing to make me better, nothing to make me a man. These people have not given me to eat and to drink, have not visited me in prison and nakedness, and here they have sent me to penal servitude. I am quits, I owe them nothing now, and owe no one anything for ever. They are wicked and I will be wicked. They are cruel and I will be cruel.' That is what he will say, gentlemen of the jury. And I swear, by finding him guilty you will only make it easier for him: you will ease his conscience, he will curse the blood he has shed and will not regret it. At the same time you will destroy in him the possibility of becoming a new man, for he will remain in his wickedness and blindness all his life.

"But do you want to punish him fearfully, terribly, with the most awful punishment that could be imagined, and at the same time to save him and regenerate his soul? If so, overwhelm him with your mercy! You will see, you will hear how he will tremble and be horror-struck. 'How can I endure this mercy? How can I endure so much love? Am I worthy of it?' That's what he will exclaim.

"Oh, I know, I know that heart, that wild but grateful heart, gentlemen of the jury! It will bow before your mercy; it thirsts for a great and loving action, it will melt and mount upwards. There are souls which, in their limitation, blame the whole world. But subdue such a soul with mercy, show it love, and it will curse its past, for there are many good impulses in it. Such a heart will expand and see that God is merciful and that men are good and just. He will be horror-stricken; he will be crushed by remorse and the vast obligation laid upon him henceforth. And he will not say then, 'I am quits,' but will say, 'I am guilty in the sight of all men and am more unworthy than all.' With tears of penitence and poignant, tender anguish, he will exclaim: 'Others are better than I, they wanted to save me, not to ruin me!' Oh, this act of mercy is so easy for you, for in the absence of anything like real evidence it will be too awful for you to pronounce: 'Yes, he is guilty.'

"Better acquit ten guilty men than punish one innocent man! Do you hear, do you hear that majestic voice from the past century of our glorious history? It is not for an insignificant person like me to remind you that the Russian court does not exist for the punishment only, but also for the salvation of the criminal! Let other nations think of retribution and the letter of the law, we will cling to the spirit and the meaning--the salvation and the reformation of the lost. If this is true, if Russia and her justice are such, she may go forward with good cheer! Do not try to scare us with your frenzied troikas from which all the nations stand aside in disgust. Not a runaway troika, but the stately chariot of Russia will move calmly and majestically to its goal. In your hands is the fate of my client, in your hands is the fate of Russian justice. You will defend it, you will save it, you will prove that there are men to watch over it, that it is in good hands!"

Chapter 14. The Peasants Stand Firm

THIS was how Fetyukovitch concluded his speech, and the enthusiasm of the audience burst like an irresistible storm. It was out of the question to stop it: the women wept, many of the men wept too, even two important personages shed tears. The President submitted, and even postponed ringing his bell. The suppression of such an enthusiasm would be the suppression of something sacred, as the ladies cried afterwards. The orator himself was genuinely touched.

And it was at this moment that Ippolit Kirillovitch got up to make certain objections. People looked at him with hatred. "What? What's the meaning of it? He positively dares to make objections," the ladies babbled. But if the whole world of ladies, including his wife, had protested he could not have been stopped at that moment. He was pale, he was shaking with emotion, his first phrases were even unintelligible, he gasped for breath, could hardly speak clearly, lost the thread. But he soon recovered himself. Of this new speech of his I will quote only a few sentences.

"...I am reproached with having woven a romance. But what is this defence if not one romance on the top of another? All that was lacking was poetry. Fyodor Pavlovitch, while waiting for his mistress, tears open the envelope and throws it on the floor. We are even told what he said while engaged in this strange act. Is not this a flight of fancy? And what proof have we that he had taken out the money? Who heard what he said? The weak-minded idiot, Smerdyakov, transformed into a Byronic hero, avenging society for his illegitimate birth--isn't this a romance in the Byronic style? And the son who breaks into his father's house and murders him without murdering him is not even a romance--this is a sphinx setting us a riddle which he cannot solve himself. If he murdered him, he murdered him, and what's the meaning of his murdering him without having murdered him-- who can make head or tail of this?

"Then we are admonished that our tribune is a tribune of true and sound ideas and from this tribune of 'sound ideas' is heard a solemn declaration that to call the murder of a father 'parricide' is nothing but a prejudice! But if parricide is a prejudice, and if every child is to ask his father why he is to love him, what will become of us?

What will become of the foundations of society? What will become of the family? Parricide, it appears, is only a bogy of Moscow merchants' wives. The most precious, the most sacred guarantees for the destiny and future of Russian justice are presented to us in a perverted and frivolous form, simply to attain an object--to obtain the justification of something which cannot be justified. 'Oh, crush him by mercy,' cries the counsel for the defence; but that's all the criminal wants, and to-morrow it will be seen how much he is crushed. And is not the counsel for the defence too modest in asking only for the acquittal of the prisoner? Why not found a charity in the honour of the parricide to commemorate his exploit among future generations? Religion and the Gospel are corrected--that's all mysticism, we are told, and ours is the only true Christianity which has been subjected to the analysis of reason and common sense. And so they set up before us a false semblance of Christ! 'What measure ye mete so it shall be meted unto you again,' cried the counsel for the defence, and instantly deduces that Christ teaches us to measure as it is measured to us and this from the tribune of truth and sound sense! We peep into the Gospel only on the eve of making speeches, in order to dazzle the audience by our acquaintance with what is, anyway, a rather original composition, which may be of use to produce a certain effect--all to serve the purpose! But what Christ commands us is something very different: He bids us beware of doing this, because the wicked world does this, but we ought to forgive and to turn the other cheek, and not to measure to our persecutors as they measure to us. This is what our God has taught us and not that to forbid children to murder their fathers is a prejudice. And we will not from the tribune of truth and good sense correct the Gospel of our Lord, Whom the counsel for the defence deigns to call only 'the crucified lover of humanity,' in opposition to all orthodox Russia, which calls to Him, 'For Thou art our God!'"

At this the President intervened and checked the over-zealous speaker, begging him not to exaggerate, not to overstep the bounds, and so on, as presidents always do in such cases. The audience, too, was uneasy. The public was restless: there were even exclamations of indignation. Fetyukovitch did not so much as reply; he only mounted the tribune to lay his hand on his heart and, with an offended voice, utter a few words full of dignity. He only touched again, lightly and ironically, on "romancing" and "psychology," and in an appropriate place quoted, "Jupiter, you are angry, therefore you are wrong," which provoked a burst of approving laughter in the audience, for Ippolit Kirillovitch was by no means like Jupiter. Then, a propos of the accusation that he was teaching the young generation to murder their fathers, Fetyukovitch observed, with great dignity, that he would not even answer. As for the prosecutor's charge of uttering unorthodox opinions, Fetyukovitch hinted that it was a personal insinuation and that he had expected in this court to be secure from accusations "damaging to my reputation as a citizen and a loyal subject." But at these words the President pulled him up, too, and Fetyukovitch concluded his speech with a bow, amid a hum of approbation in the court. And Ippolit Kirillovitch was, in the opinion of our ladies, "crushed for good."

Then the prisoner was allowed to speak. Mitya stood up, but said very little. He was fearfully exhausted, physically and mentally. The look of strength and independence with which he had entered in the morning had almost disappeared. He seemed as though he had passed through an experience that day, which had taught him for the rest of his life something very important he had not understood till then. His voice was weak, he did not shout as before. In his words there was a new note of humility, defeat and submission.

"What am I to say, gentlemen of the jury? The hour of judgment has come for me, I feel the hand of God upon me! The end has come to an erring man! But, before God, I repeat to you, I am innocent of my father's blood! For the last time I repeat, it wasn't I killed him! I was erring, but I loved what is good. Every instant I strove to reform, but I lived like a wild beast. I thank the prosecutor, he told me many things about myself that I did not know; but it's not true that I killed my father, the prosecutor is mistaken. I thank my counsel, too. I cried listening to him; but it's not true that I killed my father, and he needn't have supposed it. And don't believe the doctors. I am perfectly sane, only my heart is heavy. If you spare me, if you let me go, I will pray for you. I will be a better man. I give you my word before God I will! And if you will condemn me, I'll break my sword over my head myself and kiss the pieces. But spare me, do not rob me of my God! I know myself, I shall rebel! My heart is heavy, gentlemen...spare me!"

He almost fell back in his place: his voice broke: he could hardly articulate the last phrase. Then the judges proceeded to put the questions and began to ask both sides to formulate their conclusions. But I will not describe the details. At last the jury rose to retire for consultation. The President was very tired, and so his last charge to the jury was rather feeble. "Be impartial, don't be influenced by the eloquence of the defence, but yet weigh the arguments. Remember that there is a great responsibility laid upon you," and so on and so on.

The jury withdrew and the court adjourned. People could get up, move about, exchange their accumulated impressions, refresh themselves at the buffet. It was very late, almost one o'clock in the night, but nobody went away: the strain was so great that no one could think of repose. All waited with sinking hearts; though that is, perhaps, too much to say, for the ladies were only in a state of hysterical impatience and their hearts were untroubled. An acquittal, they thought, was inevitable. They all prepared themselves for a dramatic moment of general enthusiasm. I must own there were many among the men, too, who were convinced that an acquittal was inevitable. Some were pleased, others frowned, while some were simply dejected, not wanting him to be acquitted. Fetyukovitch himself was confident of his success. He was surrounded by people congratulating him and fawning upon him.

"There are," he said to one group, as I was told afterwards, "there are invisible threads binding the counsel for the defence with the jury. One feels during one's speech if they are being formed. I was aware of them. They exist. Our cause is won. Set your mind at rest."

"What will our peasants say now?" said one stout, cross-looking, pock-marked gentleman, a landowner of the neighbourhood, approaching a group of gentlemen engaged in conversation.

"But they are not all peasants. There are four government clerks among them."

"Yes, there are clerks," said a member of the district council, joining the group.

"And do you know that Nazaryev, the merchant with the medal, a juryman?"

"What of him?"

"He is a man with brains."

"But he never speaks."

"He is no great talker, but so much the better. There's no need for the Petersburg man to teach him: he could teach all Petersburg himself. He's the father of twelve children. Think of that!"

"Upon my word, you don't suppose they won't acquit him?" one of our young officials exclaimed in another group.

"They'll acquit him for certain," said a resolute voice.

"It would be shameful, disgraceful, not to acquit him cried the official. "Suppose he did murder him--there are fathers and fathers! And, besides, he was in such a frenzy...He really may have done nothing but swing the pestle in the air, and so knocked the old man down. But it was a pity they dragged the valet in. That was simply an absurd theory! If I'd been in Fetyukovitch's place, I should simply have said straight out: 'He murdered him; but he is not guilty, hang it all!'

"That's what he did, only without saying, 'Hang it all!'"

"No, Mihail Semyonovitch, he almost said that, too," put in a third voice.

"Why, gentlemen, in Lent an actress was acquitted in our town who had cut the throat of her lover's lawful wife."

"Oh, but she did not finish cutting it."

"That makes no difference. She began cutting it."

"What did you think of what he said about children? Splendid, wasn't it?"

"Splended!"

"And about mysticism, too!"

"Oh, drop mysticism, do!" cried someone else; "think of Ippolit and his fate from this day forth. His wife will scratch his eyes out to-morrow for Mitya's sake."

"Is she here?"

"What an idea! If she'd been here she'd have scratched them out in court. She is at home with toothache. He he he!"

"He he he!"

In a third group:

"I dare say they will acquit Mitenka, after all."

"I should not be surprised if he turns the Metropolis upside down to-morrow. He will be drinking for ten days!"

"Oh, the devil!"

"The devil's bound to have a hand in it. Where should he be if not here?"

"Well, gentlemen, I admit it was eloquent. But still it's not the thing to break your father's head with a pestle! Or what are we coming to?"

"The chariot! Do you remember the chariot?"

"Yes; he turned a cart into a chariot!"

"And to-morrow he will turn a chariot into a cart, just to suit his purpose."

"What cunning chaps there are nowadays! Is there any justice to be had in Russia?"

But the bell rang. The jury deliberated for exactly an hour, neither more nor less. A profound silence reigned in the court as soon as the public had taken their seats. I remember how the jurymen walked into the court. At last! I won't repeat the questions in order, and, indeed, I have forgotten them. I remember only the answer to the President's first and chief question: "Did the prisoner commit the murder for the sake of robbery and with premeditation?" (I don't remember the exact words.) There was a complete hush. The foreman of the jury, the youngest of the clerks, pronounced, in a clear, loud voice, amidst the deathlike stillness of the court:

"Yes, guilty!"

And the same answer was repeated to every question: "Yes, guilty!" and without the slightest extenuating comment. This no one had expected; almost everyone had reckoned upon a recommendation to mercy, at least. The death-like silence in the court was not broken--all seemed petrified: those who desired his conviction as well as those who had been eager for his acquittal. But that was only for the first instant, and it was followed by a fearful hubbub. Many of the men in the audience were pleased. Some were rubbing their hands with no attempt to conceal their joy. Those who disagreed with the verdict seemed crushed, shrugged their shoulders, whispered, but still seemed unable to realise this. But how shall I describe the state the ladies were in? I thought they would create a riot. At first they could scarcely believe their ears. Then suddenly the whole court rang with exclamations: "What's the meaning of it? What next?" They leapt up from their places. They seemed to fancy that it might be at once reconsidered and reversed. At that instant Mitya suddenly stood up and cried in a heart-rending voice, stretching his hands out before him:

"I swear by God and the dreadful Day of Judgment I am not guilty of my father's blood! Katya, I forgive you! Brothers, friends, have pity on the other woman!"

He could not go on, and broke into a terrible sobbing wail that was heard all over the court in a strange, unnatural voice unlike his own. From the farthest corner at the back of the gallery came a piercing shriek--it was Grushenka. She had succeeded in begging admittance to the court again before the beginning of the lawyers' speeches. Mitya was taken away. The passing of the sentence was deferred till next day. The whole court was in a hubbub but I did not wait to hear. I only remember a few exclamations I heard on the steps as I went out.

"He'll have a twenty years' trip to the mines!"

"Not less."

"Well, our peasants have stood firm."

"And have done for our Mitya."

EPILOGUE
Chapter 1. Plans for Mitya's Escape

VERY early, at nine o'clock in the morning, five days after the trial, Alyosha went to Katerina Ivanovna's to talk over a matter of great importance to both of them, and to give her a message. She sat and talked to him in the very room in which she had once received Grushenka. In the next room Ivan Fyodorovitch lay unconscious in a high fever. Katerina Ivanovna had immediately after the scene at the trial ordered the sick and unconscious man to be carried to her house, disregarding the inevitable gossip and general disapproval of the public. One of two relations who lived with her had departed to Moscow immediately after the scene in court, the other remained. But if both had gone away, Katerina Ivanovna would have adhered to her resolution, and would have gone on nursing the sick man and sitting by him day and night. Varvinsky and Herzenstube were attending him. The famous doctor had gone back to Moscow, refusing to give an opinion as to the probable end of the illness. Though the doctors encouraged Katerina Ivanovna and Alyosha, it was evident that they could not yet give them positive hopes of recovery.

Alyosha came to see his sick brother twice a day. But this time he had specially urgent business, and he foresaw how difficult it would be to approach the subject, yet he was in great haste. He had another engagement that could not be put off for that same morning, and there was need of haste.

They had been talking for a quarter of an hour. Katerina Ivanovna was pale and terribly fatigued, yet at the same time in a state of hysterical excitement. She had a presentiment of the reason why Alyosha had come to her.

"Don't worry about his decision," she said, with confident emphasis to Alyosha. "One way or another he is bound to come to it. He must escape. That unhappy man, that hero of honour and principle--not he, not Dmitri Fyodorovitch, but the man lying the other side of that door, who has sacrificed himself for his brother," Katya added, with flashing eyes--"told me the whole plan of escape long ago. You know he has already entered into negotiations...I've told you something already...You see, it will probably come off at the third etape from here, when the party of prisoners is being taken to Siberia. Oh, it's a long way off yet. Ivan Fyodorovitch has already visited the superintendent of the third etape. But we don't know yet who will be in charge of the party, and it's impossible to find that out so long beforehand. To-morrow, perhaps, I will show you in detail the whole plan which Ivan Fyodorovitch left me on the eve of the trial in case of need...That was when--do you remember?-- you found us quarrelling. He had just gone downstairs, but seeing you I made him come back; do you remember? Do you know what we were quarrelling about then?"

"No, I don't," said Alyosha.

"Of course he did not tell you. It was about that plan of escape. He had told me the main idea three days before, and we began quarrelling about it at once and quarrelled for three days. We quarrelled because, when he told me that if Dmitri Fyodorovitch were convicted he would escape abroad with that creature, I felt furious at once--I can't tell you why, I don't know myself why...Oh, of course, I was furious then about that creature, and that she, too, should go abroad with Dmitri!" Katerina Ivanovna exclaimed suddenly, her lips quivering with anger. "As soon as Ivan Fyodorovitch saw that I was furious about that woman, he instantly imagined I was jealous of Dmitri and that I still loved Dmitri. That is how our first quarrel began. I would not give an explanation, I could not ask forgiveness. I could not bear to think that such a man could suspect me of still loving that...and when I myself had told him long before that I did not love Dmitri, that I loved no one but him! It was only resentment against that creature that made me angry with him. Three days later, on the evening you came, he brought me a sealed envelope, which I was to open at once, if anything happened to him. Oh, he foresaw his illness! He told me that the envelope contained the details of the escape, and that if he died or was taken dangerously ill, I was to save Mitya alone. Then he left me money, nearly ten thousand--those notes to which the prosecutor referred in his speech, having learnt from someone that he had sent them to be changed. I was tremendously impressed to find that Ivan Fyodorovitch had not given up his idea of saving his brother, and was confiding this plan of escape to me, though he was still jealous of me and still convinced that I loved Mitya. Oh, that was a sacrifice! No, you cannot understand the greatness of such self-sacrifice, Alexey Fyodorovitch. I wanted to fall at his feet in reverence, but I thought at once that he would take it only for my joy at the thought of Mitya's being saved (and he certainly would have imagined that!), and I was so exasperated at the mere possibility of such an unjust thought on his part that I lost my temper again, and instead of kissing his feet, flew into a fury again! Oh, I am unhappy! It's my character, my awful, unhappy character! Oh, you will see, I shall end by driving him, too, to abandon me for another with whom he can get on better, like Dmitri. But...no, I could not bear it, I should kill myself. And when you came in then, and when I called to you and told him to come back, I was so enraged by the look of contempt and hatred he turned on me that do you remember?--I cried out to you that it was he, he alone who had persuaded me that his brother Dmitri was a murderer! I said that malicious thing on purpose to wound him again. He had never, never persuaded me that his brother was a murderer. On the contrary, it was I who persuaded him! Oh, my vile temper was the cause of everything! I paved the way to that hideous scene at the trial. He wanted to show me that he was an honourable man, and that, even if I loved his brother, he would not ruin him for revenge or jealousy. So he came to the court...I am the cause of it all, I alone am to blame!"

Katya never had made such confessions to Alyosha before, and he felt that she was now at that stage of unbearable suffering when even the proudest heart painfully crushes its pride and falls vanquished by grief. Oh, Alyosha knew another terrible reason of her present misery, though she had carefully concealed it from him during those days since the trial; but it would have been, for some reason, too painful to him if she had been brought so low as to speak to him now about that. She was suffering for her "treachery" at the trial, and Alyosha felt that her conscience was impelling her to confess it to him, to him, Alyosha, with tears and cries and hysterical writhings on the floor. But he dreaded that moment and longed to spare her. It made the commission on which he had come even more difficult. He spoke of Mitya again.

"It's all right, it's all right, don't be anxious about him! she began again, sharply and stubbornly. "All that is only momentary, I know him, I know his heart only too well. You may be sure he will consent to escape. It's not as though it would be immediately; he will have time to make up his mind to it. Ivan Fyodorovitch will be well by that time and will manage it all himself, so that I shall have nothing to do with it. Don't be anxious; he will consent to run away. He has agreed already: do you suppose he would give up that creature? And they won't let her go to him, so he is bound to escape. It's you he's most afraid of, he is afraid you won't approve of his escape on moral grounds. But you must generously allow it, if your sanction is so necessary," Katya added viciously. She paused and smiled.

"He talks about some hymn," she went on again, "some cross he has to bear, some duty; I remember Ivan Fyodorovitch told me a great deal about it, and if you knew how he talked! Katya cried suddenly, with feeling she could not repress, "If you knew how he loved that wretched man at the moment he told me, and how he hated him, perhaps, at the same moment. And I heard his story and his tears with sneering disdain. Brute! Yes, I am a brute. I am responsible for his fever. But that man in prison is incapable of suffering," Katya concluded irritably. "Can such a man suffer? Men like him never suffer!" There was a note of hatred and contemptuous repulsion in her words. And yet it was she who had betrayed him. "Perhaps because she feels how she's wronged him she hates him at moments," Alyosha thought to himself. He hoped that it was only "at moments." In Katya's last words he detected a challenging note, but he did not take it up.

"I sent for you this morning to make you promise to persuade him yourself. Or do you, too, consider that to escape would be dishonourable, cowardly, or something...unchristian, perhaps?" Katya added, even more defiantly.

"Oh, no. I'll tell him everything," muttered Alyosha. "He asks you to come and see him to-day," he blurted out suddenly, looking her steadily in the face. She started, and drew back a little from him on the sofa.

"Me? Can that be?" She faltered, turning pale.

"It can and ought to be!" Alyosha began emphatically, growing more animated. "He needs you particularly just now. I would not have opened the subject and worried you, if it were not necessary. He is ill, he is beside himself, he keeps asking for you. It is not to be reconciled with you that he wants you, but only that you would go and show yourself at his door. So much has happened to him since that day. He realises that he has injured you beyond all reckoning. He does not ask your forgiveness--'It's impossible to forgive me,' he says himself--but only that you would show yourself in his doorway."

"It's so sudden..." faltered Katya. "I've had a presentiment all these days that you would come with that message. I knew he would ask me to come. It's impossible!"

"Let it be impossible, but do it. Only think, he realises for the first time how he has wounded you, the first time in his life; he had never grasped it before so fully. He said, 'If she refuses to come I shall be unhappy all my life.' you hear? though he is condemned to penal servitude for twenty years, he is still planning to be happy--is not that piteous? Think--you must visit him; though he is ruined, he is innocent," broke like a challenge from Alyosha. "His hands are clean, there is no blood on them! For the sake of his infinite sufferings in the future visit him now. Go, greet him on his way into the darkness--stand at his door, that is all...You ought to do it, you ought to!" Alyosha concluded, laying immense stress on the word "ought."

"I ought to...but I cannot..." Katya moaned. "He will look at me...I can't."

"Your eyes ought to meet. How will you live all your life, if you don't make up your mind to do it now?"

"Better suffer all my life."

"You ought to go, you ought to go," Alyosha repeated with merciless emphasis.

"But why to-day, why at once?...I can't leave our patient-"

"You can for a moment. It will only be a moment. If you don't come, he will be in delirium by to-night. I would not tell you a lie; have pity on him!"

"Have pity on me!" Katya said, with bitter reproach, and she burst into tears.

"Then you will come," said Alyosha firmly, seeing her tears. "I'll go and tell him you will come directly."

"No, don't tell him so on any account," cried Katya in alarm. "I will come, but don't tell him beforehand, for perhaps I may go, but not go in...I don't know yet-"

Her voice failed her. She gasped for breath. Alyosha got up to go.

"And what if I meet anyone?" she said suddenly, in a low voice, turning white again.

"That's just why you must go now, to avoid meeting anyone. There will be no one there, I can tell you that for certain. We will expect you," he concluded emphatically, and went out of the room.

Chapter 2. For a Moment the Lie Becomes Truth

HE hurried to the hospital where Mitya was lying now. The day after his fate was determined, Mitya had fallen ill with nervous fever, and was sent to the prison division of the town hospital. But at the request of several persons (Alyosha, Madame Hohlakov, Lise, etc.), Doctor Varvinsky had put Mitya not with other prisoners, but in a separate little room, the one where Smerdyakov had been. It is true that there was a sentinel at the other end of the corridor, and there was a grating over the window, so that Varvinsky could be at ease about the indulgence he had shown, which was not quite legal, indeed; but he was a kind-hearted and compassionate young man. He knew how hard it would be for a man like Mitya to pass at once so suddenly into the society of robbers and murderers, and that he must get used to it by degrees. The visits of relations and friends were informally sanctioned by the doctor and overseer, and even by the police captain. But only Alyosha and Grushenka had visited Mitya. Rakitin had tried to force his way in twice, but Mitya persistently begged Varvinsky not to admit him.

Alyosha found him sitting on his bed in a hospital dressing gown, rather feverish, with a towel, soaked in vinegar and water, on his head. He looked at Alyosha as he came in with an undefined expression, but there was a shade of something like dread discernible in it. He had become terribly preoccupied since the trial; sometimes he would be silent for half an hour together, and seemed to be pondering something heavily and painfully, oblivious of everything about him. If he roused himself from his brooding and began to talk, he always spoke with a kind of abruptness and never of what he really wanted to say. He looked sometimes with a face of suffering at his brother. He seemed to be more at ease with Grushenka than with Alyosha. It is true, he scarcely spoke to her at all, but as soon as she came in, his whole face lighted up with joy.

Alyosha sat down beside him on the bed in silence. This time Mitya was waiting for Alyosha in suspense, but he did not dare ask him a question. He felt it almost unthinkable that Katya would consent to come, and at the same time he felt that if she did not come, something inconceivable would happen. Alyosha understood his feelings.

"Trifon Borissovitch," Mitya began nervously, "has pulled his whole inn to pieces, I am told. He's taken up the flooring, pulled apart the planks, split up all the gallery, I am told. He is seeking treasure all the time--the fifteen hundred roubles which the prosecutor said I'd hidden there. He began playing these tricks, they say, as soon as he got home. Serve him right, the swindler! The guard here told me yesterday; he comes from there."

"Listen," began Alyosha. "She will come, but I don't know when. Perhaps to-day, perhaps in a few days, that I can't tell. But she will come, she will, that's certain."

Mitya started, would have said something, but was silent. The news had a tremendous effect on him. It was evident that he would have liked terribly to know what had been said, but he was again afraid to ask. Something cruel and contemptuous from Katya would have cut him like a knife at that moment.

"This was what she said among other things; that I must be sure to set your conscience at rest about escaping. If Ivan is not well by then she will see to it all herself."

"You've spoken of that already," Mitya observed musingly.

"And you have repeated it to Grusha," observed Alyosha.

"Yes," Mitya admitted. "She won't come this morning." He looked timidly at his brother. "She won't come till the evening. When I told her yesterday that Katya was taking measures, she was silent, but she set her mouth. She only whispered, 'Let her!' She understood that it was important. I did not dare to try her further. She understands now, I think, that Katya no longer cares for me, but loves Ivan."

"Does she?" broke from Alyosha.

"Perhaps she does not. Only she is not coming this morning," Mitya hastened to explain again; "I asked her to do something for me. You know, Ivan is superior to all of us. He ought to live, not us. He will recover."

"Would you believe it, though Katya is alarmed about him, she scarcely doubts of his recovery," said Alyosha.

"That means that she is convinced he will die. It's because she is frightened she's so sure he will get well."

"Ivan has a strong constitution, and I, too, believe there's every hope that he will get well," Alyosha observed anxiously.

"Yes, he will get well. But she is convinced that he will die. She has a great deal of sorrow to bear..." A silence followed. A grave anxiety was fretting Mitya.

"Alyosha, I love Grusha terribly," he said suddenly in a shaking voice, full of tears.

"They won't let her go out there to you," Alyosha put in at once.

"And there is something else I wanted tell you," Mitya went on, with a sudden ring in his voice. "If they beat me on the way or out there, I won't submit to it. I shall kill someone, and shall be shot for it. And this will be going on for twenty years! They speak to me rudely as it is. I've been lying here all night, passing judgment on myself. I am not ready! I am not able to resign myself. I wanted to sing a 'hymn'; but if a guard speaks rudely to me, I have not the strength to bear it. For Grusha I would bear anything...anything except blows...But she won't be allowed to come there."

Alyosha smiled gently.

"Listen, brother, once for all," he said. "This is what I think about it. And you know that I would not tell you a lie. Listen: you are not ready, and such a cross is not for you. What's more, you don't need such a martyr's cross when you are not ready for it. If you had murdered our father, it would grieve me that you should reject your punishment. But you are innocent, and such a cross is too much for you. You wanted to make yourself another man by suffering. I say, only remember that other man always, all your life and wherever you go; and that will be enough for you. Your refusal of that great cross will only serve to make you feel all your life even greater duty, and that constant feeling will do more to make you a new man, perhaps, than if you went there. For there you would not endure it and would repine, and perhaps at last would say: 'I am quits.' The lawyer was right about that. Such heavy burdens are not for all men. For some they are impossible. These are my thoughts about it, if you want them so much. If other men would have to answer for your escape, officers or soldiers, then I would not have 'allowed' you," smiled Alyosha. "But they declare--the superintendent of that etape* told Ivan himself--that if it's well managed there will be no great inquiry, and that they can get off easily. Of course, bribing is dishonest even in such a case, but I can't undertake to judge about it, because if Ivan and Katya commissioned me to act for you, I know I should go and give bribes. I must tell you the truth. And so I can't judge of your own action. But let me assure you that I shall never condemn you. And it would be a strange thing if I could judge you in this. Now I think I've gone into everything."

* Stockade.

"But I do condemn myself!" cried Mitya. "I shall escape, that was settled apart from you; could Mitya Karamazov do anything but run away? But I shall condemn myself, and I will pray for my sin for ever. That's how the Jesuits talk, isn't it? Just as we are doing?"

"Yes." Alyosha smiled gently.

"I love you for always telling the whole truth and never hiding anything," cried Mitya, with a joyful laugh. "So I've caught my Alyosha being Jesuitical. I must kiss you for that. Now listen to the rest; I'll open the other side of my heart to you. This is what I planned and decided. If I run away, even with money and a passport, and even to America, I should be cheered up by the thought that I am not running away for pleasure, not for happiness, but to another exile as bad, perhaps, as Siberia. It is as bad, Alyosha, it is! I hate that America, damn it, already. Even though Grusha will be with me. Just look at her; is she an American? She is Russian, Russian to the marrow of her bones; she will be homesick for the mother country, and I shall see every hour that she is suffering for my sake, that she has taken up that cross for me. And what harm has she done? And how shall I, too, put up with the rabble out there, though they may be better than I, every one of them? I hate that America already! And though they may be wonderful at machinery, every one of them, damn them, they are not of my soul. I love Russia, Alyosha, I love the Russian God, though I am a scoundrel myself. I shall choke there!" he exclaimed, his eyes suddenly flashing. His voice was trembling with tears. "So this is what I've decided, Alyosha, listen," he began again, mastering his emotion. "As soon as I arrive there with Grusha, we will set to work at once on the land, in solitude, somewhere very remote, with wild bears. There must be some remote parts even there. I am told there are still Redskins there, somewhere, on the edge of the horizon. So to the country of the Last of the Mohicans, and there we'll tackle the grammar at once, Grusha and I. Work and grammar--that's how we'll spend three years. And by that time we shall speak English like any Englishman. And as soon as we've learnt it--good-bye to America! We'll run here to Russia as American citizens. Don't be uneasy--we would not come to this little town. We'd hide somewhere, a long way off, in the north or in the south. I shall be changed by that time, and she will, too, in America. The doctors shall make me some sort of wart on my face--what's the use of their being so mechanical!--or else I'll put out one eye, let my beard grow a yard, and I shall turn grey, fretting for Russia. I dare say they won't recognise us. And if they do, let them send us to Siberia--I don't care. It will show it's our fate. We'll work on the land here, too, somewhere in the wilds, and I'll make up as an American all my life. But we shall die on our own soil. That's my plan, and it shan't be altered. Do you approve?"

"Yes," said Alyosha, not wanting to contradict him. Mitya paused for a minute and said suddenly:

"And how they worked it up at the trial! Didn't they work it up!"

"If they had not, you would have been convicted just the same," said Alyosha, with a sigh.

"Yes, people are sick of me here! God bless them, but it's hard," Mitya moaned miserably. Again there was silence for a minute.

"Alyosha, put me out of my misery at once!" he exclaimed suddenly. "Tell me, is she coming now, or not? Tell me? What did she say? How did she say it?"

"She said she would come, but I don't know whether she will come to-day. It's hard for her, you know," Alyosha looked timidly at his brother.

"I should think it is hard for her! Alyosha, it will drive me out of my mind. Grusha keeps looking at me. She understands. My God, calm my heart: what is it I want? I want Katya! Do I understand what I want? It's the headstrong, evil Karamazov spirit! No, I am not fit for suffering. I am a scoundrel, that's all one can say."

"Here she is!" cried Alyosha.

At that instant Katya appeared in the doorway. For a moment she stood still, gazing at Mitya with a dazed expression. He leapt pulsively to his feet, and a scared look came into his face. He turned pale, but a timid, pleading smile appeared on his lips at once, and with an irresistible impulse he held out both hands to Katya. Seeing it, she flew impetuously to him. She seized him by the hands, and almost by force made him sit down on the bed. She sat down beside him, and still keeping his hands pressed them violently. Several times they both strove to speak, but stopped short and again gazed speechless with a strange smile, their eyes fastened on one another. So passed two minutes.

"Have you forgiven me?" Mitya faltered at last, and at the same moment turning to Alyosha, his face working with joy, he cried, "Do you hear what I am asking, do you hear?"

"That's what I loved you for, that you are generous at heart!" broke from Katya. "My forgiveness is no good to you, nor yours to me; whether you forgive me or not, you will always be a sore place in my heart, and I in yours--so it must be..." She stopped to take breath. "What have I come for?" she began again with nervous haste: "to embrace your feet, to press your hands like this, till it hurts--you remember how in Moscow I used to squeeze them--to tell you again that you are my god, my joy, to tell you that I love you madly," she moaned in anguish, and suddenly pressed his hand greedily to her lips. Tears streamed from her eyes. Alyosha stood speechless and confounded; he had never expected what he was seeing.

"Love is over, Mitya!" Katya began again, "But the past is painfully dear to me. Know that you will always be so. But now let what might have been come true for one minute," she faltered, with a drawn smile, looking into his face joyfully again. "You love another woman, and I love another man, and yet I shall love you for ever, and you will love me; do you know that? Do you hear? Love me, love me all your life!" she cried, with a quiver almost of menace in her voice.

"I shall love you, and...do you know, Katya," Mitya began, drawing a deep breath at each word, "do you know, five days ago, that same evening, I loved you...When you fell down and were carried out...All my life! So it will be, so it will always be-"

So they murmured to one another frantic words, almost meaningless, perhaps not even true, but at that moment it was all true, and they both believed what they said implicitly.

"Katya," cried Mitya suddenly, "do you believe I murdered him? I know you don't believe it now, but then...when you gave evidence...Surely, surely you did not believe it!"

"I did not believe it even then. I've never believed it. I hated you, and for a moment I persuaded myself. While I was giving evidence I persuaded myself and believed it, but when I'd finished speaking I left off believing it at once. Don't doubt that! I have forgotten that I came here to punish myself," she said, with a new expression in her voice, quite unlike the loving tones of a moment before.

"Woman, yours is a heavy burden," broke, as it were, involuntarily from Mitya.

"Let me go," she whispered. "I'll come again. It's more than I can bear now."

She was getting up from her place, but suddenly uttered a loud scream and staggered back. Grushenka walked suddenly and noiselessly into the room. No one had expected her. Katya moved swiftly to the door, but when she reached Grushenka, she stopped suddenly, turned as white as chalk and moaned softly, almost in a whisper:

"Forgive me!"

Grushenka stared at her and, pausing for an instant, in a vindictive, venomous voice, answered:

"We are full of hatred, my girl, you and I! We are both full of hatred! As though we could forgive one another! Save him, and I'll worship you all my life."

"You won't forgive her!" cried Mitya, with frantic reproach.

"Don't be anxious, I'll save him for you!" Katya whispered rapidly, and she ran out of the room.

"And you could refuse to forgive her when she begged your forgiveness herself?' Mitya exclaimed bitterly again.

"Mitya, don't dare to blame her; you have no right to!" Alyosha cried hotly.

"Her proud lips spoke, not her heart," Grushenka brought out in a tone of disgust. "If she saves you I'll forgive her everything-"

She stopped speaking, as though suppressing something. She could not yet recover herself. She had come in, as appeared afterwards, accidentally, with no suspicion of what she would meet.

"Alyosha, run after her!" Mitya cried to his brother; "tell her...I don't know...don't let her go away like this!"

"I'll come to you again at nightfall," said Alyosha, and he ran after Katya. He overtook her outside the hospital grounds. She walking fast, but as soon as Alyosha caught her up she said quickly:

"No, before that woman I can't punish myself! I asked her forgiveness because I wanted to punish myself to the bitter end. She would not forgive me...I like her for that!" she added, in an unnatural voice, and her eyes flashed with fierce resentment.

"My brother did not expect this in the least," muttered Alyosha. "He was sure she would not come-"

"No doubt. Let us leave that," she snapped. "Listen: I can't go with you to the funeral now. I've sent them flowers. I think they still have money. If necessary, tell them I'll never abandon them...Now leave me, leave me, please. You are late as it is--the bells are ringing for the service...Leave me, please!"

Chapter 3. Ilusha's Funeral. The Speech at the Stone

HE really was late. They had waited for him and had already decided to bear the pretty flower-decked little coffin to the church without him. It was the coffin of poor little Ilusha. He had died two days after Mitya was sentenced. At the gate of the house Alyosha was met by the shouts of the boys, Ilusha's schoolfellows. They had all been impatiently expecting him and were glad that he had come at last. There were about twelve of them, they all had their school-bags or satchels on their shoulders. "Father will cry, be with father," Ilusha had told them as he lay dying, and the boys remembered it. Kolya Krassotkin was the foremost of them.

"How glad I am you've come, Karamazov!" he cried, holding out his hand to Alyosha. "It's awful here. It's really horrible to see it. Snegiryov is not drunk, we know for a fact he's had nothing to drink to-day, but he seems as if he were drunk...I am always manly, but this is awful. Karamazov, if I am not keeping you, one question before you go in?"

"What is it, Kolya?" said Alyosha.

"Is your brother innocent or guilty? Was it he killed your father or was it the valet? As you say, so it will be. I haven't slept for the last four nights for thinking of it."

"The valet killed him, my brother is innocent," answered Alyosha.

"That's what I said," cried Smurov.

"So he will perish an innocent victim!" exclaimed Kolya; "though he is ruined he is happy! I could envy him!"

"What do you mean? How can you? Why?" cried Alyosha surprised.

"Oh, if I, too, could sacrifice myself some day for truth!" said Kolya with enthusiasm.

"But not in such a cause, not with such disgrace and such horrer!" said Alyosha.

"Of course...I should like to die for all humanity, and as for disgrace, I don't care about that--our names may perish. I respect your brother!"

"And so do I!" the boy, who had once declared that he knew who had founded Troy, cried suddenly and unexpectedly, and he blushed up to his ears like a peony as he had done on that occasion.

Alyosha went into the room. Ilusha lay with his hands folded and his eyes closed in a blue coffin with a white frill round it. His thin face was hardly changed at all, and strange to say there was no smell of decay from the corpse. The expression of his face was serious and, as it were, thoughtful. His hands, crossed over his breast, looked particularly beautiful, as though chiselled in marble. There were flowers in his hands and the coffin, with flowers, which had been sent early in the morning by Lise Hohlakov. But there were flowers too from Katerina Ivanovna, and when Alyosha opened the door, the captain had a bunch in his trembling hands and was strewing them again over his dear boy. He scarcely glanced at Alyosha when he came in, and he would not look at anyone, even at his crazy weeping wife, "mamma," who kept trying to stand on her crippled legs to get a nearer look at her dead boy. Nina had been pushed in her chair by the boys close up to the coffin. She sat with her head pressed to it and she too was no doubt quietly weeping. Snegiryov's face looked eager, yet bewildered and exasperated. There was something crazy about his gestures and the words that broke from him. "Old man, dear old man!" he exclaimed every minute, gazing at Ilusha. It was his habit to call Ilusha "old man," as a term of affection when he was alive.

"Father, give me a flower, too; take that white one out of his hand and give it me," the crazy mother begged, whimpering. Either because the little white rose in Ilusha's hand had caught her fancy or that she wanted one from his hand to keep in memory of him, she moved restlessly, stretching out her hands for the flower.

"I won't give it to anyone, I won't give you anything," Snegiryov cried callously. "They are his flowers, not yours! Everything is his, nothing is yours!"

"Father, give mother a flower!" said Nina, lifting her face wet with tears.

"I won't give away anything and to her less than anyone! She didn't love Ilusha. She took away his little cannon and he gave it to her," the captain broke into loud sobs at the thought of how Ilusha had given up his cannon to his mother. The poor, crazy creature was bathed in noiseless tears, hiding her face in her hands.

The boys, seeing that the father would not leave the coffin and that it was time to carry it out, stood round it in a close circle and began to lift it up.

"I don't want him to be buried in the churchyard," Snegiryov wailed suddenly; "I'll bury him by the stone, by our stone! Ilusha told me to. I won't let him be carried out!" He had been saying for the last three days that he would bury him by the stone, but Alyosha, Krassotkin, the landlady, her sister and all the boys interfered.

"What an idea, bury him by an unholy stone, as though he had hanged himself!" the old landlady said sternly. "There in the churchyard the ground has been crossed. He'll be prayed for there. One can hear the singing in church and the deacon reads so plainly and verbally that it will reach him every time just as though it were read over his grave."

At last the captain made a gesture of despair as though to say, "Take him where you will." The boys raised the coffin, but as they passed the mother, they stopped for a moment and lowered it that she might say good-bye to Ilusha. But on seeing that precious little face, which for the last three days she had only looked at from a distance, she trembled all over and her grey head began twitching spasmodically over the coffin.

"Mother, make the sign of the cross over him, give him your blessing, kiss him," Nina cried to her. But her head still twitched like an automaton and with a face contorted with bitter grief she began, without a word, beating her breast with her fist. They carried the coffin past her. Nina pressed her lips to her brother's for the last time as they bore the coffin by her. As Alyosha went out of the house he begged the landlady to look after those who were left behind, but she interrupted him before he had finished.

"To be sure, I'll stay with them, we are Christians, too." The old woman wept as she said it.

They had not far to carry the coffin to the church, not more than three hundred paces. It was a still, clear day, with a slight frost. The church bells were still ringing. Snegiryov ran fussing and distracted after the coffin, in his short old summer overcoat, with his head bare and his soft, old, wide-brimmed hat in his hand. He seemed in a state of bewildered anxiety. At one minute he stretched out his hand to support the head of the coffin and only hindered the bearers, at another he ran alongside and tried to find a place for himself there. A flower fell on the snow and he rushed to pick it up as though everything in the world depended on the loss of that flower.

"And the crust of bread, we've forgotten the crust!" he cried suddenly in dismay. But the boys reminded him at once that he had taken the crust of bread already and that it was in his pocket. He instantly pulled it out and was reassured.

"Ilusha told me to, Ilusha," he explained at once to Alyosha. "I was sitting by him one night and he suddenly told me: 'Father, when my grave is filled up crumble a piece of bread on it so that the sparrows may fly down; I shall hear and it will cheer me up not to be lying alone.'"

"That's a good thing," said Alyosha, "we must often take some."

"Every day, every day!" said the captain quickly, seeming cheered at the thought.

They reached the church at last and set the coffin in the middle of it. The boys surrounded it and remained reverently standing so, all through the service. It was an old and rather poor church; many of the ikons were without settings; but such churches are the best for praying in. During the mass Snegiryov became somewhat calmer, though at times he had outbursts of the same unconscious and, as it were, incoherent anxiety. At one moment he went up to the coffin to set straight the cover or the wreath, when a candle fell out of the candlestick he rushed to replace it and was a fearful time fumbling over it, then he subsided and stood quietly by the coffin with a look of blank uneasiness and perplexity. After the Epistle he suddenly whispered to Alyosha, who was standing beside him, that the Epistle had not been read properly but did not explain what he meant. During the prayer, "Like the Cherubim," he joined in the singing but did not go on to the end. Falling on his knees, he pressed his forehead to the stone floor and lay so for a long while.

At last came the funeral service itself and candles were distributed. The distracted father began fussing about again, but the touching and impressive funeral prayers moved and roused his soul. He seemed suddenly to shrink together and broke into rapid, short sobs, which he tried at first to smother, but at last he sobbed aloud. When they began taking leave of the dead and closing the coffin, he flung his arms about, as though he would not allow them to cover Ilusha, and began greedily and persistently kissing his dead boy on the lips. At last they succeeded in persuading him to come away from the step, but suddenly he impulsively stretched out his hand and snatched a few flowers from the coffin. He looked at them and a new idea seemed to dawn upon him, so that he apparently forgot his grief for a minute. Gradually he seemed to sink into brooding and did not resist when the coffin was lifted up and carried to the grave. It was an expensive one in the churchyard close to the church, Katerina Ivanovna had paid for it. After the customary rites the grave-diggers lowered the coffin. Snegiryov with his flowers in his hands bent down so low over the open grave that the boys caught hold of his coat in alarm and pulled him back. He did not seem to understand fully what was happening. When they began filling up the grave, he suddenly pointed anxiously at the falling earth and began trying to say something, but no one could make out what he meant, and he stopped suddenly. Then he was reminded that he must crumble the bread and he was awfully excited, snatched up the bread and began pulling it to pieces--and flinging the morsels on the grave.

"Come, fly down, birds, fly down, sparrows!" he muttered anxiously.

One of the boys observed that it was awkward for him to crumble the bread with the flowers in his hands and suggested he should give them to someone to hold for a time. But he would not do this and seemed indeed suddenly alarmed for his flowers, as though they wanted to take them from him altogether. And after looking at the grave, and as it were, satisfying himself that everything had been done and the bread had been crumbled, he suddenly, to the surprise of everyone, turned, quite composedly even, and made his way homewards. But his steps became more and more hurried, he almost ran. The boys and Alyosha kept up with him.

"The flowers are for mamma, the flowers are for mamma! I was unkind to mamma," he began exclaiming suddenly.

Someone called to him to put on his hat as it was cold. But he flung the hat in the snow as though he were angry and kept repeating, "I won't have the hat, I won't have the hat." Smurov picked it up and carried it after him. All the boys were crying, and Kolya and the boy who discovered about Troy most of all. Though Smurov, with the captain's hat in his hand, was crying bitterly too, he managed, as he ran, to snatch up a piece of red brick that lay on the snow of the path, to fling it at the flock of sparrows that was flying by. He missed them, of course, and went on crying as he ran. Half-way, Snegiryov suddenly stopped, stood still for half a minute, as though struck by something, and suddenly turning back to the church, ran towards the deserted grave. But the boys instantly overtook him and caught hold of him on all sides. Then he fell helpless on the snow as though he had been knocked down, and struggling, sobbing, and wailing, he began crying out, "Ilusha, old man, dear old man!" Alyosha and Kolya tried to make him get up, soothing and persuading him.

"Captain, give over, a brave man must show fortitude," muttered Kolya.

"You'll spoil the flowers," said Alyosha, "and mamma is expecting them, she is sitting crying because you would not give her any before. Ilusha's little bed is still there--"

"Yes, yes, mamma!" Snegiryov suddenly recollected, "they'll take away the bed, they'll take it away," he added as though alarmed that they really would. He jumped up and ran homewards again. But it was not far off and they all arrived together. Snegiryov opened the door hurriedly and called to his wife with whom he had so cruelly quarrelled just before:

"Mamma, poor crippled darling, Ilusha has sent you these flowers," he cried, holding out to her a little bunch of flowers that had been frozen and broken while he was struggling in the snow. But at that instant he saw in the corner, by the little bed, Ilusha's little boots, which the landlady had put tidily side by side. Seeing the old, patched, rusty-looking, stiff boots he flung up his hands and rushed to them, fell on his knees, snatched up one boot and, pressing his lips to it, began kissing it greedily, crying, "Ilusha, old man, dear old man, where are your little feet?"

"Where have you taken him away? Where have you taken him?" the lunatic cried in a heart-rending voice. Nina, too, broke into sobs. Kolya ran out of the room, the boys followed him. At last Alyosha too went out.

"Let them weep," he said to Kolya, "it's no use trying to comfort them just now. Let wait a minute and then go back."

"No, it's no use, it's awful," Kolya assented. "Do you know, Karamazov," he dropped his voice so that no one could hear them, "I feel dreadfully sad, and if it were only possible to bring him back, I'd give anything in the world to do it."

"Ah, so would I," said Alyosha.

"What do you think, Karamazov? Had we better come back here to-night? He'll be drunk, you know."

"Perhaps he will. Let us come together, you and I, that will be enough, to spend an hour with them, with the mother and Nina. If we all come together we shall remind them of everything again," Alyosha suggested.

"The landlady is laying the table for them now--there'll be a funeral dinner or something, the priest is coming; shall we go back to it, Karamazov?"

"Of course," said Alyosha.

"It's all so strange, Karamazov, such sorrow and then pancakes after it, it all seems so unnatural in our religion."

"They are going to have salmon, too," the boy who had discovered about Troy observed in a loud voice.

"I beg you most earnestly, Kartashov, not to interrupt again with your idiotic remarks, especially when one is not talking to you and doesn't care to know whether you exist or not!" Kolya snapped out irritably. The boy flushed crimson but did not dare to reply.

Meantime they were strolling slowly along the path and suddenly Smurov exclaimed:

"There's Ilusha's stone, under which they wanted to bury him."

They all stood still by the big stone. Alyosha looked and the whole picture of what Snegiryov had described to him that day, how Ilusha, weeping and hugging his father, had cried, "Father, father, how he insulted you," rose at once before his imagination. A sudden impulse seemed to come into his soul. With a serious and earnest expression he looked from one to another of the bright, pleasant faces of Ilusha's schoolfellows, and suddenly said to them:

"Boys, I should like to say one word to you, here at this place."

The boys stood round him and at once bent attentive and expectant eyes upon him.

"Boys, we shall soon part. I shall be for some time with my two brothers, of whom one is going to Siberia and the other is lying at death's door. But soon I shall leave this town, perhaps for a long time, so we shall part. Let us make a compact here, at Ilusha's stone, that we will never forget Ilusha and one another.

And whatever happens to us later in life, if we don't meet for twenty years afterwards, let us always remember how we buried the poor boy at whom we once threw stones, do you remember, by the bridge? and afterwards we all grew so fond of him. He was a fine boy, a kindhearted, brave boy, he felt for his father's honour and resented the cruel insult to him and stood up for him. And so in the first place, we will remember him, boys, all our lives. And even if we are occupied with most important things, if we attain to honour or fall into great misfortune--still let us remember how good it was once here, when we were all together, united by a good and kind feeling which made us, for the time we were loving that poor boy, better perhaps than we are. My little doves let me call you so, for you are very like them, those pretty blue birds, at this minute as I look at your good dear faces. My dear children, perhaps you won't understand what I am saying to you, because I often speak very unintelligibly, but you'll remember all the same and will agree with my words some time. You must know that there is nothing higher and stronger and more wholesome and good for life in the future than some good memory, especially a memory of childhood, of home. People talk to you a great deal about your education, but some good, sacred memory, preserved from childhood, is perhaps the best education. If a man carries many such memories with him into life, he is safe to the end of his days, and if one has only one good memory left in one's heart, even that may sometime be the means of saving us. Perhaps we may even grow wicked later on, may be unable to refrain from a bad action, may laugh at men's tears and at those people who say as Kolya did just now, 'I want to suffer for all men,' and may even jeer spitefully at such people. But however bad we may become--which God forbid--yet, when we recall how we buried Ilusha, how we loved him in his last days, and how we have been talking like friends all together, at this stone, the cruellest and most mocking of us--if we do become so will not dare to laugh inwardly at having been kind and good at this moment! What's more, perhaps, that one memory may keep him from great evil and he will reflect and say, 'Yes, I was good and brave and honest then!' Let him laugh to himself, that's no matter, a man often laughs at what's good and kind. That's only from thoughtlessness. But I assure you, boys, that as he laughs he will say at once in his heart, 'No, I do wrong to laugh, for that's not a thing to laugh at.'

"That will be so, I understand you, Karamazov!" cried Kolya, with flashing eyes.

The boys were excited and they, too, wanted to say something, but they restrained themselves, looking with intentness and emotion at the speaker.

"I say this in case we become bad," Alyosha went on, "but there's no reason why we should become bad, is there, boys? Let us be, first and above all, kind, then honest and then let us never forget each other! I say that again. I give you my word for my part that I'll never forget one of you. Every face looking at me now I shall remember even for thirty years. Just now Kolya said to Kartashov that we did not care to know whether he exists or not. But I cannot forget that Kartashov exists and that he is not blushing now as he did when he discovered the founders of Troy, but is looking at me with his jolly, kind, dear little eyes. Boys, my dear boys, let us all be generous and brave like Ilusha, clever, brave and generous like Kolya (though he will be ever so much cleverer when he is grown up), and let us all be as modest, as clever and sweet as Kartashov. But why am I talking about those two? You are all dear to me, boys; from this day forth, I have a place in my heart for you all, and I beg you to keep a place in your hearts for me! Well, and who has united us in this kind, good feeling which we shall remember and intend to remember all our lives? Who, if not Ilusha, the good boy, the dear boy, precious to us for ever! Let us never forget him. May his memory live for ever in our hearts from this time forth!"

"Yes, yes, for ever, for ever!" the boys cried in their ringing voices, with softened faces.

"Let us remember his face and his clothes and his poor little boots, his coffin and his unhappy, sinful father, and how boldly he stood up for him alone against the whole school."

"We will remember, we will remember," cried the boys. "He was brave, he was good!"

"Ah, how I loved him!" exclaimed Kolya.

"Ah, children, ah, dear friends, don't be afraid of life! How good life is when one does something good and just!"

"Yes, yes," the boys repeated enthusiastically.

"Karamazov, we love you!" a voice, probably Kartashov's, cried impulsively.

"We love you, we love you!" they all caught it up. There were tears in the eyes of many of them.

"Hurrah for Karamazov!" Kolya shouted ecstatically.

"And may the dead boy's memory live for ever!" Alyosha added again with feeling.

"For ever!" the boys chimed in again.

"Karamazov," cried Kolya, "can it be true what's taught us in religion, that we shall all rise again from the dead and shall live and see each other again, all, Ilusha too?"

"Certainly we shall all rise again, certainly we shall see each other and shall tell each other with joy and gladness all that has happened!" Alyosha answered, half laughing, half enthusiastic.

"Ah, how splendid it will be!" broke from Kolya.

"Well, now we will finish talking and go to his funeral dinner. Don't be put out at our eating pancakes--it's a very old custom and there's something nice in that!" laughed Alyosha. "Well, let us go! And now we go hand in hand."

"And always so, all our lives hand in hand! Hurrah for Karamazov!" Kolya cried once more rapturously, and once more the boys took up his exclamation:

"Hurrah for Karamazov!"

Crime and Punishment

PART I

CHAPTER I

On an exceptionally hot evening early in July a young man came out of the garret in which he lodged in S. Place and walked slowly, as though in hesitation, towards K. bridge.

He had successfully avoided meeting his landlady on the staircase. His garret was under the roof of a high, five-storied house and was more like a cupboard than a room. The landlady who provided him with garret, dinners, and attendance, lived on the floor below, and every time he went out he was obliged to pass her kitchen, the door of which invariably stood open. And each time he passed, the young man had a sick, frightened feeling, which made him scowl and feel ashamed. He was hopelessly in debt to his landlady, and was afraid of meeting her.

This was not because he was cowardly and abject, quite the contrary; but for some time past he had been in an overstrained irritable condition, verging on hypochondria. He had become so completely absorbed in himself, and isolated from his fellows that he dreaded meeting, not only his landlady, but anyone at all. He was crushed by poverty, but the anxieties of his position had of late ceased to weigh upon him. He had given up attending to matters of practical importance; he had lost all desire to do so. Nothing that any landlady could do had a real terror for him. But to be stopped on the stairs, to be forced to listen to her trivial, irrelevant gossip, to pestering demands for payment, threats and complaints, and to rack his brains for excuses, to prevaricate, to lie—no, rather than that, he would creep down the stairs like a cat and slip out unseen.

This evening, however, on coming out into the street, he became acutely aware of his fears.

"I want to attempt a thing *like that* and am frightened by these trifles," he thought, with an odd smile. "Hm... yes, all is in a man's hands and he lets it all slip from cowardice, that's an axiom. It would be interesting to know what it is men are most afraid of. Taking a new step, uttering a new word is what they fear most.... But I am talking too much. It's because I chatter that I do nothing. Or perhaps it is that I chatter because I do nothing. I've learned to chatter this last month, lying for days together in my den thinking... of Jack the Giant-killer. Why am I going there now? Am I capable of *that*? Is *that* serious? It is not serious at all. It's simply a fantasy to amuse myself; a plaything! Yes, maybe it is a plaything."

The heat in the street was terrible: and the airlessness, the bustle and the plaster, scaffolding, bricks, and dust all about him, and that special Petersburg stench, so familiar to all who are unable to get out of town in summer—all worked painfully upon the young man's already overwrought nerves. The insufferable stench from the pot-houses, which are particularly numerous in that part of the town, and the drunken men whom he met continually, although it was a working day, completed the revolting misery of the picture. An expression of the profoundest disgust gleamed for a moment in the young man's refined face. He was, by the way, exceptionally handsome, above the average in height, slim, well-built, with beautiful dark eyes and dark brown hair. Soon he sank into deep thought, or more accurately speaking into a complete blankness of mind; he walked along not observing what was about him and not caring to observe it. From time to time, he would mutter something, from the habit of talking to himself, to which he had just confessed. At these moments he would become conscious that his ideas were sometimes in a tangle and that he was very weak; for two days he had scarcely tasted food.

He was so badly dressed that even a man accustomed to shabbiness would have been ashamed to be seen in the street in such rags. In that quarter of the town, however, scarcely any shortcoming in dress would have created surprise. Owing to the proximity of the Hay Market, the number of establishments of bad character, the preponderance of the trading and working class population crowded in these streets and alleys in the heart of Petersburg, types so various were to be seen in the streets that no figure, however queer, would have caused surprise. But there was such accumulated bitterness and contempt in the young man's heart, that, in spite of all the fastidiousness of youth, he minded his rags least of all in the street. It was a different matter when he met with acquaintances or with former fellow students, whom, indeed, he disliked meeting at any time. And yet when a drunken man who, for some unknown reason, was being taken somewhere in a huge waggon dragged by a heavy dray horse, suddenly shouted at him as he drove past: "Hey there, German hatter" bawling at the top of his voice and pointing at him—the young man stopped suddenly and clutched tremulously at his hat. It was a tall round hat from Zimmerman's, but completely worn out, rusty with age, all torn and bespattered, brimless and bent on one side in a most unseemly fashion. Not shame, however, but quite another feeling akin to terror had overtaken him.

"I knew it," he muttered in confusion, "I thought so! That's the worst of all! Why, a stupid thing like this, the most trivial detail might spoil the whole plan. Yes, my hat is too noticeable.... It looks absurd and that makes it noticeable.... With my rags I ought to wear a cap, any sort of old pancake, but not this grotesque thing. Nobody wears such a hat, it would be noticed a mile off, it would be remembered.... What matters is that people would remember it, and that would give them a clue. For this business one should be as little conspicuous as possible.... Trifles, trifles are what matter! Why, it's just such trifles that always ruin everything...."

He had not far to go; he knew indeed how many steps it was from the gate of his lodging house: exactly seven hundred and thirty. He had counted them once when he had been lost in dreams. At the time he had put no faith in those dreams and was only tantalising himself by their hideous but daring recklessness. Now, a month later, he had begun to look upon them differently, and, in spite of the monologues in which he jeered at his own impotence and indecision, he had involuntarily come to regard this "hideous" dream as an exploit to be attempted, although he still did not realise this himself. He was positively going now for a "rehearsal" of his project, and at every step his excitement grew more and more violent.

With a sinking heart and a nervous tremor, he went up to a huge house which on one side looked on to the canal, and on the other into the street. This house was let out in tiny tenements and was inhabited by working people of all kinds—tailors, locksmiths, cooks, Germans of sorts, girls picking up a living as best they could, petty clerks, etc. There was a continual coming and going through the two gates and in the two courtyards of the house. Three or four door-keepers were employed on the building. The young man was very glad to meet none of them, and at once slipped unnoticed through the door on the right, and up the staircase. It was a back staircase, dark and narrow, but he was familiar with it already, and knew his way, and he liked all these surroundings: in such darkness even the most inquisitive eyes were not to be dreaded.

"If I am so scared now, what would it be if it somehow came to pass that I were really going to do it?" he could not help asking himself as he reached the fourth storey. There his progress was barred by some porters who were engaged in moving furniture out of a flat. He knew that the flat had been occupied by a German clerk in the civil service, and his family. This German was moving out then, and so the fourth floor on this staircase would be untenanted except by the old woman. "That's a good thing anyway," he thought to himself, as he rang the bell of the old woman's flat. The bell gave a faint tinkle as though it were made of tin and not of copper. The little flats in such houses always have bells that ring like that. He had forgotten the note of that bell, and now its peculiar tinkle seemed to remind him of something and to bring it clearly before him.... He started, his nerves were terribly overstrained by now. In a little while, the door was opened a tiny crack: the old woman eyed her visitor with evident distrust through the crack, and nothing could be seen but her little eyes, glittering in the darkness. But, seeing a number of people on the landing, she grew bolder, and opened the door wide. The young man stepped into the dark entry, which was partitioned off from the tiny kitchen. The old woman stood facing him in silence and looking inquiringly at him. She was a diminutive, withered up old woman of sixty, with sharp malignant eyes and a sharp little nose. Her colourless, somewhat grizzled hair was thickly smeared with oil, and she wore no kerchief over it. Round her thin long neck, which looked like a hen's leg, was knotted some sort of flannel rag, and, in spite of the heat, there hung flapping on her shoulders, a mangy fur cape, yellow with age. The old woman coughed and groaned at every instant. The young man must have looked at her with a rather peculiar expression, for a gleam of mistrust came into her eyes again.

"Raskolnikov, a student, I came here a month ago," the young man made haste to mutter, with a half bow, remembering that he ought to be more polite.

"I remember, my good sir, I remember quite well your coming here," the old woman said distinctly, still keeping her inquiring eyes on his face.

"And here... I am again on the same errand," Raskolnikov continued, a little disconcerted and surprised at the old woman's mistrust. "Perhaps she is always like that though, only I did not notice it the other time," he thought with an uneasy feeling.

The old woman paused, as though hesitating; then stepped on one side, and pointing to the door of the room, she said, letting her visitor pass in front of her:

"Step in, my good sir."

The little room into which the young man walked, with yellow paper on the walls, geraniums and muslin curtains in the windows, was brightly lighted up at that moment by the setting sun.

"So the sun will shine like this *then* too!" flashed as it were by chance through Raskolnikov's mind, and with a rapid glance he scanned everything in the room, trying as far as possible to notice and remember its arrangement. But there was nothing special in the room. The furniture, all very old and of yellow wood, consisted of a sofa with a huge bent wooden back, an oval table in front of the sofa, a dressing-table with a looking-glass fixed on it between the windows, chairs along the walls and two or three half-penny prints in yellow frames, representing German damsels with birds in their hands—that was all. In the corner a light was burning before a small ikon. Everything was very clean; the floor and the furniture were brightly polished; everything shone.

"Lizaveta's work," thought the young man. There was not a speck of dust to be seen in the whole flat.

"It's in the houses of spiteful old widows that one finds such cleanliness," Raskolnikov thought again, and he stole a curious glance at the cotton curtain over the door leading into another tiny room, in which stood the old woman's bed and chest of drawers and into which he had never looked before. These two rooms made up the whole flat.

"What do you want?" the old woman said severely, coming into the room and, as before, standing in front of him so as to look him straight in the face.

"I've brought something to pawn here," and he drew out of his pocket an old-fashioned flat silver watch, on the back of which was engraved a globe; the chain was of steel.

"But the time is up for your last pledge. The month was up the day before yesterday."

"I will bring you the interest for another month; wait a little."

"But that's for me to do as I please, my good sir, to wait or to sell your pledge at once."

"How much will you give me for the watch, Alyona Ivanovna?"

"You come with such trifles, my good sir, it's scarcely worth anything. I gave you two roubles last time for your ring and one could buy it quite new at a jeweler's for a rouble and a half."

"Give me four roubles for it, I shall redeem it, it was my father's. I shall be getting some money soon."

"A rouble and a half, and interest in advance, if you like!"

"A rouble and a half!" cried the young man.

"Please yourself"—and the old woman handed him back the watch. The young man took it, and was so angry that he was on the point of going away; but checked himself at once, remembering that there was nowhere else he could go, and that he had had another object also in coming.

"Hand it over," he said roughly.

The old woman fumbled in her pocket for her keys, and disappeared behind the curtain into the other room. The young man, left standing alone in the middle of the room, listened inquisitively, thinking. He could hear her unlocking the chest of drawers.

"It must be the top drawer," he reflected. "So she carries the keys in a pocket on the right. All in one bunch on a steel ring.... And there's one key there, three times as big as all the others, with deep notches; that can't be the key of the chest of drawers... then there must be some other chest or strong-box... that's worth knowing. Strong-boxes always have keys like that... but how degrading it all is."

The old woman came back.

"Here, sir: as we say ten copecks the rouble a month, so I must take fifteen copecks from a rouble and a half for the month in advance. But for the two roubles I lent you before, you owe me now twenty copecks on the same reckoning in advance. That makes thirty-five copecks altogether. So I must give you a rouble and fifteen copecks for the watch. Here it is."

"What! only a rouble and fifteen copecks now!"

"Just so."

The young man did not dispute it and took the money. He looked at the old woman, and was in no hurry to get away, as though there was still something he wanted to say or to do, but he did not himself quite know what.

"I may be bringing you something else in a day or two, Alyona Ivanovna—a valuable thing—silver—a cigarette-box, as soon as I get it back from a friend..." he broke off in confusion.

"Well, we will talk about it then, sir."

"Good-bye—are you always at home alone, your sister is not here with you?" He asked her as casually as possible as he went out into the passage.

"What business is she of yours, my good sir?"

"Oh, nothing particular, I simply asked. You are too quick.... Good-day, Alyona Ivanovna."

Raskolnikov went out in complete confusion. This confusion became more and more intense. As he went down the stairs, he even stopped short, two or three times, as though suddenly struck by some thought. When he was in the street he cried out, "Oh, God, how loathsome it all is! and can I, can I possibly.... No, it's nonsense, it's rubbish!" he added resolutely. "And how could such an atrocious thing come into my head? What filthy things my heart is capable of. Yes, filthy above all, disgusting, loathsome, loathsome!—and for a whole month I've been...." But no words, no exclamations, could express his agitation. The feeling of intense repulsion, which had begun to oppress and torture his heart while he was on his way to the old woman, had by now reached such a pitch and had taken such a definite form that he did not know what to do with himself to escape from his wretchedness. He walked along the pavement like a drunken man, regardless of the passers-by, and jostling against them, and only came to his senses when he was in the next street. Looking round, he noticed that he was standing close to a tavern which was entered by steps leading from the pavement to the basement. At that instant two drunken men came out at the door, and abusing and supporting one another, they mounted the steps. Without stopping to think, Raskolnikov went down the steps at once. Till that moment he had never been into a tavern, but now he felt giddy and was tormented by a burning thirst. He longed for a drink of cold beer, and attributed his sudden weakness to the want of food. He sat down at a sticky little table in a dark and dirty corner; ordered some beer, and eagerly drank off the first glassful. At once he felt easier; and his thoughts became clear.

"All that's nonsense," he said hopefully, "and there is nothing in it all to worry about! It's simply physical derangement. Just a glass of beer, a piece of dry bread—and in one moment the brain is stronger, the mind is clearer and the will is firm! Phew, how utterly petty it all is!"

But in spite of this scornful reflection, he was by now looking cheerful as though he were suddenly set free from a terrible burden: and he gazed round in a friendly way at the people in the room. But even at that moment he had a dim foreboding that this happier frame of mind was also not normal.

There were few people at the time in the tavern. Besides the two drunken men he had met on the steps, a group consisting of about five men and a girl with a concertina had gone out at the same time. Their departure left the room quiet and rather empty. The persons still in the tavern were a man who appeared to be an artisan, drunk, but not extremely so, sitting before a pot of beer, and his companion, a huge, stout man with a grey beard, in a short full-skirted coat. He was very drunk: and had dropped asleep on the bench; every now and then, he began as though in his sleep, cracking his fingers, with his arms wide apart and the upper part of his body bounding about on the bench, while he hummed some meaningless refrain, trying to recall some such lines as these:

"His   wife   a   year   he   fondly   loved
His wife a—a year he—fondly loved."

Or suddenly waking up again:

"Walking   along   the   crowded   row
He met the one he used to know."

But no one shared his enjoyment: his silent companion looked with positive hostility and mistrust at all these manifestations. There was another man in the room who looked somewhat like a retired government clerk. He was sitting apart, now and then sipping from his pot and looking round at the company. He, too, appeared to be in some agitation.

CHAPTER II

Raskolnikov was not used to crowds, and, as we said before, he avoided society of every sort, more especially of late. But now all at once he felt a desire to be with other people. Something new seemed to be taking place within him, and with it he felt a sort of thirst for company. He was so weary after a whole month of concentrated wretchedness and gloomy excitement that he longed to rest, if only for a moment, in some other world, whatever it might be; and, in spite of the filthiness of the surroundings, he was glad now to stay in the tavern.

The master of the establishment was in another room, but he frequently came down some steps into the main room, his jaunty, tarred boots with red turn-over tops coming into view each time before the rest of his person. He wore a full coat and a horribly greasy black satin waistcoat, with no cravat, and his whole face seemed smeared with oil like an iron lock. At the counter stood a boy of about fourteen, and there was another boy somewhat younger who handed whatever was wanted. On the counter lay some sliced cucumber, some pieces of dried black bread, and some fish, chopped up small, all smelling very bad. It was insufferably close, and so heavy with the fumes of spirits that five minutes in such an atmosphere might well make a man drunk.

There are chance meetings with strangers that interest us from the first moment, before a word is spoken. Such was the impression made on Raskolnikov by the person sitting a little distance from him, who looked like a retired clerk. The young man often recalled this impression afterwards, and even ascribed it to presentiment. He looked repeatedly at the clerk, partly no doubt because the latter was staring persistently at him, obviously anxious to enter into conversation. At the other persons in the room, including the tavern-keeper, the clerk looked as though he were used to their company, and weary of it, showing a shade of condescending contempt for them as persons of station and culture inferior to his own, with whom it would be useless for him to converse. He was a man over fifty, bald and grizzled, of medium height, and stoutly built. His face, bloated from continual drinking, was of a yellow, even greenish, tinge, with swollen eyelids out of which keen reddish eyes gleamed like little chinks. But there was something very strange in him; there was a light in his eyes as though of intense feeling—perhaps there were even thought and intelligence, but at the same time there was a gleam of something like madness. He was wearing an old and hopelessly ragged black dress coat, with all its buttons missing except one, and that one he had buttoned, evidently clinging to this last trace of respectability. A crumpled shirt front, covered with spots and stains, protruded from his canvas waistcoat. Like a clerk, he wore no beard, nor moustache, but had been so long unshaven that his chin looked like a stiff greyish brush. And there was something respectable and like an official about his manner too. But he was restless; he ruffled up his hair and from time to time let his head drop into his hands dejectedly resting his ragged elbows on the stained and sticky table. At last he looked straight at Raskolnikov, and said loudly and resolutely:

"May I venture, honoured sir, to engage you in polite conversation? Forasmuch as, though your exterior would not command respect, my experience admonishes me that you are a man of education and not accustomed to drinking. I have always respected education when in conjunction with genuine sentiments, and I am besides a titular counsellor in rank. Marmeladov—such is my name; titular counsellor. I make bold to inquire—have you been in the service?"

"No, I am studying," answered the young man, somewhat surprised at the grandiloquent style of the speaker and also at being so directly addressed. In spite of the momentary desire he had just been feeling for company of any sort, on being actually spoken to he felt immediately his habitual irritable and uneasy aversion for any stranger who approached or attempted to approach him.

"A student then, or formerly a student," cried the clerk. "Just what I thought! I'm a man of experience, immense experience, sir," and he tapped his forehead with his fingers in self-approval. "You've been a student or have attended some learned institution!... But allow me...." He got up, staggered, took up his jug and glass, and sat down beside the young man, facing him a little sideways. He was drunk, but spoke fluently and boldly, only occasionally losing the thread of his sentences and drawling his words. He pounced upon Raskolnikov as greedily as though he too had not spoken to a soul for a month.

"Honoured sir," he began almost with solemnity, "poverty is not a vice, that's a true saying. Yet I know too that drunkenness is not a virtue, and that that's even truer. But beggary, honoured sir, beggary is a vice. In poverty you may still retain your innate nobility of soul, but in beggary—never—no one. For beggary a man is not chased out of human society with a stick, he is swept out with a broom, so as to make it as humiliating as possible; and quite right, too, forasmuch as in beggary I am ready to be the first to humiliate myself. Hence the pot-house! Honoured sir, a month ago Mr. Lebeziatnikov gave my wife a beating, and my wife is a very different matter from me! Do you understand? Allow me to ask you another question out of simple curiosity: have you ever spent a night on a hay barge, on the Neva?"

"No, I have not happened to," answered Raskolnikov. "What do you mean?"

"Well, I've just come from one and it's the fifth night I've slept so...." He filled his glass, emptied it and paused. Bits of hay were in fact clinging to his clothes and sticking to his hair. It seemed quite probable that he had not undressed or washed for the last five days. His hands, particularly, were filthy. They were fat and red, with black nails.

His conversation seemed to excite a general though languid interest. The boys at the counter fell to sniggering. The innkeeper came down from the upper room, apparently on purpose to listen to the "funny fellow" and sat down at a little distance, yawning lazily, but with dignity. Evidently Marmeladov was a familiar figure here, and he had most likely acquired his weakness for high-flown speeches from the habit of frequently entering into conversation with strangers of all sorts in the tavern. This habit develops into a necessity in some drunkards, and especially in those who are looked after sharply and kept in order at home. Hence in the company of other drinkers they try to justify themselves and even if possible obtain consideration.

"Funny fellow!" pronounced the innkeeper. "And why don't you work, why aren't you at your duty, if you are in the service?"

"Why am I not at my duty, honoured sir," Marmeladov went on, addressing himself exclusively to Raskolnikov, as though it had been he who put that question to him. "Why am I not at my duty? Does not my heart ache to think what a useless worm I am? A month ago when Mr. Lebeziatnikov beat my wife with his own hands, and I lay drunk, didn't I suffer? Excuse me, young man, has it ever happened to you... hm... well, to petition hopelessly for a loan?"

"Yes, it has. But what do you mean by hopelessly?"

"Hopelessly in the fullest sense, when you know beforehand that you will get nothing by it. You know, for instance, beforehand with positive certainty that this man, this most reputable and exemplary citizen, will on no consideration give you money; and indeed I ask you why should he? For he knows of course that I shan't pay it back. From compassion? But Mr. Lebeziatnikov who keeps up with modern ideas explained the other day that compassion is forbidden nowadays by science itself, and that that's what is done now in England, where there is political economy. Why, I ask you, should he give it to me? And yet though I know beforehand that he won't, I set off to him and..."

"Why do you go?" put in Raskolnikov.

"Well, when one has no one, nowhere else one can go! For every man must have somewhere to go. Since there are times when one absolutely must go somewhere! When my own daughter first went out with a yellow ticket, then I had to go... (for my daughter has a yellow passport)," he added in parenthesis, looking with a certain uneasiness at the young man. "No matter, sir, no matter!" he went on hurriedly and with apparent composure when both the boys at the counter guffawed and even the innkeeper smiled—"No matter, I am not confounded by the wagging of their heads; for everyone knows everything about it already, and all that is secret is made open. And I accept it all, not with contempt, but with humility. So be it! So be it! 'Behold the man!' Excuse me, young man, can you.... No, to put it more strongly and more distinctly; not *can* you but *dare* you, looking upon me, assert that I am not a pig?"

The young man did not answer a word.

"Well," the orator began again stolidly and with even increased dignity, after waiting for the laughter in the room to subside. "Well, so be it, I am a pig, but she is a lady! I have the semblance of a beast, but Katerina Ivanovna, my spouse, is a person of education and an officer's daughter. Granted, granted, I am a scoundrel, but she is a woman of a noble heart, full of sentiments, refined by education. And yet... oh, if only she felt for me! Honoured sir, honoured sir, you know every man ought to have at least one place where people feel for him! But Katerina Ivanovna, though she is magnanimous, she is unjust.... And yet, although I realise that when she pulls my hair she only does it out of pity—for I repeat without being ashamed, she pulls my hair, young man," he declared with redoubled dignity, hearing the sniggering again—"but, my God, if she would but once.... But no, no! It's all in vain and it's no use talking! No use talking! For more than once, my wish did come true and more than once she has felt for me but... such is my fate and I am a beast by nature!"

"Rather!" assented the innkeeper yawning. Marmeladov struck his fist resolutely on the table.

"Such is my fate! Do you know, sir, do you know, I have sold her very stockings for drink? Not her shoes—that would be more or less in the order of things, but her stockings, her stockings I have sold for drink! Her mohair shawl I sold for drink, a present to her long ago, her own property, not mine; and we live in a cold room and she caught cold this winter and has begun coughing and spitting blood too. We have three little children and Katerina Ivanovna is at work from morning till night; she is scrubbing and cleaning and washing the children, for she's been used to cleanliness from a child. But her chest is weak and she has a tendency to consumption and I feel it! Do you suppose I don't feel it? And the more I drink the more I feel it. That's why I drink too. I try to find sympathy and feeling in drink.... I drink so that I may suffer twice as much!" And as though in despair he laid his head down on the table.

"Young man," he went on, raising his head again, "in your face I seem to read some trouble of mind. When you came in I read it, and that was why I addressed you at once. For in unfolding to you the story of my life, I do not wish to make myself a laughing-stock before these idle listeners, who indeed know all about it already, but I am looking for a man of feeling and education. Know then that my wife was educated in a high-class school for the daughters of noblemen, and on leaving she danced the shawl dance before the governor and other personages for which she was presented with a gold medal and a certificate of merit. The medal... well, the medal of course was sold—long ago, hm... but the certificate of merit is in her trunk still and not long ago she showed it to our landlady. And although she is most continually on bad terms with the landlady, yet she wanted to tell someone or other of her past honours and of the happy days that are gone. I don't condemn her for it, I don't blame her, for the one thing left her is recollection of the past, and all the rest is dust and ashes. Yes, yes, she is a lady of spirit, proud and determined. She scrubs the floors herself and has nothing but black bread to eat, but won't allow herself to be treated with disrespect. That's why she would not overlook Mr. Lebeziatnikov's rudeness to her, and so when he gave her a beating for it, she took to her bed more from the hurt to her feelings than from the blows. She was a widow when I married her, with three children, one smaller than the other. She married her first husband, an infantry officer, for love, and ran away with him from her father's house. She was exceedingly fond of her husband; but he gave way to cards, got into trouble and with that he died. He used to beat her at the end: and although she paid him back, of which I have authentic documentary evidence, to this day she speaks of him with tears and she throws him up to me; and I am glad, I am glad that, though only in imagination, she should think of herself as having once been happy.... And she was left at his death with three children in a wild and remote district where I happened to be at the time; and she was left in such hopeless poverty that, although I have seen many ups and downs of all sort, I don't feel equal to describing it even. Her relations had all thrown her off. And she was proud, too, excessively proud.... And then, honoured sir, and then, I, being at the time a widower, with a daughter of fourteen left me by my first wife, offered her my hand, for I could not bear the sight of such suffering. You can judge the extremity of her calamities, that she, a woman of education and culture and distinguished family, should have consented to be my wife. But she did! Weeping and sobbing and wringing her hands, she married me! For she had nowhere to turn! Do you understand, sir, do you understand what it means when you have absolutely nowhere to turn? No, that you don't understand yet.... And for a whole year, I performed my duties conscientiously and faithfully, and did not touch this" (he tapped the jug with his finger), "for I have feelings. But even so, I could not please her; and then I lost my place too, and that through no fault of mine but through changes in the office; and then I did touch it!... It will be a year and a half ago soon since we found ourselves at last after many wanderings and numerous calamities in this magnificent capital, adorned with innumerable monuments. Here I obtained a situation.... I obtained it and I lost it again. Do you understand? This time it was through my own fault I lost it: for my weakness had come out.... We have now part of a room at Amalia Fyodorovna Lippevechsel's; and what we live upon and what we pay our rent with, I could not say. There are a lot of people living there besides ourselves. Dirt and disorder, a perfect Bedlam... hm... yes... And meanwhile my daughter by my first wife has grown up; and what my daughter has had to put up with from her step-mother whilst she was growing up, I won't speak of. For, though Katerina Ivanovna is full of generous feelings, she is a spirited lady, irritable and short-tempered.... Yes. But it's no use going over that! Sonia, as you may well fancy, has had no education. I did make an effort four years ago to give her a course of geography and universal history, but as I was not very well up in those subjects myself and we had no suitable books, and what books we had... hm, anyway we have not even those now, so all our instruction came to an end. We stopped at Cyrus of Persia. Since she has attained years of maturity, she has read other books of romantic tendency and of late she had read with great interest a book she got through Mr. Lebeziatnikov, Lewes' Physiology—do you know it?—and even recounted extracts from it to us: and that's the whole of her education. And now may I venture to address you, honoured sir, on my own account with a private question. Do you suppose that a respectable poor girl can earn much by honest work? Not fifteen farthings a day can she earn, if she is respectable and has no special talent and that without putting her work down for an instant! And what's more, Ivan Ivanitch Klopstock the civil counsellor—have you heard of him?—has not to this day paid her for the half-dozen linen shirts she made him and drove her roughly away, stamping and reviling her, on the pretext that the shirt collars were not made like the pattern and were put in askew. And there are the little ones hungry.... And Katerina Ivanovna walking up and down and wringing her hands, her cheeks flushed red, as they always are in that disease: 'Here you live with us,' says she, 'you eat and drink and are kept warm and you do nothing to help.' And much she gets to eat and drink when there is not a crust for the little ones for three days! I was lying at the time... well, what of it! I was lying drunk and I heard my Sonia speaking (she is a gentle creature with a soft little voice... fair hair and such a pale, thin little face). She said: 'Katerina Ivanovna, am I really to do a thing like that?' And Darya Frantsovna, a woman of evil character and very well known to the police, had two or three times tried to get at her through the landlady. 'And why not?' said Katerina Ivanovna with a jeer, 'you are something mighty precious to be so careful of!' But don't blame her, don't blame her, honoured sir, don't blame her! She was not herself when she spoke, but driven to distraction by her illness and the crying of the hungry children; and it was said more to wound her than anything else.... For that's Katerina Ivanovna's character, and when children cry, even from hunger, she falls to beating them at once. At six o'clock I saw Sonia get up, put on her kerchief and her cape, and go out of the room and about nine o'clock she came back. She walked straight up to Katerina Ivanovna and she laid thirty roubles on the table before her in silence. She did not utter a word, she did not even look at her, she simply picked up our big green *drap de dames* shawl (we have a shawl, made of *drap de dames*), put it over her head and face and lay down on the bed with her face to the wall; only her little shoulders and her body kept shuddering.... And I went on lying there, just as before.... And then I saw, young man, I saw Katerina Ivanovna, in the same silence go up to Sonia's little bed; she was on her knees all the evening kissing Sonia's feet, and would not get up, and then they both fell asleep in each other's arms... together, together... yes... and I... lay drunk."

Marmeladov stopped short, as though his voice had failed him. Then he hurriedly filled his glass, drank, and cleared his throat.

"Since then, sir," he went on after a brief pause—"Since then, owing to an unfortunate occurrence and through information given by evil-intentioned persons—in all which Darya Frantsovna took a leading part on the pretext that she had been treated with want of respect—since then my daughter Sofya Semyonovna has been forced to take a yellow ticket, and owing to that she is unable to go on living with us. For our landlady, Amalia Fyodorovna would not hear of it (though she had backed up Darya Frantsovna before) and Mr. Lebeziatnikov too... hm.... All the trouble between him and Katerina Ivanovna was on Sonia's account. At first he was for making up to Sonia himself and then all of a sudden he stood on his dignity: 'how,' said he, 'can a highly educated man like me live in the same rooms with a girl like that?' And Katerina Ivanovna would not let it pass, she stood up for her... and so that's how it happened. And Sonia comes to us now, mostly after dark; she comforts Katerina Ivanovna and gives her all she can.... She has a room at the Kapernaumovs' the tailors, she lodges with them; Kapernaumov is a lame man with a cleft palate and all of his numerous family have cleft palates too. And his wife, too, has a cleft palate. They all live in one room, but Sonia has her own, partitioned off.... Hm... yes... very poor people and all with cleft palates... yes. Then I got up in the morning, and put on my rags, lifted up my hands to heaven and set off to his excellency Ivan Afanasyvitch. His excellency Ivan Afanasyvitch, do you know him? No? Well, then, it's a man of God you don't know. He is wax... wax before the face of the Lord; even as wax melteth!... His eyes were dim when he heard my story. 'Marmeladov, once already you have deceived my expectations... I'll take you once more on my own responsibility'—that's what he said, 'remember,' he said, 'and now you can go.' I kissed the dust at his feet—in thought only, for in reality he would not have allowed me to do it, being a statesman and a man of modern political and enlightened ideas. I returned home, and when I announced that I'd been taken back into the service and should receive a salary, heavens, what a to-do there was!..."

Marmeladov stopped again in violent excitement. At that moment a whole party of revellers already drunk came in from the street, and the sounds of a hired concertina and the cracked piping voice of a child of seven singing "The Hamlet" were heard in the entry. The room was filled with noise. The tavern-keeper and the boys were busy with the new-comers. Marmeladov paying no attention to the new arrivals continued his story. He appeared by now to be extremely weak, but as he became more and more drunk, he became more and more talkative. The recollection of his recent success in getting the situation seemed to revive him, and was positively reflected in a sort of radiance on his face. Raskolnikov listened attentively.

"That was five weeks ago, sir. Yes.... As soon as Katerina Ivanovna and Sonia heard of it, mercy on us, it was as though I stepped into the kingdom of Heaven. It used to be: you can lie like a beast, nothing but abuse. Now they were walking on tiptoe, hushing the children. 'Semyon Zaharovitch is tired with his work at the office, he is resting, shh!' They made me coffee before I went to work and boiled cream for me! They began to get real cream for me, do you hear that? And how they managed to get together the money for a decent outfit—eleven roubles, fifty copecks, I can't guess. Boots, cotton shirt-fronts—most magnificent, a uniform, they got up all in splendid style, for eleven roubles and a half. The first morning I came back from the office I found Katerina Ivanovna had cooked two courses for dinner—soup and salt meat with horse radish—which we had never dreamed of till then. She had not any dresses... none at all, but she got herself up as though she were going on a visit; and not that she'd anything to do it with, she smartened herself up with nothing at all, she'd done her hair nicely, put on a clean collar of some sort, cuffs, and there she was, quite a different person, she was younger and better looking. Sonia, my little darling, had only helped with money 'for the time,' she said, 'it won't do for me to come and see you too often. After dark maybe when no one can see.' Do you hear, do you hear? I lay down for a nap after dinner and what do you think: though Katerina Ivanovna had quarrelled to the last degree with our landlady Amalia Fyodorovna only a week before, she could not resist then asking her in to coffee. For two hours they were sitting, whispering together. 'Semyon Zaharovitch is in the service again, now, and receiving a salary,' says she, 'and he went himself to his excellency and his excellency himself came out to him, made all the others wait and led Semyon Zaharovitch by the hand before everybody into his study.' Do you hear, do you hear? 'To be sure,' says he, 'Semyon Zaharovitch, remembering your past services,' says he, 'and in spite of your propensity to that foolish weakness, since you promise now and since moreover we've got on badly without you,' (do you hear, do you hear;) 'and so,' says he, 'I rely now on your word as a gentleman.' And all that, let me tell you, she has simply made up for herself, and not simply out of wantonness, for the sake of bragging; no, she believes it all herself, she amuses herself with her own fancies, upon my word she does! And I don't blame her for it, no, I don't blame her!... Six days ago when I brought her my first earnings in full—twenty-three roubles forty copecks altogether—she called me her poppet: 'poppet,' said she, 'my little poppet.' And when we were by ourselves, you understand? You would not think me a beauty, you would not think much of me as a husband, would you?... Well, she pinched my cheek, 'my little poppet,' said she."

Marmeladov broke off, tried to smile, but suddenly his chin began to twitch. He controlled himself however. The tavern, the degraded appearance of the man, the five nights in the hay barge, and the pot of spirits, and yet this poignant love for his wife and children bewildered his listener. Raskolnikov listened intently but with a sick sensation. He felt vexed that he had come here.

"Honoured sir, honoured sir," cried Marmeladov recovering himself—"Oh, sir, perhaps all this seems a laughing matter to you, as it does to others, and perhaps I am only worrying you with the stupidity of all the trivial details of my home life, but it is not a laughing matter to me. For I can feel it all.... And the whole of that heavenly day of my life and the whole of that evening I passed in fleeting dreams of how I would arrange it all, and how I would dress all the children, and how I should give her rest, and how I should rescue my own daughter from dishonour and restore her to the bosom of her family.... And a great deal more.... Quite excusable, sir. Well, then, sir" (Marmeladov suddenly gave a sort of start, raised his head and gazed intently at his listener) "well, on the very next day after all those dreams, that is to say, exactly five days ago, in the evening, by a cunning trick, like a thief in the night, I stole from Katerina Ivanovna the key of her box, took out what was left of my earnings, how much it was I have forgotten, and now look at me, all of you! It's the fifth day since I left home, and they are looking for me there and it's the end of my employment, and my uniform is lying in a tavern on the Egyptian bridge. I exchanged it for the garments I have on... and it's the end of everything!"

Marmeladov struck his forehead with his fist, clenched his teeth, closed his eyes and leaned heavily with his elbow on the table. But a minute later his face suddenly changed and with a certain assumed slyness and affectation of bravado, he glanced at Raskolnikov, laughed and said:

"This morning I went to see Sonia, I went to ask her for a pick-me-up! He-he-he!"

"You don't say she gave it to you?" cried one of the new-comers; he shouted the words and went off into a guffaw.

"This very quart was bought with her money," Marmeladov declared, addressing himself exclusively to Raskolnikov. "Thirty copecks she gave me with her own hands, her last, all she had, as I saw.... She said nothing, she only looked at me without a word.... Not on earth, but up yonder... they grieve over men, they weep, but they don't blame them, they don't blame them! But it hurts more, it hurts more when they don't blame! Thirty copecks yes! And maybe she needs them now, eh? What do you think, my dear sir? For now she's got to keep up her appearance. It costs money, that smartness, that special smartness, you know? Do you understand? And there's pomatum, too, you see, she must have things; petticoats, starched ones, shoes, too, real jaunty ones to show off her foot when she has to step over a puddle. Do you understand, sir, do you understand what all that smartness means? And here I, her own father, here I took thirty copecks of that money for a drink! And I am drinking it! And I have already drunk it! Come, who will have pity on a man like me, eh? Are you sorry for me, sir, or not? Tell me, sir, are you sorry or not? He-he-he!"

He would have filled his glass, but there was no drink left. The pot was empty.

"What are you to be pitied for?" shouted the tavern-keeper who was again near them.

Shouts of laughter and even oaths followed. The laughter and the oaths came from those who were listening and also from those who had heard nothing but were simply looking at the figure of the discharged government clerk.

"To be pitied! Why am I to be pitied?" Marmeladov suddenly declaimed, standing up with his arm outstretched, as though he had been only waiting for that question.

"Why am I to be pitied, you say? Yes! there's nothing to pity me for! I ought to be crucified, crucified on a cross, not pitied! Crucify me, oh judge, crucify me but pity me! And then I will go of myself to be crucified, for it's not merry-making I seek but tears and tribulation!... Do you suppose, you that sell, that this pint of yours has been sweet to me? It was tribulation I sought at the bottom of it, tears and tribulation, and have found it, and I have tasted it; but He will pity us Who has had pity on all men, Who has understood all men and all things, He is the One, He too is the judge. He will come in that day and He will ask: 'Where is the daughter who gave herself for her cross, consumptive step-mother and for the little children of another? Where is the daughter who had pity upon the filthy drunkard, her earthly father, undismayed by his beastliness?' And He will say, 'Come to me! I have already forgiven thee once.... I have forgiven thee once.... Thy sins which are many are forgiven thee for thou hast loved much....' And he will forgive my Sonia, He will forgive, I know it... I felt it in my heart when I was with her just now! And He will judge and will forgive all, the good and the evil, the wise and the meek.... And when He has done with all of them, then He will summon us. 'You too come forth,' He will say, 'Come forth ye drunkards, come forth, ye weak ones, come forth, ye children of shame!' And we shall all come forth, without shame and shall stand before him. And He will say unto us, 'Ye are swine, made in the Image of the Beast and with his mark; but come ye also!' And the wise ones and those of understanding will say, 'Oh Lord, why dost Thou receive these men?' And He will say, 'This is why I receive them, oh ye wise, this is why I receive them, oh ye of understanding, that not one of them believed himself to be worthy of this.' And He will hold out His hands to us and we shall fall down before him... and we shall weep... and we shall understand all things! Then we shall understand all!... and all will understand, Katerina Ivanovna even... she will understand.... Lord, Thy kingdom come!" And he sank down on the bench exhausted, and helpless, looking at no one, apparently oblivious of his surroundings and plunged in deep thought. His words had created a certain impression; there was a moment of silence; but soon laughter and oaths were heard again.

"That's his notion!"

"Talked himself silly!"

"A fine clerk he is!"

And so on, and so on.

"Let us go, sir," said Marmeladov all at once, raising his head and addressing Raskolnikov—"come along with me... Kozel's house, looking into the yard. I'm going to Katerina Ivanovna—time I did."

Raskolnikov had for some time been wanting to go and he had meant to help him. Marmeladov was much unsteadier on his legs than in his speech and leaned heavily on the young man. They had two or three hundred paces to go. The drunken man was more and more overcome by dismay and confusion as they drew nearer the house.

"It's not Katerina Ivanovna I am afraid of now," he muttered in agitation—"and that she will begin pulling my hair. What does my hair matter! Bother my hair! That's what I say! Indeed it will be better if she does begin pulling it, that's not what I am afraid of... it's her eyes I am afraid of... yes, her eyes... the red on her cheeks, too, frightens me... and her breathing too.... Have you noticed how people in that disease breathe... when they are excited? I am frightened of the children's crying, too.... For if Sonia has not taken them food... I don't know what's happened! I don't know! But blows I am not afraid of.... Know, sir, that such blows are not a pain to me, but even an enjoyment. In fact I can't get on without it.... It's better so. Let her strike me, it relieves her heart... it's better so... There is the house. The house of Kozel, the cabinet-maker... a German, well-to-do. Lead the way!"

They went in from the yard and up to the fourth storey. The staircase got darker and darker as they went up. It was nearly eleven o'clock and although in summer in Petersburg there is no real night, yet it was quite dark at the top of the stairs.

A grimy little door at the very top of the stairs stood ajar. A very poor-looking room about ten paces long was lighted up by a candle-end; the whole of it was visible from the entrance. It was all in disorder, littered up with rags of all sorts, especially children's garments. Across the furthest corner was stretched a ragged sheet. Behind it probably was the bed. There was nothing in the room except two chairs and a sofa covered with American leather, full of holes, before which stood an old deal kitchen-table, unpainted and uncovered. At the edge of the table stood a smoldering tallow-candle in an iron candlestick. It appeared that the family had a room to themselves, not part of a room, but their room was practically a passage. The door leading to the other rooms, or rather cupboards, into which Amalia Lippevechsel's flat was divided stood half open, and there was shouting, uproar and laughter within. People seemed to be playing cards and drinking tea there. Words of the most unceremonious kind flew out from time to time.

Raskolnikov recognised Katerina Ivanovna at once. She was a rather tall, slim and graceful woman, terribly emaciated, with magnificent dark brown hair and with a hectic flush in her cheeks. She was pacing up and down in her little room, pressing her hands against her chest; her lips were parched and her breathing came in nervous broken gasps. Her eyes glittered as in fever and looked about with a harsh immovable stare. And that consumptive and excited face with the last flickering light of the candle-end playing upon it made a sickening impression. She seemed to Raskolnikov about thirty years old and was certainly a strange wife for Marmeladov.... She had not heard them and did not notice them coming in. She seemed to be lost in thought, hearing and seeing nothing. The room was close, but she had not opened the window; a stench rose from the staircase, but the door on to the stairs was not closed. From the inner rooms clouds of tobacco smoke floated in, she kept coughing, but did not close the door. The youngest child, a girl of six, was asleep, sitting curled up on the floor with her head on the sofa. A boy a year older stood crying and shaking in the corner, probably he had just had a beating. Beside him stood a girl of nine years old, tall and thin, wearing a thin and ragged chemise with an ancient cashmere pelisse flung over her bare shoulders, long outgrown and barely reaching her knees. Her arm, as thin as a stick, was round her brother's neck. She was trying to comfort him, whispering something to him, and doing all she could to keep him from whimpering again. At the same time her large dark eyes, which looked larger still from the thinness of her frightened face, were watching her mother with alarm. Marmeladov did not enter the door, but dropped on his knees in the very doorway, pushing Raskolnikov in front of him. The woman seeing a stranger stopped indifferently facing him, coming to herself for a moment and apparently wondering what he had come for. But evidently she decided that he was going into the next room, as he had to pass through hers to get there. Taking no further notice of him, she walked towards the outer door to close it and uttered a sudden scream on seeing her husband on his knees in the doorway.

"Ah!" she cried out in a frenzy, "he has come back! The criminal! the monster!... And where is the money? What's in your pocket, show me! And your clothes are all different! Where are your clothes? Where is the money! Speak!"

And she fell to searching him. Marmeladov submissively and obediently held up both arms to facilitate the search. Not a farthing was there.

"Where is the money?" she cried—"Mercy on us, can he have drunk it all? There were twelve silver roubles left in the chest!" and in a fury she seized him by the hair and dragged him into the room. Marmeladov seconded her efforts by meekly crawling along on his knees.

"And this is a consolation to me! This does not hurt me, but is a positive con-so-la-tion, ho-nou-red sir," he called out, shaken to and fro by his hair and even once striking the ground with his forehead. The child asleep on the floor woke up, and began to cry. The boy in the corner losing all control began trembling and screaming and rushed to his sister in violent terror, almost in a fit. The eldest girl was shaking like a leaf.

"He's drunk it! he's drunk it all," the poor woman screamed in despair—"and his clothes are gone! And they are hungry, hungry!"—and wringing her hands she pointed to the children. "Oh, accursed life! And you, are you not ashamed?"—she pounced all at once upon Raskolnikov—"from the tavern! Have you been drinking with him? You have been drinking with him, too! Go away!"

The young man was hastening away without uttering a word. The inner door was thrown wide open and inquisitive faces were peering in at it. Coarse laughing faces with pipes and cigarettes and heads wearing caps thrust themselves in at the doorway. Further in could be seen figures in dressing gowns flung open, in costumes of unseemly scantiness, some of them with cards in their hands. They were particularly diverted, when Marmeladov, dragged about by his hair, shouted that it was a consolation to him. They even began to come into the room; at last a sinister shrill outcry was heard: this came from Amalia Lippevechsel herself pushing her way amongst them and trying to restore order after her own fashion and for the hundredth time to frighten the poor woman by ordering her with coarse abuse to clear out of the room next day. As he went out, Raskolnikov had time to put his hand into his pocket, to snatch up the coppers he had received in exchange for his rouble in the tavern and to lay them unnoticed on the window. Afterwards on the stairs, he changed his mind and would have gone back.

"What a stupid thing I've done," he thought to himself, "they have Sonia and I want it myself." But reflecting that it would be impossible to take it back now and that in any case he would not have taken it, he dismissed it with a wave of his hand and went back to his lodging. "Sonia wants pomatum too," he said as he walked along the street, and he laughed malignantly—"such smartness costs money.... Hm! And maybe Sonia herself will be bankrupt to-day, for there is always a risk, hunting big game... digging for gold... then they would all be without a crust to-morrow except for my money. Hurrah for Sonia! What a mine they've dug there! And they're making the most of it! Yes, they are making the most of it! They've wept over it and grown used to it. Man grows used to everything, the scoundrel!"

He sank into thought.

"And what if I am wrong," he cried suddenly after a moment's thought. "What if man is not really a scoundrel, man in general, I mean, the whole race of mankind—then all the rest is prejudice, simply artificial terrors and there are no barriers and it's all as it should be."

CHAPTER III

He waked up late next day after a broken sleep. But his sleep had not refreshed him; he waked up bilious, irritable, ill-tempered, and looked with hatred at his room. It was a tiny cupboard of a room about six paces in length. It had a poverty-stricken appearance with its dusty yellow paper peeling off the walls, and it was so low-pitched that a man of more than average height was ill at ease in it and felt every moment that he would knock his head against the ceiling. The furniture was in keeping with the room: there were three old chairs, rather rickety; a painted table in the corner on which lay a few manuscripts and books; the dust that lay thick upon them showed that they had been long untouched. A big clumsy sofa occupied almost the whole of one wall and half the floor space of the room; it was once covered with chintz, but was now in rags and served Raskolnikov as a bed. Often he went to sleep on it, as he was, without undressing, without sheets, wrapped in his old student's overcoat, with his head on one little pillow, under which he heaped up all the linen he had, clean and dirty, by way of a bolster. A little table stood in front of the sofa.

It would have been difficult to sink to a lower ebb of disorder, but to Raskolnikov in his present state of mind this was positively agreeable. He had got completely away from everyone, like a tortoise in its shell, and even the sight of a servant girl who had to wait upon him and looked sometimes into his room made him writhe with nervous irritation. He was in the condition that overtakes some monomaniacs entirely concentrated upon one thing. His landlady had for the last fortnight given up sending him in meals, and he had not yet thought of expostulating with her, though he went without his dinner. Nastasya, the cook and only servant, was rather pleased at the lodger's mood and had entirely given up sweeping and doing his room, only once a week or so she would stray into his room with a broom. She waked him up that day.

"Get up, why are you asleep?" she called to him. "It's past nine, I have brought you some tea; will you have a cup? I should think you're fairly starving?"

Raskolnikov opened his eyes, started and recognised Nastasya.

"From the landlady, eh?" he asked, slowly and with a sickly face sitting up on the sofa.

"From the landlady, indeed!"

She set before him her own cracked teapot full of weak and stale tea and laid two yellow lumps of sugar by the side of it.

"Here, Nastasya, take it please," he said, fumbling in his pocket (for he had slept in his clothes) and taking out a handful of coppers—"run and buy me a loaf. And get me a little sausage, the cheapest, at the pork-butcher's."

"The loaf I'll fetch you this very minute, but wouldn't you rather have some cabbage soup instead of sausage? It's capital soup, yesterday's. I saved it for you yesterday, but you came in late. It's fine soup."

When the soup had been brought, and he had begun upon it, Nastasya sat down beside him on the sofa and began chatting. She was a country peasant-woman and a very talkative one.

"Praskovya Pavlovna means to complain to the police about you," she said.

He scowled.

"To the police? What does she want?"

"You don't pay her money and you won't turn out of the room. That's what she wants, to be sure."

"The devil, that's the last straw," he muttered, grinding his teeth, "no, that would not suit me... just now. She is a fool," he added aloud. "I'll go and talk to her to-day."

"Fool she is and no mistake, just as I am. But why, if you are so clever, do you lie here like a sack and have nothing to show for it? One time you used to go out, you say, to teach children. But why is it you do nothing now?"

"I am doing..." Raskolnikov began sullenly and reluctantly.

"What are you doing?"

"Work..."

"What sort of work?"

"I am thinking," he answered seriously after a pause.

Nastasya was overcome with a fit of laughter. She was given to laughter and when anything amused her, she laughed inaudibly, quivering and shaking all over till she felt ill.

"And have you made much money by your thinking?" she managed to articulate at last.

"One can't go out to give lessons without boots. And I'm sick of it."

"Don't quarrel with your bread and butter."

"They pay so little for lessons. What's the use of a few coppers?" he answered, reluctantly, as though replying to his own thought.

"And you want to get a fortune all at once?"

He looked at her strangely.

"Yes, I want a fortune," he answered firmly, after a brief pause.

"Don't be in such a hurry, you quite frighten me! Shall I get you the loaf or not?"

"As you please."

"Ah, I forgot! A letter came for you yesterday when you were out."

"A letter? for me! from whom?"

"I can't say. I gave three copecks of my own to the postman for it. Will you pay me back?"

"Then bring it to me, for God's sake, bring it," cried Raskolnikov greatly excited—"good God!"

A minute later the letter was brought him. That was it: from his mother, from the province of R——. He turned pale when he took it. It was a long while since he had received a letter, but another feeling also suddenly stabbed his heart.

"Nastasya, leave me alone, for goodness' sake; here are your three copecks, but for goodness' sake, make haste and go!"

The letter was quivering in his hand; he did not want to open it in her presence; he wanted to be left *alone* with this letter. When Nastasya had gone out, he lifted it quickly to his lips and kissed it; then he gazed intently at the address, the small, sloping handwriting, so dear and familiar, of the mother who had once taught him to read and write. He delayed; he seemed almost afraid of something. At last he opened it; it was a thick heavy letter, weighing over two ounces, two large sheets of note paper were covered with very small handwriting.

"My dear Rodya," wrote his mother—"it's two months since I last had a talk with you by letter which has distressed me and even kept me awake at night, thinking. But I am sure you will not blame me for my inevitable silence. You know how I love you; you are all we have to look to, Dounia and I, you are our all, our one hope, our one stay. What a grief it was to me when I heard that you had given up the university some months ago, for want of means to keep yourself and that you had lost your lessons and your other work! How could I help you out of my hundred and twenty roubles a year pension? The fifteen roubles I sent you four months ago I borrowed, as you know, on security of my pension, from Vassily Ivanovitch Vahrushin a merchant of this town.

He is a kind-hearted man and was a friend of your father's too. But having given him the right to receive the pension, I had to wait till the debt was paid off and that is only just done, so that I've been unable to send you anything all this time. But now, thank God, I believe I shall be able to send you something more and in fact we may congratulate ourselves on our good fortune now, of which I hasten to inform you. In the first place, would you have guessed, dear Rodya, that your sister has been living with me for the last six weeks and we shall not be separated in the future. Thank God, her sufferings are over, but I will tell you everything in order, so that you may know just how everything has happened and all that we have hitherto concealed from you. When you wrote to me two months ago that you had heard that Dounia had a great deal to put up with in the Svidrigaïlovs' house, when you wrote that and asked me to tell you all about it—what could I write in answer to you? If I had written the whole truth to you, I dare say you would have thrown up everything and have come to us, even if you had to walk all the way, for I know your character and your feelings, and you would not let your sister be insulted. I was in despair myself, but what could I do? And, besides, I did not know the whole truth myself then. What made it all so difficult was that Dounia received a hundred roubles in advance when she took the place as governess in their family, on condition of part of her salary being deducted every month, and so it was impossible to throw up the situation without repaying the debt. This sum (now I can explain it all to you, my precious Rodya) she took chiefly in order to send you sixty roubles, which you needed so terribly then and which you received from us last year. We deceived you then, writing that this money came from Dounia's savings, but that was not so, and now I tell you all about it, because, thank God, things have suddenly changed for the better, and that you may know how Dounia loves you and what a heart she has. At first indeed Mr. Svidrigaïlov treated her very rudely and used to make disrespectful and jeering remarks at table.... But I don't want to go into all those painful details, so as not to worry you for nothing when it is now all over. In short, in spite of the kind and generous behaviour of Marfa Petrovna, Mr. Svidrigaïlov's wife, and all the rest of the household, Dounia had a very hard time, especially when Mr. Svidrigaïlov, relapsing into his old regimental habits, was under the influence of Bacchus. And how do you think it was all explained later on? Would you believe that the crazy fellow had conceived a passion for Dounia from the beginning, but had concealed it under a show of rudeness and contempt. Possibly he was ashamed and horrified himself at his own flighty hopes, considering his years and his being the father of a family; and that made him angry with Dounia. And possibly, too, he hoped by his rude and sneering behaviour to hide the truth from others. But at last he lost all control and had the face to make Dounia an open and shameful proposal, promising her all sorts of inducements and offering, besides, to throw up everything and take her to another estate of his, or even abroad. You can imagine all she went through! To leave her situation at once was impossible not only on account of the money debt, but also to spare the feelings of Marfa Petrovna, whose suspicions would have been aroused: and then Dounia would have been the cause of a rupture in the family. And it would have meant a terrible scandal for Dounia too; that would have been inevitable. There were various other reasons owing to which Dounia could not hope to escape from that awful house for another six weeks. You know Dounia, of course; you know how clever she is and what a strong will she has. Dounia can endure a great deal and even in the most difficult cases she has the fortitude to maintain her firmness. She did not even write to me about everything for fear of upsetting me, although we were constantly in communication. It all ended very unexpectedly. Marfa Petrovna accidentally overheard her husband imploring Dounia in the garden, and, putting quite a wrong interpretation on the position, threw the blame upon her, believing her to be the cause of it all. An awful scene took place between them on the spot in the garden; Marfa Petrovna went so far as to strike Dounia, refused to hear anything and was shouting at her for a whole hour and then gave orders that Dounia should be packed off at once to me in a plain peasant's cart, into which they flung all her things, her linen and her clothes, all pell-mell, without folding it up and packing it. And a heavy shower of rain came on, too, and Dounia, insulted and put to shame, had to drive with a peasant in an open cart all the seventeen versts into town. Only think now what answer could I have sent to the letter I received from you two months ago and what could I have written? I was in despair; I dared not write to you the truth because you would have been very unhappy, mortified and indignant, and yet what could you do? You could only perhaps ruin yourself, and, besides, Dounia would not allow it; and fill up my letter with trifles when my heart was so full of sorrow, I could not. For a whole month the town was full of gossip about this scandal, and it came to such a pass that Dounia and I dared not even go to church on account of the contemptuous looks, whispers, and even remarks made aloud about us. All our acquaintances avoided us, nobody even bowed to us in the street, and I learnt that some shopmen and clerks were intending to insult us in a shameful way, smearing the gates of our house with pitch, so that the landlord began to tell us we must leave. All this was set going by Marfa Petrovna who managed to slander Dounia and throw dirt at her in every family. She knows everyone in the neighbourhood, and that month she was continually coming into the town, and as she is rather talkative and fond of gossiping about her family affairs and particularly of complaining to all and each of her husband—which is not at all right—so in a short time she had spread her story not only in the town, but over the whole surrounding district. It made me ill, but Dounia bore it better than I did, and if only you could have seen how she endured it all and tried to comfort me and cheer me up! She is an angel! But by God's mercy, our sufferings were cut short: Mr. Svidrigaïlov returned to his senses and repented and, probably feeling sorry for Dounia, he laid before Marfa Petrovna a complete and unmistakable proof of Dounia's innocence, in the form of a letter Dounia had been forced to write and give to him, before Marfa Petrovna came upon them in the garden. This letter, which remained in Mr. Svidrigaïlov's hands after her departure, she had written to refuse personal explanations and secret interviews, for which he was entreating her. In that letter she reproached him with great heat and indignation for the baseness of his behaviour in regard to Marfa Petrovna, reminding him that he was the father and head of a family and telling him how infamous it was of him to torment and make unhappy a defenceless girl, unhappy enough already. Indeed, dear Rodya, the letter was so nobly and touchingly written that I sobbed when I read it and to this day I cannot read it without tears. Moreover, the evidence of the servants, too, cleared Dounia's reputation; they had seen and known a great deal more than Mr. Svidrigaïlov had himself supposed—as indeed is always the case with servants. Marfa Petrovna was completely taken aback, and 'again crushed' as she said herself to us, but she was completely convinced of Dounia's innocence. The very next day, being Sunday, she went straight to the Cathedral, knelt down and prayed with tears to Our Lady to give her strength to bear this new trial and to do her duty. Then she came straight from the Cathedral to us, told us the whole story, wept bitterly and, fully penitent, she embraced Dounia and besought her to forgive her. The same morning without any delay, she went round to all the houses in the town and everywhere, shedding tears, she asserted in the most flattering terms Dounia's innocence and the nobility of her feelings and her behavior. What was more, she showed and read to everyone the letter in Dounia's own handwriting to Mr. Svidrigaïlov and even allowed them to take copies of it—which I must say I think was superfluous. In this way she was busy for several days in driving about the whole town, because some people had taken offence through precedence having been given to others. And therefore they had to take turns, so that in every house she was expected before she arrived, and everyone knew that on such and such a day Marfa Petrovna would be reading the letter in such and such a place and people assembled for every reading of it, even many who had heard it several times already both in their own houses and in other people's. In my opinion a great deal, a very great deal of all this was unnecessary; but that's Marfa Petrovna's character. Anyway she succeeded in completely re-establishing Dounia's reputation and the whole ignominy of this affair rested as an indelible disgrace upon her husband, as the only person to blame, so that I really began to feel sorry for him; it was really treating the crazy fellow too harshly. Dounia was at once asked to give lessons in several families, but she refused. All of a sudden everyone began to treat her with marked respect and all this did much to bring about the event by which, one may say, our whole fortunes are now transformed. You must know, dear Rodya, that Dounia has a suitor and that she has already consented to marry him. I hasten to tell you all about the matter, and though it has been arranged without asking your consent, I think you will not be aggrieved with me or with your sister on that account, for you will see that we could not wait and put off our decision till we heard from you. And you could not have judged all the facts without being on the spot. This was how it happened. He is already of the rank of a counsellor, Pyotr Petrovitch Luzhin, and is distantly related to Marfa Petrovna, who has been very active in bringing the match about. It began with his expressing through her his desire to make our acquaintance. He was properly received, drank coffee with us and the very next day he sent us a letter in which he very courteously made an offer and begged for a speedy and decided answer. He is a very busy man and is in a great hurry to get to Petersburg, so that every moment is precious to him. At first, of course, we were greatly surprised, as it had all happened so quickly and unexpectedly. We thought and talked it over the whole day. He is a well-to-do man, to be depended upon, he has two posts in the government and has already made his fortune. It is true that he is forty-five years old, but he is of a fairly prepossessing appearance and might still be thought attractive by women, and he is altogether a very respectable and presentable man, only he seems a little morose and somewhat conceited. But possibly that may only be the impression he makes at first sight. And beware, dear Rodya, when he comes to Petersburg, as he shortly will do, beware of judging him too hastily and severely, as your way is, if there is anything you do not like in him at first sight. I give you this warning, although I feel sure that he will make a favourable impression upon you. Moreover, in order to understand any man one must be deliberate and careful to avoid forming prejudices and mistaken ideas, which are very difficult to correct and get over afterwards. And Pyotr Petrovitch, judging by many indications, is a thoroughly estimable man. At his first visit, indeed, he told us that he was a practical man, but still he shares, as he expressed it, many of the convictions 'of our most rising generation' and he is an opponent of all prejudices. He said a good deal more, for he seems a little conceited and likes to be listened to, but this is scarcely a vice. I, of course, understood very little of it, but Dounia explained to me that, though he is not a man of great education, he is clever and seems to be good-natured. You know your sister's character, Rodya. She is a resolute, sensible, patient and generous girl, but she has a passionate heart, as I know very well. Of course, there is no great love either on his side, or on hers, but Dounia is a clever girl and has the heart of an angel, and will make it her duty to make her husband happy who on his side will make her happiness his care. Of that we have no good reason to doubt, though it must be admitted the matter has been arranged in great haste. Besides he is a man of great prudence and he will see, to be sure, of himself, that his own happiness will be the more secure, the happier Dounia is with him. And as for some defects of character, for some habits and even certain differences of opinion—which indeed are inevitable even in the happiest marriages—Dounia has said that, as regards all that, she relies on herself, that there is nothing to be uneasy about, and that she is ready to put up with a great deal, if only their future relationship can be an honourable and straightforward one. He struck me, for instance, at first, as rather abrupt, but that may well come from his being an outspoken man, and that is no doubt how it is. For instance, at his second visit, after he had received Dounia's consent, in the course of conversation, he declared that before making Dounia's acquaintance, he had made up his mind to marry a girl of good reputation, without dowry and, above all, one who had experienced poverty, because, as he explained, a man ought not to be indebted to his wife, but that it is better for a wife to look upon her husband as her benefactor. I must add that he expressed it more nicely and politely than I have done, for I have forgotten his actual phrases and only remember the meaning. And, besides, it was obviously not said of design, but slipped out in the heat of conversation, so that he tried afterwards to correct himself and smooth it over, but all the same it did strike me as somewhat rude, and I said so afterwards to Dounia. But Dounia was vexed, and answered that 'words are not deeds,' and that, of course, is perfectly true. Dounia did not sleep all night before she made up her mind, and, thinking that I was asleep, she got out of bed and was walking up and down the room all night; at last she knelt down before the ikon and prayed long and fervently and in the morning she told me that she had decided.

"I have mentioned already that Pyotr Petrovitch is just setting off for Petersburg, where he has a great deal of business, and he wants to open a legal bureau. He has been occupied for many years in conducting civil and commercial litigation, and only the other day he won an important case. He has to be in Petersburg because he has an important case before the Senate. So, Rodya dear, he may be of the greatest use to you, in every way indeed, and Dounia and I have agreed that from this very day you could definitely enter upon your career and might consider that your future is marked out and assured for you. Oh, if only this comes to pass! This would be such a benefit that we could only look upon it as a providential blessing. Dounia is dreaming of nothing else. We have even ventured already to drop a few words on the subject to Pyotr Petrovitch. He was cautious in his answer, and said that, of course, as he could not get on without a secretary, it would be better to be paying a salary to a relation than to a stranger, if only the former were fitted for the duties (as though there could be doubt of your being fitted!) but then he expressed doubts whether your studies at the university would leave you time for work at his office. The matter dropped for the time, but Dounia is thinking of nothing else now. She has been in a sort of fever for the last few days, and has already made a regular plan for your becoming in the end an associate and even a partner in Pyotr Petrovitch's business, which might well be, seeing that you are a student of law. I am in complete agreement with her, Rodya, and share all her plans and hopes, and think there is every probability of realising them. And in spite of Pyotr Petrovitch's evasiveness, very natural at present (since he does not know you), Dounia is firmly persuaded that she will gain everything by her good influence over her future husband; this she is reckoning upon. Of course we are careful not to talk of any of these more remote plans to Pyotr Petrovitch, especially of your becoming his partner. He is a practical man and might take this very coldly, it might all seem to him simply a day-dream. Nor has either Dounia or I breathed a word to him of the great hopes we have of his helping us to pay for your university studies; we have not spoken of it in the first place, because it will come to pass of itself, later on, and he will no doubt without wasting words offer to do it of himself, (as though he could refuse Dounia that) the more readily since you may by your own efforts become his right hand in the office, and receive this assistance not as a charity, but as a salary earned by your own work. Dounia wants to arrange it all like this and I quite agree with her. And we have not spoken of our plans for another reason, that is, because I particularly wanted you to feel on an equal footing when you first meet him. When Dounia spoke to him with enthusiasm about you, he answered that one could never judge of a man without seeing him close, for oneself, and that he looked forward to forming his own opinion when he makes your acquaintance. Do you know, my precious Rodya, I think that perhaps for some reasons (nothing to do with Pyotr Petrovitch though, simply for my own personal, perhaps old-womanish, fancies) I should do better to go on living by myself, apart, than with them, after the wedding. I am convinced that he will be generous and delicate enough to invite me and to urge me to remain with my daughter for the future, and if he has said nothing about it hitherto, it is simply because it has been taken for granted; but I shall refuse. I have noticed more than once in my life that husbands don't quite get on with their mothers-in-law, and I don't want to be the least bit in anyone's way, and for my own sake, too, would rather be quite independent, so long as I have a crust of bread of my own, and such children as you and Dounia. If possible, I would settle somewhere near you, for the most joyful piece of news, dear Rodya, I have kept for the end of my letter: know then, my dear boy, that we may, perhaps, be all together in a very short time and may embrace one another again after a separation of almost three years! It is settled *for certain* that Dounia and I are to set off for Petersburg, exactly when I don't know, but very, very soon, possibly in a week. It all depends on Pyotr Petrovitch who will let us know when he has had time to look round him in Petersburg. To suit his own arrangements he is anxious to have the ceremony as soon as possible, even before the fast of Our Lady, if it could be managed, or if that is too soon to be ready, immediately after. Oh, with what happiness I shall press you to my heart! Dounia is all excitement at the joyful thought of seeing you, she said one day in joke that she would be ready to marry Pyotr Petrovitch for that alone. She is an angel! She is not writing anything to you now, and has only told me to write that she has so much, so much to tell you that she is not going to take up her pen now, for a few lines would tell you nothing, and it would only mean upsetting herself; she bids me send you her love and innumerable kisses. But although we shall be meeting so soon, perhaps I shall send you as much money as I can in a day or two. Now that everyone has heard that Dounia is to marry Pyotr Petrovitch, my credit has suddenly improved and I know that Afanasy Ivanovitch will trust me now even to seventy-five roubles on the security of my pension, so that perhaps I shall be able to send you twenty-five or even thirty roubles. I would send you more, but I am uneasy about our travelling expenses; for though Pyotr Petrovitch has been so kind as to undertake part of the expenses of the journey, that is to say, he has taken upon himself the conveyance of our bags and big trunk (which will be conveyed through some acquaintances of his), we must reckon upon some expense on our arrival in Petersburg, where we can't be left without a halfpenny, at least for the first few days. But we have calculated it all, Dounia and I, to the last penny, and we see that the journey will not cost very much. It is only ninety versts from us to the railway and we have come to an agreement with a driver we know, so as to be in readiness; and from there Dounia and I can travel quite comfortably third class. So that I may very likely be able to send to you not twenty-five, but thirty roubles. But enough; I have covered two sheets already and there is no space left for more; our whole history, but so many events have happened! And now, my precious Rodya, I embrace you and send you a mother's blessing till we meet. Love Dounia your sister, Rodya; love her as she loves you and understand that she loves you beyond everything, more than herself. She is an angel and you, Rodya, you are everything to us—our one hope, our one consolation. If only you are happy, we shall be happy. Do you still say your prayers, Rodya, and believe in the mercy of our Creator and our Redeemer? I am afraid in my heart that you may have been visited by the new spirit of infidelity that is abroad to-day; If it is so, I pray for you. Remember, dear boy, how in your childhood, when your father was living, you used to lisp your prayers at my knee, and how happy we all were in those days. Good-bye, till we meet then—I embrace you warmly, warmly, with many kisses.

"Yours till death,

"PULCHERIA RASKOLNIKOV."

Almost from the first, while he read the letter, Raskolnikov's face was wet with tears; but when he finished it, his face was pale and distorted and a bitter, wrathful and malignant smile was on his lips. He laid his head down on his threadbare dirty pillow and pondered, pondered a long time. His heart was beating violently, and his brain was in a turmoil. At last he felt cramped and stifled in the little yellow room that was like a cupboard or a box. His eyes and his mind craved for space. He took up his hat and went out, this time without dread of meeting anyone; he had forgotten his dread. He turned in the direction of the Vassilyevsky Ostrov, walking along Vassilyevsky Prospect, as though hastening on some business, but he walked, as his habit was, without noticing his way, muttering and even speaking aloud to himself, to the astonishment of the passers-by. Many of them took him to be drunk.

CHAPTER IV

His mother's letter had been a torture to him, but as regards the chief fact in it, he had felt not one moment's hesitation, even whilst he was reading the letter. The essential question was settled, and irrevocably settled, in his mind: "Never such a marriage while I am alive and Mr. Luzhin be damned!" "The thing is perfectly clear," he muttered to himself, with a malignant smile anticipating the triumph of his decision. "No, mother, no, Dounia, you won't deceive me! and then they apologise for not asking my advice and for taking the decision without me! I dare say! They imagine it is arranged now and can't be broken off; but we will see whether it can or not! A magnificent excuse: 'Pyotr Petrovitch is such a busy man that even his wedding has to be in post-haste, almost by express.' No, Dounia, I see it all and I know what you want to say to me; and I know too what you were thinking about, when you walked up and down all night, and what your prayers were like before the Holy Mother of Kazan who stands in mother's bedroom. Bitter is the ascent to Golgotha.... Hm... so it is finally settled; you have determined to marry a sensible business man, Avdotya Romanovna, one who has a fortune (has *already*made his fortune, that is so much more solid and impressive) a man who holds two government posts and who shares the ideas of our most rising generation, as mother writes, and who *seems* to be kind, as Dounia herself observes. That *seems* beats everything! And that very Dounia for that very 'seems' is marrying him! Splendid! splendid!

"... But I should like to know why mother has written to me about 'our most rising generation'? Simply as a descriptive touch, or with the idea of prepossessing me in favour of Mr. Luzhin? Oh, the cunning of them! I should like to know one thing more: how far they were open with one another that day and night and all this time since? Was it all put into *words*, or did both understand that they had the same thing at heart and in their minds, so that there was no need to speak of it aloud, and better not to speak of it. Most likely it was partly like that, from mother's letter it's evident: he struck her as rude *a little*, and mother in her simplicity took her observations to Dounia. And she was sure to be vexed and 'answered her angrily.' I should think so! Who would not be angered when it was quite clear without any naïve questions and when it was understood that it was useless to discuss it. And why does she write to me, 'love Dounia, Rodya, and she loves you more than herself'? Has she a secret conscience-prick at sacrificing her daughter to her son? 'You are our one comfort, you are everything to us.' Oh, mother!"

His bitterness grew more and more intense, and if he had happened to meet Mr. Luzhin at the moment, he might have murdered him.

"Hm... yes, that's true," he continued, pursuing the whirling ideas that chased each other in his brain, "it is true that 'it needs time and care to get to know a man,' but there is no mistake about Mr. Luzhin. The chief thing is he is 'a man of business and*seems* kind,' that was something, wasn't it, to send the bags and big box for them! A kind man, no doubt after that! But his*bride* and her mother are to drive in a peasant's cart covered with sacking (I know, I have been driven in it). No matter! It is only ninety versts and then they can 'travel very comfortably, third class,' for a thousand versts! Quite right, too. One must cut one's coat according to one's cloth, but what about you, Mr. Luzhin? She is your bride.... And you must be aware that her mother has to raise money on her pension for the journey. To be sure it's a matter of business, a partnership for mutual benefit, with equal shares and expenses;—food and drink provided, but pay for your tobacco. The business man has got the better of them, too. The luggage will cost less than their fares and very likely go for nothing. How is it that they don't both see all that, or is it that they don't want to see? And they are pleased, pleased! And to think that this is only the first blossoming, and that the real fruits are to come! But what really matters is not the stinginess, is not the meanness, but the *tone* of the whole thing. For that will be the tone after marriage, it's a foretaste of it. And mother too, why should she be so lavish? What will she have by the time she gets to Petersburg? Three silver roubles or two 'paper ones' as *she* says.... that old woman... hm. What does she expect to live upon in Petersburg afterwards? She has her reasons already for guessing that she *could not* live with Dounia after the marriage, even for the first few months. The good man has no doubt let slip something on that subject also, though mother would deny it: 'I shall refuse,' says she. On whom is she reckoning then? Is she counting on what is left of her hundred and twenty roubles of pension when Afanasy Ivanovitch's debt is paid? She knits woollen shawls and embroiders cuffs, ruining her old eyes. And all her shawls don't add more than twenty roubles a year to her hundred and twenty, I know that. So she is building all her hopes all the time on Mr. Luzhin's generosity; 'he will offer it of himself, he will press it on me.' You may wait a long time for that! That's how it always is with these Schilleresque noble hearts; till the last moment every goose is a swan with them, till the last moment, they hope for the best and will see nothing wrong, and although they have an inkling of the other side of the picture, yet they won't face the truth till they are forced to; the very thought of it makes them shiver; they thrust the truth away with both hands, until the man they deck out in false colours puts a fool's cap on them with his own hands. I should like to know whether Mr. Luzhin has any orders of merit; I bet he has the Anna in his buttonhole and that he puts it on when he goes to dine with contractors or merchants. He will be sure to have it for his wedding, too! Enough of him, confound him!

"Well,... mother I don't wonder at, it's like her, God bless her, but how could Dounia? Dounia darling, as though I did not know you! You were nearly twenty when I saw you last: I understood you then. Mother writes that 'Dounia can put up with a great deal.' I know that very well. I knew that two years and a half ago, and for the last two and a half years I have been thinking about it, thinking of just that, that 'Dounia can put up with a great deal.' If she could put up with Mr. Svidrigaïlov and all the rest of it, she certainly can put up with a great deal. And now mother and she have taken it into their heads that she can put up with Mr. Luzhin, who propounds the theory of the superiority of wives raised from destitution and owing everything to their husband's bounty—who propounds it, too, almost at the first interview. Granted that he 'let it slip,' though he is a sensible man, (yet maybe it was not a slip at all, but he meant to make himself clear as soon as possible) but Dounia, Dounia? She understands the man, of course, but she will have to live with the man. Why! she'd live on black bread and water, she would not sell her soul, she would not barter her moral freedom for comfort; she would not barter it for all Schleswig-Holstein, much less Mr. Luzhin's money. No, Dounia was not that sort when I knew her and... she is still the same, of course! Yes, there's no denying, the Svidrigaïlovs are a bitter pill! It's a bitter thing to spend one's life a governess in the provinces for two hundred roubles, but I know she would rather be a nigger on a plantation or a Lett with a German master than degrade her soul, and her moral dignity, by binding herself for ever to a man whom she does not respect and with whom she has nothing in common—for her own advantage. And if Mr. Luzhin had been of unalloyed gold, or one huge diamond, she would never have consented to become his legal concubine. Why is she consenting then? What's the point of it? What's the answer? It's clear enough: for herself, for her comfort, to save her life she would not sell herself, but for someone else she is doing it! For one she loves, for one she adores, she will sell herself! That's what it all amounts to; for her brother, for her mother, she will sell herself! She will sell everything! In such cases, 'we overcome our moral feeling if necessary,' freedom, peace, conscience even, all, all are brought into the market. Let my life go, if only my dear ones may be happy! More than that, we become casuists, we learn to be Jesuitical and for a time maybe we can soothe ourselves, we can persuade ourselves that it is one's duty for a good object. That's just like us, it's as clear as daylight. It's clear that Rodion Romanovitch Raskolnikov is the central figure in the business, and no one else. Oh, yes, she can ensure his happiness, keep him in the university, make him a partner in the office, make his whole future secure; perhaps he may even be a rich man later on, prosperous, respected, and may even end his life a famous man! But my mother? It's all Rodya, precious Rodya, her first born! For such a son who would not sacrifice such a daughter! Oh, loving, over-partial hearts! Why, for his sake we would not shrink even from Sonia's fate. Sonia, Sonia Marmeladov, the eternal victim so long as the world lasts. Have you taken the measure of your sacrifice, both of you? Is it right? Can you bear it? Is it any use? Is there sense in it? And let me tell you, Dounia, Sonia's life is no worse than life with Mr. Luzhin. 'There can be no question of love,' mother writes. And what if there can be no respect either, if on the contrary there is aversion, contempt, repulsion, what then? So you will have to 'keep up your appearance,' too. Is not that so? Do you understand what that smartness means? Do you understand that the Luzhin smartness is just the same thing as Sonia's and may be worse, viler, baser, because in your case, Dounia, it's a bargain for luxuries, after all, but with Sonia it's simply a question of starvation. It has to be paid for, it has to be paid for, Dounia, this smartness. And what if it's more than you can bear afterwards, if you regret it? The bitterness, the misery, the curses, the tears hidden from all the world, for you are not a Marfa Petrovna. And how will your mother feel then? Even now she is uneasy, she is worried, but then, when she sees it all clearly? And I? Yes, indeed, what have you taken me for? I won't have your sacrifice, Dounia, I won't have it, mother! It shall not be, so long as I am alive, it shall not, it shall not! I won't accept it!"

He suddenly paused in his reflection and stood still.

"It shall not be? But what are you going to do to prevent it? You'll forbid it? And what right have you? What can you promise them on your side to give you such a right? Your whole life, your whole future, you will devote to them *when you have finished your studies and obtained a post*? Yes, we have heard all that before, and that's all *words*, but now? Now something must be done, now, do you understand that? And what are you doing now? You are living upon them. They borrow on their hundred roubles pension. They borrow from the Svidrigaïlovs. How are you going to save them from Svidrigaïlovs, from Afanasy Ivanovitch Vahrushin, oh, future millionaire Zeus who would arrange their lives for them? In another ten years? In another ten years, mother will be blind with knitting shawls, maybe with weeping too. She will be worn to a shadow with fasting; and my sister? Imagine for a moment what may have become of your sister in ten years? What may happen to her during those ten years? Can you fancy?"

So he tortured himself, fretting himself with such questions, and finding a kind of enjoyment in it. And yet all these questions were not new ones suddenly confronting him, they were old familiar aches. It was long since they had first begun to grip and rend his heart. Long, long ago his present anguish had its first beginnings; it had waxed and gathered strength, it had matured and concentrated, until it had taken the form of a fearful, frenzied and fantastic question, which tortured his heart and mind, clamouring insistently for an answer. Now his mother's letter had burst on him like a thunderclap. It was clear that he must not now suffer passively, worrying himself over unsolved questions, but that he must do something, do it at once, and do it quickly. Anyway he must decide on something, or else...

"Or throw up life altogether!" he cried suddenly, in a frenzy—"accept one's lot humbly as it is, once for all and stifle everything in oneself, giving up all claim to activity, life and love!"

"Do you understand, sir, do you understand what it means when you have absolutely nowhere to turn?" Marmeladov's question came suddenly into his mind, "for every man must have somewhere to turn...."

He gave a sudden start; another thought, that he had had yesterday, slipped back into his mind. But he did not start at the thought recurring to him, for he knew, he had *felt beforehand*, that it must come back, he was expecting it; besides it was not only yesterday's thought. The difference was that a month ago, yesterday even, the thought was a mere dream: but now... now it appeared not a dream at all, it had taken a new menacing and quite unfamiliar shape, and he suddenly became aware of this himself.... He felt a hammering in his head, and there was a darkness before his eyes.

He looked round hurriedly, he was searching for something. He wanted to sit down and was looking for a seat; he was walking along the K—— Boulevard. There was a seat about a hundred paces in front of him. He walked towards it as fast he could; but on the way he met with a little adventure which absorbed all his attention. Looking for the seat, he had noticed a woman walking some twenty paces in front of him, but at first he took no more notice of her than of other objects that crossed his path. It had happened to him many times going home not to notice the road by which he was going, and he was accustomed to walk like that. But there was at first sight something so strange about the woman in front of him, that gradually his attention was riveted upon her, at first reluctantly and, as it were, resentfully, and then more and more intently. He felt a sudden desire to find out what it was that was so strange about the woman. In the first place, she appeared to be a girl quite young, and she was walking in the great heat bareheaded and with no parasol or gloves, waving her arms about in an absurd way. She had on a dress of some light silky material, but put on strangely awry, not properly hooked up, and torn open at the top of the skirt, close to the waist: a great piece was rent and hanging loose. A little kerchief was flung about her bare throat, but lay slanting on one side. The girl was walking unsteadily, too, stumbling and staggering from side to side. She drew Raskolnikov's whole attention at last. He overtook the girl at the seat, but, on reaching it, she dropped down on it, in the corner; she let her head sink on the back of the seat and closed her eyes, apparently in extreme exhaustion. Looking at her closely, he saw at once that she was completely drunk. It was a strange and shocking sight. He could hardly believe that he was not mistaken. He saw before him the face of a quite young, fair-haired girl—sixteen, perhaps not more than fifteen, years old, pretty little face, but flushed and heavy looking and, as it were, swollen. The girl seemed hardly to know what she was doing; she crossed one leg over the other, lifting it indecorously, and showed every sign of being unconscious that she was in the street.

Raskolnikov did not sit down, but he felt unwilling to leave her, and stood facing her in perplexity. This boulevard was never much frequented; and now, at two o'clock, in the stifling heat, it was quite deserted. And yet on the further side of the boulevard, about fifteen paces away, a gentleman was standing on the edge of the pavement. He, too, would apparently have liked to approach the girl with some object of his own. He, too, had probably seen her in the distance and had followed her, but found Raskolnikov in his way. He looked angrily at him, though he tried to escape his notice, and stood impatiently biding his time, till the unwelcome man in rags should have moved away. His intentions were unmistakable. The gentleman was a plump, thickly-set man, about thirty, fashionably dressed, with a high colour, red lips and moustaches. Raskolnikov felt furious; he had a sudden longing to insult this fat dandy in some way. He left the girl for a moment and walked towards the gentleman.

"Hey! You Svidrigaïlov! What do you want here?" he shouted, clenching his fists and laughing, spluttering with rage.

"What do you mean?" the gentleman asked sternly, scowling in haughty astonishment.

"Get away, that's what I mean."

"How dare you, you low fellow!"

He raised his cane. Raskolnikov rushed at him with his fists, without reflecting that the stout gentleman was a match for two men like himself. But at that instant someone seized him from behind, and a police constable stood between them.

"That's enough, gentlemen, no fighting, please, in a public place. What do you want? Who are you?" he asked Raskolnikov sternly, noticing his rags.

Raskolnikov looked at him intently. He had a straight-forward, sensible, soldierly face, with grey moustaches and whiskers.

"You are just the man I want," Raskolnikov cried, catching at his arm. "I am a student, Raskolnikov.... You may as well know that too," he added, addressing the gentleman, "come along, I have something to show you."

And taking the policeman by the hand he drew him towards the seat.

"Look here, hopelessly drunk, and she has just come down the boulevard. There is no telling who and what she is, she does not look like a professional. It's more likely she has been given drink and deceived somewhere... for the first time... you understand? and they've put her out into the street like that. Look at the way her dress is torn, and the way it has been put on: she has been dressed by somebody, she has not dressed herself, and dressed by unpractised hands, by a man's hands; that's evident. And now look there: I don't know that dandy with whom I was going to fight, I see him for the first time, but he, too, has seen her on the road, just now, drunk, not knowing what she is doing, and now he is very eager to get hold of her, to get her away somewhere while she is in this state... that's certain, believe me, I am not wrong. I saw him myself watching her and following her, but I prevented him, and he is just waiting for me to go away. Now he has walked away a little, and is standing still, pretending to make a cigarette.... Think how can we keep her out of his hands, and how are we to get her home?"

The policeman saw it all in a flash. The stout gentleman was easy to understand, he turned to consider the girl. The policeman bent over to examine her more closely, and his face worked with genuine compassion.

"Ah, what a pity!" he said, shaking his head—"why, she is quite a child! She has been deceived, you can see that at once. Listen, lady," he began addressing her, "where do you live?" The girl opened her weary and sleepy-looking eyes, gazed blankly at the speaker and waved her hand.

"Here," said Raskolnikov feeling in his pocket and finding twenty copecks, "here, call a cab and tell him to drive her to her address. The only thing is to find out her address!"

"Missy, missy!" the policeman began again, taking the money. "I'll fetch you a cab and take you home myself. Where shall I take you, eh? Where do you live?"

"Go away! They won't let me alone," the girl muttered, and once more waved her hand.

"Ach, ach, how shocking! It's shameful, missy, it's a shame!" He shook his head again, shocked, sympathetic and indignant.

"It's a difficult job," the policeman said to Raskolnikov, and as he did so, he looked him up and down in a rapid glance. He, too, must have seemed a strange figure to him: dressed in rags and handing him money!

"Did you meet her far from here?" he asked him.

"I tell you she was walking in front of me, staggering, just here, in the boulevard. She only just reached the seat and sank down on it."

"Ah, the shameful things that are done in the world nowadays, God have mercy on us! An innocent creature like that, drunk already! She has been deceived, that's a sure thing. See how her dress has been torn too.... Ah, the vice one sees nowadays! And as likely as not she belongs to gentlefolk too, poor ones maybe.... There are many like that nowadays. She looks refined, too, as though she were a lady," and he bent over her once more.

Perhaps he had daughters growing up like that, "looking like ladies and refined" with pretensions to gentility and smartness....

"The chief thing is," Raskolnikov persisted, "to keep her out of this scoundrel's hands! Why should he outrage her! It's as clear as day what he is after; ah, the brute, he is not moving off!"

Raskolnikov spoke aloud and pointed to him. The gentleman heard him, and seemed about to fly into a rage again, but thought better of it, and confined himself to a contemptuous look. He then walked slowly another ten paces away and again halted.

"Keep her out of his hands we can," said the constable thoughtfully, "if only she'd tell us where to take her, but as it is.... Missy, hey, missy!" he bent over her once more.

She opened her eyes fully all of a sudden, looked at him intently, as though realising something, got up from the seat and walked away in the direction from which she had come. "Oh shameful wretches, they won't let me alone!" she said, waving her hand again. She walked quickly, though staggering as before. The dandy followed her, but along another avenue, keeping his eye on her.

"Don't be anxious, I won't let him have her," the policeman said resolutely, and he set off after them.

"Ah, the vice one sees nowadays!" he repeated aloud, sighing.

At that moment something seemed to sting Raskolnikov; in an instant a complete revulsion of feeling came over him.

"Hey, here!" he shouted after the policeman.

The latter turned round.

"Let them be! What is it to do with you? Let her go! Let him amuse himself." He pointed at the dandy, "What is it to do with you?"

The policeman was bewildered, and stared at him open-eyed. Raskolnikov laughed.

"Well!" ejaculated the policeman, with a gesture of contempt, and he walked after the dandy and the girl, probably taking Raskolnikov for a madman or something even worse.

"He has carried off my twenty copecks," Raskolnikov murmured angrily when he was left alone. "Well, let him take as much from the other fellow to allow him to have the girl and so let it end. And why did I want to interfere? Is it for me to help? Have I any right to help? Let them devour each other alive—what is to me? How did I dare to give him twenty copecks? Were they mine?"

In spite of those strange words he felt very wretched. He sat down on the deserted seat. His thoughts strayed aimlessly.... He found it hard to fix his mind on anything at that moment. He longed to forget himself altogether, to forget everything, and then to wake up and begin life anew....

"Poor girl!" he said, looking at the empty corner where she had sat—"She will come to herself and weep, and then her mother will find out.... She will give her a beating, a horrible, shameful beating and then maybe, turn her out of doors.... And even if she does not, the Darya Frantsovnas will get wind of it, and the girl will soon be slipping out on the sly here and there. Then there will be the hospital directly (that's always the luck of those girls with respectable mothers, who go wrong on the sly) and then... again the hospital... drink... the taverns... and more hospital, in two or three years—a wreck, and her life over at eighteen or nineteen.... Have not I seen cases like that? And how have they been brought to it? Why, they've all come to it like that. Ugh! But what does it matter? That's as it should be, they tell us. A certain percentage, they tell us, must every year go... that way... to the devil, I suppose, so that the rest may remain chaste, and not be interfered with. A percentage! What splendid words they have; they are so scientific, so consolatory.... Once you've said 'percentage' there's nothing more to worry about. If we had any other word... maybe we might feel more uneasy.... But what if Dounia were one of the percentage! Of another one if not that one?

"But where am I going?" he thought suddenly. "Strange, I came out for something. As soon as I had read the letter I came out.... I was going to Vassilyevsky Ostrov, to Razumihin. That's what it was... now I remember. What for, though? And what put the idea of going to Razumihin into my head just now? That's curious."

He wondered at himself. Razumihin was one of his old comrades at the university. It was remarkable that Raskolnikov had hardly any friends at the university; he kept aloof from everyone, went to see no one, and did not welcome anyone who came to see him, and indeed everyone soon gave him up. He took no part in the students' gatherings, amusements or conversations. He worked with great intensity without sparing himself, and he was respected for this, but no one liked him. He was very poor, and there was a sort of haughty pride and reserve about him, as though he were keeping something to himself. He seemed to some of his comrades to look down upon them all as children, as though he were superior in development, knowledge and convictions, as though their beliefs and interests were beneath him.

With Razumihin he had got on, or, at least, he was more unreserved and communicative with him. Indeed it was impossible to be on any other terms with Razumihin. He was an exceptionally good-humoured and candid youth, good-natured to the point of simplicity, though both depth and dignity lay concealed under that simplicity. The better of his comrades understood this, and all were fond of him. He was extremely intelligent, though he was certainly rather a simpleton at times. He was of striking appearance—tall, thin, blackhaired and always badly shaved. He was sometimes uproarious and was reputed to be of great physical strength. One night, when out in a festive company, he had with one blow laid a gigantic policeman on his back. There was no limit to his drinking powers, but he could abstain from drink altogether; he sometimes went too far in his pranks; but he could do without pranks altogether. Another thing striking about Razumihin, no failure distressed him, and it seemed as though no unfavourable circumstances could crush him. He could lodge anywhere, and bear the extremes of cold and hunger. He was very poor, and kept himself entirely on what he could earn by work of one sort or another. He knew of no end of resources by which to earn money. He spent one whole winter without lighting his stove, and used to declare that he liked it better, because one slept more soundly in the cold. For the present he, too, had been obliged to give up the university, but it was only for a time, and he was working with all his might to save enough to return to his studies again. Raskolnikov had not been to see him for the last four months, and Razumihin did not even know his address. About two months before, they had met in the street, but Raskolnikov had turned away and even crossed to the other side that he might not be observed. And though Razumihin noticed him, he passed him by, as he did not want to annoy him.

CHAPTER V

"Of course, I've been meaning lately to go to Razumihin's to ask for work, to ask him to get me lessons or something..." Raskolnikov thought, "but what help can he be to me now? Suppose he gets me lessons, suppose he shares his last farthing with me, if he has any farthings, so that I could get some boots and make myself tidy enough to give lessons... hm... Well and what then? What shall I do with the few coppers I earn? That's not what I want now. It's really absurd for me to go to Razumihin...."

The question why he was now going to Razumihin agitated him even more than he was himself aware; he kept uneasily seeking for some sinister significance in this apparently ordinary action.

"Could I have expected to set it all straight and to find a way out by means of Razumihin alone?" he asked himself in perplexity.

He pondered and rubbed his forehead, and, strange to say, after long musing, suddenly, as if it were spontaneously and by chance, a fantastic thought came into his head.

"Hm... to Razumihin's," he said all at once, calmly, as though he had reached a final determination. "I shall go to Razumihin's of course, but... not now. I shall go to him... on the next day after It, when It will be over and everything will begin afresh...."

And suddenly he realised what he was thinking.

"After It," he shouted, jumping up from the seat, "but is It really going to happen? Is it possible it really will happen?" He left the seat, and went off almost at a run; he meant to turn back, homewards, but the thought of going home suddenly filled him with intense loathing; in that hole, in that awful little cupboard of his, all *this* had for a month past been growing up in him; and he walked on at random.

His nervous shudder had passed into a fever that made him feel shivering; in spite of the heat he felt cold. With a kind of effort he began almost unconsciously, from some inner craving, to stare at all the objects before him, as though looking for something to distract his attention; but he did not succeed, and kept dropping every moment into brooding. When with a start he lifted his head again and looked round, he forgot at once what he had just been thinking about and even where he was going. In this way he walked right across Vassilyevsky Ostrov, came out on to the Lesser Neva, crossed the bridge and turned towards the islands. The greenness and freshness were at first restful to his weary eyes after the dust of the town and the huge houses that hemmed him in and weighed upon him. Here there were no taverns, no stifling closeness, no stench. But soon these new pleasant sensations passed into morbid irritability. Sometimes he stood still before a brightly painted summer villa standing among green foliage, he gazed through the fence, he saw in the distance smartly dressed women on the verandahs and balconies, and children running in the gardens. The flowers especially caught his attention; he gazed at them longer than at anything. He was met, too, by luxurious carriages and by men and women on horseback; he watched them with curious eyes and forgot about them before they had vanished from his sight. Once he stood still and counted his money; he found he had thirty copecks. "Twenty to the policeman, three to Nastasya for the letter, so I must have given forty-seven or fifty to the Marmeladovs yesterday," he thought, reckoning it up for some unknown reason, but he soon forgot with what object he had taken the money out of his pocket. He recalled it on passing an eating-house or tavern, and felt that he was hungry.... Going into the tavern he drank a glass of vodka and ate a pie of some sort. He finished eating it as he walked away. It was a long while since he had taken vodka and it had an effect upon him at once, though he only drank a wineglassful. His legs felt suddenly heavy and a great drowsiness came upon him. He turned homewards, but reaching Petrovsky Ostrov he stopped completely exhausted, turned off the road into the bushes, sank down upon the grass and instantly fell asleep.

In a morbid condition of the brain, dreams often have a singular actuality, vividness, and extraordinary semblance of reality. At times monstrous images are created, but the setting and the whole picture are so truth-like and filled with details so delicate, so unexpectedly, but so artistically consistent, that the dreamer, were he an artist like Pushkin or Turgenev even, could never have invented them in the waking state. Such sick dreams always remain long in the memory and make a powerful impression on the overwrought and deranged nervous system.

Raskolnikov had a fearful dream. He dreamt he was back in his childhood in the little town of his birth. He was a child about seven years old, walking into the country with his father on the evening of a holiday. It was a grey and heavy day, the country was exactly as he remembered it; indeed he recalled it far more vividly in his dream than he had done in memory. The little town stood on a level flat as bare as the hand, not even a willow near it; only in the far distance, a copse lay, a dark blur on the very edge of the horizon. A few paces beyond the last market garden stood a tavern, a big tavern, which had always aroused in him a feeling of aversion, even of fear, when he walked by it with his father. There was always a crowd there, always shouting, laughter and abuse, hideous hoarse singing and often fighting. Drunken and horrible-looking figures were hanging about the tavern. He used to cling close to his father, trembling all over when he met them. Near the tavern the road became a dusty track, the dust of which was always black. It was a winding road, and about a hundred paces further on, it turned to the right to the graveyard. In the middle of the graveyard stood a stone church with a green cupola where he used to go to mass two or three times a year with his father and mother, when a service was held in memory of his grandmother, who had long been dead, and whom he had never seen. On these occasions they used to take on a white dish tied up in a table napkin a special sort of rice pudding with raisins stuck in it in the shape of a cross. He loved that church, the old-fashioned, unadorned ikons and the old priest with the shaking head. Near his grandmother's grave, which was marked by a stone, was the little grave of his younger brother who had died at six months old. He did not remember him at all, but he had been told about his little brother, and whenever he visited the graveyard he used religiously and reverently to cross himself and to bow down and kiss the little grave. And now he dreamt that he was walking with his father past the tavern on the way to the graveyard; he was holding his father's hand and looking with dread at the tavern. A peculiar circumstance attracted his attention: there seemed to be some kind of festivity going on, there were crowds of gaily dressed townspeople, peasant women, their husbands, and riff-raff of all sorts, all singing and all more or less drunk. Near the entrance of the tavern stood a cart, but a strange cart. It was one of those big carts usually drawn by heavy cart-horses and laden with casks of wine or other heavy goods. He always liked looking at those great cart-horses, with their long manes, thick legs, and slow even pace, drawing along a perfect mountain with no appearance of effort, as though it were easier going with a load than without it. But now, strange to say, in the shafts of such a cart he saw a thin little sorrel beast, one of those peasants' nags which he had often seen straining their utmost under a heavy load of wood or hay, especially when the wheels were stuck in the mud or in a rut. And the peasants would beat them so cruelly, sometimes even about the nose and eyes, and he felt so sorry, so sorry for them that he almost cried, and his mother always used to take him away from the window. All of a sudden there was a great uproar of shouting, singing and the balalaïka, and from the tavern a number of big and very drunken peasants came out, wearing red and blue shirts and coats thrown over their shoulders.

"Get in, get in!" shouted one of them, a young thick-necked peasant with a fleshy face red as a carrot. "I'll take you all, get in!"

But at once there was an outbreak of laughter and exclamations in the crowd.

"Take us all with a beast like that!"

"Why, Mikolka, are you crazy to put a nag like that in such a cart?"

"And this mare is twenty if she is a day, mates!"

"Get in, I'll take you all," Mikolka shouted again, leaping first into the cart, seizing the reins and standing straight up in front. "The bay has gone with Matvey," he shouted from the cart—"and this brute, mates, is just breaking my heart, I feel as if I could kill her. She's just eating her head off. Get in, I tell you! I'll make her gallop! She'll gallop!" and he picked up the whip, preparing himself with relish to flog the little mare.

"Get in! Come along!" The crowd laughed. "D'you hear, she'll gallop!"

"Gallop indeed! She has not had a gallop in her for the last ten years!"

"She'll jog along!"

"Don't you mind her, mates, bring a whip each of you, get ready!"

"All right! Give it to her!"

They all clambered into Mikolka's cart, laughing and making jokes. Six men got in and there was still room for more. They hauled in a fat, rosy-cheeked woman. She was dressed in red cotton, in a pointed, beaded headdress and thick leather shoes; she was cracking nuts and laughing. The crowd round them was laughing too and indeed, how could they help laughing? That wretched nag was to drag all the cartload of them at a gallop! Two young fellows in the cart were just getting whips ready to help Mikolka. With the cry of "now," the mare tugged with all her might, but far from galloping, could scarcely move forward; she struggled with her legs, gasping and shrinking from the blows of the three whips which were showered upon her like hail. The laughter in the cart and in the crowd was redoubled, but Mikolka flew into a rage and furiously thrashed the mare, as though he supposed she really could gallop.

"Let me get in, too, mates," shouted a young man in the crowd whose appetite was aroused.

"Get in, all get in," cried Mikolka, "she will draw you all. I'll beat her to death!" And he thrashed and thrashed at the mare, beside himself with fury.

"Father, father," he cried, "father, what are they doing? Father, they are beating the poor horse!"

"Come along, come along!" said his father. "They are drunken and foolish, they are in fun; come away, don't look!" and he tried to draw him away, but he tore himself away from his hand, and, beside himself with horror, ran to the horse. The poor beast was in a bad way. She was gasping, standing still, then tugging again and almost falling.

"Beat her to death," cried Mikolka, "it's come to that. I'll do for her!"

"What are you about, are you a Christian, you devil?" shouted an old man in the crowd.

"Did anyone ever see the like? A wretched nag like that pulling such a cartload," said another.

"You'll kill her," shouted the third.

"Don't meddle! It's my property, I'll do what I choose. Get in, more of you! Get in, all of you! I will have her go at a gallop!..."

All at once laughter broke into a roar and covered everything: the mare, roused by the shower of blows, began feebly kicking. Even the old man could not help smiling. To think of a wretched little beast like that trying to kick!

Two lads in the crowd snatched up whips and ran to the mare to beat her about the ribs. One ran each side.

"Hit her in the face, in the eyes, in the eyes," cried Mikolka.

"Give us a song, mates," shouted someone in the cart and everyone in the cart joined in a riotous song, jingling a tambourine and whistling. The woman went on cracking nuts and laughing.

... He ran beside the mare, ran in front of her, saw her being whipped across the eyes, right in the eyes! He was crying, he felt choking, his tears were streaming. One of the men gave him a cut with the whip across the face, he did not feel it. Wringing his hands and screaming, he rushed up to the grey-headed old man with the grey beard, who was shaking his head in disapproval. One woman seized him by the hand and would have taken him away, but he tore himself from her and ran back to the mare. She was almost at the last gasp, but began kicking once more.

"I'll teach you to kick," Mikolka shouted ferociously. He threw down the whip, bent forward and picked up from the bottom of the cart a long, thick shaft, he took hold of one end with both hands and with an effort brandished it over the mare.

"He'll crush her," was shouted round him. "He'll kill her!"

"It's my property," shouted Mikolka and brought the shaft down with a swinging blow. There was a sound of a heavy thud.

"Thrash her, thrash her! Why have you stopped?" shouted voices in the crowd.

And Mikolka swung the shaft a second time and it fell a second time on the spine of the luckless mare. She sank back on her haunches, but lurched forward and tugged forward with all her force, tugged first on one side and then on the other, trying to move the cart. But the six whips were attacking her in all directions, and the shaft was raised again and fell upon her a third time, then a fourth, with heavy measured blows. Mikolka was in a fury that he could not kill her at one blow.

"She's a tough one," was shouted in the crowd.

"She'll fall in a minute, mates, there will soon be an end of her," said an admiring spectator in the crowd.

"Fetch an axe to her! Finish her off," shouted a third.

"I'll show you! Stand off," Mikolka screamed frantically; he threw down the shaft, stooped down in the cart and picked up an iron crowbar. "Look out," he shouted, and with all his might he dealt a stunning blow at the poor mare. The blow fell; the mare staggered, sank back, tried to pull, but the bar fell again with a swinging blow on her back and she fell on the ground like a log.

"Finish her off," shouted Mikolka and he leapt beside himself, out of the cart. Several young men, also flushed with drink, seized anything they could come across—whips, sticks, poles, and ran to the dying mare. Mikolka stood on one side and began dealing random blows with the crowbar. The mare stretched out her head, drew a long breath and died.

"You butchered her," someone shouted in the crowd.

"Why wouldn't she gallop then?"

"My property!" shouted Mikolka, with bloodshot eyes, brandishing the bar in his hands. He stood as though regretting that he had nothing more to beat.

"No mistake about it, you are not a Christian," many voices were shouting in the crowd.

But the poor boy, beside himself, made his way, screaming, through the crowd to the sorrel nag, put his arms round her bleeding dead head and kissed it, kissed the eyes and kissed the lips.... Then he jumped up and flew in a frenzy with his little fists out at Mikolka. At that instant his father, who had been running after him, snatched him up and carried him out of the crowd.

"Come along, come! Let us go home," he said to him.

"Father! Why did they... kill... the poor horse!" he sobbed, but his voice broke and the words came in shrieks from his panting chest.

"They are drunk.... They are brutal... it's not our business!" said his father. He put his arms round his father but he felt choked, choked. He tried to draw a breath, to cry out—and woke up.

He waked up, gasping for breath, his hair soaked with perspiration, and stood up in terror.

"Thank God, that was only a dream," he said, sitting down under a tree and drawing deep breaths. "But what is it? Is it some fever coming on? Such a hideous dream!"

He felt utterly broken: darkness and confusion were in his soul. He rested his elbows on his knees and leaned his head on his hands.

"Good God!" he cried, "can it be, can it be, that I shall really take an axe, that I shall strike her on the head, split her skull open... that I shall tread in the sticky warm blood, break the lock, steal and tremble; hide, all spattered in the blood... with the axe.... Good God, can it be?"

He was shaking like a leaf as he said this.

"But why am I going on like this?" he continued, sitting up again, as it were in profound amazement. "I knew that I could never bring myself to it, so what have I been torturing myself for till now? Yesterday, yesterday, when I went to make that...*experiment*, yesterday I realised completely that I could never bear to do it.... Why am I going over it again, then? Why am I hesitating? As I came down the stairs yesterday, I said myself that it was base, loathsome, vile, vile... the very thought of it made me feel sick and filled me with horror.

"No, I couldn't do it, I couldn't do it! Granted, granted that there is no flaw in all that reasoning, that all that I have concluded this last month is clear as day, true as arithmetic.... My God! Anyway I couldn't bring myself to it! I couldn't do it, I couldn't do it! Why, why then am I still...?"

He rose to his feet, looked round in wonder as though surprised at finding himself in this place, and went towards the bridge. He was pale, his eyes glowed, he was exhausted in every limb, but he seemed suddenly to breathe more easily. He felt he had cast off that fearful burden that had so long been weighing upon him, and all at once there was a sense of relief and peace in his soul. "Lord," he prayed, "show me my path—I renounce that accursed... dream of mine."

Crossing the bridge, he gazed quietly and calmly at the Neva, at the glowing red sun setting in the glowing sky. In spite of his weakness he was not conscious of fatigue. It was as though an abscess that had been forming for a month past in his heart had suddenly broken. Freedom, freedom! He was free from that spell, that sorcery, that obsession!

Later on, when he recalled that time and all that happened to him during those days, minute by minute, point by point, he was superstitiously impressed by one circumstance, which, though in itself not very exceptional, always seemed to him afterwards the predestined turning-point of his fate. He could never understand and explain to himself why, when he was tired and worn out, when it would have been more convenient for him to go home by the shortest and most direct way, he had returned by the Hay Market where he had no need to go. It was obviously and quite unnecessarily out of his way, though not much so. It is true that it happened to him dozens of times to return home without noticing what streets he passed through. But why, he was always asking himself, why had such an important, such a decisive and at the same time such an absolutely chance meeting happened in the Hay Market (where he had moreover no reason to go) at the very hour, the very minute of his life when he was just in the very mood and in the very circumstances in which that meeting was able to exert the gravest and most decisive influence on his whole destiny? As though it had been lying in wait for him on purpose!

It was about nine o'clock when he crossed the Hay Market. At the tables and the barrows, at the booths and the shops, all the market people were closing their establishments or clearing away and packing up their wares and, like their customers, were going home. Rag pickers and costermongers of all kinds were crowding round the taverns in the dirty and stinking courtyards of the Hay Market. Raskolnikov particularly liked this place and the neighbouring alleys, when he wandered aimlessly in the streets. Here his rags did not attract contemptuous attention, and one could walk about in any attire without scandalising people. At the corner of an alley a huckster and his wife had two tables set out with tapes, thread, cotton handkerchiefs, etc. They, too, had got up to go home, but were lingering in conversation with a friend, who had just come up to them. This friend was Lizaveta Ivanovna, or, as everyone called her, Lizaveta, the younger sister of the old pawnbroker, Alyona Ivanovna, whom Raskolnikov had visited the previous day to pawn his watch and make his *experiment*.... He already knew all about Lizaveta and she knew him a little too. She was a single woman of about thirty-five, tall, clumsy, timid, submissive and almost idiotic. She was a complete slave and went in fear and trembling of her sister, who made her work day and night, and even beat her. She was standing with a bundle before the huckster and his wife, listening earnestly and doubtfully. They were talking of something with special warmth. The moment Raskolnikov caught sight of her, he was overcome by a strange sensation as it were of intense astonishment, though there was nothing astonishing about this meeting.

"You could make up your mind for yourself, Lizaveta Ivanovna," the huckster was saying aloud. "Come round to-morrow about seven. They will be here too."

"To-morrow?" said Lizaveta slowly and thoughtfully, as though unable to make up her mind.

"Upon my word, what a fright you are in of Alyona Ivanovna," gabbled the huckster's wife, a lively little woman. "I look at you, you are like some little babe. And she is not your own sister either—nothing but a step-sister and what a hand she keeps over you!"

"But this time don't say a word to Alyona Ivanovna," her husband interrupted; "that's my advice, but come round to us without asking. It will be worth your while. Later on your sister herself may have a notion."

"Am I to come?"

"About seven o'clock to-morrow. And they will be here. You will be able to decide for yourself."

"And we'll have a cup of tea," added his wife.

"All right, I'll come," said Lizaveta, still pondering, and she began slowly moving away.

Raskolnikov had just passed and heard no more. He passed softly, unnoticed, trying not to miss a word. His first amazement was followed by a thrill of horror, like a shiver running down his spine. He had learnt, he had suddenly quite unexpectedly learnt, that the next day at seven o'clock Lizaveta, the old woman's sister and only companion, would be away from home and that therefore at seven o'clock precisely the old woman *would be left alone*.

He was only a few steps from his lodging. He went in like a man condemned to death. He thought of nothing and was incapable of thinking; but he felt suddenly in his whole being that he had no more freedom of thought, no will, and that everything was suddenly and irrevocably decided.

Certainly, if he had to wait whole years for a suitable opportunity, he could not reckon on a more certain step towards the success of the plan than that which had just presented itself. In any case, it would have been difficult to find out beforehand and with certainty, with greater exactness and less risk, and without dangerous inquiries and investigations, that next day at a certain time an old woman, on whose life an attempt was contemplated, would be at home and entirely alone.

CHAPTER VI

Later on Raskolnikov happened to find out why the huckster and his wife had invited Lizaveta. It was a very ordinary matter and there was nothing exceptional about it. A family who had come to the town and been reduced to poverty were selling their household goods and clothes, all women's things. As the things would have fetched little in the market, they were looking for a dealer. This was Lizaveta's business. She undertook such jobs and was frequently employed, as she was very honest and always fixed a fair price and stuck to it. She spoke as a rule little and, as we have said already, she was very submissive and timid.

But Raskolnikov had become superstitious of late. The traces of superstition remained in him long after, and were almost ineradicable. And in all this he was always afterwards disposed to see something strange and mysterious, as it were, the presence of some peculiar influences and coincidences. In the previous winter a student he knew called Pokorev, who had left for Harkov, had chanced in conversation to give him the address of Alyona Ivanovna, the old pawnbroker, in case he might want to pawn anything. For a long while he did not go to her, for he had lessons and managed to get along somehow. Six weeks ago he had remembered the address; he had two articles that could be pawned: his father's old silver watch and a little gold ring with three red stones, a present from his sister at parting. He decided to take the ring. When he found the old woman he had felt an insurmountable repulsion for her at the first glance, though he knew nothing special about her. He got two roubles from her and went into a miserable little tavern on his way home. He asked for tea, sat down and sank into deep thought. A strange idea was pecking at his brain like a chicken in the egg, and very, very much absorbed him.

Almost beside him at the next table there was sitting a student, whom he did not know and had never seen, and with him a young officer. They had played a game of billiards and began drinking tea. All at once he heard the student mention to the officer the pawnbroker Alyona Ivanovna and give him her address. This of itself seemed strange to Raskolnikov; he had just come from her and here at once he heard her name. Of course it was a chance, but he could not shake off a very extraordinary impression, and here someone seemed to be speaking expressly for him; the student began telling his friend various details about Alyona Ivanovna.

"She is first-rate," he said. "You can always get money from her. She is as rich as a Jew, she can give you five thousand roubles at a time and she is not above taking a pledge for a rouble. Lots of our fellows have had dealings with her. But she is an awful old harpy...."

And he began describing how spiteful and uncertain she was, how if you were only a day late with your interest the pledge was lost; how she gave a quarter of the value of an article and took five and even seven percent a month on it and so on. The student chattered on, saying that she had a sister Lizaveta, whom the wretched little creature was continually beating, and kept in complete bondage like a small child, though Lizaveta was at least six feet high.

"There's a phenomenon for you," cried the student and he laughed.

They began talking about Lizaveta. The student spoke about her with a peculiar relish and was continually laughing and the officer listened with great interest and asked him to send Lizaveta to do some mending for him. Raskolnikov did not miss a word and learned everything about her. Lizaveta was younger than the old woman and was her half-sister, being the child of a different mother. She was thirty-five. She worked day and night for her sister, and besides doing the cooking and the washing, she did sewing and worked as a charwoman and gave her sister all she earned. She did not dare to accept an order or job of any kind without her sister's permission. The old woman had already made her will, and Lizaveta knew of it, and by this will she would not get a farthing; nothing but the movables, chairs and so on; all the money was left to a monastery in the province of N——, that prayers might be said for her in perpetuity. Lizaveta was of lower rank than her sister, unmarried and awfully uncouth in appearance, remarkably tall with long feet that looked as if they were bent outwards.

She always wore battered goatskin shoes, and was clean in her person. What the student expressed most surprise and amusement about was the fact that Lizaveta was continually with child.

"But you say she is hideous?" observed the officer.

"Yes, she is so dark-skinned and looks like a soldier dressed up, but you know she is not at all hideous. She has such a good-natured face and eyes. Strikingly so. And the proof of it is that lots of people are attracted by her. She is such a soft, gentle creature, ready to put up with anything, always willing, willing to do anything. And her smile is really very sweet."

"You seem to find her attractive yourself," laughed the officer.

"From her queerness. No, I'll tell you what. I could kill that damned old woman and make off with her money, I assure you, without the faintest conscience-prick," the student added with warmth. The officer laughed again while Raskolnikov shuddered. How strange it was!

"Listen, I want to ask you a serious question," the student said hotly. "I was joking of course, but look here; on one side we have a stupid, senseless, worthless, spiteful, ailing, horrid old woman, not simply useless but doing actual mischief, who has not an idea what she is living for herself, and who will die in a day or two in any case. You understand? You understand?"

"Yes, yes, I understand," answered the officer, watching his excited companion attentively.

"Well, listen then. On the other side, fresh young lives thrown away for want of help and by thousands, on every side! A hundred thousand good deeds could be done and helped, on that old woman's money which will be buried in a monastery! Hundreds, thousands perhaps, might be set on the right path; dozens of families saved from destitution, from ruin, from vice, from the Lock hospitals—and all with her money. Kill her, take her money and with the help of it devote oneself to the service of humanity and the good of all. What do you think, would not one tiny crime be wiped out by thousands of good deeds? For one life thousands would be saved from corruption and decay. One death, and a hundred lives in exchange—it's simple arithmetic! Besides, what value has the life of that sickly, stupid, ill-natured old woman in the balance of existence! No more than the life of a louse, of a black-beetle, less in fact because the old woman is doing harm. She is wearing out the lives of others; the other day she bit Lizaveta's finger out of spite; it almost had to be amputated."

"Of course she does not deserve to live," remarked the officer, "but there it is, it's nature."

"Oh, well, brother, but we have to correct and direct nature, and, but for that, we should drown in an ocean of prejudice. But for that, there would never have been a single great man. They talk of duty, conscience—I don't want to say anything against duty and conscience;—but the point is, what do we mean by them? Stay, I have another question to ask you. Listen!"

"No, you stay, I'll ask you a question. Listen!"

"Well?"

"You are talking and speechifying away, but tell me, would you kill the old woman *yourself*?"

"Of course not! I was only arguing the justice of it.... It's nothing to do with me...."

"But I think, if you would not do it yourself, there's no justice about it.... Let us have another game."

Raskolnikov was violently agitated. Of course, it was all ordinary youthful talk and thought, such as he had often heard before in different forms and on different themes. But why had he happened to hear such a discussion and such ideas at the very moment when his own brain was just conceiving... *the very same ideas*? And why, just at the moment when he had brought away the embryo of his idea from the old woman had he dropped at once upon a conversation about her? This coincidence always seemed strange to him. This trivial talk in a tavern had an immense influence on him in his later action; as though there had really been in it something preordained, some guiding hint....

On returning from the Hay Market he flung himself on the sofa and sat for a whole hour without stirring. Meanwhile it got dark; he had no candle and, indeed, it did not occur to him to light up. He could never recollect whether he had been thinking about anything at that time. At last he was conscious of his former fever and shivering, and he realised with relief that he could lie down on the sofa. Soon heavy, leaden sleep came over him, as it were crushing him.

He slept an extraordinarily long time and without dreaming. Nastasya, coming into his room at ten o'clock the next morning, had difficulty in rousing him. She brought him in tea and bread. The tea was again the second brew and again in her own tea-pot.

"My goodness, how he sleeps!" she cried indignantly. "And he is always asleep."

He got up with an effort. His head ached, he stood up, took a turn in his garret and sank back on the sofa again.

"Going to sleep again," cried Nastasya. "Are you ill, eh?"

He made no reply.

"Do you want some tea?"

"Afterwards," he said with an effort, closing his eyes again and turning to the wall.

Nastasya stood over him.

"Perhaps he really is ill," she said, turned and went out. She came in again at two o'clock with soup. He was lying as before. The tea stood untouched. Nastasya felt positively offended and began wrathfully rousing him.

"Why are you lying like a log?" she shouted, looking at him with repulsion.

He got up, and sat down again, but said nothing and stared at the floor.

"Are you ill or not?" asked Nastasya and again received no answer. "You'd better go out and get a breath of air," she said after a pause. "Will you eat it or not?"

"Afterwards," he said weakly. "You can go."

And he motioned her out.

She remained a little longer, looked at him with compassion and went out.

A few minutes afterwards, he raised his eyes and looked for a long while at the tea and the soup. Then he took the bread, took up a spoon and began to eat.

He ate a little, three or four spoonfuls, without appetite, as it were mechanically. His head ached less. After his meal he stretched himself on the sofa again, but now he could not sleep; he lay without stirring, with his face in the pillow. He was haunted by day-dreams and such strange day-dreams; in one, that kept recurring, he fancied that he was in Africa, in Egypt, in some sort of oasis. The caravan was resting, the camels were peacefully lying down; the palms stood all around in a complete circle; all the party were at dinner. But he was drinking water from a spring which flowed gurgling close by. And it was so cool, it was wonderful, wonderful, blue, cold water running among the parti-coloured stones and over the clean sand which glistened here and there like gold.... Suddenly he heard a clock strike. He started, roused himself, raised his head, looked out of the window, and seeing how late it was, suddenly jumped up wide awake as though someone had pulled him off the sofa. He crept on tiptoe to the door, stealthily opened it and began listening on the staircase. His heart beat terribly. But all was quiet on the stairs as if everyone was asleep.... It seemed to him strange and monstrous that he could have slept in such forgetfulness from the previous day and had done nothing, had prepared nothing yet.... And meanwhile perhaps it had struck six. And his drowsiness and stupefaction were followed by an extraordinary, feverish, as it were distracted haste. But the preparations to be made were few. He concentrated all his energies on thinking of everything and forgetting nothing; and his heart kept beating and thumping so that he could hardly breathe. First he had to make a noose and sew it into his overcoat—a work of a moment. He rummaged under his pillow and picked out amongst the linen stuffed away under it, a worn out, old unwashed shirt. From its rags he tore a long strip, a couple of inches wide and about sixteen inches long. He folded this strip in two, took off his wide, strong summer overcoat of some stout cotton material (his only outer garment) and began sewing the two ends of the rag on the inside, under the left armhole. His hands shook as he sewed, but he did it successfully so that nothing showed outside when he put the coat on again. The needle and thread he had got ready long before and they lay on his table in a piece of paper. As for the noose, it was a very ingenious device of his own; the noose was intended for the axe. It was impossible for him to carry the axe through the street in his hands. And if hidden under his coat he would still have had to support it with his hand, which would have been noticeable. Now he had only to put the head of the axe in the noose, and it would hang quietly under his arm on the inside. Putting his hand in his coat pocket, he could hold the end of the handle all the way, so that it did not swing; and as the coat was very full, a regular sack in fact, it could not be seen from outside that he was holding something with the hand that was in the pocket. This noose, too, he had designed a fortnight before.

When he had finished with this, he thrust his hand into a little opening between his sofa and the floor, fumbled in the left corner and drew out the *pledge*, which he had got ready long before and hidden there. This pledge was, however, only a smoothly planed piece of wood the size and thickness of a silver cigarette case. He picked up this piece of wood in one of his wanderings in a courtyard where there was some sort of a workshop. Afterwards he had added to the wood a thin smooth piece of iron, which he had also picked up at the same time in the street. Putting the iron which was a little the smaller on the piece of wood, he fastened them very firmly, crossing and re-crossing the thread round them; then wrapped them carefully and daintily in clean white paper and tied up the parcel so that it would be very difficult to untie. This was in order to divert the attention of the old woman for a time, while she was trying to undo the knot, and so to gain a moment. The iron strip was added to give weight, so that the woman might not guess the first minute that the "thing" was made of wood. All this had been stored by him beforehand under the sofa. He had only just got the pledge out when he heard someone suddenly about in the yard.

"It struck six long ago."

"Long ago! My God!"

He rushed to the door, listened, caught up his hat and began to descend his thirteen steps cautiously, noiselessly, like a cat. He had still the most important thing to do—to steal the axe from the kitchen. That the deed must be done with an axe he had decided long ago. He had also a pocket pruning-knife, but he could not rely on the knife and still less on his own strength, and so resolved finally on the axe. We may note in passing, one peculiarity in regard to all the final resolutions taken by him in the matter; they had one strange characteristic: the more final they were, the more hideous and the more absurd they at once became in his eyes. In spite of all his agonising inward struggle, he never for a single instant all that time could believe in the carrying out of his plans.

And, indeed, if it had ever happened that everything to the least point could have been considered and finally settled, and no uncertainty of any kind had remained, he would, it seems, have renounced it all as something absurd, monstrous and impossible. But a whole mass of unsettled points and uncertainties remained. As for getting the axe, that trifling business cost him no anxiety, for nothing could be easier. Nastasya was continually out of the house, especially in the evenings; she would run in to the neighbours or to a shop, and always left the door ajar. It was the one thing the landlady was always scolding her about. And so, when the time came, he would only have to go quietly into the kitchen and to take the axe, and an hour later (when everything was over) go in and put it back again. But these were doubtful points. Supposing he returned an hour later to put it back, and Nastasya had come back and was on the spot. He would of course have to go by and wait till she went out again. But supposing she were in the meantime to miss the axe, look for it, make an outcry—that would mean suspicion or at least grounds for suspicion.

But those were all trifles which he had not even begun to consider, and indeed he had no time. He was thinking of the chief point, and put off trifling details, until *he could believe in it all*. But that seemed utterly unattainable. So it seemed to himself at least. He could not imagine, for instance, that he would sometime leave off thinking, get up and simply go there.... Even his late experiment (i.e. his visit with the object of a final survey of the place) was simply an attempt at an experiment, far from being the real thing, as though one should say "come, let us go and try it—why dream about it!"—and at once he had broken down and had run away cursing, in a frenzy with himself. Meanwhile it would seem, as regards the moral question, that his analysis was complete; his casuistry had become keen as a razor, and he could not find rational objections in himself. But in the last resort he simply ceased to believe in himself, and doggedly, slavishly sought arguments in all directions, fumbling for them, as though someone were forcing and drawing him to it.

At first—long before indeed—he had been much occupied with one question; why almost all crimes are so badly concealed and so easily detected, and why almost all criminals leave such obvious traces? He had come gradually to many different and curious conclusions, and in his opinion the chief reason lay not so much in the material impossibility of concealing the crime, as in the criminal himself. Almost every criminal is subject to a failure of will and reasoning power by a childish and phenomenal heedlessness, at the very instant when prudence and caution are most essential. It was his conviction that this eclipse of reason and failure of will power attacked a man like a disease, developed gradually and reached its highest point just before the perpetration of the crime, continued with equal violence at the moment of the crime and for longer or shorter time after, according to the individual case, and then passed off like any other disease. The question whether the disease gives rise to the crime, or whether the crime from its own peculiar nature is always accompanied by something of the nature of disease, he did not yet feel able to decide.

When he reached these conclusions, he decided that in his own case there could not be such a morbid reaction, that his reason and will would remain unimpaired at the time of carrying out his design, for the simple reason that his design was "not a crime...." We will omit all the process by means of which he arrived at this last conclusion; we have run too far ahead already.... We may add only that the practical, purely material difficulties of the affair occupied a secondary position in his mind. "One has but to keep all one's will-power and reason to deal with them, and they will all be overcome at the time when once one has familiarised oneself with the minutest details of the business...." But this preparation had never been begun. His final decisions were what he came to trust least, and when the hour struck, it all came to pass quite differently, as it were accidentally and unexpectedly.

One trifling circumstance upset his calculations, before he had even left the staircase. When he reached the landlady's kitchen, the door of which was open as usual, he glanced cautiously in to see whether, in Nastasya's absence, the landlady herself was there, or if not, whether the door to her own room was closed, so that she might not peep out when he went in for the axe. But what was his amazement when he suddenly saw that Nastasya was not only at home in the kitchen, but was occupied there, taking linen out of a basket and hanging it on a line. Seeing him, she left off hanging the clothes, turned to him and stared at him all the time he was passing. He turned away his eyes, and walked past as though he noticed nothing. But it was the end of everything; he had not the axe! He was overwhelmed.

"What made me think," he reflected, as he went under the gateway, "what made me think that she would be sure not to be at home at that moment! Why, why, why did I assume this so certainly?"

He was crushed and even humiliated. He could have laughed at himself in his anger.... A dull animal rage boiled within him.

He stood hesitating in the gateway. To go into the street, to go a walk for appearance' sake was revolting; to go back to his room, even more revolting. "And what a chance I have lost for ever!" he muttered, standing aimlessly in the gateway, just opposite the porter's little dark room, which was also open. Suddenly he started. From the porter's room, two paces away from him, something shining under the bench to the right caught his eye.... He looked about him—nobody. He approached the room on tiptoe, went down two steps into it and in a faint voice called the porter. "Yes, not at home! Somewhere near though, in the yard, for the door is wide open." He dashed to the axe (it was an axe) and pulled it out from under the bench, where it lay between two chunks of wood; at once, before going out, he made it fast in the noose, he thrust both hands into his pockets and went out of the room; no one had noticed him! "When reason fails, the devil helps!" he thought with a strange grin. This chance raised his spirits extraordinarily.

He walked along quietly and sedately, without hurry, to avoid awakening suspicion. He scarcely looked at the passers-by, tried to escape looking at their faces at all, and to be as little noticeable as possible. Suddenly he thought of his hat. "Good heavens! I had the money the day before yesterday and did not get a cap to wear instead!" A curse rose from the bottom of his soul.

Glancing out of the corner of his eye into a shop, he saw by a clock on the wall that it was ten minutes past seven. He had to make haste and at the same time to go someway round, so as to approach the house from the other side....

When he had happened to imagine all this beforehand, he had sometimes thought that he would be very much afraid. But he was not very much afraid now, was not afraid at all, indeed. His mind was even occupied by irrelevant matters, but by nothing for long. As he passed the Yusupov garden, he was deeply absorbed in considering the building of great fountains, and of their refreshing effect on the atmosphere in all the squares. By degrees he passed to the conviction that if the summer garden were extended to the field of Mars, and perhaps joined to the garden of the Mihailovsky Palace, it would be a splendid thing and a great benefit to the town. Then he was interested by the question why in all great towns men are not simply driven by necessity, but in some peculiar way inclined to live in those parts of the town where there are no gardens nor fountains; where there is most dirt and smell and all sorts of nastiness. Then his own walks through the Hay Market came back to his mind, and for a moment he waked up to reality. "What nonsense!" he thought, "better think of nothing at all!"

"So probably men led to execution clutch mentally at every object that meets them on the way," flashed through his mind, but simply flashed, like lightning; he made haste to dismiss this thought.... And by now he was near; here was the house, here was the gate. Suddenly a clock somewhere struck once. "What! can it be half-past seven? Impossible, it must be fast!"

Luckily for him, everything went well again at the gates. At that very moment, as though expressly for his benefit, a huge waggon of hay had just driven in at the gate, completely screening him as he passed under the gateway, and the waggon had scarcely had time to drive through into the yard, before he had slipped in a flash to the right. On the other side of the waggon he could hear shouting and quarrelling; but no one noticed him and no one met him. Many windows looking into that huge quadrangular yard were open at that moment, but he did not raise his head—he had not the strength to. The staircase leading to the old woman's room was close by, just on the right of the gateway. He was already on the stairs....

Drawing a breath, pressing his hand against his throbbing heart, and once more feeling for the axe and setting it straight, he began softly and cautiously ascending the stairs, listening every minute. But the stairs, too, were quite deserted; all the doors were shut; he met no one. One flat indeed on the first floor was wide open and painters were at work in it, but they did not glance at him. He stood still, thought a minute and went on. "Of course it would be better if they had not been here, but... it's two storeys above them."

And there was the fourth storey, here was the door, here was the flat opposite, the empty one. The flat underneath the old woman's was apparently empty also; the visiting card nailed on the door had been torn off—they had gone away!... He was out of breath. For one instant the thought floated through his mind "Shall I go back?" But he made no answer and began listening at the old woman's door, a dead silence. Then he listened again on the staircase, listened long and intently... then looked about him for the last time, pulled himself together, drew himself up, and once more tried the axe in the noose. "Am I very pale?" he wondered. "Am I not evidently agitated? She is mistrustful.... Had I better wait a little longer... till my heart leaves off thumping?"

But his heart did not leave off. On the contrary, as though to spite him, it throbbed more and more violently. He could stand it no longer, he slowly put out his hand to the bell and rang. Half a minute later he rang again, more loudly.

No answer. To go on ringing was useless and out of place. The old woman was, of course, at home, but she was suspicious and alone. He had some knowledge of her habits... and once more he put his ear to the door. Either his senses were peculiarly keen (which it is difficult to suppose), or the sound was really very distinct. Anyway, he suddenly heard something like the cautious touch of a hand on the lock and the rustle of a skirt at the very door. Someone was standing stealthily close to the lock and just as he was doing on the outside was secretly listening within, and seemed to have her ear to the door.... He moved a little on purpose and muttered something aloud that he might not have the appearance of hiding, then rang a third time, but quietly, soberly, and without impatience, Recalling it afterwards, that moment stood out in his mind vividly, distinctly, for ever; he could not make out how he had had such cunning, for his mind was as it were clouded at moments and he was almost unconscious of his body.... An instant later he heard the latch unfastened.

CHAPTER VII

The door was as before opened a tiny crack, and again two sharp and suspicious eyes stared at him out of the darkness. Then Raskolnikov lost his head and nearly made a great mistake.

Fearing the old woman would be frightened by their being alone, and not hoping that the sight of him would disarm her suspicions, he took hold of the door and drew it towards him to prevent the old woman from attempting to shut it again. Seeing this she did not pull the door back, but she did not let go the handle so that he almost dragged her out with it on to the stairs. Seeing that she was standing in the doorway not allowing him to pass, he advanced straight upon her. She stepped back in alarm, tried to say something, but seemed unable to speak and stared with open eyes at him.

"Good evening, Alyona Ivanovna," he began, trying to speak easily, but his voice would not obey him, it broke and shook. "I have come... I have brought something... but we'd better come in... to the light...."

And leaving her, he passed straight into the room uninvited. The old woman ran after him; her tongue was unloosed.

"Good heavens! What it is? Who is it? What do you want?"

"Why, Alyona Ivanovna, you know me... Raskolnikov... here, I brought you the pledge I promised the other day..." And he held out the pledge.

The old woman glanced for a moment at the pledge, but at once stared in the eyes of her uninvited visitor. She looked intently, maliciously and mistrustfully. A minute passed; he even fancied something like a sneer in her eyes, as though she had already guessed everything. He felt that he was losing his head, that he was almost frightened, so frightened that if she were to look like that and not say a word for another half minute, he thought he would have run away from her.

"Why do you look at me as though you did not know me?" he said suddenly, also with malice. "Take it if you like, if not I'll go elsewhere, I am in a hurry."

He had not even thought of saying this, but it was suddenly said of itself. The old woman recovered herself, and her visitor's resolute tone evidently restored her confidence.

"But why, my good sir, all of a minute.... What is it?" she asked, looking at the pledge.

"The silver cigarette case; I spoke of it last time, you know."

She held out her hand.

"But how pale you are, to be sure... and your hands are trembling too? Have you been bathing, or what?"

"Fever," he answered abruptly. "You can't help getting pale... if you've nothing to eat," he added, with difficulty articulating the words.

His strength was failing him again. But his answer sounded like the truth; the old woman took the pledge.

"What is it?" she asked once more, scanning Raskolnikov intently, and weighing the pledge in her hand.

"A thing... cigarette case.... Silver.... Look at it."

"It does not seem somehow like silver.... How he has wrapped it up!"

Trying to untie the string and turning to the window, to the light (all her windows were shut, in spite of the stifling heat), she left him altogether for some seconds and stood with her back to him. He unbuttoned his coat and freed the axe from the noose, but did not yet take it out altogether, simply holding it in his right hand under the coat. His hands were fearfully weak, he felt them every moment growing more numb and more wooden. He was afraid he would let the axe slip and fall.... A sudden giddiness came over him.

"But what has he tied it up like this for?" the old woman cried with vexation and moved towards him.

He had not a minute more to lose. He pulled the axe quite out, swung it with both arms, scarcely conscious of himself, and almost without effort, almost mechanically, brought the blunt side down on her head. He seemed not to use his own strength in this. But as soon as he had once brought the axe down, his strength returned to him.

The old woman was as always bareheaded. Her thin, light hair, streaked with grey, thickly smeared with grease, was plaited in a rat's tail and fastened by a broken horn comb which stood out on the nape of her neck. As she was so short, the blow fell on the very top of her skull. She cried out, but very faintly, and suddenly sank all of a heap on the floor, raising her hands to her head. In one hand she still held "the pledge." Then he dealt her another and another blow with the blunt side and on the same spot. The blood gushed as from an overturned glass, the body fell back. He stepped back, let it fall, and at once bent over her face; she was dead. Her eyes seemed to be starting out of their sockets, the brow and the whole face were drawn and contorted convulsively.

He laid the axe on the ground near the dead body and felt at once in her pocket (trying to avoid the streaming body)—the same right-hand pocket from which she had taken the key on his last visit. He was in full possession of his faculties, free from confusion or giddiness, but his hands were still trembling. He remembered afterwards that he had been particularly collected and careful, trying all the time not to get smeared with blood.... He pulled out the keys at once, they were all, as before, in one bunch on a steel ring. He ran at once into the bedroom with them. It was a very small room with a whole shrine of holy images. Against the other wall stood a big bed, very clean and covered with a silk patchwork wadded quilt. Against a third wall was a chest of drawers. Strange to say, so soon as he began to fit the keys into the chest, so soon as he heard their jingling, a convulsive shudder passed over him. He suddenly felt tempted again to give it all up and go away. But that was only for an instant; it was too late to go back. He positively smiled at himself, when suddenly another terrifying idea occurred to his mind. He suddenly fancied that the old woman might be still alive and might recover her senses. Leaving the keys in the chest, he ran back to the body, snatched up the axe and lifted it once more over the old woman, but did not bring it down. There was no doubt that she was dead. Bending down and examining her again more closely, he saw clearly that the skull was broken and even battered in on one side. He was about to feel it with his finger, but drew back his hand and indeed it was evident without that. Meanwhile there was a perfect pool of blood. All at once he noticed a string on her neck; he tugged at it, but the string was strong and did not snap and besides, it was soaked with blood. He tried to pull it out from the front of the dress, but something held it and prevented its coming. In his impatience he raised the axe again to cut the string from above on the body, but did not dare, and with difficulty, smearing his hand and the axe in the blood, after two minutes' hurried effort, he cut the string and took it off without touching the body with the axe; he was not mistaken—it was a purse. On the string were two crosses, one of Cyprus wood and one of copper, and an image in silver filigree, and with them a small greasy chamois leather purse with a steel rim and ring. The purse was stuffed very full; Raskolnikov thrust it in his pocket without looking at it, flung the crosses on the old woman's body and rushed back into the bedroom, this time taking the axe with him.

He was in terrible haste, he snatched the keys, and began trying them again. But he was unsuccessful. They would not fit in the locks. It was not so much that his hands were shaking, but that he kept making mistakes; though he saw for instance that a key was not the right one and would not fit, still he tried to put it in. Suddenly he remembered and realised that the big key with the deep notches, which was hanging there with the small keys could not possibly belong to the chest of drawers (on his last visit this had struck him), but to some strong box, and that everything perhaps was hidden in that box. He left the chest of drawers, and at once felt under the bedstead, knowing that old women usually keep boxes under their beds. And so it was; there was a good-sized box under the bed, at least a yard in length, with an arched lid covered with red leather and studded with steel nails. The notched key fitted at once and unlocked it. At the top, under a white sheet, was a coat of red brocade lined with hareskin; under it was a silk dress, then a shawl and it seemed as though there was nothing below but clothes. The first thing he did was to wipe his blood-stained hands on the red brocade. "It's red, and on red blood will be less noticeable," the thought passed through his mind; then he suddenly came to himself. "Good God, am I going out of my senses?" he thought with terror.

But no sooner did he touch the clothes than a gold watch slipped from under the fur coat. He made haste to turn them all over. There turned out to be various articles made of gold among the clothes—probably all pledges, unredeemed or waiting to be redeemed—bracelets, chains, ear-rings, pins and such things. Some were in cases, others simply wrapped in newspaper, carefully and exactly folded, and tied round with tape. Without any delay, he began filling up the pockets of his trousers and overcoat without examining or undoing the parcels and cases; but he had not time to take many....

He suddenly heard steps in the room where the old woman lay. He stopped short and was still as death. But all was quiet, so it must have been his fancy. All at once he heard distinctly a faint cry, as though someone had uttered a low broken moan. Then again dead silence for a minute or two. He sat squatting on his heels by the box and waited holding his breath. Suddenly he jumped up, seized the axe and ran out of the bedroom.

In the middle of the room stood Lizaveta with a big bundle in her arms. She was gazing in stupefaction at her murdered sister, white as a sheet and seeming not to have the strength to cry out. Seeing him run out of the bedroom, she began faintly quivering all over, like a leaf, a shudder ran down her face; she lifted her hand, opened her mouth, but still did not scream. She began slowly backing away from him into the corner, staring intently, persistently at him, but still uttered no sound, as though she could not get breath to scream. He rushed at her with the axe; her mouth twitched piteously, as one sees babies' mouths, when they begin to be frightened, stare intently at what frightens them and are on the point of screaming. And this hapless Lizaveta was so simple and had been so thoroughly crushed and scared that she did not even raise a hand to guard her face, though that was the most necessary and natural action at the moment, for the axe was raised over her face. She only put up her empty left hand, but not to her face, slowly holding it out before her as though motioning him away. The axe fell with the sharp edge just on the skull and split at one blow all the top of the head. She fell heavily at once. Raskolnikov completely lost his head, snatching up her bundle, dropped it again and ran into the entry.

Fear gained more and more mastery over him, especially after this second, quite unexpected murder. He longed to run away from the place as fast as possible. And if at that moment he had been capable of seeing and reasoning more correctly, if he had been able to realise all the difficulties of his position, the hopelessness, the hideousness and the absurdity of it, if he could have understood how many obstacles and, perhaps, crimes he had still to overcome or to commit, to get out of that place and to make his way home, it is very possible that he would have flung up everything, and would have gone to give himself up, and not from fear, but from simple horror and loathing of what he had done. The feeling of loathing especially surged up within him and grew stronger every minute. He would not now have gone to the box or even into the room for anything in the world.

But a sort of blankness, even dreaminess, had begun by degrees to take possession of him; at moments he forgot himself, or rather, forgot what was of importance, and caught at trifles. Glancing, however, into the kitchen and seeing a bucket half full of water on a bench, he bethought him of washing his hands and the axe. His hands were sticky with blood. He dropped the axe with the blade in the water, snatched a piece of soap that lay in a broken saucer on the window, and began washing his hands in the bucket. When they were clean, he took out the axe, washed the blade and spent a long time, about three minutes, washing the wood where there were spots of blood rubbing them with soap. Then he wiped it all with some linen that was hanging to dry on a line in the kitchen and then he was a long while attentively examining the axe at the window. There was no trace left on it, only the wood was still damp. He carefully hung the axe in the noose under his coat. Then as far as was possible, in the dim light in the kitchen, he looked over his overcoat, his trousers and his boots. At the first glance there seemed to be nothing but stains on the boots. He wetted the rag and rubbed the boots. But he knew he was not looking thoroughly, that there might be something quite noticeable that he was overlooking. He stood in the middle of the room, lost in thought. Dark agonising ideas rose in his mind—the idea that he was mad and that at that moment he was incapable of reasoning, of protecting himself, that he ought perhaps to be doing something utterly different from what he was now doing. "Good God!" he muttered "I must fly, fly," and he rushed into the entry. But here a shock of terror awaited him such as he had never known before.

He stood and gazed and could not believe his eyes: the door, the outer door from the stairs, at which he had not long before waited and rung, was standing unfastened and at least six inches open. No lock, no bolt, all the time, all that time! The old woman had not shut it after him perhaps as a precaution. But, good God! Why, he had seen Lizaveta afterwards! And how could he, how could he have failed to reflect that she must have come in somehow! She could not have come through the wall!

He dashed to the door and fastened the latch.

"But no, the wrong thing again! I must get away, get away...."

He unfastened the latch, opened the door and began listening on the staircase.

He listened a long time. Somewhere far away, it might be in the gateway, two voices were loudly and shrilly shouting, quarrelling and scolding. "What are they about?" He waited patiently. At last all was still, as though suddenly cut off; they had separated. He was meaning to go out, but suddenly, on the floor below, a door was noisily opened and someone began going downstairs humming a tune. "How is it they all make such a noise?" flashed through his mind. Once more he closed the door and waited. At last all was still, not a soul stirring. He was just taking a step towards the stairs when he heard fresh footsteps.

The steps sounded very far off, at the very bottom of the stairs, but he remembered quite clearly and distinctly that from the first sound he began for some reason to suspect that this was someone coming *there*, to the fourth floor, to the old woman. Why? Were the sounds somehow peculiar, significant? The steps were heavy, even and unhurried. Now *he* had passed the first floor, now he was mounting higher, it was growing more and more distinct! He could hear his heavy breathing. And now the third storey had been reached. Coming here! And it seemed to him all at once that he was turned to stone, that it was like a dream in which one is being pursued, nearly caught and will be killed, and is rooted to the spot and cannot even move one's arms.

At last when the unknown was mounting to the fourth floor, he suddenly started, and succeeded in slipping neatly and quickly back into the flat and closing the door behind him. Then he took the hook and softly, noiselessly, fixed it in the catch. Instinct helped him. When he had done this, he crouched holding his breath, by the door. The unknown visitor was by now also at the door. They were now standing opposite one another, as he had just before been standing with the old woman, when the door divided them and he was listening.

The visitor panted several times. "He must be a big, fat man," thought Raskolnikov, squeezing the axe in his hand. It seemed like a dream indeed. The visitor took hold of the bell and rang it loudly.

As soon as the tin bell tinkled, Raskolnikov seemed to be aware of something moving in the room. For some seconds he listened quite seriously. The unknown rang again, waited and suddenly tugged violently and impatiently at the handle of the door. Raskolnikov gazed in horror at the hook shaking in its fastening, and in blank terror expected every minute that the fastening would be pulled out. It certainly did seem possible, so violently was he shaking it. He was tempted to hold the fastening, but *he* might be aware of it. A giddiness came over him again. "I shall fall down!" flashed through his mind, but the unknown began to speak and he recovered himself at once.

"What's up? Are they asleep or murdered? D-damn them!" he bawled in a thick voice, "Hey, Alyona Ivanovna, old witch! Lizaveta Ivanovna, hey, my beauty! open the door! Oh, damn them! Are they asleep or what?"

And again, enraged, he tugged with all his might a dozen times at the bell. He must certainly be a man of authority and an intimate acquaintance.

At this moment light hurried steps were heard not far off, on the stairs. Someone else was approaching. Raskolnikov had not heard them at first.

"You don't say there's no one at home," the new-comer cried in a cheerful, ringing voice, addressing the first visitor, who still went on pulling the bell. "Good evening, Koch."

"From his voice he must be quite young," thought Raskolnikov.

"Who the devil can tell? I've almost broken the lock," answered Koch. "But how do you come to know me?"

"Why! The day before yesterday I beat you three times running at billiards at Gambrinus'."

"Oh!"

"So they are not at home? That's queer. It's awfully stupid though. Where could the old woman have gone? I've come on business."

"Yes; and I have business with her, too."

"Well, what can we do? Go back, I suppose, Aie—aie! And I was hoping to get some money!" cried the young man.

"We must give it up, of course, but what did she fix this time for? The old witch fixed the time for me to come herself. It's out of my way. And where the devil she can have got to, I can't make out. She sits here from year's end to year's end, the old hag; her legs are bad and yet here all of a sudden she is out for a walk!"

"Hadn't we better ask the porter?"

"What?"

"Where she's gone and when she'll be back."

"Hm.... Damn it all!... We might ask.... But you know she never does go anywhere."

And he once more tugged at the door-handle.

"Damn it all. There's nothing to be done, we must go!"

"Stay!" cried the young man suddenly. "Do you see how the door shakes if you pull it?"

"Well?"

"That shows it's not locked, but fastened with the hook! Do you hear how the hook clanks?"

"Well?"

"Why, don't you see? That proves that one of them is at home. If they were all out, they would have locked the door from the outside with the key and not with the hook from inside. There, do you hear how the hook is clanking? To fasten the hook on the inside they must be at home, don't you see. So there they are sitting inside and don't open the door!"

"Well! And so they must be!" cried Koch, astonished. "What are they about in there?" And he began furiously shaking the door.

"Stay!" cried the young man again. "Don't pull at it! There must be something wrong.... Here, you've been ringing and pulling at the door and still they don't open! So either they've both fainted or..."

"What?"

"I tell you what. Let's go fetch the porter, let him wake them up."

"All right."

Both were going down.

"Stay. You stop here while I run down for the porter."

"What for?"

"Well, you'd better."

"All right."

"I'm studying the law you see! It's evident, e-vi-dent there's something wrong here!" the young man cried hotly, and he ran downstairs.

Koch remained. Once more he softly touched the bell which gave one tinkle, then gently, as though reflecting and looking about him, began touching the door-handle pulling it and letting it go to make sure once more that it was only fastened by the hook. Then puffing and panting he bent down and began looking at the keyhole: but the key was in the lock on the inside and so nothing could be seen.

Raskolnikov stood keeping tight hold of the axe. He was in a sort of delirium. He was even making ready to fight when they should come in. While they were knocking and talking together, the idea several times occurred to him to end it all at once and shout to them through the door. Now and then he was tempted to swear at them, to jeer at them, while they could not open the door! "Only make haste!" was the thought that flashed through his mind.

"But what the devil is he about?..." Time was passing, one minute, and another—no one came. Koch began to be restless.

"What the devil?" he cried suddenly and in impatience deserting his sentry duty, he, too, went down, hurrying and thumping with his heavy boots on the stairs. The steps died away.

"Good heavens! What am I to do?"

Raskolnikov unfastened the hook, opened the door—there was no sound. Abruptly, without any thought at all, he went out, closing the door as thoroughly as he could, and went downstairs.

He had gone down three flights when he suddenly heard a loud voice below—where could he go! There was nowhere to hide. He was just going back to the flat.

"Hey there! Catch the brute!"

Somebody dashed out of a flat below, shouting, and rather fell than ran down the stairs, bawling at the top of his voice.

"Mitka! Mitka! Mitka! Mitka! Mitka! Blast him!"

The shout ended in a shriek; the last sounds came from the yard; all was still. But at the same instant several men talking loud and fast began noisily mounting the stairs. There were three or four of them. He distinguished the ringing voice of the young man. "Hey!"

Filled with despair he went straight to meet them, feeling "come what must!" If they stopped him—all was lost; if they let him pass—all was lost too; they would remember him. They were approaching; they were only a flight from him—and suddenly deliverance! A few steps from him on the right, there was an empty flat with the door wide open, the flat on the second floor where the painters had been at work, and which, as though for his benefit, they had just left. It was they, no doubt, who had just run down, shouting. The floor had only just been painted, in the middle of the room stood a pail and a broken pot with paint and brushes. In one instant he had whisked in at the open door and hidden behind the wall and only in the nick of time; they had already reached the landing. Then they turned and went on up to the fourth floor, talking loudly. He waited, went out on tiptoe and ran down the stairs.

No one was on the stairs, nor in the gateway. He passed quickly through the gateway and turned to the left in the street.

He knew, he knew perfectly well that at that moment they were at the flat, that they were greatly astonished at finding it unlocked, as the door had just been fastened, that by now they were looking at the bodies, that before another minute had passed they would guess and completely realise that the murderer had just been there, and had succeeded in hiding somewhere, slipping by them and escaping. They would guess most likely that he had been in the empty flat, while they were going upstairs. And meanwhile he dared not quicken his pace much, though the next turning was still nearly a hundred yards away. "Should he slip through some gateway and wait somewhere in an unknown street? No, hopeless! Should he fling away the axe? Should he take a cab? Hopeless, hopeless!"

At last he reached the turning. He turned down it more dead than alive. Here he was half way to safety, and he understood it; it was less risky because there was a great crowd of people, and he was lost in it like a grain of sand. But all he had suffered had so weakened him that he could scarcely move. Perspiration ran down him in drops, his neck was all wet. "My word, he has been going it!" someone shouted at him when he came out on the canal bank.

He was only dimly conscious of himself now, and the farther he went the worse it was. He remembered however, that on coming out on to the canal bank, he was alarmed at finding few people there and so being more conspicuous, and he had thought of turning back. Though he was almost falling from fatigue, he went a long way round so as to get home from quite a different direction.

He was not fully conscious when he passed through the gateway of his house! He was already on the staircase before he recollected the axe. And yet he had a very grave problem before him, to put it back and to escape observation as far as possible in doing so. He was of course incapable of reflecting that it might perhaps be far better not to restore the axe at all, but to drop it later on in somebody's yard. But it all happened fortunately, the door of the porter's room was closed but not locked, so that it seemed most likely that the porter was at home. But he had so completely lost all power of reflection that he walked straight to the door and opened it. If the porter had asked him, "What do you want?" he would perhaps have simply handed him the axe. But again the porter was not at home, and he succeeded in putting the axe back under the bench, and even covering it with the chunk of wood as before. He met no one, not a soul, afterwards on the way to his room; the landlady's door was shut. When he was in his room, he flung himself on the sofa just as he was—he did not sleep, but sank into blank forgetfulness. If anyone had come into his room then, he would have jumped up at once and screamed. Scraps and shreds of thoughts were simply swarming in his brain, but he could not catch at one, he could not rest on one, in spite of all his efforts....

PART II

CHAPTER I

So he lay a very long while. Now and then he seemed to wake up, and at such moments he noticed that it was far into the night, but it did not occur to him to get up. At last he noticed that it was beginning to get light. He was lying on his back, still dazed from his recent oblivion. Fearful, despairing cries rose shrilly from the street, sounds which he heard every night, indeed, under his window after two o'clock. They woke him up now.

"Ah! the drunken men are coming out of the taverns," he thought, "it's past two o'clock," and at once he leaped up, as though someone had pulled him from the sofa.

"What! Past two o'clock!"

He sat down on the sofa—and instantly recollected everything! All at once, in one flash, he recollected everything.

For the first moment he thought he was going mad. A dreadful chill came over him; but the chill was from the fever that had begun long before in his sleep. Now he was suddenly taken with violent shivering, so that his teeth chattered and all his limbs were shaking. He opened the door and began listening—everything in the house was asleep. With amazement he gazed at himself and everything in the room around him, wondering how he could have come in the night before without fastening the door, and have flung himself on the sofa without undressing, without even taking his hat off. It had fallen off and was lying on the floor near his pillow.

"If anyone had come in, what would he have thought? That I'm drunk but..."

He rushed to the window. There was light enough, and he began hurriedly looking himself all over from head to foot, all his clothes; were there no traces? But there was no doing it like that; shivering with cold, he began taking off everything and looking over again. He turned everything over to the last threads and rags, and mistrusting himself, went through his search three times.

But there seemed to be nothing, no trace, except in one place, where some thick drops of congealed blood were clinging to the frayed edge of his trousers. He picked up a big claspknife and cut off the frayed threads. There seemed to be nothing more.

Suddenly he remembered that the purse and the things he had taken out of the old woman's box were still in his pockets! He had not thought till then of taking them out and hiding them! He had not even thought of them while he was examining his clothes! What next? Instantly he rushed to take them out and fling them on the table. When he had pulled out everything, and turned the pocket inside out to be sure there was nothing left, he carried the whole heap to the corner. The paper had come off the bottom of the wall and hung there in tatters. He began stuffing all the things into the hole under the paper: "They're in! All out of sight, and the purse too!"

he thought gleefully, getting up and gazing blankly at the hole which bulged out more than ever. Suddenly he shuddered all over with horror; "My God!" he whispered in despair: "what's the matter with me? Is that hidden? Is that the way to hide things?"

He had not reckoned on having trinkets to hide. He had only thought of money, and so had not prepared a hiding-place.

"But now, now, what am I glad of?" he thought, "Is that hiding things? My reason's deserting me—simply!"

He sat down on the sofa in exhaustion and was at once shaken by another unbearable fit of shivering. Mechanically he drew from a chair beside him his old student's winter coat, which was still warm though almost in rags, covered himself up with it and once more sank into drowsiness and delirium. He lost consciousness.

Not more than five minutes had passed when he jumped up a second time, and at once pounced in a frenzy on his clothes again.

"How could I go to sleep again with nothing done? Yes, yes; I have not taken the loop off the armhole! I forgot it, forgot a thing like that! Such a piece of evidence!"

He pulled off the noose, hurriedly cut it to pieces and threw the bits among his linen under the pillow.

"Pieces of torn linen couldn't rouse suspicion, whatever happened; I think not, I think not, any way!" he repeated, standing in the middle of the room, and with painful concentration he fell to gazing about him again, at the floor and everywhere, trying to make sure he had not forgotten anything. The conviction that all his faculties, even memory, and the simplest power of reflection were failing him, began to be an insufferable torture.

"Surely it isn't beginning already! Surely it isn't my punishment coming upon me? It is!"

The frayed rags he had cut off his trousers were actually lying on the floor in the middle of the room, where anyone coming in would see them!

"What is the matter with me!" he cried again, like one distraught.

Then a strange idea entered his head; that, perhaps, all his clothes were covered with blood, that, perhaps, there were a great many stains, but that he did not see them, did not notice them because his perceptions were failing, were going to pieces... his reason was clouded.... Suddenly he remembered that there had been blood on the purse too. "Ah! Then there must be blood on the pocket too, for I put the wet purse in my pocket!"

In a flash he had turned the pocket inside out and, yes!—there were traces, stains on the lining of the pocket!

"So my reason has not quite deserted me, so I still have some sense and memory, since I guessed it of myself," he thought triumphantly, with a deep sigh of relief; "it's simply the weakness of fever, a moment's delirium," and he tore the whole lining out of the left pocket of his trousers. At that instant the sunlight fell on his left boot; on the sock which poked out from the boot, he fancied there were traces! He flung off his boots; "traces indeed! The tip of the sock was soaked with blood;" he must have unwarily stepped into that pool.... "But what am I to do with this now? Where am I to put the sock and rags and pocket?"

He gathered them all up in his hands and stood in the middle of the room.

"In the stove? But they would ransack the stove first of all. Burn them? But what can I burn them with? There are no matches even. No, better go out and throw it all away somewhere. Yes, better throw it away," he repeated, sitting down on the sofa again, "and at once, this minute, without lingering..."

But his head sank on the pillow instead. Again the unbearable icy shivering came over him; again he drew his coat over him.

And for a long while, for some hours, he was haunted by the impulse to "go off somewhere at once, this moment, and fling it all away, so that it may be out of sight and done with, at once, at once!" Several times he tried to rise from the sofa, but could not.

He was thoroughly waked up at last by a violent knocking at his door.

"Open, do, are you dead or alive? He keeps sleeping here!" shouted Nastasya, banging with her fist on the door. "For whole days together he's snoring here like a dog! A dog he is too. Open I tell you. It's past ten."

"Maybe he's not at home," said a man's voice.

"Ha! that's the porter's voice.... What does he want?"

He jumped up and sat on the sofa. The beating of his heart was a positive pain.

"Then who can have latched the door?" retorted Nastasya. "He's taken to bolting himself in! As if he were worth stealing! Open, you stupid, wake up!"

"What do they want? Why the porter? All's discovered. Resist or open? Come what may!..."

He half rose, stooped forward and unlatched the door.

His room was so small that he could undo the latch without leaving the bed. Yes; the porter and Nastasya were standing there.

Nastasya stared at him in a strange way. He glanced with a defiant and desperate air at the porter, who without a word held out a grey folded paper sealed with bottle-wax.

"A notice from the office," he announced, as he gave him the paper.

"From what office?"

"A summons to the police office, of course. You know which office."

"To the police?... What for?..."

"How can I tell? You're sent for, so you go."

The man looked at him attentively, looked round the room and turned to go away.

"He's downright ill!" observed Nastasya, not taking her eyes off him. The porter turned his head for a moment. "He's been in a fever since yesterday," she added.

Raskolnikov made no response and held the paper in his hands, without opening it. "Don't you get up then," Nastasya went on compassionately, seeing that he was letting his feet down from the sofa. "You're ill, and so don't go; there's no such hurry. What have you got there?"

He looked; in his right hand he held the shreds he had cut from his trousers, the sock, and the rags of the pocket. So he had been asleep with them in his hand. Afterwards reflecting upon it, he remembered that half waking up in his fever, he had grasped all this tightly in his hand and so fallen asleep again.

"Look at the rags he's collected and sleeps with them, as though he has got hold of a treasure..."

And Nastasya went off into her hysterical giggle.

Instantly he thrust them all under his great coat and fixed his eyes intently upon her. Far as he was from being capable of rational reflection at that moment, he felt that no one would behave like that with a person who was going to be arrested. "But... the police?"

"You'd better have some tea! Yes? I'll bring it, there's some left."

"No... I'm going; I'll go at once," he muttered, getting on to his feet.

"Why, you'll never get downstairs!"

"Yes, I'll go."

"As you please."

She followed the porter out.

At once he rushed to the light to examine the sock and the rags.

"There are stains, but not very noticeable; all covered with dirt, and rubbed and already discoloured. No one who had no suspicion could distinguish anything. Nastasya from a distance could not have noticed, thank God!" Then with a tremor he broke the seal of the notice and began reading; he was a long while reading, before he understood. It was an ordinary summons from the district police-station to appear that day at half-past nine at the office of the district superintendent.

"But when has such a thing happened? I never have anything to do with the police! And why just to-day?" he thought in agonising bewilderment. "Good God, only get it over soon!"

He was flinging himself on his knees to pray, but broke into laughter—not at the idea of prayer, but at himself.

He began, hurriedly dressing. "If I'm lost, I am lost, I don't care! Shall I put the sock on?" he suddenly wondered, "it will get dustier still and the traces will be gone."

But no sooner had he put it on than he pulled it off again in loathing and horror. He pulled it off, but reflecting that he had no other socks, he picked it up and put it on again—and again he laughed.

"That's all conventional, that's all relative, merely a way of looking at it," he thought in a flash, but only on the top surface of his mind, while he was shuddering all over, "there, I've got it on! I have finished by getting it on!"

But his laughter was quickly followed by despair.

"No, it's too much for me..." he thought. His legs shook. "From fear," he muttered. His head swam and ached with fever. "It's a trick! They want to decoy me there and confound me over everything," he mused, as he went out on to the stairs—"the worst of it is I'm almost light-headed... I may blurt out something stupid..."

On the stairs he remembered that he was leaving all the things just as they were in the hole in the wall, "and very likely, it's on purpose to search when I'm out," he thought, and stopped short. But he was possessed by such despair, such cynicism of misery, if one may so call it, that with a wave of his hand he went on. "Only to get it over!"

In the street the heat was insufferable again; not a drop of rain had fallen all those days. Again dust, bricks and mortar, again the stench from the shops and pot-houses, again the drunken men, the Finnish pedlars and half-broken-down cabs. The sun shone straight in his eyes, so that it hurt him to look out of them, and he felt his head going round—as a man in a fever is apt to feel when he comes out into the street on a bright sunny day.

When he reached the turning into *the* street, in an agony of trepidation he looked down it... at *the* house... and at once averted his eyes.

"If they question me, perhaps I'll simply tell," he thought, as he drew near the police-station.

The police-station was about a quarter of a mile off. It had lately been moved to new rooms on the fourth floor of a new house. He had been once for a moment in the old office but long ago. Turning in at the gateway, he saw on the right a flight of stairs which a peasant was mounting with a book in his hand. "A house-porter, no doubt; so then, the office is here," and he began ascending the stairs on the chance. He did not want to ask questions of anyone.

"I'll go in, fall on my knees, and confess everything..." he thought, as he reached the fourth floor.

The staircase was steep, narrow and all sloppy with dirty water. The kitchens of the flats opened on to the stairs and stood open almost the whole day. So there was a fearful smell and heat. The staircase was crowded with porters going up and down with their books under their arms, policemen, and persons of all sorts and both sexes. The door of the office, too, stood wide open. Peasants stood waiting within. There, too, the heat was stifling and there was a sickening smell of fresh paint and stale oil from the newly decorated rooms.

After waiting a little, he decided to move forward into the next room. All the rooms were small and low-pitched. A fearful impatience drew him on and on. No one paid attention to him. In the second room some clerks sat writing, dressed hardly better than he was, and rather a queer-looking set. He went up to one of them.

"What is it?"

He showed the notice he had received.

"You are a student?" the man asked, glancing at the notice.

"Yes, formerly a student."

The clerk looked at him, but without the slightest interest. He was a particularly unkempt person with the look of a fixed idea in his eye.

"There would be no getting anything out of him, because he has no interest in anything," thought Raskolnikov.

"Go in there to the head clerk," said the clerk, pointing towards the furthest room.

He went into that room—the fourth in order; it was a small room and packed full of people, rather better dressed than in the outer rooms. Among them were two ladies. One, poorly dressed in mourning, sat at the table opposite the chief clerk, writing something at his dictation. The other, a very stout, buxom woman with a purplish-red, blotchy face, excessively smartly dressed with a brooch on her bosom as big as a saucer, was standing on one side, apparently waiting for something. Raskolnikov thrust his notice upon the head clerk. The latter glanced at it, said: "Wait a minute," and went on attending to the lady in mourning.

He breathed more freely. "It can't be that!"

By degrees he began to regain confidence, he kept urging himself to have courage and be calm.

"Some foolishness, some trifling carelessness, and I may betray myself! Hm... it's a pity there's no air here," he added, "it's stifling.... It makes one's head dizzier than ever... and one's mind too..."

He was conscious of a terrible inner turmoil. He was afraid of losing his self-control; he tried to catch at something and fix his mind on it, something quite irrelevant, but he could not succeed in this at all. Yet the head clerk greatly interested him, he kept hoping to see through him and guess something from his face.

He was a very young man, about two and twenty, with a dark mobile face that looked older than his years. He was fashionably dressed and foppish, with his hair parted in the middle, well combed and pomaded, and wore a number of rings on his well-scrubbed fingers and a gold chain on his waistcoat. He said a couple of words in French to a foreigner who was in the room, and said them fairly correctly.

"Luise Ivanovna, you can sit down," he said casually to the gaily-dressed, purple-faced lady, who was still standing as though not venturing to sit down, though there was a chair beside her.

"Ich danke," said the latter, and softly, with a rustle of silk she sank into the chair. Her light blue dress trimmed with white lace floated about the table like an air-balloon and filled almost half the room. She smelt of scent. But she was obviously embarrassed at filling half the room and smelling so strongly of scent; and though her smile was impudent as well as cringing, it betrayed evident uneasiness.

The lady in mourning had done at last, and got up. All at once, with some noise, an officer walked in very jauntily, with a peculiar swing of his shoulders at each step. He tossed his cockaded cap on the table and sat down in an easy-chair. The small lady positively skipped from her seat on seeing him, and fell to curtsying in a sort of ecstasy; but the officer took not the smallest notice of her, and she did not venture to sit down again in his presence. He was the assistant superintendent. He had a reddish moustache that stood out horizontally on each side of his face, and extremely small features, expressive of nothing much except a certain insolence. He looked askance and rather indignantly at Raskolnikov; he was so very badly dressed, and in spite of his humiliating position, his bearing was by no means in keeping with his clothes. Raskolnikov had unwarily fixed a very long and direct look on him, so that he felt positively affronted.

"What do you want?" he shouted, apparently astonished that such a ragged fellow was not annihilated by the majesty of his glance.

"I was summoned... by a notice..." Raskolnikov faltered.

"For the recovery of money due, from *the student*," the head clerk interfered hurriedly, tearing himself from his papers. "Here!" and he flung Raskolnikov a document and pointed out the place. "Read that!"

"Money? What money?" thought Raskolnikov, "but... then... it's certainly not *that*."

And he trembled with joy. He felt sudden intense indescribable relief. A load was lifted from his back.

"And pray, what time were you directed to appear, sir?" shouted the assistant superintendent, seeming for some unknown reason more and more aggrieved. "You are told to come at nine, and now it's twelve!"

"The notice was only brought me a quarter of an hour ago," Raskolnikov answered loudly over his shoulder. To his own surprise he, too, grew suddenly angry and found a certain pleasure in it. "And it's enough that I have come here ill with fever."

"Kindly refrain from shouting!"

"I'm not shouting, I'm speaking very quietly, it's you who are shouting at me. I'm a student, and allow no one to shout at me."

The assistant superintendent was so furious that for the first minute he could only splutter inarticulately. He leaped up from his seat.

"Be silent! You are in a government office. Don't be impudent, sir!"

"You're in a government office, too," cried Raskolnikov, "and you're smoking a cigarette as well as shouting, so you are showing disrespect to all of us."

He felt an indescribable satisfaction at having said this.

The head clerk looked at him with a smile. The angry assistant superintendent was obviously disconcerted.

"That's not your business!" he shouted at last with unnatural loudness. "Kindly make the declaration demanded of you. Show him. Alexandr Grigorievitch. There is a complaint against you! You don't pay your debts! You're a fine bird!"

But Raskolnikov was not listening now; he had eagerly clutched at the paper, in haste to find an explanation. He read it once, and a second time, and still did not understand.

"What is this?" he asked the head clerk.

"It is for the recovery of money on an I O U, a writ. You must either pay it, with all expenses, costs and so on, or give a written declaration when you can pay it, and at the same time an undertaking not to leave the capital without payment, and nor to sell or conceal your property. The creditor is at liberty to sell your property, and proceed against you according to the law."

"But I... am not in debt to anyone!"

"That's not our business. Here, an I O U for a hundred and fifteen roubles, legally attested, and due for payment, has been brought us for recovery, given by you to the widow of the assessor Zarnitsyn, nine months ago, and paid over by the widow Zarnitsyn to one Mr. Tchebarov. We therefore summon you, hereupon."

"But she is my landlady!"

"And what if she is your landlady?"

The head clerk looked at him with a condescending smile of compassion, and at the same time with a certain triumph, as at a novice under fire for the first time—as though he would say: "Well, how do you feel now?" But what did he care now for an I O U, for a writ of recovery! Was that worth worrying about now, was it worth attention even! He stood, he read, he listened, he answered, he even asked questions himself, but all mechanically. The triumphant sense of security, of deliverance from overwhelming danger, that was what filled his whole soul that moment without thought for the future, without analysis, without suppositions or surmises, without doubts and without questioning. It was an instant of full, direct, purely instinctive joy. But at that very moment something like a thunderstorm took place in the office. The assistant superintendent, still shaken by Raskolnikov's disrespect, still fuming and obviously anxious to keep up his wounded dignity, pounced on the unfortunate smart lady, who had been gazing at him ever since he came in with an exceedingly silly smile.

"You shameful hussy!" he shouted suddenly at the top of his voice. (The lady in mourning had left the office.) "What was going on at your house last night? Eh! A disgrace again, you're a scandal to the whole street. Fighting and drinking again. Do you want the house of correction? Why, I have warned you ten times over that I would not let you off the eleventh! And here you are again, again, you... you...!"

The paper fell out of Raskolnikov's hands, and he looked wildly at the smart lady who was so unceremoniously treated. But he soon saw what it meant, and at once began to find positive amusement in the scandal. He listened with pleasure, so that he longed to laugh and laugh... all his nerves were on edge.

"Ilya Petrovitch!" the head clerk was beginning anxiously, but stopped short, for he knew from experience that the enraged assistant could not be stopped except by force.

As for the smart lady, at first she positively trembled before the storm. But, strange to say, the more numerous and violent the terms of abuse became, the more amiable she looked, and the more seductive the smiles she lavished on the terrible assistant. She moved uneasily, and curtsied incessantly, waiting impatiently for a chance of putting in her word: and at last she found it.

"There was no sort of noise or fighting in my house, Mr. Captain," she pattered all at once, like peas dropping, speaking Russian confidently, though with a strong German accent, "and no sort of scandal, and his honour came drunk, and it's the whole truth I am telling, Mr. Captain, and I am not to blame.... Mine is an honourable house, Mr. Captain, and honourable behaviour, Mr. Captain, and I always, always dislike any scandal myself. But he came quite tipsy, and asked for three bottles again, and then he lifted up one leg, and began playing the pianoforte with one foot, and that is not at all right in an honourable house, and he *ganz* broke the piano, and it was very bad manners indeed and I said so. And he took up a bottle and began hitting everyone with it. And then I called the porter, and Karl came, and he took Karl and hit him in the eye; and he hit Henriette in the eye, too, and gave me five slaps on the cheek. And it was so ungentlemanly in an honourable house, Mr. Captain, and I screamed. And he opened the window over the canal, and stood in the window, squealing like a little pig; it was a disgrace. The idea of squealing like a little pig at the window into the street! Fie upon him! And Karl pulled him away from the window by his coat, and it is true, Mr. Captain, he tore *sein rock*. And then he shouted that *man muss* pay him fifteen roubles damages. And I did pay him, Mr. Captain, five roubles for *sein rock*. And he is an ungentlemanly visitor and caused all the scandal. 'I will show you up,' he said, 'for I can write to all the papers about you.'"

"Then he was an author?"

"Yes, Mr. Captain, and what an ungentlemanly visitor in an honourable house...."

"Now then! Enough! I have told you already..."

"Ilya Petrovitch!" the head clerk repeated significantly.

The assistant glanced rapidly at him; the head clerk slightly shook his head.

"... So I tell you this, most respectable Luise Ivanovna, and I tell it you for the last time," the assistant went on. "If there is a scandal in your honourable house once again, I will put you yourself in the lock-up, as it is called in polite society. Do you hear? So a literary man, an author took five roubles for his coat-tail in an 'honourable house'? A nice set, these authors!"

And he cast a contemptuous glance at Raskolnikov. "There was a scandal the other day in a restaurant, too. An author had eaten his dinner and would not pay; 'I'll write a satire on you,' says he. And there was another of them on a steamer last week used the most disgraceful language to the respectable family of a civil councillor, his wife and daughter. And there was one of them turned out of a confectioner's shop the other day. They are like that, authors, literary men, students, town-criers.... Pfoo! You get along! I shall look in upon you myself one day. Then you had better be careful! Do you hear?"

With hurried deference, Luise Ivanovna fell to curtsying in all directions, and so curtsied herself to the door. But at the door, she stumbled backwards against a good-looking officer with a fresh, open face and splendid thick fair whiskers. This was the superintendent of the district himself, Nikodim Fomitch. Luise Ivanovna made haste to curtsy almost to the ground, and with mincing little steps, she fluttered out of the office.

"Again thunder and lightning—a hurricane!" said Nikodim Fomitch to Ilya Petrovitch in a civil and friendly tone. "You are aroused again, you are fuming again! I heard it on the stairs!"

"Well, what then!" Ilya Petrovitch drawled with gentlemanly nonchalance; and he walked with some papers to another table, with a jaunty swing of his shoulders at each step. "Here, if you will kindly look: an author, or a student, has been one at least, does not pay his debts, has given an I O U, won't clear out of his room, and complaints are constantly being lodged against him, and here he has been pleased to make a protest against my smoking in his presence! He behaves like a cad himself, and just look at him, please. Here's the gentleman, and very attractive he is!"

"Poverty is not a vice, my friend, but we know you go off like powder, you can't bear a slight, I daresay you took offence at something and went too far yourself," continued Nikodim Fomitch, turning affably to Raskolnikov. "But you were wrong there; he is a capital fellow, I assure you, but explosive, explosive! He gets hot, fires up, boils over, and no stopping him! And then it's all over! And at the bottom he's a heart of gold! His nickname in the regiment was the Explosive Lieutenant...."

"And what a regiment it was, too," cried Ilya Petrovitch, much gratified at this agreeable banter, though still sulky.

Raskolnikov had a sudden desire to say something exceptionally pleasant to them all. "Excuse me, Captain," he began easily, suddenly addressing Nikodim Fomitch, "will you enter into my position?... I am ready to ask pardon, if I have been ill-mannered. I am a poor student, sick and shattered (shattered was the word he used) by poverty. I am not studying, because I cannot keep myself now, but I shall get money.... I have a mother and sister in the province of X. They will send it to me, and I will pay. My landlady is a good-hearted woman, but she is so exasperated at my having lost my lessons, and not paying her for the last four months, that she does not even send up my dinner... and I don't understand this I O U at all. She is asking me to pay her on this I O U. How am I to pay her? Judge for yourselves!..."

"But that is not our business, you know," the head clerk was observing.

"Yes, yes. I perfectly agree with you. But allow me to explain..." Raskolnikov put in again, still addressing Nikodim Fomitch, but trying his best to address Ilya Petrovitch also, though the latter persistently appeared to be rummaging among his papers and to be contemptuously oblivious of him. "Allow me to explain that I have been living with her for nearly three years and at first... at first... for why should I not confess it, at the very beginning I promised to marry her daughter, it was a verbal promise, freely given... she was a girl... indeed, I liked her, though I was not in love with her... a youthful affair in fact... that is, I mean to say, that my landlady gave me credit freely in those days, and I led a life of... I was very heedless..."

"Nobody asks you for these personal details, sir, we've no time to waste," Ilya Petrovitch interposed roughly and with a note of triumph; but Raskolnikov stopped him hotly, though he suddenly found it exceedingly difficult to speak.

"But excuse me, excuse me. It is for me to explain... how it all happened... In my turn... though I agree with you... it is unnecessary. But a year ago, the girl died of typhus. I remained lodging there as before, and when my landlady moved into her present quarters, she said to me... and in a friendly way... that she had complete trust in me, but still, would I not give her an I O U for one hundred and fifteen roubles, all the debt I owed her. She said if only I gave her that, she would trust me again, as much as I liked, and that she would never, never—those were her own words—make use of that I O U till I could pay of myself... and now, when I have lost my lessons and have nothing to eat, she takes action against me. What am I to say to that?"

"All these affecting details are no business of ours." Ilya Petrovitch interrupted rudely. "You must give a written undertaking but as for your love affairs and all these tragic events, we have nothing to do with that."

"Come now... you are harsh," muttered Nikodim Fomitch, sitting down at the table and also beginning to write. He looked a little ashamed.

"Write!" said the head clerk to Raskolnikov.

"Write what?" the latter asked, gruffly.

"I will dictate to you."

Raskolnikov fancied that the head clerk treated him more casually and contemptuously after his speech, but strange to say he suddenly felt completely indifferent to anyone's opinion, and this revulsion took place in a flash, in one instant. If he had cared to think a little, he would have been amazed indeed that he could have talked to them like that a minute before, forcing his feelings upon them. And where had those feelings come from? Now if the whole room had been filled, not with police officers, but with those nearest and dearest to him, he would not have found one human word for them, so empty was his heart. A gloomy sensation of agonising, everlasting solitude and remoteness, took conscious form in his soul. It was not the meanness of his sentimental effusions before Ilya Petrovitch, nor the meanness of the latter's triumph over him that had caused this sudden revulsion in his heart. Oh, what had he to do now with his own baseness, with all these petty vanities, officers, German women, debts, police-offices? If he had been sentenced to be burnt at that moment, he would not have stirred, would hardly have heard the sentence to the end. Something was happening to him entirely new, sudden and unknown. It was not that he understood, but he felt clearly with all the intensity of sensation that he could never more appeal to these people in the police-office with sentimental effusions like his recent outburst, or with anything whatever; and that if they had been his own brothers and sisters and not police-officers, it would have been utterly out of the question to appeal to them in any circumstance of life. He had never experienced such a strange and awful sensation. And what was most agonising—it was more a sensation than a conception or idea, a direct sensation, the most agonising of all the sensations he had known in his life.

The head clerk began dictating to him the usual form of declaration, that he could not pay, that he undertook to do so at a future date, that he would not leave the town, nor sell his property, and so on.

"But you can't write, you can hardly hold the pen," observed the head clerk, looking with curiosity at Raskolnikov. "Are you ill?"

"Yes, I am giddy. Go on!"

"That's all. Sign it."

The head clerk took the paper, and turned to attend to others.

Raskolnikov gave back the pen; but instead of getting up and going away, he put his elbows on the table and pressed his head in his hands. He felt as if a nail were being driven into his skull. A strange idea suddenly occurred to him, to get up at once, to go up to Nikodim Fomitch, and tell him everything that had happened yesterday, and then to go with him to his lodgings and to show him the things in the hole in the corner. The impulse was so strong that he got up from his seat to carry it out. "Hadn't I better think a minute?" flashed through his mind. "No, better cast off the burden without thinking." But all at once he stood still, rooted to the spot. Nikodim Fomitch was talking eagerly with Ilya Petrovitch, and the words reached him:

"It's impossible, they'll both be released. To begin with, the whole story contradicts itself. Why should they have called the porter, if it had been their doing? To inform against themselves? Or as a blind? No, that would be too cunning! Besides, Pestryakov, the student, was seen at the gate by both the porters and a woman as he went in. He was walking with three friends, who left him only at the gate, and he asked the porters to direct him, in the presence of the friends. Now, would he have asked his way if he had been going with such an object? As for Koch, he spent half an hour at the silversmith's below, before he went up to the old woman and he left him at exactly a quarter to eight. Now just consider..."

"But excuse me, how do you explain this contradiction? They state themselves that they knocked and the door was locked; yet three minutes later when they went up with the porter, it turned out the door was unfastened."

"That's just it; the murderer must have been there and bolted himself in; and they'd have caught him for a certainty if Koch had not been an ass and gone to look for the porter too. *He* must have seized the interval to get downstairs and slip by them somehow. Koch keeps crossing himself and saying: 'If I had been there, he would have jumped out and killed me with his axe.' He is going to have a thanksgiving service—ha, ha!"

"And no one saw the murderer?"

"They might well not see him; the house is a regular Noah's Ark," said the head clerk, who was listening.

"It's clear, quite clear," Nikodim Fomitch repeated warmly.

"No, it is anything but clear," Ilya Petrovitch maintained.

Raskolnikov picked up his hat and walked towards the door, but he did not reach it....

When he recovered consciousness, he found himself sitting in a chair, supported by someone on the right side, while someone else was standing on the left, holding a yellowish glass filled with yellow water, and Nikodim Fomitch standing before him, looking intently at him. He got up from the chair.

"What's this? Are you ill?" Nikodim Fomitch asked, rather sharply.

"He could hardly hold his pen when he was signing," said the head clerk, settling back in his place, and taking up his work again.

"Have you been ill long?" cried Ilya Petrovitch from his place, where he, too, was looking through papers. He had, of course, come to look at the sick man when he fainted, but retired at once when he recovered.

"Since yesterday," muttered Raskolnikov in reply.

"Did you go out yesterday?"

"Yes."

"Though you were ill?"

"Yes."

"At what time?"

"About seven."

"And where did you go, my I ask?"

"Along the street."

"Short and clear."

Raskolnikov, white as a handkerchief, had answered sharply, jerkily, without dropping his black feverish eyes before Ilya Petrovitch's stare.

"He can scarcely stand upright. And you..." Nikodim Fomitch was beginning.

"No matter," Ilya Petrovitch pronounced rather peculiarly.

Nikodim Fomitch would have made some further protest, but glancing at the head clerk who was looking very hard at him, he did not speak. There was a sudden silence. It was strange.

"Very well, then," concluded Ilya Petrovitch, "we will not detain you."

Raskolnikov went out. He caught the sound of eager conversation on his departure, and above the rest rose the questioning voice of Nikodim Fomitch. In the street, his faintness passed off completely.

"A search—there will be a search at once," he repeated to himself, hurrying home. "The brutes! they suspect."

His former terror mastered him completely again.

CHAPTER II

"And what if there has been a search already? What if I find them in my room?"

But here was his room. Nothing and no one in it. No one had peeped in. Even Nastasya had not touched it. But heavens! how could he have left all those things in the hole?

He rushed to the corner, slipped his hand under the paper, pulled the things out and lined his pockets with them. There were eight articles in all: two little boxes with ear-rings or something of the sort, he hardly looked to see; then four small leather cases. There was a chain, too, merely wrapped in newspaper and something else in newspaper, that looked like a decoration.... He put them all in the different pockets of his overcoat, and the remaining pocket of his trousers, trying to conceal them as much as possible. He took the purse, too. Then he went out of his room, leaving the door open. He walked quickly and resolutely, and though he felt shattered, he had his senses about him. He was afraid of pursuit, he was afraid that in another half-hour, another quarter of an hour perhaps, instructions would be issued for his pursuit, and so at all costs, he must hide all traces before then. He must clear everything up while he still had some strength, some reasoning power left him.... Where was he to go?

That had long been settled: "Fling them into the canal, and all traces hidden in the water, the thing would be at an end." So he had decided in the night of his delirium when several times he had had the impulse to get up and go away, to make haste, and get rid of it all. But to get rid of it, turned out to be a very difficult task. He wandered along the bank of the Ekaterininsky Canal for half an hour or more and looked several times at the steps running down to the water, but he could not think of carrying out his plan; either rafts stood at the steps' edge, and women were washing clothes on them, or boats were moored there, and people were swarming everywhere. Moreover he could be seen and noticed from the banks on all sides; it would look suspicious for a man to go down on purpose, stop, and throw something into the water. And what if the boxes were to float instead of sinking? And of course they would. Even as it was, everyone he met seemed to stare and look round, as if they had nothing to do but to watch him. "Why is it, or can it be my fancy?" he thought.

At last the thought struck him that it might be better to go to the Neva. There were not so many people there, he would be less observed, and it would be more convenient in every way, above all it was further off. He wondered how he could have been wandering for a good half-hour, worried and anxious in this dangerous past without thinking of it before. And that half-hour he had lost over an irrational plan, simply because he had thought of it in delirium! He had become extremely absent and forgetful and he was aware of it. He certainly must make haste.

He walked towards the Neva along V—— Prospect, but on the way another idea struck him. "Why to the Neva? Would it not be better to go somewhere far off, to the Islands again, and there hide the things in some solitary place, in a wood or under a bush, and mark the spot perhaps?" And though he felt incapable of clear judgment, the idea seemed to him a sound one. But he was not destined to go there. For coming out of V—— Prospect towards the square, he saw on the left a passage leading between two blank walls to a courtyard. On the right hand, the blank unwhitewashed wall of a four-storied house stretched far into the court; on the left, a wooden hoarding ran parallel with it for twenty paces into the court, and then turned sharply to the left. Here was a deserted fenced-off place where rubbish of different sorts was lying. At the end of the court, the corner of a low, smutty, stone shed, apparently part of some workshop, peeped from behind the hoarding. It was probably a carriage builder's or carpenter's shed; the whole place from the entrance was black with coal dust. Here would be the place to throw it, he thought. Not seeing anyone in the yard, he slipped in, and at once saw near the gate a sink, such as is often put in yards where there are many workmen or cab-drivers; and on the hoarding above had been scribbled in chalk the time-honoured witticism, "Standing here strictly forbidden." This was all the better, for there would be nothing suspicious about his going in. "Here I could throw it all in a heap and get away!"

Looking round once more, with his hand already in his pocket, he noticed against the outer wall, between the entrance and the sink, a big unhewn stone, weighing perhaps sixty pounds. The other side of the wall was a street. He could hear passers-by, always numerous in that part, but he could not be seen from the entrance, unless someone came in from the street, which might well happen indeed, so there was need of haste.

He bent down over the stone, seized the top of it firmly in both hands, and using all his strength turned it over. Under the stone was a small hollow in the ground, and he immediately emptied his pocket into it. The purse lay at the top, and yet the hollow was not filled up. Then he seized the stone again and with one twist turned it back, so that it was in the same position again, though it stood a very little higher. But he scraped the earth about it and pressed it at the edges with his foot. Nothing could be noticed.

Then he went out, and turned into the square. Again an intense, almost unbearable joy overwhelmed him for an instant, as it had in the police-office. "I have buried my tracks! And who, who can think of looking under that stone? It has been lying there most likely ever since the house was built, and will lie as many years more. And if it were found, who would think of me? It is all over! No clue!" And he laughed. Yes, he remembered that he began laughing a thin, nervous noiseless laugh, and went on laughing all the time he was crossing the square. But when he reached the K—— Boulevard where two days before he had come upon that girl, his laughter suddenly ceased. Other ideas crept into his mind. He felt all at once that it would be loathsome to pass that seat on which after the girl was gone, he had sat and pondered, and that it would be hateful, too, to meet that whiskered policeman to whom he had given the twenty copecks: "Damn him!"

411

He walked, looking about him angrily and distractedly. All his ideas now seemed to be circling round some single point, and he felt that there really was such a point, and that now, now, he was left facing that point—and for the first time, indeed, during the last two months.

"Damn it all!" he thought suddenly, in a fit of ungovernable fury. "If it has begun, then it has begun. Hang the new life! Good Lord, how stupid it is!... And what lies I told to-day! How despicably I fawned upon that wretched Ilya Petrovitch! But that is all folly! What do I care for them all, and my fawning upon them! It is not that at all! It is not that at all!"

Suddenly he stopped; a new utterly unexpected and exceedingly simple question perplexed and bitterly confounded him.

"If it all has really been done deliberately and not idiotically, if I really had a certain and definite object, how is it I did not even glance into the purse and don't know what I had there, for which I have undergone these agonies, and have deliberately undertaken this base, filthy degrading business? And here I wanted at once to throw into the water the purse together with all the things which I had not seen either... how's that?"

Yes, that was so, that was all so. Yet he had known it all before, and it was not a new question for him, even when it was decided in the night without hesitation and consideration, as though so it must be, as though it could not possibly be otherwise.... Yes, he had known it all, and understood it all; it surely had all been settled even yesterday at the moment when he was bending over the box and pulling the jewel-cases out of it.... Yes, so it was.

"It is because I am very ill," he decided grimly at last, "I have been worrying and fretting myself, and I don't know what I am doing.... Yesterday and the day before yesterday and all this time I have been worrying myself.... I shall get well and I shall not worry.... But what if I don't get well at all? Good God, how sick I am of it all!"

He walked on without resting. He had a terrible longing for some distraction, but he did not know what to do, what to attempt. A new overwhelming sensation was gaining more and more mastery over him every moment; this was an immeasurable, almost physical, repulsion for everything surrounding him, an obstinate, malignant feeling of hatred. All who met him were loathsome to him—he loathed their faces, their movements, their gestures. If anyone had addressed him, he felt that he might have spat at him or bitten him....

He stopped suddenly, on coming out on the bank of the Little Neva, near the bridge to Vassilyevsky Ostrov. "Why, he lives here, in that house," he thought, "why, I have not come to Razumihin of my own accord! Here it's the same thing over again.... Very interesting to know, though; have I come on purpose or have I simply walked here by chance? Never mind, I said the day before yesterday that I would go and see him the day *after*; well, and so I will! Besides I really cannot go further now."

He went up to Razumihin's room on the fifth floor.

The latter was at home in his garret, busily writing at the moment, and he opened the door himself. It was four months since they had seen each other. Razumihin was sitting in a ragged dressing-gown, with slippers on his bare feet, unkempt, unshaven and unwashed. His face showed surprise.

"Is it you?" he cried. He looked his comrade up and down; then after a brief pause, he whistled. "As hard up as all that! Why, brother, you've cut me out!" he added, looking at Raskolnikov's rags. "Come sit down, you are tired, I'll be bound."

And when he had sunk down on the American leather sofa, which was in even worse condition than his own, Razumihin saw at once that his visitor was ill.

"Why, you are seriously ill, do you know that?" He began feeling his pulse. Raskolnikov pulled away his hand.

"Never mind," he said, "I have come for this: I have no lessons.... I wanted,... but I don't really want lessons...."

"But I say! You are delirious, you know!" Razumihin observed, watching him carefully.

"No, I am not."

Raskolnikov got up from the sofa. As he had mounted the stairs to Razumihin's, he had not realised that he would be meeting his friend face to face. Now, in a flash, he knew, that what he was least of all disposed for at that moment was to be face to face with anyone in the wide world. His spleen rose within him. He almost choked with rage at himself as soon as he crossed Razumihin's threshold.

"Good-bye," he said abruptly, and walked to the door.

"Stop, stop! You queer fish."

"I don't want to," said the other, again pulling away his hand.

"Then why the devil have you come? Are you mad, or what? Why, this is... almost insulting! I won't let you go like that."

"Well, then, I came to you because I know no one but you who could help... to begin... because you are kinder than anyone—cleverer, I mean, and can judge... and now I see that I want nothing. Do you hear? Nothing at all... no one's services... no one's sympathy. I am by myself... alone. Come, that's enough. Leave me alone."

"Stay a minute, you sweep! You are a perfect madman. As you like for all I care. I have no lessons, do you see, and I don't care about that, but there's a bookseller, Heruvimov—and he takes the place of a lesson. I would not exchange him for five lessons. He's doing publishing of a kind, and issuing natural science manuals and what a circulation they have! The very titles are worth the money! You always maintained that I was a fool, but by Jove, my boy, there are greater fools than I am! Now he is setting up for being advanced, not that he has an inkling of anything, but, of course, I encourage him. Here are two signatures of the German text—in my opinion, the crudest charlatanism; it discusses the question, 'Is woman a human being?' And, of course, triumphantly proves that she is. Heruvimov is going to bring out this work as a contribution to the woman question; I am translating it; he will expand these two and a half signatures into six, we shall make up a gorgeous title half a page long and bring it out at half a rouble. It will do! He pays me six roubles the signature, it works out to about fifteen roubles for the job, and I've had six already in advance. When we have finished this, we are going to begin a translation about whales, and then some of the dullest scandals out of the second part of *Les Confessions* we have marked for translation; somebody has told Heruvimov, that Rousseau was a kind of Radishchev. You may be sure I don't contradict him, hang him! Well, would you like to do the second signature of '*Is woman a human being?*' If you would, take the German and pens and paper—all those are provided, and take three roubles; for as I have had six roubles in advance on the whole thing, three roubles come to you for your share. And when you have finished the signature there will be another three roubles for you. And please don't think I am doing you a service; quite the contrary, as soon as you came in, I saw how you could help me; to begin with, I am weak in spelling, and secondly, I am sometimes utterly adrift in German, so that I make it up as I go along for the most part. The only comfort is, that it's bound to be a change for the better. Though who can tell, maybe it's sometimes for the worse. Will you take it?"

Raskolnikov took the German sheets in silence, took the three roubles and without a word went out. Razumihin gazed after him in astonishment. But when Raskolnikov was in the next street, he turned back, mounted the stairs to Razumihin's again and laying on the table the German article and the three roubles, went out again, still without uttering a word.

"Are you raving, or what?" Razumihin shouted, roused to fury at last. "What farce is this? You'll drive me crazy too... what did you come to see me for, damn you?"

"I don't want... translation," muttered Raskolnikov from the stairs.

"Then what the devil do you want?" shouted Razumihin from above. Raskolnikov continued descending the staircase in silence.

"Hey, there! Where are you living?"

No answer.

"Well, confound you then!"

But Raskolnikov was already stepping into the street. On the Nikolaevsky Bridge he was roused to full consciousness again by an unpleasant incident. A coachman, after shouting at him two or three times, gave him a violent lash on the back with his whip, for having almost fallen under his horses' hoofs. The lash so infuriated him that he dashed away to the railing (for some unknown reason he had been walking in the very middle of the bridge in the traffic). He angrily clenched and ground his teeth. He heard laughter, of course.

"Serves him right!"

"A pickpocket I dare say."

"Pretending to be drunk, for sure, and getting under the wheels on purpose; and you have to answer for him."

"It's a regular profession, that's what it is."

But while he stood at the railing, still looking angry and bewildered after the retreating carriage, and rubbing his back, he suddenly felt someone thrust money into his hand. He looked. It was an elderly woman in a kerchief and goatskin shoes, with a girl, probably her daughter wearing a hat, and carrying a green parasol.

"Take it, my good man, in Christ's name."

He took it and they passed on. It was a piece of twenty copecks. From his dress and appearance they might well have taken him for a beggar asking alms in the streets, and the gift of the twenty copecks he doubtless owed to the blow, which made them feel sorry for him.

He closed his hand on the twenty copecks, walked on for ten paces, and turned facing the Neva, looking towards the palace. The sky was without a cloud and the water was almost bright blue, which is so rare in the Neva. The cupola of the cathedral, which is seen at its best from the bridge about twenty paces from the chapel, glittered in the sunlight, and in the pure air every ornament on it could be clearly distinguished. The pain from the lash went off, and Raskolnikov forgot about it; one uneasy and not quite definite idea occupied him now completely. He stood still, and gazed long and intently into the distance; this spot was especially familiar to him. When he was attending the university, he had hundreds of times—generally on his way home—stood still on this spot, gazed at this truly magnificent spectacle and almost always marvelled at a vague and mysterious emotion it roused in him. It left him strangely cold; this gorgeous picture was for him blank and lifeless. He wondered every time at his sombre and enigmatic impression and, mistrusting himself, put off finding the explanation of it. He vividly recalled those old doubts and perplexities, and it seemed to him that it was no mere chance that he recalled them now. It struck him as strange and grotesque, that he should have stopped at the same spot as before, as though he actually imagined he could think the same thoughts, be interested in the same theories and pictures that had interested him... so short a time ago. He felt it almost amusing, and yet it wrung his heart. Deep down, hidden far away out of sight all that seemed to him now—all his old past, his old thoughts, his old problems and theories, his old impressions and that picture and himself and all, all.... He felt as though he were flying upwards, and everything were vanishing from his sight. Making an unconscious movement with his hand, he suddenly became aware of the piece of money in his fist. He opened his hand, stared at the coin, and with a sweep of his arm flung it into the water; then he turned and went home. It seemed to him, he had cut himself off from everyone and from everything at that moment.

Evening was coming on when he reached home, so that he must have been walking about six hours. How and where he came back he did not remember. Undressing, and quivering like an overdriven horse, he lay down on the sofa, drew his greatcoat over him, and at once sank into oblivion....

It was dusk when he was waked up by a fearful scream. Good God, what a scream! Such unnatural sounds, such howling, wailing, grinding, tears, blows and curses he had never heard.

He could never have imagined such brutality, such frenzy. In terror he sat up in bed, almost swooning with agony. But the fighting, wailing and cursing grew louder and louder. And then to his intense amazement he caught the voice of his landlady. She was howling, shrieking and wailing, rapidly, hurriedly, incoherently, so that he could not make out what she was talking about; she was beseeching, no doubt, not to be beaten, for she was being mercilessly beaten on the stairs. The voice of her assailant was so horrible from spite and rage that it was almost a croak; but he, too, was saying something, and just as quickly and indistinctly, hurrying and spluttering. All at once Raskolnikov trembled; he recognised the voice—it was the voice of Ilya Petrovitch. Ilya Petrovitch here and beating the landlady! He is kicking her, banging her head against the steps—that's clear, that can be told from the sounds, from the cries and the thuds. How is it, is the world topsy-turvy? He could hear people running in crowds from all the storeys and all the staircases; he heard voices, exclamations, knocking, doors banging. "But why, why, and how could it be?" he repeated, thinking seriously that he had gone mad. But no, he heard too distinctly! And they would come to him then next, "for no doubt... it's all about that... about yesterday.... Good God!" He would have fastened his door with the latch, but he could not lift his hand... besides, it would be useless. Terror gripped his heart like ice, tortured him and numbed him.... But at last all this uproar, after continuing about ten minutes, began gradually to subside. The landlady was moaning and groaning; Ilya Petrovitch was still uttering threats and curses.... But at last he, too, seemed to be silent, and now he could not be heard. "Can he have gone away? Good Lord!" Yes, and now the landlady is going too, still weeping and moaning... and then her door slammed.... Now the crowd was going from the stairs to their rooms, exclaiming, disputing, calling to one another, raising their voices to a shout, dropping them to a whisper. There must have been numbers of them—almost all the inmates of the block. "But, good God, how could it be! And why, why had he come here!"

Raskolnikov sank worn out on the sofa, but could not close his eyes. He lay for half an hour in such anguish, such an intolerable sensation of infinite terror as he had never experienced before. Suddenly a bright light flashed into his room. Nastasya came in with a candle and a plate of soup. Looking at him carefully and ascertaining that he was not asleep, she set the candle on the table and began to lay out what she had brought—bread, salt, a plate, a spoon.

"You've eaten nothing since yesterday, I warrant. You've been trudging about all day, and you're shaking with fever."

"Nastasya... what were they beating the landlady for?"

She looked intently at him.

"Who beat the landlady?"

"Just now... half an hour ago, Ilya Petrovitch, the assistant superintendent, on the stairs.... Why was he ill-treating her like that, and... why was he here?"

Nastasya scrutinised him, silent and frowning, and her scrutiny lasted a long time. He felt uneasy, even frightened at her searching eyes.

"Nastasya, why don't you speak?" he said timidly at last in a weak voice.

"It's the blood," she answered at last softly, as though speaking to herself.

"Blood? What blood?" he muttered, growing white and turning towards the wall.

Nastasya still looked at him without speaking.

"Nobody has been beating the landlady," she declared at last in a firm, resolute voice.

He gazed at her, hardly able to breathe.

"I heard it myself.... I was not asleep... I was sitting up," he said still more timidly. "I listened a long while. The assistant superintendent came.... Everyone ran out on to the stairs from all the flats."

"No one has been here. That's the blood crying in your ears. When there's no outlet for it and it gets clotted, you begin fancying things.... Will you eat something?"

He made no answer. Nastasya still stood over him, watching him.

"Give me something to drink... Nastasya."

She went downstairs and returned with a white earthenware jug of water. He remembered only swallowing one sip of the cold water and spilling some on his neck. Then followed forgetfulness.

CHAPTER III

He was not completely unconscious, however, all the time he was ill; he was in a feverish state, sometimes delirious, sometimes half conscious. He remembered a great deal afterwards. Sometimes it seemed as though there were a number of people round him; they wanted to take him away somewhere, there was a great deal of squabbling and discussing about him. Then he would be alone in the room; they had all gone away afraid of him, and only now and then opened the door a crack to look at him; they threatened him, plotted something together, laughed, and mocked at him. He remembered Nastasya often at his bedside; he distinguished another person, too, whom he seemed to know very well, though he could not remember who he was, and this fretted him, even made him cry. Sometimes he fancied he had been lying there a month; at other times it all seemed part of the same day. But of *that*—of *that* he had no recollection, and yet every minute he felt that he had forgotten something he ought to remember. He worried and tormented himself trying to remember, moaned, flew into a rage, or sank into awful, intolerable terror. Then he struggled to get up, would have run away, but someone always prevented him by force, and he sank back into impotence and forgetfulness. At last he returned to complete consciousness.

It happened at ten o'clock in the morning. On fine days the sun shone into the room at that hour, throwing a streak of light on the right wall and the corner near the door. Nastasya was standing beside him with another person, a complete stranger, who was looking at him very inquisitively. He was a young man with a beard, wearing a full, short-waisted coat, and looked like a messenger. The landlady was peeping in at the half-opened door. Raskolnikov sat up.

"Who is this, Nastasya?" he asked, pointing to the young man.

"I say, he's himself again!" she said.

"He is himself," echoed the man.

Concluding that he had returned to his senses, the landlady closed the door and disappeared. She was always shy and dreaded conversations or discussions. She was a woman of forty, not at all bad-looking, fat and buxom, with black eyes and eyebrows, good-natured from fatness and laziness, and absurdly bashful.

"Who... are you?" he went on, addressing the man. But at that moment the door was flung open, and, stooping a little, as he was so tall, Razumihin came in.

"What a cabin it is!" he cried. "I am always knocking my head. You call this a lodging! So you are conscious, brother? I've just heard the news from Pashenka."

"He has just come to," said Nastasya.

"Just come to," echoed the man again, with a smile.

"And who are you?" Razumihin asked, suddenly addressing him. "My name is Vrazumihin, at your service; not Razumihin, as I am always called, but Vrazumihin, a student and gentleman; and he is my friend. And who are you?"

"I am the messenger from our office, from the merchant Shelopaev, and I've come on business."

"Please sit down." Razumihin seated himself on the other side of the table. "It's a good thing you've come to, brother," he went on to Raskolnikov. "For the last four days you have scarcely eaten or drunk anything. We had to give you tea in spoonfuls. I brought Zossimov to see you twice. You remember Zossimov? He examined you carefully and said at once it was nothing serious—something seemed to have gone to your head. Some nervous nonsense, the result of bad feeding, he says you have not had enough beer and radish, but it's nothing much, it will pass and you will be all right. Zossimov is a first-rate fellow! He is making quite a name. Come, I won't keep you," he said, addressing the man again. "Will you explain what you want? You must know, Rodya, this is the second time they have sent from the office; but it was another man last time, and I talked to him. Who was it came before?"

"That was the day before yesterday, I venture to say, if you please, sir. That was Alexey Semyonovitch; he is in our office, too."

"He was more intelligent than you, don't you think so?"

"Yes, indeed, sir, he is of more weight than I am."

"Quite so; go on."

"At your mamma's request, through Afanasy Ivanovitch Vahrushin, of whom I presume you have heard more than once, a remittance is sent to you from our office," the man began, addressing Raskolnikov. "If you are in an intelligible condition, I've thirty-five roubles to remit to you, as Semyon Semyonovitch has received from Afanasy Ivanovitch at your mamma's request instructions to that effect, as on previous occasions. Do you know him, sir?"

"Yes, I remember... Vahrushin," Raskolnikov said dreamily.

"You hear, he knows Vahrushin," cried Razumihin. "He is in 'an intelligible condition'! And I see you are an intelligent man too. Well, it's always pleasant to hear words of wisdom."

"That's the gentleman, Vahrushin, Afanasy Ivanovitch. And at the request of your mamma, who has sent you a remittance once before in the same manner through him, he did not refuse this time also, and sent instructions to Semyon Semyonovitch some days since to hand you thirty-five roubles in the hope of better to come."

"That 'hoping for better to come' is the best thing you've said, though 'your mamma' is not bad either. Come then, what do you say? Is he fully conscious, eh?"

"That's all right. If only he can sign this little paper."

"He can scrawl his name. Have you got the book?"

"Yes, here's the book."

"Give it to me. Here, Rodya, sit up. I'll hold you. Take the pen and scribble 'Raskolnikov' for him. For just now, brother, money is sweeter to us than treacle."

"I don't want it," said Raskolnikov, pushing away the pen.

"Not want it?"

"I won't sign it."

"How the devil can you do without signing it?"

"I don't want... the money."

"Don't want the money! Come, brother, that's nonsense, I bear witness. Don't trouble, please, it's only that he is on his travels again. But that's pretty common with him at all times though.... You are a man of judgment and we will take him in hand, that is, more simply, take his hand and he will sign it. Here."

"But I can come another time."

"No, no. Why should we trouble you? You are a man of judgment.... Now, Rodya, don't keep your visitor, you see he is waiting," and he made ready to hold Raskolnikov's hand in earnest.

"Stop, I'll do it alone," said the latter, taking the pen and signing his name.

The messenger took out the money and went away.

"Bravo! And now, brother, are you hungry?"

"Yes," answered Raskolnikov.

"Is there any soup?"

"Some of yesterday's," answered Nastasya, who was still standing there.

"With potatoes and rice in it?"

"Yes."

"I know it by heart. Bring soup and give us some tea."

"Very well."

Raskolnikov looked at all this with profound astonishment and a dull, unreasoning terror. He made up his mind to keep quiet and see what would happen. "I believe I am not wandering. I believe it's reality," he thought.

In a couple of minutes Nastasya returned with the soup, and announced that the tea would be ready directly. With the soup she brought two spoons, two plates, salt, pepper, mustard for the beef, and so on. The table was set as it had not been for a long time. The cloth was clean.

"It would not be amiss, Nastasya, if Praskovya Pavlovna were to send us up a couple of bottles of beer. We could empty them."

"Well, you are a cool hand," muttered Nastasya, and she departed to carry out his orders.

Raskolnikov still gazed wildly with strained attention. Meanwhile Razumihin sat down on the sofa beside him, as clumsily as a bear put his left arm round Raskolnikov's head, although he was able to sit up, and with his right hand gave him a spoonful of soup, blowing on it that it might not burn him. But the soup was only just warm. Raskolnikov swallowed one spoonful greedily, then a second, then a third. But after giving him a few more spoonfuls of soup, Razumihin suddenly stopped, and said that he must ask Zossimov whether he ought to have more.

Nastasya came in with two bottles of beer.

"And will you have tea?"

"Yes."

"Cut along, Nastasya, and bring some tea, for tea we may venture on without the faculty. But here is the beer!" He moved back to his chair, pulled the soup and meat in front of him, and began eating as though he had not touched food for three days.

"I must tell you, Rodya, I dine like this here every day now," he mumbled with his mouth full of beef, "and it's all Pashenka, your dear little landlady, who sees to that; she loves to do anything for me. I don't ask for it, but, of course, I don't object. And here's Nastasya with the tea. She is a quick girl. Nastasya, my dear, won't you have some beer?"

"Get along with your nonsense!"

"A cup of tea, then?"

"A cup of tea, maybe."

"Pour it out. Stay, I'll pour it out myself. Sit down."

He poured out two cups, left his dinner, and sat on the sofa again. As before, he put his left arm round the sick man's head, raised him up and gave him tea in spoonfuls, again blowing each spoonful steadily and earnestly, as though this process was the principal and most effective means towards his friend's recovery. Raskolnikov said nothing and made no resistance, though he felt quite strong enough to sit up on the sofa without support and could not merely have held a cup or a spoon, but even perhaps could have walked about. But from some queer, almost animal, cunning he conceived the idea of hiding his strength and lying low for a time, pretending if necessary not to be yet in full possession of his faculties, and meanwhile listening to find out what was going on. Yet he could not overcome his sense of repugnance. After sipping a dozen spoonfuls of tea, he suddenly released his head, pushed the spoon away capriciously, and sank back on the pillow. There were actually real pillows under his head now, down pillows in clean cases, he observed that, too, and took note of it.

"Pashenka must give us some raspberry jam to-day to make him some raspberry tea," said Razumihin, going back to his chair and attacking his soup and beer again.

"And where is she to get raspberries for you?" asked Nastasya, balancing a saucer on her five outspread fingers and sipping tea through a lump of sugar.

"She'll get it at the shop, my dear. You see, Rodya, all sorts of things have been happening while you have been laid up. When you decamped in that rascally way without leaving your address, I felt so angry that I resolved to find you out and punish you. I set to work that very day. How I ran about making inquiries for you! This lodging of yours I had forgotten, though I never remembered it, indeed, because I did not know it; and as for your old lodgings, I could only remember it was at the Five Corners, Harlamov's house. I kept trying to find that Harlamov's house, and afterwards it turned out that it was not Harlamov's, but Buch's. How one muddles up sound sometimes! So I lost my temper, and I went on the chance to the address bureau next day, and only fancy, in two minutes they looked you up! Your name is down there."

"My name!"

"I should think so; and yet a General Kobelev they could not find while I was there. Well, it's a long story. But as soon as I did land on this place, I soon got to know all your affairs—all, all, brother, I know everything; Nastasya here will tell you. I made the acquaintance of Nikodim Fomitch and Ilya Petrovitch, and the house-porter and Mr. Zametov, Alexandr Grigorievitch, the head clerk in the police office, and, last, but not least, of Pashenka; Nastasya here knows...."

"He's got round her," Nastasya murmured, smiling slyly.

"Why don't you put the sugar in your tea, Nastasya Nikiforovna?"

"You are a one!" Nastasya cried suddenly, going off into a giggle. "I am not Nikiforovna, but Petrovna," she added suddenly, recovering from her mirth.

"I'll make a note of it. Well, brother, to make a long story short, I was going in for a regular explosion here to uproot all malignant influences in the locality, but Pashenka won the day. I had not expected, brother, to find her so... prepossessing. Eh, what do you think?"

Raskolnikov did not speak, but he still kept his eyes fixed upon him, full of alarm.

"And all that could be wished, indeed, in every respect," Razumihin went on, not at all embarrassed by his silence.

"Ah, the sly dog!" Nastasya shrieked again. This conversation afforded her unspeakable delight.

"It's a pity, brother, that you did not set to work in the right way at first. You ought to have approached her differently. She is, so to speak, a most unaccountable character. But we will talk about her character later.... How could you let things come to such a pass that she gave up sending you your dinner? And that I O U? You must have been mad to sign an I O U. And that promise of marriage when her daughter, Natalya Yegorovna, was alive?... I know all about it! But I see that's a delicate matter and I am an ass; forgive me. But, talking of foolishness, do you know Praskovya Pavlovna is not nearly so foolish as you would think at first sight?"

"No," mumbled Raskolnikov, looking away, but feeling that it was better to keep up the conversation.

"She isn't, is she?" cried Razumihin, delighted to get an answer out of him. "But she is not very clever either, eh? She is essentially, essentially an unaccountable character! I am sometimes quite at a loss, I assure you.... She must be forty; she says she is thirty-six, and of course she has every right to say so. But I swear I judge her intellectually, simply from the metaphysical point of view; there is a sort of symbolism sprung up between us, a sort of algebra or what not! I don't understand it! Well, that's all nonsense. Only, seeing that you are not a student now and have lost your lessons and your clothes, and that through the young lady's death she has no need to treat you as a relation, she suddenly took fright; and as you hid in your den and dropped all your old relations with her, she planned to get rid of you. And she's been cherishing that design a long time, but was sorry to lose the I O U, for you assured her yourself that your mother would pay."

"It was base of me to say that.... My mother herself is almost a beggar... and I told a lie to keep my lodging... and be fed," Raskolnikov said loudly and distinctly.

"Yes, you did very sensibly. But the worst of it is that at that point Mr. Tchebarov turns up, a business man. Pashenka would never have thought of doing anything on her own account, she is too retiring; but the business man is by no means retiring, and first thing he puts the question, 'Is there any hope of realising the I O U?' Answer: there is, because he has a mother who would save her Rodya with her hundred and twenty-five roubles pension, if she has to starve herself; and a sister, too, who would go into bondage for his sake. That's what he was building upon.... Why do you start? I know all the ins and outs of your affairs now, my dear boy—it's not for nothing that you were so open with Pashenka when you were her prospective son-in-law, and I say all this as a friend.... But I tell you what it is; an honest and sensitive man is open; and a business man 'listens and goes on eating' you up. Well, then she gave the I O U by way of payment to this Tchebarov, and without hesitation he made a formal demand for payment. When I heard of all this I wanted to blow him up, too, to clear my conscience, but by that time harmony reigned between me and Pashenka, and I insisted on stopping the whole affair, engaging that you would pay. I went security for you, brother. Do you understand? We called Tchebarov, flung him ten roubles and got the I O U back from him, and here I have the honour of presenting it to you. She trusts your word now. Here, take it, you see I have torn it."

Razumihin put the note on the table. Raskolnikov looked at him and turned to the wall without uttering a word. Even Razumihin felt a twinge.

"I see, brother," he said a moment later, "that I have been playing the fool again. I thought I should amuse you with my chatter, and I believe I have only made you cross."

"Was it you I did not recognise when I was delirious?" Raskolnikov asked, after a moment's pause without turning his head.

"Yes, and you flew into a rage about it, especially when I brought Zametov one day."

"Zametov? The head clerk? What for?" Raskolnikov turned round quickly and fixed his eyes on Razumihin.

"What's the matter with you?... What are you upset about? He wanted to make your acquaintance because I talked to him a lot about you.... How could I have found out so much except from him? He is a capital fellow, brother, first-rate... in his own way, of course. Now we are friends—see each other almost every day. I have moved into this part, you know. I have only just moved. I've been with him to Luise Ivanovna once or twice.... Do you remember Luise, Luise Ivanovna?"

"Did I say anything in delirium?"

"I should think so! You were beside yourself."

"What did I rave about?"

"What next? What did you rave about? What people do rave about.... Well, brother, now I must not lose time. To work." He got up from the table and took up his cap.

"What did I rave about?"

"How he keeps on! Are you afraid of having let out some secret? Don't worry yourself; you said nothing about a countess. But you said a lot about a bulldog, and about ear-rings and chains, and about Krestovsky Island, and some porter, and Nikodim Fomitch and Ilya Petrovitch, the assistant superintendent. And another thing that was of special interest to you was your own sock. You whined, 'Give me my sock.' Zametov hunted all about your room for your socks, and with his own scented, ring-bedecked fingers he gave you the rag. And only then were you comforted, and for the next twenty-four hours you held the wretched thing in your hand; we could not get it from you. It is most likely somewhere under your quilt at this moment. And then you asked so piteously for fringe for your trousers. We tried to find out what sort of fringe, but we could not make it out. Now to business! Here are thirty-five roubles; I take ten of them, and shall give you an account of them in an hour or two. I will let Zossimov know at the same time, though he ought to have been here long ago, for it is nearly twelve. And you, Nastasya, look in pretty often while I am away, to see whether he wants a drink or anything else. And I will tell Pashenka what is wanted myself. Good-bye!"

"He calls her Pashenka! Ah, he's a deep one!" said Nastasya as he went out; then she opened the door and stood listening, but could not resist running downstairs after him. She was very eager to hear what he would say to the landlady. She was evidently quite fascinated by Razumihin.

No sooner had she left the room than the sick man flung off the bedclothes and leapt out of bed like a madman. With burning, twitching impatience he had waited for them to be gone so that he might set to work. But to what work? Now, as though to spite him, it eluded him.

"Good God, only tell me one thing: do they know of it yet or not? What if they know it and are only pretending, mocking me while I am laid up, and then they will come in and tell me that it's been discovered long ago and that they have only... What am I to do now? That's what I've forgotten, as though on purpose; forgotten it all at once, I remembered a minute ago."

He stood in the middle of the room and gazed in miserable bewilderment about him; he walked to the door, opened it, listened; but that was not what he wanted. Suddenly, as though recalling something, he rushed to the corner where there was a hole under the paper, began examining it, put his hand into the hole, fumbled—but that was not it. He went to the stove, opened it and began rummaging in the ashes; the frayed edges of his trousers and the rags cut off his pocket were lying there just as he had thrown them. No one had looked, then! Then he remembered the sock about which Razumihin had just been telling him. Yes, there it lay on the sofa under the quilt, but it was so covered with dust and grime that Zametov could not have seen anything on it.

"Bah, Zametov! The police office! And why am I sent for to the police office? Where's the notice? Bah! I am mixing it up; that was then. I looked at my sock then, too, but now... now I have been ill. But what did Zametov come for? Why did Razumihin bring him?" he muttered, helplessly sitting on the sofa again. "What does it mean? Am I still in delirium, or is it real? I believe it is real.... Ah, I remember; I must escape! Make haste to escape. Yes, I must, I must escape! Yes... but where? And where are my clothes? I've no boots. They've taken them away! They've hidden them! I understand! Ah, here is my coat—they passed that over! And here is money on the table, thank God! And here's the I O U... I'll take the money and go and take another lodging. They won't find me!... Yes, but the address bureau? They'll find me, Razumihin will find me. Better escape altogether... far away... to America, and let them do their worst! And take the I O U... it would be of use there.... What else shall I take? They think I am ill! They don't know that I can walk, ha-ha-ha! I could see by their eyes that they know all about it! If only I could get downstairs! And what if they have set a watch there—policemen! What's this tea? Ah, and here is beer left, half a bottle, cold!"

He snatched up the bottle, which still contained a glassful of beer, and gulped it down with relish, as though quenching a flame in his breast. But in another minute the beer had gone to his head, and a faint and even pleasant shiver ran down his spine. He lay down and pulled the quilt over him. His sick and incoherent thoughts grew more and more disconnected, and soon a light, pleasant drowsiness came upon him. With a sense of comfort he nestled his head into the pillow, wrapped more closely about him the soft, wadded quilt which had replaced the old, ragged greatcoat, sighed softly and sank into a deep, sound, refreshing sleep.

He woke up, hearing someone come in. He opened his eyes and saw Razumihin standing in the doorway, uncertain whether to come in or not. Raskolnikov sat up quickly on the sofa and gazed at him, as though trying to recall something.

"Ah, you are not asleep! Here I am! Nastasya, bring in the parcel!" Razumihin shouted down the stairs. "You shall have the account directly."

"What time is it?" asked Raskolnikov, looking round uneasily.

"Yes, you had a fine sleep, brother, it's almost evening, it will be six o'clock directly. You have slept more than six hours."

"Good heavens! Have I?"

"And why not? It will do you good. What's the hurry? A tryst, is it? We've all time before us. I've been waiting for the last three hours for you; I've been up twice and found you asleep. I've called on Zossimov twice; not at home, only fancy! But no matter, he will turn up. And I've been out on my own business, too. You know I've been moving to-day, moving with my uncle. I have an uncle living with me now. But that's no matter, to business. Give me the parcel, Nastasya. We will open it directly. And how do you feel now, brother?"

"I am quite well, I am not ill. Razumihin, have you been here long?"

"I tell you I've been waiting for the last three hours."

"No, before."

"How do you mean?"

"How long have you been coming here?"

"Why I told you all about it this morning. Don't you remember?"

Raskolnikov pondered. The morning seemed like a dream to him. He could not remember alone, and looked inquiringly at Razumihin.

"Hm!" said the latter, "he has forgotten. I fancied then that you were not quite yourself. Now you are better for your sleep.... You really look much better. First-rate! Well, to business. Look here, my dear boy."

He began untying the bundle, which evidently interested him.

"Believe me, brother, this is something specially near my heart. For we must make a man of you. Let's begin from the top. Do you see this cap?" he said, taking out of the bundle a fairly good though cheap and ordinary cap. "Let me try it on."

"Presently, afterwards," said Raskolnikov, waving it off pettishly.

"Come, Rodya, my boy, don't oppose it, afterwards will be too late; and I shan't sleep all night, for I bought it by guess, without measure. Just right!" he cried triumphantly, fitting it on, "just your size! A proper head-covering is the first thing in dress and a recommendation in its own way. Tolstyakov, a friend of mine, is always obliged to take off his pudding basin when he goes into any public place where other people wear their hats or caps. People think he does it from slavish politeness, but it's simply because he is ashamed of his bird's nest; he is such a boastful fellow! Look, Nastasya, here are two specimens of headgear: this Palmerston"—he took from the corner Raskolnikov's old, battered hat, which for some unknown reason, he called a Palmerston—"or this jewel! Guess the price, Rodya, what do you suppose I paid for it, Nastasya!" he said, turning to her, seeing that Raskolnikov did not speak.

"Twenty copecks, no more, I dare say," answered Nastasya.

"Twenty copecks, silly!" he cried, offended. "Why, nowadays you would cost more than that—eighty copecks! And that only because it has been worn. And it's bought on condition that when's it's worn out, they will give you another next year. Yes, on my word! Well, now let us pass to the United States of America, as they called them at school. I assure you I am proud of these breeches," and he exhibited to Raskolnikov a pair of light, summer trousers of grey woollen material. "No holes, no spots, and quite respectable, although a little worn; and a waistcoat to match, quite in the fashion. And its being worn really is an improvement, it's softer, smoother.... You see, Rodya, to my thinking, the great thing for getting on in the world is always to keep to the seasons; if you don't insist on having asparagus in January, you keep your money in your purse; and it's the same with this purchase. It's summer now, so I've been buying summer things—warmer materials will be wanted for autumn, so you will have to throw these away in any case... especially as they will be done for by then from their own lack of coherence if not your higher standard of luxury. Come, price them! What do you say? Two roubles twenty-five copecks! And remember the condition: if you wear these out, you will have another suit for nothing! They only do business on that system at Fedyaev's; if you've bought a thing once, you are satisfied for life, for you will never go there again of your own free will. Now for the boots. What do you say? You see that they are a bit worn, but they'll last a couple of months, for it's foreign work and foreign leather; the secretary of the English Embassy sold them last week—he had only worn them six days, but he was very short of cash. Price—a rouble and a half. A bargain?"

"But perhaps they won't fit," observed Nastasya.

"Not fit? Just look!" and he pulled out of his pocket Raskolnikov's old, broken boot, stiffly coated with dry mud. "I did not go empty-handed—they took the size from this monster. We all did our best. And as to your linen, your landlady has seen to that. Here, to begin with are three shirts, hempen but with a fashionable front.... Well now then, eighty copecks the cap, two roubles twenty-five copecks the suit—together three roubles five copecks—a rouble and a half for the boots—for, you see, they are very good—and that makes four roubles fifty-five copecks; five roubles for the underclothes—they were bought in the lo—which makes exactly nine roubles fifty-five copecks. Forty-five copecks change in coppers. Will you take it? And so, Rodya, you are set up with a complete new rig-out, for your overcoat will serve, and even has a style of its own. That comes from getting one's clothes from Sharmer's! As for your socks and other things, I leave them to you; we've twenty-five roubles left. And as for Pashenka and paying for your lodging, don't you worry. I tell you she'll trust you for anything. And now, brother, let me change your linen, for I daresay you will throw off your illness with your shirt."

"Let me be! I don't want to!" Raskolnikov waved him off. He had listened with disgust to Razumihin's efforts to be playful about his purchases.

"Come, brother, don't tell me I've been trudging around for nothing," Razumihin insisted. "Nastasya, don't be bashful, but help me—that's it," and in spite of Raskolnikov's resistance he changed his linen. The latter sank back on the pillows and for a minute or two said nothing.

"It will be long before I get rid of them," he thought. "What money was all that bought with?" he asked at last, gazing at the wall.

"Money? Why, your own, what the messenger brought from Vahrushin, your mother sent it. Have you forgotten that, too?"

"I remember now," said Raskolnikov after a long, sullen silence. Razumihin looked at him, frowning and uneasy.

The door opened and a tall, stout man whose appearance seemed familiar to Raskolnikov came in.

CHAPTER IV

Zossimov was a tall, fat man with a puffy, colourless, clean-shaven face and straight flaxen hair. He wore spectacles, and a big gold ring on his fat finger. He was twenty-seven. He had on a light grey fashionable loose coat, light summer trousers, and everything about him loose, fashionable and spick and span; his linen was irreproachable, his watch-chain was massive. In manner he was slow and, as it were, nonchalant, and at the same time studiously free and easy; he made efforts to conceal his self-importance, but it was apparent at every instant. All his acquaintances found him tedious, but said he was clever at his work.

"I've been to you twice to-day, brother. You see, he's come to himself," cried Razumihin.

"I see, I see; and how do we feel now, eh?" said Zossimov to Raskolnikov, watching him carefully and, sitting down at the foot of the sofa, he settled himself as comfortably as he could.

"He is still depressed," Razumihin went on. "We've just changed his linen and he almost cried."

"That's very natural; you might have put it off if he did not wish it.... His pulse is first-rate. Is your head still aching, eh?"

"I am well, I am perfectly well!" Raskolnikov declared positively and irritably. He raised himself on the sofa and looked at them with glittering eyes, but sank back on to the pillow at once and turned to the wall. Zossimov watched him intently.

"Very good.... Going on all right," he said lazily. "Has he eaten anything?"

They told him, and asked what he might have.

"He may have anything... soup, tea... mushrooms and cucumbers, of course, you must not give him; he'd better not have meat either, and... but no need to tell you that!" Razumihin and he looked at each other. "No more medicine or anything. I'll look at him again to-morrow. Perhaps, to-day even... but never mind..."

"To-morrow evening I shall take him for a walk," said Razumihin. "We are going to the Yusupov garden and then to the Palais de Crystal."

"I would not disturb him to-morrow at all, but I don't know... a little, maybe... but we'll see."

"Ach, what a nuisance! I've got a house-warming party to-night; it's only a step from here. Couldn't he come? He could lie on the sofa. You are coming?" Razumihin said to Zossimov. "Don't forget, you promised."

"All right, only rather later. What are you going to do?"

"Oh, nothing—tea, vodka, herrings. There will be a pie... just our friends."

"And who?"

"All neighbours here, almost all new friends, except my old uncle, and he is new too—he only arrived in Petersburg yesterday to see to some business of his. We meet once in five years."

"What is he?"

"He's been stagnating all his life as a district postmaster; gets a little pension. He is sixty-five—not worth talking about.... But I am fond of him. Porfiry Petrovitch, the head of the Investigation Department here... But you know him."

"Is he a relation of yours, too?"

"A very distant one. But why are you scowling? Because you quarrelled once, won't you come then?"

"I don't care a damn for him."

"So much the better. Well, there will be some students, a teacher, a government clerk, a musician, an officer and Zametov."

"Do tell me, please, what you or he"—Zossimov nodded at Raskolnikov—"can have in common with this Zametov?"

"Oh, you particular gentleman! Principles! You are worked by principles, as it were by springs; you won't venture to turn round on your own account. If a man is a nice fellow, that's the only principle I go upon. Zametov is a delightful person."

"Though he does take bribes."

"Well, he does! and what of it? I don't care if he does take bribes," Razumihin cried with unnatural irritability. "I don't praise him for taking bribes. I only say he is a nice man in his own way! But if one looks at men in all ways—are there many good ones left? Why, I am sure I shouldn't be worth a baked onion myself... perhaps with you thrown in."

"That's too little; I'd give two for you."

"And I wouldn't give more than one for you. No more of your jokes! Zametov is no more than a boy. I can pull his hair and one must draw him not repel him. You'll never improve a man by repelling him, especially a boy. One has to be twice as careful with a boy. Oh, you progressive dullards! You don't understand. You harm yourselves running another man down.... But if you want to know, we really have something in common."

"I should like to know what."

"Why, it's all about a house-painter.... We are getting him out of a mess! Though indeed there's nothing to fear now. The matter is absolutely self-evident. We only put on steam."

"A painter?"

"Why, haven't I told you about it? I only told you the beginning then about the murder of the old pawnbroker-woman. Well, the painter is mixed up in it..."

"Oh, I heard about that murder before and was rather interested in it... partly... for one reason.... I read about it in the papers, too...."

"Lizaveta was murdered, too," Nastasya blurted out, suddenly addressing Raskolnikov. She remained in the room all the time, standing by the door listening.

"Lizaveta," murmured Raskolnikov hardly audibly.

"Lizaveta, who sold old clothes. Didn't you know her? She used to come here. She mended a shirt for you, too."

Raskolnikov turned to the wall where in the dirty, yellow paper he picked out one clumsy, white flower with brown lines on it and began examining how many petals there were in it, how many scallops in the petals and how many lines on them. He felt his arms and legs as lifeless as though they had been cut off. He did not attempt to move, but stared obstinately at the flower.

"But what about the painter?" Zossimov interrupted Nastasya's chatter with marked displeasure. She sighed and was silent.

"Why, he was accused of the murder," Razumihin went on hotly.

"Was there evidence against him then?"

"Evidence, indeed! Evidence that was no evidence, and that's what we have to prove. It was just as they pitched on those fellows, Koch and Pestryakov, at first. Foo! how stupidly it's all done, it makes one sick, though it's not one's business! Pestryakov may be coming to-night.... By the way, Rodya, you've heard about the business already; it happened before you were ill, the day before you fainted at the police office while they were talking about it."

Zossimov looked curiously at Raskolnikov. He did not stir.

"But I say, Razumihin, I wonder at you. What a busybody you are!" Zossimov observed.

"Maybe I am, but we will get him off anyway," shouted Razumihin, bringing his fist down on the table. "What's the most offensive is not their lying—one can always forgive lying—lying is a delightful thing, for it leads to truth—what is offensive is that they lie and worship their own lying.... I respect Porfiry, but... What threw them out at first? The door was locked, and when they came back with the porter it was open. So it followed that Koch and Pestryakov were the murderers—that was their logic!"

"But don't excite yourself; they simply detained them, they could not help that.... And, by the way, I've met that man Koch. He used to buy unredeemed pledges from the old woman? Eh?"

"Yes, he is a swindler. He buys up bad debts, too. He makes a profession of it. But enough of him! Do you know what makes me angry? It's their sickening rotten, petrified routine.... And this case might be the means of introducing a new method. One can show from the psychological data alone how to get on the track of the real man. 'We have facts,' they say. But facts are not everything—at least half the business lies in how you interpret them!"

"Can you interpret them, then?"

"Anyway, one can't hold one's tongue when one has a feeling, a tangible feeling, that one might be a help if only.... Eh! Do you know the details of the case?"

"I am waiting to hear about the painter."

"Oh, yes! Well, here's the story. Early on the third day after the murder, when they were still dandling Koch and Pestryakov—though they accounted for every step they took and it was as plain as a pikestaff—an unexpected fact turned up. A peasant called Dushkin, who keeps a dram-shop facing the house, brought to the police office a jeweller's case containing some gold ear-rings, and told a long rigamarole. 'The day before yesterday, just after eight o'clock'—mark the day and the hour!—'a journeyman house-painter, Nikolay, who had been in to see me already that day, brought me this box of gold ear-rings and stones, and asked me to give him two roubles for them. When I asked him where he got them, he said that he picked them up in the street. I did not ask him anything more.' I am telling you Dushkin's story. 'I gave him a note'—a rouble that is—'for I thought if he did not pawn it with me he would with another. It would all come to the same thing—he'd spend it on drink, so the thing had better be with me. The further you hide it the quicker you will find it, and if anything turns up, if I hear any rumours, I'll take it to the police.' Of course, that's all taradiddle; he lies like a horse, for I know this Dushkin, he is a pawnbroker and a receiver of stolen goods, and he did not cheat Nikolay out of a thirty-rouble trinket in order to give it to the police. He was simply afraid. But no matter, to return to Dushkin's story. 'I've known this peasant, Nikolay Dementyev, from a child; he comes from the same province and district of Zaraïsk, we are both Ryazan men. And though Nikolay is not a drunkard, he drinks, and I knew he had a job in that house, painting work with Dmitri, who comes from the same village, too. As soon as he got the rouble he changed it, had a couple of glasses, took his change and went out. But I did not see Dmitri with him then. And the next day I heard that someone had murdered Alyona Ivanovna and her sister, Lizaveta Ivanovna, with an axe. I knew them, and I felt suspicious about the ear-rings at once, for I knew the murdered woman lent money on pledges. I went to the house, and began to make careful inquiries without saying a word to anyone. First of all I asked, "Is Nikolay here?" Dmitri told me that Nikolay had gone off on the spree; he had come home at daybreak drunk, stayed in the house about ten minutes, and went out again. Dmitri didn't see him again and is finishing the job alone. And their job is on the same staircase as the murder, on the second floor. When I heard all that I did not say a word to anyone'—that's Dushkin's tale—'but I found out what I could about the murder, and went home feeling as suspicious as ever. And at eight o'clock this morning'—that was the third day, you understand—'I saw Nikolay coming in, not sober, though not to say very drunk—he could understand what was said to him. He sat down on the bench and did not speak. There was only one stranger in the bar and a man I knew asleep on a bench and our two boys. "Have you seen Dmitri?" said I. "No, I haven't," said he. "And you've not been here either?" "Not since the day before yesterday," said he. "And where did you sleep last night?" "In Peski, with the Kolomensky men." "And where did you get those ear-rings?" I asked. "I found them in the street," and the way he said it was a bit queer; he did not look at me. "Did you hear what happened that very evening, at that very hour, on that same staircase?" said I. "No," said he, "I had not heard," and all the while he was listening, his eyes were staring out of his head and he turned as white as chalk. I told him all about it and he took his hat and began getting up. I wanted to keep him. "Wait a bit, Nikolay," said I, "won't you have a drink?" And I signed to the boy to hold the door, and I came out from behind the bar; but he darted out and down the street to the turning at a run. I have not seen him since. Then my doubts were at an end—it was his doing, as clear as could be...."'

"I should think so," said Zossimov.

"Wait! Hear the end. Of course they sought high and low for Nikolay; they detained Dushkin and searched his house; Dmitri, too, was arrested; the Kolomensky men also were turned inside out. And the day before yesterday they arrested Nikolay in a tavern at the end of the town. He had gone there, taken the silver cross off his neck and asked for a dram for it. They gave it to him. A few minutes afterwards the woman went to the cowshed, and through a crack in the wall she saw in the stable adjoining he had made a noose of his sash from the beam, stood on a block of wood, and was trying to put his neck in the noose. The woman screeched her hardest; people ran in. 'So that's what you are up to!' 'Take me,' he says, 'to such-and-such a police officer; I'll confess everything.' Well, they took him to that police station—that is here—with a suitable escort. So they asked him this and that, how old he is, 'twenty-two,' and so on. At the question, 'When you were working with Dmitri, didn't you see anyone on the staircase at such-and-such a time?'—answer: 'To be sure folks may have gone up and down, but I did not notice them.' 'And didn't you hear anything, any noise, and so on?' 'We heard nothing special.' 'And did you hear, Nikolay, that on the same day Widow So-and-so and her sister were murdered and robbed?' 'I never knew a thing about it. The first I heard of it was from Afanasy Pavlovitch the day before yesterday.' 'And where did you find the ear-rings?' 'I found them on the pavement.' 'Why didn't you go to work with Dmitri the other day?' 'Because I was drinking.' 'And where were you drinking?' 'Oh, in such-and-such a place.' 'Why did you run away from Dushkin's?' 'Because I was awfully frightened.' 'What were you frightened of?' 'That I should be accused.' 'How could you be frightened, if you felt free from guilt?' Now, Zossimov, you may not believe me, that question was put literally in those words. I know it for a fact, it was repeated to me exactly! What do you say to that?"

"Well, anyway, there's the evidence."

"I am not talking of the evidence now, I am talking about that question, of their own idea of themselves. Well, so they squeezed and squeezed him and he confessed: 'I did not find it in the street, but in the flat where I was painting with Dmitri.' 'And how was that?' 'Why, Dmitri and I were painting there all day, and we were just

423

getting ready to go, and Dmitri took a brush and painted my face, and he ran off and I after him. I ran after him, shouting my hardest, and at the bottom of the stairs I ran right against the porter and some gentlemen—and how many gentlemen were there I don't remember. And the porter swore at me, and the other porter swore, too, and the porter's wife came out, and swore at us, too; and a gentleman came into the entry with a lady, and he swore at us, too, for Dmitri and I lay right across the way. I got hold of Dmitri's hair and knocked him down and began beating him. And Dmitri, too, caught me by the hair and began beating me. But we did it all not for temper but in a friendly way, for sport. And then Dmitri escaped and ran into the street, and I ran after him; but I did not catch him, and went back to the flat alone; I had to clear up my things. I began putting them together, expecting Dmitri to come, and there in the passage, in the corner by the door, I stepped on the box. I saw it lying there wrapped up in paper. I took off the paper, saw some little hooks, undid them, and in the box were the ear-rings....'"

"Behind the door? Lying behind the door? Behind the door?" Raskolnikov cried suddenly, staring with a blank look of terror at Razumihin, and he slowly sat up on the sofa, leaning on his hand.

"Yes... why? What's the matter? What's wrong?" Razumihin, too, got up from his seat.

"Nothing," Raskolnikov answered faintly, turning to the wall. All were silent for a while.

"He must have waked from a dream," Razumihin said at last, looking inquiringly at Zossimov. The latter slightly shook his head.

"Well, go on," said Zossimov. "What next?"

"What next? As soon as he saw the ear-rings, forgetting Dmitri and everything, he took up his cap and ran to Dushkin and, as we know, got a rouble from him. He told a lie saying he found them in the street, and went off drinking. He keeps repeating his old story about the murder: 'I know nothing of it, never heard of it till the day before yesterday.' 'And why didn't you come to the police till now?' 'I was frightened.' 'And why did you try to hang yourself?' 'From anxiety.' 'What anxiety?' 'That I should be accused of it.' Well, that's the whole story. And now what do you suppose they deduced from that?"

"Why, there's no supposing. There's a clue, such as it is, a fact. You wouldn't have your painter set free?"

"Now they've simply taken him for the murderer. They haven't a shadow of doubt."

"That's nonsense. You are excited. But what about the ear-rings? You must admit that, if on the very same day and hour ear-rings from the old woman's box have come into Nikolay's hands, they must have come there somehow. That's a good deal in such a case."

"How did they get there? How did they get there?" cried Razumihin. "How can you, a doctor, whose duty it is to study man and who has more opportunity than anyone else for studying human nature—how can you fail to see the character of the man in the whole story? Don't you see at once that the answers he has given in the examination are the holy truth? They came into his hand precisely as he has told us—he stepped on the box and picked it up."

"The holy truth! But didn't he own himself that he told a lie at first?"

"Listen to me, listen attentively. The porter and Koch and Pestryakov and the other porter and the wife of the first porter and the woman who was sitting in the porter's lodge and the man Kryukov, who had just got out of a cab at that minute and went in at the entry with a lady on his arm, that is eight or ten witnesses, agree that Nikolay had Dmitri on the ground, was lying on him beating him, while Dmitri hung on to his hair, beating him, too. They lay right across the way, blocking the thoroughfare. They were sworn at on all sides while they 'like children' (the very words of the witnesses) were falling over one another, squealing, fighting and laughing with the funniest faces, and, chasing one another like children, they ran into the street. Now take careful note. The bodies upstairs were warm, you understand, warm when they found them! If they, or Nikolay alone, had murdered them and broken open the boxes, or simply taken part in the robbery, allow me to ask you one question: do their state of mind, their squeals and giggles and childish scuffling at the gate fit in with axes, bloodshed, fiendish cunning, robbery? They'd just killed them, not five or ten minutes before, for the bodies were still warm, and at once, leaving the flat open, knowing that people would go there at once, flinging away their booty, they rolled about like children, laughing and attracting general attention. And there are a dozen witnesses to swear to that!"

"Of course it is strange! It's impossible, indeed, but..."

"No, brother, no *buts*. And if the ear-rings being found in Nikolay's hands at the very day and hour of the murder constitutes an important piece of circumstantial evidence against him—although the explanation given by him accounts for it, and therefore it does not tell seriously against him—one must take into consideration the facts which prove him innocent, especially as they are facts that *cannot be denied*. And do you suppose, from the character of our legal system, that they will accept, or that they are in a position to accept, this fact—resting simply on a psychological impossibility—as irrefutable and conclusively breaking down the circumstantial evidence for the prosecution? No, they won't accept it, they certainly won't, because they found the jewel-case and the man tried to hang himself, 'which he could not have done if he hadn't felt guilty.' That's the point, that's what excites me, you must understand!"

"Oh, I see you are excited! Wait a bit. I forgot to ask you; what proof is there that the box came from the old woman?"

"That's been proved," said Razumihin with apparent reluctance, frowning. "Koch recognised the jewel-case and gave the name of the owner, who proved conclusively that it was his."

"That's bad. Now another point. Did anyone see Nikolay at the time that Koch and Pestryakov were going upstairs at first, and is there no evidence about that?"

"Nobody did see him," Razumihin answered with vexation. "That's the worst of it. Even Koch and Pestryakov did not notice them on their way upstairs, though, indeed, their evidence could not have been worth much. They said they saw the flat was open, and that there must be work going on in it, but they took no special notice and could not remember whether there actually were men at work in it."

"Hm!... So the only evidence for the defence is that they were beating one another and laughing. That constitutes a strong presumption, but... How do you explain the facts yourself?"

"How do I explain them? What is there to explain? It's clear. At any rate, the direction in which explanation is to be sought is clear, and the jewel-case points to it. The real murderer dropped those ear-rings. The murderer was upstairs, locked in, when Koch and Pestryakov knocked at the door. Koch, like an ass, did not stay at the door; so the murderer popped out and ran down, too; for he had no other way of escape. He hid from Koch, Pestryakov and the porter in the flat when Nikolay and Dmitri had just run out of it. He stopped there while the porter and others were going upstairs, waited till they were out of hearing, and then went calmly downstairs at the very minute when Dmitri and Nikolay ran out into the street and there was no one in the entry; possibly he was seen, but not noticed. There are lots of people going in and out. He must have dropped the ear-rings out of his pocket when he stood behind the door, and did not notice he dropped them, because he had other things to think of. The jewel-case is a conclusive proof that he did stand there.... That's how I explain it."

"Too clever! No, my boy, you're too clever. That beats everything."

"But, why, why?"

"Why, because everything fits too well... it's too melodramatic."

"A-ach!" Razumihin was exclaiming, but at that moment the door opened and a personage came in who was a stranger to all present.

CHAPTER V

This was a gentleman no longer young, of a stiff and portly appearance, and a cautious and sour countenance. He began by stopping short in the doorway, staring about him with offensive and undisguised astonishment, as though asking himself what sort of place he had come to. Mistrustfully and with an affectation of being alarmed and almost affronted, he scanned Raskolnikov's low and narrow "cabin." With the same amazement he stared at Raskolnikov, who lay undressed, dishevelled, unwashed, on his miserable dirty sofa, looking fixedly at him. Then with the same deliberation he scrutinised the uncouth, unkempt figure and unshaven face of Razumihin, who looked him boldly and inquiringly in the face without rising from his seat. A constrained silence lasted for a couple of minutes, and then, as might be expected, some scene-shifting took place. Reflecting, probably from certain fairly unmistakable signs, that he would get nothing in this "cabin" by attempting to overawe them, the gentleman softened somewhat, and civilly, though with some severity, emphasising every syllable of his question, addressed Zossimov:

"Rodion Romanovitch Raskolnikov, a student, or formerly a student?"

Zossimov made a slight movement, and would have answered, had not Razumihin anticipated him.

"Here he is lying on the sofa! What do you want?"

This familiar "what do you want" seemed to cut the ground from the feet of the pompous gentleman. He was turning to Razumihin, but checked himself in time and turned to Zossimov again.

"This is Raskolnikov," mumbled Zossimov, nodding towards him. Then he gave a prolonged yawn, opening his mouth as wide as possible. Then he lazily put his hand into his waistcoat-pocket, pulled out a huge gold watch in a round hunter's case, opened it, looked at it and as slowly and lazily proceeded to put it back.

Raskolnikov himself lay without speaking, on his back, gazing persistently, though without understanding, at the stranger. Now that his face was turned away from the strange flower on the paper, it was extremely pale and wore a look of anguish, as though he had just undergone an agonising operation or just been taken from the rack. But the new-comer gradually began to arouse his attention, then his wonder, then suspicion and even alarm. When Zossimov said "This is Raskolnikov" he jumped up quickly, sat on the sofa and with an almost defiant, but weak and breaking, voice articulated:

"Yes, I am Raskolnikov! What do you want?"

The visitor scrutinised him and pronounced impressively:

"Pyotr Petrovitch Luzhin. I believe I have reason to hope that my name is not wholly unknown to you?"

But Raskolnikov, who had expected something quite different, gazed blankly and dreamily at him, making no reply, as though he heard the name of Pyotr Petrovitch for the first time.

"Is it possible that you can up to the present have received no information?" asked Pyotr Petrovitch, somewhat disconcerted.

In reply Raskolnikov sank languidly back on the pillow, put his hands behind his head and gazed at the ceiling. A look of dismay came into Luzhin's face. Zossimov and Razumihin stared at him more inquisitively than ever, and at last he showed unmistakable signs of embarrassment.

"I had presumed and calculated," he faltered, "that a letter posted more than ten days, if not a fortnight ago..."

"I say, why are you standing in the doorway?" Razumihin interrupted suddenly. "If you've something to say, sit down. Nastasya and you are so crowded. Nastasya, make room. Here's a chair, thread your way in!"

He moved his chair back from the table, made a little space between the table and his knees, and waited in a rather cramped position for the visitor to "thread his way in." The minute was so chosen that it was impossible to refuse, and the visitor squeezed his way through, hurrying and stumbling. Reaching the chair, he sat down, looking suspiciously at Razumihin.

"No need to be nervous," the latter blurted out. "Rodya has been ill for the last five days and delirious for three, but now he is recovering and has got an appetite. This is his doctor, who has just had a look at him. I am a comrade of Rodya's, like him, formerly a student, and now I am nursing him; so don't you take any notice of us, but go on with your business."

"Thank you. But shall I not disturb the invalid by my presence and conversation?" Pyotr Petrovitch asked of Zossimov.

"N-no," mumbled Zossimov; "you may amuse him." He yawned again.

"He has been conscious a long time, since the morning," went on Razumihin, whose familiarity seemed so much like unaffected good-nature that Pyotr Petrovitch began to be more cheerful, partly, perhaps, because this shabby and impudent person had introduced himself as a student.

"Your mamma," began Luzhin.

"Hm!" Razumihin cleared his throat loudly. Luzhin looked at him inquiringly.

"That's all right, go on."

Luzhin shrugged his shoulders.

"Your mamma had commenced a letter to you while I was sojourning in her neighbourhood. On my arrival here I purposely allowed a few days to elapse before coming to see you, in order that I might be fully assured that you were in full possession of the tidings; but now, to my astonishment..."

"I know, I know!" Raskolnikov cried suddenly with impatient vexation. "So you are the *fiancé*? I know, and that's enough!"

There was no doubt about Pyotr Petrovitch's being offended this time, but he said nothing. He made a violent effort to understand what it all meant. There was a moment's silence.

Meanwhile Raskolnikov, who had turned a little towards him when he answered, began suddenly staring at him again with marked curiosity, as though he had not had a good look at him yet, or as though something new had struck him; he rose from his pillow on purpose to stare at him. There certainly was something peculiar in Pyotr Petrovitch's whole appearance, something which seemed to justify the title of "fiancé" so unceremoniously applied to him. In the first place, it was evident, far too much so indeed, that Pyotr Petrovitch had made eager use of his few days in the capital to get himself up and rig himself out in expectation of his betrothed—a perfectly innocent and permissible proceeding, indeed. Even his own, perhaps too complacent, consciousness of the agreeable improvement in his appearance might have been forgiven in such circumstances, seeing that Pyotr Petrovitch had taken up the rôle of fiancé. All his clothes were fresh from the tailor's and were all right, except for being too new and too distinctly appropriate. Even the stylish new round hat had the same significance. Pyotr Petrovitch treated it too respectfully and held it too carefully in his hands. The exquisite pair of lavender gloves, real Louvain, told the same tale, if only from the fact of his not wearing them, but carrying them in his hand for show. Light and youthful colours predominated in Pyotr Petrovitch's attire. He wore a charming summer jacket of a fawn shade, light thin trousers, a waistcoat of the same, new and fine linen, a cravat of the lightest cambric with pink stripes on it, and the best of it was, this all suited Pyotr Petrovitch. His very fresh and even handsome face looked younger than his forty-five years at all times. His dark, mutton-chop whiskers made an agreeable setting on both sides, growing thickly upon his shining, clean-shaven chin. Even his hair, touched here and there with grey, though it had been combed and curled at a hairdresser's, did not give him a stupid appearance, as curled hair usually does, by inevitably suggesting a German on his wedding-day. If there really was something unpleasing and repulsive in his rather good-looking and imposing countenance, it was due to quite other causes. After scanning Mr. Luzhin unceremoniously, Raskolnikov smiled malignantly, sank back on the pillow and stared at the ceiling as before.

But Mr. Luzhin hardened his heart and seemed to determine to take no notice of their oddities.

"I feel the greatest regret at finding you in this situation," he began, again breaking the silence with an effort. "If I had been aware of your illness I should have come earlier. But you know what business is. I have, too, a very important legal affair in the Senate, not to mention other preoccupations which you may well conjecture. I am expecting your mamma and sister any minute."

Raskolnikov made a movement and seemed about to speak; his face showed some excitement. Pyotr Petrovitch paused, waited, but as nothing followed, he went on:

"... Any minute. I have found a lodging for them on their arrival."

"Where?" asked Raskolnikov weakly.

"Very near here, in Bakaleyev's house."

"That's in Voskresensky," put in Razumihin. "There are two storeys of rooms, let by a merchant called Yushin; I've been there."

"Yes, rooms..."

"A disgusting place—filthy, stinking and, what's more, of doubtful character. Things have happened there, and there are all sorts of queer people living there. And I went there about a scandalous business. It's cheap, though..."

"I could not, of course, find out so much about it, for I am a stranger in Petersburg myself," Pyotr Petrovitch replied huffily. "However, the two rooms are exceedingly clean, and as it is for so short a time... I have already taken a permanent, that is, our future flat," he said, addressing Raskolnikov, "and I am having it done up. And meanwhile I am myself cramped for room in a lodging with my friend Andrey Semyonovitch Lebeziatnikov, in the flat of Madame Lippevechsel; it was he who told me of Bakaleyev's house, too..."

"Lebeziatnikov?" said Raskolnikov slowly, as if recalling something.

"Yes, Andrey Semyonovitch Lebeziatnikov, a clerk in the Ministry. Do you know him?"

"Yes... no," Raskolnikov answered.

"Excuse me, I fancied so from your inquiry. I was once his guardian.... A very nice young man and advanced. I like to meet young people: one learns new things from them." Luzhin looked round hopefully at them all.

"How do you mean?" asked Razumihin.

"In the most serious and essential matters," Pyotr Petrovitch replied, as though delighted at the question. "You see, it's ten years since I visited Petersburg. All the novelties, reforms, ideas have reached us in the provinces, but to see it all more clearly one must be in Petersburg. And it's my notion that you observe and learn most by watching the younger generation. And I confess I am delighted..."

"At what?"

"Your question is a wide one. I may be mistaken, but I fancy I find clearer views, more, so to say, criticism, more practicality..."

"That's true," Zossimov let drop.

"Nonsense! There's no practicality." Razumihin flew at him. "Practicality is a difficult thing to find; it does not drop down from heaven. And for the last two hundred years we have been divorced from all practical life. Ideas, if you like, are fermenting," he said to Pyotr Petrovitch, "and desire for good exists, though it's in a childish form, and honesty you may find, although there are crowds of brigands. Anyway, there's no practicality. Practicality goes well shod."

"I don't agree with you," Pyotr Petrovitch replied, with evident enjoyment. "Of course, people do get carried away and make mistakes, but one must have indulgence; those mistakes are merely evidence of enthusiasm for the cause and of abnormal external environment. If little has been done, the time has been but short; of means I will not speak. It's my personal view, if you care to know, that something has been accomplished already. New valuable ideas, new valuable works are circulating in the place of our old dreamy and romantic authors. Literature is taking a maturer form, many injurious prejudices have been rooted up and turned into ridicule.... In a word, we have cut ourselves off irrevocably from the past, and that, to my thinking, is a great thing..."

"He's learnt it by heart to show off!" Raskolnikov pronounced suddenly.

"What?" asked Pyotr Petrovitch, not catching his words; but he received no reply.

"That's all true," Zossimov hastened to interpose.

"Isn't it so?" Pyotr Petrovitch went on, glancing affably at Zossimov. "You must admit," he went on, addressing Razumihin with a shade of triumph and superciliousness—he almost added "young man"—"that there is an advance, or, as they say now, progress in the name of science and economic truth..."

"A commonplace."

"No, not a commonplace! Hitherto, for instance, if I were told, 'love thy neighbour,' what came of it?" Pyotr Petrovitch went on, perhaps with excessive haste. "It came to my tearing my coat in half to share with my neighbour and we both were left half naked. As a Russian proverb has it, 'Catch several hares and you won't catch one.' Science now tells us, love yourself before all men, for everything in the world rests on self-interest. You love yourself and manage your own affairs properly and your coat remains whole. Economic truth adds that the better private affairs are organised in society—the more whole coats, so to say—the firmer are its foundations and the better is the common welfare organised too. Therefore, in acquiring wealth solely and exclusively for myself, I am acquiring, so to speak, for all, and helping to bring to pass my neighbour's getting a little more than a torn coat; and that not from private, personal liberality, but as a consequence of the general advance. The idea is simple, but unhappily it has been a long time reaching us, being hindered by idealism and sentimentality. And yet it would seem to want very little wit to perceive it..."

"Excuse me, I've very little wit myself," Razumihin cut in sharply, "and so let us drop it. I began this discussion with an object, but I've grown so sick during the last three years of this chattering to amuse oneself, of this incessant flow of commonplaces, always the same, that, by Jove, I blush even when other people talk like that. You are in a hurry, no doubt, to exhibit your acquirements; and I don't blame you, that's quite pardonable. I only wanted to find out what sort of man you are, for so many unscrupulous people have got hold of the progressive cause of late and have so distorted in their own interests everything they touched, that the whole cause has been dragged in the mire. That's enough!"

"Excuse me, sir," said Luzhin, affronted, and speaking with excessive dignity. "Do you mean to suggest so unceremoniously that I too..."

"Oh, my dear sir... how could I?... Come, that's enough," Razumihin concluded, and he turned abruptly to Zossimov to continue their previous conversation.

Pyotr Petrovitch had the good sense to accept the disavowal. He made up his mind to take leave in another minute or two.

"I trust our acquaintance," he said, addressing Raskolnikov, "may, upon your recovery and in view of the circumstances of which you are aware, become closer... Above all, I hope for your return to health..."

Raskolnikov did not even turn his head. Pyotr Petrovitch began getting up from his chair.

"One of her customers must have killed her," Zossimov declared positively.

"Not a doubt of it," replied Razumihin. "Porfiry doesn't give his opinion, but is examining all who have left pledges with her there."

"Examining them?" Raskolnikov asked aloud.

"Yes. What then?"

"Nothing."

"How does he get hold of them?" asked Zossimov.

"Koch has given the names of some of them, other names are on the wrappers of the pledges and some have come forward of themselves."

"It must have been a cunning and practised ruffian! The boldness of it! The coolness!"

"That's just what it wasn't!" interposed Razumihin. "That's what throws you all off the scent. But I maintain that he is not cunning, not practised, and probably this was his first crime! The supposition that it was a calculated crime and a cunning criminal doesn't work. Suppose him to have been inexperienced, and it's clear that it was only a chance that saved him—and chance may do anything. Why, he did not foresee obstacles, perhaps! And how did he set to work? He took jewels worth ten or twenty roubles, stuffing his pockets with them, ransacked the old woman's trunks, her rags—and they found fifteen hundred roubles, besides notes, in a box in the top drawer of the chest! He did not know how to rob; he could only murder. It was his first crime, I assure you, his first crime; he lost his head. And he got off more by luck than good counsel!"

"You are talking of the murder of the old pawnbroker, I believe?" Pyotr Petrovitch put in, addressing Zossimov. He was standing, hat and gloves in hand, but before departing he felt disposed to throw off a few more intellectual phrases. He was evidently anxious to make a favourable impression and his vanity overcame his prudence.

"Yes. You've heard of it?"

"Oh, yes, being in the neighbourhood."

"Do you know the details?"

"I can't say that; but another circumstance interests me in the case—the whole question, so to say. Not to speak of the fact that crime has been greatly on the increase among the lower classes during the last five years, not to speak of the cases of robbery and arson everywhere, what strikes me as the strangest thing is that in the higher classes, too, crime is increasing proportionately. In one place one hears of a student's robbing the mail on the high road; in another place people of good social position forge false banknotes; in Moscow of late a whole gang has been captured who used to forge lottery tickets, and one of the ringleaders was a lecturer in universal history; then our secretary abroad was murdered from some obscure motive of gain.... And if this old woman, the pawnbroker, has been murdered by someone of a higher class in society—for peasants don't pawn gold trinkets—how are we to explain this demoralisation of the civilised part of our society?"

"There are many economic changes," put in Zossimov.

"How are we to explain it?" Razumihin caught him up. "It might be explained by our inveterate impracticality."

"How do you mean?"

"What answer had your lecturer in Moscow to make to the question why he was forging notes? 'Everybody is getting rich one way or another, so I want to make haste to get rich too.' I don't remember the exact words, but the upshot was that he wants money for nothing, without waiting or working! We've grown used to having everything ready-made, to walking on crutches, to having our food chewed for us. Then the great hour struck,[*] and every man showed himself in his true colours."

[*] *The emancipation of the serfs in 1861 is meant.*
—*TRANSLATOR'S NOTE.*

"But morality? And so to speak, principles..."

"But why do you worry about it?" Raskolnikov interposed suddenly. "It's in accordance with your theory!"

"In accordance with my theory?"

"Why, carry out logically the theory you were advocating just now, and it follows that people may be killed..."

"Upon my word!" cried Luzhin.

"No, that's not so," put in Zossimov.

Raskolnikov lay with a white face and twitching upper lip, breathing painfully.

"There's a measure in all things," Luzhin went on superciliously. "Economic ideas are not an incitement to murder, and one has but to suppose..."

"And is it true," Raskolnikov interposed once more suddenly, again in a voice quivering with fury and delight in insulting him, "is it true that you told your *fiancée*... within an hour of her acceptance, that what pleased you most... was that she was a beggar... because it was better to raise a wife from poverty, so that you may have complete control over her, and reproach her with your being her benefactor?"

"Upon my word," Luzhin cried wrathfully and irritably, crimson with confusion, "to distort my words in this way! Excuse me, allow me to assure you that the report which has reached you, or rather, let me say, has been conveyed to you, has no foundation in truth, and I... suspect who... in a word... this arrow... in a word, your mamma... She seemed to me in other things, with all her excellent qualities, of a somewhat high-flown and romantic way of thinking.... But I was a thousand miles from supposing that she would misunderstand and misrepresent things in so fanciful a way.... And indeed... indeed..."

"I tell you what," cried Raskolnikov, raising himself on his pillow and fixing his piercing, glittering eyes upon him, "I tell you what."

"What?" Luzhin stood still, waiting with a defiant and offended face. Silence lasted for some seconds.

"Why, if ever again... you dare to mention a single word... about my mother... I shall send you flying downstairs!"

"What's the matter with you?" cried Razumihin.

"So that's how it is?" Luzhin turned pale and bit his lip. "Let me tell you, sir," he began deliberately, doing his utmost to restrain himself but breathing hard, "at the first moment I saw you you were ill-disposed to me, but I remained here on purpose to find out more. I could forgive a great deal in a sick man and a connection, but you... never after this..."

"I am not ill," cried Raskolnikov.

"So much the worse..."

"Go to hell!"

But Luzhin was already leaving without finishing his speech, squeezing between the table and the chair; Razumihin got up this time to let him pass. Without glancing at anyone, and not even nodding to Zossimov, who had for some time been making signs to him to let the sick man alone, he went out, lifting his hat to the level of his shoulders to avoid crushing it as he stooped to go out of the door. And even the curve of his spine was expressive of the horrible insult he had received.

"How could you—how could you!" Razumihin said, shaking his head in perplexity.

"Let me alone—let me alone all of you!" Raskolnikov cried in a frenzy. "Will you ever leave off tormenting me? I am not afraid of you! I am not afraid of anyone, anyone now! Get away from me! I want to be alone, alone, alone!"

"Come along," said Zossimov, nodding to Razumihin.

"But we can't leave him like this!"

"Come along," Zossimov repeated insistently, and he went out. Razumihin thought a minute and ran to overtake him.

"It might be worse not to obey him," said Zossimov on the stairs. "He mustn't be irritated."

"What's the matter with him?"

"If only he could get some favourable shock, that's what would do it! At first he was better.... You know he has got something on his mind! Some fixed idea weighing on him.... I am very much afraid so; he must have!"

"Perhaps it's that gentleman, Pyotr Petrovitch. From his conversation I gather he is going to marry his sister, and that he had received a letter about it just before his illness...."

"Yes, confound the man! he may have upset the case altogether. But have you noticed, he takes no interest in anything, he does not respond to anything except one point on which he seems excited—that's the murder?"

"Yes, yes," Razumihin agreed, "I noticed that, too. He is interested, frightened. It gave him a shock on the day he was ill in the police office; he fainted."

"Tell me more about that this evening and I'll tell you something afterwards. He interests me very much! In half an hour I'll go and see him again.... There'll be no inflammation though."

"Thanks! And I'll wait with Pashenka meantime and will keep watch on him through Nastasya...."

Raskolnikov, left alone, looked with impatience and misery at Nastasya, but she still lingered.

"Won't you have some tea now?" she asked.

"Later! I am sleepy! Leave me."

He turned abruptly to the wall; Nastasya went out.

CHAPTER VI

But as soon as she went out, he got up, latched the door, undid the parcel which Razumihin had brought in that evening and had tied up again and began dressing. Strange to say, he seemed immediately to have become perfectly calm; not a trace of his recent delirium nor of the panic fear that had haunted him of late. It was the first moment of a strange sudden calm. His movements were precise and definite; a firm purpose was evident in them. "To-day, to-day," he muttered to himself. He understood that he was still weak, but his intense spiritual concentration gave him strength and self-confidence. He hoped, moreover, that he would not fall down in the street. When he had dressed in entirely new clothes, he looked at the money lying on the table, and after a moment's thought put it in his pocket. It was twenty-five roubles. He took also all the copper change from the ten roubles spent by Razumihin on the clothes. Then he softly unlatched the door, went out, slipped downstairs and glanced in at the open kitchen door. Nastasya was standing with her back to him, blowing up the landlady's samovar. She heard nothing. Who would have dreamed of his going out, indeed? A minute later he was in the street.

It was nearly eight o'clock, the sun was setting. It was as stifling as before, but he eagerly drank in the stinking, dusty town air. His head felt rather dizzy; a sort of savage energy gleamed suddenly in his feverish eyes and his wasted, pale and yellow face. He did not know and did not think where he was going, he had one thought only: "that all *this* must be ended to-day, once for all, immediately; that he would not return home without it, because he *would not go on living like that*." How, with what to make an end? He had not an idea about it, he did not even want to think of it. He drove away thought; thought tortured him. All he knew, all he felt was that everything must be changed "one way or another," he repeated with desperate and immovable self-confidence and determination.

From old habit he took his usual walk in the direction of the Hay Market. A dark-haired young man with a barrel organ was standing in the road in front of a little general shop and was grinding out a very sentimental song. He was accompanying a girl of fifteen, who stood on the pavement in front of him. She was dressed up in a crinoline, a mantle and a straw hat with a flame-coloured feather in it, all very old and shabby. In a strong and rather agreeable voice, cracked and coarsened by street singing, she sang in hope of getting a copper from the shop. Raskolnikov joined two or three listeners, took out a five copeck piece and put it in the girl's hand. She broke off abruptly on a sentimental high note, shouted sharply to the organ grinder "Come on," and both moved on to the next shop.

"Do you like street music?" said Raskolnikov, addressing a middle-aged man standing idly by him. The man looked at him, startled and wondering.

"I love to hear singing to a street organ," said Raskolnikov, and his manner seemed strangely out of keeping with the subject—"I like it on cold, dark, damp autumn evenings—they must be damp—when all the passers-by have pale green, sickly faces, or better still when wet snow is falling straight down, when there's no wind—you know what I mean?—and the street lamps shine through it..."

"I don't know.... Excuse me..." muttered the stranger, frightened by the question and Raskolnikov's strange manner, and he crossed over to the other side of the street.

Raskolnikov walked straight on and came out at the corner of the Hay Market, where the huckster and his wife had talked with Lizaveta; but they were not there now. Recognising the place, he stopped, looked round and addressed a young fellow in a red shirt who stood gaping before a corn chandler's shop.

"Isn't there a man who keeps a booth with his wife at this corner?"

"All sorts of people keep booths here," answered the young man, glancing superciliously at Raskolnikov.

"What's his name?"

"What he was christened."

"Aren't you a Zaraïsky man, too? Which province?"

The young man looked at Raskolnikov again.

"It's not a province, your excellency, but a district. Graciously forgive me, your excellency!"

"Is that a tavern at the top there?"

"Yes, it's an eating-house and there's a billiard-room and you'll find princesses there too.... La-la!"

Raskolnikov crossed the square. In that corner there was a dense crowd of peasants. He pushed his way into the thickest part of it, looking at the faces. He felt an unaccountable inclination to enter into conversation with people. But the peasants took no notice of him; they were all shouting in groups together. He stood and thought a little and took a turning to the right in the direction of V.

He had often crossed that little street which turns at an angle, leading from the market-place to Sadovy Street. Of late he had often felt drawn to wander about this district, when he felt depressed, that he might feel more so.

Now he walked along, thinking of nothing. At that point there is a great block of buildings, entirely let out in dram shops and eating-houses; women were continually running in and out, bare-headed and in their indoor clothes. Here and there they gathered in groups, on the pavement, especially about the entrances to various festive establishments in the lower storeys. From one of these a loud din, sounds of singing, the tinkling of a guitar and shouts of merriment, floated into the street. A crowd of women were thronging round the door; some were sitting on the steps, others on the pavement, others were standing talking. A drunken soldier, smoking a cigarette, was walking near them in the road, swearing; he seemed to be trying to find his way somewhere, but had forgotten where. One beggar was quarrelling with another, and a man dead drunk was lying right across the road. Raskolnikov joined the throng of women, who were talking in husky voices. They were bare-headed and wore cotton dresses and goatskin shoes. There were women of forty and some not more than seventeen; almost all had blackened eyes.

He felt strangely attracted by the singing and all the noise and uproar in the saloon below.... someone could be heard within dancing frantically, marking time with his heels to the sounds of the guitar and of a thin falsetto voice singing a jaunty air. He listened intently, gloomily and dreamily, bending down at the entrance and peeping inquisitively in from the pavement.

"Oh,   my   handsome   soldier
Don't beat me for nothing,"

trilled the thin voice of the singer. Raskolnikov felt a great desire to make out what he was singing, as though everything depended on that.

"Shall I go in?" he thought. "They are laughing. From drink. Shall I get drunk?"

"Won't you come in?" one of the women asked him. Her voice was still musical and less thick than the others, she was young and not repulsive—the only one of the group.

"Why, she's pretty," he said, drawing himself up and looking at her.

She smiled, much pleased at the compliment.

"You're very nice looking yourself," she said.

"Isn't he thin though!" observed another woman in a deep bass. "Have you just come out of a hospital?"

"They're all generals' daughters, it seems, but they have all snub noses," interposed a tipsy peasant with a sly smile on his face, wearing a loose coat. "See how jolly they are."

"Go along with you!"

"I'll go, sweetie!"

And he darted down into the saloon below. Raskolnikov moved on.

"I say, sir," the girl shouted after him.

"What is it?"

She hesitated.

"I'll always be pleased to spend an hour with you, kind gentleman, but now I feel shy. Give me six copecks for a drink, there's a nice young man!"

Raskolnikov gave her what came first—fifteen copecks.

"Ah, what a good-natured gentleman!"

"What's your name?"

"Ask for Duclida."

"Well, that's too much," one of the women observed, shaking her head at Duclida. "I don't know how you can ask like that. I believe I should drop with shame...."

Raskolnikov looked curiously at the speaker. She was a pock-marked wench of thirty, covered with bruises, with her upper lip swollen. She made her criticism quietly and earnestly. "Where is it," thought Raskolnikov. "Where is it I've read that someone condemned to death says or thinks, an hour before his death, that if he had to live on some high rock, on such a narrow ledge that he'd only room to stand, and the ocean, everlasting darkness, everlasting solitude, everlasting tempest around him, if he had to remain standing on a square yard of space all his life, a thousand years, eternity, it were better to live so than to die at once! Only to live, to live and live! Life, whatever it may be!... How true it is! Good God, how true! Man is a vile creature!... And vile is he who calls him vile for that," he added a moment later.

He went into another street. "Bah, the Palais de Cristal! Razumihin was just talking of the Palais de Cristal. But what on earth was it I wanted? Yes, the newspapers.... Zossimov said he'd read it in the papers. Have you the papers?" he asked, going into a very spacious and positively clean restaurant, consisting of several rooms, which were, however, rather empty. Two or three people were drinking tea, and in a room further away were sitting four men drinking champagne. Raskolnikov fancied that Zametov was one of them, but he could not be sure at that distance. "What if it is?" he thought.

"Will you have vodka?" asked the waiter.

"Give me some tea and bring me the papers, the old ones for the last five days, and I'll give you something."

"Yes, sir, here's to-day's. No vodka?"

The old newspapers and the tea were brought. Raskolnikov sat down and began to look through them.

"Oh, damn... these are the items of intelligence. An accident on a staircase, spontaneous combustion of a shopkeeper from alcohol, a fire in Peski... a fire in the Petersburg quarter... another fire in the Petersburg quarter... and another fire in the Petersburg quarter.... Ah, here it is!" He found at last what he was seeking and began to read it. The lines danced before his eyes, but he read it all and began eagerly seeking later additions in the following numbers. His hands shook with nervous impatience as he turned the sheets. Suddenly someone sat down beside him at his table. He looked up, it was the head clerk Zametov, looking just the same, with the rings on his fingers and the watch-chain, with the curly, black hair, parted and pomaded, with the smart waistcoat, rather shabby coat and doubtful linen. He was in a good humour, at least he was smiling very gaily and good-humouredly. His dark face was rather flushed from the champagne he had drunk.

"What, you here?" he began in surprise, speaking as though he'd known him all his life. "Why, Razumihin told me only yesterday you were unconscious. How strange! And do you know I've been to see you?"

Raskolnikov knew he would come up to him. He laid aside the papers and turned to Zametov. There was a smile on his lips, and a new shade of irritable impatience was apparent in that smile.

"I know you have," he answered. "I've heard it. You looked for my sock.... And you know Razumihin has lost his heart to you? He says you've been with him to Luise Ivanovna's—you know, the woman you tried to befriend, for whom you winked to the Explosive Lieutenant and he would not understand. Do you remember? How could he fail to understand—it was quite clear, wasn't it?"

"What a hot head he is!"

"The explosive one?"

"No, your friend Razumihin."

"You must have a jolly life, Mr. Zametov; entrance free to the most agreeable places. Who's been pouring champagne into you just now?"

"We've just been... having a drink together.... You talk about pouring it into me!"

"By way of a fee! You profit by everything!" Raskolnikov laughed, "it's all right, my dear boy," he added, slapping Zametov on the shoulder. "I am not speaking from temper, but in a friendly way, for sport, as that workman of yours said when he was scuffling with Dmitri, in the case of the old woman...."

"How do you know about it?"

"Perhaps I know more about it than you do."

"How strange you are.... I am sure you are still very unwell. You oughtn't to have come out."

"Oh, do I seem strange to you?"

"Yes. What are you doing, reading the papers?"

"Yes."

"There's a lot about the fires."

"No, I am not reading about the fires." Here he looked mysteriously at Zametov; his lips were twisted again in a mocking smile. "No, I am not reading about the fires," he went on, winking at Zametov. "But confess now, my dear fellow, you're awfully anxious to know what I am reading about?"

"I am not in the least. Mayn't I ask a question? Why do you keep on...?"

"Listen, you are a man of culture and education?"

"I was in the sixth class at the gymnasium," said Zametov with some dignity.

"Sixth class! Ah, my cock-sparrow! With your parting and your rings—you are a gentleman of fortune. Foo! what a charming boy!" Here Raskolnikov broke into a nervous laugh right in Zametov's face. The latter drew back, more amazed than offended.

"Foo! how strange you are!" Zametov repeated very seriously. "I can't help thinking you are still delirious."

"I am delirious? You are fibbing, my cock-sparrow! So I am strange? You find me curious, do you?"

"Yes, curious."

"Shall I tell you what I was reading about, what I was looking for? See what a lot of papers I've made them bring me. Suspicious, eh?"

"Well, what is it?"

"You prick up your ears?"

"How do you mean—'prick up my ears'?"

"I'll explain that afterwards, but now, my boy, I declare to you... no, better 'I confess'... No, that's not right either; 'I make a deposition and you take it.' I depose that I was reading, that I was looking and searching...." he screwed up his eyes and paused. "I was searching—and came here on purpose to do it—for news of the murder of the old pawnbroker woman," he articulated at last, almost in a whisper, bringing his face exceedingly close to the face of Zametov. Zametov looked at him steadily, without moving or drawing his face away. What struck Zametov afterwards as the strangest part of it all was that silence followed for exactly a minute, and that they gazed at one another all the while.

"What if you have been reading about it?" he cried at last, perplexed and impatient. "That's no business of mine! What of it?"

"The same old woman," Raskolnikov went on in the same whisper, not heeding Zametov's explanation, "about whom you were talking in the police-office, you remember, when I fainted. Well, do you understand now?"

"What do you mean? Understand... what?" Zametov brought out, almost alarmed.

Raskolnikov's set and earnest face was suddenly transformed, and he suddenly went off into the same nervous laugh as before, as though utterly unable to restrain himself. And in one flash he recalled with extraordinary vividness of sensation a moment in the recent past, that moment when he stood with the axe behind the door, while the latch trembled and the men outside swore and shook it, and he had a sudden desire to shout at them, to swear at them, to put out his tongue at them, to mock them, to laugh, and laugh, and laugh!

"You are either mad, or..." began Zametov, and he broke off, as though stunned by the idea that had suddenly flashed into his mind.

"Or? Or what? What? Come, tell me!"

"Nothing," said Zametov, getting angry, "it's all nonsense!"

Both were silent. After his sudden fit of laughter Raskolnikov became suddenly thoughtful and melancholy. He put his elbow on the table and leaned his head on his hand. He seemed to have completely forgotten Zametov. The silence lasted for some time.

"Why don't you drink your tea? It's getting cold," said Zametov.

"What! Tea? Oh, yes...." Raskolnikov sipped the glass, put a morsel of bread in his mouth and, suddenly looking at Zametov, seemed to remember everything and pulled himself together. At the same moment his face resumed its original mocking expression. He went on drinking tea.

"There have been a great many of these crimes lately," said Zametov. "Only the other day I read in the *Moscow News* that a whole gang of false coiners had been caught in Moscow. It was a regular society. They used to forge tickets!"

"Oh, but it was a long time ago! I read about it a month ago," Raskolnikov answered calmly. "So you consider them criminals?" he added, smiling.

"Of course they are criminals."

"They? They are children, simpletons, not criminals! Why, half a hundred people meeting for such an object—what an idea! Three would be too many, and then they want to have more faith in one another than in themselves! One has only to blab in his cups and it all collapses. Simpletons! They engaged untrustworthy people to change the notes—what a thing to trust to a casual stranger! Well, let us suppose that these simpletons succeed and each makes a million, and what follows for the rest of their lives? Each is dependent on the others for the rest of his life! Better hang oneself at once! And they did not know how to change the notes either; the man who changed the notes took five thousand roubles, and his hands trembled. He counted the first four thousand, but did not count the fifth thousand—he was in such a hurry to get the money into his pocket and run away. Of course he roused suspicion. And the whole thing came to a crash through one fool! Is it possible?"

"That his hands trembled?" observed Zametov, "yes, that's quite possible. That, I feel quite sure, is possible. Sometimes one can't stand things."

"Can't stand that?"

"Why, could you stand it then? No, I couldn't. For the sake of a hundred roubles to face such a terrible experience? To go with false notes into a bank where it's their business to spot that sort of thing! No, I should not have the face to do it. Would you?"

Raskolnikov had an intense desire again "to put his tongue out." Shivers kept running down his spine.

"I should do it quite differently," Raskolnikov began. "This is how I would change the notes: I'd count the first thousand three or four times backwards and forwards, looking at every note and then I'd set to the second thousand; I'd count that half-way through and then hold some fifty-rouble note to the light, then turn it, then hold it to the light again—to see whether it was a good one. 'I am afraid,' I would say, 'a relation of mine lost twenty-five roubles the other day through a false note,' and then I'd tell them the whole story. And after I began counting the third, 'No, excuse me,' I would say, 'I fancy I made a mistake in the seventh hundred in that second thousand, I am not sure.' And so I would give up the third thousand and go back to the second and so on to the end. And when I had finished, I'd pick out one from the fifth and one from the second thousand and take them again to the light and ask again, 'Change them, please,' and put the clerk into such a stew that he would not know how to get rid of me. When I'd finished and had gone out, I'd come back, 'No, excuse me,' and ask for some explanation. That's how I'd do it."

"Foo! what terrible things you say!" said Zametov, laughing. "But all that is only talk. I dare say when it came to deeds you'd make a slip. I believe that even a practised, desperate man cannot always reckon on himself, much less you and I. To take an example near home—that old woman murdered in our district. The murderer seems to have been a desperate fellow, he risked everything in open daylight, was saved by a miracle—but his hands shook, too. He did not succeed in robbing the place, he couldn't stand it. That was clear from the..."

Raskolnikov seemed offended.

"Clear? Why don't you catch him then?" he cried, maliciously gibing at Zametov.

"Well, they will catch him."

"Who? You? Do you suppose you could catch him? You've a tough job! A great point for you is whether a man is spending money or not. If he had no money and suddenly begins spending, he must be the man. So that any child can mislead you."

"The fact is they always do that, though," answered Zametov. "A man will commit a clever murder at the risk of his life and then at once he goes drinking in a tavern. They are caught spending money, they are not all as cunning as you are. You wouldn't go to a tavern, of course?"

Raskolnikov frowned and looked steadily at Zametov.

"You seem to enjoy the subject and would like to know how I should behave in that case, too?" he asked with displeasure.

"I should like to," Zametov answered firmly and seriously. Somewhat too much earnestness began to appear in his words and looks.

"Very much?"

"Very much!"

"All right then. This is how I should behave," Raskolnikov began, again bringing his face close to Zametov's, again staring at him and speaking in a whisper, so that the latter positively shuddered. "This is what I should have done. I should have taken the money and jewels, I should have walked out of there and have gone straight to some deserted place with fences round it and scarcely anyone to be seen, some kitchen garden or place of that sort. I should have looked out beforehand some stone weighing a hundredweight or more which had been lying in the corner from the time the house was built. I would lift that stone—there would sure to be a hollow under it, and I would put the jewels and money in that hole. Then I'd roll the stone back so that it would look as before, would press it down with my foot and walk away. And for a year or two, three maybe, I would not touch it. And, well, they could search! There'd be no trace."

"You are a madman," said Zametov, and for some reason he too spoke in a whisper, and moved away from Raskolnikov, whose eyes were glittering. He had turned fearfully pale and his upper lip was twitching and quivering. He bent down as close as possible to Zametov, and his lips began to move without uttering a word. This lasted for half a minute; he knew what he was doing, but could not restrain himself. The terrible word trembled on his lips, like the latch on that door; in another moment it will break out, in another moment he will let it go, he will speak out.

"And what if it was I who murdered the old woman and Lizaveta?" he said suddenly and—realised what he had done.

Zametov looked wildly at him and turned white as the tablecloth. His face wore a contorted smile.

"But is it possible?" he brought out faintly. Raskolnikov looked wrathfully at him.

"Own up that you believed it, yes, you did?"

"Not a bit of it, I believe it less than ever now," Zametov cried hastily.

"I've caught my cock-sparrow! So you did believe it before, if now you believe less than ever?"

"Not at all," cried Zametov, obviously embarrassed. "Have you been frightening me so as to lead up to this?"

"You don't believe it then? What were you talking about behind my back when I went out of the police-office? And why did the explosive lieutenant question me after I fainted? Hey, there," he shouted to the waiter, getting up and taking his cap, "how much?"

"Thirty copecks," the latter replied, running up.

"And there is twenty copecks for vodka. See what a lot of money!" he held out his shaking hand to Zametov with notes in it. "Red notes and blue, twenty-five roubles. Where did I get them? And where did my new clothes come from? You know I had not a copeck. You've cross-examined my landlady, I'll be bound.... Well, that's enough! *Assez causé!* Till we meet again!"

He went out, trembling all over from a sort of wild hysterical sensation, in which there was an element of insufferable rapture. Yet he was gloomy and terribly tired. His face was twisted as after a fit. His fatigue increased rapidly. Any shock, any irritating sensation stimulated and revived his energies at once, but his strength failed as quickly when the stimulus was removed.

Zametov, left alone, sat for a long time in the same place, plunged in thought. Raskolnikov had unwittingly worked a revolution in his brain on a certain point and had made up his mind for him conclusively.

"Ilya Petrovitch is a blockhead," he decided.

Raskolnikov had hardly opened the door of the restaurant when he stumbled against Razumihin on the steps. They did not see each other till they almost knocked against each other. For a moment they stood looking each other up and down. Razumihin was greatly astounded, then anger, real anger gleamed fiercely in his eyes.

"So here you are!" he shouted at the top of his voice—"you ran away from your bed! And here I've been looking for you under the sofa! We went up to the garret. I almost beat Nastasya on your account. And here he is after all. Rodya! What is the meaning of it? Tell me the whole truth! Confess! Do you hear?"

"It means that I'm sick to death of you all and I want to be alone," Raskolnikov answered calmly.

"Alone? When you are not able to walk, when your face is as white as a sheet and you are gasping for breath! Idiot!... What have you been doing in the Palais de Cristal? Own up at once!"

"Let me go!" said Raskolnikov and tried to pass him. This was too much for Razumihin; he gripped him firmly by the shoulder.

"Let you go? You dare tell me to let you go? Do you know what I'll do with you directly? I'll pick you up, tie you up in a bundle, carry you home under my arm and lock you up!"

"Listen, Razumihin," Raskolnikov began quietly, apparently calm—"can't you see that I don't want your benevolence? A strange desire you have to shower benefits on a man who... curses them, who feels them a burden in fact! Why did you seek me out at the beginning of my illness? Maybe I was very glad to die. Didn't I tell you plainly enough to-day that you were torturing me, that I was... sick of you! You seem to want to torture people! I assure you that all that is seriously hindering my recovery, because it's continually irritating me. You saw Zossimov went away just now to avoid irritating me. You leave me alone too, for goodness' sake! What right have you, indeed, to keep me by force? Don't you see that I am in possession of all my faculties now? How, how can I persuade you not to persecute me with your kindness? I may be ungrateful, I may be mean, only let me be, for God's sake, let me be! Let me be, let me be!"

He began calmly, gloating beforehand over the venomous phrases he was about to utter, but finished, panting for breath, in a frenzy, as he had been with Luzhin.

Razumihin stood a moment, thought and let his hand drop.

"Well, go to hell then," he said gently and thoughtfully. "Stay," he roared, as Raskolnikov was about to move. "Listen to me. Let me tell you, that you are all a set of babbling, posing idiots! If you've any little trouble you brood over it like a hen over an egg. And you are plagiarists even in that! There isn't a sign of independent life in you! You are made of spermaceti ointment and you've lymph in your veins instead of blood. I don't believe in anyone of you! In any circumstances the first thing for all of you is to be unlike a human being! Stop!" he cried with redoubled fury, noticing that Raskolnikov was again making a movement—"hear me out! You know I'm having a house-warming this evening, I dare say they've arrived by now, but I left my uncle there—I just ran in—to receive the guests. And if you weren't a fool, a common fool, a perfect fool, if you were an original instead of a translation... you see, Rodya, I recognise you're a clever fellow, but you're a fool!—and if you weren't a fool you'd come round to me this evening instead of wearing out your boots in the street! Since you have gone out, there's no help for it! I'd give you a snug easy chair, my landlady has one... a cup of tea, company.... Or you could lie on the sofa—any way you would be with us.... Zossimov will be there too. Will you come?"

"No."

"R-rubbish!" Razumihin shouted, out of patience. "How do you know? You can't answer for yourself! You don't know anything about it.... Thousands of times I've fought tooth and nail with people and run back to them afterwards.... One feels ashamed and goes back to a man! So remember, Potchinkov's house on the third storey...."

"Why, Mr. Razumihin, I do believe you'd let anybody beat you from sheer benevolence."

"Beat? Whom? Me? I'd twist his nose off at the mere idea! Potchinkov's house, 47, Babushkin's flat...."

"I shall not come, Razumihin." Raskolnikov turned and walked away.

"I bet you will," Razumihin shouted after him. "I refuse to know you if you don't! Stay, hey, is Zametov in there?"

"Yes."

"Did you see him?"

"Yes."

"Talked to him?"

"Yes."

"What about? Confound you, don't tell me then. Potchinkov's house, 47, Babushkin's flat, remember!"

Raskolnikov walked on and turned the corner into Sadovy Street. Razumihin looked after him thoughtfully. Then with a wave of his hand he went into the house but stopped short of the stairs.

"Confound it," he went on almost aloud. "He talked sensibly but yet... I am a fool! As if madmen didn't talk sensibly! And this was just what Zossimov seemed afraid of." He struck his finger on his forehead. "What if... how could I let him go off alone? He may drown himself.... Ach, what a blunder! I can't." And he ran back to overtake Raskolnikov, but there was no trace of him. With a curse he returned with rapid steps to the Palais de Cristal to question Zametov.

Raskolnikov walked straight to X—— Bridge, stood in the middle, and leaning both elbows on the rail stared into the distance. On parting with Razumihin, he felt so much weaker that he could scarcely reach this place. He longed to sit or lie down somewhere in the street. Bending over the water, he gazed mechanically at the last pink flush of the sunset, at the row of houses growing dark in the gathering twilight, at one distant attic window on the left bank, flashing as though on fire in the last rays of the setting sun, at the darkening water of the canal, and the water seemed to catch his attention. At last red circles flashed before his eyes, the houses seemed moving, the passers-by, the canal banks, the carriages, all danced before his eyes. Suddenly he started, saved again perhaps from swooning by an uncanny and hideous sight. He became aware of someone standing on the right side of him; he looked and saw a tall woman with a kerchief on her head, with a long, yellow, wasted face and red sunken eyes. She was looking straight at him, but obviously she saw nothing and recognised no one. Suddenly she leaned her right hand on the parapet, lifted her right leg over the railing, then her left and threw herself into the canal. The filthy water parted and swallowed up its victim for a moment, but an instant later the drowning woman floated to the surface, moving slowly with the current, her head and legs in the water, her skirt inflated like a balloon over her back.

"A woman drowning! A woman drowning!" shouted dozens of voices; people ran up, both banks were thronged with spectators, on the bridge people crowded about Raskolnikov, pressing up behind him.

"Mercy on it! it's our Afrosinya!" a woman cried tearfully close by. "Mercy! save her! kind people, pull her out!"

"A boat, a boat" was shouted in the crowd. But there was no need of a boat; a policeman ran down the steps to the canal, threw off his great coat and his boots and rushed into the water. It was easy to reach her: she floated within a couple of yards from the steps, he caught hold of her clothes with his right hand and with his left seized a pole which a comrade held out to him; the drowning woman was pulled out at once. They laid her on the granite pavement of the embankment. She soon recovered consciousness, raised her head, sat up and began sneezing and coughing, stupidly wiping her wet dress with her hands. She said nothing.

"She's drunk herself out of her senses," the same woman's voice wailed at her side. "Out of her senses. The other day she tried to hang herself, we cut her down. I ran out to the shop just now, left my little girl to look after her—and here she's in trouble again! A neighbour, gentleman, a neighbour, we live close by, the second house from the end, see yonder...."

The crowd broke up. The police still remained round the woman, someone mentioned the police station.... Raskolnikov looked on with a strange sensation of indifference and apathy. He felt disgusted. "No, that's loathsome... water... it's not good enough," he muttered to himself. "Nothing will come of it," he added, "no use to wait. What about the police office...? And why isn't Zametov at the police office? The police office is open till ten o'clock...." He turned his back to the railing and looked about him.

"Very well then!" he said resolutely; he moved from the bridge and walked in the direction of the police office. His heart felt hollow and empty. He did not want to think. Even his depression had passed, there was not a trace now of the energy with which he had set out "to make an end of it all." Complete apathy had succeeded to it.

"Well, it's a way out of it," he thought, walking slowly and listlessly along the canal bank. "Anyway I'll make an end, for I want to.... But is it a way out? What does it matter! There'll be the square yard of space—ha! But what an end! Is it really the end? Shall I tell them or not? Ah... damn! How tired I am! If I could find somewhere to sit or lie down soon! What I am most ashamed of is its being so stupid. But I don't care about that either! What idiotic ideas come into one's head."

To reach the police office he had to go straight forward and take the second turning to the left. It was only a few paces away. But at the first turning he stopped and, after a minute's thought, turned into a side street and went two streets out of his way, possibly without any object, or possibly to delay a minute and gain time. He walked, looking at the ground; suddenly someone seemed to whisper in his ear; he lifted his head and saw that he was standing at the very gate of *the* house. He had not passed it, he had not been near it since *that* evening. An overwhelming, unaccountable prompting drew him on. He went into the house, passed through the gateway, then into the first entrance on the right, and began mounting the familiar staircase to the fourth storey. The narrow, steep staircase was very dark. He stopped at each landing and looked round him with curiosity; on the first landing the framework of the window had been taken out. "That wasn't so then," he thought. Here was the flat on the second storey where Nikolay and Dmitri had been working. "It's shut up and the door newly painted. So it's to let." Then the third storey and the fourth. "Here!" He was perplexed to find the door of the flat wide open. There were men there, he could hear voices; he had not expected that. After brief hesitation he mounted the last stairs and went into the flat. It, too, was being done up; there were workmen in it. This seemed to amaze him; he somehow fancied that he would find everything as he left it, even perhaps the corpses in the same places on the floor. And now, bare walls, no furniture; it seemed strange. He walked to the window and sat down on the window-sill. There were two workmen, both young fellows, but one much younger than the other. They were papering the walls with a new white paper covered with lilac flowers, instead of the old, dirty, yellow one. Raskolnikov for some reason felt horribly annoyed by this. He looked at the new paper with dislike, as though he felt sorry to have it all so changed. The workmen had obviously stayed beyond their time and now they were hurriedly rolling up their paper and getting ready to go home. They took no notice of Raskolnikov's coming in; they were talking. Raskolnikov folded his arms and listened.

"She comes to me in the morning," said the elder to the younger, "very early, all dressed up. 'Why are you preening and prinking?' says I. 'I am ready to do anything to please you, Tit Vassilitch!' That's a way of going on! And she dressed up like a regular fashion book!"

"And what is a fashion book?" the younger one asked. He obviously regarded the other as an authority.

"A fashion book is a lot of pictures, coloured, and they come to the tailors here every Saturday, by post from abroad, to show folks how to dress, the male sex as well as the female. They're pictures. The gentlemen are generally wearing fur coats and for the ladies' fluffles, they're beyond anything you can fancy."

"There's nothing you can't find in Petersburg," the younger cried enthusiastically, "except father and mother, there's everything!"

"Except them, there's everything to be found, my boy," the elder declared sententiously.

Raskolnikov got up and walked into the other room where the strong box, the bed, and the chest of drawers had been; the room seemed to him very tiny without furniture in it. The paper was the same; the paper in the corner showed where the case of ikons had stood. He looked at it and went to the window. The elder workman looked at him askance.

"What do you want?" he asked suddenly.

Instead of answering Raskolnikov went into the passage and pulled the bell. The same bell, the same cracked note. He rang it a second and a third time; he listened and remembered. The hideous and agonisingly fearful sensation he had felt then began to come back more and more vividly. He shuddered at every ring and it gave him more and more satisfaction.

"Well, what do you want? Who are you?" the workman shouted, going out to him. Raskolnikov went inside again.

"I want to take a flat," he said. "I am looking round."

"It's not the time to look at rooms at night! and you ought to come up with the porter."

"The floors have been washed, will they be painted?" Raskolnikov went on. "Is there no blood?"

"What blood?"

"Why, the old woman and her sister were murdered here. There was a perfect pool there."

"But who are you?" the workman cried, uneasy.

"Who am I?"

"Yes."

"You want to know? Come to the police station, I'll tell you."

The workmen looked at him in amazement.

"It's time for us to go, we are late. Come along, Alyoshka. We must lock up," said the elder workman.

"Very well, come along," said Raskolnikov indifferently, and going out first, he went slowly downstairs. "Hey, porter," he cried in the gateway.

At the entrance several people were standing, staring at the passers-by; the two porters, a peasant woman, a man in a long coat and a few others. Raskolnikov went straight up to them.

"What do you want?" asked one of the porters.

"Have you been to the police office?"

"I've just been there. What do you want?"

"Is it open?"

"Of course."

"Is the assistant there?"

"He was there for a time. What do you want?"

Raskolnikov made no reply, but stood beside them lost in thought.

"He's been to look at the flat," said the elder workman, coming forward.

"Which flat?"

"Where we are at work. 'Why have you washed away the blood?' says he. 'There has been a murder here,' says he, 'and I've come to take it.' And he began ringing at the bell, all but broke it. 'Come to the police station,' says he. 'I'll tell you everything there.' He wouldn't leave us."

The porter looked at Raskolnikov, frowning and perplexed.

"Who are you?" he shouted as impressively as he could.

"I am Rodion Romanovitch Raskolnikov, formerly a student, I live in Shil's house, not far from here, flat Number 14, ask the porter, he knows me." Raskolnikov said all this in a lazy, dreamy voice, not turning round, but looking intently into the darkening street.

"Why have you been to the flat?"

"To look at it."

"What is there to look at?"

"Take him straight to the police station," the man in the long coat jerked in abruptly.

Raskolnikov looked intently at him over his shoulder and said in the same slow, lazy tones:

"Come along."

"Yes, take him," the man went on more confidently. "Why was he going into *that*, what's in his mind, eh?"

"He's not drunk, but God knows what's the matter with him," muttered the workman.

"But what do you want?" the porter shouted again, beginning to get angry in earnest—"Why are you hanging about?"

"You funk the police station then?" said Raskolnikov jeeringly.

"How funk it? Why are you hanging about?"

"He's a rogue!" shouted the peasant woman.

"Why waste time talking to him?" cried the other porter, a huge peasant in a full open coat and with keys on his belt. "Get along! He is a rogue and no mistake. Get along!"

And seizing Raskolnikov by the shoulder he flung him into the street. He lurched forward, but recovered his footing, looked at the spectators in silence and walked away.

"Strange man!" observed the workman.

"There are strange folks about nowadays," said the woman.

"You should have taken him to the police station all the same," said the man in the long coat.

"Better have nothing to do with him," decided the big porter. "A regular rogue! Just what he wants, you may be sure, but once take him up, you won't get rid of him.... We know the sort!"

"Shall I go there or not?" thought Raskolnikov, standing in the middle of the thoroughfare at the cross-roads, and he looked about him, as though expecting from someone a decisive word. But no sound came, all was dead and silent like the stones on which he walked, dead to him, to him alone.... All at once at the end of the street, two hundred yards away, in the gathering dusk he saw a crowd and heard talk and shouts. In the middle of the crowd stood a carriage.... A light gleamed in the middle of the street. "What is it?" Raskolnikov turned to the right and went up to the crowd. He seemed to clutch at everything and smiled coldly when he recognised it, for he had fully made up his mind to go to the police station and knew that it would all soon be over.

CHAPTER VII

An elegant carriage stood in the middle of the road with a pair of spirited grey horses; there was no one in it, and the coachman had got off his box and stood by; the horses were being held by the bridle.... A mass of people had gathered round, the police standing in front. One of them held a lighted lantern which he was turning on something lying close to the wheels. Everyone was talking, shouting, exclaiming; the coachman seemed at a loss and kept repeating:

"What a misfortune! Good Lord, what a misfortune!"

Raskolnikov pushed his way in as far as he could, and succeeded at last in seeing the object of the commotion and interest. On the ground a man who had been run over lay apparently unconscious, and covered with blood; he was very badly dressed, but not like a workman. Blood was flowing from his head and face; his face was crushed, mutilated and disfigured. He was evidently badly injured.

"Merciful heaven!" wailed the coachman, "what more could I do? If I'd been driving fast or had not shouted to him, but I was going quietly, not in a hurry. Everyone could see I was going along just like everybody else. A drunken man can't walk straight, we all know.... I saw him crossing the street, staggering and almost falling. I shouted again and a second and a third time, then I held the horses in, but he fell straight under their feet! Either he did it on purpose or he was very tipsy.... The horses are young and ready to take fright... they started, he screamed... that made them worse. That's how it happened!"

"That's just how it was," a voice in the crowd confirmed.

"He shouted, that's true, he shouted three times," another voice declared.

"Three times it was, we all heard it," shouted a third.

But the coachman was not very much distressed and frightened. It was evident that the carriage belonged to a rich and important person who was awaiting it somewhere; the police, of course, were in no little anxiety to avoid upsetting his arrangements. All they had to do was to take the injured man to the police station and the hospital. No one knew his name.

Meanwhile Raskolnikov had squeezed in and stooped closer over him. The lantern suddenly lighted up the unfortunate man's face. He recognised him.

"I know him! I know him!" he shouted, pushing to the front. "It's a government clerk retired from the service, Marmeladov. He lives close by in Kozel's house.... Make haste for a doctor! I will pay, see?" He pulled money out of his pocket and showed it to the policeman. He was in violent agitation.

The police were glad that they had found out who the man was. Raskolnikov gave his own name and address, and, as earnestly as if it had been his father, he besought the police to carry the unconscious Marmeladov to his lodging at once.

"Just here, three houses away," he said eagerly, "the house belongs to Kozel, a rich German. He was going home, no doubt drunk. I know him, he is a drunkard. He has a family there, a wife, children, he has one daughter.... It will take time to take him to the hospital, and there is sure to be a doctor in the house. I'll pay, I'll pay! At least he will be looked after at home... they will help him at once. But he'll die before you get him to the hospital." He managed to slip something unseen into the policeman's hand. But the thing was straightforward and legitimate, and in any case help was closer here. They raised the injured man; people volunteered to help.

Kozel's house was thirty yards away. Raskolnikov walked behind, carefully holding Marmeladov's head and showing the way.

"This way, this way! We must take him upstairs head foremost. Turn round! I'll pay, I'll make it worth your while," he muttered.

Katerina Ivanovna had just begun, as she always did at every free moment, walking to and fro in her little room from window to stove and back again, with her arms folded across her chest, talking to herself and coughing. Of late she had begun to talk more than ever to her eldest girl, Polenka, a child of ten, who, though there was much she did not understand, understood very well that her mother needed her, and so always watched her with her big clever eyes and strove her utmost to appear to understand. This time Polenka was undressing her little brother, who had been unwell all day and was going to bed. The boy was waiting for her to take off his shirt, which had to be washed at night. He was sitting straight and motionless on a chair, with a silent, serious face, with his legs stretched out straight before him—heels together and toes turned out.

He was listening to what his mother was saying to his sister, sitting perfectly still with pouting lips and wide-open eyes, just as all good little boys have to sit when they are undressed to go to bed. A little girl, still younger, dressed literally in rags, stood at the screen, waiting for her turn. The door on to the stairs was open to relieve them a little from the clouds of tobacco smoke which floated in from the other rooms and brought on long terrible fits of coughing in the poor, consumptive woman. Katerina Ivanovna seemed to have grown even thinner during that week and the hectic flush on her face was brighter than ever.

"You wouldn't believe, you can't imagine, Polenka," she said, walking about the room, "what a happy luxurious life we had in my papa's house and how this drunkard has brought me, and will bring you all, to ruin! Papa was a civil colonel and only a step from being a governor; so that everyone who came to see him said, 'We look upon you, Ivan Mihailovitch, as our governor!' When I... when..." she coughed violently, "oh, cursed life," she cried, clearing her throat and pressing her hands to her breast, "when I... when at the last ball... at the marshal's... Princess Bezzemelny saw me—who gave me the blessing when your father and I were married, Polenka—she asked at once 'Isn't that the pretty girl who danced the shawl dance at the breaking-up?' (You must mend that tear, you must take your needle and darn it as I showed you, or to-morrow—cough, cough, cough— he will make the hole bigger," she articulated with effort.) "Prince Schegolskoy, a kammerjunker, had just come from Petersburg then... he danced the mazurka with me and wanted to make me an offer next day; but I thanked him in flattering expressions and told him that my heart had long been another's. That other was your father, Polya; papa was fearfully angry.... Is the water ready? Give me the shirt, and the stockings! Lida," said she to the youngest one, "you must manage without your chemise to-night... and lay your stockings out with it... I'll wash them together.... How is it that drunken vagabond doesn't come in? He has worn his shirt till it looks like a dish-clout, he has torn it to rags! I'd do it all together, so as not to have to work two nights running! Oh, dear! (Cough, cough, cough, cough!) Again! What's this?" she cried, noticing a crowd in the passage and the men, who were pushing into her room, carrying a burden. "What is it? What are they bringing? Mercy on us!"

"Where are we to put him?" asked the policeman, looking round when Marmeladov, unconscious and covered with blood, had been carried in.

"On the sofa! Put him straight on the sofa, with his head this way," Raskolnikov showed him.

"Run over in the road! Drunk!" someone shouted in the passage.

Katerina Ivanovna stood, turning white and gasping for breath. The children were terrified. Little Lida screamed, rushed to Polenka and clutched at her, trembling all over.

Having laid Marmeladov down, Raskolnikov flew to Katerina Ivanovna.

"For God's sake be calm, don't be frightened!" he said, speaking quickly, "he was crossing the road and was run over by a carriage, don't be frightened, he will come to, I told them bring him here... I've been here already, you remember? He will come to; I'll pay!"

"He's done it this time!" Katerina Ivanovna cried despairingly and she rushed to her husband.

Raskolnikov noticed at once that she was not one of those women who swoon easily. She instantly placed under the luckless man's head a pillow, which no one had thought of and began undressing and examining him. She kept her head, forgetting herself, biting her trembling lips and stifling the screams which were ready to break from her.

Raskolnikov meanwhile induced someone to run for a doctor. There was a doctor, it appeared, next door but one.

"I've sent for a doctor," he kept assuring Katerina Ivanovna, "don't be uneasy, I'll pay. Haven't you water?... and give me a napkin or a towel, anything, as quick as you can.... He is injured, but not killed, believe me.... We shall see what the doctor says!"

Katerina Ivanovna ran to the window; there, on a broken chair in the corner, a large earthenware basin full of water had been stood, in readiness for washing her children's and husband's linen that night. This washing was done by Katerina Ivanovna at night at least twice a week, if not oftener. For the family had come to such a pass that they were practically without change of linen, and Katerina Ivanovna could not endure uncleanliness and, rather than see dirt in the house, she preferred to wear herself out at night, working beyond her strength when the rest were asleep, so as to get the wet linen hung on a line and dry by the morning. She took up the basin of water at Raskolnikov's request, but almost fell down with her burden. But the latter had already succeeded in finding a towel, wetted it and began washing the blood off Marmeladov's face.

Katerina Ivanovna stood by, breathing painfully and pressing her hands to her breast. She was in need of attention herself. Raskolnikov began to realise that he might have made a mistake in having the injured man brought here. The policeman, too, stood in hesitation.

"Polenka," cried Katerina Ivanovna, "run to Sonia, make haste. If you don't find her at home, leave word that her father has been run over and that she is to come here at once... when she comes in. Run, Polenka! there, put on the shawl."

"Run your fastest!" cried the little boy on the chair suddenly, after which he relapsed into the same dumb rigidity, with round eyes, his heels thrust forward and his toes spread out.

Meanwhile the room had become so full of people that you couldn't have dropped a pin. The policemen left, all except one, who remained for a time, trying to drive out the people who came in from the stairs. Almost all Madame Lippevechsel's lodgers had streamed in from the inner rooms of the flat; at first they were squeezed together in the doorway, but afterwards they overflowed into the room. Katerina Ivanovna flew into a fury.

"You might let him die in peace, at least," she shouted at the crowd, "is it a spectacle for you to gape at? With cigarettes! (Cough, cough, cough!) You might as well keep your hats on.... And there is one in his hat!... Get away! You should respect the dead, at least!"

Her cough choked her—but her reproaches were not without result. They evidently stood in some awe of Katerina Ivanovna. The lodgers, one after another, squeezed back into the doorway with that strange inner feeling of satisfaction which may be observed in the presence of a sudden accident, even in those nearest and dearest to the victim, from which no living man is exempt, even in spite of the sincerest sympathy and compassion.

Voices outside were heard, however, speaking of the hospital and saying that they'd no business to make a disturbance here.

"No business to die!" cried Katerina Ivanovna, and she was rushing to the door to vent her wrath upon them, but in the doorway came face to face with Madame Lippevechsel who had only just heard of the accident and ran in to restore order. She was a particularly quarrelsome and irresponsible German.

"Ah, my God!" she cried, clasping her hands, "your husband drunken horses have trampled! To the hospital with him! I am the landlady!"

"Amalia Ludwigovna, I beg you to recollect what you are saying," Katerina Ivanovna began haughtily (she always took a haughty tone with the landlady that she might "remember her place" and even now could not deny herself this satisfaction). "Amalia Ludwigovna..."

"I have you once before told that you to call me Amalia Ludwigovna may not dare; I am Amalia Ivanovna."

"You are not Amalia Ivanovna, but Amalia Ludwigovna, and as I am not one of your despicable flatterers like Mr. Lebeziatnikov, who's laughing behind the door at this moment (a laugh and a cry of 'they are at it again' was in fact audible at the door) so I shall always call you Amalia Ludwigovna, though I fail to understand why you dislike that name. You can see for yourself what has happened to Semyon Zaharovitch; he is dying. I beg you to close that door at once and to admit no one. Let him at least die in peace! Or I warn you the Governor-General, himself, shall be informed of your conduct to-morrow. The prince knew me as a girl; he remembers Semyon Zaharovitch well and has often been a benefactor to him. Everyone knows that Semyon Zaharovitch had many friends and protectors, whom he abandoned himself from an honourable pride, knowing his unhappy weakness, but now (she pointed to Raskolnikov) a generous young man has come to our assistance, who has wealth and connections and whom Semyon Zaharovitch has known from a child. You may rest assured, Amalia Ludwigovna..."

All this was uttered with extreme rapidity, getting quicker and quicker, but a cough suddenly cut short Katerina Ivanovna's eloquence. At that instant the dying man recovered consciousness and uttered a groan; she ran to him. The injured man opened his eyes and without recognition or understanding gazed at Raskolnikov who was bending over him. He drew deep, slow, painful breaths; blood oozed at the corners of his mouth and drops of perspiration came out on his forehead. Not recognising Raskolnikov, he began looking round uneasily. Katerina Ivanovna looked at him with a sad but stern face, and tears trickled from her eyes.

"My God! His whole chest is crushed! How he is bleeding," she said in despair. "We must take off his clothes. Turn a little, Semyon Zaharovitch, if you can," she cried to him.

Marmeladov recognised her.

"A priest," he articulated huskily.

Katerina Ivanovna walked to the window, laid her head against the window frame and exclaimed in despair: "Oh, cursed life!"

"A priest," the dying man said again after a moment's silence.

"They've gone for him," Katerina Ivanovna shouted to him, he obeyed her shout and was silent. With sad and timid eyes he looked for her; she returned and stood by his pillow. He seemed a little easier but not for long.

Soon his eyes rested on little Lida, his favourite, who was shaking in the corner, as though she were in a fit, and staring at him with her wondering childish eyes.

"A-ah," he signed towards her uneasily. He wanted to say something.

"What now?" cried Katerina Ivanovna.

"Barefoot, barefoot!" he muttered, indicating with frenzied eyes the child's bare feet.

"Be silent," Katerina Ivanovna cried irritably, "you know why she is barefooted."

"Thank God, the doctor," exclaimed Raskolnikov, relieved.

The doctor came in, a precise little old man, a German, looking about him mistrustfully; he went up to the sick man, took his pulse, carefully felt his head and with the help of Katerina Ivanovna he unbuttoned the blood-stained shirt, and bared the injured man's chest. It was gashed, crushed and fractured, several ribs on the right side were broken. On the left side, just over the heart, was a large, sinister-looking yellowish-black bruise—a cruel kick from the horse's hoof. The doctor frowned. The policeman told him that he was caught in the wheel and turned round with it for thirty yards on the road.

"It's wonderful that he has recovered consciousness," the doctor whispered softly to Raskolnikov.

"What do you think of him?" he asked.

"He will die immediately."

"Is there really no hope?"

"Not the faintest! He is at the last gasp.... His head is badly injured, too... Hm... I could bleed him if you like, but... it would be useless. He is bound to die within the next five or ten minutes."

"Better bleed him then."

"If you like.... But I warn you it will be perfectly useless."

At that moment other steps were heard; the crowd in the passage parted, and the priest, a little, grey old man, appeared in the doorway bearing the sacrament. A policeman had gone for him at the time of the accident. The doctor changed places with him, exchanging glances with him. Raskolnikov begged the doctor to remain a little while. He shrugged his shoulders and remained.

All stepped back. The confession was soon over. The dying man probably understood little; he could only utter indistinct broken sounds. Katerina Ivanovna took little Lida, lifted the boy from the chair, knelt down in the corner by the stove and made the children kneel in front of her. The little girl was still trembling; but the boy, kneeling on his little bare knees, lifted his hand rhythmically, crossing himself with precision and bowed down, touching the floor with his forehead, which seemed to afford him especial satisfaction. Katerina Ivanovna bit her lips and held back her tears; she prayed, too, now and then pulling straight the boy's shirt, and managed to cover the girl's bare shoulders with a kerchief, which she took from the chest without rising from her knees or ceasing to pray. Meanwhile the door from the inner rooms was opened inquisitively again. In the passage the crowd of spectators from all the flats on the staircase grew denser and denser, but they did not venture beyond the threshold. A single candle-end lighted up the scene.

At that moment Polenka forced her way through the crowd at the door. She came in panting from running so fast, took off her kerchief, looked for her mother, went up to her and said, "She's coming, I met her in the street." Her mother made her kneel beside her.

Timidly and noiselessly a young girl made her way through the crowd, and strange was her appearance in that room, in the midst of want, rags, death and despair. She, too, was in rags, her attire was all of the cheapest, but decked out in gutter finery of a special stamp, unmistakably betraying its shameful purpose. Sonia stopped short in the doorway and looked about her bewildered, unconscious of everything. She forgot her fourth-hand, gaudy silk dress, so unseemly here with its ridiculous long train, and her immense crinoline that filled up the whole doorway, and her light-coloured shoes, and the parasol she brought with her, though it was no use at night, and the absurd round straw hat with its flaring flame-coloured feather. Under this rakishly-tilted hat was a pale, frightened little face with lips parted and eyes staring in terror. Sonia was a small thin girl of eighteen with fair hair, rather pretty, with wonderful blue eyes. She looked intently at the bed and the priest; she too was out of breath with running. At last whispers, some words in the crowd probably, reached her. She looked down and took a step forward into the room, still keeping close to the door.

The service was over. Katerina Ivanovna went up to her husband again. The priest stepped back and turned to say a few words of admonition and consolation to Katerina Ivanovna on leaving.

"What am I to do with these?" she interrupted sharply and irritably, pointing to the little ones.

"God is merciful; look to the Most High for succour," the priest began.

"Ach! He is merciful, but not to us."

"That's a sin, a sin, madam," observed the priest, shaking his head.

"And isn't that a sin?" cried Katerina Ivanovna, pointing to the dying man.

"Perhaps those who have involuntarily caused the accident will agree to compensate you, at least for the loss of his earnings."

"You don't understand!" cried Katerina Ivanovna angrily waving her hand. "And why should they compensate me? Why, he was drunk and threw himself under the horses! What earnings? He brought us in nothing but misery. He drank everything away, the drunkard! He robbed us to get drink, he wasted their lives and mine for drink! And thank God he's dying! One less to keep!"

"You must forgive in the hour of death, that's a sin, madam, such feelings are a great sin."

Katerina Ivanovna was busy with the dying man; she was giving him water, wiping the blood and sweat from his head, setting his pillow straight, and had only turned now and then for a moment to address the priest. Now she flew at him almost in a frenzy.

"Ah, father! That's words and only words! Forgive! If he'd not been run over, he'd have come home to-day drunk and his only shirt dirty and in rags and he'd have fallen asleep like a log, and I should have been sousing and rinsing till daybreak, washing his rags and the children's and then drying them by the window and as soon as it was daylight I should have been darning them. That's how I spend my nights!... What's the use of talking of forgiveness! I have forgiven as it is!"

A terrible hollow cough interrupted her words. She put her handkerchief to her lips and showed it to the priest, pressing her other hand to her aching chest. The handkerchief was covered with blood. The priest bowed his head and said nothing.

Marmeladov was in the last agony; he did not take his eyes off the face of Katerina Ivanovna, who was bending over him again. He kept trying to say something to her; he began moving his tongue with difficulty and articulating indistinctly, but Katerina Ivanovna, understanding that he wanted to ask her forgiveness, called peremptorily to him:

"Be silent! No need! I know what you want to say!" And the sick man was silent, but at the same instant his wandering eyes strayed to the doorway and he saw Sonia.

Till then he had not noticed her: she was standing in the shadow in a corner.

"Who's that? Who's that?" he said suddenly in a thick gasping voice, in agitation, turning his eyes in horror towards the door where his daughter was standing, and trying to sit up.

"Lie down! Lie do-own!" cried Katerina Ivanovna.

With unnatural strength he had succeeded in propping himself on his elbow. He looked wildly and fixedly for some time on his daughter, as though not recognising her. He had never seen her before in such attire. Suddenly he recognised her, crushed and ashamed in her humiliation and gaudy finery, meekly awaiting her turn to say good-bye to her dying father. His face showed intense suffering.

"Sonia! Daughter! Forgive!" he cried, and he tried to hold out his hand to her, but losing his balance, he fell off the sofa, face downwards on the floor. They rushed to pick him up, they put him on the sofa; but he was dying. Sonia with a faint cry ran up, embraced him and remained so without moving. He died in her arms.

"He's got what he wanted," Katerina Ivanovna cried, seeing her husband's dead body. "Well, what's to be done now? How am I to bury him! What can I give them to-morrow to eat?"

Raskolnikov went up to Katerina Ivanovna.

"Katerina Ivanovna," he began, "last week your husband told me all his life and circumstances.... Believe me, he spoke of you with passionate reverence. From that evening, when I learnt how devoted he was to you all and how he loved and respected you especially, Katerina Ivanovna, in spite of his unfortunate weakness, from that evening we became friends.... Allow me now... to do something... to repay my debt to my dead friend. Here are twenty roubles, I think—and if that can be of any assistance to you, then... I... in short, I will come again, I will be sure to come again... I shall, perhaps, come again to-morrow.... Good-bye!"

And he went quickly out of the room, squeezing his way through the crowd to the stairs. But in the crowd he suddenly jostled against Nikodim Fomitch, who had heard of the accident and had come to give instructions in person. They had not met since the scene at the police station, but Nikodim Fomitch knew him instantly.

"Ah, is that you?" he asked him.

"He's dead," answered Raskolnikov. "The doctor and the priest have been, all as it should have been. Don't worry the poor woman too much, she is in consumption as it is. Try and cheer her up, if possible... you are a kind-hearted man, I know..." he added with a smile, looking straight in his face.

"But you are spattered with blood," observed Nikodim Fomitch, noticing in the lamplight some fresh stains on Raskolnikov's waistcoat.

"Yes... I'm covered with blood," Raskolnikov said with a peculiar air; then he smiled, nodded and went downstairs.

He walked down slowly and deliberately, feverish but not conscious of it, entirely absorbed in a new overwhelming sensation of life and strength that surged up suddenly within him. This sensation might be compared to that of a man condemned to death who has suddenly been pardoned. Halfway down the staircase he was overtaken by the priest on his way home; Raskolnikov let him pass, exchanging a silent greeting with him. He was just descending the last steps when he heard rapid footsteps behind him. Someone overtook him; it was Polenka. She was running after him, calling "Wait! wait!"

He turned round. She was at the bottom of the staircase and stopped short a step above him. A dim light came in from the yard. Raskolnikov could distinguish the child's thin but pretty little face, looking at him with a bright childish smile. She had run after him with a message which she was evidently glad to give.

"Tell me, what is your name?... and where do you live?" she said hurriedly in a breathless voice.

He laid both hands on her shoulders and looked at her with a sort of rapture. It was such a joy to him to look at her, he could not have said why.

"Who sent you?"

"Sister Sonia sent me," answered the girl, smiling still more brightly.

"I knew it was sister Sonia sent you."

"Mamma sent me, too... when sister Sonia was sending me, mamma came up, too, and said 'Run fast, Polenka.'"

"Do you love sister Sonia?"

"I love her more than anyone," Polenka answered with a peculiar earnestness, and her smile became graver.

"And will you love me?"

By way of answer he saw the little girl's face approaching him, her full lips naïvely held out to kiss him. Suddenly her arms as thin as sticks held him tightly, her head rested on his shoulder and the little girl wept softly, pressing her face against him.

"I am sorry for father," she said a moment later, raising her tear-stained face and brushing away the tears with her hands. "It's nothing but misfortunes now," she added suddenly with that peculiarly sedate air which children try hard to assume when they want to speak like grown-up people.

"Did your father love you?"

"He loved Lida most," she went on very seriously without a smile, exactly like grown-up people, "he loved her because she is little and because she is ill, too. And he always used to bring her presents. But he taught us to read and me grammar and scripture, too," she added with dignity. "And mother never used to say anything, but we knew that she liked it and father knew it, too. And mother wants to teach me French, for it's time my education began."

"And do you know your prayers?"

"Of course, we do! We knew them long ago. I say my prayers to myself as I am a big girl now, but Kolya and Lida say them aloud with mother. First they repeat the 'Ave Maria' and then another prayer: 'Lord, forgive and bless sister Sonia,' and then another, 'Lord, forgive and bless our second father.' For our elder father is dead and this is another one, but we do pray for the other as well."

"Polenka, my name is Rodion. Pray sometimes for me, too. 'And Thy servant Rodion,' nothing more."

"I'll pray for you all the rest of my life," the little girl declared hotly, and suddenly smiling again she rushed at him and hugged him warmly once more.

Raskolnikov told her his name and address and promised to be sure to come next day. The child went away quite enchanted with him. It was past ten when he came out into the street. In five minutes he was standing on the bridge at the spot where the woman had jumped in.

"Enough," he pronounced resolutely and triumphantly. "I've done with fancies, imaginary terrors and phantoms! Life is real! haven't I lived just now? My life has not yet died with that old woman! The Kingdom of Heaven to her—and now enough, madam, leave me in peace! Now for the reign of reason and light... and of will, and of strength... and now we will see! We will try our strength!" he added defiantly, as though challenging some power of darkness. "And I was ready to consent to live in a square of space!

"I am very weak at this moment, but... I believe my illness is all over. I knew it would be over when I went out. By the way, Potchinkov's house is only a few steps away. I certainly must go to Razumihin even if it were not close by... let him win his bet! Let us give him some satisfaction, too—no matter! Strength, strength is what one wants, you can get nothing without it, and strength must be won by strength—that's what they don't know," he added proudly and self-confidently and he walked with flagging footsteps from the bridge. Pride and self-confidence grew continually stronger in him; he was becoming a different man every moment. What was it had happened to work this revolution in him? He did not know himself; like a man catching at a straw, he suddenly felt that he, too, 'could live, that there was still life for him, that his life had not died with the old woman.' Perhaps he was in too great a hurry with his conclusions, but he did not think of that.

"But I did ask her to remember 'Thy servant Rodion' in her prayers," the idea struck him. "Well, that was... in case of emergency," he added and laughed himself at his boyish sally. He was in the best of spirits.

He easily found Razumihin; the new lodger was already known at Potchinkov's and the porter at once showed him the way. Half-way upstairs he could hear the noise and animated conversation of a big gathering of people. The door was wide open on the stairs; he could hear exclamations and discussion. Razumihin's room was fairly large; the company consisted of fifteen people. Raskolnikov stopped in the entry, where two of the landlady's servants were busy behind a screen with two samovars, bottles, plates and dishes of pie and savouries, brought up from the landlady's kitchen. Raskolnikov sent in for Razumihin. He ran out delighted. At the first glance it was apparent that he had had a great deal to drink and, though no amount of liquor made Razumihin quite drunk, this time he was perceptibly affected by it.

"Listen," Raskolnikov hastened to say, "I've only just come to tell you you've won your bet and that no one really knows what may not happen to him. I can't come in; I am so weak that I shall fall down directly. And so good evening and good-bye! Come and see me to-morrow."

"Do you know what? I'll see you home. If you say you're weak yourself, you must..."

"And your visitors? Who is the curly-headed one who has just peeped out?"

"He? Goodness only knows! Some friend of uncle's, I expect, or perhaps he has come without being invited... I'll leave uncle with them, he is an invaluable person, pity I can't introduce you to him now. But confound them all now! They won't notice me, and I need a little fresh air, for you've come just in the nick of time—another two minutes and I should have come to blows! They are talking such a lot of wild stuff... you simply can't imagine what men will say! Though why shouldn't you imagine? Don't we talk nonsense ourselves? And let them... that's the way to learn not to!... Wait a minute, I'll fetch Zossimov."

Zossimov pounced upon Raskolnikov almost greedily; he showed a special interest in him; soon his face brightened.

"You must go to bed at once," he pronounced, examining the patient as far as he could, "and take something for the night. Will you take it? I got it ready some time ago... a powder."

"Two, if you like," answered Raskolnikov. The powder was taken at once.

"It's a good thing you are taking him home," observed Zossimov to Razumihin—"we shall see how he is to-morrow, to-day he's not at all amiss—a considerable change since the afternoon. Live and learn..."

"Do you know what Zossimov whispered to me when we were coming out?" Razumihin blurted out, as soon as they were in the street. "I won't tell you everything, brother, because they are such fools. Zossimov told me to talk freely to you on the way and get you to talk freely to me, and afterwards I am to tell him about it, for he's got a notion in his head that you are... mad or close on it. Only fancy! In the first place, you've three times the brains he has; in the second, if you are not mad, you needn't care a hang that he has got such a wild idea; and thirdly, that piece of beef whose specialty is surgery has gone mad on mental diseases, and what's brought him to this conclusion about you was your conversation to-day with Zametov."

"Zametov told you all about it?"

"Yes, and he did well. Now I understand what it all means and so does Zametov.... Well, the fact is, Rodya... the point is... I am a little drunk now.... But that's... no matter... the point is that this idea... you understand? was just being hatched in their brains... you understand? That is, no one ventured to say it aloud, because the idea is too absurd and especially since the arrest of that painter, that bubble's burst and gone for ever. But why are they such fools? I gave Zametov a bit of a thrashing at the time—that's between ourselves, brother; please don't let out a hint that you know of it; I've noticed he is a ticklish subject; it was at Luise Ivanovna's. But to-day, to-day it's all cleared up. That Ilya Petrovitch is at the bottom of it! He took advantage of your fainting at the police station, but he is ashamed of it himself now; I know that..."

Raskolnikov listened greedily. Razumihin was drunk enough to talk too freely.

"I fainted then because it was so close and the smell of paint," said Raskolnikov.

"No need to explain that! And it wasn't the paint only: the fever had been coming on for a month; Zossimov testifies to that! But how crushed that boy is now, you wouldn't believe! 'I am not worth his little finger,' he says. Yours, he means. He has good feelings at times, brother. But the lesson, the lesson you gave him to-day in the Palais de Cristal, that was too good for anything! You frightened him at first, you know, he nearly went into convulsions! You almost convinced him again of the truth of all that hideous nonsense, and then you suddenly—put out your tongue at him: 'There now, what do you make of it?' It was perfect! He is crushed, annihilated now! It was masterly, by Jove, it's what they deserve! Ah, that I wasn't there! He was hoping to see you awfully. Porfiry, too, wants to make your acquaintance..."

"Ah!... he too... but why did they put me down as mad?"

"Oh, not mad. I must have said too much, brother.... What struck him, you see, was that only that subject seemed to interest you; now it's clear why it did interest you; knowing all the circumstances... and how that irritated you and worked in with your illness... I am a little drunk, brother, only, confound him, he has some idea of his own... I tell you, he's mad on mental diseases. But don't you mind him..."

For half a minute both were silent.

"Listen, Razumihin," began Raskolnikov, "I want to tell you plainly: I've just been at a death-bed, a clerk who died... I gave them all my money... and besides I've just been kissed by someone who, if I had killed anyone, would just the same... in fact I saw someone else there... with a flame-coloured feather... but I am talking nonsense; I am very weak, support me... we shall be at the stairs directly..."

"What's the matter? What's the matter with you?" Razumihin asked anxiously.

"I am a little giddy, but that's not the point, I am so sad, so sad... like a woman. Look, what's that? Look, look!"

"What is it?"

"Don't you see? A light in my room, you see? Through the crack..."

They were already at the foot of the last flight of stairs, at the level of the landlady's door, and they could, as a fact, see from below that there was a light in Raskolnikov's garret.

"Queer! Nastasya, perhaps," observed Razumihin.

"She is never in my room at this time and she must be in bed long ago, but... I don't care! Good-bye!"

"What do you mean? I am coming with you, we'll come in together!"

"I know we are going in together, but I want to shake hands here and say good-bye to you here. So give me your hand, good-bye!"

"What's the matter with you, Rodya?"

"Nothing... come along... you shall be witness."

They began mounting the stairs, and the idea struck Razumihin that perhaps Zossimov might be right after all. "Ah, I've upset him with my chatter!" he muttered to himself.

When they reached the door they heard voices in the room.

"What is it?" cried Razumihin. Raskolnikov was the first to open the door; he flung it wide and stood still in the doorway, dumbfoundered.

His mother and sister were sitting on his sofa and had been waiting an hour and a half for him. Why had he never expected, never thought of them, though the news that they had started, were on their way and would arrive immediately, had been repeated to him only that day? They had spent that hour and a half plying Nastasya with questions. She was standing before them and had told them everything by now. They were beside themselves with alarm when they heard of his "running away" to-day, ill and, as they understood from her story, delirious! "Good Heavens, what had become of him?" Both had been weeping, both had been in anguish for that hour and a half.

A cry of joy, of ecstasy, greeted Raskolnikov's entrance. Both rushed to him. But he stood like one dead; a sudden intolerable sensation struck him like a thunderbolt. He did not lift his arms to embrace them, he could not. His mother and sister clasped him in their arms, kissed him, laughed and cried. He took a step, tottered and fell to the ground, fainting.

Anxiety, cries of horror, moans... Razumihin who was standing in the doorway flew into the room, seized the sick man in his strong arms and in a moment had him on the sofa.

"It's nothing, nothing!" he cried to the mother and sister—"it's only a faint, a mere trifle! Only just now the doctor said he was much better, that he is perfectly well! Water! See, he is coming to himself, he is all right again!"

And seizing Dounia by the arm so that he almost dislocated it, he made her bend down to see that "he is all right again." The mother and sister looked on him with emotion and gratitude, as their Providence. They had heard already from Nastasya all that had been done for their Rodya during his illness, by this "very competent young man," as Pulcheria Alexandrovna Raskolnikov called him that evening in conversation with Dounia.

PART III

CHAPTER I

Raskolnikov got up, and sat down on the sofa. He waved his hand weakly to Razumihin to cut short the flow of warm and incoherent consolations he was addressing to his mother and sister, took them both by the hand and for a minute or two gazed from one to the other without speaking. His mother was alarmed by his expression. It revealed an emotion agonisingly poignant, and at the same time something immovable, almost insane. Pulcheria Alexandrovna began to cry.

Avdotya Romanovna was pale; her hand trembled in her brother's.

"Go home... with him," he said in a broken voice, pointing to Razumihin, "good-bye till to-morrow; to-morrow everything... Is it long since you arrived?"

"This evening, Rodya," answered Pulcheria Alexandrovna, "the train was awfully late. But, Rodya, nothing would induce me to leave you now! I will spend the night here, near you..."

"Don't torture me!" he said with a gesture of irritation.

"I will stay with him," cried Razumihin, "I won't leave him for a moment. Bother all my visitors! Let them rage to their hearts' content! My uncle is presiding there."

"How, how can I thank you!" Pulcheria Alexandrovna was beginning, once more pressing Razumihin's hands, but Raskolnikov interrupted her again.

"I can't have it! I can't have it!" he repeated irritably, "don't worry me! Enough, go away... I can't stand it!"

"Come, mamma, come out of the room at least for a minute," Dounia whispered in dismay; "we are distressing him, that's evident."

"Mayn't I look at him after three years?" wept Pulcheria Alexandrovna.

"Stay," he stopped them again, "you keep interrupting me, and my ideas get muddled.... Have you seen Luzhin?"

"No, Rodya, but he knows already of our arrival. We have heard, Rodya, that Pyotr Petrovitch was so kind as to visit you today," Pulcheria Alexandrovna added somewhat timidly.

"Yes... he was so kind... Dounia, I promised Luzhin I'd throw him downstairs and told him to go to hell...."

"Rodya, what are you saying! Surely, you don't mean to tell us..." Pulcheria Alexandrovna began in alarm, but she stopped, looking at Dounia.

Avdotya Romanovna was looking attentively at her brother, waiting for what would come next. Both of them had heard of the quarrel from Nastasya, so far as she had succeeded in understanding and reporting it, and were in painful perplexity and suspense.

"Dounia," Raskolnikov continued with an effort, "I don't want that marriage, so at the first opportunity to-morrow you must refuse Luzhin, so that we may never hear his name again."

"Good Heavens!" cried Pulcheria Alexandrovna.

"Brother, think what you are saying!" Avdotya Romanovna began impetuously, but immediately checked herself. "You are not fit to talk now, perhaps; you are tired," she added gently.

"You think I am delirious? No... You are marrying Luzhin for *my* sake. But I won't accept the sacrifice. And so write a letter before to-morrow, to refuse him... Let me read it in the morning and that will be the end of it!"

"That I can't do!" the girl cried, offended, "what right have you..."

"Dounia, you are hasty, too, be quiet, to-morrow... Don't you see..." the mother interposed in dismay. "Better come away!"

"He is raving," Razumihin cried tipsily, "or how would he dare! To-morrow all this nonsense will be over... to-day he certainly did drive him away. That was so. And Luzhin got angry, too.... He made speeches here, wanted to show off his learning and he went out crest-fallen...."

"Then it's true?" cried Pulcheria Alexandrovna.

"Good-bye till to-morrow, brother," said Dounia compassionately—"let us go, mother... Good-bye, Rodya."

"Do you hear, sister," he repeated after them, making a last effort, "I am not delirious; this marriage is—an infamy. Let me act like a scoundrel, but you mustn't... one is enough... and though I am a scoundrel, I wouldn't own such a sister. It's me or Luzhin! Go now...."

"But you're out of your mind! Despot!" roared Razumihin; but Raskolnikov did not and perhaps could not answer. He lay down on the sofa, and turned to the wall, utterly exhausted. Avdotya Romanovna looked with interest at Razumihin; her black eyes flashed; Razumihin positively started at her glance.

Pulcheria Alexandrovna stood overwhelmed.

"Nothing would induce me to go," she whispered in despair to Razumihin. "I will stay somewhere here... escort Dounia home."

"You'll spoil everything," Razumihin answered in the same whisper, losing patience—"come out on to the stairs, anyway. Nastasya, show a light! I assure you," he went on in a half whisper on the stairs—"that he was almost beating the doctor and me this afternoon! Do you understand? The doctor himself! Even he gave way and left him, so as not to irritate him. I remained downstairs on guard, but he dressed at once and slipped off. And he will slip off again if you irritate him, at this time of night, and will do himself some mischief...."

"What are you saying?"

"And Avdotya Romanovna can't possibly be left in those lodgings without you. Just think where you are staying! That blackguard Pyotr Petrovitch couldn't find you better lodgings... But you know I've had a little to drink, and that's what makes me... swear; don't mind it...."

"But I'll go to the landlady here," Pulcheria Alexandrovna insisted, "I'll beseech her to find some corner for Dounia and me for the night. I can't leave him like that, I cannot!"

This conversation took place on the landing just before the landlady's door. Nastasya lighted them from a step below. Razumihin was in extraordinary excitement. Half an hour earlier, while he was bringing Raskolnikov home, he had indeed talked too freely, but he was aware of it himself, and his head was clear in spite of the vast quantities he had imbibed. Now he was in a state bordering on ecstasy, and all that he had drunk seemed to fly to his head with redoubled effect. He stood with the two ladies, seizing both by their hands, persuading them, and giving them reasons with astonishing plainness of speech, and at almost every word he uttered, probably to emphasise his arguments, he squeezed their hands painfully as in a vise. He stared at Avdotya Romanovna without the least regard for good manners. They sometimes pulled their hands out of his huge bony paws, but far from noticing what was the matter, he drew them all the closer to him. If they'd told him to jump head foremost from the staircase, he would have done it without thought or hesitation in their service. Though Pulcheria Alexandrovna felt that the young man was really too eccentric and pinched her hand too much, in her anxiety over her Rodya she looked on his presence as providential, and was unwilling to notice all his peculiarities. But though Avdotya Romanovna shared her anxiety, and was not of timorous disposition, she could not see the glowing light in his eyes without wonder and almost alarm. It was only the unbounded confidence inspired by Nastasya's account of her brother's queer friend, which prevented her from trying to run away from him, and to persuade her mother to do the same. She realised, too, that even running away was perhaps impossible now. Ten minutes later, however, she was considerably reassured; it was characteristic of Razumihin that he showed his true nature at once, whatever mood he might be in, so that people quickly saw the sort of man they had to deal with.

"You can't go to the landlady, that's perfect nonsense!" he cried. "If you stay, though you are his mother, you'll drive him to a frenzy, and then goodness knows what will happen! Listen, I'll tell you what I'll do: Nastasya will stay with him now, and I'll conduct you both home, you can't be in the streets alone; Petersburg is an awful place in that way.... But no matter! Then I'll run straight back here and a quarter of an hour later, on my word of honour, I'll bring you news how he is, whether he is asleep, and all that. Then, listen! Then I'll run home in a twinkling—I've a lot of friends there, all drunk—I'll fetch Zossimov—that's the doctor who is looking after him, he is there, too, but he is not drunk; he is not drunk, he is never drunk! I'll drag him to Rodya, and then to you, so that you'll get two reports in the hour—from the doctor, you understand, from the doctor himself, that's a very different thing from my account of him! If there's anything wrong, I swear I'll bring you here myself, but, if it's all right, you go to bed. And I'll spend the night here, in the passage, he won't hear me, and I'll tell Zossimov to sleep at the landlady's, to be at hand. Which is better for him: you or the doctor? So come home then! But the landlady is out of the question; it's all right for me, but it's out of the question for you: she wouldn't take you, for she's... for she's a fool... She'd be jealous on my account of Avdotya Romanovna and of you, too, if you want to know... of Avdotya Romanovna certainly. She is an absolutely, absolutely unaccountable character! But I am a fool, too!... No matter! Come along! Do you trust me? Come, do you trust me or not?"

"Let us go, mother," said Avdotya Romanovna, "he will certainly do what he has promised. He has saved Rodya already, and if the doctor really will consent to spend the night here, what could be better?"

"You see, you... you... understand me, because you are an angel!" Razumihin cried in ecstasy, "let us go! Nastasya! Fly upstairs and sit with him with a light; I'll come in a quarter of an hour."

Though Pulcheria Alexandrovna was not perfectly convinced, she made no further resistance. Razumihin gave an arm to each and drew them down the stairs. He still made her uneasy, as though he was competent and good-natured, was he capable of carrying out his promise? He seemed in such a condition....

"Ah, I see you think I am in such a condition!" Razumihin broke in upon her thoughts, guessing them, as he strolled along the pavement with huge steps, so that the two ladies could hardly keep up with him, a fact he did not observe, however. "Nonsense! That is... I am drunk like a fool, but that's not it; I am not drunk from wine. It's seeing you has turned my head... But don't mind me! Don't take any notice: I am talking nonsense, I am not worthy of you.... I am utterly unworthy of you! The minute I've taken you home, I'll pour a couple of pailfuls of water over my head in the gutter here, and then I shall be all right.... If only you knew how I love you both! Don't laugh, and don't be angry! You may be angry with anyone, but not with me! I am his friend, and therefore I am your friend, too, I want to be... I had a presentiment... Last year there was a moment... though it wasn't a presentiment really, for you seem to have fallen from heaven. And I expect I shan't sleep all night... Zossimov was afraid a little time ago that he would go mad... that's why he mustn't be irritated."

"What do you say?" cried the mother.

"Did the doctor really say that?" asked Avdotya Romanovna, alarmed.

"Yes, but it's not so, not a bit of it. He gave him some medicine, a powder, I saw it, and then your coming here.... Ah! It would have been better if you had come to-morrow. It's a good thing we went away. And in an hour Zossimov himself will report to you about everything. He is not drunk! And I shan't be drunk.... And what made me get so tight? Because they got me into an argument, damn them! I've sworn never to argue! They talk such trash! I almost came to blows! I've left my uncle to preside. Would you believe, they insist on complete absence of individualism and that's just what they relish! Not to be themselves, to be as unlike themselves as they can. That's what they regard as the highest point of progress. If only their nonsense were their own, but as it is..."

"Listen!" Pulcheria Alexandrovna interrupted timidly, but it only added fuel to the flames.

"What do you think?" shouted Razumihin, louder than ever, "you think I am attacking them for talking nonsense? Not a bit! I like them to talk nonsense. That's man's one privilege over all creation. Through error you come to the truth! I am a man because I err! You never reach any truth without making fourteen mistakes and very likely a hundred and fourteen. And a fine thing, too, in its way; but we can't even make mistakes on our own account! Talk nonsense, but talk your own nonsense, and I'll kiss you for it. To go wrong in one's own way is better than to go right in someone else's. In the first case you are a man, in the second you're no better than a bird. Truth won't escape you, but life can be cramped. There have been examples. And what are we doing now? In science, development, thought, invention, ideals, aims, liberalism, judgment, experience and everything, everything, everything, we are still in the preparatory class at school. We prefer to live on other people's ideas, it's what we are used to! Am I right, am I right?" cried Razumihin, pressing and shaking the two ladies' hands.

"Oh, mercy, I do not know," cried poor Pulcheria Alexandrovna.

"Yes, yes... though I don't agree with you in everything," added Avdotya Romanovna earnestly and at once uttered a cry, for he squeezed her hand so painfully.

"Yes, you say yes... well after that you... you..." he cried in a transport, "you are a fount of goodness, purity, sense... and perfection. Give me your hand... you give me yours, too! I want to kiss your hands here at once, on my knees..." and he fell on his knees on the pavement, fortunately at that time deserted.

"Leave off, I entreat you, what are you doing?" Pulcheria Alexandrovna cried, greatly distressed.

"Get up, get up!" said Dounia laughing, though she, too, was upset.

"Not for anything till you let me kiss your hands! That's it! Enough! I get up and we'll go on! I am a luckless fool, I am unworthy of you and drunk... and I am ashamed.... I am not worthy to love you, but to do homage to you is the duty of every man who is not a perfect beast! And I've done homage.... Here are your lodgings, and for that alone Rodya was right in driving your Pyotr Petrovitch away.... How dare he! how dare he put you in such lodgings! It's a scandal! Do you know the sort of people they take in here? And you his betrothed! You are his betrothed? Yes? Well, then, I'll tell you, your *fiancé* is a scoundrel."

"Excuse me, Mr. Razumihin, you are forgetting..." Pulcheria Alexandrovna was beginning.

"Yes, yes, you are right, I did forget myself, I am ashamed of it," Razumihin made haste to apologise. "But... but you can't be angry with me for speaking so! For I speak sincerely and not because... hm, hm! That would be disgraceful; in fact not because I'm in... hm! Well, anyway, I won't say why, I daren't.... But we all saw to-day when he came in that that man is not of our sort. Not because he had his hair curled at the barber's, not because he was in such a hurry to show his wit, but because he is a spy, a speculator, because he is a skin-flint and a buffoon. That's evident. Do you think him clever? No, he is a fool, a fool. And is he a match for you? Good heavens! Do you see, ladies?" he stopped suddenly on the way upstairs to their rooms, "though all my friends there are drunk, yet they are all honest, and though we do talk a lot of trash, and I do, too, yet we shall talk our way to the truth at last, for we are on the right path, while Pyotr Petrovitch... is not on the right path. Though I've been calling them all sorts of names just now, I do respect them all... though I don't respect Zametov, I like him, for he is a puppy, and that bullock Zossimov, because he is an honest man and knows his work. But enough, it's all said and forgiven. Is it forgiven? Well, then, let's go on. I know this corridor, I've been here, there was a scandal here at Number 3.... Where are you here? Which number? eight? Well, lock yourselves in for the night, then. Don't let anybody in. In a quarter of an hour I'll come back with news, and half an hour later I'll bring Zossimov, you'll see! Good-bye, I'll run."

"Good heavens, Dounia, what is going to happen?" said Pulcheria Alexandrovna, addressing her daughter with anxiety and dismay.

"Don't worry yourself, mother," said Dounia, taking off her hat and cape. "God has sent this gentleman to our aid, though he has come from a drinking party. We can depend on him, I assure you. And all that he has done for Rodya...."

"Ah. Dounia, goodness knows whether he will come! How could I bring myself to leave Rodya?... And how different, how different I had fancied our meeting! How sullen he was, as though not pleased to see us...."

Tears came into her eyes.

"No, it's not that, mother. You didn't see, you were crying all the time. He is quite unhinged by serious illness—that's the reason."

"Ah, that illness! What will happen, what will happen? And how he talked to you, Dounia!" said the mother, looking timidly at her daughter, trying to read her thoughts and, already half consoled by Dounia's standing up for her brother, which meant that she had already forgiven him. "I am sure he will think better of it to-morrow," she added, probing her further.

"And I am sure that he will say the same to-morrow... about that," Avdotya Romanovna said finally. And, of course, there was no going beyond that, for this was a point which Pulcheria Alexandrovna was afraid to discuss. Dounia went up and kissed her mother. The latter warmly embraced her without speaking. Then she sat down to wait anxiously for Razumihin's return, timidly watching her daughter who walked up and down the room with her arms folded, lost in thought. This walking up and down when she was thinking was a habit of Avdotya Romanovna's and the mother was always afraid to break in on her daughter's mood at such moments.

Razumihin, of course, was ridiculous in his sudden drunken infatuation for Avdotya Romanovna. Yet apart from his eccentric condition, many people would have thought it justified if they had seen Avdotya Romanovna, especially at that moment when she was walking to and fro with folded arms, pensive and melancholy. Avdotya Romanovna was remarkably good looking; she was tall, strikingly well-proportioned, strong and self-reliant—the latter quality was apparent in every gesture, though it did not in the least detract from the grace and softness of her movements. In face she resembled her brother, but she might be described as really beautiful. Her hair was dark brown, a little lighter than her brother's; there was a proud light in her almost black eyes and yet at times a look of extraordinary kindness. She was pale, but it was a healthy pallor; her face was radiant with freshness and vigour. Her mouth was rather small; the full red lower lip projected a little as did her chin; it was the only irregularity in her beautiful face, but it gave it a peculiarly individual and almost haughty expression. Her face was always more serious and thoughtful than gay; but how well smiles, how well youthful, lighthearted, irresponsible, laughter suited her face! It was natural enough that a warm, open, simple-hearted, honest giant like Razumihin, who had never seen anyone like her and was not quite sober at the time, should lose his head immediately. Besides, as chance would have it, he saw Dounia for the first time transfigured by her love for her brother and her joy at meeting him. Afterwards he saw her lower lip quiver with indignation at her brother's insolent, cruel and ungrateful words—and his fate was sealed.

He had spoken the truth, moreover, when he blurted out in his drunken talk on the stairs that Praskovya Pavlovna, Raskolnikov's eccentric landlady, would be jealous of Pulcheria Alexandrovna as well as of Avdotya Romanovna on his account. Although Pulcheria Alexandrovna was forty-three, her face still retained traces of her former beauty; she looked much younger than her age, indeed, which is almost always the case with women who retain serenity of spirit, sensitiveness and pure sincere warmth of heart to old age. We may add in parenthesis that to preserve all this is the only means of retaining beauty to old age. Her hair had begun to grow grey and thin, there had long been little crow's foot wrinkles round her eyes, her cheeks were hollow and sunken from anxiety and grief, and yet it was a handsome face. She was Dounia over again, twenty years older, but without the projecting underlip. Pulcheria Alexandrovna was emotional, but not sentimental, timid and yielding, but only to a certain point. She could give way and accept a great deal even of what was contrary to her convictions, but there was a certain barrier fixed by honesty, principle and the deepest convictions which nothing would induce her to cross.

Exactly twenty minutes after Razumihin's departure, there came two subdued but hurried knocks at the door: he had come back.

"I won't come in, I haven't time," he hastened to say when the door was opened. "He sleeps like a top, soundly, quietly, and God grant he may sleep ten hours. Nastasya's with him; I told her not to leave till I came. Now I am fetching Zossimov, he will report to you and then you'd better turn in; I can see you are too tired to do anything...."

And he ran off down the corridor.

"What a very competent and... devoted young man!" cried Pulcheria Alexandrovna exceedingly delighted.

"He seems a splendid person!" Avdotya Romanovna replied with some warmth, resuming her walk up and down the room.

It was nearly an hour later when they heard footsteps in the corridor and another knock at the door. Both women waited this time completely relying on Razumihin's promise; he actually had succeeded in bringing Zossimov. Zossimov had agreed at once to desert the drinking party to go to Raskolnikov's, but he came reluctantly and with the greatest suspicion to see the ladies, mistrusting Razumihin in his exhilarated condition. But his vanity was at once reassured and flattered; he saw that they were really expecting him as an oracle. He stayed just ten minutes and succeeded in completely convincing and comforting Pulcheria Alexandrovna. He spoke with marked sympathy, but with the reserve and extreme seriousness of a young doctor at an important consultation. He did not utter a word on any other subject and did not display the slightest desire to enter into more personal relations with the two ladies. Remarking at his first entrance the dazzling beauty of Avdotya Romanovna, he endeavoured not to notice her at all during his visit and addressed himself solely to Pulcheria Alexandrovna. All this gave him extraordinary inward satisfaction. He declared that he thought the invalid at this moment going on very satisfactorily. According to his observations the patient's illness was due partly to his unfortunate material surroundings during the last few months, but it had partly also a moral origin, "was, so to speak, the product of several material and moral influences, anxieties, apprehensions, troubles, certain ideas... and so on." Noticing stealthily that Avdotya Romanovna was following his words with close attention, Zossimov allowed himself to enlarge on this theme. On Pulcheria Alexandrovna's anxiously and timidly inquiring as to "some suspicion of insanity," he replied with a composed and candid smile that his words had been exaggerated; that certainly the patient had some fixed idea, something approaching a monomania—he, Zossimov, was now particularly studying this interesting branch of medicine—but that it must be recollected that until to-day the patient had been in delirium and... and that no doubt the presence of his family would have a favourable effect on his recovery and distract his mind, "if only all fresh shocks can be avoided," he added significantly. Then he got up, took leave with an impressive and affable bow, while blessings, warm gratitude, and entreaties were showered upon him, and Avdotya Romanovna spontaneously offered her hand to him. He went out exceedingly pleased with his visit and still more so with himself.

"We'll talk to-morrow; go to bed at once!" Razumihin said in conclusion, following Zossimov out. "I'll be with you to-morrow morning as early as possible with my report."

"That's a fetching little girl, Avdotya Romanovna," remarked Zossimov, almost licking his lips as they both came out into the street.

"Fetching? You said fetching?" roared Razumihin and he flew at Zossimov and seized him by the throat. "If you ever dare.... Do you understand? Do you understand?" he shouted, shaking him by the collar and squeezing him against the wall. "Do you hear?"

"Let me go, you drunken devil," said Zossimov, struggling and when he had let him go, he stared at him and went off into a sudden guffaw. Razumihin stood facing him in gloomy and earnest reflection.

"Of course, I am an ass," he observed, sombre as a storm cloud, "but still... you are another."

"No, brother, not at all such another. I am not dreaming of any folly."

They walked along in silence and only when they were close to Raskolnikov's lodgings, Razumihin broke the silence in considerable anxiety.

"Listen," he said, "you're a first-rate fellow, but among your other failings, you're a loose fish, that I know, and a dirty one, too. You are a feeble, nervous wretch, and a mass of whims, you're getting fat and lazy and can't deny yourself anything—and I call that dirty because it leads one straight into the dirt. You've let yourself get so slack that I don't know how it is you are still a good, even a devoted doctor. You—a doctor—sleep on a feather bed and get up at night to your patients! In another three or four years you won't get up for your patients... But hang it all, that's not the point!... You are going to spend to-night in the landlady's flat here. (Hard work I've had to persuade her!) And I'll be in the kitchen. So here's a chance for you to get to know her better.... It's not as you think! There's not a trace of anything of the sort, brother...!"

"But I don't think!"

"Here you have modesty, brother, silence, bashfulness, a savage virtue... and yet she's sighing and melting like wax, simply melting! Save me from her, by all that's unholy! She's most prepossessing... I'll repay you, I'll do anything...."

Zossimov laughed more violently than ever.

"Well, you are smitten! But what am I to do with her?"

"It won't be much trouble, I assure you. Talk any rot you like to her, as long as you sit by her and talk. You're a doctor, too; try curing her of something. I swear you won't regret it. She has a piano, and you know, I strum a little. I have a song there, a genuine Russian one: 'I shed hot tears.' She likes the genuine article—and well, it all began with that song; Now you're a regular performer, a *maître*, a Rubinstein.... I assure you, you won't regret it!"

"But have you made her some promise? Something signed? A promise of marriage, perhaps?"

"Nothing, nothing, absolutely nothing of the kind! Besides she is not that sort at all.... Tchebarov tried that...."

"Well then, drop her!"

"But I can't drop her like that!"

"Why can't you?"

"Well, I can't, that's all about it! There's an element of attraction here, brother."

"Then why have you fascinated her?"

"I haven't fascinated her; perhaps I was fascinated myself in my folly. But she won't care a straw whether it's you or I, so long as somebody sits beside her, sighing.... I can't explain the position, brother... look here, you are good at mathematics, and working at it now... begin teaching her the integral calculus; upon my soul, I'm not joking, I'm in earnest, it'll be just the same to her. She will gaze at you and sigh for a whole year together. I talked to her once for two days at a time about the Prussian House of Lords (for one must talk of something)— she just sighed and perspired! And you mustn't talk of love—she's bashful to hysterics—but just let her see you can't tear yourself away—that's enough. It's fearfully comfortable; you're quite at home, you can read, sit, lie about, write. You may even venture on a kiss, if you're careful."

"But what do I want with her?"

"Ach, I can't make you understand! You see, you are made for each other! I have often been reminded of you!... You'll come to it in the end! So does it matter whether it's sooner or later? There's the feather-bed element here, brother—ach! and not only that! There's an attraction here—here you have the end of the world, an anchorage, a quiet haven, the navel of the earth, the three fishes that are the foundation of the world, the essence of pancakes, of savoury fish-pies, of the evening samovar, of soft sighs and warm shawls, and hot stoves to sleep on—as snug as though you were dead, and yet you're alive—the advantages of both at once! Well, hang it, brother, what stuff I'm talking, it's bedtime! Listen. I sometimes wake up at night; so I'll go in and look at him. But there's no need, it's all right. Don't you worry yourself, yet if you like, you might just look in once, too. But if you notice anything—delirium or fever—wake me at once. But there can't be...."

CHAPTER II

Razumihin waked up next morning at eight o'clock, troubled and serious. He found himself confronted with many new and unlooked-for perplexities. He had never expected that he would ever wake up feeling like that. He remembered every detail of the previous day and he knew that a perfectly novel experience had befallen him, that he had received an impression unlike anything he had known before. At the same time he recognised clearly that the dream which had fired his imagination was hopelessly unattainable—so unattainable that he felt positively ashamed of it, and he hastened to pass to the other more practical cares and difficulties bequeathed him by that "thrice accursed yesterday."

The most awful recollection of the previous day was the way he had shown himself "base and mean," not only because he had been drunk, but because he had taken advantage of the young girl's position to abuse her *fiancé* in his stupid jealousy, knowing nothing of their mutual relations and obligations and next to nothing of the man himself. And what right had he to criticise him in that hasty and unguarded manner? Who had asked for his opinion? Was it thinkable that such a creature as Avdotya Romanovna would be marrying an unworthy man for money? So there must be something in him. The lodgings? But after all how could he know the character of the lodgings? He was furnishing a flat... Foo! how despicable it all was! And what justification was it that he was drunk? Such a stupid excuse was even more degrading! In wine is truth, and the truth had all come out, "that is, all the uncleanness of his coarse and envious heart"! And would such a dream ever be permissible to him, Razumihin? What was he beside such a girl—he, the drunken noisy braggart of last night? Was it possible to imagine so absurd and cynical a juxtaposition? Razumihin blushed desperately at the very idea and suddenly the recollection forced itself vividly upon him of how he had said last night on the stairs that the landlady would be jealous of Avdotya Romanovna... that was simply intolerable. He brought his fist down heavily on the kitchen stove, hurt his hand and sent one of the bricks flying.

"Of course," he muttered to himself a minute later with a feeling of self-abasement, "of course, all these infamies can never be wiped out or smoothed over... and so it's useless even to think of it, and I must go to them in silence and do my duty... in silence, too... and not ask forgiveness, and say nothing... for all is lost now!"

And yet as he dressed he examined his attire more carefully than usual. He hadn't another suit—if he had had, perhaps he wouldn't have put it on. "I would have made a point of not putting it on." But in any case he could not remain a cynic and a dirty sloven; he had no right to offend the feelings of others, especially when they were in need of his assistance and asking him to see them. He brushed his clothes carefully. His linen was always decent; in that respect he was especially clean.

He washed that morning scrupulously—he got some soap from Nastasya—he washed his hair, his neck and especially his hands. When it came to the question whether to shave his stubbly chin or not (Praskovya Pavlovna had capital razors that had been left by her late husband), the question was angrily answered in the negative. "Let it stay as it is! What if they think that I shaved on purpose to...? They certainly would think so! Not on any account!"

"And... the worst of it was he was so coarse, so dirty, he had the manners of a pothouse; and... and even admitting that he knew he had some of the essentials of a gentleman... what was there in that to be proud of? Everyone ought to be a gentleman and more than that... and all the same (he remembered) he, too, had done little things... not exactly dishonest, and yet.... And what thoughts he sometimes had; hm... and to set all that beside Avdotya Romanovna! Confound it! So be it! Well, he'd make a point then of being dirty, greasy, pothouse in his manners and he wouldn't care! He'd be worse!"

He was engaged in such monologues when Zossimov, who had spent the night in Praskovya Pavlovna's parlour, came in.

He was going home and was in a hurry to look at the invalid first. Razumihin informed him that Raskolnikov was sleeping like a dormouse. Zossimov gave orders that they shouldn't wake him and promised to see him again about eleven.

"If he is still at home," he added. "Damn it all! If one can't control one's patients, how is one to cure them? Do you know whether *he* will go to them, or whether *they* are coming here?"

"They are coming, I think," said Razumihin, understanding the object of the question, "and they will discuss their family affairs, no doubt. I'll be off. You, as the doctor, have more right to be here than I."

"But I am not a father confessor; I shall come and go away; I've plenty to do besides looking after them."

"One thing worries me," interposed Razumihin, frowning. "On the way home I talked a lot of drunken nonsense to him... all sorts of things... and amongst them that you were afraid that he... might become insane."

"You told the ladies so, too."

"I know it was stupid! You may beat me if you like! Did you think so seriously?"

"That's nonsense, I tell you, how could I think it seriously? You, yourself, described him as a monomaniac when you fetched me to him... and we added fuel to the fire yesterday, you did, that is, with your story about the painter; it was a nice conversation, when he was, perhaps, mad on that very point! If only I'd known what happened then at the police station and that some wretch... had insulted him with this suspicion! Hm... I would not have allowed that conversation yesterday. These monomaniacs will make a mountain out of a mole-hill... and see their fancies as solid realities.... As far as I remember, it was Zametov's story that cleared up half the mystery, to my mind. Why, I know one case in which a hypochondriac, a man of forty, cut the throat of a little boy of eight, because he couldn't endure the jokes he made every day at table! And in this case his rags, the insolent police officer, the fever and this suspicion! All that working upon a man half frantic with hypochondria, and with his morbid exceptional vanity! That may well have been the starting-point of illness. Well, bother it all!... And, by the way, that Zametov certainly is a nice fellow, but hm... he shouldn't have told all that last night. He is an awful chatterbox!"

"But whom did he tell it to? You and me?"

"And Porfiry."

"What does that matter?"

"And, by the way, have you any influence on them, his mother and sister? Tell them to be more careful with him to-day...."

"They'll get on all right!" Razumihin answered reluctantly.

"Why is he so set against this Luzhin? A man with money and she doesn't seem to dislike him... and they haven't a farthing, I suppose? eh?"

"But what business is it of yours?" Razumihin cried with annoyance. "How can I tell whether they've a farthing? Ask them yourself and perhaps you'll find out...."

"Foo! what an ass you are sometimes! Last night's wine has not gone off yet.... Good-bye; thank your Praskovya Pavlovna from me for my night's lodging. She locked herself in, made no reply to my *bonjour* through the door; she was up at seven o'clock, the samovar was taken into her from the kitchen. I was not vouchsafed a personal interview...."

At nine o'clock precisely Razumihin reached the lodgings at Bakaleyev's house. Both ladies were waiting for him with nervous impatience. They had risen at seven o'clock or earlier. He entered looking as black as night, bowed awkwardly and was at once furious with himself for it. He had reckoned without his host: Pulcheria Alexandrovna fairly rushed at him, seized him by both hands and was almost kissing them. He glanced timidly at Avdotya Romanovna, but her proud countenance wore at that moment an expression of such gratitude and friendliness, such complete and unlooked-for respect (in place of the sneering looks and ill-disguised contempt he had expected), that it threw him into greater confusion than if he had been met with abuse. Fortunately there was a subject for conversation, and he made haste to snatch at it.

Hearing that everything was going well and that Rodya had not yet waked, Pulcheria Alexandrovna declared that she was glad to hear it, because "she had something which it was very, very necessary to talk over beforehand." Then followed an inquiry about breakfast and an invitation to have it with them; they had waited to have it with him. Avdotya Romanovna rang the bell: it was answered by a ragged dirty waiter, and they asked him to bring tea which was served at last, but in such a dirty and disorderly way that the ladies were ashamed. Razumihin vigorously attacked the lodgings, but, remembering Luzhin, stopped in embarrassment and was greatly relieved by Pulcheria Alexandrovna's questions, which showered in a continual stream upon him.

He talked for three quarters of an hour, being constantly interrupted by their questions, and succeeded in describing to them all the most important facts he knew of the last year of Raskolnikov's life, concluding with a circumstantial account of his illness. He omitted, however, many things, which were better omitted, including the scene at the police station with all its consequences. They listened eagerly to his story, and, when he thought he had finished and satisfied his listeners, he found that they considered he had hardly begun.

"Tell me, tell me! What do you think...? Excuse me, I still don't know your name!" Pulcheria Alexandrovna put in hastily.

"Dmitri Prokofitch."

"I should like very, very much to know, Dmitri Prokofitch... how he looks... on things in general now, that is, how can I explain, what are his likes and dislikes? Is he always so irritable? Tell me, if you can, what are his hopes and, so to say, his dreams? Under what influences is he now? In a word, I should like..."

"Ah, mother, how can he answer all that at once?" observed Dounia.

"Good heavens, I had not expected to find him in the least like this, Dmitri Prokofitch!"

"Naturally," answered Razumihin. "I have no mother, but my uncle comes every year and almost every time he can scarcely recognise me, even in appearance, though he is a clever man; and your three years' separation means a great deal. What am I to tell you? I have known Rodion for a year and a half; he is morose, gloomy, proud and haughty, and of late—and perhaps for a long time before—he has been suspicious and fanciful. He has a noble nature and a kind heart. He does not like showing his feelings and would rather do a cruel thing than open his heart freely. Sometimes, though, he is not at all morbid, but simply cold and inhumanly callous; it's as though he were alternating between two characters. Sometimes he is fearfully reserved! He says he is so busy that everything is a hindrance, and yet he lies in bed doing nothing. He doesn't jeer at things, not because he hasn't the wit, but as though he hadn't time to waste on such trifles. He never listens to what is said to him. He is never interested in what interests other people at any given moment. He thinks very highly of himself and perhaps he is right. Well, what more? I think your arrival will have a most beneficial influence upon him."

"God grant it may," cried Pulcheria Alexandrovna, distressed by Razumihin's account of her Rodya.

And Razumihin ventured to look more boldly at Avdotya Romanovna at last. He glanced at her often while he was talking, but only for a moment and looked away again at once. Avdotya Romanovna sat at the table, listening attentively, then got up again and began walking to and fro with her arms folded and her lips compressed, occasionally putting in a question, without stopping her walk. She had the same habit of not listening to what was said. She was wearing a dress of thin dark stuff and she had a white transparent scarf round her neck. Razumihin soon detected signs of extreme poverty in their belongings. Had Avdotya Romanovna been dressed like a queen, he felt that he would not be afraid of her, but perhaps just because she was poorly dressed and that he noticed all the misery of her surroundings, his heart was filled with dread and he began to be afraid of every word he uttered, every gesture he made, which was very trying for a man who already felt diffident.

"You've told us a great deal that is interesting about my brother's character... and have told it impartially. I am glad. I thought that you were too uncritically devoted to him," observed Avdotya Romanovna with a smile. "I think you are right that he needs a woman's care," she added thoughtfully.

"I didn't say so; but I daresay you are right, only..."

"What?"

"He loves no one and perhaps he never will," Razumihin declared decisively.

"You mean he is not capable of love?"

"Do you know, Avdotya Romanovna, you are awfully like your brother, in everything, indeed!" he blurted out suddenly to his own surprise, but remembering at once what he had just before said of her brother, he turned as red as a crab and was overcome with confusion. Avdotya Romanovna couldn't help laughing when she looked at him.

"You may both be mistaken about Rodya," Pulcheria Alexandrovna remarked, slightly piqued. "I am not talking of our present difficulty, Dounia. What Pyotr Petrovitch writes in this letter and what you and I have supposed may be mistaken, but you can't imagine, Dmitri Prokofitch, how moody and, so to say, capricious he is. I never could depend on what he would do when he was only fifteen. And I am sure that he might do something now that nobody else would think of doing... Well, for instance, do you know how a year and a half ago he astounded me and gave me a shock that nearly killed me, when he had the idea of marrying that girl—what was her name—his landlady's daughter?"

"Did you hear about that affair?" asked Avdotya Romanovna.

"Do you suppose——" Pulcheria Alexandrovna continued warmly. "Do you suppose that my tears, my entreaties, my illness, my possible death from grief, our poverty would have made him pause? No, he would calmly have disregarded all obstacles. And yet it isn't that he doesn't love us!"

"He has never spoken a word of that affair to me," Razumihin answered cautiously. "But I did hear something from Praskovya Pavlovna herself, though she is by no means a gossip. And what I heard certainly was rather strange."

"And what did you hear?" both the ladies asked at once.

"Well, nothing very special. I only learned that the marriage, which only failed to take place through the girl's death, was not at all to Praskovya Pavlovna's liking. They say, too, the girl was not at all pretty, in fact I am told positively ugly... and such an invalid... and queer. But she seems to have had some good qualities. She must have had some good qualities or it's quite inexplicable.... She had no money either and he wouldn't have considered her money.... But it's always difficult to judge in such matters."

"I am sure she was a good girl," Avdotya Romanovna observed briefly.

"God forgive me, I simply rejoiced at her death. Though I don't know which of them would have caused most misery to the other—he to her or she to him," Pulcheria Alexandrovna concluded. Then she began tentatively questioning him about the scene on the previous day with Luzhin, hesitating and continually glancing at Dounia, obviously to the latter's annoyance. This incident more than all the rest evidently caused her uneasiness, even consternation. Razumihin described it in detail again, but this time he added his own conclusions: he openly blamed Raskolnikov for intentionally insulting Pyotr Petrovitch, not seeking to excuse him on the score of his illness.

"He had planned it before his illness," he added.

"I think so, too," Pulcheria Alexandrovna agreed with a dejected air. But she was very much surprised at hearing Razumihin express himself so carefully and even with a certain respect about Pyotr Petrovitch. Avdotya Romanovna, too, was struck by it.

"So this is your opinion of Pyotr Petrovitch?" Pulcheria Alexandrovna could not resist asking.

"I can have no other opinion of your daughter's future husband," Razumihin answered firmly and with warmth, "and I don't say it simply from vulgar politeness, but because... simply because Avdotya Romanovna has of her own free will deigned to accept this man. If I spoke so rudely of him last night, it was because I was disgustingly drunk and... mad besides; yes, mad, crazy, I lost my head completely... and this morning I am ashamed of it."

He crimsoned and ceased speaking. Avdotya Romanovna flushed, but did not break the silence. She had not uttered a word from the moment they began to speak of Luzhin.

Without her support Pulcheria Alexandrovna obviously did not know what to do. At last, faltering and continually glancing at her daughter, she confessed that she was exceedingly worried by one circumstance.

"You see, Dmitri Prokofitch," she began. "I'll be perfectly open with Dmitri Prokofitch, Dounia?"

"Of course, mother," said Avdotya Romanovna emphatically.

"This is what it is," she began in haste, as though the permission to speak of her trouble lifted a weight off her mind. "Very early this morning we got a note from Pyotr Petrovitch in reply to our letter announcing our arrival. He promised to meet us at the station, you know; instead of that he sent a servant to bring us the address of these lodgings and to show us the way; and he sent a message that he would be here himself this morning. But this morning this note came from him. You'd better read it yourself; there is one point in it which worries me very much... you will soon see what that is, and... tell me your candid opinion, Dmitri Prokofitch! You know Rodya's character better than anyone and no one can advise us better than you can. Dounia, I must tell you, made her decision at once, but I still don't feel sure how to act and I... I've been waiting for your opinion."

Razumihin opened the note which was dated the previous evening and read as follows:

"Dear Madam, Pulcheria Alexandrovna, I have the honour to inform you that owing to unforeseen obstacles I was rendered unable to meet you at the railway station; I sent a very competent person with the same object in view. I likewise shall be deprived of the honour of an interview with you to-morrow morning by business in the Senate that does not admit of delay, and also that I may not intrude on your family circle while you are meeting your son, and Avdotya Romanovna her brother. I shall have the honour of visiting you and paying you my respects at your lodgings not later than to-morrow evening at eight o'clock precisely, and herewith I venture to present my earnest and, I may add, imperative request that Rodion Romanovitch may not be present at our interview—as he offered me a gross and unprecedented affront on the occasion of my visit to him in his illness yesterday, and, moreover, since I desire from you personally an indispensable and circumstantial explanation upon a certain point, in regard to which I wish to learn your own interpretation. I have the honour to inform you, in anticipation, that if, in spite of my request, I meet Rodion Romanovitch, I shall be compelled to withdraw immediately and then you have only yourself to blame. I write on the assumption that Rodion Romanovitch who appeared so ill at my visit, suddenly recovered two hours later and so, being able to leave the house, may visit you also. I was confirmed in that belief by the testimony of my own eyes in the lodging of a drunken man who was run over and has since died, to whose daughter, a young woman of notorious behaviour, he gave twenty-five roubles on the pretext of the funeral, which gravely surprised me knowing what pains you were at to raise that sum. Herewith expressing my special respect to your estimable daughter, Avdotya Romanovna, I beg you to accept the respectful homage of

"Your humble servant,

"P. LUZHIN."

"What am I to do now, Dmitri Prokofitch?" began Pulcheria Alexandrovna, almost weeping. "How can I ask Rodya not to come? Yesterday he insisted so earnestly on our refusing Pyotr Petrovitch and now we are ordered not to receive Rodya! He will come on purpose if he knows, and... what will happen then?"

"Act on Avdotya Romanovna's decision," Razumihin answered calmly at once.

"Oh, dear me! She says... goodness knows what she says, she doesn't explain her object! She says that it would be best, at least, not that it would be best, but that it's absolutely necessary that Rodya should make a point of being here at eight o'clock and that they must meet.... I didn't want even to show him the letter, but to prevent him from coming by some stratagem with your help... because he is so irritable.... Besides I don't understand about that drunkard who died and that daughter, and how he could have given the daughter all the money... which..."

"Which cost you such sacrifice, mother," put in Avdotya Romanovna.

"He was not himself yesterday," Razumihin said thoughtfully, "if you only knew what he was up to in a restaurant yesterday, though there was sense in it too.... Hm! He did say something, as we were going home yesterday evening, about a dead man and a girl, but I didn't understand a word.... But last night, I myself..."

"The best thing, mother, will be for us to go to him ourselves and there I assure you we shall see at once what's to be done. Besides, it's getting late—good heavens, it's past ten," she cried looking at a splendid gold enamelled watch which hung round her neck on a thin Venetian chain, and looked entirely out of keeping with the rest of her dress. "A present from her *fiancé*," thought Razumihin.

"We must start, Dounia, we must start," her mother cried in a flutter. "He will be thinking we are still angry after yesterday, from our coming so late. Merciful heavens!"

While she said this she was hurriedly putting on her hat and mantle; Dounia, too, put on her things. Her gloves, as Razumihin noticed, were not merely shabby but had holes in them, and yet this evident poverty gave the two ladies an air of special dignity, which is always found in people who know how to wear poor clothes. Razumihin looked reverently at Dounia and felt proud of escorting her. "The queen who mended her stockings in prison," he thought, "must have looked then every inch a queen and even more a queen than at sumptuous banquets and levées."

"My God!" exclaimed Pulcheria Alexandrovna, "little did I think that I should ever fear seeing my son, my darling, darling Rodya! I am afraid, Dmitri Prokofitch," she added, glancing at him timidly.

"Don't be afraid, mother," said Dounia, kissing her, "better have faith in him."

"Oh, dear, I have faith in him, but I haven't slept all night," exclaimed the poor woman.

They came out into the street.

"Do you know, Dounia, when I dozed a little this morning I dreamed of Marfa Petrovna... she was all in white... she came up to me, took my hand, and shook her head at me, but so sternly as though she were blaming me.... Is that a good omen? Oh, dear me! You don't know, Dmitri Prokofitch, that Marfa Petrovna's dead!"

"No, I didn't know; who is Marfa Petrovna?"

"She died suddenly; and only fancy..."

"Afterwards, mamma," put in Dounia. "He doesn't know who Marfa Petrovna is."

"Ah, you don't know? And I was thinking that you knew all about us. Forgive me, Dmitri Prokofitch, I don't know what I am thinking about these last few days. I look upon you really as a providence for us, and so I took it for granted that you knew all about us. I look on you as a relation.... Don't be angry with me for saying so. Dear me, what's the matter with your right hand? Have you knocked it?"

"Yes, I bruised it," muttered Razumihin overjoyed.

"I sometimes speak too much from the heart, so that Dounia finds fault with me.... But, dear me, what a cupboard he lives in! I wonder whether he is awake? Does this woman, his landlady, consider it a room? Listen, you say he does not like to show his feelings, so perhaps I shall annoy him with my... weaknesses? Do advise me, Dmitri Prokofitch, how am I to treat him? I feel quite distracted, you know."

"Don't question him too much about anything if you see him frown; don't ask him too much about his health; he doesn't like that."

"Ah, Dmitri Prokofitch, how hard it is to be a mother! But here are the stairs.... What an awful staircase!"

"Mother, you are quite pale, don't distress yourself, darling," said Dounia caressing her, then with flashing eyes she added: "He ought to be happy at seeing you, and you are tormenting yourself so."

"Wait, I'll peep in and see whether he has waked up."

The ladies slowly followed Razumihin, who went on before, and when they reached the landlady's door on the fourth storey, they noticed that her door was a tiny crack open and that two keen black eyes were watching them from the darkness within. When their eyes met, the door was suddenly shut with such a slam that Pulcheria Alexandrovna almost cried out.

CHAPTER III

"He is well, quite well!" Zossimov cried cheerfully as they entered.

He had come in ten minutes earlier and was sitting in the same place as before, on the sofa. Raskolnikov was sitting in the opposite corner, fully dressed and carefully washed and combed, as he had not been for some time past. The room was immediately crowded, yet Nastasya managed to follow the visitors in and stayed to listen.

Raskolnikov really was almost well, as compared with his condition the day before, but he was still pale, listless, and sombre. He looked like a wounded man or one who has undergone some terrible physical suffering. His brows were knitted, his lips compressed, his eyes feverish. He spoke little and reluctantly, as though performing a duty, and there was a restlessness in his movements.

He only wanted a sling on his arm or a bandage on his finger to complete the impression of a man with a painful abscess or a broken arm. The pale, sombre face lighted up for a moment when his mother and sister entered, but this only gave it a look of more intense suffering, in place of its listless dejection. The light soon died away, but the look of suffering remained, and Zossimov, watching and studying his patient with all the zest of a young doctor beginning to practise, noticed in him no joy at the arrival of his mother and sister, but a sort of bitter, hidden determination to bear another hour or two of inevitable torture. He saw later that almost every word of the following conversation seemed to touch on some sore place and irritate it. But at the same time he marvelled at the power of controlling himself and hiding his feelings in a patient who the previous day had, like a monomaniac, fallen into a frenzy at the slightest word.

"Yes, I see myself now that I am almost well," said Raskolnikov, giving his mother and sister a kiss of welcome which made Pulcheria Alexandrovna radiant at once. "And I don't say this *as I did yesterday*," he said, addressing Razumihin, with a friendly pressure of his hand.

"Yes, indeed, I am quite surprised at him to-day," began Zossimov, much delighted at the ladies' entrance, for he had not succeeded in keeping up a conversation with his patient for ten minutes. "In another three or four days, if he goes on like this, he will be just as before, that is, as he was a month ago, or two... or perhaps even three. This has been coming on for a long while.... eh? Confess, now, that it has been perhaps your own fault?" he added, with a tentative smile, as though still afraid of irritating him.

"It is very possible," answered Raskolnikov coldly.

"I should say, too," continued Zossimov with zest, "that your complete recovery depends solely on yourself. Now that one can talk to you, I should like to impress upon you that it is essential to avoid the elementary, so to speak, fundamental causes tending to produce your morbid condition: in that case you will be cured, if not, it will go from bad to worse. These fundamental causes I don't know, but they must be known to you. You are an intelligent man, and must have observed yourself, of course. I fancy the first stage of your derangement coincides with your leaving the university. You must not be left without occupation, and so, work and a definite aim set before you might, I fancy, be very beneficial."

"Yes, yes; you are perfectly right.... I will make haste and return to the university: and then everything will go smoothly...."

Zossimov, who had begun his sage advice partly to make an effect before the ladies, was certainly somewhat mystified, when, glancing at his patient, he observed unmistakable mockery on his face. This lasted an instant,

457

however. Pulcheria Alexandrovna began at once thanking Zossimov, especially for his visit to their lodging the previous night.

"What! he saw you last night?" Raskolnikov asked, as though startled. "Then you have not slept either after your journey."

"Ach, Rodya, that was only till two o'clock. Dounia and I never go to bed before two at home."

"I don't know how to thank him either," Raskolnikov went on, suddenly frowning and looking down. "Setting aside the question of payment—forgive me for referring to it (he turned to Zossimov)—I really don't know what I have done to deserve such special attention from you! I simply don't understand it... and... and... it weighs upon me, indeed, because I don't understand it. I tell you so candidly."

"Don't be irritated." Zossimov forced himself to laugh. "Assume that you are my first patient—well—we fellows just beginning to practise love our first patients as if they were our children, and some almost fall in love with them. And, of course, I am not rich in patients."

"I say nothing about him," added Raskolnikov, pointing to Razumihin, "though he has had nothing from me either but insult and trouble."

"What nonsense he is talking! Why, you are in a sentimental mood to-day, are you?" shouted Razumihin.

If he had had more penetration he would have seen that there was no trace of sentimentality in him, but something indeed quite the opposite. But Avdotya Romanovna noticed it. She was intently and uneasily watching her brother.

"As for you, mother, I don't dare to speak," he went on, as though repeating a lesson learned by heart. "It is only to-day that I have been able to realise a little how distressed you must have been here yesterday, waiting for me to come back."

When he had said this, he suddenly held out his hand to his sister, smiling without a word. But in this smile there was a flash of real unfeigned feeling. Dounia caught it at once, and warmly pressed his hand, overjoyed and thankful. It was the first time he had addressed her since their dispute the previous day. The mother's face lighted up with ecstatic happiness at the sight of this conclusive unspoken reconciliation. "Yes, that is what I love him for," Razumihin, exaggerating it all, muttered to himself, with a vigorous turn in his chair. "He has these movements."

"And how well he does it all," the mother was thinking to herself. "What generous impulses he has, and how simply, how delicately he put an end to all the misunderstanding with his sister—simply by holding out his hand at the right minute and looking at her like that.... And what fine eyes he has, and how fine his whole face is!... He is even better looking than Dounia.... But, good heavens, what a suit—how terribly he's dressed!... Vasya, the messenger boy in Afanasy Ivanitch's shop, is better dressed! I could rush at him and hug him... weep over him—but I am afraid.... Oh, dear, he's so strange! He's talking kindly, but I'm afraid! Why, what am I afraid of?..."

"Oh, Rodya, you wouldn't believe," she began suddenly, in haste to answer his words to her, "how unhappy Dounia and I were yesterday! Now that it's all over and done with and we are quite happy again—I can tell you. Fancy, we ran here almost straight from the train to embrace you and that woman—ah, here she is! Good morning, Nastasya!... She told us at once that you were lying in a high fever and had just run away from the doctor in delirium, and they were looking for you in the streets. You can't imagine how we felt! I couldn't help thinking of the tragic end of Lieutenant Potanchikov, a friend of your father's—you can't remember him, Rodya—who ran out in the same way in a high fever and fell into the well in the court-yard and they couldn't pull him out till next day. Of course, we exaggerated things. We were on the point of rushing to find Pyotr Petrovitch to ask him to help.... Because we were alone, utterly alone," she said plaintively and stopped short, suddenly, recollecting it was still somewhat dangerous to speak of Pyotr Petrovitch, although "we are quite happy again."

"Yes, yes.... Of course it's very annoying...." Raskolnikov muttered in reply, but with such a preoccupied and inattentive air that Dounia gazed at him in perplexity.

"What else was it I wanted to say?" He went on trying to recollect. "Oh, yes; mother, and you too, Dounia, please don't think that I didn't mean to come and see you to-day and was waiting for you to come first."

"What are you saying, Rodya?" cried Pulcheria Alexandrovna. She, too, was surprised.

"Is he answering us as a duty?" Dounia wondered. "Is he being reconciled and asking forgiveness as though he were performing a rite or repeating a lesson?"

"I've only just waked up, and wanted to go to you, but was delayed owing to my clothes; I forgot yesterday to ask her... Nastasya... to wash out the blood... I've only just dressed."

"Blood! What blood?" Pulcheria Alexandrovna asked in alarm.

"Oh, nothing—don't be uneasy. It was when I was wandering about yesterday, rather delirious, I chanced upon a man who had been run over... a clerk..."

"Delirious? But you remember everything!" Razumihin interrupted.

"That's true," Raskolnikov answered with special carefulness. "I remember everything even to the slightest detail, and yet—why I did that and went there and said that, I can't clearly explain now."

"A familiar phenomenon," interposed Zossimov, "actions are sometimes performed in a masterly and most cunning way, while the direction of the actions is deranged and dependent on various morbid impressions—it's like a dream."

"Perhaps it's a good thing really that he should think me almost a madman," thought Raskolnikov.

"Why, people in perfect health act in the same way too," observed Dounia, looking uneasily at Zossimov.

"There is some truth in your observation," the latter replied. "In that sense we are certainly all not infrequently like madmen, but with the slight difference that the deranged are somewhat madder, for we must draw a line. A normal man, it is true, hardly exists. Among dozens—perhaps hundreds of thousands—hardly one is to be met with."

At the word "madman," carelessly dropped by Zossimov in his chatter on his favourite subject, everyone frowned.

Raskolnikov sat seeming not to pay attention, plunged in thought with a strange smile on his pale lips. He was still meditating on something.

"Well, what about the man who was run over? I interrupted you!" Razumihin cried hastily.

"What?" Raskolnikov seemed to wake up. "Oh... I got spattered with blood helping to carry him to his lodging. By the way, mamma, I did an unpardonable thing yesterday. I was literally out of my mind. I gave away all the money you sent me... to his wife for the funeral. She's a widow now, in consumption, a poor creature... three little children, starving... nothing in the house... there's a daughter, too... perhaps you'd have given it yourself if you'd seen them. But I had no right to do it I admit, especially as I knew how you needed the money yourself. To help others one must have the right to do it, or else *Crevez, chiens, si vous n'êtes pas contents*." He laughed, "That's right, isn't it, Dounia?"

"No, it's not," answered Dounia firmly.

"Bah! you, too, have ideals," he muttered, looking at her almost with hatred, and smiling sarcastically. "I ought to have considered that.... Well, that's praiseworthy, and it's better for you... and if you reach a line you won't overstep, you will be unhappy... and if you overstep it, maybe you will be still unhappier.... But all that's nonsense," he added irritably, vexed at being carried away. "I only meant to say that I beg your forgiveness, mother," he concluded, shortly and abruptly.

"That's enough, Rodya, I am sure that everything you do is very good," said his mother, delighted.

"Don't be too sure," he answered, twisting his mouth into a smile.

A silence followed. There was a certain constraint in all this conversation, and in the silence, and in the reconciliation, and in the forgiveness, and all were feeling it.

"It is as though they were afraid of me," Raskolnikov was thinking to himself, looking askance at his mother and sister. Pulcheria Alexandrovna was indeed growing more timid the longer she kept silent.

"Yet in their absence I seemed to love them so much," flashed through his mind.

"Do you know, Rodya, Marfa Petrovna is dead," Pulcheria Alexandrovna suddenly blurted out.

"What Marfa Petrovna?"

"Oh, mercy on us—Marfa Petrovna Svidrigaïlov. I wrote you so much about her."

"A-a-h! Yes, I remember.... So she's dead! Oh, really?" he roused himself suddenly, as if waking up. "What did she die of?"

"Only imagine, quite suddenly," Pulcheria Alexandrovna answered hurriedly, encouraged by his curiosity. "On the very day I was sending you that letter! Would you believe it, that awful man seems to have been the cause of her death. They say he beat her dreadfully."

"Why, were they on such bad terms?" he asked, addressing his sister.

"Not at all. Quite the contrary indeed. With her, he was always very patient, considerate even. In fact, all those seven years of their married life he gave way to her, too much so indeed, in many cases. All of a sudden he seems to have lost patience."

"Then he could not have been so awful if he controlled himself for seven years? You seem to be defending him, Dounia?"

"No, no, he's an awful man! I can imagine nothing more awful!" Dounia answered, almost with a shudder, knitting her brows, and sinking into thought.

"That had happened in the morning," Pulcheria Alexandrovna went on hurriedly. "And directly afterwards she ordered the horses to be harnessed to drive to the town immediately after dinner. She always used to drive to the town in such cases. She ate a very good dinner, I am told...."

"After the beating?"

"That was always her... habit; and immediately after dinner, so as not to be late in starting, she went to the bath-house.... You see, she was undergoing some treatment with baths. They have a cold spring there, and she used to bathe in it regularly every day, and no sooner had she got into the water when she suddenly had a stroke!"

"I should think so," said Zossimov.

"And did he beat her badly?"

"What does that matter!" put in Dounia.

"H'm! But I don't know why you want to tell us such gossip, mother," said Raskolnikov irritably, as it were in spite of himself.

"Ah, my dear, I don't know what to talk about," broke from Pulcheria Alexandrovna.

"Why, are you all afraid of me?" he asked, with a constrained smile.

"That's certainly true," said Dounia, looking directly and sternly at her brother. "Mother was crossing herself with terror as she came up the stairs."

His face worked, as though in convulsion.

"Ach, what are you saying, Dounia! Don't be angry, please, Rodya.... Why did you say that, Dounia?" Pulcheria Alexandrovna began, overwhelmed—"You see, coming here, I was dreaming all the way, in the train, how we should meet, how we should talk over everything together.... And I was so happy, I did not notice the journey! But what am I saying? I am happy now.... You should not, Dounia.... I am happy now—simply in seeing you, Rodya...."

"Hush, mother," he muttered in confusion, not looking at her, but pressing her hand. "We shall have time to speak freely of everything!"

As he said this, he was suddenly overwhelmed with confusion and turned pale. Again that awful sensation he had known of late passed with deadly chill over his soul. Again it became suddenly plain and perceptible to him that he had just told a fearful lie—that he would never now be able to speak freely of everything—that he would never again be able to *speak* of anything to anyone. The anguish of this thought was such that for a moment he almost forgot himself. He got up from his seat, and not looking at anyone walked towards the door.

"What are you about?" cried Razumihin, clutching him by the arm.

He sat down again, and began looking about him, in silence. They were all looking at him in perplexity.

"But what are you all so dull for?" he shouted, suddenly and quite unexpectedly. "Do say something! What's the use of sitting like this? Come, do speak. Let us talk.... We meet together and sit in silence.... Come, anything!"

"Thank God; I was afraid the same thing as yesterday was beginning again," said Pulcheria Alexandrovna, crossing herself.

"What is the matter, Rodya?" asked Avdotya Romanovna, distrustfully.

"Oh, nothing! I remembered something," he answered, and suddenly laughed.

"Well, if you remembered something; that's all right!... I was beginning to think..." muttered Zossimov, getting up from the sofa. "It is time for me to be off. I will look in again perhaps... if I can..." He made his bows, and went out.

"What an excellent man!" observed Pulcheria Alexandrovna.

"Yes, excellent, splendid, well-educated, intelligent," Raskolnikov began, suddenly speaking with surprising rapidity, and a liveliness he had not shown till then. "I can't remember where I met him before my illness.... I believe I have met him somewhere——... And this is a good man, too," he nodded at Razumihin. "Do you like him, Dounia?" he asked her; and suddenly, for some unknown reason, laughed.

"Very much," answered Dounia.

"Foo!—what a pig you are!" Razumihin protested, blushing in terrible confusion, and he got up from his chair. Pulcheria Alexandrovna smiled faintly, but Raskolnikov laughed aloud.

"Where are you off to?"

"I must go."

"You need not at all. Stay. Zossimov has gone, so you must. Don't go. What's the time? Is it twelve o'clock? What a pretty watch you have got, Dounia. But why are you all silent again? I do all the talking."

"It was a present from Marfa Petrovna," answered Dounia.

"And a very expensive one!" added Pulcheria Alexandrovna.

"A-ah! What a big one! Hardly like a lady's."

"I like that sort," said Dounia.

"So it is not a present from her *fiancé*," thought Razumihin, and was unreasonably delighted.

"I thought it was Luzhin's present," observed Raskolnikov.

"No, he has not made Dounia any presents yet."

"A-ah! And do you remember, mother, I was in love and wanted to get married?" he said suddenly, looking at his mother, who was disconcerted by the sudden change of subject and the way he spoke of it.

"Oh, yes, my dear."

Pulcheria Alexandrovna exchanged glances with Dounia and Razumihin.

"H'm, yes. What shall I tell you? I don't remember much indeed. She was such a sickly girl," he went on, growing dreamy and looking down again. "Quite an invalid. She was fond of giving alms to the poor, and was always dreaming of a nunnery, and once she burst into tears when she began talking to me about it. Yes, yes, I remember. I remember very well. She was an ugly little thing. I really don't know what drew me to her then—I think it was because she was always ill. If she had been lame or hunchback, I believe I should have liked her better still," he smiled dreamily. "Yes, it was a sort of spring delirium."

"No, it was not only spring delirium," said Dounia, with warm feeling.

He fixed a strained intent look on his sister, but did not hear or did not understand her words. Then, completely lost in thought, he got up, went up to his mother, kissed her, went back to his place and sat down.

"You love her even now?" said Pulcheria Alexandrovna, touched.

"Her? Now? Oh, yes.... You ask about her? No... that's all now, as it were, in another world... and so long ago. And indeed everything happening here seems somehow far away." He looked attentively at them. "You, now... I seem to be looking at you from a thousand miles away... but, goodness knows why we are talking of that! And what's the use of asking about it?" he added with annoyance, and biting his nails, fell into dreamy silence again.

"What a wretched lodging you have, Rodya! It's like a tomb," said Pulcheria Alexandrovna, suddenly breaking the oppressive silence. "I am sure it's quite half through your lodging you have become so melancholy."

"My lodging," he answered, listlessly. "Yes, the lodging had a great deal to do with it.... I thought that, too.... If only you knew, though, what a strange thing you said just now, mother," he said, laughing strangely.

A little more, and their companionship, this mother and this sister, with him after three years' absence, this intimate tone of conversation, in face of the utter impossibility of really speaking about anything, would have been beyond his power of endurance. But there was one urgent matter which must be settled one way or the other that day—so he had decided when he woke. Now he was glad to remember it, as a means of escape.

"Listen, Dounia," he began, gravely and drily, "of course I beg your pardon for yesterday, but I consider it my duty to tell you again that I do not withdraw from my chief point. It is me or Luzhin. If I am a scoundrel, you must not be. One is enough. If you marry Luzhin, I cease at once to look on you as a sister."

"Rodya, Rodya! It is the same as yesterday again," Pulcheria Alexandrovna cried, mournfully. "And why do you call yourself a scoundrel? I can't bear it. You said the same yesterday."

"Brother," Dounia answered firmly and with the same dryness. "In all this there is a mistake on your part. I thought it over at night, and found out the mistake. It is all because you seem to fancy I am sacrificing myself to someone and for someone. That is not the case at all. I am simply marrying for my own sake, because things are hard for me. Though, of course, I shall be glad if I succeed in being useful to my family. But that is not the chief motive for my decision...."

"She is lying," he thought to himself, biting his nails vindictively. "Proud creature! She won't admit she wants to do it out of charity! Too haughty! Oh, base characters! They even love as though they hate.... Oh, how I... hate them all!"

"In fact," continued Dounia, "I am marrying Pyotr Petrovitch because of two evils I choose the less. I intend to do honestly all he expects of me, so I am not deceiving him.... Why did you smile just now?" She, too, flushed, and there was a gleam of anger in her eyes.

"All?" he asked, with a malignant grin.

"Within certain limits. Both the manner and form of Pyotr Petrovitch's courtship showed me at once what he wanted. He may, of course, think too well of himself, but I hope he esteems me, too.... Why are you laughing again?"

"And why are you blushing again? You are lying, sister. You are intentionally lying, simply from feminine obstinacy, simply to hold your own against me.... You cannot respect Luzhin. I have seen him and talked with him. So you are selling yourself for money, and so in any case you are acting basely, and I am glad at least that you can blush for it."

"It is not true. I am not lying," cried Dounia, losing her composure. "I would not marry him if I were not convinced that he esteems me and thinks highly of me. I would not marry him if I were not firmly convinced that I can respect him. Fortunately, I can have convincing proof of it this very day... and such a marriage is not a vileness, as you say! And even if you were right, if I really had determined on a vile action, is it not merciless on your part to speak to me like that? Why do you demand of me a heroism that perhaps you have not either? It is despotism; it is tyranny. If I ruin anyone, it is only myself.... I am not committing a murder. Why do you look at me like that? Why are you so pale? Rodya, darling, what's the matter?"

"Good heavens! You have made him faint," cried Pulcheria Alexandrovna.

"No, no, nonsense! It's nothing. A little giddiness—not fainting. You have fainting on the brain. H'm, yes, what was I saying? Oh, yes. In what way will you get convincing proof to-day that you can respect him, and that he... esteems you, as you said. I think you said to-day?"

"Mother, show Rodya Pyotr Petrovitch's letter," said Dounia.

With trembling hands, Pulcheria Alexandrovna gave him the letter. He took it with great interest, but, before opening it, he suddenly looked with a sort of wonder at Dounia.

"It is strange," he said, slowly, as though struck by a new idea. "What am I making such a fuss for? What is it all about? Marry whom you like!"

He said this as though to himself, but said it aloud, and looked for some time at his sister, as though puzzled. He opened the letter at last, still with the same look of strange wonder on his face. Then, slowly and attentively, he began reading, and read it through twice. Pulcheria Alexandrovna showed marked anxiety, and all indeed expected something particular.

"What surprises me," he began, after a short pause, handing the letter to his mother, but not addressing anyone in particular, "is that he is a business man, a lawyer, and his conversation is pretentious indeed, and yet he writes such an uneducated letter."

They all started. They had expected something quite different.

"But they all write like that, you know," Razumihin observed, abruptly.

"Have you read it?"

"Yes."

"We showed him, Rodya. We... consulted him just now," Pulcheria Alexandrovna began, embarrassed.

"That's just the jargon of the courts," Razumihin put in. "Legal documents are written like that to this day."

"Legal? Yes, it's just legal—business language—not so very uneducated, and not quite educated—business language!"

"Pyotr Petrovitch makes no secret of the fact that he had a cheap education, he is proud indeed of having made his own way," Avdotya Romanovna observed, somewhat offended by her brother's tone.

"Well, if he's proud of it, he has reason, I don't deny it. You seem to be offended, sister, at my making only such a frivolous criticism on the letter, and to think that I speak of such trifling matters on purpose to annoy you. It is quite the contrary, an observation apropos of the style occurred to me that is by no means irrelevant as things stand. There is one expression, 'blame yourselves' put in very significantly and plainly, and there is besides a threat that he will go away at once if I am present. That threat to go away is equivalent to a threat to abandon you both if you are disobedient, and to abandon you now after summoning you to Petersburg. Well, what do you think? Can one resent such an expression from Luzhin, as we should if he (he pointed to Razumihin) had written it, or Zossimov, or one of us?"

"N-no," answered Dounia, with more animation. "I saw clearly that it was too naïvely expressed, and that perhaps he simply has no skill in writing... that is a true criticism, brother. I did not expect, indeed..."

"It is expressed in legal style, and sounds coarser than perhaps he intended. But I must disillusion you a little. There is one expression in the letter, one slander about me, and rather a contemptible one. I gave the money last night to the widow, a woman in consumption, crushed with trouble, and not 'on the pretext of the funeral,' but simply to pay for the funeral, and not to the daughter—a young woman, as he writes, of notorious behaviour (whom I saw last night for the first time in my life)—but to the widow. In all this I see a too hasty desire to slander me and to raise dissension between us. It is expressed again in legal jargon, that is to say, with a too obvious display of the aim, and with a very naïve eagerness. He is a man of intelligence, but to act sensibly, intelligence is not enough. It all shows the man and... I don't think he has a great esteem for you. I tell you this simply to warn you, because I sincerely wish for your good..."

Dounia did not reply. Her resolution had been taken. She was only awaiting the evening.

"Then what is your decision, Rodya?" asked Pulcheria Alexandrovna, who was more uneasy than ever at the sudden, new businesslike tone of his talk.

"What decision?"

"You see Pyotr Petrovitch writes that you are not to be with us this evening, and that he will go away if you come. So will you... come?"

"That, of course, is not for me to decide, but for you first, if you are not offended by such a request; and secondly, by Dounia, if she, too, is not offended. I will do what you think best," he added, drily.

"Dounia has already decided, and I fully agree with her," Pulcheria Alexandrovna hastened to declare.

"I decided to ask you, Rodya, to urge you not to fail to be with us at this interview," said Dounia. "Will you come?"

"Yes."

"I will ask you, too, to be with us at eight o'clock," she said, addressing Razumihin. "Mother, I am inviting him, too."

"Quite right, Dounia. Well, since you have decided," added Pulcheria Alexandrovna, "so be it. I shall feel easier myself. I do not like concealment and deception. Better let us have the whole truth.... Pyotr Petrovitch may be angry or not, now!"

CHAPTER IV

At that moment the door was softly opened, and a young girl walked into the room, looking timidly about her. Everyone turned towards her with surprise and curiosity. At first sight, Raskolnikov did not recognise her. It was Sofya Semyonovna Marmeladov. He had seen her yesterday for the first time, but at such a moment, in such surroundings and in such a dress, that his memory retained a very different image of her. Now she was a modestly and poorly-dressed young girl, very young, indeed, almost like a child, with a modest and refined manner, with a candid but somewhat frightened-looking face. She was wearing a very plain indoor dress, and had on a shabby old-fashioned hat, but she still carried a parasol. Unexpectedly finding the room full of people, she was not so much embarrassed as completely overwhelmed with shyness, like a little child. She was even about to retreat. "Oh... it's you!" said Raskolnikov, extremely astonished, and he, too, was confused. He at once recollected that his mother and sister knew through Luzhin's letter of "some young woman of notorious behaviour." He had only just been protesting against Luzhin's calumny and declaring that he had seen the girl last night for the first time, and suddenly she had walked in. He remembered, too, that he had not protested against the expression "of notorious behaviour." All this passed vaguely and fleetingly through his brain, but looking at her more intently, he saw that the humiliated creature was so humiliated that he felt suddenly sorry for her. When she made a movement to retreat in terror, it sent a pang to his heart.

"I did not expect you," he said, hurriedly, with a look that made her stop. "Please sit down. You come, no doubt, from Katerina Ivanovna. Allow me—not there. Sit here...."

At Sonia's entrance, Razumihin, who had been sitting on one of Raskolnikov's three chairs, close to the door, got up to allow her to enter. Raskolnikov had at first shown her the place on the sofa where Zossimov had been sitting, but feeling that the sofa which served him as a bed, was too *familiar* a place, he hurriedly motioned her to Razumihin's chair.

"You sit here," he said to Razumihin, putting him on the sofa.

Sonia sat down, almost shaking with terror, and looked timidly at the two ladies. It was evidently almost inconceivable to herself that she could sit down beside them. At the thought of it, she was so frightened that she hurriedly got up again, and in utter confusion addressed Raskolnikov.

"I... I... have come for one minute. Forgive me for disturbing you," she began falteringly. "I come from Katerina Ivanovna, and she had no one to send. Katerina Ivanovna told me to beg you... to be at the service... in the morning... at Mitrofanievsky... and then... to us... to her... to do her the honour... she told me to beg you..." Sonia stammered and ceased speaking.

"I will try, certainly, most certainly," answered Raskolnikov. He, too, stood up, and he, too, faltered and could not finish his sentence. "Please sit down," he said, suddenly. "I want to talk to you. You are perhaps in a hurry, but please, be so kind, spare me two minutes," and he drew up a chair for her.

Sonia sat down again, and again timidly she took a hurried, frightened look at the two ladies, and dropped her eyes. Raskolnikov's pale face flushed, a shudder passed over him, his eyes glowed.

"Mother," he said, firmly and insistently, "this is Sofya Semyonovna Marmeladov, the daughter of that unfortunate Mr. Marmeladov, who was run over yesterday before my eyes, and of whom I was just telling you."

Pulcheria Alexandrovna glanced at Sonia, and slightly screwed up her eyes. In spite of her embarrassment before Rodya's urgent and challenging look, she could not deny herself that satisfaction. Dounia gazed gravely and intently into the poor girl's face, and scrutinised her with perplexity. Sonia, hearing herself introduced, tried to raise her eyes again, but was more embarrassed than ever.

"I wanted to ask you," said Raskolnikov, hastily, "how things were arranged yesterday. You were not worried by the police, for instance?"

"No, that was all right... it was too evident, the cause of death... they did not worry us... only the lodgers are angry."

"Why?"

"At the body's remaining so long. You see it is hot now. So that, to-day, they will carry it to the cemetery, into the chapel, until to-morrow. At first Katerina Ivanovna was unwilling, but now she sees herself that it's necessary..."

"To-day, then?"

"She begs you to do us the honour to be in the church to-morrow for the service, and then to be present at the funeral lunch."

"She is giving a funeral lunch?"

"Yes... just a little.... She told me to thank you very much for helping us yesterday. But for you, we should have had nothing for the funeral."

All at once her lips and chin began trembling, but, with an effort, she controlled herself, looking down again.

During the conversation, Raskolnikov watched her carefully. She had a thin, very thin, pale little face, rather irregular and angular, with a sharp little nose and chin. She could not have been called pretty, but her blue eyes were so clear, and when they lighted up, there was such a kindliness and simplicity in her expression that one could not help being attracted. Her face, and her whole figure indeed, had another peculiar characteristic. In spite of her eighteen years, she looked almost a little girl—almost a child. And in some of her gestures, this childishness seemed almost absurd.

"But has Katerina Ivanovna been able to manage with such small means? Does she even mean to have a funeral lunch?" Raskolnikov asked, persistently keeping up the conversation.

"The coffin will be plain, of course... and everything will be plain, so it won't cost much. Katerina Ivanovna and I have reckoned it all out, so that there will be enough left... and Katerina Ivanovna was very anxious it should be so. You know one can't... it's a comfort to her... she is like that, you know...."

"I understand, I understand... of course... why do you look at my room like that? My mother has just said it is like a tomb."

"You gave us everything yesterday," Sonia said suddenly, in reply, in a loud rapid whisper; and again she looked down in confusion. Her lips and chin were trembling once more. She had been struck at once by Raskolnikov's poor surroundings, and now these words broke out spontaneously. A silence followed. There was a light in Dounia's eyes, and even Pulcheria Alexandrovna looked kindly at Sonia.

"Rodya," she said, getting up, "we shall have dinner together, of course. Come, Dounia.... And you, Rodya, had better go for a little walk, and then rest and lie down before you come to see us.... I am afraid we have exhausted you...."

"Yes, yes, I'll come," he answered, getting up fussily. "But I have something to see to."

"But surely you will have dinner together?" cried Razumihin, looking in surprise at Raskolnikov. "What do you mean?"

"Yes, yes, I am coming... of course, of course! And you stay a minute. You do not want him just now, do you, mother? Or perhaps I am taking him from you?"

"Oh, no, no. And will you, Dmitri Prokofitch, do us the favour of dining with us?"

"Please do," added Dounia.

Razumihin bowed, positively radiant. For one moment, they were all strangely embarrassed.

"Good-bye, Rodya, that is till we meet. I do not like saying good-bye. Good-bye, Nastasya. Ah, I have said good-bye again."

Pulcheria Alexandrovna meant to greet Sonia, too; but it somehow failed to come off, and she went in a flutter out of the room.

But Avdotya Romanovna seemed to await her turn, and following her mother out, gave Sonia an attentive, courteous bow. Sonia, in confusion, gave a hurried, frightened curtsy. There was a look of poignant discomfort in her face, as though Avdotya Romanovna's courtesy and attention were oppressive and painful to her.

"Dounia, good-bye," called Raskolnikov, in the passage. "Give me your hand."

"Why, I did give it to you. Have you forgotten?" said Dounia, turning warmly and awkwardly to him.

"Never mind, give it to me again." And he squeezed her fingers warmly.

Dounia smiled, flushed, pulled her hand away, and went off quite happy.

"Come, that's capital," he said to Sonia, going back and looking brightly at her. "God give peace to the dead, the living have still to live. That is right, isn't it?"

Sonia looked surprised at the sudden brightness of his face. He looked at her for some moments in silence. The whole history of the dead father floated before his memory in those moments....

***

"Heavens, Dounia," Pulcheria Alexandrovna began, as soon as they were in the street, "I really feel relieved myself at coming away—more at ease. How little did I think yesterday in the train that I could ever be glad of that."

"I tell you again, mother, he is still very ill. Don't you see it? Perhaps worrying about us upset him. We must be patient, and much, much can be forgiven."

"Well, you were not very patient!" Pulcheria Alexandrovna caught her up, hotly and jealously. "Do you know, Dounia, I was looking at you two. You are the very portrait of him, and not so much in face as in soul. You are both melancholy, both morose and hot-tempered, both haughty and both generous.... Surely he can't be an egoist, Dounia. Eh? When I think of what is in store for us this evening, my heart sinks!"

"Don't be uneasy, mother. What must be, will be."

"Dounia, only think what a position we are in! What if Pyotr Petrovitch breaks it off?" poor Pulcheria Alexandrovna blurted out, incautiously.

"He won't be worth much if he does," answered Dounia, sharply and contemptuously.

"We did well to come away," Pulcheria Alexandrovna hurriedly broke in. "He was in a hurry about some business or other. If he gets out and has a breath of air... it is fearfully close in his room.... But where is one to get a breath of air here? The very streets here feel like shut-up rooms. Good heavens! what a town!... stay... this side... they will crush you—carrying something. Why, it is a piano they have got, I declare... how they push!... I am very much afraid of that young woman, too."

"What young woman, mother?

"Why, that Sofya Semyonovna, who was there just now."

"Why?"

"I have a presentiment, Dounia. Well, you may believe it or not, but as soon as she came in, that very minute, I felt that she was the chief cause of the trouble...."

"Nothing of the sort!" cried Dounia, in vexation. "What nonsense, with your presentiments, mother! He only made her acquaintance the evening before, and he did not know her when she came in."

"Well, you will see.... She worries me; but you will see, you will see! I was so frightened. She was gazing at me with those eyes. I could scarcely sit still in my chair when he began introducing her, do you remember? It seems so strange, but Pyotr Petrovitch writes like that about her, and he introduces her to us—to you! So he must think a great deal of her."

"People will write anything. We were talked about and written about, too. Have you forgotten? I am sure that she is a good girl, and that it is all nonsense."

"God grant it may be!"

"And Pyotr Petrovitch is a contemptible slanderer," Dounia snapped out, suddenly.

Pulcheria Alexandrovna was crushed; the conversation was not resumed.

"I will tell you what I want with you," said Raskolnikov, drawing Razumihin to the window.

"Then I will tell Katerina Ivanovna that you are coming," Sonia said hurriedly, preparing to depart.

"One minute, Sofya Semyonovna. We have no secrets. You are not in our way. I want to have another word or two with you. Listen!" he turned suddenly to Razumihin again. "You know that... what's his name... Porfiry Petrovitch?"

"I should think so! He is a relation. Why?" added the latter, with interest.

"Is not he managing that case... you know, about that murder?... You were speaking about it yesterday."

"Yes... well?" Razumihin's eyes opened wide.

"He was inquiring for people who had pawned things, and I have some pledges there, too—trifles—a ring my sister gave me as a keepsake when I left home, and my father's silver watch—they are only worth five or six roubles altogether... but I value them. So what am I to do now? I do not want to lose the things, especially the watch. I was quaking just now, for fear mother would ask to look at it, when we spoke of Dounia's watch. It is the only thing of father's left us. She would be ill if it were lost. You know what women are. So tell me what to do. I know I ought to have given notice at the police station, but would it not be better to go straight to Porfiry? Eh? What do you think? The matter might be settled more quickly. You see, mother may ask for it before dinner."

"Certainly not to the police station. Certainly to Porfiry," Razumihin shouted in extraordinary excitement. "Well, how glad I am. Let us go at once. It is a couple of steps. We shall be sure to find him."

"Very well, let us go."

"And he will be very, very glad to make your acquaintance. I have often talked to him of you at different times. I was speaking of you yesterday. Let us go. So you knew the old woman? So that's it! It is all turning out splendidly.... Oh, yes, Sofya Ivanovna..."

"Sofya Semyonovna," corrected Raskolnikov. "Sofya Semyonovna, this is my friend Razumihin, and he is a good man."

"If you have to go now," Sonia was beginning, not looking at Razumihin at all, and still more embarrassed.

"Let us go," decided Raskolnikov. "I will come to you to-day, Sofya Semyonovna. Only tell me where you live."

He was not exactly ill at ease, but seemed hurried, and avoided her eyes. Sonia gave her address, and flushed as she did so. They all went out together.

"Don't you lock up?" asked Razumihin, following him on to the stairs.

"Never," answered Raskolnikov. "I have been meaning to buy a lock for these two years. People are happy who have no need of locks," he said, laughing, to Sonia. They stood still in the gateway.

"Do you go to the right, Sofya Semyonovna? How did you find me, by the way?" he added, as though he wanted to say something quite different. He wanted to look at her soft clear eyes, but this was not easy.

"Why, you gave your address to Polenka yesterday."

"Polenka? Oh, yes; Polenka, that is the little girl. She is your sister? Did I give her the address?"

"Why, had you forgotten?"

"No, I remember."

"I had heard my father speak of you... only I did not know your name, and he did not know it. And now I came... and as I had learnt your name, I asked to-day, 'Where does Mr. Raskolnikov live?' I did not know you had only a room too.... Good-bye, I will tell Katerina Ivanovna."

She was extremely glad to escape at last; she went away looking down, hurrying to get out of sight as soon as possible, to walk the twenty steps to the turning on the right and to be at last alone, and then moving rapidly along, looking at no one, noticing nothing, to think, to remember, to meditate on every word, every detail. Never, never had she felt anything like this. Dimly and unconsciously a whole new world was opening before her. She remembered suddenly that Raskolnikov meant to come to her that day, perhaps at once!

"Only not to-day, please, not to-day!" she kept muttering with a sinking heart, as though entreating someone, like a frightened child. "Mercy! to me... to that room... he will see... oh, dear!"

She was not capable at that instant of noticing an unknown gentleman who was watching her and following at her heels. He had accompanied her from the gateway. At the moment when Razumihin, Raskolnikov, and she stood still at parting on the pavement, this gentleman, who was just passing, started on hearing Sonia's words: "and I asked where Mr. Raskolnikov lived?" He turned a rapid but attentive look upon all three, especially upon Raskolnikov, to whom Sonia was speaking; then looked back and noted the house. All this was done in an instant as he passed, and trying not to betray his interest, he walked on more slowly as though waiting for something. He was waiting for Sonia; he saw that they were parting, and that Sonia was going home.

"Home? Where? I've seen that face somewhere," he thought. "I must find out."

At the turning he crossed over, looked round, and saw Sonia coming the same way, noticing nothing. She turned the corner. He followed her on the other side. After about fifty paces he crossed over again, overtook her and kept two or three yards behind her.

He was a man about fifty, rather tall and thickly set, with broad high shoulders which made him look as though he stooped a little. He wore good and fashionable clothes, and looked like a gentleman of position. He carried a handsome cane, which he tapped on the pavement at each step; his gloves were spotless. He had a broad, rather pleasant face with high cheek-bones and a fresh colour, not often seen in Petersburg. His flaxen hair was still abundant, and only touched here and there with grey, and his thick square beard was even lighter than his hair. His eyes were blue and had a cold and thoughtful look; his lips were crimson. He was a remarkedly well-preserved man and looked much younger than his years.

When Sonia came out on the canal bank, they were the only two persons on the pavement. He observed her dreaminess and preoccupation. On reaching the house where she lodged, Sonia turned in at the gate; he followed her, seeming rather surprised. In the courtyard she turned to the right corner. "Bah!" muttered the unknown gentleman, and mounted the stairs behind her. Only then Sonia noticed him. She reached the third storey, turned down the passage, and rang at No. 9. On the door was inscribed in chalk, "Kapernaumov, Tailor." "Bah!" the stranger repeated again, wondering at the strange coincidence, and he rang next door, at No. 8. The doors were two or three yards apart.

"You lodge at Kapernaumov's," he said, looking at Sonia and laughing. "He altered a waistcoat for me yesterday. I am staying close here at Madame Resslich's. How odd!" Sonia looked at him attentively.

"We are neighbours," he went on gaily. "I only came to town the day before yesterday. Good-bye for the present."

Sonia made no reply; the door opened and she slipped in. She felt for some reason ashamed and uneasy.

On the way to Porfiry's, Razumihin was obviously excited.

"That's capital, brother," he repeated several times, "and I am glad! I am glad!"

"What are you glad about?" Raskolnikov thought to himself.

"I didn't know that you pledged things at the old woman's, too. And... was it long ago? I mean, was it long since you were there?"

"What a simple-hearted fool he is!"

"When was it?" Raskolnikov stopped still to recollect. "Two or three days before her death it must have been. But I am not going to redeem the things now," he put in with a sort of hurried and conspicuous solicitude about the things. "I've not more than a silver rouble left... after last night's accursed delirium!"

He laid special emphasis on the delirium.

"Yes, yes," Razumihin hastened to agree—with what was not clear. "Then that's why you... were stuck... partly... you know in your delirium you were continually mentioning some rings or chains! Yes, yes... that's clear, it's all clear now."

"Hullo! How that idea must have got about among them. Here this man will go to the stake for me, and I find him delighted at having it *cleared up* why I spoke of rings in my delirium! What a hold the idea must have on all of them!"

"Shall we find him?" he asked suddenly.

"Oh, yes," Razumihin answered quickly. "He is a nice fellow, you will see, brother. Rather clumsy, that is to say, he is a man of polished manners, but I mean clumsy in a different sense. He is an intelligent fellow, very much so indeed, but he has his own range of ideas.... He is incredulous, sceptical, cynical... he likes to impose on people, or rather to make fun of them. His is the old, circumstantial method.... But he understands his work... thoroughly.... Last year he cleared up a case of murder in which the police had hardly a clue. He is very, very anxious to make your acquaintance!"

"On what grounds is he so anxious?"

"Oh, it's not exactly... you see, since you've been ill I happen to have mentioned you several times.... So, when he heard about you... about your being a law student and not able to finish your studies, he said, 'What a pity!' And so I concluded... from everything together, not only that; yesterday Zametov... you know, Rodya, I talked some nonsense on the way home to you yesterday, when I was drunk... I am afraid, brother, of your exaggerating it, you see."

"What? That they think I am a madman? Maybe they are right," he said with a constrained smile.

"Yes, yes.... That is, pooh, no!... But all that I said (and there was something else too) it was all nonsense, drunken nonsense."

"But why are you apologising? I am so sick of it all!" Raskolnikov cried with exaggerated irritability. It was partly assumed, however.

"I know, I know, I understand. Believe me, I understand. One's ashamed to speak of it."

"If you are ashamed, then don't speak of it."

Both were silent. Razumihin was more than ecstatic and Raskolnikov perceived it with repulsion. He was alarmed, too, by what Razumihin had just said about Porfiry.

"I shall have to pull a long face with him too," he thought, with a beating heart, and he turned white, "and do it naturally, too. But the most natural thing would be to do nothing at all. Carefully do nothing at all! No, *carefully* would not be natural again.... Oh, well, we shall see how it turns out.... We shall see... directly. Is it a good thing to go or not? The butterfly flies to the light. My heart is beating, that's what's bad!"

"In this grey house," said Razumihin.

"The most important thing, does Porfiry know that I was at the old hag's flat yesterday... and asked about the blood? I must find that out instantly, as soon as I go in, find out from his face; otherwise... I'll find out, if it's my ruin."

"I say, brother," he said suddenly, addressing Razumihin, with a sly smile, "I have been noticing all day that you seem to be curiously excited. Isn't it so?"

"Excited? Not a bit of it," said Razumihin, stung to the quick.

"Yes, brother, I assure you it's noticeable. Why, you sat on your chair in a way you never do sit, on the edge somehow, and you seemed to be writhing all the time. You kept jumping up for nothing. One moment you were angry, and the next your face looked like a sweetmeat. You even blushed; especially when you were invited to dinner, you blushed awfully."

"Nothing of the sort, nonsense! What do you mean?"

"But why are you wriggling out of it, like a schoolboy? By Jove, there he's blushing again."

"What a pig you are!"

"But why are you so shamefaced about it? Romeo! Stay, I'll tell of you to-day. Ha-ha-ha! I'll make mother laugh, and someone else, too..."

"Listen, listen, listen, this is serious.... What next, you fiend!" Razumihin was utterly overwhelmed, turning cold with horror. "What will you tell them? Come, brother... foo! what a pig you are!"

"You are like a summer rose. And if only you knew how it suits you; a Romeo over six foot high! And how you've washed to-day—you cleaned your nails, I declare. Eh? That's something unheard of! Why, I do believe you've got pomatum on your hair! Bend down."

"Pig!"

Raskolnikov laughed as though he could not restrain himself. So laughing, they entered Porfiry Petrovitch's flat. This is what Raskolnikov wanted: from within they could be heard laughing as they came in, still guffawing in the passage.

"Not a word here or I'll... brain you!" Razumihin whispered furiously, seizing Raskolnikov by the shoulder.

CHAPTER V

Raskolnikov was already entering the room. He came in looking as though he had the utmost difficulty not to burst out laughing again. Behind him Razumihin strode in gawky and awkward, shamefaced and red as a peony, with an utterly crestfallen and ferocious expression. His face and whole figure really were ridiculous at that moment and amply justified Raskolnikov's laughter. Raskolnikov, not waiting for an introduction, bowed to Porfiry Petrovitch, who stood in the middle of the room looking inquiringly at them. He held out his hand and shook hands, still apparently making desperate efforts to subdue his mirth and utter a few words to introduce himself. But he had no sooner succeeded in assuming a serious air and muttering something when he suddenly glanced again as though accidentally at Razumihin, and could no longer control himself: his stifled laughter broke out the more irresistibly the more he tried to restrain it. The extraordinary ferocity with which Razumihin received this "spontaneous" mirth gave the whole scene the appearance of most genuine fun and naturalness. Razumihin strengthened this impression as though on purpose.

"Fool! You fiend," he roared, waving his arm which at once struck a little round table with an empty tea-glass on it. Everything was sent flying and crashing.

"But why break chairs, gentlemen? You know it's a loss to the Crown," Porfiry Petrovitch quoted gaily.

Raskolnikov was still laughing, with his hand in Porfiry Petrovitch's, but anxious not to overdo it, awaited the right moment to put a natural end to it. Razumihin, completely put to confusion by upsetting the table and smashing the glass, gazed gloomily at the fragments, cursed and turned sharply to the window where he stood looking out with his back to the company with a fiercely scowling countenance, seeing nothing. Porfiry Petrovitch laughed and was ready to go on laughing, but obviously looked for explanations. Zametov had been sitting in the corner, but he rose at the visitors' entrance and was standing in expectation with a smile on his lips, though he looked with surprise and even it seemed incredulity at the whole scene and at Raskolnikov with a certain embarrassment. Zametov's unexpected presence struck Raskolnikov unpleasantly.

"I've got to think of that," he thought. "Excuse me, please," he began, affecting extreme embarrassment. "Raskolnikov."

"Not at all, very pleasant to see you... and how pleasantly you've come in.... Why, won't he even say good-morning?" Porfiry Petrovitch nodded at Razumihin.

"Upon my honour I don't know why he is in such a rage with me. I only told him as we came along that he was like Romeo... and proved it. And that was all, I think!"

"Pig!" ejaculated Razumihin, without turning round.

"There must have been very grave grounds for it, if he is so furious at the word," Porfiry laughed.

"Oh, you sharp lawyer!... Damn you all!" snapped Razumihin, and suddenly bursting out laughing himself, he went up to Porfiry with a more cheerful face as though nothing had happened. "That'll do! We are all fools. To come to business. This is my friend Rodion Romanovitch Raskolnikov; in the first place he has heard of you and wants to make your acquaintance, and secondly, he has a little matter of business with you. Bah! Zametov, what brought you here? Have you met before? Have you known each other long?"

"What does this mean?" thought Raskolnikov uneasily.

Zametov seemed taken aback, but not very much so.

"Why, it was at your rooms we met yesterday," he said easily.

"Then I have been spared the trouble. All last week he was begging me to introduce him to you. Porfiry and you have sniffed each other out without me. Where is your tobacco?"

Porfiry Petrovitch was wearing a dressing-gown, very clean linen, and trodden-down slippers. He was a man of about five and thirty, short, stout even to corpulence, and clean shaven. He wore his hair cut short and had a large round head, particularly prominent at the back. His soft, round, rather snub-nosed face was of a sickly yellowish colour, but had a vigorous and rather ironical expression. It would have been good-natured except for a look in the eyes, which shone with a watery, mawkish light under almost white, blinking eyelashes. The expression of those eyes was strangely out of keeping with his somewhat womanish figure, and gave it something far more serious than could be guessed at first sight.

As soon as Porfiry Petrovitch heard that his visitor had a little matter of business with him, he begged him to sit down on the sofa and sat down himself on the other end, waiting for him to explain his business, with that careful and over-serious attention which is at once oppressive and embarrassing, especially to a stranger, and especially if what you are discussing is in your opinion of far too little importance for such exceptional solemnity. But in brief and coherent phrases Raskolnikov explained his business clearly and exactly, and was so well satisfied with himself that he even succeeded in taking a good look at Porfiry. Porfiry Petrovitch did not once take his eyes off him. Razumihin, sitting opposite at the same table, listened warmly and impatiently, looking from one to the other every moment with rather excessive interest.

"Fool," Raskolnikov swore to himself.

"You have to give information to the police," Porfiry replied, with a most businesslike air, "that having learnt of this incident, that is of the murder, you beg to inform the lawyer in charge of the case that such and such things belong to you, and that you desire to redeem them... or... but they will write to you."

"That's just the point, that at the present moment," Raskolnikov tried his utmost to feign embarrassment, "I am not quite in funds... and even this trifling sum is beyond me... I only wanted, you see, for the present to declare that the things are mine, and that when I have money...."

"That's no matter," answered Porfiry Petrovitch, receiving his explanation of his pecuniary position coldly, "but you can, if you prefer, write straight to me, to say, that having been informed of the matter, and claiming such and such as your property, you beg..."

"On an ordinary sheet of paper?" Raskolnikov interrupted eagerly, again interested in the financial side of the question.

"Oh, the most ordinary," and suddenly Porfiry Petrovitch looked with obvious irony at him, screwing up his eyes and, as it were, winking at him. But perhaps it was Raskolnikov's fancy, for it all lasted but a moment. There was certainly something of the sort, Raskolnikov could have sworn he winked at him, goodness knows why.

"He knows," flashed through his mind like lightning.

"Forgive my troubling you about such trifles," he went on, a little disconcerted, "the things are only worth five roubles, but I prize them particularly for the sake of those from whom they came to me, and I must confess that I was alarmed when I heard..."

"That's why you were so much struck when I mentioned to Zossimov that Porfiry was inquiring for everyone who had pledges!" Razumihin put in with obvious intention.

This was really unbearable. Raskolnikov could not help glancing at him with a flash of vindictive anger in his black eyes, but immediately recollected himself.

"You seem to be jeering at me, brother?" he said to him, with a well-feigned irritability. "I dare say I do seem to you absurdly anxious about such trash; but you mustn't think me selfish or grasping for that, and these two things may be anything but trash in my eyes. I told you just now that the silver watch, though it's not worth a cent, is the only thing left us of my father's. You may laugh at me, but my mother is here," he turned suddenly to Porfiry, "and if she knew," he turned again hurriedly to Razumihin, carefully making his voice tremble, "that the watch was lost, she would be in despair! You know what women are!"

"Not a bit of it! I didn't mean that at all! Quite the contrary!" shouted Razumihin distressed.

"Was it right? Was it natural? Did I overdo it?" Raskolnikov asked himself in a tremor. "Why did I say that about women?"

"Oh, your mother is with you?" Porfiry Petrovitch inquired.

"Yes."

"When did she come?"

"Last night."

Porfiry paused as though reflecting.

"Your things would not in any case be lost," he went on calmly and coldly. "I have been expecting you here for some time."

And as though that was a matter of no importance, he carefully offered the ash-tray to Razumihin, who was ruthlessly scattering cigarette ash over the carpet. Raskolnikov shuddered, but Porfiry did not seem to be looking at him, and was still concerned with Razumihin's cigarette.

"What? Expecting him? Why, did you know that he had pledges *there*?" cried Razumihin.

Porfiry Petrovitch addressed himself to Raskolnikov.

"Your things, the ring and the watch, were wrapped up together, and on the paper your name was legibly written in pencil, together with the date on which you left them with her..."

"How observant you are!" Raskolnikov smiled awkwardly, doing his very utmost to look him straight in the face, but he failed, and suddenly added:

"I say that because I suppose there were a great many pledges... that it must be difficult to remember them all.... But you remember them all so clearly, and... and..."

"Stupid! Feeble!" he thought. "Why did I add that?"

"But we know all who had pledges, and you are the only one who hasn't come forward," Porfiry answered with hardly perceptible irony.

"I haven't been quite well."

"I heard that too. I heard, indeed, that you were in great distress about something. You look pale still."

"I am not pale at all.... No, I am quite well," Raskolnikov snapped out rudely and angrily, completely changing his tone. His anger was mounting, he could not repress it. "And in my anger I shall betray myself," flashed through his mind again. "Why are they torturing me?"

"Not quite well!" Razumihin caught him up. "What next! He was unconscious and delirious all yesterday. Would you believe, Porfiry, as soon as our backs were turned, he dressed, though he could hardly stand, and gave us the slip and went off on a spree somewhere till midnight, delirious all the time! Would you believe it! Extraordinary!"

"Really delirious? You don't say so!" Porfiry shook his head in a womanish way.

"Nonsense! Don't you believe it! But you don't believe it anyway," Raskolnikov let slip in his anger. But Porfiry Petrovitch did not seem to catch those strange words.

"But how could you have gone out if you hadn't been delirious?" Razumihin got hot suddenly. "What did you go out for? What was the object of it? And why on the sly? Were you in your senses when you did it? Now that all danger is over I can speak plainly."

"I was awfully sick of them yesterday." Raskolnikov addressed Porfiry suddenly with a smile of insolent defiance, "I ran away from them to take lodgings where they wouldn't find me, and took a lot of money with me. Mr. Zametov there saw it. I say, Mr. Zametov, was I sensible or delirious yesterday; settle our dispute."

He could have strangled Zametov at that moment, so hateful were his expression and his silence to him.

"In my opinion you talked sensibly and even artfully, but you were extremely irritable," Zametov pronounced dryly.

"And Nikodim Fomitch was telling me to-day," put in Porfiry Petrovitch, "that he met you very late last night in the lodging of a man who had been run over."

"And there," said Razumihin, "weren't you mad then? You gave your last penny to the widow for the funeral. If you wanted to help, give fifteen or twenty even, but keep three roubles for yourself at least, but he flung away all the twenty-five at once!"

"Maybe I found a treasure somewhere and you know nothing of it? So that's why I was liberal yesterday.... Mr. Zametov knows I've found a treasure! Excuse us, please, for disturbing you for half an hour with such trivialities," he said, turning to Porfiry Petrovitch, with trembling lips. "We are boring you, aren't we?"

"Oh no, quite the contrary, quite the contrary! If only you knew how you interest me! It's interesting to look on and listen... and I am really glad you have come forward at last."

"But you might give us some tea! My throat's dry," cried Razumihin.

"Capital idea! Perhaps we will all keep you company. Wouldn't you like... something more essential before tea?"

"Get along with you!"

Porfiry Petrovitch went out to order tea.

Raskolnikov's thoughts were in a whirl. He was in terrible exasperation.

"The worst of it is they don't disguise it; they don't care to stand on ceremony! And how if you didn't know me at all, did you come to talk to Nikodim Fomitch about me? So they don't care to hide that they are tracking me like a pack of dogs. They simply spit in my face." He was shaking with rage. "Come, strike me openly, don't play with me like a cat with a mouse. It's hardly civil, Porfiry Petrovitch, but perhaps I won't allow it! I shall get up and throw the whole truth in your ugly faces, and you'll see how I despise you." He could hardly breathe. "And what if it's only my fancy? What if I am mistaken, and through inexperience I get angry and don't keep up my nasty part? Perhaps it's all unintentional. All their phrases are the usual ones, but there is something about them.... It all might be said, but there is something. Why did he say bluntly, 'With her'? Why did Zametov add that I spoke artfully? Why do they speak in that tone? Yes, the tone.... Razumihin is sitting here, why does he see nothing? That innocent blockhead never does see anything! Feverish again! Did Porfiry wink at me just now? Of course it's nonsense! What could he wink for? Are they trying to upset my nerves or are they teasing me? Either it's ill fancy or they know! Even Zametov is rude.... Is Zametov rude? Zametov has changed his mind. I foresaw he would change his mind! He is at home here, while it's my first visit. Porfiry does not consider him a visitor; sits with his back to him. They're as thick as thieves, no doubt, over me! Not a doubt they were talking about me before we came. Do they know about the flat? If only they'd make haste! When I said that I ran away to take a flat he let it pass.... I put that in cleverly about a flat, it may be of use afterwards.... Delirious, indeed... ha-ha-ha! He knows all about last night! He didn't know of my mother's arrival! The hag had written the date on in pencil! You are wrong, you won't catch me! There are no facts... it's all supposition! You produce facts! The flat even isn't a fact but delirium. I know what to say to them.... Do they know about the flat? I won't go without finding out. What did I come for? But my being angry now, maybe is a fact! Fool, how irritable I am! Perhaps that's right; to play the invalid.... He is feeling me. He will try to catch me. Why did I come?"

All this flashed like lightning through his mind.

Porfiry Petrovitch returned quickly. He became suddenly more jovial.

"Your party yesterday, brother, has left my head rather.... And I am out of sorts altogether," he began in quite a different tone, laughing to Razumihin.

"Was it interesting? I left you yesterday at the most interesting point. Who got the best of it?"

"Oh, no one, of course. They got on to everlasting questions, floated off into space."

"Only fancy, Rodya, what we got on to yesterday. Whether there is such a thing as crime. I told you that we talked our heads off."

"What is there strange? It's an everyday social question," Raskolnikov answered casually.

"The question wasn't put quite like that," observed Porfiry.

"Not quite, that's true," Razumihin agreed at once, getting warm and hurried as usual. "Listen, Rodion, and tell us your opinion, I want to hear it. I was fighting tooth and nail with them and wanted you to help me. I told them you were coming.... It began with the socialist doctrine. You know their doctrine; crime is a protest against the abnormality of the social organisation and nothing more, and nothing more; no other causes admitted!...."

"You are wrong there," cried Porfiry Petrovitch; he was noticeably animated and kept laughing as he looked at Razumihin, which made him more excited than ever.

"Nothing is admitted," Razumihin interrupted with heat.

"I am not wrong. I'll show you their pamphlets. Everything with them is 'the influence of environment,' and nothing else. Their favourite phrase! From which it follows that, if society is normally organised, all crime will cease at once, since there will be nothing to protest against and all men will become righteous in one instant. Human nature is not taken into account, it is excluded, it's not supposed to exist! They don't recognise that humanity, developing by a historical living process, will become at last a normal society, but they believe that a social system that has come out of some mathematical brain is going to organise all humanity at once and make it just and sinless in an instant, quicker than any living process! That's why they instinctively dislike history, 'nothing but ugliness and stupidity in it,' and they explain it all as stupidity! That's why they so dislike the *living* process of life; they don't want a *living soul*! The living soul demands life, the soul won't obey the rules of mechanics, the soul is an object of suspicion, the soul is retrograde! But what they want though it smells of death and can be made of India-rubber, at least is not alive, has no will, is servile and won't revolt! And it comes in the end to their reducing everything to the building of walls and the planning of rooms and passages in a phalanstery! The phalanstery is ready, indeed, but your human nature is not ready for the phalanstery—it wants life, it hasn't completed its vital process, it's too soon for the graveyard! You can't skip over nature by logic. Logic presupposes three possibilities, but there are millions! Cut away a million, and reduce it all to the question of comfort! That's the easiest solution of the problem! It's seductively clear and you musn't think about it. That's the great thing, you mustn't think! The whole secret of life in two pages of print!"

"Now he is off, beating the drum! Catch hold of him, do!" laughed Porfiry. "Can you imagine," he turned to Raskolnikov, "six people holding forth like that last night, in one room, with punch as a preliminary! No, brother, you are wrong, environment accounts for a great deal in crime; I can assure you of that."

"Oh, I know it does, but just tell me: a man of forty violates a child of ten; was it environment drove him to it?"

"Well, strictly speaking, it did," Porfiry observed with noteworthy gravity; "a crime of that nature may be very well ascribed to the influence of environment."

Razumihin was almost in a frenzy. "Oh, if you like," he roared. "I'll prove to you that your white eyelashes may very well be ascribed to the Church of Ivan the Great's being two hundred and fifty feet high, and I will prove it clearly, exactly, progressively, and even with a Liberal tendency! I undertake to! Will you bet on it?"

"Done! Let's hear, please, how he will prove it!"

"He is always humbugging, confound him," cried Razumihin, jumping up and gesticulating. "What's the use of talking to you? He does all that on purpose; you don't know him, Rodion! He took their side yesterday, simply to make fools of them. And the things he said yesterday! And they were delighted! He can keep it up for a fortnight together. Last year he persuaded us that he was going into a monastery: he stuck to it for two months. Not long ago he took it into his head to declare he was going to get married, that he had everything ready for the wedding. He ordered new clothes indeed. We all began to congratulate him. There was no bride, nothing, all pure fantasy!"

"Ah, you are wrong! I got the clothes before. It was the new clothes in fact that made me think of taking you in."

"Are you such a good dissembler?" Raskolnikov asked carelessly.

"You wouldn't have supposed it, eh? Wait a bit, I shall take you in, too. Ha-ha-ha! No, I'll tell you the truth. All these questions about crime, environment, children, recall to my mind an article of yours which interested me at the time. 'On Crime'... or something of the sort, I forget the title, I read it with pleasure two months ago in the *Periodical Review*."

"My article? In the *Periodical Review*?" Raskolnikov asked in astonishment. "I certainly did write an article upon a book six months ago when I left the university, but I sent it to the *Weekly Review*."

"But it came out in the *Periodical*."

"And the *Weekly Review* ceased to exist, so that's why it wasn't printed at the time."

"That's true; but when it ceased to exist, the *Weekly Review* was amalgamated with the *Periodical*, and so your article appeared two months ago in the latter. Didn't you know?"

Raskolnikov had not known.

"Why, you might get some money out of them for the article! What a strange person you are! You lead such a solitary life that you know nothing of matters that concern you directly. It's a fact, I assure you."

"Bravo, Rodya! I knew nothing about it either!" cried Razumihin. "I'll run to-day to the reading-room and ask for the number. Two months ago? What was the date? It doesn't matter though, I will find it. Think of not telling us!"

"How did you find out that the article was mine? It's only signed with an initial."

"I only learnt it by chance, the other day. Through the editor; I know him.... I was very much interested."

"I analysed, if I remember, the psychology of a criminal before and after the crime."

"Yes, and you maintained that the perpetration of a crime is always accompanied by illness. Very, very original, but... it was not that part of your article that interested me so much, but an idea at the end of the article which I regret to say you merely suggested without working it out clearly. There is, if you recollect, a suggestion that there are certain persons who can... that is, not precisely are able to, but have a perfect right to commit breaches of morality and crimes, and that the law is not for them."

Raskolnikov smiled at the exaggerated and intentional distortion of his idea.

"What? What do you mean? A right to crime? But not because of the influence of environment?" Razumihin inquired with some alarm even.

"No, not exactly because of it," answered Porfiry. "In his article all men are divided into 'ordinary' and 'extraordinary.' Ordinary men have to live in submission, have no right to transgress the law, because, don't you see, they are ordinary. But extraordinary men have a right to commit any crime and to transgress the law in any way, just because they are extraordinary. That was your idea, if I am not mistaken?"

"What do you mean? That can't be right?" Razumihin muttered in bewilderment.

Raskolnikov smiled again. He saw the point at once, and knew where they wanted to drive him. He decided to take up the challenge.

"That wasn't quite my contention," he began simply and modestly. "Yet I admit that you have stated it almost correctly; perhaps, if you like, perfectly so." (It almost gave him pleasure to admit this.) "The only difference is that I don't contend that extraordinary people are always bound to commit breaches of morals, as you call it. In fact, I doubt whether such an argument could be published. I simply hinted that an 'extraordinary' man has the right... that is not an official right, but an inner right to decide in his own conscience to overstep... certain obstacles, and only in case it is essential for the practical fulfilment of his idea (sometimes, perhaps, of benefit to the whole of humanity). You say that my article isn't definite; I am ready to make it as clear as I can. Perhaps I am right in thinking you want me to; very well. I maintain that if the discoveries of Kepler and Newton could not have been made known except by sacrificing the lives of one, a dozen, a hundred, or more men, Newton would have had the right, would indeed have been in duty bound... to *eliminate* the dozen or the hundred men for the sake of making his discoveries known to the whole of humanity. But it does not follow from that that Newton had a right to murder people right and left and to steal every day in the market. Then, I remember, I maintain in my article that all... well, legislators and leaders of men, such as Lycurgus, Solon, Mahomet,

Napoleon, and so on, were all without exception criminals, from the very fact that, making a new law, they transgressed the ancient one, handed down from their ancestors and held sacred by the people, and they did not stop short at bloodshed either, if that bloodshed—often of innocent persons fighting bravely in defence of ancient law—were of use to their cause. It's remarkable, in fact, that the majority, indeed, of these benefactors and leaders of humanity were guilty of terrible carnage. In short, I maintain that all great men or even men a little out of the common, that is to say capable of giving some new word, must from their very nature be criminals—more or less, of course. Otherwise it's hard for them to get out of the common rut; and to remain in the common rut is what they can't submit to, from their very nature again, and to my mind they ought not, indeed, to submit to it. You see that there is nothing particularly new in all that. The same thing has been printed and read a thousand times before. As for my division of people into ordinary and extraordinary, I acknowledge that it's somewhat arbitrary, but I don't insist upon exact numbers. I only believe in my leading idea that men are *in general* divided by a law of nature into two categories, inferior (ordinary), that is, so to say, material that serves only to reproduce its kind, and men who have the gift or the talent to utter *a new word*. There are, of course, innumerable sub-divisions, but the distinguishing features of both categories are fairly well marked. The first category, generally speaking, are men conservative in temperament and law-abiding; they live under control and love to be controlled. To my thinking it is their duty to be controlled, because that's their vocation, and there is nothing humiliating in it for them. The second category all transgress the law; they are destroyers or disposed to destruction according to their capacities. The crimes of these men are of course relative and varied; for the most part they seek in very varied ways the destruction of the present for the sake of the better. But if such a one is forced for the sake of his idea to step over a corpse or wade through blood, he can, I maintain, find within himself, in his conscience, a sanction for wading through blood—that depends on the idea and its dimensions, note that. It's only in that sense I speak of their right to crime in my article (you remember it began with the legal question). There's no need for such anxiety, however; the masses will scarcely ever admit this right, they punish them or hang them (more or less), and in doing so fulfil quite justly their conservative vocation. But the same masses set these criminals on a pedestal in the next generation and worship them (more or less). The first category is always the man of the present, the second the man of the future. The first preserve the world and people it, the second move the world and lead it to its goal. Each class has an equal right to exist. In fact, all have equal rights with me—and *vive la guerre éternelle*—till the New Jerusalem, of course!"

"Then you believe in the New Jerusalem, do you?"

"I do," Raskolnikov answered firmly; as he said these words and during the whole preceding tirade he kept his eyes on one spot on the carpet.

"And... and do you believe in God? Excuse my curiosity."

"I do," repeated Raskolnikov, raising his eyes to Porfiry.

"And... do you believe in Lazarus' rising from the dead?"

"I... I do. Why do you ask all this?"

"You believe it literally?"

"Literally."

"You don't say so.... I asked from curiosity. Excuse me. But let us go back to the question; they are not always executed. Some, on the contrary..."

"Triumph in their lifetime? Oh, yes, some attain their ends in this life, and then..."

"They begin executing other people?"

"If it's necessary; indeed, for the most part they do. Your remark is very witty."

"Thank you. But tell me this: how do you distinguish those extraordinary people from the ordinary ones? Are there signs at their birth? I feel there ought to be more exactitude, more external definition. Excuse the natural anxiety of a practical law-abiding citizen, but couldn't they adopt a special uniform, for instance, couldn't they wear something, be branded in some way? For you know if confusion arises and a member of one category imagines that he belongs to the other, begins to 'eliminate obstacles' as you so happily expressed it, then..."

"Oh, that very often happens! That remark is wittier than the other."

"Thank you."

"No reason to; but take note that the mistake can only arise in the first category, that is among the ordinary people (as I perhaps unfortunately called them). In spite of their predisposition to obedience very many of them, through a playfulness of nature, sometimes vouchsafed even to the cow, like to imagine themselves advanced people, 'destroyers,' and to push themselves into the 'new movement,' and this quite sincerely. Meanwhile the really *new* people are very often unobserved by them, or even despised as reactionaries of grovelling tendencies. But I don't think there is any considerable danger here, and you really need not be uneasy for they never go very far. Of course, they might have a thrashing sometimes for letting their fancy run away with them and to teach them their place, but no more; in fact, even this isn't necessary as they castigate themselves, for they are very conscientious: some perform this service for one another and others chastise themselves with their own hands.... They will impose various public acts of penitence upon themselves with a beautiful and edifying effect; in fact you've nothing to be uneasy about.... It's a law of nature."

"Well, you have certainly set my mind more at rest on that score; but there's another thing worries me. Tell me, please, are there many people who have the right to kill others, these extraordinary people? I am ready to bow down to them, of course, but you must admit it's alarming if there are a great many of them, eh?"

"Oh, you needn't worry about that either," Raskolnikov went on in the same tone. "People with new ideas, people with the faintest capacity for saying something *new*, are extremely few in number, extraordinarily so in fact. One thing only is clear, that the appearance of all these grades and sub-divisions of men must follow with unfailing regularity some law of nature. That law, of course, is unknown at present, but I am convinced that it exists, and one day may become known. The vast mass of mankind is mere material, and only exists in order by some great effort, by some mysterious process, by means of some crossing of races and stocks, to bring into the world at last perhaps one man out of a thousand with a spark of independence. One in ten thousand perhaps—I speak roughly, approximately—is born with some independence, and with still greater independence one in a hundred thousand. The man of genius is one of millions, and the great geniuses, the crown of humanity, appear on earth perhaps one in many thousand millions. In fact I have not peeped into the retort in which all this takes place. But there certainly is and must be a definite law, it cannot be a matter of chance."

"Why, are you both joking?" Razumihin cried at last. "There you sit, making fun of one another. Are you serious, Rodya?"

Raskolnikov raised his pale and almost mournful face and made no reply. And the unconcealed, persistent, nervous, and *discourteous* sarcasm of Porfiry seemed strange to Razumihin beside that quiet and mournful face.

"Well, brother, if you are really serious... You are right, of course, in saying that it's not new, that it's like what we've read and heard a thousand times already; but what is really original in all this, and is exclusively your own, to my horror, is that you sanction bloodshed *in the name of conscience*, and, excuse my saying so, with such fanaticism.... That, I take it, is the point of your article. But that sanction of bloodshed *by conscience* is to my mind... more terrible than the official, legal sanction of bloodshed...."

"You are quite right, it is more terrible," Porfiry agreed.

"Yes, you must have exaggerated! There is some mistake, I shall read it. You can't think that! I shall read it."

"All that is not in the article, there's only a hint of it," said Raskolnikov.

"Yes, yes." Porfiry couldn't sit still. "Your attitude to crime is pretty clear to me now, but... excuse me for my impertinence (I am really ashamed to be worrying you like this), you see, you've removed my anxiety as to the two grades getting mixed, but... there are various practical possibilities that make me uneasy! What if some man or youth imagines that he is a Lycurgus or Mahomet—a future one of course—and suppose he begins to remove all obstacles.... He has some great enterprise before him and needs money for it... and tries to get it... do you see?"

Zametov gave a sudden guffaw in his corner. Raskolnikov did not even raise his eyes to him.

"I must admit," he went on calmly, "that such cases certainly must arise. The vain and foolish are particularly apt to fall into that snare; young people especially."

"Yes, you see. Well then?"

"What then?" Raskolnikov smiled in reply; "that's not my fault. So it is and so it always will be. He said just now (he nodded at Razumihin) that I sanction bloodshed. Society is too well protected by prisons, banishment, criminal investigators, penal servitude. There's no need to be uneasy. You have but to catch the thief."

"And what if we do catch him?"

"Then he gets what he deserves."

"You are certainly logical. But what of his conscience?"

"Why do you care about that?"

"Simply from humanity."

"If he has a conscience he will suffer for his mistake. That will be his punishment—as well as the prison."

"But the real geniuses," asked Razumihin frowning, "those who have the right to murder? Oughtn't they to suffer at all even for the blood they've shed?"

"Why the word *ought*? It's not a matter of permission or prohibition. He will suffer if he is sorry for his victim. Pain and suffering are always inevitable for a large intelligence and a deep heart. The really great men must, I think, have great sadness on earth," he added dreamily, not in the tone of the conversation.

He raised his eyes, looked earnestly at them all, smiled, and took his cap. He was too quiet by comparison with his manner at his entrance, and he felt this. Everyone got up.

"Well, you may abuse me, be angry with me if you like," Porfiry Petrovitch began again, "but I can't resist. Allow me one little question (I know I am troubling you). There is just one little notion I want to express, simply that I may not forget it."

"Very good, tell me your little notion," Raskolnikov stood waiting, pale and grave before him.

"Well, you see... I really don't know how to express it properly.... It's a playful, psychological idea.... When you were writing your article, surely you couldn't have helped, he-he! fancying yourself... just a little, an 'extraordinary' man, uttering a *new word* in your sense.... That's so, isn't it?"

"Quite possibly," Raskolnikov answered contemptuously.

Razumihin made a movement.

"And, if so, could you bring yourself in case of worldly difficulties and hardship or for some service to humanity—to overstep obstacles?... For instance, to rob and murder?"

And again he winked with his left eye, and laughed noiselessly just as before.

"If I did I certainly should not tell you," Raskolnikov answered with defiant and haughty contempt.

"No, I was only interested on account of your article, from a literary point of view..."

"Foo! how obvious and insolent that is!" Raskolnikov thought with repulsion.

"Allow me to observe," he answered dryly, "that I don't consider myself a Mahomet or a Napoleon, nor any personage of that kind, and not being one of them I cannot tell you how I should act."

"Oh, come, don't we all think ourselves Napoleons now in Russia?" Porfiry Petrovitch said with alarming familiarity.

Something peculiar betrayed itself in the very intonation of his voice.

"Perhaps it was one of these future Napoleons who did for Alyona Ivanovna last week?" Zametov blurted out from the corner.

Raskolnikov did not speak, but looked firmly and intently at Porfiry. Razumihin was scowling gloomily. He seemed before this to be noticing something. He looked angrily around. There was a minute of gloomy silence. Raskolnikov turned to go.

"Are you going already?" Porfiry said amiably, holding out his hand with excessive politeness. "Very, very glad of your acquaintance. As for your request, have no uneasiness, write just as I told you, or, better still, come to me there yourself in a day or two... to-morrow, indeed. I shall be there at eleven o'clock for certain. We'll arrange it all; we'll have a talk. As one of the last to be *there*, you might perhaps be able to tell us something," he added with a most good-natured expression.

"You want to cross-examine me officially in due form?" Raskolnikov asked sharply.

"Oh, why? That's not necessary for the present. You misunderstand me. I lose no opportunity, you see, and... I've talked with all who had pledges.... I obtained evidence from some of them, and you are the last.... Yes, by the way," he cried, seemingly suddenly delighted, "I just remember, what was I thinking of?" he turned to Razumihin, "you were talking my ears off about that Nikolay... of course, I know, I know very well," he turned to Raskolnikov, "that the fellow is innocent, but what is one to do? We had to trouble Dmitri too.... This is the point, this is all: when you went up the stairs it was past seven, wasn't it?"

"Yes," answered Raskolnikov, with an unpleasant sensation at the very moment he spoke that he need not have said it.

"Then when you went upstairs between seven and eight, didn't you see in a flat that stood open on a second storey, do you remember? two workmen or at least one of them? They were painting there, didn't you notice them? It's very, very important for them."

"Painters? No, I didn't see them," Raskolnikov answered slowly, as though ransacking his memory, while at the same instant he was racking every nerve, almost swooning with anxiety to conjecture as quickly as possible where the trap lay and not to overlook anything. "No, I didn't see them, and I don't think I noticed a flat like that open.... But on the fourth storey" (he had mastered the trap now and was triumphant) "I remember now that someone was moving out of the flat opposite Alyona Ivanovna's.... I remember... I remember it clearly. Some porters were carrying out a sofa and they squeezed me against the wall. But painters... no, I don't remember that there were any painters, and I don't think that there was a flat open anywhere, no, there wasn't."

"What do you mean?" Razumihin shouted suddenly, as though he had reflected and realised. "Why, it was on the day of the murder the painters were at work, and he was there three days before? What are you asking?"

"Foo! I have muddled it!" Porfiry slapped himself on the forehead. "Deuce take it! This business is turning my brain!" he addressed Raskolnikov somewhat apologetically. "It would be such a great thing for us to find out whether anyone had seen them between seven and eight at the flat, so I fancied you could perhaps have told us something.... I quite muddled it."

"Then you should be more careful," Razumihin observed grimly.

The last words were uttered in the passage. Porfiry Petrovitch saw them to the door with excessive politeness.

They went out into the street gloomy and sullen, and for some steps they did not say a word. Raskolnikov drew a deep breath.

CHAPTER VI

"I don't believe it, I can't believe it!" repeated Razumihin, trying in perplexity to refute Raskolnikov's arguments.

They were by now approaching Bakaleyev's lodgings, where Pulcheria Alexandrovna and Dounia had been expecting them a long while. Razumihin kept stopping on the way in the heat of discussion, confused and excited by the very fact that they were for the first time speaking openly about *it*.

"Don't believe it, then!" answered Raskolnikov, with a cold, careless smile. "You were noticing nothing as usual, but I was weighing every word."

"You are suspicious. That is why you weighed their words... h'm... certainly, I agree, Porfiry's tone was rather strange, and still more that wretch Zametov!... You are right, there was something about him—but why? Why?"

"He has changed his mind since last night."

"Quite the contrary! If they had that brainless idea, they would do their utmost to hide it, and conceal their cards, so as to catch you afterwards.... But it was all impudent and careless."

"If they had had facts—I mean, real facts—or at least grounds for suspicion, then they would certainly have tried to hide their game, in the hope of getting more (they would have made a search long ago besides). But they have no facts, not one. It is all mirage—all ambiguous. Simply a floating idea. So they try to throw me out by impudence. And perhaps, he was irritated at having no facts, and blurted it out in his vexation—or perhaps he has some plan... he seems an intelligent man. Perhaps he wanted to frighten me by pretending to know. They have a psychology of their own, brother. But it is loathsome explaining it all. Stop!"

"And it's insulting, insulting! I understand you. But... since we have spoken openly now (and it is an excellent thing that we have at last—I am glad) I will own now frankly that I noticed it in them long ago, this idea. Of course the merest hint only—an insinuation—but why an insinuation even? How dare they? What foundation have they? If only you knew how furious I have been. Think only! Simply because a poor student, unhinged by poverty and hypochondria, on the eve of a severe delirious illness (note that), suspicious, vain, proud, who has not seen a soul to speak to for six months, in rags and in boots without soles, has to face some wretched policemen and put up with their insolence; and the unexpected debt thrust under his nose, the I.O.U. presented by Tchebarov, the new paint, thirty degrees Reaumur and a stifling atmosphere, a crowd of people, the talk about the murder of a person where he had been just before, and all that on an empty stomach—he might well have a fainting fit! And that, that is what they found it all on! Damn them! I understand how annoying it is, but in your place, Rodya, I would laugh at them, or better still, spit in their ugly faces, and spit a dozen times in all directions. I'd hit out in all directions, neatly too, and so I'd put an end to it. Damn them! Don't be downhearted. It's a shame!"

"He really has put it well, though," Raskolnikov thought.

"Damn them? But the cross-examination again, to-morrow?" he said with bitterness. "Must I really enter into explanations with them? I feel vexed as it is, that I condescended to speak to Zametov yesterday in the restaurant...."

"Damn it! I will go myself to Porfiry. I will squeeze it out of him, as one of the family: he must let me know the ins and outs of it all! And as for Zametov..."

"At last he sees through him!" thought Raskolnikov.

"Stay!" cried Razumihin, seizing him by the shoulder again. "Stay! you were wrong. I have thought it out. You are wrong! How was that a trap? You say that the question about the workmen was a trap. But if you had done *that*, could you have said you had seen them painting the flat... and the workmen? On the contrary, you would have seen nothing, even if you had seen it. Who would own it against himself?"

"If I had done *that thing*, I should certainly have said that I had seen the workmen and the flat," Raskolnikov answered, with reluctance and obvious disgust.

"But why speak against yourself?"

"Because only peasants, or the most inexperienced novices deny everything flatly at examinations. If a man is ever so little developed and experienced, he will certainly try to admit all the external facts that can't be avoided, but will seek other explanations of them, will introduce some special, unexpected turn, that will give them another significance and put them in another light. Porfiry might well reckon that I should be sure to answer so, and say I had seen them to give an air of truth, and then make some explanation."

"But he would have told you at once that the workmen could not have been there two days before, and that therefore you must have been there on the day of the murder at eight o'clock. And so he would have caught you over a detail."

"Yes, that is what he was reckoning on, that I should not have time to reflect, and should be in a hurry to make the most likely answer, and so would forget that the workmen could not have been there two days before."

"But how could you forget it?"

"Nothing easier. It is in just such stupid things clever people are most easily caught. The more cunning a man is, the less he suspects that he will be caught in a simple thing. The more cunning a man is, the simpler the trap he must be caught in. Porfiry is not such a fool as you think...."

"He is a knave then, if that is so!"

Raskolnikov could not help laughing. But at the very moment, he was struck by the strangeness of his own frankness, and the eagerness with which he had made this explanation, though he had kept up all the preceding conversation with gloomy repulsion, obviously with a motive, from necessity.

"I am getting a relish for certain aspects!" he thought to himself. But almost at the same instant he became suddenly uneasy, as though an unexpected and alarming idea had occurred to him. His uneasiness kept on increasing. They had just reached the entrance to Bakaleyev's.

"Go in alone!" said Raskolnikov suddenly. "I will be back directly."

"Where are you going? Why, we are just here."

"I can't help it.... I will come in half an hour. Tell them."

"Say what you like, I will come with you."

"You, too, want to torture me!" he screamed, with such bitter irritation, such despair in his eyes that Razumihin's hands dropped. He stood for some time on the steps, looking gloomily at Raskolnikov striding rapidly away in the direction of his lodging. At last, gritting his teeth and clenching his fist, he swore he would squeeze Porfiry like a lemon that very day, and went up the stairs to reassure Pulcheria Alexandrovna, who was by now alarmed at their long absence.

When Raskolnikov got home, his hair was soaked with sweat and he was breathing heavily. He went rapidly up the stairs, walked into his unlocked room and at once fastened the latch. Then in senseless terror he rushed to the corner, to that hole under the paper where he had put the things; put his hand in, and for some minutes felt carefully in the hole, in every crack and fold of the paper. Finding nothing, he got up and drew a deep breath. As he was reaching the steps of Bakaleyev's, he suddenly fancied that something, a chain, a stud or even a bit of paper in which they had been wrapped with the old woman's handwriting on it, might somehow have slipped out and been lost in some crack, and then might suddenly turn up as unexpected, conclusive evidence against him.

He stood as though lost in thought, and a strange, humiliated, half senseless smile strayed on his lips. He took his cap at last and went quietly out of the room. His ideas were all tangled. He went dreamily through the gateway.

"Here he is himself," shouted a loud voice.

He raised his head.

The porter was standing at the door of his little room and was pointing him out to a short man who looked like an artisan, wearing a long coat and a waistcoat, and looking at a distance remarkably like a woman. He stooped, and his head in a greasy cap hung forward. From his wrinkled flabby face he looked over fifty; his little eyes were lost in fat and they looked out grimly, sternly and discontentedly.

"What is it?" Raskolnikov asked, going up to the porter.

The man stole a look at him from under his brows and he looked at him attentively, deliberately; then he turned slowly and went out of the gate into the street without saying a word.

"What is it?" cried Raskolnikov.

"Why, he there was asking whether a student lived here, mentioned your name and whom you lodged with. I saw you coming and pointed you out and he went away. It's funny."

The porter too seemed rather puzzled, but not much so, and after wondering for a moment he turned and went back to his room.

Raskolnikov ran after the stranger, and at once caught sight of him walking along the other side of the street with the same even, deliberate step with his eyes fixed on the ground, as though in meditation. He soon overtook him, but for some time walked behind him. At last, moving on to a level with him, he looked at his face. The man noticed him at once, looked at him quickly, but dropped his eyes again; and so they walked for a minute side by side without uttering a word.

"You were inquiring for me... of the porter?" Raskolnikov said at last, but in a curiously quiet voice.

The man made no answer; he didn't even look at him. Again they were both silent.

"Why do you... come and ask for me... and say nothing.... What's the meaning of it?"

Raskolnikov's voice broke and he seemed unable to articulate the words clearly.

The man raised his eyes this time and turned a gloomy sinister look at Raskolnikov.

"Murderer!" he said suddenly in a quiet but clear and distinct voice.

Raskolnikov went on walking beside him. His legs felt suddenly weak, a cold shiver ran down his spine, and his heart seemed to stand still for a moment, then suddenly began throbbing as though it were set free. So they walked for about a hundred paces, side by side in silence.

The man did not look at him.

"What do you mean... what is.... Who is a murderer?" muttered Raskolnikov hardly audibly.

"*You* are a murderer," the man answered still more articulately and emphatically, with a smile of triumphant hatred, and again he looked straight into Raskolnikov's pale face and stricken eyes.

They had just reached the cross-roads. The man turned to the left without looking behind him. Raskolnikov remained standing, gazing after him. He saw him turn round fifty paces away and look back at him still standing there. Raskolnikov could not see clearly, but he fancied that he was again smiling the same smile of cold hatred and triumph.

With slow faltering steps, with shaking knees, Raskolnikov made his way back to his little garret, feeling chilled all over. He took off his cap and put it on the table, and for ten minutes he stood without moving. Then he sank exhausted on the sofa and with a weak moan of pain he stretched himself on it. So he lay for half an hour.

He thought of nothing. Some thoughts or fragments of thoughts, some images without order or coherence floated before his mind—faces of people he had seen in his childhood or met somewhere once, whom he would never have recalled, the belfry of the church at V., the billiard table in a restaurant and some officers playing billiards, the smell of cigars in some underground tobacco shop, a tavern room, a back staircase quite dark, all sloppy with dirty water and strewn with egg-shells, and the Sunday bells floating in from somewhere.... The images followed one another, whirling like a hurricane. Some of them he liked and tried to clutch at, but they faded and all the while there was an oppression within him, but it was not overwhelming, sometimes it was even pleasant.... The slight shivering still persisted, but that too was an almost pleasant sensation.

He heard the hurried footsteps of Razumihin; he closed his eyes and pretended to be asleep. Razumihin opened the door and stood for some time in the doorway as though hesitating, then he stepped softly into the room and went cautiously to the sofa. Raskolnikov heard Nastasya's whisper:

"Don't disturb him! Let him sleep. He can have his dinner later."

"Quite so," answered Razumihin. Both withdrew carefully and closed the door. Another half-hour passed. Raskolnikov opened his eyes, turned on his back again, clasping his hands behind his head.

"Who is he? Who is that man who sprang out of the earth? Where was he, what did he see? He has seen it all, that's clear. Where was he then? And from where did he see? Why has he only now sprung out of the earth? And how could he see? Is it possible? Hm..." continued Raskolnikov, turning cold and shivering, "and the jewel case Nikolay found behind the door—was that possible? A clue? You miss an infinitesimal line and you can build it into a pyramid of evidence! A fly flew by and saw it! Is it possible?" He felt with sudden loathing how weak, how physically weak he had become. "I ought to have known it," he thought with a bitter smile. "And how dared I, knowing myself, knowing how I should be, take up an axe and shed blood! I ought to have known beforehand.... Ah, but I did know!" he whispered in despair. At times he came to a standstill at some thought.

"No, those men are not made so. The real *Master* to whom all is permitted storms Toulon, makes a massacre in Paris, *forgets* an army in Egypt, *wastes* half a million men in the Moscow expedition and gets off with a jest at Vilna. And altars are set up to him after his death, and so *all* is permitted. No, such people, it seems, are not of flesh but of bronze!"

One sudden irrelevant idea almost made him laugh. Napoleon, the pyramids, Waterloo, and a wretched skinny old woman, a pawnbroker with a red trunk under her bed—it's a nice hash for Porfiry Petrovitch to digest! How can they digest it! It's too inartistic. "A Napoleon creep under an old woman's bed! Ugh, how loathsome!"

At moments he felt he was raving. He sank into a state of feverish excitement. "The old woman is of no consequence," he thought, hotly and incoherently. "The old woman was a mistake perhaps, but she is not what matters! The old woman was only an illness.... I was in a hurry to overstep.... I didn't kill a human being, but a principle! I killed the principle, but I didn't overstep, I stopped on this side.... I was only capable of killing. And it seems I wasn't even capable of that... Principle? Why was that fool Razumihin abusing the socialists? They are industrious, commercial people; 'the happiness of all' is their case. No, life is only given to me once and I shall never have it again; I don't want to wait for 'the happiness of all.' I want to live myself, or else better not live at all. I simply couldn't pass by my mother starving, keeping my rouble in my pocket while I waited for the 'happiness of all.' I am putting my little brick into the happiness of all and so my heart is at peace. Ha-ha! Why have you let me slip? I only live once, I too want.... Ech, I am an æsthetic louse and nothing more," he added suddenly, laughing like a madman. "Yes, I am certainly a louse," he went on, clutching at the idea, gloating over it and playing with it with vindictive pleasure. "In the first place, because I can reason that I am one, and secondly, because for a month past I have been troubling benevolent Providence, calling it to witness that not for my own fleshly lusts did I undertake it, but with a grand and noble object—ha-ha! Thirdly, because I aimed at carrying it out as justly as possible, weighing, measuring and calculating. Of all the lice I picked out the most useless one and proposed to take from her only as much as I needed for the first step, no more nor less (so the rest would have gone to a monastery, according to her will, ha-ha!). And what shows that I am utterly a louse," he added, grinding his teeth, "is that I am perhaps viler and more loathsome than the louse I killed, and *I felt beforehand* that I should tell myself so *after* killing her. Can anything be compared with the horror of that? The vulgarity! The abjectness! I understand the 'prophet' with his sabre, on his steed: Allah commands and 'trembling' creation must obey! The 'prophet' is right, he is right when he sets a battery across the street and blows up the innocent and the guilty without deigning to explain! It's for you to obey, trembling creation, and not *to have desires*, for that's not for you!... I shall never, never forgive the old woman!"

His hair was soaked with sweat, his quivering lips were parched, his eyes were fixed on the ceiling.

"Mother, sister—how I loved them! Why do I hate them now? Yes, I hate them, I feel a physical hatred for them, I can't bear them near me.... I went up to my mother and kissed her, I remember.... To embrace her and think if she only knew... shall I tell her then? That's just what I might do.... *She* must be the same as I am," he added, straining himself to think, as it were struggling with delirium. "Ah, how I hate the old woman now! I feel I should kill her again if she came to life! Poor Lizaveta! Why did she come in?... It's strange though, why is it I scarcely ever think of her, as though I hadn't killed her? Lizaveta! Sonia! Poor gentle things, with gentle eyes.... Dear women! Why don't they weep? Why don't they moan? They give up everything... their eyes are soft and gentle.... Sonia, Sonia! Gentle Sonia!"

He lost consciousness; it seemed strange to him that he didn't remember how he got into the street. It was late evening. The twilight had fallen and the full moon was shining more and more brightly; but there was a peculiar breathlessness in the air. There were crowds of people in the street; workmen and business people were making their way home; other people had come out for a walk; there was a smell of mortar, dust and stagnant water. Raskolnikov walked along, mournful and anxious; he was distinctly aware of having come out with a purpose, of having to do something in a hurry, but what it was he had forgotten. Suddenly he stood still and saw a man standing on the other side of the street, beckoning to him. He crossed over to him, but at once the man turned and walked away with his head hanging, as though he had made no sign to him. "Stay, did he really beckon?" Raskolnikov wondered, but he tried to overtake him. When he was within ten paces he recognised him and was frightened; it was the same man with stooping shoulders in the long coat. Raskolnikov followed him at a distance; his heart was beating; they went down a turning; the man still did not look round. "Does he know I am following him?" thought Raskolnikov. The man went into the gateway of a big house. Raskolnikov hastened to the gate and looked in to see whether he would look round and sign to him. In the court-yard the man did turn round and again seemed to beckon him. Raskolnikov at once followed him into the yard, but the man was gone. He must have gone up the first staircase. Raskolnikov rushed after him. He heard slow measured steps two flights above. The staircase seemed strangely familiar. He reached the window on the first floor; the moon shone through the panes with a melancholy and mysterious light; then he reached the second floor. Bah! this is the flat where the painters were at work... but how was it he did not recognise it at once? The steps of the man above had died away. "So he must have stopped or hidden somewhere." He reached the third storey, should he go on? There was a stillness that was dreadful.... But he went on. The sound of his own footsteps scared and frightened him. How dark it was! The man must be hiding in some corner here. Ah! the flat was standing wide open, he hesitated and went in. It was very dark and empty in the passage, as though everything had been removed; he crept on tiptoe into the parlour which was flooded with moonlight. Everything there was as before, the chairs, the looking-glass, the yellow sofa and the pictures in the frames. A huge, round, copper-red moon looked in at the windows. "It's the moon that makes it so still, weaving some mystery," thought Raskolnikov. He stood and waited, waited a long while, and the more silent the moonlight, the more violently his heart beat, till it was painful. And still the same hush. Suddenly he heard a momentary sharp crack like the snapping of a splinter and all was still again. A fly flew up suddenly and struck the window pane with a plaintive buzz. At that moment he noticed in the corner between the window and the little cupboard something like a cloak hanging on the wall. "Why is that cloak here?" he thought, "it wasn't there before...." He went up to it quietly and felt that there was someone hiding behind it. He cautiously moved the cloak and saw, sitting on a chair in the corner, the old woman bent double so that he couldn't see her face; but it was she. He stood over her. "She is afraid," he thought. He stealthily took the axe from the noose and struck her one blow, then another on the skull. But strange to say she did not stir, as though she were made of wood. He was frightened, bent down nearer and tried to look at her; but she, too, bent her head lower. He bent right down to the ground and peeped up into her face from below, he peeped and turned cold with horror: the old woman was sitting and laughing, shaking with noiseless laughter, doing her utmost that he should not hear it. Suddenly he fancied that the door from the bedroom was opened a little and that there was laughter and whispering within. He was overcome with frenzy and he began hitting the old woman on the head with all his force, but at every blow of the axe the laughter and whispering from the bedroom grew louder and the old woman was simply shaking with mirth. He was rushing away, but the passage was full of people, the doors of the flats stood open and on the landing, on the stairs and everywhere below there were people, rows of heads, all looking, but huddled together in silence and expectation. Something gripped his heart, his legs were rooted to the spot, they would not move.... He tried to scream and woke up.

He drew a deep breath—but his dream seemed strangely to persist: his door was flung open and a man whom he had never seen stood in the doorway watching him intently.

Raskolnikov had hardly opened his eyes and he instantly closed them again. He lay on his back without stirring.

"Is it still a dream?" he wondered and again raised his eyelids hardly perceptibly; the stranger was standing in the same place, still watching him.

He stepped cautiously into the room, carefully closing the door after him, went up to the table, paused a moment, still keeping his eyes on Raskolnikov, and noiselessly seated himself on the chair by the sofa; he put his hat on the floor beside him and leaned his hands on his cane and his chin on his hands. It was evident that he was prepared to wait indefinitely. As far as Raskolnikov could make out from his stolen glances, he was a man no longer young, stout, with a full, fair, almost whitish beard.

Ten minutes passed. It was still light, but beginning to get dusk. There was complete stillness in the room. Not a sound came from the stairs. Only a big fly buzzed and fluttered against the window pane. It was unbearable at last. Raskolnikov suddenly got up and sat on the sofa.

"Come, tell me what you want."

"I knew you were not asleep, but only pretending," the stranger answered oddly, laughing calmly. "Arkady Ivanovitch Svidrigaïlov, allow me to introduce myself...."

PART IV

CHAPTER I

"Can this be still a dream?" Raskolnikov thought once more.

He looked carefully and suspiciously at the unexpected visitor.

"Svidrigaïlov! What nonsense! It can't be!" he said at last aloud in bewilderment.

His visitor did not seem at all surprised at this exclamation.

"I've come to you for two reasons. In the first place, I wanted to make your personal acquaintance, as I have already heard a great deal about you that is interesting and flattering; secondly, I cherish the hope that you may not refuse to assist me in a matter directly concerning the welfare of your sister, Avdotya Romanovna. For without your support she might not let me come near her now, for she is prejudiced against me, but with your assistance I reckon on..."

"You reckon wrongly," interrupted Raskolnikov.

"They only arrived yesterday, may I ask you?"

Raskolnikov made no reply.

"It was yesterday, I know. I only arrived myself the day before. Well, let me tell you this, Rodion Romanovitch, I don't consider it necessary to justify myself, but kindly tell me what was there particularly criminal on my part in all this business, speaking without prejudice, with common sense?"

Raskolnikov continued to look at him in silence.

"That in my own house I persecuted a defenceless girl and 'insulted her with my infamous proposals'—is that it? (I am anticipating you.) But you've only to assume that I, too, am a man *et nihil humanum*... in a word, that I am capable of being attracted and falling in love (which does not depend on our will), then everything can be explained in the most natural manner. The question is, am I a monster, or am I myself a victim? And what if I am a victim? In proposing to the object of my passion to elope with me to America or Switzerland, I may have cherished the deepest respect for her and may have thought that I was promoting our mutual happiness! Reason is the slave of passion, you know; why, probably, I was doing more harm to myself than anyone!"

"But that's not the point," Raskolnikov interrupted with disgust. "It's simply that whether you are right or wrong, we dislike you. We don't want to have anything to do with you. We show you the door. Go out!"

Svidrigaïlov broke into a sudden laugh.

"But you're... but there's no getting round you," he said, laughing in the frankest way. "I hoped to get round you, but you took up the right line at once!"

"But you are trying to get round me still!"

"What of it? What of it?" cried Svidrigaïlov, laughing openly. "But this is what the French call *bonne guerre*, and the most innocent form of deception!... But still you have interrupted me; one way or another, I repeat again: there would never have been any unpleasantness except for what happened in the garden. Marfa Petrovna..."

"You have got rid of Marfa Petrovna, too, so they say?" Raskolnikov interrupted rudely.

"Oh, you've heard that, too, then? You'd be sure to, though.... But as for your question, I really don't know what to say, though my own conscience is quite at rest on that score. Don't suppose that I am in any apprehension about it. All was regular and in order; the medical inquiry diagnosed apoplexy due to bathing immediately after a heavy dinner and a bottle of wine, and indeed it could have proved nothing else. But I'll tell you what I have been thinking to myself of late, on my way here in the train, especially: didn't I contribute to all that... calamity, morally, in a way, by irritation or something of the sort. But I came to the conclusion that that, too, was quite out of the question."

Raskolnikov laughed.

"I wonder you trouble yourself about it!"

"But what are you laughing at? Only consider, I struck her just twice with a switch—there were no marks even... don't regard me as a cynic, please; I am perfectly aware how atrocious it was of me and all that; but I know for certain, too, that Marfa Petrovna was very likely pleased at my, so to say, warmth. The story of your sister had been wrung out to the last drop; for the last three days Marfa Petrovna had been forced to sit at home; she had nothing to show herself with in the town. Besides, she had bored them so with that letter (you heard about her reading the letter). And all of a sudden those two switches fell from heaven! Her first act was to order the carriage to be got out.... Not to speak of the fact that there are cases when women are very, very glad to be insulted in spite of all their show of indignation. There are instances of it with everyone; human beings in general, indeed, greatly love to be insulted, have you noticed that? But it's particularly so with women. One might even say it's their only amusement."

At one time Raskolnikov thought of getting up and walking out and so finishing the interview. But some curiosity and even a sort of prudence made him linger for a moment.

"You are fond of fighting?" he asked carelessly.

"No, not very," Svidrigaïlov answered, calmly. "And Marfa Petrovna and I scarcely ever fought. We lived very harmoniously, and she was always pleased with me. I only used the whip twice in all our seven years (not counting a third occasion of a very ambiguous character). The first time, two months after our marriage, immediately after we arrived in the country, and the last time was that of which we are speaking. Did you suppose I was such a monster, such a reactionary, such a slave driver? Ha, ha! By the way, do you remember, Rodion Romanovitch, how a few years ago, in those days of beneficent publicity, a nobleman, I've forgotten his name, was put to shame everywhere, in all the papers, for having thrashed a German woman in the railway train. You remember? It was in those days, that very year I believe, the 'disgraceful action of the *Age*' took place (you know, 'The Egyptian Nights,' that public reading, you remember? The dark eyes, you know! Ah, the golden days of our youth, where are they?). Well, as for the gentleman who thrashed the German, I feel no sympathy with him, because after all what need is there for sympathy? But I must say that there are sometimes such provoking 'Germans' that I don't believe there is a progressive who could quite answer for himself. No one looked at the subject from that point of view then, but that's the truly humane point of view, I assure you."

After saying this, Svidrigaïlov broke into a sudden laugh again. Raskolnikov saw clearly that this was a man with a firm purpose in his mind and able to keep it to himself.

"I expect you've not talked to anyone for some days?" he asked.

"Scarcely anyone. I suppose you are wondering at my being such an adaptable man?"

"No, I am only wondering at your being too adaptable a man."

"Because I am not offended at the rudeness of your questions? Is that it? But why take offence? As you asked, so I answered," he replied, with a surprising expression of simplicity. "You know, there's hardly anything I take interest in," he went on, as it were dreamily, "especially now, I've nothing to do.... You are quite at liberty to imagine though that I am making up to you with a motive, particularly as I told you I want to see your sister about something. But I'll confess frankly, I am very much bored. The last three days especially, so I am delighted to see you.... Don't be angry, Rodion Romanovitch, but you seem to be somehow awfully strange yourself. Say what you like, there's something wrong with you, and now, too... not this very minute, I mean, but now, generally.... Well, well, I won't, I won't, don't scowl! I am not such a bear, you know, as you think."

Raskolnikov looked gloomily at him.

"You are not a bear, perhaps, at all," he said. "I fancy indeed that you are a man of very good breeding, or at least know how on occasion to behave like one."

"I am not particularly interested in anyone's opinion," Svidrigaïlov answered, dryly and even with a shade of haughtiness, "and therefore why not be vulgar at times when vulgarity is such a convenient cloak for our climate... and especially if one has a natural propensity that way," he added, laughing again.

"But I've heard you have many friends here. You are, as they say, 'not without connections.' What can you want with me, then, unless you've some special object?"

"That's true that I have friends here," Svidrigaïlov admitted, not replying to the chief point. "I've met some already. I've been lounging about for the last three days, and I've seen them, or they've seen me. That's a matter of course. I am well dressed and reckoned not a poor man; the emancipation of the serfs hasn't affected me; my property consists chiefly of forests and water meadows. The revenue has not fallen off; but... I am not going to see them, I was sick of them long ago. I've been here three days and have called on no one.... What a town it is! How has it come into existence among us, tell me that? A town of officials and students of all sorts. Yes, there's a great deal I didn't notice when I was here eight years ago, kicking up my heels.... My only hope now is in anatomy, by Jove, it is!"

"Anatomy?"

"But as for these clubs, Dussauts, parades, or progress, indeed, maybe—well, all that can go on without me," he went on, again without noticing the question. "Besides, who wants to be a card-sharper?"

"Why, have you been a card-sharper then?"

"How could I help being? There was a regular set of us, men of the best society, eight years ago; we had a fine time. And all men of breeding, you know, poets, men of property. And indeed as a rule in our Russian society the best manners are found among those who've been thrashed, have you noticed that? I've deteriorated in the country. But I did get into prison for debt, through a low Greek who came from Nezhin. Then Marfa Petrovna turned up; she bargained with him and bought me off for thirty thousand silver pieces (I owed seventy thousand). We were united in lawful wedlock and she bore me off into the country like a treasure. You know she was five years older than I. She was very fond of me. For seven years I never left the country. And, take note, that all my life she held a document over me, the IOU for thirty thousand roubles, so if I were to elect to be restive about anything I should be trapped at once! And she would have done it! Women find nothing incompatible in that."

"If it hadn't been for that, would you have given her the slip?"

"I don't know what to say. It was scarcely the document restrained me. I didn't want to go anywhere else. Marfa Petrovna herself invited me to go abroad, seeing I was bored, but I've been abroad before, and always felt sick there. For no reason, but the sunrise, the bay of Naples, the sea—you look at them and it makes you sad. What's most revolting is that one is really sad! No, it's better at home. Here at least one blames others for everything and excuses oneself. I should have gone perhaps on an expedition to the North Pole, because *j'ai le vin mauvais* and hate drinking, and there's nothing left but wine. I have tried it. But, I say, I've been told Berg is going up in a great balloon next Sunday from the Yusupov Garden and will take up passengers at a fee. Is it true?"

"Why, would you go up?"

"I... No, oh, no," muttered Svidrigaïlov really seeming to be deep in thought.

"What does he mean? Is he in earnest?" Raskolnikov wondered.

"No, the document didn't restrain me," Svidrigaïlov went on, meditatively. "It was my own doing, not leaving the country, and nearly a year ago Marfa Petrovna gave me back the document on my name-day and made me a present of a considerable sum of money, too. She had a fortune, you know. 'You see how I trust you, Arkady Ivanovitch'—that was actually her expression. You don't believe she used it? But do you know I managed the estate quite decently, they know me in the neighbourhood. I ordered books, too. Marfa Petrovna at first approved, but afterwards she was afraid of my over-studying."

"You seem to be missing Marfa Petrovna very much?"

"Missing her? Perhaps. Really, perhaps I am. And, by the way, do you believe in ghosts?"

"What ghosts?"

"Why, ordinary ghosts."

"Do you believe in them?"

"Perhaps not, *pour vous plaire*.... I wouldn't say no exactly."

"Do you see them, then?"

Svidrigaïlov looked at him rather oddly.

"Marfa Petrovna is pleased to visit me," he said, twisting his mouth into a strange smile.

"How do you mean 'she is pleased to visit you'?"

"She has been three times. I saw her first on the very day of the funeral, an hour after she was buried. It was the day before I left to come here. The second time was the day before yesterday, at daybreak, on the journey at the station of Malaya Vishera, and the third time was two hours ago in the room where I am staying. I was alone."

"Were you awake?"

"Quite awake. I was wide awake every time. She comes, speaks to me for a minute and goes out at the door—always at the door. I can almost hear her."

"What made me think that something of the sort must be happening to you?" Raskolnikov said suddenly.

At the same moment he was surprised at having said it. He was much excited.

"What! Did you think so?" Svidrigaïlov asked in astonishment. "Did you really? Didn't I say that there was something in common between us, eh?"

"You never said so!" Raskolnikov cried sharply and with heat.

"Didn't I?"

"No!"

"I thought I did. When I came in and saw you lying with your eyes shut, pretending, I said to myself at once, 'Here's the man.'"

"What do you mean by 'the man?' What are you talking about?" cried Raskolnikov.

"What do I mean? I really don't know...." Svidrigaïlov muttered ingenuously, as though he, too, were puzzled.

For a minute they were silent. They stared in each other's faces.

"That's all nonsense!" Raskolnikov shouted with vexation. "What does she say when she comes to you?"

"She! Would you believe it, she talks of the silliest trifles and—man is a strange creature—it makes me angry. The first time she came in (I was tired you know: the funeral service, the funeral ceremony, the lunch afterwards. At last I was left alone in my study. I lighted a cigar and began to think), she came in at the door. 'You've been so busy to-day, Arkady Ivanovitch, you have forgotten to wind the dining-room clock,' she said. All those seven years I've wound that clock every week, and if I forgot it she would always remind me. The next day I set off on my way here. I got out at the station at daybreak; I'd been asleep, tired out, with my eyes half open, I was drinking some coffee. I looked up and there was suddenly Marfa Petrovna sitting beside me with a pack of cards in her hands. 'Shall I tell your fortune for the journey, Arkady Ivanovitch?' She was a great hand at telling fortunes. I shall never forgive myself for not asking her to. I ran away in a fright, and, besides, the bell rang. I was sitting to-day, feeling very heavy after a miserable dinner from a cookshop; I was sitting smoking, all of a sudden Marfa Petrovna again. She came in very smart in a new green silk dress with a long train. 'Good day, Arkady Ivanovitch! How do you like my dress? Aniska can't make like this.' (Aniska was a dressmaker in the country, one of our former serf girls who had been trained in Moscow, a pretty wench.) She stood turning round before me. I looked at the dress, and then I looked carefully, very carefully, at her face. 'I wonder you trouble to come to me about such trifles, Marfa Petrovna.' 'Good gracious, you won't let one disturb you about anything!' To tease her I said, 'I want to get married, Marfa Petrovna.' 'That's just like you, Arkady Ivanovitch; it does you very little credit to come looking for a bride when you've hardly buried your wife. And if you could make a good choice, at least, but I know it won't be for your happiness or hers, you will only be a laughing-stock to all good people.' Then she went out and her train seemed to rustle. Isn't it nonsense, eh?"

"But perhaps you are telling lies?" Raskolnikov put in.

"I rarely lie," answered Svidrigaïlov thoughtfully, apparently not noticing the rudeness of the question.

"And in the past, have you ever seen ghosts before?"

"Y-yes, I have seen them, but only once in my life, six years ago. I had a serf, Filka; just after his burial I called out forgetting 'Filka, my pipe!' He came in and went to the cupboard where my pipes were. I sat still and thought 'he is doing it out of revenge,' because we had a violent quarrel just before his death. 'How dare you come in with a hole in your elbow?' I said. 'Go away, you scamp!' He turned and went out, and never came again. I didn't tell Marfa Petrovna at the time. I wanted to have a service sung for him, but I was ashamed."

"You should go to a doctor."

"I know I am not well, without your telling me, though I don't know what's wrong; I believe I am five times as strong as you are. I didn't ask you whether you believe that ghosts are seen, but whether you believe that they exist."

"No, I won't believe it!" Raskolnikov cried, with positive anger.

"What do people generally say?" muttered Svidrigaïlov, as though speaking to himself, looking aside and bowing his head. "They say, 'You are ill, so what appears to you is only unreal fantasy.' But that's not strictly logical. I agree that ghosts only appear to the sick, but that only proves that they are unable to appear except to the sick, not that they don't exist."

"Nothing of the sort," Raskolnikov insisted irritably.

"No? You don't think so?" Svidrigaïlov went on, looking at him deliberately. "But what do you say to this argument (help me with it): ghosts are, as it were, shreds and fragments of other worlds, the beginning of them. A man in health has, of course, no reason to see them, because he is above all a man of this earth and is bound for the sake of completeness and order to live only in this life. But as soon as one is ill, as soon as the normal earthly order of the organism is broken, one begins to realise the possibility of another world; and the more seriously ill one is, the closer becomes one's contact with that other world, so that as soon as the man dies he steps straight into that world. I thought of that long ago. If you believe in a future life, you could believe in that, too."

"I don't believe in a future life," said Raskolnikov.

Svidrigaïlov sat lost in thought.

"And what if there are only spiders there, or something of that sort," he said suddenly.

"He is a madman," thought Raskolnikov.

"We always imagine eternity as something beyond our conception, something vast, vast! But why must it be vast? Instead of all that, what if it's one little room, like a bath house in the country, black and grimy and spiders in every corner, and that's all eternity is? I sometimes fancy it like that."

"Can it be you can imagine nothing juster and more comforting than that?" Raskolnikov cried, with a feeling of anguish.

"Juster? And how can we tell, perhaps that is just, and do you know it's what I would certainly have made it," answered Svidrigaïlov, with a vague smile.

This horrible answer sent a cold chill through Raskolnikov. Svidrigaïlov raised his head, looked at him, and suddenly began laughing.

"Only think," he cried, "half an hour ago we had never seen each other, we regarded each other as enemies; there is a matter unsettled between us; we've thrown it aside, and away we've gone into the abstract! Wasn't I right in saying that we were birds of a feather?"

"Kindly allow me," Raskolnikov went on irritably, "to ask you to explain why you have honoured me with your visit... and... and I am in a hurry, I have no time to waste. I want to go out."

"By all means, by all means. Your sister, Avdotya Romanovna, is going to be married to Mr. Luzhin, Pyotr Petrovitch?"

"Can you refrain from any question about my sister and from mentioning her name? I can't understand how you dare utter her name in my presence, if you really are Svidrigaïlov."

"Why, but I've come here to speak about her; how can I avoid mentioning her?"

"Very good, speak, but make haste."

"I am sure that you must have formed your own opinion of this Mr. Luzhin, who is a connection of mine through my wife, if you have only seen him for half an hour, or heard any facts about him. He is no match for Avdotya Romanovna. I believe Avdotya Romanovna is sacrificing herself generously and imprudently for the sake of... for the sake of her family. I fancied from all I had heard of you that you would be very glad if the match could be broken off without the sacrifice of worldly advantages. Now I know you personally, I am convinced of it."

"All this is very naïve... excuse me, I should have said impudent on your part," said Raskolnikov.

"You mean to say that I am seeking my own ends. Don't be uneasy, Rodion Romanovitch, if I were working for my own advantage, I would not have spoken out so directly. I am not quite a fool. I will confess something psychologically curious about that: just now, defending my love for Avdotya Romanovna, I said I was myself the victim. Well, let me tell you that I've no feeling of love now, not the slightest, so that I wonder myself indeed, for I really did feel something..."

"Through idleness and depravity," Raskolnikov put in.

"I certainly am idle and depraved, but your sister has such qualities that even I could not help being impressed by them. But that's all nonsense, as I see myself now."

"Have you seen that long?"

"I began to be aware of it before, but was only perfectly sure of it the day before yesterday, almost at the moment I arrived in Petersburg. I still fancied in Moscow, though, that I was coming to try to get Avdotya Romanovna's hand and to cut out Mr. Luzhin."

"Excuse me for interrupting you; kindly be brief, and come to the object of your visit. I am in a hurry, I want to go out..."

"With the greatest pleasure. On arriving here and determining on a certain... journey, I should like to make some necessary preliminary arrangements. I left my children with an aunt; they are well provided for; and they have no need of me personally. And a nice father I should make, too! I have taken nothing but what Marfa Petrovna gave me a year ago. That's enough for me. Excuse me, I am just coming to the point. Before the journey which may come off, I want to settle Mr. Luzhin, too. It's not that I detest him so much, but it was through him I quarrelled with Marfa Petrovna when I learned that she had dished up this marriage. I want now to see Avdotya Romanovna through your mediation, and if you like in your presence, to explain to her that in the first place she will never gain anything but harm from Mr. Luzhin. Then, begging her pardon for all past unpleasantness, to make her a present of ten thousand roubles and so assist the rupture with Mr. Luzhin, a rupture to which I believe she is herself not disinclined, if she could see the way to it."

"You are certainly mad," cried Raskolnikov not so much angered as astonished. "How dare you talk like that!"

"I knew you would scream at me; but in the first place, though I am not rich, this ten thousand roubles is perfectly free; I have absolutely no need for it. If Avdotya Romanovna does not accept it, I shall waste it in some more foolish way. That's the first thing. Secondly, my conscience is perfectly easy; I make the offer with no ulterior motive. You may not believe it, but in the end Avdotya Romanovna and you will know. The point is, that I did actually cause your sister, whom I greatly respect, some trouble and unpleasantness, and so, sincerely regretting it, I want—not to compensate, not to repay her for the unpleasantness, but simply to do something to her advantage, to show that I am not, after all, privileged to do nothing but harm. If there were a millionth fraction of self-interest in my offer, I should not have made it so openly; and I should not have offered her ten thousand only, when five weeks ago I offered her more, Besides, I may, perhaps, very soon marry a young lady, and that alone ought to prevent suspicion of any design on Avdotya Romanovna. In conclusion, let me say that in marrying Mr. Luzhin, she is taking money just the same, only from another man. Don't be angry, Rodion Romanovitch, think it over coolly and quietly."

Svidrigaïlov himself was exceedingly cool and quiet as he was saying this.

"I beg you to say no more," said Raskolnikov. "In any case this is unpardonable impertinence."

"Not in the least. Then a man may do nothing but harm to his neighbour in this world, and is prevented from doing the tiniest bit of good by trivial conventional formalities. That's absurd. If I died, for instance, and left that sum to your sister in my will, surely she wouldn't refuse it?"

"Very likely she would."

"Oh, no, indeed. However, if you refuse it, so be it, though ten thousand roubles is a capital thing to have on occasion. In any case I beg you to repeat what I have said to Avdotya Romanovna."

"No, I won't."

"In that case, Rodion Romanovitch, I shall be obliged to try and see her myself and worry her by doing so."

"And if I do tell her, will you not try to see her?"

"I don't know really what to say. I should like very much to see her once more."

"Don't hope for it."

"I'm sorry. But you don't know me. Perhaps we may become better friends."

"You think we may become friends?"

"And why not?" Svidrigaïlov said, smiling. He stood up and took his hat. "I didn't quite intend to disturb you and I came here without reckoning on it... though I was very much struck by your face this morning."

"Where did you see me this morning?" Raskolnikov asked uneasily.

"I saw you by chance.... I kept fancying there is something about you like me.... But don't be uneasy. I am not intrusive; I used to get on all right with card-sharpers, and I never bored Prince Svirbey, a great personage who is a distant relation of mine, and I could write about Raphael's *Madonna* in Madam Prilukov's album, and I never left Marfa Petrovna's side for seven years, and I used to stay the night at Viazemsky's house in the Hay Market in the old days, and I may go up in a balloon with Berg, perhaps."

"Oh, all right. Are you starting soon on your travels, may I ask?"

"What travels?"

"Why, on that 'journey'; you spoke of it yourself."

"A journey? Oh, yes. I did speak of a journey. Well, that's a wide subject.... if only you knew what you are asking," he added, and gave a sudden, loud, short laugh. "Perhaps I'll get married instead of the journey. They're making a match for me."

"Here?"

"Yes."

"How have you had time for that?"

485

"But I am very anxious to see Avdotya Romanovna once. I earnestly beg it. Well, good-bye for the present. Oh, yes. I have forgotten something. Tell your sister, Rodion Romanovitch, that Marfa Petrovna remembered her in her will and left her three thousand roubles. That's absolutely certain. Marfa Petrovna arranged it a week before her death, and it was done in my presence. Avdotya Romanovna will be able to receive the money in two or three weeks."

"Are you telling the truth?"

"Yes, tell her. Well, your servant. I am staying very near you."

As he went out, Svidrigaïlov ran up against Razumihin in the doorway.

CHAPTER II

It was nearly eight o'clock. The two young men hurried to Bakaleyev's, to arrive before Luzhin.

"Why, who was that?" asked Razumihin, as soon as they were in the street.

"It was Svidrigaïlov, that landowner in whose house my sister was insulted when she was their governess. Through his persecuting her with his attentions, she was turned out by his wife, Marfa Petrovna. This Marfa Petrovna begged Dounia's forgiveness afterwards, and she's just died suddenly. It was of her we were talking this morning. I don't know why I'm afraid of that man. He came here at once after his wife's funeral. He is very strange, and is determined on doing something.... We must guard Dounia from him... that's what I wanted to tell you, do you hear?"

"Guard her! What can he do to harm Avdotya Romanovna? Thank you, Rodya, for speaking to me like that.... We will, we will guard her. Where does he live?"

"I don't know."

"Why didn't you ask? What a pity! I'll find out, though."

"Did you see him?" asked Raskolnikov after a pause.

"Yes, I noticed him, I noticed him well."

"You did really see him? You saw him clearly?" Raskolnikov insisted.

"Yes, I remember him perfectly, I should know him in a thousand; I have a good memory for faces."

They were silent again.

"Hm!... that's all right," muttered Raskolnikov. "Do you know, I fancied... I keep thinking that it may have been an hallucination."

"What do you mean? I don't understand you."

"Well, you all say," Raskolnikov went on, twisting his mouth into a smile, "that I am mad. I thought just now that perhaps I really am mad, and have only seen a phantom."

"What do you mean?"

"Why, who can tell? Perhaps I am really mad, and perhaps everything that happened all these days may be only imagination."

"Ach, Rodya, you have been upset again!... But what did he say, what did he come for?"

Raskolnikov did not answer. Razumihin thought a minute.

"Now let me tell you my story," he began, "I came to you, you were asleep. Then we had dinner and then I went to Porfiry's, Zametov was still with him. I tried to begin, but it was no use. I couldn't speak in the right way. They don't seem to understand and can't understand, but are not a bit ashamed. I drew Porfiry to the window, and began talking to him, but it was still no use. He looked away and I looked away. At last I shook my fist in his ugly face, and told him as a cousin I'd brain him. He merely looked at me, I cursed and came away. That was all. It was very stupid. To Zametov I didn't say a word. But, you see, I thought I'd made a mess of it, but as I went downstairs a brilliant idea struck me: why should we trouble? Of course if you were in any danger or anything, but why need you care? You needn't care a hang for them. We shall have a laugh at them afterwards, and if I were in your place I'd mystify them more than ever. How ashamed they'll be afterwards! Hang them! We can thrash them afterwards, but let's laugh at them now!"

"To be sure," answered Raskolnikov. "But what will you say to-morrow?" he thought to himself. Strange to say, till that moment it had never occurred to him to wonder what Razumihin would think when he knew. As he thought it, Raskolnikov looked at him. Razumihin's account of his visit to Porfiry had very little interest for him, so much had come and gone since then.

In the corridor they came upon Luzhin; he had arrived punctually at eight, and was looking for the number, so that all three went in together without greeting or looking at one another. The young men walked in first, while Pyotr Petrovitch, for good manners, lingered a little in the passage, taking off his coat. Pulcheria Alexandrovna came forward at once to greet him in the doorway, Dounia was welcoming her brother. Pyotr Petrovitch walked in and quite amiably, though with redoubled dignity, bowed to the ladies. He looked, however, as though he were a little put out and could not yet recover himself. Pulcheria Alexandrovna, who seemed also a little embarrassed, hastened to make them all sit down at the round table where a samovar was boiling. Dounia and Luzhin were facing one another on opposite sides of the table. Razumihin and Raskolnikov were facing Pulcheria Alexandrovna, Razumihin was next to Luzhin and Raskolnikov was beside his sister.

A moment's silence followed. Pyotr Petrovitch deliberately drew out a cambric handkerchief reeking of scent and blew his nose with an air of a benevolent man who felt himself slighted, and was firmly resolved to insist on an explanation. In the passage the idea had occurred to him to keep on his overcoat and walk away, and so give the two ladies a sharp and emphatic lesson and make them feel the gravity of the position. But he could not bring himself to do this. Besides, he could not endure uncertainty, and he wanted an explanation: if his request had been so openly disobeyed, there was something behind it, and in that case it was better to find it out beforehand; it rested with him to punish them and there would always be time for that.

"I trust you had a favourable journey," he inquired officially of Pulcheria Alexandrovna.

"Oh, very, Pyotr Petrovitch."

"I am gratified to hear it. And Avdotya Romanovna is not over-fatigued either?"

"I am young and strong, I don't get tired, but it was a great strain for mother," answered Dounia.

"That's unavoidable! our national railways are of terrible length. 'Mother Russia,' as they say, is a vast country.... In spite of all my desire to do so, I was unable to meet you yesterday. But I trust all passed off without inconvenience?"

"Oh, no, Pyotr Petrovitch, it was all terribly disheartening," Pulcheria Alexandrovna hastened to declare with peculiar intonation, "and if Dmitri Prokofitch had not been sent us, I really believe by God Himself, we should have been utterly lost. Here, he is! Dmitri Prokofitch Razumihin," she added, introducing him to Luzhin.

"I had the pleasure... yesterday," muttered Pyotr Petrovitch with a hostile glance sidelong at Razumihin; then he scowled and was silent.

Pyotr Petrovitch belonged to that class of persons, on the surface very polite in society, who make a great point of punctiliousness, but who, directly they are crossed in anything, are completely disconcerted, and become more like sacks of flour than elegant and lively men of society. Again all was silent; Raskolnikov was obstinately mute, Avdotya Romanovna was unwilling to open the conversation too soon. Razumihin had nothing to say, so Pulcheria Alexandrovna was anxious again.

"Marfa Petrovna is dead, have you heard?" she began having recourse to her leading item of conversation.

"To be sure, I heard so. I was immediately informed, and I have come to make you acquainted with the fact that Arkady Ivanovitch Svidrigaïlov set off in haste for Petersburg immediately after his wife's funeral. So at least I have excellent authority for believing."

"To Petersburg? here?" Dounia asked in alarm and looked at her mother.

"Yes, indeed, and doubtless not without some design, having in view the rapidity of his departure, and all the circumstances preceding it."

"Good heavens! won't he leave Dounia in peace even here?" cried Pulcheria Alexandrovna.

"I imagine that neither you nor Avdotya Romanovna have any grounds for uneasiness, unless, of course, you are yourselves desirous of getting into communication with him. For my part I am on my guard, and am now discovering where he is lodging."

"Oh, Pyotr Petrovitch, you would not believe what a fright you have given me," Pulcheria Alexandrovna went on: "I've only seen him twice, but I thought him terrible, terrible! I am convinced that he was the cause of Marfa Petrovna's death."

"It's impossible to be certain about that. I have precise information. I do not dispute that he may have contributed to accelerate the course of events by the moral influence, so to say, of the affront; but as to the general conduct and moral characteristics of that personage, I am in agreement with you. I do not know whether he is well off now, and precisely what Marfa Petrovna left him; this will be known to me within a very short period; but no doubt here in Petersburg, if he has any pecuniary resources, he will relapse at once into his old ways. He is the most depraved, and abjectly vicious specimen of that class of men. I have considerable reason to believe that Marfa Petrovna, who was so unfortunate as to fall in love with him and to pay his debts eight years ago, was of service to him also in another way. Solely by her exertions and sacrifices, a criminal charge, involving an element of fantastic and homicidal brutality for which he might well have been sentenced to Siberia, was hushed up. That's the sort of man he is, if you care to know."

"Good heavens!" cried Pulcheria Alexandrovna. Raskolnikov listened attentively.

"Are you speaking the truth when you say that you have good evidence of this?" Dounia asked sternly and emphatically.

"I only repeat what I was told in secret by Marfa Petrovna. I must observe that from the legal point of view the case was far from clear. There was, and I believe still is, living here a woman called Resslich, a foreigner, who lent small sums of money at interest, and did other commissions, and with this woman Svidrigaïlov had for a long while close and mysterious relations. She had a relation, a niece I believe, living with her, a deaf and dumb girl of fifteen, or perhaps not more than fourteen. Resslich hated this girl, and grudged her every crust; she used to beat her mercilessly. One day the girl was found hanging in the garret. At the inquest the verdict was suicide. After the usual proceedings the matter ended, but, later on, information was given that the child had been... cruelly outraged by Svidrigaïlov. It is true, this was not clearly established, the information was given by another German woman of loose character whose word could not be trusted; no statement was actually made to the police, thanks to Marfa Petrovna's money and exertions; it did not get beyond gossip. And yet the story is a very significant one. You heard, no doubt, Avdotya Romanovna, when you were with them the story of the servant Philip who died of ill treatment he received six years ago, before the abolition of serfdom."

"I heard, on the contrary, that this Philip hanged himself."

"Quite so, but what drove him, or rather perhaps disposed him, to suicide was the systematic persecution and severity of Mr. Svidrigaïlov."

"I don't know that," answered Dounia, dryly. "I only heard a queer story that Philip was a sort of hypochondriac, a sort of domestic philosopher, the servants used to say, 'he read himself silly,' and that he hanged himself partly on account of Mr. Svidrigaïlov's mockery of him and not his blows. When I was there he behaved well to the servants, and they were actually fond of him, though they certainly did blame him for Philip's death."

"I perceive, Avdotya Romanovna, that you seem disposed to undertake his defence all of a sudden," Luzhin observed, twisting his lips into an ambiguous smile, "there's no doubt that he is an astute man, and insinuating where ladies are concerned, of which Marfa Petrovna, who has died so strangely, is a terrible instance. My only desire has been to be of service to you and your mother with my advice, in view of the renewed efforts which may certainly be anticipated from him. For my part it's my firm conviction, that he will end in a debtor's prison again. Marfa Petrovna had not the slightest intention of settling anything substantial on him, having regard for his children's interests, and, if she left him anything, it would only be the merest sufficiency, something insignificant and ephemeral, which would not last a year for a man of his habits."

"Pyotr Petrovitch, I beg you," said Dounia, "say no more of Mr. Svidrigaïlov. It makes me miserable."

"He has just been to see me," said Raskolnikov, breaking his silence for the first time.

There were exclamations from all, and they all turned to him. Even Pyotr Petrovitch was roused.

"An hour and a half ago, he came in when I was asleep, waked me, and introduced himself," Raskolnikov continued. "He was fairly cheerful and at ease, and quite hopes that we shall become friends. He is particularly anxious, by the way, Dounia, for an interview with you, at which he asked me to assist. He has a proposition to make to you, and he told me about it. He told me, too, that a week before her death Marfa Petrovna left you three thousand roubles in her will, Dounia, and that you can receive the money very shortly."

"Thank God!" cried Pulcheria Alexandrovna, crossing herself. "Pray for her soul, Dounia!"

"It's a fact!" broke from Luzhin.

"Tell us, what more?" Dounia urged Raskolnikov.

"Then he said that he wasn't rich and all the estate was left to his children who are now with an aunt, then that he was staying somewhere not far from me, but where, I don't know, I didn't ask...."

"But what, what does he want to propose to Dounia?" cried Pulcheria Alexandrovna in a fright. "Did he tell you?"

"Yes."

"What was it?"

"I'll tell you afterwards."

Raskolnikov ceased speaking and turned his attention to his tea.

Pyotr Petrovitch looked at his watch.

"I am compelled to keep a business engagement, and so I shall not be in your way," he added with an air of some pique and he began getting up.

"Don't go, Pyotr Petrovitch," said Dounia, "you intended to spend the evening. Besides, you wrote yourself that you wanted to have an explanation with mother."

"Precisely so, Avdotya Romanovna," Pyotr Petrovitch answered impressively, sitting down again, but still holding his hat. "I certainly desired an explanation with you and your honoured mother upon a very important point indeed. But as your brother cannot speak openly in my presence of some proposals of Mr. Svidrigaïlov, I, too, do not desire and am not able to speak openly... in the presence of others... of certain matters of the greatest gravity. Moreover, my most weighty and urgent request has been disregarded...."

Assuming an aggrieved air, Luzhin relapsed into dignified silence.

"Your request that my brother should not be present at our meeting was disregarded solely at my instance," said Dounia. "You wrote that you had been insulted by my brother; I think that this must be explained at once, and you must be reconciled. And if Rodya really has insulted you, then he *should* and *will* apologise."

Pyotr Petrovitch took a stronger line.

"There are insults, Avdotya Romanovna, which no goodwill can make us forget. There is a line in everything which it is dangerous to overstep; and when it has been overstepped, there is no return."

"That wasn't what I was speaking of exactly, Pyotr Petrovitch," Dounia interrupted with some impatience. "Please understand that our whole future depends now on whether all this is explained and set right as soon as possible. I tell you frankly at the start that I cannot look at it in any other light, and if you have the least regard for me, all this business must be ended to-day, however hard that may be. I repeat that if my brother is to blame he will ask your forgiveness."

"I am surprised at your putting the question like that," said Luzhin, getting more and more irritated. "Esteeming, and so to say, adoring you, I may at the same time, very well indeed, be able to dislike some member of your family. Though I lay claim to the happiness of your hand, I cannot accept duties incompatible with..."

"Ah, don't be so ready to take offence, Pyotr Petrovitch," Dounia interrupted with feeling, "and be the sensible and generous man I have always considered, and wish to consider, you to be. I've given you a great promise, I am your betrothed. Trust me in this matter and, believe me, I shall be capable of judging impartially. My assuming the part of judge is as much a surprise for my brother as for you. When I insisted on his coming to our interview to-day after your letter, I told him nothing of what I meant to do. Understand that, if you are not reconciled, I must choose between you—it must be either you or he. That is how the question rests on your side and on his. I don't want to be mistaken in my choice, and I must not be. For your sake I must break off with my brother, for my brother's sake I must break off with you. I can find out for certain now whether he is a brother to me, and I want to know it; and of you, whether I am dear to you, whether you esteem me, whether you are the husband for me."

"Avdotya Romanovna," Luzhin declared huffily, "your words are of too much consequence to me; I will say more, they are offensive in view of the position I have the honour to occupy in relation to you. To say nothing of your strange and offensive setting me on a level with an impertinent boy, you admit the possibility of breaking your promise to me. You say 'you or he,' showing thereby of how little consequence I am in your eyes... I cannot let this pass considering the relationship and... the obligations existing between us."

"What!" cried Dounia, flushing. "I set your interest beside all that has hitherto been most precious in my life, what has made up the *whole* of my life, and here you are offended at my making too *little* account of you."

Raskolnikov smiled sarcastically, Razumihin fidgeted, but Pyotr Petrovitch did not accept the reproof; on the contrary, at every word he became more persistent and irritable, as though he relished it.

"Love for the future partner of your life, for your husband, ought to outweigh your love for your brother," he pronounced sententiously, "and in any case I cannot be put on the same level.... Although I said so emphatically that I would not speak openly in your brother's presence, nevertheless, I intend now to ask your honoured mother for a necessary explanation on a point of great importance closely affecting my dignity. Your son," he turned to Pulcheria Alexandrovna, "yesterday in the presence of Mr. Razsudkin (or... I think that's it? excuse me I have forgotten your surname," he bowed politely to Razumihin) "insulted me by misrepresenting the idea I expressed to you in a private conversation, drinking coffee, that is, that marriage with a poor girl who has had experience of trouble is more advantageous from the conjugal point of view than with one who has lived in luxury, since it is more profitable for the moral character. Your son intentionally exaggerated the significance of my words and made them ridiculous, accusing me of malicious intentions, and, as far as I could see, relied upon your correspondence with him. I shall consider myself happy, Pulcheria Alexandrovna, if it is possible for you to convince me of an opposite conclusion, and thereby considerably reassure me. Kindly let me know in what terms precisely you repeated my words in your letter to Rodion Romanovitch."

"I don't remember," faltered Pulcheria Alexandrovna. "I repeated them as I understood them. I don't know how Rodya repeated them to you, perhaps he exaggerated."

"He could not have exaggerated them, except at your instigation."

"Pyotr Petrovitch," Pulcheria Alexandrovna declared with dignity, "the proof that Dounia and I did not take your words in a very bad sense is the fact that we are here."

"Good, mother," said Dounia approvingly.

"Then this is my fault again," said Luzhin, aggrieved.

"Well, Pyotr Petrovitch, you keep blaming Rodion, but you yourself have just written what was false about him," Pulcheria Alexandrovna added, gaining courage.

"I don't remember writing anything false."

"You wrote," Raskolnikov said sharply, not turning to Luzhin, "that I gave money yesterday not to the widow of the man who was killed, as was the fact, but to his daughter (whom I had never seen till yesterday). You wrote this to make dissension between me and my family, and for that object added coarse expressions about the conduct of a girl whom you don't know. All that is mean slander."

"Excuse me, sir," said Luzhin, quivering with fury. "I enlarged upon your qualities and conduct in my letter solely in response to your sister's and mother's inquiries, how I found you, and what impression you made on me. As for what you've alluded to in my letter, be so good as to point out one word of falsehood, show, that is, that you didn't throw away your money, and that there are not worthless persons in that family, however unfortunate."

"To my thinking, you, with all your virtues, are not worth the little finger of that unfortunate girl at whom you throw stones."

"Would you go so far then as to let her associate with your mother and sister?"

"I have done so already, if you care to know. I made her sit down to-day with mother and Dounia."

"Rodya!" cried Pulcheria Alexandrovna. Dounia crimsoned, Razumihin knitted his brows. Luzhin smiled with lofty sarcasm.

"You may see for yourself, Avdotya Romanovna," he said, "whether it is possible for us to agree. I hope now that this question is at an end, once and for all. I will withdraw, that I may not hinder the pleasures of family intimacy, and the discussion of secrets." He got up from his chair and took his hat. "But in withdrawing, I venture to request that for the future I may be spared similar meetings, and, so to say, compromises. I appeal particularly to you, honoured Pulcheria Alexandrovna, on this subject, the more as my letter was addressed to you and to no one else."

Pulcheria Alexandrovna was a little offended.

"You seem to think we are completely under your authority, Pyotr Petrovitch. Dounia has told you the reason your desire was disregarded, she had the best intentions. And indeed you write as though you were laying commands upon me. Are we to consider every desire of yours as a command? Let me tell you on the contrary that you ought to show particular delicacy and consideration for us now, because we have thrown up everything, and have come here relying on you, and so we are in any case in a sense in your hands."

"That is not quite true, Pulcheria Alexandrovna, especially at the present moment, when the news has come of Marfa Petrovna's legacy, which seems indeed very apropos, judging from the new tone you take to me," he added sarcastically.

"Judging from that remark, we may certainly presume that you were reckoning on our helplessness," Dounia observed irritably.

"But now in any case I cannot reckon on it, and I particularly desire not to hinder your discussion of the secret proposals of Arkady Ivanovitch Svidrigaïlov, which he has entrusted to your brother and which have, I perceive, a great and possibly a very agreeable interest for you."

"Good heavens!" cried Pulcheria Alexandrovna.

Razumihin could not sit still on his chair.

"Aren't you ashamed now, sister?" asked Raskolnikov.

"I am ashamed, Rodya," said Dounia. "Pyotr Petrovitch, go away," she turned to him, white with anger.

Pyotr Petrovitch had apparently not at all expected such a conclusion. He had too much confidence in himself, in his power and in the helplessness of his victims. He could not believe it even now. He turned pale, and his lips quivered.

"Avdotya Romanovna, if I go out of this door now, after such a dismissal, then, you may reckon on it, I will never come back. Consider what you are doing. My word is not to be shaken."

"What insolence!" cried Dounia, springing up from her seat. "I don't want you to come back again."

"What! So that's how it stands!" cried Luzhin, utterly unable to the last moment to believe in the rupture and so completely thrown out of his reckoning now. "So that's how it stands! But do you know, Avdotya Romanovna, that I might protest?"

"What right have you to speak to her like that?" Pulcheria Alexandrovna intervened hotly. "And what can you protest about? What rights have you? Am I to give my Dounia to a man like you? Go away, leave us altogether! We are to blame for having agreed to a wrong action, and I above all...."

"But you have bound me, Pulcheria Alexandrovna," Luzhin stormed in a frenzy, "by your promise, and now you deny it and... besides... I have been led on account of that into expenses...."

This last complaint was so characteristic of Pyotr Petrovitch, that Raskolnikov, pale with anger and with the effort of restraining it, could not help breaking into laughter. But Pulcheria Alexandrovna was furious.

"Expenses? What expenses? Are you speaking of our trunk? But the conductor brought it for nothing for you. Mercy on us, we have bound you! What are you thinking about, Pyotr Petrovitch, it was you bound us, hand and foot, not we!"

"Enough, mother, no more please," Avdotya Romanovna implored. "Pyotr Petrovitch, do be kind and go!"

"I am going, but one last word," he said, quite unable to control himself. "Your mamma seems to have entirely forgotten that I made up my mind to take you, so to speak, after the gossip of the town had spread all over the district in regard to your reputation. Disregarding public opinion for your sake and reinstating your reputation, I certainly might very well reckon on a fitting return, and might indeed look for gratitude on your part. And my eyes have only now been opened! I see myself that I may have acted very, very recklessly in disregarding the universal verdict...."

"Does the fellow want his head smashed?" cried Razumihin, jumping up.

"You are a mean and spiteful man!" cried Dounia.

"Not a word! Not a movement!" cried Raskolnikov, holding Razumihin back; then going close up to Luzhin, "Kindly leave the room!" he said quietly and distinctly, "and not a word more or..."

Pyotr Petrovitch gazed at him for some seconds with a pale face that worked with anger, then he turned, went out, and rarely has any man carried away in his heart such vindictive hatred as he felt against Raskolnikov. Him, and him alone, he blamed for everything. It is noteworthy that as he went downstairs he still imagined that his case was perhaps not utterly lost, and that, so far as the ladies were concerned, all might "very well indeed" be set right again.

CHAPTER III

The fact was that up to the last moment he had never expected such an ending; he had been overbearing to the last degree, never dreaming that two destitute and defenceless women could escape from his control. This conviction was strengthened by his vanity and conceit, a conceit to the point of fatuity. Pyotr Petrovitch, who had made his way up from insignificance, was morbidly given to self-admiration, had the highest opinion of his intelligence and capacities, and sometimes even gloated in solitude over his image in the glass. But what he loved and valued above all was the money he had amassed by his labour, and by all sorts of devices: that money made him the equal of all who had been his superiors.

When he had bitterly reminded Dounia that he had decided to take her in spite of evil report, Pyotr Petrovitch had spoken with perfect sincerity and had, indeed, felt genuinely indignant at such "black ingratitude." And yet, when he made Dounia his offer, he was fully aware of the groundlessness of all the gossip. The story had been everywhere contradicted by Marfa Petrovna, and was by then disbelieved by all the townspeople, who were warm in Dounia'a defence. And he would not have denied that he knew all that at the time. Yet he still thought highly of his own resolution in lifting Dounia to his level and regarded it as something heroic. In speaking of it to Dounia, he had let out the secret feeling he cherished and admired, and he could not understand that others should fail to admire it too. He had called on Raskolnikov with the feelings of a benefactor who is about to reap the fruits of his good deeds and to hear agreeable flattery. And as he went downstairs now, he considered himself most undeservedly injured and unrecognised.

Dounia was simply essential to him; to do without her was unthinkable. For many years he had had voluptuous dreams of marriage, but he had gone on waiting and amassing money. He brooded with relish, in profound secret, over the image of a girl—virtuous, poor (she must be poor), very young, very pretty, of good birth and education, very timid, one who had suffered much, and was completely humbled before him, one who would all her life look on him as her saviour, worship him, admire him and only him. How many scenes, how many amorous episodes he had imagined on this seductive and playful theme, when his work was over! And, behold, the dream of so many years was all but realised; the beauty and education of Avdotya Romanovna had impressed him; her helpless position had been a great allurement; in her he had found even more than he dreamed of. Here was a girl of pride, character, virtue, of education and breeding superior to his own (he felt that), and this creature would be slavishly grateful all her life for his heroic condescension, and would humble herself in the dust before him, and he would have absolute, unbounded power over her!... Not long before, he had, too, after long reflection and hesitation, made an important change in his career and was now entering on a wider circle of business. With this change his cherished dreams of rising into a higher class of society seemed likely to be realised.... He was, in fact, determined to try his fortune in Petersburg. He knew that women could do a very great deal. The fascination of a charming, virtuous, highly educated woman might make his way easier, might do wonders in attracting people to him, throwing an aureole round him, and now everything was in ruins! This sudden horrible rupture affected him like a clap of thunder; it was like a hideous joke, an absurdity. He had only been a tiny bit masterful, had not even time to speak out, had simply made a joke, been carried away—and it had ended so seriously. And, of course, too, he did love Dounia in his own way; he already possessed her in his dreams—and all at once! No! The next day, the very next day, it must all be set right, smoothed over, settled. Above all he must crush that conceited milksop who was the cause of it all. With a sick feeling he could not help recalling Razumihin too, but, he soon reassured himself on that score; as though a fellow like that could be put on a level with him! The man he really dreaded in earnest was Svidrigaïlov.... He had, in short, a great deal to attend to....

"No, I, I am more to blame than anyone!" said Dounia, kissing and embracing her mother. "I was tempted by his money, but on my honour, brother, I had no idea he was such a base man. If I had seen through him before, nothing would have tempted me! Don't blame me, brother!"

"God has delivered us! God has delivered us!" Pulcheria Alexandrovna muttered, but half consciously, as though scarcely able to realise what had happened.

They were all relieved, and in five minutes they were laughing. Only now and then Dounia turned white and frowned, remembering what had passed. Pulcheria Alexandrovna was surprised to find that she, too, was glad: she had only that morning thought rupture with Luzhin a terrible misfortune. Razumihin was delighted. He did not yet dare to express his joy fully, but he was in a fever of excitement as though a ton-weight had fallen off his heart. Now he had the right to devote his life to them, to serve them.... Anything might happen now! But he felt afraid to think of further possibilities and dared not let his imagination range. But Raskolnikov sat still in the same place, almost sullen and indifferent. Though he had been the most insistent on getting rid of Luzhin, he seemed now the least concerned at what had happened. Dounia could not help thinking that he was still angry with her, and Pulcheria Alexandrovna watched him timidly.

"What did Svidrigaïlov say to you?" said Dounia, approaching him.

"Yes, yes!" cried Pulcheria Alexandrovna.

Raskolnikov raised his head.

"He wants to make you a present of ten thousand roubles and he desires to see you once in my presence."

"See her! On no account!" cried Pulcheria Alexandrovna. "And how dare he offer her money!"

Then Raskolnikov repeated (rather dryly) his conversation with Svidrigaïlov, omitting his account of the ghostly visitations of Marfa Petrovna, wishing to avoid all unnecessary talk.

"What answer did you give him?" asked Dounia.

"At first I said I would not take any message to you. Then he said that he would do his utmost to obtain an interview with you without my help. He assured me that his passion for you was a passing infatuation, now he has no feeling for you. He doesn't want you to marry Luzhin.... His talk was altogether rather muddled."

"How do you explain him to yourself, Rodya? How did he strike you?"

"I must confess I don't quite understand him. He offers you ten thousand, and yet says he is not well off. He says he is going away, and in ten minutes he forgets he has said it. Then he says is he going to be married and has already fixed on the girl.... No doubt he has a motive, and probably a bad one. But it's odd that he should be so clumsy about it if he had any designs against you.... Of course, I refused this money on your account, once for all. Altogether, I thought him very strange.... One might almost think he was mad. But I may be mistaken; that may only be the part he assumes. The death of Marfa Petrovna seems to have made a great impression on him."

"God rest her soul," exclaimed Pulcheria Alexandrovna. "I shall always, always pray for her! Where should we be now, Dounia, without this three thousand! It's as though it had fallen from heaven! Why, Rodya, this morning we had only three roubles in our pocket and Dounia and I were just planning to pawn her watch, so as to avoid borrowing from that man until he offered help."

Dounia seemed strangely impressed by Svidrigaïlov's offer. She still stood meditating.

"He has got some terrible plan," she said in a half whisper to herself, almost shuddering.

Raskolnikov noticed this disproportionate terror.

"I fancy I shall have to see him more than once again," he said to Dounia.

"We will watch him! I will track him out!" cried Razumihin, vigorously. "I won't lose sight of him. Rodya has given me leave. He said to me himself just now. 'Take care of my sister.' Will you give me leave, too, Avdotya Romanovna?"

Dounia smiled and held out her hand, but the look of anxiety did not leave her face. Pulcheria Alexandrovna gazed at her timidly, but the three thousand roubles had obviously a soothing effect on her.

A quarter of an hour later, they were all engaged in a lively conversation. Even Raskolnikov listened attentively for some time, though he did not talk. Razumihin was the speaker.

"And why, why should you go away?" he flowed on ecstatically. "And what are you to do in a little town? The great thing is, you are all here together and you need one another—you do need one another, believe me. For a time, anyway.... Take me into partnership, and I assure you we'll plan a capital enterprise. Listen! I'll explain it all in detail to you, the whole project! It all flashed into my head this morning, before anything had happened... I tell you what; I have an uncle, I must introduce him to you (a most accommodating and respectable old man). This uncle has got a capital of a thousand roubles, and he lives on his pension and has no need of that money. For the last two years he has been bothering me to borrow it from him and pay him six per cent. interest. I know what that means; he simply wants to help me. Last year I had no need of it, but this year I resolved to borrow it as soon as he arrived. Then you lend me another thousand of your three and we have enough for a start, so we'll go into partnership, and what are we going to do?"

Then Razumihin began to unfold his project, and he explained at length that almost all our publishers and booksellers know nothing at all of what they are selling, and for that reason they are usually bad publishers, and that any decent publications pay as a rule and give a profit, sometimes a considerable one. Razumihin had, indeed, been dreaming of setting up as a publisher. For the last two years he had been working in publishers' offices, and knew three European languages well, though he had told Raskolnikov six days before that he was "schwach" in German with an object of persuading him to take half his translation and half the payment for it. He had told a lie then, and Raskolnikov knew he was lying.

"Why, why should we let our chance slip when we have one of the chief means of success—money of our own!" cried Razumihin warmly. "Of course there will be a lot of work, but we will work, you, Avdotya Romanovna, I, Rodion.... You get a splendid profit on some books nowadays! And the great point of the business is that we shall know just what wants translating, and we shall be translating, publishing, learning all at once. I can be of use because I have experience. For nearly two years I've been scuttling about among the publishers, and now I know every detail of their business. You need not be a saint to make pots, believe me! And why, why should we let our chance slip! Why, I know—and I kept the secret—two or three books which one might get a hundred roubles simply for thinking of translating and publishing. Indeed, and I would not take five hundred for the very idea of one of them. And what do you think? If I were to tell a publisher, I dare say he'd hesitate—they are such blockheads! And as for the business side, printing, paper, selling, you trust to me, I know my way about. We'll begin in a small way and go on to a large. In any case it will get us our living and we shall get back our capital."

Dounia's eyes shone.

"I like what you are saying, Dmitri Prokofitch!" she said.

"I know nothing about it, of course," put in Pulcheria Alexandrovna, "it may be a good idea, but again God knows. It's new and untried. Of course, we must remain here at least for a time." She looked at Rodya.

"What do you think, brother?" said Dounia.

"I think he's got a very good idea," he answered. "Of course, it's too soon to dream of a publishing firm, but we certainly might bring out five or six books and be sure of success. I know of one book myself which would be sure to go well. And as for his being able to manage it, there's no doubt about that either. He knows the business.... But we can talk it over later...."

"Hurrah!" cried Razumihin. "Now, stay, there's a flat here in this house, belonging to the same owner. It's a special flat apart, not communicating with these lodgings. It's furnished, rent moderate, three rooms. Suppose you take them to begin with. I'll pawn your watch to-morrow and bring you the money, and everything can be arranged then. You can all three live together, and Rodya will be with you. But where are you off to, Rodya?"

"What, Rodya, you are going already?" Pulcheria Alexandrovna asked in dismay.

"At such a minute?" cried Razumihin.

Dounia looked at her brother with incredulous wonder. He held his cap in his hand, he was preparing to leave them.

"One would think you were burying me or saying good-bye for ever," he said somewhat oddly. He attempted to smile, but it did not turn out a smile. "But who knows, perhaps it is the last time we shall see each other..." he let slip accidentally. It was what he was thinking, and it somehow was uttered aloud.

"What is the matter with you?" cried his mother.

"Where are you going, Rodya?" asked Dounia rather strangely.

"Oh, I'm quite obliged to..." he answered vaguely, as though hesitating what he would say. But there was a look of sharp determination in his white face.

"I meant to say... as I was coming here... I meant to tell you, mother, and you, Dounia, that it would be better for us to part for a time. I feel ill, I am not at peace.... I will come afterwards, I will come of myself... when it's possible. I remember you and love you.... Leave me, leave me alone. I decided this even before... I'm absolutely resolved on it. Whatever may come to me, whether I come to ruin or not, I want to be alone. Forget me altogether, it's better. Don't inquire about me. When I can, I'll come of myself or... I'll send for you. Perhaps it will all come back, but now if you love me, give me up... else I shall begin to hate you, I feel it.... Good-bye!"

"Good God!" cried Pulcheria Alexandrovna. Both his mother and his sister were terribly alarmed. Razumihin was also.

"Rodya, Rodya, be reconciled with us! Let us be as before!" cried his poor mother.

He turned slowly to the door and slowly went out of the room. Dounia overtook him.

"Brother, what are you doing to mother?" she whispered, her eyes flashing with indignation.

He looked dully at her.

"No matter, I shall come.... I'm coming," he muttered in an undertone, as though not fully conscious of what he was saying, and he went out of the room.

"Wicked, heartless egoist!" cried Dounia.

"He is insane, but not heartless. He is mad! Don't you see it? You're heartless after that!" Razumihin whispered in her ear, squeezing her hand tightly. "I shall be back directly," he shouted to the horror-stricken mother, and he ran out of the room.

Raskolnikov was waiting for him at the end of the passage.

"I knew you would run after me," he said. "Go back to them—be with them... be with them to-morrow and always.... I... perhaps I shall come... if I can. Good-bye."

And without holding out his hand he walked away.

"But where are you going? What are you doing? What's the matter with you? How can you go on like this?" Razumihin muttered, at his wits' end.

Raskolnikov stopped once more.

"Once for all, never ask me about anything. I have nothing to tell you. Don't come to see me. Maybe I'll come here.... Leave me, but *don't leave* them. Do you understand me?"

It was dark in the corridor, they were standing near the lamp. For a minute they were looking at one another in silence. Razumihin remembered that minute all his life. Raskolnikov's burning and intent eyes grew more penetrating every moment, piercing into his soul, into his consciousness. Suddenly Razumihin started. Something strange, as it were, passed between them.... Some idea, some hint, as it were, slipped, something awful, hideous, and suddenly understood on both sides.... Razumihin turned pale.

"Do you understand now?" said Raskolnikov, his face twitching nervously. "Go back, go to them," he said suddenly, and turning quickly, he went out of the house.

I will not attempt to describe how Razumihin went back to the ladies, how he soothed them, how he protested that Rodya needed rest in his illness, protested that Rodya was sure to come, that he would come every day, that he was very, very much upset, that he must not be irritated, that he, Razumihin, would watch over him, would get him a doctor, the best doctor, a consultation.... In fact from that evening Razumihin took his place with them as a son and a brother.

CHAPTER IV

Raskolnikov went straight to the house on the canal bank where Sonia lived. It was an old green house of three storeys. He found the porter and obtained from him vague directions as to the whereabouts of Kapernaumov, the tailor. Having found in the corner of the courtyard the entrance to the dark and narrow staircase, he mounted to the second floor and came out into a gallery that ran round the whole second storey over the yard. While he was wandering in the darkness, uncertain where to turn for Kapernaumov's door, a door opened three paces from him; he mechanically took hold of it.

"Who is there?" a woman's voice asked uneasily.

"It's I... come to see you," answered Raskolnikov and he walked into the tiny entry.

On a broken chair stood a candle in a battered copper candlestick.

"It's you! Good heavens!" cried Sonia weakly, and she stood rooted to the spot.

"Which is your room? This way?" and Raskolnikov, trying not to look at her, hastened in.

A minute later Sonia, too, came in with the candle, set down the candlestick and, completely disconcerted, stood before him inexpressibly agitated and apparently frightened by his unexpected visit. The colour rushed suddenly to her pale face and tears came into her eyes... She felt sick and ashamed and happy, too.... Raskolnikov turned away quickly and sat on a chair by the table. He scanned the room in a rapid glance.

It was a large but exceedingly low-pitched room, the only one let by the Kapernaumovs, to whose rooms a closed door led in the wall on the left. In the opposite side on the right hand wall was another door, always kept locked. That led to the next flat, which formed a separate lodging. Sonia's room looked like a barn; it was a very irregular quadrangle and this gave it a grotesque appearance. A wall with three windows looking out on to the canal ran aslant so that one corner formed a very acute angle, and it was difficult to see in it without very strong light. The other corner was disproportionately obtuse. There was scarcely any furniture in the big room: in the corner on the right was a bedstead, beside it, nearest the door, a chair. A plain, deal table covered by a blue cloth stood against the same wall, close to the door into the other flat. Two rush-bottom chairs stood by the table. On the opposite wall near the acute angle stood a small plain wooden chest of drawers looking, as it were, lost in a desert. That was all there was in the room. The yellow, scratched and shabby wall-paper was black in the corners. It must have been damp and full of fumes in the winter. There was every sign of poverty; even the bedstead had no curtain.

Sonia looked in silence at her visitor, who was so attentively and unceremoniously scrutinising her room, and even began at last to tremble with terror, as though she was standing before her judge and the arbiter of her destinies.

"I am late.... It's eleven, isn't it?" he asked, still not lifting his eyes.

"Yes," muttered Sonia, "oh yes, it is," she added, hastily, as though in that lay her means of escape. "My landlady's clock has just struck... I heard it myself...."

"I've come to you for the last time," Raskolnikov went on gloomily, although this was the first time. "I may perhaps not see you again..."

"Are you... going away?"

"I don't know... to-morrow...."

"Then you are not coming to Katerina Ivanovna to-morrow?" Sonia's voice shook.

"I don't know. I shall know to-morrow morning.... Never mind that: I've come to say one word...."

He raised his brooding eyes to her and suddenly noticed that he was sitting down while she was all the while standing before him.

"Why are you standing? Sit down," he said in a changed voice, gentle and friendly.

She sat down. He looked kindly and almost compassionately at her.

"How thin you are! What a hand! Quite transparent, like a dead hand."

He took her hand. Sonia smiled faintly.

"I have always been like that," she said.

"Even when you lived at home?"

"Yes."

"Of course, you were," he added abruptly and the expression of his face and the sound of his voice changed again suddenly.

He looked round him once more.

"You rent this room from the Kapernaumovs?"

"Yes...."

"They live there, through that door?"

"Yes.... They have another room like this."

"All in one room?"

"Yes."

"I should be afraid in your room at night," he observed gloomily.

"They are very good people, very kind," answered Sonia, who still seemed bewildered, "and all the furniture, everything... everything is theirs. And they are very kind and the children, too, often come to see me."

"They all stammer, don't they?"

"Yes.... He stammers and he's lame. And his wife, too.... It's not exactly that she stammers, but she can't speak plainly. She is a very kind woman. And he used to be a house serf. And there are seven children... and it's only the eldest one that stammers and the others are simply ill... but they don't stammer.... But where did you hear about them?" she added with some surprise.

"Your father told me, then. He told me all about you.... And how you went out at six o'clock and came back at nine and how Katerina Ivanovna knelt down by your bed."

Sonia was confused.

"I fancied I saw him to-day," she whispered hesitatingly.

"Whom?"

"Father. I was walking in the street, out there at the corner, about ten o'clock and he seemed to be walking in front. It looked just like him. I wanted to go to Katerina Ivanovna...."

"You were walking in the streets?"

"Yes," Sonia whispered abruptly, again overcome with confusion and looking down.

"Katerina Ivanovna used to beat you, I dare say?"

"Oh no, what are you saying? No!" Sonia looked at him almost with dismay.

"You love her, then?"

"Love her? Of course!" said Sonia with plaintive emphasis, and she clasped her hands in distress. "Ah, you don't.... If you only knew! You see, she is quite like a child.... Her mind is quite unhinged, you see... from sorrow. And how clever she used to be... how generous... how kind! Ah, you don't understand, you don't understand!"

Sonia said this as though in despair, wringing her hands in excitement and distress. Her pale cheeks flushed, there was a look of anguish in her eyes. It was clear that she was stirred to the very depths, that she was longing to speak, to champion, to express something. A sort of *insatiable* compassion, if one may so express it, was reflected in every feature of her face.

"Beat me! how can you? Good heavens, beat me! And if she did beat me, what then? What of it? You know nothing, nothing about it.... She is so unhappy... ah, how unhappy! And ill.... She is seeking righteousness, she is pure. She has such faith that there must be righteousness everywhere and she expects it.... And if you were to torture her, she wouldn't do wrong. She doesn't see that it's impossible for people to be righteous and she is angry at it. Like a child, like a child. She is good!"

"And what will happen to you?"

Sonia looked at him inquiringly.

"They are left on your hands, you see. They were all on your hands before, though.... And your father came to you to beg for drink. Well, how will it be now?"

"I don't know," Sonia articulated mournfully.

"Will they stay there?"

"I don't know.... They are in debt for the lodging, but the landlady, I hear, said to-day that she wanted to get rid of them, and Katerina Ivanovna says that she won't stay another minute."

"How is it she is so bold? She relies upon you?"

"Oh, no, don't talk like that.... We are one, we live like one." Sonia was agitated again and even angry, as though a canary or some other little bird were to be angry. "And what could she do? What, what could she do?" she persisted, getting hot and excited. "And how she cried to-day! Her mind is unhinged, haven't you noticed it? At one minute she is worrying like a child that everything should be right to-morrow, the lunch and all that.... Then she is wringing her hands, spitting blood, weeping, and all at once she will begin knocking her head against the wall, in despair. Then she will be comforted again. She builds all her hopes on you; she says that you will help her now and that she will borrow a little money somewhere and go to her native town with me and set up a boarding school for the daughters of gentlemen and take me to superintend it, and we will begin a new splendid life. And she kisses and hugs me, comforts me, and you know she has such faith, such faith in her fancies! One can't contradict her. And all the day long she has been washing, cleaning, mending. She dragged the wash tub into the room with her feeble hands and sank on the bed, gasping for breath. We went this morning to the shops to buy shoes for Polenka and Lida for theirs are quite worn out. Only the money we'd reckoned wasn't enough, not nearly enough. And she picked out such dear little boots, for she has taste, you don't know. And there in the shop she burst out crying before the shopmen because she hadn't enough.... Ah, it was sad to see her...."

"Well, after that I can understand your living like this," Raskolnikov said with a bitter smile.

"And aren't you sorry for them? Aren't you sorry?" Sonia flew at him again. "Why, I know, you gave your last penny yourself, though you'd seen nothing of it, and if you'd seen everything, oh dear! And how often, how often I've brought her to tears! Only last week! Yes, I! Only a week before his death. I was cruel! And how often I've done it! Ah, I've been wretched at the thought of it all day!"

Sonia wrung her hands as she spoke at the pain of remembering it.

"You were cruel?"

"Yes, I—I. I went to see them," she went on, weeping, "and father said, 'read me something, Sonia, my head aches, read to me, here's a book.' He had a book he had got from Andrey Semyonovitch Lebeziatnikov, he lives there, he always used to get hold of such funny books. And I said, 'I can't stay,' as I didn't want to read, and I'd gone in chiefly to show Katerina Ivanovna some collars. Lizaveta, the pedlar, sold me some collars and cuffs cheap, pretty, new, embroidered ones. Katerina Ivanovna liked them very much; she put them on and looked at herself in the glass and was delighted with them. 'Make me a present of them, Sonia,' she said, 'please do.' '*Please do*,' she said, she wanted them so much. And when could she wear them? They just reminded her of her old happy days. She looked at herself in the glass, admired herself, and she has no clothes at all, no things of her own, hasn't had all these years! And she never asks anyone for anything; she is proud, she'd sooner give away everything. And these she asked for, she liked them so much. And I was sorry to give them. 'What use are they to you, Katerina Ivanovna?' I said. I spoke like that to her, I ought not to have said that! She gave me such a look. And she was so grieved, so grieved at my refusing her. And it was so sad to see.... And she was not grieved for the collars, but for my refusing, I saw that. Ah, if only I could bring it all back, change it, take back those words! Ah, if I... but it's nothing to you!"

"Did you know Lizaveta, the pedlar?"

"Yes.... Did you know her?" Sonia asked with some surprise.

"Katerina Ivanovna is in consumption, rapid consumption; she will soon die," said Raskolnikov after a pause, without answering her question.

"Oh, no, no, no!"

And Sonia unconsciously clutched both his hands, as though imploring that she should not.

"But it will be better if she does die."

"No, not better, not at all better!" Sonia unconsciously repeated in dismay.

"And the children? What can you do except take them to live with you?"

"Oh, I don't know," cried Sonia, almost in despair, and she put her hands to her head.

It was evident that that idea had very often occurred to her before and he had only roused it again.

"And, what, if even now, while Katerina Ivanovna is alive, you get ill and are taken to the hospital, what will happen then?" he persisted pitilessly.

"How can you? That cannot be!"

And Sonia's face worked with awful terror.

"Cannot be?" Raskolnikov went on with a harsh smile. "You are not insured against it, are you? What will happen to them then? They will be in the street, all of them, she will cough and beg and knock her head against some wall, as she did to-day, and the children will cry.... Then she will fall down, be taken to the police station and to the hospital, she will die, and the children..."

"Oh, no.... God will not let it be!" broke at last from Sonia's overburdened bosom.

She listened, looking imploringly at him, clasping her hands in dumb entreaty, as though it all depended upon him.

Raskolnikov got up and began to walk about the room. A minute passed. Sonia was standing with her hands and her head hanging in terrible dejection.

"And can't you save? Put by for a rainy day?" he asked, stopping suddenly before her.

"No," whispered Sonia.

"Of course not. Have you tried?" he added almost ironically.

"Yes."

"And it didn't come off! Of course not! No need to ask."

And again he paced the room. Another minute passed.

"You don't get money every day?"

Sonia was more confused than ever and colour rushed into her face again.

"No," she whispered with a painful effort.

"It will be the same with Polenka, no doubt," he said suddenly.

"No, no! It can't be, no!" Sonia cried aloud in desperation, as though she had been stabbed. "God would not allow anything so awful!"

"He lets others come to it."

"No, no! God will protect her, God!" she repeated beside herself.

"But, perhaps, there is no God at all," Raskolnikov answered with a sort of malignance, laughed and looked at her.

Sonia's face suddenly changed; a tremor passed over it. She looked at him with unutterable reproach, tried to say something, but could not speak and broke into bitter, bitter sobs, hiding her face in her hands.

"You say Katerina Ivanovna's mind is unhinged; your own mind is unhinged," he said after a brief silence.

Five minutes passed. He still paced up and down the room in silence, not looking at her. At last he went up to her; his eyes glittered. He put his two hands on her shoulders and looked straight into her tearful face. His eyes were hard, feverish and piercing, his lips were twitching. All at once he bent down quickly and dropping to the ground, kissed her foot. Sonia drew back from him as from a madman. And certainly he looked like a madman.

"What are you doing to me?" she muttered, turning pale, and a sudden anguish clutched at her heart.

He stood up at once.

"I did not bow down to you, I bowed down to all the suffering of humanity," he said wildly and walked away to the window. "Listen," he added, turning to her a minute later. "I said just now to an insolent man that he was not worth your little finger... and that I did my sister honour making her sit beside you."

"Ach, you said that to them! And in her presence?" cried Sonia, frightened. "Sit down with me! An honour! Why, I'm... dishonourable.... Ah, why did you say that?"

"It was not because of your dishonour and your sin I said that of you, but because of your great suffering. But you are a great sinner, that's true," he added almost solemnly, "and your worst sin is that you have destroyed and betrayed yourself *for nothing*. Isn't that fearful? Isn't it fearful that you are living in this filth which you loathe so, and at the same time you know yourself (you've only to open your eyes) that you are not helping anyone by it, not saving anyone from anything? Tell me," he went on almost in a frenzy, "how this shame and degradation can exist in you side by side with other, opposite, holy feelings? It would be better, a thousand times better and wiser to leap into the water and end it all!"

"But what would become of them?" Sonia asked faintly, gazing at him with eyes of anguish, but not seeming surprised at his suggestion.

Raskolnikov looked strangely at her. He read it all in her face; so she must have had that thought already, perhaps many times, and earnestly she had thought out in her despair how to end it and so earnestly, that now she scarcely wondered at his suggestion. She had not even noticed the cruelty of his words. (The significance of his reproaches and his peculiar attitude to her shame she had, of course, not noticed either, and that, too, was clear to him.) But he saw how monstrously the thought of her disgraceful, shameful position was torturing her and had long tortured her. "What, what," he thought, "could hitherto have hindered her from putting an end to it?" Only then he realised what those poor little orphan children and that pitiful half-crazy Katerina Ivanovna, knocking her head against the wall in her consumption, meant for Sonia.

But, nevertheless, it was clear to him again that with her character and the amount of education she had after all received, she could not in any case remain so. He was still confronted by the question, how could she have remained so long in that position without going out of her mind, since she could not bring herself to jump into the water? Of course he knew that Sonia's position was an exceptional case, though unhappily not unique and not infrequent, indeed; but that very exceptionalness, her tinge of education, her previous life might, one would have thought, have killed her at the first step on that revolting path. What held her up—surely not depravity? All that infamy had obviously only touched her mechanically, not one drop of real depravity had penetrated to her heart; he saw that. He saw through her as she stood before him....

"There are three ways before her," he thought, "the canal, the madhouse, or... at last to sink into depravity which obscures the mind and turns the heart to stone."

The last idea was the most revolting, but he was a sceptic, he was young, abstract, and therefore cruel, and so he could not help believing that the last end was the most likely.

"But can that be true?" he cried to himself. "Can that creature who has still preserved the purity of her spirit be consciously drawn at last into that sink of filth and iniquity? Can the process already have begun? Can it be that she has only been able to bear it till now, because vice has begun to be less loathsome to her? No, no, that cannot be!" he cried, as Sonia had just before. "No, what has kept her from the canal till now is the idea of sin and they, the children.... And if she has not gone out of her mind... but who says she has not gone out of her mind? Is she in her senses? Can one talk, can one reason as she does? How can she sit on the edge of the abyss of loathsomeness into which she is slipping and refuse to listen when she is told of danger? Does she expect a miracle? No doubt she does. Doesn't that all mean madness?"

He stayed obstinately at that thought. He liked that explanation indeed better than any other. He began looking more intently at her.

"So you pray to God a great deal, Sonia?" he asked her.

Sonia did not speak; he stood beside her waiting for an answer.

"What should I be without God?" she whispered rapidly, forcibly, glancing at him with suddenly flashing eyes, and squeezing his hand.

"Ah, so that is it!" he thought.

"And what does God do for you?" he asked, probing her further.

Sonia was silent a long while, as though she could not answer. Her weak chest kept heaving with emotion.

"Be silent! Don't ask! You don't deserve!" she cried suddenly, looking sternly and wrathfully at him.

"That's it, that's it," he repeated to himself.

"He does everything," she whispered quickly, looking down again.

"That's the way out! That's the explanation," he decided, scrutinising her with eager curiosity, with a new, strange, almost morbid feeling. He gazed at that pale, thin, irregular, angular little face, those soft blue eyes, which could flash with such fire, such stern energy, that little body still shaking with indignation and anger— and it all seemed to him more and more strange, almost impossible. "She is a religious maniac!" he repeated to himself.

There was a book lying on the chest of drawers. He had noticed it every time he paced up and down the room. Now he took it up and looked at it. It was the New Testament in the Russian translation. It was bound in leather, old and worn.

"Where did you get that?" he called to her across the room.

She was still standing in the same place, three steps from the table.

"It was brought me," she answered, as it were unwillingly, not looking at him.

"Who brought it?"

"Lizaveta, I asked her for it."

"Lizaveta! strange!" he thought.

Everything about Sonia seemed to him stranger and more wonderful every moment. He carried the book to the candle and began to turn over the pages.

"Where is the story of Lazarus?" he asked suddenly.

Sonia looked obstinately at the ground and would not answer. She was standing sideways to the table.

"Where is the raising of Lazarus? Find it for me, Sonia."

She stole a glance at him.

"You are not looking in the right place.... It's in the fourth gospel," she whispered sternly, without looking at him.

"Find it and read it to me," he said. He sat down with his elbow on the table, leaned his head on his hand and looked away sullenly, prepared to listen.

"In three weeks' time they'll welcome me in the madhouse! I shall be there if I am not in a worse place," he muttered to himself.

Sonia heard Raskolnikov's request distrustfully and moved hesitatingly to the table. She took the book however.

"Haven't you read it?" she asked, looking up at him across the table.

Her voice became sterner and sterner.

"Long ago.... When I was at school. Read!"

"And haven't you heard it in church?"

"I... haven't been. Do you often go?"

"N-no," whispered Sonia.

Raskolnikov smiled.

"I understand.... And you won't go to your father's funeral to-morrow?"

"Yes, I shall. I was at church last week, too... I had a requiem service."

"For whom?"

"For Lizaveta. She was killed with an axe."

His nerves were more and more strained. His head began to go round.

"Were you friends with Lizaveta?"

"Yes.... She was good... she used to come... not often... she couldn't.... We used to read together and... talk. She will see God."

The last phrase sounded strange in his ears. And here was something new again: the mysterious meetings with Lizaveta and both of them—religious maniacs.

"I shall be a religious maniac myself soon! It's infectious!"

"Read!" he cried irritably and insistently.

Sonia still hesitated. Her heart was throbbing. She hardly dared to read to him. He looked almost with exasperation at the "unhappy lunatic."

"What for? You don't believe?..." she whispered softly and as it were breathlessly.

"Read! I want you to," he persisted. "You used to read to Lizaveta."

Sonia opened the book and found the place. Her hands were shaking, her voice failed her. Twice she tried to begin and could not bring out the first syllable.

"Now a certain man was sick named Lazarus of Bethany..." she forced herself at last to read, but at the third word her voice broke like an overstrained string. There was a catch in her breath.

Raskolnikov saw in part why Sonia could not bring herself to read to him and the more he saw this, the more roughly and irritably he insisted on her doing so. He understood only too well how painful it was for her to betray and unveil all that was her *own*. He understood that these feelings really were her *secret treasure*, which she had kept perhaps for years, perhaps from childhood, while she lived with an unhappy father and a distracted stepmother crazed by grief, in the midst of starving children and unseemly abuse and reproaches. But at the same time he knew now and knew for certain that, although it filled her with dread and suffering, yet she had a tormenting desire to read and to read to *him* that he might hear it, and to read *now* whatever might come of it!...

He read this in her eyes, he could see it in her intense emotion. She mastered herself, controlled the spasm in her throat and went on reading the eleventh chapter of St. John. She went on to the nineteenth verse:

"And many of the Jews came to Martha and Mary to comfort them concerning their brother.

"Then Martha as soon as she heard that Jesus was coming went and met Him: but Mary sat still in the house.

"Then said Martha unto Jesus, Lord, if Thou hadst been here, my brother had not died.

"But I know that even now whatsoever Thou wilt ask of God, God will give it Thee...."

Then she stopped again with a shamefaced feeling that her voice would quiver and break again.

"Jesus said unto her, thy brother shall rise again.

"Martha saith unto Him, I know that he shall rise again in the resurrection, at the last day.

"Jesus said unto her, I am the resurrection and the life: he that believeth in Me though he were dead, yet shall he live.

"And whosoever liveth and believeth in Me shall never die. Believest thou this?

"She saith unto Him,"

(And drawing a painful breath, Sonia read distinctly and forcibly as though she were making a public confession of faith.)

"Yea, Lord: I believe that Thou art the Christ, the Son of God Which should come into the world."

She stopped and looked up quickly at him, but controlling herself went on reading. Raskolnikov sat without moving, his elbows on the table and his eyes turned away. She read to the thirty-second verse.

"Then when Mary was come where Jesus was and saw Him, she fell down at His feet, saying unto Him, Lord if Thou hadst been here, my brother had not died.

"When Jesus therefore saw her weeping, and the Jews also weeping which came with her, He groaned in the spirit and was troubled,

"And said, Where have ye laid him? They said unto Him, Lord, come and see.

"Jesus wept.

"Then said the Jews, behold how He loved him!

"And some of them said, could not this Man which opened the eyes of the blind, have caused that even this man should not have died?"

Raskolnikov turned and looked at her with emotion. Yes, he had known it! She was trembling in a real physical fever. He had expected it. She was getting near the story of the greatest miracle and a feeling of immense triumph came over her. Her voice rang out like a bell; triumph and joy gave it power. The lines danced before her eyes, but she knew what she was reading by heart. At the last verse "Could not this Man which opened the eyes of the blind..." dropping her voice she passionately reproduced the doubt, the reproach and censure of the blind disbelieving Jews, who in another moment would fall at His feet as though struck by thunder, sobbing and believing.... "And *he, he*—too, is blinded and unbelieving, he, too, will hear, he, too, will believe, yes, yes! At once, now," was what she was dreaming, and she was quivering with happy anticipation.

"Jesus therefore again groaning in Himself cometh to the grave. It was a cave, and a stone lay upon it.

"Jesus said, Take ye away the stone. Martha, the sister of him that was dead, saith unto Him, Lord by this time he stinketh: for he hath been dead four days."

She laid emphasis on the word *four*.

"Jesus saith unto her, Said I not unto thee that if thou wouldest believe, thou shouldest see the glory of God?

"Then they took away the stone from the place where the dead was laid. And Jesus lifted up His eyes and said, Father, I thank Thee that Thou hast heard Me.

"And I knew that Thou hearest Me always; but because of the people which stand by I said it, that they may believe that Thou hast sent Me.

"And when He thus had spoken, He cried with a loud voice, Lazarus, come forth.

"And he that was dead came forth."

(She read loudly, cold and trembling with ecstasy, as though she were seeing it before her eyes.)

"Bound hand and foot with graveclothes; and his face was bound about with a napkin. Jesus saith unto them, Loose him and let him go.

"Then many of the Jews which came to Mary and had seen the things which Jesus did believed on Him."

She could read no more, closed the book and got up from her chair quickly.

"That is all about the raising of Lazarus," she whispered severely and abruptly, and turning away she stood motionless, not daring to raise her eyes to him. She still trembled feverishly. The candle-end was flickering out in the battered candlestick, dimly lighting up in the poverty-stricken room the murderer and the harlot who had so strangely been reading together the eternal book. Five minutes or more passed.

"I came to speak of something," Raskolnikov said aloud, frowning. He got up and went to Sonia. She lifted her eyes to him in silence. His face was particularly stern and there was a sort of savage determination in it.

"I have abandoned my family to-day," he said, "my mother and sister. I am not going to see them. I've broken with them completely."

"What for?" asked Sonia amazed. Her recent meeting with his mother and sister had left a great impression which she could not analyse. She heard his news almost with horror.

"I have only you now," he added. "Let us go together.... I've come to you, we are both accursed, let us go our way together!"

His eyes glittered "as though he were mad," Sonia thought, in her turn.

"Go where?" she asked in alarm and she involuntarily stepped back.

"How do I know? I only know it's the same road, I know that and nothing more. It's the same goal!"

She looked at him and understood nothing. She knew only that he was terribly, infinitely unhappy.

"No one of them will understand, if you tell them, but I have understood. I need you, that is why I have come to you."

"I don't understand," whispered Sonia.

"You'll understand later. Haven't you done the same? You, too, have transgressed... have had the strength to transgress. You have laid hands on yourself, you have destroyed a life... *your own* (it's all the same!). You might have lived in spirit and understanding, but you'll end in the Hay Market.... But you won't be able to stand it, and if you remain alone you'll go out of your mind like me. You are like a mad creature already. So we must go together on the same road! Let us go!"

"What for? What's all this for?" said Sonia, strangely and violently agitated by his words.

"What for? Because you can't remain like this, that's why! You must look things straight in the face at last, and not weep like a child and cry that God won't allow it. What will happen, if you should really be taken to the hospital to-morrow? She is mad and in consumption, she'll soon die and the children? Do you mean to tell me Polenka won't come to grief? Haven't you seen children here at the street corners sent out by their mothers to beg? I've found out where those mothers live and in what surroundings. Children can't remain children there! At seven the child is vicious and a thief. Yet children, you know, are the image of Christ: 'theirs is the kingdom of Heaven.' He bade us honour and love them, they are the humanity of the future...."

"What's to be done, what's to be done?" repeated Sonia, weeping hysterically and wringing her hands.

"What's to be done? Break what must be broken, once for all, that's all, and take the suffering on oneself. What, you don't understand? You'll understand later.... Freedom and power, and above all, power! Over all trembling creation and all the ant-heap!... That's the goal, remember that! That's my farewell message. Perhaps it's the last time I shall speak to you. If I don't come to-morrow, you'll hear of it all, and then remember these words. And some day later on, in years to come, you'll understand perhaps what they meant. If I come to-morrow, I'll tell you who killed Lizaveta.... Good-bye."

Sonia started with terror.

"Why, do you know who killed her?" she asked, chilled with horror, looking wildly at him.

"I know and will tell... you, only you. I have chosen you out. I'm not coming to you to ask forgiveness, but simply to tell you. I chose you out long ago to hear this, when your father talked of you and when Lizaveta was alive, I thought of it. Good-bye, don't shake hands. To-morrow!"

He went out. Sonia gazed at him as at a madman. But she herself was like one insane and felt it. Her head was going round.

"Good heavens, how does he know who killed Lizaveta? What did those words mean? It's awful!" But at the same time *the idea* did not enter her head, not for a moment! "Oh, he must be terribly unhappy!... He has abandoned his mother and sister.... What for? What has happened? And what had he in his mind? What did he say to her? He had kissed her foot and said... said (yes, he had said it clearly) that he could not live without her.... Oh, merciful heavens!"

Sonia spent the whole night feverish and delirious. She jumped up from time to time, wept and wrung her hands, then sank again into feverish sleep and dreamt of Polenka, Katerina Ivanovna and Lizaveta, of reading the gospel and him... him with pale face, with burning eyes... kissing her feet, weeping.

On the other side of the door on the right, which divided Sonia's room from Madame Resslich's flat, was a room which had long stood empty. A card was fixed on the gate and a notice stuck in the windows over the canal advertising it to let. Sonia had long been accustomed to the room's being uninhabited. But all that time Mr. Svidrigaïlov had been standing, listening at the door of the empty room. When Raskolnikov went out he stood still, thought a moment, went on tiptoe to his own room which adjoined the empty one, brought a chair and noiselessly carried it to the door that led to Sonia's room. The conversation had struck him as interesting and remarkable, and he had greatly enjoyed it—so much so that he brought a chair that he might not in the future, to-morrow, for instance, have to endure the inconvenience of standing a whole hour, but might listen in comfort.

CHAPTER V

When next morning at eleven o'clock punctually Raskolnikov went into the department of the investigation of criminal causes and sent his name in to Porfiry Petrovitch, he was surprised at being kept waiting so long: it was at least ten minutes before he was summoned. He had expected that they would pounce upon him. But he stood in the waiting-room, and people, who apparently had nothing to do with him, were continually passing to and fro before him. In the next room which looked like an office, several clerks were sitting writing and obviously they had no notion who or what Raskolnikov might be. He looked uneasily and suspiciously about him to see whether there was not some guard, some mysterious watch being kept on him to prevent his escape. But there was nothing of the sort: he saw only the faces of clerks absorbed in petty details, then other people, no one seemed to have any concern with him. He might go where he liked for them. The conviction grew stronger in him that if that enigmatic man of yesterday, that phantom sprung out of the earth, had seen everything, they would not have let him stand and wait like that. And would they have waited till he elected to appear at eleven? Either the man had not yet given information, or... or simply he knew nothing, had seen nothing (and how could he have seen anything?) and so all that had happened to him the day before was again a phantom exaggerated by his sick and overstrained imagination. This conjecture had begun to grow strong the day before, in the midst of all his alarm and despair. Thinking it all over now and preparing for a fresh conflict, he was suddenly aware that he was trembling—and he felt a rush of indignation at the thought that he was trembling with fear at facing that hateful Porfiry Petrovitch. What he dreaded above all was meeting that man again; he hated him with an intense, unmitigated hatred and was afraid his hatred might betray him. His indignation was such that he ceased trembling at once; he made ready to go in with a cold and arrogant bearing and vowed to himself to keep as silent as possible, to watch and listen and for once at least to control his overstrained nerves. At that moment he was summoned to Porfiry Petrovitch.

He found Porfiry Petrovitch alone in his study. His study was a room neither large nor small, furnished with a large writing-table, that stood before a sofa, upholstered in checked material, a bureau, a bookcase in the corner and several chairs—all government furniture, of polished yellow wood. In the further wall there was a closed door, beyond it there were no doubt other rooms. On Raskolnikov's entrance Porfiry Petrovitch had at once closed the door by which he had come in and they remained alone. He met his visitor with an apparently genial and good-tempered air, and it was only after a few minutes that Raskolnikov saw signs of a certain awkwardness in him, as though he had been thrown out of his reckoning or caught in something very secret.

"Ah, my dear fellow! Here you are... in our domain"... began Porfiry, holding out both hands to him. "Come, sit down, old man... or perhaps you don't like to be called 'my dear fellow' and 'old man!'—*tout court*? Please don't think it too familiar.... Here, on the sofa."

Raskolnikov sat down, keeping his eyes fixed on him. "In our domain," the apologies for familiarity, the French phrase *tout court*, were all characteristic signs.

"He held out both hands to me, but he did not give me one—he drew it back in time," struck him suspiciously. Both were watching each other, but when their eyes met, quick as lightning they looked away.

"I brought you this paper... about the watch. Here it is. Is it all right or shall I copy it again?"

"What? A paper? Yes, yes, don't be uneasy, it's all right," Porfiry Petrovitch said as though in haste, and after he had said it he took the paper and looked at it. "Yes, it's all right. Nothing more is needed," he declared with the same rapidity and he laid the paper on the table.

A minute later when he was talking of something else he took it from the table and put it on his bureau.

"I believe you said yesterday you would like to question me... formally... about my acquaintance with the murdered woman?" Raskolnikov was beginning again. "Why did I put in 'I believe'" passed through his mind in a flash. "Why am I so uneasy at having put in that '*I believe*'?" came in a second flash. And he suddenly felt that his uneasiness at the mere contact with Porfiry, at the first words, at the first looks, had grown in an instant to monstrous proportions, and that this was fearfully dangerous. His nerves were quivering, his emotion was increasing. "It's bad, it's bad! I shall say too much again."

"Yes, yes, yes! There's no hurry, there's no hurry," muttered Porfiry Petrovitch, moving to and fro about the table without any apparent aim, as it were making dashes towards the window, the bureau and the table, at one moment avoiding Raskolnikov's suspicious glance, then again standing still and looking him straight in the face.

His fat round little figure looked very strange, like a ball rolling from one side to the other and rebounding back.

"We've plenty of time. Do you smoke? have you your own? Here, a cigarette!" he went on, offering his visitor a cigarette. "You know I am receiving you here, but my own quarters are through there, you know, my government quarters. But I am living outside for the time, I had to have some repairs done here. It's almost finished now.... Government quarters, you know, are a capital thing. Eh, what do you think?"

"Yes, a capital thing," answered Raskolnikov, looking at him almost ironically.

"A capital thing, a capital thing," repeated Porfiry Petrovitch, as though he had just thought of something quite different. "Yes, a capital thing," he almost shouted at last, suddenly staring at Raskolnikov and stopping short two steps from him.

This stupid repetition was too incongruous in its ineptitude with the serious, brooding and enigmatic glance he turned upon his visitor.

But this stirred Raskolnikov's spleen more than ever and he could not resist an ironical and rather incautious challenge.

"Tell me, please," he asked suddenly, looking almost insolently at him and taking a kind of pleasure in his own insolence. "I believe it's a sort of legal rule, a sort of legal tradition—for all investigating lawyers—to begin their attack from afar, with a trivial, or at least an irrelevant subject, so as to encourage, or rather, to divert the man they are cross-examining, to disarm his caution and then all at once to give him an unexpected knock-down blow with some fatal question. Isn't that so? It's a sacred tradition, mentioned, I fancy, in all the manuals of the art?"

"Yes, yes.... Why, do you imagine that was why I spoke about government quarters... eh?"

And as he said this Porfiry Petrovitch screwed up his eyes and winked; a good-humoured, crafty look passed over his face. The wrinkles on his forehead were smoothed out, his eyes contracted, his features broadened and he suddenly went off into a nervous prolonged laugh, shaking all over and looking Raskolnikov straight in the face. The latter forced himself to laugh, too, but when Porfiry, seeing that he was laughing, broke into such a guffaw that he turned almost crimson, Raskolnikov's repulsion overcame all precaution; he left off laughing, scowled and stared with hatred at Porfiry, keeping his eyes fixed on him while his intentionally prolonged laughter lasted. There was lack of precaution on both sides, however, for Porfiry Petrovitch seemed to be laughing in his visitor's face and to be very little disturbed at the annoyance with which the visitor received it. The latter fact was very significant in Raskolnikov's eyes: he saw that Porfiry Petrovitch had not been embarrassed just before either, but that he, Raskolnikov, had perhaps fallen into a trap; that there must be something, some motive here unknown to him; that, perhaps, everything was in readiness and in another moment would break upon him...

He went straight to the point at once, rose from his seat and took his cap.

"Porfiry Petrovitch," he began resolutely, though with considerable irritation, "yesterday you expressed a desire that I should come to you for some inquiries" (he laid special stress on the word "inquiries"). "I have come and if you have anything to ask me, ask it, and if not, allow me to withdraw. I have no time to spare.... I have to be at the funeral of that man who was run over, of whom you... know also," he added, feeling angry at once at having made this addition and more irritated at his anger. "I am sick of it all, do you hear? and have long been. It's partly what made me ill. In short," he shouted, feeling that the phrase about his illness was still more out of place, "in short, kindly examine me or let me go, at once. And if you must examine me, do so in the proper form! I will not allow you to do so otherwise, and so meanwhile, good-bye, as we have evidently nothing to keep us now."

"Good heavens! What do you mean? What shall I question you about?" cackled Porfiry Petrovitch with a change of tone, instantly leaving off laughing. "Please don't disturb yourself," he began fidgeting from place to place and fussily making Raskolnikov sit down. "There's no hurry, there's no hurry, it's all nonsense. Oh, no, I'm very glad you've come to see me at last... I look upon you simply as a visitor. And as for my confounded laughter, please excuse it, Rodion Romanovitch. Rodion Romanovitch? That is your name?... It's my nerves, you tickled me so with your witty observation; I assure you, sometimes I shake with laughter like an india-rubber ball for half an hour at a time.... I'm often afraid of an attack of paralysis. Do sit down. Please do, or I shall think you are angry..."

Raskolnikov did not speak; he listened, watching him, still frowning angrily. He did sit down, but still held his cap.

"I must tell you one thing about myself, my dear Rodion Romanovitch," Porfiry Petrovitch continued, moving about the room and again avoiding his visitor's eyes. "You see, I'm a bachelor, a man of no consequence and not used to society; besides, I have nothing before me, I'm set, I'm running to seed and... and have you noticed, Rodion Romanovitch, that in our Petersburg circles, if two clever men meet who are not intimate, but respect each other, like you and me, it takes them half an hour before they can find a subject for conversation—they are dumb, they sit opposite each other and feel awkward. Everyone has subjects of conversation, ladies for instance... people in high society always have their subjects of conversation,*c'est de rigueur*, but people of the middle sort like us, thinking people that is, are always tongue-tied and awkward. What is the reason of it? Whether it is the lack of public interest, or whether it is we are so honest we don't want to deceive one another, I don't know. What do you think? Do put down your cap, it looks as if you were just going, it makes me uncomfortable... I am so delighted..."

Raskolnikov put down his cap and continued listening in silence with a serious frowning face to the vague and empty chatter of Porfiry Petrovitch. "Does he really want to distract my attention with his silly babble?"

"I can't offer you coffee here; but why not spend five minutes with a friend?" Porfiry pattered on, "and you know all these official duties... please don't mind my running up and down, excuse it, my dear fellow, I am very much afraid of offending you, but exercise is absolutely indispensable for me. I'm always sitting and so glad to be moving about for five minutes... I suffer from my sedentary life... I always intend to join a gymnasium; they say that officials of all ranks, even Privy Councillors, may be seen skipping gaily there; there you have it, modern science... yes, yes.... But as for my duties here, inquiries and all such formalities... you mentioned inquiries yourself just now... I assure you these interrogations are sometimes more embarrassing for the interrogator than for the interrogated.... You made the observation yourself just now very aptly and wittily." (Raskolnikov had made no observation of the kind.) "One gets into a muddle! A regular muddle! One keeps harping on the same note, like a drum! There is to be a reform and we shall be called by a different name, at least, he-he-he! And as for our legal tradition, as you so wittily called it, I thoroughly agree with you. Every prisoner on trial, even the rudest peasant, knows that they begin by disarming him with irrelevant questions (as you so happily put it) and then deal him a knock-down blow, he-he-he!—your felicitous comparison, he-he! So you really imagined that I meant by 'government quarters'... he-he! You are an ironical person. Come. I won't go on! Ah, by the way, yes! One word leads to another. You spoke of formality just now, apropos of the inquiry, you know. But what's the use of formality? In many cases it's nonsense. Sometimes one has a friendly chat and gets a good deal more out of it. One can always fall back on formality, allow me to assure you. And after all, what does it amount to? An examining lawyer cannot be bounded by formality at every step. The work of investigation is, so to speak, a free art in its own way, he-he-he!"

Porfiry Petrovitch took breath a moment. He had simply babbled on uttering empty phrases, letting slip a few enigmatic words and again reverting to incoherence. He was almost running about the room, moving his fat little legs quicker and quicker, looking at the ground, with his right hand behind his back, while with his left making gesticulations that were extraordinarily incongruous with his words. Raskolnikov suddenly noticed that as he ran about the room he seemed twice to stop for a moment near the door, as though he were listening.

"Is he expecting anything?"

"You are certainly quite right about it," Porfiry began gaily, looking with extraordinary simplicity at Raskolnikov (which startled him and instantly put him on his guard); "certainly quite right in laughing so wittily at our legal forms, he-he! Some of these elaborate psychological methods are exceedingly ridiculous and perhaps useless, if one adheres too closely to the forms. Yes... I am talking of forms again. Well, if I recognise, or more strictly speaking, if I suspect someone or other to be a criminal in any case entrusted to me... you're reading for the law, of course, Rodion Romanovitch?"

"Yes, I was..."

"Well, then it is a precedent for you for the future—though don't suppose I should venture to instruct you after the articles you publish about crime! No, I simply make bold to state it by way of fact, if I took this man or that for a criminal, why, I ask, should I worry him prematurely, even though I had evidence against him? In one case I may be bound, for instance, to arrest a man at once, but another may be in quite a different position, you know, so why shouldn't I let him walk about the town a bit? he-he-he! But I see you don't quite understand, so I'll give you a clearer example. If I put him in prison too soon, I may very likely give him, so to speak, moral support, he-he! You're laughing?"

Raskolnikov had no idea of laughing. He was sitting with compressed lips, his feverish eyes fixed on Porfiry Petrovitch's.

"Yet that is the case, with some types especially, for men are so different. You say 'evidence'. Well, there may be evidence. But evidence, you know, can generally be taken two ways. I am an examining lawyer and a weak man, I confess it. I should like to make a proof, so to say, mathematically clear. I should like to make a chain of evidence such as twice two are four, it ought to be a direct, irrefutable proof! And if I shut him up too soon—even though I might be convinced *he* was the man, I should very likely be depriving myself of the means of getting further evidence against him. And how? By giving him, so to speak, a definite position, I shall put him out of suspense and set his mind at rest, so that he will retreat into his shell. They say that at Sevastopol, soon after Alma, the clever people were in a terrible fright that the enemy would attack openly and take Sevastopol at once. But when they saw that the enemy preferred a regular siege, they were delighted, I am told and reassured, for the thing would drag on for two months at least. You're laughing, you don't believe me again? Of course, you're right, too. You're right, you're right. These are special cases, I admit. But you must observe this, my dear Rodion Romanovitch, the general case, the case for which all legal forms and rules are intended, for which they are calculated and laid down in books, does not exist at all, for the reason that every case, every crime, for instance, so soon as it actually occurs, at once becomes a thoroughly special case and sometimes a case unlike any that's gone before. Very comic cases of that sort sometimes occur. If I leave one man quite alone, if I don't touch him and don't worry him, but let him know or at least suspect every moment that I know all about it and am watching him day and night, and if he is in continual suspicion and terror, he'll be bound to lose his head. He'll come of himself, or maybe do something which will make it as plain as twice two are four—it's delightful. It may be so with a simple peasant, but with one of our sort, an intelligent man cultivated on a certain side, it's a dead certainty. For, my dear fellow, it's a very important matter to know on what side a man is cultivated. And then there are nerves, there are nerves, you have overlooked them! Why, they are all sick, nervous and irritable!... And then how they all suffer from spleen! That I assure you is a regular gold-mine for us. And it's no anxiety to me, his running about the town free! Let him, let him walk about for a bit! I know well enough that I've caught him and that he won't escape me. Where could he escape to, he-he? Abroad, perhaps? A Pole will escape abroad, but not here, especially as I am watching and have taken measures. Will he escape into the depths of the country perhaps? But you know, peasants live there, real rude Russian peasants. A modern cultivated man would prefer prison to living with such strangers as our peasants. He-he! But that's all nonsense, and on the surface. It's not merely that he has nowhere to run to, he is *psychologically* unable to escape me, he-he! What an expression! Through a law of nature he can't escape me if he had anywhere to go. Have you seen a butterfly round a candle? That's how he will keep circling and circling round me. Freedom will lose its attractions. He'll begin to brood, he'll weave a tangle round himself, he'll worry himself to death! What's more he will provide me with a mathematical proof—if I only give him long enough interval.... And he'll keep circling round me, getting nearer and nearer and then—flop! He'll fly straight into my mouth and I'll swallow him, and that will be very amusing, he-he-he! You don't believe me?"

Raskolnikov made no reply; he sat pale and motionless, still gazing with the same intensity into Porfiry's face.

"It's a lesson," he thought, turning cold. "This is beyond the cat playing with a mouse, like yesterday. He can't be showing off his power with no motive... prompting me; he is far too clever for that... he must have another object. What is it? It's all nonsense, my friend, you are pretending, to scare me! You've no proofs and the man I saw had no real existence. You simply want to make me lose my head, to work me up beforehand and so to crush me. But you are wrong, you won't do it! But why give me such a hint? Is he reckoning on my shattered nerves? No, my friend, you are wrong, you won't do it even though you have some trap for me... let us see what you have in store for me."

And he braced himself to face a terrible and unknown ordeal. At times he longed to fall on Porfiry and strangle him. This anger was what he dreaded from the beginning. He felt that his parched lips were flecked with foam, his heart was throbbing. But he was still determined not to speak till the right moment. He realised that this was the best policy in his position, because instead of saying too much he would be irritating his enemy by his silence and provoking him into speaking too freely. Anyhow, this was what he hoped for.

"No, I see you don't believe me, you think I am playing a harmless joke on you," Porfiry began again, getting more and more lively, chuckling at every instant and again pacing round the room. "And to be sure you're right: God has given me a figure that can awaken none but comic ideas in other people; a buffoon; but let me tell you, and I repeat it, excuse an old man, my dear Rodion Romanovitch, you are a man still young, so to say, in your first youth and so you put intellect above everything, like all young people. Playful wit and abstract arguments fascinate you and that's for all the world like the old Austrian *Hof-kriegsrath*, as far as I can judge of military matters, that is: on paper they'd beaten Napoleon and taken him prisoner, and there in their study they worked it all out in the cleverest fashion, but look you, General Mack surrendered with all his army, he-he-he! I see, I see, Rodion Romanovitch, you are laughing at a civilian like me, taking examples out of military history! But I can't help it, it's my weakness. I am fond of military science. And I'm ever so fond of reading all military histories. I've certainly missed my proper career. I ought to have been in the army, upon my word I ought. I shouldn't have been a Napoleon, but I might have been a major, he-he! Well, I'll tell you the whole truth, my dear fellow, about this *special case*, I mean: actual fact and a man's temperament, my dear sir, are weighty matters and it's astonishing how they sometimes deceive the sharpest calculation! I—listen to an old man—am speaking seriously, Rodion Romanovitch" (as he said this Porfiry Petrovitch, who was scarcely five-and-thirty, actually seemed to have grown old; even his voice changed and he seemed to shrink together) "Moreover, I'm a candid man... am I a candid man or not? What do you say? I fancy I really am: I tell you these things for nothing and don't even expect a reward for it, he-he! Well, to proceed, wit in my opinion is a splendid thing, it is, so to say, an adornment of nature and a consolation of life, and what tricks it can play! So that it sometimes is hard for a poor examining lawyer to know where he is, especially when he's liable to be carried away by his own fancy, too, for you know he is a man after all! But the poor fellow is saved by the criminal's temperament, worse luck for him! But young people carried away by their own wit don't think of that 'when they overstep all obstacles,' as you wittily and cleverly expressed it yesterday. He will lie—that is, the man who is a *special case*, the incognito, and he will lie well, in the cleverest fashion; you might think he would triumph and enjoy the fruits of his wit, but at the most interesting, the most flagrant moment he will faint. Of course there may be illness and a stuffy room as well, but anyway! Anyway he's given us the idea! He lied incomparably, but he didn't reckon on his temperament. That's what betrays him! Another time he will be carried away by his playful wit into making fun of the man who suspects him, he will turn pale as it were on purpose to mislead, but his paleness will be *too natural*, too much like the real thing, again he has given us an idea! Though his questioner may be deceived at first, he will think differently next day if he is not a fool, and, of course, it is like that at every step! He puts himself forward where he is not wanted, speaks continually when he ought to keep silent, brings in all sorts of allegorical allusions, he-he! Comes and asks why didn't you take me long ago? he-he-he! And that can happen, you know, with the cleverest man, the psychologist, the literary man. The temperament reflects everything like a mirror! Gaze into it and admire what you see! But why are you so pale, Rodion Romanovitch? Is the room stuffy? Shall I open the window?"

"Oh, don't trouble, please," cried Raskolnikov and he suddenly broke into a laugh. "Please don't trouble."

Porfiry stood facing him, paused a moment and suddenly he too laughed. Raskolnikov got up from the sofa, abruptly checking his hysterical laughter.

"Porfiry Petrovitch," he began, speaking loudly and distinctly, though his legs trembled and he could scarcely stand. "I see clearly at last that you actually suspect me of murdering that old woman and her sister Lizaveta. Let me tell you for my part that I am sick of this. If you find that you have a right to prosecute me legally, to arrest me, then prosecute me, arrest me. But I will not let myself be jeered at to my face and worried..."

His lips trembled, his eyes glowed with fury and he could not restrain his voice.

"I won't allow it!" he shouted, bringing his fist down on the table. "Do you hear that, Porfiry Petrovitch? I won't allow it."

"Good heavens! What does it mean?" cried Porfiry Petrovitch, apparently quite frightened. "Rodion Romanovitch, my dear fellow, what is the matter with you?"

"I won't allow it," Raskolnikov shouted again.

"Hush, my dear man! They'll hear and come in. Just think, what could we say to them?" Porfiry Petrovitch whispered in horror, bringing his face close to Raskolnikov's.

"I won't allow it, I won't allow it," Raskolnikov repeated mechanically, but he too spoke in a sudden whisper.

Porfiry turned quickly and ran to open the window.

"Some fresh air! And you must have some water, my dear fellow. You're ill!" and he was running to the door to call for some when he found a decanter of water in the corner. "Come, drink a little," he whispered, rushing up to him with the decanter. "It will be sure to do you good."

Porfiry Petrovitch's alarm and sympathy were so natural that Raskolnikov was silent and began looking at him with wild curiosity. He did not take the water, however.

"Rodion Romanovitch, my dear fellow, you'll drive yourself out of your mind, I assure you, ach, ach! Have some water, do drink a little."

He forced him to take the glass. Raskolnikov raised it mechanically to his lips, but set it on the table again with disgust.

"Yes, you've had a little attack! You'll bring back your illness again, my dear fellow," Porfiry Petrovitch cackled with friendly sympathy, though he still looked rather disconcerted. "Good heavens, you must take more care of yourself! Dmitri Prokofitch was here, came to see me yesterday—I know, I know, I've a nasty, ironical temper, but what they made of it!... Good heavens, he came yesterday after you'd been. We dined and he talked and talked away, and I could only throw up my hands in despair! Did he come from you? But do sit down, for mercy's sake, sit down!"

"No, not from me, but I knew he went to you and why he went," Raskolnikov answered sharply.

"You knew?"

"I knew. What of it?"

"Why this, Rodion Romanovitch, that I know more than that about you; I know about everything. I know how you went *to take a flat* at night when it was dark and how you rang the bell and asked about the blood, so that the workmen and the porter did not know what to make of it. Yes, I understand your state of mind at that time... but you'll drive yourself mad like that, upon my word! You'll lose your head! You're full of generous indignation at the wrongs you've received, first from destiny, and then from the police officers, and so you rush from one thing to another to force them to speak out and make an end of it all, because you are sick of all this suspicion and foolishness. That's so, isn't it? I have guessed how you feel, haven't I? Only in that way you'll lose your head and Razumihin's, too; he's too *good* a man for such a position, you must know that. You are ill and he is good and your illness is infectious for him... I'll tell you about it when you are more yourself.... But do sit down, for goodness' sake. Please rest, you look shocking, do sit down."

Raskolnikov sat down; he no longer shivered, he was hot all over. In amazement he listened with strained attention to Porfiry Petrovitch who still seemed frightened as he looked after him with friendly solicitude. But he did not believe a word he said, though he felt a strange inclination to believe. Porfiry's unexpected words about the flat had utterly overwhelmed him. "How can it be, he knows about the flat then," he thought suddenly, "and he tells it me himself!"

"Yes, in our legal practice there was a case almost exactly similar, a case of morbid psychology," Porfiry went on quickly. "A man confessed to murder and how he kept it up! It was a regular hallucination; he brought forward facts, he imposed upon everyone and why? He had been partly, but only partly, unintentionally the cause of a murder and when he knew that he had given the murderers the opportunity, he sank into dejection, it got on his mind and turned his brain, he began imagining things and he persuaded himself that he was the murderer. But at last the High Court of Appeal went into it and the poor fellow was acquitted and put under proper care. Thanks to the Court of Appeal! Tut-tut-tut! Why, my dear fellow, you may drive yourself into delirium if you have the impulse to work upon your nerves, to go ringing bells at night and asking about blood! I've studied all this morbid psychology in my practice. A man is sometimes tempted to jump out of a window or from a belfry. Just the same with bell-ringing.... It's all illness, Rodion Romanovitch! You have begun to neglect your illness. You should consult an experienced doctor, what's the good of that fat fellow? You are lightheaded! You were delirious when you did all this!"

For a moment Raskolnikov felt everything going round.

"Is it possible, is it possible," flashed through his mind, "that he is still lying? He can't be, he can't be." He rejected that idea, feeling to what a degree of fury it might drive him, feeling that that fury might drive him mad.

"I was not delirious. I knew what I was doing," he cried, straining every faculty to penetrate Porfiry's game, "I was quite myself, do you hear?"

"Yes, I hear and understand. You said yesterday you were not delirious, you were particularly emphatic about it! I understand all you can tell me! A-ach!... Listen, Rodion Romanovitch, my dear fellow. If you were actually a criminal, or were somehow mixed up in this damnable business, would you insist that you were not delirious but in full possession of your faculties? And so emphatically and persistently? Would it be possible? Quite impossible, to my thinking. If you had anything on your conscience, you certainly ought to insist that you were delirious. That's so, isn't it?"

There was a note of slyness in this inquiry. Raskolnikov drew back on the sofa as Porfiry bent over him and stared in silent perplexity at him.

"Another thing about Razumihin—you certainly ought to have said that he came of his own accord, to have concealed your part in it! But you don't conceal it! You lay stress on his coming at your instigation."

Raskolnikov had not done so. A chill went down his back.

"You keep telling lies," he said slowly and weakly, twisting his lips into a sickly smile, "you are trying again to show that you know all my game, that you know all I shall say beforehand," he said, conscious himself that he was not weighing his words as he ought. "You want to frighten me... or you are simply laughing at me..."

He still stared at him as he said this and again there was a light of intense hatred in his eyes.

"You keep lying," he said. "You know perfectly well that the best policy for the criminal is to tell the truth as nearly as possible... to conceal as little as possible. I don't believe you!"

"What a wily person you are!" Porfiry tittered, "there's no catching you; you've a perfect monomania. So you don't believe me? But still you do believe me, you believe a quarter; I'll soon make you believe the whole, because I have a sincere liking for you and genuinely wish you good."

Raskolnikov's lips trembled.

"Yes, I do," went on Porfiry, touching Raskolnikov's arm genially, "you must take care of your illness. Besides, your mother and sister are here now; you must think of them. You must soothe and comfort them and you do nothing but frighten them..."

"What has that to do with you? How do you know it? What concern is it of yours? You are keeping watch on me and want to let me know it?"

"Good heavens! Why, I learnt it all from you yourself! You don't notice that in your excitement you tell me and others everything. From Razumihin, too, I learnt a number of interesting details yesterday. No, you interrupted me, but I must tell you that, for all your wit, your suspiciousness makes you lose the common-sense view of things. To return to bell-ringing, for instance. I, an examining lawyer, have betrayed a precious thing like that, a real fact (for it is a fact worth having), and you see nothing in it! Why, if I had the slightest suspicion of you, should I have acted like that? No, I should first have disarmed your suspicions and not let you see I knew of that fact, should have diverted your attention and suddenly have dealt you a knock-down blow (your expression) saying: 'And what were you doing, sir, pray, at ten or nearly eleven at the murdered woman's flat and why did you ring the bell and why did you ask about blood? And why did you invite the porters to go with you to the police station, to the lieutenant?' That's how I ought to have acted if I had a grain of suspicion of you. I ought to have taken your evidence in due form, searched your lodging and perhaps have arrested you, too... so I have no suspicion of you, since I have not done that! But you can't look at it normally and you see nothing, I say again."

Raskolnikov started so that Porfiry Petrovitch could not fail to perceive it.

"You are lying all the while," he cried, "I don't know your object, but you are lying. You did not speak like that just now and I cannot be mistaken!"

"I am lying?" Porfiry repeated, apparently incensed, but preserving a good-humoured and ironical face, as though he were not in the least concerned at Raskolnikov's opinion of him. "I am lying... but how did I treat you just now, I, the examining lawyer? Prompting you and giving you every means for your defence; illness, I said, delirium, injury, melancholy and the police officers and all the rest of it? Ah! He-he-he! Though, indeed, all those psychological means of defence are not very reliable and cut both ways: illness, delirium, I don't remember—that's all right, but why, my good sir, in your illness and in your delirium were you haunted by just those delusions and not by any others? There may have been others, eh? He-he-he!"

Raskolnikov looked haughtily and contemptuously at him.

"Briefly," he said loudly and imperiously, rising to his feet and in so doing pushing Porfiry back a little, "briefly, I want to know, do you acknowledge me perfectly free from suspicion or not? Tell me, Porfiry Petrovitch, tell me once for all and make haste!"

"What a business I'm having with you!" cried Porfiry with a perfectly good-humoured, sly and composed face. "And why do you want to know, why do you want to know so much, since they haven't begun to worry you? Why, you are like a child asking for matches! And why are you so uneasy? Why do you force yourself upon us, eh? He-he-he!"

"I repeat," Raskolnikov cried furiously, "that I can't put up with it!"

"With what? Uncertainty?" interrupted Porfiry.

"Don't jeer at me! I won't have it! I tell you I won't have it. I can't and I won't, do you hear, do you hear?" he shouted, bringing his fist down on the table again.

"Hush! Hush! They'll overhear! I warn you seriously, take care of yourself. I am not joking," Porfiry whispered, but this time there was not the look of old womanish good nature and alarm in his face. Now he was peremptory, stern, frowning and for once laying aside all mystification.

But this was only for an instant. Raskolnikov, bewildered, suddenly fell into actual frenzy, but, strange to say, he again obeyed the command to speak quietly, though he was in a perfect paroxysm of fury.

"I will not allow myself to be tortured," he whispered, instantly recognising with hatred that he could not help obeying the command and driven to even greater fury by the thought. "Arrest me, search me, but kindly act in due form and don't play with me! Don't dare!"

"Don't worry about the form," Porfiry interrupted with the same sly smile, as it were, gloating with enjoyment over Raskolnikov. "I invited you to see me quite in a friendly way."

"I don't want your friendship and I spit on it! Do you hear? And, here, I take my cap and go. What will you say now if you mean to arrest me?"

He took up his cap and went to the door.

"And won't you see my little surprise?" chuckled Porfiry, again taking him by the arm and stopping him at the door.

He seemed to become more playful and good-humoured which maddened Raskolnikov.

"What surprise?" he asked, standing still and looking at Porfiry in alarm.

"My little surprise, it's sitting there behind the door, he-he-he!" (He pointed to the locked door.) "I locked him in that he should not escape."

"What is it? Where? What?..."

Raskolnikov walked to the door and would have opened it, but it was locked.

"It's locked, here is the key!"

And he brought a key out of his pocket.

"You are lying," roared Raskolnikov without restraint, "you lie, you damned punchinello!" and he rushed at Porfiry who retreated to the other door, not at all alarmed.

"I understand it all! You are lying and mocking so that I may betray myself to you..."

"Why, you could not betray yourself any further, my dear Rodion Romanovitch. You are in a passion. Don't shout, I shall call the clerks."

"You are lying! Call the clerks! You knew I was ill and tried to work me into a frenzy to make me betray myself, that was your object! Produce your facts! I understand it all. You've no evidence, you have only wretched rubbishly suspicions like Zametov's! You knew my character, you wanted to drive me to fury and then to knock me down with priests and deputies.... Are you waiting for them? eh! What are you waiting for? Where are they? Produce them?"

"Why deputies, my good man? What things people will imagine! And to do so would not be acting in form as you say, you don't know the business, my dear fellow.... And there's no escaping form, as you see," Porfiry muttered, listening at the door through which a noise could be heard.

"Ah, they're coming," cried Raskolnikov. "You've sent for them! You expected them! Well, produce them all: your deputies, your witnesses, what you like!... I am ready!"

But at this moment a strange incident occurred, something so unexpected that neither Raskolnikov nor Porfiry Petrovitch could have looked for such a conclusion to their interview.

CHAPTER VI

When he remembered the scene afterwards, this is how Raskolnikov saw it.

The noise behind the door increased, and suddenly the door was opened a little.

"What is it?" cried Porfiry Petrovitch, annoyed. "Why, I gave orders..."

For an instant there was no answer, but it was evident that there were several persons at the door, and that they were apparently pushing somebody back.

"What is it?" Porfiry Petrovitch repeated, uneasily.

"The prisoner Nikolay has been brought," someone answered.

"He is not wanted! Take him away! Let him wait! What's he doing here? How irregular!" cried Porfiry, rushing to the door.

"But he..." began the same voice, and suddenly ceased.

Two seconds, not more, were spent in actual struggle, then someone gave a violent shove, and then a man, very pale, strode into the room.

This man's appearance was at first sight very strange. He stared straight before him, as though seeing nothing. There was a determined gleam in his eyes; at the same time there was a deathly pallor in his face, as though he were being led to the scaffold. His white lips were faintly twitching.

He was dressed like a workman and was of medium height, very young, slim, his hair cut in round crop, with thin spare features. The man whom he had thrust back followed him into the room and succeeded in seizing him by the shoulder; he was a warder; but Nikolay pulled his arm away.

Several persons crowded inquisitively into the doorway. Some of them tried to get in. All this took place almost instantaneously.

"Go away, it's too soon! Wait till you are sent for!... Why have you brought him so soon?" Porfiry Petrovitch muttered, extremely annoyed, and as it were thrown out of his reckoning.

But Nikolay suddenly knelt down.

"What's the matter?" cried Porfiry, surprised.

"I am guilty! Mine is the sin! I am the murderer," Nikolay articulated suddenly, rather breathless, but speaking fairly loudly.

For ten seconds there was silence as though all had been struck dumb; even the warder stepped back, mechanically retreated to the door, and stood immovable.

"What is it?" cried Porfiry Petrovitch, recovering from his momentary stupefaction.

"I... am the murderer," repeated Nikolay, after a brief pause.

"What... you... what... whom did you kill?" Porfiry Petrovitch was obviously bewildered.

Nikolay again was silent for a moment.

"Alyona Ivanovna and her sister Lizaveta Ivanovna, I... killed... with an axe. Darkness came over me," he added suddenly, and was again silent.

He still remained on his knees. Porfiry Petrovitch stood for some moments as though meditating, but suddenly roused himself and waved back the uninvited spectators. They instantly vanished and closed the door. Then he looked towards Raskolnikov, who was standing in the corner, staring wildly at Nikolay and moved towards him, but stopped short, looked from Nikolay to Raskolnikov and then again at Nikolay, and seeming unable to restrain himself darted at the latter.

"You're in too great a hurry," he shouted at him, almost angrily. "I didn't ask you what came over you.... Speak, did you kill them?"

"I am the murderer.... I want to give evidence," Nikolay pronounced.

"Ach! What did you kill them with?"

"An axe. I had it ready."

"Ach, he is in a hurry! Alone?"

Nikolay did not understand the question.

"Did you do it alone?"

"Yes, alone. And Mitka is not guilty and had no share in it."

"Don't be in a hurry about Mitka! A-ach! How was it you ran downstairs like that at the time? The porters met you both!"

"It was to put them off the scent... I ran after Mitka," Nikolay replied hurriedly, as though he had prepared the answer.

"I knew it!" cried Porfiry, with vexation. "It's not his own tale he is telling," he muttered as though to himself, and suddenly his eyes rested on Raskolnikov again.

He was apparently so taken up with Nikolay that for a moment he had forgotten Raskolnikov. He was a little taken aback.

"My dear Rodion Romanovitch, excuse me!" he flew up to him, "this won't do; I'm afraid you must go... it's no good your staying... I will... you see, what a surprise!... Good-bye!"

And taking him by the arm, he showed him to the door.

"I suppose you didn't expect it?" said Raskolnikov who, though he had not yet fully grasped the situation, had regained his courage.

"You did not expect it either, my friend. See how your hand is trembling! He-he!"

"You're trembling, too, Porfiry Petrovitch!"

"Yes, I am; I didn't expect it."

They were already at the door; Porfiry was impatient for Raskolnikov to be gone.

"And your little surprise, aren't you going to show it to me?" Raskolnikov said, sarcastically.

"Why, his teeth are chattering as he asks, he-he! You are an ironical person! Come, till we meet!"

"I believe we can say *good-bye*!"

"That's in God's hands," muttered Porfiry, with an unnatural smile.

As he walked through the office, Raskolnikov noticed that many people were looking at him. Among them he saw the two porters from *the* house, whom he had invited that night to the police station. They stood there waiting. But he was no sooner on the stairs than he heard the voice of Porfiry Petrovitch behind him. Turning round, he saw the latter running after him, out of breath.

"One word, Rodion Romanovitch; as to all the rest, it's in God's hands, but as a matter of form there are some questions I shall have to ask you... so we shall meet again, shan't we?"

And Porfiry stood still, facing him with a smile.

"Shan't we?" he added again.

He seemed to want to say something more, but could not speak out.

"You must forgive me, Porfiry Petrovitch, for what has just passed... I lost my temper," began Raskolnikov, who had so far regained his courage that he felt irresistibly inclined to display his coolness.

"Don't mention it, don't mention it," Porfiry replied, almost gleefully. "I myself, too... I have a wicked temper, I admit it! But we shall meet again. If it's God's will, we may see a great deal of one another."

"And will get to know each other through and through?" added Raskolnikov.

"Yes; know each other through and through," assented Porfiry Petrovitch, and he screwed up his eyes, looking earnestly at Raskolnikov. "Now you're going to a birthday party?"

"To a funeral."

"Of course, the funeral! Take care of yourself, and get well."

"I don't know what to wish you," said Raskolnikov, who had begun to descend the stairs, but looked back again. "I should like to wish you success, but your office is such a comical one."

"Why comical?" Porfiry Petrovitch had turned to go, but he seemed to prick up his ears at this.

"Why, how you must have been torturing and harassing that poor Nikolay psychologically, after your fashion, till he confessed! You must have been at him day and night, proving to him that he was the murderer, and now that he has confessed, you'll begin vivisecting him again. 'You are lying,' you'll say. 'You are not the murderer! You can't be! It's not your own tale you are telling!' You must admit it's a comical business!"

"He-he-he! You noticed then that I said to Nikolay just now that it was not his own tale he was telling?"

"How could I help noticing it!"

"He-he! You are quick-witted. You notice everything! You've really a playful mind! And you always fasten on the comic side... he-he! They say that was the marked characteristic of Gogol, among the writers."

"Yes, of Gogol."

"Yes, of Gogol.... I shall look forward to meeting you."

"So shall I."

Raskolnikov walked straight home. He was so muddled and bewildered that on getting home he sat for a quarter of an hour on the sofa, trying to collect his thoughts. He did not attempt to think about Nikolay; he was stupefied; he felt that his confession was something inexplicable, amazing—something beyond his understanding. But Nikolay's confession was an actual fact. The consequences of this fact were clear to him at once, its falsehood could not fail to be discovered, and then they would be after him again. Till then, at least, he was free and must do something for himself, for the danger was imminent.

But how imminent? His position gradually became clear to him. Remembering, sketchily, the main outlines of his recent scene with Porfiry, he could not help shuddering again with horror. Of course, he did not yet know all Porfiry's aims, he could not see into all his calculations. But he had already partly shown his hand, and no one knew better than Raskolnikov how terrible Porfiry's "lead" had been for him. A little more and he *might* have given himself away completely, circumstantially. Knowing his nervous temperament and from the first glance seeing through him, Porfiry, though playing a bold game, was bound to win. There's no denying that Raskolnikov had compromised himself seriously, but no *facts* had come to light as yet; there was nothing positive. But was he taking a true view of the position? Wasn't he mistaken? What had Porfiry been trying to get at? Had he really some surprise prepared for him? And what was it? Had he really been expecting something or not? How would they have parted if it had not been for the unexpected appearance of Nikolay?

Porfiry had shown almost all his cards—of course, he had risked something in showing them—and if he had really had anything up his sleeve (Raskolnikov reflected), he would have shown that, too. What was that "surprise"? Was it a joke? Had it meant anything? Could it have concealed anything like a fact, a piece of positive evidence? His yesterday's visitor? What had become of him? Where was he to-day? If Porfiry really had any evidence, it must be connected with him....

He sat on the sofa with his elbows on his knees and his face hidden in his hands. He was still shivering nervously. At last he got up, took his cap, thought a minute, and went to the door.

He had a sort of presentiment that for to-day, at least, he might consider himself out of danger. He had a sudden sense almost of joy; he wanted to make haste to Katerina Ivanovna's. He would be too late for the funeral, of course, but he would be in time for the memorial dinner, and there at once he would see Sonia.

He stood still, thought a moment, and a suffering smile came for a moment on to his lips.

"To-day! To-day," he repeated to himself. "Yes, to-day! So it must be...."

But as he was about to open the door, it began opening of itself. He started and moved back. The door opened gently and slowly, and there suddenly appeared a figure—yesterday's visitor *from underground*.

The man stood in the doorway, looked at Raskolnikov without speaking, and took a step forward into the room. He was exactly the same as yesterday; the same figure, the same dress, but there was a great change in his face; he looked dejected and sighed deeply. If he had only put his hand up to his cheek and leaned his head on one side he would have looked exactly like a peasant woman.

"What do you want?" asked Raskolnikov, numb with terror. The man was still silent, but suddenly he bowed down almost to the ground, touching it with his finger.

"What is it?" cried Raskolnikov.

"I have sinned," the man articulated softly.

"How?"

"By evil thoughts."

They looked at one another.

"I was vexed. When you came, perhaps in drink, and bade the porters go to the police station and asked about the blood, I was vexed that they let you go and took you for drunken. I was so vexed that I lost my sleep. And remembering the address we came here yesterday and asked for you...."

"Who came?" Raskolnikov interrupted, instantly beginning to recollect.

"I did, I've wronged you."

"Then you come from that house?"

"I was standing at the gate with them... don't you remember? We have carried on our trade in that house for years past. We cure and prepare hides, we take work home... most of all I was vexed...."

And the whole scene of the day before yesterday in the gateway came clearly before Raskolnikov's mind; he recollected that there had been several people there besides the porters, women among them. He remembered one voice had suggested taking him straight to the police-station. He could not recall the face of the speaker, and even now he did not recognise it, but he remembered that he had turned round and made him some answer....

So this was the solution of yesterday's horror. The most awful thought was that he had been actually almost lost, had almost done for himself on account of such a *trivial* circumstance. So this man could tell nothing except his asking about the flat and the blood stains. So Porfiry, too, had nothing but that *delirium*, no facts but this *psychology* which *cuts both ways*, nothing positive. So if no more facts come to light (and they must not, they must not!) then... then what can they do to him? How can they convict him, even if they arrest him? And Porfiry then had only just heard about the flat and had not known about it before.

"Was it you who told Porfiry... that I'd been there?" he cried, struck by a sudden idea.

"What Porfiry?"

"The head of the detective department?"

"Yes. The porters did not go there, but I went."

"To-day?"

"I got there two minutes before you. And I heard, I heard it all, how he worried you."

"Where? What? When?"

"Why, in the next room. I was sitting there all the time."

"What? Why, then you were the surprise? But how could it happen? Upon my word!"

"I saw that the porters did not want to do what I said," began the man; "for it's too late, said they, and maybe he'll be angry that we did not come at the time. I was vexed and I lost my sleep, and I began making inquiries. And finding out yesterday where to go, I went to-day. The first time I went he wasn't there, when I came an hour later he couldn't see me. I went the third time, and they showed me in. I informed him of everything, just as it happened, and he began skipping about the room and punching himself on the chest. 'What do you scoundrels mean by it? If I'd known about it I should have arrested him!' Then he ran out, called somebody and began talking to him in the corner, then he turned to me, scolding and questioning me. He scolded me a great deal; and I told him everything, and I told him that you didn't dare to say a word in answer to me yesterday and that you didn't recognise me. And he fell to running about again and kept hitting himself on the chest, and getting angry and running about, and when you were announced he told me to go into the next room. 'Sit there a bit,' he said. 'Don't move, whatever you may hear.' And he set a chair there for me and locked me in. 'Perhaps,' he said, 'I may call you.' And when Nikolay'd been brought he let me out as soon as you were gone. 'I shall send for you again and question you,' he said."

"And did he question Nikolay while you were there?"

"He got rid of me as he did of you, before he spoke to Nikolay."

The man stood still, and again suddenly bowed down, touching the ground with his finger.

"Forgive me for my evil thoughts, and my slander."

"May God forgive you," answered Raskolnikov.

And as he said this, the man bowed down again, but not to the ground, turned slowly and went out of the room.

"It all cuts both ways, now it all cuts both ways," repeated Raskolnikov, and he went out more confident than ever.

"Now we'll make a fight for it," he said, with a malicious smile, as he went down the stairs. His malice was aimed at himself; with shame and contempt he recollected his "cowardice."

PART V

CHAPTER I

The morning that followed the fateful interview with Dounia and her mother brought sobering influences to bear on Pyotr Petrovitch. Intensely unpleasant as it was, he was forced little by little to accept as a fact beyond recall what had seemed to him only the day before fantastic and incredible. The black snake of wounded vanity had been gnawing at his heart all night. When he got out of bed, Pyotr Petrovitch immediately looked in the looking-glass. He was afraid that he had jaundice. However his health seemed unimpaired so far, and looking at his noble, clear-skinned countenance which had grown fattish of late, Pyotr Petrovitch for an instant was positively comforted in the conviction that he would find another bride and, perhaps, even a better one. But coming back to the sense of his present position, he turned aside and spat vigorously, which excited a sarcastic smile in Andrey Semyonovitch Lebeziatnikov, the young friend with whom he was staying. That smile Pyotr Petrovitch noticed, and at once set it down against his young friend's account. He had set down a good many points against him of late. His anger was redoubled when he reflected that he ought not to have told Andrey Semyonovitch about the result of yesterday's interview. That was the second mistake he had made in temper, through impulsiveness and irritability.... Moreover, all that morning one unpleasantness followed another. He even found a hitch awaiting him in his legal case in the senate. He was particularly irritated by the owner of the flat which had been taken in view of his approaching marriage and was being redecorated at his own expense; the owner, a rich German tradesman, would not entertain the idea of breaking the contract which had just been signed and insisted on the full forfeit money, though Pyotr Petrovitch would be giving him back the flat practically redecorated. In the same way the upholsterers refused to return a single rouble of the instalment paid for the furniture purchased but not yet removed to the flat.

"Am I to get married simply for the sake of the furniture?" Pyotr Petrovitch ground his teeth and at the same time once more he had a gleam of desperate hope. "Can all that be really so irrevocably over? Is it no use to make another effort?" The thought of Dounia sent a voluptuous pang through his heart. He endured anguish at that moment, and if it had been possible to slay Raskolnikov instantly by wishing it, Pyotr Petrovitch would promptly have uttered the wish.

"It was my mistake, too, not to have given them money," he thought, as he returned dejectedly to Lebeziatnikov's room, "and why on earth was I such a Jew? It was false economy! I meant to keep them without a penny so that they should turn to me as their providence, and look at them! foo! If I'd spent some fifteen hundred roubles on them for the trousseau and presents, on knick-knacks, dressing-cases, jewellery, materials, and all that sort of trash from Knopp's and the English shop, my position would have been better and... stronger! They could not have refused me so easily! They are the sort of people that would feel bound to return money and presents if they broke it off; and they would find it hard to do it! And their conscience would prick them: how can we dismiss a man who has hitherto been so generous and delicate?.... H'm! I've made a blunder."

And grinding his teeth again, Pyotr Petrovitch called himself a fool—but not aloud, of course.

He returned home, twice as irritated and angry as before. The preparations for the funeral dinner at Katerina Ivanovna's excited his curiosity as he passed. He had heard about it the day before; he fancied, indeed, that he had been invited, but absorbed in his own cares he had paid no attention. Inquiring of Madame Lippevechsel who was busy laying the table while Katerina Ivanovna was away at the cemetery, he heard that the entertainment was to be a great affair, that all the lodgers had been invited, among them some who had not known the dead man, that even Andrey Semyonovitch Lebeziatnikov was invited in spite of his previous quarrel with Katerina Ivanovna, that he, Pyotr Petrovitch, was not only invited, but was eagerly expected as he was the most important of the lodgers. Amalia Ivanovna herself had been invited with great ceremony in spite of the recent unpleasantness, and so she was very busy with preparations and was taking a positive pleasure in them; she was moreover dressed up to the nines, all in new black silk, and she was proud of it. All this suggested an idea to Pyotr Petrovitch and he went into his room, or rather Lebeziatnikov's, somewhat thoughtful. He had learnt that Raskolnikov was to be one of the guests.

Andrey Semyonovitch had been at home all the morning. The attitude of Pyotr Petrovitch to this gentleman was strange, though perhaps natural. Pyotr Petrovitch had despised and hated him from the day he came to stay with him and at the same time he seemed somewhat afraid of him. He had not come to stay with him on his arrival in Petersburg simply from parsimony, though that had been perhaps his chief object. He had heard of Andrey Semyonovitch, who had once been his ward, as a leading young progressive who was taking an important part in certain interesting circles, the doings of which were a legend in the provinces. It had impressed Pyotr Petrovitch. These powerful omniscient circles who despised everyone and showed everyone up had long inspired in him a peculiar but quite vague alarm. He had not, of course, been able to form even an approximate notion of what they meant. He, like everyone, had heard that there were, especially in Petersburg, progressives of some sort, nihilists and so on, and, like many people, he exaggerated and distorted the significance of those words to an absurd degree. What for many years past he had feared more than anything was *being shown up* and this was the chief ground for his continual uneasiness at the thought of transferring his business to Petersburg. He was afraid of this as little children are sometimes panic-stricken. Some years before, when he was just entering on his own career, he had come upon two cases in which rather important personages in the province, patrons of his, had been cruelly shown up. One instance had ended in great scandal for the person attacked and the other had very nearly ended in serious trouble. For this reason Pyotr Petrovitch intended to go into the subject as soon as he reached Petersburg and, if necessary, to anticipate contingencies by seeking the favour of "our younger generation." He relied on Andrey Semyonovitch for this and before his visit to Raskolnikov he had succeeded in picking up some current phrases. He soon discovered that Andrey Semyonovitch was a commonplace simpleton, but that by no means reassured Pyotr Petrovitch. Even if he had been certain that all the progressives were fools like him, it would not have allayed his uneasiness. All the doctrines, the ideas, the systems, with which Andrey Semyonovitch pestered him had no interest for him. He had his own object—he simply wanted to find out at once what was happening *here*. Had these people any power or not? Had he anything to fear from them? Would they expose any enterprise of his? And what precisely was now the object of their attacks? Could he somehow make up to them and get round them if they really were powerful? Was this the thing to do or not? Couldn't he gain something through them? In fact hundreds of questions presented themselves.

Andrey Semyonovitch was an anæmic, scrofulous little man, with strangely flaxen mutton-chop whiskers of which he was very proud. He was a clerk and had almost always something wrong with his eyes. He was rather soft-hearted, but self-confident and sometimes extremely conceited in speech, which had an absurd effect, incongruous with his little figure. He was one of the lodgers most respected by Amalia Ivanovna, for he did not get drunk and paid regularly for his lodgings. Andrey Semyonovitch really was rather stupid; he attached himself to the cause of progress and "our younger generation" from enthusiasm. He was one of the numerous and varied legion of dullards, of half-animate abortions, conceited, half-educated coxcombs, who attach themselves to the idea most in fashion only to vulgarise it and who caricature every cause they serve, however sincerely.

Though Lebeziatnikov was so good-natured, he, too, was beginning to dislike Pyotr Petrovitch. This happened on both sides unconsciously. However simple Andrey Semyonovitch might be, he began to see that Pyotr Petrovitch was duping him and secretly despising him, and that "he was not the right sort of man." He had tried expounding to him the system of Fourier and the Darwinian theory, but of late Pyotr Petrovitch began to listen too sarcastically and even to be rude. The fact was he had begun instinctively to guess that Lebeziatnikov was not merely a commonplace simpleton, but, perhaps, a liar, too, and that he had no connections of any consequence even in his own circle, but had simply picked things up third-hand; and that very likely he did not even know much about his own work of propaganda, for he was in too great a muddle. A fine person he would be to show anyone up! It must be noted, by the way, that Pyotr Petrovitch had during those ten days eagerly accepted the strangest praise from Andrey Semyonovitch; he had not protested, for instance, when Andrey Semyonovitch belauded him for being ready to contribute to the establishment of the new "commune," or to abstain from christening his future children, or to acquiesce if Dounia were to take a lover a month after marriage, and so on. Pyotr Petrovitch so enjoyed hearing his own praises that he did not disdain even such virtues when they were attributed to him.

Pyotr Petrovitch had had occasion that morning to realise some five-per-cent bonds and now he sat down to the table and counted over bundles of notes. Andrey Semyonovitch who hardly ever had any money walked about the room pretending to himself to look at all those bank notes with indifference and even contempt. Nothing would have convinced Pyotr Petrovitch that Andrey Semyonovitch could really look on the money unmoved, and the latter, on his side, kept thinking bitterly that Pyotr Petrovitch was capable of entertaining such an idea about him and was, perhaps, glad of the opportunity of teasing his young friend by reminding him of his inferiority and the great difference between them.

He found him incredibly inattentive and irritable, though he, Andrey Semyonovitch, began enlarging on his favourite subject, the foundation of a new special "commune." The brief remarks that dropped from Pyotr Petrovitch between the clicking of the beads on the reckoning frame betrayed unmistakable and discourteous irony. But the "humane" Andrey Semyonovitch ascribed Pyotr Petrovitch's ill-humour to his recent breach with Dounia and he was burning with impatience to discourse on that theme. He had something progressive to say on the subject which might console his worthy friend and "could not fail" to promote his development.

"There is some sort of festivity being prepared at that... at the widow's, isn't there?" Pyotr Petrovitch asked suddenly, interrupting Andrey Semyonovitch at the most interesting passage.

"Why, don't you know? Why, I was telling you last night what I think about all such ceremonies. And she invited you too, I heard. You were talking to her yesterday..."

"I should never have expected that beggarly fool would have spent on this feast all the money she got from that other fool, Raskolnikov. I was surprised just now as I came through at the preparations there, the wines! Several people are invited. It's beyond everything!" continued Pyotr Petrovitch, who seemed to have some object in pursuing the conversation. "What? You say I am asked too? When was that? I don't remember. But I shan't go. Why should I? I only said a word to her in passing yesterday of the possibility of her obtaining a year's salary as a destitute widow of a government clerk. I suppose she has invited me on that account, hasn't she? He-he-he!"

"I don't intend to go either," said Lebeziatnikov.

"I should think not, after giving her a thrashing! You might well hesitate, he-he!"

"Who thrashed? Whom?" cried Lebeziatnikov, flustered and blushing.

"Why, you thrashed Katerina Ivanovna a month ago. I heard so yesterday... so that's what your convictions amount to... and the woman question, too, wasn't quite sound, he-he-he!" and Pyotr Petrovitch, as though comforted, went back to clicking his beads.

"It's all slander and nonsense!" cried Lebeziatnikov, who was always afraid of allusions to the subject. "It was not like that at all, it was quite different. You've heard it wrong; it's a libel. I was simply defending myself. She rushed at me first with her nails, she pulled out all my whiskers.... It's permissable for anyone, I should hope, to defend himself and I never allow anyone to use violence to me on principle, for it's an act of despotism. What was I to do? I simply pushed her back."

"He-he-he!" Luzhin went on laughing maliciously.

"You keep on like that because you are out of humour yourself.... But that's nonsense and it has nothing, nothing whatever to do with the woman question! You don't understand; I used to think, indeed, that if women are equal to men in all respects, even in strength (as is maintained now) there ought to be equality in that, too. Of course, I reflected afterwards that such a question ought not really to arise, for there ought not to be fighting and in the future society fighting is unthinkable... and that it would be a queer thing to seek for equality in fighting. I am not so stupid... though, of course, there is fighting... there won't be later, but at present there is... confound it! How muddled one gets with you! It's not on that account that I am not going. I am not going on principle, not to take part in the revolting convention of memorial dinners, that's why! Though, of course, one might go to laugh at it.... I am sorry there won't be any priests at it. I should certainly go if there were."

"Then you would sit down at another man's table and insult it and those who invited you. Eh?"

"Certainly not insult, but protest. I should do it with a good object. I might indirectly assist the cause of enlightenment and propaganda. It's a duty of every man to work for enlightenment and propaganda and the more harshly, perhaps, the better. I might drop a seed, an idea.... And something might grow up from that seed. How should I be insulting them? They might be offended at first, but afterwards they'd see I'd done them a service. You know, Terebyeva (who is in the community now) was blamed because when she left her family and... devoted... herself, she wrote to her father and mother that she wouldn't go on living conventionally and was entering on a free marriage and it was said that that was too harsh, that she might have spared them and have written more kindly. I think that's all nonsense and there's no need of softness; on the contrary, what's wanted is protest. Varents had been married seven years, she abandoned her two children, she told her husband straight out in a letter: 'I have realised that I cannot be happy with you. I can never forgive you that you have deceived me by concealing from me that there is another organisation of society by means of the communities. I have only lately learned it from a great-hearted man to whom I have given myself and with whom I am establishing a community. I speak plainly because I consider it dishonest to deceive you. Do as you think best. Do not hope to get me back, you are too late. I hope you will be happy.' That's how letters like that ought to be written!"

"Is that Terebyeva the one you said had made a third free marriage?"

"No, it's only the second, really! But what if it were the fourth, what if it were the fifteenth, that's all nonsense! And if ever I regretted the death of my father and mother, it is now, and I sometimes think if my parents were living what a protest I would have aimed at them! I would have done something on purpose... I would have shown them! I would have astonished them! I am really sorry there is no one!"

"To surprise! He-he! Well, be that as you will," Pyotr Petrovitch interrupted, "but tell me this; do you know the dead man's daughter, the delicate-looking little thing? It's true what they say about her, isn't it?"

"What of it? I think, that is, it is my own personal conviction that this is the normal condition of women. Why not? I mean, *distinguons*. In our present society it is not altogether normal, because it is compulsory, but in the future society it will be perfectly normal, because it will be voluntary. Even as it is, she was quite right: she was suffering and that was her asset, so to speak, her capital which she had a perfect right to dispose of. Of course, in the future society there will be no need of assets, but her part will have another significance, rational and in harmony with her environment. As to Sofya Semyonovna personally, I regard her action as a vigorous protest against the organisation of society, and I respect her deeply for it; I rejoice indeed when I look at her!"

"I was told that you got her turned out of these lodgings."

Lebeziatnikov was enraged.

"That's another slander," he yelled. "It was not so at all! That was all Katerina Ivanovna's invention, for she did not understand! And I never made love to Sofya Semyonovna! I was simply developing her, entirely

515

disinterestedly, trying to rouse her to protest.... All I wanted was her protest and Sofya Semyonovna could not have remained here anyway!"

"Have you asked her to join your community?"

"You keep on laughing and very inappropriately, allow me to tell you. You don't understand! There is no such rôle in a community. The community is established that there should be no such rôles. In a community, such a rôle is essentially transformed and what is stupid here is sensible there, what, under present conditions, is unnatural becomes perfectly natural in the community. It all depends on the environment. It's all the environment and man himself is nothing. And I am on good terms with Sofya Semyonovna to this day, which is a proof that she never regarded me as having wronged her. I am trying now to attract her to the community, but on quite, quite a different footing. What are you laughing at? We are trying to establish a community of our own, a special one, on a broader basis. We have gone further in our convictions. We reject more! And meanwhile I'm still developing Sofya Semyonovna. She has a beautiful, beautiful character!"

"And you take advantage of her fine character, eh? He-he!"

"No, no! Oh, no! On the contrary."

"Oh, on the contrary! He-he-he! A queer thing to say!"

"Believe me! Why should I disguise it? In fact, I feel it strange myself how timid, chaste and modern she is with me!"

"And you, of course, are developing her... he-he! trying to prove to her that all that modesty is nonsense?"

"Not at all, not at all! How coarsely, how stupidly—excuse me saying so—you misunderstand the word development! Good heavens, how... crude you still are! We are striving for the freedom of women and you have only one idea in your head.... Setting aside the general question of chastity and feminine modesty as useless in themselves and indeed prejudices, I fully accept her chastity with me, because that's for her to decide. Of course if she were to tell me herself that she wanted me, I should think myself very lucky, because I like the girl very much; but as it is, no one has ever treated her more courteously than I, with more respect for her dignity... I wait in hopes, that's all!"

"You had much better make her a present of something. I bet you never thought of that."

"You don't understand, as I've told you already! Of course, she is in such a position, but it's another question. Quite another question! You simply despise her. Seeing a fact which you mistakenly consider deserving of contempt, you refuse to take a humane view of a fellow creature. You don't know what a character she is! I am only sorry that of late she has quite given up reading and borrowing books. I used to lend them to her. I am sorry, too, that with all the energy and resolution in protesting—which she has already shown once—she has little self-reliance, little, so to say, independence, so as to break free from certain prejudices and certain foolish ideas. Yet she thoroughly understands some questions, for instance about kissing of hands, that is, that it's an insult to a woman for a man to kiss her hand, because it's a sign of inequality. We had a debate about it and I described it to her. She listened attentively to an account of the workmen's associations in France, too. Now I am explaining the question of coming into the room in the future society."

"And what's that, pray?"

"We had a debate lately on the question: Has a member of the community the right to enter another member's room, whether man or woman, at any time... and we decided that he has!"

"It might be at an inconvenient moment, he-he!"

Lebeziatnikov was really angry.

"You are always thinking of something unpleasant," he cried with aversion. "Tfoo! How vexed I am that when I was expounding our system, I referred prematurely to the question of personal privacy! It's always a stumbling-block to people like you, they turn it into ridicule before they understand it. And how proud they are of it, too! Tfoo! I've often maintained that that question should not be approached by a novice till he has a firm faith in the system. And tell me, please, what do you find so shameful even in cesspools? I should be the first to be ready to clean out any cesspool you like. And it's not a question of self-sacrifice, it's simply work, honourable, useful work which is as good as any other and much better than the work of a Raphael and a Pushkin, because it is more useful."

"And more honourable, more honourable, he-he-he!"

"What do you mean by 'more honourable'? I don't understand such expressions to describe human activity. 'More honourable,' 'nobler'—all those are old-fashioned prejudices which I reject. Everything which is *of use* to mankind is honourable. I only understand one word: *useful*! You can snigger as much as you like, but that's so!"

Pyotr Petrovitch laughed heartily. He had finished counting the money and was putting it away. But some of the notes he left on the table. The "cesspool question" had already been a subject of dispute between them. What was absurd was that it made Lebeziatnikov really angry, while it amused Luzhin and at that moment he particularly wanted to anger his young friend.

"It's your ill-luck yesterday that makes you so ill-humoured and annoying," blurted out Lebeziatnikov, who in spite of his "independence" and his "protests" did not venture to oppose Pyotr Petrovitch and still behaved to him with some of the respect habitual in earlier years.

"You'd better tell me this," Pyotr Petrovitch interrupted with haughty displeasure, "can you... or rather are you really friendly enough with that young person to ask her to step in here for a minute? I think they've all come back from the cemetery... I heard the sound of steps... I want to see her, that young person."

"What for?" Lebeziatnikov asked with surprise.

"Oh, I want to. I am leaving here to-day or to-morrow and therefore I wanted to speak to her about.... However, you may be present during the interview. It's better you should be, indeed. For there's no knowing what you might imagine."

"I shan't imagine anything. I only asked and, if you've anything to say to her, nothing is easier than to call her in. I'll go directly and you may be sure I won't be in your way."

Five minutes later Lebeziatnikov came in with Sonia. She came in very much surprised and overcome with shyness as usual. She was always shy in such circumstances and was always afraid of new people, she had been as a child and was even more so now.... Pyotr Petrovitch met her "politely and affably," but with a certain shade of bantering familiarity which in his opinion was suitable for a man of his respectability and weight in dealing with a creature so young and so *interesting* as she. He hastened to "reassure" her and made her sit down facing him at the table. Sonia sat down, looked about her—at Lebeziatnikov, at the notes lying on the table and then again at Pyotr Petrovitch and her eyes remained riveted on him. Lebeziatnikov was moving to the door. Pyotr Petrovitch signed to Sonia to remain seated and stopped Lebeziatnikov.

"Is Raskolnikov in there? Has he come?" he asked him in a whisper.

"Raskolnikov? Yes. Why? Yes, he is there. I saw him just come in.... Why?"

"Well, I particularly beg you to remain here with us and not to leave me alone with this... young woman. I only want a few words with her, but God knows what they may make of it. I shouldn't like Raskolnikov to repeat anything.... You understand what I mean?"

"I understand!" Lebeziatnikov saw the point. "Yes, you are right.... Of course, I am convinced personally that you have no reason to be uneasy, but... still, you are right. Certainly I'll stay. I'll stand here at the window and not be in your way... I think you are right..."

Pyotr Petrovitch returned to the sofa, sat down opposite Sonia, looked attentively at her and assumed an extremely dignified, even severe expression, as much as to say, "don't you make any mistake, madam." Sonia was overwhelmed with embarrassment.

"In the first place, Sofya Semyonovna, will you make my excuses to your respected mamma.... That's right, isn't it? Katerina Ivanovna stands in the place of a mother to you?" Pyotr Petrovitch began with great dignity, though affably.

It was evident that his intentions were friendly.

"Quite so, yes; the place of a mother," Sonia answered, timidly and hurriedly.

"Then will you make my apologies to her? Through inevitable circumstances I am forced to be absent and shall not be at the dinner in spite of your mamma's kind invitation."

"Yes... I'll tell her... at once."

And Sonia hastily jumped up from her seat.

"Wait, that's not all," Pyotr Petrovitch detained her, smiling at her simplicity and ignorance of good manners, "and you know me little, my dear Sofya Semyonovna, if you suppose I would have ventured to trouble a person like you for a matter of so little consequence affecting myself only. I have another object."

Sonia sat down hurriedly. Her eyes rested again for an instant on the grey-and-rainbow-coloured notes that remained on the table, but she quickly looked away and fixed her eyes on Pyotr Petrovitch. She felt it horribly indecorous, especially for *her*, to look at another person's money. She stared at the gold eye-glass which Pyotr Petrovitch held in his left hand and at the massive and extremely handsome ring with a yellow stone on his middle finger. But suddenly she looked away and, not knowing where to turn, ended by staring Pyotr Petrovitch again straight in the face. After a pause of still greater dignity he continued.

"I chanced yesterday in passing to exchange a couple of words with Katerina Ivanovna, poor woman. That was sufficient to enable me to ascertain that she is in a position—preternatural, if one may so express it."

"Yes... preternatural..." Sonia hurriedly assented.

"Or it would be simpler and more comprehensible to say, ill."

"Yes, simpler and more comprehen... yes, ill."

"Quite so. So then from a feeling of humanity and so to speak compassion, I should be glad to be of service to her in any way, foreseeing her unfortunate position. I believe the whole of this poverty-stricken family depends now entirely on you?"

"Allow me to ask," Sonia rose to her feet, "did you say something to her yesterday of the possibility of a pension? Because she told me you had undertaken to get her one. Was that true?"

"Not in the slightest, and indeed it's an absurdity! I merely hinted at her obtaining temporary assistance as the widow of an official who had died in the service—if only she has patronage... but apparently your late parent had not served his full term and had not indeed been in the service at all of late. In fact, if there could be any hope, it would be very ephemeral, because there would be no claim for assistance in that case, far from it.... And she is dreaming of a pension already, he-he-he!... A go-ahead lady!"

"Yes, she is. For she is credulous and good-hearted, and she believes everything from the goodness of her heart and... and... and she is like that... yes... You must excuse her," said Sonia, and again she got up to go.

"But you haven't heard what I have to say."

"No, I haven't heard," muttered Sonia.

"Then sit down." She was terribly confused; she sat down again a third time.

"Seeing her position with her unfortunate little ones, I should be glad, as I have said before, so far as lies in my power, to be of service, that is, so far as is in my power, not more. One might for instance get up a subscription for her, or a lottery, something of the sort, such as is always arranged in such cases by friends or even outsiders desirous of assisting people. It was of that I intended to speak to you; it might be done."

"Yes, yes... God will repay you for it," faltered Sonia, gazing intently at Pyotr Petrovitch.

"It might be, but we will talk of it later. We might begin it to-day, we will talk it over this evening and lay the foundation so to speak. Come to me at seven o'clock. Mr. Lebeziatnikov, I hope, will assist us. But there is one circumstance of which I ought to warn you beforehand and for which I venture to trouble you, Sofya Semyonovna, to come here. In my opinion money cannot be, indeed it's unsafe to put it into Katerina Ivanovna's own hands. The dinner to-day is a proof of that. Though she has not, so to speak, a crust of bread for to-morrow and... well, boots or shoes, or anything; she has bought to-day Jamaica rum, and even, I believe, Madeira and... and coffee. I saw it as I passed through. To-morrow it will all fall upon you again, they won't have a crust of bread. It's absurd, really, and so, to my thinking, a subscription ought to be raised so that the unhappy widow should not know of the money, but only you, for instance. Am I right?"

"I don't know... this is only to-day, once in her life.... She was so anxious to do honour, to celebrate the memory.... And she is very sensible... but just as you think and I shall be very, very... they will all be... and God will reward... and the orphans..."

Sonia burst into tears.

"Very well, then, keep it in mind; and now will you accept for the benefit of your relation the small sum that I am able to spare, from me personally. I am very anxious that my name should not be mentioned in connection with it. Here... having so to speak anxieties of my own, I cannot do more..."

And Pyotr Petrovitch held out to Sonia a ten-rouble note carefully unfolded. Sonia took it, flushed crimson, jumped up, muttered something and began taking leave. Pyotr Petrovitch accompanied her ceremoniously to the door. She got out of the room at last, agitated and distressed, and returned to Katerina Ivanovna, overwhelmed with confusion.

All this time Lebeziatnikov had stood at the window or walked about the room, anxious not to interrupt the conversation; when Sonia had gone he walked up to Pyotr Petrovitch and solemnly held out his hand.

"I heard and *saw* everything," he said, laying stress on the last verb. "That is honourable, I mean to say, it's humane! You wanted to avoid gratitude, I saw! And although I cannot, I confess, in principle sympathise with private charity, for it not only fails to eradicate the evil but even promotes it, yet I must admit that I saw your action with pleasure—yes, yes, I like it."

"That's all nonsense," muttered Pyotr Petrovitch, somewhat disconcerted, looking carefully at Lebeziatnikov.

"No, it's not nonsense! A man who has suffered distress and annoyance as you did yesterday and who yet can sympathise with the misery of others, such a man... even though he is making a social mistake—is still deserving of respect! I did not expect it indeed of you, Pyotr Petrovitch, especially as according to your ideas... oh, what a drawback your ideas are to you! How distressed you are for instance by your ill-luck yesterday," cried the simple-hearted Lebeziatnikov, who felt a return of affection for Pyotr Petrovitch. "And, what do you want with marriage, with *legal* marriage, my dear, noble Pyotr Petrovitch? Why do you cling to this *legality* of marriage? Well, you may beat me if you like, but I am glad, positively glad it hasn't come off, that you are free, that you are not quite lost for humanity.... you see, I've spoken my mind!"

"Because I don't want in your free marriage to be made a fool of and to bring up another man's children, that's why I want legal marriage," Luzhin replied in order to make some answer.

He seemed preoccupied by something.

"Children? You referred to children," Lebeziatnikov started off like a warhorse at the trumpet call. "Children are a social question and a question of first importance, I agree; but the question of children has another solution. Some refuse to have children altogether, because they suggest the institution of the family. We'll speak of children later, but now as to the question of honour, I confess that's my weak point. That horrid, military, Pushkin expression is unthinkable in the dictionary of the future. What does it mean indeed? It's nonsense, there will be no deception in a free marriage! That is only the natural consequence of a legal marriage, so to say, its corrective, a protest. So that indeed it's not humiliating... and if I ever, to suppose an absurdity, were to be legally married, I should be positively glad of it. I should say to my wife: 'My dear, hitherto I have loved you, now I respect you, for you've shown you can protest!' You laugh! That's because you are of incapable of getting away from prejudices. Confound it all! I understand now where the unpleasantness is of being deceived in a legal marriage, but it's simply a despicable consequence of a despicable position in which both are humiliated. When the deception is open, as in a free marriage, then it does not exist, it's unthinkable. Your wife will only prove how she respects you by considering you incapable of opposing her happiness and avenging yourself on her for her new husband. Damn it all! I sometimes dream if I were to be married, pfoo! I mean if I were to marry, legally or not, it's just the same, I should present my wife with a lover if she had not found one for herself. 'My dear,' I should say, 'I love you, but even more than that I desire you to respect me. See!' Am I not right?"

Pyotr Petrovitch sniggered as he listened, but without much merriment. He hardly heard it indeed. He was preoccupied with something else and even Lebeziatnikov at last noticed it. Pyotr Petrovitch seemed excited and rubbed his hands. Lebeziatnikov remembered all this and reflected upon it afterwards.

CHAPTER II

It would be difficult to explain exactly what could have originated the idea of that senseless dinner in Katerina Ivanovna's disordered brain. Nearly ten of the twenty roubles, given by Raskolnikov for Marmeladov's funeral, were wasted upon it. Possibly Katerina Ivanovna felt obliged to honour the memory of the deceased "suitably," that all the lodgers, and still more Amalia Ivanovna, might know "that he was in no way their inferior, and perhaps very much their superior," and that no one had the right "to turn up his nose at him." Perhaps the chief element was that peculiar "poor man's pride," which compels many poor people to spend their last savings on some traditional social ceremony, simply in order to do "like other people," and not to "be looked down upon." It is very probable, too, that Katerina Ivanovna longed on this occasion, at the moment when she seemed to be abandoned by everyone, to show those "wretched contemptible lodgers" that she knew "how to do things, how to entertain" and that she had been brought up "in a genteel, she might almost say aristocratic colonel's family" and had not been meant for sweeping floors and washing the children's rags at night. Even the poorest and most broken-spirited people are sometimes liable to these paroxysms of pride and vanity which take the form of an irresistible nervous craving. And Katerina Ivanovna was not broken-spirited; she might have been killed by circumstance, but her spirit could not have been broken, that is, she could not have been intimidated, her will could not be crushed. Moreover Sonia had said with good reason that her mind was unhinged. She could not be said to be insane, but for a year past she had been so harassed that her mind might well be overstrained. The later stages of consumption are apt, doctors tell us, to affect the intellect.

There was no great variety of wines, nor was there Madeira; but wine there was. There was vodka, rum and Lisbon wine, all of the poorest quality but in sufficient quantity. Besides the traditional rice and honey, there were three or four dishes, one of which consisted of pancakes, all prepared in Amalia Ivanovna's kitchen. Two samovars were boiling, that tea and punch might be offered after dinner. Katerina Ivanovna had herself seen to purchasing the provisions, with the help of one of the lodgers, an unfortunate little Pole who had somehow been stranded at Madame Lippevechsel's. He promptly put himself at Katerina Ivanovna's disposal and had been all that morning and all the day before running about as fast as his legs could carry him, and very anxious that everyone should be aware of it. For every trifle he ran to Katerina Ivanovna, even hunting her out at the bazaar, at every instant called her "*Pani*." She was heartily sick of him before the end, though she had declared at first that she could not have got on without this "serviceable and magnanimous man." It was one of Katerina Ivanovna's characteristics to paint everyone she met in the most glowing colours. Her praises were so exaggerated as sometimes to be embarrassing; she would invent various circumstances to the credit of her new acquaintance and quite genuinely believe in their reality. Then all of a sudden she would be disillusioned and would rudely and contemptuously repulse the person she had only a few hours before been literally adoring. She was naturally of a gay, lively and peace-loving disposition, but from continual failures and misfortunes she had come to desire so *keenly* that all should live in peace and joy and should not *dare* to break the peace, that the slightest jar, the smallest disaster reduced her almost to frenzy, and she would pass in an instant from the brightest hopes and fancies to cursing her fate and raving, and knocking her head against the wall.

Amalia Ivanovna, too, suddenly acquired extraordinary importance in Katerina Ivanovna's eyes and was treated by her with extraordinary respect, probably only because Amalia Ivanovna had thrown herself heart and soul into the preparations. She had undertaken to lay the table, to provide the linen, crockery, etc., and to cook the dishes in her kitchen, and Katerina Ivanovna had left it all in her hands and gone herself to the cemetery. Everything had been well done. Even the table-cloth was nearly clean; the crockery, knives, forks and glasses were, of course, of all shapes and patterns, lent by different lodgers, but the table was properly laid at the time fixed, and Amalia Ivanovna, feeling she had done her work well, had put on a black silk dress and a cap with new mourning ribbons and met the returning party with some pride. This pride, though justifiable, displeased Katerina Ivanovna for some reason: "as though the table could not have been laid except by Amalia Ivanovna!" She disliked the cap with new ribbons, too. "Could she be stuck up, the stupid German, because she was mistress of the house, and had consented as a favour to help her poor lodgers! As a favour! Fancy that! Katerina Ivanovna's father who had been a colonel and almost a governor had sometimes had the table set for forty persons, and then anyone like Amalia Ivanovna, or rather Ludwigovna, would not have been allowed into the kitchen."

Katerina Ivanovna, however, put off expressing her feelings for the time and contented herself with treating her coldly, though she decided inwardly that she would certainly have to put Amalia Ivanovna down and set her in her proper place, for goodness only knew what she was fancying herself. Katerina Ivanovna was irritated too by the fact that hardly any of the lodgers invited had come to the funeral, except the Pole who had just managed to run into the cemetery, while to the memorial dinner the poorest and most insignificant of them had turned up, the wretched creatures, many of them not quite sober. The older and more respectable of them all, as if by common consent, stayed away. Pyotr Petrovitch Luzhin, for instance, who might be said to be the most respectable of all the lodgers, did not appear, though Katerina Ivanovna had the evening before told all the world, that is Amalia Ivanovna, Polenka, Sonia and the Pole, that he was the most generous, noble-hearted man with a large property and vast connections, who had been a friend of her first husband's, and a guest in her father's house, and that he had promised to use all his influence to secure her a considerable pension. It must be noted that when Katerina Ivanovna exalted anyone's connections and fortune, it was without any ulterior motive, quite disinterestedly, for the mere pleasure of adding to the consequence of the person praised. Probably "taking his cue" from Luzhin, "that contemptible wretch Lebeziatnikov had not turned up either. What did he fancy himself? He was only asked out of kindness and because he was sharing the same room with Pyotr Petrovitch and was a friend of his, so that it would have been awkward not to invite him."

Among those who failed to appear were "the genteel lady and her old-maidish daughter," who had only been lodgers in the house for the last fortnight, but had several times complained of the noise and uproar in Katerina Ivanovna's room, especially when Marmeladov had come back drunk. Katerina Ivanovna heard this from Amalia Ivanovna who, quarrelling with Katerina Ivanovna, and threatening to turn the whole family out of doors, had shouted at her that they "were not worth the foot" of the honourable lodgers whom they were disturbing. Katerina Ivanovna determined now to invite this lady and her daughter, "whose foot she was not worth," and who had turned away haughtily when she casually met them, so that they might know that "she was more noble in her thoughts and feelings and did not harbour malice," and might see that she was not accustomed to her way of living. She had proposed to make this clear to them at dinner with allusions to her late father's governorship, and also at the same time to hint that it was exceedingly stupid of them to turn away on meeting her. The fat colonel-major (he was really a discharged officer of low rank) was also absent, but it appeared that he had been "not himself" for the last two days. The party consisted of the Pole, a wretched looking clerk with a spotty face and a greasy coat, who had not a word to say for himself, and smelt abominably, a deaf and almost blind old man who had once been in the post office and who had been from immemorial ages maintained by someone at Amalia Ivanovna's.

A retired clerk of the commissariat department came, too; he was drunk, had a loud and most unseemly laugh and only fancy—was without a waistcoat! One of the visitors sat straight down to the table without even greeting Katerina Ivanovna. Finally one person having no suit appeared in his dressing-gown, but this was too much, and the efforts of Amalia Ivanovna and the Pole succeeded in removing him. The Pole brought with him, however, two other Poles who did not live at Amalia Ivanovna's and whom no one had seen here before. All this irritated Katerina Ivanovna intensely. "For whom had they made all these preparations then?" To make room for the visitors the children had not even been laid for at the table; but the two little ones were sitting on a bench in the furthest corner with their dinner laid on a box, while Polenka as a big girl had to look after them, feed them, and keep their noses wiped like well-bred children's.

Katerina Ivanovna, in fact, could hardly help meeting her guests with increased dignity, and even haughtiness. She stared at some of them with special severity, and loftily invited them to take their seats. Rushing to the conclusion that Amalia Ivanovna must be responsible for those who were absent, she began treating her with extreme nonchalance, which the latter promptly observed and resented. Such a beginning was no good omen for the end. All were seated at last.

Raskolnikov came in almost at the moment of their return from the cemetery. Katerina Ivanovna was greatly delighted to see him, in the first place, because he was the one "educated visitor, and, as everyone knew, was in two years to take a professorship in the university," and secondly because he immediately and respectfully apologised for having been unable to be at the funeral. She positively pounced upon him, and made him sit on her left hand (Amalia Ivanovna was on her right). In spite of her continual anxiety that the dishes should be passed round correctly and that everyone should taste them, in spite of the agonising cough which interrupted her every minute and seemed to have grown worse during the last few days, she hastened to pour out in a half whisper to Raskolnikov all her suppressed feelings and her just indignation at the failure of the dinner, interspersing her remarks with lively and uncontrollable laughter at the expense of her visitors and especially of her landlady.

"It's all that cuckoo's fault! You know whom I mean? Her, her!" Katerina Ivanovna nodded towards the landlady. "Look at her, she's making round eyes, she feels that we are talking about her and can't understand. Pfoo, the owl! Ha-ha! (Cough-cough-cough.) And what does she put on that cap for? (Cough-cough-cough.) Have you noticed that she wants everyone to consider that she is patronising me and doing me an honour by being here? I asked her like a sensible woman to invite people, especially those who knew my late husband, and look at the set of fools she has brought! The sweeps! Look at that one with the spotty face. And those wretched Poles, ha-ha-ha! (Cough-cough-cough.) Not one of them has ever poked his nose in here, I've never set eyes on them. What have they come here for, I ask you? There they sit in a row. Hey, *pan*!" she cried suddenly to one of them, "have you tasted the pancakes? Take some more! Have some beer! Won't you have some vodka? Look, he's jumped up and is making his bows, they must be quite starved, poor things. Never mind, let them eat! They don't make a noise, anyway, though I'm really afraid for our landlady's silver spoons... Amalia Ivanovna!" she addressed her suddenly, almost aloud, "if your spoons should happen to be stolen, I won't be responsible, I warn you! Ha-ha-ha!" She laughed turning to Raskolnikov, and again nodding towards the landlady, in high glee at her sally. "She didn't understand, she didn't understand again! Look how she sits with her mouth open! An owl, a real owl! An owl in new ribbons, ha-ha-ha!"

Here her laugh turned again to an insufferable fit of coughing that lasted five minutes. Drops of perspiration stood out on her forehead and her handkerchief was stained with blood. She showed Raskolnikov the blood in silence, and as soon as she could get her breath began whispering to him again with extreme animation and a hectic flush on her cheeks.

"Do you know, I gave her the most delicate instructions, so to speak, for inviting that lady and her daughter, you understand of whom I am speaking? It needed the utmost delicacy, the greatest nicety, but she has managed things so that that fool, that conceited baggage, that provincial nonentity, simply because she is the widow of a major, and has come to try and get a pension and to fray out her skirts in the government offices, because at fifty she paints her face (everybody knows it)... a creature like that did not think fit to come, and has not even answered the invitation, which the most ordinary good manners required! I can't understand why Pyotr Petrovitch has not come? But where's Sonia? Where has she gone? Ah, there she is at last! what is it, Sonia, where have you been? It's odd that even at your father's funeral you should be so unpunctual. Rodion Romanovitch, make room for her beside you. That's your place, Sonia... take what you like. Have some of the cold entrée with jelly, that's the best. They'll bring the pancakes directly. Have they given the children some? Polenka, have you got everything? (Cough-cough-cough.) That's all right. Be a good girl, Lida, and, Kolya, don't fidget with your feet; sit like a little gentleman. What are you saying, Sonia?"

Sonia hastened to give her Pyotr Petrovitch's apologies, trying to speak loud enough for everyone to hear and carefully choosing the most respectful phrases which she attributed to Pyotr Petrovitch. She added that Pyotr Petrovitch had particularly told her to say that, as soon as he possibly could, he would come immediately to discuss *business* alone with her and to consider what could be done for her, etc., etc.

Sonia knew that this would comfort Katerina Ivanovna, would flatter her and gratify her pride. She sat down beside Raskolnikov; she made him a hurried bow, glancing curiously at him. But for the rest of the time she seemed to avoid looking at him or speaking to him. She seemed absent-minded, though she kept looking at Katerina Ivanovna, trying to please her. Neither she nor Katerina Ivanovna had been able to get mourning; Sonia was wearing dark brown, and Katerina Ivanovna had on her only dress, a dark striped cotton one.

The message from Pyotr Petrovitch was very successful. Listening to Sonia with dignity, Katerina Ivanovna inquired with equal dignity how Pyotr Petrovitch was, then at once whispered almost aloud to Raskolnikov that it certainly would have been strange for a man of Pyotr Petrovitch's position and standing to find himself in such "extraordinary company," in spite of his devotion to her family and his old friendship with her father.

"That's why I am so grateful to you, Rodion Romanovitch, that you have not disdained my hospitality, even in such surroundings," she added almost aloud. "But I am sure that it was only your special affection for my poor husband that has made you keep your promise."

Then once more with pride and dignity she scanned her visitors, and suddenly inquired aloud across the table of the deaf man: "Wouldn't he have some more meat, and had he been given some wine?" The old man made no answer and for a long while could not understand what he was asked, though his neighbours amused themselves by poking and shaking him. He simply gazed about him with his mouth open, which only increased the general mirth.

"What an imbecile! Look, look! Why was he brought? But as to Pyotr Petrovitch, I always had confidence in him," Katerina Ivanovna continued, "and, of course, he is not like..." with an extremely stern face she addressed Amalia Ivanovna so sharply and loudly that the latter was quite disconcerted, "not like your dressed up draggletails whom my father would not have taken as cooks into his kitchen, and my late husband would have done them honour if he had invited them in the goodness of his heart."

"Yes, he was fond of drink, he was fond of it, he did drink!" cried the commissariat clerk, gulping down his twelfth glass of vodka.

"My late husband certainly had that weakness, and everyone knows it," Katerina Ivanovna attacked him at once, "but he was a kind and honourable man, who loved and respected his family. The worst of it was his good nature made him trust all sorts of disreputable people, and he drank with fellows who were not worth the sole of his shoe. Would you believe it, Rodion Romanovitch, they found a gingerbread cock in his pocket; he was dead drunk, but he did not forget the children!"

"A cock? Did you say a cock?" shouted the commissariat clerk.

Katerina Ivanovna did not vouchsafe a reply. She sighed, lost in thought.

"No doubt you think, like everyone, that I was too severe with him," she went on, addressing Raskolnikov. "But that's not so! He respected me, he respected me very much! He was a kind-hearted man! And how sorry I was for him sometimes! He would sit in a corner and look at me, I used to feel so sorry for him, I used to want to be kind to him and then would think to myself: 'Be kind to him and he will drink again,' it was only by severity that you could keep him within bounds."

"Yes, he used to get his hair pulled pretty often," roared the commissariat clerk again, swallowing another glass of vodka.

"Some fools would be the better for a good drubbing, as well as having their hair pulled. I am not talking of my late husband now!" Katerina Ivanovna snapped at him.

The flush on her cheeks grew more and more marked, her chest heaved. In another minute she would have been ready to make a scene. Many of the visitors were sniggering, evidently delighted. They began poking the commissariat clerk and whispering something to him. They were evidently trying to egg him on.

"Allow me to ask what are you alluding to," began the clerk, "that is to say, whose... about whom... did you say just now... But I don't care! That's nonsense! Widow! I forgive you.... Pass!"

And he took another drink of vodka.

Raskolnikov sat in silence, listening with disgust. He only ate from politeness, just tasting the food that Katerina Ivanovna was continually putting on his plate, to avoid hurting her feelings. He watched Sonia intently. But Sonia became more and more anxious and distressed; she, too, foresaw that the dinner would not end peaceably, and saw with terror Katerina Ivanovna's growing irritation. She knew that she, Sonia, was the chief reason for the 'genteel' ladies' contemptuous treatment of Katerina Ivanovna's invitation. She had heard from Amalia Ivanovna that the mother was positively offended at the invitation and had asked the question: "How could she let her daughter sit down beside *that young person*?" Sonia had a feeling that Katerina Ivanovna had already heard this and an insult to Sonia meant more to Katerina Ivanovna than an insult to herself, her children, or her father, Sonia knew that Katerina Ivanovna would not be satisfied now, "till she had shown those draggletails that they were both..." To make matters worse someone passed Sonia, from the other end of the table, a plate with two hearts pierced with an arrow, cut out of black bread. Katerina Ivanovna flushed crimson and at once said aloud across the table that the man who sent it was "a drunken ass!"

Amalia Ivanovna was foreseeing something amiss, and at the same time deeply wounded by Katerina Ivanovna's haughtiness, and to restore the good-humour of the company and raise herself in their esteem she began, apropos of nothing, telling a story about an acquaintance of hers "Karl from the chemist's," who was driving one night in a cab, and that "the cabman wanted him to kill, and Karl very much begged him not to kill, and wept and clasped hands, and frightened and from fear pierced his heart." Though Katerina Ivanovna smiled, she observed at once that Amalia Ivanovna ought not to tell anecdotes in Russian; the latter was still more offended, and she retorted that her "*Vater aus Berlin* was a very important man, and always went with his hands in pockets." Katerina Ivanovna could not restrain herself and laughed so much that Amalia Ivanovna lost patience and could scarcely control herself.

"Listen to the owl!" Katerina Ivanovna whispered at once, her good-humour almost restored, "she meant to say he kept his hands in his pockets, but she said he put his hands in people's pockets. (Cough-cough.) And have you noticed, Rodion Romanovitch, that all these Petersburg foreigners, the Germans especially, are all stupider than we! Can you fancy anyone of us telling how 'Karl from the chemist's' 'pierced his heart from fear' and that the idiot, instead of punishing the cabman, 'clasped his hands and wept, and much begged.' Ah, the fool! And you know she fancies it's very touching and does not suspect how stupid she is! To my thinking that drunken commissariat clerk is a great deal cleverer, anyway one can see that he has addled his brains with drink, but you know, these foreigners are always so well behaved and serious.... Look how she sits glaring! She is angry, ha-ha! (Cough-cough-cough.)"

Regaining her good-humour, Katerina Ivanovna began at once telling Raskolnikov that when she had obtained her pension, she intended to open a school for the daughters of gentlemen in her native town T——. This was the first time she had spoken to him of the project, and she launched out into the most alluring details. It suddenly appeared that Katerina Ivanovna had in her hands the very certificate of honour of which Marmeladov had spoken to Raskolnikov in the tavern, when he told him that Katerina Ivanovna, his wife, had danced the shawl dance before the governor and other great personages on leaving school. This certificate of honour was obviously intended now to prove Katerina Ivanovna's right to open a boarding-school; but she had armed herself with it chiefly with the object of overwhelming "those two stuck-up draggletails" if they came to the dinner, and proving incontestably that Katerina Ivanovna was of the most noble, "she might even say aristocratic family, a colonel's daughter and was far superior to certain adventuresses who have been so much to the fore of late." The certificate of honour immediately passed into the hands of the drunken guests, and Katerina Ivanovna did not try to retain it, for it actually contained the statement *en toutes lettres*, that her father was of the rank of a major, and also a companion of an order, so that she really was almost the daughter of a colonel.

Warming up, Katerina Ivanovna proceeded to enlarge on the peaceful and happy life they would lead in T——, on the gymnasium teachers whom she would engage to give lessons in her boarding-school, one a most respectable old Frenchman, one Mangot, who had taught Katerina Ivanovna herself in old days and was still living in T——, and would no doubt teach in her school on moderate terms. Next she spoke of Sonia who would go with her to T—— and help her in all her plans. At this someone at the further end of the table gave a sudden guffaw.

Though Katerina Ivanovna tried to appear to be disdainfully unaware of it, she raised her voice and began at once speaking with conviction of Sonia's undoubted ability to assist her, of "her gentleness, patience, devotion, generosity and good education," tapping Sonia on the cheek and kissing her warmly twice. Sonia flushed crimson, and Katerina Ivanovna suddenly burst into tears, immediately observing that she was "nervous and silly, that she was too much upset, that it was time to finish, and as the dinner was over, it was time to hand round the tea."

At that moment, Amalia Ivanovna, deeply aggrieved at taking no part in the conversation, and not being listened to, made one last effort, and with secret misgivings ventured on an exceedingly deep and weighty observation, that "in the future boarding-school she would have to pay particular attention to *die Wäsche*, and that there certainly must be a good *dame* to look after the linen, and secondly that the young ladies must not novels at night read."

Katerina Ivanovna, who certainly was upset and very tired, as well as heartily sick of the dinner, at once cut short Amalia Ivanovna, saying "she knew nothing about it and was talking nonsense, that it was the business of the laundry maid, and not of the directress of a high-class boarding-school to look after *die Wäsche*, and as for novel-reading, that was simply rudeness, and she begged her to be silent." Amalia Ivanovna fired up and getting angry observed that she only "meant her good," and that "she had meant her very good," and that "it was long since she had paid her *gold* for the lodgings."

Katerina Ivanovna at once "set her down," saying that it was a lie to say she wished her good, because only yesterday when her dead husband was lying on the table, she had worried her about the lodgings. To this Amalia Ivanovna very appropriately observed that she had invited those ladies, but "those ladies had not come, because those ladies *are* ladies and cannot come to a lady who is not a lady." Katerina Ivanovna at once pointed out to her, that as she was a slut she could not judge what made one really a lady. Amalia Ivanovna at once declared that her "*Vater aus Berlin* was a very, very important man, and both hands in pockets went, and always used to say: 'Poof! poof!'" and she leapt up from the table to represent her father, sticking her hands in her pockets, puffing her cheeks, and uttering vague sounds resembling "poof! poof!" amid loud laughter from all the lodgers, who purposely encouraged Amalia Ivanovna, hoping for a fight.

But this was too much for Katerina Ivanovna, and she at once declared, so that all could hear, that Amalia Ivanovna probably never had a father, but was simply a drunken Petersburg Finn, and had certainly once been a cook and probably something worse. Amalia Ivanovna turned as red as a lobster and squealed that perhaps Katerina Ivanovna never had a father, "but she had a *Vater aus Berlin* and that he wore a long coat and always said poof-poof-poof!"

Katerina Ivanovna observed contemptuously that all knew what her family was and that on that very certificate of honour it was stated in print that her father was a colonel, while Amalia Ivanovna's father—if she really had one—was probably some Finnish milkman, but that probably she never had a father at all, since it was still uncertain whether her name was Amalia Ivanovna or Amalia Ludwigovna.

At this Amalia Ivanovna, lashed to fury, struck the table with her fist, and shrieked that she was Amalia Ivanovna, and not Ludwigovna, "that her *Vater* was named Johann and that he was a burgomeister, and that Katerina Ivanovna's *Vater* was quite never a burgomeister." Katerina Ivanovna rose from her chair, and with a stern and apparently calm voice (though she was pale and her chest was heaving) observed that "if she dared for one moment to set her contemptible wretch of a father on a level with her papa, she, Katerina Ivanovna, would tear her cap off her head and trample it under foot." Amalia Ivanovna ran about the room, shouting at the top of her voice, that she was mistress of the house and that Katerina Ivanovna should leave the lodgings that minute; then she rushed for some reason to collect the silver spoons from the table. There was a great outcry and uproar, the children began crying. Sonia ran to restrain Katerina Ivanovna, but when Amalia Ivanovna shouted something about "the yellow ticket," Katerina Ivanovna pushed Sonia away, and rushed at the landlady to carry out her threat.

At that minute the door opened, and Pyotr Petrovitch Luzhin appeared on the threshold. He stood scanning the party with severe and vigilant eyes. Katerina Ivanovna rushed to him.

CHAPTER III

"Pyotr Petrovitch," she cried, "protect me... you at least! Make this foolish woman understand that she can't behave like this to a lady in misfortune... that there is a law for such things.... I'll go to the governor-general himself.... She shall answer for it.... Remembering my father's hospitality protect these orphans."

"Allow me, madam.... Allow me." Pyotr Petrovitch waved her off. "Your papa as you are well aware I had not the honour of knowing" (someone laughed aloud) "and I do not intend to take part in your everlasting squabbles with Amalia Ivanovna.... I have come here to speak of my own affairs... and I want to have a word with your stepdaughter, Sofya... Ivanovna, I think it is? Allow me to pass."

Pyotr Petrovitch, edging by her, went to the opposite corner where Sonia was.

Katerina Ivanovna remained standing where she was, as though thunderstruck. She could not understand how Pyotr Petrovitch could deny having enjoyed her father's hospitality. Though she had invented it herself, she believed in it firmly by this time. She was struck too by the businesslike, dry and even contemptuous menacing tone of Pyotr Petrovitch. All the clamour gradually died away at his entrance. Not only was this "serious business man" strikingly incongruous with the rest of the party, but it was evident, too, that he had come upon some matter of consequence, that some exceptional cause must have brought him and that therefore something was going to happen. Raskolnikov, standing beside Sonia, moved aside to let him pass; Pyotr Petrovitch did not seem to notice him. A minute later Lebeziatnikov, too, appeared in the doorway; he did not come in, but stood still, listening with marked interest, almost wonder, and seemed for a time perplexed.

"Excuse me for possibly interrupting you, but it's a matter of some importance," Pyotr Petrovitch observed, addressing the company generally. "I am glad indeed to find other persons present. Amalia Ivanovna, I humbly beg you as mistress of the house to pay careful attention to what I have to say to Sofya Ivanovna. Sofya Ivanovna," he went on, addressing Sonia, who was very much surprised and already alarmed, "immediately after your visit I found that a hundred-rouble note was missing from my table, in the room of my friend Mr. Lebeziatnikov. If in any way whatever you know and will tell us where it is now, I assure you on my word of honour and call all present to witness that the matter shall end there. In the opposite case I shall be compelled to have recourse to very serious measures and then... you must blame yourself."

Complete silence reigned in the room. Even the crying children were still. Sonia stood deadly pale, staring at Luzhin and unable to say a word. She seemed not to understand. Some seconds passed.

"Well, how is it to be then?" asked Luzhin, looking intently at her.

"I don't know.... I know nothing about it," Sonia articulated faintly at last.

"No, you know nothing?" Luzhin repeated and again he paused for some seconds. "Think a moment, mademoiselle," he began severely, but still, as it were, admonishing her. "Reflect, I am prepared to give you time for consideration. Kindly observe this: if I were not so entirely convinced I should not, you may be sure, with my experience venture to accuse you so directly. Seeing that for such direct accusation before witnesses, if false or even mistaken, I should myself in a certain sense be made responsible, I am aware of that. This morning I changed for my own purposes several five-per-cent securities for the sum of approximately three thousand roubles. The account is noted down in my pocket-book. On my return home I proceeded to count the money— as Mr. Lebeziatnikov will bear witness—and after counting two thousand three hundred roubles I put the rest in my pocket-book in my coat pocket. About five hundred roubles remained on the table and among them three notes of a hundred roubles each. At that moment you entered (at my invitation)—and all the time you were present you were exceedingly embarrassed; so that three times you jumped up in the middle of the conversation and tried to make off. Mr. Lebeziatnikov can bear witness to this. You yourself, mademoiselle, probably will not refuse to confirm my statement that I invited you through Mr. Lebeziatnikov, solely in order to discuss with you the hopeless and destitute position of your relative, Katerina Ivanovna (whose dinner I was unable to attend), and the advisability of getting up something of the nature of a subscription, lottery or the like, for her benefit. You thanked me and even shed tears. I describe all this as it took place, primarily to recall it to your mind and secondly to show you that not the slightest detail has escaped my recollection. Then I took a ten-rouble note from the table and handed it to you by way of first instalment on my part for the benefit of your relative. Mr. Lebeziatnikov saw all this. Then I accompanied you to the door—you being still in the same state of embarrassment—after which, being left alone with Mr. Lebeziatnikov I talked to him for ten minutes—then Mr. Lebeziatnikov went out and I returned to the table with the money lying on it, intending to count it and to put it aside, as I proposed doing before. To my surprise one hundred-rouble note had disappeared. Kindly consider the position. Mr. Lebeziatnikov I cannot suspect. I am ashamed to allude to such a supposition. I cannot have made a mistake in my reckoning, for the minute before your entrance I had finished my accounts and found the total correct. You will admit that recollecting your embarrassment, your eagerness to get away and the fact that you kept your hands for some time on the table, and taking into consideration your social position and the habits associated with it, I was, so to say, with horror and positively against my will, *compelled* to entertain a suspicion—a cruel, but justifiable suspicion! I will add further and repeat that in spite of my positive conviction, I realise that I run a certain risk in making this accusation, but as you see, I could not let it pass. I have taken action and I will tell you why: solely, madam, solely, owing to your black ingratitude! Why! I invite you for the benefit of your destitute relative, I present you with my donation of ten roubles and you, on the spot, repay me for all that with such an action. It is too bad! You need a lesson. Reflect! Moreover, like a true friend I beg you—and you could have no better friend at this moment—think what you are doing, otherwise I shall be immovable! Well, what do you say?"

"I have taken nothing," Sonia whispered in terror, "you gave me ten roubles, here it is, take it."

Sonia pulled her handkerchief out of her pocket, untied a corner of it, took out the ten-rouble note and gave it to Luzhin.

"And the hundred roubles you do not confess to taking?" he insisted reproachfully, not taking the note.

Sonia looked about her. All were looking at her with such awful, stern, ironical, hostile eyes. She looked at Raskolnikov... he stood against the wall, with his arms crossed, looking at her with glowing eyes.

"Good God!" broke from Sonia.

"Amalia Ivanovna, we shall have to send word to the police and therefore I humbly beg you meanwhile to send for the house porter," Luzhin said softly and even kindly.

"*Gott der Barmherzige*! I knew she was the thief," cried Amalia Ivanovna, throwing up her hands.

"You knew it?" Luzhin caught her up, "then I suppose you had some reason before this for thinking so. I beg you, worthy Amalia Ivanovna, to remember your words which have been uttered before witnesses."

There was a buzz of loud conversation on all sides. All were in movement.

"What!" cried Katerina Ivanovna, suddenly realising the position, and she rushed at Luzhin. "What! You accuse her of stealing? Sonia? Ah, the wretches, the wretches!"

And running to Sonia she flung her wasted arms round her and held her as in a vise.

"Sonia! how dared you take ten roubles from him? Foolish girl! Give it to me! Give me the ten roubles at once—here!"

And snatching the note from Sonia, Katerina Ivanovna crumpled it up and flung it straight into Luzhin's face. It hit him in the eye and fell on the ground. Amalia Ivanovna hastened to pick it up. Pyotr Petrovitch lost his temper.

"Hold that mad woman!" he shouted.

At that moment several other persons, besides Lebeziatnikov, appeared in the doorway, among them the two ladies.

"What! Mad? Am I mad? Idiot!" shrieked Katerina Ivanovna. "You are an idiot yourself, pettifogging lawyer, base man! Sonia, Sonia take his money! Sonia a thief! Why, she'd give away her last penny!" and Katerina Ivanovna broke into hysterical laughter. "Did you ever see such an idiot?" she turned from side to side. "And you too?" she suddenly saw the landlady, "and you too, sausage eater, you declare that she is a thief, you trashy Prussian hen's leg in a crinoline! She hasn't been out of this room: she came straight from you, you wretch, and sat down beside me, everyone saw her. She sat here, by Rodion Romanovitch. Search her! Since she's not left the room, the money would have to be on her! Search her, search her! But if you don't find it, then excuse me, my dear fellow, you'll answer for it! I'll go to our Sovereign, to our Sovereign, to our gracious Tsar himself, and throw myself at his feet, to-day, this minute! I am alone in the world! They would let me in! Do you think they wouldn't? You're wrong, I will get in! I will get in! You reckoned on her meekness! You relied upon that! But I am not so submissive, let me tell you! You've gone too far yourself. Search her, search her!"

And Katerina Ivanovna in a frenzy shook Luzhin and dragged him towards Sonia.

"I am ready, I'll be responsible... but calm yourself, madam, calm yourself. I see that you are not so submissive!... Well, well, but as to that..." Luzhin muttered, "that ought to be before the police... though indeed there are witnesses enough as it is.... I am ready.... But in any case it's difficult for a man... on account of her sex.... But with the help of Amalia Ivanovna... though, of course, it's not the way to do things.... How is it to be done?"

"As you will! Let anyone who likes search her!" cried Katerina Ivanovna. "Sonia, turn out your pockets! See! Look, monster, the pocket is empty, here was her handkerchief! Here is the other pocket, look! D'you see, d'you see?"

And Katerina Ivanovna turned—or rather snatched—both pockets inside out. But from the right pocket a piece of paper flew out and describing a parabola in the air fell at Luzhin's feet. Everyone saw it, several cried out. Pyotr Petrovitch stooped down, picked up the paper in two fingers, lifted it where all could see it and opened it. It was a hundred-rouble note folded in eight. Pyotr Petrovitch held up the note showing it to everyone.

"Thief! Out of my lodging. Police, police!" yelled Amalia Ivanovna. "They must to Siberia be sent! Away!"

Exclamations arose on all sides. Raskolnikov was silent, keeping his eyes fixed on Sonia, except for an occasional rapid glance at Luzhin. Sonia stood still, as though unconscious. She was hardly able to feel surprise. Suddenly the colour rushed to her cheeks; she uttered a cry and hid her face in her hands.

"No, it wasn't I! I didn't take it! I know nothing about it," she cried with a heartrending wail, and she ran to Katerina Ivanovna, who clasped her tightly in her arms, as though she would shelter her from all the world.

"Sonia! Sonia! I don't believe it! You see, I don't believe it!" she cried in the face of the obvious fact, swaying her to and fro in her arms like a baby, kissing her face continually, then snatching at her hands and kissing them, too, "you took it! How stupid these people are! Oh dear! You are fools, fools," she cried, addressing the whole room, "you don't know, you don't know what a heart she has, what a girl she is! She take it, she? She'd sell her last rag, she'd go barefoot to help you if you needed it, that's what she is! She has the yellow passport because my children were starving, she sold herself for us! Ah, husband, husband! Do you see? Do you see? What a memorial dinner for you! Merciful heavens! Defend her, why are you all standing still? Rodion Romanovitch, why don't you stand up for her? Do you believe it, too? You are not worth her little finger, all of you together! Good God! Defend her now, at least!"

The wail of the poor, consumptive, helpless woman seemed to produce a great effect on her audience. The agonised, wasted, consumptive face, the parched blood-stained lips, the hoarse voice, the tears unrestrained as a child's, the trustful, childish and yet despairing prayer for help were so piteous that everyone seemed to feel for her. Pyotr Petrovitch at any rate was at once moved to *compassion*.

"Madam, madam, this incident does not reflect upon you!" he cried impressively, "no one would take upon himself to accuse you of being an instigator or even an accomplice in it, especially as you have proved her guilt by turning out her pockets, showing that you had no previous idea of it. I am most ready, most ready to show compassion, if poverty, so to speak, drove Sofya Semyonovna to it, but why did you refuse to confess, mademoiselle? Were you afraid of the disgrace? The first step? You lost your head, perhaps? One can quite understand it.... But how could you have lowered yourself to such an action? Gentlemen," he addressed the whole company, "gentlemen! Compassionate and, so to say, commiserating these people, I am ready to overlook it even now in spite of the personal insult lavished upon me! And may this disgrace be a lesson to you for the future," he said, addressing Sonia, "and I will carry the matter no further. Enough!"

Pyotr Petrovitch stole a glance at Raskolnikov. Their eyes met, and the fire in Raskolnikov's seemed ready to reduce him to ashes. Meanwhile Katerina Ivanovna apparently heard nothing. She was kissing and hugging

Sonia like a madwoman. The children, too, were embracing Sonia on all sides, and Polenka—though she did not fully understand what was wrong—was drowned in tears and shaking with sobs, as she hid her pretty little face, swollen with weeping, on Sonia's shoulder.

"How vile!" a loud voice cried suddenly in the doorway.

Pyotr Petrovitch looked round quickly.

"What vileness!" Lebeziatnikov repeated, staring him straight in the face.

Pyotr Petrovitch gave a positive start—all noticed it and recalled it afterwards. Lebeziatnikov strode into the room.

"And you dared to call me as witness?" he said, going up to Pyotr Petrovitch.

"What do you mean? What are you talking about?" muttered Luzhin.

"I mean that you... are a slanderer, that's what my words mean!" Lebeziatnikov said hotly, looking sternly at him with his short-sighted eyes.

He was extremely angry. Raskolnikov gazed intently at him, as though seizing and weighing each word. Again there was a silence. Pyotr Petrovitch indeed seemed almost dumbfounded for the first moment.

"If you mean that for me,..." he began, stammering. "But what's the matter with you? Are you out of your mind?"

"I'm in my mind, but you are a scoundrel! Ah, how vile! I have heard everything. I kept waiting on purpose to understand it, for I must own even now it is not quite logical.... What you have done it all for I can't understand."

"Why, what have I done then? Give over talking in your nonsensical riddles! Or maybe you are drunk!"

"You may be a drunkard, perhaps, vile man, but I am not! I never touch vodka, for it's against my convictions. Would you believe it, he, he himself, with his own hands gave Sofya Semyonovna that hundred-rouble note—I saw it, I was a witness, I'll take my oath! He did it, he!" repeated Lebeziatnikov, addressing all.

"Are you crazy, milksop?" squealed Luzhin. "She is herself before you—she herself here declared just now before everyone that I gave her only ten roubles. How could I have given it to her?"

"I saw it, I saw it," Lebeziatnikov repeated, "and though it is against my principles, I am ready this very minute to take any oath you like before the court, for I saw how you slipped it in her pocket. Only like a fool I thought you did it out of kindness! When you were saying good-bye to her at the door, while you held her hand in one hand, with the other, the left, you slipped the note into her pocket. I saw it, I saw it!"

Luzhin turned pale.

"What lies!" he cried impudently, "why, how could you, standing by the window, see the note? You fancied it with your short-sighted eyes. You are raving!"

"No, I didn't fancy it. And though I was standing some way off, I saw it all. And though it certainly would be hard to distinguish a note from the window—that's true—I knew for certain that it was a hundred-rouble note, because, when you were going to give Sofya Semyonovna ten roubles, you took up from the table a hundred-rouble note (I saw it because I was standing near then, and an idea struck me at once, so that I did not forget you had it in your hand). You folded it and kept it in your hand all the time. I didn't think of it again until, when you were getting up, you changed it from your right hand to your left and nearly dropped it! I noticed it because the same idea struck me again, that you meant to do her a kindness without my seeing. You can fancy how I watched you and I saw how you succeeded in slipping it into her pocket. I saw it, I saw it, I'll take my oath."

Lebeziatnikov was almost breathless. Exclamations arose on all hands chiefly expressive of wonder, but some were menacing in tone. They all crowded round Pyotr Petrovitch. Katerina Ivanovna flew to Lebeziatnikov.

"I was mistaken in you! Protect her! You are the only one to take her part! She is an orphan. God has sent you!"

Katerina Ivanovna, hardly knowing what she was doing, sank on her knees before him.

"A pack of nonsense!" yelled Luzhin, roused to fury, "it's all nonsense you've been talking! 'An idea struck you, you didn't think, you noticed'—what does it amount to? So I gave it to her on the sly on purpose? What for? With what object? What have I to do with this...?"

"What for? That's what I can't understand, but that what I am telling you is the fact, that's certain! So far from my being mistaken, you infamous criminal man, I remember how, on account of it, a question occurred to me at once, just when I was thanking you and pressing your hand. What made you put it secretly in her pocket? Why you did it secretly, I mean? Could it be simply to conceal it from me, knowing that my convictions are opposed to yours and that I do not approve of private benevolence, which effects no radical cure? Well, I decided that you really were ashamed of giving such a large sum before me. Perhaps, too, I thought, he wants to give her a surprise, when she finds a whole hundred-rouble note in her pocket. (For I know, some benevolent people are very fond of decking out their charitable actions in that way.) Then the idea struck me, too, that you wanted to test her, to see whether, when she found it, she would come to thank you. Then, too, that you wanted to avoid thanks and that, as the saying is, your right hand should not know... something of that sort, in fact. I thought of so many possibilities that I put off considering it, but still thought it indelicate to show you that I knew your secret. But another idea struck me again that Sofya Semyonovna might easily lose the money before she noticed it, that was why I decided to come in here to call her out of the room and to tell her that you put a hundred roubles in her pocket. But on my way I went first to Madame Kobilatnikov's to take them the 'General Treatise on the Positive Method' and especially to recommend Piderit's article (and also Wagner's); then I come on here and what a state of things I find! Now could I, could I, have all these ideas and reflections if I had not seen you put the hundred-rouble note in her pocket?"

When Lebeziatnikov finished his long-winded harangue with the logical deduction at the end, he was quite tired, and the perspiration streamed from his face. He could not, alas, even express himself correctly in Russian, though he knew no other language, so that he was quite exhausted, almost emaciated after this heroic exploit. But his speech produced a powerful effect. He had spoken with such vehemence, with such conviction that everyone obviously believed him. Pyotr Petrovitch felt that things were going badly with him.

"What is it to do with me if silly ideas did occur to you?" he shouted, "that's no evidence. You may have dreamt it, that's all! And I tell you, you are lying, sir. You are lying and slandering from some spite against me, simply from pique, because I did not agree with your free-thinking, godless, social propositions!"

But this retort did not benefit Pyotr Petrovitch. Murmurs of disapproval were heard on all sides.

"Ah, that's your line now, is it!" cried Lebeziatnikov, "that's nonsense! Call the police and I'll take my oath! There's only one thing I can't understand: what made him risk such a contemptible action. Oh, pitiful, despicable man!"

"I can explain why he risked such an action, and if necessary, I, too, will swear to it," Raskolnikov said at last in a firm voice, and he stepped forward.

He appeared to be firm and composed. Everyone felt clearly, from the very look of him that he really knew about it and that the mystery would be solved.

"Now I can explain it all to myself," said Raskolnikov, addressing Lebeziatnikov. "From the very beginning of the business, I suspected that there was some scoundrelly intrigue at the bottom of it. I began to suspect it from some special circumstances known to me only, which I will explain at once to everyone: they account for everything. Your valuable evidence has finally made everything clear to me. I beg all, all to listen. This gentleman (he pointed to Luzhin) was recently engaged to be married to a young lady—my sister, Avdotya Romanovna Raskolnikov. But coming to Petersburg he quarrelled with me, the day before yesterday, at our first meeting and I drove him out of my room—I have two witnesses to prove it. He is a very spiteful man.... The day before yesterday I did not know that he was staying here, in your room, and that consequently on the very day we quarrelled—the day before yesterday—he saw me give Katerina Ivanovna some money for the funeral, as a friend of the late Mr. Marmeladov. He at once wrote a note to my mother and informed her that I had given away all my money, not to Katerina Ivanovna but to Sofya Semyonovna, and referred in a most contemptible way to the... character of Sofya Semyonovna, that is, hinted at the character of my attitude to Sofya Semyonovna. All this you understand was with the object of dividing me from my mother and sister, by insinuating that I was squandering on unworthy objects the money which they had sent me and which was all they had. Yesterday evening, before my mother and sister and in his presence, I declared that I had given the money to Katerina Ivanovna for the funeral and not to Sofya Semyonovna and that I had no acquaintance with Sofya Semyonovna and had never seen her before, indeed. At the same time I added that he, Pyotr Petrovitch Luzhin, with all his virtues, was not worth Sofya Semyonovna's little finger, though he spoke so ill of her. To his question—would I let Sofya Semyonovna sit down beside my sister, I answered that I had already done so that day. Irritated that my mother and sister were unwilling to quarrel with me at his insinuations, he gradually began being unpardonably rude to them. A final rupture took place and he was turned out of the house. All this happened yesterday evening. Now I beg your special attention: consider: if he had now succeeded in proving that Sofya Semyonovna was a thief, he would have shown to my mother and sister that he was almost right in his suspicions, that he had reason to be angry at my putting my sister on a level with Sofya Semyonovna, that, in attacking me, he was protecting and preserving the honour of my sister, his betrothed. In fact he might even, through all this, have been able to estrange me from my family, and no doubt he hoped to be restored to favour with them; to say nothing of revenging himself on me personally, for he has grounds for supposing that the honour and happiness of Sofya Semyonovna are very precious to me. That was what he was working for! That's how I understand it. That's the whole reason for it and there can be no other!"

It was like this, or somewhat like this, that Raskolnikov wound up his speech which was followed very attentively, though often interrupted by exclamations from his audience. But in spite of interruptions he spoke clearly, calmly, exactly, firmly. His decisive voice, his tone of conviction and his stern face made a great impression on everyone.

"Yes, yes, that's it," Lebeziatnikov assented gleefully, "that must be it, for he asked me, as soon as Sofya Semyonovna came into our room, whether you were here, whether I had seen you among Katerina Ivanovna's guests. He called me aside to the window and asked me in secret. It was essential for him that you should be here! That's it, that's it!"

Luzhin smiled contemptuously and did not speak. But he was very pale. He seemed to be deliberating on some means of escape. Perhaps he would have been glad to give up everything and get away, but at the moment this was scarcely possible. It would have implied admitting the truth of the accusations brought against him. Moreover, the company, which had already been excited by drink, was now too much stirred to allow it. The commissariat clerk, though indeed he had not grasped the whole position, was shouting louder than anyone and was making some suggestions very unpleasant to Luzhin. But not all those present were drunk; lodgers came in from all the rooms. The three Poles were tremendously excited and were continually shouting at him: "The *pan* is a *lajdak*!" and muttering threats in Polish. Sonia had been listening with strained attention, though she too seemed unable to grasp it all; she seemed as though she had just returned to consciousness. She did not take her eyes off Raskolnikov, feeling that all her safety lay in him. Katerina Ivanovna breathed hard and painfully and seemed fearfully exhausted. Amalia Ivanovna stood looking more stupid than anyone, with her mouth wide open, unable to make out what had happened. She only saw that Pyotr Petrovitch had somehow come to grief.

Raskolnikov was attempting to speak again, but they did not let him. Everyone was crowding round Luzhin with threats and shouts of abuse. But Pyotr Petrovitch was not intimidated. Seeing that his accusation of Sonia had completely failed, he had recourse to insolence:

"Allow me, gentlemen, allow me! Don't squeeze, let me pass!" he said, making his way through the crowd. "And no threats, if you please! I assure you it will be useless, you will gain nothing by it. On the contrary, you'll have to answer, gentlemen, for violently obstructing the course of justice. The thief has been more than unmasked, and I shall prosecute. Our judges are not so blind and... not so drunk, and will not believe the testimony of two notorious infidels, agitators, and atheists, who accuse me from motives of personal revenge which they are foolish enough to admit.... Yes, allow me to pass!"

"Don't let me find a trace of you in my room! Kindly leave at once, and everything is at an end between us! When I think of the trouble I've been taking, the way I've been expounding... all this fortnight!"

"I told you myself to-day that I was going, when you tried to keep me; now I will simply add that you are a fool. I advise you to see a doctor for your brains and your short sight. Let me pass, gentlemen!"

He forced his way through. But the commissariat clerk was unwilling to let him off so easily: he picked up a glass from the table, brandished it in the air and flung it at Pyotr Petrovitch; but the glass flew straight at Amalia Ivanovna. She screamed, and the clerk, overbalancing, fell heavily under the table. Pyotr Petrovitch made his way to his room and half an hour later had left the house. Sonia, timid by nature, had felt before that day that she could be ill-treated more easily than anyone, and that she could be wronged with impunity. Yet till that moment she had fancied that she might escape misfortune by care, gentleness and submissiveness before everyone. Her disappointment was too great. She could, of course, bear with patience and almost without murmur anything, even this. But for the first minute she felt it too bitter. In spite of her triumph and her justification—when her first terror and stupefaction had passed and she could understand it all clearly—the feeling of her helplessness and of the wrong done to her made her heart throb with anguish and she was overcome with hysterical weeping. At last, unable to bear any more, she rushed out of the room and ran home, almost immediately after Luzhin's departure. When amidst loud laughter the glass flew at Amalia Ivanovna, it was more than the landlady could endure. With a shriek she rushed like a fury at Katerina Ivanovna, considering her to blame for everything.

"Out of my lodgings! At once! Quick march!"

And with these words she began snatching up everything she could lay her hands on that belonged to Katerina Ivanovna, and throwing it on the floor. Katerina Ivanovna, pale, almost fainting, and gasping for breath, jumped up from the bed where she had sunk in exhaustion and darted at Amalia Ivanovna. But the battle was too unequal: the landlady waved her away like a feather.

"What! As though that godless calumny was not enough—this vile creature attacks me! What! On the day of my husband's funeral I am turned out of my lodging! After eating my bread and salt she turns me into the street, with my orphans! Where am I to go?" wailed the poor woman, sobbing and gasping. "Good God!" she cried with flashing eyes, "is there no justice upon earth? Whom should you protect if not us orphans? We shall see! There is law and justice on earth, there is, I will find it! Wait a bit, godless creature! Polenka, stay with the children, I'll come back. Wait for me, if you have to wait in the street. We will see whether there is justice on earth!"

And throwing over her head that green shawl which Marmeladov had mentioned to Raskolnikov, Katerina Ivanovna squeezed her way through the disorderly and drunken crowd of lodgers who still filled the room, and, wailing and tearful, she ran into the street—with a vague intention of going at once somewhere to find justice. Polenka with the two little ones in her arms crouched, terrified, on the trunk in the corner of the room, where she waited trembling for her mother to come back. Amalia Ivanovna raged about the room, shrieking, lamenting and throwing everything she came across on the floor. The lodgers talked incoherently, some commented to the best of their ability on what had happened, others quarrelled and swore at one another, while others struck up a song....

"Now it's time for me to go," thought Raskolnikov. "Well, Sofya Semyonovna, we shall see what you'll say now!"

And he set off in the direction of Sonia's lodgings.

CHAPTER IV

Raskolnikov had been a vigorous and active champion of Sonia against Luzhin, although he had such a load of horror and anguish in his own heart. But having gone through so much in the morning, he found a sort of relief in a change of sensations, apart from the strong personal feeling which impelled him to defend Sonia. He was agitated too, especially at some moments, by the thought of his approaching interview with Sonia: he *had* to tell her who had killed Lizaveta. He knew the terrible suffering it would be to him and, as it were, brushed away the thought of it. So when he cried as he left Katerina Ivanovna's, "Well, Sofya Semyonovna, we shall see what you'll say now!" he was still superficially excited, still vigorous and defiant from his triumph over Luzhin. But, strange to say, by the time he reached Sonia's lodging, he felt a sudden impotence and fear. He stood still in hesitation at the door, asking himself the strange question: "Must he tell her who killed Lizaveta?" It was a strange question because he felt at the very time not only that he could not help telling her, but also that he could not put off the telling. He did not yet know why it must be so, he only *felt* it, and the agonising sense of his impotence before the inevitable almost crushed him. To cut short his hesitation and suffering, he quickly opened the door and looked at Sonia from the doorway. She was sitting with her elbows on the table and her face in her hands, but seeing Raskolnikov she got up at once and came to meet him as though she were expecting him.

"What would have become of me but for you?" she said quickly, meeting him in the middle of the room.

Evidently she was in haste to say this to him. It was what she had been waiting for.

Raskolnikov went to the table and sat down on the chair from which she had only just risen. She stood facing him, two steps away, just as she had done the day before.

"Well, Sonia?" he said, and felt that his voice was trembling, "it was all due to 'your social position and the habits associated with it.' Did you understand that just now?"

Her face showed her distress.

"Only don't talk to me as you did yesterday," she interrupted him. "Please don't begin it. There is misery enough without that."

She made haste to smile, afraid that he might not like the reproach.

"I was silly to come away from there. What is happening there now? I wanted to go back directly, but I kept thinking that... you would come."

He told her that Amalia Ivanovna was turning them out of their lodging and that Katerina Ivanovna had run off somewhere "to seek justice."

"My God!" cried Sonia, "let's go at once...."

And she snatched up her cape.

"It's everlastingly the same thing!" said Raskolnikov, irritably. "You've no thought except for them! Stay a little with me."

"But... Katerina Ivanovna?"

"You won't lose Katerina Ivanovna, you may be sure, she'll come to you herself since she has run out," he added peevishly. "If she doesn't find you here, you'll be blamed for it...."

Sonia sat down in painful suspense. Raskolnikov was silent, gazing at the floor and deliberating.

"This time Luzhin did not want to prosecute you," he began, not looking at Sonia, "but if he had wanted to, if it had suited his plans, he would have sent you to prison if it had not been for Lebeziatnikov and me. Ah?"

"Yes," she assented in a faint voice. "Yes," she repeated, preoccupied and distressed.

"But I might easily not have been there. And it was quite an accident Lebeziatnikov's turning up."

Sonia was silent.

"And if you'd gone to prison, what then? Do you remember what I said yesterday?"

Again she did not answer. He waited.

"I thought you would cry out again 'don't speak of it, leave off.'" Raskolnikov gave a laugh, but rather a forced one. "What, silence again?" he asked a minute later. "We must talk about something, you know. It would be interesting for me to know how you would decide a certain 'problem' as Lebeziatnikov would say." (He was beginning to lose the thread.) "No, really, I am serious. Imagine, Sonia, that you had known all Luzhin's intentions beforehand. Known, that is, for a fact, that they would be the ruin of Katerina Ivanovna and the children and yourself thrown in—since you don't count yourself for anything—Polenka too... for she'll go the same way. Well, if suddenly it all depended on your decision whether he or they should go on living, that is whether Luzhin should go on living and doing wicked things, or Katerina Ivanovna should die? How would you decide which of them was to die? I ask you?"

Sonia looked uneasily at him. There was something peculiar in this hesitating question, which seemed approaching something in a roundabout way.

"I felt that you were going to ask some question like that," she said, looking inquisitively at him.

"I dare say you did. But how is it to be answered?"

"Why do you ask about what could not happen?" said Sonia reluctantly.

"Then it would be better for Luzhin to go on living and doing wicked things? You haven't dared to decide even that!"

"But I can't know the Divine Providence.... And why do you ask what can't be answered? What's the use of such foolish questions? How could it happen that it should depend on my decision—who has made me a judge to decide who is to live and who is not to live?"

"Oh, if the Divine Providence is to be mixed up in it, there is no doing anything," Raskolnikov grumbled morosely.

"You'd better say straight out what you want!" Sonia cried in distress. "You are leading up to something again.... Can you have come simply to torture me?"

She could not control herself and began crying bitterly. He looked at her in gloomy misery. Five minutes passed.

"Of course you're right, Sonia," he said softly at last. He was suddenly changed. His tone of assumed arrogance and helpless defiance was gone. Even his voice was suddenly weak. "I told you yesterday that I was not coming to ask forgiveness and almost the first thing I've said is to ask forgiveness.... I said that about Luzhin and Providence for my own sake. I was asking forgiveness, Sonia...."

He tried to smile, but there was something helpless and incomplete in his pale smile. He bowed his head and hid his face in his hands.

And suddenly a strange, surprising sensation of a sort of bitter hatred for Sonia passed through his heart. As it were wondering and frightened of this sensation, he raised his head and looked intently at her; but he met her uneasy and painfully anxious eyes fixed on him; there was love in them; his hatred vanished like a phantom. It was not the real feeling; he had taken the one feeling for the other. It only meant that *that* minute had come.

He hid his face in his hands again and bowed his head. Suddenly he turned pale, got up from his chair, looked at Sonia, and without uttering a word sat down mechanically on her bed.

His sensations that moment were terribly like the moment when he had stood over the old woman with the axe in his hand and felt that "he must not lose another minute."

"What's the matter?" asked Sonia, dreadfully frightened.

He could not utter a word. This was not at all, not at all the way he had intended to "tell" and he did not understand what was happening to him now. She went up to him, softly, sat down on the bed beside him and waited, not taking her eyes off him. Her heart throbbed and sank. It was unendurable; he turned his deadly pale face to her. His lips worked, helplessly struggling to utter something. A pang of terror passed through Sonia's heart.

"What's the matter?" she repeated, drawing a little away from him.

"Nothing, Sonia, don't be frightened.... It's nonsense. It really is nonsense, if you think of it," he muttered, like a man in delirium. "Why have I come to torture you?" he added suddenly, looking at her. "Why, really? I keep asking myself that question, Sonia...."

He had perhaps been asking himself that question a quarter of an hour before, but now he spoke helplessly, hardly knowing what he said and feeling a continual tremor all over.

"Oh, how you are suffering!" she muttered in distress, looking intently at him.

"It's all nonsense.... Listen, Sonia." He suddenly smiled, a pale helpless smile for two seconds. "You remember what I meant to tell you yesterday?"

Sonia waited uneasily.

"I said as I went away that perhaps I was saying good-bye for ever, but that if I came to-day I would tell you who... who killed Lizaveta."

She began trembling all over.

"Well, here I've come to tell you."

"Then you really meant it yesterday?" she whispered with difficulty. "How do you know?" she asked quickly, as though suddenly regaining her reason.

Sonia's face grew paler and paler, and she breathed painfully.

"I know."

She paused a minute.

"Have they found him?" she asked timidly.

"No."

"Then how do you know about *it*?" she asked again, hardly audibly and again after a minute's pause.

He turned to her and looked very intently at her.

"Guess," he said, with the same distorted helpless smile.

A shudder passed over her.

"But you... why do you frighten me like this?" she said, smiling like a child.

"I must be a great friend of *his*... since I know," Raskolnikov went on, still gazing into her face, as though he could not turn his eyes away. "He... did not mean to kill that Lizaveta... he... killed her accidentally.... He meant to kill the old woman when she was alone and he went there... and then Lizaveta came in... he killed her too."

Another awful moment passed. Both still gazed at one another.

"You can't guess, then?" he asked suddenly, feeling as though he were flinging himself down from a steeple.

"N-no..." whispered Sonia.

"Take a good look."

As soon as he had said this again, the same familiar sensation froze his heart. He looked at her and all at once seemed to see in her face the face of Lizaveta. He remembered clearly the expression in Lizaveta's face, when he approached her with the axe and she stepped back to the wall, putting out her hand, with childish terror in her face, looking as little children do when they begin to be frightened of something, looking intently and uneasily at what frightens them, shrinking back and holding out their little hands on the point of crying. Almost the same thing happened now to Sonia. With the same helplessness and the same terror, she looked at him for a while and, suddenly putting out her left hand, pressed her fingers faintly against his breast and slowly began to get up from the bed, moving further from him and keeping her eyes fixed even more immovably on him. Her terror infected him. The same fear showed itself on his face. In the same way he stared at her and almost with the same *childish* smile.

"Have you guessed?" he whispered at last.

"Good God!" broke in an awful wail from her bosom.

She sank helplessly on the bed with her face in the pillows, but a moment later she got up, moved quickly to him, seized both his hands and, gripping them tight in her thin fingers, began looking into his face again with the same intent stare. In this last desperate look she tried to look into him and catch some last hope. But there was no hope; there was no doubt remaining; it was all true! Later on, indeed, when she recalled that moment, she thought it strange and wondered why she had seen at once that there was no doubt. She could not have said, for instance, that she had foreseen something of the sort—and yet now, as soon as he told her, she suddenly fancied that she had really foreseen this very thing.

"Stop, Sonia, enough! don't torture me," he begged her miserably.

It was not at all, not at all like this he had thought of telling her, but this is how it happened.

She jumped up, seeming not to know what she was doing, and, wringing her hands, walked into the middle of the room; but quickly went back and sat down again beside him, her shoulder almost touching his. All of a sudden she started as though she had been stabbed, uttered a cry and fell on her knees before him, she did not know why.

"What have you done—what have you done to yourself?" she said in despair, and, jumping up, she flung herself on his neck, threw her arms round him, and held him tightly.

Raskolnikov drew back and looked at her with a mournful smile.

"You are a strange girl, Sonia—you kiss me and hug me when I tell you about that.... You don't think what you are doing."

"There is no one—no one in the whole world now so unhappy as you!" she cried in a frenzy, not hearing what he said, and she suddenly broke into violent hysterical weeping.

A feeling long unfamiliar to him flooded his heart and softened it at once. He did not struggle against it. Two tears started into his eyes and hung on his eyelashes.

"Then you won't leave me, Sonia?" he said, looking at her almost with hope.

"No, no, never, nowhere!" cried Sonia. "I will follow you, I will follow you everywhere. Oh, my God! Oh, how miserable I am!... Why, why didn't I know you before! Why didn't you come before? Oh, dear!"

"Here I have come."

"Yes, now! What's to be done now?... Together, together!" she repeated as it were unconsciously, and she hugged him again. "I'll follow you to Siberia!"

He recoiled at this, and the same hostile, almost haughty smile came to his lips.

"Perhaps I don't want to go to Siberia yet, Sonia," he said.

Sonia looked at him quickly.

Again after her first passionate, agonising sympathy for the unhappy man the terrible idea of the murder overwhelmed her. In his changed tone she seemed to hear the murderer speaking. She looked at him bewildered. She knew nothing as yet, why, how, with what object it had been. Now all these questions rushed at once into her mind. And again she could not believe it: "He, he is a murderer! Could it be true?"

"What's the meaning of it? Where am I?" she said in complete bewilderment, as though still unable to recover herself. "How could you, you, a man like you.... How could you bring yourself to it?... What does it mean?"

"Oh, well—to plunder. Leave off, Sonia," he answered wearily, almost with vexation.

Sonia stood as though struck dumb, but suddenly she cried:

"You were hungry! It was... to help your mother? Yes?"

"No, Sonia, no," he muttered, turning away and hanging his head. "I was not so hungry.... I certainly did want to help my mother, but... that's not the real thing either.... Don't torture me, Sonia."

Sonia clasped her hands.

"Could it, could it all be true? Good God, what a truth! Who could believe it? And how could you give away your last farthing and yet rob and murder! Ah," she cried suddenly, "that money you gave Katerina Ivanovna... that money.... Can that money..."

"No, Sonia," he broke in hurriedly, "that money was not it. Don't worry yourself! That money my mother sent me and it came when I was ill, the day I gave it to you.... Razumihin saw it... he received it for me.... That money was mine—my own."

Sonia listened to him in bewilderment and did her utmost to comprehend.

"And *that* money.... I don't even know really whether there was any money," he added softly, as though reflecting. "I took a purse off her neck, made of chamois leather... a purse stuffed full of something... but I didn't look in it; I suppose I hadn't time.... And the things—chains and trinkets—I buried under a stone with the purse next morning in a yard off the V—— Prospect. They are all there now...."

Sonia strained every nerve to listen.

"Then why... why, you said you did it to rob, but you took nothing?" she asked quickly, catching at a straw.

"I don't know.... I haven't yet decided whether to take that money or not," he said, musing again; and, seeming to wake up with a start, he gave a brief ironical smile. "Ach, what silly stuff I am talking, eh?"

The thought flashed through Sonia's mind, wasn't he mad? But she dismissed it at once. "No, it was something else." She could make nothing of it, nothing.

"Do you know, Sonia," he said suddenly with conviction, "let me tell you: if I'd simply killed because I was hungry," laying stress on every word and looking enigmatically but sincerely at her, "I should be *happy* now. You must believe that! What would it matter to you," he cried a moment later with a sort of despair, "what would it matter to you if I were to confess that I did wrong? What do you gain by such a stupid triumph over me? Ah, Sonia, was it for that I've come to you to-day?"

Again Sonia tried to say something, but did not speak.

"I asked you to go with me yesterday because you are all I have left."

"Go where?" asked Sonia timidly.

"Not to steal and not to murder, don't be anxious," he smiled bitterly. "We are so different.... And you know, Sonia, it's only now, only this moment that I understand *where* I asked you to go with me yesterday! Yesterday when I said it I did not know where. I asked you for one thing, I came to you for one thing—not to leave me. You won't leave me, Sonia?"

She squeezed his hand.

"And why, why did I tell her? Why did I let her know?" he cried a minute later in despair, looking with infinite anguish at her. "Here you expect an explanation from me, Sonia; you are sitting and waiting for it, I see that. But what can I tell you? You won't understand and will only suffer misery... on my account! Well, you are crying and embracing me again. Why do you do it? Because I couldn't bear my burden and have come to throw it on another: you suffer too, and I shall feel better! And can you love such a mean wretch?"

"But aren't you suffering, too?" cried Sonia.

Again a wave of the same feeling surged into his heart, and again for an instant softened it.

"Sonia, I have a bad heart, take note of that. It may explain a great deal. I have come because I am bad. There are men who wouldn't have come. But I am a coward and... a mean wretch. But... never mind! That's not the point. I must speak now, but I don't know how to begin."

He paused and sank into thought.

"Ach, we are so different," he cried again, "we are not alike. And why, why did I come? I shall never forgive myself that."

"No, no, it was a good thing you came," cried Sonia. "It's better I should know, far better!"

He looked at her with anguish.

"What if it were really that?" he said, as though reaching a conclusion. "Yes, that's what it was! I wanted to become a Napoleon, that is why I killed her.... Do you understand now?"

"N-no," Sonia whispered naïvely and timidly. "Only speak, speak, I shall understand, I shall understand *in myself*!" she kept begging him.

"You'll understand? Very well, we shall see!" He paused and was for some time lost in meditation.

"It was like this: I asked myself one day this question—what if Napoleon, for instance, had happened to be in my place, and if he had not had Toulon nor Egypt nor the passage of Mont Blanc to begin his career with, but instead of all those picturesque and monumental things, there had simply been some ridiculous old hag, a pawnbroker, who had to be murdered too to get money from her trunk (for his career, you understand). Well, would he have brought himself to that if there had been no other means? Wouldn't he have felt a pang at its being so far from monumental and... and sinful, too? Well, I must tell you that I worried myself fearfully over that 'question' so that I was awfully ashamed when I guessed at last (all of a sudden, somehow) that it would not have given him the least pang, that it would not even have struck him that it was not monumental... that he would not have seen that there was anything in it to pause over, and that, if he had had no other way, he would have strangled her in a minute without thinking about it! Well, I too... left off thinking about it... murdered her, following his example. And that's exactly how it was! Do you think it funny? Yes, Sonia, the funniest thing of all is that perhaps that's just how it was."

Sonia did not think it at all funny.

"You had better tell me straight out... without examples," she begged, still more timidly and scarcely audibly.

He turned to her, looked sadly at her and took her hands.

"You are right again, Sonia. Of course that's all nonsense, it's almost all talk! You see, you know of course that my mother has scarcely anything, my sister happened to have a good education and was condemned to drudge as a governess. All their hopes were centered on me. I was a student, but I couldn't keep myself at the university and was forced for a time to leave it. Even if I had lingered on like that, in ten or twelve years I might (with luck) hope to be some sort of teacher or clerk with a salary of a thousand roubles" (he repeated it as though it were a lesson) "and by that time my mother would be worn out with grief and anxiety and I could not succeed in keeping her in comfort while my sister... well, my sister might well have fared worse! And it's a hard thing to pass everything by all one's life, to turn one's back upon everything, to forget one's mother and decorously accept the insults inflicted on one's sister. Why should one? When one has buried them to burden oneself with others—wife and children—and to leave them again without a farthing? So I resolved to gain possession of the old woman's money and to use it for my first years without worrying my mother, to keep myself at the university and for a little while after leaving it—and to do this all on a broad, thorough scale, so as to build up a completely new career and enter upon a new life of independence.... Well... that's all.... Well, of course in killing the old woman I did wrong.... Well, that's enough."

He struggled to the end of his speech in exhaustion and let his head sink.

"Oh, that's not it, that's not it," Sonia cried in distress. "How could one... no, that's not right, not right."

"You see yourself that it's not right. But I've spoken truly, it's the truth."

"As though that could be the truth! Good God!"

"I've only killed a louse, Sonia, a useless, loathsome, harmful creature."

"A human being—a louse!"

"I too know it wasn't a louse," he answered, looking strangely at her. "But I am talking nonsense, Sonia," he added. "I've been talking nonsense a long time.... That's not it, you are right there. There were quite, quite other causes for it! I haven't talked to anyone for so long, Sonia.... My head aches dreadfully now."

His eyes shone with feverish brilliance. He was almost delirious; an uneasy smile strayed on his lips. His terrible exhaustion could be seen through his excitement. Sonia saw how he was suffering. She too was growing dizzy. And he talked so strangely; it seemed somehow comprehensible, but yet... "But how, how! Good God!" And she wrung her hands in despair.

"No, Sonia, that's not it," he began again suddenly, raising his head, as though a new and sudden train of thought had struck and as it were roused him—"that's not it! Better... imagine—yes, it's certainly better—imagine that I am vain, envious, malicious, base, vindictive and... well, perhaps with a tendency to insanity. (Let's have it all out at once! They've talked of madness already, I noticed.) I told you just now I could not keep myself at the university. But do you know that perhaps I might have done? My mother would have sent me what I needed for the fees and I could have earned enough for clothes, boots and food, no doubt. Lessons had turned up at half a rouble. Razumihin works! But I turned sulky and wouldn't. (Yes, sulkiness, that's the right word for it!) I sat in my room like a spider. You've been in my den, you've seen it.... And do you know, Sonia, that low ceilings and tiny rooms cramp the soul and the mind? Ah, how I hated that garret! And yet I wouldn't go out of it! I wouldn't on purpose! I didn't go out for days together, and I wouldn't work, I wouldn't even eat, I just lay there doing nothing. If Nastasya brought me anything, I ate it, if she didn't, I went all day without; I wouldn't ask, on purpose, from sulkiness! At night I had no light, I lay in the dark and I wouldn't earn money for candles. I ought to have studied, but I sold my books; and the dust lies an inch thick on the notebooks on my table. I preferred lying still and thinking. And I kept thinking.... And I had dreams all the time, strange dreams of all sorts, no need to describe! Only then I began to fancy that... No, that's not it! Again I am telling you wrong! You see I kept asking myself then: why am I so stupid that if others are stupid—and I know they are—yet I won't be wiser? Then I saw, Sonia, that if one waits for everyone to get wiser it will take too long.... Afterwards I understood that that would never come to pass, that men won't change and that nobody can alter it and that it's not worth wasting effort over it. Yes, that's so. That's the law of their nature, Sonia,... that's so!... And I know now, Sonia, that whoever is strong in mind and spirit will have power over them. Anyone who is greatly daring is right in their eyes. He who despises most things will be a lawgiver among them and he who dares most of all will be most in the right! So it has been till now and so it will always be. A man must be blind not to see it!"

Though Raskolnikov looked at Sonia as he said this, he no longer cared whether she understood or not. The fever had complete hold of him; he was in a sort of gloomy ecstasy (he certainly had been too long without talking to anyone). Sonia felt that his gloomy creed had become his faith and code.

"I divined then, Sonia," he went on eagerly, "that power is only vouchsafed to the man who dares to stoop and pick it up. There is only one thing, one thing needful: one has only to dare! Then for the first time in my life an idea took shape in my mind which no one had ever thought of before me, no one! I saw clear as daylight how strange it is that not a single person living in this mad world has had the daring to go straight for it all and send it flying to the devil! I... I wanted *to have the daring*... and I killed her. I only wanted to have the daring, Sonia! That was the whole cause of it!"

"Oh hush, hush," cried Sonia, clasping her hands. "You turned away from God and God has smitten you, has given you over to the devil!"

"Then Sonia, when I used to lie there in the dark and all this became clear to me, was it a temptation of the devil, eh?"

"Hush, don't laugh, blasphemer! You don't understand, you don't understand! Oh God! He won't understand!"

"Hush, Sonia! I am not laughing. I know myself that it was the devil leading me. Hush, Sonia, hush!" he repeated with gloomy insistence. "I know it all, I have thought it all over and over and whispered it all over to myself, lying there in the dark.... I've argued it all over with myself, every point of it, and I know it all, all! And how sick, how sick I was then of going over it all! I have kept wanting to forget it and make a new beginning, Sonia, and leave off thinking. And you don't suppose that I went into it headlong like a fool? I went into it like a wise man, and that was just my destruction. And you mustn't suppose that I didn't know, for instance, that if I began to question myself whether I had the right to gain power—I certainly hadn't the right—or that if I asked myself whether a human being is a louse it proved that it wasn't so for me, though it might be for a man who would go straight to his goal without asking questions.... If I worried myself all those days, wondering whether Napoleon would have done it or not, I felt clearly of course that I wasn't Napoleon. I had to endure all the agony of that battle of ideas, Sonia, and I longed to throw it off: I wanted to murder without casuistry, to murder for my own sake, for myself alone! I didn't want to lie about it even to myself. It wasn't to help my mother I did the murder—that's nonsense—I didn't do the murder to gain wealth and power and to become a benefactor of mankind. Nonsense! I simply did it; I did the murder for myself, for myself alone, and whether I became a benefactor to others, or spent my life like a spider catching men in my web and sucking the life out of men, I couldn't have cared at that moment.... And it was not the money I wanted, Sonia, when I did it. It was not so much the money I wanted, but something else.... I know it all now.... Understand me! Perhaps I should never have committed a murder again. I wanted to find out something else; it was something else led me on. I wanted to find out then and quickly whether I was a louse like everybody else or a man. Whether I can step over barriers or not, whether I dare stoop to pick up or not, whether I am a trembling creature or whether I have the *right*..."

535

"To kill? Have the right to kill?" Sonia clasped her hands.

"Ach, Sonia!" he cried irritably and seemed about to make some retort, but was contemptuously silent. "Don't interrupt me, Sonia. I want to prove one thing only, that the devil led me on then and he has shown me since that I had not the right to take that path, because I am just such a louse as all the rest. He was mocking me and here I've come to you now! Welcome your guest! If I were not a louse, should I have come to you? Listen: when I went then to the old woman's I only went to *try*.... You may be sure of that!"

"And you murdered her!"

"But how did I murder her? Is that how men do murders? Do men go to commit a murder as I went then? I will tell you some day how I went! Did I murder the old woman? I murdered myself, not her! I crushed myself once for all, for ever.... But it was the devil that killed that old woman, not I. Enough, enough, Sonia, enough! Let me be!" he cried in a sudden spasm of agony, "let me be!"

He leaned his elbows on his knees and squeezed his head in his hands as in a vise.

"What suffering!" A wail of anguish broke from Sonia.

"Well, what am I to do now?" he asked, suddenly raising his head and looking at her with a face hideously distorted by despair.

"What are you to do?" she cried, jumping up, and her eyes that had been full of tears suddenly began to shine. "Stand up!" (She seized him by the shoulder, he got up, looking at her almost bewildered.) "Go at once, this very minute, stand at the cross-roads, bow down, first kiss the earth which you have defiled and then bow down to all the world and say to all men aloud, 'I am a murderer!' Then God will send you life again. Will you go, will you go?" she asked him, trembling all over, snatching his two hands, squeezing them tight in hers and gazing at him with eyes full of fire.

He was amazed at her sudden ecstasy.

"You mean Siberia, Sonia? I must give myself up?" he asked gloomily.

"Suffer and expiate your sin by it, that's what you must do."

"No! I am not going to them, Sonia!"

"But how will you go on living? What will you live for?" cried Sonia, "how is it possible now? Why, how can you talk to your mother? (Oh, what will become of them now?) But what am I saying? You have abandoned your mother and your sister already. He has abandoned them already! Oh, God!" she cried, "why, he knows it all himself. How, how can he live by himself! What will become of you now?"

"Don't be a child, Sonia," he said softly. "What wrong have I done them? Why should I go to them? What should I say to them? That's only a phantom.... They destroy men by millions themselves and look on it as a virtue. They are knaves and scoundrels, Sonia! I am not going to them. And what should I say to them—that I murdered her, but did not dare to take the money and hid it under a stone?" he added with a bitter smile. "Why, they would laugh at me, and would call me a fool for not getting it. A coward and a fool! They wouldn't understand and they don't deserve to understand. Why should I go to them? I won't. Don't be a child, Sonia...."

"It will be too much for you to bear, too much!" she repeated, holding out her hands in despairing supplication.

"Perhaps I've been unfair to myself," he observed gloomily, pondering, "perhaps after all I am a man and not a louse and I've been in too great a hurry to condemn myself. I'll make another fight for it."

A haughty smile appeared on his lips.

"What a burden to bear! And your whole life, your whole life!"

"I shall get used to it," he said grimly and thoughtfully. "Listen," he began a minute later, "stop crying, it's time to talk of the facts: I've come to tell you that the police are after me, on my track...."

"Ach!" Sonia cried in terror.

"Well, why do you cry out? You want me to go to Siberia and now you are frightened? But let me tell you: I shall not give myself up. I shall make a struggle for it and they won't do anything to me. They've no real evidence. Yesterday I was in great danger and believed I was lost; but to-day things are going better. All the facts they know can be explained two ways, that's to say I can turn their accusations to my credit, do you understand? And I shall, for I've learnt my lesson. But they will certainly arrest me. If it had not been for something that happened, they would have done so to-day for certain; perhaps even now they will arrest me to-day.... But that's no matter, Sonia; they'll let me out again... for there isn't any real proof against me, and there won't be, I give you my word for it. And they can't convict a man on what they have against me. Enough.... I only tell you that you may know.... I will try to manage somehow to put it to my mother and sister so that they won't be frightened.... My sister's future is secure, however, now, I believe... and my mother's must be too.... Well, that's all. Be careful, though. Will you come and see me in prison when I am there?"

"Oh, I will, I will."

They sat side by side, both mournful and dejected, as though they had been cast up by the tempest alone on some deserted shore. He looked at Sonia and felt how great was her love for him, and strange to say he felt it suddenly burdensome and painful to be so loved. Yes, it was a strange and awful sensation! On his way to see Sonia he had felt that all his hopes rested on her; he expected to be rid of at least part of his suffering, and now, when all her heart turned towards him, he suddenly felt that he was immeasurably unhappier than before.

"Sonia," he said, "you'd better not come and see me when I am in prison."

Sonia did not answer, she was crying. Several minutes passed.

"Have you a cross on you?" she asked, as though suddenly thinking of it.

He did not at first understand the question.

"No, of course not. Here, take this one, of cypress wood. I have another, a copper one that belonged to Lizaveta. I changed with Lizaveta: she gave me her cross and I gave her my little ikon. I will wear Lizaveta's now and give you this. Take it... it's mine! It's mine, you know," she begged him. "We will go to suffer together, and together we will bear our cross!"

"Give it me," said Raskolnikov.

He did not want to hurt her feelings. But immediately he drew back the hand he held out for the cross.

"Not now, Sonia. Better later," he added to comfort her.

"Yes, yes, better," she repeated with conviction, "when you go to meet your suffering, then put it on. You will come to me, I'll put it on you, we will pray and go together."

At that moment someone knocked three times at the door.

"Sofya Semyonovna, may I come in?" they heard in a very familiar and polite voice.

Sonia rushed to the door in a fright. The flaxen head of Mr. Lebeziatnikov appeared at the door.

CHAPTER V

Lebeziatnikov looked perturbed.

"I've come to you, Sofya Semyonovna," he began. "Excuse me... I thought I should find you," he said, addressing Raskolnikov suddenly, "that is, I didn't mean anything... of that sort... But I just thought... Katerina Ivanovna has gone out of her mind," he blurted out suddenly, turning from Raskolnikov to Sonia.

Sonia screamed.

"At least it seems so. But... we don't know what to do, you see! She came back—she seems to have been turned out somewhere, perhaps beaten.... So it seems at least,... She had run to your father's former chief, she didn't find him at home: he was dining at some other general's.... Only fancy, she rushed off there, to the other general's, and, imagine, she was so persistent that she managed to get the chief to see her, had him fetched out from dinner, it seems. You can imagine what happened. She was turned out, of course; but, according to her own story, she abused him and threw something at him. One may well believe it.... How it is she wasn't taken up, I can't understand! Now she is telling everyone, including Amalia Ivanovna; but it's difficult to understand her, she is screaming and flinging herself about.... Oh yes, she shouts that since everyone has abandoned her, she will take the children and go into the street with a barrel-organ, and the children will sing and dance, and she too, and collect money, and will go every day under the general's window... 'to let everyone see well-born children, whose father was an official, begging in the street.' She keeps beating the children and they are all crying. She is teaching Lida to sing 'My Village,' the boy to dance, Polenka the same. She is tearing up all the clothes, and making them little caps like actors; she means to carry a tin basin and make it tinkle, instead of music.... She won't listen to anything.... Imagine the state of things! It's beyond anything!"

Lebeziatnikov would have gone on, but Sonia, who had heard him almost breathless, snatched up her cloak and hat, and ran out of the room, putting on her things as she went. Raskolnikov followed her and Lebeziatnikov came after him.

"She has certainly gone mad!" he said to Raskolnikov, as they went out into the street. "I didn't want to frighten Sofya Semyonovna, so I said 'it seemed like it,' but there isn't a doubt of it. They say that in consumption the tubercles sometimes occur in the brain; it's a pity I know nothing of medicine. I did try to persuade her, but she wouldn't listen."

"Did you talk to her about the tubercles?"

"Not precisely of the tubercles. Besides, she wouldn't have understood! But what I say is, that if you convince a person logically that he has nothing to cry about, he'll stop crying. That's clear. Is it your conviction that he won't?"

"Life would be too easy if it were so," answered Raskolnikov.

"Excuse me, excuse me; of course it would be rather difficult for Katerina Ivanovna to understand, but do you know that in Paris they have been conducting serious experiments as to the possibility of curing the insane, simply by logical argument? One professor there, a scientific man of standing, lately dead, believed in the possibility of such treatment. His idea was that there's nothing really wrong with the physical organism of the insane, and that insanity is, so to say, a logical mistake, an error of judgment, an incorrect view of things. He gradually showed the madman his error and, would you believe it, they say he was successful? But as he made use of douches too, how far success was due to that treatment remains uncertain.... So it seems at least."

Raskolnikov had long ceased to listen. Reaching the house where he lived, he nodded to Lebeziatnikov and went in at the gate. Lebeziatnikov woke up with a start, looked about him and hurried on.

Raskolnikov went into his little room and stood still in the middle of it. Why had he come back here? He looked at the yellow and tattered paper, at the dust, at his sofa.... From the yard came a loud continuous knocking; someone seemed to be hammering... He went to the window, rose on tiptoe and looked out into the yard for a long time with an air of absorbed attention. But the yard was empty and he could not see who was hammering. In the house on the left he saw some open windows; on the window-sills were pots of sickly-looking geraniums. Linen was hung out of the windows... He knew it all by heart. He turned away and sat down on the sofa.

Never, never had he felt himself so fearfully alone!

Yes, he felt once more that he would perhaps come to hate Sonia, now that he had made her more miserable.

"Why had he gone to her to beg for her tears? What need had he to poison her life? Oh, the meanness of it!"

"I will remain alone," he said resolutely, "and she shall not come to the prison!"

Five minutes later he raised his head with a strange smile. That was a strange thought.

"Perhaps it really would be better in Siberia," he thought suddenly.

He could not have said how long he sat there with vague thoughts surging through his mind. All at once the door opened and Dounia came in. At first she stood still and looked at him from the doorway, just as he had done at Sonia; then she came in and sat down in the same place as yesterday, on the chair facing him. He looked silently and almost vacantly at her.

"Don't be angry, brother; I've only come for one minute," said Dounia.

Her face looked thoughtful but not stern. Her eyes were bright and soft. He saw that she too had come to him with love.

"Brother, now I know all, *all*. Dmitri Prokofitch has explained and told me everything. They are worrying and persecuting you through a stupid and contemptible suspicion.... Dmitri Prokofitch told me that there is no danger, and that you are wrong in looking upon it with such horror. I don't think so, and I fully understand how indignant you must be, and that that indignation may have a permanent effect on you. That's what I am afraid of. As for your cutting yourself off from us, I don't judge you, I don't venture to judge you, and forgive me for having blamed you for it. I feel that I too, if I had so great a trouble, should keep away from everyone. I shall tell mother nothing *of this*, but I shall talk about you continually and shall tell her from you that you will come very soon. Don't worry about her; *I* will set her mind at rest; but don't you try her too much—come once at least; remember that she is your mother. And now I have come simply to say" (Dounia began to get up) "that if you should need me or should need... all my life or anything... call me, and I'll come. Good-bye!"

She turned abruptly and went towards the door.

"Dounia!" Raskolnikov stopped her and went towards her. "That Razumihin, Dmitri Prokofitch, is a very good fellow."

Dounia flushed slightly.

"Well?" she asked, waiting a moment.

"He is competent, hardworking, honest and capable of real love.... Good-bye, Dounia."

Dounia flushed crimson, then suddenly she took alarm.

"But what does it mean, brother? Are we really parting for ever that you... give me such a parting message?"

"Never mind.... Good-bye."

He turned away, and walked to the window. She stood a moment, looked at him uneasily, and went out troubled.

No, he was not cold to her. There was an instant (the very last one) when he had longed to take her in his arms and *say good-bye* to her, and even *to tell* her, but he had not dared even to touch her hand.

"Afterwards she may shudder when she remembers that I embraced her, and will feel that I stole her kiss."

"And would *she* stand that test?" he went on a few minutes later to himself. "No, she wouldn't; girls like that can't stand things! They never do."

And he thought of Sonia.

There was a breath of fresh air from the window. The daylight was fading. He took up his cap and went out.

He could not, of course, and would not consider how ill he was. But all this continual anxiety and agony of mind could not but affect him. And if he were not lying in high fever it was perhaps just because this continual inner strain helped to keep him on his legs and in possession of his faculties. But this artificial excitement could not last long.

He wandered aimlessly. The sun was setting. A special form of misery had begun to oppress him of late. There was nothing poignant, nothing acute about it; but there was a feeling of permanence, of eternity about it; it brought a foretaste of hopeless years of this cold leaden misery, a foretaste of an eternity "on a square yard of space." Towards evening this sensation usually began to weigh on him more heavily.

"With this idiotic, purely physical weakness, depending on the sunset or something, one can't help doing something stupid! You'll go to Dounia, as well as to Sonia," he muttered bitterly.

He heard his name called. He looked round. Lebeziatnikov rushed up to him.

"Only fancy, I've been to your room looking for you. Only fancy, she's carried out her plan, and taken away the children. Sofya Semyonovna and I have had a job to find them. She is rapping on a frying-pan and making the children dance. The children are crying. They keep stopping at the cross-roads and in front of shops; there's a crowd of fools running after them. Come along!"

"And Sonia?" Raskolnikov asked anxiously, hurrying after Lebeziatnikov.

"Simply frantic. That is, it's not Sofya Semyonovna's frantic, but Katerina Ivanovna, though Sofya Semyonova's frantic too. But Katerina Ivanovna is absolutely frantic. I tell you she is quite mad. They'll be taken to the police. You can fancy what an effect that will have.... They are on the canal bank, near the bridge now, not far from Sofya Semyonovna's, quite close."

On the canal bank near the bridge and not two houses away from the one where Sonia lodged, there was a crowd of people, consisting principally of gutter children. The hoarse broken voice of Katerina Ivanovna could be heard from the bridge, and it certainly was a strange spectacle likely to attract a street crowd. Katerina Ivanovna in her old dress with the green shawl, wearing a torn straw hat, crushed in a hideous way on one side, was really frantic. She was exhausted and breathless. Her wasted consumptive face looked more suffering than ever, and indeed out of doors in the sunshine a consumptive always looks worse than at home. But her excitement did not flag, and every moment her irritation grew more intense. She rushed at the children, shouted at them, coaxed them, told them before the crowd how to dance and what to sing, began explaining to them why it was necessary, and driven to desperation by their not understanding, beat them.... Then she would make a rush at the crowd; if she noticed any decently dressed person stopping to look, she immediately appealed to him to see what these children "from a genteel, one may say aristocratic, house" had been brought to. If she heard laughter or jeering in the crowd, she would rush at once at the scoffers and begin squabbling with them. Some people laughed, others shook their heads, but everyone felt curious at the sight of the madwoman with the frightened children. The frying-pan of which Lebeziatnikov had spoken was not there, at least Raskolnikov did not see it. But instead of rapping on the pan, Katerina Ivanovna began clapping her wasted hands, when she made Lida and Kolya dance and Polenka sing. She too joined in the singing, but broke down at the second note with a fearful cough, which made her curse in despair and even shed tears. What made her most furious was the weeping and terror of Kolya and Lida. Some effort had been made to dress the children up as street singers are dressed. The boy had on a turban made of something red and white to look like a Turk. There had been no costume for Lida; she simply had a red knitted cap, or rather a night cap that had belonged to Marmeladov, decorated with a broken piece of white ostrich feather, which had been Katerina Ivanovna's grandmother's and had been preserved as a family possession. Polenka was in her everyday dress; she looked in timid perplexity at her mother, and kept at her side, hiding her tears. She dimly realised her mother's condition, and looked uneasily about her. She was terribly frightened of the street and the crowd. Sonia followed Katerina Ivanovna, weeping and beseeching her to return home, but Katerina Ivanovna was not to be persuaded.

"Leave off, Sonia, leave off," she shouted, speaking fast, panting and coughing. "You don't know what you ask; you are like a child! I've told you before that I am not coming back to that drunken German. Let everyone, let all Petersburg see the children begging in the streets, though their father was an honourable man who served all his life in truth and fidelity, and one may say died in the service." (Katerina Ivanovna had by now invented this fantastic story and thoroughly believed it.) "Let that wretch of a general see it! And you are silly, Sonia: what have we to eat? Tell me that. We have worried you enough, I won't go on so! Ah, Rodion Romanovitch, is that you?" she cried, seeing Raskolnikov and rushing up to him. "Explain to this silly girl, please, that nothing better could be done! Even organ-grinders earn their living, and everyone will see at once that we are different, that we are an honourable and bereaved family reduced to beggary. And that general will lose his post, you'll see! We shall perform under his windows every day, and if the Tsar drives by, I'll fall on my knees, put the children before me, show them to him, and say 'Defend us father.' He is the father of the fatherless, he is merciful, he'll protect us, you'll see, and that wretch of a general.... Lida, *tenez vous droite!* Kolya, you'll dance again. Why are you whimpering? Whimpering again! What are you afraid of, stupid? Goodness, what am I to do with them, Rodion Romanovitch? If you only knew how stupid they are! What's one to do with such children?"

And she, almost crying herself—which did not stop her uninterrupted, rapid flow of talk—pointed to the crying children. Raskolnikov tried to persuade her to go home, and even said, hoping to work on her vanity, that it was unseemly for her to be wandering about the streets like an organ-grinder, as she was intending to become the principal of a boarding-school.

"A boarding-school, ha-ha-ha! A castle in the air," cried Katerina Ivanovna, her laugh ending in a cough. "No, Rodion Romanovitch, that dream is over! All have forsaken us!... And that general.... You know, Rodion Romanovitch, I threw an inkpot at him—it happened to be standing in the waiting-room by the paper where you sign your name. I wrote my name, threw it at him and ran away. Oh, the scoundrels, the scoundrels! But enough of them, now I'll provide for the children myself, I won't bow down to anybody! She has had to bear enough for us!" she pointed to Sonia. "Polenka, how much have you got? Show me! What, only two farthings! Oh, the mean wretches! They give us nothing, only run after us, putting their tongues out. There, what is that blockhead laughing at?" (She pointed to a man in the crowd.) "It's all because Kolya here is so stupid; I have such a bother with him. What do you want, Polenka? Tell me in French, *parlez-moi français*. Why, I've taught you, you know some phrases. Else how are you to show that you are of good family, well brought-up children, and not at all like other organ-grinders? We aren't going to have a Punch and Judy show in the street, but to sing a genteel song.... Ah, yes,... What are we to sing? You keep putting me out, but we... you see, we are standing here, Rodion Romanovitch, to find something to sing and get money, something Kolya can dance to.... For, as you can fancy, our performance is all impromptu.... We must talk it over and rehearse it all thoroughly, and then we shall go to Nevsky, where there are far more people of good society, and we shall be noticed at once. Lida knows 'My Village' only, nothing but 'My Village,' and everyone sings that. We must sing something far more genteel.... Well, have you thought of anything, Polenka? If only you'd help your mother! My memory's quite gone, or I should have thought of something. We really can't sing 'An Hussar.' Ah, let us sing in French, 'Cinq sous,' I have taught it you, I have taught it you. And as it is in French, people will see at once that you are children of good family, and that will be much more touching.... You might sing 'Marlborough s'en va-t-en guerre,' for that's quite a child's song and is sung as a lullaby in all the aristocratic houses.

"*Marlborough s'en va-t-en guerre Ne sait quand reviendra...*" she began singing. "But no, better sing 'Cinq sous.' Now, Kolya, your hands on your hips, make haste, and you, Lida, keep turning the other way, and Polenka and I will sing and clap our hands!

"*Cinq sous, cinq sous Pour monter notre menage.*"

(Cough-cough-cough!) "Set your dress straight, Polenka, it's slipped down on your shoulders," she observed, panting from coughing. "Now it's particularly necessary to behave nicely and genteelly, that all may see that you are well-born children. I said at the time that the bodice should be cut longer, and made of two widths. It was your fault, Sonia, with your advice to make it shorter, and now you see the child is quite deformed by it.... Why, you're all crying again! What's the matter, stupids? Come, Kolya, begin. Make haste, make haste! Oh, what an unbearable child!

"Cinq sous, cinq sous.

"A policeman again! What do you want?"

A policeman was indeed forcing his way through the crowd. But at that moment a gentleman in civilian uniform and an overcoat—a solid-looking official of about fifty with a decoration on his neck (which delighted Katerina Ivanovna and had its effect on the policeman)—approached and without a word handed her a green three-rouble note. His face wore a look of genuine sympathy. Katerina Ivanovna took it and gave him a polite, even ceremonious, bow.

"I thank you, honoured sir," she began loftily. "The causes that have induced us (take the money, Polenka: you see there are generous and honourable people who are ready to help a poor gentlewoman in distress). You see, honoured sir, these orphans of good family—I might even say of aristocratic connections—and that wretch of a general sat eating grouse... and stamped at my disturbing him. 'Your excellency,' I said, 'protect the orphans, for you knew my late husband, Semyon Zaharovitch, and on the very day of his death the basest of scoundrels slandered his only daughter.'... That policeman again! Protect me," she cried to the official. "Why is that policeman edging up to me? We have only just run away from one of them. What do you want, fool?"

"It's forbidden in the streets. You mustn't make a disturbance."

"It's you're making a disturbance. It's just the same as if I were grinding an organ. What business is it of yours?"

"You have to get a licence for an organ, and you haven't got one, and in that way you collect a crowd. Where do you lodge?"

"What, a license?" wailed Katerina Ivanovna. "I buried my husband to-day. What need of a license?"

"Calm yourself, madam, calm yourself," began the official. "Come along; I will escort you.... This is no place for you in the crowd. You are ill."

"Honoured sir, honoured sir, you don't know," screamed Katerina Ivanovna. "We are going to the Nevsky.... Sonia, Sonia! Where is she? She is crying too! What's the matter with you all? Kolya, Lida, where are you going?" she cried suddenly in alarm. "Oh, silly children! Kolya, Lida, where are they off to?..."

Kolya and Lida, scared out of their wits by the crowd, and their mother's mad pranks, suddenly seized each other by the hand, and ran off at the sight of the policeman who wanted to take them away somewhere. Weeping and wailing, poor Katerina Ivanovna ran after them. She was a piteous and unseemly spectacle, as she ran, weeping and panting for breath. Sonia and Polenka rushed after them.

"Bring them back, bring them back, Sonia! Oh stupid, ungrateful children!... Polenka! catch them.... It's for your sakes I..."

She stumbled as she ran and fell down.

"She's cut herself, she's bleeding! Oh, dear!" cried Sonia, bending over her.

All ran up and crowded around. Raskolnikov and Lebeziatnikov were the first at her side, the official too hastened up, and behind him the policeman who muttered, "Bother!" with a gesture of impatience, feeling that the job was going to be a troublesome one.

"Pass on! Pass on!" he said to the crowd that pressed forward.

"She's dying," someone shouted.

"She's gone out of her mind," said another.

"Lord have mercy upon us," said a woman, crossing herself. "Have they caught the little girl and the boy? They're being brought back, the elder one's got them.... Ah, the naughty imps!"

When they examined Katerina Ivanovna carefully, they saw that she had not cut herself against a stone, as Sonia thought, but that the blood that stained the pavement red was from her chest.

"I've seen that before," muttered the official to Raskolnikov and Lebeziatnikov; "that's consumption; the blood flows and chokes the patient. I saw the same thing with a relative of my own not long ago... nearly a pint of blood, all in a minute.... What's to be done though? She is dying."

"This way, this way, to my room!" Sonia implored. "I live here!... See, that house, the second from here.... Come to me, make haste," she turned from one to the other. "Send for the doctor! Oh, dear!"

Thanks to the official's efforts, this plan was adopted, the policeman even helping to carry Katerina Ivanovna. She was carried to Sonia's room, almost unconscious, and laid on the bed. The blood was still flowing, but she seemed to be coming to herself. Raskolnikov, Lebeziatnikov, and the official accompanied Sonia into the room and were followed by the policeman, who first drove back the crowd which followed to the very door. Polenka came in holding Kolya and Lida, who were trembling and weeping. Several persons came in too from the Kapernaumovs' room; the landlord, a lame one-eyed man of strange appearance with whiskers and hair that stood up like a brush, his wife, a woman with an everlastingly scared expression, and several open-mouthed children with wonder-struck faces. Among these, Svidrigaïlov suddenly made his appearance. Raskolnikov looked at him with surprise, not understanding where he had come from and not having noticed him in the crowd. A doctor and priest wore spoken of. The official whispered to Raskolnikov that he thought it was too late now for the doctor, but he ordered him to be sent for. Kapernaumov ran himself.

Meanwhile Katerina Ivanovna had regained her breath. The bleeding ceased for a time. She looked with sick but intent and penetrating eyes at Sonia, who stood pale and trembling, wiping the sweat from her brow with a handkerchief. At last she asked to be raised. They sat her up on the bed, supporting her on both sides.

"Where are the children?" she said in a faint voice. "You've brought them, Polenka? Oh the sillies! Why did you run away.... Och!"

Once more her parched lips were covered with blood. She moved her eyes, looking about her.

"So that's how you live, Sonia! Never once have I been in your room."

She looked at her with a face of suffering.

"We have been your ruin, Sonia. Polenka, Lida, Kolya, come here! Well, here they are, Sonia, take them all! I hand them over to you, I've had enough! The ball is over." (Cough!) "Lay me down, let me die in peace."

They laid her back on the pillow.

"What, the priest? I don't want him. You haven't got a rouble to spare. I have no sins. God must forgive me without that. He knows how I have suffered.... And if He won't forgive me, I don't care!"

She sank more and more into uneasy delirium. At times she shuddered, turned her eyes from side to side, recognised everyone for a minute, but at once sank into delirium again. Her breathing was hoarse and difficult, there was a sort of rattle in her throat.

"I said to him, your excellency," she ejaculated, gasping after each word. "That Amalia Ludwigovna, ah! Lida, Kolya, hands on your hips, make haste! *Glissez, glissez! pas de basque!* Tap with your heels, be a graceful child!

"*Du hast Diamanten und Perlen*

"What next? That's the thing to sing.

"*Du hast die schonsten Augen Madchen, was willst du mehr?*

"What an idea! *Was willst du mehr?* What things the fool invents! Ah, yes!

"In the heat of midday in the vale of Dagestan.

"Ah, how I loved it! I loved that song to distraction, Polenka! Your father, you know, used to sing it when we were engaged.... Oh those days! Oh that's the thing for us to sing! How does it go? I've forgotten. Remind me! How was it?"

She was violently excited and tried to sit up. At last, in a horribly hoarse, broken voice, she began, shrieking and gasping at every word, with a look of growing terror.

"In the heat of midday!... in the vale!... of Dagestan!... With lead in my breast!..."

"Your excellency!" she wailed suddenly with a heart-rending scream and a flood of tears, "protect the orphans! You have been their father's guest... one may say aristocratic...." She started, regaining consciousness, and gazed at all with a sort of terror, but at once recognised Sonia.

"Sonia, Sonia!" she articulated softly and caressingly, as though surprised to find her there. "Sonia darling, are you here, too?"

They lifted her up again.

"Enough! It's over! Farewell, poor thing! I am done for! I am broken!" she cried with vindictive despair, and her head fell heavily back on the pillow.

She sank into unconsciousness again, but this time it did not last long. Her pale, yellow, wasted face dropped back, her mouth fell open, her leg moved convulsively, she gave a deep, deep sigh and died.

Sonia fell upon her, flung her arms about her, and remained motionless with her head pressed to the dead woman's wasted bosom. Polenka threw herself at her mother's feet, kissing them and weeping violently. Though Kolya and Lida did not understand what had happened, they had a feeling that it was something terrible; they put their hands on each other's little shoulders, stared straight at one another and both at once opened their mouths and began screaming. They were both still in their fancy dress; one in a turban, the other in the cap with the ostrich feather.

And how did "the certificate of merit" come to be on the bed beside Katerina Ivanovna? It lay there by the pillow; Raskolnikov saw it.

He walked away to the window. Lebeziatnikov skipped up to him.

"She is dead," he said.

"Rodion Romanovitch, I must have two words with you," said Svidrigaïlov, coming up to them. Lebeziatnikov at once made room for him and delicately withdrew. Svidrigaïlov drew Raskolnikov further away.

"I will undertake all the arrangements, the funeral and that. You know it's a question of money and, as I told you, I have plenty to spare. I will put those two little ones and Polenka into some good orphan asylum, and I will settle fifteen hundred roubles to be paid to each on coming of age, so that Sofya Semyonovna need have no anxiety about them. And I will pull her out of the mud too, for she is a good girl, isn't she? So tell Avdotya Romanovna that that is how I am spending her ten thousand."

"What is your motive for such benevolence?" asked Raskolnikov.

"Ah! you sceptical person!" laughed Svidrigaïlov. "I told you I had no need of that money. Won't you admit that it's simply done from humanity? She wasn't 'a louse,' you know" (he pointed to the corner where the dead woman lay), "was she, like some old pawnbroker woman? Come, you'll agree, is Luzhin to go on living, and doing wicked things or is she to die? And if I didn't help them, Polenka would go the same way."

He said this with an air of a sort of gay winking slyness, keeping his eyes fixed on Raskolnikov, who turned white and cold, hearing his own phrases, spoken to Sonia. He quickly stepped back and looked wildly at Svidrigaïlov.

"How do you know?" he whispered, hardly able to breathe.

"Why, I lodge here at Madame Resslich's, the other side of the wall. Here is Kapernaumov, and there lives Madame Resslich, an old and devoted friend of mine. I am a neighbour."

"You?"

"Yes," continued Svidrigaïlov, shaking with laughter. "I assure you on my honour, dear Rodion Romanovitch, that you have interested me enormously. I told you we should become friends, I foretold it. Well, here we have. And you will see what an accommodating person I am. You'll see that you can get on with me!"

PART VI

CHAPTER I

A strange period began for Raskolnikov: it was as though a fog had fallen upon him and wrapped him in a dreary solitude from which there was no escape. Recalling that period long after, he believed that his mind had been clouded at times, and that it had continued so, with intervals, till the final catastrophe. He was convinced that he had been mistaken about many things at that time, for instance as to the date of certain events. Anyway, when he tried later on to piece his recollections together, he learnt a great deal about himself from what other people told him. He had mixed up incidents and had explained events as due to circumstances which existed only in his imagination. At times he was a prey to agonies of morbid uneasiness, amounting sometimes to panic. But he remembered, too, moments, hours, perhaps whole days, of complete apathy, which came upon him as a reaction from his previous terror and might be compared with the abnormal insensibility, sometimes seen in the dying. He seemed to be trying in that latter stage to escape from a full and clear understanding of his position. Certain essential facts which required immediate consideration were particularly irksome to him. How glad he would have been to be free from some cares, the neglect of which would have threatened him with complete, inevitable ruin.

He was particularly worried about Svidrigaïlov, he might be said to be permanently thinking of Svidrigaïlov. From the time of Svidrigaïlov's too menacing and unmistakable words in Sonia's room at the moment of Katerina Ivanovna's death, the normal working of his mind seemed to break down. But although this new fact caused him extreme uneasiness, Raskolnikov was in no hurry for an explanation of it. At times, finding himself in a solitary and remote part of the town, in some wretched eating-house, sitting alone lost in thought, hardly knowing how he had come there, he suddenly thought of Svidrigaïlov. He recognised suddenly, clearly, and with dismay that he ought at once to come to an understanding with that man and to make what terms he could. Walking outside the city gates one day, he positively fancied that they had fixed a meeting there, that he was waiting for Svidrigaïlov. Another time he woke up before daybreak lying on the ground under some bushes and could not at first understand how he had come there.

But during the two or three days after Katerina Ivanovna's death, he had two or three times met Svidrigaïlov at Sonia's lodging, where he had gone aimlessly for a moment. They exchanged a few words and made no reference to the vital subject, as though they were tacitly agreed not to speak of it for a time.

Katerina Ivanovna's body was still lying in the coffin, Svidrigaïlov was busy making arrangements for the funeral. Sonia too was very busy. At their last meeting Svidrigaïlov informed Raskolnikov that he had made an arrangement, and a very satisfactory one, for Katerina Ivanovna's children; that he had, through certain connections, succeeded in getting hold of certain personages by whose help the three orphans could be at once placed in very suitable institutions; that the money he had settled on them had been of great assistance, as it is much easier to place orphans with some property than destitute ones. He said something too about Sonia and promised to come himself in a day or two to see Raskolnikov, mentioning that "he would like to consult with him, that there were things they must talk over...."

This conversation took place in the passage on the stairs. Svidrigaïlov looked intently at Raskolnikov and suddenly, after a brief pause, dropping his voice, asked: "But how is it, Rodion Romanovitch; you don't seem yourself? You look and you listen, but you don't seem to understand. Cheer up! We'll talk things over; I am only sorry, I've so much to do of my own business and other people's. Ah, Rodion Romanovitch," he added suddenly, "what all men need is fresh air, fresh air... more than anything!"

He moved to one side to make way for the priest and server, who were coming up the stairs. They had come for the requiem service. By Svidrigaïlov's orders it was sung twice a day punctually. Svidrigaïlov went his way. Raskolnikov stood still a moment, thought, and followed the priest into Sonia's room. He stood at the door. They began quietly, slowly and mournfully singing the service. From his childhood the thought of death and the presence of death had something oppressive and mysteriously awful; and it was long since he had heard the requiem service. And there was something else here as well, too awful and disturbing. He looked at the children:

they were all kneeling by the coffin; Polenka was weeping. Behind them Sonia prayed, softly and, as it were, timidly weeping.

"These last two days she hasn't said a word to me, she hasn't glanced at me," Raskolnikov thought suddenly. The sunlight was bright in the room; the incense rose in clouds; the priest read, "Give rest, oh Lord...." Raskolnikov stayed all through the service. As he blessed them and took his leave, the priest looked round strangely. After the service, Raskolnikov went up to Sonia. She took both his hands and let her head sink on his shoulder. This slight friendly gesture bewildered Raskolnikov. It seemed strange to him that there was no trace of repugnance, no trace of disgust, no tremor in her hand. It was the furthest limit of self-abnegation, at least so he interpreted it.

Sonia said nothing. Raskolnikov pressed her hand and went out. He felt very miserable. If it had been possible to escape to some solitude, he would have thought himself lucky, even if he had to spend his whole life there. But although he had almost always been by himself of late, he had never been able to feel alone. Sometimes he walked out of the town on to the high road, once he had even reached a little wood, but the lonelier the place was, the more he seemed to be aware of an uneasy presence near him. It did not frighten him, but greatly annoyed him, so that he made haste to return to the town, to mingle with the crowd, to enter restaurants and taverns, to walk in busy thoroughfares. There he felt easier and even more solitary. One day at dusk he sat for an hour listening to songs in a tavern and he remembered that he positively enjoyed it. But at last he had suddenly felt the same uneasiness again, as though his conscience smote him. "Here I sit listening to singing, is that what I ought to be doing?" he thought. Yet he felt at once that that was not the only cause of his uneasiness; there was something requiring immediate decision, but it was something he could not clearly understand or put into words. It was a hopeless tangle. "No, better the struggle again! Better Porfiry again... or Svidrigaïlov.... Better some challenge again... some attack. Yes, yes!" he thought. He went out of the tavern and rushed away almost at a run. The thought of Dounia and his mother suddenly reduced him almost to a panic. That night he woke up before morning among some bushes in Krestovsky Island, trembling all over with fever; he walked home, and it was early morning when he arrived. After some hours' sleep the fever left him, but he woke up late, two o'clock in the afternoon.

He remembered that Katerina Ivanovna's funeral had been fixed for that day, and was glad that he was not present at it. Nastasya brought him some food; he ate and drank with appetite, almost with greediness. His head was fresher and he was calmer than he had been for the last three days. He even felt a passing wonder at his previous attacks of panic.

The door opened and Razumihin came in.

"Ah, he's eating, then he's not ill," said Razumihin. He took a chair and sat down at the table opposite Raskolnikov.

He was troubled and did not attempt to conceal it. He spoke with evident annoyance, but without hurry or raising his voice. He looked as though he had some special fixed determination.

"Listen," he began resolutely. "As far as I am concerned, you may all go to hell, but from what I see, it's clear to me that I can't make head or tail of it; please don't think I've come to ask you questions. I don't want to know, hang it! If you begin telling me your secrets, I dare say I shouldn't stay to listen, I should go away cursing. I have only come to find out once for all whether it's a fact that you are mad? There is a conviction in the air that you are mad or very nearly so. I admit I've been disposed to that opinion myself, judging from your stupid, repulsive and quite inexplicable actions, and from your recent behavior to your mother and sister. Only a monster or a madman could treat them as you have; so you must be mad."

"When did you see them last?"

"Just now. Haven't you seen them since then? What have you been doing with yourself? Tell me, please. I've been to you three times already. Your mother has been seriously ill since yesterday. She had made up her mind to come to you; Avdotya Romanovna tried to prevent her; she wouldn't hear a word. 'If he is ill, if his mind is giving way, who can look after him like his mother?' she said. We all came here together, we couldn't let her come alone all the way. We kept begging her to be calm. We came in, you weren't here; she sat down, and stayed ten minutes, while we stood waiting in silence. She got up and said: 'If he's gone out, that is, if he is well, and has forgotten his mother, it's humiliating and unseemly for his mother to stand at his door begging for kindness.' She returned home and took to her bed; now she is in a fever. 'I see,' she said, 'that he has time for *his girl*.' She means by *your girl* Sofya Semyonovna, your betrothed or your mistress, I don't know. I went at once to Sofya Semyonovna's, for I wanted to know what was going on. I looked round, I saw the coffin, the children crying, and Sofya Semyonovna trying them on mourning dresses. No sign of you. I apologised, came away, and reported to Avdotya Romanovna. So that's all nonsense and you haven't got a girl; the most likely thing is that you are mad. But here you sit, guzzling boiled beef as though you'd not had a bite for three days. Though as far as that goes, madmen eat too, but though you have not said a word to me yet... you are not mad! That I'd swear!

Above all, you are not mad! So you may go to hell, all of you, for there's some mystery, some secret about it, and I don't intend to worry my brains over your secrets. So I've simply come to swear at you," he finished, getting up, "to relieve my mind. And I know what to do now."

"What do you mean to do now?"

"What business is it of yours what I mean to do?"

"You are going in for a drinking bout."

"How... how did you know?"

"Why, it's pretty plain."

Razumihin paused for a minute.

"You always have been a very rational person and you've never been mad, never," he observed suddenly with warmth. "You're right: I shall drink. Good-bye!"

And he moved to go out.

"I was talking with my sister—the day before yesterday, I think it was—about you, Razumihin."

"About me! But... where can you have seen her the day before yesterday?" Razumihin stopped short and even turned a little pale.

One could see that his heart was throbbing slowly and violently.

"She came here by herself, sat there and talked to me."

"She did!"

"Yes."

"What did you say to her... I mean, about me?"

"I told her you were a very good, honest, and industrious man. I didn't tell her you love her, because she knows that herself."

"She knows that herself?"

"Well, it's pretty plain. Wherever I might go, whatever happened to me, you would remain to look after them. I, so to speak, give them into your keeping, Razumihin. I say this because I know quite well how you love her, and am convinced of the purity of your heart. I know that she too may love you and perhaps does love you already. Now decide for yourself, as you know best, whether you need go in for a drinking bout or not."

"Rodya! You see... well.... Ach, damn it! But where do you mean to go? Of course, if it's all a secret, never mind.... But I... I shall find out the secret... and I am sure that it must be some ridiculous nonsense and that you've made it all up. Anyway you are a capital fellow, a capital fellow!..."

"That was just what I wanted to add, only you interrupted, that that was a very good decision of yours not to find out these secrets. Leave it to time, don't worry about it. You'll know it all in time when it must be. Yesterday a man said to me that what a man needs is fresh air, fresh air, fresh air. I mean to go to him directly to find out what he meant by that."

Razumihin stood lost in thought and excitement, making a silent conclusion.

"He's a political conspirator! He must be. And he's on the eve of some desperate step, that's certain. It can only be that! And... and Dounia knows," he thought suddenly.

"So Avdotya Romanovna comes to see you," he said, weighing each syllable, "and you're going to see a man who says we need more air, and so of course that letter... that too must have something to do with it," he concluded to himself.

"What letter?"

"She got a letter to-day. It upset her very much—very much indeed. Too much so. I began speaking of you, she begged me not to. Then... then she said that perhaps we should very soon have to part... then she began warmly thanking me for something; then she went to her room and locked herself in."

"She got a letter?" Raskolnikov asked thoughtfully.

"Yes, and you didn't know? hm..."

They were both silent.

"Good-bye, Rodion. There was a time, brother, when I.... Never mind, good-bye. You see, there was a time.... Well, good-bye! I must be off too. I am not going to drink. There's no need now.... That's all stuff!"

He hurried out; but when he had almost closed the door behind him, he suddenly opened it again, and said, looking away:

"Oh, by the way, do you remember that murder, you know Porfiry's, that old woman? Do you know the murderer has been found, he has confessed and given the proofs. It's one of those very workmen, the painter, only fancy! Do you remember I defended them here? Would you believe it, all that scene of fighting and laughing with his companions on the stairs while the porter and the two witnesses were going up, he got up on purpose to disarm suspicion. The cunning, the presence of mind of the young dog! One can hardly credit it; but it's his own explanation, he has confessed it all. And what a fool I was about it! Well, he's simply a genius of hypocrisy and resourcefulness in disarming the suspicions of the lawyers—so there's nothing much to wonder at, I suppose! Of course people like that are always possible. And the fact that he couldn't keep up the character, but confessed, makes him easier to believe in. But what a fool I was! I was frantic on their side!"

"Tell me, please, from whom did you hear that, and why does it interest you so?" Raskolnikov asked with unmistakable agitation.

"What next? You ask me why it interests me!... Well, I heard it from Porfiry, among others... It was from him I heard almost all about it."

"From Porfiry?"

"From Porfiry."

"What... what did he say?" Raskolnikov asked in dismay.

"He gave me a capital explanation of it. Psychologically, after his fashion."

"He explained it? Explained it himself?"

"Yes, yes; good-bye. I'll tell you all about it another time, but now I'm busy. There was a time when I fancied... But no matter, another time!... What need is there for me to drink now? You have made me drunk without wine. I am drunk, Rodya! Good-bye, I'm going. I'll come again very soon."

He went out.

"He's a political conspirator, there's not a doubt about it," Razumihin decided, as he slowly descended the stairs. "And he's drawn his sister in; that's quite, quite in keeping with Avdotya Romanovna's character. There are interviews between them!... She hinted at it too... So many of her words.... and hints... bear that meaning! And how else can all this tangle be explained? Hm! And I was almost thinking... Good heavens, what I thought! Yes, I took leave of my senses and I wronged him! It was his doing, under the lamp in the corridor that day. Pfoo! What a crude, nasty, vile idea on my part! Nikolay is a brick, for confessing.... And how clear it all is now! His illness then, all his strange actions... before this, in the university, how morose he used to be, how gloomy.... But what's the meaning now of that letter? There's something in that, too, perhaps. Whom was it from? I suspect...! No, I must find out!"

He thought of Dounia, realising all he had heard and his heart throbbed, and he suddenly broke into a run.

As soon as Razumihin went out, Raskolnikov got up, turned to the window, walked into one corner and then into another, as though forgetting the smallness of his room, and sat down again on the sofa. He felt, so to speak, renewed; again the struggle, so a means of escape had come.

"Yes, a means of escape had come! It had been too stifling, too cramping, the burden had been too agonising. A lethargy had come upon him at times. From the moment of the scene with Nikolay at Porfiry's he had been suffocating, penned in without hope of escape. After Nikolay's confession, on that very day had come the scene with Sonia; his behaviour and his last words had been utterly unlike anything he could have imagined beforehand; he had grown feebler, instantly and fundamentally! And he had agreed at the time with Sonia, he had agreed in his heart he could not go on living alone with such a thing on his mind!

"And Svidrigaïlov was a riddle... He worried him, that was true, but somehow not on the same point. He might still have a struggle to come with Svidrigaïlov. Svidrigaïlov, too, might be a means of escape; but Porfiry was a different matter.

"And so Porfiry himself had explained it to Razumihin, had explained it *psychologically*. He had begun bringing in his damned psychology again! Porfiry? But to think that Porfiry should for one moment believe that Nikolay was guilty, after what had passed between them before Nikolay's appearance, after that tête-à-tête interview, which could have only *one*explanation? (During those days Raskolnikov had often recalled passages in that scene with Porfiry; he could not bear to let his mind rest on it.) Such words, such gestures had passed between them, they had exchanged such glances, things had been said in such a tone and had reached such a pass, that Nikolay, whom Porfiry had seen through at the first word, at the first gesture, could not have shaken his conviction.

"And to think that even Razumihin had begun to suspect! The scene in the corridor under the lamp had produced its effect then. He had rushed to Porfiry.... But what had induced the latter to receive him like that? What had been his object in putting Razumihin off with Nikolay? He must have some plan; there was some design, but what was it? It was true that a long time had passed since that morning—too long a time—and no sight nor sound of Porfiry. Well, that was a bad sign...."

Raskolnikov took his cap and went out of the room, still pondering. It was the first time for a long while that he had felt clear in his mind, at least. "I must settle Svidrigaïlov," he thought, "and as soon as possible; he, too, seems to be waiting for me to come to him of my own accord." And at that moment there was such a rush of hate in his weary heart that he might have killed either of those two—Porfiry or Svidrigaïlov. At least he felt that he would be capable of doing it later, if not now.

"We shall see, we shall see," he repeated to himself.

But no sooner had he opened the door than he stumbled upon Porfiry himself in the passage. He was coming in to see him. Raskolnikov was dumbfounded for a minute, but only for one minute. Strange to say, he was not very much astonished at seeing Porfiry and scarcely afraid of him. He was simply startled, but was quickly, instantly, on his guard. "Perhaps this will mean the end? But how could Porfiry have approached so quietly, like a cat, so that he had heard nothing? Could he have been listening at the door?"

"You didn't expect a visitor, Rodion Romanovitch," Porfiry explained, laughing. "I've been meaning to look in a long time; I was passing by and thought why not go in for five minutes. Are you going out? I won't keep you long. Just let me have one cigarette."

"Sit down, Porfiry Petrovitch, sit down." Raskolnikov gave his visitor a seat with so pleased and friendly an expression that he would have marvelled at himself, if he could have seen it.

The last moment had come, the last drops had to be drained! So a man will sometimes go through half an hour of mortal terror with a brigand, yet when the knife is at his throat at last, he feels no fear.

Raskolnikov seated himself directly facing Porfiry, and looked at him without flinching. Porfiry screwed up his eyes and began lighting a cigarette.

"Speak, speak," seemed as though it would burst from Raskolnikov's heart. "Come, why don't you speak?"

CHAPTER II

"Ah these cigarettes!" Porfiry Petrovitch ejaculated at last, having lighted one. "They are pernicious, positively pernicious, and yet I can't give them up! I cough, I begin to have tickling in my throat and a difficulty in breathing. You know I am a coward, I went lately to Dr. B———n; he always gives at least half an hour to each patient. He positively laughed looking at me; he sounded me: 'Tobacco's bad for you,' he said, 'your lungs are affected.' But how am I to give it up? What is there to take its place? I don't drink, that's the mischief, he-he-he, that I don't. Everything is relative, Rodion Romanovitch, everything is relative!"

"Why, he's playing his professional tricks again," Raskolnikov thought with disgust. All the circumstances of their last interview suddenly came back to him, and he felt a rush of the feeling that had come upon him then.

"I came to see you the day before yesterday, in the evening; you didn't know?" Porfiry Petrovitch went on, looking round the room. "I came into this very room. I was passing by, just as I did to-day, and I thought I'd return your call. I walked in as your door was wide open, I looked round, waited and went out without leaving my name with your servant. Don't you lock your door?"

Raskolnikov's face grew more and more gloomy. Porfiry seemed to guess his state of mind.

"I've come to have it out with you, Rodion Romanovitch, my dear fellow! I owe you an explanation and must give it to you," he continued with a slight smile, just patting Raskolnikov's knee.

But almost at the same instant a serious and careworn look came into his face; to his surprise Raskolnikov saw a touch of sadness in it. He had never seen and never suspected such an expression in his face.

"A strange scene passed between us last time we met, Rodion Romanovitch. Our first interview, too, was a strange one; but then... and one thing after another! This is the point: I have perhaps acted unfairly to you; I feel it. Do you remember how we parted? Your nerves were unhinged and your knees were shaking and so were mine. And, you know, our behaviour was unseemly, even ungentlemanly. And yet we are gentlemen, above all, in any case, gentlemen; that must be understood. Do you remember what we came to?... and it was quite indecorous."

"What is he up to, what does he take me for?" Raskolnikov asked himself in amazement, raising his head and looking with open eyes on Porfiry.

"I've decided openness is better between us," Porfiry Petrovitch went on, turning his head away and dropping his eyes, as though unwilling to disconcert his former victim and as though disdaining his former wiles. "Yes, such suspicions and such scenes cannot continue for long. Nikolay put a stop to it, or I don't know what we might not have come to. That damned workman was sitting at the time in the next room—can you realise that? You know that, of course; and I am aware that he came to you afterwards. But what you supposed then was not true: I had not sent for anyone, I had made no kind of arrangements. You ask why I hadn't? What shall I say to you? it had all come upon me so suddenly. I had scarcely sent for the porters (you noticed them as you went out, I dare say). An idea flashed upon me; I was firmly convinced at the time, you see, Rodion Romanovitch. Come, I thought—even if I let one thing slip for a time, I shall get hold of something else—I shan't lose what I want, anyway. You are nervously irritable, Rodion Romanovitch, by temperament; it's out of proportion with other qualities of your heart and character, which I flatter myself I have to some extent divined. Of course I did reflect even then that it does not always happen that a man gets up and blurts out his whole story. It does happen sometimes, if you make a man lose all patience, though even then it's rare. I was capable of realising that. If I only had a fact, I thought, the least little fact to go upon, something I could lay hold of, something tangible, not merely psychological. For if a man is guilty, you must be able to get something substantial out of him; one may reckon upon most surprising results indeed. I was reckoning on your temperament, Rodion Romanovitch, on your temperament above all things! I had great hopes of you at that time."

"But what are you driving at now?" Raskolnikov muttered at last, asking the question without thinking.

"What is he talking about?" he wondered distractedly, "does he really take me to be innocent?"

"What am I driving at? I've come to explain myself, I consider it my duty, so to speak. I want to make clear to you how the whole business, the whole misunderstanding arose. I've caused you a great deal of suffering, Rodion Romanovitch. I am not a monster. I understand what it must mean for a man who has been unfortunate, but who is proud, imperious and above all, impatient, to have to bear such treatment! I regard you in any case as a man of noble character and not without elements of magnanimity, though I don't agree with all your convictions. I wanted to tell you this first, frankly and quite sincerely, for above all I don't want to deceive you. When I made your acquaintance, I felt attracted by you. Perhaps you will laugh at my saying so. You have a right to. I know you disliked me from the first and indeed you've no reason to like me. You may think what you like, but I desire now to do all I can to efface that impression and to show that I am a man of heart and conscience. I speak sincerely."

Porfiry Petrovitch made a dignified pause. Raskolnikov felt a rush of renewed alarm. The thought that Porfiry believed him to be innocent began to make him uneasy.

"It's scarcely necessary to go over everything in detail," Porfiry Petrovitch went on. "Indeed, I could scarcely attempt it. To begin with there were rumours. Through whom, how, and when those rumours came to me... and how they affected you, I need not go into. My suspicions were aroused by a complete accident, which might just as easily not have happened. What was it? Hm! I believe there is no need to go into that either. Those rumours and that accident led to one idea in my mind. I admit it openly—for one may as well make a clean breast of it— I was the first to pitch on you. The old woman's notes on the pledges and the rest of it—that all came to nothing. Yours was one of a hundred. I happened, too, to hear of the scene at the office, from a man who described it capitally, unconsciously reproducing the scene with great vividness. It was just one thing after another, Rodion Romanovitch, my dear fellow! How could I avoid being brought to certain ideas? From a hundred rabbits you can't make a horse, a hundred suspicions don't make a proof, as the English proverb says, but that's only from the rational point of view—you can't help being partial, for after all a lawyer is only human. I thought, too, of your article in that journal, do you remember, on your first visit we talked of it? I jeered at you at the time, but that was only to lead you on. I repeat, Rodion Romanovitch, you are ill and impatient. That you were bold, headstrong, in earnest and... had felt a great deal I recognised long before. I, too, have felt the same, so that your article seemed familiar to me. It was conceived on sleepless nights, with a throbbing heart, in ecstasy and suppressed enthusiasm. And that proud suppressed enthusiasm in young people is dangerous! I jeered at you then, but let me tell you that, as a literary amateur, I am awfully fond of such first essays, full of the heat of youth. There is a mistiness and a chord vibrating in the mist. Your article is absurd and fantastic, but there's a transparent sincerity, a youthful incorruptible pride and the daring of despair in it. It's a gloomy article, but that's what's fine in it. I read your article and put it aside, thinking as I did so 'that man won't go the common way.' Well, I ask you, after that as a preliminary, how could I help being carried away by what followed? Oh, dear, I am not saying anything, I am not making any statement now. I simply noted it at the time. What is there in it? I reflected. There's nothing in it, that is really nothing and perhaps absolutely nothing. And it's not at all the thing for the prosecutor to let himself be carried away by notions: here I have Nikolay on my hands with actual evidence against him—you may think what you like of it, but it's evidence. He brings in his psychology, too; one has to consider him, too, for it's a matter of life and death. Why am I explaining this to you? That you may understand, and not blame my malicious behaviour on that occasion. It was not malicious, I assure you, he-he! Do you suppose I didn't come to search your room at the time? I did, I did, he-he! I was here when you were lying ill in bed, not officially, not in my own person, but I was here. Your room was searched to the last thread at the first suspicion; but *umsonst*! I thought to myself, now that man will come, will come of himself and quickly, too; if he's guilty, he's sure to come. Another man wouldn't, but he will. And you remember how Mr. Razumihin began discussing the subject with you? We arranged that to excite you, so we purposely spread rumours, that he might discuss the case with you, and Razumihin is not a man to restrain his indignation. Mr. Zametov was tremendously struck by your anger and your open daring. Think of blurting out in a restaurant 'I killed her.' It was too daring, too reckless. I thought so myself, if he is guilty he will be a formidable opponent. That was what I thought at the time. I was expecting you. But you simply bowled Zametov over and... well, you see, it all lies in this—that this damnable psychology can be taken two ways! Well, I kept expecting you, and so it was, you came! My heart was fairly throbbing. Ach!

"Now, why need you have come? Your laughter, too, as you came in, do you remember? I saw it all plain as daylight, but if I hadn't expected you so specially, I should not have noticed anything in your laughter. You see what influence a mood has! Mr. Razumihin then—ah, that stone, that stone under which the things were hidden! I seem to see it somewhere in a kitchen garden. It was in a kitchen garden, you told Zametov and afterwards you repeated that in my office? And when we began picking your article to pieces, how you explained it! One could take every word of yours in two senses, as though there were another meaning hidden.

"So in this way, Rodion Romanovitch, I reached the furthest limit, and knocking my head against a post, I pulled myself up, asking myself what I was about. After all, I said, you can take it all in another sense if you like, and it's more natural so, indeed. I couldn't help admitting it was more natural. I was bothered! 'No, I'd better get hold of some little fact' I said. So when I heard of the bell-ringing, I held my breath and was all in a tremor. 'Here is my little fact,' thought I, and I didn't think it over, I simply wouldn't. I would have given a thousand roubles at that minute to have seen you with my own eyes, when you walked a hundred paces beside that workman, after he had called you murderer to your face, and you did not dare to ask him a question all the way. And then what about your trembling, what about your bell-ringing in your illness, in semi-delirium?

"And so, Rodion Romanovitch, can you wonder that I played such pranks on you? And what made you come at that very minute? Someone seemed to have sent you, by Jove! And if Nikolay had not parted us... and do you remember Nikolay at the time? Do you remember him clearly? It was a thunderbolt, a regular thunderbolt! And how I met him! I didn't believe in the thunderbolt, not for a minute. You could see it for yourself; and how could I? Even afterwards, when you had gone and he began making very, very plausible answers on certain points, so that I was surprised at him myself, even then I didn't believe his story! You see what it is to be as firm as a rock! No, thought I, *Morgenfrüh*. What has Nikolay got to do with it!"

"Razumihin told me just now that you think Nikolay guilty and had yourself assured him of it...."

His voice failed him, and he broke off. He had been listening in indescribable agitation, as this man who had seen through and through him, went back upon himself. He was afraid of believing it and did not believe it. In those still ambiguous words he kept eagerly looking for something more definite and conclusive.

"Mr. Razumihin!" cried Porfiry Petrovitch, seeming glad of a question from Raskolnikov, who had till then been silent. "He-he-he! But I had to put Mr. Razumihin off; two is company, three is none. Mr. Razumihin is not the right man, besides he is an outsider. He came running to me with a pale face.... But never mind him, why bring him in? To return to Nikolay, would you like to know what sort of a type he is, how I understand him, that is? To begin with, he is still a child and not exactly a coward, but something by way of an artist. Really, don't laugh at my describing him so. He is innocent and responsive to influence. He has a heart, and is a fantastic fellow. He sings and dances, he tells stories, they say, so that people come from other villages to hear him. He attends school too, and laughs till he cries if you hold up a finger to him; he will drink himself senseless—not as a regular vice, but at times, when people treat him, like a child. And he stole, too, then, without knowing it himself, for 'How can it be stealing, if one picks it up?' And do you know he is an Old Believer, or rather a dissenter? There have been Wanderers[*] in his family, and he was for two years in his village under the spiritual guidance of a certain elder. I learnt all this from Nikolay and from his fellow villagers. And what's more, he wanted to run into the wilderness! He was full of fervour, prayed at night, read the old books, 'the true' ones, and read himself crazy.

[*] A religious sect.—TRANSLATOR'S NOTE.

"Petersburg had a great effect upon him, especially the women and the wine. He responds to everything and he forgot the elder and all that. I learnt that an artist here took a fancy to him, and used to go and see him, and now this business came upon him.

"Well, he was frightened, he tried to hang himself! He ran away! How can one get over the idea the people have of Russian legal proceedings? The very word 'trial' frightens some of them. Whose fault is it? We shall see what the new juries will do. God grant they do good! Well, in prison, it seems, he remembered the venerable elder; the Bible, too, made its appearance again. Do you know, Rodion Romanovitch, the force of the word 'suffering' among some of these people! It's not a question of suffering for someone's benefit, but simply, 'one must suffer.' If they suffer at the hands of the authorities, so much the better. In my time there was a very meek and mild prisoner who spent a whole year in prison always reading his Bible on the stove at night and he read himself crazy, and so crazy, do you know, that one day, apropos of nothing, he seized a brick and flung it at the governor; though he had done him no harm. And the way he threw it too: aimed it a yard on one side on purpose, for fear of hurting him. Well, we know what happens to a prisoner who assaults an officer with a weapon. So 'he took his suffering.'

"So I suspect now that Nikolay wants to take his suffering or something of the sort. I know it for certain from facts, indeed. Only he doesn't know that I know. What, you don't admit that there are such fantastic people among the peasants? Lots of them. The elder now has begun influencing him, especially since he tried to hang himself. But he'll come and tell me all himself. You think he'll hold out? Wait a bit, he'll take his words back. I am waiting from hour to hour for him to come and abjure his evidence. I have come to like that Nikolay and am studying him in detail. And what do you think? He-he! He answered me very plausibly on some points, he obviously had collected some evidence and prepared himself cleverly. But on other points he is simply at sea, knows nothing and doesn't even suspect that he doesn't know!

"No, Rodion Romanovitch, Nikolay doesn't come in! This is a fantastic, gloomy business, a modern case, an incident of to-day when the heart of man is troubled, when the phrase is quoted that blood 'renews,' when comfort is preached as the aim of life. Here we have bookish dreams, a heart unhinged by theories. Here we see resolution in the first stage, but resolution of a special kind: he resolved to do it like jumping over a precipice or from a bell tower and his legs shook as he went to the crime. He forgot to shut the door after him, and murdered two people for a theory. He committed the murder and couldn't take the money, and what he did manage to snatch up he hid under a stone. It wasn't enough for him to suffer agony behind the door while they battered at the door and rung the bell, no, he had to go to the empty lodging, half delirious, to recall the bell-ringing, he wanted to feel the cold shiver over again.... Well, that we grant, was through illness, but consider this: he is a murderer, but looks upon himself as an honest man, despises others, poses as injured innocence. No, that's not the work of a Nikolay, my dear Rodion Romanovitch!"

All that had been said before had sounded so like a recantation that these words were too great a shock. Raskolnikov shuddered as though he had been stabbed.

"Then... who then... is the murderer?" he asked in a breathless voice, unable to restrain himself.

Porfiry Petrovitch sank back in his chair, as though he were amazed at the question.

"Who is the murderer?" he repeated, as though unable to believe his ears. "Why, *you*, Rodion Romanovitch! You are the murderer," he added, almost in a whisper, in a voice of genuine conviction.

Raskolnikov leapt from the sofa, stood up for a few seconds and sat down again without uttering a word. His face twitched convulsively.

"Your lip is twitching just as it did before," Porfiry Petrovitch observed almost sympathetically. "You've been misunderstanding me, I think, Rodion Romanovitch," he added after a brief pause, "that's why you are so surprised. I came on purpose to tell you everything and deal openly with you."

"It was not I murdered her," Raskolnikov whispered like a frightened child caught in the act.

"No, it was you, you Rodion Romanovitch, and no one else," Porfiry whispered sternly, with conviction.

They were both silent and the silence lasted strangely long, about ten minutes. Raskolnikov put his elbow on the table and passed his fingers through his hair. Porfiry Petrovitch sat quietly waiting. Suddenly Raskolnikov looked scornfully at Porfiry.

"You are at your old tricks again, Porfiry Petrovitch! Your old method again. I wonder you don't get sick of it!"

"Oh, stop that, what does that matter now? It would be a different matter if there were witnesses present, but we are whispering alone. You see yourself that I have not come to chase and capture you like a hare. Whether you confess it or not is nothing to me now; for myself, I am convinced without it."

"If so, what did you come for?" Raskolnikov asked irritably. "I ask you the same question again: if you consider me guilty, why don't you take me to prison?"

"Oh, that's your question! I will answer you, point for point. In the first place, to arrest you so directly is not to my interest."

"How so? If you are convinced you ought...."

"Ach, what if I am convinced? That's only my dream for the time. Why should I put you in safety? You know that's it, since you ask me to do it. If I confront you with that workman for instance and you say to him 'were you drunk or not? Who saw me with you? I simply took you to be drunk, and you were drunk, too.' Well, what could I answer, especially as your story is a more likely one than his? for there's nothing but psychology to support his evidence—that's almost unseemly with his ugly mug, while you hit the mark exactly, for the rascal is an inveterate drunkard and notoriously so. And I have myself admitted candidly several times already that that psychology can be taken in two ways and that the second way is stronger and looks far more probable, and that apart from that I have as yet nothing against you. And though I shall put you in prison and indeed have come—quite contrary to etiquette—to inform you of it beforehand, yet I tell you frankly, also contrary to etiquette, that it won't be to my advantage. Well, secondly, I've come to you because..."

"Yes, yes, secondly?" Raskolnikov was listening breathless.

"Because, as I told you just now, I consider I owe you an explanation. I don't want you to look upon me as a monster, as I have a genuine liking for you, you may believe me or not. And in the third place I've come to you with a direct and open proposition—that you should surrender and confess. It will be infinitely more to your advantage and to my advantage too, for my task will be done. Well, is this open on my part or not?"

Raskolnikov thought a minute.

"Listen, Porfiry Petrovitch. You said just now you have nothing but psychology to go on, yet now you've gone on mathematics. Well, what if you are mistaken yourself, now?"

"No, Rodion Romanovitch, I am not mistaken. I have a little fact even then, Providence sent it me."

"What little fact?"

"I won't tell you what, Rodion Romanovitch. And in any case, I haven't the right to put it off any longer, I must arrest you. So think it over: it makes no difference to me *now* and so I speak only for your sake. Believe me, it will be better, Rodion Romanovitch."

Raskolnikov smiled malignantly.

"That's not simply ridiculous, it's positively shameless. Why, even if I were guilty, which I don't admit, what reason should I have to confess, when you tell me yourself that I shall be in greater safety in prison?"

"Ah, Rodion Romanovitch, don't put too much faith in words, perhaps prison will not be altogether a restful place. That's only theory and my theory, and what authority am I for you? Perhaps, too, even now I am hiding something from you? I can't lay bare everything, he-he! And how can you ask what advantage? Don't you know how it would lessen your sentence? You would be confessing at a moment when another man has taken the crime on himself and so has muddled the whole case. Consider that! I swear before God that I will so arrange that your confession shall come as a complete surprise. We will make a clean sweep of all these psychological points, of a suspicion against you, so that your crime will appear to have been something like an aberration, for in truth it was an aberration. I am an honest man, Rodion Romanovitch, and will keep my word."

Raskolnikov maintained a mournful silence and let his head sink dejectedly. He pondered a long while and at last smiled again, but his smile was sad and gentle.

"No!" he said, apparently abandoning all attempt to keep up appearances with Porfiry, "it's not worth it, I don't care about lessening the sentence!"

"That's just what I was afraid of!" Porfiry cried warmly and, as it seemed, involuntarily. "That's just what I feared, that you wouldn't care about the mitigation of sentence."

Raskolnikov looked sadly and expressively at him.

"Ah, don't disdain life!" Porfiry went on. "You have a great deal of it still before you. How can you say you don't want a mitigation of sentence? You are an impatient fellow!"

"A great deal of what lies before me?"

"Of life. What sort of prophet are you, do you know much about it? Seek and ye shall find. This may be God's means for bringing you to Him. And it's not for ever, the bondage...."

"The time will be shortened," laughed Raskolnikov.

"Why, is it the bourgeois disgrace you are afraid of? It may be that you are afraid of it without knowing it, because you are young! But anyway *you* shouldn't be afraid of giving yourself up and confessing."

"Ach, hang it!" Raskolnikov whispered with loathing and contempt, as though he did not want to speak aloud.

He got up again as though he meant to go away, but sat down again in evident despair.

"Hang it, if you like! You've lost faith and you think that I am grossly flattering you; but how long has your life been? How much do you understand? You made up a theory and then were ashamed that it broke down and turned out to be not at all original! It turned out something base, that's true, but you are not hopelessly base. By no means so base! At least you didn't deceive yourself for long, you went straight to the furthest point at one bound. How do I regard you? I regard you as one of those men who would stand and smile at their torturer while he cuts their entrails out, if only they have found faith or God. Find it and you will live. You have long needed a change of air. Suffering, too, is a good thing. Suffer! Maybe Nikolay is right in wanting to suffer. I know you don't believe in it—but don't be over-wise; fling yourself straight into life, without deliberation; don't be afraid—the flood will bear you to the bank and set you safe on your feet again. What bank? How can I tell? I only believe that you have long life before you. I know that you take all my words now for a set speech prepared beforehand, but maybe you will remember them after. They may be of use some time. That's why I speak. It's as well that you only killed the old woman. If you'd invented another theory you might perhaps have done something a thousand times more hideous. You ought to thank God, perhaps. How do you know? Perhaps God is saving you for something. But keep a good heart and have less fear! Are you afraid of the great expiation before you? No, it would be shameful to be afraid of it. Since you have taken such a step, you must harden your heart. There is justice in it. You must fulfil the demands of justice. I know that you don't believe it, but indeed, life will bring you through. You will live it down in time. What you need now is fresh air, fresh air, fresh air!"

Raskolnikov positively started.

"But who are you? what prophet are you? From the height of what majestic calm do you proclaim these words of wisdom?"

"Who am I? I am a man with nothing to hope for, that's all. A man perhaps of feeling and sympathy, maybe of some knowledge too, but my day is over. But you are a different matter, there is life waiting for you. Though, who knows? maybe your life, too, will pass off in smoke and come to nothing. Come, what does it matter, that you will pass into another class of men? It's not comfort you regret, with your heart! What of it that perhaps no one will see you for so long? It's not time, but yourself that will decide that. Be the sun and all will see you. The sun has before all to be the sun. Why are you smiling again? At my being such a Schiller? I bet you're imagining that I am trying to get round you by flattery. Well, perhaps I am, he-he-he! Perhaps you'd better not believe my word, perhaps you'd better never believe it altogether—I'm made that way, I confess it. But let me add, you can judge for yourself, I think, how far I am a base sort of man and how far I am honest."

"When do you mean to arrest me?"

"Well, I can let you walk about another day or two. Think it over, my dear fellow, and pray to God. It's more in your interest, believe me."

"And what if I run away?" asked Raskolnikov with a strange smile.

"No, you won't run away. A peasant would run away, a fashionable dissenter would run away, the flunkey of another man's thought, for you've only to show him the end of your little finger and he'll be ready to believe in anything for the rest of his life. But you've ceased to believe in your theory already, what will you run away with? And what would you do in hiding? It would be hateful and difficult for you, and what you need more than anything in life is a definite position, an atmosphere to suit you. And what sort of atmosphere would you have? If you ran away, you'd come back to yourself. *You can't get on without us.* And if I put you in prison—say you've been there a month, or two, or three—remember my word, you'll confess of yourself and perhaps to your own surprise. You won't know an hour beforehand that you are coming with a confession. I am convinced that you will decide, 'to take your suffering.' You don't believe my words now, but you'll come to it of yourself. For suffering, Rodion Romanovitch, is a great thing. Never mind my having grown fat, I know all the same. Don't laugh at it, there's an idea in suffering, Nokolay is right. No, you won't run away, Rodion Romanovitch."

Raskolnikov got up and took his cap. Porfiry Petrovitch also rose.

"Are you going for a walk? The evening will be fine, if only we don't have a storm. Though it would be a good thing to freshen the air."

He, too, took his cap.

"Porfiry Petrovitch, please don't take up the notion that I have confessed to you to-day," Raskolnikov pronounced with sullen insistence. "You're a strange man and I have listened to you from simple curiosity. But I have admitted nothing, remember that!"

"Oh, I know that, I'll remember. Look at him, he's trembling! Don't be uneasy, my dear fellow, have it your own way. Walk about a bit, you won't be able to walk too far. If anything happens, I have one request to make of you," he added, dropping his voice. "It's an awkward one, but important. If anything were to happen (though indeed I don't believe in it and think you quite incapable of it), yet in case you were taken during these forty or fifty hours with the notion of putting an end to the business in some other way, in some fantastic fashion—laying hands on yourself—(it's an absurd proposition, but you must forgive me for it) do leave a brief but precise note, only two lines, and mention the stone. It will be more generous. Come, till we meet! Good thoughts and sound decisions to you!"

Porfiry went out, stooping and avoiding looking at Raskolnikov. The latter went to the window and waited with irritable impatience till he calculated that Porfiry had reached the street and moved away. Then he too went hurriedly out of the room.

CHAPTER III

He hurried to Svidrigaïlov's. What he had to hope from that man he did not know. But that man had some hidden power over him. Having once recognised this, he could not rest, and now the time had come.

On the way, one question particularly worried him: had Svidrigaïlov been to Porfiry's?

As far as he could judge, he would swear to it, that he had not. He pondered again and again, went over Porfiry's visit; no, he hadn't been, of course he hadn't.

But if he had not been yet, would he go? Meanwhile, for the present he fancied he couldn't. Why? He could not have explained, but if he could, he would not have wasted much thought over it at the moment. It all worried him and at the same time he could not attend to it. Strange to say, none would have believed it perhaps, but he only felt a faint vague anxiety about his immediate future. Another, much more important anxiety tormented him—it concerned himself, but in a different, more vital way. Moreover, he was conscious of immense moral fatigue, though his mind was working better that morning than it had done of late.

And was it worth while, after all that had happened, to contend with these new trivial difficulties? Was it worth while, for instance, to manoeuvre that Svidrigaïlov should not go to Porfiry's? Was it worth while to investigate, to ascertain the facts, to waste time over anyone like Svidrigaïlov?

Oh, how sick he was of it all!

And yet he was hastening to Svidrigaïlov; could he be expecting something *new* from him, information, or means of escape? Men will catch at straws! Was it destiny or some instinct bringing them together? Perhaps it was only fatigue, despair; perhaps it was not Svidrigaïlov but some other whom he needed, and Svidrigaïlov had simply presented himself by chance. Sonia? But what should he go to Sonia for now? To beg her tears again? He was afraid of Sonia, too. Sonia stood before him as an irrevocable sentence. He must go his own way or hers. At that moment especially he did not feel equal to seeing her. No, would it not be better to try Svidrigaïlov? And he could not help inwardly owning that he had long felt that he must see him for some reason.

But what could they have in common? Their very evil-doing could not be of the same kind. The man, moreover, was very unpleasant, evidently depraved, undoubtedly cunning and deceitful, possibly malignant. Such stories were told about him. It is true he was befriending Katerina Ivanovna's children, but who could tell with what motive and what it meant? The man always had some design, some project.

There was another thought which had been continually hovering of late about Raskolnikov's mind, and causing him great uneasiness. It was so painful that he made distinct efforts to get rid of it. He sometimes thought that Svidrigaïlov was dogging his footsteps. Svidrigaïlov had found out his secret and had had designs on Dounia. What if he had them still? Wasn't it practically certain that he had? And what if, having learnt his secret and so having gained power over him, he were to use it as a weapon against Dounia?

This idea sometimes even tormented his dreams, but it had never presented itself so vividly to him as on his way to Svidrigaïlov. The very thought moved him to gloomy rage. To begin with, this would transform everything, even his own position; he would have at once to confess his secret to Dounia. Would he have to give himself up perhaps to prevent Dounia from taking some rash step? The letter? This morning Dounia had received a letter. From whom could she get letters in Petersburg? Luzhin, perhaps? It's true Razumihin was there to protect her, but Razumihin knew nothing of the position. Perhaps it was his duty to tell Razumihin? He thought of it with repugnance.

In any case he must see Svidrigaïlov as soon as possible, he decided finally. Thank God, the details of the interview were of little consequence, if only he could get at the root of the matter; but if Svidrigaïlov were capable... if he were intriguing against Dounia—then...

Raskolnikov was so exhausted by what he had passed through that month that he could only decide such questions in one way; "then I shall kill him," he thought in cold despair.

A sudden anguish oppressed his heart, he stood still in the middle of the street and began looking about to see where he was and which way he was going. He found himself in X. Prospect, thirty or forty paces from the Hay Market, through which he had come. The whole second storey of the house on the left was used as a tavern. All the windows were wide open; judging from the figures moving at the windows, the rooms were full to overflowing. There were sounds of singing, of clarionet and violin, and the boom of a Turkish drum. He could hear women shrieking. He was about to turn back wondering why he had come to the X. Prospect, when suddenly at one of the end windows he saw Svidrigaïlov, sitting at a tea-table right in the open window with a pipe in his mouth. Raskolnikov was dreadfully taken aback, almost terrified. Svidrigaïlov was silently watching and scrutinising him and, what struck Raskolnikov at once, seemed to be meaning to get up and slip away unobserved. Raskolnikov at once pretended not to have seen him, but to be looking absent-mindedly away, while he watched him out of the corner of his eye. His heart was beating violently. Yet, it was evident that Svidrigaïlov did not want to be seen. He took the pipe out of his mouth and was on the point of concealing himself, but as he got up and moved back his chair, he seemed to have become suddenly aware that Raskolnikov had seen him, and was watching him. What had passed between them was much the same as what happened at their first meeting in Raskolnikov's room. A sly smile came into Svidrigaïlov's face and grew broader and broader. Each knew that he was seen and watched by the other. At last Svidrigaïlov broke into a loud laugh.

"Well, well, come in if you want me; I am here!" he shouted from the window.

Raskolnikov went up into the tavern. He found Svidrigaïlov in a tiny back room, adjoining the saloon in which merchants, clerks and numbers of people of all sorts were drinking tea at twenty little tables to the desperate bawling of a chorus of singers. The click of billiard balls could be heard in the distance. On the table before Svidrigaïlov stood an open bottle and a glass half full of champagne. In the room he found also a boy with a little hand organ, a healthy-looking red-cheeked girl of eighteen, wearing a tucked-up striped skirt, and a

Tyrolese hat with ribbons. In spite of the chorus in the other room, she was singing some servants' hall song in a rather husky contralto, to the accompaniment of the organ.

"Come, that's enough," Svidrigaïlov stopped her at Raskolnikov's entrance. The girl at once broke off and stood waiting respectfully. She had sung her guttural rhymes, too, with a serious and respectful expression in her face.

"Hey, Philip, a glass!" shouted Svidrigaïlov.

"I won't drink anything," said Raskolnikov.

"As you like, I didn't mean it for you. Drink, Katia! I don't want anything more to-day, you can go." He poured her out a full glass, and laid down a yellow note.

Katia drank off her glass of wine, as women do, without putting it down, in twenty gulps, took the note and kissed Svidrigaïlov's hand, which he allowed quite seriously. She went out of the room and the boy trailed after her with the organ. Both had been brought in from the street. Svidrigaïlov had not been a week in Petersburg, but everything about him was already, so to speak, on a patriarchal footing; the waiter, Philip, was by now an old friend and very obsequious.

The door leading to the saloon had a lock on it. Svidrigaïlov was at home in this room and perhaps spent whole days in it. The tavern was dirty and wretched, not even second-rate.

"I was going to see you and looking for you," Raskolnikov began, "but I don't know what made me turn from the Hay Market into the X. Prospect just now. I never take this turning. I turn to the right from the Hay Market. And this isn't the way to you. I simply turned and here you are. It is strange!"

"Why don't you say at once 'it's a miracle'?"

"Because it may be only chance."

"Oh, that's the way with all you folk," laughed Svidrigaïlov. "You won't admit it, even if you do inwardly believe it a miracle! Here you say that it may be only chance. And what cowards they all are here, about having an opinion of their own, you can't fancy, Rodion Romanovitch. I don't mean you, you have an opinion of your own and are not afraid to have it. That's how it was you attracted my curiosity."

"Nothing else?"

"Well, that's enough, you know," Svidrigaïlov was obviously exhilarated, but only slightly so, he had not had more than half a glass of wine.

"I fancy you came to see me before you knew that I was capable of having what you call an opinion of my own," observed Raskolnikov.

"Oh, well, it was a different matter. Everyone has his own plans. And apropos of the miracle let me tell you that I think you have been asleep for the last two or three days. I told you of this tavern myself, there is no miracle in your coming straight here. I explained the way myself, told you where it was, and the hours you could find me here. Do you remember?"

"I don't remember," answered Raskolnikov with surprise.

"I believe you. I told you twice. The address has been stamped mechanically on your memory. You turned this way mechanically and yet precisely according to the direction, though you are not aware of it. When I told you then, I hardly hoped you understood me. You give yourself away too much, Rodion Romanovitch. And another thing, I'm convinced there are lots of people in Petersburg who talk to themselves as they walk. This is a town of crazy people. If only we had scientific men, doctors, lawyers and philosophers might make most valuable investigations in Petersburg each in his own line. There are few places where there are so many gloomy, strong and queer influences on the soul of man as in Petersburg. The mere influences of climate mean so much. And it's the administrative centre of all Russia and its character must be reflected on the whole country. But that is neither here nor there now. The point is that I have several times watched you. You walk out of your house— holding your head high—twenty paces from home you let it sink, and fold your hands behind your back. You look and evidently see nothing before nor beside you. At last you begin moving your lips and talking to yourself, and sometimes you wave one hand and declaim, and at last stand still in the middle of the road. That's not at all the thing. Someone may be watching you besides me, and it won't do you any good. It's nothing really to do with me and I can't cure you, but, of course, you understand me."

"Do you know that I am being followed?" asked Raskolnikov, looking inquisitively at him.

"No, I know nothing about it," said Svidrigaïlov, seeming surprised.

"Well, then, let us leave me alone," Raskolnikov muttered, frowning.

"Very good, let us leave you alone."

"You had better tell me, if you come here to drink, and directed me twice to come here to you, why did you hide, and try to get away just now when I looked at the window from the street? I saw it."

"He-he! And why was it you lay on your sofa with closed eyes and pretended to be asleep, though you were wide awake while I stood in your doorway? I saw it."

"I may have had... reasons. You know that yourself."

"And I may have had my reasons, though you don't know them."

Raskolnikov dropped his right elbow on the table, leaned his chin in the fingers of his right hand, and stared intently at Svidrigaïlov. For a full minute he scrutinised his face, which had impressed him before. It was a strange face, like a mask; white and red, with bright red lips, with a flaxen beard, and still thick flaxen hair. His eyes were somehow too blue and their expression somehow too heavy and fixed. There was something awfully unpleasant in that handsome face, which looked so wonderfully young for his age. Svidrigaïlov was smartly dressed in light summer clothes and was particularly dainty in his linen. He wore a huge ring with a precious stone in it.

"Have I got to bother myself about you, too, now?" said Raskolnikov suddenly, coming with nervous impatience straight to the point. "Even though perhaps you are the most dangerous man if you care to injure me, I don't want to put myself out any more. I will show you at once that I don't prize myself as you probably think I do. I've come to tell you at once that if you keep to your former intentions with regard to my sister and if you think to derive any benefit in that direction from what has been discovered of late, I will kill you before you get me locked up. You can reckon on my word. You know that I can keep it. And in the second place if you want to tell me anything—for I keep fancying all this time that you have something to tell me—make haste and tell it, for time is precious and very likely it will soon be too late."

"Why in such haste?" asked Svidrigaïlov, looking at him curiously.

"Everyone has his plans," Raskolnikov answered gloomily and impatiently.

"You urged me yourself to frankness just now, and at the first question you refuse to answer," Svidrigaïlov observed with a smile. "You keep fancying that I have aims of my own and so you look at me with suspicion. Of course it's perfectly natural in your position. But though I should like to be friends with you, I shan't trouble myself to convince you of the contrary. The game isn't worth the candle and I wasn't intending to talk to you about anything special."

"What did you want me, for, then? It was you who came hanging about me."

"Why, simply as an interesting subject for observation. I liked the fantastic nature of your position—that's what it was! Besides you are the brother of a person who greatly interested me, and from that person I had in the past heard a very great deal about you, from which I gathered that you had a great influence over her; isn't that enough? Ha-ha-ha! Still I must admit that your question is rather complex, and is difficult for me to answer. Here, you, for instance, have come to me not only for a definite object, but for the sake of hearing something new. Isn't that so? Isn't that so?" persisted Svidrigaïlov with a sly smile. "Well, can't you fancy then that I, too, on my way here in the train was reckoning on you, on your telling me something new, and on my making some profit out of you! You see what rich men we are!"

"What profit could you make?"

"How can I tell you? How do I know? You see in what a tavern I spend all my time and it's my enjoyment, that's to say it's no great enjoyment, but one must sit somewhere; that poor Katia now—you saw her?... If only I had been a glutton now, a club gourmand, but you see I can eat this."

He pointed to a little table in the corner where the remnants of a terrible-looking beef-steak and potatoes lay on a tin dish.

"Have you dined, by the way? I've had something and want nothing more. I don't drink, for instance, at all. Except for champagne I never touch anything, and not more than a glass of that all the evening, and even that is enough to make my head ache. I ordered it just now to wind myself up, for I am just going off somewhere and you see me in a peculiar state of mind. That was why I hid myself just now like a schoolboy, for I was afraid you would hinder me. But I believe," he pulled out his watch, "I can spend an hour with you. It's half-past four now. If only I'd been something, a landowner, a father, a cavalry officer, a photographer, a journalist... I am nothing, no specialty, and sometimes I am positively bored. I really thought you would tell me something new."

"But what are you, and why have you come here?"

"What am I? You know, a gentleman, I served for two years in the cavalry, then I knocked about here in Petersburg, then I married Marfa Petrovna and lived in the country. There you have my biography!"

"You are a gambler, I believe?"

"No, a poor sort of gambler. A card-sharper—not a gambler."

"You have been a card-sharper then?"

"Yes, I've been a card-sharper too."

"Didn't you get thrashed sometimes?"

"It did happen. Why?"

"Why, you might have challenged them... altogether it must have been lively."

"I won't contradict you, and besides I am no hand at philosophy. I confess that I hastened here for the sake of the women."

"As soon as you buried Marfa Petrovna?"

"Quite so," Svidrigaïlov smiled with engaging candour. "What of it? You seem to find something wrong in my speaking like that about women?"

"You ask whether I find anything wrong in vice?"

"Vice! Oh, that's what you are after! But I'll answer you in order, first about women in general; you know I am fond of talking. Tell me, what should I restrain myself for? Why should I give up women, since I have a passion for them? It's an occupation, anyway."

"So you hope for nothing here but vice?"

"Oh, very well, for vice then. You insist on its being vice. But anyway I like a direct question. In this vice at least there is something permanent, founded indeed upon nature and not dependent on fantasy, something present in the blood like an ever-burning ember, for ever setting one on fire and, maybe, not to be quickly extinguished, even with years. You'll agree it's an occupation of a sort."

"That's nothing to rejoice at, it's a disease and a dangerous one."

"Oh, that's what you think, is it! I agree, that it is a disease like everything that exceeds moderation. And, of course, in this one must exceed moderation. But in the first place, everybody does so in one way or another, and in the second place, of course, one ought to be moderate and prudent, however mean it may be, but what am I to do? If I hadn't this, I might have to shoot myself. I am ready to admit that a decent man ought to put up with being bored, but yet..."

"And could you shoot yourself?"

"Oh, come!" Svidrigaïlov parried with disgust. "Please don't speak of it," he added hurriedly and with none of the bragging tone he had shown in all the previous conversation. His face quite changed. "I admit it's an unpardonable weakness, but I can't help it. I am afraid of death and I dislike its being talked of. Do you know that I am to a certain extent a mystic?"

"Ah, the apparitions of Marfa Petrovna! Do they still go on visiting you?"

"Oh, don't talk of them; there have been no more in Petersburg, confound them!" he cried with an air of irritation. "Let's rather talk of that... though... H'm! I have not much time, and can't stay long with you, it's a pity! I should have found plenty to tell you."

"What's your engagement, a woman?"

"Yes, a woman, a casual incident.... No, that's not what I want to talk of."

"And the hideousness, the filthiness of all your surroundings, doesn't that affect you? Have you lost the strength to stop yourself?"

"And do you pretend to strength, too? He-he-he! You surprised me just now, Rodion Romanovitch, though I knew beforehand it would be so. You preach to me about vice and æsthetics! You—a Schiller, you—an idealist! Of course that's all as it should be and it would be surprising if it were not so, yet it is strange in reality.... Ah, what a pity I have no time, for you're a most interesting type! And, by-the-way, are you fond of Schiller? I am awfully fond of him."

"But what a braggart you are," Raskolnikov said with some disgust.

"Upon my word, I am not," answered Svidrigaïlov laughing. "However, I won't dispute it, let me be a braggart, why not brag, if it hurts no one? I spent seven years in the country with Marfa Petrovna, so now when I come across an intelligent person like you—intelligent and highly interesting—I am simply glad to talk and, besides, I've drunk that half-glass of champagne and it's gone to my head a little. And besides, there's a certain fact that has wound me up tremendously, but about that I... will keep quiet. Where are you off to?" he asked in alarm.

Raskolnikov had begun getting up. He felt oppressed and stifled and, as it were, ill at ease at having come here. He felt convinced that Svidrigaïlov was the most worthless scoundrel on the face of the earth.

"A-ach! Sit down, stay a little!" Svidrigaïlov begged. "Let them bring you some tea, anyway. Stay a little, I won't talk nonsense, about myself, I mean. I'll tell you something. If you like I'll tell you how a woman tried 'to save' me, as you would call it? It will be an answer to your first question indeed, for the woman was your sister. May I tell you? It will help to spend the time."

"Tell me, but I trust that you..."

"Oh, don't be uneasy. Besides, even in a worthless low fellow like me, Avdotya Romanovna can only excite the deepest respect."

"You know perhaps—yes, I told you myself," began Svidrigaïlov, "that I was in the debtors' prison here, for an immense sum, and had not any expectation of being able to pay it. There's no need to go into particulars how Marfa Petrovna bought me out; do you know to what a point of insanity a woman can sometimes love? She was an honest woman, and very sensible, although completely uneducated. Would you believe that this honest and jealous woman, after many scenes of hysterics and reproaches, condescended to enter into a kind of contract with me which she kept throughout our married life? She was considerably older than I, and besides, she always kept a clove or something in her mouth. There was so much swinishness in my soul and honesty too, of a sort, as to tell her straight out that I couldn't be absolutely faithful to her. This confession drove her to frenzy, but yet she seems in a way to have liked my brutal frankness. She thought it showed I was unwilling to deceive her if I warned her like this beforehand and for a jealous woman, you know, that's the first consideration. After many tears an unwritten contract was drawn up between us: first, that I would never leave Marfa Petrovna and would always be her husband; secondly, that I would never absent myself without her permission; thirdly, that I would never set up a permanent mistress; fourthly, in return for this, Marfa Petrovna gave me a free hand with the maidservants, but only with her secret knowledge; fifthly, God forbid my falling in love with a woman of our class; sixthly, in case I—which God forbid—should be visited by a great serious passion I was bound to reveal it to Marfa Petrovna. On this last score, however, Marfa Petrovna was fairly at ease. She was a sensible woman and so she could not help looking upon me as a dissolute profligate incapable of real love. But a sensible woman and a jealous woman are two very different things, and that's where the trouble came in. But to judge some people impartially we must renounce certain preconceived opinions and our habitual attitude to the ordinary people about us. I have reason to have faith in your judgment rather than in anyone's. Perhaps you have already heard a great deal that was ridiculous and absurd about Marfa Petrovna. She certainly had some very ridiculous ways, but I tell you frankly that I feel really sorry for the innumerable woes of which I was the cause. Well, and that's enough, I think, by way of a decorous *oraison funèbre* for the most tender wife of a most tender husband. When we quarrelled, I usually held my tongue and did not irritate her and that gentlemanly conduct rarely failed to attain its object, it influenced her, it pleased her, indeed. These were times when she was positively proud of me. But your sister she couldn't put up with, anyway. And however she came to risk taking such a beautiful creature into her house as a governess. My explanation is that Marfa Petrovna was an ardent and impressionable woman and simply fell in love herself—literally fell in love—with your sister. Well, little wonder—look at Avdotya Romanovna! I saw the danger at the first glance and what do you think, I resolved not to look at her even. But Avdotya Romanovna herself made the first step, would you believe it? Would you believe it too that Marfa Petrovna was positively angry with me at first for my persistent silence about your sister, for my careless reception of her continual adoring praises of Avdotya Romanovna. I don't know what it was she wanted! Well, of course, Marfa Petrovna told Avdotya Romanovna every detail about me. She had the unfortunate habit of telling literally everyone all our family secrets and continually complaining of me; how could she fail to confide in such a delightful new friend? I expect they talked of nothing else but me and no doubt Avdotya Romanovna heard all those dark mysterious rumours that were current about me.... I don't mind betting that you too have heard something of the sort already?"

"I have. Luzhin charged you with having caused the death of a child. Is that true?"

"Don't refer to those vulgar tales, I beg," said Svidrigaïlov with disgust and annoyance. "If you insist on wanting to know about all that idiocy, I will tell you one day, but now..."

"I was told too about some footman of yours in the country whom you treated badly."

"I beg you to drop the subject," Svidrigaïlov interrupted again with obvious impatience.

"Was that the footman who came to you after death to fill your pipe?... you told me about it yourself." Raskolnikov felt more and more irritated.

Svidrigaïlov looked at him attentively and Raskolnikov fancied he caught a flash of spiteful mockery in that look. But Svidrigaïlov restrained himself and answered very civilly:

"Yes, it was. I see that you, too, are extremely interested and shall feel it my duty to satisfy your curiosity at the first opportunity. Upon my soul! I see that I really might pass for a romantic figure with some people. Judge how grateful I must be to Marfa Petrovna for having repeated to Avdotya Romanovna such mysterious and interesting gossip about me. I dare not guess what impression it made on her, but in any case it worked in my interests. With all Avdotya Romanovna's natural aversion and in spite of my invariably gloomy and repellent aspect—she did at least feel pity for me, pity for a lost soul. And if once a girl's heart is moved to *pity*, it's more dangerous than anything. She is bound to want to 'save him,' to bring him to his senses, and lift him up and draw him to nobler aims, and restore him to new life and usefulness—well, we all know how far such dreams can go. I saw at once that the bird was flying into the cage of herself. And I too made ready. I think you are frowning, Rodion Romanovitch? There's no need. As you know, it all ended in smoke. (Hang it all, what a lot I am drinking!) Do you know, I always, from the very beginning, regretted that it wasn't your sister's fate to be born in the second or third century A.D., as the daughter of a reigning prince or some governor or pro-consul in Asia Minor. She would undoubtedly have been one of those who would endure martyrdom and would have smiled when they branded her bosom with hot pincers. And she would have gone to it of herself. And in the fourth or fifth century she would have walked away into the Egyptian desert and would have stayed there thirty years living on roots and ecstasies and visions. She is simply thirsting to face some torture for someone, and if she can't get her torture, she'll throw herself out of a window. I've heard something of a Mr. Razumihin—he's said to be a sensible fellow; his surname suggests it, indeed. He's probably a divinity student. Well, he'd better look after your sister! I believe I understand her, and I am proud of it. But at the beginning of an acquaintance, as you know, one is apt to be more heedless and stupid. One doesn't see clearly. Hang it all, why is she so handsome? It's not my fault. In fact, it began on my side with a most irresistible physical desire. Avdotya Romanovna is awfully chaste, incredibly and phenomenally so. Take note, I tell you this about your sister as a fact. She is almost morbidly chaste, in spite of her broad intelligence, and it will stand in her way. There happened to be a girl in the house then, Parasha, a black-eyed wench, whom I had never seen before—she had just come from another village—very pretty, but incredibly stupid: she burst into tears, wailed so that she could be heard all over the place and caused scandal. One day after dinner Avdotya Romanovna followed me into an avenue in the garden and with flashing eyes *insisted* on my leaving poor Parasha alone. It was almost our first conversation by ourselves. I, of course, was only too pleased to obey her wishes, tried to appear disconcerted, embarrassed, in fact played my part not badly. Then came interviews, mysterious conversations, exhortations, entreaties, supplications, even tears—would you believe it, even tears? Think what the passion for propaganda will bring some girls to! I, of course, threw it all on my destiny, posed as hungering and thirsting for light, and finally resorted to the most powerful weapon in the subjection of the female heart, a weapon which never fails one. It's the well-known resource—flattery. Nothing in the world is harder than speaking the truth and nothing easier than flattery. If there's the hundredth part of a false note in speaking the truth, it leads to a discord, and that leads to trouble. But if all, to the last note, is false in flattery, it is just as agreeable, and is heard not without satisfaction. It may be a coarse satisfaction, but still a satisfaction. And however coarse the flattery, at least half will be sure to seem true. That's so for all stages of development and classes of society. A vestal virgin might be seduced by flattery. I can never remember without laughter how I once seduced a lady who was devoted to her husband, her children, and her principles. What fun it was and how little trouble! And the lady really had principles—of her own, anyway. All my tactics lay in simply being utterly annihilated and prostrate before her purity. I flattered her shamelessly, and as soon as I succeeded in getting a pressure of the hand, even a glance from her, I would reproach myself for having snatched it by force, and would declare that she had resisted, so that I could never have gained anything but for my being so unprincipled. I maintained that she was so innocent that she could not foresee my treachery, and yielded to me unconsciously, unawares, and so on. In fact, I triumphed, while my lady remained firmly convinced that she was innocent, chaste, and faithful to all her duties and obligations and had succumbed quite by accident. And how angry she was with me when I explained to her at last that it was my sincere conviction that she was just as eager as I. Poor Marfa Petrovna was awfully weak on the side of flattery, and if I had only cared to, I might have had all her property settled on me during her lifetime. (I am drinking an awful lot of wine now and talking too much.) I hope you won't be angry if I mention now that I was beginning to produce the same effect on Avdotya Romanovna. But I was stupid and impatient and spoiled it all. Avdotya Romanovna had several times—and one time in particular—been greatly displeased by the expression of my eyes, would you believe it? There was sometimes a light in them which frightened her and grew stronger and stronger and more unguarded till it was hateful to her. No need to go into detail, but we parted. There I acted stupidly again. I fell to jeering in the coarsest way at all such propaganda and efforts to convert me; Parasha came on to the scene again, and not she alone; in fact there was a tremendous to-do. Ah, Rodion Romanovitch, if you could only see how your sister's eyes can flash sometimes! Never mind my being drunk at this moment and having had a whole glass of wine. I am speaking the truth. I assure you that this glance has haunted my dreams; the very rustle of her dress was more than I could stand at last. I really began to think that I might become epileptic. I could never have believed that I could be moved to such a frenzy. It was essential, indeed, to be reconciled, but by then it was impossible. And imagine what I did then! To what a pitch of stupidity a man can be brought by frenzy! Never undertake anything in a frenzy, Rodion Romanovitch. I reflected that Avdotya Romanovna was after all a beggar (ach, excuse me, that's not the word... but does it matter if it expresses the meaning?), that she lived by her work, that she had her mother and you to keep (ach, hang it, you are frowning again), and I resolved to offer her all my money—thirty thousand roubles I could have realised then—if she would run away with me here, to Petersburg. Of course I should have vowed eternal love, rapture, and so on. Do you know, I was so wild about her at that time that if she had told me to poison Marfa Petrovna or to cut her throat and to marry herself, it would have been done at once! But it ended in the catastrophe of which you know already. You can fancy how frantic I was when I heard that Marfa Petrovna had got hold of that scoundrelly attorney, Luzhin, and had almost made a match between them—which would really have been just the same thing as I was proposing. Wouldn't it? Wouldn't it? I notice that you've begun to be very attentive... you interesting young man...."

Svidrigaïlov struck the table with his fist impatiently. He was flushed. Raskolnikov saw clearly that the glass or glass and a half of champagne that he had sipped almost unconsciously was affecting him—and he resolved to take advantage of the opportunity. He felt very suspicious of Svidrigaïlov.

"Well, after what you have said, I am fully convinced that you have come to Petersburg with designs on my sister," he said directly to Svidrigaïlov, in order to irritate him further.

"Oh, nonsense," said Svidrigaïlov, seeming to rouse himself. "Why, I told you... besides your sister can't endure me."

"Yes, I am certain that she can't, but that's not the point."

"Are you so sure that she can't?" Svidrigaïlov screwed up his eyes and smiled mockingly. "You are right, she doesn't love me, but you can never be sure of what has passed between husband and wife or lover and mistress. There's always a little corner which remains a secret to the world and is only known to those two. Will you answer for it that Avdotya Romanovna regarded me with aversion?"

"From some words you've dropped, I notice that you still have designs—and of course evil ones—on Dounia and mean to carry them out promptly."

"What, have I dropped words like that?" Svidrigaïlov asked in naïve dismay, taking not the slightest notice of the epithet bestowed on his designs.

"Why, you are dropping them even now. Why are you so frightened? What are you so afraid of now?"

"Me—afraid? Afraid of you? You have rather to be afraid of me, *cher ami*. But what nonsense.... I've drunk too much though, I see that. I was almost saying too much again. Damn the wine! Hi! there, water!"

He snatched up the champagne bottle and flung it without ceremony out of the window. Philip brought the water.

"That's all nonsense!" said Svidrigaïlov, wetting a towel and putting it to his head. "But I can answer you in one word and annihilate all your suspicions. Do you know that I am going to get married?"

"You told me so before."

"Did I? I've forgotten. But I couldn't have told you so for certain for I had not even seen my betrothed; I only meant to. But now I really have a betrothed and it's a settled thing, and if it weren't that I have business that can't be put off, I would have taken you to see them at once, for I should like to ask your advice. Ach, hang it, only ten minutes left! See, look at the watch. But I must tell you, for it's an interesting story, my marriage, in its own way. Where are you off to? Going again?"

"No, I'm not going away now."

"Not at all? We shall see. I'll take you there, I'll show you my betrothed, only not now. For you'll soon have to be off. You have to go to the right and I to the left. Do you know that Madame Resslich, the woman I am lodging with now, eh? I know what you're thinking, that she's the woman whose girl they say drowned herself in the winter. Come, are you listening? She arranged it all for me. You're bored, she said, you want something to fill up your time. For, you know, I am a gloomy, depressed person. Do you think I'm light-hearted? No, I'm gloomy. I do no harm, but sit in a corner without speaking a word for three days at a time. And that Resslich is a sly hussy, I tell you. I know what she has got in her mind; she thinks I shall get sick of it, abandon my wife and depart, and she'll get hold of her and make a profit out of her—in our class, of course, or higher. She told me the father was a broken-down retired official, who has been sitting in a chair for the last three years with his legs paralysed. The mamma, she said, was a sensible woman. There is a son serving in the provinces, but he doesn't help; there is a daughter, who is married, but she doesn't visit them. And they've two little nephews on their hands, as though their own children were not enough, and they've taken from school their youngest daughter, a girl who'll be sixteen in another month, so that then she can be married. She was for me. We went there. How funny it was! I present myself—a landowner, a widower, of a well-known name, with connections, with a fortune. What if I am fifty and she is not sixteen? Who thinks of that? But it's fascinating, isn't it? It is fascinating, ha-ha! You should have seen how I talked to the papa and mamma. It was worth paying to have seen me at that moment. She comes in, curtseys, you can fancy, still in a short frock—an unopened bud! Flushing like a sunset—she had been told, no doubt. I don't know how you feel about female faces, but to my mind these sixteen years, these childish eyes, shyness and tears of bashfulness are better than beauty; and she is a perfect little picture, too. Fair hair in little curls, like a lamb's, full little rosy lips, tiny feet, a charmer!... Well, we made friends. I told them I was in a hurry owing to domestic circumstances, and the next day, that is the day before yesterday, we were betrothed. When I go now I take her on my knee at once and keep her there.... Well, she flushes like a sunset and I kiss her every minute. Her mamma of course impresses on her that this is her husband and that this must be so. It's simply delicious! The present betrothed condition is perhaps better than marriage. Here you have what is called *la nature et la vérité*, ha-ha! I've talked to her twice, she is far from a fool. Sometimes she steals a look at me that positively scorches me. Her face is like Raphael's Madonna. You know, the Sistine Madonna's face has something fantastic in it, the face of mournful religious ecstasy. Haven't you noticed it? Well, she's something in that line. The day after we'd been betrothed, I bought her presents to the value of fifteen hundred roubles—a set of diamonds and another of pearls and a silver dressing-case as large as this, with all sorts of things in it, so that even my Madonna's face glowed. I sat her on my knee, yesterday, and I suppose rather too unceremoniously—she flushed crimson and the tears started, but she didn't want to show it. We were left alone, she suddenly flung herself on my neck (for the first time of her own accord), put her little arms round me, kissed me, and vowed that she would be an obedient, faithful, and good wife, would make me happy, would devote all her life, every minute of her life, would sacrifice everything, everything, and that all she asks in return is my *respect*, and that she wants 'nothing, nothing more from me, no presents.' You'll admit that to hear such a confession, alone, from an angel of sixteen in a muslin frock, with little curls, with a flush of maiden shyness in her cheeks and tears of enthusiasm in her eyes is rather fascinating! Isn't it fascinating? It's worth paying for, isn't it? Well... listen, we'll go to see my betrothed, only not just now!"

"The fact is this monstrous difference in age and development excites your sensuality! Will you really make such a marriage?"

"Why, of course. Everyone thinks of himself, and he lives most gaily who knows best how to deceive himself. Ha-ha! But why are you so keen about virtue? Have mercy on me, my good friend. I am a sinful man. Ha-ha-ha!"

"But you have provided for the children of Katerina Ivanovna. Though... though you had your own reasons.... I understand it all now."

"I am always fond of children, very fond of them," laughed Svidrigaïlov. "I can tell you one curious instance of it. The first day I came here I visited various haunts, after seven years I simply rushed at them. You probably notice that I am not in a hurry to renew acquaintance with my old friends. I shall do without them as long as I can. Do you know, when I was with Marfa Petrovna in the country, I was haunted by the thought of these places where anyone who knows his way about can find a great deal. Yes, upon my soul! The peasants have vodka, the educated young people, shut out from activity, waste themselves in impossible dreams and visions and are crippled by theories; Jews have sprung up and are amassing money, and all the rest give themselves up to debauchery. From the first hour the town reeked of its familiar odours. I chanced to be in a frightful den—I like my dens dirty—it was a dance, so called, and there was a *cancan* such as I never saw in my day. Yes, there you have progress. All of a sudden I saw a little girl of thirteen, nicely dressed, dancing with a specialist in that line, with another one *vis-à-vis*. Her mother was sitting on a chair by the wall. You can't fancy what a *cancan* that was! The girl was ashamed, blushed, at last felt insulted, and began to cry. Her partner seized her and began whirling her round and performing before her; everyone laughed and—I like your public, even the *cancan* public—they laughed and shouted, 'Serves her right—serves her right! Shouldn't bring children!' Well, it's not my business whether that consoling reflection was logical or not. I at once fixed on my plan, sat down by the mother, and began by saying that I too was a stranger and that people here were ill-bred and that they couldn't distinguish decent folks and treat them with respect, gave her to understand that I had plenty of money, offered to take them home in my carriage. I took them home and got to know them. They were lodging in a miserable little hole and had only just arrived from the country. She told me that she and her daughter could only regard my acquaintance as an honour. I found out that they had nothing of their own and had come to town upon some legal business. I proffered my services and money. I learnt that they had gone to the dancing saloon by mistake, believing that it was a genuine dancing class. I offered to assist in the young girl's education in French and dancing. My offer was accepted with enthusiasm as an honour—and we are still friendly.... If you like, we'll go and see them, only not just now."

"Stop! Enough of your vile, nasty anecdotes, depraved vile, sensual man!"

"Schiller, you are a regular Schiller! *O la vertu va-t-elle se nicher?* But you know I shall tell you these things on purpose, for the pleasure of hearing your outcries!"

"I dare say. I can see I am ridiculous myself," muttered Raskolnikov angrily.

Svidrigaïlov laughed heartily; finally he called Philip, paid his bill, and began getting up.

"I say, but I am drunk, *assez causé*," he said. "It's been a pleasure."

"I should rather think it must be a pleasure!" cried Raskolnikov, getting up. "No doubt it is a pleasure for a worn-out profligate to describe such adventures with a monstrous project of the same sort in his mind—especially under such circumstances and to such a man as me.... It's stimulating!"

"Well, if you come to that," Svidrigaïlov answered, scrutinising Raskolnikov with some surprise, "if you come to that, you are a thorough cynic yourself. You've plenty to make you so, anyway. You can understand a great deal... and you can do a great deal too. But enough. I sincerely regret not having had more talk with you, but I shan't lose sight of you.... Only wait a bit."

Svidrigaïlov walked out of the restaurant. Raskolnikov walked out after him. Svidrigaïlov was not however very drunk, the wine had affected him for a moment, but it was passing off every minute. He was preoccupied with something of importance and was frowning. He was apparently excited and uneasy in anticipation of something. His manner to Raskolnikov had changed during the last few minutes, and he was ruder and more sneering every moment. Raskolnikov noticed all this, and he too was uneasy. He became very suspicious of Svidrigaïlov and resolved to follow him.

They came out on to the pavement.

"You go to the right, and I to the left, or if you like, the other way. Only *adieu, mon plaisir*, may we meet again."

And he walked to the right towards the Hay Market.

CHAPTER V

Raskolnikov walked after him.

"What's this?" cried Svidrigaïlov turning round, "I thought I said..."

"It means that I am not going to lose sight of you now."

"What?"

Both stood still and gazed at one another, as though measuring their strength.

"From all your half tipsy stories," Raskolnikov observed harshly, "I am *positive* that you have not given up your designs on my sister, but are pursuing them more actively than ever. I have learnt that my sister received a letter this morning. You have hardly been able to sit still all this time.... You may have unearthed a wife on the way, but that means nothing. I should like to make certain myself."

Raskolnikov could hardly have said himself what he wanted and of what he wished to make certain.

"Upon my word! I'll call the police!"

"Call away!"

Again they stood for a minute facing each other. At last Svidrigaïlov's face changed. Having satisfied himself that Raskolnikov was not frightened at his threat, he assumed a mirthful and friendly air.

"What a fellow! I purposely refrained from referring to your affair, though I am devoured by curiosity. It's a fantastic affair. I've put it off till another time, but you're enough to rouse the dead.... Well, let us go, only I warn you beforehand I am only going home for a moment, to get some money; then I shall lock up the flat, take a cab and go to spend the evening at the Islands. Now, now are you going to follow me?"

"I'm coming to your lodgings, not to see you but Sofya Semyonovna, to say I'm sorry not to have been at the funeral."

"That's as you like, but Sofya Semyonovna is not at home. She has taken the three children to an old lady of high rank, the patroness of some orphan asylums, whom I used to know years ago. I charmed the old lady by depositing a sum of money with her to provide for the three children of Katerina Ivanovna and subscribing to the institution as well. I told her too the story of Sofya Semyonovna in full detail, suppressing nothing. It produced an indescribable effect on her. That's why Sofya Semyonovna has been invited to call to-day at the X. Hotel where the lady is staying for the time."

"No matter, I'll come all the same."

"As you like, it's nothing to me, but I won't come with you; here we are at home. By the way, I am convinced that you regard me with suspicion just because I have shown such delicacy and have not so far troubled you with questions... you understand? It struck you as extraordinary; I don't mind betting it's that. Well, it teaches one to show delicacy!"

"And to listen at doors!"

"Ah, that's it, is it?" laughed Svidrigaïlov. "Yes, I should have been surprised if you had let that pass after all that has happened. Ha-ha! Though I did understand something of the pranks you had been up to and were telling Sofya Semyonovna about, what was the meaning of it? Perhaps I am quite behind the times and can't understand. For goodness' sake, explain it, my dear boy. Expound the latest theories!"

"You couldn't have heard anything. You're making it all up!"

"But I'm not talking about that (though I did hear something). No, I'm talking of the way you keep sighing and groaning now. The Schiller in you is in revolt every moment, and now you tell me not to listen at doors. If that's how you feel, go and inform the police that you had this mischance: you made a little mistake in your theory.

But if you are convinced that one mustn't listen at doors, but one may murder old women at one's pleasure, you'd better be off to America and make haste. Run, young man! There may still be time. I'm speaking sincerely. Haven't you the money? I'll give you the fare."

"I'm not thinking of that at all," Raskolnikov interrupted with disgust.

"I understand (but don't put yourself out, don't discuss it if you don't want to). I understand the questions you are worrying over—moral ones, aren't they? Duties of citizen and man? Lay them all aside. They are nothing to you now, ha-ha! You'll say you are still a man and a citizen. If so you ought not to have got into this coil. It's no use taking up a job you are not fit for. Well, you'd better shoot yourself, or don't you want to?"

"You seem trying to enrage me, to make me leave you."

"What a queer fellow! But here we are. Welcome to the staircase. You see, that's the way to Sofya Semyonovna. Look, there is no one at home. Don't you believe me? Ask Kapernaumov. She leaves the key with him. Here is Madame de Kapernaumov herself. Hey, what? She is rather deaf. Has she gone out? Where? Did you hear? She is not in and won't be till late in the evening probably. Well, come to my room; you wanted to come and see me, didn't you? Here we are. Madame Resslich's not at home. She is a woman who is always busy, an excellent woman I assure you.... She might have been of use to you if you had been a little more sensible. Now, see! I take this five-per-cent bond out of the bureau—see what a lot I've got of them still—this one will be turned into cash to-day. I mustn't waste any more time. The bureau is locked, the flat is locked, and here we are again on the stairs. Shall we take a cab? I'm going to the Islands. Would you like a lift? I'll take this carriage. Ah, you refuse? You are tired of it! Come for a drive! I believe it will come on to rain. Never mind, we'll put down the hood...."

Svidrigaïlov was already in the carriage. Raskolnikov decided that his suspicions were at least for that moment unjust. Without answering a word he turned and walked back towards the Hay Market. If he had only turned round on his way he might have seen Svidrigaïlov get out not a hundred paces off, dismiss the cab and walk along the pavement. But he had turned the corner and could see nothing. Intense disgust drew him away from Svidrigaïlov.

"To think that I could for one instant have looked for help from that coarse brute, that depraved sensualist and blackguard!" he cried.

Raskolnikov's judgment was uttered too lightly and hastily: there was something about Svidrigaïlov which gave him a certain original, even a mysterious character. As concerned his sister, Raskolnikov was convinced that Svidrigaïlov would not leave her in peace. But it was too tiresome and unbearable to go on thinking and thinking about this.

When he was alone, he had not gone twenty paces before he sank, as usual, into deep thought. On the bridge he stood by the railing and began gazing at the water. And his sister was standing close by him.

He met her at the entrance to the bridge, but passed by without seeing her. Dounia had never met him like this in the street before and was struck with dismay. She stood still and did not know whether to call to him or not. Suddenly she saw Svidrigaïlov coming quickly from the direction of the Hay Market.

He seemed to be approaching cautiously. He did not go on to the bridge, but stood aside on the pavement, doing all he could to avoid Raskolnikov's seeing him. He had observed Dounia for some time and had been making signs to her. She fancied he was signalling to beg her not to speak to her brother, but to come to him.

That was what Dounia did. She stole by her brother and went up to Svidrigaïlov.

"Let us make haste away," Svidrigaïlov whispered to her, "I don't want Rodion Romanovitch to know of our meeting. I must tell you I've been sitting with him in the restaurant close by, where he looked me up and I had great difficulty in getting rid of him. He has somehow heard of my letter to you and suspects something. It wasn't you who told him, of course, but if not you, who then?"

"Well, we've turned the corner now," Dounia interrupted, "and my brother won't see us. I have to tell you that I am going no further with you. Speak to me here. You can tell it all in the street."

"In the first place, I can't say it in the street; secondly, you must hear Sofya Semyonovna too; and, thirdly, I will show you some papers.... Oh well, if you won't agree to come with me, I shall refuse to give any explanation and go away at once. But I beg you not to forget that a very curious secret of your beloved brother's is entirely in my keeping."

Dounia stood still, hesitating, and looked at Svidrigaïlov with searching eyes.

"What are you afraid of?" he observed quietly. "The town is not the country. And even in the country you did me more harm than I did you."

"Have you prepared Sofya Semyonovna?"

"No, I have not said a word to her and am not quite certain whether she is at home now. But most likely she is. She has buried her stepmother to-day: she is not likely to go visiting on such a day. For the time I don't want to speak to anyone about it and I half regret having spoken to you. The slightest indiscretion is as bad as betrayal in a thing like this. I live there in that house, we are coming to it. That's the porter of our house—he knows me very well; you see, he's bowing; he sees I'm coming with a lady and no doubt he has noticed your face already and you will be glad of that if you are afraid of me and suspicious. Excuse my putting things so coarsely. I haven't a flat to myself; Sofya Semyonovna's room is next to mine—she lodges in the next flat. The whole floor is let out in lodgings. Why are you frightened like a child? Am I really so terrible?"

Svidrigaïlov's lips were twisted in a condescending smile; but he was in no smiling mood. His heart was throbbing and he could scarcely breathe. He spoke rather loud to cover his growing excitement. But Dounia did not notice this peculiar excitement, she was so irritated by his remark that she was frightened of him like a child and that he was so terrible to her.

"Though I know that you are not a man... of honour, I am not in the least afraid of you. Lead the way," she said with apparent composure, but her face was very pale.

Svidrigaïlov stopped at Sonia's room.

"Allow me to inquire whether she is at home.... She is not. How unfortunate! But I know she may come quite soon. If she's gone out, it can only be to see a lady about the orphans. Their mother is dead.... I've been meddling and making arrangements for them. If Sofya Semyonovna does not come back in ten minutes, I will send her to you, to-day if you like. This is my flat. These are my two rooms. Madame Resslich, my landlady, has the next room. Now, look this way. I will show you my chief piece of evidence: this door from my bedroom leads into two perfectly empty rooms, which are to let. Here they are... You must look into them with some attention."

Svidrigaïlov occupied two fairly large furnished rooms. Dounia was looking about her mistrustfully, but saw nothing special in the furniture or position of the rooms. Yet there was something to observe, for instance, that Svidrigaïlov's flat was exactly between two sets of almost uninhabited apartments. His rooms were not entered directly from the passage, but through the landlady's two almost empty rooms. Unlocking a door leading out of his bedroom, Svidrigaïlov showed Dounia the two empty rooms that were to let. Dounia stopped in the doorway, not knowing what she was called to look upon, but Svidrigaïlov hastened to explain.

"Look here, at this second large room. Notice that door, it's locked. By the door stands a chair, the only one in the two rooms. I brought it from my rooms so as to listen more conveniently. Just the other side of the door is Sofya Semyonovna's table; she sat there talking to Rodion Romanovitch. And I sat here listening on two successive evenings, for two hours each time—and of course I was able to learn something, what do you think?"

"You listened?"

"Yes, I did. Now come back to my room; we can't sit down here."

He brought Avdotya Romanovna back into his sitting-room and offered her a chair. He sat down at the opposite side of the table, at least seven feet from her, but probably there was the same glow in his eyes which had once frightened Dounia so much. She shuddered and once more looked about her distrustfully. It was an involuntary gesture; she evidently did not wish to betray her uneasiness. But the secluded position of Svidrigaïlov's lodging had suddenly struck her. She wanted to ask whether his landlady at least were at home, but pride kept her from asking. Moreover, she had another trouble in her heart incomparably greater than fear for herself. She was in great distress.

"Here is your letter," she said, laying it on the table. "Can it be true what you write? You hint at a crime committed, you say, by my brother. You hint at it too clearly; you daren't deny it now. I must tell you that I'd heard of this stupid story before you wrote and don't believe a word of it. It's a disgusting and ridiculous suspicion. I know the story and why and how it was invented. You can have no proofs. You promised to prove it. Speak! But let me warn you that I don't believe you! I don't believe you!"

Dounia said this, speaking hurriedly, and for an instant the colour rushed to her face.

"If you didn't believe it, how could you risk coming alone to my rooms? Why have you come? Simply from curiosity?"

"Don't torment me. Speak, speak!"

"There's no denying that you are a brave girl. Upon my word, I thought you would have asked Mr. Razumihin to escort you here. But he was not with you nor anywhere near. I was on the look-out. It's spirited of you, it proves you wanted to spare Rodion Romanovitch. But everything is divine in you.... About your brother, what am I to say to you? You've just seen him yourself. What did you think of him?"

"Surely that's not the only thing you are building on?"

"No, not on that, but on his own words. He came here on two successive evenings to see Sofya Semyonovna. I've shown you where they sat. He made a full confession to her. He is a murderer. He killed an old woman, a pawnbroker, with whom he had pawned things himself. He killed her sister too, a pedlar woman called Lizaveta, who happened to come in while he was murdering her sister. He killed them with an axe he brought with him. He murdered them to rob them and he did rob them. He took money and various things.... He told all this, word for word, to Sofya Semyonovna, the only person who knows his secret. But she has had no share by word or deed in the murder; she was as horrified at it as you are now. Don't be anxious, she won't betray him."

"It cannot be," muttered Dounia, with white lips. She gasped for breath. "It cannot be. There was not the slightest cause, no sort of ground.... It's a lie, a lie!"

"He robbed her, that was the cause, he took money and things. It's true that by his own admission he made no use of the money or things, but hid them under a stone, where they are now. But that was because he dared not make use of them."

"But how could he steal, rob? How could he dream of it?" cried Dounia, and she jumped up from the chair. "Why, you know him, and you've seen him, can he be a thief?"

She seemed to be imploring Svidrigaïlov; she had entirely forgotten her fear.

"There are thousands and millions of combinations and possibilities, Avdotya Romanovna. A thief steals and knows he is a scoundrel, but I've heard of a gentleman who broke open the mail. Who knows, very likely he thought he was doing a gentlemanly thing! Of course I should not have believed it myself if I'd been told of it as you have, but I believe my own ears. He explained all the causes of it to Sofya Semyonovna too, but she did not believe her ears at first, yet she believed her own eyes at last."

"What... were the causes?"

"It's a long story, Avdotya Romanovna. Here's... how shall I tell you?—A theory of a sort, the same one by which I for instance consider that a single misdeed is permissible if the principal aim is right, a solitary wrongdoing and hundreds of good deeds! It's galling too, of course, for a young man of gifts and overweening pride to know that if he had, for instance, a paltry three thousand, his whole career, his whole future would be differently shaped and yet not to have that three thousand. Add to that, nervous irritability from hunger, from lodging in a hole, from rags, from a vivid sense of the charm of his social position and his sister's and mother's position too. Above all, vanity, pride and vanity, though goodness knows he may have good qualities too.... I am not blaming him, please don't think it; besides, it's not my business. A special little theory came in too—a theory of a sort—dividing mankind, you see, into material and superior persons, that is persons to whom the law does not apply owing to their superiority, who make laws for the rest of mankind, the material, that is. It's all right as a theory, *une théorie comme une autre*. Napoleon attracted him tremendously, that is, what affected him was that a great many men of genius have not hesitated at wrongdoing, but have overstepped the law without thinking about it. He seems to have fancied that he was a genius too—that is, he was convinced of it for a time. He has suffered a great deal and is still suffering from the idea that he could make a theory, but was incapable of boldly overstepping the law, and so he is not a man of genius. And that's humiliating for a young man of any pride, in our day especially...."

"But remorse? You deny him any moral feeling then? Is he like that?"

"Ah, Avdotya Romanovna, everything is in a muddle now; not that it was ever in very good order. Russians in general are broad in their ideas, Avdotya Romanovna, broad like their land and exceedingly disposed to the fantastic, the chaotic. But it's a misfortune to be broad without a special genius. Do you remember what a lot of talk we had together on this subject, sitting in the evenings on the terrace after supper? Why, you used to reproach me with breadth! Who knows, perhaps we were talking at the very time when he was lying here thinking over his plan. There are no sacred traditions amongst us, especially in the educated class, Avdotya Romanovna. At the best someone will make them up somehow for himself out of books or from some old chronicle. But those are for the most part the learned and all old fogeys, so that it would be almost ill-bred in a man of society. You know my opinions in general, though. I never blame anyone. I do nothing at all, I persevere in that. But we've talked of this more than once before. I was so happy indeed as to interest you in my opinions.... You are very pale, Avdotya Romanovna."

"I know his theory. I read that article of his about men to whom all is permitted. Razumihin brought it to me."

"Mr. Razumihin? Your brother's article? In a magazine? Is there such an article? I didn't know. It must be interesting. But where are you going, Avdotya Romanovna?"

"I want to see Sofya Semyonovna," Dounia articulated faintly. "How do I go to her? She has come in, perhaps. I must see her at once. Perhaps she..."

Avdotya Romanovna could not finish. Her breath literally failed her.

"Sofya Semyonovna will not be back till night, at least I believe not. She was to have been back at once, but if not, then she will not be in till quite late."

"Ah, then you are lying! I see... you were lying... lying all the time.... I don't believe you! I don't believe you!" cried Dounia, completely losing her head.

Almost fainting, she sank on to a chair which Svidrigaïlov made haste to give her.

"Avdotya Romanovna, what is it? Control yourself! Here is some water. Drink a little...."

He sprinkled some water over her. Dounia shuddered and came to herself.

"It has acted violently," Svidrigaïlov muttered to himself, frowning. "Avdotya Romanovna, calm yourself! Believe me, he has friends. We will save him. Would you like me to take him abroad? I have money, I can get a ticket in three days. And as for the murder, he will do all sorts of good deeds yet, to atone for it. Calm yourself. He may become a great man yet. Well, how are you? How do you feel?"

"Cruel man! To be able to jeer at it! Let me go..."

"Where are you going?"

"To him. Where is he? Do you know? Why is this door locked? We came in at that door and now it is locked. When did you manage to lock it?"

"We couldn't be shouting all over the flat on such a subject. I am far from jeering; it's simply that I'm sick of talking like this. But how can you go in such a state? Do you want to betray him? You will drive him to fury, and he will give himself up. Let me tell you, he is already being watched; they are already on his track. You will simply be giving him away. Wait a little: I saw him and was talking to him just now. He can still be saved. Wait a bit, sit down; let us think it over together. I asked you to come in order to discuss it alone with you and to consider it thoroughly. But do sit down!"

"How can you save him? Can he really be saved?"

Dounia sat down. Svidrigaïlov sat down beside her.

"It all depends on you, on you, on you alone," he began with glowing eyes, almost in a whisper and hardly able to utter the words for emotion.

Dounia drew back from him in alarm. He too was trembling all over.

"You... one word from you, and he is saved. I... I'll save him. I have money and friends. I'll send him away at once. I'll get a passport, two passports, one for him and one for me. I have friends... capable people.... If you like, I'll take a passport for you... for your mother.... What do you want with Razumihin? I love you too.... I love you beyond everything.... Let me kiss the hem of your dress, let me, let me.... The very rustle of it is too much for me. Tell me, 'do that,' and I'll do it. I'll do everything. I will do the impossible. What you believe, I will believe. I'll do anything—anything! Don't, don't look at me like that. Do you know that you are killing me?..."

He was almost beginning to rave.... Something seemed suddenly to go to his head. Dounia jumped up and rushed to the door.

"Open it! Open it!" she called, shaking the door. "Open it! Is there no one there?"

Svidrigaïlov got up and came to himself. His still trembling lips slowly broke into an angry mocking smile.

"There is no one at home," he said quietly and emphatically. "The landlady has gone out, and it's waste of time to shout like that. You are only exciting yourself uselessly."

"Where is the key? Open the door at once, at once, base man!"

"I have lost the key and cannot find it."

"This is an outrage," cried Dounia, turning pale as death. She rushed to the furthest corner, where she made haste to barricade herself with a little table.

She did not scream, but she fixed her eyes on her tormentor and watched every movement he made.

Svidrigaïlov remained standing at the other end of the room facing her. He was positively composed, at least in appearance, but his face was pale as before. The mocking smile did not leave his face.

"You spoke of outrage just now, Avdotya Romanovna. In that case you may be sure I've taken measures. Sofya Semyonovna is not at home. The Kapernaumovs are far away—there are five locked rooms between. I am at least twice as strong as you are and I have nothing to fear, besides. For you could not complain afterwards. You surely would not be willing actually to betray your brother? Besides, no one would believe you. How should a girl have come alone to visit a solitary man in his lodgings? So that even if you do sacrifice your brother, you could prove nothing. It is very difficult to prove an assault, Avdotya Romanovna."

"Scoundrel!" whispered Dounia indignantly.

"As you like, but observe I was only speaking by way of a general proposition. It's my personal conviction that you are perfectly right—violence is hateful. I only spoke to show you that you need have no remorse even if... you were willing to save your brother of your own accord, as I suggest to you. You would be simply submitting to circumstances, to violence, in fact, if we must use that word. Think about it. Your brother's and your mother's fate are in your hands. I will be your slave... all my life... I will wait here."

Svidrigaïlov sat down on the sofa about eight steps from Dounia. She had not the slightest doubt now of his unbending determination. Besides, she knew him. Suddenly she pulled out of her pocket a revolver, cocked it and laid it in her hand on the table. Svidrigaïlov jumped up.

"Aha! So that's it, is it?" he cried, surprised but smiling maliciously. "Well, that completely alters the aspect of affairs. You've made things wonderfully easier for me, Avdotya Romanovna. But where did you get the revolver? Was it Mr. Razumihin? Why, it's my revolver, an old friend! And how I've hunted for it! The shooting lessons I've given you in the country have not been thrown away."

"It's not your revolver, it belonged to Marfa Petrovna, whom you killed, wretch! There was nothing of yours in her house. I took it when I began to suspect what you were capable of. If you dare to advance one step, I swear I'll kill you." She was frantic.

"But your brother? I ask from curiosity," said Svidrigaïlov, still standing where he was.

"Inform, if you want to! Don't stir! Don't come nearer! I'll shoot! You poisoned your wife, I know; you are a murderer yourself!" She held the revolver ready.

"Are you so positive I poisoned Marfa Petrovna?"

"You did! You hinted it yourself; you talked to me of poison.... I know you went to get it... you had it in readiness.... It was your doing.... It must have been your doing.... Scoundrel!"

"Even if that were true, it would have been for your sake... you would have been the cause."

"You are lying! I hated you always, always...."

"Oho, Avdotya Romanovna! You seem to have forgotten how you softened to me in the heat of propaganda. I saw it in your eyes. Do you remember that moonlight night, when the nightingale was singing?"

"That's a lie," there was a flash of fury in Dounia's eyes, "that's a lie and a libel!"

"A lie? Well, if you like, it's a lie. I made it up. Women ought not to be reminded of such things," he smiled. "I know you will shoot, you pretty wild creature. Well, shoot away!"

Dounia raised the revolver, and deadly pale, gazed at him, measuring the distance and awaiting the first movement on his part. Her lower lip was white and quivering and her big black eyes flashed like fire. He had never seen her so handsome. The fire glowing in her eyes at the moment she raised the revolver seemed to kindle him and there was a pang of anguish in his heart. He took a step forward and a shot rang out. The bullet grazed his hair and flew into the wall behind. He stood still and laughed softly.

"The wasp has stung me. She aimed straight at my head. What's this? Blood?" he pulled out his handkerchief to wipe the blood, which flowed in a thin stream down his right temple. The bullet seemed to have just grazed the skin.

Dounia lowered the revolver and looked at Svidrigaïlov not so much in terror as in a sort of wild amazement. She seemed not to understand what she was doing and what was going on.

"Well, you missed! Fire again, I'll wait," said Svidrigaïlov softly, still smiling, but gloomily. "If you go on like that, I shall have time to seize you before you cock again."

Dounia started, quickly cocked the pistol and again raised it.

"Let me be," she cried in despair. "I swear I'll shoot again. I... I'll kill you."

"Well... at three paces you can hardly help it. But if you don't... then." His eyes flashed and he took two steps forward. Dounia shot again: it missed fire.

"You haven't loaded it properly. Never mind, you have another charge there. Get it ready, I'll wait."

He stood facing her, two paces away, waiting and gazing at her with wild determination, with feverishly passionate, stubborn, set eyes. Dounia saw that he would sooner die than let her go. "And... now, of course she would kill him, at two paces!" Suddenly she flung away the revolver.

"She's dropped it!" said Svidrigaïlov with surprise, and he drew a deep breath. A weight seemed to have rolled from his heart—perhaps not only the fear of death; indeed he may scarcely have felt it at that moment. It was the deliverance from another feeling, darker and more bitter, which he could not himself have defined.

He went to Dounia and gently put his arm round her waist. She did not resist, but, trembling like a leaf, looked at him with suppliant eyes. He tried to say something, but his lips moved without being able to utter a sound.

"Let me go," Dounia implored. Svidrigaïlov shuddered. Her voice now was quite different.

"Then you don't love me?" he asked softly. Dounia shook her head.

"And... and you can't? Never?" he whispered in despair.

"Never!"

There followed a moment of terrible, dumb struggle in the heart of Svidrigaïlov. He looked at her with an indescribable gaze. Suddenly he withdrew his arm, turned quickly to the window and stood facing it. Another moment passed.

"Here's the key."

He took it out of the left pocket of his coat and laid it on the table behind him, without turning or looking at Dounia.

"Take it! Make haste!"

He looked stubbornly out of the window. Dounia went up to the table to take the key.

"Make haste! Make haste!" repeated Svidrigaïlov, still without turning or moving. But there seemed a terrible significance in the tone of that "make haste."

Dounia understood it, snatched up the key, flew to the door, unlocked it quickly and rushed out of the room. A minute later, beside herself, she ran out on to the canal bank in the direction of X. Bridge.

Svidrigaïlov remained three minutes standing at the window. At last he slowly turned, looked about him and passed his hand over his forehead. A strange smile contorted his face, a pitiful, sad, weak smile, a smile of despair. The blood, which was already getting dry, smeared his hand. He looked angrily at it, then wetted a towel and washed his temple. The revolver which Dounia had flung away lay near the door and suddenly caught his eye. He picked it up and examined it. It was a little pocket three-barrel revolver of old-fashioned construction. There were still two charges and one capsule left in it. It could be fired again. He thought a little, put the revolver in his pocket, took his hat and went out.

CHAPTER VI

He spent that evening till ten o'clock going from one low haunt to another. Katia too turned up and sang another gutter song, how a certain

"villain and tyrant,"

"began kissing Katia."

Svidrigaïlov treated Katia and the organ-grinder and some singers and the waiters and two little clerks. He was particularly drawn to these clerks by the fact that they both had crooked noses, one bent to the left and the other to the right. They took him finally to a pleasure garden, where he paid for their entrance. There was one lanky three-year-old pine-tree and three bushes in the garden, besides a "Vauxhall," which was in reality a drinking-bar where tea too was served, and there were a few green tables and chairs standing round it. A chorus of wretched singers and a drunken but exceedingly depressed German clown from Munich with a red nose entertained the public. The clerks quarrelled with some other clerks and a fight seemed imminent. Svidrigaïlov was chosen to decide the dispute. He listened to them for a quarter of an hour, but they shouted so loud that there was no possibility of understanding them. The only fact that seemed certain was that one of them had stolen something and had even succeeded in selling it on the spot to a Jew, but would not share the spoil with his companion. Finally it appeared that the stolen object was a teaspoon belonging to the Vauxhall. It was missed and the affair began to seem troublesome. Svidrigaïlov paid for the spoon, got up, and walked out of the garden. It was about six o'clock. He had not drunk a drop of wine all this time and had ordered tea more for the sake of appearances than anything.

It was a dark and stifling evening. Threatening storm-clouds came over the sky about ten o'clock. There was a clap of thunder, and the rain came down like a waterfall. The water fell not in drops, but beat on the earth in streams. There were flashes of lightning every minute and each flash lasted while one could count five.

Drenched to the skin, he went home, locked himself in, opened the bureau, took out all his money and tore up two or three papers. Then, putting the money in his pocket, he was about to change his clothes, but, looking out of the window and listening to the thunder and the rain, he gave up the idea, took up his hat and went out of the room without locking the door. He went straight to Sonia. She was at home.

She was not alone: the four Kapernaumov children were with her. She was giving them tea. She received Svidrigaïlov in respectful silence, looking wonderingly at his soaking clothes. The children all ran away at once in indescribable terror.

Svidrigaïlov sat down at the table and asked Sonia to sit beside him. She timidly prepared to listen.

"I may be going to America, Sofya Semyonovna," said Svidrigaïlov, "and as I am probably seeing you for the last time, I have come to make some arrangements. Well, did you see the lady to-day? I know what she said to you, you need not tell me." (Sonia made a movement and blushed.) "Those people have their own way of doing things. As to your sisters and your brother, they are really provided for and the money assigned to them I've put into safe keeping and have received acknowledgments. You had better take charge of the receipts, in case anything happens. Here, take them! Well now, that's settled. Here are three 5-per-cent bonds to the value of three thousand roubles. Take those for yourself, entirely for yourself, and let that be strictly between ourselves, so that no one knows of it, whatever you hear. You will need the money, for to go on living in the old way, Sofya Semyonovna, is bad, and besides there is no need for it now."

"I am so much indebted to you, and so are the children and my stepmother," said Sonia hurriedly, "and if I've said so little... please don't consider..."

"That's enough! that's enough!"

"But as for the money, Arkady Ivanovitch, I am very grateful to you, but I don't need it now. I can always earn my own living. Don't think me ungrateful. If you are so charitable, that money...."

"It's for you, for you, Sofya Semyonovna, and please don't waste words over it. I haven't time for it. You will want it. Rodion Romanovitch has two alternatives: a bullet in the brain or Siberia." (Sonia looked wildly at him, and started.) "Don't be uneasy, I know all about it from himself and I am not a gossip; I won't tell anyone. It was good advice when you told him to give himself up and confess. It would be much better for him. Well, if it turns out to be Siberia, he will go and you will follow him. That's so, isn't it? And if so, you'll need money. You'll need it for him, do you understand? Giving it to you is the same as my giving it to him. Besides, you promised Amalia Ivanovna to pay what's owing. I heard you. How can you undertake such obligations so heedlessly, Sofya Semyonovna? It was Katerina Ivanovna's debt and not yours, so you ought not to have taken any notice of the German woman. You can't get through the world like that. If you are ever questioned about me—to-morrow or the day after you will be asked—don't say anything about my coming to see you now and don't show the money to anyone or say a word about it. Well, now good-bye." (He got up.) "My greetings to Rodion Romanovitch. By the way, you'd better put the money for the present in Mr. Razumihin's keeping. You know Mr. Razumihin? Of course you do. He's not a bad fellow. Take it to him to-morrow or... when the time comes. And till then, hide it carefully."

Sonia too jumped up from her chair and looked in dismay at Svidrigaïlov. She longed to speak, to ask a question, but for the first moments she did not dare and did not know how to begin.

"How can you... how can you be going now, in such rain?"

"Why, be starting for America, and be stopped by rain! Ha, ha! Good-bye, Sofya Semyonovna, my dear! Live and live long, you will be of use to others. By the way... tell Mr. Razumihin I send my greetings to him. Tell him Arkady Ivanovitch Svidrigaïlov sends his greetings. Be sure to."

He went out, leaving Sonia in a state of wondering anxiety and vague apprehension.

It appeared afterwards that on the same evening, at twenty past eleven, he made another very eccentric and unexpected visit. The rain still persisted. Drenched to the skin, he walked into the little flat where the parents of his betrothed lived, in Third Street in Vassilyevsky Island. He knocked some time before he was admitted, and his visit at first caused great perturbation; but Svidrigaïlov could be very fascinating when he liked, so that the first, and indeed very intelligent surmise of the sensible parents that Svidrigaïlov had probably had so much to drink that he did not know what he was doing vanished immediately. The decrepit father was wheeled in to see Svidrigaïlov by the tender and sensible mother, who as usual began the conversation with various irrelevant questions. She never asked a direct question, but began by smiling and rubbing her hands and then, if she were obliged to ascertain something—for instance, when Svidrigaïlov would like to have the wedding—she would begin by interested and almost eager questions about Paris and the court life there, and only by degrees brought the conversation round to Third Street. On other occasions this had of course been very impressive, but this time Arkady Ivanovitch seemed particularly impatient, and insisted on seeing his betrothed at once, though he had been informed, to begin with, that she had already gone to bed. The girl of course appeared.

Svidrigaïlov informed her at once that he was obliged by very important affairs to leave Petersburg for a time, and therefore brought her fifteen thousand roubles and begged her accept them as a present from him, as he had long been intending to make her this trifling present before their wedding. The logical connection of the present with his immediate departure and the absolute necessity of visiting them for that purpose in pouring rain at midnight was not made clear. But it all went off very well; even the inevitable ejaculations of wonder and regret, the inevitable questions were extraordinarily few and restrained. On the other hand, the gratitude expressed was most glowing and was reinforced by tears from the most sensible of mothers. Svidrigaïlov got up, laughed, kissed his betrothed, patted her cheek, declared he would soon come back, and noticing in her eyes, together with childish curiosity, a sort of earnest dumb inquiry, reflected and kissed her again, though he felt sincere anger inwardly at the thought that his present would be immediately locked up in the keeping of the most sensible of mothers. He went away, leaving them all in a state of extraordinary excitement, but the tender mamma, speaking quietly in a half whisper, settled some of the most important of their doubts, concluding that Svidrigaïlov was a great man, a man of great affairs and connections and of great wealth—there was no knowing what he had in his mind. He would start off on a journey and give away money just as the fancy took him, so that there was nothing surprising about it. Of course it was strange that he was wet through, but Englishmen, for instance, are even more eccentric, and all these people of high society didn't think of what was said of them and didn't stand on ceremony. Possibly, indeed, he came like that on purpose to show that he was not afraid of anyone. Above all, not a word should be said about it, for God knows what might come of it, and the money must be locked up, and it was most fortunate that Fedosya, the cook, had not left the kitchen. And above all not a word must be said to that old cat, Madame Resslich, and so on and so on. They sat up whispering till two o'clock, but the girl went to bed much earlier, amazed and rather sorrowful.

Svidrigaïlov meanwhile, exactly at midnight, crossed the bridge on the way back to the mainland. The rain had ceased and there was a roaring wind. He began shivering, and for one moment he gazed at the black waters of the Little Neva with a look of special interest, even inquiry. But he soon felt it very cold, standing by the water; he turned and went towards Y. Prospect. He walked along that endless street for a long time, almost half an hour, more than once stumbling in the dark on the wooden pavement, but continually looking for something on the right side of the street. He had noticed passing through this street lately that there was a hotel somewhere towards the end, built of wood, but fairly large, and its name he remembered was something like Adrianople. He was not mistaken: the hotel was so conspicuous in that God-forsaken place that he could not fail to see it even in the dark. It was a long, blackened wooden building, and in spite of the late hour there were lights in the windows and signs of life within. He went in and asked a ragged fellow who met him in the corridor for a room. The latter, scanning Svidrigaïlov, pulled himself together and led him at once to a close and tiny room in the distance, at the end of the corridor, under the stairs. There was no other, all were occupied. The ragged fellow looked inquiringly.

"Is there tea?" asked Svidrigaïlov.

"Yes, sir."

"What else is there?"

"Veal, vodka, savouries."

"Bring me tea and veal."

"And you want nothing else?" he asked with apparent surprise.

"Nothing, nothing."

The ragged man went away, completely disillusioned.

"It must be a nice place," thought Svidrigaïlov. "How was it I didn't know it? I expect I look as if I came from a café chantant and have had some adventure on the way. It would be interesting to know who stay here?"

He lighted the candle and looked at the room more carefully. It was a room so low-pitched that Svidrigaïlov could only just stand up in it; it had one window; the bed, which was very dirty, and the plain-stained chair and table almost filled it up. The walls looked as though they were made of planks, covered with shabby paper, so torn and dusty that the pattern was indistinguishable, though the general colour—yellow—could still be made out. One of the walls was cut short by the sloping ceiling, though the room was not an attic but just under the stairs.

Svidrigaïlov set down the candle, sat down on the bed and sank into thought. But a strange persistent murmur which sometimes rose to a shout in the next room attracted his attention. The murmur had not ceased from the moment he entered the room. He listened: someone was upbraiding and almost tearfully scolding, but he heard only one voice.

Svidrigaïlov got up, shaded the light with his hand and at once he saw light through a crack in the wall; he went up and peeped through. The room, which was somewhat larger than his, had two occupants. One of them, a very curly-headed man with a red inflamed face, was standing in the pose of an orator, without his coat, with his legs wide apart to preserve his balance, and smiting himself on the breast. He reproached the other with being a beggar, with having no standing whatever. He declared that he had taken the other out of the gutter and he could turn him out when he liked, and that only the finger of Providence sees it all. The object of his reproaches was sitting in a chair, and had the air of a man who wants dreadfully to sneeze, but can't. He sometimes turned sheepish and befogged eyes on the speaker, but obviously had not the slightest idea what he was talking about and scarcely heard it. A candle was burning down on the table; there were wine-glasses, a nearly empty bottle of vodka, bread and cucumber, and glasses with the dregs of stale tea. After gazing attentively at this, Svidrigaïlov turned away indifferently and sat down on the bed.

The ragged attendant, returning with the tea, could not resist asking him again whether he didn't want anything more, and again receiving a negative reply, finally withdrew. Svidrigaïlov made haste to drink a glass of tea to warm himself, but could not eat anything. He began to feel feverish. He took off his coat and, wrapping himself in the blanket, lay down on the bed. He was annoyed. "It would have been better to be well for the occasion," he thought with a smile. The room was close, the candle burnt dimly, the wind was roaring outside, he heard a mouse scratching in the corner and the room smelt of mice and of leather. He lay in a sort of reverie: one thought followed another. He felt a longing to fix his imagination on something. "It must be a garden under the window," he thought. "There's a sound of trees. How I dislike the sound of trees on a stormy night, in the dark! They give one a horrid feeling." He remembered how he had disliked it when he passed Petrovsky Park just now. This reminded him of the bridge over the Little Neva and he felt cold again as he had when standing there. "I never have liked water," he thought, "even in a landscape," and he suddenly smiled again at a strange idea: "Surely now all these questions of taste and comfort ought not to matter, but I've become more particular, like an animal that picks out a special place... for such an occasion. I ought to have gone into the Petrovsky Park! I suppose it seemed dark, cold, ha-ha! As though I were seeking pleasant sensations!... By the way, why haven't I put out the candle?" he blew it out. "They've gone to bed next door," he thought, not seeing the light at the crack. "Well, now, Marfa Petrovna, now is the time for you to turn up; it's dark, and the very time and place for you. But now you won't come!"

He suddenly recalled how, an hour before carrying out his design on Dounia, he had recommended Raskolnikov to trust her to Razumihin's keeping. "I suppose I really did say it, as Raskolnikov guessed, to tease myself. But what a rogue that Raskolnikov is! He's gone through a good deal. He may be a successful rogue in time when he's got over his nonsense. But now he's *too* eager for life. These young men are contemptible on that point. But, hang the fellow! Let him please himself, it's nothing to do with me."

He could not get to sleep. By degrees Dounia's image rose before him, and a shudder ran over him. "No, I must give up all that now," he thought, rousing himself. "I must think of something else. It's queer and funny. I never had a great hatred for anyone, I never particularly desired to avenge myself even, and that's a bad sign, a bad sign, a bad sign. I never liked quarrelling either, and never lost my temper—that's a bad sign too. And the promises I made her just now, too—Damnation! But—who knows?—perhaps she would have made a new man of me somehow...."

He ground his teeth and sank into silence again. Again Dounia's image rose before him, just as she was when, after shooting the first time, she had lowered the revolver in terror and gazed blankly at him, so that he might have seized her twice over and she would not have lifted a hand to defend herself if he had not reminded her. He recalled how at that instant he felt almost sorry for her, how he had felt a pang at his heart...

"Aïe! Damnation, these thoughts again! I must put it away!"

He was dozing off; the feverish shiver had ceased, when suddenly something seemed to run over his arm and leg under the bedclothes. He started. "Ugh! hang it! I believe it's a mouse," he thought, "that's the veal I left on the table." He felt fearfully disinclined to pull off the blanket, get up, get cold, but all at once something unpleasant ran over his leg again. He pulled off the blanket and lighted the candle. Shaking with feverish chill he bent down to examine the bed: there was nothing. He shook the blanket and suddenly a mouse jumped out on the sheet. He tried to catch it, but the mouse ran to and fro in zigzags without leaving the bed, slipped between his fingers, ran over his hand and suddenly darted under the pillow. He threw down the pillow, but in one instant felt something leap on his chest and dart over his body and down his back under his shirt. He trembled nervously and woke up.

The room was dark. He was lying on the bed and wrapped up in the blanket as before. The wind was howling under the window. "How disgusting," he thought with annoyance.

He got up and sat on the edge of the bedstead with his back to the window. "It's better not to sleep at all," he decided. There was a cold damp draught from the window, however; without getting up he drew the blanket over him and wrapped himself in it. He was not thinking of anything and did not want to think. But one image rose after another, incoherent scraps of thought without beginning or end passed through his mind. He sank into drowsiness. Perhaps the cold, or the dampness, or the dark, or the wind that howled under the window and tossed the trees roused a sort of persistent craving for the fantastic. He kept dwelling on images of flowers, he fancied a charming flower garden, a bright, warm, almost hot day, a holiday—Trinity day. A fine, sumptuous country cottage in the English taste overgrown with fragrant flowers, with flower beds going round the house; the porch, wreathed in climbers, was surrounded with beds of roses. A light, cool staircase, carpeted with rich rugs, was decorated with rare plants in china pots. He noticed particularly in the windows nosegays of tender, white, heavily fragrant narcissus bending over their bright, green, thick long stalks. He was reluctant to move away from them, but he went up the stairs and came into a large, high drawing-room and again everywhere—at the windows, the doors on to the balcony, and on the balcony itself—were flowers. The floors were strewn with freshly-cut fragrant hay, the windows were open, a fresh, cool, light air came into the room. The birds were chirruping under the window, and in the middle of the room, on a table covered with a white satin shroud, stood a coffin. The coffin was covered with white silk and edged with a thick white frill; wreaths of flowers surrounded it on all sides. Among the flowers lay a girl in a white muslin dress, with her arms crossed and pressed on her bosom, as though carved out of marble. But her loose fair hair was wet; there was a wreath of roses on her head. The stern and already rigid profile of her face looked as though chiselled of marble too, and the smile on her pale lips was full of an immense unchildish misery and sorrowful appeal. Svidrigaïlov knew that girl; there was no holy image, no burning candle beside the coffin; no sound of prayers: the girl had drowned herself. She was only fourteen, but her heart was broken. And she had destroyed herself, crushed by an insult that had appalled and amazed that childish soul, had smirched that angel purity with unmerited disgrace and torn from her a last scream of despair, unheeded and brutally disregarded, on a dark night in the cold and wet while the wind howled....

Svidrigaïlov came to himself, got up from the bed and went to the window. He felt for the latch and opened it. The wind lashed furiously into the little room and stung his face and his chest, only covered with his shirt, as though with frost. Under the window there must have been something like a garden, and apparently a pleasure garden. There, too, probably there were tea-tables and singing in the daytime. Now drops of rain flew in at the window from the trees and bushes; it was dark as in a cellar, so that he could only just make out some dark blurs of objects. Svidrigaïlov, bending down with elbows on the window-sill, gazed for five minutes into the darkness; the boom of a cannon, followed by a second one, resounded in the darkness of the night. "Ah, the signal! The river is overflowing," he thought. "By morning it will be swirling down the street in the lower parts, flooding the basements and cellars. The cellar rats will swim out, and men will curse in the rain and wind as they drag their rubbish to their upper storeys. What time is it now?" And he had hardly thought it when, somewhere near, a clock on the wall, ticking away hurriedly, struck three.

"Aha! It will be light in an hour! Why wait? I'll go out at once straight to the park. I'll choose a great bush there drenched with rain, so that as soon as one's shoulder touches it, millions of drops drip on one's head."

He moved away from the window, shut it, lighted the candle, put on his waistcoat, his overcoat and his hat and went out, carrying the candle, into the passage to look for the ragged attendant who would be asleep somewhere in the midst of candle-ends and all sorts of rubbish, to pay him for the room and leave the hotel. "It's the best minute; I couldn't choose a better."

He walked for some time through a long narrow corridor without finding anyone and was just going to call out, when suddenly in a dark corner between an old cupboard and the door he caught sight of a strange object which seemed to be alive. He bent down with the candle and saw a little girl, not more than five years old, shivering and crying, with her clothes as wet as a soaking house-flannel. She did not seem afraid of Svidrigaïlov, but looked at him with blank amazement out of her big black eyes. Now and then she sobbed as children do when they have been crying a long time, but are beginning to be comforted. The child's face was pale and tired, she was numb with cold. "How can she have come here? She must have hidden here and not slept all night." He began questioning her. The child suddenly becoming animated, chattered away in her baby language, something about "mammy" and that "mammy would beat her," and about some cup that she had "bwoken." The child chattered on without stopping. He could only guess from what she said that she was a neglected child, whose mother, probably a drunken cook, in the service of the hotel, whipped and frightened her; that the child had broken a cup of her mother's and was so frightened that she had run away the evening before, had hidden for a long while somewhere outside in the rain, at last had made her way in here, hidden behind the cupboard and spent the night there, crying and trembling from the damp, the darkness and the fear that she would be badly beaten for it. He took her in his arms, went back to his room, sat her on the bed, and began undressing her. The torn shoes which she had on her stockingless feet were as wet as if they had been standing in a puddle all night. When he had undressed her, he put her on the bed, covered her up and wrapped her in the blanket from her head downwards. She fell asleep at once. Then he sank into dreary musing again.

"What folly to trouble myself," he decided suddenly with an oppressive feeling of annoyance. "What idiocy!" In vexation he took up the candle to go and look for the ragged attendant again and make haste to go away. "Damn the child!" he thought as he opened the door, but he turned again to see whether the child was asleep. He raised the blanket carefully. The child was sleeping soundly, she had got warm under the blanket, and her pale cheeks were flushed. But strange to say that flush seemed brighter and coarser than the rosy cheeks of childhood. "It's a flush of fever," thought Svidrigaïlov. It was like the flush from drinking, as though she had been given a full glass to drink. Her crimson lips were hot and glowing; but what was this? He suddenly fancied that her long black eyelashes were quivering, as though the lids were opening and a sly crafty eye peeped out with an unchildlike wink, as though the little girl were not asleep, but pretending. Yes, it was so. Her lips parted in a smile. The corners of her mouth quivered, as though she were trying to control them. But now she quite gave up all effort, now it was a grin, a broad grin; there was something shameless, provocative in that quite unchildish face; it was depravity, it was the face of a harlot, the shameless face of a French harlot. Now both eyes opened wide; they turned a glowing, shameless glance upon him; they laughed, invited him.... There was something infinitely hideous and shocking in that laugh, in those eyes, in such nastiness in the face of a child. "What, at five years old?" Svidrigaïlov muttered in genuine horror. "What does it mean?" And now she turned to him, her little face all aglow, holding out her arms.... "Accursed child!" Svidrigaïlov cried, raising his hand to strike her, but at that moment he woke up.

He was in the same bed, still wrapped in the blanket. The candle had not been lighted, and daylight was streaming in at the windows.

"I've had nightmare all night!" He got up angrily, feeling utterly shattered; his bones ached. There was a thick mist outside and he could see nothing. It was nearly five. He had overslept himself! He got up, put on his still damp jacket and overcoat. Feeling the revolver in his pocket, he took it out and then he sat down, took a notebook out of his pocket and in the most conspicuous place on the title page wrote a few lines in large letters. Reading them over, he sank into thought with his elbows on the table. The revolver and the notebook lay beside him. Some flies woke up and settled on the untouched veal, which was still on the table. He stared at them and at last with his free right hand began trying to catch one. He tried till he was tired, but could not catch it. At last, realising that he was engaged in this interesting pursuit, he started, got up and walked resolutely out of the room. A minute later he was in the street.

A thick milky mist hung over the town. Svidrigaïlov walked along the slippery dirty wooden pavement towards the Little Neva. He was picturing the waters of the Little Neva swollen in the night, Petrovsky Island, the wet paths, the wet grass, the wet trees and bushes and at last the bush.... He began ill-humouredly staring at the houses, trying to think of something else. There was not a cabman or a passer-by in the street. The bright yellow, wooden, little houses looked dirty and dejected with their closed shutters. The cold and damp penetrated his whole body and he began to shiver. From time to time he came across shop signs and read each carefully. At last he reached the end of the wooden pavement and came to a big stone house. A dirty, shivering dog crossed his path with its tail between its legs. A man in a greatcoat lay face downwards; dead drunk, across the pavement. He looked at him and went on. A high tower stood up on the left. "Bah!" he shouted, "here is a place. Why should it be Petrovsky? It will be in the presence of an official witness anyway...."

He almost smiled at this new thought and turned into the street where there was the big house with the tower. At the great closed gates of the house, a little man stood with his shoulder leaning against them, wrapped in a grey soldier's coat, with a copper Achilles helmet on his head. He cast a drowsy and indifferent glance at Svidrigaïlov. His face wore that perpetual look of peevish dejection, which is so sourly printed on all faces of Jewish race without exception. They both, Svidrigaïlov and Achilles, stared at each other for a few minutes without speaking. At last it struck Achilles as irregular for a man not drunk to be standing three steps from him, staring and not saying a word.

"What do you want here?" he said, without moving or changing his position.

"Nothing, brother, good morning," answered Svidrigaïlov.

"This isn't the place."

"I am going to foreign parts, brother."

"To foreign parts?"

"To America."

"America."

Svidrigaïlov took out the revolver and cocked it. Achilles raised his eyebrows.

"I say, this is not the place for such jokes!"

"Why shouldn't it be the place?"

"Because it isn't."

"Well, brother, I don't mind that. It's a good place. When you are asked, you just say he was going, he said, to America."

He put the revolver to his right temple.

"You can't do it here, it's not the place," cried Achilles, rousing himself, his eyes growing bigger and bigger.

Svidrigaïlov pulled the trigger.

CHAPTER VII

The same day, about seven o'clock in the evening, Raskolnikov was on his way to his mother's and sister's lodging—the lodging in Bakaleyev's house which Razumihin had found for them. The stairs went up from the street. Raskolnikov walked with lagging steps, as though still hesitating whether to go or not. But nothing would have turned him back: his decision was taken.

"Besides, it doesn't matter, they still know nothing," he thought, "and they are used to thinking of me as eccentric."

He was appallingly dressed: his clothes torn and dirty, soaked with a night's rain. His face was almost distorted from fatigue, exposure, the inward conflict that had lasted for twenty-four hours. He had spent all the previous night alone, God knows where. But anyway he had reached a decision.

He knocked at the door which was opened by his mother. Dounia was not at home. Even the servant happened to be out. At first Pulcheria Alexandrovna was speechless with joy and surprise; then she took him by the hand and drew him into the room.

"Here you are!" she began, faltering with joy. "Don't be angry with me, Rodya, for welcoming you so foolishly with tears: I am laughing not crying. Did you think I was crying? No, I am delighted, but I've got into such a stupid habit of shedding tears. I've been like that ever since your father's death. I cry for anything. Sit down, dear boy, you must be tired; I see you are. Ah, how muddy you are."

"I was in the rain yesterday, mother...." Raskolnikov began.

"No, no," Pulcheria Alexandrovna hurriedly interrupted, "you thought I was going to cross-question you in the womanish way I used to; don't be anxious, I understand, I understand it all: now I've learned the ways here and truly I see for myself that they are better. I've made up my mind once for all: how could I understand your plans and expect you to give an account of them? God knows what concerns and plans you may have, or what ideas you are hatching; so it's not for me to keep nudging your elbow, asking you what you are thinking about? But, my goodness! why am I running to and fro as though I were crazy...? I am reading your article in the magazine for the third time, Rodya. Dmitri Prokofitch brought it to me. Directly I saw it I cried out to myself: 'There, foolish one,' I thought, 'that's what he is busy about; that's the solution of the mystery! Learned people are always like that. He may have some new ideas in his head just now; he is thinking them over and I worry him and upset him.' I read it, my dear, and of course there was a great deal I did not understand; but that's only natural—how should I?"

"Show me, mother."

Raskolnikov took the magazine and glanced at his article. Incongruous as it was with his mood and his circumstances, he felt that strange and bitter sweet sensation that every author experiences the first time he sees himself in print; besides, he was only twenty-three. It lasted only a moment. After reading a few lines he frowned and his heart throbbed with anguish. He recalled all the inward conflict of the preceding months. He flung the article on the table with disgust and anger.

"But, however foolish I may be, Rodya, I can see for myself that you will very soon be one of the leading—if not the leading man—in the world of Russian thought. And they dared to think you were mad! You don't know, but they really thought that. Ah, the despicable creatures, how could they understand genius! And Dounia, Dounia was all but believing it—what do you say to that? Your father sent twice to magazines—the first time poems (I've got the manuscript and will show you) and the second time a whole novel (I begged him to let me copy it out) and how we prayed that they should be taken—they weren't! I was breaking my heart, Rodya, six or seven days ago over your food and your clothes and the way you are living. But now I see again how foolish I was, for you can attain any position you like by your intellect and talent. No doubt you don't care about that for the present and you are occupied with much more important matters...."

"Dounia's not at home, mother?"

"No, Rodya. I often don't see her; she leaves me alone. Dmitri Prokofitch comes to see me, it's so good of him, and he always talks about you. He loves you and respects you, my dear. I don't say that Dounia is very wanting in consideration. I am not complaining. She has her ways and I have mine; she seems to have got some secrets of late and I never have any secrets from you two. Of course, I am sure that Dounia has far too much sense, and besides she loves you and me... but I don't know what it will all lead to. You've made me so happy by coming now, Rodya, but she has missed you by going out; when she comes in I'll tell her: 'Your brother came in while you were out. Where have you been all this time?' You mustn't spoil me, Rodya, you know; come when you can, but if you can't, it doesn't matter, I can wait. I shall know, anyway, that you are fond of me, that will be enough for me. I shall read what you write, I shall hear about you from everyone, and sometimes you'll come yourself to see me. What could be better? Here you've come now to comfort your mother, I see that."

Here Pulcheria Alexandrovna began to cry.

"Here I am again! Don't mind my foolishness. My goodness, why am I sitting here?" she cried, jumping up. "There is coffee and I don't offer you any. Ah, that's the selfishness of old age. I'll get it at once!"

"Mother, don't trouble, I am going at once. I haven't come for that. Please listen to me."

Pulcheria Alexandrovna went up to him timidly.

"Mother, whatever happens, whatever you hear about me, whatever you are told about me, will you always love me as you do now?" he asked suddenly from the fullness of his heart, as though not thinking of his words and not weighing them.

"Rodya, Rodya, what is the matter? How can you ask me such a question? Why, who will tell me anything about you? Besides, I shouldn't believe anyone, I should refuse to listen."

"I've come to assure you that I've always loved you and I am glad that we are alone, even glad Dounia is out," he went on with the same impulse. "I have come to tell you that though you will be unhappy, you must believe that your son loves you now more than himself, and that all you thought about me, that I was cruel and didn't care about you, was all a mistake. I shall never cease to love you.... Well, that's enough: I thought I must do this and begin with this...."

Pulcheria Alexandrovna embraced him in silence, pressing him to her bosom and weeping gently.

"I don't know what is wrong with you, Rodya," she said at last. "I've been thinking all this time that we were simply boring you and now I see that there is a great sorrow in store for you, and that's why you are miserable. I've foreseen it a long time, Rodya. Forgive me for speaking about it. I keep thinking about it and lie awake at nights. Your sister lay talking in her sleep all last night, talking of nothing but you. I caught something, but I couldn't make it out. I felt all the morning as though I were going to be hanged, waiting for something, expecting something, and now it has come! Rodya, Rodya, where are you going? You are going away somewhere?"

"Yes."

"That's what I thought! I can come with you, you know, if you need me. And Dounia, too; she loves you, she loves you dearly—and Sofya Semyonovna may come with us if you like. You see, I am glad to look upon her as a daughter even... Dmitri Prokofitch will help us to go together. But... where... are you going?"

"Good-bye, mother."

"What, to-day?" she cried, as though losing him for ever.

"I can't stay, I must go now...."

"And can't I come with you?"

"No, but kneel down and pray to God for me. Your prayer perhaps will reach Him."

"Let me bless you and sign you with the cross. That's right, that's right. Oh, God, what are we doing?"

Yes, he was glad, he was very glad that there was no one there, that he was alone with his mother. For the first time after all those awful months his heart was softened. He fell down before her, he kissed her feet and both wept, embracing. And she was not surprised and did not question him this time. For some days she had realised that something awful was happening to her son and that now some terrible minute had come for him.

"Rodya, my darling, my first born," she said sobbing, "now you are just as when you were little. You would run like this to me and hug me and kiss me. When your father was living and we were poor, you comforted us simply by being with us and when I buried your father, how often we wept together at his grave and embraced, as now. And if I've been crying lately, it's that my mother's heart had a foreboding of trouble. The first time I saw you, that evening, you remember, as soon as we arrived here, I guessed simply from your eyes. My heart sank at once, and to-day when I opened the door and looked at you, I thought the fatal hour had come. Rodya, Rodya, you are not going away to-day?"

"No!"

"You'll come again?"

"Yes... I'll come."

"Rodya, don't be angry, I don't dare to question you. I know I mustn't. Only say two words to me—is it far where you are going?"

"Very far."

"What is awaiting you there? Some post or career for you?"

"What God sends... only pray for me." Raskolnikov went to the door, but she clutched him and gazed despairingly into his eyes. Her face worked with terror.

"Enough, mother," said Raskolnikov, deeply regretting that he had come.

"Not for ever, it's not yet for ever? You'll come, you'll come to-morrow?"

"I will, I will, good-bye." He tore himself away at last.

It was a warm, fresh, bright evening; it had cleared up in the morning. Raskolnikov went to his lodgings; he made haste. He wanted to finish all before sunset. He did not want to meet anyone till then. Going up the stairs he noticed that Nastasya rushed from the samovar to watch him intently. "Can anyone have come to see me?" he wondered. He had a disgusted vision of Porfiry. But opening his door he saw Dounia. She was sitting alone, plunged in deep thought, and looked as though she had been waiting a long time. He stopped short in the doorway. She rose from the sofa in dismay and stood up facing him. Her eyes, fixed upon him, betrayed horror and infinite grief. And from those eyes alone he saw at once that she knew.

"Am I to come in or go away?" he asked uncertainly.

"I've been all day with Sofya Semyonovna. We were both waiting for you. We thought that you would be sure to come there."

Raskolnikov went into the room and sank exhausted on a chair.

"I feel weak, Dounia, I am very tired; and I should have liked at this moment to be able to control myself."

He glanced at her mistrustfully.

"Where were you all night?"

"I don't remember clearly. You see, sister, I wanted to make up my mind once for all, and several times I walked by the Neva, I remember that I wanted to end it all there, but... I couldn't make up my mind," he whispered, looking at her mistrustfully again.

"Thank God! That was just what we were afraid of, Sofya Semyonovna and I. Then you still have faith in life? Thank God, thank God!"

Raskolnikov smiled bitterly.

"I haven't faith, but I have just been weeping in mother's arms; I haven't faith, but I have just asked her to pray for me. I don't know how it is, Dounia, I don't understand it."

"Have you been at mother's? Have you told her?" cried Dounia, horror-stricken. "Surely you haven't done that?"

"No, I didn't tell her... in words; but she understood a great deal. She heard you talking in your sleep. I am sure she half understands it already. Perhaps I did wrong in going to see her. I don't know why I did go. I am a contemptible person, Dounia."

"A contemptible person, but ready to face suffering! You are, aren't you?"

"Yes, I am going. At once. Yes, to escape the disgrace I thought of drowning myself, Dounia, but as I looked into the water, I thought that if I had considered myself strong till now I'd better not be afraid of disgrace," he said, hurrying on. "It's pride, Dounia."

"Pride, Rodya."

There was a gleam of fire in his lustreless eyes; he seemed to be glad to think that he was still proud.

"You don't think, sister, that I was simply afraid of the water?" he asked, looking into her face with a sinister smile.

"Oh, Rodya, hush!" cried Dounia bitterly. Silence lasted for two minutes. He sat with his eyes fixed on the floor; Dounia stood at the other end of the table and looked at him with anguish. Suddenly he got up.

"It's late, it's time to go! I am going at once to give myself up. But I don't know why I am going to give myself up."

Big tears fell down her cheeks.

"You are crying, sister, but can you hold out your hand to me?"

"You doubted it?"

She threw her arms round him.

"Aren't you half expiating your crime by facing the suffering?" she cried, holding him close and kissing him.

"Crime? What crime?" he cried in sudden fury. "That I killed a vile noxious insect, an old pawnbroker woman, of use to no one!... Killing her was atonement for forty sins. She was sucking the life out of poor people. Was that a crime? I am not thinking of it and I am not thinking of expiating it, and why are you all rubbing it in on all sides? 'A crime! a crime!' Only now I see clearly the imbecility of my cowardice, now that I have decided to face this superfluous disgrace. It's simply because I am contemptible and have nothing in me that I have decided to, perhaps too for my advantage, as that... Porfiry... suggested!"

"Brother, brother, what are you saying? Why, you have shed blood?" cried Dounia in despair.

"Which all men shed," he put in almost frantically, "which flows and has always flowed in streams, which is spilt like champagne, and for which men are crowned in the Capitol and are called afterwards benefactors of mankind. Look into it more carefully and understand it! I too wanted to do good to men and would have done hundreds, thousands of good deeds to make up for that one piece of stupidity, not stupidity even, simply clumsiness, for the idea was by no means so stupid as it seems now that it has failed.... (Everything seems stupid when it fails.) By that stupidity I only wanted to put myself into an independent position, to take the first step, to obtain means, and then everything would have been smoothed over by benefits immeasurable in comparison.... But I... I couldn't carry out even the first step, because I am contemptible, that's what's the matter! And yet I won't look at it as you do. If I had succeeded I should have been crowned with glory, but now I'm trapped."

"But that's not so, not so! Brother, what are you saying?"

"Ah, it's not picturesque, not æsthetically attractive! I fail to understand why bombarding people by regular siege is more honourable. The fear of appearances is the first symptom of impotence. I've never, never recognised this more clearly than now, and I am further than ever from seeing that what I did was a crime. I've never, never been stronger and more convinced than now."

The colour had rushed into his pale exhausted face, but as he uttered his last explanation, he happened to meet Dounia's eyes and he saw such anguish in them that he could not help being checked. He felt that he had, anyway, made these two poor women miserable, that he was, anyway, the cause...

"Dounia darling, if I am guilty forgive me (though I cannot be forgiven if I am guilty). Good-bye! We won't dispute. It's time, high time to go. Don't follow me, I beseech you, I have somewhere else to go.... But you go at once and sit with mother. I entreat you to! It's my last request of you. Don't leave her at all; I left her in a state of anxiety, that she is not fit to bear; she will die or go out of her mind. Be with her! Razumihin will be with you. I've been talking to him.... Don't cry about me: I'll try to be honest and manly all my life, even if I am a murderer. Perhaps I shall some day make a name. I won't disgrace you, you will see; I'll still show.... Now good-bye for the present," he concluded hurriedly, noticing again a strange expression in Dounia's eyes at his last words and promises. "Why are you crying? Don't cry, don't cry: we are not parting for ever! Ah, yes! Wait a minute, I'd forgotten!"

He went to the table, took up a thick dusty book, opened it and took from between the pages a little water-colour portrait on ivory. It was the portrait of his landlady's daughter, who had died of fever, that strange girl who had wanted to be a nun. For a minute he gazed at the delicate expressive face of his betrothed, kissed the portrait and gave it to Dounia.

"I used to talk a great deal about it to her, only to her," he said thoughtfully. "To her heart I confided much of what has since been so hideously realised. Don't be uneasy," he returned to Dounia, "she was as much opposed to it as you, and I am glad that she is gone. The great point is that everything now is going to be different, is going to be broken in two," he cried, suddenly returning to his dejection. "Everything, everything, and am I prepared for it? Do I want it myself? They say it is necessary for me to suffer! What's the object of these senseless sufferings? shall I know any better what they are for, when I am crushed by hardships and idiocy, and weak as an old man after twenty years' penal servitude? And what shall I have to live for then? Why am I consenting to that life now? Oh, I knew I was contemptible when I stood looking at the Neva at daybreak to-day!"

At last they both went out. It was hard for Dounia, but she loved him. She walked away, but after going fifty paces she turned round to look at him again. He was still in sight. At the corner he too turned and for the last time their eyes met; but noticing that she was looking at him, he motioned her away with impatience and even vexation, and turned the corner abruptly.

"I am wicked, I see that," he thought to himself, feeling ashamed a moment later of his angry gesture to Dounia. "But why are they so fond of me if I don't deserve it? Oh, if only I were alone and no one loved me and I too had never loved anyone! *Nothing of all this would have happened.* But I wonder shall I in those fifteen or twenty years grow so meek that I shall humble myself before people and whimper at every word that I am a criminal? Yes, that's it, that's it, that's what they are sending me there for, that's what they want. Look at them running to and fro about the streets, every one of them a scoundrel and a criminal at heart and, worse still, an idiot. But try to get me off and they'd be wild with righteous indignation. Oh, how I hate them all!"

He fell to musing by what process it could come to pass, that he could be humbled before all of them, indiscriminately—humbled by conviction. And yet why not? It must be so. Would not twenty years of continual bondage crush him utterly? Water wears out a stone. And why, why should he live after that? Why should he go now when he knew that it would be so? It was the hundredth time perhaps that he had asked himself that question since the previous evening, but still he went.

CHAPTER VIII

When he went into Sonia's room, it was already getting dark. All day Sonia had been waiting for him in terrible anxiety. Dounia had been waiting with her. She had come to her that morning, remembering Svidrigaïlov's words that Sonia knew. We will not describe the conversation and tears of the two girls, and how friendly they became. Dounia gained one comfort at least from that interview, that her brother would not be alone. He had gone to her, Sonia, first with his confession; he had gone to her for human fellowship when he needed it; she would go with him wherever fate might send him. Dounia did not ask, but she knew it was so. She looked at Sonia almost with reverence and at first almost embarrassed her by it. Sonia was almost on the point of tears. She felt herself, on the contrary, hardly worthy to look at Dounia. Dounia's gracious image when she had bowed to her so attentively and respectfully at their first meeting in Raskolnikov's room had remained in her mind as one of the fairest visions of her life.

Dounia at last became impatient and, leaving Sonia, went to her brother's room to await him there; she kept thinking that he would come there first. When she had gone, Sonia began to be tortured by the dread of his committing suicide, and Dounia too feared it. But they had spent the day trying to persuade each other that that could not be, and both were less anxious while they were together. As soon as they parted, each thought of nothing else. Sonia remembered how Svidrigaïlov had said to her the day before that Raskolnikov had two alternatives—Siberia or... Besides she knew his vanity, his pride and his lack of faith.

"Is it possible that he has nothing but cowardice and fear of death to make him live?" she thought at last in despair.

Meanwhile the sun was setting. Sonia was standing in dejection, looking intently out of the window, but from it she could see nothing but the unwhitewashed blank wall of the next house. At last when she began to feel sure of his death—he walked into the room.

She gave a cry of joy, but looking carefully into his face she turned pale.

"Yes," said Raskolnikov, smiling. "I have come for your cross, Sonia. It was you told me to go to the cross-roads; why is it you are frightened now it's come to that?"

Sonia gazed at him astonished. His tone seemed strange to her; a cold shiver ran over her, but in a moment she guessed that the tone and the words were a mask. He spoke to her looking away, as though to avoid meeting her eyes.

"You see, Sonia, I've decided that it will be better so. There is one fact.... But it's a long story and there's no need to discuss it. But do you know what angers me? It annoys me that all those stupid brutish faces will be gaping at me directly, pestering me with their stupid questions, which I shall have to answer—they'll point their fingers at me.... Tfoo! You know I am not going to Porfiry, I am sick of him. I'd rather go to my friend, the Explosive Lieutenant; how I shall surprise him, what a sensation I shall make! But I must be cooler; I've become too irritable of late. You know I was nearly shaking my fist at my sister just now, because she turned to take a last look at me. It's a brutal state to be in! Ah! what am I coming to! Well, where are the crosses?"

He seemed hardly to know what he was doing. He could not stay still or concentrate his attention on anything; his ideas seemed to gallop after one another, he talked incoherently, his hands trembled slightly.

Without a word Sonia took out of the drawer two crosses, one of cypress wood and one of copper. She made the sign of the cross over herself and over him, and put the wooden cross on his neck.

"It's the symbol of my taking up the cross," he laughed. "As though I had not suffered much till now! The wooden cross, that is the peasant one; the copper one, that is Lizaveta's—you will wear yourself, show me! So she had it on... at that moment? I remember two things like these too, a silver one and a little ikon. I threw them back on the old woman's neck. Those would be appropriate now, really, those are what I ought to put on now.... But I am talking nonsense and forgetting what matters; I'm somehow forgetful.... You see I have come to warn you, Sonia, so that you might know... that's all—that's all I came for. But I thought I had more to say. You wanted me to go yourself. Well, now I am going to prison and you'll have your wish. Well, what are you crying for? You too? Don't. Leave off! Oh, how I hate it all!"

But his feeling was stirred; his heart ached, as he looked at her. "Why is she grieving too?" he thought to himself. "What am I to her? Why does she weep? Why is she looking after me, like my mother or Dounia? She'll be my nurse."

"Cross yourself, say at least one prayer," Sonia begged in a timid broken voice.

"Oh certainly, as much as you like! And sincerely, Sonia, sincerely...."

But he wanted to say something quite different.

He crossed himself several times. Sonia took up her shawl and put it over her head. It was the green *drap de dames* shawl of which Marmeladov had spoken, "the family shawl." Raskolnikov thought of that looking at it, but he did not ask. He began to feel himself that he was certainly forgetting things and was disgustingly agitated. He was frightened at this. He was suddenly struck too by the thought that Sonia meant to go with him.

"What are you doing? Where are you going? Stay here, stay! I'll go alone," he cried in cowardly vexation, and almost resentful, he moved towards the door. "What's the use of going in procession?" he muttered going out.

Sonia remained standing in the middle of the room. He had not even said good-bye to her; he had forgotten her. A poignant and rebellious doubt surged in his heart.

"Was it right, was it right, all this?" he thought again as he went down the stairs. "Couldn't he stop and retract it all... and not go?"

But still he went. He felt suddenly once for all that he mustn't ask himself questions. As he turned into the street he remembered that he had not said good-bye to Sonia, that he had left her in the middle of the room in her green shawl, not daring to stir after he had shouted at her, and he stopped short for a moment. At the same instant, another thought dawned upon him, as though it had been lying in wait to strike him then.

"Why, with what object did I go to her just now? I told her—on business; on what business? I had no sort of business! To tell her I was *going*; but where was the need? Do I love her? No, no, I drove her away just now like a dog. Did I want her crosses? Oh, how low I've sunk! No, I wanted her tears, I wanted to see her terror, to see how her heart ached! I had to have something to cling to, something to delay me, some friendly face to see! And I dared to believe in myself, to dream of what I would do! I am a beggarly contemptible wretch, contemptible!"

He walked along the canal bank, and he had not much further to go. But on reaching the bridge he stopped and turning out of his way along it went to the Hay Market.

He looked eagerly to right and left, gazed intently at every object and could not fix his attention on anything; everything slipped away. "In another week, another month I shall be driven in a prison van over this bridge, how shall I look at the canal then? I should like to remember this!" slipped into his mind. "Look at this sign! How shall I read those letters then? It's written here 'Campany,' that's a thing to remember, that letter *a*, and to look at it again in a month—how shall I look at it then? What shall I be feeling and thinking then?... How trivial it all must be, what I am fretting about now! Of course it must all be interesting... in its way... (Ha-ha-ha! What am I thinking about?) I am becoming a baby, I am showing off to myself; why am I ashamed? Foo! how people shove! that fat man—a German he must be—who pushed against me, does he know whom he pushed? There's a peasant woman with a baby, begging. It's curious that she thinks me happier than she is. I might give her something, for the incongruity of it. Here's a five copeck piece left in my pocket, where did I get it? Here, here... take it, my good woman!"

"God bless you," the beggar chanted in a lachrymose voice.

He went into the Hay Market. It was distasteful, very distasteful to be in a crowd, but he walked just where he saw most people. He would have given anything in the world to be alone; but he knew himself that he would not have remained alone for a moment. There was a man drunk and disorderly in the crowd; he kept trying to dance and falling down. There was a ring round him. Raskolnikov squeezed his way through the crowd, stared for some minutes at the drunken man and suddenly gave a short jerky laugh. A minute later he had forgotten him and did not see him, though he still stared. He moved away at last, not remembering where he was; but when he got into the middle of the square an emotion suddenly came over him, overwhelming him body and mind.

He suddenly recalled Sonia's words, "Go to the cross-roads, bow down to the people, kiss the earth, for you have sinned against it too, and say aloud to the whole world, 'I am a murderer.'" He trembled, remembering that. And the hopeless misery and anxiety of all that time, especially of the last hours, had weighed so heavily upon him that he positively clutched at the chance of this new unmixed, complete sensation. It came over him like a fit; it was like a single spark kindled in his soul and spreading fire through him. Everything in him softened at once and the tears started into his eyes. He fell to the earth on the spot....

He knelt down in the middle of the square, bowed down to the earth, and kissed that filthy earth with bliss and rapture. He got up and bowed down a second time.

"He's boozed," a youth near him observed.

There was a roar of laughter.

"He's going to Jerusalem, brothers, and saying good-bye to his children and his country. He's bowing down to all the world and kissing the great city of St. Petersburg and its pavement," added a workman who was a little drunk.

"Quite a young man, too!" observed a third.

"And a gentleman," someone observed soberly.

"There's no knowing who's a gentleman and who isn't nowadays."

These exclamations and remarks checked Raskolnikov, and the words, "I am a murderer," which were perhaps on the point of dropping from his lips, died away. He bore these remarks quietly, however, and, without looking round, he turned down a street leading to the police office. He had a glimpse of something on the way which did not surprise him; he had felt that it must be so. The second time he bowed down in the Hay Market he saw, standing fifty paces from him on the left, Sonia. She was hiding from him behind one of the wooden shanties in the market-place. She had followed him then on his painful way! Raskolnikov at that moment felt and knew once for all that Sonia was with him for ever and would follow him to the ends of the earth, wherever fate might take him. It wrung his heart... but he was just reaching the fatal place.

He went into the yard fairly resolutely. He had to mount to the third storey. "I shall be some time going up," he thought. He felt as though the fateful moment was still far off, as though he had plenty of time left for consideration.

Again the same rubbish, the same eggshells lying about on the spiral stairs, again the open doors of the flats, again the same kitchens and the same fumes and stench coming from them. Raskolnikov had not been here since that day. His legs were numb and gave way under him, but still they moved forward. He stopped for a moment to take breath, to collect himself, so as to enter *like a man*. "But why? what for?" he wondered, reflecting. "If I must drink the cup what difference does it make? The more revolting the better." He imagined for an instant the figure of the "explosive lieutenant," Ilya Petrovitch. Was he actually going to him? Couldn't he go to someone else? To Nikodim Fomitch? Couldn't he turn back and go straight to Nikodim Fomitch's lodgings? At least then it would be done privately.... No, no! To the "explosive lieutenant"! If he must drink it, drink it off at once.

Turning cold and hardly conscious, he opened the door of the office. There were very few people in it this time—only a house porter and a peasant. The doorkeeper did not even peep out from behind his screen. Raskolnikov walked into the next room. "Perhaps I still need not speak," passed through his mind. Some sort of clerk not wearing a uniform was settling himself at a bureau to write. In a corner another clerk was seating himself. Zametov was not there, nor, of course, Nikodim Fomitch.

"No one in?" Raskolnikov asked, addressing the person at the bureau.

"Whom do you want?"

"A-ah! Not a sound was heard, not a sight was seen, but I scent the Russian... how does it go on in the fairy tale... I've forgotten! 'At your service!'" a familiar voice cried suddenly.

Raskolnikov shuddered. The Explosive Lieutenant stood before him. He had just come in from the third room. "It is the hand of fate," thought Raskolnikov. "Why is he here?"

"You've come to see us? What about?" cried Ilya Petrovitch. He was obviously in an exceedingly good humour and perhaps a trifle exhilarated. "If it's on business you are rather early.[*] It's only a chance that I am here... however I'll do what I can. I must admit, I... what is it, what is it? Excuse me...."

[*] *Dostoevsky appears to have forgotten that it is after*
sunset, and that the last time Raskolnikov visited the
police office at two in the afternoon he was reproached for
coming too late.—TRANSLATOR.

"Raskolnikov."

"Of course, Raskolnikov. You didn't imagine I'd forgotten? Don't think I am like that... Rodion Ro—Ro—Rodionovitch, that's it, isn't it?"

"Rodion Romanovitch."

"Yes, yes, of course, Rodion Romanovitch! I was just getting at it. I made many inquiries about you. I assure you I've been genuinely grieved since that... since I behaved like that... it was explained to me afterwards that you were a literary man... and a learned one too... and so to say the first steps... Mercy on us! What literary or scientific man does not begin by some originality of conduct! My wife and I have the greatest respect for literature, in my wife it's a genuine passion! Literature and art! If only a man is a gentleman, all the rest can be gained by talents, learning, good sense, genius. As for a hat—well, what does a hat matter? I can buy a hat as easily as I can a bun; but what's under the hat, what the hat covers, I can't buy that! I was even meaning to come and apologise to you, but thought maybe you'd... But I am forgetting to ask you, is there anything you want really? I hear your family have come?"

"Yes, my mother and sister."

"I've even had the honour and happiness of meeting your sister—a highly cultivated and charming person. I confess I was sorry I got so hot with you. There it is! But as for my looking suspiciously at your fainting fit—that affair has been cleared up splendidly! Bigotry and fanaticism! I understand your indignation. Perhaps you are changing your lodging on account of your family's arriving?"

"No, I only looked in... I came to ask... I thought that I should find Zametov here."

"Oh, yes! Of course, you've made friends, I heard. Well, no, Zametov is not here. Yes, we've lost Zametov. He's not been here since yesterday... he quarrelled with everyone on leaving... in the rudest way. He is a feather-headed youngster, that's all; one might have expected something from him, but there, you know what they are, our brilliant young men. He wanted to go in for some examination, but it's only to talk and boast about it, it will go no further than that. Of course it's a very different matter with you or Mr. Razumihin there, your friend. Your career is an intellectual one and you won't be deterred by failure. For you, one may say, all the attractions of life *nihil est*—you are an ascetic, a monk, a hermit!... A book, a pen behind your ear, a learned research—that's where your spirit soars! I am the same way myself.... Have you read Livingstone's Travels?"

"No."

"Oh, I have. There are a great many Nihilists about nowadays, you know, and indeed it is not to be wondered at. What sort of days are they? I ask you. But we thought... you are not a Nihilist of course? Answer me openly, openly!"

"N-no..."

"Believe me, you can speak openly to me as you would to yourself! Official duty is one thing but... you are thinking I meant to say *friendship* is quite another? No, you're wrong! It's not friendship, but the feeling of a man and a citizen, the feeling of humanity and of love for the Almighty. I may be an official, but I am always bound to feel myself a man and a citizen.... You were asking about Zametov. Zametov will make a scandal in the French style in a house of bad reputation, over a glass of champagne... that's all your Zametov is good for! While I'm perhaps, so to speak, burning with devotion and lofty feelings, and besides I have rank, consequence, a post! I am married and have children, I fulfil the duties of a man and a citizen, but who is he, may I ask? I appeal to you as a man ennobled by education... Then these midwives, too, have become extraordinarily numerous."

Raskolnikov raised his eyebrows inquiringly. The words of Ilya Petrovitch, who had obviously been dining, were for the most part a stream of empty sounds for him. But some of them he understood. He looked at him inquiringly, not knowing how it would end.

"I mean those crop-headed wenches," the talkative Ilya Petrovitch continued. "Midwives is my name for them. I think it a very satisfactory one, ha-ha! They go to the Academy, study anatomy. If I fall ill, am I to send for a young lady to treat me? What do you say? Ha-ha!" Ilya Petrovitch laughed, quite pleased with his own wit. "It's an immoderate zeal for education, but once you're educated, that's enough. Why abuse it? Why insult honourable people, as that scoundrel Zametov does? Why did he insult me, I ask you? Look at these suicides, too, how common they are, you can't fancy! People spend their last halfpenny and kill themselves, boys and girls and old people. Only this morning we heard about a gentleman who had just come to town. Nil Pavlitch, I say, what was the name of that gentleman who shot himself?"

"Svidrigaïlov," someone answered from the other room with drowsy listlessness.

Raskolnikov started.

"Svidrigaïlov! Svidrigaïlov has shot himself!" he cried.

"What, do you know Svidrigaïlov?"

"Yes... I knew him.... He hadn't been here long."

"Yes, that's so. He had lost his wife, was a man of reckless habits and all of a sudden shot himself, and in such a shocking way.... He left in his notebook a few words: that he dies in full possession of his faculties and that no one is to blame for his death. He had money, they say. How did you come to know him?"

"I... was acquainted... my sister was governess in his family."

"Bah-bah-bah! Then no doubt you can tell us something about him. You had no suspicion?"

"I saw him yesterday... he... was drinking wine; I knew nothing."

Raskolnikov felt as though something had fallen on him and was stifling him.

"You've turned pale again. It's so stuffy here..."

"Yes, I must go," muttered Raskolnikov. "Excuse my troubling you...."

"Oh, not at all, as often as you like. It's a pleasure to see you and I am glad to say so."

Ilya Petrovitch held out his hand.

"I only wanted... I came to see Zametov."

"I understand, I understand, and it's a pleasure to see you."

"I... am very glad... good-bye," Raskolnikov smiled.

He went out; he reeled, he was overtaken with giddiness and did not know what he was doing. He began going down the stairs, supporting himself with his right hand against the wall. He fancied that a porter pushed past him on his way upstairs to the police office, that a dog in the lower storey kept up a shrill barking and that a woman flung a rolling-pin at it and shouted. He went down and out into the yard. There, not far from the entrance, stood Sonia, pale and horror-stricken. She looked wildly at him. He stood still before her. There was a look of poignant agony, of despair, in her face. She clasped her hands. His lips worked in an ugly, meaningless smile. He stood still a minute, grinned and went back to the police office.

Ilya Petrovitch had sat down and was rummaging among some papers. Before him stood the same peasant who had pushed by on the stairs.

"Hulloa! Back again! have you left something behind? What's the matter?"

Raskolnikov, with white lips and staring eyes, came slowly nearer. He walked right to the table, leaned his hand on it, tried to say something, but could not; only incoherent sounds were audible.

"You are feeling ill, a chair! Here, sit down! Some water!"

Raskolnikov dropped on to a chair, but he kept his eyes fixed on the face of Ilya Petrovitch, which expressed unpleasant surprise. Both looked at one another for a minute and waited. Water was brought.

"It was I..." began Raskolnikov.

"Drink some water."

Raskolnikov refused the water with his hand, and softly and brokenly, but distinctly said:

"*It was I killed the old pawnbroker woman and her sister Lizaveta with an axe and robbed them.*"

Ilya Petrovitch opened his mouth. People ran up on all sides.

Raskolnikov repeated his statement.

EPILOGUE

I

Siberia. On the banks of a broad solitary river stands a town, one of the administrative centres of Russia; in the town there is a fortress, in the fortress there is a prison. In the prison the second-class convict Rodion Raskolnikov has been confined for nine months. Almost a year and a half has passed since his crime.

There had been little difficulty about his trial. The criminal adhered exactly, firmly, and clearly to his statement. He did not confuse nor misrepresent the facts, nor soften them in his own interest, nor omit the smallest detail. He explained every incident of the murder, the secret of *the pledge* (the piece of wood with a strip of metal) which was found in the murdered woman's hand. He described minutely how he had taken her keys, what they were like, as well as the chest and its contents; he explained the mystery of Lizaveta's murder; described how Koch and, after him, the student knocked, and repeated all they had said to one another; how he afterwards had run downstairs and heard Nikolay and Dmitri shouting; how he had hidden in the empty flat and afterwards gone home. He ended by indicating the stone in the yard off the Voznesensky Prospect under which the purse and the trinkets were found. The whole thing, in fact, was perfectly clear. The lawyers and the judges were very much struck, among other things, by the fact that he had hidden the trinkets and the purse under a stone, without making use of them, and that, what was more, he did not now remember what the trinkets were like, or even how many there were. The fact that he had never opened the purse and did not even know how much was in it seemed incredible. There turned out to be in the purse three hundred and seventeen roubles and sixty copecks. From being so long under the stone, some of the most valuable notes lying uppermost had suffered from the damp. They were a long while trying to discover why the accused man should tell a lie about this, when about everything else he had made a truthful and straightforward confession. Finally some of the lawyers more versed in psychology admitted that it was possible he had really not looked into the purse, and so didn't know what was in it when he hid it under the stone. But they immediately drew the deduction that the crime could only have been committed through temporary mental derangement, through homicidal mania, without object or the pursuit of gain. This fell in with the most recent fashionable theory of temporary insanity, so often applied in our days in criminal cases. Moreover Raskolnikov's hypochondriacal condition was proved by many witnesses, by Dr. Zossimov, his former fellow students, his landlady and her servant. All this pointed strongly to the conclusion that Raskolnikov was not quite like an ordinary murderer and robber, but that there was another element in the case.

To the intense annoyance of those who maintained this opinion, the criminal scarcely attempted to defend himself. To the decisive question as to what motive impelled him to the murder and the robbery, he answered very clearly with the coarsest frankness that the cause was his miserable position, his poverty and helplessness, and his desire to provide for his first steps in life by the help of the three thousand roubles he had reckoned on finding. He had been led to the murder through his shallow and cowardly nature, exasperated moreover by privation and failure. To the question what led him to confess, he answered that it was his heartfelt repentance. All this was almost coarse....

The sentence however was more merciful than could have been expected, perhaps partly because the criminal had not tried to justify himself, but had rather shown a desire to exaggerate his guilt. All the strange and peculiar circumstances of the crime were taken into consideration. There could be no doubt of the abnormal and poverty-stricken condition of the criminal at the time. The fact that he had made no use of what he had stolen was put down partly to the effect of remorse, partly to his abnormal mental condition at the time of the crime. Incidentally the murder of Lizaveta served indeed to confirm the last hypothesis: a man commits two murders and forgets that the door is open! Finally, the confession, at the very moment when the case was hopelessly muddled by the false evidence given by Nikolay through melancholy and fanaticism, and when, moreover, there were no proofs against the real criminal, no suspicions even (Porfiry Petrovitch fully kept his word)—all this did much to soften the sentence. Other circumstances, too, in the prisoner's favour came out quite unexpectedly. Razumihin somehow discovered and proved that while Raskolnikov was at the university he had helped a poor consumptive fellow student and had spent his last penny on supporting him for six months, and when this student died, leaving a decrepit old father whom he had maintained almost from his thirteenth year, Raskolnikov had got the old man into a hospital and paid for his funeral when he died. Raskolnikov's landlady bore witness, too, that when they had lived in another house at Five Corners, Raskolnikov had rescued two little children from a house on fire and was burnt in doing so. This was investigated and fairly well confirmed by many witnesses. These facts made an impression in his favour.

And in the end the criminal was, in consideration of extenuating circumstances, condemned to penal servitude in the second class for a term of eight years only.

At the very beginning of the trial Raskolnikov's mother fell ill. Dounia and Razumihin found it possible to get her out of Petersburg during the trial. Razumihin chose a town on the railway not far from Petersburg, so as to be able to follow every step of the trial and at the same time to see Avdotya Romanovna as often as possible. Pulcheria Alexandrovna's illness was a strange nervous one and was accompanied by a partial derangement of her intellect.

When Dounia returned from her last interview with her brother, she had found her mother already ill, in feverish delirium. That evening Razumihin and she agreed what answers they must make to her mother's questions about Raskolnikov and made up a complete story for her mother's benefit of his having to go away to a distant part of Russia on a business commission, which would bring him in the end money and reputation.

But they were struck by the fact that Pulcheria Alexandrovna never asked them anything on the subject, neither then nor thereafter. On the contrary, she had her own version of her son's sudden departure; she told them with tears how he had come to say good-bye to her, hinting that she alone knew many mysterious and important facts, and that Rodya had many very powerful enemies, so that it was necessary for him to be in hiding. As for his future career, she had no doubt that it would be brilliant when certain sinister influences could be removed. She assured Razumihin that her son would be one day a great statesman, that his article and brilliant literary talent proved it. This article she was continually reading, she even read it aloud, almost took it to bed with her, but scarcely asked where Rodya was, though the subject was obviously avoided by the others, which might have been enough to awaken her suspicions.

They began to be frightened at last at Pulcheria Alexandrovna's strange silence on certain subjects. She did not, for instance, complain of getting no letters from him, though in previous years she had only lived on the hope of letters from her beloved Rodya. This was the cause of great uneasiness to Dounia; the idea occurred to her that her mother suspected that there was something terrible in her son's fate and was afraid to ask, for fear of hearing something still more awful. In any case, Dounia saw clearly that her mother was not in full possession of her faculties.

It happened once or twice, however, that Pulcheria Alexandrovna gave such a turn to the conversation that it was impossible to answer her without mentioning where Rodya was, and on receiving unsatisfactory and suspicious answers she became at once gloomy and silent, and this mood lasted for a long time. Dounia saw at last that it was hard to deceive her and came to the conclusion that it was better to be absolutely silent on certain points; but it became more and more evident that the poor mother suspected something terrible. Dounia remembered her brother's telling her that her mother had overheard her talking in her sleep on the night after her interview with Svidrigaïlov and before the fatal day of the confession: had not she made out something from that? Sometimes days and even weeks of gloomy silence and tears would be succeeded by a period of hysterical animation, and the invalid would begin to talk almost incessantly of her son, of her hopes of his future.... Her fancies were sometimes very strange. They humoured her, pretended to agree with her (she saw perhaps that they were pretending), but she still went on talking.

Five months after Raskolnikov's confession, he was sentenced. Razumihin and Sonia saw him in prison as often as it was possible. At last the moment of separation came. Dounia swore to her brother that the separation should not be for ever, Razumihin did the same. Razumihin, in his youthful ardour, had firmly resolved to lay the foundations at least of a secure livelihood during the next three or four years, and saving up a certain sum, to emigrate to Siberia, a country rich in every natural resource and in need of workers, active men and capital. There they would settle in the town where Rodya was and all together would begin a new life. They all wept at parting.

Raskolnikov had been very dreamy for a few days before. He asked a great deal about his mother and was constantly anxious about her. He worried so much about her that it alarmed Dounia. When he heard about his mother's illness he became very gloomy. With Sonia he was particularly reserved all the time. With the help of the money left to her by Svidrigaïlov, Sonia had long ago made her preparations to follow the party of convicts in which he was despatched to Siberia. Not a word passed between Raskolnikov and her on the subject, but both knew it would be so. At the final leave-taking he smiled strangely at his sister's and Razumihin's fervent anticipations of their happy future together when he should come out of prison. He predicted that their mother's illness would soon have a fatal ending. Sonia and he at last set off.

Two months later Dounia was married to Razumihin. It was a quiet and sorrowful wedding; Porfiry Petrovitch and Zossimov were invited however. During all this period Razumihin wore an air of resolute determination. Dounia put implicit faith in his carrying out his plans and indeed she could not but believe in him. He displayed a rare strength of will. Among other things he began attending university lectures again in order to take his degree. They were continually making plans for the future; both counted on settling in Siberia within five years at least. Till then they rested their hopes on Sonia.

Pulcheria Alexandrovna was delighted to give her blessing to Dounia's marriage with Razumihin; but after the marriage she became even more melancholy and anxious. To give her pleasure Razumihin told her how Raskolnikov had looked after the poor student and his decrepit father and how a year ago he had been burnt and injured in rescuing two little children from a fire. These two pieces of news excited Pulcheria Alexandrovna's disordered imagination almost to ecstasy. She was continually talking about them, even entering into conversation with strangers in the street, though Dounia always accompanied her. In public conveyances and shops, wherever she could capture a listener, she would begin the discourse about her son, his article, how he had helped the student, how he had been burnt at the fire, and so on! Dounia did not know how to restrain her. Apart from the danger of her morbid excitement, there was the risk of someone's recalling Raskolnikov's name and speaking of the recent trial. Pulcheria Alexandrovna found out the address of the mother of the two children her son had saved and insisted on going to see her.

At last her restlessness reached an extreme point. She would sometimes begin to cry suddenly and was often ill and feverishly delirious. One morning she declared that by her reckoning Rodya ought soon to be home, that she remembered when he said good-bye to her he said that they must expect him back in nine months. She began to prepare for his coming, began to do up her room for him, to clean the furniture, to wash and put up new hangings and so on. Dounia was anxious, but said nothing and helped her to arrange the room. After a fatiguing day spent in continual fancies, in joyful day-dreams and tears, Pulcheria Alexandrovna was taken ill in the night and by morning she was feverish and delirious. It was brain fever. She died within a fortnight. In her delirium she dropped words which showed that she knew a great deal more about her son's terrible fate than they had supposed.

For a long time Raskolnikov did not know of his mother's death, though a regular correspondence had been maintained from the time he reached Siberia. It was carried on by means of Sonia, who wrote every month to the Razumihins and received an answer with unfailing regularity. At first they found Sonia's letters dry and unsatisfactory, but later on they came to the conclusion that the letters could not be better, for from these letters they received a complete picture of their unfortunate brother's life. Sonia's letters were full of the most matter-of-fact detail, the simplest and clearest description of all Raskolnikov's surroundings as a convict. There was no word of her own hopes, no conjecture as to the future, no description of her feelings. Instead of any attempt to interpret his state of mind and inner life, she gave the simple facts—that is, his own words, an exact account of his health, what he asked for at their interviews, what commission he gave her and so on. All these facts she gave with extraordinary minuteness. The picture of their unhappy brother stood out at last with great clearness and precision. There could be no mistake, because nothing was given but facts.

But Dounia and her husband could get little comfort out of the news, especially at first. Sonia wrote that he was constantly sullen and not ready to talk, that he scarcely seemed interested in the news she gave him from their letters, that he sometimes asked after his mother and that when, seeing that he had guessed the truth, she told him at last of her death, she was surprised to find that he did not seem greatly affected by it, not externally at any rate. She told them that, although he seemed so wrapped up in himself and, as it were, shut himself off from everyone—he took a very direct and simple view of his new life; that he understood his position, expected nothing better for the time, had no ill-founded hopes (as is so common in his position) and scarcely seemed surprised at anything in his surroundings, so unlike anything he had known before. She wrote that his health was satisfactory; he did his work without shirking or seeking to do more; he was almost indifferent about food, but except on Sundays and holidays the food was so bad that at last he had been glad to accept some money from her, Sonia, to have his own tea every day. He begged her not to trouble about anything else, declaring that all this fuss about him only annoyed him. Sonia wrote further that in prison he shared the same room with the rest, that she had not seen the inside of their barracks, but concluded that they were crowded, miserable and unhealthy; that he slept on a plank bed with a rug under him and was unwilling to make any other arrangement. But that he lived so poorly and roughly, not from any plan or design, but simply from inattention and indifference.

Sonia wrote simply that he had at first shown no interest in her visits, had almost been vexed with her indeed for coming, unwilling to talk and rude to her. But that in the end these visits had become a habit and almost a necessity for him, so that he was positively distressed when she was ill for some days and could not visit him. She used to see him on holidays at the prison gates or in the guard-room, to which he was brought for a few minutes to see her. On working days she would go to see him at work either at the workshops or at the brick kilns, or at the sheds on the banks of the Irtish.

About herself, Sonia wrote that she had succeeded in making some acquaintances in the town, that she did sewing, and, as there was scarcely a dressmaker in the town, she was looked upon as an indispensable person in many houses. But she did not mention that the authorities were, through her, interested in Raskolnikov; that his task was lightened and so on.

At last the news came (Dounia had indeed noticed signs of alarm and uneasiness in the preceding letters) that he held aloof from everyone, that his fellow prisoners did not like him, that he kept silent for days at a time and was becoming very pale. In the last letter Sonia wrote that he had been taken very seriously ill and was in the convict ward of the hospital.

II

He was ill a long time. But it was not the horrors of prison life, not the hard labour, the bad food, the shaven head, or the patched clothes that crushed him. What did he care for all those trials and hardships! he was even glad of the hard work. Physically exhausted, he could at least reckon on a few hours of quiet sleep. And what was the food to him—the thin cabbage soup with beetles floating in it? In the past as a student he had often not had even that. His clothes were warm and suited to his manner of life. He did not even feel the fetters. Was he ashamed of his shaven head and parti-coloured coat? Before whom? Before Sonia? Sonia was afraid of him, how could he be ashamed before her? And yet he was ashamed even before Sonia, whom he tortured because of it with his contemptuous rough manner. But it was not his shaven head and his fetters he was ashamed of: his pride had been stung to the quick. It was wounded pride that made him ill. Oh, how happy he would have been if he could have blamed himself! He could have borne anything then, even shame and disgrace. But he judged himself severely, and his exasperated conscience found no particularly terrible fault in his past, except a simple*blunder* which might happen to anyone. He was ashamed just because he, Raskolnikov, had so hopelessly, stupidly come to grief through some decree of blind fate, and must humble himself and submit to "the idiocy" of a sentence, if he were anyhow to be at peace.

Vague and objectless anxiety in the present, and in the future a continual sacrifice leading to nothing—that was all that lay before him. And what comfort was it to him that at the end of eight years he would only be thirty-two and able to begin a new life! What had he to live for? What had he to look forward to? Why should he strive? To live in order to exist? Why, he had been ready a thousand times before to give up existence for the sake of an idea, for a hope, even for a fancy. Mere existence had always been too little for him; he had always wanted more. Perhaps it was just because of the strength of his desires that he had thought himself a man to whom more was permissible than to others.

And if only fate would have sent him repentance—burning repentance that would have torn his heart and robbed him of sleep, that repentance, the awful agony of which brings visions of hanging or drowning! Oh, he would have been glad of it! Tears and agonies would at least have been life. But he did not repent of his crime.

At least he might have found relief in raging at his stupidity, as he had raged at the grotesque blunders that had brought him to prison. But now in prison, *in freedom*, he thought over and criticised all his actions again and by no means found them so blundering and so grotesque as they had seemed at the fatal time.

"In what way," he asked himself, "was my theory stupider than others that have swarmed and clashed from the beginning of the world? One has only to look at the thing quite independently, broadly, and uninfluenced by commonplace ideas, and my idea will by no means seem so... strange. Oh, sceptics and halfpenny philosophers, why do you halt half-way!

"Why does my action strike them as so horrible?" he said to himself. "Is it because it was a crime? What is meant by crime? My conscience is at rest. Of course, it was a legal crime, of course, the letter of the law was broken and blood was shed. Well, punish me for the letter of the law... and that's enough. Of course, in that case many of the benefactors of mankind who snatched power for themselves instead of inheriting it ought to have been punished at their first steps. But those men succeeded and so *they were right*, and I didn't, and so I had no right to have taken that step."

It was only in that that he recognised his criminality, only in the fact that he had been unsuccessful and had confessed it.

He suffered too from the question: why had he not killed himself? Why had he stood looking at the river and preferred to confess? Was the desire to live so strong and was it so hard to overcome it? Had not Svidrigaïlov overcome it, although he was afraid of death?

In misery he asked himself this question, and could not understand that, at the very time he had been standing looking into the river, he had perhaps been dimly conscious of the fundamental falsity in himself and his convictions. He didn't understand that that consciousness might be the promise of a future crisis, of a new view of life and of his future resurrection.

He preferred to attribute it to the dead weight of instinct which he could not step over, again through weakness and meanness. He looked at his fellow prisoners and was amazed to see how they all loved life and prized it. It seemed to him that they loved and valued life more in prison than in freedom. What terrible agonies and privations some of them, the tramps for instance, had endured! Could they care so much for a ray of sunshine, for the primeval forest, the cold spring hidden away in some unseen spot, which the tramp had marked three years before, and longed to see again, as he might to see his sweetheart, dreaming of the green grass round it and the bird singing in the bush? As he went on he saw still more inexplicable examples.

In prison, of course, there was a great deal he did not see and did not want to see; he lived as it were with downcast eyes. It was loathsome and unbearable for him to look. But in the end there was much that surprised him and he began, as it were involuntarily, to notice much that he had not suspected before. What surprised him most of all was the terrible impossible gulf that lay between him and all the rest. They seemed to be a different species, and he looked at them and they at him with distrust and hostility. He felt and knew the reasons of his isolation, but he would never have admitted till then that those reasons were so deep and strong. There were some Polish exiles, political prisoners, among them. They simply looked down upon all the rest as ignorant churls; but Raskolnikov could not look upon them like that. He saw that these ignorant men were in many respects far wiser than the Poles. There were some Russians who were just as contemptuous, a former officer and two seminarists. Raskolnikov saw their mistake as clearly. He was disliked and avoided by everyone; they even began to hate him at last—why, he could not tell. Men who had been far more guilty despised and laughed at his crime.

"You're a gentleman," they used to say. "You shouldn't hack about with an axe; that's not a gentleman's work."

The second week in Lent, his turn came to take the sacrament with his gang. He went to church and prayed with the others. A quarrel broke out one day, he did not know how. All fell on him at once in a fury.

"You're an infidel! You don't believe in God," they shouted. "You ought to be killed."

He had never talked to them about God nor his belief, but they wanted to kill him as an infidel. He said nothing. One of the prisoners rushed at him in a perfect frenzy. Raskolnikov awaited him calmly and silently; his eyebrows did not quiver, his face did not flinch. The guard succeeded in intervening between him and his assailant, or there would have been bloodshed.

There was another question he could not decide: why were they all so fond of Sonia? She did not try to win their favour; she rarely met them, sometimes only she came to see him at work for a moment. And yet everybody knew her, they knew that she had come out to follow *him*, knew how and where she lived. She never gave them money, did them no particular services. Only once at Christmas she sent them all presents of pies and rolls. But by degrees closer relations sprang up between them and Sonia. She would write and post letters for them to their relations. Relations of the prisoners who visited the town, at their instructions, left with Sonia presents and money for them. Their wives and sweethearts knew her and used to visit her. And when she visited Raskolnikov at work, or met a party of the prisoners on the road, they all took off their hats to her. "Little mother Sofya Semyonovna, you are our dear, good little mother," coarse branded criminals said to that frail little creature. She would smile and bow to them and everyone was delighted when she smiled. They even admired her gait and turned round to watch her walking; they admired her too for being so little, and, in fact, did not know what to admire her most for. They even came to her for help in their illnesses.

He was in the hospital from the middle of Lent till after Easter. When he was better, he remembered the dreams he had had while he was feverish and delirious. He dreamt that the whole world was condemned to a terrible new strange plague that had come to Europe from the depths of Asia. All were to be destroyed except a very few chosen. Some new sorts of microbes were attacking the bodies of men, but these microbes were endowed with intelligence and will. Men attacked by them became at once mad and furious. But never had men considered themselves so intellectual and so completely in possession of the truth as these sufferers, never had they considered their decisions, their scientific conclusions, their moral convictions so infallible. Whole villages, whole towns and peoples went mad from the infection. All were excited and did not understand one another. Each thought that he alone had the truth and was wretched looking at the others, beat himself on the breast, wept, and wrung his hands. They did not know how to judge and could not agree what to consider evil and what good; they did not know whom to blame, whom to justify. Men killed each other in a sort of senseless spite. They gathered together in armies against one another, but even on the march the armies would begin attacking each other, the ranks would be broken and the soldiers would fall on each other, stabbing and cutting, biting and devouring each other. The alarm bell was ringing all day long in the towns; men rushed together, but why they were summoned and who was summoning them no one knew. The most ordinary trades were abandoned, because everyone proposed his own ideas, his own improvements, and they could not agree. The land too was abandoned. Men met in groups, agreed on something, swore to keep together, but at once began on something quite different from what they had proposed. They accused one another, fought and killed each other. There were conflagrations and famine. All men and all things were involved in destruction. The plague spread and moved further and further. Only a few men could be saved in the whole world. They were a pure chosen people, destined to found a new race and a new life, to renew and purify the earth, but no one had seen these men, no one had heard their words and their voices.

Raskolnikov was worried that this senseless dream haunted his memory so miserably, the impression of this feverish delirium persisted so long. The second week after Easter had come. There were warm bright spring days; in the prison ward the grating windows under which the sentinel paced were opened. Sonia had only been able to visit him twice during his illness; each time she had to obtain permission, and it was difficult. But she often used to come to the hospital yard, especially in the evening, sometimes only to stand a minute and look up at the windows of the ward.

One evening, when he was almost well again, Raskolnikov fell asleep. On waking up he chanced to go to the window, and at once saw Sonia in the distance at the hospital gate. She seemed to be waiting for someone. Something stabbed him to the heart at that minute. He shuddered and moved away from the window. Next day Sonia did not come, nor the day after; he noticed that he was expecting her uneasily. At last he was discharged.

On reaching the prison he learnt from the convicts that Sofya Semyonovna was lying ill at home and was unable to go out.

He was very uneasy and sent to inquire after her; he soon learnt that her illness was not dangerous. Hearing that he was anxious about her, Sonia sent him a pencilled note, telling him that she was much better, that she had a slight cold and that she would soon, very soon come and see him at his work. His heart throbbed painfully as he read it.

Again it was a warm bright day. Early in the morning, at six o'clock, he went off to work on the river bank, where they used to pound alabaster and where there was a kiln for baking it in a shed. There were only three of them sent. One of the convicts went with the guard to the fortress to fetch a tool; the other began getting the wood ready and laying it in the kiln. Raskolnikov came out of the shed on to the river bank, sat down on a heap of logs by the shed and began gazing at the wide deserted river. From the high bank a broad landscape opened before him, the sound of singing floated faintly audible from the other bank. In the vast steppe, bathed in sunshine, he could just see, like black specks, the nomads' tents. There there was freedom, there other men were living, utterly unlike those here; there time itself seemed to stand still, as though the age of Abraham and his flocks had not passed. Raskolnikov sat gazing, his thoughts passed into day-dreams, into contemplation; he thought of nothing, but a vague restlessness excited and troubled him. Suddenly he found Sonia beside him; she had come up noiselessly and sat down at his side. It was still quite early; the morning chill was still keen. She wore her poor old burnous and the green shawl; her face still showed signs of illness, it was thinner and paler. She gave him a joyful smile of welcome, but held out her hand with her usual timidity. She was always timid of holding out her hand to him and sometimes did not offer it at all, as though afraid he would repel it. He always took her hand as though with repugnance, always seemed vexed to meet her and was sometimes obstinately silent throughout her visit. Sometimes she trembled before him and went away deeply grieved. But now their hands did not part. He stole a rapid glance at her and dropped his eyes on the ground without speaking. They were alone, no one had seen them. The guard had turned away for the time.

How it happened he did not know. But all at once something seemed to seize him and fling him at her feet. He wept and threw his arms round her knees. For the first instant she was terribly frightened and she turned pale. She jumped up and looked at him trembling. But at the same moment she understood, and a light of infinite happiness came into her eyes. She knew and had no doubt that he loved her beyond everything and that at last the moment had come....

They wanted to speak, but could not; tears stood in their eyes. They were both pale and thin; but those sick pale faces were bright with the dawn of a new future, of a full resurrection into a new life. They were renewed by love; the heart of each held infinite sources of life for the heart of the other.

They resolved to wait and be patient. They had another seven years to wait, and what terrible suffering and what infinite happiness before them! But he had risen again and he knew it and felt it in all his being, while she—she only lived in his life.

On the evening of the same day, when the barracks were locked, Raskolnikov lay on his plank bed and thought of her. He had even fancied that day that all the convicts who had been his enemies looked at him differently; he had even entered into talk with them and they answered him in a friendly way. He remembered that now, and thought it was bound to be so. Wasn't everything now bound to be changed?

He thought of her. He remembered how continually he had tormented her and wounded her heart. He remembered her pale and thin little face. But these recollections scarcely troubled him now; he knew with what infinite love he would now repay all her sufferings. And what were all, *all* the agonies of the past! Everything, even his crime, his sentence and imprisonment, seemed to him now in the first rush of feeling an external, strange fact with which he had no concern. But he could not think for long together of anything that evening, and he could not have analysed anything consciously; he was simply feeling. Life had stepped into the place of theory and something quite different would work itself out in his mind.

Under his pillow lay the New Testament. He took it up mechanically. The book belonged to Sonia; it was the one from which she had read the raising of Lazarus to him. At first he was afraid that she would worry him about religion, would talk about the gospel and pester him with books. But to his great surprise she had not once approached the subject and had not even offered him the Testament. He had asked her for it himself not long before his illness and she brought him the book without a word. Till now he had not opened it.

He did not open it now, but one thought passed through his mind: "Can her convictions not be mine now? Her feelings, her aspirations at least...."

She too had been greatly agitated that day, and at night she was taken ill again. But she was so happy—and so unexpectedly happy—that she was almost frightened of her happiness. Seven years, *only* seven years! At the beginning of their happiness at some moments they were both ready to look on those seven years as though they were seven days. He did not know that the new life would not be given him for nothing, that he would have to pay dearly for it, that it would cost him great striving, great suffering.

But that is the beginning of a new story—the story of the gradual renewal of a man, the story of his gradual regeneration, of his passing from one world into another, of his initiation into a new unknown life. That might be the subject of a new story, but our present story is ended.

Made in the USA
Coppell, TX
06 December 2020